Praise for Robert Littell's
The Company

"Besides being hugely entertaining, *The Company* is a serious look at how our nation exercised power, for good and ill, in the second half of the twentieth century. . . . Once I picked it up I did not want to put it down. . . . This is popular fiction at its finest."
— *The Washington Post Book World*

"[Littell] never lost this reader for even a single page. . . . The U.S. [has] a genre writer as good as the best England could offer. Over the last three decades, Littell has been true to his craft, bringing out novel after entertaining novel at a level consistently far above that of pulp writers like Ludlum . . . giving us psychologically interesting thrillers that rival in their intensity and the delivery of their plots the best work of John le Carré."
— *Chicago Tribune*

"Robert Littell's book ranges widely and at great length, nearly fifty years of postwar espionage, offering perspectives on alarums and excursions as varied as the Rosenberg trial, the Bay of Pigs invasion, the alleged 'assassination' of Pope John Paul I in 1978 and the great winding down of perestroika. . . . A gold mine for true conspiracy theorists."
— *The New York Times Book Review*

"Robert Littell's *The Company* reads like a breeze and is guaranteed to suck you right back into the Alice-in-Wonderland world of spy vs. spy. It's a ripping good yarn—entertaining, chilling and insightful."
— *Newsweek*

"*The Company* . . . is wonderfully rich. . . . It is compulsive reading from start to finish. . . . Littell seduces the reader."
— *The Boston Globe*

"This massively ambitious page-turner covers the entire Cold War through several generations of CIA agents and what amounts to the greatest hits (and failures) of the Company. . . . *The Company* is a humanizing history of the Cold War."
— *New York Post*

"It may be more accurate to refer to it as 'THE novel of the CIA.' . . . Convincing enough to provide a new perspective on history." — *The Oregonian* (Portland)

"The best read you're ever going to find on how the Central Intelligence Agency waged—and helped win—the Cold War. *The Company* weighs in at almost 900 pages, and I wish it could have been twice that length. . . . Move over Mr. le Carré, the Cold War might be over, but it still can produce good yarns."
— *The Washington Times*

"True to the genre [*The Company*], ends with brave, noble heroes saving the day. The Brothers Grimm couldn't have done it better." — *New York Daily News*

PENGUIN BOOKS

THE COMPANY

Connoisseurs of the literary spy thriller have elevated Robert Littell to the genre's highest ranks—along with John le Carré, Len Deighton, and Graham Greene. Littell's novels include *The Defection of A. J. Lewinter*, *The October Circle*, *Mother Russia*, *The Amateur* (which was made into a feature film), and *The Once and Future Spy*. A former *Newsweek* journalist, he is an American currently living in France.

Also by Robert Littell

FICTION

WALKING BACK THE CAT

THE VISITING PROFESSOR

AN AGENT IN PLACE

THE ONCE AND FUTURE SPY

THE REVOLUTIONIST

THE SISTERS

THE AMATEUR

THE DEBRIEFING

MOTHER RUSSIA

THE OCTOBER CIRCLE

SWEET REASON

THE DEFECTION OF A. J. LEWINTER

NONFICTION

FOR THE FUTURE OF ISRAEL (with Shimon Peres)

THE COMPANY

A NOVEL OF THE CIA

ROBERT LITTELL

PENGUIN BOOKS

PENGUIN BOOKS

Published by the Penguin Group

Penguin Putnam Inc., 375 Hudson Street, New York, New York 10014, U.S.A.
Penguin Books Ltd, 80 Strand, London WC2R 0RL, England
Penguin Books Australia Ltd, 250 Camberwell Road, Camberwell, Victoria 3124, Australia
Penguin Books Canada Ltd, 10 Alcorn Avenue, Toronto, Ontario, Canada M4V 3B2
Penguin Books India (P) Ltd, 11 Community Centre, Panchsheel Park, New Delhi – 110 017, India
Penguin Books (N.Z.) Ltd, Cnr Rosedale and Airborne Roads, Albany, Auchland, New Zealand
Penguin Books (South Africa) (Pty) Ltd, 24 Sturdee Avenue,
Rosebank, Johannesburg 2196, South Africa

Penguin Books Ltd, Registered Offices:
Harmondsworth, Middlesex, England

First published in the United States of America by the Overlook Press,
Peter Mayer Publishers, Inc. 2002
Published in Penguin Books 2003

3 5 7 9 10 8 6 4 2

PUBLISHER'S NOTE
This is a work of fiction. Names, characters, places, and incidents either are the product
of the author's imagination or are used fictitiously, and any resemblance to actual persons,
living or dead, business establishments, events, or locales is entirely coincidental.

THE LIBRARY OF CONGRESS HAS CATALOGUED THE HARDCOVER EDITION AS FOLLOWS:
Littell, Robert.
The company : a novel of the CIA / Robert Littell.
p. cm.
ISBN 1-58567-197-5 (hc.)
ISBN 0 14 20.0262 3 (pbk.)
1. United States. Central Intelligence Agency—Fiction.
2. International relations—Fiction. 3. Intelligence officers—Fiction. I. Title
PS3562.I7827 C66   2002   813'.54—dc21   2001051383

Printed in the United States of America

For the witnesses, Michael and Jimmie Ritchie

And the guardian angel, Ed Victor

AUTHOR'S NOTE:

Since its creation in 1917, the Soviet intelligence service has changed names several times. It started out as the Cheka, then became the GPU, OGPU, NKVD, NKGB, MGB, and finally, in March 1954, the KGB. In order to keep readers from drowning in an alphabet soup, I have used the appellation KGB, even in the parts of the story set prior to March 1954. Similarly, before March 1973, the CIA's clandestine service was known as the Directorate of Plans, headed by the Deputy Director for Plans, or DD/P. After March 1973, the name was changed to Directorate of Operations, headed by the Deputy Director for Operations, or DD/O. Again, to avoid confusion, I have used the current appellation, DD/O, throughout the book.

THE CALABRIAN

"This must be the wood," she said thoughtfully to herself, "where things have no name."

HIGH OVER THE CITY, A RACK OF CLOUDS DRIFTED ACROSS THE hunter's moon so rapidly it looked as if a motion picture had been speeded up. On a deserted avenue near a long wall, a dirty yellow Fiat mini-taxi cut its lights and its motor and coasted to the curb at Porta Angelica. A lean figure wearing the rough ankle-length cassock and hood of a Dominican friar emerged from the back seat. He had been raised in the toe of the boot of Italy and was known as the Calabrian by the shadowy organizations that from time to time employed his services. As a teenager, the Calabrian, a beautiful young man with the angelic face of a Renaissance castrato, had trained for several years as an equilibrist in a circus academy but abandoned it when he fell from a high wire and shattered an ankle. Now, despite a perceptible limp, he still moved with the catlike elegance of a tightrope walker. From the hills above the Tiber, a church bell that had recently been hooked up to an electric timer sounded the half-hour half a minute early. The Calabrian checked the luminous dial of his wristwatch, then walked the fifty meters alongside the colonnade to the heavy wooden doors. Pulling on a pair of surgeon's latex gloves, he scratched at the tradesmen's entrance. Immediately a heavy bolt on the inside was thrown and the small blue door set into the larger doors opened just enough for him to slip through. A pale, middle-aged man, dressed in mufti but with the ramrod bearing of an army officer, held up five fingers and nodded toward the only window of the guard barracks out of which light streamed. The Calabrian nodded once. With the officer leading the way, the two started down the alley, ducking when they came to the lighted window. The Calabrian peered over the sill; inside the orderly room two young soldiers in uniform were playing cards, three others dozed in easy chairs. Automatic weapons and clips of ammunition were visible on the table next to a small refrigerator.

The Calabrian trailed after the officer in mufti, past the Institute for

Religious Works, to a servants' door in the back of the sprawling palazzo. The officer produced a large skeleton key from his jacket pocket and inserted it into the lock. The door clicked open. He dropped a second skeleton key into the Calabrian's palm. "For the door on the landing," he whispered. He spoke Italian with the flat elongated vowels of someone who came from one of the mountainous cantons of Switzerland bordering the Dolomite Alps. "Impossible to get the key to the apartment without attracting attention."

"No matter," the Calabrian said. "I will pick the lock. What about the milk? What about the alarms?"

"The milk was delivered. You will soon see whether it was consumed. As for the alarms, I disconnected the three doors on the control panel in the officers' ready room."

As the Calabrian started through the door, the officer touched his arm. "You have twelve minutes before the guards begin their next patrol."

"I am able to slow time down or speed it up," remarked the Calabrian, looking up at the moon. "Twelve minutes, spent carefully, can be made to last an eternity." With that, he vanished into the building.

He knew the floor plan of the palazzo as well as he knew the lifelines on the palms of his hands. Hiking his cassock, taking the steps three at a time, he climbed the narrow servants' staircase to the third floor, opened the door with the skeleton key and let himself into the dimly lit corridor. A long tongue of violet drugget, faded and worn in the middle, ran from the far end of the corridor to the small table facing the antiquated elevator and the central staircase next to it. Moving soundlessly, the Calabrian made his way down the corridor to the table. A plump nun, one of the Sisters of the Handmaids of Jesus Crucified, sat slumped over the table, her head directly under the pale circle of light from a silver desk lamp almost as if she were drying her hair. An empty tumbler with the last of the drugged milk was next to the old-fashioned telephone perched high on its cradle.

The Calabrian pulled an identical tumbler, with a film of uncontaminated milk at the bottom, from one of the deep pockets of his cassock and retrieved the nun's glass containing traces of the doped milk. Then he headed back up the corridor, counting doors. At the third door, he inserted a length of stiff wire with a hook on the end into the keyhole and expertly stroked the inside until the first pin moved up into position, then repeated the gesture with the other pins. When the last pin moved up, the lock snapped open. The Calabrian eased open the door and listened for a moment. Hearing nothing, he padded through the foyer into a large rectangular drawing room with a marble fireplace on each end and ornate furniture scattered around. The slatted shutters on all four windows had been pulled closed. A single table lamp with a low wattage bulb served, as the briefing report had predicted, as a night-light.

Gliding soundlessly across the room and down a hallway on rubber-soled shoes, the Calabrian came to the bedroom door. He turned the ceramic knob and carefully pushed the door open and listened again. A stifling stuffiness, the stench of an old man's room, emerged from the bedchamber; the person who occupied it obviously didn't sleep with a window open. Flicking on a penlight, the Calabrian inspected the room. Unlike the drawing room, the furnishings were spartan: there was a sturdy brass bed, a night table, two wooden chairs, one piled with neatly folded clothing, the other with dossiers, a wash basin with a single tap over it, a naked electric bulb dangling from the ceiling, a simple wooden crucifix on the wall over the head of the bed. He crossed the room and looked down at the figure sleeping with a sheet drawn up to its chin. A thickset man with a peasant's rugged features, he had been in his new job only thirty-four days, barely enough time to learn his way around the palazzo. His breathing was regular and intense, causing the hairs protruding from his nostrils to quiver; he was deep in a drugged sleep. There was a tumbler on the night table with traces of milk at the bottom, and a photograph in a silver frame—it showed a prince of the church making the sign of the cross over a young priest prostrate on the ground before him. The inscription, written in a bold hand across the bottom of the photograph, read "Per Albino Luciani, Venizia, 1933." A signature was scrawled under the inscription: "Ambrogio Ratti, Pius XI." Next to the photograph was a pair of reading spectacles, a worn bible filled with place markers, and a bound and numbered copy of *Humani Generis Unitas*, Pius XI's never-promulgated encyclical condemning racism and anti-Semitism that had been on the Pope's desk awaiting his signature the day he died in 1939.

The Calabrian checked his wristwatch and set to work. He rinsed the milk glass in the wash basin, dried it on the hem of his cassock and replaced it in precisely the same place on the night table. He produced the phial filled with milk from his pocket and emptied the contents into the glass so there would be a trace of uncontaminated milk in it. Clamping the penlight between his lips, the Calabrian turned to the drugged man in the bed, stripped back the sheet and heaved him over onto his stomach. Then he pulled up the white cotton nightgown, exposing the saphenous vein behind the knee. The people who had hired the Calabrian had gotten their hands on Albino Luciani's medical report after a routine colonoscopy the previous winter; because of the varicose nature of the vein running the length of his right leg, the patient had been given preventive treatment against phlebitis. The Calabrian fetched the small metal kit from his pocket and opened it on the bed next to the knee. Working rapidly—after his high-wire accident, he had spent several years as a male nurse—he inserted a 30-gauge, 0.3 millimeter needle into the syringe filled with extract from a castor oil plant, then deftly stabbed the needle into the *saphenae* behind the knee and injected the four-milliliter dose of fluid into the bloodstream. According to his employer, cardiovascular collapse would occur within minutes; within hours the toxin would dissipate, leaving no trace in the unlikely event an autopsy were to be performed. Carefully extracting the incredibly thin needle, the Calabrian wiped away the pinpoint of blood with a small moist sponge, then bent close to see if he could detect the puncture wound. There was a slight reddening, the size of a grain of sand but that, too, would disappear by the time the body was discovered in the morning. Satisfied with his handiwork, he went over to the chair piled high with dossiers and shuffled through them until he came to the one marked, in Roman letters, KHOLSTOMER. Lifting the hem of his cassock, he wedged the file folder under his belt, then looked around to see if he had forgotten anything.

Back in the corridor, the Calabrian pulled the apartment door shut and heard the pins in the lock click closed. Checking his watch—he had four minutes remaining before the guards started on their rounds—he hurried down the stairs and through the alleyway to the tradesmen's entrance. The officer in mufti, looking quite shaken, stared at him, afraid to pose the question. The Calabrian smiled the answer as he handed back the skeleton key. The officer's lips parted and he sucked in a quick gulp of air; the thing that had no name was accomplished. He pulled open the small blue door wide enough for the Calabrian to slip through and bolted it after him.

The taxi was waiting at the curb, its door ajar. The Calabrian settled into the back seat and slowly began to peel away the latex gloves, finger by finger. The driver, a young Corsican with a broken, badly-set nose, started down the still deserted street, moving cautiously at first so as not to attract attention, then picking up speed as he turned onto a broad boulevard and headed for Civitavecchia, the port of Rome on the Tyrrhenian Sea, thirty-five minutes away. There, in a dockside warehouse a stone's throw from the *Vladimir Ilyich*, a Russian freighter due to sail on the morning tide, the Calabrian would meet his controller, a reed-like man with a scraggly pewter beard and brooding eyes, known only as Starik. He would return the paraphernalia of assassination— the gloves, the lock-pick, the metal kit, the tumbler with the last drops of doped milk in it, even the empty phial—and deliver the dossier marked KHOLSTOMER. And he would take possession of the bag containing a king's ransom, $1 million in used bills of various denominations; not a bad wage for fifteen minutes' work. About the time first light stained the eastern horizon, when the Sister of the Handmaids of Jesus Crucified (emerging from a drugged sleep) discovered Albino Luciani dead in his bed, the victim of a heart attack, the Calabrian would board the small fishing boat at a wharf that would take him, in two days' time, into exile on the sun-drenched beaches of Palermo.

THE ANATOMY OF AN EXFILTRATION

"But I don't want to go among mad people," Alice remarked.
"Oh, you can't help that," said the Cat:
"we're all mad here. I'm mad. You're mad."
"How do you know I'm mad?" said Alice.
"You must be," said the Cat, "or you wouldn't have come here."

FROM ITS PERCH OVER THE MANTELSHELF A MUTILATED BAVARIAN cuckoo clock, its hour hand mangled, its minute hand missing, sent the seconds ricocheting from wall to wall of the shabby room. The Sorcerer, his face contorted in chronic constipation, sniffed tentatively at the air, which was bitterly cold and stung his nostrils. "Someday the goddamn fiction writers will get around to describing what we did here—"

"I love spy stories," the Fallen Angel giggled from the door of the adjoining room.

"They'll turn it into melodrama," Jack McAuliffe said. "They'll make it sound as if we played cowboys and Indians to brighten our dull lives."

"Spying—if that's what I been doing all these years—don't brighten my life none," remarked the Fallen Angel. "I always get stomach cramps before an operation."

"I'm not here in this dry-rotted rain-wash of a city because it brightens my life," the Sorcerer said, preempting the question an apprentice with balls would have posed by now. "I'm here because the goddamn Goths are at the goddamn gate." He tugged a threadbare scarf up over his numb earlobes, tap-danced his scruffy cowboy boots on the floor to keep up the circulation in his toes. "Are you reading me loud and clear, sport? This isn't alcohol talking, this is the honcho of Berlin Base talking. Someone has to man the goddamn ramparts." He sucked on a soggy Camel and washed down the smoke with a healthy gulp of what he called medicinal whiskey. "I drink what my fitness report describes as a toxic amount of booze," he rambled on, addressing the problem Jack didn't have the guts to raise, articulating each syllable as if he were patrolling the fault line between soused and sober, "because the goddamn Goths happen to be winning the goddamn war."

· Harvey Torriti, a.k.a. the Sorcerer, scraped back the chair and made his way to the single small oriel window of the safe house two floors above the East Berlin neighborhood cinema. From under the floorboards came the distant shriek of incoming mortars, then a series of dull explosions as they slammed into the German positions. Several of Torriti's hookers had seen the Soviet war film the week before. The Ukrainian girl who bleached her hair the color of chrome claimed the movie had been shot, with the usual cast of thousands, on a studio lot in Alma-Ata; in the background she recognized, so she'd said, the snow-capped Ala-Tau mountain range, where she used to sleigh ride when she was evacuated to Central Asia during the war. Snorting to clear a tingling sinus, the Sorcerer parted the slats of an imaginary Venetian blind with two thick fingers of his gloved hand and gazed through the grime on the pane. At sunset a mustard-color haze had drifted in from the Polish steppe, a mere thirty miles east, shrouding the Soviet Sector of Berlin in an eerie stillness, coating its intestine-like cobble gutters with what looked like an algae that reeked, according to Torriti's conceit, of intrigue. Down the block jackdaws beat into the air and cawed savagely as they wheeled around the steeple of a dilapidated church that had been converted into a dilapidated warehouse. (The Sorcerer, an aficionado of cause-and-effect, listened for the echo of the pistol shot he'd surely missed.) In the narrow street outside the cinema Silwan I, known as Sweet Jesus, one of the two Rumanian gypsies employed by Torriti as bodyguards, could be seen, a sailor's watch cap pulled low over his head, dragging a muzzled lap dog through the brackish light of a vapor lamp. Except for Sweet Jesus, the streets of what the Company pros called "West Moscow" appeared to be deserted. "If there are *Homo sapiens* out there celebrating the end of the year," Torriti muttered gloomily, "they sure are being discreet about it."

Suffering from a mild case of first operation adrenalin jitters, Jack McAuliffe, a.k.a. the Sorcerer's Apprentice, called from the door with elaborate laziness, "The quiet gives me the willies, Harvey. Back in the States everyone honks their horns on New Year's Eve."

The second gypsy, Silwan II, dubbed the Fallen Angel by Torriti after he detected in his dark eyes an ugly hint of things the Rumanian was desperately trying to forget, stuck his head in from the next room. A gangly young man with a smallpox-scarred face, he had been reading for the Rumanian Orthodox church and wound up in the business of espionage when the Communists shut down his seminary. "Blowing horns is against the law in the German Democratic Republic," Silwan II announced in the precise accented English of someone who had picked up the language from textbooks. "Also in our capitalist Germany."

At the window, the Sorcerer fogged a pane with his whiskey breath and rubbed it clean with a heavy forearm. Across the roofs the top floors of several high-rise apartment buildings, their windows flickering with light, loomed through the murky cityscape like the tips of icebergs. "It's not a matter of German law," Torriti reckoned moodily, "it's a matter of German character." He wheeled away from the window so abruptly he almost lost his balance. Grabbing the back of the chair to steady himself, he cautiously shoehorned his heavy carcass onto the wooden seat. "I happen to be the god-damn Company specialist on German character," he insisted, his voice pitched high but curiously melodic. "I was a member of the debriefing team that inter-rogated the SS *Obersturmführer* of Auschwitz night before the fucker was strung up for war crimes. What was his goddamn name? Höss. Rudolf Höss. Fucker claimed he couldn't have killed five thousand Jews a day because the trains could only bring in two thousand. Talk about an airtight defense! We were all smoking like concentration camp chimneys and you could see Herr Höss was dying for a goddamn cigarette, so I offered him one of my Camels." Torriti swallowed a sour giggle. "You know what Rudy did, sport?"

"What did Rudy do, Harvey?"

"*The night before his execution* he turned down the fucking cigarette because there was a 'No Smoking' sign on the wall. Now *that's* what I call German character."

"Lenin once said the only way you could get Germans to storm a rail-way station was to buy them tickets to the quay," ventured the Fallen Angel.

Jack laughed—a shade too quickly, a shade too heartily for Torriti's taste.

The Sorcerer was dressed in the shapeless trousers and ankle-length rumpled green overcoat of an East German worker. The tips of a wide and flowery Italian tie were tucked, military style, between two buttons of his shirt. His thin hair was sweat-pasted onto his glistening skull. Eying his apprentice across the room, he began to wonder how Jack would perform in a crunch; he himself had barely made it through a small Midwestern com-munity college and then had clawed his way up through the ranks to finish the war with the fool's gold oak leaves of a major pinned to the frayed col-lar of his faded khaki shirt, which left him with a low threshold of tolerance for the Harvard-Yale-Princeton crowd—what he called "the boys from HYP." It was a bias that grew during a brief stint running organized crime investigations for the FBI right after the war (employment that ended abruptly when J. Edgar Hoover himself spotted Torriti in the corridor wear-ing tight trousers and an untied tie and fired him on the spot). What the hell! Nobody in the Company bothered consulting the folks on the firing line when they press-ganged the Ivy League for recruits and came up with jokers like Jack McAuliffe, a Yalie so green behind the ears he'd forgotten to get his ashes hauled when he was sent to debrief Torriti's hookers the week the Sorcerer came down with the clap. Well, what could you expect from a college graduate with a degree in rowing?

Clutching the bottle of PX whiskey by its throat, closing one eye and squinting through the other, the Sorcerer painstakingly filled the kitchen tumbler to the brim. "Not the same without ice," he mumbled, belching as he carefully maneuvered his thick lips over the glass. He felt the alcohol scald the back of his throat. "No ice, no tinkle. No tinkle, *schlecht!*" He jerked his head up and called across to Jack, "So what time do you make it, sport?"

Jack, anxious to put on a good show, glanced nonchalantly at the Bulova his parents had given him on his graduation from Yale. "He should have been here twelve, fifteen minutes ago," he said.

The Sorcerer scratched absently at the two-day stubble on his overlapping chins. He hadn't had time to shave since the high priority message had sizzled into Berlin Base forty-two hours earlier. The heading had been crammed with in-house codes indicating it had come directly from counterintelligence; from Mother himself. Like all messages from counterintelligence it had been flagged "CRITIC," which meant you were expected to drop whatever you were doing and concentrate on the matter at hand. Like some messages from counterintelligence—usually the ones dealing with defectors—it had been encoded in one of Mother's unbreakable polyalphabetic systems that used two cipher alphabets to provide multiple substitutes for any given letter in the text.

TOP SECRET
WARNING NOTICE: SENSITIVE COMPARTMENTED INFORMATION
Intelligence sources and methods involved

FROM: Hugh Ashmead [Mother's in-house cryptonym]
TO: Alice Reader [the Sorcerer's in-house cryptonym]
SUBJECT: Bringing home the bacon

The message had gone on to inform Torriti that someone claiming to be a high-ranking Russian intelligence officer had put out feelers that had landed in one of the several in-boxes on Mother's desk. (In the Sorcerer's experience everything landed in one of the in-boxes on Mother's desk but that was another story.) Mother's cable identified the would-be defector by the random cryptonym SNOWDROP, preceded by the digraph AE to indicate the matter was being handled by the Soviet Russia Division, and went on to quote the entire contents of the Company's 201—the file in Central Registry—on the Russian.

> Vishnevsky, Konstantin: born either 1898 or 1899 in Kiev; father, a chemical engineer and Party member, died when subject was a teenager; at age 17 enrolled as cadet in Kiev Military Academy; graduated four years later as an artillery officer; did advanced studies at the Odessa Artillery School for officers; coopted into military intelligence at the start of Second World War; believed to be a member of the Soviet Communist Party; married, one son born 1940; after war transferred to the Committee for State Security (KGB); studied counterintelligence at the High Intelligence School (one-year short course); on graduation posted to Brest-Litovsk for four months; attended the KGB Diplomatic Institute in Moscow for one year; on successfully completing course assigned to Moscow Centre for six months as analyst in US order of battle section of the KGB's Information Department; posted to Stockholm summer 1948–January 1950 where he believed to have specialized in military affairs; subsequent assignment unknown. No record of anti-Soviet opinions. Conclusion: considered poor candidate for recruitment.

Always maternally protective of his sources, Mother had been careful not to identify where the original tip had come from, but the Sorcerer was able to make an educated guess when Berlin Base asked the Germans— "our" Germans, which was to say Reinhard Gehlen's Sud-Deutsche Industrie-Verwertungs GmbH, working out of a secret compound in the Munich suburb of Pullach—for routine background traces on a baker's dozen KGB officers stationed at the Soviet Karlshorst enclave in East Berlin. Gehlen's people, always eager to please their American masters, quickly provided a bulky briefing book on the Russians in question. Buried in the report was a detail missing from the Company's 201: AESNOWDROP was thought to have had a Jewish mother. That, in turn, led the Sorcerer to suspect that it was the Israeli Mossad agent in West Berlin known as the Rabbi who had been whispering in Mother's ear; nine times out of ten anything that even remotely concerned a Jew passed through the Rabbi's hands. (The Israelis had their own agenda, of course, but high on it was scoring Brownie points in Washington against the day when they needed to cash in their IOUs.) According to Mother the potential KGB defector wanted to come over with a wife and a child. The Sorcerer was to meet with him in the safe house designated MARLBOROUGH at such and such a date, at such and such an hour, establish his *bona fides* to make absolutely certain he wasn't what Mother called a "bad 'un"—a dispatched agent sent across with a briefcase full of KGB disinformation—at which point he was to "press the orange" and find out what goodies he had to offer in exchange for political asylum. After which the Sorcerer would report back to Mother to see if Washington wanted to go ahead with the actual defection.

In the next room the Fallen Angel's radio crackled into life. Surfing on a burst of static came the codewords *Morgenstunde hat Gold im Mund* ("the morning hour has gold in its mouth"). Jack, startled, snapped to attention. Silwan II appeared at the door again. "He's on the way up," he hissed. Kissing the fingernail of his thumb, he hurriedly crossed himself.

One of the Sorcerer's Watchers, a German woman in her seventies sitting in the back row of the theater, had seen the dark figure of a man slipping into the toilet at the side of the cinema and mumbled the news into a small battery-powered radio hidden in her knitting bag. Inside the toilet the Russian would open the door of a broom closet, shove aside the mops and carpet sweepers and push through the hidden panel in the back wall of the closet, then start up the ridiculously narrow wooden stairs that led to the top floor and the safe house.

The Sorcerer, suddenly cold sober, shuddered like a Labrador shaking off rain water and shook his head to clear his vision. He waved Silwan II into the adjoining room, then leaned toward the spine of *God and Man at Yale— the Superstition of Academic Freedom* and whispered "Testing five, four, three, two, one." Silwan popped through the door, flashed a thumbs-up sign and disappeared again, shutting and locking the door behind him.

Jack felt his pulse speed up. He flattened himself against the wall so that the door to the corridor, once opened, would conceal him. Pulling a Walther PPK from the holster strapped to the belt in the hollow of his back, he thumbed off the safety and held the weapon out of sight behind his overcoat. Looking across the room, he was unnerved to see the Sorcerer rocking back and forth in mock admiration.

"Oh, neat trick," Torriti said, his face straight, his small beady eyes flashing in derision. "Hiding the handgun behind you like that, I mean. Rules out the possibility of frightening off the defector before the fucker has a chance to give us his name, rank, and serial number." Torriti himself carried a pearl-handled revolver under one sweaty armpit and a snub-nosed .38 Detective Special in a holster taped to an ankle, but he made it a rule never to reach for a weapon unless there was a strong possibility he would eventually pull the trigger. It was a bit of tradecraft McAuliffe would pick up if he stuck around

Berlin Base long enough: the sight of handguns made the nervous people in the business of espionage nervouser; the nervouser they got the more likely it was that someone would wind up shooting someone, which was from everyone's point of view a disagreeable dénouement to any operation.

The fact of the matter was that Torriti, for all his griping about greenhorns, got a charge out of breaking in the virgins. He thought of tradecraft as a kind of religion—it was said of the Sorcerer that he could blend into a crowd even when there wasn't one—and took a visceral pleasure in baptizing his disciples. And, all things considered, he judged McAuliffe—with his tinted aviator sunglasses, his unkempt Cossack mustache, his flaming-red hair slicked back and parted in the middle, the unfailing politeness that masked an affinity for violence—to be a cut above the usual cannon fodder sent out from Washington these days, and this despite the handicap of a Yale education. There was something almost comically Irish about him: the progeny of the undefeated bareknuckle lightweight champion of the world, a McAuliffe whose motto had been "Once down is no battle"; the lapsed moralist who came out laughing and swinging and wouldn't stop either simply because a gong sounded; the lapsed Catholic capable of making a lifelong friend of someone he met over breakfast and consigning him to everlasting purgatory by teatime.

At the door Jack sheepishly slipped the Walther back into its holster. The Sorcerer rapped a knuckle against his forehead. "Get it into your thick skull we're the good guys, sport."

"Jesus H. Christ, Harvey, I know who the good guys are or I wouldn't be here."

In the corridor outside the room, the floorboards groaned. A fist drummed against the door. The Sorcerer closed his eyes and nodded. Jack pulled open the door.

A short, powerfully built man with close-cropped charcoal hair, an oval Slavic face, and skin the color and texture of moist candle wax stood on the threshold. Visibly edgy, he looked quickly at Jack, then turned to study through narrowed, vaguely Asiatic eyes the Buddha-like figure who appeared to be lost in meditation at the small table. Suddenly showing signs of life, the Sorcerer greeted the Russian with a cheery salute and waved him toward the free chair. The Russian walked over to the oriel window and peered down at the street as one of those newfangled East German cars, its sorethroated motor coughing like a tubercular man, lurched past the cinema and disappeared around a corner. Reassured by the lack of activity outside, the Russian took a turn around the room, running the tips of his finger over the surface of a cracked mirror, trying the handle on the door of the adjoining room. He wound up in front of the cuckoo clock. "What happened to his hands?" he asked.

"The first time I set foot in Berlin," the Sorcerer said, "which was one week after the end of what you jokers call the Great Patriotic War, the Ring Road was crammed with emaciated horses pulling farm wagons. The scrawny German kids watching them were eating acorn cakes. The horses were being led by Russian soldiers. The wagons were piled high with loot—four-poster beds, toilets, radiators, faucets, kitchen sinks and stoves, just about anything that could be unscrewed. I remember seeing soldiers carrying sofas out of Hermann Goering's villa. Nothing was too big or too small. I'll lay odds the minute hand of the cuckoo clock was in one of those wagons."

An acrid smirk made its way onto the Russian's lips. "It was me leading one of the wagons," he said. "I served as an intelligence officer in an infantry regiment that battled, in four winters, from the faubourg of Moscow to the rubble of the Reichstag in the Tiergarten. On the way we passed hundreds of our villages razed to the ground by the fleeing Nazis. We buried the mutilated corpses of our partisan fighters—there were women and children who had been executed with flame throwers. Only forty-two of the original twelve hundred sixty men in my battalion reached Berlin. The hands of your cuckoo clock, Mister American Central Intelligence agent, were small repay for what the Germans did to us during the war."

The Russian pulled the seat back from the table so that from it he could watch both Jack and the Sorcerer, and sat down. Torriti's nostrils flared as he nodded his chins toward the bottle of whiskey. The Russian, who reeked of a trashy eau de cologne, shook his head no.

"Okay, let's start down the yellow brick road. I've been told to expect someone name of Konstantin Vishnevsky."

"I am Vishnevsky."

"Funny part is we couldn't find a Vishnevsky, Konstantin, on the KGB Berlin roster."

"That is because I am carried on the register under the name Volkov. How, please, is your name?"

The Sorcerer was in his element now and thoroughly enjoying himself. "Tweedledum is how my name is."

"Tweedle-Dum how?"

"Just Tweedledum." Torriti wagged a forefinger at the Russian sitting an arm's length from the table. "Look, friend, you're obviously not new at this game we're playing—you know the ground rules like I know the ground rules."

Jack leaned back against the wall next to the door and watched in fascination as Vishnevsky unbuttoned his overcoat and produced a battered tin cigarette case from which he extracted a long, thin paper-tipped *papyrosi*. From another pocket he brought out an American Army Air Corps lighter. Both his hand and the cigarette between his lips trembled as he bent his head to the flame. The act of lighting up appeared to soothe his nerves. The room filled with the foul-smelling Herzegovina Flor that the Russian officers smoked in the crowded cabarets along the Kurfürstendamm. "Please to answer me a single question," Vishnevsky said. "Is there a microphone? Are you recording our conversation?"

The Sorcerer sensed a great deal was riding on his answer. Keeping his unblinking eyes fixed on the Russian, he decided to wing it. "I am. We are. Yes."

Vishnevsky actually breathed a sigh of relief. "Most certainly you are. In your position I would do the same. If you said me no I would get up and exit. A defection is a high-wire act performed without benefit of safety net. I am putting my life in your hands, Mr. Tweedle however your name is. I must be able to trust you." He dragged on the cigarette and exhaled through his nostrils. "I hold the rank of lieutenant colonel in our KGB."

The Sorcerer accepted this with a curt nod. There was a dead silence while the Russian concentrated on the cigarette. Torriti made no effort to fill the void. He had been through this drill more times than he could remember. He understood that it was crucial for him to set the agenda, to impose a pace that violated the defector's expectations; it was important to demonstrate, in subtle ways, who was running the show. If there was going to be a defection it would be on the Sorcerer's terms and at the Sorcerer's pleasure.

"I am listed as a cultural attaché and function under the cover of a diplomatic passport," the Russian added.

The Sorcerer reached out and caressed the side of the whiskey bottle with the backs of his gloved fingers. "Okay, here's the deal," he finally said. "Think of me as a fisherman trawling the continental shelf off the Prussian coast. When I feel there is something in the net I pull it up and examine it. I throw the little ones back because I am under strict orders to only keep big fish. Nothing personal, it goes without saying. Are you a big fish, Comrade Vishnevsky?"

The Russian squirmed on his seat. "So: I am the deputy to the chief of the First Chief Directorate at the KGB's Berlin base in Karlshorst."

The Sorcerer produced a small notebook from an inside pocket and thumbed through it to a page filled with minuscule writing in Sicilian. He regularly debriefed the sister of a cleaning woman who worked at the hotel a stone's throw from Karlshorst where KGB officers from Moscow Centre stayed when they visited Berlin. "On 22 December 1950 KGB Karlshorst had its books inspected by an auditor sent out from the Central Committee Control Commission. What was his name?"

"Evpraksein, Fyodor Eremeyevich. He ended up at the spare desk in the office next to mine."

The Sorcerer arched his eyebrows as if to say: Fine, you work at Karlshorst, but you'll have to do a lot better if you want to qualify as a big fish. "What exactly do you want from me?" Torriti asked suddenly.

The defector cleared his throat. "I am ready to come over," he announced, "but only if I can bring with me my wife, my son."

"Why?"

"What does it change, the why?"

"Trust me. It changes everything. Why?"

"My career is arrived to a dead end. I am"—he struggled to find a word in English, then settled for the German—"*desillusioniert* with system. I am not talking about Communism, I am talking about the KGB. The *rezident* tried to seduce my wife. I said him face to face about this. He denied the thing, he accused me of trying to blackmail him into giving me a good end-year report. Moscow Centre believed his version, not mine. So: this is my last foreign posting. I am fifty-two years old—I will be put out like a sheep to graze in some obscure pasture. I will spend the rest of my life in Kazakhstan typewriting in triplicate reports from informers. I dreamed of more important things...This is my last chance to make a new life for myself, for my wife, for my son."

"Is your *rezident* aware that you are half-Jewish?"

Vishnevsky started. "How can you know..." He sighed. "My *rezident* discovered it, which is to say Moscow Centre discovered it, when my mother died last summer. She left a testament saying she wished to be buried in the Jewish cemetery of Kiev. I tried to suppress the testament before it was filed but—"

"Your fear of being put out to pasture—is it because Moscow found out you were half-Jewish or your dispute with the Berlin *rezident*?"

The Russian shrugged wearily. "I said you what I think."

"Does your wife know you've contacted us?"

"I will tell her when the time arrives to leave."

"How can you be sure she'll want to go?"

Vishnevsky considered the question. "There are things a husband knows about a wife...things he does not have to ask in words."

Grunting from the effort, the Sorcerer pushed himself to his feet and came around the table. He leaned back against it and looked down at the Russian. "If we were to bring you and your family out, say to Florida, we would want to throw you a party." Torriti's face twisted into an unpleasant smile as he held out his hands, palms up. "In the US of A it's considered rude to come to a party empty-handed. Before I can get the folks I work for to agree to help you, you need to tell me what you plan to bring to the party, Comrade Vishnevsky."

The Russian glanced at the clock over the mantle, then looked back at Torriti. "I was stationed in Stockholm for two years and two months before being posted to Berlin. I can give you the names of our operatives in Stockholm, the addresses of our safe houses—"

"Exfiltrating three people from East Germany is extremely complicated."

"I can bring with me the order of battle of the KGB Karlshorst *residentura* in Berlin."

Jack noticed the Sorcerer's eyes misting over with disinterest; he made a mental note to add this piece of playacting to his repertoire. The Russian must have seen it, too, because he blurted out, "The KGB works under cover of Inspektsiia po voprosam bezopasnosti—what you call the Inspectorate for Security Questions. The Inspektsiia took over the Saint Antonius Hospital and has a staff of six hundred thirty full-time employees. The *resident*, General Ilichev, works under the cover of counselor to the Soviet Control Commission. The deputy *resident* is Ugor-Molody, Oskar— he is listed as chief of the visa section. General Ilichev is creating a separate illegals directorate within the Karlshorst-based First Chief Directorate—the designation is Directorate S. It will train and provide documents for KGB illegals assigned to Westwork."

The Sorcerer's lids seemed to close over his eyes out of sheer boredom.

The Russian dropped his cigarette on the floor and ground it out under a heel. "I can give you microphones...phone taps...listening posts."

The Sorcerer glanced across the room at Jack in obvious disappointment. Under the floorboards heavy caliber machine guns spat out bullets as the Russians stormed Guderian's tanks dug in along the Oder-Neisse line. "For us to get a KGB officer, assuming that's what you are, his wife, his son into West Berlin and then fly them out to the West will take an enormous effort. People will be asked to put their lives in jeopardy. An extremely large sum of money will be spent. Once in the West the officer in question will need to be taken care of, and generously. He will require a new identity, a bank account, a monthly stipend, a house on a quiet street in a remote city, an automobile." The Sorcerer stuffed his notebook back into a pocket. "If that's all you have, friend, I'm afraid we're both wasting our time. They say there are seven thousand spies in Berlin ready to put down cold cash for what our German friends call *Spielmaterial*. Peddle your wares to one of them. Maybe the French or the Israelis—"

Following every word from the wall, Jack grasped that Torriti was an artiste at this delectable game of espionage.

The Russian lowered his voice to a whisper. "For the last several months I have been assigned as the KGB liaison with the new German Democratic Republic intelligence service. They are setting up an office in a former school in the Pankow district of East Berlin near the restricted area where the Party and government leaders live. The new intelligence service, part of the Ministerium fuer Staatssicherheit, goes by a cover name—Institut fuer Wirtschaftswissenschaftliche Forschung, the Institute for Economic and Scientific Research. I can deliver you its order of battle down to the last paper clip. The chief is Ackermann, Anton, but it is said that his second in command, who is twenty-eight years of age, is being groomed as the eventual boss. His name is Wolf, Marcus. You can maybe find photographs of him—he covered the Nuremberg war crimes trials in 1945 for the Berlin radio station Berliner Rundfunk."

Jack, who had been pouring over the Berlin Base morgue files in the six weeks since he'd been posted to Germany, interrupted in what he hoped was a bored voice. "Wolf spent the war years in Moscow and speaks perfect Russian. Everyone at Karlshorst calls him by his Russian name, Misha."

Vishnevsky plunged on, dredging up names and dates and places in a desperate attempt to impress the Sorcerer. "The Main Directorate started out with eight Germans and four Soviet advisors but they are expanding rapidly. Within the Main Directorate there is a small independent unit called Abwehr, what you call counterintelligence. Its brief is to monitor and penetrate the West German security services. The Abwehr staff plans to use captured Nazi archives to blackmail prominent people in the West who have suppressed their Nazi pasts. High on their list of targets is Filbinger, Hans, the Baden-Württemberg political figure who, as a Nazi prosecutor, handed down death sentences for soldiers and civilians. The architect of this Westwork program is the current head of the Main Directorate, Stahlmann, Richard—"

Jack interrupted again. "Stahlmann's real name is Artur Illner. He's been a member of the German Communist Party since the First World War. He's operated under a cover alias for so long even his wife calls him Stahlmann."

The Sorcerer, pleased with Jack's ability to pick up on the game, rewarded him with a faint smile.

Jack's comments had rattled the Russian. He dragged an oversized hand-kerchief from a trouser pocket and mopped the back of his neck. "I am able to give you—" Vishnevsky hesitated. He had planned to dole out what he had, an increment of information in exchange for an increment of protection; he had planned to keep the best for when he was safely in the West and then use it to pry a generous settlement package out of his hosts. When he spoke again his words were barely audible. "I am able to reveal to you the identity of a Soviet agent in Britain's intelligence service. Someone high up in their MI6...."

To Jack, watching from the wall, it appeared as if the Sorcerer had frozen in place.

"You know his name?" Torriti asked casually.

"I know things about him that will allow you to identify him."

"Such as?"

"The precise date he was debriefed in Stockholm last summer. The approximate date he was debriefed in Zurich the previous winter. Two oper-ations that were exposed because of him—one involved an agent, the second involved a microphone. With these details even a child would be capable of identifying him."

"How do you happen to have this information?"

"I was serving in Stockholm last February when a KGB officer from Moscow Centre turned up. He traveled under the cover of a sports journal-ist from *Pravda*. He was flying in and out for a highly secret one-time con-tact. It was a cutout operation—he debriefed a Swedish national who debriefed the British mole. The KGB officer was the husband of my wife's sister. One night we invited him to dinner. He drank a great deal of Swedish vodka. He is my age and very competitive—he wanted to impress me. He boasted about his mission."

"What was the name of the KGB agent who came to Stockholm?"

"Zhitkin, Markel Sergeyevich."

"I would like to help you but I must have more than that to nibble on..."

The Russian agonized about it for a moment. "I will give you the micro-phone that went dry."

The Sorcerer, all business, returned to his seat, opened his notebook, uncapped a pen and looked up at the Russian. "Okay, let's talk turkey."

The hand-lettered sign taped to the armor-plated door of the Sorcerer's Berlin Base sanctum, two levels below ground in a brick building on a quiet, tree-lined street in the upper-crust suburb of Berlin-Dahlem, proclaimed the gospel according to Torriti: "Territory needs to be defended at the frontier, sport." Silwan II, his eyes pink with grogginess, his shoulder holster sagging into view under his embroidered Tyrolean jacket, sat slumped on a stool, the guardian of the Sorcerer's door and the water cooler filled with moonshine slivovitz across from it. From inside the office came the scratchy sound of a 78-rpm record belting out Björling arias; the Sorcerer, who had taken to describing himself as a certified paranoid with real enemies, kept the Victrola running at full blast on the off chance the Russians had succeeded in bugging the room. The walls on either side of his vast desk were lined with racks of loaded rifles and machine pistols he'd "liberated" over the years; one desk drawer was stuffed with hand-guns, another with boxes of cartridges. A round red-painted thermite bomb sat atop each of the three large office safes for the emergency destruction of files if the balloon went up and the Russians, a mortar shot away, invaded.

Hunched like a parenthesis over the message board on his blotter, the Sorcerer was putting the finishing touches on the overnight report to Washington. Jack, back from emptying the Sorcerer's burn bag into the incinerator, pushed through the door and flopped onto the couch under some gun racks. Looking up, Torriti squinted at Jack as if he were trying to place him. Then his eyes brightened. "So what did you make of him, sport?" he called over the music, his trigger finger absently stirring the ice in the whiskey glass.

"He worries me, Harvey," Jack called back. "It seems to me he hemmed and hawed his way through his biography when you put him through the wringer. Like when you asked him to describe the street he lived on during his first KGB posting in Brest-Litovsk. Like when you asked him the names of the instructors at the KGB's Diplomatic Institute in Moscow."

"So where were you raised, sport?"

"In a backwater called Jonestown, Pennsylvania. I went to high school in nearby Lebanon."

"And then, for the paltry sum of three-thousand-odd dollars per, which happens to be more than my secretary makes, you got what the hoi polloi call a higher education at Yale U."

Jack smoothed back the wings of his Cossack mustache with his fore-fingers. "'Hoi' already means 'the,' Harvey. So you don't really need to put a 'the' before 'hoi polloi' because there's already..." His voice trailed off as he spotted the pained expression lurking in the creases around the Sorcerer's eyes.

"Stop busting my balls, sport, and describe the street your high school was on."

"The street my high school was on. Sure. Well, I seem to recall it was lined with trees on which we used to tack dirty Burma-Shave limericks."

"What kind of trees were they? Was it a one-way street or a two-way street? What was on the corner, a stop sign or a stoplight? Was it a no-parking zone? What was across the street from the school?"

Jack examined the ceiling. "Houses were across the street. No, it must have been the public school in Jonestown that had houses across the street. Across from the high school in Lebanon was a playground. Or was that behind the school? The street was—" Jack screwed up his face. "I guess I see what you're driving at, Harvey."

Torriti took a swig of whiskey. "Let's say for argument's sake that Vishnevsky is a disinformation operation. When we walked him through his legend, he'd have it down pat, he'd be able to give you chapter and verse without sounding as if he made it up as he went along."

"How do you know the Russians aren't one jump ahead of you? How do you know they haven't programmed their plants to hem and haw their way through the legend?"

"The Russians are street-smart, sport, but they're not sidewalk-smart, which happens to be an expression I invented that means sophisticated. Besides which, my nose didn't twitch. My nose always twitches when it gets a whiff of a phony."

"Did you swallow the story about the *rezident* making a play for his wife?"

"Hey, on both sides of the Iron Curtain rank has its privileges. I mean, what's the point of being the head honcho at Karlshorst if you can't make a pass at the wife of one of your minions, especially one who's already in hot water for hiding the fact that he's part-Jewish? Listen up, sport, most of the defectors who come over try to tell us what they think we want to hear—how they've become disenchanted with Communism, how they're being suffocated by the lack of freedom, how they've come to understand that old Joe Stalin is a tyrant, that sort of bullshit."

"So what are you telling Washington, Harvey? That your nose didn't twitch?"

"I'm saying there is a seventy percent chance the fucker is who he says he is, so we should exfiltrate him. I'm saying I'll have the infrastructure ready in forty-eight hours. I'm saying the serial about the mole in MI6 needs to be explored because, if it's true, we're in a pretty fucking pickle; we've been sharing all our shit with the cousins forever, which means our secrets may be winding up, via the Brits, on some joker's desk in Moscow. And I'm reminding Washington, in case they get cold feet, that even if the defector is a black agent, it's still worth while bringing him across."

"I don't follow you there, Harvey."

The Sorcerer's fist hit a buzzer on the telephone console. His Night Owl, Miss Sipp, a thirtyish brunette with somnolent eyes that blinked very occasionally and very slowly, stuck her head into the office; she was something of a legend at Berlin Base for having fallen into a dead faint the day Torriti peeled off his shirt to show her the shrapnel wound that had decapitated the naked lady tattooed on his arm. Since then she had treated him as if he suffered from a communicable sexual disease, which is to say she held her breath in his presence and spent as little time as possible in his office. The Sorcerer pushed the message board across the desk. "Happy 1951, Miss Sipp. Have you made any New Year's resolutions?"

"I've promised myself I won't be working for you this time next year," she retorted.

Torriti nodded happily; he appreciated the female of the species who came equipped with a sharp tongue. "Do me a favor, honey, take this up to the radio shack. Tell Meech I want it enciphered on a one-time pad and sent priority. I want the cipher text filed in a burn bag and the original back on my desk in half an hour." As the Night Owl scurried from the office, Torriti splashed more whiskey into his glass, melted back into the leather chair he'd bought for a song on the black market and propped his pointed cowboy boots up on the desk. "So now I'll walk you through the delicate business of dealing with a defection, sport. Because you have a degree from Yale I'll talk real slow. Let's take the worst case scenario: let's say our Russian friend is a black agent come across to make us nibble at some bad information. If you want to make him seem like the real McCoy you send him over with a wife and kid but we're smart-assed Central Intelligence officers, right? We're not impressed by window dressing. When all is said and done there is only one way for a defector to establish his *bona fides*— he has to bring with him a certain amount of true information."

"So far so good. Once he delivers true information, especially true information that's important, we know he's a real defector, right?"

"Wrong, sport. A defector who delivers true information could still be a black agent. Which is another way of saying that a black agent also has to deliver a reasonable amount of true information in order to convince us that he is a genuine defector so that we'll swallow the shit he slips in between the true information."

Jack, intrigued by how intricate the game was, sat up on the couch and leaned forward. "They sure didn't teach us this in Washington, Harvey. So the fact that the defector delivers true information doesn't tell us if he's a true defector."

"Something like that."

"Question, Harvey. If all this is so, why do we bother taking defectors?"

"Because, first off, the defector may be genuine and his true information may be useful. The identity of a Russian mole in MI6 doesn't fall into your lap every day. Even if the defector's not genuine, if we play the game skillfully we can take the true information he brings with him and avoid the deception."

"My head's spinning, Harvey."

The Sorcerer snickered. "Yeah, well, basically what we do is we go round and round the mulberry bush until we become stark raving mad. In the end it's all a crazy intellectual game—to become a player you need to cross the frontier into what Mother calls a wilderness of mirrors."

Jack thought about this for a moment. "So who's this Mother you're always talking about?"

But the Sorcerer's head had already nodded onto his chest; balancing the whiskey glass on the bulge of his stomach, he had fallen asleep for the first time in two white nights.

The Sorcerer's overnight report, addressed—like all cables to Washington originating with Company stations abroad—to the Director, Central Intelligence, was hand-delivered to the desk of Jim Angleton in a metal folder with a distinctive red slash across it indicating that the material stashed between the covers was so incredibly sensitive it ought (as the mock directive posted on a second floor bulletin board put it) to be burned before reading. The single copy of the deciphered text had already been initialed by the Director and routed on for "Immediate Action" to Angleton, known by his in-house code name, Mother. The Director, Walter Bedell Smith, Eisenhower's crusty chief of staff at the Normandy invasion whose mood swings were said to alternate between anger and outrage, had scrawled across the message in a nearly illegible script that resembled hieroglyphics: "Sounds kosher to me. WBS." His Deputy Director/Operations, the World War II OSS spymaster Allen Dulles, had added: "For crying out loud, Jim, let's not let this one wriggle off the hook. AD."

The Sorcerer's report began with the usual Company rigmarole:

FROM:	Alice Reader
TO:	DCI
COPY TO:	Hugh Ashmead
SUBJECT:	AESNOWDROP
REFERENCE:	Your 28/12/50 re bringing home the bacon

Angleton, the Company's gaunt, stoop-shouldered, chain-smoking counterintelligence wizard, worked out of a large corner office in "L" building, one of the "temporary" wooden hulks that had washed up like jetsam next to the Reflecting Pool between the Lincoln and Washington monuments during World War II and had since been nicknamed, for reasons that were painfully apparent to the current tenants, "Cockroach Alley." From Angleton's windows there would have been a magnificent view of the Lincoln Memorial if anybody had bothered to crack the Venetian blinds. Thousands of three-by-five index cards crammed with trivia Mother had accumulated during his years on the counterintelligence beat—the 1935 graduating class of a Brest-Litovsk gymnasium, the pre-war curriculum of the Odessa Artillery School, the license plate numbers on the Zil limousines that ferried members of the Soviet elite to and from their Kremlin offices—lay scattered across the desk and tables and shelves. If there was a method to the madness, only Angleton himself had the key to it. Sorting through his precious cards, he was quickly able to come up with the answers to the Sorcerer's questions:

1. Yes, there is a street in Brest-Litovsk named after the Russian hero of the Napoleonic war, Mikhail Kutuzov; yes, there is a large statue of a blind-folded partisan woman tied to a stake and awaiting execution in the small park across Kutuzov Street from the apartment building complex where the local KGB officers are housed.

2. Yes, instructors named Piotr Maslov, Gennady Brykin and Johnreed Arkhangelsky were listed on the roster of the KGB Diplomatic Institute in Moscow in 1947.

3. Yes, the deputy *rezident* at KGB Karlshorst is named Oskar Ugor-Molody.

4. Yes, an entity using the appellation Institute for Economic and Scientific Research has set up shop in a former school in the Pankow district of East Berlin.

5. Yes, there is a sports journalist writing for *Pravda* under the byline M. Zhitkin. Unable to confirm the patronymic Sergeyevich. He is said to be married but unable to confirm that his wife is AESNOWDROP's sister-in-law.

6. No, we have no record of Zhitkin traveling to Stockholm last February, although his weekly *Pravda* column failed to appear during the third week of February.

7. Yes, the audio device Division D embedded in the arm of an easy chair purchased by the Soviet Embassy in The Hague and delivered to the ambassador's office was operational until 2245 hours on 12 November 1949, at which point it suddenly went dry. A friendly national subsequently visiting the Soviet Ambassador reported finding a small cavity in the under-

side of the arm of the chair, leading us to conclude that KGB counterintelligence had stumbled on the microphone during a routine sweep of the office and removed it. Transcripts of the Soviet Ambassador's conversations that dealt with Kremlin plans to pressure the Americans into withdrawing occupation forces from West Berlin had been narrowly circulated in American and British intelligence circles.

8. The consensus here is that AESNOWDROP has sufficiently established his *bona fides* to justify an exfiltration operation. He is being notified by my source to turn up at MARLBOROUGH with his wife and son, no valises, forty-eight hours from time of his last meeting.

Angleton signed off on the message and left it with his girl Friday to be enciphered using one of his departments private polyalphabetic codes. Back in his corner office, he frisked himself for cigarettes, stabbed one between his delicate lips and stared off into space without lighting it, a distracted scowl on his brow. For Angleton, the essence of counterintelligence was penetration: you penetrated the enemy's ranks, either by defections such as the one being organized now in Berlin or, more rarely, through the occasional agent in place who sent back material directly from the KGB inner sanctums, to get at their secrets. And the secret you most wanted to get at was whether they had penetrated you. The Russians had already succeeded in penetrating the American government and scientific communities; Elisabeth Bentley, a dowdy American Communist serving as a courier for her Soviet handler in Washington, had reeled off under FBI questioning the names of a hundred or so people linked to Soviet spy rings in the states and in Canada, among them Hiss, Fuchs, Gold, Sobell, Greenglass, the Rosenbergs. There was good reason to believe that the blueprint for the atomic bomb the Russians successfully tested in 1949 had been swiped from American A-bomb labs in Los Alamos. Angleton's job was to circle the Company with the counterintelligence wagons and make sure the Russians never got a toe in the CIA's door. Which is how Mother, riding high on his reputation as a World War II counterintelligence ace for the Office of Strategic Services, America's wartime spy agency, wound up looking over everyone's shoulder to monitor clandestine operations—a situation that rubbed a lot of people, including Torriti, the wrong way.

Angleton and Torriti had crossed paths—and swords—in 1944 when Mother, at twenty-seven already considered a master of the subtleties of the espionage game, had been in charge of rounding up stay-behind fascist agents as the Germans retreated up the boot of Italy. Torriti, who spoke the Sicilian dialect fluently and went out of his way to look like a Sicilian *caid*, had been acting as liaison with the Mafia clans that aided the allies in the invasion of Sicily and, later, the landings in Italy. In the months after the German surrender the Sorcerer was all for nurturing the Italian Social Democrats as a way of outflanking the local Communists, who received considerable support from Moscow and were threatening to make a strong showing in the next elections. Angleton, who was convinced that World War III started the day World War II ended, argued that if you scratched a Social Democrat you uncovered a Communist who took orders from the Kremlin. Angleton's reasoning prevailed with what the Sorcerer called the "poison Ivy League" crowd in Washington; the Company threw its considerable weight—in the form of tens of millions of dollars in cold cash, propaganda campaigns, and the occasional blackmail caper—behind the Christian Democrats, who eventually came out on top in the elections.

From Angleton's vantage point, the Sorcerer had enough experience with nuts-and-bolts field operations to put in the plumbing for a defection but was over his head in a situation requiring geopolitical sophistication; and he was too dense—and, in recent months, too drunk—to follow Mother into what T.S. Eliot had called, in his poem "Gerontion," "the wilderness of mirrors." Oh, Torriti grasped the first level of ambiguity well enough: that even black defectors brought with them real secrets to establish their *bona fides*. But there were other, more elegant, scenarios that only a handful of Company officers, Angleton foremost among them, could fathom. When you were dealing with a defector bearing true information, it was Mother's fervent conviction that you were obliged to keep in the back of your head the possibility that the greater the importance of the true information he brought with him, the bigger the deception the other side was trying to pull off. If you grasped this, it followed, as night the day, that you had to treat every success as if it were a potential calamity. There were OSS veterans working for the Company who just couldn't get a handle on the many levels of ambiguity involved in espionage operations; who whispered that Mother was a stark raving paranoid. "Ignore the old farts," Angleton's great British buddy would cackle when, over one of the regular weekly lunches at their Washington watering hole, Mother would allow that the whispering occasionally got him down. "Their m-m-mentalities grow inward like t-t-toenails."

A buzz on Angleton's intercom snapped him out of his reverie. A moment later a familiar face materialized at the door. It belonged to Mother's British friend and mentor, the MI6 liaison man in Washington. "Hello t-t-to you, Jimbo," Adrian cried with the exuberant upper-class stutter Angleton had first heard when the two had shared a cubbyhole in the Rose Garden Hotel on London's Ryder Street during the war. At the time

the ramshackle hotel had served as the nerve center for the combined counterintelligence operations of the American OSS and the British Secret Service,
MI6. The Brit, five years Angleton's senior and MI6's wartime counterintelligence specialist for the Iberian peninsula, had initiated the young American
corporal, fresh out of Yale and a virgin when it came to the business of
spying, into the mysteries of counterintelligence. Now, with a long string
of first rate exploits to his credit, both during the war and after, Adrian was a
rising star in the British intelligence firmament; office scuttlebutt touted him
as the next "C," the code-letter designation for the head of MI6.

"Speak of the devil, I was just thinking about you," Angleton said. "Take
a load off your feet and tell me what worlds you've conquered this morning."

The Brit cleared several shoe boxes filled with index cards off a government-issue chair and settled onto it across the desk from his American friend.
Angleton found a match and lit up. Between them an antique Tiffany lamp
beamed a pale yellow oval of light onto the reams of paper spilling from the
in-baskets. Angleton's thin face, coming in and out of focus behind a swirling
mist of cigarette smoke, appeared unusually satanic, or so the Brit thought.

"Just came from breakfast with your lord and master," Adrian
announced. "Meager fare—would have thought we were b-b-back at the
Connaught during rationing. He gave me a sales-cackle on some cockamamie scheme to infiltrate émigré agents into Alb-b-bania, of all places.
Seems as if the Yanks are counting on us to turn Malta into a staging base
and lay on a Spanish Armada of small boats. You'll want a copy of the
p-p-paper work if you're going to vet the operation?"

"Damn right I'll want a copy."

The Brit pulled two thick envelopes from the breast pocket of his
blazer. "Why don't you have these put through the p-p-pants presser while
we chew the fat."

Angleton buzzed for his secretary and nodded toward the envelopes in
his friend's hand. "Gloria, will you get these Thermofaxed right away and
give him back the originals on his way out." Half-Chicano by birth but an
Anglophile by dint of his wartime service in London and his affinity for the
Brits, Mother waved a hole in the smoke and spoke through it with the
barest trace of a clipped English accent acquired during a three-year stint at
an English college. "So what's your fix on our Bedell Smith?" he asked.

"Between you, me and the wall, Jimbo, I think he has a cool fishy eye and
a precision-tooled brain. He flipped through twenty-odd p-p-paragraphs on
the Albanian caper, dropped the paper onto his blotter and started quoting
chapter and verse from the d-d-damn thing. The bugger even referred to the

paragraphs by their bloody numbers. Christ, I had to spend the whole night memorizing the ropey d-d-document."

"No one denies he's smart—"

"The problem is he's a military man. Military men take it on faith that the shortest distance between two p-p-points is a straight line, which you and I, old boy, in our infinite wisdom, know to be a dodgy proposition. Me, I am an orthodox anti-Euclidean. There simply is no short distance between two points. There's only a meander. Bob's never your uncle; you leave p-p-point *A* and only the devil knows where you're going to wind up. To dot the *I*s, your 'Beetle' Smith started griping about how his operational chaps tell him one thing about resistance groups in Albania and his analysts, another."

"Knowing you, I'll lay odds you set him straight."

The Brit tilted the chair back until it was balanced on its hind legs. "As a matter of fact I did. I quoted chapter and verse from our illustrious former naval p-p-person. True genius, Churchill taught us, resides in the capacity to evaluate conflicting information. You have true genius, Jimbo. You have the ability to look at a mass of what seems like conflicting trivia and discern patterns. And patterns, as any spy worth his salt grasps, are the outer shells of conspiracies."

Angleton flashed one of his rare smiles. "You taught me everything I know," he said. And the two of them recited E.M. Forster's dictum, which had been posted over the Brit's desk during the Ryder Street days, in chorus: "Only connect!" And then they laughed together like public school boys caught in the act.

Angleton suppressed the start of a hacking cough by sucking air through his nostrils. "You're buttering me up," he finally decided, "which means you want something."

"To you, Jimbo, I'm the proverbial open book." Adrian righted his chair. "Your General Smith allowed as how he had an exfiltration in the works that would be of keen interest to me and mine. When I asked him for the dirty details he gave me leave to try and p-p-pry them out of you. So come clean, Jimbo. What do you have cooking on that notorious front b-b-burner of yours?"

Angleton began rummaging through the small mountain of paper on his desk for the Sorcerer's overnight cable. He found it under another cable from the Mexico City CIA Station; signed by two Company officers, E. Howard Hunt and William F. Buckley, Jr., it provided the outline for what was euphemistically called a "tangential special project."

"Frankly, you're the only Brit I'd trust with this," Angleton said, flapping Torriti's cable in the air to disperse the cigarette smoke.

"Thanks for that, Jimbo."

"Which means you'll have to give me your word you won't spill the beans to London before I say so."

"Must be bloody important for you to take that line."

"It is."

"You have my word, old boy. My lips are sealed until you unseal them."

Angleton slipped the cable across the desk to his British friend, who fitted a pair of National Health spectacles over his nose and held the report under the Tiffany lamp. After a moment his eyes tightened. "Christ, no wonder you don't want me to cable London. Handle with care, Jimbo—there's always the chance the Russian bloke is a dangle and his serial is p-p-part of a scheme to set my shop and yours at each other's throats. Remember when I scattered serials across Spain to convince the Germans we had a high-level mole *chez-eux*? The Abwehr spent half a year chasing their tails before they figured out the serials were phony."

"Everything Torriti pried out of him at their first meeting checked out."

"Including the microphone that went dry?"

Behind the cloud of smoke Angleton nodded. "I've already assigned a team to walk back the cat on the microphone in the Soviet Ambassador's chair in The Hague—the product was circulated narrowly but circulated all the same. You can count the people who knew where the product came from on the fingers of two hands."

Angleton's Brit, an old hand at defections, was all business. "We'll have to tread on eggshells, Jimbo. If there really is a mole in MI6, he'll jump ship the instant he smells trouble. The KGB will have contingency p-p-plans for this sort of thing. The trick'll be to keep the defection under wraps for as long as p-p-possible."

Angleton pulled another cigarette from the pack and lit it from the bitter end of the old one. "Torriti's going to smuggle the Russian and his family into West Berlin and fly them straight back to the states out of Tempelhof," he said. "I'll put people on the plane so that we can start sorting through the serials before word of the defection leaks. With any luck we'll be able to figure out the identity of the mole before KGB Karlshorst realizes the deputy to the chief of the First Chief Directorate has gone AWOL. Then the ball will be in MI6's court—you'll have to move fast on your end."

"Give me a name to go on," the Brit insisted, "we'll draw and quarter the son of a b-b-bitch."

Torriti had gone on the wagon for the exfiltration, which probably was a bad idea inasmuch as the lack of booze left him edgier than usual. He skulked through the small room of the safe house over the cinema the way a lion prowls a cage, plunging round and round so obsessively that Jack became

giddy watching him. At the oriel window the Fallen Angel kept an eye on
Sweet Jesus walking his muzzled lap dog in endless ovals in the street below.
Every now and then he'd remove his watch cap and scratch at the bald spot
on the top of his head, which meant he hadn't seen hide nor hair of the
Russian defector, hide nor hair of his wife or eleven year old son either.
Silwan II's radio, set on the floor against one wall, the antenna strung across
the room like a laundry line, burst into life and the voice of the Watcher in
the back row of the cinema could be heard whispering: "*Der Film ist fertig...*
in eight minutes. Where is somebody?"

"My nose is twitching to beat the band," the Sorcerer growled as he pulled
up short in front of the clock over the mantle. "Something's not right.
Russians, in my experience, always come late for meetings and early for defections." The pounding pulse of the imperturbable cuckoo ticking off the
seconds was suddenly more than Torriti could stomach. Snatching his pearl-
handled revolver from the shoulder holster, he grasped it by the long barrel
and slammed the grip into the clock, decapitating the cuckoo, shattering the
mechanism. "At least it's quiet enough to think straight," he announced, preempting the question Jack would have posed if he had worked up the nerve.

They had made their way into the Soviet Sector of East Berlin in the
usual way: Torriti and Jack lying prone in the false compartment under the
roof of a small Studebaker truck that had passed through a little-used checkpoint on one of its regular runs delivering sacks of bone meal fertilizer;
Sweet Jesus and the Fallen Angel, dressed as German workers, mingling with
the river of people returning through the Friedrichstrasse Station after a day
of digging sewage trenches in the western part of the city. Sweet Jesus had
had a close call when one of the smartly dressed East German *Volkspolizei*
patrolling beyond the turnstiles demanded his workplace pass and then
thumbed through its pages to make sure it bore the appropriate stamps.
Sweet Jesus, who once worked as a cook for an SS unit in Rumania during
the war and spoke flawless German, had mumbled the right answers to
the *Volkspolizei*'s brittle questions and was sent on his way.

Now the plumbing for the exfiltration was in place. The defector
Vishnevsky and his wife would be smuggled out in the fertilizer truck, which
was waiting for them in an unlighted alleyway around the corner from the cinema; the driver, a Polish national rumored to have a German wife in West
Berlin and a Russian mistress in the eastern part of the city, had often returned
from one of his fertilizer runs well after midnight, provoking ribald quips from
the German frontier guards. An agent of the French Service de
Documentation Extérieure et de Contre-Espionnage (SDECE), carrying a

diplomatic passport identifying him as an assistant cultural attaché, was scheduled to pass close to the cinema at midnight on his way back from a dinner at the Soviet embassy. Allied diplomats refused to recognize the authority of the East German police and never stopped for passport controls. His Citroën, with diplomatic license plates and a small French flag flying from one of its teardrop fenders, would spirit the Sorcerer and Jack past the border guards back into West Berlin. The two Rumanians would go to ground in East Berlin and return to the west in the morning when the workers began to cross over for the day. Which left Vishnevsky's eleven-year-old son: the Sorcerer had arranged for the boy to be smuggled across by a Dutch Egyptologist who had come into East Germany, accompanied by his wife, to date artifacts in an East Berlin museum. The Dutch couple would cross back into West Berlin on a forged family passport with a blurred photo taken when the boy was supposed to have been five years younger, and a visa for the Dutch father, his wife and 10-year-old boy stamped into its very frayed pages. The Sorcerer had been through this drill half a dozen times; the sleepy East German *Volkspolizei* manning the checkpoints had always waved the family through with a perfunctory glance at the passport photo. Once over the border, the three Russians would be whisked to the Tempelhof airport in West Berlin and flown in a US Air Force cargo plane to the defector reception center in Frankfurt, Germany, and from there on to Andrews Air Force Base in Maryland.

But the success of the exfiltration hinged on Vishnevsky and his family shaking off their Watchers—there were KGB people at Karlshorst who did nothing but keep track of the other KGB people—and making their way to the safe house over the cinema. Torriti resumed his prowl, stopping once every orbit to peer over the Fallen Angel's shoulder at the street.

Another burst of static came from the radio on the floor. "Film *ist zu Ende*. All must leave. *Gute Nacht* to you. Please for God's sake remember to deposit the *Geld* in my account."

In the street below figures bundled into long overcoats hurried away from the cinema. Sweet Jesus, stamping his feet under a vapor lamp, glanced up at the faint light in the oriel window under the eaves and hiked his shoulders in an apprehensive shrug. Jack pulled the antenna down and started packing it away in the radio's carrying case. "How long do you figure on waiting, Harvey?" he asked.

The Sorcerer, sweating from alcohol deprivation, turned on Jack. "We wait until I decide to stop waiting," he snapped.

The Irishman in Jack stood his ground. "He was supposed to get here before the film ended." And he added quietly, "If he hasn't shown up by now chances are he's not going to show. If he hasn't been blown we can reschedule the exfiltration for another night."

The Fallen Angel said anxiously, "If the Russian was blown, the safe house maybe was blown. Which leaves us up the creek filled with shit, chief."

Torriti screwed up his face until his eyes were reduced to slits. He knew they were right; not only was the Russian not going to turn up but it had become imprudent for them to hang in there. "Okay, we give him five minutes and we head for home," he said.

Time passed with excruciating slowness, or so it seemed to Jack as he kept his eyes fixed on the second hand of his Bulova. At the window, Silwan II, rolling his head from side to side, humming an ancient Rumanian liturgical chant under his breath, surveyed the street. Suddenly he pressed his forehead against the pane and grabbed his stomach. "Holy Mother of God," he rasped, "Sweet Jesus went and picked up the dog."

"Damnation," cried Jack, who knew what the signal meant.

The Sorcerer, freezing in mid-prowl, decided he badly needed a swig of medicinal whiskey to clear the cobwebs from his head. "Into every life a little rain must fall," he groaned.

The Fallen Angel called, "Oh, yeah, here they come—one, two, oh shit, seven, wait, eight *Volkspolizei* wagons have turned into the street. Sweet Jesus is disappearing himself around the corner."

"Time for us to disappear ourselves around a corner, too," Torriti announced. He grabbed his rumpled overcoat off the back of a chair, Jack crammed the radio into its satchel and the three of them, with Jack in the lead and the Sorcerer puffing along behind him, ducked through the door and started up the narrow stairs. It was the route they would have taken if the Russian defectors had turned up. From three floors below came the clamor of rifle butts pounding on the heavy double doors of the cinema, then muffled shouts in German as the *Volkspolizei*—accompanied by a handful of KGB agents—spread out through the building.

At the top of the stairs Jack unbolted the steel door and pushed it open with his shoulder. A gust of wintry night air slammed into his face, bringing tears to his eyes. Overhead a half moon filled the rooftop with shadows. Below, in the toilet off the cinema, heavy boots kicked in the false door at the back of the broom closet and started lumbering up the narrow stairs. Once Jack and Torriti were on the roof, the Fallen Angel eased the door closed and quietly slid home the two bolts on it. The Sorcerer, breathing heavily from the exertion, managed to spit out, "That'll slow the fuckers down." The three made their way diagonally across the slippery shingles. Silwan II helped the Sorcerer over a low wall and led the way across the next roof to a line of brick chimneys, then swung a leg over the side of a wall and scrambled down the wooden ladder he had planted there when the Sorcerer had laid in the plumbing for the exfiltration. When his turn came Jack started down the ladder, then jumped the rest of the way to the roof below. The Sorcerer, gingerly stabbing the air with his foot to locate the next rung, climbed down after them.

The three of them squatted for a moment, listening to the icy wind whistling over the rooftops. With the adrenalin flowing and a pulse pounding in his ear, Jack asked himself if he was frightened; he was quite pleased to discover that he wasn't. From somewhere below came guttural explicatives in German. Then a door leading to the roof was flung open and two silvery silhouettes appeared. The beams from two flashlights swept across the chimneys and illuminated the wooden ladder. One of the silhouettes grunted something in Russian. From a pocket the Fallen Angel produced an old 9 mm Beretta he had once stripped from the body of an Italian fascist whose throat he'd slit near Patras in Greece. A subsonic handgun suited to in-fighting, the Beretta was fitted with a stubby silencer on the end of the barrel. Torriti scratched Silwan II on the back of the neck and, pressing his lips to his ear, whispered, "Only shoot the one in uniform."

Bracing his right wrist in his left hand, the Fallen Angel drew a bead on the taller of the two figures and pulled back on the hairpin trigger. Jack heard a quick hiss, as if air had been let out of a tire. One of the two flashlights clattered to the roof. The figure who had been holding it seemed to melt into the shadow of the ground. Breathing heavily, the other man thrust his two arms, one holding the flashlight, the other a pistol, high over his head. "I know it is you, Torriti," he called in a husky voice. "Not to shoot. I am KGB."

Jack's blood was up. "Jesus H. Christ, shoot the fucker!"

The Sorcerer pressed Silwan II's gun arm down. "Germans are fair game but KGB is another story. We don't shoot them, they don't shoot us." To the Russian he called, "Drop your weapon."

The Russian, a burly figure wearing a civilian overcoat and a fedora, must have known what was coming because he turned around and carefully set his flashlight and handgun on the ground. Straightening, he removed his fedora and waited.

Moving on the balls of his feet, the Fallen Angel crossed the roof and stepped up behind the Russian and brought the butt of the Beretta sharply down across his skull over an ear—hard enough to give him splitting headaches for the rest of his life but not hard enough to kill him. The Rumanian deftly caught the Russian under the armpits and lowered him to the roof.

Moments later the three of them were clambering down the dimly lit staircase of the apartment building, then darting through a corridor reeking of urine and out a back door to an alley filled with garbage cans piled one on top of another. Hidden behind the garbage cans was the fertilizer truck. Without a word the Fallen Angel vanished down the alley into the darkness. Torriti and Jack climbed up into the compartment under the false roof of the vehicle and pulled the trap-ladder closed after them. The engine coughed softly into life and the truck, running on parking lights, eased out of the alley and headed through the silent back streets of East Berlin toward a Pankow crossing point and the French sector of the divided city beyond it.

Even the old hands at Berlin Base had never seen the Sorcerer so worked up. "I don't fucking believe it," he railed, his hoarse cries echoing through the underground corridors, "the KGB fucker on the roof even knew my *name*." Torriti slopped some whiskey into a glass, tossed it into the back of his throat and gargled before swallowing. The sting of the booze calmed him down. "Okay," he instructed his Night Owl, "walk me through it real slow-like."

Miss Sipp, sitting on the couch, crossed her legs and began citing chapter and verse from the raw operations log clipped to the message board. She had to raise her voice to make herself heard over Tito Gobbi's 78-rpm interpretation of Scarpia. It was an indication of Torriti's mental state that he didn't seem to catch a glimpse of the erotic frontier where the top of her stocking fastened to the strap of a garter belt.

"Item number one," began Miss Sipp, her voice vibrating with suppressed musicality. (She had actually signed on as Torriti's Night Owl in order to pay for singing lessons at the Berlin Opera, which ended when her teacher informed her that she had almost as much talent as his rooster.) "The listening post at Berlin Base noticed an increase in radio traffic between Moscow and Karlshorst, and vice versa, eighty-five minutes before the defector and his family were due to show up at the safe house."

"Bastards were getting their marching orders from Uncle Joe," the Sorcerer snarled.

"Item number two: The sister of the cleaning woman who works at the hotel near Karlshorst called her contact in West Berlin, who called us to say the Russians were running around like chickens without a head, i.e., something was up."

"What time was that?" Jack, leaning against a wall, wanted to know.

"D-hour minus sixty minutes, give or take."

"The fuckers knew there was going to be a defection," figured the

Sorcerer, talking more to himself than to the eight people who had crowded into his office for the wake-like postmortem. "But they didn't get ahold of that information until late in the game."

"Maybe Vishnevsky lost his nerve," Jack suggested. "Maybe he was perspiring so much he drew attention to himself."

The Sorcerer batted the possibility away with the back of his hand. "He was a tough cookie, sport. He didn't come that far to fink out at the last moment."

"Maybe he told his wife and she lost her nerve."

Torriti's brow wrinkled in concentration. Then he shook his head once. "He'd thought it all through. Remember when he asked me if I had a microphone running? He was testing me. He would have tested his wife before he brought her in on the defection. If he thought she'd lose her nerve he would have skipped without her. As for the kid, all he had to know was that they were going to see a late movie."

"There's another angle," Jack said. "The wife may or may not have gone to bed with the *rezident*—either way she was probably afraid of him, not to mention ashamed of the trouble she'd brought down on her husband after he confronted the *rezident*. All of which could have given her enough motivation to defect with Vishnevsky."

"There's smoke coming out your ears, sport," Torriti said, but it was easy to see he was pleased with his Apprentice. The Sorcerer closed his eyes and raised his nose in the direction of Miss Sipp. She glanced down at the log sheet balanced on her knees.

"Oh dear, where was I? Ah. Item number three: The Rabbi reported in from the German-Jewish Cultural Center to say that East Germany's Hauptverwaltung Aufklärung troops were mustering next to vehicles parked in the courtyard behind the school in the Pankow district. That was D-hour minus thirty-five minutes."

"The time frame would seem to suggest that the Russians were the ones who were tipped off, as opposed to the Germans."

All heads turned toward the speaker, a relative newcomer to Berlin Base, E. Winstrom Ebbitt II. A big, broad-shouldered New York attorney who had seen action with the OSS during the last months of the war, Ebby, as his friends called him, had recently signed on with the Company and had been posted to Berlin to run émigré agents into the "denied areas" of Eastern Europe and the Soviet Union. He had spent the entire night in the base's radio shack, waiting for two of his "Joes" who had parachuted into Poland to come on the air. Curious to hear about the aborted defection, he'd drifted into the Sorcerer's office when he learned there would be an early morning wake. "My guess is the Russians probably brought *their* Germans in at the last moment," Ebby added, "because they don't trust them any more than we trust our Germans."

The Sorcerer fixed a malevolent eye on the young man with long wavy hair and fancy wide suspenders sitting atop one of the office safes and toying with a red thermite canister. "Elementary deduction, my dear Watson," Torriti said mockingly. "Careful that doohickey doesn't blow up in your puss. By the way, did you get ahold of the lambs you sent to the slaughter?"

"Afraid I haven't, Harvey. They missed the time slot. There's another one tomorrow night."

"Like I said, it's the goddamn Goths who are winning the goddamn war." Torriti turned his attention back to Miss Sipp.

"Item number four: Gehlen's night duty officer at Pullach rang us on the red phone to say that one of their agents in the Soviet zone who is good at *Augenerkundung*"—the Night Owl raised her eyes and translated for the benefit of those in the room who didn't speak German—"that means 'eye spying'; the *Augenerkundung* had just spotted wagons filled with *Volkspolizei* throwing up roadblocks across the approaches to the Soviet air base at Eberswalde. Minutes later—just about the time the defector was supposed to present his warm body at your safe house, Mr. Torriti—the *Augenerkundung* spotted a convoy of Tatra limousines pulling on to the runway from a little used entrance in the chainlink fence. Sandwiched in the middle of the convoy was a brown military ambulance. Dozens of civilians—KGB heavies, judging by the cut of their trousers, so said the Watcher—spilled out of the Tatras. Two stretchers with bodies strapped onto them were taken out of the ambulance and carried up a ramp into the plane parked, with its engines revving, at the end of the runway." Miss Sipp looked up and said with a bright smile, "That means Vishnevsky and his wife were still alive at this point. I mean"—her smile faded, her voice faltered—"if they were deceased they wouldn't have needed to strap them onto stretchers, would they have?"

"That still leaves the kid unaccounted for," noted Jack.

"If you'd let me finish," the Night Owl said huffily, "I'll give you the kid, too." She turned back toward the Sorcerer and recrossed her legs; this time the gesture provoked a flicker of interest from his restless eyes. "A boy—the Watcher estimated he was somewhere between ten and fifteen years of age; he said it was difficult to tell because of all the clothing the child was wearing—was pulled from one of the Tatras and, accompanied by two heavies, one holding him under each armpit, led up the ramp onto the plane. The boy was sobbing and crying out 'papa' in Russian, which led Gehlen's duty officer to conclude that the two people strapped onto the stretchers must have been Russians."

The Sorcerer palm came down on his desk in admiration. "Fucking Gehlen gives good value for the bucks we provide. Just think of it, he had a Watcher close enough to *hear* the boy call out for his papa. Probably has one of the fucking Hauptverwaltung Aufklärung storm troopers on his payroll. We fucking pay through the nose, how come we don't get Watchers of this quality?"

"Gehlen was supposed to have planted one of his Fremde Heere Ost agents in Stalin's inner circle during the war," remarked the Berlin Base archivist, a former Yale librarian named Rosemarie Kitchen.

"Lot of good it did him," quipped Ebby, which got a titter around the room.

"I don't fucking see what there is to laugh about," Torriti exploded. His eyes, suddenly blazing, were fixed on Ebby. "The frigging Russians were tipped off—the KGB pricks know when and where and who. Vishnevsky's got a rendezvous with a bullet fired at point blank range into the nape of his neck, and that bothers me, okay? It bothers me that he counted on me to get him out and I didn't do it. It bothers me that I almost didn't get myself and Jack and the two Silwans out neither. All of which means we're being jerked off by a fucking mole. How come almost all the agents we drop into Czechoslovakia or Rumania wind up in front of firing squads? How come the émigrés we slip into Poland don't radio back to say they're having a nice vacation, PS regards to Uncle Harvey? How come the fucking KGB seems to know what we're doing before we know what we're doing?"

Torriti breathed deeply through his nostrils; to the people crowded into the room it came across like a bugle call to action. "Okay, here's what we do. For starters I want the names of everyone, from fucking Bedell Smith on down, in Washington and in Berlin Base, who knew we were going to pull out a defector who claimed he could identify a Soviet mole in MI6. I want the names of the secretaries who typed the fucking messages, I want the names of the code clerks who enciphered or deciphered them, I want the names of the housekeepers who burned the fucking typewriter ribbons."

Miss Sipp, scrawling shorthand across the lined pages of the night order book, looked up, her eyes watery with fatigue. "What kind of priority should I put on this, Mr. Torriti? It's seven hours earlier in DC. They're fast asleep there."

"Ticket it *Flash*," snapped the Sorcerer. "Wake the fuckers up."

Holding fort at table number 41, seated facing a large mirror on the back wall so that he could keep track of the other customers in La Niçoise, his watering hole on Wisconsin Avenue in upper Georgetown, Mother polished off the Harper bourbon and, catching the waiter's eye, signaled that he was ready to switch to double martinis. Adrian, no slouch when it came to lunchtime lubricants, clinked glasses with him when the first ones were set on the table. "Those were the d-d-days," he told the visiting fireman from London, a junior minister who had just gotten the Company to foot the bill for turning Malta into an Albania ops staging base. "We all used to climb up to the roof of the Rose Garden, whiskeys in our p-p-paws, to watch the German doodlebugs coming in. Christ, if one of them had come down in Ryder Street it would have wiped out half our spooks."

"From a distance the V-1s sounded like sewing machines," Angleton recalled. "There was a moment of utter silence before they started down. Then came the explosion. If it landed close enough you'd feel the building quake."

"It was the silence I detested most," Adrian said emotionally. "To this day I can't stand utter silence. Which I suppose is why I talk so damn much."

"All that before my time, I'm afraid," the visiting fireman muttered. "Rough war, was it?" He pushed back a very starched cuff and glanced quickly at a very expensive watch that kept track of the phase of the moon. Leaning toward Adrian, he inquired, "Oughtn't we to order?"

Adrian ignored the question. "Nights were b-b-best," he prattled on. "Remember how our searchlights would stab at the sky stalking the Hun bombers? When they locked onto one it looked like a giant bloody moth pinned in the beam."

"I say, isn't that your Mr. Hoover who's just come in? Who's the chap with him?"

Adrian peered over the top of his National Health spectacles. "Search me."

Angleton studied the newcomer in the mirror. "It's Senator Kefauver," he said. He raised three fingers for another round of drinks. "I had a bachelor flat at Craven Hill near Paddington," he reminded Adrian. "Hardly ever went there. Spent most nights on a cot in my cubbyhole."

"He was nose to the grindstone even then," Adrian told the visiting fireman. "Couldn't pry him away. Poke your head in any hour day or night, he'd be puzzling over those bloody file cards of his, trying to solve the riddle."

"Know what they say about all work and no play," the visiting fireman observed brightly.

Adrian cocked his head. "Quite frankly, I don't," he said. "What do they say?"

"Well, I'm actually not quite sure myself—something about Jack turning into a dull chap. Some such thing."

"Jack who?" Mother asked with a bewildered frown.

"Did I say Jack?" the fireman inquired with a flustered half-smile. "Oh dear, I suppose any Jack will do."

"Christ, Jimbo, I thought I'd split my trousers when you asked him who Jack was," Adrian said after the visiting fireman, his cuff worn from glancing at his wristwatch, was put out of his misery and allowed to head to Foggy Bottom for an important four o'clock meeting.

They were sampling a Calvados that the sommelier had laid in especially for Angleton. After a moment Mother excused himself and darted from the restaurant to call his secretary from the tailor's shop next door; he didn't want to risk talking on one of the restaurant's phones for fear it might have been tapped by the Russians. On his way back to the table he was waylaid by Monsieur Andrieux, the Washington station chief for the French SDECE, who sprang to his feet and pumped Mother's hand as he funneled secrets into his ear. It was several minutes before Angleton could pry his fingers free and make his way to table 41. Sliding onto the chair, holding up the Calvados glass for a refill, he murmured to Adrian, "French've been treating me like a big wheel ever since they pinned a Légion d'Honneur on my chest."

"Frogs are a race apart," Adrian crabbed as he jammed the back of his hand against his mouth to stifle a belch. "Heard one of their senior spooks vet an op we were proposing to run against the French Communists—he allowed as how it would probably work in practice but he doubted it would work in theory. Sorry about my junior minister, Jimbo. They say he's very good at what he does. Not sure what he does, actually. Someone had to give him grub. Now that he's gone we can talk shop. Any news from Berlin?"

Mother studied his friend across the table. "You're not going to like it."

"Try me."

"*Amicitia nostra dissoluta est.* 'Our friendship is dissolved.' I am on to you and your KGB friends!"

The Brit, who knew a joke when he heard one, chortled with pleasure as he identified the quotation. "Nero's telegram to Seneca when he decided time had come for his tutor to commit hari-kari. Christ, Jimbo, only surprised I was able to p-p-pull the wool over your eyes this long. Seriously, what happened to your Russian coming across in Berlin?"

"The Sorcerer woke me up late last night with a cable marked *Flash*—been going back and forth with him since. Vishnevsky never showed up. The KGB did. Things turned nasty. Torriti hung around longer than he should have—had to shoot one of the Germans and hit a Russian over the head to get himself out of a tight corner. Vishnevsky and his wife, drugged probably, were hauled back to Moscow to face the music. Kid, too."

"Christ, what went wrong?"

"You tell me."

"What about Vishnevsky's serials? What about the mole in MI6?"

For answer, one of Mother's nicotine-stained fingers went round and round the rim of the snifter until a melancholy moan emerged from the glass.

After a moment Adrian said thoughtfully, "Hard cheese, this. I'd better p-p-pass Vishnevsky's serials on to C—there's not enough to dine out on but he can work up an appetite. Do I have it right, Jimbo? The Russian chaps debriefed someone from MI6 in Stockholm last summer, in Zurich the winter before. There were two blown operations that could finger him—one involved an agent, the other a microphone in The Hague—"

"I haven't unsealed your lips," Angleton reminded his friend.

"He'll take my guts for garters if he gets wind I knew and didn't tell him."

"He won't hear it from me."

"What's to be gained waiting?"

"If Vishnevsky wasn't feeding us drivel, if there is a mole in MI6, it could be anybody, up to and including C himself."

"I would have thought C was above and beyond." The Brit shrugged. "I hope to Christ you know what you're doing."

A waiter brought over a silver salver with their bill folded on it . Adrian reached for the check but Angleton was quicker. "King got the last one," he said. "Let me get this."

Angleton's luncheon partner, Harold Adrian Russell Philby—Kim to his colleagues in MI6, Adrian to a handful of old Ryder Street pals like Angleton—managed a faint smiled. "First Malta. Now lunch. Seems as if we're fated to live off Yankee largess."

Jack McAuliffe had taken Ebby slumming to a posh cabaret called Die Pfeffermühle—The Peppermill—off the Kurfürstendamm, West Berlin's main drag sizzling with neon. The joint was crawling with diplomats and spies and businessmen from the four powers that occupied Berlin. On the small stage a transvestite, wearing what the Germans called a *Fahne,* a cheap gaudy dress, rattled off one-liners and then laughed at them so hard his stomach rippled. "For God's sake, don't laugh at anti-Soviet jokes," the comic warned, wagging a finger at an imaginary companion. "You'll get three years in jail." Raising his voice half an octave, he mimicked the friend's reply. "That's better than three years in one of those new high-rise apartments in Friedrichsmain." Some upper-class Brits drinking at a corner table roared at a joke one of them had told. The comedian, thinking the laughter was for him, curtsied in their direction.

At a small table near the toilets Jack scraped the foam off a mug with his forefinger, angled back his head and, his Adam's apple bobbing, drained off the beer in one long swig. Wiping his lips with the back of his hand, he carefully set the empty mug down next to the two others he'd already knocked back. "Jesus H. Christ, Ebby, you're coming down too hard on him," he told his friend. "The Sorcerer's like a wild dog you come across in the field. You need to stand dead still and let him sniff your trousers, your shoes, before he'll start to accept you."

"It's the drinking that rubs me the wrong way," Ebby said. "I don't see how a drunk can run Berlin Base."

"The booze is his pain killer. He hurts, Ebby. He was in Bucharest at the end of the war—he served under the Wiz when Wisner ran the OSS station there. He saw the Soviet boxcars hauling off Rumanians who had sided with Germany to Siberian prison camps. He heard the cries of the prisoners, he helped bury the ones who killed themselves rather than board the trains. It marked him for life. For him the battle against Communism is a personal crusade—it's the forces of good versus the forces of evil. Right now evil's got the upper hand and it's killing him."

"So he drinks."

"Yeah. He drinks. But that doesn't stop him from performing on a very high level. The alcohol feeds his genius. If the KGB ever cornered me on an East Berlin rooftop, Harvey's the man I'd want next to me."

The two exchanged knowing looks; Ebby had heard scuttlebutt about the close call on the roof after the aborted defection.

On the other side of the room a middle-aged Russian attaché wearing a double-breasted suit jacket with enormous lapels staggered drunkenly to his feet and began belting out, in Russian, a popular song called "Moscow Nights." At the bar two American foreign service officers, both recent graduates of Yale, pushed themselves off their stools and started singing Kipling's original words to what later became the Yale Whiffenpoof song.

We have done with Hope and Honor,
we are lost to Love and Truth...

Jack leaped to his feet and sang along with them.

We are dropping down the ladder rung by rung...

Ebby, who had done his undergraduate work at Yale before going on to Columbia Law, stood up and joined them.

And the measure of our torment is the measure of our youth,
God help us, for we knew the worst too young!

Half a dozen American civilians sitting around a large table in a corner turned to listen. Several added their voices to the chorus.

Our shame is clean repentance
for the crime that brought the sentence,
Our pride it is to know no spur of pride.

As they neared the end of the song others around the cabaret joined in. The transvestite comic, furious, stalked off the stage.

And the Curse of Reuben holds us
till an alien turf enfolds us
And we die, and none can tell Them where we died.

By now Americans all over the cabaret were on their feet, waving mugs over their heads as they bellowed out the refrain. The Russian and East European diplomats looked on in amused bewilderment.

GENTLEMEN-RANKERS OUT ON THE SPREE,
DAMNED FROM HERE TO ETERNITY,
GOD HA' MERCI ON SUCH AS WE,
BAA! YAH! BAH!

"We're all mad here, Ebby." Jack had to holler to be heard over the riotous applause. "I'm mad. You're mad. Question is: How the hell did I end up in this madhouse?"

"From what you told me back at the Cloud Club," Ebby shouted, "your big mistake was saying yes when the coach offered you and your rowing pal the Green Cup down at Mory's."

PART ONE

PRIMING THE GUN

In another moment down went Alice after it, never once considering how in the world she was to get out again.

Snapshot: a three-by-five-inch black-and-white photograph turned sepia with age. Hand-printed across the scalloped white border is a faded caption: "Jack & Leo & Stella after The Race but before The Fall." There is a date but it has been smudged and is illegible. In the photograph two men in their early twenties, brandishing long oars draped with the shirts they won off the backs of the Harvard crew, are posing in front of a slender racing shell. Standing slightly apart, a thin woman wearing a knee-length skirt and a man's varsity sweater has been caught brushing the hair out of her wide, anxious eyes with the splayed fingers of her left hand. The two young men are dressed identically in boating sneakers, shorts, and sleeveless undershirts, each with a large Y on the chest. The taller of the young men, sporting a Cossack mustache, clutches an open bottle of Champagne by its throat. His head is angled toward the shirt flying like a captured pennant from the blade of his oar but his eyes are devouring the girl.

1

RACING NECK AND NECK BETWEEN THE BUOYS, THE TWO SLEEK-SCULLED coxed eights skidded down the mirror-still surface of the Thames. Languid gusts impregnated with the salty aroma of the sea and the hoarse shrieks from the students on the bank of the river drifted across their bows. Rowing stroke for Yale, Jack McAuliffe feathered an instant too soon and caught a crab and heard the cox, Leo Kritzky, swear under his breath. At the four-fifths mark Leo pushed the pace to a sprint. Several of the oarsman crewing behind Jack started punctuating each stroke with rasping grunts. Sliding on the seat until his knees grazed his armpits, Jack made a clean catch and felt the blade lock onto a swell of river water. A splinter of pain stabbed at the rib that had mended and broken and mended again. Blinking away the ache in his rib cage, he hauled back on the haft of the oar slick with blood from a burst blister. Slivers of sunlight glancing off the river blinded him for an instant. When he was able to see he caught a glimpse of the Harvard eight riding on its inverted reflection, its oars catching and feathering and squaring in flawless synchronization. The cox must have decided the Harvard boat was slipping ahead because he notched up the strokes to forty-eight per minute. Balanced on the knife edge of the keel, coiling and uncoiling his limbs in long fluid motions, Jack abandoned himself to the cadence of pain. When the Yale scull soared across the finish line just ahead of the Crimson's hull, he slumped over his oar and tried to recollect what whim of craziness had pushed him to go out for Crew.

"Rowing," Skip Waltz shouted over the din of the New Haven railroad station, "is a great training ground for real life in the sense that you're taking something that is essentially very simple and perfecting it."

"In your view, Coach Waltz, what's the most difficult moment of a race?" called the reporter from the Yale student newspaper.

Waltz screwed up his lips. "I'd say it's when you reach for the next stroke, because you're actually going in one direction and the hull's going in the opposite direction. I always tell my men that rowing is a metaphor for life. If you're not perfectly balanced over the keel the boat will wobble and the race will slip through your fingers." The coach glanced at the station clock and said, "What do you say we wrap this up, boys," and made his way across the platform to his crew, who were pulling their duffle bags off a low baggage cart. Waltz rummaged in his trouser pocket for a dime and gave it to the Negro porter, who touched the brim of his red cap in thanks. "Anyone for a Green Cup down at Mory's?" Waltz said.

"Mind if I take a rain check, coach?" one of the oarsman asked. "I have a philosophy oral at the crack of eleven tomorrow and I still haven't read Kant's *Critique of Pure Reason*."

One after another the rowers begged off and headed back to college with their duffel bags slung from their shoulders. Only Jack and Leo and Leo's girl, Stella, took the coach up on his invitation. Waltz collected his Frazer Vagabond from the parking lot down the street and brought it around to the station entrance. Leo and Jack tossed their duffle bags into the trunk and the three of them piled in.

Mory's was nearly deserted when they got there. Two waiters and a handful of students, all wearing ties and jackets, applauded the victory over the arch enemy, Harvard. "A Green Cup for my people," the coach called as the four of them pulled up high-backed wooden chairs around a small table. For a while they talked about scull weights and blade shapes and the ideal length of the slide along which the oarsman travels with each stroke.

"Is it true that Yale rowers invented the slide?" Jack inquired.

"You bet," Coach Waltz said. "It was back in the 1880s. Before then oarsmen used to grease their trousers and slide their butts up and back along a wooden plank set in the hull."

When the Green Cup arrived Coach Waltz raised the cup and saluted the two crewmen. Cocking his head, he casually asked them if they spoke any foreign languages. It turned out that Jack was fluent in German and could get by in Spanish; Leo, an ardent, angry young man who had been raised in a family of anti-Communist Russian-Jewish immigrants and was majoring in Slavic languages and history, on a full scholarship, spoke Russian and Yiddish like a native and Italian like a tourist. The coach took this in with a nod, then asked whether they found time to keep up with the international situation, and when they both said yes he steered the conversation to the 1948 Communist coup d'état in Czechoslovakia and Cardinal Mindszenty's recent death sentence in Red Hungary. Both young men agreed that if the Americans and the British didn't draw a line across Europe and defend it, Russian tanks would sweep through Germany and France to the English Channel. Waltz asked what they thought about the Russian attempt to squeeze the allies out of Berlin.

Jack offered an impassioned defense of Truman's airlift that had forced Stalin to back down on the blockade. "If Berlin proves anything," he said, "it's that Joe Stalin understands only one thing, and that's force."

Leo believed that America ought to go to war rather than abandon Berlin to the Reds. "The Cold War is bound to turn into a shooting war eventually," he said, leaning over the table. "America disarmed too soon after the Germans and Japs surrendered and that was a big mistake. We should be rearming and fast, for God's sake. We need to stop watching the Cold War and start fighting it. We need to stop pussyfooting around while they're turning the satellite countries into slave states and sabotaging free elections in France and Italy."

The coach said, "I'm curious to know how you men see this McCarthy business?"

Jack said, "All right, maybe Joe McCarthy's overstating his case when he says the government is crawling with card-carrying Commies. But like the man says, where there's smoke, there's fire."

"The way I see it," Leo said, "we need to put some pizzazz into this new Central Intelligence Agency that Truman concocted. We need to spy on them the way they're spying on us."

"That's the ticket," Jack heartily agreed.

Stella, a New Haven social worker seven years older than Leo, shook her head in disgust. "Well, I don't agree with a word you boys are saying. There's a song on the hit parade...it's called, 'Enjoy Yourself (It's Later Than You Think).' The title says it all: we ought to be enjoying ourselves *because* it is later than we think." When everyone looked at her she blushed. "Hey, I'm entitled to my opinion."

"Coach Waltz is talking seriously, Stella," Leo said.

"Well, so am I. Talking seriously, I mean. We'd better enjoy ourselves before the war breaks out because after it breaks out we won't be able to—the ones who're still alive will be living like worms in underground fallout shelters."

On the way back to the off-campus apartment that Leo and Jack shared (when they weren't bunking at the Yale boathouse on the Housatonic) with a Russian exchange student named Yevgeny Alexandrovich Tsipin, Leo tried to argue with Stella but she stuck to her guns. "I don't see the sense of starting the shooting all over again just to stay in some godforsaken city like Berlin."

This exasperated Leo. "This pacifism of yours plays right into Stalin's hands."

Stella slipped her arm through Jack's, lightly brushing a breast against his elbow. "Leo's angry with me, Jacky," she said with a mock pout, "but you see my point."

"To tell the truth, I see two of them," Jack said with a leer.

"I hope you're not trying to beat my time," Leo warned.

"I thought crew shared everything," Jack said.

Leo stopped in his tracks. "So what are you asking, Jack? Are you asking me to lend you Stella for the night?"

"You're doing it again," Jack warned good-naturedly, "exposing the chip on your shoulder."

"When is it going to sink in?" Stella told Jack. "The chip on his shoulder is what he's all about." She turned on Leo. "Let's get something straight," she said, her face a mask of seriousness. "You don't own me, Leo, you only have the franchise. Which means that nobody borrows Stella unless Stella decides to be borrowed."

The three started walking again. Jack was shaking his head. "Damnation! Leo, old pal, old buddy, are we numskulls—I think we've been on the receiving end of a pitch!"

"Stella's not making a pitch—"

"I don't mean Stella. I mean Coach Waltz. When's the last time coach talked politics with any of his rowers? Remember what he asked us just before we headed for the Roach Ranch? Do we think patriotism is out of fashion? Do we think one man can make a difference in a world threatened by atomic wars? And remember his parting words—about how, what with Yevgeny being the son of a Russian diplomat and all, it'd be better if we kept the conversation under our hats."

"For cryin' out loud, Yevgeny's not a *Communist*," Stella declared.

"Jesus H. Christ, I'm not saying he's a Communist," Jack said. "Though, come to think of it, his father would probably have to be, to be where he is." He turned back to Leo. "How could we miss it? The coach's got to be a talent scout. And we're the talent."

Leo flashed one of his famous sour smiles. "So who do you think he's scouting for? The New Haven Shore Line?"

"It's got to be something connected with government. And I'll lay you odds it's not the National Forest Service." Jack's Cossack mustache twitched in satisfaction. "Well, damnation," he said again. "Skull and Bones didn't tap us, Leo, but I have a hunch a society a lot more mysterious than one of Yale's secret societies may be about to."

"How can any society be more secret than Skull and Bones?" Stella wanted to know but by now both of her companions were absorbed in their own thoughts.

Making their way single file up the narrow, dimly lit staircase in a seedy building on Dwight Street, pushing open the door of a fifth-floor walkup, tossing their duffels into a corner, they found their Russian apartment-mate slumped over the kitchen table, his head on Trevelyan's *American Revolution*. When Jack shook his shoulder Yevgeny yawned and stretched and said, "I dreamed you guys became the first boat in the Harvard-Yale classic to come in third."

"Leo went to a sprint at the four-fifths mark," Jack said. "Yale won by a nose. The two oarsmen who died of exhaustion were buried in the river with full honors."

Stella set the kettle to boiling. Jack threw on a 78-rpm Cole Porter record. The "troika," as the three roommates styled themselves, pushed the rowing machine into a corner and settled onto the floor of the tiny living room for one of their regular late-night bull sessions. Yevgeny, a sturdy, sandy-haired young man whose pale eyes seemed to change color with his moods, was majoring in American history and had become something of a Revolutionary War buff; he had pored over Pennypacker's *General Washington's Spies* and Trevelyan's *The American Revolution* and had actually followed in Washington's footsteps, walking during winter recess the route the Continental Army had taken from Valley Forge across the frozen Delaware to Trenton. "I've figured out the big difference between the American Revolution and the Bolshevik revolution," he was saying now. "The American version lacked a central unifying vision."

"The Americans were against tyranny and taxation without representation," Jack reminded his Russian friend. "They were for individual rights, especially the right to express minority views without being oppressed by the majority. Those are unifying visions."

Yevgeny flashed a wrinkled smile. "Jefferson's 'All men are created equal' didn't include the Negroes who worked in his nail factory at Monticello. Even Washington's supposedly idealistic Continental Army was run along elitist principles—if you were called up you could pay someone to take your place or send your Negro slave."

Stella spooned instant coffee into mugs, filled them with boiling water from the kettle and handed them around. "America's central vision was to spread the American way of life from coast to shining coast," she commented. "It's called Manifest Destiny."

Jack said, "The American way of life hasn't been all that bad for a hundred fifty million Americans—especially when you see how the rest of the world scrapes by."

Stella said, "Hey, I work with Negro families in downtown New Haven that don't have enough money for one square meal a day. Are you counting them in your hundred fifty million?"

Yevgeny spiked his coffee from a small flask of cheap cooking cognac and passed the bottle around. "What motivated Washington and Jefferson, what motivates Americans today, is a kind of sentimental imperialism," he said, stirring his coffee with the eraser end of a pencil. "The original eastern seaboard revolution spread from coast to shining coast over the bodies of two million Indians. You Americans carry on about making the world safe for democracy but the sub text is you want to make the world safe for the United Fruit Company."

Leo turned moody. "So what image would you reshape the world in, Yevgeny?"

Jack climbed to his feet to put on a new record. "Yeah, tell us about the unifying vision of Stalin."

"My central vision doesn't come from Stalin. It doesn't even come from Marx. It comes from Leon Tolstoy. He spent most of his life searching for a unifying theory, the single key that would unlock every door, the universal explanation for our passions and economics and poverty and politics. What I really am is a Tolstoyist."

Leo said, "The universal explanation—the force that conditions all human choice—turns out, according to Marx, to be economics."

Stella nudged Jack in the ribs with an elbow. "I thought sex was behind all our choices," she teased.

Jack wagged a finger in Stella's face. "You've been reading Freud again."

"Freud's mistake was to generalize from a particular," Yevgeny went on, bending forward, caught up in his own narrative. "And the particular in his case was himself. Don't forget that many of the dreams he analyzed were his own. Tolstoy moved far beyond himself—he caught a glimpse of a force, a fate, a scheme of things that was behind all of history; 'Something incomprehensible but which is nevertheless the only thing that matters,' as he has his Prince Andrei say."

Leo poured the last of their open bottle of cooking cognac into his cup. "Human experience is too complex and too inconsistent to be explained by any one law or any one truth."

Jack said flatly, "All visions which lead to concentration camps are flat-out wrong."

Stella waved her hand as if she were in a classroom. "What about America's concentration camps? They're harder to identify because they don't have walls or barbed wire. We call them Negro ghettos and Indian reservations."

Yevgeny said, "Stella's got it right, of course—"

"What about the Iron Curtain?" Jack blurted out. "What about the slave nations imprisoned behind it? Damnation, a Negro can walk out of the ghetto any time he wants, which is more than you can say for a Pole or a Hungarian."

"Negro soldiers fought World War II in segregated units run by white officers," Yevgeny said sharply. "Your Mr. Truman finally got around to inte-grating the armed forces last year, eighty-four years after the end of your Civil War."

"Arguing with the two of you has a lot in common with beating your head against a wall," Jack said wearily.

Yevgeny climbed to his feet and produced another bottle of cooking cognac from behind a stack of books on a shelf and passed it around. The members of the troika each poured a shot of cognac onto the coffee dregs at the bottom of their respective cups. Yevgeny raised his cup aloft and called out his trademark slogan in Russian: *"Za uspiekh nashevo beznadiozhnovo diela!"*

"Za uspiekh nashevo beznadiozhnovo diela," Jack and Leo repeated.

Stella said, "You've told me before but I always forget. What's that mean again?"

Leo supplied the English translation: "To the success of our hopeless task!"

Stella swallowed a yawn. "Right now my hopeless task is to keep my eyes open. I'm going to hit the hay. Are you coming, Leo, baby?"

"Are you coming, Leo, baby?" Jack cooed, mimicking Stella.

Leo threw a dark look in Jack's direction as he trailed after Stella and dis-appeared into the room at the end of the hallway.

In the early hours of the morning, as the first ash-gray streaks of first light broke against the Harkness Quadrangle, Leo came awake to discover Stella missing from the narrow bed. Padding sleepily through the silent apartment he heard the scratching of a needle going round and round in the end grooves of a record in the living room. Yevgeny was fast asleep on the old couch under the window with the torn shade, his arm trailing down to the linoleum, the tips of his fingers wedged in Trevelyan's masterpiece on the American Revolution so he wouldn't lose his place. Leo gently lifted the needle from the record and switched off Yevgeny's reading lamp. As his eyes became accustomed to the darkness he noticed a flicker of light under Jack's door on one side of the living room. Expecting to catch Jack burning the midnight oil, he gripped the knob and softly turned it and inched the door open.

Inside a sputtering candle splashed quivering shadows onto the peeling wallpaper. One of the shadows belonged to Stella. She was wearing one of Leo's sleeveless Yale rowing shirts and slouched on the bed, her back against the wall, her long bare legs stretched out and parted wide. Another shadow was cast by Jack. He was kneeling on the floor between Stella's silvery thighs, his head bent forward. Sifting through the murky images, Leo's sleep-fogged brain decided it had stumbled on Jack worshipping at an altar.

In the half-darkness, Leo could make out Stella's face. She was looking straight at him, a faint smile of complicity on her slightly parted lips.

Working out of an empty office that his old law firm put at his disposition whenever he came to Manhattan, Frank Wisner wound up the meeting with E. (for Elliott) Winstrom Ebbitt II and walked him over to the bank of elevators. "I'm real pleased Bill Donovan made sure our paths crossed," he drawled, stretching his Mississippi vowels like rubber bands and letting them snap back on the consonants. The Wiz, as Wisner was affectionately nicknamed in the Company, was the deputy head, behind Allen Dulles, of what some journalists had dubbed the dirty tricks department of the fledgling Central Intelligence Agency. A ruggedly handsome OSS veteran, he favored his visitor with one of his legendary gap-toothed smiles. "Welcome aboard, Ebby," he declared, offering a resolute paw.

Nodding, Ebby took it. "It was flattering to be asked to join such a distinguished team."

As Ebby climbed into the elevator, the Wiz slapped him on the back. "We'll see how flattered you feel when I kick ass over some operation that didn't end up the way I thought it should. Cloud Club, sixteen thirty tomorrow."

Ebby got off the elevator two floors below to pick up a briefcase full of legal briefs from his desk. He pushed through the double doors with "Donovan, Leisure, Newton, Lumbard & Irvine" and "Attorneys at Law" etched in gold letters across the thick glass. Except for the two Negro cleaning ladies vacuuming the wall-to-wall carpets, the offices were deserted. Heading back to the elevators, Ebby stopped to pen a note in his small, precise handwriting to his secretary. "Kindly cancel my four o'clock and keep my calendar clear for the afternoon. Try and get me fifteen minutes with Mr. Donovan anytime in the morning. Also, please Thermofax my outstanding dossiers and leave the copies on Ken Brill's desk. Tell him I'd take it as a favor if he could bring himself up to speed on all the material by Monday latest." He scribbled "E.E." across the bottom of the page and stuck it under a paperweight on the blotter.

Moments later the revolving door at Number Two Wall Street spilled Ebby into a late afternoon heat wave. Loosening his tie, he flagged down a cab, gave the driver an address on Park and Eighty-eighth and told him to take his sweet time getting there. He wasn't looking forward to the storm that was about to burst.

Eleonora (pronounced with an Italian lilt ever since the young Eleanor Krandal had spent a junior semester at Radcliffe studying Etruscan jewelry at the Villa Giulia in Rome) was painting her fingernails for the dinner party that night when Ebby, stirring an absinth and water with a silver swizzle stick, wandered into the bedroom. "Darling, where *have* you been?" she cried with a frown. "The Wilsons invited us for eight, which means we have to cross their threshold not a split second later than eight-thirtyish. I heard Mr. Harriman was coming—"

"Manny have a good day?"

"When Miss Utterback picked him up, the teacher told her Manny'd been frightened when the air raid siren shrieked and all the children had to take cover under their little tables. These atomic alerts scare me, too. How was your day?"

"Frank Wisner asked me up to Carter Ledyard for a chat this afternoon."

Eleonora glanced up from her nails in mild interest. "Did he?"

Ebby noticed that every last hair on his wife's gorgeous head was in place, which meant that she'd stopped by the hairdresser's after the lunch with her Radcliffe girlfriends at the Automat on Broadway. He wondered, not for the first time, what had happened to the eager girl who'd been waiting when the banana boat back from the war had deposited him on a Manhattan dock draped with an enormous banner reading "Welcome Home—Well Done." In those days she had been filled with impatience—to have herself folded into his arms, no matter they hadn't seen each other in four years; to climb into the rack with him, no matter she was a virgin; to walk down the aisle on her father's arm and agree to love and honor and obey, though she'd made it crystal clear from day one that the obey part was a mere formality. During the first years of their marriage it was her money—

from a trust fund, from her salary as a part-time jewelry buyer for Bergdorf's—that had put him through Columbia Law. Once he had his degree and had been hired by "Wild" Bill Donovan, his old boss at OSS who was back practicing law in New York, Eleonora more or less decided to retire and begin living in the style to which she wanted to become accustomed.

Across the bedroom, Eleonora held up one hand to the light and examined her nails. Ebby decided there was no point in beating around the bush. "The Wiz offered me a job. I accepted."

"Is Frank Wisner back at Carter Ledyard? I suppose that Washington thing didn't work out for him. I hope you talked salary? Knowing you, darling, I'm sure you would never be the first to raise the ugly subject of money. Did he say anything about an eventual partnership? You ought to play your cards carefully—Mr. Donovan might be willing to give you a junior partnership to keep from losing you. On the other hand, Daddy won't be disappointed if you go to Carter Ledyard. He and Mr. Wisner know each other from Yale—they were both Skull and Bones. He could put in a good word—"

Ebby puffed up two pillows and stretched out on the cream-colored bedspread. "Frank Wisner hasn't gone back to Carter Ledyard."

"Darling, you might take your shoes off."

He undid his laces and kicked off his shoes. "The Wiz's still in government service."

"I thought you said you saw him at Carter Ledyard."

Ebby started over again. "Frank has the use of an office there when he's in town. He asked me up and offered me a job. I'm joining him in Washington. You'll be pleased to know I did raise the ugly subject of money. I'll be starting at GS-12, which pays six-thousand four-hundred dollars."

Eleonora concentrated on screwing the cap back onto the nail polish. "Darling, if this is some sort of silly prank..." She began waving her fingers in the air to dry her nails but stopped when she caught sight of his eyes. "You're being serious, Eb, aren't you? You're not becoming involved with that ridiculous Central Agency Mr. Donovan and you were talking about over brandy the other night, for heaven's sake."

"I'm afraid I am."

Eleonora undid the knot on the belt of the silk robe and shrugged it off her delicate shoulders; it fell in a heap on the floor, where it would stay until the Cuban maid straightened up the room the next morning. Ebby noticed his wife was wearing one of those newfangled slips that doubled as a brassiere and pushed up her small pointed breasts. "I thought you'd grown up, Eb," she was saying as she slipped into a black Fogarty number with a pinched waist and a frilly skirt. Taking it for granted that she could talk him out of this silly idea, she backed up to him so he could close the zipper.

"That's just it," Ebby said, sitting up to wrestle with the zipper. "I have grown up. I've had it up to here with company mergers and stock issues and trust funds for spoiled grandchildren. Frank Wisner says the country is at peril and he's not the only one to think so. Mr. Luce called this the American century, but at the halfway mark it's beginning to look more and more like the Soviet century. The Czechoslovak President, Mr. Masaryk, was thrown out of a window and the last free East European country went down the drain. Then we lost China to the Reds. If we don't get cracking France and Italy will go Communist and our whole position in Europe will be in jeopardy." He gave up on the zipper and touched the back of his hand to the nape of her neck. "A lot of the old OSS crowd are signing on, Eleonora. The Wiz was very convincing—he said he couldn't find people with my experience in clandestine operations on every street corner. I couldn't refuse him. You do see that?"

Eleonora pulled free from his clumsy fingers and padded across the room in her stockinged feet to study herself in the full-length mirror. "I married a brilliant attorney with a bright future—"

"Do you love me or my law degree?"

She regarded him in the mirror. "To be perfectly honest, darling, both. I love you in the context of your work. Daddy is an attorney, my two uncles are attorneys, my brother has one more year at Harvard Law and then he'll join Daddy's firm. How could I possibly explain to them that my husband has decided to throw away a thirty-seven-thousand-dollar-a-year position in one of the smartest firms on Wall Street for a six-thousand-a-year job—doing what? You've fought your war, Eb. Let someone else fight this one. How many times do you need to be a hero in one lifetime?" Her skirt flaring above her delicate ankles, Eleonora wheeled around to face her husband. "Look, let's both of us simmer down and enjoy ourselves at the Wilsons. Then you'll sleep on it, Eb. Things will look clearer in the cold light of morning."

"I've accepted Frank's offer," Ebby insisted. "I don't intend to go back on that."

Eleonora's beautiful eyes turned flinty. "Whatever you do, you'll never match your father unless someone stands you in front of a firing squad."

"My father has nothing to do with this."

She looked around for her shoes. "You really don't expect me to transplant Immanuel to a semi-attached stucco house in some dingy Washington suburb so you can take a six-thousand-a-year job spying on Communists who are spying on Americans who are spying on Communists."

Ebby said dryly, "It's sixty-four-hundred, and that doesn't include the two-hundred-dollar longevity increase for my two years in the OSS."

Eleonora let her voice grow husky. "If you abandon a promising career you'll be abandoning a wife and a son with it. I'm just not the 'Whither thou goest' type."

"I don't suppose you are," Ebby remarked in a voice hollow with melancholy for what might have been.

With a deft gesture that, as far as Ebby could see, only the female of the species had mastered, Eleonora reached behind her shoulders blades with both hands and did up the zipper. "You'd better throw something on if you don't want us to be late for the Wilsons," she snapped. She spotted her stiletto-heeled pumps under a chair. Slipping her feet into them, she stomped from the bedroom.

The Otis elevator lifting Ebby with motionless speed to the sixty-sixth floor of the Chrysler Building was thick with cigar smoke and the latest news bulletins. "It's not a rumor," a middle-aged woman reported excitedly. "I caught it on the hackie's radio—the North Koreans have invaded South Korea. It's our nightmare come true—masses of them poured across the thirty-eighth parallel this morning."

"Moscow obviously put them up to it," said one man. "Stalin is testing our mettle."

"Do you think Mr. Truman will fight?" asked a young woman whose black veil masked the upper half of her face.

"He was solid as bedrock on Berlin," observed another man.

"Berlin happens to be in the heart of Europe," noted an elderly gentleman. "South Korea is a suburb of Japan. Any idiot can see this is the wrong war in the wrong place."

"I heard the President's ordered the Seventh Fleet to sea," the first man said.

"My fiancé is a reserve naval aviator," the young woman put in. "I just spoke with him on the telephone. He's worried sick he's going to be called back to service."

The operator, an elderly Negro wearing a crisp brown uniform with gold piping, braked the elevator to a smooth stop and slid back the heavy gold grill with a gloved hand. "Eighty-second Airborne's been put on alert," he announced. "Reason I know, got a nephew happens to be a radio operator with the Eighty-second." Without missing a beat he added, "Final stop, Chrysler Cloud Club."

Ebby, half an hour early, shouldered through the crowd milling excitedly around the bar and ordered a scotch on the rocks. He was listening to the ice crackle in the glass, rehashing the waspish conversation he'd had with Eleonora over breakfast, when he felt a tug on his elbow. He glanced over his shoulder. "Berkshire!" he cried, calling Bill Colby by his wartime OSS code name. "I thought you were in Washington with the Labor Relations people. Don't tell me the Wiz snared you, too."

Colby nodded. "I was with the NLRB until the old warlock worked his magic on me. You've heard the news?"

"Difficult not to hear it. People who generally clam up in elevators were holding a seminar on whether Truman's going to take the country to war."

Carrying their drinks, the two men made their way to one of the tall windows that offered a breathtaking view of Manhattan's grid-like streets and the two rivers bracketing the island. Ebby waved at the smog swirling across their line of sight as if he expected to dispel it. "Hudson's out there somewhere. On a clear day you can see across those parklands trailing off to the horizon behind the Palisades. Eleonora and I used to picnic there before we could afford restaurants."

"How is Eleonora? How's Immanuel?"

"They're both fine." Ebby touched his glass against Colby's. "Good to see you again, Bill. What's the word from the District of Columbia?"

Colby glanced around to make sure they couldn't be overheard. "We're going to war, Eb, that's what the Wiz told me and he ought to know." The pale eyes behind Colby's military-issue spectacles were, as always, imperturbable. The half smile that appeared on his face was the expression of a poker player who didn't want to give away his cards, or his lack of them. "Let the Communists get away with this," he added, "they're only going to test us somewhere else. And that somewhere else could be the Iranian oil fields or the English Channel."

Ebby knew the imperturbable eyes and the poker player's smile well. He and Colby and another young American named Stewart Alsop had studied Morse from the same instructor at an English manor house before being parachuted into France as part of three-man Jedburgh teams (the name came from the Scottish town near the secret OSS training camp). Long after he'd returned to the states and married, Ebby would come awake in the early hours of the morning convinced he could hear the throttled-back drone of the Liberator banking toward England and the snap of the parachute spilling and catching the air as he drifted down toward the triangle of fires the *maquis* had ignited in a field. Ebby and Colby, assigned to different Jedburgh teams, had crossed paths as they scurried around the French countryside, blowing up bridges to protect Patton's exposed right flank as his tanks raced north of the Yonne for the Rhine. Ebby's Jedburgh mission had ended with him inching his way through the jammed, jubilant streets of the newly liberated Paris in a shiny black Cadillac that had once belonged to Vichy Premier Pierre Laval. After the German surrender Ebby had tried to talk the OSS into transferring him to the Pacific theater but had wound up at a debriefing center the Americans had set up in a German Champagne factory outside Wiesbaden, trying to piece together the Soviet order of battle from Russian defectors. He might have stayed on in the postwar OSS if there had been a postwar OSS. When the Japanese capitulated, Truman decided America didn't need a central intelligence organization and disbanded it. The Presidential ax sent the OSS's analysts to the State Department (where they were as welcome as fleas in a rug), the cowboys to the War Department and Ebby, by then married to his pre-war sweetheart, back to Columbia Law School. And who did he come across there but his old sidekick from the Jedburgh days, Berkshire, one year ahead of him but already talking vaguely of abandoning law when the Cold War intensified and Truman reckoned, in 1947, that America could use a central intelligence agency after all.

"I heard on the grapevine that Truman's flipped his lid at the CIA," Colby said. "He blames them for not providing early warning of the North Korean attack. He's right, of course. But with the nickel-and-dime budget Congress provides, they're lucky if they can predict anything beside Truman's moods. Heads are going to roll, you can believe it. The buzz on Capitol Hill is that the Admiral"—he was referring to the current DCI, Rear Admiral Roscoe Hillenkoetter—"will be job hunting before the year's out. The Wiz thinks Eisenhower's Chief of Staff at Normandy, Bedell Smith, may get the nod." Colby glanced at a wall clock, clicked glasses with Ebby again and they both tossed off their drinks. "We'd better be getting in," he said. "When the Wiz says sixteen thirty he doesn't mean sixteen thirty-one."

Near the bank of elevators a small sign directed visitors attending the S.M. Craw Management Symposium to a suite of private rooms at the far end of the corridor. Inside a vestibule two unsmiling young men in three-piece suits checked Colby's identification, then scrutinized Ebby's driver's license and his old laminated OSS ID card (which he'd retrieved from a shoebox filled with his wartime citations, medals and discharge papers). Ticking off names on a clipboard, they motioned Ebby and Colby though the door with a sign on it reading, "S.M. Craw Symposium."

Several dozen men and a single woman were crowded around a makeshift bar. The only other woman in sight, wearing slacks and a man's vest over a ruffled shirt, was busy ladling punch into glasses and setting them out on the table. Ebby helped himself to a glass of punch, then turned to chat with a young man sporting a Cossack mustache. "My name's Elliott Ebbitt," he told him. "Friends call me Ebby."

"I'm John McAuliffe," said the young man, a flamboyant six-footer wearing an expensive three-piece linen suit custom-tailored by Bernard Witherill of New York. "Friends call me a lot of things behind my back and Jack to my face." He nodded toward the thin-faced, lean young man in a rumpled off-the-rack suit from the R.H. Macy Company. "This is my former friend Leo Kritzky."

Ebby took the bait. "Why former?"

"His former girlfriend crept into my bed late one night," Jack said with disarming frankness. "He figures I should have sent her packing. I keep reminding him that she's a terrific piece of ass and I'm a perfectly normal *Homo erectus*."

"I was angry, but I'm not any more," Leo commented dryly. "I decided to leave the pretty girls to the men without imagination." He offered a hand to Ebby. "Pleased to meet you."

For a second Ebby thought Jack was putting him on but the brooding darkness in Leo's eyes and the frown-creases on his high forehead convinced him otherwise. Never comfortable with discussions of other people's private lives, he quickly changed the subject. "Where are you fellows coming from? And how did you wind up here?"

Leo said, "We're both graduating from Yale at the end of the month."

Jack said with a laugh, "We wound up here because we said yes when our rowing coach offered us cups down at Mory's. Turns out he was head hunting for—" Jack was unsure whether you were supposed to pronounce the words "Central Intelligence Agency" out loud, so he simply waved his hand at the crowd.

Leo asked, "How about you, Elliott?"

"I went from Yale to OSS the last year of the war. I suppose you could say I'm reenlisting."

"Did you see action?" Jack wanted to know.

"Some."

"Where?"

"France, mostly. By the time I crossed the Rhine, Hitler had shot a bullet into his brain and the Germans had thrown in the sponge."

The young woman who had been serving drinks tapped a spoon against a glass and the two dozen young men—what Jack called the "Arrow-shirt-cum-starched-collar-crowd"—gravitated toward the folding chairs that had been set up in rows facing the floor-to-ceiling picture window with a view of the Empire State Building and downtown Manhattan. She stepped up to the glass lectern and tapped a long fingernail against the microphone to make sure it was working. "My name is Mildred Owen-Brack," she began. Clearly used to dealing with men who weren't used to dealing with women, she plowed on, "I'm going to walk you through the standard secrecy form which those of you who are alert will have discovered on your seats; those of you who are a bit slower will find you're sitting on them." There was a ripple of nervous laughter at Owen-Brack's attempt to break the ice. "When you came into this room you entered what the sociologists call a closed culture. The form commits you to submit to the CIA for prior review everything and anything you may write for publication about the CIA while you're serving and after you leave it. That includes articles, books of fact or fiction, screenplays, epic poems, opera librettos, Hallmark card verses, et cetera. It goes without saying but I will say it all the same: Only those who sign the agreement will remain in the room. Questions?"

Owen-Brack surveyed the faces in front of her. The lone female amid all the male recruits, a particularly good-looking dark-haired young woman wearing a knee-length skirt and a torso-hugging jacket lifted a very manicured hand. "I'm Millicent Pearlstein from Cincinnati." She cleared her throat in embarrassment when she realized there had been no reason to say where she came from. "Okay. You're probably aware that your agreement imposes prior restraint on the First Amendment right of free speech, and as such it would stand a good chance of being thrown out by the courts."

Owen-Brack smiled sweetly. "You're obviously a lawyer, but you're missing the point," she explained with exaggerated politeness. "We're asking you to sign this form for your own safety. We're a secret organization protecting our secrets from the occasional employee who might be tempted to describe his employment in print. If someone tried to do that, he—or she—would certainly rub us the wrong way and we'd have to seriously consider terminating the offender along with the contract. So we're trying to make it legally uninviting for someone to rub us the wrong way. Hopefully the intriguing question of whether the Company's absolute need to protect its secrets outweighs the First Amendment right of free speech will never be put to the test."

Ebby leaned over to Colby, who was sitting on the aisle next to him. "Who's the man-eater?"

"She's the Company *consigliere*," he whispered back. "The Wiz says she's not someone whose feathers you want to ruffle."

Owen-Brack proceeded to read the two-paragraph contract aloud.

Afterward she went around collecting the signed forms, stuffed them in a folder and took a seat in the back of the room.

Frank Wisner strode up the lectern. "Welcome to the Pickle Factory," he drawled, using the in-house jargon for the Company. "My name is Frank Wisner. I'm the deputy to Allen Dulles, who is the Deputy Director/ Operations—that's DD-slash-O in Companyese. DD/O refers both to the man who runs the Clandestine Service as well as the service itself." The Wiz wet his lips from a glass of punch. "The Truman Doctrine of 1947 promised that America would aid free peoples everywhere in the struggle against total-itarianism. The principal instrument of American foreign policy in this struggle is the Central Intelligence Agency. And the cutting edge of the CIA is the DD/O. So far we have a mixed record. We lost Czechoslovakia to the Communists but we saved France from economic collapse after the war, we saved Italy from an almost certain Communist victory in the elections and the Czech-style putsch that would have surely followed, we saved Greece from a Soviet-backed insurgency. Make no mistake about it—Western civi-lization is being attacked and a very thin line of patriots is manning the ramparts. We badly need to reinforce this line of patriots, which is why you've been invited here today. We're looking for driven, imaginative men and women"—the Wiz acknowledged Millicent Pearlstein with a gallant nod—"who are aggressive in pursuit of their goals and not afraid of taking risks—who, like Alice in Wonderland, can plunge into the unknown with-out worrying about how they are going to get out again. The bottom line is: There aren't any textbooks on spying, you have to invent it as you go along. I'll give you a case in point. Ten days ago, one of our officers who'd been try-ing to recruit a woman for five months discovered that she religiously read the astrology column in her local newspaper. So the morning he made his pitch, he arranged for the section on Capricorns to say that a financial offer that day would change their lives and solve their money problems—don't refuse it. The woman in question listened to the pitch and signed on the dotted line and is now reporting to us from a very sensitive embassy in a Communist country."

In the back of the room Wisner's minder began tapping his wristwatch. At the lectern, Wisner nodded imperceptibly. "You people have no doubt read a lot of cloak-and-dagger novels. If the impression you have of the Central Intelligence Agency comes from them you'll find you are seriously mistaken. The real world of espionage is less glamorous and more dangerous than those novels would lead you to believe. If you make it through our training program, you will spend your professional lives doing things you can't talk about to anyone outside the office, and that includes wives and girlfriends. We're looking for people who are comfortable living in the shad- ows and who can conduct imaginative operations that the US government can plausibly disclaim any responsibility for if things go right *or* wrong. What you do won't turn up in headlines on the front page—it won't appear on *any* page—unless you foul up. You'll be operating in the killing fields of the Cold War and you'll be playing for keeps. If you aren't completely com- fortable with this, my advice to you is to seek employment with the Fuller Brush Company."

Wisner checked his own watch. "So much for the sermon from the Cloud Club. Owen-Brack will walk you though the nitty-gritty part of today's get-together—where and when you are to report, what you are to bring with you, when you will start to draw salary, what you are to tell peo- ple if they ask you what you're doing. She'll also give you a backstop, which is to say a mailing address and a phone number where a secretary will say you are away from your desk and offer to take a message. In the months ahead you're going to be away from your desk an awful lot."

The new recruits in the room laughed at this. At the lectern Wisner had a whispered conversation with Owen-Brack, after which he ducked out of the room one step behind his minder. Leaning toward the microphone, Owen-Brack said, "I'll begin by saying that the Company singled you out— and went to the trouble and expense of ordering up background security checks—because we need street-smart people who can burgle a safe and drink tea without rattling the cup. Chances are you're coming to us with only the second of these skills. We plan to teach you the first, along with the nuts and bolts of the espionage business, when you report for duty. For the record, you are S.M. Craw Management trainees from Sears, Roebuck. The first phase of your training—which will actually include a course in management in case you ever need to explain in detail what you were doing—will take place at the Craw offices behind the Hilton Inn off Route 95 in Springfield, Virginia, starting at 7:30 A.M. on the first Monday in July."

Pausing every now and then to hand out printed matter, Owen-Brack droned on for another twenty minutes. "That's more or less it," she finally said. She flashed another of her guileless smiles. "With any luck I'll never see any of you again."

Jack lingered in the room after the others left. Owen-Brack was collect- ing her papers. "Forget something?" she inquired.

"Name's McAuliffe. John J. McAuliffe. Jack to my friends. I just thought what a crying shame to come all the way up to the Cloud Club and not take in the view. And the best way to take in the view is with a cup of Champagne in your fist—"

Tilting her head, Owen-Brack sized up Jack. She took in the three-piece linen suit, the cowboy boots, the tinted glasses, the dark hair slicked back and parted in the middle. "What's the *J* stand for?" she asked.

"It doesn't stand for anything. I only use it when I'm trying to impress people. My father wrote it in on the birth certificate because he thought it made you look important if you had a middle initial."

"I happen to be on the review board that examines the 201s—the personal files—of potential recruits. I remember yours, John J. McAuliffe. During your junior semester abroad you served as an intern in the American embassy in Moscow—"

"My father knew someone in the State Department—he pulled strings," Jack explained.

"The ambassador sent you back to the states when it was discovered that you were using the diplomatic pouch to smuggle Finnish lobsters in from Helsinki."

"Your background checks are pretty thorough. I was afraid I'd wash out if that became known."

"I suppose there's no harm in telling you—your college record is fairly mediocre. You were taken *because* of the incident. The Company wants people who are not afraid to bend the rules."

"That being the case, what about the cup of Champagne?" Jack turned on the charm. "The way I see it, men and women are accomplices in the great game of sex. You lean forward, the top of your blouse falls open, it's a gesture you've practiced in front of a mirror, there is a glimpse of a breast, a nipple—you'd think something was wrong with me if I don't notice."

Owen-Brack screwed up her lips. "You beautiful boys never get it right, and you won't get it right until you lose your beauty. It's not your beauty that seduces us but your voices, your words; we are seduced by your heads, not your hands." She glanced impatiently at a tiny watch on her wrist. "Look, you need to know that Owen is my maiden name," she informed him, "Brack is my married name."

"Hell, nobody's perfect—I won't hold your being married against you."

Owen-Brack didn't think Jack was funny. "My husband worked for the Company—he was killed in a border skirmish you never read about in the *New York Times*. Stop me if I'm wrong but the view from the sixty-sixth floor, the drink in my fist—that's not what you have in mind. You're asking me if I'd be willing to sleep with you. The answer is: Yeah, I can see how I might enjoy that. If my husband were alive I'd be tempted to go ahead and cheat on him. Hell, he cheated enough on me. But his being dead changes the chemistry of the situation. I don't need a one-night stand, I need a love affair. And that rules you out—you're obviously not the love affair type. Bye-bye, John J. McAuliffe. And good luck to you. You're going to need it."

"Spies," the instructor was saying, his voice reduced to stifled gasps because his scarred vocal cords strained easily, "are perfectly sane human beings who become neurotically obsessed with trivia." Robert Andrews, as he was listed on the S.M. Craw roster in the lobby, had captured the attention of the management trainees the moment he shuffled into the classroom eight weeks before. Only the bare bones of his illustrious OSS career were known. He had been parachuted into Germany in 1944 to contact the Abwehr clique planning to assassinate Hitler, and what was left of him after months of Gestapo interrogation was miraculously liberated from Buchenwald by Patton's troops at the end of the war. Sometime between the two events the skin on the right side of his face had been branded with a series of small round welts and his left arm had been literally torn from its shoulder socket on some sort of medieval torture rack. Now the empty sleeve of his sports jacket, pinned neatly back, flapped gently against his rib cage as he paced in front of the trainees. "Spies," he went on, "file away the details that may one day save their lives. Such as which side of any given street will be in the shadows cast by a rising moon. Such as under what atmospheric conditions a pistol shot sounds like an automobile backfiring."

Enthralled by the whine of a police siren that reached his good ear through the windows, Mr. Andrews ambled over to the sill and stared through his reflection at the traffic on Route 95. The sound appeared to transport him to another time and another place and only with a visible effort was he able to snap himself out of a fearful reverie. "We have tried to drum into your heads what the people who employ us are pleased to call the basics of tradecraft," he said, turning back to his students. "Letter drops, cut-out agents, invisible writing techniques, microdots, miniature cameras, shaking a tail, planting bugs—you are all proficient in these matters. We have tried to teach you KGB tradecraft—how they send over handsome young men to seduce secretaries with access to secrets, how their handlers prefer to meet their agents in open areas as opposed to safe houses, how East Germans spies operating in the West employ the serial numbers on American ten-dollar bills to break out telephone numbers from lottery numbers broadcast over the local radio stations. But the truth is that these so-called basics will take you only so far. To go beyond, you have to invent yourself for each assignment; you have to become the person the enemy would never suspect you of being, which involves doing things the enemy would never suspect an intelligence officer of doing. I know of an agent who limped when he was assigned to follow someone—he calculated that nobody would suspect a lame man of working the street for an intelligence organization. I shall add that the agent was apprehended when the Abwehr man he was following noticed that he was favoring his right foot one day and his left the next. I was that agent. Which makes me uniquely qualified to pass on to you the ultimate message of tradecraft." Here Mr. Andrews turned back toward the window to stare at his own image in the glass.

"For the love of God," the reflection said, "don't make mistakes."

Several hours had been set aside after classes let out for meetings with representatives of the various Company departments who had come down from Cockroach Alley on the Reflecting Pool to recruit for their divisions. As usual the deputy head of the elite Soviet Russia Division, Felix Etz, was allowed to skim off the cream of the crop. To nobody's surprise the first person he homed in on turned out to be Millicent Pearlstein, the lawyer from Cincinnati who had earned a bachelor's degree from the University of Chicago in Russian language and literature before she went on to law school. She had done extremely well in Flaps and Seals as well as Picks and Locks, and had scored high marks in the Essentials of Recruitment and Advanced Ciphers and Communist Theory and Practice. Jack had a so-so record in the course work but he had aced a field exercise; on a training run to Norfolk he had used a phony State of West Virginia Operator's license and a bogus letter with a forged signature of the Chief of Naval Ordinance to talk his way onto the USS *John R. Pierce* and into the destroyer's Combat Information Center, and come away with top-secret training manuals for the ship's surface and air radars. His gung-ho attitude, plus his knowledge of German and Spanish, caught Etz's eye and he was offered a plum berth. Ebby, with his operational experience in OSS and his excellent grades in the refresher courses, was high on Etz's list, too. When Leo's interview came he practically talked his way into the Soviet Russia Division. It wasn't his knowledge of Russian and Yiddish or his high grades that impressed Etz so much as his motivation; Leo had inherited the ardent and lucid anti-Communism of his parents, who had fled Russia one step ahead of the Bolsheviks after the 1917 revolution.

In the early evening the management trainees drifted over to an Italian restaurant in downtown Springfield to celebrate the end of the grueling twelve-week Craw curriculum. "Looks as if I'm going to Germany," Ebby was telling the others at his end of the long banquet table. He half-filled Millicent's wine glass, and then his own, with Chianti. "Say, you're not going to believe me when I tell you what attracted them to me."

"Fact that you're at home in German might have had something to do with it," Jack guessed.

"Not everyone who speaks German winds up in Germany," Ebby noted. "It was something else. When I was sixteen my grandfather died and my grandmother, who was a bit of an eccentric, decided to celebrate her new-found widowhood by taking me on a grand tour of Europe that included a night in a Parisian *maison close* and a week in King Zog's Albania. We made it out of the country in the nick of time when Mussolini's troops invaded— my grandmother used gold coins sewn into her girdle to get us two berths on a tramp steamer to Marseille. Turns out that some bright soul in the Company spotted Albania under the list of 'countries visited' on my personnel file and decided that that qualified me for Albanian ops, which are run out of Germany."

Across the room one of the locals from Springfield slipped a nickel into the jukebox and began dancing the crab walk with a teenage girl in crinolines.

"I'm headed for the Washington Campus," Leo confided. "Mr. Etz told me that Bill Colby could use someone with fluent Russian on his team."

"I'm being sent to an Army language school to brush up on my Italian," Millicent told the others, "after which I'm off to Rome to bat my eyelashes at Communist diplomats." Millicent looked across the table. "What about you, Jack?"

"It's the Soviet Russia division for me too, guys. They're sending me off to some hush-hush Marine base for three weeks of training in weaponry and demolition, after which they're offering me the choice of starting out in Madrid or working for someone nicknamed the Sorcerer in Berlin, which I suppose would make me the Sorcerer's Apprentice. I decided on Berlin because German girls are supposed to give good head."

"Oh, Jack, with you everything boils down to sex," complained Millicent.

"He's just trying to get a rise out of you," Ebby told her.

"I'm not trying to get a rise out of her," Jack insisted. "I'm trying to get her to pay attention to the rise out of me."

"Fat chance of you succeeding," she groaned.

"'Mad, bad and dangerous to know'—that's what they put under Jack's senior photo in the Yale yearbook," Leo informed the others. "It was in quotation marks because the original described Lord Byron, which deep down is how Jack sees himself. Isn't that a fact, Jack?"

Slightly drunk by now, Jack threw his head back and declaimed some lines from Byron. "When Love's delirium haunts the glowing mind, Limping Decorum lingers far behind."

"That's what your code name ought to be, Jack—Limping Decorum," quipped Millicent.

By eleven most of the trainees had left to catch a late-night showing of *Sunset Boulevard* in a nearby cinema. Ebby, Jack, Leo, and Millicent stuck around to polish off the Chianti and gossip about their division assignments. Since this was to be their last meal in the restaurant, the proprietor offered a round of grappa on the house. As they filed past the cash register on their way out he said, "You're the third trainee group to come through here since Christmas. What exactly do you Craw Management folks do?"

"Why, we *manage*," Millicent said with a grin.

"We don't actually work for S.M. Craw," Leo said, coming up with the cover story. "We work for Sears, Roebuck. Sears sent us to attend the Craw management course."

"Management could be just the ticket for my restaurant," the owner said. "Where the heck do you manage when you leave Springfield?"

"All over," Millicent told him. "Some of us have been assigned to the head office in Chicago, others will go to branches around the country."

"Well, good luck to you young people in your endeavors."

"*Auguri*," Millicent said with a smile.

An evening drizzle had turned the gutter outside the restaurant into a glistening mirror. The mewl of a cat in heat reverberated through the narrow street as the group started back toward the Hilton Inn. Ebby stopped under a street light to reread the letter from his lawyer announcing that the divorce finally had come through. Folding it away, he caught up with the others, who were arguing about Truman's decision a few days before to have the Army seize the railroads to avoid a general strike. "That Harry Truman," Jack was saying, "is one tough article."

"He's one tough strikebreaker," Millicent declared.

"A President worth his salt can't knuckle under to strikers while the country's fighting in Korea," Ebby said.

Engrossed in conversation, the four took no notice of the small newspaper delivery van parked in front of the fire hydrant just ahead. As they drew abreast of it, the van's back doors flew open and four men armed with handguns spilled onto the sidewalk behind them. Other dark figures appeared out of an alleyway and blocked their path. Leo managed a startled "What the hell is go—" as a burlap sack came down over his head. His hands were jerked behind his back and bound with a length of electrical wire. Leo heard a fist punch the air out of a rib cage and Jack's muffled gasp. Strong hands bundled the four recruits into the van and shoved them roughly onto stacks of newspapers scattered on the floor. The doors slammed closed, the motor kicked into life and the van veered sharply away from the curb, throwing the prisoners hard against one wall. Leo started to ask if the others were all right but shut up when he felt something metallic pressing against an ear. He heard Jack's angry "case of mistaken iden—" cut off by another gasp.

The van swerved sharply left and then left again, then with its motor revving it picked up speed on a straightaway. There were several stops, probably for red lights, and more turns. At first Leo tried to memorize them in the hope of eventually reconstructing the route, but he soon got confused and lost track. After what seemed like forty or fifty minutes but could easily have been twice that the van eased to a stop. The hollow bleating of what Leo took to be foghorns reached his ears through the burlap. He heard the sharp snap of a cigarette lighter and had to fight back the panic that rose like bile to the back of his throat—were his captors about to set fire to the newspapers in the van and burn them alive? Only when Leo got a whiff of tobacco smoke did he begin to dominate the terror. He told himself that this was certainly an exercise, a mock kidnapping—it had to be that; anything else was unthinkable—organized by the Soviet Russia people to test the mettle of their new recruits. But a seed of doubt planted itself in his brain. Mr. Andrews remark about becoming obsessed with trivia came back to him. Suddenly his antenna was tuned to details. Why were his captors being so silent? Was it because they didn't speak English, or spoke it with an accent? Or spoke it *without* an accent, which could have been the case if they had been kidnapped by CIA agents? But if they had been kidnapped by CIA agents, how come the odor of tobacco that reached his nostrils reminded him of the rough-cut Herzegovina Flor that his father had smoked until the day he shot himself? Weighing possibilities in the hope that one of them would lead to a probability, Leo's thoughts began to drift—only afterward did it occur to him that he had actually dozed—and he found himself sorting through a scrapbook of faded images: his father's coffin being lowered into the ground in a wind-washed Jewish cemetery on Long Island; the rain drumming on the black umbrellas; the car backfire that sounded like the crack of a pistol; the pigeons that beat in panic into the air from the dry branches of dead trees; the drone of his father's brother blundering through a transliterated text of the *Kaddish*; the anguished whimper of his mother repeating over and over, "What will become of us? What will become of us?"

Leo came back to his senses with a start when the back doors were jerked open and a fresh sea breeze swept through the stuffy van. Strong hands pulled him and the others from their bed of newspapers and guided them across a gangplank into the cabin of a small boat. There they were obliged to lie down on a wooden deck that reeked of fish, and they were covered with a heavy tarpaulin saturated with motor oil. The deck vibrated beneath them as the boat, its bow pitching into the swells, headed to sea. The engines droned monotonously for a quarter of an hour, then slowed to an idle as the boat bumped repeatedly against something solid. With the boat rising and falling under his feet, Leo felt himself being pulled onto a wooden landing and pushed up a long flight of narrow steps and onto the deck of a ship, then led down two flights of steps. He tripped going through a hatch and thought he heard one of the captors swear under his breath in Polish. As he descended into the bowels of the ship the stale air that reached Leo's nose through the burlap smelled of *flour*. Someone forced Leo through another hatch into a sweltering compartment. He felt rough hands drag the shoes off his feet and then strip him to his skivvies. His wrists, aching from the wire biting into them, were cut free and he was shoved onto a chair and tied to it, his wrists behind the back of the chair, with rope that was passed several times across his chest and behind the chair. Then the burlap hood was pulled off his head.

Blinking hard to keep the spotlights on the bulkheads from stinging his eyes, Leo looked around. The others, also stripped to their socks and underwear, were angling their heads away from the bright light. Millicent, in a lace brassiere and underpants, appeared pale and disoriented. Three sailors in stained dungarees and turtleneck sweaters were removing wallets and papers from the pockets of the garments and throwing the clothing into a heap in a corner. An emaciated man in an ill-fitting suit studied them from the door through eyes that were bulging out of a skull so narrow it looked deformed. A trace of a smile appeared on his thin lips. "Hello to you," he said, speaking English in what sounded to Leo's ear like an Eastern European—perhaps Latvian, perhaps Polish—accent. "So: I am saying to myself, the sooner you are talking to me in the things I want to knowledge, the sooner this unhappy episode is being located behind us. Please to talk now between yourself. Myself, I am hungry. After a time I am coming back and we will be talking together to see if you are coming out of this thing maybe alive, maybe dead, who knows?"

The civilian ducked through the hatch, followed by the sailors. Then the door clanged shut. The bolts that locked it could be seen turning in the bulkhead.

"Oh, my God," Millicent breathed, her voice quivering, spittle dribbling from a corner of lips swollen from biting on them, "this isn't happening."

Ebby gestured toward the bulkhead with his chin. "They'll have microphones," he whispered. "They'll be listening to everything we say."

Jack was absolutely positive this was another Company training drill but he played the game, hoping to make a good impression on the Company spooks who monitored the exercise. "Why would thugs want to kidnap Craw trainees?" he asked, sticking to the cover legend they had worked out in the first week of the course.

Ebby took his cue from Jack. "It's a case of mistaken identity—there's no other explanation."

"Maybe someone has a grudge against Craw," Jack offered.

"Or Sears, Roebuck, for that matter," Leo said.

Millicent was in a world of her own. "It's a training exercise," she said, talking to herself. "They want to see how we behave under fire." Squinting because of the spotlights, it suddenly dawned on her that she was practically naked and she began to moan softly. "I don't mind admitting it, I'm frightened out of my skin."

Breathing carefully through his nostrils to calm himself, Leo tried to distinguish the thread of logic buried somewhere in the riot of thoughts. In the end there were really only two possibilities. The most likely was that it was a very realistic training exercise; a rite of passage for those who had signed on to work for the elite Soviet Russia Division. The second possibility—that the four of them had really been kidnapped by Soviet agents who wanted information about CIA recruiting and training—struck him as ludicrous. But was Leo dismissing it out of wishful thinking? What if it were true? What if the Russians had discovered that Craw Management was a Company front and were trawling for trainees? What if the luck of the draw had deposited the four stragglers from the Italian restaurant in their net?

Leo tried to remember what they'd been taught in the seminar on interrogation techniques. Bits and pieces came back to him. All interrogators tried to convince their prisoners that they knew more than they actually did; that any information you provided was only confirming what they already knew. You were supposed to stick to your cover story even in the face of evidence that the interrogators were familiar with details of your work for the CIA. Mr. Andrews had turned up unexpectedly at the last session on interrogation techniques; in his mind's eye Leo could see the infinitely sad smile creeping over his instructor's face as he wrapped up the course but, for the life of him, he couldn't remember what Mr. Andrews had said.

After what seemed like an eternity Leo became aware of a grinding noise. He noticed the hatch-bolts turning in the bulkhead. The door swung open on greased hinges. The emaciated man, his eyes hidden behind oval sunglasses, stepped into the room. He had changed clothing and was wearing a white jumpsuit with washed-out orange stains on it. One of the sailors came in behind him carrying a wooden bucket half filled with water. The sailor set it in a corner, filled a wooden ladle with brackish water from the bucket, and spilled some down the throat of each of the parched prisoners. The emaciated man scraped over a chair, turned it so that the back was to the prisoners and straddled the seat facing them. He extracted a cigarette from a steel case, tapped down the tobacco and held the flame of a lighter to the tip; Leo got another whiff of the Russian tobacco. Sucking on the cigarette, the emaciated man seemed lost in thought. "Call me Oskar," he announced abruptly. "Admit it," he went on, "you are hoping this is a CIA training exercise but you are not sure." A taunting cackle emerged from the back of his throat. "It falls to me to pass on to you displeasant news—you are on the Latvian freighter *Liepaja* anchored in your Chesapeake Bay while we wait for clearance to put to sea with a cargo of flour, destination Riga. The ship has already been searched by your Coastal Guard. They usually keep us waiting many hours to torment us, but we play cards and listen to Negro jazz on the radio and sometime question CIA agents who have fallen into our hands." He pulled a small spiral notebook from a pocket, moistened a thumb on his tongue and started leafing through the pages. "So," he said when he found what he was looking for. "Which one of you is Ebbitt?"

Ebby cleared his throat. "I'm Ebbitt." His voice sounded unnaturally hoarse.

"I see that you have a divorce decree signed by a judge in the city of Las Vegas." Oskar looked up. "You carry a laminated card identifying you as an employee of Sears, Roebuck and a second card admitting you to the S.M. Craw Management course in Springfield, Virginia."

"That's right."

"What exactly is your work at Sears, Roebuck?"

"I am a lawyer. I write contracts."

"So: I ask you this question, Mr. Ebbitt—why would an employee of Sears, Roebuck tell his friends"—Oskar looked down at the notebook—"'They will have microphones. They will be listening to everything we say.'"

Ebby raised his chin and squinted into the spotlights as if he were sunning himself. "I read too many spy novels."

"My colleagues and I, we know that S.M. Craw Management is a spy school run by your Central Intelligence Agency. We know that the four of you are conscripted into the CIA's curiously named Soviet Russia Division—curious because Russia is only one of fifteen republics in the Union of Soviet Socialist Republics. Before your famous espionage agency can learn secrets it should study a Rand McNally atlas."

Leo asked, "What do you want from us?"

Oskar sized up Leo. "For beginning, I want you to abandon the legend of working for the Sears, Roebuck. For next, I want you to abandon the fiction that S.M. Craw teaches management techniques. When you have primed the pump with these admittances many other things will spill from the spigot— the names of your instructors and the details of their instruction, the names and descriptions of your classmates, the details of the cipher systems you learned at the spy school, the names and descriptions of the espionage agents who recruited you or you have met in the course of your training."

Oskar, it turned out, was the first in a series of interrogators who took turns questioning the prisoners without a break. With the spotlights burning into their eyes, the captives quickly lost track of time. At one point Millicent pleaded for permission to go to the toilet. A fat interrogator with a monocle stuck in one eye jerked aside her brassiere and pinched a nipple and then, laughing, motioned for one of the sailors to untie her and lead her to a filthy toilet in the passageway; this turned out to be particularly humiliating for Millicent because the sailor insisted on keeping the door wide open to watch her. If any of the four nodded off during the interrogation, a sailor would jar the sleeper awake with a sharp kick to an ankle. Working from handwritten notes scribbled across the pages of their notebooks, the interrogators walked the captives through the cover stories that had been worked up, sticking wherever possible to actual biographies, during the first week at Craw.

"You claim you worked for the law firm of Donovan, Leisure, Newton, Lumbard and Irvine," Oskar told Ebby at one point.

"How many times are you going to cover the same ground? Working for Donovan, Leisure, Newton, Lumbard and Irvine isn't the same thing as working for a government agency, damn it."

The cigarette Oskar held between his thumb and middle finger was burning dangerously close to both. When he felt the heat on his skin he flicked it across the room. "Your Mr. Donovan is the same William Donovan who was the chief of the American Office of Strategic Services during the Great Patriotic War?"

"One and the same," Ebby said wearily.

"Mr. Donovan is also the William Donovan who eagerly pushed your President Truman to construct a central intelligence agency after the war."

"I read the same newspapers you do," Ebby shot back.

"As you are a former member of Mr. Donovan's OSS, it would have been logical for him to recommend you to the people who run this new central intelligence agency."

"He would not have recommended me without first asking me if I wanted to return to government service. Why in the world would I give up a thirty-seven-thousand-dollar-a-year job in a prestigious law firm for a six-thousand-four-hundred-dollar job with an intelligence agency? It doesn't make sense."

Ebby realized he had made a mistake the instant the numbers passed his lips. He knew what Oskar's next question would be before he asked it.

"So: Please, how do you know that an agent for the Central Intelligence Agency earns six-thousand-four-hundred-dollars a year?"

Ebby's shoulders lifted in an irritated shrug. "I must have read it in a newspaper."

"And the precise figure of six-thousand-four-hundred lodged in your memory?"

"I suppose it did, yes."

"Why did you give up the thirty-seven-thousand-dollar job to join Sears, Roebuck?"

"Because Mr. Donovan wasn't holding out the prospect of a partnership. Because the Sears people were pleased with the contracts I drew up for them when I was working at Donovan. Because they were paying an arm and a leg for legal work and figured they could come out ahead even if they paid me more than Mr. Donovan paid me."

"Who do you work for at Sears?"

Ebby named names and Oskar copied them into his notebook. He was about to ask another question when one of the sailors came into the room and whispered in his ear. Oskar said, "So: Your Coastal Guard has at last given us permission to get underway." Beneath the feet of the prisoners the deck plates began to vibrate, faintly at first, then with a distinct throb. "It can be hoped none of you suffer from sea sickness," Oskar said. He switched to Russian and barked an order to one of the sailors. Leo understood what he was saying—Oskar wanted buckets brought around in case anyone should throw up—but he kept his eyes empty of expression.

Slumped in her chair, Millicent held up better than the others had expected; she seemed to take strength from the tenacity with which they stuck to their legends. Again and again the interrogator returned to the Craw Management course; he even described the class in tradecraft given by a one-armed instructor named Andrews, but Millicent only shook her head. She couldn't say what the others had been doing at Craw, she could only speak for herself; she had been studying techniques of management. Yes, she vaguely remembered seeing a one-armed man in the room where mail was sorted but she had never taken a course with him. No, there had never been a field trip to Norfolk to try and steal secrets from military bases. Why on earth would someone studying management want to steal military secrets? What would they do with them after they had stolen them?

And then suddenly there was a commotion in the passageway. The door was ajar and men in uniform could be seen lumbering past. The two interrogators in the room at that moment exchanged puzzled looks. Oskar gestured with his head. They both stepped outside and had a hushed conversation in Russian with a heavy-set man wearing the gold braid of a naval officer on his sleeves. Leo thought he heard "cipher machine" and "lead-weighted bag," and he was sure he heard "overboard if the Americans try to intercept us."

"What are they saying?" Jack growled. He was beginning to wonder if they had been caught up in a Company exercise after all.

"They talking about putting their cipher machine in a weighted bag and throwing it into the sea if the Americans try to intercept the ship," Leo whispered.

"Jesus," Ebby said. "The last order that reached the Japanese embassy in Washington on December sixth, 1941 was to destroy the ciphers, along with their cipher machines."

"Damnation, the Russians must be going to war," Jack said.

Millicent's chin sank forward onto her chest and she began to tremble.

Oskar, still in the passageway, could be heard talking about "the four Americans," but what he said was lost in the wail of a siren. The naval officer snapped angrily, *"Nyet, nyet."* The officer raised his voice and Leo distinctly heard him say, "I am the one who decides...the *Liepaja* is under my...in half an...sunrise...by radio...cement and throw them over..."

Ebby and Jack turned to Leo for a translation. They could tell from the wild look in his eyes that the news was calamitous. "They're saying something about cement," Leo whispered. "They're talking about throwing us into the sea if we don't talk."

"It's part of the exercise," Ebby declared, forgetting about the microphones in the bulkhead. "They're trying to terrorize us."

His face ashen, his brow furrowed, Oskar returned to the room alone. "Very unsatisfactory news," he announced. "There has been a confrontation in Berlin. Shots were fired. Soldiers on both sides were killed. Our Politburo has given your President Truman an ultimatum: Withdraw your troops from Berlin in twelve hours or we will consider ourselves to be in a state of war."

Half a dozen sailors barged into the room. Some were carrying sacks of cement, others empty twenty-five-gallon paint cans. Another sailor ran a length of hose into the room, then darted out to hook it up to a faucet in the toilet. Oskar shook his head in despair. "Please believe me—it was never my intention that it should come to this," he said in a hollow voice. He unhooked his sunglasses from his ears; his bulging eyes were moist with emotion. "The ones we kidnapped before, we frightened them but we always let them go in the end."

Tears ran from Millicent's eyes and she started to shiver uncontrollably despite the stifling heat in the room. Ebby actually stopped breathing for a long moment and then panicked when, for a terrifying instant, he couldn't immediately remember *how* to start again. Leo desperately tried to think of something he could tell Oskar—he remembered Mr. Andrews's saying you had to become the person the enemy would never suspect you of being. Who could he become? Suddenly he had a wild idea—he would tell them he was a Soviet agent under instructions to infiltrate the CIA? Would Oskar fall for it? Would he even take the time to check it out with his superiors in Moscow?

Water began to trickle from the end of the hose and the sailors gashed open the paper sacks and started filling the four paint cans with cement. Oskar said, "I ask you, I beg you, give me what I need to save your lives. If you are CIA recruits I can countermand the orders, I can insist that we take you back to Latvia so our experts can interrogate you." Rolling his head from side to side in misery, Oskar pleaded, "Only help me and I will do everything in my power to save you."

Millicent blurted out, "I will—"

Oskar stabbed the air with a finger and one of the sailors untied the rope that bound her to the chair. Shaking convulsively, she slumped forward onto her knees. Between sobs, words welled up from the back of her throat. "Yes, yes, it's true...all of us...I was recruited out of law school... because of my looks, because I spoke Italian...Craw to take courses..." She started to gag on words, then sucked in a great gulp of air and began spitting out names and dates and places. When Oskar tried to interrupt her she clamped her palms over her ears and plunged on, describing down to the last detail the pep talk the Wiz had delivered at the Cloud Club, describing Owen-Brack's threat to terminate anyone who gave away Company secrets. Scraping the back of her mind, she came up with details of the courses she had taken at Craw. "The man who taught tradecraft, he's a great hero at the Pickle Factory—"

"Pickle Factory?"

A watery rheum seeped from Millicent's nostrils onto her upper lip. She flicked it away with the back of her hand. "More, more—I can tell you more. I was supposed to lure them, money, flattery, fuck them, picks and locks, his name is Andrew but, oh God, I can't remember if that's his first name or family name." Oskar tried to interrupt her again but she pleaded, "More, much more, please for Christ's sake—"

And she looked up and saw, through her tears, Mr. Andrews standing in the doorway, the sleeve of his sports jacked folded back, his eyes flickering in mortification, and she fell silent and swallowed hard and then screamed "Bastard...bastard...PRICK!" and pitched forward to pound her forehead against the deck plates until Oskar and one of the sailors restrained her. Her body twitching, she kept murmuring something to herself that sounded like "Bread-and-butter, bread-and-butter."

Watching Mr. Andrews avert his eyes from Millicent's near-naked body, Leo suddenly remembered what he had said that last day in the seminar on interrogation techniques; in his mind's ear he could hear Mr. Andrew's voice. "Believe me, I am speaking from experience when I tell you that anyone can be broken in *six hours*. Tops. Without exception. *Anyone.*" An infinitely sad expression had superimposed itself on the ugly scars of Mr. Andrews's face. "Curiously, it's not the pain that breaks you—you get so accustomed to it, so accustomed to your own voice yowling like an animal, that you are incapable of remembering what the absence of pain felt like. No, it's not the pain but the fear that breaks you. And there are a hundred ways of instilling fear. There is only sure one way to avoid being broken: for the love of God, observe the Eleventh Commandment of intelligence work—never, never get caught."

There was no postmortem, at least not a formal one. News of the mock-kidnapping had spread, as it was meant to; the Company wanted it clearly understood that the Marquess of Queensberry rules didn't apply to the great game of espionage. Classmates accosted the three principals in the corridors to ask if it were true and when they said yes, it had happened more or less the way they'd heard it, the others shook their heads in disbelief. Leo discovered that Millicent Pearlstein had been taken away in an unmarked ambulance to a Company clinic somewhere on the Piedmont plateau of Virginia; there was no question of keeping her on board, it was said, not because she had cracked, but because the fault line could never be repaired and the Company needed to weed out the people with fault lines. Mr. Andrews took Leo aside one afternoon and told him he felt terrible about Millicent but he thought it was better this way. She hadn't been cut out for the life of a field officer; when she was back on her feet she would be paid a small indemnity and steered to another, tamer, government security agency—both the State Department and the Defense Department ran intelligence collecting operations of their own.

At the end of the week the recruits began packing their bags—they were being accorded a two-week holiday before reporting for their assignments. By chance, a new batch of recruits was checking into the Hilton Inn. Jack and Leo recognized two of them from Yale.

"Holy shit, you guys look as if you've been through the Maytag wringer," one of them said.

"So how tough is it?" the other wanted to know.

"It's a pushover," Jack said. "I didn't work up a sweat."

"Easy as falling off a log," Leo agreed.

Both of them tried to smile. Neither of them could locate the muscles that did that sort of thing.

2

MUSCOVITES COULDN'T REMEMBER ANYTHING LIKE IT IN THIS century. Drifts of heat had clawed their way up from the Kara Kum Desert in Turkmenistan, asphyxiating the sprawling capital, cooking the asphalt of the streets until it felt gummy under the soles of summer shoes. The sweltering temperatures had driven thousands of Muscovites, stripped to their underwear, into the polluted waters of the Moscow River for relief. Yevgeny found shelter in the bar of the Metropole Hotel near Red Square, where he'd gone for a late afternoon drink with the gorgeous Austrian exchange student he'd flirted with on the flight back from the States. Not for the first time Yevgeny took a mordant pleasure in passing himself off as an American; he thought of it as an indoor sport. The Austrian girl, a dyed-in-the-wool socialist overdosing on Marxism at Lomonosov University, was ecstatic at the daily reports of North Korean victories and American defeats, and it took a while before Yevgeny managed to steer the conversation away from politics and onto sex. It turned out the girl was willing but not able—she was afraid to invite him up to her dormitory room for fear a KGB informer would eavesdrop on their lovemaking and she would be expelled from Russia for anti-socialist behavior. And no amount of coaxing ("In *Das Kapital*, volume two," Yevgeny—ad libbing with a straight face—said at one point, "Marx makes the case that chastity is a bourgeoisie vice that will not survive the class struggle") could convince her otherwise. Yevgeny eventually gave up on her and, suddenly aware of the hour, tried to flag down a taxi in front of the Bolshoi. When that didn't work out he ducked into the metro and rode it across the river to the Maksim

Gorky Embankment and jogged the hundred-fifty meters uphill toward the new nine-story apartment complex where his father had gone to ground after his retirement from the United Nations Secretariat. At the walled entrance to the complex, three high-rise buildings dominating the Moscow River, a militiaman stepped out of the booth and crisply demanded Yevgeny's internal passport. The complex on the Lenin Hills had been set aside for high-ranking Party secretaries and senior diplomats and important editors and was guarded round the clock, which only added to the aura of the *nomenklatura* lucky enough to be allotted apartments in any of the buildings. The star resident, so Yevgeny's father had boasted on the phone, was none other than Nikita Sergeyevich Khrushchev, the tubby Ukrainian peasant who had made a name for himself in the '30s supervising the building of the Moscow metro and was now one of the "kittens" in Stalin's Politburo; Khrushchev occupied what the Russians (even writing in Cyrillic) called the "*bel étage*" and had a private elevator that served his floor only. The militiaman examined the photograph in the passport and, looking up, carefully matched it against Yevgeny's face, then ran a finger down the list on his clipboard until he came to the name Yevgeny Aleksandrovich Tsipin. "You are expected," he announced in the toneless pitch of self-importance common to policemen the world over, and waved Yevgeny toward the building. There was another militiaman inside the lobby and a third operating the elevator; the latter let the visitor off on the eighth floor and waited, with the elevator door open, until Aleksandr Timofeyevich Tsipin answered Yevgeny's ring and signalled that he recognized the guest. Yevgeny's father, still wearing a black mourning band on the sleeve of his suit jacket eleven months after his wife's death, drew his oldest son into the air-conditioned apartment and embraced him awkwardly, planting a scratchy kiss on each check.

It was difficult to say who felt more self-conscious at this show of affection, the father or the son.

"I apologize for not seeing you sooner," mumbled the elder Tsipin. "There were conferences, there were reports to finish."

"The usual things. How is your rheumatism?"

"It comes, it goes, depending on the weather. Since when have you been cultivating a goatee?"

"Since I last saw you, which was at my mother's funeral."

Tsipin avoided his son's eye. "Sorry I was unable to offer you a bed. Where did you wind up living?"

"A friend has a room in a communal apartment. He is putting me up on a couch."

Through the double door of the vast living room, Yevgeny caught a glimpse of the immense picture window with its breathtaking view of the river and of Moscow sprawling beyond it. *"Ochen khorosho,"* he said. "The Soviet Union treats its former senior diplomats like tsars."

"Grinka is here," the elder Tsipin said, hooking an arm through Yevgeny's and leading him into the living room. "He took the overnight train down from Leningrad when he heard you were coming. I also invited a friend, and my friend brought along a friend of his." He favored his son with a mysterious grin. "I am sure you will find my friend interesting." He lowered his voice and leaned toward his son's ear. "If he asks you about America I count on you to emphasize the faults."

Yevgeny spotted his younger brother through the double door and bounded across the room to wrap Grinka in a bear hug. Tsipin's longtime servant, a lean middle-aged Uzbek woman with the delicate features of a bird, was serving *zakuski* to the two guests near the window. A sigh of pure elation escaped her lips when she saw Yevgeny. She cried out to him in Uzbek and, pulling his head down, planted kisses on his forehead and both shoulders.

Yevgeny said, "Hello to you, Nyura."

"Thanks to God you are returned from America alive," she exclaimed. "It is said the cities are under the command of armed gangsters."

"Our journalists tend to see the worst," he told her with a smile. He leaned over and kissed her on both cheeks, causing her to bow her head and blush.

"Nyura practically raised Yevgeny during the war years when his mother and I were posted to Turkey," Tsipin explained to his guests.

"I spent several days in Istanbul on a secret mission before the war started," the older of the two remarked. "My memory is that it was a chaotic city."

Yevgeny noticed that the guest spoke Russian with an accent he took to be German. "It was my dream to be allowed to live with my parents in Istanbul," he said, "but Turkey in those days was a center of international intrigue—there were kidnappings, even murders—and I was obliged to remain in Alma-Ata with Nyura and Grinka for safety's sake."

Tsipin did the introductions. "Yevgeny, I present to you Martin Dietrich. Comrade Dietrich, please meet my oldest son recently returned from his American university. And this is Pavel Semyonovich Zhilov, Pasha for short, a great friend to me for more years than I care to remember. Pasha is known to the comrades—"

"Perhaps you will have the good fortune to become one," Dietrich told Yevgeny with elaborate formality.

"—as Starik."

Yevgeny shook hands with both men, then flung an arm over the shoulder of his younger brother as he inspected his father's guests. Martin Dietrich was on the short side, stocky, in his early fifties with a washed-out complexion, tired humorless eyes and surgical scars on his cheeks where skin had been grafted over the facial bones. Pasha Semyonovich Zhilov was a tall, reed-like man who looked as if he had stepped out of another century and was ill at ease in the present one. In his mid or late thirties, he had the scraggy pewter beard of a priest and brooding blue eyes that narrowed slightly and fixed on you with unnerving intensity. His fingernails were thick and long and cropped squarely, in the manner of peasants'. He was dressed in baggy trousers and a rough white shirt whose broad collar, open at the neck, offered a glimpse of a finely wrought silver chain. A dark peasant's jacket plunged to his knees. He stood there cracking open toasted Samarkand apricot pits with thick thumbnails and popping the nuts into his mouth. Half a dozen small silk rosettes were pinned on his lapel. Yevgeny, who had learned to identify the rosettes during a stint in the Komsomol Youth Organization, recognized several: the Hero of the Soviet Union, the Order of the Red Banner, the Order of Aleksandr Nevsky, the Order of the Red Star. Nodding toward the rosettes, Yevgeny said, with just a trace of mockery, "You are clearly a great war hero. Perhaps one day you will tell me the story behind each of your medals."

Starik, puffing on a Bulgarian cigarette with a long hollow tip, eyed his host's son. "Contrary to appearances, I do not live in the past," he said flatly.

"That alone sets you apart from everyone else in Russia," Yevgeny said. He helped himself to a cracker spread with caviar. "Starik—*the old man*—was what the comrades called Lenin, wasn't it? How did you come to be called by such a name?"

Yevgeny's father answered for him. "In Lenin's case it was because he was so much older than the others around him at the time of the Revolution. In Pasha's case it was because he talked like Tolstoy long before he let his beard grow."

Yevgeny, who had acquired the American gift for insouciance, asked with an insolent grin, "And what do you talk about when you talk like Tolstoy?"

His father tried to divert the conversation. "How was your flight back from America, Yevgeny?"

Starik waved off his host. "There is no harm done, Aleksandr Timofeyevich. I prefer curious young men to those who, at twenty-one, know all there is to know."

He turned a guarded smirk on Yevgeny for the first time; Yevgeny recognized it for what it was—the enigmatic expression of someone who thought of life as an intricate game of chess. Another member of the Communist *nomenklatura* who climbed over the bodies of his colleagues to get ahead!

Starik spit a spoiled Samarkand nut onto the Persian carpet. "What I talk about," he told Yevgeny, articulating his words carefully, "is a state secret."

Later, over dinner, Starik steered the subject to America and asked Yevgeny for his impressions. Did he believe racial tensions would lead to a Negro uprising? Would the exploited Caucasian proletariat support such a revolt? Yevgeny responded by saying that he hadn't really been in America—he'd been in Yale, a ghetto populated by members of the privileged classes who could afford tuition, or the occasional scholarship student who aspired to join the privileged class. "As for the Negroes revolting," he added, "man will walk on the moon before that happens. Whoever is telling you such things simply doesn't know what he's talking about."

"I read it in *Pravda*," Starik said, watching his host's son to see if he would back down.

Yevgeny suddenly felt as if he were taking an oral exam. "The journalists of *Pravda* are telling you what they think you should hear," he said. "If we hope to compete successfully with the immense power of capitalist America we must first understand what makes it tick."

"Do you understand what makes it tick?"

"I begin to understand America well enough to know there is no possibility that its Negroes will revolt."

"And what do you plan to do with this knowledge you have of America?" Starik inquired.

"I have not figured that out yet."

Grinka asked his father if he had seen the *Pravda* story about the TASS journalist in Washington who had been drugged and photographed in bed with a stark-naked teenage girl, after which the American CIA had tried to blackmail him into spying for it. Yevgeny commented that there was a good chance the TASS man had been a KGB agent to begin with. His father, refilling the glasses from a chilled bottle of Hungarian white wine, remarked that the Americans regularly accused Soviet journalists and diplomats of being spies.

Yevgeny regarded his father. "Aren't they?" he asked with a laugh in his eyes.

Starik raised his wineglass to eye level and studied Yevgeny over the rim as he turned the stem in his fingers. "Let us be frank: Sometimes they are," he said evenly. "But Socialism, if it is to survive, must defend itself."

"And don't we try the same tricks on them that they try on us?" Yevgeny persisted.

Martin Dietrich turned out to have a mild sense of humor after all. "With all my heart, I hope so," he announced. "Considering the dangers they run, spies are underpaid and occasionally need to be compensated with something other than money."

"To an outsider, I can see how the business of spying sometimes appears to be an amusing game," Starik conceded, his eyes riveted on Yevgeny across the table. Turning to his host, he launched into the story of a French military attaché who had been seduced by a young woman who worked at the Ministry of Internal Affairs. "One night he visited her in the single room she shared with one other girl. Before you knew it he and the two girls had removed their clothing and jumped into bed. Of course the girls worked for our KGB. They filmed the whole thing through a two-way mirror. When they discreetly confronted the attaché with still photographs, he burst into laughter and asked them if they could supply him with copies to send to his wife in Paris to prove that his virility had not diminished during his two years in Moscow."

Yevgeny's eyes widened slightly. How was it that his father's friend knew such a story? Was Pasha Semyonovich Zhilov connected with the KGB? Yevgeny glanced at his father—he had always assumed he had some sort of relationship with the KGB. After all, diplomats abroad were expected to keep their eyes and ears open and report back to their handlers. *Their handlers!* Could it be that Starik was his father's conducting officer? The elder Tsipin had introduced Starik as his great friend. If Starik was his handler, his father may have played a more active role in Soviet intelligence than his son imagined; Zhilov simply didn't seem like someone who merely debriefed returning diplomats.

There was another riddle that intrigued Yevgeny: Who was the quiet German who went by the name Martin Dietrich and looked as if his features had been burned—or altered by plastic surgery? And what had he done for the Motherland to merit wearing over his breast pocket a ribbon indicating that he, too, was a Hero of the Soviet Union?

Back in the living room, Nyura set out Napoleon brandy and snifters, which the host half-filled and Grinka handed around. Zhilov and Tsipin were in the middle of an argument about what had stopped the seemingly invincible Germans when they attacked the Soviet Union. Grinka, a second-year student of history and Marxist theory at Leningrad University, said, "The same thing that stopped Napoleon—Russian bayonets and Russian winter."

"We had a secret weapon against both Napoleon's Grand Army and Hitler's Wehrmacht," Aleksandr instructed his youngest son. "It was the *rasputitsa*—the rivers of melting snow in the spring, the torrents of rain in the autumn—that transform the Steppe into an impassable swamp. I remember that the *rasputitsa* was especially severe in March of '41, preventing the Germans from attacking for several crucial weeks. It was severe again in October of '41 and the winter frost that hardens the ground enough for tanks to operate came late, which left the Wehrmacht bogged down within sight of the spires of Moscow when the full force of winter struck."

"Aleksandr is correct—we had a secret weapon. But it was neither our bayonets nor the Russian winter, nor the *rasputitsa*," Zhilov said. "It was our spies who told us which of the German thrusts were feints and which were real; who told us how much petrol stocks their tanks had on hand so we could figure out how long they could run; who told us that the Wehrmacht, calculating that the Red Army could not resist the German onslaught, had not brought up winter lubricants, which meant their battle tanks would be useless once the weather turned cold."

Yevgeny felt the warmth of the brandy invade his chest. "I have never understood how the Motherland lost twenty million killed in the Great Patriotic War—a suffering so enormous it defies description—yet those who participated in the blood bath speak of it with nostalgia?"

"Do you remember the stories of the Ottoman sultans ruling an empire that stretched from the Danube to the Indian Ocean?" Starik inquired. "They would recline on cushions in the lush garden pavilions of Istanbul wearing archer's rings on their thumbs to remind them of battles they could only dimly remember." His large head swung round slowly in Yevgeny's direction. "In a manner of speaking, all of us who fought the Great Patriotic War wear archer's rings on our thumbs or rosettes on our lapels. When our memories fade all we will have left of that heroic moment will be our rings and our medals."

Later, waiting for the elevator to arrive, Starik talked in an undertone with his host. As the elevator door opened Zhilov turned back toward Yevgeny and casually offered him a small calling card. "I invite you to take tea with me," he murmured. "Perhaps I will tell you the story behind one of my medals after all."

If the dinner had been a test, Yevgeny understood that he had passed it. Almost against his will he found himself being drawn to this unkempt peasant of a man who—judging from his bearing; judging, too, from the deference with which his father had treated him—clearly outranked a former Under Secretary-General of the United Nations. And much to his surprise he heard himself say, "I would consider it a privilege."

"Tomorrow at four-thirty." Starik wasn't asking, he was informing. "Leave word with your father where you will be and I will send a car for you. The calling card will serve as a *laissez-passer*"—Starik used the French phrase—"for the militiamen guarding the outer gate."

"The outer gate of what?" Yevgeny asked, but Starik had disappeared into the elevator.

Yevgeny was turning the card in his fingers when Grinka snatched it out of his hand. "He's a *general polkovnik*—a colonel general—in the KGB," he said with a whistle. "What do you think he wants with you?"

"Perhaps he wants me to follow in our father's footsteps," Yevgeny told his brother.

"Become a diplomat!"

"Is that what you were, father?" Yevgeny asked with an insolent smile.

"What I was, was a servant of my country," the elder Tsipin responded in irritation. He turned abruptly and left the room.

Yevgeny saw his brother off at the Leningrad Railway Station, then crossed Komsomolskaya Square to the kiosk with the distinctive red-tiled roof and waited in the shade. As the station clock struck four a black Zil with gleaming chrome and tinted windows pulled to a stop in front of him. The windows were closed, which meant that the car was ventilated. A round-faced man wearing sunglasses and a bright Kazakh hat rolled down the front window.

"Are you from—" Yevgeny began.

"Don't be thick," the man said impatiently. "Get in."

Yevgeny climbed into the back. The Zil turned around the Ring Road and sped out of the city heading southwest on the Kaluga Road. Yevgeny rapped his knuckles on the thick glass partition separating him from the two men in the front seat. The one with the Kazakh hat glanced over his shoulder.

"How long will it take to get where we are going?" Yevgeny called through the partition. The man flashed five fingers three times and turned back.

Yevgeny sank into the cool leather of the seat and passed the time studying the people along the street. He remembered the elation he'd felt as a child when his father had taken him and Grinka for excursions in the family's Volga limousine. His father's car had been chauffeured by one of the uniformed militiamen from the Ministry of Foreign Affairs, a dark man with slanting eyes and a peach-shaped face who called the boys "Little Sirs" when he held the door for them. Peering from behind the car's curtains, Yevgeny would pretend that he and his brother were heroes of Mother Russia who had been decorated by the Great Helmsman, Comrade Stalin, himself; from time to time the two boys would wave imperiously at some peasants along the route to Peredelkino, where his father had purchased a Ministry dacha. Now, in the Zil, the driver leaned on the horn and pedestrians scattered out of his way. The car slowed, but never stopped, for red lights. When they spotted the Zil, militiamen sweating in tunics buttoned up to the neck brought cross traffic to a standstill with their batons and prevented the swarm of pedestrians from surging across the boulevard. As the car flew by people gazed at the tinted windows, trying to figure out which member of the Politburo or Central Committee might be behind them.

After a time the Zil turned onto a narrow one-lane road with a sign at the edge reading, "Center for Study—No Admittance." They drove for three or four minutes through a forest of white birches, the bark peeling from the trunks like discarded paper wrapping. Through the trees Yevgeny caught sight of a small abandoned church, its door and windows gaping open, its single onion-shaped dome leaning into the heat wave from Central Asia. The limousine swung into a driveway paved with fine white gravel and pulled up in front of a small brick building. A high chain-link fence topped with coils of barbed wire stretched as far as the eye could see in either direction. Two gray-and-tan Siberian huskies prowled back and forth at the end of long ropes fastened to trees. An Army officer came around to the rear window. A soldier with a PPD-34 under his arm, its round clip inserted, watched from behind a pile of sandbags. Yevgeny rolled the window down just enough to pass Starik's calling card to the officer. A hot blast of outside air filled the back of the car. The officer looked at the card, then handed it back and waved the driver on. At the end of the gravel driveway loomed a pre-revolutionary three-story mansion. Around the side of the house, two little girls, barefoot and wearing short smock-like dresses, were crying out in mock fright as they soared high or dipped low on a seesaw. Nearby, a mottled white-and-brown horse, reins hanging loose on his neck, cropped the grass. A young man in a tight suit, alerted by the guards at the gate, was waiting at the open door, his arms folded self-importantly across his chest, his shoulders hunched against the heat. "You are invited to follow me," he said when Yevgeny came up the steps. He preceded the visitor down a marble hallway and up a curving flight of stairs covered with a worn red runner, rapped twice on a door on the second floor, threw it open and stepped back to let Yevgeny through.

Pasha Semyonovich Zhilov, cooling himself in front of a Westinghouse air conditioner fixed in a window of the antechamber, was reading aloud from a thin book to two small girls curled up on a sofa, their knees parted shamelessly, their thin limbs askew. Starik broke off reading when he caught sight of Yevgeny. "Oh, do continue, uncle," one of the little girls pleaded. The other sucked sulkily on her thumb. Ignoring the girls, Starik strode across the room and clasped the hand of his visitor in both of his. Behind Yevgeny the door clicked closed.

"Do you have any idea where you are?" Starik inquired as he gripped Yevgeny's elbow and steered him through a door into a large sitting room.

"Not the slightest," Yevgeny admitted.

"I may tell you that you are in the Southwestern District near the village of Cheryomuski. The estate, originally tens of thousands of hectares, belonged to the Apatov family but, it was taken over by the CHEKA in the early 1920s and has been used as a secret retreat since." He gestured with his head for Yevgeny to follow him as he made his way through a billiard room and into a dining room with a large oval table set with fine china and Czech glass. "The mansion is actually divided into three apartments — one is used by Viktor Abakumov, who is the head of our SMERSH organization. The second is set aside for the Minister of Internal Security, Comrade Beria. He uses it as a hideaway when he wants to escape from the bedlam of Moscow." Starik collected a bottle of Narzan mineral water and two glasses, each with a slice of lemon in it, and continued on to a spacious wood-paneled library filled with hundreds of leather-covered volumes and several dozen small gold- and silver-inlaid icons. On the single stretch of wall not covered with bookcases hung a life-sized portrait of L.N. Tolstoy. The painter's name—I.E. Repin—and the date 1887 were visible at the bottom right. Tolstoy, wearing a rough peasant's shirt and a long white beard, had been posed sitting in a chair, a book open in his left hand. Yevgeny noticed that the great writer's fingernails, like Starik's, were thick and long and cut off squarely.

A large wooden table containing a neat pile of file folders stood in the center of the room. Starik set the mineral water and glasses on the table and slipped into a seat. He motioned for Yevgeny to take the seat across from him. "Comrade Beria claims that the calm and the country air are an analgesic for his ulcers—more effective than the hot-water bottles he keeps applying to his stomach. Who can say he is not right?" Starik lit one of his Bulgarian cigarettes. "You don't smoke?"

Yevgeny shook his head.

A man with a shaven head, wearing a black jacket and black trousers, appeared carrying a tray. He set a saucer of sugar cubes and another with slices of apple on the table, filled two glasses with steaming tea from a thermos and set the thermos down. When he had left, closing the door behind him, Starik wedged a cube of sugar between his teeth and, straining the liquid through it, began noisily drinking the tea. Yevgeny could see the Adam's apple bobbing in his sinewy neck. After a moment Starik asked, "Do Americans think there will be war?"

"Some do, some don't. In any case there is a general reluctance to go to war. Americans are a frontier people who have grown soft buying on credit whatever their hearts desire and paying off their mortgages for the rest of their lives."

Starik opened the file folder on top of the pile and began to leaf through the report as he sipped his tea. "I do not agree with your analysis. The American Pentagon thinks there will be war—they have actually predicted that it will start on the first of July 1952. A great many in the American Congress agree with the Pentagon forecast. When it was organized in 1947, the CIA was treated as a stepchild in matters of financing; now it is getting unlimited funds and recruiting agents at a feverish pace. And there is nothing *soft* about the training phase. The Soviet Russia Division, which is our *glavni protivnik*—how would you say that in American?"

"Principal adversary."

Starik tried out the words in English. "The principal adversary"—and quickly switched back to Russian—"organizes realistic kidnappings of their own officers by Russians on its staff pretending to be KGB agents, who then menace the recruits with death if they refuse to confess that they work for the CIA. The test is shrewd in as much as it establishes which of the new officers can survive the psychological shock of the episode and move on."

Starik looked up from the folder. "I am impressed by the questions you don't ask."

"If I asked how you knew such a thing you would not tell me, so why bother?"

Starik gulped more tea. "I propose that we speak as if we have known each other as long as I have known your father." When Yevgeny nodded assent he continued: "You come from a distinguished family with a long history of service to Soviet intelligence organs. In the twenties, at the time of the Civil War, your father's father was a Chekist, fighting alongside Feliks Edmundovich Dzerzhinsky when he created the All-Russian Extraordinary Commission for Combating Counterrevolution and Sabotage. Your father's brother is head of a department in the Second Chief Directorate of the KGB—ah, I see you were not aware of that."

"I was told that he worked for...but it doesn't matter what I was told."

"And your father—"

"My father?"

"He has worked for First Chief Directorate for years while he held diplomatic posts, the most recent of which, as you know, was an Under Secretary-Generalship in the United Nations Secretariat. For the past twelve years I have been his conducting officer, so I can personally attest to his enormous contribution to our cause. I have been told you take a rather cynical view of this cause. At its core what is Communism? A crazy idea that there is a side to us we have not yet explored. The tragedy of what we call Marxism-Leninism is that Lenin's hope and Zinoviev's expectation that the German revolution would lead to the establishment of a Soviet Germany were foiled. The first country to try the experiment was not proletarian-rich Germany but peasant-poor Russia. The capitalists never tire of throwing in our faces that we are a backward country, but look where we come from. I hold the view that our Communists can be divided into two groups: tsars who promote Mother Russia and Soviet *vlast*, and dreamers who promote the genius and generosity of the human spirit."

"My mother spoke often about the genius and generosity of the human spirit."

"I have nothing against expanding Soviet power but, in my heart of hearts I belong, like your mother, to the second category. Are you at all familiar with Leon Tolstoy, Yevgeny? Somewhere in one of his letters he says"—Starik threw back his head and closed his eyes and recited in a melodious voice—"'the changes in our life must come, not from our mental resolution to try a new form of life, but rather from the impossibility to live otherwise than according to the demands of our conscience.'" When he opened his eyes they were burning with fervor. "Our political system, in as much as it comes from a mental resolution to try a new form of life, is flawed. (I speak to you frankly; if you were to repeat what I tell you I could be prosecuted for treason.) The flaw has led to aberrations. But which political system hasn't its aberrations? In the previous century Americans collected blankets from soldiers who died of smallpox and distributed them to the native Indians. Southerners exploited their Negro slaves and lynched the ones who rebelled against this exploitation. French Catholics tied weights to the ankles of French Protestants and threw them into rivers. The Spanish Inquisition burned Hebrew and Muslim converts to Christianity at the stake because it doubted the sincerity of the conversions. Catholic Crusaders, waging holy war against Islam, locked Jews in temples in Jerusalem and burned them alive. All of which is to say that our system of Communism, like other political systems before it, will survive the aberrations of our tsars." Starik refilled his glass from the thermos. "How long were you in America?"

"My father began working for the UN immediately after the war. Which means I was in the states, let's see, almost five-and-a-half years—three and a half years at Erasmus High School in Brooklyn, then my junior and senior year at Yale thanks to the strings my father got Secretary-General Lie to pull."

Starik extracted a folder from the middle of the pile and held it so that Yevgeny could see the cover. His name—"Yevgeny Aleksandrovich Tsipin" was written across it, with the notation: "Very secret. No distribution whatsoever." He opened the folder and pulled out a sheet filled with handwritten notes. "Your father was not the one who got Secretary-General Lie to pull strings. It was me, working through Foreign Minister Molotov, who pulled the strings. You obviously have no memory of it but you and I have met before, Yevgeny. It was at your father's dacha in Peredelkino six years ago. You were not quite fifteen years of age at the time and attending Special School Number 19 in Moscow. You were eager, bright, with an ear for languages; you already spoke American well enough to converse with your mother—it was, I remember, your secret language so that your brother would not understand what you were saying."

Yevgeny smiled at the memory. Talking with Starik, he understood what it must be like to confess to a priest; you felt the urge to tell him things you didn't normally reveal to a stranger. "For obvious reasons it was not something that was spoken of, but my mother was descended from the aristocracy that traces is lineage back to Peter the Great—like Peter she was forever turning her eyes toward the West. She loved foreign languages—she herself spoke French as well as English. She had studied painting at La Grande Chaumière in Paris as a young woman and it marked her for life. I suspect that her marriage turned out to be a great disappointment to my mother, though she was thrilled when my father was sent abroad."

"That day at Peredelkino six years ago your father had just learned of the United Nations posting. Your mother talked him into taking you and your brother with them to America—he was reluctant at first, but your mother turned to me and I helped convince him. Your brother wound up studying at the Soviet Consulate school in New York. As you were older than Grinka your mother dreamed of enrolling you in an American high school, but the Foreign Ministry *apparatchiki* refused to waive the standing rules against such things. Once again your mother turned to me. I went over their heads and appealed directly to Molotov. I told him that we desperately needed people who were educated in America and were steeped in its language and culture. I remember Molotov's asking me whether you could survive an American education to become a good Soviet citizen. I gave him my pledge that you would."

"Why were you so sure?"

"I was not, but I was willing to take the risk for your mother's sake. She and I were distant cousins, you see, but there was more than a vague family tie between us. Over the years we had become...friends. It was the friendship of what I shall call, for want of a better expression, kindred spirits. We didn't see eye to eye at all on everything, and most especially on Marxism; but on other matters we saw heart to heart. And then...then there was something about you, a lust lurking in the pupils of your eyes. You *wanted* to believe—in a cause, in a mission, in a person." Starik's eyes narrowed. "You were like your mother in many ways. You both had a superstitious streak." He laughed to himself at a memory. "You were always spitting over your shoulder for good luck. Your mother always sat on her valise before starting on a voyage—it was something right out of Dostoyevsky. She never turned back once she crossed the threshold or, if she did, she looked at herself in a mirror before starting out again."

"I still do these things." Yevgeny thought a moment. "At Erasmus High we were not sure I would get permission to apply to Yale; not sure, when they accepted me, that my father could raise the hard currency to pay the tuition."

"It was *me* who organized for you to receive permission to apply to Yale. It was *me* who arranged for your father's book—*From the Soviet Point of View*—to be published by left-wing houses in several European and Third World countries, after which I made sure that the book earned enough for him to afford the tuition."

Yevgeny said, in a muffled voice, "What you are telling me takes my breath away."

Starik sprang to his feet and came around the table and gazed down at his young visitor. His peasant jacket swung open and Yevgeny caught a glimpse of the worn butt of a heavy naval pistol tucked into his waistband. The sight made his heart beat faster.

"Have I misjudged you, Yevgeny?" Starik demanded, abandoning the formal "*vui*," switching to the intimate "*ti*." "Have I misjudged your courage and your conscience? Your command of the American language, your knowledge of America, your ability to pass for an American, give you the possibility of making a unique contribution. You know only what you have read in books; I will teach you things that are not in books. Will you follow in your grandfather's and your father's footsteps? Will you enlist in the ranks of our Chekists and work with the dreamers who promote the genius and generosity of the human spirit?"

Yevgeny cried out, "With all my heart, yes." Then he repeated it with an urgency he had never felt before. "Yes, yes, I will follow where you lead me."

Starik, an austere man who seldom permitted himself the luxury of expressing emotions, reached over and clasped Yevgeny's hand in both of his large hands. His lips curled into an unaccustomed smile. "There are many rites of passage into my world, but by far the greatest is to demonstrate to you how much I trust you—with the lives of our agents, with state secrets, with my own well-being. Now I will relate to you the story behind my Order of the Red Banner. The tale is a state secret of the highest magnitude—so high that even your father does not know it. Once you hear it there will be no turning back."

"Tell me this secret."

"It concerns the German Martin Dietrich," he began in a hoarse whisper. "He was a Soviet spy in the Great Patriotic War. His real name"— Starik's eyes burned into Yevgeny's—"was Martin Bormann. Yes, the Martin Bormann who was Hitler's deputy. He was a Soviet agent from the late twenties; in 1929 we pushed him to marry the daughter of a Nazi close to Hitler and thus gain access to the Führer's inner circle. When the war started Bormann betrayed Hitler's strategy to us. He told us which of the German thrusts were feints, he told us how much petrol their tanks had on hand, he told us that the Wehrmacht had not brought up winter lubricants for their tanks in 1941. From the time of the great German defeat at Stalingrad Bormann was instrumental in pushing Hitler, over the objections of the generals, to make irrational decisions—the Führer's refusal to permit von Paulus to break out of the Stalingrad trap resulted in the loss of eight hundred and fifty thousand Fascist troops. And during all that time I was Martin's conducting officer."

"But Bormann was said to have died during the final battle for Berlin!"

"Some weeks before the end of the war German intelligence officers stumbled across deciphered intercepts that suggested Martin could be a

Soviet spy. They confided in Goebbels, but Goebbels was unable to work up the nerve tell Hitler, who by then was a ranting madman. In the final hours of the final battle Martin made his way across the Tiergarten toward the Lehrter Station. For a time he was pinned down in a crossfire between advance units of Chuikov's 8th Guards and an SS unit dug in next to the station, but during the night of first to second of May he finally managed to cross the line. I had arranged to meet Martin at the station. Our front line troops were told to be on the alert for a German officer dressed in a long leather coat with a camouflage uniform underneath. I took him to safety."

"Why have you kept the story secret?"

"Martin brought with him microdots containing German files on Western espionage services. We decided it was to our advantage to have the world think that Bormann had been loyal to Hitler to the end and had been killed while trying to escape Berlin. We changed his appearance with plastic surgery. He is retired now but for years he was a high-ranking officer of our intelligence service."

Starik released Yevgeny's hand and returned to his seat. "Now," he said in a triumphant voice, "we will, together, take the first steps in a long journey."

In the weeks that followed, Yevgeny Alexandrovich Tsipin disappeared through the looking glass into a clandestine world peopled by eccentric characters who had mastered bizarre skills. The trip was exhilarating; for the first time in memory he felt as if the attention being showered on him had nothing to do with the fact that he was his father's son. He was given the code name Gregory; he himself selected the surname Ozolin, which Starik immediately recognized as the name of the stationmaster at Astapovo, the godforsaken backwater where Tolstoy, on the lam from his wife, had breathed his last. ("And what were his last words?" Starik, who had been something of a Tolstoy scholar in his youth, challenged his protégé. "'The truth—I care a great deal,'" Yevgeny shot back. "Bravo!" cried Starik. "Bravo!") Without fanfare Gregory Ozolin was inducted into the Communist Party of the Soviet Union, card number 01783753 and assigned to a small Interior Ministry safe house on Granovskiy Street, *batiment* number 3, second entrance, flat 71, which came with a refrigerator (a rarity in the Soviet Union) filled with pasteurized koumis belonging to the Tajik maid with a mustache on her upper lip. Six mornings a week a bread-delivery van fetched Yevgeny from the alleyway behind the building and whisked him to an underground entrance of the First Chief Directorate's Shkloa Osobogo Naznacheniva (Special Purpose School) in the middle of a woods at Balashikha, some fifteen miles east of the Moscow Ring Road. There Yevgeny, segregated for reasons of security from the scores of male and female students attending classes in the main part of the compound, was given intensive courses in selecting and servicing *tayniki* (which the Americans called dead drops), secret writing, wireless telegraphy, cryptography in general and one-time pads in particular, photography, Marxist theory, and the glorious history of the Cheka from Feliks Dzerzhinsky down to the present. The curriculum for this last course consisted mostly of maxims, which were supposed to be memorized and regurgitated on demand.

"What was the dictum of the Cheka in 1934?" the instructor, a zealous time-server whose shaven skull glistened under the neon lamp in the classroom, demanded at one session.

"A spy in hand is worth two in the bush?"

Pursing his lips, clucking his tongue, the time-server scolded his student. "Comrade Ozolin will simply have to take this more seriously if he expects to earn a passing grade." And he recited the correct response, obliging Yevgeny to repeat each phrase after him.

"In our work, boldness, daring and audacity..."

"In our work, boldness, daring and audacity..."

"...must be combined..."

"...must be combined..."

"...with prudence."

"...with prudence."

"In other words, dialectics."

"In other words, dialectics."

"I honestly don't see what dialectics has to do with being a successful espionage agent," Yevgeny groaned when Starik turned up, as usual, at midday to share the sandwiches and cold kvass sent over from the canteen.

"It is the heart of the matter," Starik explained patiently. "We cannot teach you everything, but we *can* teach you how to think. The successful agent is invariably one who has mastered Marxist methodology. Which is to say, he perfects the art of thinking conventionally and then systematically challenges the conventional thinking to develop alternatives that will take the"—his eyes sparkling, Yevgeny's conducting officer dredged up the English term—"'principal adversary' by surprise. The short name for this process is dialectics. You came across it when you studied Hegel and Marx. You develop a thesis, you contradict it with an anthesis and then you resolve the contradiction with a synthesis. I am told that the practical side of the curriculum comes quickly to you. You must make more of an effort on the theoretical side."

On the even days of the month, a sinewy Ossete with a clubfoot and incredibly powerful arms would lead Yevgeny to a windowless room with mattresses propped up against the walls and wrestling mats on the floor, and teach him seven different ways to kill with his bare hands; the absolute precision of the Ossete's gestures convinced Yevgeny that he had diligently practiced the subject he now instructed. On the odd days, Yevgeny was taken down to a soundproofed sub-basement firing range and shown how to strip and clean and shoot a variety of small arms of American manufacture. When he had mastered that he was taken on a field trip to a KGB special laboratory at the edge of a village near Moscow and allowed to test fire one of the exotic weapons that had been developed there, a cigarette case concealing a silent pistol that shot platinum-alloy pellets the size of a pinhead; indentations in the pinhead contained a poisonous extract from the castor oil plant, which (so Yevgeny was assured by a short, myopic man in a white smock) invariably led to cardiovascular collapse.

Evenings, Yevgeny was driven back to his apartment to eat the warm meal that had been set out for him by the Tajik maid. After dinner he was expected to do several hours of homework, which involved keeping abreast of all things American, and most especially sports, by carefully reading *Time* and *Life* and *Newsweek*. He was also ordered to study a series of lectures entitled "Characteristics of Agent Communications and Agent Handling in the USA," written by Lieutenant Colonel I. Ye. Prikhodko, an intelligence officer who had served in New York under diplomatic cover. Fortifying himself with a stiff cognac, Yevgeny would settle into a soft chair with a lamp directed over his shoulder and skim the Prikhodko material. "New York is divided into five sections," one chapter, clearly intended for neophytes, began, "which are called boroughs. Because of its isolation from the main city—one can reach the island only by ferry from Manhattan and from Brooklyn—Richmond is the least suitable of the five boroughs for organizing agent communications. New York's other four sections—named Manhattan, Bronx, Brooklyn, and Queens—are widely used by our intelligence officers. Department stores, with their dozens of entrances and exits, some directly into the subway system, are ideal meeting places. Prospect Park in the borough of Brooklyn or cemeteries in the borough of Queens are also excellent places to meet with agents. When organizing such meetings do not specify a spot (for example, the southwest corner of Fourteenth Street and Seventh Avenue) but a route, preferably a small street along which he is to walk at a prearranged time.

This permits the Soviet intelligence officer to observe the agent to determine whether or not he is under surveillance before establishing contact."

"I skimmed several of the Prikhodko lectures last night," Yevgeny told Starik one morning. They were in a brand new Volga from the First Chief Directorate's motor pool, heading out of Moscow toward Peredelkino for a Sunday picnic at Yevgeny's father's dacha. As Starik had never learned to drive, Yevgeny was behind the wheel. "They strike me as being fairly primitive."

"They are intended for agents who have never set foot in America, not graduates of Yale University," Starik explained. "Still, there are things in them that can be useful to you. The business about meetings with agents, for example. The CIA is known to favor safe houses because of the possibility of controlling access and egress, and of tape recording or filming what happens during the meeting. We, on the other hand, prefer doing things in open areas because of the opportunities to make sure that you are not being followed."

On the car radio, the sonorous voice of a newscaster reporting from the North Korean capital of Pyongyang could be heard saying that the American aggressors, who had debarked the day before at Inchon, were being contained by the North Koreans.

"What do you make of the American landing?" Yevgeny asked his conducting officer.

"I have seen very secret briefings—there is no possibility the Americans will be thrown back into the sea. But this outflanking stratagem of the American General MacArthur is a perilous gambit. In fact the Americans are threatening to cut off the North Korean troops in the south, which will oblige the North Koreans to pull back rapidly if they hope to avoid encirclement. The strategic question is whether the Americans will stop at the thirty-eighth parallel, or pursue the Communist armies north to the Yalu River in order to reunify Korea under the puppet regime in Seoul."

"If the Americans continue on to the Yalu what will the Chinese do?"

"They will certainly feel obliged to attack across the river, in which case they will overpower the American divisions with sheer numbers. If the Americans are facing defeat they might bomb China with atomic weapons, in which case we will be obliged to step in."

"In other words we could be in the verge of a world war."

"I hope not; I hope the Americans will have the good sense to stop before they reach the Yalu or, if they don't, I hope they will be able to arrest the inevitable Chinese attack without resorting to atomic weapons. A Chinese attack across the Yalu that eventually fails to defeat the Americans will benefit Sino-Soviet relations, which are showing signs of fraying."

Yevgeny understood that Starik's analysis of the situation was not one that would appear in *Pravda*. "How would a Chinese setback benefit Sino-Soviet relations?"

"For the simple reason that it will demonstrate to the Chinese leadership that they remain vulnerable to Western arms and need to remain under the Soviet atomic umbrella."

Yevgeny drove through the village of Peredelkino, which consisted mostly of a wide unpaved road, a Party building with a red star over its door and a statue of Stalin in front, a farmer's cooperative and a local school. At the first road marker beyond the village he turned off and pulled up next to a line of cars already parked in the shade of some trees. A dozen chauffeurs were dozing in the back seats of cars or on newspapers spread out on the ground. Yevgeny led the way along a narrow grassy path to his father's country house. As they approached they could hear the sound of music and laughter drifting through the woods. Four unsmiling civilians wearing dark suits and fedoras stood at the wooden gate; they parted to let Yevgeny past when they spotted Starik behind him. Two dozen or so men and women stood around the lawn watching a young man playing a tiny concertina. Bottles of Armenian cognac and a hard-to-find aged vodka called *starka* were set out on a long table covered with white sailcloth. Maids wearing white aprons over their long peasant dresses passed around plates filled with potato salad and cold chicken. Munching on a drumstick, Yevgeny wandered around to the back of the dacha and discovered his father, naked from the waist up, sitting on a milking stool inside the tool shed. An old man with a pinched face was pressing the open mouth of a bottle filled with bees against the skin on Tsipin's back. "The peasants say that bee stings can alleviate rheumatism," Tsipin told his son, wincing as the bees planted their darts in him. "Where have you disappeared to, Yevgeny? What hole have you fallen into?"

"Your friend Pasha Semyonovich has given me work translating American newspaper articles and the Congressional Record into Russian," Yevgeny replied, repeating the cover story Starik had worked out for him.

"If only you had a decent Party record," his father said with a sigh, "they might have given you more important things to do." He gasped from a new sting. "Enough, enough, Dmitri," he told the peasant. "I'm beginning to think I prefer the rheumatism."

The old man capped the bottle and, tipping his hat, departed. Yevgeny rubbed a salve on the rash of red welts across his father's bony neck and shoulders to sooth the ache of the stings. "Even with a good record I wouldn't get far in your world," Yevgeny remarked. "You have to be schizophrenic to live two lives."

His father looked back over his shoulder. "Why do you call it *my* world?"

Yevgeny regarded his father with wide-eyed innocence. "I have always presumed—"

"You would do well to stop presuming, especially where it concerns connections with our Chekists."

By late afternoon the nonstop drinking had taken its toll on the guests, who were stretched out on ottomans or dozing in Danish deck chairs scattered around the garden. Starik had disappeared into the dacha with Tsipin. Sitting on the grass with his back to a tree, enjoying the warmth of the sun through the canopy of foliage over his head, Yevgeny caught sight of a barefoot young woman talking with an older man who looked vaguely familiar. At one point the older man put an arm around the waist of the girl and the two of them strolled off through the woods. Yevgeny noticed that two of the unsmiling men at the gate detached themselves from the group and followed at a discreet distance. For a time Yevgeny could see the girl and her companion fleetingly through the trees, deep in conversation as they appeared and disappeared from view. He finished his cognac and closed his eyes, intending only to rest them for a few moments. He came awake with a start when he sensed that someone had come between him and the sun. A musical voice speaking a very precise English announced: "I dislike summer so very much."

Yevgeny batted away a swarm of insects and found himself staring at a very shapely pair of bare ankles. He saluted them respectfully. "Why would anyone in his right mind dislike summer?" he responded in English.

"For the reason that it is too short. For the reason that our Arctic winter will be upon us before our skin has had its provision of summer sunshine. You must excuse me if I have awaked you."

"An American would say *woken you*, not *awaked you*." Yevgeny blinked away the drowsiness and brought her into focus. The young woman looked to be in her early or middle twenties and tall for a female of the species, at least five-eleven in her bare feet. Two rowboat-sized flat-soled sandals dangled from a forefinger, a small cloth knapsack hung off one shoulder. She had a slight offset to an otherwise presentable nose, a gap between two front teeth, faint worry lines around her eyes and mouth. Her hair was short and straight and dark, and tucked neatly back behind her ears.

"I work as a historian and on the side, for the pleasure of it, I translate English language books that interest me," the girl said. "I have read the novels of E. Hemingway and F. Fitzgerald—I am in the process of translating a novel entitled *For Whom the Bell Tolls*. Have you by chance read it? I have been informed that you attended a university in the state of Connecticut. I am pleased to talk English with someone who has actually been to America."

Yevgeny patted the grass alongside him. She smiled shyly and settled cross-legged onto the ground and held out a hand. "My name is Azalia Isanova. There are some who call me Aza."

Yevgeny took her hand in his. "I will call you Aza, too. Are you here with a husband?" he asked, thinking of the older gentleman she had been talking to. "Or a lover?"

She laughed lightly. "I am the apartment-mate of Comrade Beria's daughter."

Yevgeny whistled. "Now I know where I've seen the man you were with before—in the newspapers!" He decided to impress her. "Did you know that Comrade Beria suffers from ulcers? That he applies hot water bottles to his stomach to ease the pain?"

She cocked her head. "Who are you?"

"My name is...Gregory. Gregory Ozolin."

Her face darkened. "No, you're not. You are Yevgeny Alexandrovich, the oldest son of Aleksandr Timofeyevich Tsipin. Lavrenti Pavlovich himself pointed you out to me. Why do you invent a name?"

"For the pleasure of seeing your frown when you unmask me."

"Are you familiar with the work of Hemingway and Fitzgerald? Speaking from a stylistical point of view, I was struck by the dissimilarity of Hemingway's short, declarative sentence structure and Fitzgerald's more complex network of interconnected sentences. Do you agree with this distinction?"

"Definitely."

"How is it that two American writers living during the same period and on occasion in the same place—I refer, of course, to Paris—can end up writing so differently?"

"I suppose it's because different folks have different strokes."

"I beg your pardon?"

"That's an American slang epigram—"

"Different folks have different strokes? Ah, I see what you are driving at. Strokes refers to rowing. Different people row differently. Do you mind if I copy that down." She produced a fountain pen and pad from her knapsack and carefully copied the epigram into it.

A black chauffeur-driven Zil drew up to the wooden gate. A second car filled with men in dark suits pulled up right behind it. On the porch of the dacha Lavrenti Pavlovich Beria shook hands with Tsipin and Starik and waved to his daughter, who was deep in conversation with three women. Beria's daughter, in turn, called, "Aza, come quickly. Papa is starting back to Moscow."

Aza sprang to her feet and brushed the grass off of her skirt. Yevgeny asked with some urgency, "Can I see you again?" He added quickly, "To talk more of Hemingway and Fitzgerald."

She looked down at him for a moment, her brow creased in thought. Then she said, "It is possible." She scribbled a number on the pad, tore off the sheet and let it flutter down to Yevgeny. "You may telephone me."

"I will," he said with undisguised eagerness.

The next morning Yevgeny's tradecraft classes started to taper off and he began the long, tedious process of creating (with the help of identical twin sisters who didn't look at all alike) two distinct legends that he could slip into and out of at will. It was painstaking work because every detail had to be compartmentalized in Yevgeny's brain so that he would never confuse his two identities. "It is vital," the sister whose name was Agrippina told him as they set out two thick loose-leaf books on the table, "not to memorize a legend—you must *become* the legend."

"You must shed your real identity," the other sister, whose name was Serafima, explained, "the way a snake sheds its skin. You must settle into each legend as if it were a new skin. If you were to hear someone call out your old name, the thought must flash across your mind: Who can that be? Certainly not me! With time and many many hours of very difficult work you will be able to put a mental distance between the person known as Yevgeny Alexandrovich Tsipin and your new identities."

"Why two legends?" Yevgeny asked.

"One will be a primary operating legend, the second will be a fallback legend in the event the first legend is compromised and you must disappear into a new identity," Agrippina said. She smiled in a motherly fashion and motioned for Serafima to commence.

"Thank you, dear. Now, in building each legend we will start from the cradle and work up to the young man who will be roughly your present age, or at least near enough to it so as not to arouse suspicion. To distinguish the two legends from each other, and from your genuine identity, it will be helpful if you develop different ways of walking and speaking for each persona—"

"It will be helpful if you comb your hair differently, carry your wallet in a different pocket, wear clothing which reflects different tastes," her sister added.

"Eventually," Serafima offered, blushing slightly, "you might even make love differently."

Working from their loose-leaf books, the sisters—both senior researchers in Starik's Directorate S, the department within the First Chief Directorate that ran illegals operating under deep cover abroad—began to set out the rough outlines of what they dubbed "Legend A" and "Legend B." "A" had spent his childhood in New Haven, which Yevgeny knew well; "B" had grown up in the Crown Heights section of Brooklyn, which Yevgeny—with the help of maps and slides and personal accounts published in the American press—would come to know intimately. In each case, the sisters would use the addresses of buildings that had been torn down so that it would be practically impossible for the American FBI to verify who had lived there. The foundation for the legends would be birth certificates that were actually on record in New Haven and in New York in the names of two young Caucasian males who, unbeknownst to the American authorities, had been lost at sea when the Allies ran convoys to Murmansk during the war. Two frayed Social Security cards were the next building blocks of the legends. Serafima was an expert on the American social security system; the first three digits of the numbers, she explained, indicated the state in which the number had been issued; the middle two digits, when it had been issued. The cards Yevgeny would carry were actually on file with the United States government. As he would be passing for men two or three years older, there would be voter registration cards in addition to the usual paper identification—driver's licenses, library cards, laminated American Youth Hostel cards with photographs, that sort of thing. The legends would be backstopped by educational records in existence at a New Haven high school and at Erasmus in Brooklyn (which Yevgeny knew well), along with an employment history that would ring true but would also be unverifiable. Medical and dental histories would be built into each legend—they would involve doctors who were dead, which would make the stories impossible to check. And each legend would have a working passport with travel stamps on its pages.

"You have obviously thought of everything," Yevgeny commented.

"We hope for your sake that we have," Agrippina said. "Still, I must draw your attention to two minor problems."

"According to your dental records," Serafima said, "the majority of your cavities were filled by American dentists in the United States. But you have two cavities that were filled in the Soviet Union, one before you first went to join your parents in New York after the war, the second when you were in Moscow during a summer vacation. These cavities will have to be redone by Centre dentists who are familiar with American dental techniques and have access to American materials."

"And the second problem?"

Starik suddenly appeared at the door carrying sandwiches and a bottle of kvass. "There is no hurry about the second problem," he said. He was clearly annoyed at the sisters for having raised it now. "We will tell him at a later date."

Yevgeny telephoned Aza the first time he had a free evening and the two met (after Yevgeny, trying out his newfound tradecraft, ditched the man who was tailing him from across the street) in Gorky Park. They wandered along a path that ran parallel to the Moscow River, talking of American literature at first, then nibbling at the edge of matters that were more personal. No, she said, she was an orphan; both her mother, a writer of radio plays, and her father, an actor in the Yiddish theater, had disappeared in the late 1940s. No, she couldn't be more precise because the authorities who had notified her of their deaths had not been more precise. She had been befriended by Beria's daughter, Natasha, at a summer camp in the Urals. They had become pen pals, had written to each other for years. It seemed only natural, when her application to study history and languages at Lomonosov University was, against all odds, accepted, that she would move in with her friend. Yes, she had met Natasha's father on many occasions; he was a warm, friendly man who doted on his daughter but otherwise seemed preoccupied with important matters. He had three phones on his desk, one of them red, which sometimes rang day and night. Tiring of the quiz, Aza pulled typed sheets containing several of Anna Akhmatova's early love poems, along with the first rough draft of her attempts to translate the poems into English, from the pocket of her blouse. She absently plucked wild berries off bushes and popped them in her mouth as Yevgeny read aloud, first in Russian, then in English:

> What syrupy witches' brew was prepared
> On that bleak January day?
> What concealed passion drove us mad
> All night until dawn—who can say?

"I can identify the witches' brew," Yevgeny insisted. "It was lust."

Aza turned her grave eyes on the young man. "Lust fuels the passions of men, so I am told, but women are driven by other, more subtle desires that come from..."

"Come from?"

"...the uncertainty that can be seen in a man's regard, the hesitancy that can be felt in his touch, and most especially the tentativeness that can be heard in his voice, which after all are reflections of his innermost self." She added very seriously, "I am pleased with your voice, Yevgeny."

"I am pleased that you are pleased," he said, and he meant it.

The following Sunday Yevgeny, using a phone number reserved for high-ranking members of the Foreign Office, managed to reserve rare tickets to the Moscow Art Theater and took Aza to see the great Tarasova in the role of Anna Karenina. He reached for Aza's hand as the narrator's opening line echoed through the theater: "All happy families resemble one another but each unhappy family is unhappy in its own way." Afterwards he invited her to dinner in a small restaurant off Trubnaya Square. When the bill came she insisted on paying according to the German principle. Yevgeny told her that the Americans called it the Dutch principle, or Dutch treat, and she jotted down the expression on her pad. After dinner they strolled arm in arm down Tsvetnoy Boulevard into the heart of Moscow. "Do you know Chekhov's essay, 'On Trubnaya Square'?" she asked him. "In it he describes the old Birds Market, which was not far from where we are standing now. My grandparents lived in a room over the market when they were first married. I offer you a question, Yevgeny Alexandrovich: Are all things, like the Birds Market, fleeting phenomena?"

Yevgeny's mind raced; he understood that she wanted to know if the feelings she had for him—and he appeared to have for her—would suffer the same fate as the Birds Market on Trubnaya Square. "I cannot say yet what is lasting in this world and what is not."

"You answer honestly. For that I thank you."

On an impulse he crossed to the center strip of the boulevard and bought Aza a bouquet of white carnations from one of the old peasant women in blue canvas jackets selling flowers there. Later, at the door of her building on Nizhny Kizlovsky Lane, she buried her nose in the carnations and breathed in the fragrance. Then she flung her arms around Yevgeny's neck, kissed him with great passion on the lips and darted off through the doors into the building before he could utter a word.

He telephoned her in the morning before he left for his rendezvous with the twin sisters. "It's me," he announced.

"I recognize the tentativeness of your voice," she replied. "I recognize even the ring of the telephone."

"Aza, each time I see you I leave a bit of me with you."

"Oh, I hope this is not true," she said softly. "For if you see me too often there will be nothing left of you." She was silent for a moment; he could hear her breathing into the mouthpiece. Finally she said in a firm voice:

"Next Sunday Natasha is voyaging to the Crimea with her father. I will bring you back here with me. We will together explore whether your lust and my desire are harmonious in bed." She said something else that was lost in a burst of static. Then the connection was cut.

Gradually Yevgeny became the legends that the sisters had devised—brushing his hair forward into his eyes; speaking in a rapid-fire fashion in sentences he often didn't bother to finish; striding around the room in loud, sure steps as he spoke; rattling off the details of his life from the cradle to the present. Starik, who was sitting in on the sessions, would occasionally interrupt with a question. "Precisely where was the drugstore in which you worked?"

"On Kingston Avenue just off Eastern Parkway. I sold comic books—Captain Marvel, Superman, Batman—and made egg creams for the kids for a nickel."

The sisters were pleased with their pupil. "I suppose there is nothing left for us to do now except destroy all the loose-leaf books," Agrippina said.

"There is still the matter of the second problem," Serafima said. They looked at Starik, who nodded in agreement. The sisters exchanged embarrassed looks. "You must tell him," Serafima informed her sister. "You are the one who stumbled across it."

Agrippina cleared her throat. "Both of your legends are built around young men who were born in the United States of America, which means that like the overwhelming majority of Americans they will have been circumcised at birth. We have examined your birth records at"—here she named a small and exclusive Kremlin clinic that was used by ranking Party people. "They make no mention of a circumcision. I apologize for posing such a personal question but are we correct in assuming you were not circumcised?"

Yevgeny pulled a face. "I see where this is leading."

Starik said, "We once lost an agent who was passing himself off as a Canadian businessman. The Royal Canadian Mounted Police found the businessman's medical records and discovered he had been circumcised. Our agent was not." He pulled a slip of paper from a shirt pocket and read it. "The operation, which will be performed in a private Centre clinic in a Moscow suburb, is scheduled for nine tomorrow morning." The sisters stood up. Starik signaled for Yevgeny to remain. The two women bid goodbye to their student and left the room.

"There is one more matter that needs to be cleared up," Starik said. "I am talking about the girl, Azalia Isanova. You shook the man who was tailing you from across the street, but you did not lose the one who was assigned to follow you from in front. Your street craft needs work. Your faculty of discretion, too. We have been monitoring your telephone calls. We know that you slept with the girl—"

Yevgeny blurted out, "She can be trusted—she shares an apartment with the daughter of Comrade Beria—"

Starik, his face contorted, his eyes bulging, blurted out, "But don't you see it? She is too *old* for you!"

Yevgeny was startled. "She is two years older than me, it is true, but what does that amount to? The question of age must be seen as—"

Starik, hissing now, cut him off. "There is something else. Her surname is Lebowitz. Her patronymic is a version of Isaiah. She is a *zhid*!"

The word struck Yevgeny like a slap across the face. "But Comrade Beria must have known about her when he took her in..."

Starik eyes narrowed dangerously. "Of course Beria knows. A great many in the superstructure are careful to include one or two Jews in their entourage to counter Western propaganda about anti-Semitism. Molotov went too far—he actually married one of them. Stalin decided it was an impossible situation—the Foreign Minister married to a Jewess—and had her shipped off to a detention camp." Starik's bony fingers gripped Yevgeny's wrist. "For someone in your position any liaison with a girl would pose delicate problems. A liaison with a *zhid* is out of the realm of possibility."

"Surely I have a say—"

For Starik there was no middle ground. "You have no say," he declared, switching to the formal "*vui*" and spitting it into the conversation. "*You* must choose between the girl and a brilliant career—*you* must choose between her and me." He shot to his feet and dropped a card with the address of the clinic on the table in front of Yevgeny. "If *you* do not turn up for the operation our paths will never cross again."

That night Yevgeny climbed to the roof of his building and gazed for hours at the red-hazed glow hovering over the Kremlin. He knew he was walking a tightrope; he understood he could jump off one side as easily as the other. If he had been asked to give up Aza for operational reasons he would have understood; to give her up because she was a Jewess was a bitter pill to swallow. For all his talk about the genius and generosity of the human spirit, Starik—*Yevgeny's* Tolstoy—had turned out to be a rabid anti-Semite. Yevgeny could hear the word *zhid* festering in his brain. And then it dawned on him that the voice he heard wasn't Starik's; it was a thinner voice, quivering with age and pessimism and panic, seeping from the back of the throat of someone who feared growing old, who welcomed death but dreaded dying. The word *zhid* resounding in Yevgeny's ear came from the great Tolstoy himself; scratch the lofty idealist of the spirit and underneath you discovered an anti-Semite who believed, so Tolstoy had affirmed, that the flaw of Christianity, the tragedy of mankind, came from the racial incompatibility between Christ, who was not a Jew, and Paul, who was a Jew.

Yevgeny laughed under his breath. Then he laughed out loud. And then he opened his mouth and bellowed into the night: *"Za uspiekh nashevo beznadiozhnovo diela!* To the success of our hopeless task!"

The circumcision, performed under a local anesthetic, was over in minutes. Yevgeny was given pills to ease the pain and an antiseptic cream to guard against infection. He retreated to his apartment and buried himself in the Prikhodko lectures, making lists of neighborhoods and parks and department stores in various East Coast American cities that could be used for meetings with agents. The telephone rang seven times on Saturday, four times on Sunday and twice on Monday. Once or twice the maid plucked the receiver off its hook. Hearing a female voice on the other end of the line she muttered a curse in Tajik and slammed down the phone. After a few days the burning sensation in Yevgeny's penis dulled to an ache and gradually disappeared. One morning a motorcycle messenger brought Yevgeny a sealed envelope. Inside was a second sealed envelope containing a passport in the name of Gregory Ozolin and a plane ticket to Oslo. There, Ozolin would disappear from the face of the earth and a young American named Eugene Dodgson, who had been backpacking in Scandinavia, would buy passage on a Norwegian freighter bound for Halifax, Canada, the staging area for Soviet illegals bound for assignments in the United States.

On the evening before Yevgeny's departure, Starik, smiling thinly, turned up with a tin of imported herring and a cold bottle of Polish vodka. The two talked about everything under the sun late into the night; everything except the girl. After Starik had departed Yevgeny found himself staring at the telephone, half-hoping it would ring; half-hoping there would be a musical voice on the other end saying "I dislike summer so very much."

When, just before six in the morning, it finally did ring, Yevgeny leapt from the bed and stood staring at the receiver. With the phone's discordant peal still echoing through the apartment, his eye fell on the packed valise near the door. He could feel a magnetic force pulling him toward his quest on the American continent. Accepting his destiny with a grudging smile, he sat down on the valise in preparation for a long, long voyage.

3

THE OVERHEAD LIGHTS DIMMED AND THE TWO CHICKEN COLONELS attached to the Joint Chiefs materialized in the spotlight. Endless rows of campaign ribbons shimmered over the breast pockets of their starched uniforms. Company scuttlebutt had it that they'd passed the time on the flight out from Washington spit-shining their shoes until they resembled mirrors. "Gentlemen," the colonel with the cropped mustache began.

"Seems as how he's giving us the benefit of the doubt," Frank Wisner, his shirtsleeves rolled up, muttered in his inimitable southern drawl, and the officers within earshot, Ebby among them, laughed under their breaths.

They had gathered in Frankfurt Station's sloping auditorium on the second floor of the huge, drearily modern I.G. Farben complex in the Frankfurt suburb of Höchst to hear the Pentagon's latest Cassandra-like forebodings. For Wisner, Allen Dulles's deputy in the Dirty Tricks Department who was passing through Germany on a whirlwind tour of the CIA's European stations, the briefing was another installment in the "pissing contest" between the Joint Chiefs and the Company over Cold War priorities. The chicken colonels who had turned up in Frankfurt before had agonized over the Soviet order of battle as if it were the entrails of a slaughtered ram, counting and recounting the armored divisions that could punch on six hours notice through the *cordon sanitaire* the Allies had strung like a laundry line across Europe. In the great tradition of military mindset, they had made the delicate leap from *capabilities* to *intentions*; from *could* to *would*. Like Delphic oracles predicting the end of the world, they had even identified D-day (in a top-secret "Eyes Only" memo with extremely limited distribution; the last thing they wanted was for this kind of information to fall into the hands of the Russians). World War III would break out on Tuesday, 1 July 1952.

Now they had come back with details of the Soviet assault. Tapping a large map of Europe with a pointer, the chicken colonel with the mustache reeled off the names and effective strengths of the Soviet divisions in East Germany and Poland, and asserted that the Kremlin had massed three times as many troops as it needed for occupation duties. A slim, crewcut sergeant major who walked as if he had a ramrod up his butt changed maps, and the colonel briefed the audience on the route the two-pronged Soviet armored blitzkrieg would follow across the northern plain; in a Pentagon war game simulation, the colonel said, the Soviet attack had reached the English Channel in a matter of weeks. Still a third map was thumbtacked to the easel, this one showing Soviet airfields in Poland and East Germany and the western Bohemian area of Czechoslovakia that would provide close air support for the assault. Signaling for the house-lights, the colonel strode to the edge of the stage and looked out at Wisner, who was slouched in the third row next to General Lucian Truscott IV, the Company's Chief of Station in Germany. "What the Joint Chiefs want," the colonel announced, his jaw elevated a notch, his eyes steely, "is for you to plant an agent at every one of these airfields before July first, 1952 in order to sabotage them when the balloon goes up and the fun starts."

Wisner pulled at an earlobe. "Well now, Lucian, we damn well ought to be able to handle that," he remarked. There was no hint in his tone or expression that he was being anything but serious. "How many airfields did you say there were, colonel?"

The chicken colonel had the figure at the tip of his tongue. "Two thousand, give or take half a hundred. Some of them have got tarmac runways, some dirt." He grinned at his colleague; he was sure they would be returning to Washington with upbeat news.

Wisner nodded thoughtfully. "Two thousand, some tarmac, some dirt," he repeated. He twisted in his seat to speak to his deputy, Dick Helms, sitting directly behind him. "I'll bite, Dick—how does an agent on the ground go about sabotaging a runway?"

Helms looked blank. "Beats me, Frank."

Wisner looked around at his troops. "Anyone here have an inkling how you put a runway out of action?" When nobody spoke up Wisner turned back to the colonel. "Maybe you can enlighten us, colonel. How *do* you sabotage a runway?"

The two colonels exchanged looks. "We'll have to get back to you with an answer," one of them said.

When the chicken colonels had wrapped up the briefing and beat a tactical retreat, Wisner settled onto the back of the seat in front of him and chatted with his people. "I'll be goddamned surprised if we ever hear from them again," he said with a belly laugh. "Carpet bombing can put an airfield out of action two hours, three tops. What a single agent on the ground could do is beyond me. To turn to more serious matters than planting two thousand agents at two thousand airfields—"

There were guffaws around the auditorium.

"Back in the insulated offices of the District of Columbia, the Pentagon is trying to figure out how to blunt a Soviet attack across Europe that is highly unlikely, given our superiority in atomic weaponry and delivery capacity, not to mention that some divisions in the satellite armies are more likely to attack the Russians than the Americans if war breaks out. The Washington civilians, led by our erstwhile specialist on all things Soviet, George Kennan, are rambling on about containment, though nobody has made the case *why* the Russians would want to add another dozen satellites to their fragile empire. And make no mistake about it—the Soviet empire is a house of cards. One good puff in the right place at the right time and the whole thing will come crashing down. I am not presiding over the clandestine service in order to sabotage airfields or contain Communism. Our mission is to *roll back* Communism and liberate the captive nations of East Europe. Am I getting through to you, gentlemen? Our mission is to destroy Communism, as opposed to dirt runways on airfields."

Ebby had been deeply involved in Wisner's roll-back campaign from the day he reported for duty in Germany the previous November. His first assignment, at Berlin Base, had ended abruptly when Ebby's gripe about a "pathological dipsomaniac" being in charge of a Company base reached the Sorcerer's ear and he had whipped off one of his notorious "It's him or me" cables to the DD/O. Bowing to the inevitable, Ebby had put in for a transfer to Frankfurt Station, where he wound up working as an assistant case officer in the Internal Operations Groups of the SE (Soviet/Eastern Europe) Division, cutting his teeth on a new and risky campaign: agent drops into the Russian Carpathians.

It was the first of these drops that almost broke Ebby's heart—and led to an incident that came within a hairsbreadth of cutting short his Company career.

He was unpacking his valise in an upstairs bedroom of a private house in the "Compound," an entire residential neighborhood commandeered by the Army a mile down the road from the I.G. Farben building, when his immediate superior, a grizzly, curly-haired Russian-speaking former OSS officer named Anthony Spink, came around to collect him. They were off, he explained, gunning the engine of a motor pool Ford as he sped west out of Frankfurt, to meet an agent code-named SUMMERSAULT, a Ukrainian being trained at a secret Army base for infiltration into the denied areas behind the Iron Curtain. Jockeying in and out of heavy truck traffic, Spink briefed Ebby on the agent: he was a twenty-three-year-old from the west-central Ukrainian city of Lutsk who had fought for the Germans under the turncoat Russian General Vlasov during the war. Vlasov himself, along with hundreds of his officers, had been hanged by the Russians after V-E Day. SUMMERSAULT, whose real name was Alyosha Kulakov, had been one of the lucky few who had been able to flee west with the retreating Germans and eventually wound up in one of the Displaced Persons camps teeming with refugees from the Soviet Union and the satellite countries. There he had been spotted by a Company recruiter and interviewed by Spink. SUMMERSAULT had maintained that there were thousands of armed Ukrainian nationalists still battling the Russians in the Carpathian Mountains, a claim supported by a deciphered intercept from the Communist boss of the Ukraine, a little known *apparatchik* named Nikita Khrushchev, who had cabled Moscow: "From behind every bush, from behind every tree, at every turn of the road, a government official is in danger of a terrorist attack." The Company decided to train SUMMERSAULT in radio and ciphers, and to drop him into the Carpathians to establish a link between the CIA and the resistance movement.

On paper the operation looked propitious.

Spink drove the Ford along a winding unpaved road through endless fields planted with winter wheat to an isolated dairy farm. Pulling up in front of a stone barn, they could see a young man with a baby face and blond hair drawing water from a well. He greeted Spink with a broad smile, pounding him on the back. "When you sending me home to my Carpathians?" he asked eagerly.

"Pretty soon now," Spink promised.

Spink explained that he had come out to introduce Ebby (for security reasons, he used a pseudonym), who was going to be working with SUMMERSAULT in devising a legend and fabricating the official Soviet documents to go with it. "I got a birthday present for you, son," he added. With Alyosha dancing behind him excitedly, he opened the Ford's trunk and gave SUMMERSAULT a Minox camera disguised as a cigarette lighter, and a book-size battery-powered shortwave radio with a built-in Morse key and an external antenna that could be strung between trees; the transmitter, German war surplus, had a range of eight hundred kilometers.

When Spink headed back to Frankfurt, Ebby and SUMMERSAULT circled each other cautiously. As a prelude to creating a workable legend, Ebby began to walk Alyosha through his biography; when they constructed a legend they wanted as much of it as possible to be true. At first, the young Ukrainian seemed reluctant to tell his story and Ebby had to worm details out of him: his childhood on the banks of the Styr River in Lutsk with his father deeply involved in a clandestine circle of Ukrainian nationalists; an adolescence filled with terror and suffering when his father and he wound up fighting against the Russians ("because they are Russians, not because they are Communists") in Vlasov's Army of Liberation. When Alyosha finally came to talk about his father's execution by the Russians, his eyes brimmed with tears and he had difficulty finishing his sentences. Ebby's eyes misted over, too, and he found himself telling Alyosha about the death of *his* father, a legendary OSS officer who had parachuted into Bulgaria at the end of the war to pry that country out of the Axis alliance. Winstrom Ebbitt had been betrayed by a supposed partisan and tortured by the Germans until he had agreed to radio back false information; he had included in the report a prearranged signal to indicate he was being "played back" by German intelligence. After a while the Germans realized that the OSS hadn't taken the bait. On the day the Red Army crossed the Danube into Bulgaria, Ebbitt had been hauled out on a stretcher—because both of his ankles had been broken—to a soccer field on the edge of Sofia, lashed to a goal post and bayonetted to death by a German firing squad that was short of ammunition. One of the executioners, on trial for war crimes after the end of hostilities, remembered a curious detail: the American OSS officer had died with a smile on his lips.

The telling of the story broke the ice between the two young men and, for the better part of two weeks, they became inseparable companions. During sessions that went on into the early hours of the morning, on long walks through the fields of waist-high winter wheat, Alyosha related the details of his life to the person he came to call "my American brother." Using the main lines of the Ukrainian's biography, filling in the gaps with plausible fictions (Alyosha had to account for the years in Vlasov's army and the post-war years in Western DP camps), Ebby painstakingly constructed a persona that could pass all but the most careful examination by trained KGB investigators. Seeing that Alyosha was chafing at the bit, he took him for a night on the town in Frankfurt that included a visit to a local brothel (paid for with a pair of nylon stockings from the station's PX) and a meal in a black-market restaurant, where a dinner and a bottle of Rhine wine could be had in exchange for several packs of American cigarettes.

Back at the farm Alyosha polished his Morse "fist," memorized the silhouettes of Soviet planes from flash cards and plowed through thick briefing books to bring himself up to date on life in the Soviet Union—trolley fares, the price of a loaf of black bread, the latest regulations on changing jobs or traveling between cities, the most recent Russian slang expressions. Ebby, meanwhile, began the last phase of the legend-building: creating the Soviet documents that would support the legend. Which is how he came in contact with the shadowy West German intelligence "Org" run by Reinhard Gehlen.

Over lunch in the "Casino," a dollar-a-day mess in one of the enormous I.G. Farben buildings, Tony Spink told Ebby more about the man whose unofficial Company code name was "Strange Bedfellow." General Gehlen, it seemed, had been the commander of Fremde Heere Ost, a World War II German intelligence unit that had targeted the Soviet Union. With the war winding down, Gehlen had microfilmed his archives (including invaluable profiles of Soviet political and military leaders), destroyed the originals and buried fifty-two cases of files near an alpine hut in the Bavarian mountains. "The microfilmed files were Gehlen's life insurance policy," Spink explained. "He put out feelers to Western intelligence and offered to give his files to the Americans."

"In exchange for?"

One of the Casino waiters, recruited from a nearby Displaced Persons camp, cleared off the empty plates and carefully emptied the butts in the ashtray into an envelope, which he put in the pocket of his white jacket. Spink made sure the waiter was out of earshot before he answered the question.

"Gehlen wanted to set up a West German intelligence entity, with him as its *Führer*, and he expected the CIA to fund it. There was a lot of soul searching. Putting a German general back in business—especially one who had remained loyal to Der Führer to the bitter end—rubbed a lot of people the wrong way. Sure, we wanted his files and his assets, but Gehlen came with the package. Take it or leave it, that was his attitude. To make a long story shorter, the Cold War was starting to heat up and Gehlen's microfilms contained a gold mine of information on the enemy. Besides which Gehlen had stay-behind teams along the railway line from Vologda to Moscow, he claimed to be in contact with survivors of Vlasov's army scattered across the Oriol Mountains, he could identify anti-Soviet Ukrainian units around Kiev and Lvov, he even had assets in the part of Germany occupied by Soviet armies." Spink shrugged philosophically. "Without Gehlen and his microfilm we would have been up shit's creek as far as the Ruskies were concerned." He pulled two cigarettes from a pack and left them on the table as a tip. "I know how your old man bought it, Ebby. So here's some unsolicited advice: grit your teeth and get the job done."

The next afternoon Ebby checked out a car from the motor pool and drove the two hundred miles down to the village of Pullach, some eight miles from downtown Munich. Arriving at dark, he found Heilmannstrasse, with a ten-foot-high gray concrete wall running along one side, then turned and followed the narrow road that ran parallel to the thick hedges with the electrified fence behind it until he came to the small guardhouse manned by sentries wearing green Bavarian gameskeepers' uniforms. A naked electric bulb illuminated a sign in four languages that read: "SUD-DEUTSCHE INDUSTRIE-VERWERTUNGS GmbH—Switch off your headlights and switch on your inside lights." Only when Ebby had complied did one of the guards approach the car. Ebby cracked the window and passed him his American passport and Company ID card. The guard took them back to the house, dialed a number and read the documents to someone on the other end. Moments later a jeep roared up to the gate and a lean, balding man with a distinctive military bearing pushed through a turnstile and let himself into the passengers seat of Ebby's car. "I am Doktor Uppmann of the Records Department," he announced. He never offered his hand. "You may switch on the headlights now."

"What about my ID?" Ebby asked.

"They will be returned to you when you leave. I will accompany you until then."

The gate in the electrified fence swung open and Ebby followed Herr Uppmann's directions through the Compound. "This is your first visit here, yes?" Uppmann commented.

"Yes," Ebby said. He could feel a tingling at the back of his neck.

"We are, be assured, eager to be of service to our American friends," his guide said, gesturing with an open palm toward a lighted road to the right.

Ebby turned into the road. "Does anyone fall for the South German Industries Utilization Company sign back at the gate?" he inquired.

The German managed a thin smile. "Doktor Schneider"—Gehlen's cover name—"has a hypothesis: If you want to keep a big secret, disguise it as a boring and inconsequential secret rather then try to convince people it is not a secret at all. You would be astonished how many Germans think we steal industrial secrets from the Americans or the French."

Following his guide's hand signals, Ebby pulled up on the side of a long one-story building. Doktor Uppmann produced a metal ring with half a dozen keys attached to it. With one he turned off the alarm system, with another he opened the two locks on a heavy metal door. Ebby followed him down a lighted corridor. "How long have you been here?" he asked, waving toward the Compound.

"We moved in soon after the end of hostilities. Except for some under-ground vaults that were added, the compound existed much as you see it today. It was originally built for SS officers and their families and by good fortune survived your bombers." Uppmann let himself into a lighted office and locked the door behind them. Looking around, Ebby took in the sturdy furniture and the gray walls encrusted with squashed insects. He noticed an American poster taped to the back of the door. It read: "Watched from a safe dis-tance an atomic explosion is one of the most beautiful sights ever seen by man."

"Do you really believe that?" Ebby asked his guide.

Doktor Uppmann looked flustered. "It is merely a joke."

"I have heard it said a German joke is no laughing matter," Ebby muttered.

"I beg your pardon?"

"Nothing."

Uppmann crouched in front of a large safe and fiddled with the dial until the door clicked open. From a shelf in the safe he withdrew a manila folder. He swung the safe's door closed and spun the dial to make sure it was locked, then, straightening, emptied the contents of the manila folder onto a table. "All of these were fabricated by the Abwehr in the last months of the great struggle against Bolshevism," Uppmann informed his visitor. "They are first-class forgeries, in some ways superior to the documents we fabricated ear-lier in the war. Many of the agents we dropped behind Bolshevik lines were executed because we made the error of using our own stainless steel staples and not the Russian staples which rust after a very short period of time. You Americans have a saying we Germans appreciate—live and learn. Take a close look at the stamps—they are small masterpieces. Only a Russian trained in credentials could distinguish them from the real thing." He slid the docu-ments across the table, one by one. "An internal passport for the Ukrainian Republic, a labor book, a military status book, an officer's identity book, a Ukrainian ration book. When filling in the documents you must bear in mind certain Russian idiosyncracies. Whereas the internal passport, the military sta-tus and officer's identity books would normally be filled in by secretaries with a more or less elaborate bureaucratic penmanship, the labor book would be signed by the factory managers who, if they rose from the ranks, might be quite illiterate and would scratch their initials in place of a readable signature. There is also the matter of which inks are used in Russia. But I am confident your experts in Frankfurt are familiar with these details, Herr Ebbitt."

Herr Doktor Uppmann led Ebby to a lounge at the end of the corridor. Waving him toward an easy chair, he fetched a bottle of three-star French cognac and two small glasses from a painted Bavarian cabinet. He filled them to the brim and handed one to Ebby. "*Prosit*," he said, smiling, carefully clicking glasses. "To the next war—this time we get them together."

Ebby, trembling with anger, rose to his feet and set the glass down on a table without drinking. "I must tell you, Herr Doktor Uppmann—" He took a deep breath to control his temper.

Uppmann cocked his head. "You must tell me what, Herr Ebbitt? That your father was killed in the war? I see you are surprised to discover I am familiar with your pedigree. As a matter of absolute routine we perform background checks on all visitors to the compound. My father, too, was a casualty of the war—he was taken captive at Stalingrad and did not survive the long march through the snow to the prison camp. My younger brother, Ludwig, stepped on a land mine and returned from the war with both of his legs amputated above the knees. My mother cares for him at our family estate in the Black Forest."

Ebby murmured, "Did you know?"

"Did I know what?"

"Did you know about the Final Solution?"

The German rested a finger along the bridge of his nose. "Of course not."

Ebby said, "How could you *not* know? A little girl named Anne Frank hiding in an attic in Amsterdam wrote in her diary that the Jews were being packed off in cattle cars. How come she knew and you didn't?"

"I was not involved with the Jewish question. I did then what I do now—I fought Bolsheviks. I served on the intelligence staff of General Gehlen—three and one-half years on the Russian front. One thousand two hundred and seventy-seven days, *thirty thousand six hundred hours* in purgatory! *Bolshevism* is the common enemy, Herr Ebbitt. If we had had the good sense to join forces earlier your father and my father might still be alive, the Bolsheviks would not have swallowed up the nations of Eastern Europe as well as a large portion of Greater Germany—"

"*You* swallowed up the nations of Eastern Europe before the Bolsheviks—Poland, the Sudetenland, Yugoslavia."

Uppmann bridled. "We created a buffer between the Christian West and the atheistic Bolsheviks." He turned to stare out the window at the lighted streets of the Compound. "Hitler," he whispered, his hollow voice drifting back over a shoulder, "betrayed Germany. He confused the priorities—he was more concerned with eliminating the Jews than eliminating the Bolsheviks." Uppmann turned back abruptly to face his visitor and spoke with quiet emotion. "You make the mistake of judging us without knowing what really happened, Herr Ebbitt. My class—the German military class—

despised the crude corporal but we agreed with his goals. After the Versailles *Diktat* we Germans were a *Volk ohne Raum*—a nation without space to develop. I tell you frankly, German patriots were seduced by Hitler's denunciation of the odious Versailles Treaty, we were drawn to his promise of *Lebensraum* for the Third Reich, we shared his passionate anti-Bolshevism. Our mistake was to see Hitler's chancellorship as a passing phase in chaotic German politics. Do you know what Herr Hindenburg said after he met Hitler for the first time? I shall tell you what he said. '*Germany could never be ruled by a Bohemian corporal.*' That is what he said." Uppmann threw back his head and gulped down the entire glass of cognac. Then he poured himself a refill. "I personally saw Hitler at the end in his bunker—Herr Gehlen sent me to deliver an appreciation of the Russian offensive against Berlin. You cannot imagine...a stooped figure with a swollen face, one eye inflamed, sat hunched in a chair. His hands trembled. He tried without success to conceal the twitching of his left arm. When he walked to the map room he dragged his left leg behind him. The one we called the Angel of Death, the Braun woman, was present also: pale, pretty, frightened to die and afraid not to. And what did Hitler have to offer the German people at this tragic hour? He issued an order, I myself heard him, to record the sound of tanks rolling over roads, cut gramophone records and distribute them to the front line commands to play over loudspeakers for the Russians. We were reduced to stopping the Bolsheviks with *gramophone records*, Herr Ebbitt. This will never—I repeat to you the word *never*—happen again."

Ebby covered his mouth with a palm to keep from speaking. Herr Doktor Uppmann took this as a sign of sympathy for the story he had told. "You maybe begin to see things in the new light."

"*No!*" Ebby closed the gap between him and the German. "It makes me want to throw up. You didn't wage war, Doktor Uppmann, you inflicted holocausts. Your solutions to Germany's problems were Final Solutions."

Uppmann appeared to address his words directly to a photograph of Gehlen hanging on the wall. "The Jews won the war and then wrote the history of the war. This number of six million—they picked it out of a hat and the victors swallowed it to diabolize Germany."

"The only thing left of your thousand-year Reich, Herr Doktor Uppmann, is the memory of the crimes you committed—and the memory will last a thousand years. It makes me sick to my stomach to be on the same side as you—to be in the same room with you. If you will conduct me to the main gate—"

The German stiffened. A muscle in his neck twitched. "The sooner you are gone from here the sooner we can get on with the struggle against

Bolshevism, Herr Ebbitt." He downed the last of his cognac and flung the empty glass against a wall, shattering it into pieces. Crunching the shards under foot, he stalked from the room.

The official complaint was not long in working its way up the German chain of command and back down the American chain of command. Summoned to explain what had happened, Ebby appeared before a three-man board of inquiry. The Wiz came up from Vienna to sit in on the hearing. Ebby made no effort to water down what the officers in Frankfurt Station were calling "The Affair." It turned out that Ebby had punctured the abscess. Company officers across Germany heard the story on the grapevine and slipped him memos and Ebby boiled them down to an indictment, which he read aloud to the board of inquiry. "When General Gehlen was allowed to get back into the business of intelligence," he began, "he agreed in writing not to employ former Gestapo officers or war criminals. Yet he has surrounded himself with ex-Nazis, all of whom are listed on his masthead under false identities."

"I assume you are prepared to name names," snapped the CIA officer presiding over the hearing.

"I can name names, yes. There are SS Obersturmführers Franz Goring and Hans Sommer. Sommer's name will ring a bell—he got into trouble with his Gestapo superiors for organizing the 1941 burning of seven Paris synagogues. There is SS Sturmbannführer Fritz Schmidt, who was involved in the executions of slave labor workers at the Friedrich Ott camp near Kiel in 1944. There is Franz Alfred Six, the SS Brigadeführer of Section VII of Himmler's RSHA, convicted at Nuremberg to twenty years imprisonment for having ordered executions of hundreds of Jews when he commanded a Jajdkommando in July and August 1941; he was released after four years and immediately employed by Gehlen's Org. There is Standartenführer Emil Augsburg, who headed a section in Adolf Eichmann's department handling the so-called Jewish problem. My guide when I turned up at Gehlen's compound goes by the name of Doktor Uppmann. His real name is Gustav Pohl. He was a staff officer in Gehlen's Foreign Armies East but he wore second hat—he was the German Foreign Office's liaison to the SS during the invasion of Russia. According to evidence presented at Nuremberg, Pohl participated in the creation of the SS Einsatzgruppen mobile killing squads that shot Jews, including women and children, as well as Commissars, into the graves that the condemned had been forced to dig."

At the side of the room Frank Wisner appeared to be dozing in a wooden chair tilted back against a wall. "Now I did warn you, Ebby," he called out, his eyes still closed. "You can't say I didn't. I warned you I'd kick ass when things didn't work out the way I thought they ought to." The Wiz righted his chair and came ambling across the room. "I'm 'bout to kick ass, Ebby. Let me fill you in on some facts of life—you know who the OSS officer was who negotiated with Gehlen to get hold of his goddamned microfilms? It was me, Ebby. I negotiated with him. I swallowed my pride and I swallowed my bile and I swallowed whatever scruples the weak-kneed crowd came up with and I made a deal with one devil the better to fight another devil. Do you really believe we don't know that Gehlen employs ex-Nazis? Come off it, Ebby—we pick up the tab over in Pullach. Jesus Christ Almighty, here you got a Joe 'bout to jump out of an aeroplane into Communist Russia and you suddenly have qualms about where you're getting the ID your Joe needs to avoid a firing squad. Myself, I'd *crawl* through dog shit on all fours and kiss Hermann Goering's fat ass if he could supply me with what my Joe needed to survive. In what ostrich hole have you been hiding your head, Ebby? In Berlin Station you got all hot under the collar because Harvey Torriti—who happens to be one of the most competent officers in the field—needs a ration of booze to get through the day. In Frankfurt Station you get all hot under the collar because of the company the Company keeps. Didn't your Daddy ever teach you that the enemy of your enemy is your friend? And while we're on the subject of your Daddy let me tell you something else. Before he parachuted into Bulgaria he was hanging out in Madrid doing deals with Spanish fascists to get the skinny on German raw material shipments. Hell, your Daddy was made of harder stuff than his son, that's for damn sure. So which way you gonna jump, boy? You gonna go all out for your Joe or you gonna fill our ears with slop about the occasional ex-Nazi in the woodpile?"

In a large corner office in "L" building next to the Reflecting Pool, James Angleton leafed through the day's field reports clamped between the metal covers of the top-secret folder.

"Anything happening I need to write home ab-b-bout, Jimbo?" asked his friend Adrian, the MI6 liaison man in Washington.

Angleton plucked a sheet from the folder and slid it across the blotter. Stirring a whiskey and branch water with one of the wooden tongue depressors he'd swiped from a doctor's office, Kim Philby leaned over the report and sniffed at it. "*Smells* top secret," he said with a snicker. He read it quickly, then read it a second time more slowly. A whistle seeped through his front teeth. "You want a second opinion? We should have gotten round to this kind of shenanigans months ago. If there really is a Ukrainian resistance movement in the Carpathians we'd be b-b-bloody fools not to hook up with them."

"Do me a favor, Adrian, keep this under your hat until we hear our man's safely on the ground," Angleton said.

"Ayatollah Angleton's every wish is his servant's command," Philby shot back, bowing obsequiously toward his friend. They both laughed and, clinking glasses, sat back to polish off their drinks.

SUMMERSAULT had to shout to be heard over the roar of the C-47's engines. "I thank you, I thank President Truman, I thank America for sending me back. If my father sees me now, for sure he turns over in his grave—his son Alyosha comes home in a plane where he is the only passenger."

Ebby had brought SUMMERSAULT to the secret air strip in the American zone of Germany at sunset to meet the two pilots, Czech airmen who had flown Spitfires during the Battle of Britain. The C-47 had been "sheep-dipped"—stripped of all its markings—and fitted with extra fuel tanks under the wings for the round trip to the Ukrainian Carpathians and back. An Air Force sergeant had personally folded the main parachute and the emergency chute into their packs and had shown the young Ukrainian how to tighten the straps over his shoulder blades. "The plane's going to descend to six hundred feet for the drop," he instructed Alyosha, who had seen training films but had never jumped himself. "When the yellow light comes on, you position yourself at the open door. When the green light comes on, you jump. Remember to count to five before you pull the rip cord. Count slow-like. One one-hundredth. Two one-hundredth. Like that, awright?"

"Awright," Alyosha had replied, imitating the sergeant's New York accent.

Ebby had helped SUMMERSAULT lug his gear out to the plane—the heavy parachute pack, the small suitcase (containing worn Russian clothing, the shortwave radio and several dozen German wristwatches that could be used to bribe people), a lunchbox with sandwiches and beer. Now, with the engines revving, Ebby carefully removed the poison capsule from a matchbox and forced it through the tiny rip in the fabric under SUMMERSAULT's collar. He wrapped his arms around his Joe in a bear hug and yelled into his ear, "Good luck to you, Alyosha." He would have said more if he could have trusted himself to speak.

SUMMERSAULT grinned back. "Good luck to both of us and lousy luck to Joe Stalin!"

Moments later the plane climbed into the night sky and, banking as it gained altitude, disappeared into the east. Ebby used a base bicycle to peddle over to the Quonset hut that served as the flight center. If everything went according to plan the C-47 would be droning in for a landing in roughly six hours. The Czech pilots were under strict orders to maintain radio silence; the hope was that the Russians would take the flight for one of the aerial surveillance missions that regularly cut across the "denied areas" in a great rainbow arc. An Air Force duty officer brought Ebby a tray filled with warmed Spam and dehydrated mashed potatoes and offered him the use of a cot in a back room. He lay in the darkness, unable to cat-nap because of the disjointed thoughts tearing through his brain. Had he and Spink overlooked anything? The labels in Alyosha's clothing—they were all Russian. The soles on his shoes—Russian too. The wristwatches—anyone who had served in a Russian unit in Germany (Alyosha's military status book bore the forged signature of an officer who was dead) could explain away a packet of stolen wristwatches. The radio and the one-time pads and the Minox camera—they would be buried immediately after SUMMERSAULT sent word that he had landed safely. But what if he broke an ankle while landing? What if he was knocked unconscious and some peasants turned him in to the militia? Would the legend that Ebby had devised—that Alyosha had worked for two-and-a-half-years at a dam construction project in the northern Ukraine—stand up under scrutiny? The doubts crowded in, one behind the other, a long succession of them jostling each other to reach the head of the line.

An hour or so before dawn Ebby, braving the icy air outside the Quonset hut, thought he heard the distant drone of engines. He climbed on the bicycle and pedaled across the field to the giant hangar, arriving just as two wing lights snapped on and the C-47 touched down at the end of the strip. The plane taxied up to the hangar. Spotting Ebby, one of the Czech pilots slid back a cockpit window and gave him the thumbs-up sign. Ebby, exhilarated, sliced the air with his palm in response. All that remained now was to pick up the first cipher message announcing that the landing had gone off without a hitch.

Back at Frankfurt Station later that morning, Ebby was catnapping on an office cot when Tony Spink shook him awake. Ebby sat straight up. "Did he check in?" he demanded.

"Yeah. The kid said he'd landed, no bones broken. He said he was going to bury the radio and head for the hills to find his friends. He said he was happy to be home. He said he'd get in touch again in a few days. He said...he said 'I love you guys.'"

Ebby searched Spink's face. "What's wrong, Tony? The fist was Alyosha's, wasn't it?"

"The fist was right. My man who taught him Morse swears it was Alyosha sending. But the kid inserted the danger signal in the message—he signed it Alyosha instead of SUMMERSAULT."

Ebby clutched at a straw. "Maybe he forgot—"

"No way, Ebby. He's being played back. We'll act as if we don't suspect anything for as long as they want to play him. But the kid is a dead man walking."

4

JACK'S AFTER-HOURS HAUNT, DIE PFEFFERMÜHLE, WAS FILLED WITH what the Vichy police chief in Mr. Humphrey Bogart's motion picture *Casablanca* would have called "the usual suspects." Freddie Leigh-Asker, the MI6 Chief of Station, sidled up to the bar to chase down a refill. "Two doubles, no rocks," he hollered to the harried bartender. "Heard the latest?" he asked Jack, who was nursing a double *with* rocks before meandering toward the small dance theater for his semi-weekly session with the agent known as RAINBOW. It was Jack's third double of the afternoon; he was beginning to understand what pushed the Sorcerer to drown his angst in alcohol. Freddie's hot breath defrosted Jack's eardrum. "The psych warfare crazies have come up with a pisser—they want us to bombard Russia with zillions of extra-large condoms."

On the small stage an all-female jazz band dressed in tight lederhosen was belting out number three on the American top ten, "Kisses Sweeter Than Wine." "Not sure I follow you," Jack called over what in other circumstances would have passed for music.

"The condoms will all be stamped 'medium' in *English*!" Freddie explained. "Do I need to draw you a diagram, old boy? It'll demoralize every Russian female of the species who hasn't reached menopause. Never look at their blokes again without wondering what they've been missing out on. Absolutely wizard scheme, what?"

Groping in an inside pocket of his blazer for some loose marks, Freddie flung them on the bar, grabbed his drinks and drifted off into a smog of cigarette smoke. Jack was glad to be rid of him. He knew the Sorcerer couldn't stand the sight of Leigh-Asker; Torriti claimed to be leery of people with hyphenated names but his Night Owl, Miss Sipp, had come up with a better take on the situation.

"It's not the silly little hyphen, oh, dear, no," she had confided in Jack late one night. "Poor Freddie Leigh-Asker had what the Brits call a good war—he parachuted into the burning fiery furnace and wasn't even singed. He's absolutely positive that if he hasn't bought it by now he's home free to die of old age. It's said of him that he doesn't know what the word fear means. Mr. Torriti prefers to work with people who are afraid—he feels they have a better chance of staying one jump ahead of the opposition. He likes you, Jack, because he reckons that behind your bravado—behind your 'Once down is no battle' mantra—there's a healthy trepidation."

A lean, muscular man in his mid twenties with short-cropped hair climbed onto the stool next to Jack and lifted a finger to get the attention of the bartender. "Draft beer," he called. He caught sight of Jack's face in the mirror behind the bar. "McAuliffe!" he cried. "Jacko McAuliffe!"

Jack raised his eyes to the mirror. He recognized the young man sitting next to him and wagged a finger at his reflection, trying to dredge up the name that went with the familiar face. The young man helped him. "The European championship? Munich? Forty-eight? I was rowing stroke in the Russian coxed four? You and me we fell crazy in love with Australian peacenik twins but broke off romance when the sun came up?"

Jack slapped his forehead in recognition. "Borisov!" he said. He glanced sideways, genuinely delighted to stumble across an old bar-hopping pal from Munich. "Vanka Borisov! Damnation! What the hell are you doing here?"

The bartender shaved the head off the beer with the back of his forefinger and set the mug down in front of Borisov. The two young men clinked glasses. "I am working for the Soviet import-export commission," the Russian said. "We conduct trade negotiations with the German Democratic Republic. What about yourself, Jacko?"

"I landed a soft job with the State Department information bureau— I'm the guy in charge of what we call boilerplate. I write up news releases describing how well *our* Germans are making out under capitalism and how badly *your* Germans are faring under Communism."

"The last time I saw you you had a bad case of blood blisters under your calluses."

Jack showed the Russian his palms, which were covered with thick calluses. "When we beat Harvard last Spring I was pulling so hard I thought the rib I cracked in Munich would crack again. The pain was something else."

"What ever happened to your cox? Leon something-or-other?"

A faint current buzzed in Jack's brain. "Leo Kritzky. I lost track of him," he said, a grin plastered on his face. He wondered if the Russian really worked in import-export. "We had a falling out over a girl."

"You always had an eye for the ladies," the Russian said with a broad smile.

The two young men talked rowing for a while. The Russians, it seemed, had developed a new slide that ran on self-lubricating ball bearings. Borisov had been one of the first to test it during trial runs on the Moscow River; the mechanism worked so smoothly, he told Jack, it allowed the rower to reduce the exaggerated body work and concentrate on blade work. The result, Borisov guessed, was worth one or two strokes every hundred meters. Still smiling, the Russian looked sideways at Jack. "I have never been to the States," he said nonchalantly. "Tell me something, Jacko—what is a lot of money in America?"

The buzzing in Jack's head grew stronger. It depended, he replied evenly, on a great many things—whether you lived in the city or the countryside, whether you drove a Studebaker or a Cadillac, whether you bought ready-made suits or had them custom-tailored.

"Give me an approximate idea," Borisov insisted. "Twenty-five thousand dollars? Fifty? A hundred thousand?"

Jack began to think the question might be innocent after all—everybody in Europe was curious about how Americans lived. He allowed as how $25,000 was an awful lot of bucks; $50,000, a fortune. Borisov let that sink in for a moment. When he turned back to Jack the smile had faded from his face. "Tell me something else, Jacko—how much do you earn a year producing boilerplate stories for the State Department?"

"Somewhere in the neighborhood of six thousand dollars."

The Russian jutted out his lower lip in thought. "What if somebody was to come up to you—right now, right here—and offer you a hundred and fifty thousand dollars in cash?"

The buzzing in Jack's head was so strong now it almost drowned out the conversation. He heard himself ask, "In return for what?"

"In return for the odd piece of information about a Mr. Harvey Torriti."

"What makes you think I know anyone named Harvey Torriti?"

Borisov gulped down the last of the beer and carefully blotted his lips on the back of a wrist. "If a hundred fifty thousand is not enough, name a figure."

Jack wondered how Vanka had gotten involved with the KGB; probably much the same way he'd gotten involved with the CIA—a talent scout, an interview, several months of intensive training and whoops, there you were, baiting a hook and casting it into the pitchy waters of Die Pfeffermühle.

"You tell *me* something," Jack said. "How much is a lot of money in the Soviet Union?" Vanka squirmed uncomfortably on his stool. "Would a Russian with five thousand United States of America dollars stashed in a numbered Swiss bank account be considered rich? No? How about twenty-five thousand? Still no? Okay, let's say somebody walked up to you—right here, right now—and wrote down the number of a secret Swiss bank account in which a hundred and fifty thousand US dollars had been deposited in your name."

The Russian let out an uncomfortable laugh. "In exchange for what?"

"In exchange for the odd bit of information from Karlshorst—import-export data, the names of the Russians who are doing the importing and exporting."

Borisov slid off his stool. "It has been a pleasure seeing you again, Jacko. Good luck to you at your State Department information bureau."

"Nice bumping into you, too, Vanka. Good luck with your import-export commission. Hey, stay in touch."

Lurking in the shadows of a doorway across Hardenbergstrasse, Jack kept an eye on the stage door of the ugly little modern dance theater. He had spent an hour and a half roaming the labyrinthian limbs of the S-Bahn, jumping into and out of trains a moment before the doors closed, lingering until everyone had passed and then doubling back on his route, finally emerging at the Zoo Station and meandering against traffic through a tangle of side streets until he was absolutely sure he wasn't being followed. Mr. Andrews, he thought, would be proud of his tradecraft. At 8 P.M. the street filled with people, their heads angled into the cold air, hurrying home from work, many carrying sacks of coal they had picked up at an Allied distribution center in the Tiergarten; something about the way they walked suggested to Jack that they weren't dying to get where they were going. At 9:10 the first students began coming out of the theater, scrawny teenagers striding off in the distinctive duck-walk of ballet dancers, great clouds of breath billowing from their mouths as they giggled excitedly. Jack waited another ten minutes, then crossed the street and let himself into the narrow hallway that smelled of perspiration and talcum powder. The watchman, an old Pomeranian named Aristide, was sitting in the shabby chair in his glass-enclosed cubbyhole, one ear glued to a small radio; von Karajan, who had played for the Führer and once arranged for audience seating in the form of a swastika, was conducting Beethoven's Fifth live from Vienna. Aristide, his eyes shaded by a visor, never looked up as Jack pushed two packs of

American cigarettes through the window. With the wooden planks creaking under his weight, he climbed the staircase at the back of the hallway to the top floor rehearsal hall and listened for a moment. Hearing no other sound in the building, he opened the door.

As she always did after her Tuesday and Friday classes, RAINBOW had lingered behind to work out at the barre after her students had gone. Barefoot, wearing purple tights and a loose-fitting washed-out sweat shirt, she leaned forward and folded her body in half to plant her palms flat on the floor, then straightened and arched her back and easily stretched one long leg flat along the barre and then leaned over it, all the while studying herself in the mirror. Her dark hair, which seemed to have trapped some of the last rays of the previous night's setting sun, was pulled back and plaited with strands of wool into a long braid that plunged to the small hollow of her back—the spot where Jack wore his Walther PPK. This was the fifth time Jack had met with her and the sheer physical beauty of her body in motion still managed to take his breath away. At some point in her life her nose had been broken and badly set, but what would have disfigured another woman on her served as an enigmatic ornament.

"What do you see when you watch yourself dance in the mirror?" Jack asked from the door.

Startled, she grabbed a towel from the barre and flung it around her neck, and with her feet barely touching the ground—so it appeared to Jack—came across the room. She dried her long delicate fingers on the towel and formally offered a hand. He shook it. She led him to the pile of clothing neatly folded on one of the wooden chairs lining the wall. "What I see are my faults—the mirror reflects only faults."

"Something tells me you're being too hard on yourself."

She smiled in disagreement. "When I was eighteen I aspired to be a great dancer, yes? Now I am twenty-eight and I aspire only to dance."

The Sorcerer had purchased RAINBOW from a Polish freelancer, a dapper man in a black undertaker's suit who pasted the last strands of hair across his scalp with an ointment designed to stimulate the *folliculus*. Like dozens of others who worked the hypogean world of Berlin, he made a handsome living selling the odd scrap of information or the occasional source who was said to have access to secrets. Warning Jack to be leery of a KGB dangle operation, Torriti—brooding full time over the aborted defection of Vishnevsky—had handed RAINBOW over to his Apprentice with instructions to fuck her if he could and tape record what she whispered in his ear. Tickled to be running his first full-fledged agent, Jack had set up a rendezvous.

RAINBOW turned out to be an East German classical dancer who crossed into West Berlin twice a week to give ballet classes at a small out-of-the-way theater. At their first meeting Jack had started to question her in German but she had cut him off, saying she preferred to conduct the meetings in English in order to perfect her grammar and vocabulary; it was her dream, she had confessed, to one day see Margot Fonteyn dance at London's Royal Ballet. RAINBOW had identified herself only as Lili and had warned Jack that if he attempted to follow her when she returned to the eastern zone of the city she would break off all contact. She had turned her back to Jack and had extracted from her brassiere a small square of silk covered with minuscule handwriting. When Jack took it from her he had discovered the silk was still warm from her breast. He had offered to pay for the information she brought but she had flatly refused. "I am hateful of the Communists, yes?" she had said, her bruised eyes staring unblinkingly into his. "My mother was a Spanish Communist—she was killed in the struggle against the fascist Franco; because of this detail I am trusted by the East German authorities," she had explained at that first meeting. "I loathe the Russian soldiers because of what they did to me when they captured Berlin. I loathe the Communists because of what they are doing to my Germany. We live in a country where phones are allotted on the basis of how often they want to call you; where you think one thing, say another and do a third. Someone must make a stand against this, yes?"

Lili had claimed to be courier for an important figure in the East German hierarchy whom she referred to as "Herr Professor," but otherwise refused to identify. Back at Berlin Base, Jack had arranged for the patch of silk to be photographed and translated. When he showed the "get" from Lili's Herr Professor (now code-named SNIPER) to the Sorcerer, Torriti had opened a bottle of Champagne to celebrate tapping into the mother lode. For Lili had provided them with a synopsis of the minutes of an East German cabinet meeting, plain-text copies of several messages that had been exchanged between the East German government and the local Soviet military leaders (Berlin Station already had enciphered versions of the same messages, which meant the Americans could work backwards and break the codes that had been used for encryption), along with a partial list of the KGB officers working out of Karlshorst. For the past six months Torriti had been running an East German agent, code-named MELODY, who worked in the Soviet office that handled freight shipments between Moscow and Berlin. Using the shipping registry, MELODY (debriefed personally by Torriti when the agent managed to visit the Sorcerer's whorehouse above a nightclub on the Grunewaldstrasse in Berlin-Schoneberg) had been able to identify many of the officers and personnel posted to Karlshorst by their real names. Comparing the names supplied by Lili with those supplied by MELODY provided confirmation that Lili's Herr Professor was genuine.

"Who the fuck is she, sport?" Torriti had demanded after Jack returned from the second rendezvous with another square of silk filled with tiny handwriting. "More important, who the fuck is her goddamn professor chum?"

"She says if I try to find out the well will go dry," Jack had reminded Torriti. "From the way she talks about him I get the feeling he's some sort of scientist. When I asked her where exactly the Communists were going wrong in East Germany, she answered by quoting the professor quoting Albert Einstein—something about our age being characterized by a perfection of means and a confusion of goals. Also, she speaks of him with great formality, more or less the way someone speaks about a much older person. I get the feeling he could be her father or an uncle. Whoever it is, he's someone close to the summit."

"More likely to be her lover," Torriti had muttered. "More often than not sex and espionage are birds of a feather." The Sorcerer had dropped an empty whiskey bottle into a government-issue wire wastebasket filled with cigarette butts and had reached into an open safe behind him for another bottle. He had poured himself a stiff drink, had splashed in a thimbleful of water, had stirred the contents with his middle finger, then had carefully licked the finger before downing half the drink in one long swallow. "Listen up, sport, there's an old Russian proverb that says you're supposed to wash the bear without getting its fur wet. That's what I want you to do with RAINBOW."

In order to wash the bear without getting its fur wet, Jack had to organize a tedious surveillance operation designed to track RAINBOW back into East Berlin and discover where she lived and who she was. Once they discovered her identity, it would be a matter of time before they found out who SNIPER was. If the Professor turned out to be a senior Communist with access to East German and Soviet secrets, some serious consideration would be given to using him in a more creative way; he could be obliged (under threat of exposure; under threat of having his courier exposed) to plant disinformation in places where it could do the most harm, or steer policy discussions in a direction that did the most good for Western interests. If he really was a member of the ruling elite over in the Soviet zone, the few people above him could be discredited or eliminated and SNIPER might even wind up running the show.

The Sorcerer had given Jack the services of the two Silwans, the Fallen Angel and Sweet Jesus, and half a dozen other Watchers. Each time Jack met with RAINBOW, one of the Silwans would take up position where Lili had last been seen when she headed back toward East Berlin. No single Watcher would follow her for more than a hundred meters. Using walkie-talkies, members of the surveillance team would position themselves ahead of Lili and, blending in with the tens of thousands of East Berliners returning home to the Soviet Sector after working in West Berlin, keep her in sight for a few minutes before passing her on to the next Watcher. When the team ran out of agents the operation would be called off for the night. Each time Jack met RAINBOW the radius of the operation would be extended.

On the first night of the operation, Jack's third meeting with RAINBOW, the Fallen Angel had watched Lili buy some sheer stockings in one of the luxury stores on the Kurfürstendamm and tracked her to the gutted Kaiser Wilhelm Memorial Church at the top of West Berlin's six-lane main drag; Sweet Jesus, walking his muzzled lap dog, had kept her in sight until she disappeared in the crowd at Potsdamer Platz, where the four Allied sectors converged. She was last seen crossing into the eastern sector near the enormous electric sign, like the one in Times Square, that beamed news into the Communist-controlled half of the city. The second night of the operation one of the Silwans picked her up in front of the Handelorganization, a giant state store on the Soviet side of Potsdamer Platz, and handed her on to the second Watcher as she passed the battle-scarred Reichstag and the grassy mound over the underground bunker where Hitler and Eva Braun committed suicide. Two uniformed policemen from the Communist Bereitschaftspolizisten stopped her near the grassy mound to check her identity booklet. Lili, glancing nervously over her shoulder every now and then to make sure she wasn't being followed, turned down a side street filled with four-story buildings gutted in the war; the few apartments where Germans still lived had their windows boarded over and stovepipes jutting through the walls. The Watcher peeled off and the next Watcher, alerted by radio, picked her up when she emerged onto Unter den Linden. He lost her moments later when a formation of Freie Deutsche Jugund, Communist boy scouts wearing blue shirts and blue bandannas and short pants even in winter, came between them; drums beating, the scouts were marching down the center of the Unter den Linden carrying large photographs of Stalin and East German leader Otto Grotewohl and a banner that read: "Forward with Stalin."

On the night of Jack's sixth rendezvous with RAINBOW on the top floor of the ugly little theater, Lili delivered the still-warm square of silk filled with writing and then offered her hand. "You have never said me your name, yes?" she remarked.

"I am called Jack," he said, gripping her hand in his.

"That sounds very American to my ears. Jackknife. Jack-in-the-box. Jack-of-all-trades."

"That's me," Jack agreed with a laugh. "Jack-of-all-trades and master of none." He was still holding her hand. She looked down at it with a cheerless smile and gently slid her fingers free. "Look," Jack said quickly, "I just happen to have two tickets to a Bartók ballet being performed at the Municipal Opera House in British Sector—Melissa Hayden is dancing in something called *The Miraculous Mandarin*." He pulled the tickets from his overcoat pocket and offered her one of them. "The curtain goes up tomorrow at six—they begin early so the East Germans can get home before midnight." She started to shake her head. "Hey," Jack said, "no strings attached—we'll watch the ballet, afterwards I'll buy you a beer at the bar and then you'll duck like a spider back into your crack in the wall." When she still didn't take the ticket he reached over and dropped it into her handbag.

"I am tempted," she admitted. "I have heard it said that Melissa Hayden is not restricted by gravity. I do not know..."

The next evening the Watchers, spread strategically through the streets surrounding Humbolt University at the end of the Unter den Linden, picked RAINBOW up coming from the direction of the Gorky Theater, behind the university. Queuing with a crowd of relatively well-dressed Berliners waiting for the Opera House doors to open, Jack was handed a note that read: "We are almost there—tonight should do it."

When the curtain rose the balcony seat next to Jack was still empty. Every now and then he cast a glance at the door behind him. In the darkness he thought he saw a figure slip in. An instant later Lili, looking ravishing in a helmet-like hat made of felt and a threadbare fur coat that dusted the tops of her flat-soled shoes, settled into the seat. Shrugging the coat off her shoulders, she smiled faintly at Jack, then produced ancient opera glasses and gazed through them at the stage. Her lips parted slightly and her chest rose and fell in quiet rapture. When the prima ballerina finally pushed through the curtain and curtsied to the audience, tears appeared in Lili's eyes as she applauded wildly.

Jack steered her through the crowd in the hallway and down the wide steps to a long bar on the ground floor. "I would very much like a *Berliner Weisse mit Schuss*—a light beer with raspberry syrup," she informed him. She took a small change purse from the pocket of her fur coat. Jack smiled and said, "Please." She smiled back and returned the change purse to her pocket. After he had ordered she leaned toward him and he could feel the feather's weight of her torso against his arm. "In the east raspberries in winter are more expensive than gold," she murmured.

They carried their beers to an empty table. Lili hiked her long skirt and sat down; Jack caught a glimpse of gray cotton stockings and slender ankles. Lili said, "Given your occupation, I am in bewilderment to discover that you are an aficionado of ballet." She cocked her head. "Perhaps you will tell me biographical things of yourself, yes?"

Jack laughed. "Yes, sure." He touched his glass to hers and drank off some of the beer. "I'll start at the start. I was raised in a small town in Pennsylvania—you will never have heard of it—called Jonestown. My parents had a house with a wraparound porch where the town stopped and the fields of corn started. When I was a kid I thought the fields went on forever, or at least until they reached the edge of the flat earth. If the wind was right you could hear the church bells ringing in the convent beyond the corn, beyond a hill. My father made a small fortune producing underwear for the army in his factory up the road from our house. I learned to drive when I was fourteen on his 1937 Pierce Arrow. My father kept saddle horses in the barn next to the house and chickens in a shed behind it. My mother played the organ at the Catholic church in Lebanon, near Jonestown. Twice a year we vacationed in New York City. We stayed at a hotel called the Waldorf-Astoria on Park Avenue. Every time we visited the city my father disappeared with some of his schoolmates and came back roaring drunk in the middle of the night. My mother took me to the ballet—I remember seeing Prokofiev's *Prodigal Son* and his *Romeo and Juliet* performed at the Metropolitan Opera House."

"And how did you become what you are? How did you..."

He took another sip of beer. "There are Americans who understand that we are involved in a life and death struggle with the Communists. When it is over only one side will survive. I was invited by these Americans to join the battle." He reached over and touched the fur on the collar of her coat with his knuckles. "Tell me about yourself, Lili. What is your real name?"

She was immediately wary. "Lili is what my father always called me as a child because my mother often played the song 'Lili Marlene' on the gramophone. As for myself, there is not much to tell—I survived the Nazis, I survived your American bombers, I survived the Russian soldiers who rampaged like crazy people across Germany." She pulled the collar of her fur coat up around her long neck. "With the assistance of these ancient squirrels I even survived the bitter winter of '47."

"At what age did you begin dancing?"

"There was never a time when I was not dancing. As a child I discovered a way to use my body to get outside my body, I discovered the secret places where gravity didn't exist, I discovered a secret language that wasn't verbal.

The adults around me said I would become a ballet dancer, but it was years before I understood what they were talking about."

Jack blurted out very softly, "Jesus H. Christ, you are a wonderfully beautiful woman, Lili."

She closed her lids wearily and kept them closed for a moment. "I am not beautiful but I am not ugly either."

Screwing up his courage, Jack asked her if she lived alone or with a man.

"Why do you ask me such a thing?" she demanded angrily. "I have told you, I tell you again, if you try to find out who I am, or who the Professor is, you will never see me again."

"I asked because I was hoping against hope you would say you lived alone, which could mean that there might be room for me in your life."

"My life is too crowded with emptiness for there to be room for you in it, Jack-of-all-trades and master of none." She sipped her raspberry-flavored beer and licked her lips, which had turned the color of raspberry, with her tongue. "Since you live and work in the universe of secrets I will add to your collection of secrets: The moments I treasure the most come when I wake up from a drugged sleep and I do not know where I am or who I am—I drift for a few delicious seconds in a gravity-less void. At such moments I dance like I have never been able to in my earthbound life. I dance *almost* the way Melissa Hayden danced before our eyes this night."

Returning home after the ballet, RAINBOW was picked up by the Fallen Angel as she turned into a street behind the Gorky Theater lined with vacant lots filled with rubble bulldozed into giant heaps on which children played king of mountain. Dozens of wild cats, meowing furiously, prowled the war-gutted buildings stalking emaciated mice. In the middle of this devastation a single structure stood untouched. Set back from the street, it was planted in the midst of a small park whose trees had all been cut down for firewood. Giant steel girders shored up the side walls that had once been joined to the adjacent buildings. The Fallen Angel watched from the shadows of a deserted kiosk as Lili took a latch key from her purse. She looked back and, seeing the street was deserted, unlocked the heavy front door and let herself into the vestibule.

The building was pitch-dark except for a large bay window on the second floor. The Fallen Angel snapped open a small telescope and focused it on the window. An older man could be seen parting a filmy curtain with the back of his left hand and peering down into the street. He had snow-white hair and wore a shirt with an old-fashioned starched collar, a necktie and a suit jacket with rounded lapels. He must have heard a door opening behind him because he turned back into the room and spread wide his arms.

Through the gauzy curtains Lili could be seen coming into them.

Jack burst into the Sorcerer's office the next afternoon. "...right about SNIPER...scientist...much older than RAINBOW," he cried excitedly, raising his voice to make himself heard over a grating 78-rpm rendition of Caruso singing an aria from Bizet's *Les Pêcheurs de Perles*.

"Simmer down, sport. I can't understand your jabberwocky."

Jack caught his breath. "I took your advice and tried out the address on your Mossad friend—the Rabbi leafed through some very thick loose-leaf books and came up with two names to go with the address. RAINBOW's real name is Helga Agnes Mittag de la Fuente. Mittag was her German father; de la Fuente was Mittag's Spanish wife and RAINBOW's mother. The Rabbi even confirmed there was a Spanish journalist named Agnes de la Fuente who was caught spying for the Republicans during the Spanish Civil War and put in front of a firing squad."

"What about SNIPER?"

"The Professor is Ernst Ludwig Löffler. He teaches theoretical physics at the Humbolt University Institute of Physics. Before the war, when Humbolt was still known as the University of Berlin, Löffler hung out with Max Planck and Albert Einstein."

Torriti settled back into his chair and stirred a whiskey and water with his forefinger. "A fucking theoretical physicist! Wait'll the Wiz gets wind of this."

"That's only the icing on the cake, Harvey. There's more. Right after the war Grotewohl's Socialist Unity Party let several small parties into the National Front for window dressing—that way he could claim East Germany was a genuine democracy. One of these parties is the Liberal Democratic Party. SNIPER is deputy head of that party and a deputy prime minister of the German Democratic Republic!"

"Eureka!" exalted Torriti. "Do me a favor, sport. Put a teardrop in SNIPER's wall."

"Why do you want to bug him? He's sending you whatever he gets his hands on."

"Motivation, sport. I want to know *why* he's sending it."

"A teardrop."

"Uh-huh."

5

BERLIN, TUESDAY, MARCH 6, 1951

Is face screwed up in revulsion, the Sorcerer spilled into the whiskey and water the sodium bicarbonate his Night Owl had bought back from an all-night pharmacy. He stirred the mixture with his pinky until the whitish powder dissolved.

"Down the hatch, Mr. Torriti," Miss Sipp coaxed. "It won't kill you. Think of it as one for the road."

Harvey Torriti pinched his nostrils between a thumb and forefinger and drained off the concoction in one long disgruntled gulp. He shivered as he scraped his mouth dry on the wrinkled sleeve of his shirt. Stomach cramps, constipation, loss of appetite, a permanent soreness in his solar plexus, the end of one dull hangover overlapping the beginning of another even when he cut back to one and a half bottles of booze a day—these were the plagues that had afflicted the Sorcerer since the aborted exfiltration of the Russian Vishnevsky. Slivovitz from the water cooler tasted tasteless, cigarette smoke burned the back of his throat; on any given night he would come wide awake before he actually fell asleep, sweating bullets and blinking away images of a heavy caliber pistol spitting hot metal into the nape of a thick neck. The short Russian with his central casting Slavic mask of a face, the mind-scarred veteran of the four brutal winters that took the Red Army from Moscow to Berlin, had deposited his life in the Sorcerer's perspiring hands. Also his wife's. Also his son's. Torriti had put in the plumbing for the defection and come away with zilch. In the days that followed he had agonized over the Berlin end of the operation to see if there could have been a weak link; he had scoured the personnel folders of everyone who had been within shouting distance of the operation: Jack McAuliffe, Sweet Jesus and the Fallen Angel, the Night Owl, the code clerk who had enciphered and deciphered the messages to and from Angleton.

If Vishnevsky had bought it because of a leak, it hadn't originated in Berlin.

The Sorcerer had dispatched a discreetly worded message to Mother suggesting he take a hard look at his end of the operation. Angleton's vinegary reply was on his desk the next morning. In two tart paragraphs Angleton informed Torriti that: (1) it wasn't clear the exfiltration had fallen through because of a leak; Vishnevsky could have been betrayed by his wife or son or a friend who had been let in on the secret; alternatively, Vishnevsky could have given himself away by words or actions that aroused suspicions; (2) if there was a leak it had not originated in Mother's shop, which was uncontaminated, but rather in the Berlin end of the operation. Period. End of discussion.

In plain English: fuck off.

Several days after the debacle the Sorcerer—staggering into the office after another sleepless night—had stumbled across hard evidence that someone had, in fact, betrayed Vishnevsky. Torriti had been rummaging through the "get" from one of his most productive operations: a teardrop-sized high-tech electronic microphone secreted in the wall of the communications shack of the Karlshorst *rezidentura*. The KGB communicated with Moscow Centre using one-time pads which, given the limited distribution of the cipher keys and the fact that they were utilized only once before being discarded, were impossible to break. Very occasionally, to speed up the process, two KGB communications officers did the enciphering—one read out the clear text as the other enciphered. The night of Vishnevsky's aborted exfiltration two KGB officers had enciphered an "Urgent Immediate" message to Moscow Centre that had been picked up by the Sorcerer's minuscule microphone. The translation from the Russian read: "Ref: Your Urgent Immediate zero zero one of 2 January 1951 Stop Early warning from Moscow Centre prevented defection of Lieutenant Colonel Volkov-Vishnevsky his wife and son Stop Berlin Station offers sincere congratulations to all concerned Stop Volkov-Vishnevsky his wife and son being put aboard military flight Eberswalde Air Force Base immediately Stop Estimated time of arrival Moscow zero six forty five."

The reference to an "early warning" in the congratulatory message from Karlshorst to Moscow confirmed that the KGB had been tipped off about the impending defection. The $64,000 question was: tipped off by whom?

Vishnevsky's words came back to haunt the Sorcerer. "I am able to reveal to you the identity of a Soviet agent in Britain," he had said. "Someone high up in their MI6."

Torriti checked out the distribution of the ciphered messages that had passed between Angleton in Washington and Berlin Station but could find no evidence that anyone from MI6—or any Brit, for that matter—had been in on the secret. It was inconceivable that the Russians had cracked Angleton's unbreakable polyalphabetic ciphers. Was it possible...could the Soviet agent high up in MI6 have gotten wind of the defection through a back channel?

Finding the answer to the riddle—avenging the Russian who had trusted Torriti and lost his life because of it—became the Sorcerer's obsession. His mind sprinting ahead, his aching body trailing along behind, he began the long tedious job of walking back the cat on the aborted defection.

He started with the Israeli Mossad agent in West Berlin who had picked up a "vibration" (his shorthand for a possible defection) from East Berlin and immediately alerted Angleton, who (in addition to the counterintelligence portfolio) ran the Company's Israeli account out of his hip pocket. Known to the local spooks as the Rabbi because of his straggly steel wool beard and side-burns, he was in his early forties and wore windowpane-thick glasses that magnified his already bulging eyes so much his face appeared to be deformed. He dressed in what the spook community took to be a Mossad uniform because nobody could recall seeing him wearing anything else: a baggy black suit with ritual zizith dangling below the hem of the jacket, a white shirt without tie buttoned up to a majestic Adam's apple, a black fedora (worn indoors because he was afraid of drafts) and basketball sneakers. "You see before you a very distressed man," the Rabbi confided once Torriti had suc-cessfully lowered his bulk into one of the wobbly wooden chairs lining the wall of Ezra Ben Ezra's musty inner sanctum in the French zone of Berlin.

"Try sodium bicarbonate," the Sorcerer advised. He knew from experi-ence that there would be a certain amount of polite prattle before they got down to brass tacks.

"My distress is mental as opposed to physical. It has to do with the trial of the Rosenbergs that began in New York this morning. If the judge was a goy they would get twenty years and be out in ten. Mark my words, Harvey, remember you heard it here first: the miserable protagonists, Julius and Ethel, will be sentenced to the electric chair because the federal judge is a Jew-hating Jew named Kaufman."

"They did steal the plans for the atomic bomb, Ezra."

"They passed on to the Russians some rough sketches—"

"There are people who think the North Koreans would never have invaded the south if the Russians hadn't been behind them with the A-bomb."

"*Genug shoyn*, Harvey! Enough already! The North Koreans invaded the south because Communist *China*, with its six hundred million souls, was behind them, not a Tinkertoy Russian A-bomb that could maybe explode in the bomb rack of the airplane as it rattles down the runway."

The Rabbi stopped talking abruptly as a young man with shaved eyebrows came in carrying a tray with two steaming cups of an herbal infusion. Without a word he cleared a space on the Rabbi's chaotic desk, set down the tray and disappeared.

Torriti gestured with his head. "He's new."

"Hamlet—which, believe it or not, is his given name—is Georgian by birth and my *Shabbas goy* by vocation. There are things I cannot do because someone in my position, which is to say a representative of the State of Israel, albeit a secret representative, is expected to be observant, so Hamlet turns on the lights and answers the telephone and kills people for me on Saturdays."

The Sorcerer suspected that the Rabbi was passing the truth off as a joke. "I didn't know you were religious, Ezra."

"I live by the Mossad manual: eye for eye, tooth for tooth, hand for hand, foot for foot, burning for burning, wound for wound, bruise for bruise."

"But do you actually believe in God? Do you believe in life after death or any of that rigmarole?"

"Definitely not."

"In what sense are you Jewish, then?"

"In the sense that if I should happen to forget, the world will remind me every ten or twenty years the way it is currently reminding the Rosenbergs. Read the *New York Times* and weep: two dumb but idealistic schleps pass the odd sketch on to the Russians and all of a sudden, Harvey, *all of a sudden* the number one topic of conversation in the world is the international Jewish conspiracy. There is an international Jewish conspiracy, thanks to God it exists. It's a conspiracy to save the Jews from Stalin—he wants to pack the ones he hasn't murdered off to Siberia to make a Jewish state. A Jewish state on a tundra in Siberia! We already have a Jewish state on the land that God gave to Abraham. It's called Israel." Without missing a beat the Rabbi asked, "To what do I owe the pleasure, Harvey?"

"It was you who got wind of the Vishnevsky defection and passed it on to Angleton, right?"

"'*Datta. Dayadhvam. Damyata.* These fragments I have shored against my ruins.' I am quoting from the gospel according to that major poet and minor anti-Semite, Thomas Stearns Eliot. The Company owes me one."

"The exfiltration went sour. There was a leak, Ezra."

The Rabbi sucked in his cheeks. "You think so?"

"I know so. Any chance one of your *Shabbas goys* moonlights for the opposition?"

"Everyone here has walked through fire, Harvey. Hamlet is missing all the fingernails on his right hand; they were extracted by a KGB pliers when he declined to reveal to them the names of some local anti-Stalinists in Georgia. If there was a chink in my armor I wouldn't be around to guarantee to you there is no chink in my armor. I run a small but efficient shop. I trade or sell information, I keep track of Nazi missile engineers who go to ground in Egypt or Syria, I doctor passports and smuggle them into the denied areas and smuggle Jews out to Israel. If there was a leak, if Vishnevsky didn't give the game away by stammering when he asked for permission to take his family out for a night on the town, it took place somewhere between Mother and you."

"I took a hard look at the distribution, Ezra. I couldn't see a weak link."

The Rabbi shrugged his bony shoulders.

The Sorcerer reached for the herbal tea, took a whiff of it, pulled a face and set the cup back on the desk. "The night I vetted Vishnevsky he told me there was a Soviet mole in Britain's Six."

The Rabbi perked up. "In MI6! That is an earthshaking possibility."

"The Brits were never brought into the Vishnevsky picture. Which leaves me holding the bag. There are eighty intelligence agencies, with a tangle of branches and front organizations, operating out of Berlin. Where do I grab the wool to make the sweater unravel, Ezra? I thought of asking the French to give me a list of SDECE operations blown in the last year or two."

The Rabbi held up his hands and studied his fingernails, which had recently been manicured. After a while he said, "Forget Berlin. Forget the French— they're so traumatized from losing the war they won't give the winners the time of day." Ben Ezra pulled a number two pencil from an inside breast pocket and a small metal pencil sharpener from another pocket. He carefully sharpened the pencil, then scrawled a phone number on a pad open on his desk. He tore off the page, folded it and passed it to Torriti. The Rabbi then tore off the next page and dropped it into a burn bag. "If I were you I'd start in London," he said. "Look up Elihu Epstein—he's a walking cyclopedia. Maybe Elihu can assist you with your inquiries, as our English friends like to say."

"How do I jog his memory?"

"Prime the pump by telling him something he doesn't know. Then get him to tell you about a Russian general named Krivitsky. After that keep him talking. If anyone knows where the bodies are buried it will be Elihu."

Luxuriating in the relative vastness of the British public phone booth, the Sorcerer force fed some coins into the slot and dialed the unlisted number the Rabbi had given him.

A crabby voice on the other end demanded, "And then what?"

Torriti pushed the button to speak. "Mr. Epstein, please."

"Whom shall is say is calling?"

"Swan Song."

Dripping with derision, the voice said, "Please do hold on, Mr. Song." The line crackled as the call was transferred. Then the unmistakable whinny of Torriti's old OSS friend came down the pipe. "Harvey, dear boy. Heard on my grapevine you were hoeing the Company's furrows in Krautville. What brings you to my neck of the British woods?"

"We need to talk."

"Do we? Where? When?"

"Kite Hill, overlooking the bandstand on Hampstead Heath. There are benches facing downtown London. I'll be on one of them admiring the pollution hovering like a cloud over the city. Noon suit you?"

"Noon's wizard."

On the slope below, a very tall man in a pinstripe suit played out the line that trailed off to a Chinese dragon kite, which dipped and balked and soared in the updrafts with acrobatic deftness. An Asian woman stood nearby with one hand on the back of a bench, trying to clean dog droppings off the sole of her shoe by rinsing it in a shoal of rainwater. Somewhere in Highgate a church bell pealed the hour. A shortish, round-shouldered man, his teeth dark with decay, strolled up the hill and settled with a wheeze onto the bench next to Sorcerer.

"Expecting someone, are you?" he asked, removing his bowler and setting it on the bench next to him.

"As a matter of fact, yes," the Sorcerer said. "It's been a while, Elihu."

"Understatement of the century. Glad to see you're still kicking, Harv."

Elihu Epstein and Harvey Torriti had been billeted in the same house for several months in Palermo, Sicily during the war. Elihu had been an officer in one of Britain's most ruthless units, called 3 Commando, which was using the former German submarine base at Augusta Bay as a staging area for raids on the boot of Italy. The Sorcerer, working under the code name SWAN SONG, had been running an OSS operation to enlist the Mafia dons of the island on the side of the Allies. Making use of his private Mafia sources, Torriti had been able to provide Elihu with the German order of battle in towns along the mainland coast. Elihu had given the Sorcerer credit for saving dozens of 3 Commando lives and never forgotten the favor.

"What brings you London town?" Elihu inquired now.

"The Cold War."

Elihu let fly one of his distinctive whinnies, a bleating that came from having perpetually clogged sinuses. "I have come around to the view of your General W. Tecumseh Sherman when he said that war is hell; its glory, moonshine." Elihu, who was a deputy to Roger Hollis, the head of the MI5 section investigating Soviet espionage in England, sized up his wartime buddy. "You look fat but fit. Are you?"

"Fit enough. You?"

"I have a touch of that upper class malady, gout. I have problems with a quack pretending to be a National Health dentist—he takes the view that tooth decay is a sign of moral degeneracy and advises me to circumcise my heart. Oh, I do wish it were true, Harv! Always wanted to try my hand at moral degeneracy. To square the circle, there is a buzzing in my left ear that refuses to go away unless I drown it out with a louder buzzing. Had it since a very large land mine went off too close for comfort in the war, actually."

"Are you wired, Elihu?"

"'Fraid I am, Harv. It's about my pension. I don't mind meeting you away from the madding mob for a confabulation, just don't want it to blow up in my face afterward. You do see what I mean? There's an old Yiddish aphorism: *Me ken nit tantzen auf tsvai chassenes mit ain mol*—you can't dance at two weddings at the same time. Our wonky civil service minders take the injunction very seriously. Cross a line and you will be put out to graze without the pound sterling to keep you in fresh green grass. If I can keep my nose clean, twenty-nine more months will see me off to pasture."

"Where will you retire to? What will you do?"

"To your first question: I have had the good luck to snaffle a small gatehouse on an estate in Hampshire. It's not much but then every house is someone's dream house. I shall retire to the dull plodding intercourse of country life where secrets are intended to be spread, like jam over toast, on the rumor mill. The local farmers will touch their hats and call me squire. I shall be so vague about the career I am retiring from they will assume I want them to assume I was some sort of spook, which will lead them to conclude I wasn't. To your second question: I have bought half a gun at a local club. Weather permitting I shall shoot at anything that beats the air with its wings. With luck I may occasionally pot something. Between shoots I shall come out of the closet. I am a latent heterosexual, Harv. I shall serve myself, and lavishly, instead of the Crown. With any luck I shall prove my dentist right."

A scrawny teenage boy pitched a stick downhill and called, "Go fetch, Mozart." A drooling sheepdog watched it land, then lazily turned an expressionless gaze on his young master, who trotted off to retrieve the stick and try again.

"Old dogs are slow to pick up new tricks," the Sorcerer remarked.

"Heart of the problem," Elihu agreed grumpily.

Torriti badly needed a midday ration of booze. He scratched at a nostril and bit the bullet. "I have reason to believe there may be a Soviet mole in your Six."

"In MI6? Good lord!"

Keeping his account as sketchy as possible, the Sorcerer walked Elihu through the aborted defection: there had been a KGB lieutenant colonel who wanted to come across in Berlin; to establish his *bona fides* and convince the Americans to take him, he told the Sorcerer he could give them serials that would lead to a Soviet mole in MI6; the night of the exfiltration the Russian had been seen strapped to a stretcher on his way into a Soviet plane. No, the Russian didn't give himself away; the Sorcerer had a communications intercept—surely Elihu would understand if he was not more forthcoming—indicating that the Russian had been betrayed.

Elihu, an old hand when it came to defections, asked all the right questions and Torriti tried to make it sound as if he were answering them: no, the Brits had been deliberately left off the distribution list of the cipher traffic concerning the defection; no, even the Brits in Berlin who had their ear to the ground wouldn't have ticked to it; no, the aborted defection didn't smell like a KGB disinformation op to sow dissension between the American and British cousins.

"Assuming your Russian chap was betrayed," Elihu asked thoughtfully, "how can you be absolutely certain the villain of the piece isn't in the American end of the pipeline?"

"The Company flutters its people, Elihu. You Brits just make sure they're sporting the right school tie."

"Your polygraph is about as accurate as the Chinese rice test. Remember that one? If the Mandarins thought someone was fibbing they'd stuff his mouth with rice. Rice stayed dry, meant the bugger was a liar. Oh Jesus, you really do think it was a Brit. Achilles once allowed as how he felt like an eagle which'd been struck by an arrow fledged with its own feathers." Elihu blushed apologetically. "I read what was left of the ancient poets at Oxford when I was a virgin. That's why they recruited me into MI5..."

"Because you were a virgin?"

"Because I could read Greek."

"I'm missing something."

"Don't you see, Harv? The ex-Oxford don who ran MI5 at the time reckoned anyone able to make heads or tails of a dead language ought to be able to bury the enemies of the house of Windsor." Elihu shook his head in despair. "A Brit? Shit! We could muddle through if the Soviet mole were a Yank. If you're right—oh, I hate to think of the consequences. A Brit? A yawning gap will open between your CIA and us."

"Mind the gap," Torriti snapped, imitating the warning the conductor shouted every time a train pulled into a London tube station.

"Yes, we will need to, won't we? We will be consigned to Coventry by your very clever Mr. Angleton. He won't return our calls."

"There's another reason I think the leaky faucet is British, Elihu."

"I assumed there was," Elihu muttered to himself. "The question is: Do I really want to hear it?"

The Sorcerer slumped toward the Englishman until their shoulders were rubbing. *Prime the pump by telling him something he doesn't know,* the Rabbi had said. "Listen up, Elihu: Your MI5 technical people have come up with an amazing breakthrough. Every radio receiver has an oscillator that beats down the signal it's tuned to into a frequency that can be more easily filtered. Your technicians discovered that this oscillator gives off sound waves that can be detected two hundred yards away; you even have equipment that can read the frequency to which the receiver is tuned. Which means you can send a laundry truck meandering through a neighborhood and home in on a Soviet agent's *receiver* tuned to one of Moscow Centre's burst frequencies."

Elihu blanched. "That is one of the most closely held secrets in my shop," he breathed. "We never shared it with the American cousins. How in the world did you find out about it?"

"I know it because the Russians know it. Do me a favor, turn off your tape, Elihu."

Elihu hesitated, then reached into his overcoat pocket and removed a pack of Pall Malls. He opened the lid and pressed down on one cigarette. Torriti heard a distinct click. "I fear I shall live to regret this," the Englishman announced with a sigh.

The Sorcerer said, "There is a Soviet underground telephone cable linking Moscow Centre to the KGB's Karlshorst station in the Soviet sector of Berlin. The KGB uses this so-called Ve-Che cable, named for the Russian abbreviation for 'high frequency,' *vysokaya chastota*. Russian technicians invented a foolproof safety device—they filled the wires inside the cable with pressurized air. Any bug on the wire would cause the current going through it to dip and this dip could be read off a meter, tipping off the Russians to the existence of a bug. Our people invented a foolproof way to tap into the wire without causing the pressurized air to leak or the current to dip."

"You are reading Soviet traffic to and from Karlshorst!"

"We are reading all of the traffic. We are deciphering bits and pieces of it. One of the bits we managed to decipher had Moscow Centre urgently warning Karlshorst that its agents in the Western sectors of Germany could be located by a new British device that homed in on the oscillator beating down the signal bursts out of Karlshorst."

"My head is spinning, Harv. If what you say is true—"

Torriti finished the sentence for his British pal. "—the Russians have a mole inside the British intelligence establishment. I need your help, Elihu."

"I don't see what exactly—"

"Does the name Walter Krivitsky ring a gong?"

Elihu's brow crinkled up. "Ah, it does indeed. Krivitsky was the Red Army bloke who ran Soviet military intelligence in Western Europe during the thirties out of the Holland *rezidentura*. Defected in '36, or was it '37? Wound up killing himself in the States a few years later, though the Yanks did give us a crack at him before they lured him across the Atlantic with their fast cars and their fast ladies and their fast food. All happened before my time, of course, but I read the minutes. Krivitsky gave us a titillating serial about a young English journalist code-named PARSIFAL. The Englishman had been recruited somewhere down the line by his then wife, who was a rabid Red, and then packed off to Spain during the Spanish dustup by his Soviet handler, a legendary case officer known only by the nickname Starik."

"Were you able to run down the serial?"

"'Fraid the answer to that is negative. There were three or four dozen

dozen young Englishmen from Fleet Street who covered the Spanish War at one time or another."

"Did your predecessors share the Krivitsky serial with the Americans?"

"Certainly not. There was talk of having another go at Krivitsky but that was when he bought it—a bullet in the head, if memory serves me—in a Washington hotel room in 1941. His serial died with him. How could anyone be sure Krivitsky wasn't inventing serials that would inflate his importance in our eyes? Why give our American cousins grounds to mistrust us? That was the party line at the time."

The Sorcerer scraped some wax out of an ear with a fingernail and examined it, hoping to find a clue to why good PX whiskey all of a sudden tasted tasteless. "Krivitsky wasn't inventing serials, Elihu. I worked with Jim Angleton in Italy after the war," he reminded him. "We rubbed each other the wrong way but that's another story. In those days we had an understanding with the Jews from Palestine—they were desperately trying to run guns and ammunition and people through the British blockade. We didn't get in their way, in return for which they let us debrief the Jewish refugees escaping from East Europe. One of the Jews from Palestine was a Viennese joker named Kollek. Teddy Kollek. Turned out he'd been in Vienna in the early thirties. I remember Kollek describing a wedding—it stuck in my head because the bridegroom had been Angleton's MI6 guru at Ryder Street during the war; he'd taught him chapter and verse about counterintelligence."

Elihu tossed his head back and bleated like a goat. "Kim Philby! Oh, dear, I can feel my pension slipping through my fingers already."

"Happen to know him personally, Elihu?"

"Good lord, yes. We've been trading serials on the Bolsheviks for eons, much the way children trade rugby cards. I talk with Kim two, three times a week on the phone—I've more or less become the go-between between him and my chief, Roger Hollis."

"The marriage Kollek described took place in Vienna in 1934. Philby, then a young Cambridge grad who'd come to Austria to help the socialists riot against the government, apparently got himself hitched to a Communist broad name of Litzi Friedman. Kollek had a nodding acquaintance with both the bride and the groom, which is how he knew about the wedding. Marriage didn't last long and people never attached much importance to it. Philby was only twenty-two at the time and everyone assumed he'd married the first girl who gave him a blow job. He eventually returned to England and talked himself into an assignment covering Franco's side of the war for *The Times* of London."

Elihu set the balls of the fingers of his right hand on his left wrist to monitor his racing pulse. "God, Harv, do you at all grasp what you're suggesting—that the head of our Section IX, the chap who until quite recently ran our counterintelligence ops against the Russians, is actually a Soviet mole!" Elihu's eyelids sagged and he seemed to go into mourning. "You simply cannot be serious."

"I've never been seriouser."

"I will need time to digest all this. Say twenty-nine months."

"Time is what's running out on us, Elihu. The Barbarians are at the gate just as surely as they were when they crossed the frozen Rhine and clobbered what passed for civilized Europe."

"That happened before my time, too," Elihu muttered.

"The Iron Curtain is our Rhine, Elihu."

"So people say. So people say."

Elihu leaned back and closed his eyes and turned his face into the sun. "'Move him into the sun—Gently its touch awoke him once,'" he murmured. "I am a great admirer of the late Wilfred Owen," he explained. Then he fell silent, neither speaking nor moving. A couple of men Torriti tagged as homosexuals ambled up the walkway to the crest of the hill and down the other side, whispering fiercely in the way people did when they argued in public. Elihu's eyes finally came open; he had come to a decision. "I could be keel-hauled for telling you what I'm going to tell you. As they say, in for a penny, in for a pound. Years before Kim Philby became involved in Soviet-targeted counterintelligence ops he was an underling in Section V, which was tracking German ops on his old London *Times* stamping ground, the Iberian peninsular. MI6 had and has a very secret Central Registry with source books containing the records of British agents world-wide. The source books are organized geographically. On a great number of occasions Philby signed out the Iberian book, which was consistent with his area of expertise. One day not long ago I went down to Central Registry to take a look at the source book on the Soviet Union, which was consistent with my area of expertise. While the clerk went off to fetch it I leafed through the logbook—I was curious to see who had been exploring that sinkhole before me. I was quite startled to discover that Philby had signed out the source book on the Soviet Union long before he became chief of our Soviet Division. He was supposed to be chivvying Germans in Spain, not reading up on British agents in Russia."

"Who beside me knows about your source book saga, Elihu?"

"I've actually only told it to one other living soul," Elihu replied.

"Let me climb out on a limb—Ezra Ben Ezra, better known as the Rabbi."

Elihu was genuinely surprised. "How'd you guess?"

"The Rabbi once told me there was an international Jewish conspiracy and I believed him." Torriti shook with quiet laughter. "Now I understand why Ben Ezra sent me to see you. Tell me something—why didn't you take your suspicions to Roger Hollis?"

The suggestion appalled Elihu. "Because I am not yet stark raving, that's why. And what does it all add up to, Harv? A KGB defector who tries to whip up some excitement by claiming he can finger a Soviet mole in MI6, a marriage in Austria, a Russian General who dropped dark hints about a British journalist in Spain, some easily explainable Central Registry logs—Philby could have been gearing up for the Cold War before anyone else felt the temperature drop. Hardly enough evidence to accuse MI6's next ataman of being a Soviet spy! Dear me, I hate to think what would happen to the poor prole who dropped that spanner into the works. Forget about being put out to pasture, he'd be *disemboweled*, Harv. Oh, dear me, his entrails would be ground up and fed to the hogs, his carcass would be left to rot in some muddy ha-ha."

"Pure and simple truth carries weight, Elihu."

Elihu retrieved his bowler from the bench and fitted it squarely onto his nearly hairless head. "Oscar Wilde said that truth is rarely pure and never simple and I am inclined to take his point." He gazed toward London in the hazy distance. "I was born and raised in Hampshire, in a village called Palestine—had the damnedest time convincing the mandarins not to post me to the Middle East because they assumed I had an affinity for the miserable place." Elihu pursed his lips and shook his head. "Yes. Well. What you could do is feed out a series of barium meals. We did it once or twice during the war."

"Barium meals! That's something I haven't thought of."

"Yes, indeed. Tricky business. Can't feed out junk, mind you—the Russian mole will recognize it as junk and won't be bothered to pass it on. Got to be top-grade stuff. Takes a bit of nerve, it does, giving away secrets in order to learn a secret." Climbing to his feet, Elihu removed a slip of paper from his fob pocket and handed it to the Sorcerer. "I take supper weekdays at the Lion and Last in Kentish Town. Here's the phone number. Be a good fellow, don't call me at the office again. Ah, yes, and if anybody should inquire, this meeting never took place. Do I have that right, Harv?"

Torriti, lost in the myriad tangle of barium meals, nodded absently. "Nobody's going to hear any different from me, Elihu."

"Ta."

"Ta to you."

6

WASHINGTON, DC, FRIDAY, MARCH 30, 1951

FIFTEEN EARNEST YOUNG SECTION HEADS HAD SQUEEZED INTO BILL Colby's office for the semi-weekly coffee-and-doughnut klatsch on the stay-behind networks being set up across Scandinavia. "The infrastructure in Norway is ninety per cent in place," reported a young woman with bleached blonde hair and painted fingernails. "Within the next several weeks we expect to cache radio equipment in a dozen pre-selected locations, which will give the leaders of our clandestine cells the capability of communicating with NATO and their governments-in-exile when the Russians overrun the country."

Colby corrected her with a soft chuckle. "*If* the Russians overrun the country, Margaret. *If.*" He turned to the others, who were sprawled on radiators and green four-drawer government-issue filing cabinets or, like Leo Kritzky, leaning against one of the pitted partitions that separated Colby's office from the warren of cubbyholes around it. "Let me break in here to underscore two critical points," Colby said. "First, even where the local government is cooperating in setting up stay-behind cells, which is the case in most Scandinavian countries, we want to create our own independent assets. The reason for this is simple: No one can be sure that some governments won't accept Soviet occupation under pressure; no one can be sure that elements in those governments won't collaborate with that occupation and betray the stay-behind network. Secondly, I can't stress too much the matter of security. If word of the stay-behind networks leaks, the Russians could wipe out the cells *if* they overrun the country. Perhaps even more important, if the public gets wind of the existence of a stay-behind network, it would undermine morale, inasmuch as it would indicate that the CIA doesn't have much faith in NATO's chances of stopping a full-fledged Soviet invasion."

"But we don't have much faith," Margaret quipped.

"Agreed," Colby said. "But we don't have to advertise the fact." Colby, in shirtsleeves and suspenders, swiveled his wooden chair toward Kritzky. "How are you doing with your choke points, Leo?"

Leo's particular assignment when he turned up for duty in Colby's shop on the Reflecting Pool had been to identify vulnerable geographic choke points—key bridges, rail lines, locomotive repair facilities, canal locks, hub terminals—across Scandinavia, assign them to individual stay-behind cells and then squirrel away enough explosives in each area so the cells could destroy the choke points in the event of war. "*If* the balloon goes up," Leo was saying, "my team reckons that with what we already have on the ground, we could bring half the rail and river traffic in Scandinavia to a dead stop."

"Half is ten percent better than I expected and half as good as we need to be," Colby commented from behind his desk. "Keep at it, Leo." He addressed everyone in the room. "It's not an easy matter to prepare for war during what appears to be peacetime. There is a general tendency to feel you have all the time in the world. We don't. General MacArthur is privately trying to convince the Joint Chiefs to let him bomb targets in China. The final decision, of course, will be Truman's. But it doesn't take much imagination to see the Korean War escalating into World War III if we send our planes north of the Yalu and bomb China. We're on track with our stay-behind nets but don't ease up. Okay, gentlemen and ladies, that's it for today."

"Want to put some salve on the whip marks on your back, Leo?" his "cellmate" inquired when Leo returned to his corner cubbyhole. Maud was a heavyset, middle-aged woman who chain-smoked small Schimelpenick cigars. Four large filing cabinets and the drawers of her desk were overflowing with documents "liberated" from the Abwehr in 1945. New piles were brought in almost daily. Maud, a historian by training who had served as an OSS researcher during the war, pored over the documents looking for the telltale traces of Soviet intelligence operations in the areas that had been occupied by German troops. She was hoping to discover if any of the famous Soviet spy rings had had agents in England or France during the war—agents who might still be loyal to the Kremlin and spying for Russia.

Leo settled down behind his second hand wooden desk and stared for a long moment at the ceiling, which was streaked with stains from the rain and snow that had seeped through the roof. "No matter how much we give Colby, he wants more," he griped.

"Which is why he is the leader and you are a follower," Maud observed dryly.

"Which is why," Leo agreed.

"Courier service left this for you," Maud said. She tossed a sealed letter onto his desk and, lighting a fresh Schimelpenick, went back to her Abwehr documents.

Leo ripped open the envelope and extracted a tissue-thin letter, which turned out to be from Jack. "Leo, you old fart," it began.

"Thanks for the note, which arrived in yesterday's overnight pouch. I'm rushing to get this into tonight's overnight so excuse the penmanship or lack of same. Your work in Washington sounds tedious but important. Regarding Colby, the word in Germany is that he's headed for big things, so hang on to his coattails, old buddy. There's not much I can tell about Berlin Base because (as we say in the trade) you don't need to know. Things are pretty feverish here. You see a lot of people running around like chickens without heads. Remember the OSS lawyer-type we met at the Cloud Club—'Ebby' Ebbitt? He got the old heave-ho for saying out loud what a lot of people (though not me) were thinking, which is that the honcho of Berlin Base drinks too much. Ebby was palmed off on Frankfurt Station and I haven't heard hide nor hair since. The Sorcerer, meanwhile, is going up the wall over a defection that turned sour—he is sure the opposition was tipped off. Question is: by whom? As for yours truly, I've been given my first agent to run. Luck of the draw, she's what you'd call a raving beauty. Enormous sad eyes and long legs that simply don't end. My honcho wants me to seduce her so he can tune in on the pillow talk. I am more than willing to make this sacrifice for my country but I can't seem to get to first base with her. Which is a new experience for me. Win some, lose some. Keep in touch. Hopefully our paths will cross when I get home leave."

There was a postscript scrawled down one side of the letter. "Came across an old comrade (the term, as you'll see, is appropriate) in a Berlin bar the other night. Remember Vanka Borisov? He was the bruiser rowing stroke for the Russians at the European championships in Munich in '48. You, me, and Vanka spent a night bar-hopping, we picked up those Australian sisters—peaceniks who told us with tears in their eyes that our friendship was beautiful because it was sabotaging the Cold War. After you went back to the hotel the sisters took turns screwing us as their contribution to world peace. I had a broken rib so the girls had to do everything. Imagine a vast peace movement made up of gorgeous nymphets fucking to stop the Cold War! Vanka, who's put on weight, knew about my working for the Pickle Factory, which makes him KGB. Looked around the bar but there were no Australian girls in sight!"

Leo clasped his hands behind his neck and leaned back into them. He almost wished he had landed an assignment in someplace like Berlin. Washington seemed tame by comparison. Still, this was the eye of the storm—he had been given to understand that this was where he could contribute the most. His gaze fell on the framed copy of National Security Council Memorandum 68, which had been drafted by Paul Nitze and called for a national crusade against global Communism. Leo wondered if the knights starting on the long trek to the Holy Land nine centuries earlier had been spurred on by equivalent papal memoranda. His gaze drifted to the government executive calendar tacked to the wall. Like all Fridays, March 30 was circled in red to remind him that it was payday; it was also circled in blue to remind him to take his dog to the vet when he got off from work for the day.

With the ancient arthritic dog hobbling alongside, Leo pushed through the door into the waiting room of the Maryland Veterinary Hospital and took a seat. The dog, mostly but not entirely German Shepherd, slumped with a thud onto the linoleum. Reaching down, Leo stroked his head.

"So what's wrong with him?"

He glanced across the room. A young woman, slightly overweight, on the short side with short curly hair that fell in bangs over a high forehead, was watching him. Her eyelids were pink and swollen from crying. She was dressed in a black turtleneck sweater, faded orange overalls with a bib top and tennis shoes. A tan-and-white Siamese cat stained with dried blood lay limply across her knees.

"He's starting to lead a dog's life, which is a new experience for him," Leo said morosely. "I've decided to put him out of his misery."

"Oh," the young woman said, "you must be very sad. How long have you had him?"

Leo looked down at the dog. "Sometimes it seems as if he's been with me forever."

The woman absently laced her fingers through the fur on the cat's neck. "I know what you mean."

There was an awkward silence. Leo nodded toward the cat on her knees. "What's its name?"

"Her full name is Once in a Blue Moon. Her friends call her Blue Moon for short. I'm her best friend."

"What happened to Once in a Blue Moon?"

The story spilled out; she seemed eager to tell it, almost as if the telling would dull the pain. "Blue Moon was raised on my Dad's farm in the Maryland countryside. When I got a job in Washington and moved to Georgetown last year I took her with me. Big error. She hated being cooped up—she would gaze out the window hours on end. In the summer she used to climb out the open window and sit on a sill watching the birds fly and I knew she wanted to fly, too. I sleep with my bedroom window open even in winter—I could have sworn I'd closed it when I left for work this morning but I guess I must have forgotten." The young woman couldn't speak for a moment. Then, her voice grown husky, she said, "Blue Moon forgot she was a cat and decided to fly like a bird but she didn't know how, did she? You hear all these stories about cats jumping off tall buildings and landing unharmed on their feet. But she jumped from the fourth floor and landed on her back. She seems to be paralyzed. I'm going to have them give her an injection—"

The vets took Leo first. When he came back to the waiting room ten minutes later carrying the still-warm corpse of his dog in a supermarket paper bag, the young woman was gone. He sat down and waited for her. After a while she pushed through the door holding a paper bag of her own. Tears were streaming down her cheeks. Leo stood up.

She looked at the paper bag in her hands. "Blue Moon is still warm," she whispered.

Leo nodded. "Do you have a car?" he asked suddenly.

She said she did.

"What are you going to do with Once in a Blue Moon?"

"I was planning to drive out to Daddy's farm—"

"Look, what if we were to stop by that big hardware store on the mall and buy a shovel, and then drive into the country and find a hill with a great view and bury the two of them together?" Leo shifted his weight from foot to foot in embarrassment. "Maybe it's a crazy idea. I mean, you don't even know me—"

"What sign are you?"

"I was born the day of the great stock market crash, October twenty-ninth, 1929. My father used to joke that my birth brought on the crash. I could never work out how my being born could affect the stock market but until I was nine or ten I actually believed him."

"October twenty-ninth—that makes you a Scorpio. I'm a Gemini." The young woman regarded Leo through her tears. "Burying them together strikes me as a fine idea," she decided. Clutching her paper bag under her left arm, she stepped forward and offered her hand. "I'm Adelle Swett."

Somewhat clumsily, Leo clasped it. "Leo. Leo Kritzky."

"I am glad to make your acquaintance, Leo Kritzky."

He nodded. "Likewise."

She smiled through her tears because he had not let go of her hand. The smile lingered in her normally solemn eyes after it had faded from her lips. He smiled back at her.

Leo and Adelle had what the screen magazines referred to as a whirlwind romance. After they buried his dog and her cat on a hill in Maryland he took her to a roadside tavern he knew near Annapolis. Dinner—fried clams and shrimps fresh from the Maryland shore—was served on a table covered with the front page of the *Baltimore Sun* bearing a banner headline announcing that the Rosenbergs had been convicted of espionage. Leo sprinted up a narrow flight of steps to the smoke-filled bar and came back with two giant mugs of light tap beer. For a time he and Adelle circled each other warily, talking about the Rosenberg trial, talking about books they'd read recently: James Jones's *From Here to Eternity* (which he liked), Truman Capote's *The Grass Harp* (which she liked), J.D. Salinger's *Catcher in the Rye* (which they both loved because they shared the hero's loathing of phonies). After that first date they fell easily into the habit of talking on the phone almost daily. Adelle had earned a bachelor's degree in political science from Johns Hopkins in Baltimore and had found work as a legislative assistant to a first-term senator, a Texas Democrat named Lyndon Johnson who was considered a comer in Democratic circles. Johnson spent hours each day on the phone working the Washington rumor mill, so Adelle always had a lot of hot political gossip to pass on. Leo, for his part, claimed to be a junior researcher at the State Department but when she tried to pin him down about what exactly he researched, he remained vague, which convinced Adelle, wise in the ways of Washington, that he was engaged in some sort of secret work.

Two weeks after they met Leo took Adelle to see a new film called *The African Queen,* starring Hepburn and Bogart, and afterward, to a steakhouse in Virginia. Over medium-rare inch-thick sirloins Adelle inquired with great formality whether Leo's intentions were honorable. He asked her to define the word. She flushed but her eyes never strayed from his. She told him she was a virgin and only planned to sleep with the man she would marry. Leo promptly proposed to her. Adelle promised to think about it seriously. When dessert came she reached across the table and ran her fingers over the back of his wrist. She said she had given the matter a great deal of thought and had decided to accept.

"Long about now you should be inviting me home with you," she announced.

Leo allowed as how he was kind of frightened. She asked if he was a virgin and when he said no, he had lived for a time with a girl some years older than he was, she asked: Then where's the problem? Leo said he was in love with her and didn't want it to go wrong in bed. She raised a wine glass and toasted him across the table. Nothing can go wrong, she whispered.

And nothing did.

There was still one height to scale: her Daddy, who turned out to be none other than Philip Swett, a self-made St. Paul wheeler-dealer who had moved to Chicago and earned a fortune in commodity futures. More recently he had become a heavy hitter in the Democratic Party and a crony of Harry Truman's, breakfasting with the President twice a week, sometimes striding alongside him on his brisk morning constitutionals. To drive home that the young man courting Adelle was out of his depth, Swett invited Leo to one of his notorious Saturday night Georgetown suppers. The guests included the Alsop brothers, the Bohlens (just back from Moscow), the Nitzes, Phil and Kay Graham, Randolph Churchill and Malcolm Muggeridge (over from London for the weekend), along with several senior people Leo recognized from the corridors of the Company—the Wiz was there with his wife, as well as the DD/O, Allen Dulles, who most Washington pundits figured would wind up running the CIA one day soon. Leo found himself seated below the salt, a table-length away from Adelle, who kept casting furtive looks in his direction to see how he was faring. Dulles, sitting next to her, wowed the guests with one yarn after another. Phil Graham asked Dulles if his relationship with Truman had improved any.

"Not so you'd notice," Dulles said. "He's never forgiven me for siding with Dewey in forty-eight. He likes to pull my leg whenever he can. I stood in for Bedell Smith at the regular intelligence meeting this week. As I was leaving, Truman called me over and said he wanted the CIA to provide a wall map for the Oval Office with pins stuck in it showing the location of our secret agents around the world. I started to sputter about how we couldn't do anything like that because not everyone who came into the Oval Office had the appropriate security clearance." Dulles smiled at his own story. "At which point Truman burst out laughing and I realized he was having fun at my expense."

After dinner the guests retired to the spacious living room, pushed back the furniture and began dancing to Big Band records blasting from the phonograph. Leo was trying to catch Adelle's eye when Swett crooked a forefinger at both of them.

"Join me in the study," he ordered Leo. He waved for Adelle to follow them.

Fearing the worst, Leo trailed after him up the carpeted stairs to a paneled room with a log fire burning in the fireplace. Adelle slipped in and closed the door. Opening a mahogany humidor, Swett motioned Leo into a leather-upholstered chair and offered him a very phallic-looking Havana cigar.

"Don't smoke," Leo said, feeling as if he were admitting to an unforgivable lapse of character. Adelle settled onto the arm of his chair. Together they confronted her father.

"By golly, you don't know what you're missing," Swett said. Half sitting on the edge of a table, he snipped off the tip with a silver scissor, struck a match with his thumbnail and held the flame to the end of the cigar. Great clouds of dusky smoke billowed from his mouth. Swett's raspy sentences seemed to emerge from the smoke. "Grab the bull by the horns, that's what I say. Adelle tells me she's been seeing a lot of you."

Leo nodded carefully.

"What do you do? For income, I mean."

"Daddy, you've seen too many of those Hollywood movies."

"I work for the government," Leo replied.

Swett snickered. "When a man 'round here says something fuzzy like he works for the government, that means he's Pickle Factory. You with Allen Dulles and the Wiz over at Operations?"

Leo dug in his heels. "I work for the State Department, Mr. Swett." He named an office, a superior, an area of expertise. His offer to supply a telephone number was backhanded away.

Swett sucked on his cigar. "What's your salary, son?"

"Daddy, you promised me you wouldn't browbeat him."

"Where I come from man's got the right to ask a fellow who's courting his daughter what his prospects are." He focused on Leo. "How much?"

Leo sensed that more was riding on the manner in which he answered Swett's question than the answer itself. Adelle was impulsive but he doubted she would marry someone against her father's will. He needed to be smart; to grab the bull by the horns, as Swett put it. "How much do you earn a year, sir?"

Adelle held her breath. Her father took several staccato puffs on his cigar and scrutinized Leo through the smoke. "Roughly one point four million, give or take a couple of dozen thousand. That's *after* taxes."

"I make six thousand four hundred dollars, sir. That's *before* taxes."

A weighty silence filled the room. "Tarnation, I'm not one to pussyfoot around, son. It's not the money that worries me—when I got hitched I was making forty a week. Here's where I stand: I'm dead blast set against mixed marriages. Mind you, I got nothing against Jewish people but I figure Jews should marry Jews and white Anglo-Saxon Protestants need to go and marry white Anglo-Saxon Protestants."

"When you get right down to it, all marriages are mixed," Leo said. "One male, one female."

Adelle rested a hand on his shoulder. "They sure are, Daddy. Look at you and mom. More mixed, you'd melt."

"Sir," Leo said, leaning forward, "I'm in love with your daughter. I wasn't aware that we were asking your permission to marry." He reached over and laced his fingers through Adelle's. "We're informing you. We'd both prefer to have your blessing, me as much as Adelle. If not"—he tightened his grip on Adelle—"not."

Swett eyed Leo with grudging respect. "I'll give you this much, young fellah—you have better taste than my little gal here."

"Oh, Daddy!" cried Adelle, "I knew you'd like him." And she bounded across the room into her father's arms.

The wedding was performed by a female justice of the peace in Annapolis on the young couple's first anniversary, which was to say one month to the day after they had met in the waiting room of the veterinary hospital. Adelle had squirmed and wriggled into one of her kid sister's lace Mainbochers for the occasion. Adelle's sister, Sydney, was the maid of honor. Bill Colby stood up for Leo. Adelle's employer, Lyndon Johnson, gave away the bride when Philip Swett, who had been dispatched by Truman to mend political fences in Texas, couldn't make it back in time for the ceremony. Adelle's mother broke into tears when the justice of the peace pronounced the couple man and wife until death did them part. Colby broke open a bottle of New York State Champagne. As Leo was kissing his mother-in-law goodbye she slipped an envelope into the pocket of his spanking new suit jacket. In it was a check for $5,000 and a note that said, "Live happily ever after or I'll break your neck." It was signed: "P. Swett."

The couple had a one-night honeymoon at an inn with a majestic view of the sun rising over Chesapeake Bay. The next morning Leo reported back to work; there were choke points in Norway waiting to be classified according to their vulnerability and assigned to stay behind cells. Adelle had been given three days off by Lyndon Johnson. She used the time to shuttle back and forth, in her two-door Plymouth, between her apartment in Georgetown and the top floor of the house that Leo had rented on Bradley Lane, behind the Chevy Chase Club in Maryland. The last thing she brought over was the wedding present from her boss, the Senator. It was a baby kitten with a gnarled snout. Adelle had instantly dubbed her new pet Sour Pickles.

In short order the newlyweds settled into a rut of routines. Mornings, Leo caught a lift to the Campus with Dick Helms, a Company colleague who lived down Bradley Lane. Helms, another OSS alumnus who was working in clandestine operations under the Wiz, always took a roundabout route to the Reflecting Pool, crossing Connecticut Avenue and going up the Brookville Road in order to mask his destination. On the drives into town they talked shop. Leo filled Helms in on Colby's stay behind operation. Helms told him about a chief of station in Iran who was "ringing the gong"—warning that an Arab radical named Mohammed Mossadegh was likely to take over as premier in the next few weeks; Mossadegh, the head of the extremist National Front, was threatening to nationalize the British-owned oil industry. If that happened, Helms said, the Company would have to explore ways of pulling the rug out from under him.

One night every two weeks Leo pulled the graveyard shift, reporting to work on the Reflecting Pool at four in the morning as the Clandestine Service's representative to the team producing the President's *Daily Brief.* For the next three hours he and the others sifted through the overnight cables from bases overseas and culled the items that ought to be brought to Mr. Truman's attention. The Book, as it was called—an eight- or ten-page letter-size briefing document arranged in a newspaper column format and marked "For the President's Eyes Only"—was delivered by the senior member of the Daily Brief committee to the White House every morning in time for Mr. Truman to read it over his oatmeal breakfast.

One Sunday morning not long after Leo's marriage the officer who was supposed to deliver the Book got a last minute phone call from his wife. Labor pains had begun and she was on her way to the hospital. The officer asked Leo to stand in for him and raced off to witness the birth of his first child. Leo's Company credentials were checked at the south gate of the White House. A secret service officer led him through the First Family's entrance under the South Portico and took him up in a private elevator to the President's living quarters on the second floor. Leo recognized the only person in sight from photographs he'd seen in *Life* magazine; it was Mr.

Truman's daughter, Margaret, just back from a concert she'd given in New York. Of course she'd be glad to take the book in to the President, she said. Leo settled onto a couch in the corridor to wait. Soon the door to what turned out to be the President's private dining room opened a crack and a short man wearing a double-breasted suit and a dapper bow tie gestured for him to come on in. Quite startled to be in the presence of the President himself, Leo followed Truman into the room. To his surprise he saw Philip Swett sitting across from Margaret Truman at the breakfast table.

"So you work for the Pickle Factory after all," Swett growled, his forehead wrinkling in amusement.

"You two gents know each other?" Mr. Truman inquired, a distinctly Midwestern twang to his nasal voice.

"He's the fellow who upped and married my girl, which I suppose makes him my son-in-law," Swett told the President. "First time we talked he had the gumption to ask me how much I earned a year."

Mr. Truman looked at Leo. "I admire a man with mettle." There was a playful twinkle in the President's eye. "What did Phil reply?"

"I'm afraid I don't remember, sir."

"Good for you!" Mr. Truman said. "I am a great admirer of discretion, too."

The President took out a fountain pen, uncapped it and started to underline an item in the briefing book. "When you get back tell Wisner I want a personal briefing on this Mossadegh fellow." Truman scribbled cryptic questions in the margin as he talked. "Want to know where he comes from. What the heck do these Islam fundamentalists want anyhow? What kind of support does he have in the country? What kind of contingency plans are you fellows working up if he takes over and tries to nationalize British Petroleum?"

The President closed the cover and handed the briefing book to Leo. "Adelle's a fine woman," Mr. Truman said. "Know her personally. You're a lucky young man."

From the table, Swett observed in a not unkindly tone, "Lucky is what he sure as shooting is."

7

WASHINGTON, DC, THURSDAY, APRIL 5, 1951

IN THE SMALL PITCHED-CEILING ATTIC STUDIO ABOVE KAHN'S WINE AND Beverage on M Street at the Washington side of Key Bridge, Eugene Dodgson, the young American recently returned from backpacking in Scandinavia, clipped one end of the shortwave antenna to a water pipe. Unreeling the wire across the room, he attached the other end to a screw in the back of what looked like an ordinary Motorola kitchen radio. Pulling up a wooden stool, he turned on the radio and simultaneously depressed the first and third buttons—one ostensibly controlled the tone, the other tuned the radio to a pre-set station—transforming the Motorola into a sophisticated short wave receiver. Checking the Elgin on his wrist, Eugene tuned the radio dial to Moscow's 11 P.M. frequency and waited, hunched over the set, a pencil poised in his fingers, to see if the station would broadcast his personal code phrase during the English language cultural quiz program. The woman emcee posed the question. "In what well-known book would you find the lines: 'And the moral of that is—The more there is of mine, the less there is of yours?'" The literature student from Moscow University thought a moment and then said, "Lewis Carroll's *Alice's Adventures in Wonderland*!" Eugene's heart literally started pounding in his chest. Suddenly he felt connected to the Motherland; he felt as if he were on one end of a long umbilical cord that reached from the Motorola across continents and seas to remind him that he was not alone. He jotted down the winning lottery number that was repeated twice at the end of the program. A feeling of elation swept through Eugene—he leapt from the stool and stood with his back flat against a wall that smelled of fresh paint, breathing as if he'd just run the hundred-meter dash. He held in his hand the first message from Starik!

Laughing out loud, shaking his head in awe—all these codes, all these frequencies actually worked!—Eugene tuned the radio to a popular local AM music station, then carefully coiled the antenna and stashed it in the cavity under the floorboard in the closet. He retrieved the "lucky" ten-dollar bill (with "For Eugene, from his dad, on his eighth birthday" scrawled across it in ink) from his billfold and subtracted the serial number on it from the lottery number in the Moscow broadcast.

What he was left with was the ten-digit Washington telephone number of his cutout to the *resident*. When he dialed the number from a pay phone at the stroke of midnight, the cutout, a woman who spoke with a thick Eastern European accent, would give him the home phone number of the Soviet agent he had come to America to contact and conduct: the high-level mole code-named PARSIFAL.

The Atlantic crossing—eleven days from Kristiansand to Halifax on a tramp steamer bucking the Brobdingnagian swells of the North Atlantic—had not been out of the ordinary, or so the ship's bearded captain had explained the single time his young American passenger managed to join the officers for supper in the wardroom. The tablecloth had been doused with water to keep the dishes from sliding with each roll and pitch of the ship's rusted hull; Eugene Dodgson's plate hadn't moved but on one wild pitch the boiled beef and noodles on it had come cascading down into his lap, much to the amusement of the ship's officers. When Eugene finally staggered down the gangway in Halifax, it took several hours before the cement under the soles of his hiking boots ceased to heave and recede like the sea under the vessel.

Strapping on his backpack, Eugene had hitched rides with truckers from Halifax to Caribou, Maine in four days. At the frontier a Canadian officer had stuck his head into the cab and had asked him where he was from.

"Brooklyn," Eugene had replied with a broad smile.

"Think the Giants will take the pennant this year?" the Canadian had asked, testing Eugene's English as well as his claim to be from Brooklyn.

"You are not being serious," Eugene had burst out. "Look at the Dodger lineup—Jackie Robinson and Pee Wee Reese cover the infield like a blanket, Roy Campanella has the MVP in his sights, Don Newcombe's fast ball is sizzling, the way Carl Furillo is going he's bound to break .330. The pennant belongs to Brooklyn, the Series, too."

From Caribou, Eugene had caught a Greyhound bus to Boston and another to New York. He had taken a room at the Saint George Hotel in

Brooklyn Heights. From a nearby phone booth he had dialed the number Starik had obliged him to memorize before he left Moscow. The disgruntled voice of someone speaking English with an accent came on the line.

"Can I speak to Mr. Goodpaster?" asked Eugene.

"What number you want?"

Eugene read off the number he was calling from.

"You got a wrong number." The line went dead.

Seven minutes later, the time it took for the man on the other end to reach a pay phone, the telephone rang in Eugene's booth. He snatched it off the hook and said, "If you dine with the devil use a long spoon."

"I was told to expect you three days ago," the man complained. "What took you so long?"

"The crossing took eleven days instead of nine. I lost another day hitchhiking down."

"Ever hear of the Brooklyn Botanical Garden?"

"Sure I have."

"I'll be sitting on the fourth bench down from the main entrance off Eastern Parkway at ten tomorrow morning feeding the pigeons. I will have a Leica around my neck and a package wrapped in red-and-gold Christmas paper on the bench next to me."

"Ten tomorrow," Eugene confirmed, and he severed the connection.

Eugene instantly recognized the thin, balding, hawk-faced man, a Leica dangling from a strap around his neck, from the photograph Starik had shown him; Colonel Rudolf Ivanovich Abel had entered the United States the previous year and was living under deep cover somewhere in Brooklyn. The colonel, tearing slices of bread and scattering the crumbs to the pigeons milling at his feet, didn't look up when Eugene slumped onto the park bench next to him. The Christmas-wrapped package—containing the Motorola, an antenna and a flashlight that worked despite a hollowed-out battery concealing a microdot reader; the passport, driver's license and other documents for Legend B in case Eugene needed to adopt a new identity; a hollowed-out silver dollar with a microfilm positive transparency filled with Eugene's personal identification codes, one-time cipher pads and phone numbers in Washington and New York to call in an emergency; along with an envelope containing $20,000 in small-denomination bills—was on the bench between them.

Eugene started to repeat the code phrase: "If you dine with the devil—" but Abel, raising his eyes, cut him off.

"I recognize you from your passport photograph." A forlorn smile appeared on his unshaven face. "I am Rudolf Abel," he announced.

"Starik sends you warm comradely greetings," Eugene said.

"No one can overhear us but the pigeons," Abel said. "How I hate the little bastards. Do me a favor, talk Russian."

Eugene repeated his message in Russian. The Soviet espionage officer was eager for news of the homeland. What had the weather been like in Moscow when Eugune left? Were there more automobiles on the streets these days? What motion picture films had Eugene seen recently? What books had he read? Was there any truth to American propaganda about shortages of consumer goods in the state-owned stores? About bread riots in Krasnoyarsk? About the arrest of Yiddish poets and actors who had been conspiring against Comrade Stalin?

Twenty minutes later Eugene got up and offered his hand. Colonel Abel seemed loath to see him leave. "The worst part is the loneliness," he told Eugene. "That and the prospect that the Motherland will attack America and kill me with one of its A-bombs."

Eugene spent ten days at the Saint George Hotel, roaming through Crown Heights to familiarize himself with the neighborhood, drinking egg creams in the candy store he was supposed to have hung out in, visiting the laundromat and the Chinese restaurant he was supposed to have frequented. One drizzly afternoon he took the F train out to Coney Island and rode the great Ferris wheel, another time he caught the IRT into Manhattan and wandered around Times Square. He purchased two valises at a discount store on Broadway and filled them with used clothing— a sports jacket and trousers, a pair of loafers, four shirts, a tie, a leather jacket and a raincoat—from Gentleman's Resale on Madison Avenue. On April Fool's Day, Starik's newest agent in America packed his valises and sat down on one of them to bring him luck for the trip ahead. Then he settled his bill at the Saint George in cash, took the subway to Grand Central and boarded a train bound for Washington and his new life as a Soviet illegal.

From Washington's Union Station, Eugene made his way by taxi to the Washington end of Key Bridge and arrived at the liquor store just as Max Kahn was locking up for the night.

A short stocky man in his early fifties with a mane of unruly white hair, Kahn looked startled when he heard someone rapping his knuckles on the glass of the front door. He waved an open palm and called, "Sorry but I'm already—" Then his expression changed to one of pure delight as he caught sight of the two valises. He strode across the store and unlocked the door and wrapped Eugene in a bear hug. "I thought you would be here days ago," he said in a hoarse whisper. "Come on in, comrade. The upstairs studio is at your disposal—I repainted it last week so it would be ready for your arrival." Plucking one of Eugene's valises off the floor, he led the way up the narrow staircase at the back of the store.

When he talked about himself, which was infrequently, Kahn liked to say that his life had been transformed the evening he wandered into a Jewish intellectual discussion group on upper Broadway in the early 1920s. At the time, enrolled under his father's family name, Cohen, he had been taking accounting courses in Columbia University night school. The Marxist critique of the capitalist system had opened his eyes to a world he had only dimly perceived before. With a degree from Columbia in his pocket, he had become a card-carrying member of the American Communist Party and had joined the staff of the Party's newspaper, The *Daily Worker*, selling subscriptions and setting type there until the German attack on the USSR in June, 1941. At that point he had "dropped out": Acting under orders from a Soviet diplomat, he had ceased all Party activity, broken off all Party contacts, changed his name to Kahn and relocated to Washington. Using funds supplied by his conducting officer, he had bought out an existing liquor franchise and had changed its name to Kahn's Wine and Beverage. "Several of us were selected to go underground," he told Eugene over a spaghetti and beer supper the night he turned up at Kahn's store. "We didn't carry Party cards but we were under Party discipline—we were good soldiers, we obeyed orders. My control pointed me in a given direction and I marched out, no questions asked, to do battle for the motherland of world socialism. I'm still fighting the good fight," he added proudly.

Kahn had been told only that he would be sheltering a young Communist Party comrade from New York who was being harassed by FBI. The visitor would be taking night courses at Georgetown University; days he would be available to deliver liquor in Kahn's beat-up Studebaker station wagon in exchange for the use of the studio over the store.

"Can you give me a ballpark figure how long he'll be staying?" Kahn had asked his conducting officer when they met in a men's room at Washington's Smithsonian Institution.

"He will be living in the apartment until he is told to stop living in the apartment," the Russian had answered matter-of-factly.

"I understand," Kahn had replied. And he did.

"I know you are under Party discipline," Kahn was saying now as he carefully poured what was left of the beer into Eugene's mug. "I know there are things you can't talk about." He lowered his voice. "This business with the Rosenbergs—it makes me sick to my stomach." When Eugene looked blank he said, "Didn't you catch the news bulletins—they were sentenced today. *To the electric chair*, for God's sake! I knew the Rosenbergs in the late thirties—I used to run across them at Party meetings before I dropped out. I can tell you that Ethel was a complete innocent. Julius was the Marxist. I bumped into him once in the New York Public Library after the war. He told me he'd dropped out in forty-three. He was being controlled by a Russian case officer working out of the Soviet Consulate in New York. Later I heard on the grapevine that they used Julius as a clearing house for messages. He was like all of us—a soldier in the army of liberation of America. He would receive envelopes and pass them on, sure, though I doubt he knew what was in them. Ethel cooked and cleaned house and took care of the kids and darned socks while the men talked politics. If she grasped half of what she heard, I'd be surprised. *Sentenced to death!* In the electric chair. What is this world coming to?"

"Do you think they'll actually carry out the sentences?" Eugene asked.

Kahn reached back under his starched collar to scratch between his shoulder blades. "The anti-Soviet hysteria in the country has gotten out of hand. The Rosenbergs are being used as scapegoats for the Korean War. Someone had to be blamed. For political reasons it may become impossible for the President to spare their lives." Kahn got up to leave. "We must all be vigilant. Bernice will bring you the newspapers tomorrow morning."

"Who is Bernice?"

Kahn's face lit up as he repeated the question to emphasize its absurdity. "Who's Bernice? Bernice is Bernice. Bernice is practically my adopted daughter, and one of us—Bernice is a real comrade, a proletarian fighter. Along with everything else she does, Bernice opens the store, I close it. Good night to you, Eugene."

"Good night to you, Max."

Eugene could hear Max Kahn laughing under his breath and repeating "Who's Bernice?" as he padded down the steps.

Shaving in the cracked mirror over the sink in the closet-sized bathroom the next morning, Eugene heard someone moving cartons in the liquor store under the floorboards. Soon there were muffled footfalls on the back steps and a soft rap on the door.

"Anyone home?" a woman called.

Toweling the last of the shaving cream from his face, Eugene opened the door a crack.

"Hi," said a young woman. She was holding the front page of the

Washington Star up so he could see the photograph of Julius and Ethel Rosenberg.

"You must be Bernice."

"Right as rain."

Bernice turned out to be a lean, dark Semitic beauty with a beaklike nose and bushy brows and deep-set eyes that flashed with belligerence whenever she got onto the subject that obsessed her. "Purple mountain majesty, my ass," she would cry, knotting her thin fingers into small fists, hunching her bony shoulders until she looked like a prizefighter lowering his profile for combat. "America the Beautiful was built on two crimes that are never mentioned in polite conversation: the crime against the Indians, who were driven off their lands and practically exterminated; the crime against the Negroes, who were kidnapped from Africa and auctioned off to the highest bidder like so many cattle."

It didn't take Eugene long to discover that Bernice's rebellion against the capitalist system had sexual implications. She wore neither makeup nor undergarments and laughingly boasted that she considered stripping to the skin to be an honest proletarian activity, since it permitted her to shed, if only for a while, the clothes and image with which capitalism had tarred and feathered her. She described herself as a Marxist feminist following in the footsteps of Aleksandra Kollontai, the Russian Bolshevik who had abandoned a husband and children to serve Lenin and the Revolution. Bernice, too, was ready to abandon the bourgeois morality and offer her body to the Revolution—if only someone would issue an invitation.

Bernice was nobody's fool. Eugene made such a point about having been born and raised in Brooklyn that she began to wonder if he was really American; several times she thought she caught trivial slips in grammar or pronunciation that reminded her of the way her grandfather, a Jewish immigrant from Vilnus, had talked even after years of living in the States. She found herself drawn to what she sensed was Eugene's secret self. She assumed that he was under Party discipline; she supposed he was on a mission, which made him a warrior in the Party's struggle against the red-baiting McCarthyism that had gripped America.

"Oh, I have your number, Eugene," she told him when he parked the station wagon in the alley behind the liquor store after a round of deliveries and slipped in the back door. She was wearing flowery toreador pants and a torso-hugging white jersey through which the dark nipples of her almost nonexistent breasts were plainly visible. She sucked on her thumb for a moment, then came out with it: "You are a Canadian Communist, one of the organizers of those strikes last year where the longshoremen tried to stop

Marshall Plan aid from leaving Canadian ports. You're on the lam from those awful Mounted Police people. Am I right?"

"You won't spill the beans?"

"I'd die before I'd tell anyone. Even Max."

"The Party knows it can count on you."

"Oh, it can, it can," she insisted. She came across the store and kissed him hungrily on the mouth. Reaching down with her left hand, she worked her fingers between the buttons of his fly. Coming up for air she announced, "Tonight I will take you home with me and we will do some peyote and fuck our heads off until dawn."

Eugene, who had spurned one Jewess in Russia only to find himself in the arms of another in America, didn't contradict her.

Eugene discovered the X chalked in blue on the side of the giant metal garbage bin in the parking lot behind Kahn's Wine and Beverage the next morning. After class that evening (on the American novel since Melville) he drifted over to the Georgetown University library reading room, pulled three books on Melville from the stacks and found a free seat at a corner table. He pulled a paperback edition of Melville's *Billy Budd* from his cloth satchel and began to underline passages that interested him, referring now and then to the reference books he had opened on the table. From time to time students in the reading room would drift into the stacks to put back or take down books. As the clock over the door clicked onto 9 P.M., a tall, thin woman with rust-color hair tied back in a sloppy chignon slid noiselessly out of a chair at another table and made her way into the stacks carrying a pile of books. She returned minutes later without the books, worked her arms into the sleeves of a cloth overcoat and disappeared through the exit.

Eugene waited until just before the 10:30 closing bell before making his move. By that time the only people left in the reading room were the two librarians and a crippled old man who walked with the aid of two crutches. One of the librarians caught Eugene's eye and pointed with her nose toward the wall clock. Nodding, he closed *Billy Budd* and put it away in his satchel. With the reference books under his arm and the satchel slung over one shoulder, he made his way back into the stacks to return what he had borrowed. Sitting on the shelf in the middle of the Melville section was a thick book on knitting. Checking to be sure no one was observing him, Eugene dropped the knitting book into his satchel, retrieved his leather jacket from the back of his chair and headed for the door. The librarian, peering over the rims of reading glasses, recognized him as a night school student and smiled. Eugene opened the satchel and held it up so she could see he wasn't making off with reference material.

The librarian noticed the knitting book. "You must be the only student in the night school studying Melville *and* knitting," she said with a laugh.

Eugene managed to look embarrassed. "It's my girlfriend's—"

"Pity. The world would be a better place if men took up knitting."

Max had loaned Eugene the store's station wagon for the evening. Instead of heading back to the studio over the store, he drove into Virginia for half an hour and pulled into an all-night gas station. While the attendant was filling the tank, he went into the office and fed a dime and a nickel into the slots of the wall phone. Bell Telephone had recently introduced direct long-distance dialing. Eugene dialed the Washington number that Starik had passed on to him over the shortwave radio.

A sleepy voice answered. "Hullo?"

Eugene said, "I'm calling about your ad in the *Washington Post*—how many miles do you have on the Ford you're selling?"

The man on the other end, speaking with the clipped inflections of an upper-class Englishman, said, "I'm afraid you have the wrong p-p-party. I am not selling a Ford. Or any other automobile for that matter."

"Damn, I dialed the wrong number."

The Englishman snapped, "I accept the apology you didn't offer" and cut the connection.

The order for four bottles of Lagavulin Malt Whisky was phoned in at mid-morning the next day. The caller said he wanted it delivered before noon. Was that within the realm of possibility? Can do, Bernice said and she jotted down the address with the stub of a pencil she kept tucked over one ear.

Piloting the store's station wagon through the dense mid-morning Washington traffic, Eugene took Canal Road and then headed up Arizona Avenue until it intersected with Nebraska Avenue, a quiet tree-lined street with large homes set back on both sides. Turning onto Nebraska, he got stuck behind a garbage truck for several minutes. A team of Negroes dressed in white overalls was collecting metal garbage cans from the back doors and carrying them down the driveways to the sidewalk, where a second crew emptied the contents into the dump truck. Eugene checked the address on Bernice's order sheet and pulled up to number 4100, a two-story brick building with a large bay window, at the stroke of eleven. The customer who had ordered the Lagavulin must have been watching from the narrow vestibule window because the front door opened as Eugene reached for the bell.

"I say, that's a spiffy wagon you have out at the curb. Please d-d-do come in."

The Englishman in the doorway had long wavy hair and was wearing a baggy blue blazer with tarnished gold buttons and an ascot around his neck in place of a tie. His eyes had the puffy look of someone who drank a great deal of alcohol. Drawing Eugene inside the vestibule, he remarked in an off-hand way, "You are supp-p-posed to have a calling card."

Eugene took out the half of the carton that had been torn from a package of Jell-O (it had been in the hollowed-out knitting book he'd retrieved from the stacks the night before). The Englishman whipped out from his pocket the other half. The two halves matched perfectly. The Englishman offered a hand. "Awfully glad," he mumbled. A nervous tic of a smile appeared on his beefy face. "To tell the truth, didn't expect Starik to send me someone as young as you. I'm P-P-PARSIFAL...but you know that already."

Eugene caught whiff of bourbon on the Englishman's breath. "My working name is Eugene."

"American, are you? Thought Starik was going to fix me up with a Russian this time round."

"I speak English like an American," Eugene informed him. "But I am Russian." And he recited his motto in perfect Russian: *"Za uspiekh nashevo beznadiozhnovo diela!"*

The Englishman brightened considerably. "Don't speak Russian myself. Like the sound of it, though. Much prefer to deal with Starik's Russians than one of those antsy American Commies." He took four exposed Minox cartridges from his pocket and handed them to Eugene. "April Fool's present for Starik—do pass the stuff on as quickly as you can. Took some awfully good shots of some awfully secret documents spelling out which Soviet cities the Americans plan to A-bomb if war starts. Got some goodies for me in exchange?"

Eugene set the bottles of Lagavulin down on the floor and took out the other items that had been in the hollowed-out knitting book: a dozen cartridges of 50-exposure film for a Minox miniature camera, new one-time cipher pads printed in minuscule letters on the inside cover of ordinary matchbooks, a new microdot reader disguised as a wide-angle lens for a 35 millimeter camera and a personal letter from Starik enciphered on the last of the Englishman's old one-time pads and rolled up inside a hollowed-out bolt.

"Thanks awfully," the man said. "Will you be getting in touch with the *rezident* anytime soon?"

"I can."

"I should think you had b-b-better do that sooner rather than later. Tell him we have a bit of a headache looming. Angleton has been on to the fact that we have had a mole in the British Foreign Service, code-named HOMER, for donkey's years." The Englishman's stutter dissipated as he became caught up in his tale. "Yesterday he told me that his cryptoanalyst chaps have broken an additional detail out of some old intercepts: when HOMER was posted to Washington he'd meet twice a week in New York with your predecessor, his cutout. It won't take Angleton long to work out that this pattern corresponds to Don Maclean—he used to go up to New York twice a week to see his wife, Melinda, who was pregnant and living there with her American mother. Maclean's running the FO's American Department in London now. Someone has got to warn him the Americans are getting warmer; someone has got to set up an exfiltration if and when. Can you remember all that?"

Eugene had been briefed by Starik about Angleton and HOMER and Maclean. "Where is Burgess hanging his hat these days?" he asked, referring to Philby's old Trinity College sidekick, the long-time Soviet agent Guy Burgess, who originally recruited Philby into MI6 during the war.

"He's been using me as a B and B, which has come to mean bed and booze, since he was posted to the British embassy in Washington. Why do you ask?"

"Burgess is an old buddy of Maclean's, isn't he?"

"Yes, as a matter of fact."

"Starik said that in an emergency you might want to think about sending Burgess back to warn Maclean."

Philby saw the advantages instantly. "Wizard idea! What could be more natural than the two of them going for a pub crawl? If things get cheesy I suppose Guy *could* tear himself away from his poofter DC friends long enough to head home and give Maclean a warning holler."

"Cover your trail—if Maclean runs for it someone might work backward from Maclean to Burgess, and from Burgess to you."

The Englishman's shoulders heaved in resignation. "Guy can bluff his way out of a tight corner," he guessed. "Besides which I have a sensible line of defense—last thing I'd do if I were really spying for the Russians would be to give bed and booze to another Russian spy."

Eugene had to smile at the Englishman's nerve. "You ought to pay me for the whiskey," he said, handing him the invoice.

Kim Philby counted out bills from a woman's change purse. "B-b-by all means keep the change," he suggested, his stutter back again and, along with it, the brooding filmy gaze of a tightrope artist trying to anticipate missteps on the high-wire stretched across his mind's eye.

8

FROM THE NARROW STREET, THE PROPYLÄEN, AN INN NAMED AFTER THE periodical founded by the German poet Goethe, looked dark and deserted. A stone's throw from Heidelberg's austere time-warped university, its restaurant normally offered students a city-subsidized potato-and-cabbage menu. Now its metal shutters were closed, the naked electric bulb over its sign was extinguished and a hand-lettered notice tacked to the door read, in German, English and French, "Exceptionally Not Open Today." Ebby had rented out the inn's dining room for a farewell banquet for his Albanian commando unit and supplied the alcohol and canned meat from the Company's PX in Frankfurt. In a back room flickering with candlelight and warmed by a small coal-burning stove, he sat at the head of the long table, refilling brandy glasses and passing out filter-tipped cigarettes. The thin clean-shaven faces of the seven young Albanians and two female trans-lators on both sides of the table glistened with perspiration and pride.

At the other end of the table, Adil Azizi, the commando leader, a beau-tiful young man with smooth skin and long fine blond hair, was peeling an orange using a razor-sharp bayonet. The man next to him, who wore a black turtleneck sweater, made a comment and everyone laughed. The translator sitting at Ebby's elbow explained: "Mehmet tells Adil not to dull his blade on orange skin but save it for Communist skin."

A grandfather clock near the door struck midnight. One of the candles, burned down to its wick, sizzled and died. Kapo, at twenty-four the oldest member of the commando and the only one to speak even broken English, pushed himself to his feet and raised his brandy glass to Ebby. The second translator repeated his words in Albanian for the others. "I can tell you, Mr.

Trabzon, that we will not fail you or our American sponsors or our people, for sure," he vowed. Mehmet coached him in Albanian and Kapo rolled his head from side to side, which in the Balkans meant he agreed. "I can tell you again of my father—a member of the before-war regime who was trialed and decided culpable and locked in cage like wild animal and thrown from deck of ship at sea. All here tell alike stories."

Adil murmured to Kapo in Albanian. Kapo said, "Adil tells that his half brother called Hsynitk was trialed for listening American music on radio and shot dead in parking lot of Tiranë soccer stadium half of one hour later. Our blood enemy is Enver Hoxha, for sure."

Kapo pulled a small package wrapped in newspaper and string from the pocket of the leather jacket hanging over the back of his chair. He held it aloft. Everyone smiled. "Me and everyone, we want give you present so you remember us, remember time we spending together in great German city of Heidelberg."

The package was passed from hand to hand until it reached Ebby. He flushed with embarrassment. "I don't know what to say—"

"So don't say nothing, Mr. Trabzon. Only open it," Kapo called. The others laughed excitedly.

Ebby tore off the string and pulled away the paper. His face lit up when he saw the present; it was a British Webley Mark VI revolver with a date—1915—engraved in the polished wood of the grip. The weapon looked to be in mint condition. "I am very pleased to have this beautiful gun," Ebby said softly. He held the gun to his heart. "I thank you."

At the head of the table, Adil said something in Albanian. The translator said: "Adil tells that the next present they bring you will be the scalp of Enver Hoxha." Around the table everyone nodded gravely. Adil tossed back his glass of brandy. The others followed suit, then drummed their glasses on the table in unison. No one smiled.

Ebby stood up. The translator next to him rose to her feet. When she translated Ebby's words, she unconsciously imitated his gestures and even some of his facial expressions. "It has been an honor for me to work with you," Ebby began. He paused between sentences. "A great deal is riding on this commando raid. We are sure that the death of Hoxha will lead to an uprising of the democratic elements in Albania. The anti-Communist Balli Kombëtar forces in the north can put thousands of armed partisans in the field. An uprising in Albania could ignite revolts elsewhere in the Balkans and the other countries of Eastern Europe and eventually—why not?—in the Ukraine and the Baltics and the Central Asian Republics. The Soviet

Union is like a set of dominoes—topple the first one and they will all come crashing down." Ebby peered the length of the table at the eager faces. "To you falls the honor and the danger of toppling the first domino." He grinned as he added, "For sure." The young Albanians roared with laughter. When they had quieted down, Ebby added solemnly: "Good luck and Godspeed to you all."

9

ROCKING ON A PAINTED HOBBYHORSE THAT ONE OF THE BERLIN BASE officers had bought on the black market and parked in the hallway, the Fallen Angel was a-twitter over "Dennis the Menace," the new comic strip that had recently turned up in the pages of *Die Neue Zeitung,* an American newspaper written in German. Leaning against the water cooler filled with slivovitz across from the Sorcerer's partly open door, Miss Sipp and Jack were engrossed in the newspaper's front page that Silwan II had passed on to them; there was the usual box score of how many East German *Volkespolizei* had defected in the past twenty-four hours (an office pool was riding on the number), and banner-headlines above the lead story on Truman's decision to relieve Douglas MacArthur of his command in Korea after the General publicly called for air strikes on Chinese cities. Absorbed as they were in various pages of the newspaper, the Fallen Angel, the Sorcerer's Apprentice and Torriti's Night Owl were oblivious to the bleating hullabaloo emanating from the Sorcerer's office, clearly audible over an orchestral version of Bellini's *Norma.*

"Even the French come up with better intelligence than you," the Company's Chief of Station in Germany, General Lucian Truscott IV, was complaining in a raucous bellow.

The Sorcerer could be heard retorting with a lewd doggerel. "The French are a creative race—they talk with their hands and fuck with their face."

"Last week they came up with the Soviet order of battle in Poland."

"Their numbers are flaky."

"At least they have numbers."

"We have our triumphs."

"Name one recent one."

"I got my hands on a sample of Walter Ulbrecht's shit—we sent it back to Washington for analysis."

"Oh, cripes, next thing you'll tell me that the rumors about Ulbrecht being allergic to ragweed are true!"

In the hallway the Fallen Angel glanced up from "Dennis the Menace" and caught Miss Sipp's eye. She hiked her shoulders and curled out her lower lip. Since he'd come on board, General Truscott, a tough cookie who could turn abusive after three or four whiskeys, had cleaned up the Company's act in Germany: a lot of the dumber clandestine service ops (like the idea of bombarding Russia with extra-large condoms stamped "medium") had been permanently shelved, some of the more amateur officers had been sent to the boondocks. But despite the occasional verbal shootout, Truscott—a gruff soldier from the old school who had once spilled a pitcher of water over the head of a CIA officer to "cool him down"—seemed to have a healthy respect for the Sorcerer. Ulbrecht's excrement wasn't the only thing Torriti had come up with, and the General knew it.

"'Nother thing," the General was shouting over the music, his words strung together with a slurred grumpiness. "Air Force people've been bellyaching 'bout having to identify bombing targets from old German World War II Abwehr files. Can't we supply them with some up-to-date targeting, Torriti?"

Miss Sipp thought she heard another empty bottle crash land in her boss's wastebasket. Jack must have heard it, too, because he asked, "How many today?"

"If you love," the Night Owl pointed out with a sheepish grin, "you don't count."

"I thought you hated him," Silwan II said from the hobbyhorse.

"I hate him but I don't dislike him."

"Ah," he said, nodding as if he understood, which he didn't. He went back to the saner world of "Dennis the Menace."

"Not my fault if there's a demon cloud cover over East Europe," the Sorcerer was telling Truscott.

"It's *because* of the demon cloud cover that we need more agents on the ground, damn it."

The door to Torriti's office flew open and the two men, both clutching tumblers half-filled with whiskey, stumbled into the corridor. Truscott was bringing the Sorcerer up to date on the latest nightmare scenario from the

Pentagon war gamers: the Russians would block off the 100-mile-long umbilical corridor between the Western sectors of Berlin and West Germany; French, British and American units drawn from the 400,000 allied troops in West Germany would start down the *Autobahn* to test Soviet mettle; local Russian commanders would panic and blow up a bridge in front of them and another behind; rattled, the West would send in a tank division to rescue the stranded units; someone, somewhere would lose his nerve and pull a trigger; the shot would be heard 'round the world.

Torriti closed one very red eye to sooth a twitching lid. "Bastards won't take me alive, General," he boasted, and he flicked a fingernail against the poison-coated pin he kept stuck in the whiskey-stained lapel of his shapeless sports jacket.

With his hand on the knob of the heavy fire door leading to the staircase, Truscott suddenly spun around. "What's this I hear about you walking back a cat?"

"Who told you that?"

"I keep my ear to the ground."

The Sorcerer suddenly got the hiccups. "Fact is...I had an exfiltration that turned...turned sour," he moaned.

"Spoonful of sugar—it works every time," the General suggested.

Torriti looked confused. "For an exfiltration?"

"For the hiccups, damn it."

Miss Sipp looked up from the newspaper. "Try drinking water out of a glass with a spoon in it," she called.

"Maybe slivovitz in a glass with a...spoon might work," Torriti called, pointing to the water cooler. He turned back to Truscott. "The Russians were...tipped off. If it's the last...thing I do, I'm gonna find...find out where the tip...tip came from."

"How?"

"Barium...meals."

"Barium meals?" Jack repeated to Miss Sipp. "What the hell is that?"

"Not something you'll find at one of those fast food kiosks on the Kurfürstendamm," she said with a knowing frown.

"Barium what?" Truscott demanded.

"Meals. I'm gonna feed...feed stuff back to a single addressee at a time. It will be radioactive, in a manner of speaking—I'll be able to trace...it and see who saw what, when. I'll stamp everything...ORCON—dissemination controlled by originator. All copies numbered. Then we'll...we'll see which operations get blown and...figure out from that who's betraying us...us."

THE COMPANY

"You're giving away some of the family jewels," Truscott noted uneasily.

"Goddamn mole will give away more of them if we don't catch him."

"I suppose you know what you're doing," the General mumbled.

"I suppose...I do," the Sorcerer agreed.

The Sorcerer had begun the arduous process of walking back his cat with the distribution list on the Vishnevsky exfiltration. As far as he could figure, there had been nine warm bodies on the Washington end who were party to the operation: the director of Central Intelligence and his deputy director, four people in the Operations Directorate, the cipher clerk who had deciphered the Sorcerer's cables, the routing officer in Communications who controlled the physical distribution of traffic inside Cockroach Alley, and of course Jim Angleton, the counterintelligence swami who vetted all would-be defectors to weed out the "bad 'uns."

The permutations weren't limited to the people on the in-house distribution list. Kim Philby, as MI6's broker in Washington, was known to have access to all the top Company brass, up to and including the director, whose door was always open to the official nuncio from the British cousins. Any of them might have confided in Philby even though he wasn't on the distribution list. If someone had whispered in Philby's ear, he might have passed on to the head of MI6 the information that the Yanks were bringing across a defector who claimed to be able to finger a Soviet mole in MI6. "C," as the chief was called, might then have convened a small war council to deal with what could only be described as a seismic event in the secret Cold War struggle of intelligence services. If Philby wasn't the culprit—Torriti understood that the evidence pointing to him was only circumstantial—the mole could be anyone who learned of the Vishnevsky affair on a back channel.

Philby was also known to be bosom buddies with Jim Angleton, his sidekick from their Ryder Street days. According to what the Sorcerer had picked up (during casual phone conversations with several old cronies toiling in the dungeons on the Reflecting Pool), the birds of a feather, Philby and Angleton, flocked to a Georgetown watering hole for lunch most Fridays. Angleton obviously trusted Philby. Would he have passed on the meat of a "Flash" cable to his British pal? Would his pal have quietly passed it on to "C?" Would "C" have let the cat out of the bag to prepare for the worst?

Torriti meant to find out.

Burning midnight oil, devouring quantities of PX whiskey that had even Miss Sipp counting the empties in the wastebasket, Torriti meticulously prepared his barium meals.

Item: The Sorcerer had recently managed to have a hand-carved wooden bust of Stalin delivered to an office in the Pankow headquarters of the East German Intelligence Service. Hidden inside the base of the bust was a battery-operated microphone, a tiny tape machine and a burst-transmitter that broadcast, at 2 A.M. every second day, the conversations on the tape. The initial "get" from the microphone revealed that the East Germans had initiated a program, code-named ACTION J, to discredit the Allied-zone Germans by sending threatening letters purporting to come from West Germany to Holocaust survivors. The letters, signed "A German SS officer," would say: "We didn't gas enough Jews. Some day we'll finish what we started." Revealing ACTION J would blow the existence of the microphone hidden in the room in which the operation was being planned.

Item: The Rabbi had traded the names of two KGB case officers working under diplomatic cover out of the Soviet embassy in Washington for the whereabouts of a former Nazi germ warfare specialist in Syria, which the Sorcerer had acquired from the Gehlen Org (which, in turn, had purchased the information from a member of the Muhabarat, the Egyptian Intelligence Service). Judging from past experience, if the identity of the KGB officers fell into the hands of the Soviet mole, the Russians would find excuses (a death in the family, a son broke a leg skiing) to quickly pull the two back to the Soviet Union. If the two remained in Washington it would mean the Sorcerer's cable containing the names had not been blown.

Item: The Sorcerer had organized a phone tap in the office of Walter Ulbricht's closest collaborator, his wife, Lotte, who worked in the Central Committee building at the intersection of Lothringerstrasse and Prenzlauer Allee in the center of East Berlin. One of the barium meals would contain a transcript of a conversation between Ulbricht and his wife in which Ulbricht said rude things about his Socialist Unity Party rival Wilhelm Zaisser. The Russians, if they got wind of the tap via the Soviet mole, would make a "routine" security check on Lotte's office and discover the phone tap.

Item: An East German agent who had fled West with the tens of thousands of East German émigrés streaming across the open border had eventually landed a job working for the Messerschmidt Company. Berlin Base had stumbled across his identity while debriefing a low level Karlshorst defector and Gehlen's Org had "doubled" the agent, who now delivered to his East German handlers technical reports filled with disinformation. The East German agent was debriefed by his Karlshorst handlers during monthly visits to his aging mother in East Berlin. A barium meal from the Sorcerer identifying the doubled agent would blow the operation; the agent in question would undoubtedly fail to return to West Berlin the next time he visited his mother.

Item: The Sorcerer had personally recruited a maid who worked at the Blue House, the East German government dacha in Prerow, which was the Security Ministry's official resort on the Baltic coast. The maid turned out to be a sister of one of the prostitutes in the West German whorehouse above the nightclub in Berlin-Schoneberg that Torriti visited whenever he had a free hour to debrief the hookers. If a barium meal reporting snippets of conversation from bigwigs vacationing at the Blue House was passed on to the Soviets by their mole, the maid would certainly be arrested and her reports would dry up.

Item: The Sorcerer had a Watcher in an attic taking photographs with a long telephoto lens of the personnel who appeared at the windows in the KGB base in the former hospital at Karlshorst on the outskirts of Berlin. Using these photos, Berlin Base was compiling a "Who's Who in Soviet Intelligence" scrapbook. A barium meal status report on this operation that fell into Soviet hands would lead to the arrest of the photographer and the end of Berlin Base's scrapbook project.

Item: The Sorcerer had seen a copy of a field report prepared by E. Winstrom Ebbitt II, the CIA officer he'd kicked out of Berlin Base for shooting off his mouth about Torriti's medicinal alcohol habit. Ebbitt, now working out of Frankfurt Station, had recently been put in charge of Albania ops because of some obscure qualification relating to Albania. He was currently training a group of Albanian émigrés in a secret base near Heidelberg. In the next few days, Ebbitt planned to fly his commando group to the British base near Mdina on Malta and then sneak them onto the Albanian coast near Durrës from a sailing yacht. From there they were supposed to work their way inland to Tiranë and assassinate Enver Hoxha, the malevolent Stalinist leader of the People's Republic of Albania. Torriti's barium meal would take the form of a private "Eyes Only" cable to the Special Policy Committee that coordinated British-American operations against Albania; Kim Philby, as the ranking MI6 man in Washington, happened to be the British member of this committee. The Sorcerer would warn the committee that Ebbitt had gotten his priorities ass-backward. Hoxha lived and worked in "Le Bloc," a sealed compound in Tiranë. He was said to pass between his villa and his office through a secret tunnel. A far better (not to mention more realistic) target, Torriti would suggest, would be the submarine pens that the Soviets were constructing at the Albanian port of Saseno which, if completed, would give the Russians control of the Adriatic. If Ebbitt's commando found a reception committee waiting for them on the beach when they came ashore, it would indicate that this message had leaked, via the mole, to the Russians in Washington.

Item: Last but not least, he would send off a barium meal to Angleton giving details of the latest "get" that the courier code-named RAINBOW had delivered from her source, known as SNIPER. One of the items was particularly intriguing: SNIPER was important enough in the East German hierarchy to have been invited to hear a pep talk given by none other than Marshal Georgi Konstantinovich Zhukov during a recent visit to East Berlin; in the course of the talk, Zhukov—who had masterminded the Soviet assault on Berlin in 1945—let slip that, in the event of war, senior troop commanders expected to reach the English Channel on the tenth day of hostilities. If the Russians got wind of a leak at this level of the East German superstructure, the SNIPER source would dry up very quickly, and RAINBOW would fail to turn up for her dance course in the small theater on Hardenbergstrasse in West Berlin.

10

BERLIN, TUESDAY, APRIL 17, 1951

IN ORDER TO HAVE DIPLOMATIC IMMUNITY, JACK—LIKE ALL COMPANY officers in Berlin—was carried on the books as a Foreign Service officer working out of the American consulate. With Secretary of State Dean Acheson, the architect of America's policy of containing Soviet expansionism, passing through Berlin on a hit-and-run tour of front line consulates and embassies, Jack received one of the ambassador's notorious "your presence is requested and required" invitations to a "happy hour" pour in the Secretary's honor. Milling around with the other junior CIA officers, Jack listened as one of the Company's Technical Service Division "elves," recently back from Washington, described the new Remington Rand Univac computer being installed in the Pickle Factory. "It's going to revolutionize information retrieval," the technician was explaining excitedly. "The disadvantage is that Univac's not very portable—as a matter of fact it fills a very large room. The advantage is that it can swallow all the phone books of all the cities in America. You punch in a name, the rotors whir and four or five minutes later it spits out a phone number."

"Damn machines," someone cracked, "are going to take all the fun out of spying."

Jack laughed along with the others but only halfheartedly; his thoughts were on tonight's rendezvous in the rehearsal hall with RAINBOW, his sixteenth meeting with her since their paths first crossed two months before. Over time the snatches of conversation between them had turned into a kind of coded shorthand; the things left unspoken loomed larger than the things said, and they both knew it. Tonight Jack meant to screw up his courage and say what was on his mind; in his guts. He wasn't sure she would stand still long enough to hear him out; if she heard him out, he didn't know if she would sock him in the solar plexus or melt into his arms.

Drifting away from the group, Jack wandered over to the bar and helped himself to a fistful of pretzels and another whiskey sour. Turning back toward the room, rehearsing in his head what he would say to Lili if she gave him an opening, he suddenly found himself eyeball to eyeball with the austere Secretary of State.

"Good afternoon, I'm Dean Acheson."

The American ambassador (who had helicoptered in from the embassy in Bonn), the consul general from Berlin, two senators and a bevy of high-ranking State Department political officers crowded around.

"Sir, my name is John McAuliffe."

"What do you do here?"

Jack cleared his throat. "I work for you, Mr. Secretary," he said weakly.

"I didn't catch that."

"I work for you. In the embassy."

The ambassador tried to take Acheson's elbow and steer him toward the buffet of popcorn and open sandwiches but the Secretary of State wasn't finished quizzing Jack. "And what do you do in the embassy, Mr. McAuliffe?"

Jack looked around for help. The two senators were staring off into space. The political officers were concentrating on their fingernails. "I work in the political section, sir."

Acheson was starting to get annoyed. "And what precisely do you do in the political section, young man?"

Jack swallowed hard. "I write reports, Mr. Secretary, that I hope will be useful..."

Suddenly the penny dropped. Acheson's mouth fell open and he nodded. "I think I see. Well, good luck to you, Mr. McAuliffe." The Secretary of State mouthed the words "Sorry about that" and turned quickly away.

RAINBOW had come to look forward to her twice weekly meetings with Jack; living as she did in the bleak Soviet side of the city, locked into a relationship with a man twenty-seven years her senior, she savored the brief encounters during which she was made to feel desirable, and desired. For the past several weeks Lili had no longer turned modestly away when she reached under her sweat shirt and into her brassiere to pull out the small square of silk filled with minuscule handwriting. Now, for the first time, Jack snatched the silk, warm from her breast, and pressed it to his lips. Lili, startled, lowered her eyes for an instant, then looked up questioningly into his as Jack grazed one of her small breasts with his knuckles and kissed her softly on the corner of her thin lips. "Please, oh, please, understand that you have arrived at the frontier of our intimacy," she pleaded, her voice reduced to a husky whisper. "There can be no crossing over. In another world, in another life..." She managed a forlorn smile and Jack caught a glimpse of what her face would look like when she had grown old. "Jack the Ripper," she murmured. "Jackhammer. Jack rabbit."

"Jesus H. Christ, where do you discover all these Jacks?"

"Herr Professor has a wonderful dictionary of American slang, yes? It has long been my habit to learn several new words every day. I was up to *grab forty winks* when I met you. I skipped ahead to the *Jacks.*"

"Have you told Herr Professor about me?"

"He has never asked me and I have not raised the subject. What he does—the information he sends to you—it is out of an antique idealism. Herr Professor wears shirts with studs instead of buttons, and old-fashioned starched collars that he changes daily; he is clearly ill at ease with the latest fashions in clothing and political ideas. He gathers the information and writes it out meticulously on the silk in order to turn the clock back. He counts on me take care of the details of the delivery."

"We could become lovers," Jack breathed.

"In mysterious ways we are already lovers," Lili corrected him.

"I want you—"

"You have as much of me as I can give to you—"

"I want more. I want what any man wants. I want you in bed."

"I say it to you without ambiguity—this can never be."

"Because of Herr Professor?"

"He saved my life at the end of the war. In my dictionary *gang-rape* comes before *grab forty winks*. I was what you call gang-raped by drunken Russian soldiers. I filled the pockets of my overcoat with bricks in order to throw myself into the Spree, I could not wait for the dark waters to close over my head. Herr Professor prevented me...through the night he talked to me of another Germany...of Thomas Mann, of Heinrich Böll...at dawn he took me to the roof of the building to watch the sun rise. He convinced me that it was the first day of the rest of my life. I do not pretend, Jack, to be...indifferent to you. I only say that my first loyalty is to him. I say also that this loyalty takes the form of sexual fidelity..."

Lili stepped into a skirt and peeled off her dancing tights from under it. She folded them into her satchel and reached to turn out the lights in the rehearsal hall. "I must begin back, yes?"

Jack gripped her shoulder. "He lets you run risks."

Lili pulled away. "That is unfair—there is a hierarchy to the world we live in. Because he considers some things more important does not mean he needs me less."

"I need you more."

"You do not need me as he needs me. Without me—" She looked away, her face suddenly stony.

"Finish the sentence, damnation—without you what?"

"Without me he cannot remain alive. You can."

"You want to spell that out?"

"No."

"You owe it to yourself—"

"Whatever I owe to myself, I owe more to him. Please let me go now, Jack-o'-lantern."

Sorting through emotions that were not familiar to him, Jack nodded gloomily. "Will you come again Friday?"

"Friday, yes. Depart ahead of me, if you please. We should not be seen coming out of the theater together."

Jack put a hand on the back of her neck and drew her to him. She let her forehead rest for a moment against his shoulder. Then she stepped back and turned off the lights and opened the door and waited at the top of the staircase while he descended the steps.

He looked back once. Four floors above him Lili was lost in the shadows of the landing. "Lily of the valley?" he called. When she didn't respond he turned and, hurrying past Aristide dozing in his glass-enclosed cubbyhole, fled from the theater.

"Do me a favor, sport," the Sorcerer had said as casually as if he'd been asking Jack to break some ice cubes out of the office fridge. "Put a teardrop in SNIPER's wall."

Bugging the Professor's house had turned out to be easier said than done. Jack had dispatched some German freelancers to scout the street behind the Gorky Theater. It was filled with war-gutted buildings and rubble and the single house standing in the middle of what had once been a garden. It took them ten days to work out when both RAINBOW and SNIPER were away from home. As a deputy prime minister, Lili's Herr Professor went to a government office weekday mornings and taught seminars in particle and plasma physics at Humbolt University in the afternoons.

Six mornings a week Lili took the U-Bahn to Alexanderplatz, where she taught classical dance classes at one of the last private schools in the Soviet zone; three afternoons a week she spent in a windowless Gorky Theater rehearsal hall taking lessons from a crippled Russian woman who had danced with the Kirov before the war. Even when both RAINBOW and SNIPER were away, there was still a stumbling block to the planting of a microphone: Herr Professor had a caretaker living in two gloomy ground floor rooms of the house, an old woman who had once been his nanny and now, confined by arthritis to a wicker wheelchair, spent most of her waking hours staring through the windowpane at the deserted street.

Jack had brought the problem to the Sorcerer: how to get the caretaker out of the house long enough for a team to break into her rooms and install a bug in the ceiling?

The Sorcerer, sorting through barium meals and the people to whom they would be addressed, had grunted. His eyes were puffier than usual, and heavy-lidded; he looked as if had come out second best in a street brawl, which in itself defied logic. Jack couldn't imagine the Sorcerer coming out second best in anything.

"Kill her?" the Sorcerer had suggested.

For an instant Jack had actually taken him seriously. "We can't just up and kill her, Harvey—we're the good guys, remember?"

"Don't you know a joke when you hear one, sport? Lure her out of the house with a free ticket to a Communist Party shindig. Whatever."

"She's an old lady. And she's tied to a wheelchair."

The Sorcerer had shaken his head in despair. "I got problems of my own," he had grumbled, his double chins quivering. "Use your goddamn imagination for once."

It had taken Jack the better part of a week to figure out the answer, and three days to lay in the plumbing. One morning, soon after Herr Professor and Lili had left the apartment, an East German ambulance with two young men in white coats sitting on either side of a muzzled lap dog had eased up to the curb in front of the house. The men had knocked on the caretaker's door. When she opened it the width of the safety chain, they had explained that they had been sent by the Communist Party's Ministry of Public Health to transport her to a doctor's office off Strausberger Platz for a free medical examination. It was part of a new government social program to aid the elderly and the infirm. If she qualified—and judging from the wheelchair they suspected she might—she would be given the latest Western pills to alleviate her pain and a brand new Czech radio. The caretaker, her peasant eyes narrowing in suspi-

cion, had wanted to know how much all this would cost. Silwan II had favored
her with one of his angelic smiles and had assured her that the service was free
of charge. Scratching the hair on her upper lip, the caretaker had thought
about this for a long time. Finally she had removed the safety chain.

No sooner had Sweet Jesus and the Fallen Angel carted the caretaker off
to visit the doctor (hired for the occasion) than a small pickup truck with
the logo of the East German Electrical Collective on its doors drew up in
front of the house. Three of the Company's "plumbers," dressed in blue coveralls, carrying a wooden ladder and two wooden boxes filled with tools and
equipment, went up the walkway and let themselves into the caretaker's
rooms; a fourth plumber waited in the driver's seat. The pickup's radio was
tuned to the East German police frequency. A fist-sized radio transmitter on
the seat buzzed into life. "We are operational," a voice speaking Hungarian
said, "and starting the work."

The team inside used a silent drill—the sound of the bit working its way into
the ceiling was muted by a tiny spray of water—in case the KGB had planted
microphones in SNIPER's apartment. Jack's people worked the bit up to within
a centimeter of the surface of the floor, then switched drills to one that turned so
slowly it could punch a pinhole in the floor without pushing any telltale sawdust
up into the room. A tiny microphone the size of the tip of one of those newfangled ballpoint pens was inserted into the pinhole and then wired up to the
electric supply in the caretaker's overhead lighting fixture. The small hole in the
ceiling was filled with quick-drying plaster and repainted the same color as the
rest of the ceiling with quick-drying paint. A miniature transmitter was fitted
inside the fixture so that it was invisible from below, and hooked up to the house's
electricity. The transmitter, programmed to be sound-activated, beamed signals to
a more powerful transmitter buried in the crest of the rubble in the vacant lot next
door; this second transmitter, which ran on a mercury dry-cell battery, broadcast
in turn to an antenna on the roof of a building in the American sector of Berlin.

"Did you work something out, sport?" Torriti mumbled when he
bumped into Jack in the Berlin-Dahlem PX.

"As a matter of fact I did, Harvey. I sent in your Hungarian plumbers—"

The Sorcerer held up a palm, cutting him off. "Don't give me the details,
kid. That way I can't give your game away if I'm ever tortured by the Russians."

Torriti said it with such a straight face that Jack could only nod dumbly
in agreement. Watching the Sorcerer lumber off with a bottle of whiskey
under each arm, he began to suspect that the honcho of Berlin Base had
been putting him on. On the other hand, knowing Torriti, he could have
been serious.

11

FRANKFURT, MONDAY, APRIL 23, 1951

L OOKING LIKE WITNESSES AT A WAKE, EBBY, TONY SPINK AND HALF A dozen other officers from the Soviet/Eastern Europe Division crowded around the bulky reel-to-reel tape machine on Spink's desk. The technician, who had recorded the special radio program from Tiranë earlier that afternoon, threaded the tape through the capsun and locked it into the pickup spool. Spink looked at the translator who had been sitting next to Ebby the night of the farewell dinner for the Albanian commandoes in the Heidelberg inn. "Ready?" he asked. She nodded once. He hit the "Play" button.

At first there was a great deal of static. "We had trouble tuning in the station," the technician explained. "We had to orient our antenna. Here it comes."

Ebby could hear the high-pitched voice of a man speaking in Albanian. He seemed to be delivering a tirade. "So he is what we call the Procurator and you call the Prosecutor," announced the translator, a short, middle-aged woman with short-cropped hair. "He sums up the prosecution case against the accused terrorists. He says that they landed on the coast from two small, motorized rubber rafts immediately after midnight on April the twenty. He says a routine border patrol stumbled across them as they were deflating and burying the rafts in the sand." The translator cocked her head as another voice called out a question. "The chief judge asks the Procurator what the terrorists did when the border soldiers attempted to apprehend them. The Procurator says that the terrorists opened fire without warning, killing three border soldiers, wounding two additional border soldiers. In the exchange of gunfire four of the terrorists were killed and the three, on trial today, were apprehended." The translator wiped tears from her eyes with the back of her finger. "Now the judge asks if incriminating evidence was captured with the terrorists."

"They sound like they're reading from a goddamn script," Spink muttered angrily.

"The Procurator puts into evidence objects labelled with the letters of the alphabet. The labels arrive at the letter *V* for Victor. Items A and B consist of two American manufacture rafts and seven American air force inflatable life jackets. In addition there are five British manufacture Lee-Enfield rifles, two American manufacture Winchester Model 74 rifles fitted with British manufacture Parker-Hale silencers and Enfield telescopic sights, three American manufacture Browning pistols fitted with primitive home-made silencers, one small leather valise containing a British manufacture Type A dash Mark Roman numeral two radio transmitter and receiver with Morse key and earphones, a map of Albania and another of Tiranë printed on cotton and sewn into the lining of a jacket, seven cyanide vials in small brass containers that were attached by safety pins to the insides of lapels...Here the chief judge interrupts to ask if communications codes were discovered on the terrorists. The Procurator says the terrorists arrived to destruct the envelope containing the codes before they were captured. He goes on to explain that the envelopes were coated with a chemical that made them burn immediately a match was touched to the paper. He says also..."

The Procurator's shrill voice, trailed by the muted voice of the translator, droned on. Spink pulled Ebby away from the tape recorder. "You mustn't blame yourself," he whispered. "It's a dirty game. These things happen all the time." He patted Ebby on the shoulder. Together they turned back to the tape and the translator.

"...asks if the terrorists have anything to say."

A growl of anger from the public attending the trial could be heard on the tape. Then someone breathed heavily into the microphone. A young man began to speak in a robot-like voice. "He says—" The translator sucked in her breath. She unconsciously brought a hand to her breast as she forced herself to continue. "He says his name is Adil Azizi. He says he is the leader of the commando group. He says he and his comrades were trained in a secret base near Heidelberg, Germany by agents of the American Central Intelligence Agency. Their mission was to land on the coast of the Albanian Democratic Republic, bury their rubber boats, work their way across country to the capital of Tiranë and, with the help of local terrorist cells, assassinate comrade Enver Hoxha, who holds the post of Premier and Foreign

Minister. The chief judge asks the terrorist Azizi if there are mitigating circumstances to be taken into consideration before the court passes sentence.
Adil Azizi says there are none. Adil Azizi says that he and the two surviving
terrorists deserve the supreme penalty for betraying the motherland...The
shouts you hear in the background are from people in the courtroom
demanding the death sentence."

The technician punched the fast-forward button and kept an eye on the
tape counter. When it reached a number he had marked on a slip of paper,
he started the tape again. "The radio station played twelve minutes of patriotic music while the judges deliberated," the translator explained. "Now is
the sentence. The chief judge orders the three terrorists to stand. He says
them that they have been convicted of high treason and terrorism against the
People's Republic of Albania and its supreme leader, Enver Hoxha. He says
them that the court sentences the three terrorists to execution. Ah, I cannot
continue—"

"Translate, damn it," Ebby snapped.

"He says them there is no appeal in capital crimes. He orders that the
sentence is carried out immediately."

"When they say 'immediately,' they mean immediately," the technician
warned. Several of the CIA officers drifted away from the table and casually
lit cigarettes. Ebby noticed that the hands of one officer trembled.

"Now is the voice of the radio announcer," the translator went on very
quietly. "He describes the three terrorist as shaking with fear when their
wrists are bound behind their backs and they are led by soldiers from the
courtroom. He describes—" The translator bit her lip. "He describes following them down two flights of steps to the rear door of the courthouse
which opens onto the parking lot. He describes that there are no cars parked
in the parking lot this day. He describes that a large crowd is assembled at
the edge of the parking lot, that above his head all the windows are filled
with people watching. He describes that the three terrorists are tied to iron
rings projecting from the wall that were once used to attach horses when the
building was constructed in the previous century. He describes a man in
civilian clothing giving each terrorist a sip of peach brandy. He describes
now the peloton of execution charging their rifles and one of the terrorists
begging for mercy."

Unable to continue, sobbing into her sleeve, the translator stumbled
away from the table.

From the tape machine came the crackle of rifle fire, then three sharp
reports from smaller caliber weapons.

"Revolvers," Spink said professionally. "Twenty-two caliber, by the sound."

"They were kids," Ebby said tightly. His right hand dipped into his jacket pocket and closed over the wooden grip of the antique Webley revolver the young Albanians had given him in Heidelberg. "They never had time to liberate Albania, did they?"

Spink shrugged fatalistically. "To their everlasting credit at least they tried. God bless them for that."

"God bless them," Ebby agreed, and he came up with a sliver of a Byron poem that had once lodged in his brain at Yale:

Let there be light! said God, and there was light!
Let there be blood! says man, and there's a sea!

12

J ACK HAD HITCHED A RIDE INTO FRANKFURT ON AN AIR FORCE FILM-
exchange run to hand-deliver the Sorcerer's "For Your Eyes Only"
envelope into the fleshy hands of General Truscott, after which he was
supposed to personally burn the contents in the Frankfurt Station incinerator and return to Berlin with Truscott's yes or no. The General, in one of his
foul moods, could be heard chewing out someone through the shut door of
his office as Jack cooled his heels outside. The two secretaries, one typing
letters from a dictaphone belt, the other manicuring her fingernails, acted as
if nothing out of the ordinary were happening. "And you have the gumption," Truscott could be heard bellowing, "to stand there and tell me you
launched five hundred and sixteen balloons into Russian air space and only
managed to retrieve forty?"

A muffled voice could be heard stumbling through an explanation. The
General cut it off in mid-sentence. "I don't give a flying fart if the prevailing
winds weren't prevailing. You were supposed to send reconnaissance balloons
fitted with cameras and take photos of Soviet installations. Instead you seem
to have spilled eight hundred thousand of the taxpayers greenbacks down
the proverbial drain. From where I'm sitting that looks suspiciously like
unadulterated incompetence."

The door opened and a drawn Company officer emerged from the
General's office. Truscott's wrath trailed after him like a contrail. "Goddamn
it, man, I don't want excuses, I want results. If you can't give 'em to me I'll
find people who can. You out there, Miss Mitchel? Send in the Sorcerer's
goddamn Apprentice."

The young woman working on her nails nodded toward the General's door. Jack rolled his eyes in mock fright. "Is the front office in friendly hands?" he asked.

The secretary bared her teeth in a nasty smile. "His bark is nothing compared to his bite," she remarked.

"Thanks for the encouragement," Jack said.

"Oh, you're very welcome, I'm sure."

"What's the Sorcerer cooking up that it needs to be hand-delivered?" Truscott demanded when he caught sight of Jack in the doorway.

"Sir, I am not familiar with the contents."

He gave the sealed envelope to the General, who slit it open with the flick of a finger and pulled out the single sheet of yellow legal paper. He flattened the page on the blotter with his palms, put on a pair of spectacles and, frowning, began to read the message, which had been handwritten by Torriti. Glancing around the vast office, Jack took in the framed photographs showing Truscott with various presidents and prime ministers and field marshals. He thought he heard Truscott mutter under his breath as he jotted something on the blotter; it sounded like "Thirty, twelve, forty-five."

Truscott looked up. "Here's what you tell him: The answer to his barely legible bulletin from Berlin is affirmative."

"Affirmative," Jack repeated.

"While you're at it, remind him I'd take it as a personal favor if he'd learn to typewrite."

"You would like him to typewrite future messages," Jack repeated.

"Make tracks," Truscott snapped. He brayed through the open door, "Goddamn it, Miss Mitchel, haven't they deciphered the overnight from the Joint Chiefs yet?"

"They said it'd be another twenty minutes," the secretary called back.

"What are they doing down in the communications shack," the General groaned, "taking a coffee break between each sentence?"

Jack retrieved the Sorcerer's message from Truscott's desk and made his way down a staircase to the second-level sub-basement incinerator room. The walls and doors had been freshly painted in battleship gray, and smelled it. In the corridor outside the "Central Intelligence Agency Only" door, curiosity got the best of Jack and he sneaked a look at Torriti's note. "General," it said. "I've decided to send out one last barium meal to my prime suspect saying Torriti knows the identity of the Soviet mole who betrayed the Vishnevsky exfiltration. At which point, if I've hit the nail on the head, my suspect will get word to his KGB handlers and the Russians will try to kidnap or murder me. If they succeed you'll find a letter addressed to you in the small safe in the corner of my office. The combination is: thirty, then left past thirty to twelve, then right to forty-five. Copy the numbers on your blotter, please. The letter will identify the mole and spell out the evidence, including my last barium meal. If the attempt to 'murder or kidnap me fails I'll fly to Washington and drive home the spike myself. Okay? Torriti."

Jack folded the Sorcerer's letter back into the envelope and went into the burn room. An Army staff sergeant with sixteen years worth of hash marks on the sleeve of his field jacket hanging on the back of the door glanced at the laminated ID card Jack held up, then pointed to a metal trash bin. "Throw it in—I'll take care of it."

"I've been ordered to burn it personally," Jack told him.

"Suit yourself, chum."

Jack crumbled the envelope, opened the grate of the furnace and dropped it in. "Talk about balls," he said as the envelope went up in flames.

"Beg pardon?"

"No, nothing. I was just thinking out loud."

With an hour and a quarter to kill before he could catch a ride back to Berlin on the film-exchange plane, Jack wandered up to the fifth floor cubby-hole occupied by Ebby. Finding the door ajar, he rapped on it with his knuckles and pushed through to discover Ebby sitting with his feet propped up on the sill. He was staring gloomily out over the roofs of Frankfurt as he absently spun the cylinder of what looked like an antique revolver. Ebby's occasional office mate, a young CIA case officer named William Sloane Coffin, assigned at the time to a leaflet distribution project, was on his way out. "Maybe you can cheer him up," Coffin told Jack as they brushed past each other.

Ebby waved Jack into Bill Coffin's chair. "Hey, what brings you down to Frankfurt?"

Jack noticed that the lines around Ebby's eyes had deepened, making him look not only grimmer but older. "Needed to ferry some 'Eyes-Only' stuff to your general." Jack scraped Coffin's vacated seat over to Ebby's desk. "You look like death warmed over," he said. "Want to talk about it?"

Ebby gnawed on a lip. "I was the case officer for a team going into Albania," he finally said. He shook his head disconsolately. "My Albanians, all seven of them, bought it—four were gunned down on the beach, the other three were hauled in front of judge and treated to a mock trial, then put up against a wall and shot."

"I'm sorry to hear that, Ebby. Look, I don't mean to soft-pedal your sense of loss—"

"—of failure. Use the right word."

"What I want to say is that we all take hits," Jack said softly. He was think-ing of the would-be Russian defector Vishnevsky and his wife strapped onto stretchers. He was thinking of Vishnevsky's boy being pulled up the ramp onto a plane sobbing and crying out "papa." "It comes with the territory."

"I lost the two guys I parachuted into Poland—we never heard from them again. I lost a kid named Alyosha whom we parachuted into the Carpathians. He radioed back using the danger signal. He still checks in every week or two but he always uses the danger signal—we figure he's being played back. When they get tired of the radio game they'll shoot him, too." Ebby heaved himself out of the chair and walked over to the door and slammed it shut so hard the empty coffee cups on his desk rattled in their saucers. "It's one thing to put your own life at risk, Jack," he went on, settling onto the sill, leaning back against the windowpanes. "It's another to send simple young men into harm's way. We seduce them and train them and use them as cannon fodder. They're expendable. I don't mean to wax corny, honest to God, I really don't but I feel—oh, Christ, I feel awful. I feel I've somehow let them down."

Jack heard Ebby out—he knew there weren't many people his friend could talk to, and talking was good for him. From time to time Jack came up with what he thought would be a comforting cliché: You're not the only one in this situation, Ebby; if you didn't do it someone else would have to; we'll only know if our efforts to roll back Communism are quixotic when they write about this period in the history books.

Eventually Jack glanced at his Bulova. "Oh, shit, I gotta run if I don't want to miss the flight back."

Ebby walked him down to the lobby. "Thanks for stopping by," he said.

"Misery loves company," Jack said.

"Yeah, something along those lines," Ebby admitted. They shook hands.

Back at Berlin Base late in the afternoon, Jack tore down the steps to the Sorcerer's bunker only to be brought up short by the Night Owl standing in front of Torriti's closed door with her arms folded across her imperious chest. From inside came the melodic strains of a soprano coughing her way through the *Traviata* end game. "He's in a funk," she announced; the way she said it made it sound as if the funk were terminal.

"How can you tell?" Jack asked.

"He's drinking V-8 Cocktail Vegetable juice instead of whiskey."

"What caused it?" Jack asked.

"I brought him a couple of bottles with his afternoon messages."

"I mean, what caused the *funk*?"

"I'm not really sure. Something about barium meals giving him stomach cramps. You're his Apprentice, Jack. You have any idea what that could mean?"

"Maybe." He motioned for her to let him pass and knocked on the door. When Torriti didn't answer, he knocked louder. Then he opened the door and let himself into the room. Miss Sipp hadn't been exaggerating about the Sorcerer's funk: his thinning hair was drifting off in all directions, the tails of his shirt were trailing out of his trousers, his fly was half-unbuttoned, one of his cowboy boots was actually on the desk and the grips of two handguns were protruding from it. *Traviata* came to an end. Gesturing for Jack to keep silent until the music started again, Torriti swiveled around to his Victrola and fitted a new record onto the turntable. Then, angling his head and squinting, he cautiously lowered the needle onto the groove. There was a skin-tingling scratchy sound, followed by the angelic voice of Galli-Curci singing "Ah! non credea mirarti" from *La Sonnambula*.

Sighting along the top of an outstretched index finger, Torriti—looking like an antiaircraft gun tracking a target—swiveled his bulk around in the chair. Jack turned out to be the target. "So what'd the General have to say?"

"He said affirmative. He said you ought to typewrite your messages from now on."

"Hunt and peck is not my style, sport." He refilled a glass with V-8 juice and drank half of it off in one long painful swallow. Then he shivered. "How the mighty have fallen," he moaned. "When my Night Owl brought up the subject of vegetable juice, I thought the V-8 she was talking about was the new, improved German V-2 buzz bomb. What's going on in Frankfurt that I ought to know about?"

Jack described the dressing-down Truscott had delivered to a hapless subordinate who had been playing with balloons over the Soviet Union but Torriti, who normally relished Company gossip, didn't crack a smile. Jack mentioned having looked in on Ebby. "You remember Elliott Ebbitt—he spent a month or two here before being reassigned to Frankfurt Station."

"He wasn't *reassigned* to Frankfurt," Torriti snapped. "He was *sent packing* by yours truly for shooting off his goddamn mouth about alcohol consumption. Good thing he's not here now—he'd be shooting off his goddamn mouth about vegetable juice consumption. What's the fucker up to these days?"

"He was in mourning," Jack reported. "The Soviet-East Europe folks just infiltrated a bunch of émigré agents and lost every one of them. Ebby was the case officer."

The Sorcerer, shuffling absently through file cards in a folder labelled "Barium Meals," looked up, an ember of interest burning in his pupils. "Where did this happen? And when?"

"Albania. Nine days ago."

Torriti mouth slowly slackened into a silly grin. "Albania! Nine days ago! How come nobody tells me these things?"

"It was a Frankfurt operation, Harvey."

"You're sure the émigrés bought it?"

"That's what the man said. Four died on the beach, three in front of a firing squad."

"Eureka!" cried Torriti. "That narrows it down to the Special Policy Committee that coordinates operations against Albania." He drew his handguns out of the cowboy boot and fitted one into his shoulder holster, the other into his ankle holster. He pulled on the boot, combed his hair with his fingers, tucked his shirt back into his trousers, swept the V-8 bottle into the burn basket and produced a bottle of PX whiskey from the seemingly bottomless bottom drawer of his desk. "This needs to be anointed," he exclaimed, splashing alcohol into two glasses. He pushed one across to Jack. "Here's to the beauty of barium, sport," he declared, hiking his hand in a toast.

"Harvey, people were killed! I don't see what there is to celebrate."

The Sorcerer checked his wristwatch. "London's two hours earlier or later than us?"

"Earlier."

"An Englishman worth his salt would be sitting down to supper in a pub right about now," he said. Torriti flailed around in a frantic search of his pockets, turning some of them inside out until he found what he was looking for—a slip of paper with a number on it. He snatched the interoffice phone off its hook. "Have the Fallen Angel bring my car around to the side door," he ordered Miss Sipp. Knocking back his whiskey, he waved for Jack to come along and headed for the door.

"Uh-oh—where we off to in such a panic, Harvey?"

"I need to narrow it down ever further. To do that I need to make a phone call."

"Why don't you use the office phone—the line is secure."

"Russians thought their lines out of Karlshorst were secure, too," he muttered, "until I figured out how to make them insecure. This is fucking earthshaking—I don't want to take any chances."

Torriti sat on the edge of an unmade bed in a top-floor room of the whorehouse on the Grunewaldstrasse in Berlin-Schoneberg, the old-fashioned phone glued to his ear as he drummed on the cradle with a finger. From somewhere below came the muffled echo of a singer crooning in the night-club. One of the prostitutes, a reedy teenager wearing a gauzy slip and nothing under it, peeked in the door. She had purple-painted eyelids and frowzy hair tinted the color of chrome. When Jack waved her away, the prostitute pouted. "But Uncle Harvey always has his ashes hauled—"

"Not tonight, sweetheart," Jack told her. He went over and shooed her out and closed the door and stood with his back to it, gazing up at the Sorcerer's upside-down reflection in the mirror fixed to the ceiling over the bed.

"The Lion and Last in Kentish Town?" the Sorcerer was shouting into the phone. "Can you hear me? I need to speak to a Mr. Epstein. Elihu Epstein. He eats supper in your pub weekday nights. Yeah, I'd certainly appreciate that, thanks. Could you shake a leg? I'm calling from a very long distance."

The Sorcerer drummed his fingernails on the table top. Then the drumming stopped. "Elihu, you recognize my voice? I'm the chum you didn't meet on Hampstead Heath. Ha-ha-ha. Listen up, Elihu—you remember who we were talking about that day...the joker who got hitched to the Communist broad in Austria...I need to get a news bulletin to him but I don't want it to come from me...you told me you speak to him on the phone two or three times a week...yeah, people have been heard to say I got a memory like an elephant's...could you sort of slip my bulletin into the conversation next time you talk to him...tell him an old pal from your 3 Commando days in Sicily called you to pick your brain, he wanted to know how the *apparatchiks* at MI5 would react if he delivered an atomic bomb of a serial into their hot hands. Your man in Washington will ask if you have any idea of the contents of the serial. You hem and haw, you swear him to secrecy, you tell him it's way off the record, you tell him that your pal—be absolutely sure to give him my name—your pal says he can identify the Soviet mole who tipped the KGB off to the Vishnevsky exfiltration...Of course it's a barium meal, Elihu...Me too, I hope I know what I'm doing...Sorry to interrupt your supper...Shalom to you, Elihu."

The Sorcerer's people had gone on a war footing. Torriti's automatic weapons had been taken down from the wall racks and set out neatly on a makeshift table in the corridor; Sweet Jesus and the Fallen Angel stuffed bullets into clips and taped them back to back so the weapons could be reloaded rapidly. Jack and Miss Sipp tried out a spanking new miniature walkie-talkie system that employed a tiny microphone attached to the inside of their collars and a hearing-aid-size speaker in their respective auricles. "Testing ten, nine, eight, seven, six," Jack whispered, speaking into the collar of his shirt. The Night Owl's voice, sounding as if it originated at the bottom of a mineshaft, came back tinny but crystal clear. "Oh, swell, Jack. I am reading you loud and clear."

Several of the newer Berlin Base recruits who happened on the sub-basement preparations wondered if it meant the Russians were about to invade. "Sir, how will we know when to set off the thermite bombs in the safes?" one of them asked Jack. The Sorcerer, washing down his grub with some water-cooler slivovitz, overheard the question. "Loose lips sink ships," he bellowed down the corridor. "Don't forget to jab yourself with a poison needle so you won't be taken alive."

The recruit nodded dumbly.

"He is making a joke," Jack said.

"Un-huh." The young Company officer, a Yale midterm graduate who had turned up at Berlin Base only days before, beat a hasty retreat from the sub-basement madhouse.

For two days and two nights Torriti and his people—catnapping on couches and cots, surviving on sandwiches the Night Owl brought down from the canteen, shaving at the dirty sink in the small toilet at the end of the corridor—waited. The Sorcerer kept his office door ajar; aria after aria reverberating through the corridor and up the staircase. Every time the phone rang Jack would duck his head into the office to discover Torriti talking into the receiver while he fussed with his pearl-handled revolver, twirling it on a trigger finger, cocking and uncocking it, sighting on a bird painted on a wall calendar. "That wasn't it," he would say with a shake of his head when he had hung up.

"How will you know which one *is* it?" Jack asked in exasperation.

"My goddamn nose will twitch, sport."

And then, at the start of the third day, it did.

"Otto, long time no see," Torriti muttered into the phone he had just plucked from its hook. When Jack turned up at the door, he waved excitedly for him to pick up the extension. "Where have you been hiding yourself?" the Sorcerer asked the caller.

Jack eased the second phone off its hook. "...phone line secure?" said the voice at the other end.

"You are actually asking me if my line is secure? Otto, Otto, in your wildest imagination do you think you could reach me on a line that wasn't?"

"I may have something delicious for you, my dear Harv."

"Ach so?" Torriti said, and he laughed into the phone.

Otto laughed back. "You are again—how do you say it?—pulling my leg with your terrible German accent."

"I am again pulling your leg, right. What's the something delicious you have for me?"

"One of my people is only just back from a highly successful mission in the East. You have heard of the poisoning of seven thousand cows at a cooperative dairy near Fürstenberg, have you not? That was the work of my agent."

"Heartfelt congratulations," Torriti gushed. "Another blow struck against fucking international Communism."

"You are being ironical, correct? No matter. You fight your war your way, my dear Harv, we fight our war our way. Before returning to the West my agent spent the night with a cousin. The cousin has a female cousin on his wife's side who works as a stenographer in the office of the chief of the Ministerium fuer Staatssicherheit, what you call the Stassi. She takes dictation from Anton Ackermann. She must raise money quickly to send her husband to the West for an expensive eye operation. She is offering to sell Thermofax copies of all of Ackermann's outgoing letters for the past three months."

"Why don't you act as the middleman, Otto? Middlemen clean up in this dry rotted city."

"Two reasonments, my dear Harv. Reasonment number one: She wants many too many US dollars. Reasonment number two: She flatly refuses to deal with a German. She will only talk with the chief of the American CIA in Berlin. With Herr Torriti, Harv. And only if you come alone."

"How come she knows my name?"

"Ackermann knows your name. She reads Ackermann's mail."

"How many US dollars does the lady want, Otto?"

"Twenty-five thousand of them in small and very used bank notes. She offers to come across tonight and meet you in the British sector, she offers to supply you with a sample. If you like the quality of what she is selling, you can arrange a second meeting and conclude the deal."

Looking over at Jack, Torriti twanged at the tip of his nose with a finger. "Where? When?"

Otto suggested a small Catholic church off Reformations Platz in Spandau, not far from the Spandau U-Bahn station. Say about eleven.

"If this works out I'll owe you," Torriti told the caller.

"Harv, Harv, it is already in the ledger books."

Using his thumb and forefinger, the Sorcerer lowered the phone back onto its cradle as if a sudden gesture would cause it to explode. "Harv, Harv, it's already in the goddamn ledger books," he cheeped, mimicking Otto's voice. "I fucking know what's in the ledger books." A flaccid smile of utter bliss plastered itself across his limp jowls. He took a deep breath, peered at the wallclock, then rubbed his hands together in anticipation. "All hands on deck!" he bawled.

"What is it about Otto that makes your nose twitch?" Jack wanted to know.

The Sorcerer was happy to fill in the blanks. "My friend Otto is Herr Doktor Otto Zaisser, the second in command of an organization called Kampfgruppe gegen Unmenschlichkeit—Fighting Group against Inhumanity —set up, with a little financial help from their friends in the Pickle Factory, maybe two, maybe three years back. They work out of two tumbledown stucco houses in a back street"—Torriti waved his hand in the general direction of the American Sector—"crammed with packing crates. The packing crates are filled with index cards; each card contains the name of someone who's gone missing behind the Iron Curtain. If we need to get a line on someone in particular, Kampfgruppe can be useful. Otto himself specializes in pranks. Last year he counterfeited goddamn postage stamps bearing the portrait of Joe Stalin with a noose around his neck and stuck them on thousands of goddamn letters mailed eastward. On quiet months Kampfgruppe sends in agents to blow up the occasional Communist railroad bridge or poison the occasional herd of Communist cows."

"You still haven't explained why your nose twitched," Jack noted.

"If Otto could really put his hands on Thermofax copies of Anton Ackermann's outgoing letters, he would have begged or borrowed the twenty-five thousand and bought them himself, then turned around and peddled the collection to the Rabbi for a cool fifty grand. The Rabbi would have passed the stuff on to us for a modest seventy-five grand; he would have offered to give it to us free if we could tell him where in South America he could put his paws on Israel's Public Enemy Number One, the former head of the Gestapo's Jewish section named Adolf Eichmann."

"The Thermofaxes could be real—you won't know for sure until you see one."

With a twinkle in his eye, the Sorcerer shook his head. "I happen to know that Comrade Ackermann doesn't dictate his letters to a secretary—he is paranoid about microphones, he is paranoid about leaks, so he writes them out in longhand and seals them in envelopes that leave traces if they are tampered with."

"So your friend Otto is not your friend?"

"Knowingly or unknowingly, he's baiting a trap."

"What do you do now, Harvey?"

"I walk into it, sport."

Torriti, the tradecraft shaman capable of blending into a nonexistent crowd, shed the lazy pose of a fat man who drowned his sense of doom and gloom in PX booze and swung into action. The two Silwans and the four others chosen for the mission, along with Jack, were convoked. Miss Sipp produced a large map of Spandau, located in the British zone of Berlin, and taped it to a wall. "We have six hours to play with," Torriti told them. "All hardware will be carried out of sight. When it gets dark you will trickle one at a time into the area and take up positions. The Silwans, dressed in sackcloth and ashes, sawed-off shotguns hidden under their scapulars, will be inside the church; when I turn up I expect to see you on your knees praying for my salvation. You four will install yourselves in the darkest doorways you can find on the four corners outside the church. Jack, wearing a beat-up leather jacket and a cloth cap so that anyone spotting him will not mistake him for a Yale graduate, will drive the taxi. You'll drop me off at the door and pick me up if and when I come out. You'll have an M3 and a pile of clips on the seat next to you covered with a raincoat. Everyone will be connected to everyone by the gizmos that Miss Sipp, bless her delicate hands, will now attach to your lapels. Questions?"

Sweet Jesus wanted to know if he could take his lap dog with him.

"Priests don't usually go around with dogs on a leash," Torriti told him.

"Are we going to draw hazardous duty bonuses for this operation?" Sweet Jesus inquired.

"If there is gunfire."

Sweet Jesus persisted. "For the purposes of the bonus, will the gunfire be considered gunfire if we shoot and they don't?"

"You're squandering your natural talents in espionage," the Sorcerer told him. "You're cut out to be a lawyer who chases ambulances."

"I completed three years of law studies in Bucharest before the Communists came to power and I ran for it," Sweet Jesus reminded him.

"So much for my elephant's memory," Torriti told Jack. But nothing could dampen his high spirits.

Jack eased the taxi to the curb in front of the Catholic church as the bells in the tower began tolling eleven. He angled his jaw down to his shirt collar and said, "Whiskey leader—everyone outside set?"

One by one the Watchers in the street reported in.

"Whiskey one, roger."

"Whiskey two, roger."

"Whiskey three and four, on station."

"How about inside?" Jack asked.

There was a burst of static. "Whiskey five and six, ditto."

Torriti, wearing an old loose-fitting raincoat and clutching a bottle of gin in a paper bag, pushed open the back door of the small taxi and stumbled onto the sidewalk. He tilted his head, downed what was left in the bottle, tossed it into the back seat and slammed the car door shut with his foot. Jack leaned over and rolled down the passenger window. Torriti dragged a wallet from the hip pocket of his trousers and, holding it close to his eyes, counted out some bills. "Wait for me," he barked, gesturing with a palm.

Jack asked, *"Um wieviel Uhr?"*

"Later, goddamn it. *Später.*" Torriti straightened and belched and, walking as if he were having trouble keeping his balance, staggered toward the double door of the church.

Pulling his cap down low over his eyes, resting his hand on the stock of the M3 hidden under the raincoat on the next seat, Jack settled back to wait; from under the visor he had a good view of the two side view mirrors and the rear view mirror. From the tiny earphone he heard the progress reports:

"Whiskey two—he's gone in," one of the Americans across the street said.

"Whiskey five—I see him," Sweet Jesus was heard to mutter.

"Whiskey six—me, too, I see him," said the Fallen Angel.

Inside, the Sorcerer stopped at the shell-shaped font to dip the fingers of both hands in and splash water on his face. Shuddering, he started down the center aisle. There were a dozen or so people scattered around on the benches, praying silently. Two slender men in cowls and scapulars could be seen rocking back and forth in prayer, kneeling on either side of the aisle beside the last row; Torriti made a mental note to tell them that their style of communing with God made them look more like Hasidic Jews than Roman Catholics. As the Sorcerer headed toward the altar, a woman bundled into a man's faded green loden coat, wearing a scarf over her head and sturdy East German walking shoes, started back up the aisle. When they came abreast of each other the woman whispered, "Herr Torriti?"

The Sorcerer mimicked answering a telephone. "Speaking," he said. *"Sprechen Sie Englisch?"*

The woman said, "I am speaking some little English. Where can we go to be talking?"

Tugging at the elbow of her coat, Torriti led her into the shadows of an altar at the side of the church. He surveyed the people praying on the benches; only the two cowled figures in the back row seemed to be paying attention to them.

The Sorcerer said, "A mutual friend told me you might have some delicious goodies for sale."

"I will exhibit you *zvei* samples," the woman said. She seemed very ill at ease and anxious to get through the business at hand as quickly as possible. "You are liking what you see, we are meeting again and performing the exchange—my letters, your twenty-five thousand American dollars."

"How can you be sure I won't take the letters and refuse to pay you?"

The woman puckered her lips. "You are doing such, you are never seeing more letters, *ja*?" She thought a moment, then added, "Twenty-five thousand American dollars *billig* for what I bringing you."

"*Cheap* my balls," Torriti grunted, but he said it with a humorless smile and the woman half-smiled back.

Reaching under her coat, she pulled two folded sheets of paper from the folds of her thick skirt and handed them to Torriti. He glanced around again, then opened one and held it up to the light of a candle burning before the statue of the Madonna. He could make out a clean typescript that began with a businesslike salutation to Comrade Ulbricht and ended with the German for "Comradely greetings." The name A. Ackermann was typed at the bottom of the letter. Over the typed name was Ackermann's clearly legible signature. The second letter was addressed to the deputy Soviet *rezident* at Karlshorst, Comrade Oskar Ugor-Molody, and ended with the same comradely greetings over Ackermann's signature.

"Smells kosher to me," the Sorcerer said, pocketing the two letters. He looked around again and saw two older gentlemen leave their seats and start up the center aisle toward the back of the church. The two Silwans must have noticed them at the same moment because they began fingering the stiff objects hidden under their scapulars; Torriti knew it wasn't erections they were caressing. When the two older men reached the last row, they turned to face the altar, genuflected and crossed themselves and then, whispering intently to each other, left the church. Torriti said to the woman. "Where? When?" He scraped the bottom of the barrel for some high school German. "*Wo? Wann?*"

"*Hier,*" she replied, pointing to the Madonna. "Tomorrow *nacht*. Okay? Do you comprehend?"

"I comprehend," Torriti said. He blinked rapidly and put a hand on the statue as if to steady himself.

The woman wasn't sure what to do next, which led the Sorcerer to con-clude she was a neophyte; someone hired for a one-shot mission. She backed away, then stepped forward and offered her gloved hand. The Sorcerer scooped it up to his lips and kissed it. The woman appeared stunned. Giggling nervously, she fled between the benches and disappeared out a side door. In the back row, Sweet Jesus and the Fallen Angel looked at each other uncertainly.

The tiny speaker buried in the Sorcerer's ear purred. "Whiskey three— a female just now came out the side entrance. Subject is walking very rapidly in the direction of Breitestrasse. Wait—an old Mercedes has turned in from Breitestrasse and pulled up alongside her—she's gotten in, the car's making a U-turn, it's picking up speed, it's turned into Breitestrasse. Okay, I've lost it."

"Whiskey leader —what's next on the menu?"

The Sorcerer muttered into his collar: "This is Barfly—if something's going to happen, now is when. Stay on your toes."

He reached under his raincoat and patted the pearl handle of his revolver for luck, then ambled a bit drunkenly across the stone floor toward the double door of the church. He didn't bother to look behind him; he knew the two Silwans would be covering his back. In his ear he could hear one of the Watchers burst on the air. "Whiskey one—two males have turned in from Carl Schurzstrasse," he reported breathlessly. Jack's voice, unruffled, came over the earpiece. "Whiskey leader—everyone keep calm. I see them in my sideview, Harvey. They're passing under a street light. One is wearing a long leather coat, the other a leather jacket. They're walking toward the church very slowly."

The Sorcerer remembered Jack's jittery comportment the night they were waiting for Vishnevsky to turn up in the safe house over the movie-theater. He'd ripened on the vine in the four months since then; Torriti's original judgement—that Jack was a cut above the usual cannon fodder that came out from Washington—had been on the money. Torriti growled soft-ly into his microphone: "Whiskey three and four—come around behind them but don't crowd them. I want them to make the first move."

Pushing through the doors into the darkened street, Torriti saw the two men passing under another vapor lamp about fifty yards down the road; light glinted off the bald crown of one of them. They must have spotted the Sorcerer because they separated slightly and quickened their pace. Shuffling his feet, Torriti drifted toward the taxi parked at the curb. He could make out Jack; he seemed to be asleep behind the wheel but his right arm was reaching for something on the seat next to him. Whiskey Three and Four turned the corner and appeared behind the two figures coming up the street.

The two men were only yards away when the Sorcerer arrived at the rear door of the taxi. As he grasped the door handle one of the two pulled something metallic from his belt and lunged clumsily toward him. Moving with the grace and lightness of a fat man who had survived more street brawls than he could count, Torriti bounded to one side and melted into a crouch. The pearl-handled beauty of a revolver materialized in his fist and kicked back into it as he pulled the trigger. The shot, amplified by the darkness, reverberated through the cobblestone street as the bullet punched into his attacker's shoulder, sending him sprawling. A butcher's knife clattered to the gutter at Jack's feet as he came around the back of the taxi, running low with the M3 under an armpit, and sighted on the second man, who had the good sense to freeze in his tracks. Whiskey Three and Four, pistols drawn, came up on the run. One of them kicked the knife away from the wounded man, who was sitting with his back against the bumper, whimpering. The other frisked the bald man, standing stock-still with his hands raised over his head, and relieved him of a handgun and a small walkie-talkie.

"This was the attack, Harvey?" Jack shook his head in disbelief. "It was amateur hour—"

A small car with a blue police light flashing on its roof suddenly appeared at the end of the street. It sped toward the taxi and, with a screech of brakes, came to a stop a dozen yards away. Two doors were flung open and two men wearing the dark blue uniforms of West German *Polizei* came toward them. Both had Schmeisser submachine pistols tucked under their arms and their fingers on the triggers.

"How'd they know to get here so fast?" Jack whispered.

"Maybe it's not amateur hour after all," Torriti said under his breath.

"You having trouble?" one of the policemen called.

Jack would forever be proud of the fact that he noticed they weren't speaking German at the same instant the Sorcerer, with incredible laziness, remarked, "They're talking the King's English, sport. Shoot them."

Jack's M3 and Torriti's revolver opened fire as the two policemen, separating their feet to absorb the kick of their Schmeissers, started shooting. Jack's bullets cut down one of them, Torriti's single shot took out the other. The bald attacker standing with his hands over his head grasped his stomach and sank to his knees, hit by a stray bullet from a Schmeisser. Along the street shutters clanged open.

"Was ist hier los?" someone shouted.

"Schliesse die Fensterläden—das geht uns nichts an," a woman cried.

"Rufen Sie die Polizei," a man yelled.

"Das ist ein Polizeiauto," a teenage girl in another window yelled back.

"Time to skedaddle," the Sorcerer ordered, an elated smile spreading across his face.

"Why do you look so pleased with yourself?" Jack demanded.

"Don't you get it, kid? The fuckers tried to kidnap me!" He threw himself onto the front seat alongside Jack as the taxi sped away from the curb and, skidding around the corner, vanished into the ghostly stillness of the Berlin night.

13

BERLIN, FRIDAY, MAY 11, 1951

Holding the fort in the Sorcerer's absence, Jack had to raise his voice to be heard over the aria playing on the phonograph. He was describing the showdown in the street outside the church to two new-comers who had reported for duty in Berlin Base. "It's an old East German ruse that you should know about," he was saying. He pushed two tumblers filled with Torriti's PX whiskey across the desk, raised his glass to salute them and downed his drink in one go. "Some heavies menace you, you fight them off or beat a hasty retreat, then a police car or a taxi or an ambulance arrives on the scene, you naturally run over to it for help, they pick you up—and that's the last anybody sees of you in the Western sector. Next thing we know you are appearing before a news conference in the Soviet zone, your eyes glassy from drugs, to tell the world you have asked for political asylum in Joe Stalin's proletarian Shangri-la."

"I never came across anything like this in the newspapers," remarked one of the new recruits, his eyes wide in wonder.

"There are too many kidnappings for the newspapers to cover them all—dozens every month in Berlin alone. And they almost always follow the same pattern."

"Will that thermonuclear reaction we just set off at Eniwetok change anything in Berlin?" the other recruit asked.

"The Russians broke our monopoly on the atomic bomb," Jack said. "It won't take them long to break our monopoly on the H-bomb. Don't worry, the Cold War's not going to end before you've gotten your feet wet."

"How long you been here?" the first recruit inquired respectfully.

Jack loosened his tie and let his sports jacket fall open as he sank back into the Sorcerer's chair. He had recently taken to wearing a shoulder holster in addition to the one in the small of his back. The mahogany grip of an Italian Beretta projected from it. "A week shy of six months." He shook his head. "Damnation, time does have a way of flying here in Berlin."

"Are there any...you know, distractions," the first recruit asked.

"There are some night clubs on the Kurfürstendamm but you want to watch your ass—the place is crawling with Russians and East Germans."

Miss Sipp came in with the morning's transcripts from the Watchers monitoring assorted microphones scattered around East Berlin from the safe house near Checkpoint Charlie. "If you have questions, problems, whatever, the door is always open," Jack called. As the two recruits departed he began to leaf through the transcripts, looking for the take from the teardrop the Hungarian plumbers had embedded in Herr Professor's floorboards. There had been long rambling SNIPER transcripts every morning since the microphone was put into service twelve days before; of limited value from an intelligence point of view, the transcripts had come out of the Watcher's typewriters looking vaguely like dialogue for a radio soap opera. This morning, inexplicably, there was zilch from SNIPER. Jack sat up straight and went through the transcripts again.

"How come there's nothing from the SNIPER microphone?" he hollered out to Miss Sipp.

She stuck her head in the Sorcerer's door. "I was curious, too, so I got one of the Watchers on the horn—he said that particular teardrop has dried up."

"Check again, huh?"

"Still no joy," Miss Sipp reported later in the morning. "They're telling me there are two possibilities. Possibility number one: Someone discovered the microphone and removed it. Possibility number two: RAINBOW and/or SNIPER may be in the hands of the KGB."

"The sons of bitches left out possibility number three," Jack blurted out, his words infused with seething irritability. "The microphone and/or one of the transmitters may be defective."

"They tested the material before they installed it," Miss Sipp said quietly. Ironing out the wrinkles in her skirt with a palm, she came around the desk and touched her finger tips to the back of Jack's wrist in a sisterly way. "Face the music, Jack. You've become emotionally involved with your courier. This is definitely not a healthy situation."

Jack shook off her hand. "I never figured out why Harvey wanted me to bug them in the first place—he's getting everything SNIPER knows spelled out on pieces of silk."

"Mr. Torriti is a very methodical person, Jack. Count on him to cover angles others don't know exist."

Jack turned up early at the rehearsal hall on Hardenbergstrasse for the regular Friday night rendezvous with Lili, only to discover a hand-printed sign taped to Aristide's cubbyhole. It announced that Lili's dance classes had been cancelled until further notice. At wit's end, Jack dispatched an all-points enquiry to Berlin Base's army of informers asking if anyone had gotten wind of an important arrest in the Soviet sector. The answers that came filtering back reassured him slightly: There had been no visible signs of any earth-shaking arrests. The KGB officers at Karlshorst were preoccupied with a new Moscow Centre regulation requiring officers being rotated back to the Motherland to pay a stiff duty on furniture, clothing, automobiles, motor scooters and bicycles imported from the German Democratic Republic; there even had been some talk of circulating a petition but the *rezident*, General Ilichev, had chewed out the ringleaders and nipped the proto-rebellion in the bud. Still not satisfied, Jack got hold of the Berlin Base listening-station logs recording radio traffic into and out of Karlshorst. Again, there was nothing out of the ordinary. He read through the last few days of reports from Watchers keeping an eye on Soviet airports. There were the usual flights, all scheduled. Jack even had the Fallen Angel check the private dance school on Alexanderplatz where Lili taught mornings; a note on the concierge's window said that, until further notice, Fraülein Mittag's class would be taught by Frau Haeckler. On the way back to the American zone the Fallen Angel had dropped by the caretaker's flat under the Professor's apartment to see if her spanking new Czech radio was functioning properly; to see, also, if he could pry out of her news of the whereabouts of the couple who lived overhead. The radio, the Fallen Angel told Jack, had been tuned to the Radio Liberty wavelength in Munich. The arthritis medicine hadn't had much of an effect on the pain. The people who lived upstairs were away. Period.

Hoping against hope that there was an innocent explanation for RAINBOW's dropping from sight, Jack went to the Tuesday night rendezvous. The sign posted on Aristide's cubbyhole cancelling dance lessons was gone. As suddenly as she had disappeared, Lili reappeared. Watching from the shadows of the doorway across from the stage entrance, Jack monitored her arrival. Nobody seemed to be following her. Two hours later her students duck-walked off after the class. Rushing into the narrow corridor that reeked of sweat and talcum powder, taking the steps three at a time, Jack burst into the top floor rehearsal hall to discover Lili standing with her back arched and one long leg stretched out along the barre.

Gripping her wrist, he pried her away from the barre. "Where have you been?" he demanded harshly.

"Please, you are hurting me—"

"I was afraid you'd been—"

"I could not think of how to get word to you—"

"If you'd been arrested—"

Jack let go of her wrist. They both took a deep breath. "Jack-in-the-box," Lili whispered. She placed the flat of her palm on his solar plexus and pushed him back and shook her head once and then, sighing like a child, folded herself into his arms. "Herr Professor's brother died suddenly...we had to go to Dresden for the funeral. We stayed a few days in order to help his wife put things in order...there were bank accounts, there was an insurance policy. Oh, Jack, this is not possible. What are we to do?"

"Give me time," he said. "I'll think of something."

"What permits you to hope that time exist for us?" she murmured, breathing words into his ear that were as moist and as warm as a square of silk.

Jack crushed her to him. "Spend a night with me, Lili," he pleaded. "Only one."

"No," she said, clinging to him. "I must not..." Her voice trailed off weakly.

Lili twisted in the narrow wooden bed so that her back was toward Jack. Pressing into her, he buried his mouth in the nape of her neck and ran a calloused palm along the curve of her hip. Her voice, husky from hours of love-making, drifted back over a lean shoulder. "Did you ever notice how, when a train goes very quickly, everything close to the tracks becomes blurred? But if you blink your eyes rapidly you can stop the motion for an instant, you can freeze the images. You are going by me tonight with the speed of light, Jacklight. In the eye of my mind—"

"In your mind's eye—"

"Yes, in my mind's eye I blink to stop the motion and freeze the images of us copulating."

Jack could feel the sleekness and hardness of a dancer's muscles along her thigh. "Describe what you see."

"I have, of course, experienced physical love before...but it has been a long long while since..."

Jack thought of the Fallen Angel snapping open his small telescope and seeing Lili fall into the embrace of an older man with snow-white hair. "Start at the start," Jack said. "We'll relive tonight together."

Lili shuddered. "I consent, the last time we see each other in the rehearsal hall, to meet you at this small hotel for voyagers in the French sector. I tell Herr Professor I am spending the night with my childhood girl-friend in Potsdam; I am surprised not so much by the lie as the fact that it passes effortlessly through my lips. I do as you instructed me—I walk the wrong way down single-direction streets to be positive I am not being followed. Then, my heart beating wildly, I walk directly here."

Jack laughed into her neck. "I also made sure you weren't being followed."

"The clerk at the desk smiles knowingly when she gives me the key but I do not feel embarrassed. The opposite is true—I feel proud...proud that someone as beautiful as you, Jackstraw, has so much desire for me."

"Desire is a weak word, Lili."

"I wait in the room until I hear the sound of your steps on the landing. I have listened for them so many times in the theater that I recognize them immediately. I open the door. This is the precise point at which things began to move quickly...to blur."

"Blink. Describe the snapshots."

"Snap? Shots?"

"That's what cameras do—they freeze images. We call them snapshots."

"I will attempt it. I see me, unable to find words with which to greet you, reaching up to unfasten my earrings."

"The gesture took my breath away, Lili. It seemed to me that all life can offer in the way of intimacy begins with you taking off your earrings."

"I see you pulling your shirt over your head. I see you removing an ugly object from your belt and sliding it under the pillow. I watch you unbut-toning my dress. I fold my garments as you take them off and place them carefully on a chair, which amuses you—I can suppose, in the style of Americans, you would prefer to have me throw them on the floor. I feel the back of your hand brush against the skin of my breast. Oh, I see the melt-ing together of our clothes-less bodies, I see your eyes wide open as you press your mouth against my mouth—"

"Your eyes must have been open to notice."

"I did not want to miss any part of the ballet."

"Give me more images, Lili."

"More snapshots, yes. I possess images for a lifetime of remembering. You carry me to this bed, you loom over me in the faint light coming from the left-open door of the closet, you caress my unused body with your enor-mous hands and your famished mouth." Lili sighed into the pillow. "You enter slowly into me, you manipulate me this way and that, now you are fac-ing me, now you are behind me, now I am on top of you or alongside you.

You are very good at this business of love-making."

"It is the woman who makes the man good at the business of love-making," Jack said, discovering a truth when he heard himself say it. "We are good lovers with a very few, unremarkable lovers with most and lousy lovers with some. It is not something to be taken for granted, being a good lover. It is never for sure."

"We do not have a long time together," Lili warned him.

"Whatever time we have is enough to persuade me that your images are more powerful than my fantasies."

They dozed for a while, then came awake as the first sounds of traffic reached their ears and the first gray streaks of dawn reached their eyes. Jack started to make love to her again but she murmured that she was sore and he was hurting her and he stopped. Lili got out of bed and washed at the bidet behind the screen in the corner of the room and dressed. They had breakfast, stale rolls and margarine and jelly and hot chocolate made with powdered milk, in the small room behind the concierge's office.

Out on the sidewalk Lili's face darkened. "And how shall we say goodbye?"

"We won't," Jack said. "When I was a kid my mother used to take me to Atlantic City every Thanksgiving. I remember standing on the beach at the edge of the ocean, my knickerbockers pulled up above my knees, watching as the tide washed the sand out from under my bare feet each time it receded. It left me feeling dizzy, lightheaded. Your going, like the tide's, gives me the same feeling."

"I am the sand under your bare feet." Lili turned away to look at men with blackened faces, who were carting sacks of coal from a truck into the basement of an apartment building. "Life is an accumulation of small mistakes," she said suddenly.

"Why do you speak of mistakes?" Jack asked in annoyance. "To tell me that our night together was a mistake?"

"That is not at all what I meant. It is my way of telling you in one or two sentences the story of my life," she explained. "I have concluded that the problem is not so much the accumulation of small mistakes but the big ones we make trying to correct them."

Later that night the teardrop planted in SNIPER's floorboards detected the sound of voices, activating the transmitter hidden in the lighting fixture below. In the morning a transcript arrived on Jack's desk. It was filled with half-garbled fragments of sentences from people walking into and out of the room, rumors of a famous marriage on the rocks, a hurried declaration of undying devotion from an older man to a younger woman, the punch line of an anti-Soviet joke, a flowery tribute to someone's cooking. It was pretty much what the microphone had been picking up from the start: the inconsequential prattle of a couple in the privacy of their own apartment, as opposed to intelligence secrets, which SNIPER collected at the university or in government offices. After a while there was a long silence, followed by a quiet and intense conversation between what sounded like a German (obviously SNIPER) and a Pole talking in the only language they had in common, which was English.

It was the transcription of this conversation that intrigued Jack. The text contained details of bacteriological warfare testing on the Baltic island of Rügen, uranium production in the Joachimstal area of the Harz Mountains and the latest Soviet nuclear fission experiments in Central Asia. Then the two men chatted about friends they had in common and what had happened to them over the years; one had died of colon cancer, another had left his wife for a younger woman, still another had defected to the French and now lived in Paris. Suddenly the Pole mentioned that he supposed the Russians had an important spy in British intelligence. How could he know such a thing, asked the older man, obviously surprised. The conversation broke off when a woman's footsteps came back into the room. There was some murmured thanks for the brandy, the clink of glass against glass. The microphone picked up the woman's cat-like footfalls as she quit the room. The older man repeated his question: how could his guest possibly know the Russians had a spy in British intelligence. Because the Polish intelligence service, the UB, was in possession of a highly classified British intelligence document, the Pole said. He had seen the document with his own eyes. It was a copy of the British MI6's "watch list" for Poland. What is a watch list? the older man inquired. It was a list of Polish nationals that MI6's Warsaw Station considered potential assets and worth cultivating. The list could have been stolen from British intelligence agents in Warsaw, the older man suggested. No, no, the Pole maintained. The copy he had seen bore internal routing marks and initials indicating it had been circulated to a limited number of MI6 intelligence officers, none of whom was serving in Warsaw.

The conversation moved on to other things—news of friction between the Polish Communists and the Russians, the suppression of a Warsaw magazine for publishing an article about the massacre of thousands of Polish officers in Katyn Forest near Smolensk in 1943, a spirited discussion of whether the Germans or the Russians had killed the Poles (both men agreed it had been the Russians), a promise to keep in touch, a warning that letters on both sides were likely to be opened. Then RAINBOW's voice could be heard saying goodbye to the Pole. There were heavy footsteps on the staircase, followed by the sound of glasses being cleared away and a door closing.

Looking up from the transcript, Jack produced a new series of snapshots: he could see SNIPER removing his old-fashioned starched collar and the studs from his shirt; he could see RAINBOW reaching up to take off her earrings, he could see the smile on her lips as she remembered the effect the gesture had had on Jack; he could see her coming back from the toilet in a shapeless cotton nightdress; he could see her turning down the cover of the four poster bed and slipping under the sheets next to the man to whom she owed so much.

Shaking off the images, Jack reread the passages concerning the Soviet spy in MI6. If the Sorcerer wasn't already on his way to Washington to flaunt his barium meals in Mother's face and unmask the Soviet mole, he would have delivered this new serial to him right away. No matter. The gist of the conversation would turn up in SNIPER's distinctive handwriting on the warm silk that Jack would extract with his own fingers from Lili's brassiere.

14

WEARING A SOILED GARDENER'S APRON OVER AN OLD SHIRT AND washed-out chinos, James Jesus Angleton was sweeping the aisles of the greenhouse he had recently installed in the back yard of his suburban Arlington house, across the Potomac from the District of Columbia and the Pickle Factory on the Reflecting Pool. "What I'm doing," he said, a soggy cigarette glued to his lower lip, a hacking cough scratching at the back of his throat, a dormant migraine lurking under his eyelids, "is breeding a hybrid orchid known as a 'Cattleya cross.' Cattleya is a big corsage orchid that comes in a rainbow of colors. If I succeed in crossing a new Cattleya, I plan to call it the Cicely Angleton after my wife."

The Sorcerer loosened the knot of his tie and slung his sports jacket over the back of a bamboo chair. He shrugged out of his shoulder holster, and hung it and the pearl-handled revolver from the knob of a ventilation window. "I'm a goddamn Neanderthal when it comes to flowers, Jim. So I'll bite—how does someone cross an orchid?"

"For God's sake, don't *sit* on it," Angleton cried when he saw Torriti starting to back his bulky body into the chair. "The bamboo won't hold your weight. Sorry. Sorry."

"It's all right."

"I am sorry." Angleton went back to his sweeping. Out of the corner of his eye he kept track of Torriti, who began meandering aimlessly around the aisles running his finger tips over clay pots and small jars and gardening tools set out on a bamboo table. "Crossing orchids is a very long and very tedious process," Angleton called across the greenhouse, "not unlike the business of counterespionage."

"You don't say."

Angleton abruptly stopped sweeping. "I do say. Trying to come up with a hybrid involves taking the pollen from one flower and inseminating it into another. Ever read any of Rex Stout's mystery novels? He's got a detective named Nero Wolfe who breeds orchids in his spare time. Terrific writer, Rex Stout. You ought to get hold of him."

"I'm too busy solving goddamn mysteries to read goddamn mystery novels," Torriti remarked. "So what makes crossing orchids like counterespionage?"

Leaning on the broom handle, Angleton bent his head and lit a fresh cigarette from the embers of the one in his mouth. Then he flicked the butt into a porcelain spittoon overflowing with cigarette stubs. "It can take twelve months for the seedpod to develop," he explained, "at which point you plant the seed in one of those small jars there. Please don't knock any of them over, Harvey. It takes another twelve months for the seed to grow an inch or two. The eventual flowering, if there is a flowering, could take another five years. Counterespionage is like that—you nurture seeds in small jars for years, you keep the temperature moist and hot, you hope the seeds will flower one day but there's no guarantee. You need the patience of a saint, which is what you don't have, Harvey. Orchid breeding and counterintelligence are not your cup of tea."

Torriti came around an aisle to confront Angleton. "Why do you say that, Jim?"

"I remember you back in Italy right after the war. You were guilty of the capital crime of impatience." Angleton's rasping voice, the phrases he used, suddenly had a whetted edge to them. "You were obsessed about getting even with anybody who was perceived to have crossed you—your friends in the Mafia, the Russians, me."

"And people say *I* have the memory of an elephant!"

"Remember Rome, Harvey? Summer, nineteen forty-six? You lost an agent, he turned up in a garbage dump with his fingers and head missing. You identified him from an old bullet wound that the doctors who performed the autopsy mistook for an appendicitis scar. You were quite wild, you took it personally, as if someone had spit in your face. You didn't sleep for weeks while you walked back the cat on the affair. You narrowed the suspects down to eight, then four, then two, then one. You decided it had been the mistress of the dead man. Funny thing is you may have been right. We never got a chance to question her, to find out whom she worked for, to play her back. She drowned under what the *carabinieri* described as mysterious circumstances—she apparently stripped to the skin and went swimming off a boat at midnight. Curious part was she didn't own a boat and couldn't swim."

"She couldn't swim because there was a goddamn chunk of scrap iron tied to her goddamn ankle," Torriti said. He laughed under his alcoholic breath. "I was young and impetuous in those days. Now that I've grown up I'd use her. When she'd been used up, *that's* when I'd tie the goddamn iron to her goddamn ankle and throw her overboard." Torriti hiked up his baggy trousers, which tapered and came to a point at the ankles; Angleton caught a glimpse of another holster strapped to one ankle. "There's a bond between an agent and his handler, an umbilical cord, the kind of thing that exists between a father and a son," Torriti was saying. "You're too analytical to get a handle on it, Jim. You've got dazzling theories into which you fit everything. I don't have theories. What I know I pick up the hard way—I get my hands and knees dirty working in the goddamn field."

"You operate on the surface of things. I dig deeper." Angleton wearied of the sparring. "What did you have to tell me that couldn't wait until Monday morning?"

"I'm in the process of writing a memorandum to the Director laying out the case that your pal Philby is a Soviet spy. Has been since the early thirties. As you're the Company's counterintelligence honcho, I thought it was only fair to give you some advance warning. On top of that, I thought we ought to take precautions to make sure Philby doesn't blow the coop."

"You'll only make a fool of yourself, Harvey."

"I have the son-of-a-bitch by the balls, Jim."

"You want to lay out the case for me."

"That's what brought me across the goddamn Potomac on a drizzly Sunday afternoon when I could be drinking in my goddamn hotel room."

Angleton leaned the broom against the side of the greenhouse and produced a small pad from his hip pocket. "Mind if I make notes?"

"No skin off my goddamn nose."

Pulling the bamboo chair up to the bamboo table, pushing aside his gardening tools to make room for the pad, Angleton fingered the pencil he used for filling in his gardening log and looked up, the barest trace of a condescending smile on his lips.

The Sorcerer, patrolling behind him, began with the story of Philby's membership in the Cambridge Socialist Society in the early thirties, his pilgrimage to riot-torn Vienna, his marriage to a rabid Red (Angleton's Israeli friend, Teddy Kollek, had known about the wedding), his efforts after he returned to England to paper over his left-wing leanings by turning up at German embassy parties and nursing a reputation for being pro-German. Then came the *Times* assignment to cover Franco's side during the Spanish Civil War.

Angleton glanced up. "Adrian has been vetted a dozen times over the years—none of this breaks new ground."

Torriti rambled on, raising the Krivitsky serial which, according to Elihu Epstein, the Brits had never shared with their American cousins.

"Krivitsky was debriefed when he reached this side of the Atlantic," Angleton remembered. He closed his eyes and quoted the serial from memory. "There is a Soviet mole, code named PARSIFAL and handled by a master spy known by the nickname Starik, working in British intelligence. The mole worked for a time as a journalist in Spain during the Civil War." Opening his eyes, Angleton snickered. "Krivitsky was telling us there was a needle in the haystack in the hope we'd take him seriously."

"Somebody took him seriously—he was murdered in Washington in 1941."

"The official police report listed his death as a suicide."

Torriti turned in a complete circle, as if he were winding himself up, then asked if Angleton was aware that Philby had signed out MI6 Source Books on the Soviet Union long before he became involved in Soviet counterespionage.

"No, I didn't know that but, knowing Adrian, knowing how thorough he is, I would have been surprised if he hadn't signed out those Source Books."

Which brings us to Vishnevsky, the Sorcerer said, the would-be defector who told us he could finger a Soviet mole in MI6.

"Which brings us to Vishnevsky," Angleton agreed.

The night of the aborted exfiltration, Torriti plunged on, KGB Karlshorst sent Moscow Centre an Urgent Immediate—the Sorcerer happened to have a copy of the clear text—thanking Moscow for the early warning that prevented the defection of Lieutenant Colonel Volkov/Vishnevsky, his wife and his son. "Once Vishnevsky claimed he could identify a Soviet mole in MI6," Torriti said, "I was careful not to include any Brits on the Vishnevsky distribution list. So tell me something, Jim. I'm told you hang out with Philby at La Niçoise, not to mention that he drops by your office whenever he shows up at the Pickle Factory. Did you mention Vishnevsky to your British pal? Spill the beans, Jim. Did you tell him we had someone claiming he could identify a Soviet mole in MI6?"

Angleton set down his pencil. He appeared to be talking to himself. "To begin with, there is no hard evidence that there is a Soviet mole in MI6—"

"Vishnevsky claimed there was—"

"Vishnevsky wouldn't have been the first defector to make himself appear valuable by claiming to have a gold ingot."

"All the pieces fit," Torriti insisted.

"All the pieces are circumstantial," Angleton said coolly; he was talking down to Torriti again. "All the pieces could point to any one of two or three dozen Brits." Sucking on his cigarette, he twisted in the bamboo chair until he was facing Torriti. "I *know* Adrian as well as I know anyone in the world," he announced with sudden vehemence. "I know what makes him tick, I know what he's going to say, the attitude he'll take in a given situation, before he opens his mouth and starts to stutter. I'd trust Adrian with my life. He couldn't be spying for the Russians! He represents everything I admire in the British." A haze of cigarette smoke obscured the expression on Angleton's face as he confessed, "Adrian is the person I would have liked to be."

Torriti produced a rumpled handkerchief and mopped the humidity off his palms. "Would you trust him with your *Cattleya* if it ever blooms?" Smirking at his own joke, he raised the matter of the agent drops into Poland and the Ukraine that had all ended in disaster. Philby, as MI6's liaison in Washington, had known about these drops.

"You parachute a bunch of courageous but amateur recruits into the lion's den and then you're surprised to discover they've been eaten alive."

Torriti wandered off and picked up a small jar with a tiny bud breaking through the earth in it.

"I'd appreciate it if you wouldn't handle the merchandise," Angleton called over. "They are extremely fragile."

The Sorcerer set the jar in its rack and ambled back. Pulling out his own notebook, wetting a thumb and leafing back the pages, he began to walk Angleton through his series of barium meals. He had sent one off to every single person on the Washington end who might have betrayed the Vishnevsky exfiltration. All of the barium messages had looked as if they were distributed widely but the distribution had been limited in each case to a single person or a single office. All of the operations he had exposed in the meals remained in place—all, that is, except the Albanian operation. The barium meal spelling out the Albanian caper had gone to the inter-agency Special Policy Committee, of which Philby was a member.

"There are sixteen members of the Special Policy Committee," Angleton noted, "not counting aides and secretaries who are cleared to read everything that passes through the committee's hands."

"Know that," Torriti said. "That's why I narrowed the field down with a last barium meal. I had it sent to Philby himself. I let him know that I *knew* the identity of the Soviet mole in MI6. Two days later the Russians set me up for a kidnapping."

Angleton shook his head. "Russians kidnap people all the time—not surprising they'd try to get their hands on the head of Berlin Base." Suddenly a gleam appeared in Angleton's dark Mexican eyes. He snapped shut his notebook and stood up. "There was one more barium meal you haven't mentioned, Harvey. Unfortunately for you it punctures a gaping hole in your case against Adrian. What's your single best intelligence source in the Soviet zone of Berlin? SNIPER, by far. He is not only a theoretical physicist who has access to Soviet atomic secrets but a Deputy Prime Minister of the German Democratic Republic, someone extremely high up in the *nomen-klatura*—someone who one day could conceivably become Prime Minister. Who services SNIPER? A courier code-named RAINBOW. You fed me this information in one of your so-called barium meals. I don't mind telling you I shared it with Adrian. If Adrian is your Soviet mole, how come SNIPER and RAINBOW weren't blown?"

The Sorcerer retrieved his holster and, dipping his left arm through the loop, buckled it across his barrel chest. "You never did say whether you passed on the Vishnevsky serial to your pal."

Angleton, tracing a series of petals in the film of humidity coating a pane of greenhouse glass, appeared to be in the middle of a conversation he was having with himself. "Adrian can't be a Soviet mole—all these years, all these operations. It is inconceivable."

15

GETTYSBURG, SATURDAY, MAY 26, 1951

EUGENE STOOD ON THE CREST OF CEMETERY HILL, GAZING ACROSS the killing ground that sloped down to Seminary Ridge. "They came from there," he said, pointing with the flat of his hand to the woods at the bottom of the fields. "Pickett's lunatic charge—the high water mark of the Confederacy. At midafternoon thirteen thousand Rebels started across the no-man's land, muskets leveled at their waists, bayonets fixed, battle flags flying, drums beating, dogs barking, half the men pissing in their trousers. If they had been Russian soldiers, they would have shouted: 'To the success of our hopeless task!' The objective was the Union line, stretched out along this ridge over to the Big Round Top. The Union gunners held their fire until they could hear the Rebels calling encouragement to each other. Then seventeen hundred muskets fired at once. A moan went up from the soldiers in the fields. Union grapeshot raked the Confederate ranks; the Yankee cannons became so hot their gunners burned their fingers firing and loading, firing and loading. When the cannons and the muskets fell silent, the battlefield was strewn with limbs and awash with blood. Only half of those who started out made it back to the woods. General Lee is supposed to have ridden up to Pickett and ordered him to rally his division against the counterattack that was sure to chase him back across the Potomac. Pickett is supposed to have told Lee that he no longer had a division to rally."

Philby raised a palm to shield his eyes from the bright sun and squinted across the Gettysburg countryside. "Where did a B-b-bolshevik like you learn about the American Civil War?"

Given the situation, Eugene didn't want to pass on personal information that, if divulged, could one day help the FBI identify him. After all, how many Russian exchange students had studied American history at Yale? "At Lomonosov State University in Moscow," he replied evenly.

Philby snickered. "There's a ropey story if I ever heard one. Forget I asked."

A guide leading a group of visitors up the hill could be heard reciting Lincoln's Gettysburg address. "'...are engaged in a great Civil War, testing whether that nation or any nation so conceived and so dedicated can long endure.'"

"Bloody pertinent question, you want my view." Philby, a paper grocery bag tucked under one arm, took Eugene's elbow and steered him away from the group. They strolled along the ridge, past children spooning ice cream out of Dixie Cups, past a family picnicking in the shade of a tree, until they were out of earshot. Eugene asked, "You're sure you weren't followed?"

"That's why I was late," Philby said. "I went round in bloody circles better p-p-part of an hour playing lost. Stopped to ask a gas station attendant directions to Antietam in Maryland, just in case. What you have to tell me must be bloody important to drag me away from my creature comforts on a Saturday, Eugene."

"The news isn't good," Eugene admitted.

Surveying the battlefield, Philby let this sink in. "Didn't think it would be," he muttered.

Tuning in the Moscow frequency on the Motorola the night before, Eugene had picked up one of his personal codes ("That's correct. 'But if I'm not the same, the next question is, Who in the world am I? Ah, that's the great puzzle!' is definitely from *Alice in Wonderland*") on the cultural quiz program. Using the lucky ten-dollar bill, he had transformed the winning lottery number into a Washington-area telephone number and called it at midnight from a public phone booth. He found himself talking to the woman with the thick Polish accent. "Gene, is that you? A small packet has been attached to the back of the garbage bin in the parking lot," she said, all business. "In it is an envelope. Memorize the contents, burn the instructions and carry them out immediately." The woman cleared her throat. "Your mentor, the Old Man, wishes you to tell our mutual friend that he regrets things turned out this way. Say to him the Old Man wishes him a safe journey and looks forward eagerly to seeing him again. I would be pleased to talk more with you but I have been instructed not to." Then the line went dead.

Eugene dialed Bernice's number. "I had a fantastic day," she said breathlessly. "I got forty-four new signatures on my Rosenberg petition."

"I won't be coming over tonight," he told her.

"Oh?"

"Something important came up."

He could hear the disappointment in her voice. "Naturally I understand. Tomorrow, then."

"Tomorrow for sure."

Eugene went out behind the liquor store and felt around between the back of the garbage bin and the wall until he discovered the packet taped to the bin. Locking himself in the attic apartment, he tore open the envelope and extracted a sheet of paper crammed with four-number code groups. Working from a one-time pad hidden inside the cover of a matchbook, he deciphered the message, which had come from Starik himself. Eugene committed the contents to memory, repeating it several times to be sure he had it down pat, then burned the letter and the one-time pad in a saucepan and flushed the ashes down the toilet. Grabbing two bottles of Lagavulin Malt Whisky from a shelf in the liquor store, jumping into the station wagon parked in the alley, he headed along Canal Road to Arizona Avenue, then turned onto Nebraska and pulled up in front of the two-story brick house with the large bay window. Another automobile was parked behind Philby's car in the driveway. Eugene left the motor running and went up the walkway and rang the bell. After a moment the vestibule light came on and the front door opened. A disheveled Philby, wine stains on his shirt front, peered out at him, his eyes puffy from alcohol and lack of sleep. For an instant he couldn't seem to place Eugene. When it dawned on him who his visitor was, he seemed startled. "I d-d-didn't order anything—" he mumbled, half-looking back over his shoulder.

"Yes, you did," Eugene insisted.

"Who is it, Adrian?" someone called from inside the house.

"Liquor delivery, Jimbo. D-d-didn't want the river to run dry on us, did I?"

Through the open door Eugene caught a glimpse of a gaunt, stoop-shouldered figure pulling a book from a shelf and leafing through it. "There's a time, a place, some instructions written in plain text on the inside cover of one of the cartons," Eugene whispered. "Don't forget to burn it." He handed Philby an invoice. Philby disappeared into the house and returned counting out bills from a woman's snap purse. "Keep the change, old boy," he said in a voice loud enough to be overheard.

"In a hundred years you'd never guess who was visiting me when you d-d-dropped by so unexpectedly last night." Philby was saying now. They had reached the commemorative stone marking the furthest Confederate advance of Pickett's charge on July 3, 1863. "It was the illustrious Jimbo Angleton himself, Mr. Counterintelligence in the flesh, come to commiserate with me—seems like one of the Company underlings, a rum chap from Berlin with an Italian-sounding name, has d-d-decided I'm the rotter who's been giving away CIA secrets to the ghastly KGB."

"Angleton told you that!"

"Jimbo and I go back to the Creation," Philby explained. "He knows I couldn't be a Soviet mole." He had a good chuckle at this, though it was easy to see his heart wasn't in it.

"I'm afraid it's not a laughing matter," Eugene remarked. "Did you bring all your paraphernalia with you."

"Stuff's here in the bag," Philby said morosely.

"You didn't leave anything behind? Sorry, but I was told to ask you this." Philby shook his head.

Eugene took the paper bag filled with the objects that would doom Philby if the Americans discovered them—one-time pads, miniature cameras, film canisters, microdot readers, a volume of poems by William Blake with instructions for emergency dead drops rolled up in a hollow in the binding. "I'll get rid of this—I'll go home on back roads and bury it somewhere."

"Why all the alarums? Just b-b-because one cheeky bugger comes out of the woodwork and wags a finger at me is no reason to p-p-push the bloody p-p-p-p"—Philby, clearly unnerved, had trouble spitting out the words. "Panic button." Annoyed with himself, he took a deep breath. "Dodgy business, living on the cutting edge," he muttered. "Hard on the nerves. Time to let the bloody cat out of the bloody bag, hey? What's up? Didn't Burgess warn Maclean in time? Didn't Maclean get off ahead of the coppers?"

"Maclean left England last night. He's on his way to Moscow via East Germany."

"Wizard. Where's the bloody p-p-problem?"

"Burgess lost his nerve and went with him."

"Burgess buggered off!" Philby looked away quickly. Breathing in little gasps, he scrubbed his lips with the back of his hand. "The bloody little bastard! That *is* hard cheese."

"The British will discover Maclean is missing when they turn up Monday morning to question him about the HOMER business. Won't take them long to figure out Burgess has skipped with him. At which point the alarm bells will go off in London and Washington."

"And all those beady eyes will focus on yours truly," Philby said gloomily.

"Burgess got you into this business," Eugene agreed. "Until he headed back to England to warn Maclean, he was boarding with you in Washington. On top of that there are half a dozen serials that point in your direction. You knew from Angleton that the Americans had deciphered bits of text that identified Maclean as the Soviet agent HOMER. You knew the British were going to take him into custody and begin questioning him Monday morning. Then there are the émigré operations that ended in disaster. There is the business of the Vishnevsky defection." Eugene thought he had made his case. "The *rezident* figures you have thirty-six hours to get out of the country. You brought your backup passport with you, I hope."

"So Starik wants me to run for it, then?"

"He doesn't think you have a choice." Eugene pulled the small package from his jacket. "There's hair dye, a mustache, eyeglasses, forty-eight hundred dollars in ten- and twenty-dollar bills. I have an old raincoat for you in the station wagon. We'll remove your license plates and leave your car here—it'll take the local police a couple of days to trace it to you, by which time you'll be far away. I'll drop you at the Greyhound terminal in Harrisburg. The route is written out in the package—Harrisburg to Buffalo to Niagara Falls, where you cross to the Canadian side. A car will be waiting to take you to a safe house in Halifax. Starik's people will put you on a freighter bound for Poland."

Eugene could see trouble coming; Philby's eyes were clouding over. He put a hand on the Englishman's shoulder. "You've been on the firing line for twenty years. It's time for you to come home."

"Home!" Philby took a step back. "I am a C-c-communist and a M-m-marxist but Russia is not my *home*. England is."

Eugene started to say something but Philby cut him off. "Sorry, old boy, but I don't see myself living in Moscow, do I? What I relished all these years, aside from serving the great Cause, was the great *game*. In Moscow there will be no game, only airless offices and stale routines and dull bureaucrats who know whose side I'm on."

Eugene's instructions had not dealt with the possibility that Philby would refuse Starik's order to run for it. He decided to reason with him. "Their interrogators are skillful—they will offer you immunity if you cooperate, they will try and turn you into a triple agent—"

Philby bristled. "I have never been a double agent—I have served one master from the beginning—so how can I become a triple agent?"

"I didn't mean to suggest they would succeed..."

Philby, his eyes narrowed, his jaw thrust forward, was weighing his chances and beginning to like what he saw. A thin smile illuminated his face;

it made him look almost healthy. His stutter vanished. "All the government have to go on is circumstantial evidence. A bitch of a Communist wife twenty years back, governor, where's the tort? Half a dozen moldy serials, some coincidences that I can explain away as coincidences. And I have an ace up my sleeve, don't I?"

"An ace up your sleeve?"

"Berlin Base has a big operation going—a highly placed defector delivering them goodies twice a week. I passed this on to Moscow Centre but for reasons that are a mystery to me they didn't close it down. I can hear the dialogue now: do you really think this operation would still be running, governor, if I were on the KGB payroll? Not bloody likely! Christ, man, when you boil off the bouillon *there is no hard evidence*. All I need to do is keep my nerve and bluff it out."

"They broke Klaus Fuchs—they managed to get him to confess."

"You are relatively new at this business, Eugene," Philby said. He was standing straighter, gathering confidence from the sound of his own voice. "What you do not appreciate is that the inquisitors are in a desperately weak position. Without a confession, old boy, their evidence is conjectural—too bloody vague to be used in court. Besides which, if they were to take my case to court, they'd have to blow agents and operations." Philby, shifting his weight onto the balls of his feet and circling Eugene, was almost prancing with excitement now. "As long as I refuse to confess, the jammy bastards won't be able to lay a glove on me, will they? Oh, my career will be out onto the hard but I will be free as a lark. The great game can go on."

Eugene played his last card. "You and I are foot soldiers in a war," he told Philby. "Our vision is limited—we only see the part of the battlefield that is right in front of our eyes. Starik sees the big picture—the whole war, the complex maneuvers and counter-maneuvers of each side. Starik has given you an order. As a soldier you have no choice in the matter. You must obey it." He held out the package. "Take it and run," he said.

16

THE DIRECTOR'S REGULAR NOON POWWOW HAD BEEN CANCELLED and an ad hoc war council had been hurriedly convened in the small, windowless conference room across the hall from his office. The DCI, Bedell Smith, sitting under a framed copy of one of his favorite Churchill dictums ("Men occasionally stumble over the truth but most of them pick themselves up and hurry off as if nothing had happened"), presided from the head of the oval table. Present were the Barons who could be rounded up on short notice: the DD/O, Allen Dulles; his chief of operations, Frank Wisner; Wisner's number two, Dick Helms; General Truscott, who happened to be in Washington on Pentagon business; Jim Angleton; and (in Angleton's words, muttered as the participants queued for coffee in the corridor while the Technical Service's housekeepers swept the conference room for bugs) "the star of the show, the one and only...Har*vey* Tor*riti*!"

General Smith, who had spent the weekend reviewing the Sorcerer's memorandum and Angleton's written rebuttal, wasn't "tickled pink," as he delicately put it, to discover he had been on the receiving end of one of Torriti's barium meals. "Nothing's sacred round here," he griped, "if you think the leak could come from the DCI's office."

Torriti, shaved, shined, decked out in a tie and sports jacket and a freshly laundered shirt, was uncommonly low-keyed, not to mention sober. "Couldn't make my case that the leaks came from Philby," he pointed out, "if I hadn't foreclosed the alternatives."

Dulles, puffing away on his pipe, remarked pleasantly, "According to Jim, you haven't made your case." He slipped his toes out of the bedroom slippers he always wore in the office because of gout and propped his stockinged feet up on an empty chair. "We need to tread carefully on this one," he continued, reaching over to massage his ankles. "Our relations with the cousins can only survive this kind of accusation if we're dead right."

Helms, a cool, aloof bureaucrat who had more in common with the patient intelligence gatherers than the clandestine service's cowboys, leaned toward Angleton's point of view. "Your line of reasoning is intriguing," he told Torriti, "but Jim is right—when you strip it down to the nitty-gritty, what you're left with could easily be a series of coincidences."

"In our line of work," Torriti argued, "coincidences don't exist."

The Wiz, his shirtsleeves rolled up above his elbows, his chair tilted back against the wall, his eyes half closed, allowed as how the Sorcerer might be on to something there. A coincidence was like a matador's red cape; if you spotted one, your instinct told you to do more than stand there and paw at the ground in frustration. Which is why, Wisner added, he'd taken a gander at various logs after he'd read the Sorcerer's memorandum. Wiz flashed one of his guileless gap-toothed smiles in Angleton's direction. "On Monday, 1 January," he said, reading from a note he'd jotted to himself on the back of an envelope, "Torriti's cable arrived on Jim's desk. On Tuesday, 2 January, security logs in the lobby show Philby visiting both General Smith and Jim here. Starting in late afternoon on Tuesday, 2 January, radio intercept logs show a dramatic increase in the volume of cipher wireless traffic between the Soviet embassy and Moscow." The Wiz peered down the table at General Smith. "Seems to me like someone might have gone and pushed the panic button over there."

Torriti positioned a forefinger along the side of a nostril. It almost appeared as if he were asking permission to speak. "When all the pieces lock into place," he said, "we'd need to be off our rockers to go on trusting Philby. All I'm saying is we ought to ship him back to England COD, then get ahold of the Brits and lay out what we have and let them grill the shit out of him. They broke Fuchs. They'll break Philby."

"We'll look like horse's asses if we go out there with accusations we can't prove," Helms said lazily.

"I don't believe I'm hearing what I'm hearing," Torriti groaned, struggling to keep the cap on his pressure cooker of a temper. "Here we have a guy who began his adult life as a Cambridge socialist, who got hitched to a Communist activist in Vienna..." He looked around the table to see if anything alcoholic had somehow ended up amid all the bottles of seltzer. "Holy shit, the fucker's been betraying one operation after another—"

"There are operations he knew about that weren't betrayed," Angleton snapped.

The Sorcerer exploded. "He knew I knew the identity of the Soviet mole who had compromised the Vishnevsky defection *because I sent him a barium meal to that effect.* Next thing you know some jokers lure me to a church and try to take me out of circulation. What does that add up to?"

Angleton dragged on his cigarette. "Philby knew that your hottest source in East Germany—"

General Smith ran his thumb down the numbered paragraphs in Angleton's rebuttal. "Here it is—number three—you're talking about SNIPER."

"Philby was privy to the SNIPER material from day one," Angleton said. "Backtracking from what was passed on to us, the KGB could have easily figured out the identity of SNIPER. When Harvey discovered that SNIPER was a theoretical physicist and a deputy prime minister in the East German Government, this information was passed on as a matter of routine to the MI6 liaison man in Washington, Philby." He turned toward the Sorcerer. "SNIPER is still delivering, isn't he, Harvey?"

"Yeah, he is, Jim."

Angleton almost smiled, as if to say: I rest my case.

Torriti said, very quietly, "He's delivering because he's a Soviet disinformation operation."

The Barons around the table exchanged glances. Truscott leaned back in his chair and eyed the Sorcerer through the haze of pipe and cigarette smoke. "I suppose you're prepared to elaborate on that."

"I suppose I am," Torriti agreed. He tugged two crumpled message blanks from the breast pocket of his sports jacket, ironed them open on the table with the flat of his hand and began reading from the first one. "This is a 'Flash—Eyes Only' that reached me here Saturday morning. 'From: The Sorcerer's Apprentice. To: The Sorcerer. Subject: AESNIPER. One: Something fishy's going on here, Harvey.'"

General Smith leaned forward. "It starts off with 'Something fishy's going on here, Harvey?'"

"That's what it says, General."

"Is that a cryptogram?"

"No, sir. It's plain English."

The DCI nodded dubiously. "I see. And precisely what is the *something fishy* that was going on?"

Torriti smiled for the first time that morning. "It's like this," he began. "A while back, acting on my instructions, my Apprentice, name of John

McAullife, planted a teardrop microphone in the floorboards of SNIPER's apartment. McAullife is the officer who's been running SNIPER's courier, code-named RAINBOW..."

At their Friday night meeting in the rehearsal hall, Jack had dipped two fingers into Lili's brassiere and pressed the backs of them against her flesh as he kissed her. When his fingers came out, the square of silk filled with minuscule writing was between them. Later, at Berlin-Dahlem, Jack slipped the silk between two pieces of glass, adjusted the desk lamp and, leaning over a magnifying glass, slowly worked his way through the latest "get" from SNIPER. Not surprisingly, he found details of bacteriological warfare testing on the Baltic island of Rügen, uranium production in the Joachimstal area of the Harz Mountains, the most recent Soviet nuclear fission experiments in Central Asia. That was followed by a long quotation from a letter from Walter Ulbricht to the Soviet ambassador complaining about comments supposedly made about his, Ulbricht's, commitment to Communism by his Party rival, Wilhelm Zaisser. After that came a long list of Soviet Army units that, according to an internal Soviet study, were quietly being rotated through a training program designed to prepare combat troops for bacteriological warfare. The Friday "get" from SNIPER ended with the names of middle-level West German government and private enterprise functionaries who were hiding compromising Nazi-party pasts and were thus vulnerable to blackmail.

Bone tired after a long day, Jack switched off the desk lamp and rubbed his eyes. Then, suddenly, he found himself staring into the darkness, thinking hard. Something fishy was going on! He snapped on the desk lamp and, dialing the combination of a small safe, retrieved the most recent transcript of the conversations recorded by the teardrop microphone in SNIPER's floorboards. Leaning over the desk, he compared the microphone's "get" with the latest material from SNIPER. Slowly, his mouth gaped open. The details of bacteriological warfare testing on Rügen, of uranium production in the Harz Mountains, of the recent Soviet nuclear fission experiments in Central Asia *had all been subtly altered.* The teardrop and the silk were delivering two different versions of the same information. Even more crucial, the silk made no mention at all of the MI6 watch list in the hands of the Polish intelligence service, UB, or the presumption that there might be an important Soviet spy in British intelligence who had provided it.

Did this mean what he thought it meant?

Jack grabbed a message blank and began scrawling a "Flash—Eyes Only" for the Sorcerer in Washington. "Something fishy's going on here, Harvey," he began.

Dressed in the cobalt blue coveralls of an East German state electrical worker, Jack leaned against the kiosk on the south side of Alexanderplatz, eating a sandwich made with ersatz Swiss cheese and skimming the editorial page of Saturday's Communist Party newspaper, *Neues Deutschland.* Surveilling the far side of Alexanderplatz over the top of his newspaper, he repeated from memory the Sorcerer's answer to his overnight "Something fishy" bulletin. "Hit RAINBOW over the head with it," Torriti had ordered. "Today. I want her answer in my hands when I go into the lion's den Monday at nine."

Jack saw Lili emerge from the private dance school minutes after the noon siren had sounded. She stood for a moment as the lunch hour crowd flowed around her, angling her face toward the sun, relishing its warmth. Then she slung her net catchall over a shoulder and set off down Mühlendammstrasse. She queued to buy beets from an open farm truck, then ducked into a pharmacy before continuing on her way. Jack waved to the Fallen Angel, who seemed to be dozing behind the wheel of the small Studebaker truck that transported bone meal fertilizer into the Soviet zone. He spotted Lili and started the motor. Cutting diagonally across Alexanderplatz, Jack came abreast of her as she waited for the light to change.

"*Guten Morgen,* Helga," Jack said tensely, slipping his arm through hers. "*Wie geht es Dir?*"

Lili turned her head. A look of pure animal dread filled what Jack had always thought of as her bruised eyes. She glanced around frantically, as if she would take flight, then looked back at him. "You know my real name?" she whispered.

"I know more than that," he said under his breath. He raised his voice and asked, "*Wie geht es Herr Löffler?*"

Lili pulled free from his grip. "How do you know these things?"

Jack snapped his head in the direction of a workers' café across the street. It was evident from his manner that he was very agitated. "I invite you for coffee and cake *mit Schlagsahne.*"

Feeling giddy, afraid her knees would give way if she couldn't sit down, Lili let Jack lead her through traffic to the café, a spacious high-ceilinged neighborhood canteen with one Bauhaus stained-glass window that had miraculously survived the war. Neon lights suspended from long electrical cords illuminated tables covered in Formica. Middle-aged waiters in black trousers and white shirts and black vests, balancing trays brimming with coffee and cakes on palms raised high over their heads, plied the room. Jack steered Lili up the steps to a table at the back of the almost deserted mezzanine and slid onto the bench catty-corner to hers, his back to a tarnished mirror. He signalled the waiter for two coffees and two cakes and then reached across the table to touch her knuckles.

She jerked her hand away as if it had been scorched. "Why do you risk coming here in daylight?"

"What I have to say couldn't wait. All hell is going to break loose. I don't want you to be in the Soviet zone when it does."

"How long have you known our real names, Herr Professor and me?"

"That's not important," Jack said.

"What *is* important?"

"It is about your Professor Löffler, Lili—I stumbled across the truth. He has betrayed you. He works for the Soviet KGB, he is what we call a disinformation agent."

Lili's chin sank onto her chest and she began to breathe through her mouth. The waiter, thinking they were having a marital spat, set the coffee and cakes between them. "Some clouds have silver linings, some do not," he intoned as he slipped the check under a saucer.

Lili looked up, her eyes blinking rapidly as if she were trying to freeze an image. "Jack, I am not able to understand what you say?"

"Yes, you do, Lili," he said fiercely. "I can see it on your face, I can read it in your eyes. You understand very well. The silk I pulled from your breast Friday night—"

"It was filled with information. I read some of it before I gave it to you, yes?"

"It was filled with leftovers from a lousy supper. It was filled with things we already knew or weren't true. The good stuff had been edited out."

Now she really did look puzzled. "How could you know what was edited out?"

"We have a microphone in Löffler's apartment. It records everything that's said in the dining room. Six days ago it picked up his hurried declaration of love to you. You haven't forgotten what he told you, have you?"

Lili, unable to speak, shook her head miserably.

"You had a visitor that night, a man speaking English with a Polish accent. You do remember the evening, don't you, Lili? The three of you had supper together. Then you went out to clean up and let them talk. The microphone recorded a conversation in English between Herr Professor and his Polish friend. You came back with brandy and then left again. What they talked about when you were out of the room was incredibly interesting to us. The trouble was that it had been left off the piece of silk you delivered. The heart of the conversation in the room that night—*the secrets*, Lili—were missing. It is not something Herr Professor would have omitted if he was really working for us. Which means he is working for the Communists. Either he or the person who handles him laundered the text before the Professor wrote out his report on the silk."

Lili dipped her middle finger into her coffee and carefully ran it over her lips as if she were applying lipstick. Jack said, "Lili, this is bad news for the people I work for—but good news for us. For you and me."

"How is it possible to see this as good news for us?" she managed to ask.

"The debt you owe Herr Professor is cancelled. He has betrayed you." Jack leaned toward her and touched her knuckles again. This time she didn't pull away. "Come across to the American sector, Lili. Come across to me. Right now. Come across and don't look back. I have a small truck waiting on a side street—we will squeeze into its secret compartment and cross the frontier at a little-used check-point."

"I must think—"

"You will start life over. I'll take you to London to see the Royal Ballet. You can try out your English in America. You can use it to tell the justice of the peace that you agree to take me for your wedded husband."

Lili's mask of a face was disfigured by a bitter smile. "Dear Jack-in-the-box, it has slipped from your mind that I am the sand under your bare feet. I make you lightheaded, yes? If only the thing was as simple as you say. You understand nothing. *Nothing*."

Lili's fingertips passed across her eyelids. Then she sighed and looked Jack in the eye. "It is not the Professor who is a Soviet agent," she told him. "It is me, the Soviet agent. It is me who, in a certain sense, betrayed *him*."

Jack felt spasms shoot through his rib cage as sharp as any he had felt while rowing. It occurred to him that he might be having a heart attack; curiously, it seemed like a solution to his problems. He took a sip of coffee and forced himself to swallow. Then he heard himself say, "Okay, tell me what happened" even though he wasn't sure he wanted to hear it.

"What happened? I ask myself, again and again, what happened." She stared off into space for a moment. "Ernst is a German patriot. After much contemplation he came to the conclusion that the Communists—the

Russian Communists and their German puppets—were crippling Germany. He decided to work for reunification of the two Germanies by passing information to the West that would discredit the Communists. He thought it through very carefully—he was too well known, both at the University and as a deputy prime minister, to move about freely. I, on the other hand, crossed to the American sector twice each week to give my dance class. So we decided together—the decision was also mine, Jack—that he would collect the information and write it out on silk and I would act as the mail deliverer..."

Jack leaned toward her. "Go on," he whispered.

Lili shuddered. "The KGB found out about it. To this day I do not know how. Perhaps they, too, have microphones buried in the apartments of deputy prime ministers. Perhaps they overheard our conversations in bed late in the night. When I left for my first meeting with you—oh, it seems to me a lifetime ago, Jack—I was stopped a block from our apartment, I was forced into the back of a limousine and blindfolded and taken to a building and up an elevator and pushed into a room that smelled of insect repellent. Five men..." She caught her breath. "Five men stood around me—one spoke in Russian, four spoke in German. The Russian was clearly in charge. He was short with fat ankles and the eyes of an insect, and it crossed my brain that the repellent was there to keep him away but hadn't worked. He spoke German like a German. He ordered me to take off all my clothing. When I hesitated he said they would do it for me if I refused. In that room, before the eyes of men I did not know, I became naked. They discovered the square of silk—they seemed to know it would be in my brassiere. They said that Ernst would be tried for high treason and shot. They said I would certainly go to prison for many years. They said I would never dance again because they would see to it that my knees...my knees—"

"Lili!"

"I was standing before them completely naked, you see. If I could have crawled under a table and died I would have. Then the Russian told me to put my clothes back on. And he said...he said there was a way out for Ernst, for me. I would deliver Ernst's piece of silk to them and they would substitute another piece, rewritten, edited, things taken out, other things added, and I would deliver the second square to the American spy who would come to meet me Tuesday and Friday after my class. They promised that my service to the cause of Communism would be taken into consideration. Ernst would not be harmed as long as I cooperated—"

Jack's heart sank—he remembered Lili's saying, "Without me he cannot remain alive." At the time it had seemed a phrase with a simple meaning—the description of a lover who could not support the departure of the person he loved. Now Jack understood that she had meant it literally; she *could not* defect to the West because Ernst Ludwig Löffler would be arrested and tried and shot.

"After each meeting," she was saying, her voice thick with anger, "I wrote a report—I had to tell them who I met, and where, and what was said. They know your identity, Jack."

"Did you tell them about—"

"Not a word. They know nothing about us..."

Jack racked his brain for things he could say to convince her to come with him to the West. "The Professor—Herr Löffler—is condemned, Lili. You must see that. This game couldn't go on forever. And when it came to an end they would punish him, if only as an example to others who might be tempted to follow in his footsteps. You can still be saved. Come with me now—we will live happily ever after."

"There is no such thing as happily ever after. It is a child's tale. If I would leave, my going would kill him before they came to kill him."

So Lili's "Without me he cannot remain alive" had two meanings after all.

Jack knew he was running out of arguments. "Take him where there are no microphones and tell him what you've told me—tell him the KGB has been using him. Tell him I can get the both of you out."

"You do not understand Ernst. He will never leave his University, his work, his friends, the Germany he was born in and his parents are buried in. Not even to save his life." Her eyes clouded over. "He always said if it came to that, he had a small caliber handgun. He would joke about how the bullet was so small, the only way you could kill yourself was to fill your mouth with water and insert the pistol and explode your head..."

"He loves you—he'll want you to save yourself."

Lili nodded dumbly. "I will ask his advice..."

"Which explains why SNIPER *wasn't* closed down when Philby passed word of it on to his handlers," Torriti was telling the ad hoc war council. "The KGB already knew about SNIPER—the whole thing was a KGB disinformation operation."

There was a restless silence in the conference room when the Sorcerer came to the end of his story. The point of Truscott's pencil could be heard doodling on a yellow pad. Dulles aimed a flame from a Zippo lighter into the bowl of his pipe and sucked it back into life. Wisner drummed his fingers on the metal band of his wristwatch.

Angleton reached up and massaged his forehead, which was throbbing with a full-blown migraine. "There are two, five, seven ways of looking at any given set of facts," he said. "I will need time to tease the real meaning out of this, to—"

There was a sharp knock on the door. General Smith called out gruffly, "Come."

A secretary poked her head in. "I have a 'Flash—Eyes Only' for you, General. It's from the station chief, London."

Helms took the message board and passed it along the table to the Director. Smith fitted on a pair of reading glasses, opened the metal cover and scanned the message. Looking up, he waved the secretary out of the room. "Well, gentlemen, the shit has hit the fan," he announced. "On Friday the British Foreign Office authorized MI5 to begin interrogating Maclean regarding the HOMER serials first thing Monday. The interrogators turned up at dawn this morning and they discovered he'd jumped ship. I'm afraid that's not all. Guy Burgess seems to have disappeared with him."

Angleton, pale as a corpse, sagged back into his seat, stunned. General Truscott whistled through his front teeth. "Burgess—a Soviet agent!" he said. "Son of a bitch! He obviously went back to England to warn Maclean we'd broken the HOMER serials. At the last second he lost his nerve and went with him."

Wisner pushed his chair off the wall. "How'd Burgess find out we'd broken into the HOMER serials?"

"Burgess was living with Philby in Washington," Torriti said pointedly.

General Smith shook his head in disgust. "Burgess rented an Austin and drove to Maclean's home in the suburb of Tatsfield," he said, running his finger down the message from London station. "At 11:45 Friday night Burgess and Maclean boarded the cross-Channel boat *Falaise* bound for Saint-Malo. A sailor asked them what they planed to do with the Austin on the pier. 'Back on Monday,' Burgess called. On the French side, MI5 found a taxicab driver who remembered driving two men that he identified from photographs as Burgess and Maclean from Saint-Malo to Rennes, where they caught a train for Paris. The trail ends there."

"The trail ends in Moscow," Wisner said.

General Truscott frowned. "If Philby *is* a Soviet agent he may have run also."

Torriti turned on Angleton. "I warned you we should have taken goddamn precautions."

The Barons around the table studiously avoided Angleton's eye.

"Philby didn't run for it," Angleton said huskily, "because he is not a Soviet agent."

Truscott reached for the phone on a table behind him and pushed it across to Angleton. General Smith nodded. "Call him, Jim," he ordered.

Angleton produced a small black address book from the breast pocket of his suit jacket. He thumbed through to the P's and dialed a number. He held the phone slightly away from his ear; everyone in the room could hear it ringing on the other end. After twelve or fourteen rings he gave up. "He's not at his home," he said. The two generals, Smith and Truscott, exchanged looks. Angleton dialed the MI6 offices in Washington. A woman answered on the first ring. She repeated the phone number, her voice rising to a question mark at the end. Angleton said, "Let me speak to Mr. Philby, please."

"Would you care to give a name?"

"Hugh Ashmead."

"One moment, Mr. Ashmead."

Around the table the Barons hardly dared to breath.

A jovial voice burst onto the line. "That you, Jimbo? Assume you've heard the not-so-glad tidings. Phone hasn't stopped ringing over here. Christ, who would've thought it? Guy Burgess, of all people! He and I go way back."

"That may pose a problem," Angleton said carefully.

"Figured it would, old boy. Not to worry, I have a thick pelt against the slings and arrows—I won't take it personally."

"Let's meet for a drink," Angleton suggested.

Philby could be heard swallowing a laugh. "Sure you want to be seen with me? I may be contagious."

"Hay-Adams bar? One-thirty suit you?"

"You're calling the shots, Jimbo."

Preoccupied, Angleton set the phone back on its hook. Torriti remarked, "Give the fucker credit—he has moxie."

"If Philby were a Soviet mole," Angleton said, thinking out loud, "the KGB would have brought him home along with Maclean and Burgess." To the others in the room he sounded as if he were trying to convince himself.

General Smith scraped back his chair and stood up. "Here's the bottom line, Jim. Philby is contaminated. I want him barred from our buildings as of right now. I want him out of America within twenty-four hours. Let the cousins put him through the ringer and figure out whether he's been spying for the Ruskies." He looked down at Angleton. "Understood?"

Angleton nodded once. "Understood, General."

"As for you, Torriti: you have to be the most unconventional officer on the Company payroll. Knowing what I know, I'm not sure I would have hired you but I'm certainly not going to be the one to fire you. Understood?"

Torriti stifled a smile. "Understood, General."

In the executive lavatory down the hall from the DCI's bailiwick, the Sorcerer flexed his knees and undid the zipper of his fly and, groaning with relief, peed into the urinal. "So what does it tell us about the human condition, that taking a leak turns out to be one of life's great pleasures?" he asked the person at the next urinal.

Torriti's short, round-shouldered MI5 friend, Elihu Epstein, chortled under his breath. "Never thought of it quite like that," he admitted. "Now that you mention it, I can see that it is one of the more Elysian moments in one's day." Epstein did up the buttons of his fly and went over to the line of sinks to wash his hands. "How did things go this morning?" he asked, eyeing the Sorcerer in the mirror.

Torriti flexed his knees again and then joined Epstein at the sinks. "Are you wired, Elihu?"

"Afraid so."

"Are you taping or broadcasting?"

"I'm broadcasting. My pals on the other end are taping."

"What are you using for a microphone these days?"

Epstein let his eyes drift to the discreet Victoria Cross rosette on his lapel.

Grinning like a maniac, Torriti leaned toward Epstein and barked into the rosette: "Harold Adrian Russell Philby, known as Kim to his sidekicks in the rancid precincts of British intelligence, has been declared *persona non grata*. The fucker has twenty-four hours to get his ass out of our country, after which he'll be all yours. Persuading him to help you with your inquiries is not going to be a cakewalk—you may have to twist his old school tie around his neck to get him to talk."

Torriti spun back to the mirror and splashed water on his face. He had been up most of the night rehearsing the case he would make against Philby. Now the tension and the fatigue were hitting him.

Epstein held his hands under a hot air dryer and raised his voice to be heard over it. "By the by, how did your James Jesus Angleton take it?"

"Hard. I don't see him looking at the world the same way again."

"Hmmmm. Yes. Well. Not sure whether one ought to bless you or curse you, Harvey. Relations between our sister services will go from bad to non-existent, won't they? Still, I suppose it's better to have loved and lost. Whatever."

"Whatever," Torriti agreed. He desperately needed a drink.

The lunch hour crowd was queuing up at the Hay-Adams, across Lafayette Park from the White House, when Angleton sank onto the stool next to Philby at the low end of the bar. The bartender had set out three double martinis in front of the Englishman. Philby had polished off the first two and, squinting along his nose, was trying to impale one of the olives in a saucer on a toothpick. "Did you spot the three-piece suits at the door, Jimbo?" he asked under his breath. "J. Edgar's eunuchs. They haven't let me out of their sight. There's two cars full of 'em parked out front. Bloody FBI! You'd think I'd knocked over your Fort Knox."

"Some of my associates think you have," Angleton said. He raised a finger to get the bartender's eye, pointed at Philby's martinis and held up two fingers. "They think you sent Burgess back to warn Maclean. They think that's only the tip of the iceberg."

Philby came up with a bad imitation of a Texas accent. "That a fact, pardner?"

"Did you, Adrian? Send Burgess back to warn Maclean?"

Philby slowly turned his red-rimmed eyes on Angleton. "That cuts, Jim. Coming from you..." He shook his head. "'There is a tide in the affairs of men'...My world is coming apart at the seams, isn't it?"

"Bedell Smith sent a stinging cable to your 'C' saying he wanted you out of the country. Your Five is going to rake you over the coals, Adrian."

"Don't I know it." He gripped the third martini and threw down most of it in one gulp. "I would have run for it if I was one of theirs," he told the glass.

"I remember one night back on Ryder Street when the buzz bombs were exploding around us," Angleton said. "We were talking theory, Adrian, and suddenly you said that theory was fine as far as it went. You quoted the founder of British Secret Service back in the sixteenth century—"

"Francis Walsingham, old boy."

"I never could remember his name but I never forgot what you said he said."

Philby managed a smirk. "'Espionage is an effort to find windows into men's souls.'"

"That's it, Adrian. Windows into men's souls."

The bartender set two double martinis down on the bar. Angleton started to stir the first one with a pretzel. "Haven't found the window into your soul, Adrian. Who are you?"

"I thought you knew."

"Thought I did, too. Not so sure now."

"I swear to you, Jimbo, I never betrayed my side—"

"Which is your side, Adrian?"

The question knocked the wind out of Philby. After a moment he said, with mock lightness, "Well, have to be toddling, don't I? Sorry I can't do lunch. Bags to pack, house to close, plane to catch, that sort of thing." He more or less fell off his stool. Clutching the bar with one hand, he wedged a folded fiver under the saucer filled with olives, then held out his hand. Angleton shook it. Philby nodded, as if something he had just thought of had reinforced something he already knew. "Hang in there, Jimbo."

"I expect to."

Angleton watched Philby stumble through the swinging door. Hoover's three-piece suits fell in behind him. Turning back to his drink, he took a long swallow and pulled a face; too much vermouth but what the hell. Finishing off the martini, he started to reflect on the almost infinite number of interpretations that could be put on any set of facts, the ambiguities waiting to be discovered in patterns of behavior. Say, for argument's sake, that Adrian had been spying for the Russians. Someone that important would have been handled by the senior controller; by the one known as Starik. Angleton had started a dossier on Starik the first time he came across a reference to him in the serial provided by the Russian defector Krivitsky. The file was pretty thin but there was enough to convince him that the mysterious Starik was a cunning and meticulous planner, someone who prided himself on staying one jump ahead of the enemy. Which meant that the real question was not what Philby had given away—let the MI5 interrogators wrestle with that one—but who was taking his place. It was inconceivable that Starik would let the pipeline run dry, inconceivable that Soviet penetration operations would come to a grinding halt on 28 May 1951.

Torriti's accusations against Philby had initially unnerved Angleton but now he felt a surge of energy; now more than ever he had his work cut out for him. Attacking the second martini, he felt himself slip across a fault into a stygian mindscape where subtleties proliferated, where variations on a theme roared in the ear like an infernal chorus. Grimacing, Angleton made a silent vow: He would never trust another mortal the way he had trusted Philby. No one. Not ever. In the end, anyone could be a Soviet mole.

Or everyone.

17

THE SORCERER SCRATCHED HIS KNUCKLES ACROSS JACK'S OPEN DOOR. "Can I, eh, come in?" he asked, the balls of his feet on the threshold, his oversized body curling forward deferentially.

The question astonished Jack. "Be my guest," he said from behind the small desk that had been liberated from a Wehrmacht post office at the end of the war. He pointed to the only other place to sit in his cubicle of an office, a metal barber's stool on castors. Jack pulled a bottle of whiskey from a carton at his feet, set out two glasses and half-filled them, careful to be sure they both held the same amount. Distributing his weight carefully on the stool, Torriti wheeled closer to the desk and wrapped his fingers around one glass. "You wouldn't happen to have ice?" he asked.

"Fridge in the hall is on the fritz."

"No ice, no tinkle. No tinkle, *schlecht!*"

"That what you said the night we were waiting for Vishnevsky to show up," Jack remembered. "No tinkle, *schlecht!*"

The Sorcerer scraped dandruff out of an eyebrow with a fingernail. "Lot of water's passed under the bridge in five months."

"An awful lot, yeah."

"You played heads-up ball on the SNIPER business," the Sorcerer said. "To you."

They downed their whiskeys.

"First time I've been up to the top floor," the Sorcerer said. He took in Jack's cubicle. "Nice place."

"Small."

"Small but nice. Least you have a window. What does it look out on when the shade's up?"

"Brick wall of the building across the alley."

Torriti snickered. "Well, you didn't come to Germany for the view."

"Where are they with Philby?"

"MI5's Torquemadas are stretching him on the rack. So far he's pleading coincidence."

"Will they break him?"

"My pal in Five, Elihu Epstein, is sitting in on it. He says Philby's going to be a tough nut to crack."

For a moment neither of them could think of anything to say. Then Jack remarked, "She missed two meetings, Harvey."

Torriti nodded uncomfortably.

"The teardrop in SNIPER's floorboard's gone dry. The silence is deafening."

The Sorcerer looked around the small room as if he were trying to find a way out. "Jack, I have some unpleasant news for you."

"About RAINBOW?"

"About RAINBOW. About SNIPER."

"Un-huh."

"Remember that tap we have on the phone of Ulbricht's wife in her Central Committee office?"

"Yeah. As a matter of fact, I do."

Torriti pushed the glass across the desk for a refill. His Apprentice obliged. The Sorcerer downed the second whiskey, then patted his pockets in search of a folded sheet of paper. He found it hidden in a shirt pocket under his shoulder holster. "This is a transcript of a conversation—took place two days ago—between Ulbricht and his wife, Lotte."

Torriti started to set the sheet down on the desk but Jack said, "What's it say, Harvey?"

The Sorcerer nodded. "Ulbricht tells her the jokers from Karlshorst tracked Ernst Ludwig Löffler to his brother's house in Dresden. They went around to arrest him for high treason, they broke down the door when nobody opened it, they found Löffler's sister-in-law cowering in a closet, they found Löffler hanging from a curtain rod. He'd climbed a stepladder and tied a bunch of neckties around his neck and kicked the ladder away. He'd been dead for two days."

"Un-huh."

"Lotte asks Ulbricht about Helga Agnes."

"Un-huh."

"He tells her she'd locked herself in the john. The boys from Karlshorst ordered her to come out. They heard a shot," Torriti cleared his throat. "There are details in the transcript you don't want to know....You listening, sport?"

Jack ran his finger around the rim of his glass. "She went into it never once considering how the hell she was going to get out again."

"So I guess you kind of fell for her."

"We couldn't spend time. Neither of us had any to spare."

The Sorcerer pushed himself to his feet. "What can I say?"

"Win some, lose some."

"That's the spirit, Jack. Wasn't your fault. You offered her a ticket out. Her problem she didn't take it."

"Her problem," Jack agreed. "Solved it with a mouth full of water and a small-caliber pistol."

The Sorcerer eyed his Apprentice. "How'd you know about the mouth full of water? How'd you know the pistol was small-caliber?"

"Shot in the dark."

Torriti started for the door. Jack said, "Tell me something, Harvey."

The Sorcerer turned back. "Sure, kid. What do you want to know?"

"Were SNIPER and RAINBOW one of your barium meals? Because if they were, Harvey, if they were, I'm not sure I can go on—"

Torriti spread his hands wide. "SNIPER was Berlin Base's crown jewel, sport. I was ready to give a lot of crap away. I was ready to give Lotte's phone tap away. But not SNIPER." He shook his head for emphasis. "No way I'd put him on the line." He raised his right hand. "Hey, I swear it to you, kid. On my mother's grave."

"That makes me feel better, Harvey."

"Onward and upward, sport."

"Yeah. Onward. Whichever."

18

CHERYOMUSKI, MOSCOW DISTRICT, MONDAY, JUNE 4, 1951

STARIK HAD CLAMBERED UP THE SPIRAL IRON STAIRCASE TO THE FLAT roof of the three-story mansion to get a respite from the telephones that never stopped ringing. Was it true, Beria wanted to know, that the two Englishmen who had been spying for the Soviet Union had already arrived in Moscow? At what point, *Pravda's* editor asked, would the two be available for interviews by Western journalists in order to prove to the world that they had defected of their own free will? The Politburo needed to know, Nikita Khrushchev insisted, whether the rumors circulating in the Kremlin about there being a third English defector were based on fact or wishful thinking.

Grinding a Bulgarian cigarette out under his foot, Starik made his way across the roof to the southeast corner and hiked himself onto the balustrade. From beyond the forest of white birches came the pungent aroma of the dung that had been scattered from horse-drawn carts in the fields that the Cheryomuski collective would sow with feed corn if the weather held. Pasha Zhilov, a.k.a. Starik, had been born and raised in the Caucuses. His father, an acolyte who fasted on the Sabbath and read to his six children from the Book of Revelation before bedtime every night, died in a typhus epidemic when Starik was sixteen, and he had been sent to live with his father's brother in the Ukraine. Before the collect-ivization campaign of the early thirties, he used to accompany his uncle, a minor Bolshevik official charged with ensuring that private farms delivered the correct quotas to the state, on his trips through the countryside. The thing that Starik remembered most about these expeditions was the pure odors that reached his nostrils from the piles of manure steaming after a sudden summer cloudburst. Because Starik's uncle was extremely unpopular with the Ukrainian peasants—there were occasions when the tires of his car had been slit or sand had been thrown into its petrol tank—he was accompanied by a second automobile filled with armed militiamen who sometimes let the young Starik fire their Nagant rifles at beer bottles set out on a fence.

The boy had turned out to be a terrible shot; try as he would he couldn't prevent himself from wincing *before* he pulled the trigger. Clearly, his uncle would say with a laugh, Pasha's talents lay in other directions.

Gazing out over the birch trees, Starik smiled at the memory; how prophetic his uncle had been!

In the pale break between the dark storm clouds and the horizon, Starik could make out a large passenger airplane, its propellers droning in a throaty growl, descending toward the military runway that few in Moscow knew existed. If everything had gone according to plan, the Englishmen Burgess and Maclean would be aboard. They would be welcomed by a handful of generals in full regalia in order to make the defectors feel important, then whisked to a secret KGB training school for a long and detailed debriefing, the phase that Starik referred to as "the squeezing of the sponge." After which they would be turned over to the Party people and trotted out in front of the world's journalists to extract whatever propaganda benefits were to be had from the defections.

Starik's talents *had* lain in other directions, though there were not three people in all of the Soviet Union—in all the world!—who understood in a deep way what he was orchestrating.

What he was orchestrating was the demolition of the American Central Intelligence Agency *from the inside*.

The first stage of the meticulous campaign had involved letting selected cipher keys fall into the hands of the CIA's experts, permitting them to break out chunks of text concerning the Soviet agent code-named HOMER; the text led the Americans to the British diplomat Maclean. From Starik's point of view Maclean was expendable. His exposure had only been a matter of months; Starik had just accelerated the process.

The timing was critical. Starik knew that Philby would learn from Angleton that the Americas were closing in on Maclean. With the British gearing up for the interrogation process, Starik had planted the idea in Philby's head of sending Burgess back to warn Maclean. Then had come the stroke of genius: Burgess hadn't lost his nerve, as the Western newspapers reported; Starik had *ordered* him to defect with Maclean. Burgess had protested to the London *resident* when he was informed of the order; he was afraid his defection would lead to the exposure of his old friend Philby, since he had been the one who introduced Philby into the British Secret Service to begin with; more recently, the two had even been sharing a house in Washington. The *resident*, following Starik's instructions to the letter, had convinced Burgess that Philby's days as a spy were numbered: that, since the aborted Vishnevsky defection in Berlin, the noose had been tightening around his neck; that it was only a matter of days before he, too, would have to run for it; that he would be brought home before the Americans could arrest him; that the three Englishmen would be triumphantly reunited in Moscow for all the world to see.

By bringing Burgess in, Starik wasn't giving up much; Burgess, a pariah who exasperated many of his British and American colleagues, was drunk most of the time, frightened all of the time, and delivering little intelligence of value.

Which narrowed the game down to Kim Philby. He was close to Angleton and had access to other top people in the CIA, and was still delivering a fair amount of secrets. But Starik knew from communication intercepts that the Vishnevsky affair had set off alarm bells. The shrewd American who ran the CIA's Berlin Base, Torriti, had picked up the scent; Philby's panicky message to Moscow Centre warning that Torriti was onto him could have been the result of a barium meal planted by Torriti to smoke Philby out. In any case, it would only be a matter of time before someone would make a case against Philby based on the Krivitsky serials and the dozens of recent CIA émigré infiltrations that had ended in failure.

The enigma in intelligence work was the wear and tear on the nerves and the intellect of the successful agent—there was no way to measure it or to alleviate it. Philby put on a good show but after twenty years in the field he was anaesthetized by alcohol consumption and frayed nerves. It was high time to bring him home.

And the bringing in of Philby would serve a greater purpose.

Starik was playing a more subtle game than anyone suspected. Counterintelligence was at the heart of any intelligence service. Angleton was at the heart of American counterintelligence. Starik had been studying Angleton since Philby had first reported his presence at Ryder Street during the war. Starik had continued to observe him from afar when Angleton was in Italy after the war, and later when he returned to Washington to run the counterintelligence arm of the CIA. He had pored over Philby's reports of their rambling late-night conversations. Angleton talked endlessly about theory; about teasing seven layers of meaning out of any given situation. But Angleton had an Achilles heel—he could not imagine someone being more subtle than him, more *elegant* than him. Which meant that the person who could descend to an eighth layer of meaning had an enormous advantage over Angleton.

Like all counterintelligence operatives Angleton had a streak of paranoia; paranoia went with the terrain of counterintelligence. Every defector was a potential plant; every intelligence officer was a potential traitor. Everyone, that is, *except* his mentor and close friend, Kim Philby.

By exposing Philby, Starik would push Angleton over the edge into real paranoia. Paranoia would infect his skull. He would chase shadows, suspect everyone. From time to time Starik would send over a "defector" to feed his paranoia; to drop dark hints of Soviet moles in the CIA and in government. If Starik orchestrated it carefully, Angleton would serve Soviet interests better than a real Soviet agent inside the CIA—he would tear the CIA apart looking for elusive Soviet moles, he would mangle the CIA's anti-Soviet elite in the process.

Only one thing hadn't gone according to plan: Philby had decided on his own not to run for it. He obviously preferred the creature comforts of capitalism; he lived to pull the wool over people's eyes, which fed his feelings of superiority. Playing the great game, Philby would protest his innocence from now to doomsday. And the MI5 interrogators might not be able to prove otherwise to the satisfaction of a judge and jury in a court of law.

But Angleton knew!

And Angleton was Starik's target. Exposing Philby would break Angleton. And a broken Angleton would cripple the CIA. At which point there would be nothing standing in the way of the operation dubbed KHOLSTOMER, Starik's epic long-term machination to break the back of the Western industrial democracies, to bring them to their knees and clear the way for the spread of Marxism-Leninism to the far corners of the planet earth.

There was one other reason for pushing Philby to the sidelines—Starik had positioned his last, his best, mole, code-named SASHA, in Washington. He was someone with access to the Washington elite, including the CIA and the White House. His nerves intact, SASHA would pick up where Philby had left off.

A warm whisper of air drifted in from the fertilized fields, bringing with it the rich aroma of dung and freshly turned earth. Starik savored the redolence for a moment. Then he started back towards the phones ringing off their hooks in his office downstairs.

It was going to be a long Cold War.

Three of the girls sprawled on the oversized bed, their long white limbs entwined, their dark nipples pushing through filmy blouses, their bare toes playfully tickling Starik's thighs and penis under his long rough peasant robe. The fourth girl lay stretched on the sofa, one leg hooked over the back. Her dress had ridden up her skinny body, revealing a pair of worn cotton underpants.

"Shhhhh, girlies," Starik groaned. "How are you going to concentrate on what I'm reading if you fidget all the time."

"It's working," one of the girls tittered. "It's getting hard."

The girl on the couch, who had been with Starik the longest, taunted the others with a pink tongue. "How many times must I tell you," she called across the room. "It only gets hard when you talk directly to it."

The youngest of the girls, a curly-haired blonde who had celebrated her tenth birthday the previous week, crept under the hem of his robe. "Oh my dears, it's not hard at all," she called back to her stepcousins. "It looks ever so much like the trunk of an elephant."

"Speak to it, then," called the girl from the couch.

"But what in heaven's name shall I say?"

Starik grabbed an ankle and pulled her out from under the robe onto the bed. "I am not going to tell you again," he declared, wagging a finger at each of the girls in turn.

"Shhhhh," the girl on the couch instructed the others.

"Shhhhh," the curly-haired blonde agreed.

"We must all shhhhh," a porcelain-skinned girl with granny glasses declared, "or Uncle will become angry with us."

"Now, then," Starik said. He opened the book to the page where he'd left off the previous day and began to read aloud.

"Of all the strange things that Alice saw in her journey Through The Looking-Glass, this was the one that she always remembered most clearly. Years afterwards she could bring the whole scene back again, as if it had been only yesterday—the mild blue eyes and kindly smile of the Knight—"

"Oh, I did love the Knight," sighed the girl with blonde hair.

"You must not interrupt while Uncle is reading," instructed the girl from the sofa.

"—the setting sun gleaming through his hair, and shining on his armor in a blaze of light that quite dazzled her—the horse quietly moving about, with the reins hanging loose on his neck, cropping the grass at her feet—and the black shadows of the forest behind..."

"I am frightened of black shadows," the girl wearing granny glasses announced with a shiver.

"And I am frightened of forests," confessed the blonde.

"As for me, I am frightened of war," the girl on the sofa admitted, and she shut her eyes and covered them with her small palms to keep bad visions at bay.

"*Dadya* Stalin thinks there will be a war," the girl who had been silent up to now told the others. "I heard him say as much in the newsreel before the film."

"Uncle, will there be a war, do you suppose?" asked the curly-haired blonde.

"There won't have to be," Starik replied. "Some months ago I came across a thesis by a clever economist. The idea seemed outrageous when I first read it but then I began to see the possibilities—"

"What is a thesis?"

"And what is an economist?"

"You ask too many questions, girlies."

"How can we be expected to learn, then, if we don't ask questions?"

"You can learn by sitting still as a church mouse and paying attention to what I say." Starik was thinking out loud now. "The thesis I discovered could be the answer..."

"A thesis is a weapon," guessed the girl in the granny glasses. "Something like a tank, only larger. Something like a submarine, only smaller. Aren't I right?"

Before he could reply, the girl on the sofa asked, "And what will become of our enemies, Uncle?"

Starik ran his fingers through the blonde curls of his niece. "Why, it's as simple as rice pudding, girlies—it may take quite a time but if we are patient enough we will defeat them without shooting at them."

"How can that be, Uncle?"

"Yes, how can you be so certain of such a thing?"

Starik almost managed a smile as he recited from memory one of his all-time favorite lines: "I am older than you and must know better."

PART TWO

THE END OF INNOCENCE

"They're dreadfully fond of beheading people here:
the great wonder is that there's any one left alive!" said Alice.

Snapshot: an old Life *magazine page proof originally intended for publication in mid-November 1956 but spiked at the request of the Central Intelligence Agency, which claimed that it had identified several employees in the full-page photograph and its publication could compromise their missions and ultimately endanger their lives. The photo, taken with a powerful telephoto lens and accordingly grainy, shows a group of people dressed in heavy winter overcoats—Deputy Director Operations Frank Wisner, Jack McAuliffe, and CIA counselor Mildred Owen-Brack among them—standing on a rise watching a line of refugees trudge along a dirt rut of a road. Some of the refugees carry heavy suitcases, others clutch children by their collars or hands. Jack seems to have recognized someone through the morning ground-mist and raised a hand in salute. Diagonally across the page a big man carrying a small girl on his shoulders appears to be waving back.*

1

MOSCOW, SATURDAY, FEBRUARY 25, 1956

IN AN OVERHEATED OFFICE ON THE TOP FLOOR OF THE LUBYANKA headquarters in Moscow, a group of senior officers and Directorate chiefs of the Komitét Gosudárstvennoi Bezopásnosti, their eyes riveted on an Army radio on the table, listened through a closed-circuit military channel to the rough peasant caterwaul of the First Secretary of the Communist Party, Nikita Sergeyevich Khrushchev, as he wound up his speech to the secret session of the Twentieth Party Congress. Staring out a window at the ice-shimmering statue of Feliks Dzerzhinsky in the middle of the square below, Starik sucked absently on one of his hollow-tipped Bulgarian cigarettes, trying to calculate the likely effect of Khrushchev's secret speech on the Cold War in general; on the operation code named KHOLSTOMER in particular. His gut instinct told him that Khrushchev's decision to catalogue the crimes of the late and (at least in KGB circles) lamented Joseph Vissarionovich Dzhugashvili, known to the world by his nom de guerre, Stalin, would shake the Communist world to its foundations.

About time, that was Starik's view; the more you were committed to an idea, to an institution, *to a theory of life*, the harder it was to live with its imperfections.

Which is what he told Khrushchev when the First Secretary had casually raised the idea of a reckoning. The two, who knew each other from the Great Patriotic War, had been strolling along a bluff not far from where Europe's longest river, the Volga, plunges into the Caspian Sea. Four security guards armed with shotguns were trailing discreetly behind. Khrushchev had recently outmaneuvered his Politburo colleagues in the long struggle for power that followed Stalin's death in March 1953 and had taken control of the Party. "So what opinion do you hold on the question, Pasha Semyonovich?" Khrushchev had asked. "For too many years all of Stalin's kittens lived in dread, waiting to see whose head would be lopped off next. I myself never went to sleep without a satchel filled with toilet articles and spare socks under my bed. I would lay awake for hours listening for the sound of the Black Marias screeching to a stop in front of my building, come to cart me off to a camp in Vorkuta where the prisoners who are still alive in the morning suck on icicles of frozen milk." Khrushchev stabbed at the air with a stubby forefinger. "There is something to be said for setting the record straight. But can I survive such revelations?"

Starik had considered the question. Denouncing Stalin as error prone— hinting that he was terror prone—would rock the Party that had delivered absolute power into his hands and then had failed to stand up to him when he abused it; when he executed scores of his closest associates after a series of show trials; when he sent hundreds of thousands, even millions, of so-called counterrevolutionists to rot in the Siberian gulag. "I cannot say whether you will survive," Starik had finally replied. "But neither you nor the Leninist system can survive"—he had searched for a phrase that would resonate with the peasant-politico who had risen through the ranks to become the Party's First Secretary—"without turning over the ground before you sow new seeds."

"Everyone can err," Khrushchev could be heard saying over the Army radio now, "but Stalin considered that he never erred, that he was always right. He never acknowledged to anyone that he made a mistake, large or small, despite the fact that he made not a few mistakes in the matter of theory and in his practical activity."

"What can he be thinking of!" one of the Directorate chiefs exclaimed.

"Dangerous business, the washing of dirty linen in public," muttered another. "Once you start where do you stop?"

"Stalin was consolidating a revolution," snapped a tall man cleaning the lenses of his steel-rimmed eyeglasses with a silk handkerchief. "Mao got it right when he said revolution was not a dinner party."

"To make an omelet," someone else agreed, "one is obliged to crack eggs."

"Stalin," a bloated KGB general lieutenant growled, "taught us that revolutionists who refuse to use terror as a political weapon are vegetarians. As for me, I am addicted to red meat."

"If Stalin's hands were stained with blood," one of the younger chiefs said, "so are Khrushchev's. What was he doing in the Ukraine all those years? The same thing Stalin was doing in Moscow—eliminating enemies of the people."

Over the radio Khrushchev rambled on, his voice rising like that of a woman in lament. "Stalin was the principal exponent of the cult of the individual by the glorification of his own person. Comrades, we must abolish the cult of the individual decisively, once and for all."

From the radio came a sharp burst of what sounded like static but was actually an ovation from the delegates to the Party Congress. After a moment the closed circuit went dead. The sudden silence unnerved the men gathered around the radio and they turned away, carefully avoiding each other's eye. Several wandered over to a sideboard and poured themselves stiff whiskeys. A short, nearly bald man in his sixties, an old Bolshevik who presided over the Thirteenth Department of the First Chief Directorate, nicknamed the Wetwork Department because it specialized in kidnappings and killings, strolled across the room to join Starik at the window.

"Good thing the speech was secret," he remarked. "I do not see how the Communist Party leaders who rule the Socialist states of Eastern Europe in Stalin's name—and using Stalin's methodology—could survive the publication of Khrushchev's revelations."

Starik, the Centre's presbyter by dint of his exploits and experience, dragged the cigarette from his lips and stared at the bitter end of it as if there were a message concealed in the burning embers. "It will not remain secret for long," he told his colleague. "When the story becomes known it will break over the Soviet camp like a tidal wave. Communism will either be washed clean—or washed away."

Half an hour after the formal closing of the Twentieth Party Congress, Ezra Ben Ezra, the Mossad's man in Berlin known as the Rabbi, picked up a "tremor" from a Communist source in East Berlin: a political event registering nine on the Richter scale had occurred in Moscow; delegates to the Congress, sworn to secrecy, were scurrying back to their various bailiwicks to brief the second echelon people on what had taken place.

As it was a Saturday the Rabbi had his *Shabbas goy*, Hamlet, dial the Sorcerer's private number in Berlin-Dahlem and hold the phone to his ear. "That you, Harvey?" the Rabbi asked.

Torriti's whiskey-slurred voice came crackling down the line. "Jesus, Ezra, I'm surprised to get ahold of you on the Sabbath. Do you realize the risk you're running? Talking on the phone on Saturday could get you in hot water with the Creator."

"I am definitely not talking on the telephone," the Rabbi insisted defensively. "I'm talking into thin air. By an absolute coincidence my *Shabbas goy* happens to be holding the phone near my mouth."

"What's cooking?" the Sorcerer asked.

The Rabbi explained about the tremor from his Communist in East Berlin. The Sorcerer grunted appreciatively. "I owe you one, Ezra," he said.

"You do, don't you? As soon as the sun sets and Shabbat ends, I shall mark it in the little notebook I keep under my pillow." The Rabbi chuckled into the phone. "In indelible ink, Harvey."

Working the phone, Torriti made some discreet inquiries of his own, then dispatched a CRITIC to the Wiz, who had succeeded Allen Dulles as the Deputy Director for Operations when Dulles moved up to become Director, Central Intelligence. The Moscow rumor mill was abuzz, the Sorcerer informed Wisner. Nikita Khrushchev had made a secret speech to the Twentieth Party Congress during which he had criticized the cult of the individual, which was said to be a euphemism for Stalin's twenty-seven-year reign of terror. The revelations were bound to send a shudder through the Communist world and have a profound impact on the Cold War.

In Washington, the Wiz was impressed enough to hand-carry Torriti's CRITIC directly to Dulles, who was winding up an off-the-record briefing to the *New York Times*'s James "Scotty" Reston. The DCI, puffing on a pipe, waved Wisner to a couch while he finished his pitch. "To sum up, Scotty: Anybody looking at the big picture would have to give the Company points for its triumphs. We got rid of that Mossadegh fellow over in Iran—when he nationalized British Petroleum we installed the pro-American Shah in his place, thereby securing oil supplies for the foreseeable future. Two years ago we gave moral support to the people who ousted that Arbenz fellow in Guatemala after he took Communists into his government. The Wiz here had a hand in that."

Reston turned a guileless grin on Wisner. "Care to define 'moral support,' Frank?"

The Wiz smiled back. "We held the hands of the rebels who were afraid of the dark."

"Nothing material?"

"We may have provided war-surplus combat boots when the folks who invaded from Honduras got their feet wet. I'd have to check the records on that to be sure."

Reston, still grinning, said, "Fact that Arbenz, a democratically elected leader, expropriated four hundred thousand acres of a banana plantation owned by an American company didn't have anything to do with the coup, right?"

"Climb down off your high horse, Scotty," Wisner told Reston, his Mississippi drawl subverting the smile stitched to his face. "The Company wasn't defending United *Fruit* interests, and you damn well know it. We were defending United *States* interests. You've heard speak of the Monroe Doctrine. We need to draw the line when it comes to letting Communists into this hemisphere."

"It's cut-and-dried," Dulles interjected. "Both Iran and Guatemala are squarely in our camp now."

Reston started screwing the cap back onto his fountain pen. "You guys must have heard the story about Chou En-lai—someone asked him about the impact of the French Revolution on France. He's supposed to have formed his hands into a pyramid, his fingertips touching, and said, 'Too soon to tell.' Let's see what's happening in Iran and Guatemala twenty-five years down the pike before we list them on the credit side of the CIA's ledger."

"Thought Scotty was supposed to be one of the Company's friends," the Wiz complained when Reston had departed.

"He's a no-nonsense journalist," Dulles said, slipping his stockinged feet back into bedroom slippers. "You make a strong case, you can usually count on him being in your corner. He's peeved because the *Times* bought our 'supplied moral support' cover story two years back. A lot of ink's been spilled on Guatemala since then—people are aware that we stage-managed the invasion and frightened Arbenz into running for it." Relighting his pipe, Dulles gestured with his chin toward the piece of paper in Wisner's fist. "Must be a hell of a dog for you to be walking it personally?"

Wisner told the DCI that the Sorcerer had picked up rumors of a secret Khrushchev speech denouncing the errors—and perhaps the crimes—of Joe Stalin. Dulles, bored to tears by administrative chores and budget charts, always open to an imaginative operation, immediately grasped the propaganda potential: If the Company could get its hands on the text of the Khrushchev speech they could play it back into the satellite states, into Russia itself. The result would be incalculable: rank-and-file Communists the world over would become disillusioned with the Soviet Union; the French and Italian Communist Parties, once so powerful there was a question of them sharing political power, could be permanently crippled; the Stalinist leaders in Eastern Europe, especially in Poland and Hungary, could become vulnerable to revisionist forces.

Dulles instructed Wisner to send a top-secret cable to all Company stations abroad alerting them to the existence of the speech and ordering them to leave no stone unturned to get a copy of it.

In the end it wasn't the Company that got its hands on Khrushchev's secret speech; it was the Israeli Mossad. A Polish Jew spotted a Polish translation of

Khrushchev's speech on a desk in the Stalin Gothic Communist Party head-quarters in Warsaw and managed to smuggle it into the Israeli embassy long enough for Mossad people there to photograph it and send it on to Israel.

In Washington, James Angleton had set up a long table as an extension to his desk and filled it with boxes overflowing with file folders on CIA officers and agents; so many of the documents in the folders were flagged with red priority stickers—each sticker signaled an operation gone awry, a curious remark, a suspicious meeting—that one of the rare visitors to Mother's sanctum sanctorum had described them as poppies in a field of snow. Some two weeks after the Twentieth Party Congress, Angleton (who, in addition to his counterintelligence chores, handled liaison with the Israelis) had returned from one of his regular three-martini lunches and was poring over the Central Registry file on a Company officer who claimed to have sweet-talked a Soviet diplomat in Turkey into spying in place for the Americans. Under the best of circumstances Angleton would have been leery of anything or anybody that fell into the Company's lap. Which prompted him to take a closer look at the person who had done the recruiting. Angleton noticed that the officer in question had belonged briefly to a socialist study group at Cornell, and had fudged the episode when it was brought up during an early interview. Philby, Angleton remembered, had joined a socialist society at Cambridge but had later severed his ties with the socialists and covered his tracks by associating with rightist groups and people. The CIA officer who had recruited the Russian diplomat in Turkey needed to be brought back to Washington and grilled; the possibility that he was a Soviet mole and had "dropped out" of the socialist study group on orders from his KGB controlling officer had to be explored. If the shadow of a doubt persisted, the officer would be encouraged to resign from the CIA. In any case, the Soviet diplomat in Turkey would be kept at arm's length lest he turn out to be a KGB disinformation agent.

Angleton was tacking one of the red priority stickers to the CIA officer's Central Registry file when there was a knock on the door. His secretary opened it a crack and held up a sealed pouch that had just been brought over by a young Israeli diplomat. Waving her in, Angleton broke the seal with a wire cutter and extracted a large manila envelope. Scrawled across the face of the envelope was a note from the head of the Israeli Mossad: "Jim—consider this a down payment on the briefing you promised re: the Egyptian order of battle along the Suez Canal." Opening the envelope, Angleton discovered a bound typescript with the words "Secret Speech of the Soviet First Party Secretary N. Khrushchev to the Twentieth Party Congress" on the title page.

Days later, Dulles (over the strenuous objections of Angleton, who wanted to "doctor" the speech to further embarrass the Russians and then leak it in dribs and drabs to spin out the impact) released the text of the secret speech to the *New York Times*.

Then he and the Wiz sat back to watch the Soviets squirm.

A friend of Azalia Isanova's who worked as a headline writer for the Party newspaper, *Pravda*, let her in on the secret as they queued for tea and cakes at a canteen on a back street behind the Kremlin: the American newspaper, the *New York Times*, had published the text of a secret speech that Nikita Sergeyevich Khrushchev delivered to a closed session of the Twentieth Party Congress. Khrushchev had created a sensation at the Congress, so the American newspaper claimed, by reproving "real crimes" committed by Joseph Stalin, and accusing the Great Helmsman of abusing power and promoting a cult of the individual. At first Azalia didn't believe the news; she suggested that the American Central Intelligence Agency might have planted the story to embarrass Khrushchev and sow dissension within the Communist hierarchy. No, no, the story was accurate, her friend insisted. His brother's wife had a sister whose husband had attended a close meeting of his Party cell in Minsk; Khrushchev's secret speech had been dissected line by line for the Party faithful. Things in Russia were going to thaw, her friend predicted gleefully, now that Khrushchev himself had broken the ice. "It might even become possible," he added, his voice reduced to a whisper, "for you to publish your—"

Azalia brought a finger to her lips, cutting him off before he could finish the sentence.

In fact, Azalia—trained as a historian and working for the last four years as a researcher at the Historical Archives Institute in Moscow, thanks to a letter of introduction from her girlfriend's father, the KGB chief Lavrenti Pavlovich Beria—had been compiling index card files on Stalin's victims. She had been enormously moved, years before, by two lines from Akhmatova's poem, "Requiem," which she had come across in an underground *samizdat* edition passed from hand to hand:

I should like to call you all by name,
But they have lost the lists...

Azalia had celebrated the death of Stalin in March of 1953 by beginning to compile the lost lists; cataloguing Stalin's victims became the secret passion

of her life. The first two index cards in her collection bore the names of her
mother and father, both arrested by the secret police in the late forties and
(as she discovered from dossiers she unearthed in the Historical Archives
Institute) summarily executed as "enemies of the people" in one of the basements of the massive KGB headquarters on Lubyanskaya Square. Their bodies, along with the dozens of others executed that day, had been incinerated
in a city crematorium (there would have been a small mountain of corpses
piled in the courtyard, and dogs had been seen gnawing on human arms or
legs in a nearby field), and their ashes thrown into a common trench on the
outskirts of Moscow. The great majority of her index cards were based on
files she came across in cartons gathering dust in the Institute. Other information came from personal contacts with writers and artists and colleagues;
almost everyone had lost a parent or a relative or a friend in the Stalinist
purges, or knew someone who had. By the time of Khrushchev's secret
speech, Azalia had quietly accumulated 12,500 index cards, listing the
names, dates of birth and arrest and execution or disappearance, of the up-
to-then nameless victims of Stalin's tyrannical rule.

Unlike Akhmatova, Azalia would be able to call them by their names.

Spurred on by her Pravda friend's suggestion, Azalia arranged a meeting
with the cousin of a cousin who worked as an editor at the weekly *Ogonyok*, a
magazine noted for its relatively liberal point of view. Azalia hinted that she had
stumbled across long forgotten dossiers at the Historical Archives Institute. In
view of Khrushchev's denunciation of the crimes of Stalin, she was prepared to
write an article naming names and providing details of the summary trials and
executions or deaths in prison camps of some of the victims of Stalinism.

Like other Moscow intellectuals, the editor had heard rumors of
Khrushchev's attack on Stalin. But he was wary of actually publishing details
of Stalin's crimes; editors who went out on limbs often fell to their deaths.
Without identifying her, he would sound out members of the magazine's
editorial board, he said. Even if they agreed to her proposition, it was unlikely that a final decision would be taken without first clearing the matter with
high ranking Party officials.

That night Azalia Isanova was woken by the thud of feet pounding up the
stairwell. She knew instantly what it meant: Even in buildings equipped with
working elevators, the KGB always used the stairs in the belief that their noisy
arrival would serve as a warning to everyone within earshot. A fist pounded on
her door. Azalia was ordered to throw on some clothing and was hauled off to
a stuffy room in Lubyanka, where until noon the following day she was questioned about her work at the Institute. Was it correct, the interrogators wanted

to know, that she had acquired data on enemies of the people who had died in prison camps during the thirties and forties? Was it correct that she was exploring the possibility of publishing an article on the subject? Glancing at a dossier, another interrogator casually inquired whether she was the same Isanova, Azalia, a female of the Hebrew race, who had been summoned to a KGB station in 1950 and quizzed about her relationship with a certain Yevgeny Alexandrovich Tsipin? Thoroughly frightened but lucid, Azalia kept her answers as vague as possible. Yes, she had once known Tsipin; had been told that continuing to see him was not in the state's best interests; by that time the relationship, if that is what it was, had long since ended. Her interrogators didn't appear to know about her index cards (which she kept hidden in a metal trunk in an attic in the countryside). After twelve and a half hours of interrogation, she was let off with a crisp warning: Mind your own business, she was sternly instructed, and let the Party mind the Party's business.

One of her interrogators, a coldly polite round-faced man who squinted at her through rimless spectacles, escorted Aza down two flights of wide stairs to a back entrance of Lubyanka. "Trust us," he told her at the door. "Any rectifications to the official history of the Soviet Union would be made by the Party's historians acting in the interests of the masses. Stalin may have made minor mistakes," he added. "What leader doesn't? But it should not be forgotten that Stalin had come to power when Russian fields were plowed by oxen; by the time of his death, Russia had become a world power armed with atomic weapons and missiles."

Aza got the message; Khrushchev's speech notwithstanding, real reform in Russia would only come when history was restored to the professional, as opposed to the Party, historians. And as long as the KGB had a say in the matter, that was not about to happen anytime soon. Aza vowed to keep adding to her index cards. But until things changed, and drastically, they would have to remain hidden in the metal trunk.

Lying awake in bed late that night, watching the shadows from the street four floors below flit across the outside of her lace window-curtains, Aza let her thoughts drift to the mysterious young man who had come into her life six years before, and gone out of it just as suddenly, leaving no forwarding address; he had disappeared so completely it was almost as if he never existed. Aza had only the haziest memory of what he looked like but she was still able to recreate the timbre and pitch of his voice. Each time I see you I seem to leave a bit of me with you, he had told her over the phone. To which she had responded, Oh, I hope this is not true. For if you see me too often there will be nothing left of you. On the spur of the moment, stirred by a riptide of emotion, she had invited him to come home with her to explore whether his lust and her desire were harmonious in bed.

They had turned out to be lusciously harmonious, which made his disappearance from the face of the earth all the harder for her to bear. She had tried to find him; had casually sounded out some of the people who had been at the Perdelkino dacha the day they met; had even worked up the nerve to ask Comrade Beria if he could discover where the young man had gone to. A few days later she had found a hand-penned note from Beria under her door. Continuing a relationship with Tsipin was not in the state's best interests, it had said. Forget him. Several weeks later, when the KGB called her in to ask about her relationship with Tsipin, she had managed to put him out of mind; all that remained was the occasional echo of his voice in her brain.

I am pleased with your voice, Yevgeny, she had told him.

I am pleased that you are pleased, he had responded.

2

NEW YORK, MONDAY, SEPTEMBER 17, 1956

A COLD WAR-WEARY E. WINSTROM EBBITT II, BACK IN THE STATES on his first home leave in nineteen months, had a three-week fling with an attractive State Department attorney that ended abruptly when she weighed her options and decided on the bird in hand, which turned out to be a promotion and a posting to the Philippines. Weekdays, Ebby briefed Company analysts on the increasingly tense political situation in the satellite states in the wake of Khrushchev's secret speech. (In June, Polish workers had rioted against the Communist regime in the streets of Poznan.) Weekends, he commuted to Manhattan to spend time with his son, Manny, a thin boy with solemn eyes who had recently turned nine. Ebby's ex-wife, Eleonora, remarried to a successful divorce lawyer and living in a sumptuous Fifth Avenue apartment, made no bones about the fact that she preferred the absentee father to the one turning up on her doorstep Saturdays and Sundays to bond with Immanuel. As for Manny, he greeted his father with timid curiosity but gradually warmed to Ebby, who (acting on the advice of divorced friends, of which there were many in the Company) kept the meetings low-key. One weekend they went to see Sandy Koufax pitch the Brooklyn Dodgers to victory over the Giants at Ebbets Field. Another time they took the subway to Coney Island (an adventure in itself, since Manny was driven to his private school in a limousine) and rode the giant Ferris wheel and the roller-coaster.

Later, on the way back to Manhattan, Manny was gnawing on a frozen Milky Way when, out of the blue, he said, "What's a Center Intelligence Agency?"

"What makes you ask?"

"Mommy says that's what you work for. She says that's why you spend so much time outside America."

Ebby glanced around. The two women within earshot seemed to be concentrating on their reflections in the door windows. "I work for the American government—"

"Not this Center Intelligence thingamajig?"

Ebby swallowed hard. "Look, maybe we ought to discuss this another time."

"So what kind of stuff do you do for the government?"

"I'm a lawyer—"

"I know thaaaat."

"I do legal work for the State Department."

"Do you sue people?"

"Not exactly."

"Then what?"

"I help protect America from its enemies."

"Why does America have enemies?"

"Not every country sees eye to eye on things."

"What things?"

"Things like the existence of different political parties, things like honest trials and free elections, things like the freedom of newspapers to publish what they want, things like the right of people to criticize the government without going to jail. Things like that."

Manny thought about this for a moment. "Know what I'm going to do when I grow up?"

"What?"

Manny slipped his hand into his father's. "I'm going to protect America from its enemies same as you—if it still has any."

Ebby had to swallow a smile. "I don't think we're going to run out of enemies any time soon, Manny."

"He told me he wanted to protect America from its enemies but he was afraid there'd be none left by the time he grew up," Ebby explained.

The Wiz tossed off his Bloody Mary and signaled a passing waiter for two more. "Not much chance of that," he said, chuckling under his breath.

"That's what I told him," Ebby said. "He seemed relieved."

Ebby and the DD/O, Frank Wisner, were having a working lunch at a corner table in a private dining room of the Cloud Club atop the Chrysler Building. When two more drinks were delivered to the table, the Wiz, looking more drawn and worried than Ebby remembered him, wrapped his paw around one of them. "To you and yours," he said, clinking glasses with Ebby. "Are you surviving home leave, Eb?"

"I suppose I am." Ebby shook his head in dismay. "Sometimes I feel as if I landed on a different planet. I had dinner with three lawyers from my old firm the other day. They've grown rich and soft—big apartments in the city, weekend homes in Connecticut, country clubs in Westchester. One guy I worked with's been named a junior partner. He pulls down more in one month than I make in a year."

"Having second thoughts about the choice you made?"

"No, I'm not, Frank. There's a war on out there. People here just don't seem concerned about it. The energy they invest in working out stock options and mergers...hell, I keep thinking about those Albanian kids who were executed in Tiranë."

"Lot of people will tell you it's the folks in academia who're wrestling with the really big questions—like whether Joyce ever used a semicolon after 1919."

The comment drew an appreciative snicker from Ebby.

"Sounds to me like you're 'bout ready to get back into harness," Wisner said. "Which brings me to the subject of this lunch. I'm offering you a new assignment, Eb."

"*Offering* implies I can refuse."

"You'll have to volunteer. It'll be dangerous. If you nibble at the bait I'll tell you more."

Ebby leaned forward. "I'm nibbling, Frank."

"Thought you might. The mission's right up your alley. I want you to get your ass to Budapest, Eb."

Ebby whistled under his breath. "Budapest! Don't we have assets there already—under diplomatic cover, in the embassy?"

The Wiz looked off to the side. "All of our embassy people are tailed, their offices and apartments are bugged. Ten days back the station chief thought he'd shaken his tail, so he slipped a letter into a public mail box addressed to one of the dissidents who'd been supplying us with information. They must have emptied the box and opened all the letters, and that led them to the dissident. The poor bastard was arrested that night and wound up on a meat hook in a prison refrigerator." Wisner turned back to Ebby. "I'm speaking literally. We badly need to send in a new face, Eb. Because of security considerations, because sending someone in from the outside will emphasize the seriousness of the message being delivered."

"Why me?"

"Fair question. First off, you operated behind German lines in the war; in our business there's no substitute for experience. Secondly, you're a bona fide lawyer, which means we can work up a watertight cover story that gives you a good reason to be in Budapest. Here's the deal: there's a State

Department delegation going into Hungary mid-October to negotiate the issue of compensation for Hungarian assets that were frozen in America when Hungary came in on the side of the Germans in World War II. Your old law firm has been representing some of the claims of Hungarian-Americans who lost assets when Hungary went Communist after the war—we're talking about factories, businesses, large tracts of land, art collections, apartments, the like. Your old boss, Bill Donovan, has set aside an office and a secretary—the desk is piled high with the claims of Hungarian-Americans. The idea is for you to hole up there for a couple of weeks to establish a cover story while you familiarize yourself with the claims, after which you'll go in with the State Department folks and argue that any settlement needs to include compensation for the Hungarian-Americans. Anybody wants to check you out, Donovan's people will backstop you—you've been working there since Eve nibbled on the apple, so your secretary will tell anyone who asks."

"You haven't spelled out the real mission," Ebby noted.

Wisner glanced at his watch; Ebby noticed a slight twitch in one of his eyes. "The DCI specifically said he wanted to brief you himself."

"Dulles?"

"They don't call him the Great White Case Officer for nothing. From here on out, Eb, we want you to stay away from Cockroach Alley. Dulles is expecting us to join him for a drink at the Alibi Club in Washington day after tomorrow at six."

Ebby began chewing on a piece of ice from his glass. "You were pretty damn sure I'd accept."

The Wiz grinned. "I guess I was. I guess I counted on your commitment to protecting America from its enemies."

His brush mustache dancing on his upper lip, his eyes glinting behind silver spectacles, DCI Allen Welsh Dulles was regaling the men gathered around him at the bar of the Alibi Club, an all-male hangout in a narrow brick building a few blocks from the White House that was so exclusive only a handful of people in Washington had ever heard of it. "It happened in Switzerland right after the first war," he was saying. "I got word that some-one was waiting to see me in my office but I decided the hell with him and played tennis instead. Which is how I missed out meeting Vladimir Ilyich Ulyanov, whom you gents know by the name of Lenin."

Spotting the Wiz and Ebby at the door, Dulles waded through the crowd and steered them into a tiny office off the cloakroom that he often commandeered for private meetings. Wisner introduced Ebby and then took a back seat; he knew from experience that Dulles relished the operations side of the Company's work.

"So you're Ebbitt," Dulles said, motioning his guest toward a chair, settling into another so close to him that their knees were scraping. Puffing away on a pipe, he walked Ebby through his curriculum vitae; he wanted to know what universities he'd attended, what undergraduate clubs he'd belonged to, how he'd ended up in the OSS, precisely what he'd done during his mission behind German lines in France to win the Croix de Guerre. He quizzed Ebby about his two Company tours in Germany; about the agent infiltration ops into the Carpathians and Albania that had turned sour, about the possibility that Gehlen's Org in Pullach had been infiltrated by the KGB. Then, suddenly, he changed the subject. "The Wiz tells me you're volunteering for this mission to Budapest," he said. "Do you have an idea why we're sending you in?"

"That's above my pay grade."

"Take a stab at it anyway."

"I've been doing my homework," Ebby admitted. "Khrushchev's secret speech pulled the rug out from under the Stalinists in the satellite states. Poland is seething with insurrection. Hungary looks a lot like a powder keg waiting to explode—a totalitarian state run by an unpopular Stalinist with the help of forty thousand secret police and a million and a half informers. I assume you want me to get in touch with the Hungarian firebrands and light the fuse."

Dulles, who was jovial enough in social situations, could be icily shrewd in private. His eyes narrowing, he glanced at Wisner, then looked intently at Ebby. "You're one hundred eighty degrees out of whack, Ebbitt. We want you to go in and tell these people to simmer down."

"Radio Free Europe has been encouraging them to rise up—" Ebby started to say.

Dulles cut him off. "Radio Free Europe is not an organ of the United States government. The bottom line is: We don't want Hungary exploding until we're good and ready. Don't get me wrong: roll-back is still the official line—"

The Wiz put in a word. "You mean it's still the official *policy*, Allen, don't you?"

Dulles didn't take kindly to correction. "Line, policy, it amounts to the same thing," he said impatiently. He turned back to Ebby. "We figure we'll need a year and a half to lay in the plumbing. General Gehlen's Org has a Hungarian Section up and running but it will take a while to organize arms caches inside Hungary, train and infiltrate teams of Hungarian émigrés with communications skills and equipment so that an uprising can be coordinated."

"You're assuming that the firebrands can control their troops," Ebby said. "From the background papers I've been reading, it doesn't seem as if a spontaneous uprising can be ruled out."

"I don't buy that," Dulles shot back. "A demonstration on a street corner can be spontaneous. A popular uprising is another kettle of fish."

"Our immediate worry," Wisner chimed in, "is that the firebrands may reckon that the United States will be obliged to come in and save their hides once they bring the cauldron to a boil. Or at the very least we'll threaten to come in to keep the Russians at arm's length."

"This would be a dangerous miscalculation on their part," Dulles warned. "Neither President Eisenhower nor his Secretary of State, my brother Foster, are ready to start World War III over Hungary. Your job is to convince the firebrands of this fact of life. As long as they understand that, we're off the hook if they decide to go ahead and stir things up. On the other hand, if they can keep the lid on for, say, eighteen months—"

"A year would probably do it," Wisner suggested.

"A year, eighteen months, when the Hungarians—with our covert help—have an infrastructure in place for an uprising, the situation may be more propitious."

"There's another problem you need to be aware of," the Wiz said. "The situation in the Near East is heating up. Nasser's seizure of the Suez Canal last July, his rejection last week of that eighteen-nation proposal to internationalize the Canal, are pushing the British and French into a corner. Israeli teams have been shuttling between Tel Aviv and Paris. They're cooking up something, you can bet on it; the Israelis would do almost anything to get the French to supply them with a nuclear reactor. Cipher traffic between the Israeli Army central command in Tel Aviv and the French General Staff is way up. Feeling here is that the Israelis might spearhead a British-French attack on Nasser with a blitzkrieg across the Sinai to capture the Canal."

"In which case a revolution in Hungary would get lost in the shuffle," Dulles said. He climbed to his feet and extended a hand. "Good luck to you, Ebbitt."

Outside the Alibi Club, a newspaper vender hawking the *Washington Post* was wading into oncoming traffic backed up at a red light. "Read all about it," he cried in a sing-song voice. "Dow Jones peaks at five hundred twenty-one."

"The rich grow richer," Wisner said with a sardonic grin.

"And the soft grow softer," Ebby added.

3

BUDAPEST, TUESDAY, OCTOBER 16, 1956

THE PÁRIS-ISTANBUL ORIENT EXPRESS HURTLED ACROSS THE FLATLANDS bordering the chalky Danube toward Budapest. Drinking hot black coffee from a thermos lid, Ebby gazed through the window of the first-class compartment at the herds of squat, wide-horned cattle guarded by *czikos*, the Hungarian cowboys riding wiry horses. Stone houses and barns flitted past, along with neat vegetable gardens and fenced yards teeming with chickens and geese. Soon the first low brick-and-mortar factories came into view. As the train slipped through the suburbs of Buda, the narrow highway alongside the tracks became clogged with dilapidated open trucks spewing diesel exhaust from their tailpipes. Minutes later the Orient-Express eased into the West Station behind Castle Hill.

Carrying a bulging attaché case and a leather two-suiter, Ebby discouraged the uniformed porter with a shake of his head and made his way through the glass-domed station and down the steps to the street. A fresh-faced embassy counselor waiting next to a car-pool Ford came forward to meet him. "Sir, I'll wager you're Mr. Ebbitt," he said.

"How could you tell?"

"No offense intended but your luggage looks too posh for anyone but a New York lawyer," the young man said with a broad grin. He took Ebby's two-suiter and dropped it into the trunk compartment. "Name's Doolittle," he announced, offering a hand as he introduced himself. "Jim Doolittle, no relation whatsoever to the aviator of the same name. Welcome to Budapest, Mr. Ebbitt."

"Elliott."

"Elliott it is." He slid behind the wheel of the Ford and Ebby settled

into the passenger seat. The young counselor deftly maneuvered the car
into traffic and headed in a southeasterly direction toward the Danube.
"You've been booked into the Gellért Hotel, along with the delegation from
the State Department. They flew in yesterday. Ambassador charged me to
tell you if you need assistance in any shape or form, you only need to say
'hey.' The first negotiating session is scheduled for ten A.M. tomorrow. The
State Department people will be ferried over to the Foreign Ministry in one
of our minibuses. You're welcome to hitch a ride. Do you know Hungary
at all?"

"Only what I read in my guide book," Ebby said. "How long have you
been posted here?"

"Twenty-three months."

"Do you get to mix much with the natives?"

"Meet Hungarians! Elliott, I can see you don't know much about life
behind the Iron Curtain. Hungary is a Communist country. The only
natives you meet are the ones who work for the Allamvédelmi Hatóság, what
we call the AVH, which is their secret police. The others are too frightened.
Which reminds me, the embassy security officer wanted me to caution you
to be wary..."

"Be wary of what?"

"Of Hungarian women who seem ready and willing, if you see what
I mean. Of Hungarian men who are eager to take you to some off-the-
beaten-track night spot. Whatever you do, for God's sake don't change
money on the black market. And don't accept packages to deliver to someone's cousin in America—they could be filled with secret documents. Next
thing you know you'll be arrested as a spy and I'll be talking to you through
the bars of a prison."

"Thanks for the tips," Ebby said. "All that spy rigamarole is not up my
alley."

Doolittle glanced at his passenger with a certain amount of amusement.
"I don't suppose it is. I don't suppose you noticed the small blue Skoda
behind us, did you?"

As a matter of fact he had but he didn't want Jim Doolittle to know it.
Ebby made a show of looking over his shoulder. The blue Skoda, with two
passengers visible in the front seat, was two car lengths behind the Ford's rear
bumper. Doolittle laughed. "All of us at the embassy are followed all the
time," he said. "You get kind of used to it. I'll be mighty surprised if you're
not assigned a chaperon."

Driving parallel to the Danube, the embassy counselor sped past the

green girders of the Szabadság Bridge, then threaded through the yellow
trolley cars swarming at the corner and dropped off the New York attorney
in front of the Art Nouveau entrance to the Gellért at the foot of the Buda
hills. Watching Ebby make his way through the great revolving door into the
hotel, Doolittle shook his head. "Another innocent abroad," he muttered.
And he threw the Ford into gear and headed back toward the embassy.

The small blue Skoda with a long whip antenna attached to the rear fender
pulled into the driveway of the Gellért's outdoor swimming pool and parked
behind the hedges, giving it a view of the hotel's main entrance down the
block. The Hungarian in the passenger seat removed a small microphone
from the glove compartment and plugged it into the transceiver under the
dashboard. He flicked on the switch, let the vacuum tubes warm up for a
half a minute, then spoke into the microphone.

   "*Szervusz, szervusz.* Mobile twenty-seven reporting. The *amerikai* Ebbitt
has entered the Gellért Hotel. Activate microphones in room two zero three.
We will stand by and pick him up if he emerges from the Gellért. Over to you."

   "*Viszlát,*" a voice said.

   "*Viszlát,*" the man in the car repeated. He switched off the transceiver.

For Ebby, the week passed in a haze of wearisome negotiations that went
over the same ground again and again and seemed to go nowhere fast.
During the long morning and afternoon sessions around a shabby oval table
at the Ministry of Foreign Affairs, the Hungarian negotiators appeared to be
following a script. Sipping mineral water, puffing on cigarettes mooched
from their American counterparts, they read in droning tones from long lists
of Hungarian assets that they said were frozen in America fifteen years earlier, and supplied outrageous estimates of the value of those assets. The State
Department people, used to dealing with Communist *apparatchiki* who had
no mandate to settle for anything less than their initial demands, treated the
whole exercise as an indoor sport. One of the State Department economic
experts dryly pointed out that several dozen companies on the Hungarian
list had actually gone bust during or immediately after the 1929 stock market
crash but the Hungarians, without batting an eyelash, continued to include
these companies on their list of frozen assets. On the second afternoon,
Ebby finally got to argue his case that any agreement to compensate
Hungary for Hungarian assets lost in America must include provisions to

compensate Hungarian-Americans—here Ebby hefted a thick pile of dossiers—who lost assets when the Communists assumed power in Hungary. The chief of the Hungarian delegation, a stocky timeserver who picked at his teeth while Ebby's words were being translated, suppressed a yawn. To suggest that the People's Republic of Hungary had confiscated assets, he said stiffly, was to distort history. Under Hungarian law, those who fled Hungary after the Communist regime assumed power in 1947 forfeited any claim to compensation for nationalized assets if they failed to file the appropriate forms.

"Could such claims still be filed?" Ebby asked.

"The legal deadline established by law expired on December 31, 1950," the Hungarian responded.

"Who had passed that law?" Ebby asked.

"The legitimately elected government of the People's Republic of Hungary," the bureaucrat replied.

"In other words," Ebby said, "having confiscated assets, your government then passed a law ex post facto denying compensation to those who had fled the country."

"We never denied compensation to those who left the country," the Hungarian insisted. "We denied compensation to those who failed to file claims before the legal deadline."

"You need to simmer down," the head of the State Department delegation, an old hand at dealing with the Communists, told Ebby at an embassy reception that evening. "We're just goin' through motions here. The United States is not about to hand over gold ingots to a Soviet satellite so they can build more tanks and planes."

Saturday morning Ebby ordered a car with an English-speaking chauffeur and set out (with the small blue Skoda trailing behind him) to see something of Budapest. He roamed the Buda hills, inspecting the Buda Castle where Hungarian Kings and Habsburg royalty had once held court, visiting the Coronation Church that had been converted to a mosque during the Ottoman period; he peered over the ramparts of the Fishermen's Bastion at the massive Parliament building, a neogothic relic from the Austro-Hungarian epoch that loomed across the Danube in the Pest skyline. At one-thirty in the afternoon he dismissed the driver and ducked into an ornate coffee house on the Pest side of the river for an open sandwich and a beer; he shared a table with a bird-like old woman who wore a frayed fox fur twisted around her gaunt neck and a ski cap on her skull. Sipping a glass of Tokaj, a white wine from the slopes of the Carpathians, she whispered something to Ebby in Hungarian. Seeing his confusion, she inquired politely in German if was a foreigner. When he said yes, he was an American, she became flustered. "Oh, dear, you will have to excuse me," she whispered. Leaving her wine unfinished, she dropped some coins on the table and fled from the coffee house. Through the plate-glass window Ebby could see one of the men in the blue Skoda gesturing toward the old lady as she hurried across Stalin Avenue. On the other side of the street, two men in dark ankle-length overcoats and fedoras approached her. The old woman rummaged in her handbag for documents, which were snatched out of her hand. One of the men stuffed the woman's papers in a pocket and, with a snap of his head, indicated that she was to come with them. The two men, with the tiny woman almost lost between them, disappeared down a side street.

Ebby had a pang of concern for the old woman whose only crime was that she had found herself sharing a table with an American. Or was there more to it than that? Obviously a team of AVH men had been assigned to keep tabs on him. But were they following him because they routinely kept track of every American on Hungarian soil, or had they been alerted to his presence—and his identity—by one of the dissidents he had come to meet? Slipping a bank note under a saucer, Ebby pulled on his overcoat and set off up Stalin Avenue, stopping now and then to window-shop—and use the window to see what was happening behind him in the street. The blue Skoda was following him at a crawl but there was only one figure in it now; Ebby spotted the second man walking ahead of him. A younger man in hiking boots stopped to study a newspaper every time Ebby stopped. A middle-aged woman window-shopping across the street proceeded up the avenue at a pace that matched Ebby's.

With a tight knot forming in the pit of his stomach—a sensation he first felt the night he parachuted behind German lines during the war—Ebby continued along Stalin Avenue. He hesitated at an intersection called Octagon to consult the fold-out map in his guide book. At the top of the avenue he skirted Hero's Park, where an enormous statue of Stalin stood on its pink marble pedestal. Off to the left he could see the Fine Art Museum. He stopped to check his guide-book again, then went up the steps; as he reached the top he saw, in the glass door, the reflection of the Skoda easing to the curb in the street below.

Inside, Ebby queued at the booth to buy a ticket. A sign in English taped to the window confirmed what he had been told back in Washington: there was an English-language tour of the museum daily at 2:30 P.M. Ebby joined the dozen or so English tourists milling at the foot of the staircase.

Promptly at 2:30 a door opened and a slim young woman emerged from an office. Somewhere in her early thirties, she was dressed entirely in black—a skin-hugging ribbed turtleneck sweater, a flannel skirt flaring around delicate ankles, thick winter stockings and solid shoes with flat heels—and had a mop of unruly dirty-blonde hair that looked as if it had been hacked off at the nape of her neck by a shearing scissors. As far as Ebby could make out she wore no makeup. Pinned to the sweater over her left breast was a nametag that read: "E. Németh."

"Hullo—I am to be your guide," she announced in the crisp, flawless English of an upper-class Sloane Square bird. A nervous trace of a smile appeared on her face as she let her eyes flit over the crowd; they lingered for an instant, not longer, on Ebby before moving on. She said something in fluent Hungarian to the man guarding the turnstile, and he swung it back to let the tourists through. "If you will be kind enough to follow me," said E. Németh. With that, she turned on a heel and set off into the long hall filled with enormous canvases depicting in gory detail some of the epic battles Hungarians had fought against the Ottoman Turks.

Ebby trailed along at the fringe of the group, catching bits and pieces of the battles and the painters. Climbing the steps to the second floor, he overheard one of the tourists, a matronly woman who walked with the aid of a cane, ask the guide, "My dear, wherever did you learn to speak English so beautifully?"

"I am half-English," E. Németh told her. "I was born in Tuscany but raised and educated in Britain." She glanced quickly over her shoulder and her eyes grazed Ebby's. Again the tense half-smile flickered on her face, a flag hoisted to announce the existence of anxiety and her determination not to give in to it.

"And may I ask how an English woman like you wound up living in Budapest?"

"I married it," E. Németh replied.

"Bully for you, my dear. Bully for you."

When they reached the last room in the guided tour, fifty minutes later, E. Németh turned toward her charges. "Here you see six paintings by the renowned Spanish artist El Greco," she announced. "There is actually a seventh painting but it is currently in a basement workshop for cleaning. The museum is very proud of these paintings—this is the largest collection of El Grecos in the world outside of Spain. El Greco was born Domenikos Theotokopoulos on the Greek island of Crete in 1541. He studied under the Venetian master Titian before establishing himself in Toledo. Over the years his use of vibrant colors and deep shadows, his distorted figures, contributed to his reputation as a master painter of religious ecstasy. Many of the figures you see here were actually Spanish noblemen—"

Ebby stepped around the side of the group. "Is there any truth to the notion that El Greco's eye trouble led him to see—and to paint—his figures with elongated faces?"

Her head angled slightly, several fingers (with the nails bitten to the quick, Ebby noticed) kneading her lower lip, E. Németh slowly focused on Ebby. "I have, of course, heard that theory," she replied evenly, "but as far as I know it is based on guesswork, not medical evidence."

As the group started down the long staircase toward the main entrance of the museum, Ebby found himself trailing behind, alongside the guide. He detected the scent of attar of roses in the air.

"You seem to know a good deal about El Greco," she remarked.

"I am a great admirer of his work."

"Would it interest you to see the El Greco that is being restored in the basement workshop?"

"Very much."

They were halfway down the long flight of steps and passing a narrow door on the landing. The guide glanced back. Seeing no one behind them, she stepped quickly to the door, opened it, pulled Ebby through, and jammed it closed behind him. "You were followed when you arrived at the museum," she informed him. "I saw them through the window. There seemed to be an entire team spread out behind you—a car, at least three people on foot."

"I saw them, too," Ebby said. "It is probably standard operating procedure for them to keep tabs on visiting Americans."

E. Németh started down a wooden staircase no wider than her body and lit by weak bulbs on every landing. Under her feet the raw wood of the floorboards in the little used stairs creaked. At the bottom she pushed open another door and stuck her head through. Seeing the coast was clear, she motioned for Ebby to follow her. They made their way across the cement floor of a vast storage room filled with busts and paintings to a door locked and bolted on the inside.

"What does the *E* stand for on your nametag?" Ebby whispered.

"Elizabet."

"My name is Elliott."

She fixed her dark eyes on him. "I was sure you were the one even before you spoke the prearranged sentence," she told him. She grabbed a duffle coat off a hook and flung it over her shoulders as if it were a cape. Producing

a large skeleton key from a pocket, she threw the bolt on the door. As they
emerged from the basement into a sunken patio at the rear of the museum,
she locked the door behind them, then led the way up a flight of steel steps
to a door in the high iron fence, which she unlocked with a second skeleton
key and locked again when they had passed through it. Crossing the street,
she led the way down a narrow alleyway to a beat-up two-door Fiat parked
in a shed. Elizabet unlocked the door, slid behind the wheel, then reached
across to unlock the passenger door. Gunning the motor, she set off down
the alley and melted into the traffic on the thoroughfare at the end of it.

Elizabet piloted the tiny car through the crowded streets of Pest with
utter concentration. After a while Ebby broke the silence. "Where are you
taking me?"

"Arpád and his friends are waiting for you in an apartment in Buda,
behind the South Station."

"What will happen back at the museum when I don't turn up at the
front door?"

"They will wait a while and then come looking for you. When they realize you are no longer in the museum, they will return to the Gellért Hotel
and wait for you to show up there. We have seen this sort of thing many
times—to protect themselves from the wrath of their superiors, they are
unlikely to report your disappearance. After your meeting with Arpád I will
drop you at one of the bridges and you can make your way back to the
Gellért on foot as if nothing out of the ordinary has taken place."

"I heard you tell that woman in the museum that you were married to
Arpád."

She glanced quickly at him. "I did not say I was married to Arpád. I am
married to another Hungarian. I am Arpád's mistress."

Ebby winced. "I didn't mean to pry—"

"Of course you did. You are a spy from the Central Intelligence Agency.
Prying is your business."

Gusts of icy wind knifing in from the Danube buckled the mullions and
rattled the panes in the corner apartment on the top floor of the house lost
in the labyrinthine streets of the Buda hills. When Ebby appeared at the
door, a heavyset man in his late thirties, with a mane of prematurely grey
hair and the flat forehead and knuckled nose of a Roman Centurion, strode
across the room to greet him. He was wearing the heavy lace-up shoes and
rough corduroy trousers and worn woolen pullover of a laborer. "I welcome

you with all my heart to Budapest," he declared, burying the visitor's outstretched hand in both of his, scrutinizing him with dark, restless eyes.

"This is Arpád Zelk," Elizabet murmured.

"It is an honor to meet such a distinguished poet," Ebby said.

Arpád snorted bitterly. "As I compose my poems in my native Hungarian, a language spoken by a mere ten million of the two and a half billion people on the planet Earth, my distinction resembles that of a bird chirping at the top of his lungs in a soundproof cage."

Arpád turned away to hold a hurried conference in Hungarian with Elizabet and the two young men sitting at the glass-covered dining table. Ebby took in the room: there was an enormous 1930s radio (big enough to house a small dog) on a table, wooden beams overhead, heavy rug-like drapes drawn across the windows, a fireplace stuffed with paper waiting to be burned, two buckets filled with coal, a small mountain of pamphlets stacked against a wall. Elizabet glanced back at Ebby. "Excuse me for a moment—I am telling them about the AVH men who were following you. Arpád wants to be sure they did not follow us here."

Arpád switched off the overhead light and went to a window, where he parted the heavy drapes the width of two fingers and surveyed the street below. "It does not appear that you were followed," he announced. "In any case I have people watching the street from another apartment—they will alert us by telephone if there is danger." Arpád motioned for Ebby to take the empty chair at the table. He nodded toward the two other men sitting around it and pointedly introduced them by their first names only. "Meet, please, Mátyás; meet, also, Ulrik," he said. "They are comrades in the Hungarian Resistance Movement."

Ebby reached to shake the hand of each man—Mátyás wore the distinctive short jacket of a university student; Ulrik, the suit and vest and detachable-collar shirt and steel-rimmed eyeglasses of a white-collar worker—and then sat down in the empty chair. Elizabet settled onto a couch.

Arpád filled a demitasse with a pale liquid and pushed it across the table to his guest. "Are you familiar with our Magyar Torkoly? Ah, I did not think so. It is a brandy fabricated from the skins of grapes after they have been crushed to make wine. Egészségedre," he said, hoisting his own demitasse.

"Egészségedre," the two men at the table echoed, saluting Ebby with raised glasses.

"Cheers," Ebby said.

They downed their cups. The brandy scalded Ebby's throat. He opened his mouth wide and exhaled and pulled a face. The others smiled.

"If you please," Arpád said with great formality, "what word do you bring to us from the United States of America?"

"I bring you the good wishes of people highly placed in the American government. I bring you their respect for your courage and their sympathy for your cause—"

Arpád's palm came down on the glass of the table so hard that Ebby was astonished it didn't shatter under the blow. Mátyás said something in Hungarian and Arpád answered him irritably. When Mátyás persisted, Arpád nodded reluctantly. He looked back at Ebby. "My friends and I are not diplomats at a tea party," he said gruffly, stirring the air with his thick fingers. "We do not need your good wishes or your sympathy or your respect. We need your pledge of material assistance if the situation explodes."

"The American government is wary of pushing the Soviets too far—"

"Over something as inconsequential as Hungary," Arpád snapped, finishing the sentence for him. "That is what you dare not say."

"Hungary is not inconsequential to us. Which is why we want you to postpone any uprising until the groundwork has been laid; until Khrushchev, who has a tendency toward dovishness in these matters, has consolidated his hold on the Politburo hawks."

"How long?"

"Somewhere between a year and eighteen months."

Ulrik repeated this in Hungarian to make sure he had understood it correctly. *"Igen,"* Elizabet told him. "Between a year and eighteen months."

"Reménytelen!" sneered the young man.

Elizabet translated for Ebby. "Ulrik says the word *hopeless.*"

"It is not hopeless," Ebby said. "It is a matter of prudence and patience. The American government is not interested in being drawn into a war with the Soviets—"

"I will say you what Trotsky said to the Russians before the 1917 revolution," Arpád declared, his eyes fixed unblinkingly on Ebby's. "'You may not be interested in war but war is interested in you.'" Mátyás muttered something and Arpád nodded in agreement. "Mátyás says we can neither start nor stop an uprising against the Communists, and I hold the same view. Whatever will happen will happen with or without us, and with or without you. We live in a country sick with what we call *esengofrasz—*"

Arpád looked at Elizabet for a translation. "Doorbell fever," she said.

"Yes, yes. Doorbell fever. Everyone waits for AVH agents to ring his bell at midnight and take him away for questioning or torture. I myself have been arrested five times in my life, twice by the fascists who brought

Hungary into the world war on the side of the Germans, three times by the Communists who seized power with the help of the Red Army after the war. I have spent eleven years and four months of my life in prisons—that is fifteen years less than Sade and six years more than Dostoyevsky. I have lived for months at a time in airless subterranean cells crawling with rats in the fortress prison of Vac north of Budapest. Over one particularly bitter winter I tamed several of the rats; they used to come out to visit me in the evening and I would warm my fingers against their bodies. I was tortured in the same prison—*in the same cell*—by the Hungarian fascists before the war and the Communists after. The difference between the two ideologies is instructive. The fascists tortured you to make you confess to crimes you really committed. The Communists torture you to make you confess to imagined crimes; they want you to sign a confession they have already written—admitting to contacts with fascist elements of foreign countries, admitting to plots to assassinate the Communist leaders, admitting to putting ground glass in the supply of farina to cause economic sabotage." Sinking back into his chair, Arpád sucked air through his nostrils to calm himself. "Once, to avoid more torture, I confessed to passing state secrets to the chief of American intelligence in Vienna named Edgar Allen Poe. For this crime I was sentenced to fifteen years in prison, but I was quietly pardoned when someone in the superstructure recognized the name of Poe."

Waving a hand in scorn, Ulrik spoke at length to Arpád in Hungarian. Arpád nodded several times in agreement. "He would have me say you that your Radio Free Europe has spoken endlessly in its broadcasts to us about rolling back Communism," he told Ebby.

"Radio Free Europe is not an organ of the United States government," Ebby insisted. "It's an independent enterprise staffed by émigrés from the Communist countries. Its broadcasts don't necessarily represent official American policy—"

"If you please, who pays for Radio Free Europe?" Arpád demanded.

The question reduced Ebby to silence. Drumming a knuckle on the table top, Ulrik spoke again in Hungarian. Arpád nodded in vehement agreement. "He says the moment of truth approaches. He says you must be ready to assist an uprising, if one occurs, materially and morally. He says that if you can keep the Russians from intervening, only that, nothing more, Communism in Hungary will be swept onto the dust-heap of history."

Here the young student spoke for a moment to the others with a certain shyness. Smiling, Arpád reached across the table and gave him a mock punch in the shoulder. Elizabet said from the couch, "Mátyás quotes the

Bertold Brecht poem on the brief uprising of the East Germans against the Communist regime in 1953."

Closing his eyes, collecting his thoughts, tilting back his large head, Arpád recited four lines in English:

> Would it not be simpler
> If the government
> Dissolved the people
> And elected another?

Out of the corner of his eye Ebby caught a glimpse of Elizabet curled into a contorted position on the couch, her legs tucked under her, one arm flung back over the back of the couch. He could feel her eyes on him. "No one in the American camp doubts your determination to rid yourselves of the Stalinist dictatorship," he told Arpád. "But you must, in our view, put realities above romanticism. The realities are stark and speak for themselves. Two Soviet tank units, the second and the seventeenth Mechanized Divisions, are stationed forty miles from Budapest; they could be in the capital in an hour's time. We have abundant evidence that the Soviets are not blind to the explosiveness of the situation here. They clearly have contingency plans to rush reserves into the country in the event of unrest. I can tell you that we have information that they are in the process of assembling large mobile reserves on the Ukrainian side of the Hungarian frontier. I can tell you that they are constructing floating pontoon bridges across the Tisza River so that these reserves can reach Hungary at a moment's notice."

Arpád and Elizabet exchanged dark looks; Ebby's information apparently came as a surprise to them. Elizabet quickly translated what Ebby had said for the others. "The Soviet General Konev," Ebby went on, "who led Russian ground forces in the capture of Berlin and is considered to be one of their best tacticians, is the operational commander of the Soviet reserves. The Soviet General Zhukov, the current Minister of Defense, is pushing Khrushchev and the Politburo to be ready to intervene in Hungary for strategic reasons: the Russians are secretly constructing intermediate range ballistic missiles which eventually must be based in Hungary if they are to menace NATO's southern flank in Italy and Greece."

With Elizabet translating phrase by phrase, Ulrik, who worked as a political analyst in a government ministry, conceded they hadn't known about the pontoon bridges, but he challenged Ebby's assessment that Khrushchev would send Soviet armor across the Tisza if there were to be an uprising. "The Kremlin," Ulrik argued, "has its hands full with its own domestic worries."

Arpád produced a cloth pouch from the pocket of his corduroys. "Which is why," he agreed as he absently started to roll a cigarette, "the Russians accepted Austrian neutrality in 1955; which is why Khrushchev publicly recognized Yugoslavia as a country on the road to Socialism this year despite it being outside the Soviet bloc. In Poland, the threat of popular unrest has led to the Communist reformer Gomulka being released from prison; there is a good chance he will be named first Secretary of the Polish Communist Party any day now." He deftly licked the cigarette paper closed with his tongue, twisted the tip with his fingertips, tapped the cigarette on the table to pack down the tobacco and, thrusting it between his lips, began searching his pockets for a match. "Even the hawks on Khrushchev's Politburo seem resigned to living with the situation in Poland," he added. He found a match and, igniting it with a thick thumbnail, held the flame to the twisted end of the cigarette. Smoke billowed from his nostrils. "Why should Hungarian reformers cringe at the menace of Soviet tanks when the Polish reformers have succeeded?" he asked rhetorically.

"Because the situation in Hungary is different from the situation in Poland," Ebby argued. "The Polish reformers are clearly Communists who don't plan to sweep away Communism or take Poland out of the Soviet bloc."

"We'd be fools to settle for half a loaf," Mátyás exploded.

"You have put your finger on the heart of the problem," Ebby grimly suggested.

When Elizabet translated Ebby's remark, Mátyás angrily scraped back his chair and came around the table to flop onto the couch next to her. The two, whispering in Hungarian, got into a lively argument. It was obvious that Elizabet was trying to convince him of something but was having little success.

At the table, Arpád stared past Ebby at a calendar on the wall for a long moment. When he finally turned back to his visitor, his eyes appeared to be burning with fever. "You come to us with your Western logic and your Western realities," he began, "but neither takes into account the desperateness of our situation, nor the quirk of Hungarian character that will drive us to battle against overwhelming odds. We have been at war more or less constantly since my namesake, the Hungarian chieftain Arpád, led the Magyar horsemen out of the Urals twelve hundred years ago to eventually conquer, and later defend, the great Hungarian steppe. For Hungarians, the fact that a situation is hopeless only makes it more interesting."

Ebby decided not to mince words. "I was sent here to make certain that you calculate the risks correctly. If you decide to encourage an armed uprising, you should do so knowing that the West will not be drawn in to save you from Konev's tanks massing on the frontier."

The three men around the table exchanged faint smiles and Ebby understood that he had failed in his mission. "I and my friends thank you for coming, at great personal risk, to Budapest," Arpád said. "I will give you a message to take back to America. The Athenian historian Thucydides, speaking twenty-four hundred years ago about the terrible conflict between Athens and Sparta, wrote that three things push men to war—honor, fear and self interest. If we go to war, for Hungarians it will be a matter of honor and fear. We cling to the view that the American leaders, motivated by self-interest, will then calculate the advantages to helping us."

The conversation around the glass-covered table rambled on into early evening. From behind the thick curtains came the muted jingle of ambulance bells or the mournful shriek of a distant police siren. As a sooty twilight blanketed the city, Elizabet disappeared into the kitchen and turned up twenty minutes later carrying a tray filled with steaming bowls of marrow soup and thick slices of dark bread. Arpád quoted two lines from the legendary Hungarian poet Sándor Petöfi, who had been killed fighting the Russians in 1849:

Fine food, fine wine, both sweet and dry,
A Magyar nobleman am I.

Lifting his bowl in both palms, he gulped down the soup, then lugged a heavy German watch from the coin pocket of his trousers. He'd been asked to read poems to a group at the Technological University, he told Ebby. The students there were considered to be among the most defiant in Budapest. If it would interest him, Ebby was welcome to come along. Elizabet could translate some of what was said.

Ebby eagerly accepted; if he wanted to get a feeling for the mood of the students, a poetry reading was as good a place as any to start.

Arpád dialed a phone number and mumbled something to the comrades surveying the street from another apartment. Then, with Arpád leading the way, Ebby, Elizabet, and the others filed down a narrow corridor to a bedroom in the back of the apartment. Mátyás and Ulrik pushed aside a large armoire, revealing a narrow rug-covered break in the brick wall of the building that opened into a storage room in a vacant apartment in the adjoining building. The two young men remained behind to shoulder the armoire back into place and block the secret passage as Arpád, Elizabet, and Ebby entered the adjoining apartment and let themselves out of its back door, then descended five flights to a cellar door that gave onto a completely different street than the one Ebby and Elizabet had arrived on hours earlier. Making their way on foot through the meandering dimly lit side streets of Buda, avoiding the main thoroughfares, the three crossed Karinthy Frigyes Road and moments later entered the sprawling Technical School through a basement coal delivery ramp. A young student with a mop of curly hair was waiting for them inside. He led them through the furnace room to an employees' canteen crammed with students sitting on rows of benches or standing along the walls. There must have been a hundred and fifty of them crowded into the narrow room. They greeted the poet with an ovation, tapping their feet on the cement in unison and chanting his name: "Ar-pád, Ar-pád, Ar-pád."

At the head of the room, Arpád blew into the microphone to make sure it was alive, then flung his head back. "'Without father without mother,'" he declaimed.

> Without God or homeland either
> without crib or coffin-cover
> without kisses or a lover.

The students recognized the poem and roared their approval. Elizabet pressed her lips to Ebby's ear. "Those are lines from a poem by Attila József," she told him. "He wrote around the turn of the century...his subject was crazy Hungarian individualism..."

"Your friend Arpád broke the mold," Ebby said into her ear.

Elizabet turned on him. "He is not my friend, he is my lover. The two are worlds apart." The admission broke a logjam and disjointed phrases spilled through the breach. "You are right about Arpád...he is one crazy Hungarian...a chaos of emotions...a glutton for words and the spaces between them...addicted to the pandemonium and pain he stirs in the women who love him." (Her use of the plural *women* was not lost on Ebby.) She looked away, her fingers kneading her lower lip, then came back at him, her dark eyes fierce with resentment. "He is the poet-surgeon who distracts you from old wounds by opening new ones."

The students quieted down and Arpád, reciting in a droning matter-of-fact manner, launched into a long poem. "This is the one that made him famous," Elizabet whispered to Ebby. "It's called '*E* for *Ertelmiségi*'—which is Hungarian for 'Intellectual.' Arpád wound up spending three years in prison because of this poem. By the time he was released, it has been passed from hand to hand until half the country seemed to know it by heart. Arpád describes how he tried to slip across the frontier into Austria when the Communists came to power in 1947; he was betrayed by his peasant-guide, given an eight-minute summary trial and jailed at the notorious prison Vac, where the dead are not buried but thrown to the vultures. When he was finally set free, at the age of twenty-nine, he discovered that his internal passport had been stamped with a red E for '*Ertelmisegi*,' which meant he could no longer teach at a university." She concentrated on the poem for a moment. "In this part he describes how he worked as a mason, a carpenter, a plumber, a dish washer, a truck driver, even a dance instructor when he could no longer find literary magazines willing to publish his essays or poems."

The students crowded into the canteen appeared spellbound, leaning forward on the benches, hanging on the poet's words. When he stumbled over a phrase voices would call out the missing words and Arpád, laughing, would plunge on. "Here," Elizabet whispered, "he explains that in the prison of Vac the half of him that is Jewish—Arpád's mother was a Bulgarian Jew—transformed itself into an angel. He explains that Jews have a tradition that angels have no articulation in their knees—they can't bend them to someone. He explains that this inability to kneel can be a fatal handicap in a Communist country."

The poem ended with what Arpád styled a postlude. Raising his arms over his head, he cried: *"Ne bántsd a Magyart!"*

The students, each with one fist raised in pledge, leapt to their feet and began stamping the ground as they repeated the refrain. *"Ne bántsd a Magyart! Ne bántsd a Magyart! Ne bántsd a Magyart!"*

Elizabet, caught up in the general excitement, shouted the translation into Ebby's ear. "Let the Magyars alone!" Then she joined the Hungarians in the battle cry. *"Ne bántsd a Magyart! Ne bántsd a Magyart!"*

As the bells in the Paulist monastery on Gellért Hill struck eleven, one of the AVH man in the blue Skoda spotted a male figure on the walkway of the Szabadság Bridge. For a moment a passing trolley car hid him. When the figure reappeared the AVH man, peering through binoculars, was able to make a positive identification. The vacuum tubes in the transceiver were warm, so he flicked on the microphone. "*Szervusz, szervusz*, mobile twenty-seven. I announce quarry in sight on the Szabadság walkway. Execute operational plan ZARVA. I repeat: execute operational plan ZARVA."

Clawing his way out of an aching lethargy, Ebby toyed with the comfortable fiction that the whole thing had been a bad dream—the scream of brakes, the men who materialized from the shadows of the girders to fling him into the back of a car, the darkened warehouse looming ahead on the Pest bank of the Danube, the endless corridor along which he was half-dragged, the spotlights that burned into his eyes even when they were shut, the questions hurled at him from the darkness, the precise blows to his stomach that spilled the air out of his lungs. But the ringing in his ears, the leathery dryness in his mouth, the throb in his rib cage, the knot of fear in the pit of his stomach brought him back to a harder reality. Flat on his back on a wooden plank, he tried to will his eyes open. After what seemed like an eternity he managed to raise the one eyelid that was not swollen shut. The sun appeared high over head but, curiously, didn't seem to warm him. The sight of the sun transported him back to his stepfather's seventeen-foot Herreshoff, sailing close hauled off Penobscot Bay in Maine. He had been testing the boat to see how far it could heel without capsizing when a sudden squall had caused the wind to veer and the boom, coming over without warning, had caught Ebby in the back of the head. When he came to, he was lying on the deck in the cockpit with the orb of the sun swinging like a pendulum high over the mast. Stretched out now on the plank, it dawned on Ebby that the light over his head wasn't the sun but a naked bulb suspended from the ceiling at the end of an electric cord. With an effort he managed to drag himself into a sitting position on the plank, his back against the cement wall. Gradually things drifted into a kind of two-dimensional focus. He was in a large cell with a small barred slit of a window high in the wall, which meant it was a basement cell. In one corner there was a wooden bucket that reeked from urine and vomit. The door to the cell was made of wood crisscrossed with rusted metal belts. Through a slot high in the door, an unblinking eye observed him.

It irritated him that he couldn't tell whether it was a left eye or a right eye.

He concentrated on composing pertinent questions. He didn't bother with the answers; assuming they existed, they could come later.

How long had he been in custody?

Had he said anything during the interrogation to compromise his cover story?

Would the Americans at the Gellért notice he was missing?

Would they inform the embassy?

At what point would the embassy cable Washington?

Would Arpád discover he had been arrested?

Could he do anything about it if he did?

And, of course, the crucial question: Why had the Hungarians arrested him? Had the AVH infiltrated the Hungarian Resistance Movement? Did they know the CIA had sent someone into Budapest to contact Arpád? Did they know that he was that someone?

Formulating the questions exhausted Ebby and he drifted off, his chin nodding onto his chest, into a shallow and fitful sleep.

The squealing of hinges startled him awake. Two men and a massive woman who could have passed for a Japanese sumo wrestler appeared on the threshold of the cell, the men dressed in crisp blue uniforms, the woman wearing a sweat suit and a long white butcher's smock with what looked like dried blood stains on it. Grinning, the woman shambled over to the wooden plank and, grasping Ebby's jaw, jerked his head up to the light and deftly pressed back the eyelid of his unswollen eye with the ball of her thumb. Then she took his pulse. She kept her coal-black eyes on the second hand of a wristwatch she pulled from the pocket of her smock, then grunted something in Hungarian to the two policemen. They pulled Ebby to his feet and half-dragged, half-walked him down a long corridor to a room filled with spotlights aimed at the stool bolted to the floor in the middle of it. Ebby was deposited on the stool. A voice he remembered from the previous interrogation came out of the darkness.

"Be so kind as to state your full name."

Ebby massaged his jaw bone. "You already know my name."

"State your full name, if you please."

Ebby sighed. "Elliott Winstrom Ebbitt."

"What is your rank?"

"I don't have a rank. I am an attorney with—"

"Please, please, Mr. Ebbitt. Last night you mistook us for imbeciles. It was my hope that with reflection you would realize the futility of your predicament and collaborate with us, if only to save yourself from the sanctions that await you if you defy us. You have not practiced law since 1950. You are an employee of the American Central Intelligence Agency, a member of the Soviet Russia Division in Mr. Frank Wisner's Directorate for

Operations. Since the early 1950s you have worked in the CIA's station at Frankfurt in Western Germany running émigré agents, with great persistence but a notable lack of success, into Poland and Soviet Russia and Albania. Your immediate superior when you arrived at Frankfurt was Anthony Spink. When he was transferred back to Washington in 1954, you yourself became head of the agent-running operation."

Ebby's mind raced so rapidly he had trouble keeping up with the fragments of thoughts flitting through his brain. Clearly he had been betrayed, and by someone who knew him personally or had access to his Central Registry file. Which seemed to rule out the possibility that he had been betrayed by an informer in the Hungarian Resistance Movement. Shading his open eye with a palm, he squinted into the beams of light. He thought he could make out the feet of half a dozen or so men standing around the room. They all wore trousers with deep cuffs and shoes that were black and shining like mirrors. "I must tell you," Ebby said, his voice rasping from the back of a sore throat, "that you are confusing me with someone else. I was with the OSS during the war, that's true. After the war I finished my law studies and went to work for Donovan, Leisure, Newton, Lumbard and Irvine at number two Wall—"

Ebby could make out one set of black shoes ambling toward him from the rim of darkness in a kind of deliberate duck-walk. An instant later, a heavy man dressed in a baggy civilian suit blotted out several of the spotlights and a short, sharp blow landed in Ebby's peritoneal cavity, knocking the wind out of his lungs, dispatching an electric current of pain down to the tips of his toes. Rough hands hauled him off the floor and set him back on the stool, where he sat, doubled over, his arms hugging his stomach.

Again the soothing voice came out of the darkness. "Kindly state your full name."

Ebby's breath came in ragged gasps. "Elliott...Winstrom...Ebbitt."

"Perhaps now you will tell us your rank."

It seemed like such an inconsequential question. Why was he making such a fuss? He would tell them his name and rank and pay grade and they would let him curl up on the wooden plank in the damp cell that smelled of urine and vomit. He would open his good eye and peer up at the naked bulb hanging from the ceiling and remember the sun swinging back and forth like a pendulum high over the mast; he would feel the calming lift and slide of the Atlantic ground swell under the deck, he would taste the salt of the sea breeze on his lips. "My rank—"

Suddenly he caught a glimpse of his ex-wife's flinty eyes boring into him. He could hear Eleonora's throaty voice laced with exasperation. "Whatever you do," she said, "you'll never catch up to your father unless someone stands you in front of a firing squad."

"My father has nothing to do with this," Ebby cried out. Even as he uttered these words, he understood that his father had everything to do with it.

"Why do you speak of your father?" the soothing voice inquired from the murkiness beyond the spotlights. "We are not psychoanalysts—we only want to know your rank. Nothing more."

Ebby forced words one by one through his parched lips. "You...can...go...to...hell."

The baggy civilian suit started toward him again but the soothing voice barked a word in Hungarian and the heavy man melted back into the shadows. The spotlights went out and the entire room was plunged into inky blackness. Two hands wrenched Ebby off the stool by his armpits, propelled him across the room to a wall and propped him upright. A heavy curtain in front of his face parted, revealing a thick pane of glass and a spotlit room beyond it. There was a stool bolted to the floor in the middle of the room, and a ghostly porcelain figure on the stool. Ebby blinked his open eye hard. With the languidness of underwater motion the figure swam into focus.

The guide from the museum, the wife of a Hungarian named Németh, the lover of the poet Arpád Zelk, sat hunched on the stool. She was naked except for a pair of dirty faded-pink bloomers that sagged over one hip because of a torn elastic waistband. One arm was raised across her breasts. The fingers of her other hand played with a chipped front tooth. The dark figures of men standing around the room were obviously questioning her, although no sound reached Ebby through the thick glass. Elizabet fended off the questions with a nervous shake of her head. One of the figures came up behind her and, grabbing her elbows, pinned her arms behind her back. Then the massive woman wearing the long white butcher's smock lumbered up to her. She was brandishing a pair of pliers. Ebby tried to turn away but strong hands pinned his head to the glass.

Elizabet's swollen lips howled for a release from the pain as the woman mutilated the nipple of a breast.

Ebby started to retch but all that came up from the back of his throat was phlegm.

"My name," Ebby announced after two men had dragged him back to the stool, "is Elliott Winstrom Ebbitt. I am an officer of the United States Central Intelligence Agency. My pay grade is GS-15."

Barely concealing his sense of triumph, the interrogator asked from the darkness, "What was your mission in Budapest? What message did you bring to the counterrevolutionist Arpád Zelk?"

The spotlights caused tears to trickle from the corner of Ebby's open eye. Blotting them with the back of a hand, he detected another voice murmuring in his brain. It belonged to Mr. Andrews, the one-armed instructor back at the Company's training school. "It's not the pain but the fear that breaks you." He heard Mr. Andrews repeat the warning over and over, like a needle stuck in a grove. "Not the pain but the fear! Not the pain but the fear!"

The words reverberating through his brain grew fainter and Ebby, frantic to hang on to them, reached deep into himself. To his everlasting mystification, he discovered he wasn't afraid of the pain, the dying, the nothingness beyond death; he was *afraid of being afraid*.

The discovery exhilarated him—and liberated him.

Had his father experienced this exhilarating revelation the day he was lashed to the goal post of a soccer field? Was that the explanation for the smile on his lips when the Germans bayoneted him to death because they were short of ammunition?

Ebby felt as if a great malignant knot had been extracted from his gut.

"The message, if you please?" the voice prompted him from the darkness. "I want to remind you that you do not have diplomatic immunity."

Again Ebby forced words through his lips. "Fuck...you...pal."

4

THE MOOD IN THE CORRIDORS OF COCKROACH ALLEY WAS SUBDUED. Junior officers milled around the coffee-and-doughnut wagons, talking in undertones. There was a crisis brewing. Details were scarce. One of the Company's people somewhere in the field appeared to be in jeopardy. Leo Kritzky, whose recent promotion to the post of deputy to the head of the Soviet Russia Division in the Directorate for Operations had coincided with the birth of twin daughters, knew more than most. The DCI, Allen Dulles, who had been woken at three in the morning by the duty officer reading an "Eyes-Only" CRITIC from the CIA station chief in Budapest, brought key people in on Sunday for an early morning war council. Leo, standing in for his boss who was away on sick leave, attended it. Leaning back into the soft leather of his Eames chair, his eyeglasses turned opaque by the sun streaming through a window, Dulles brought everyone up to speed: E. Winstrom Ebbitt II, on a mission to Budapest under deep cover (and without diplomatic immunity), had failed to turn up at his hotel the previous evening. A check of hospitals and city police precincts had drawn a blank. The Hungarian AVH, which as a matter of routine monitored visiting Americans, was playing dumb: yes, they were aware that a New York attorney named Ebbitt had joined the State Department negotiating team at the Gellért Hotel; no, they didn't have any information on his whereabouts; it went without saying, they would look into the matter and get back to the Americans if they learned anything.

"The bastards are lying through their teeth," Dulles told the men gathered in his spacious corner office. "If for some reason Ebbitt went to ground of his own accord, first thing he'd do would be to send us word—before he left Washington he committed to memory the whereabouts of a Hungarian cutout equipped with a radio and ciphers. Christ, we even laid on emergency procedures to exfiltrate him out of Hungary if his cover was blown."

Half an hour into the meeting the DD/O, Frank Wisner, came on the squawk box from London, his first stopover on a tour of European stations, to remind everyone that the Hungarian AVH were the step children of the Soviet KGB. "Bear in mind the relationship," he advised from across the Atlantic in his inimitable drawl. "If the KGB sneezes, it's the AVH that catches cold."

"The Wiz may be on to something," Bill Colby allowed when the squawk box went dead. "We won't get to first base with the AVH. On the other hand the KGB has a vested interest in preserving the unspoken modus vivendi between our intelligence services."

The department heads kicked around ideas for another twenty minutes. The State Department would be encouraged to file a formal complaint with the Hungarian Ministry of Foreign Affairs, though none of the people who had pulled up chairs around Dulles's desk held out hope that this would produce results. A channel would be opened, via the Hungarian cutout, to determine if Ebby had actually met with this Arpád Zelk fellow and other members of the Resistance Movement. A sometime-asset in the AVH would be contacted through his handler in Austria but this would take time; if the Hungarians had snagged Ebbitt, the asset might have gotten wind of it. Leo, still junior enough in the presence of the DCI and the various department heads to raise a finger when he wanted to say something, felt Dulles's hard gaze lock onto him when he came up with the idea of putting the Sorcerer on the case; he could meet in Berlin with his KGB counterpart and point out the disadvantages to both sides if they allowed their client services to take scalps, Leo suggested. One of the analysts wondered aloud whether an approach to the Russians on behalf of Ebbitt would undermine whatever chance he had of sticking to the cover story about being a New York attorney.

Leo shook his head thoughtfully. "If they've seized Ebbitt," he said, "it's because they've penetrated his cover story. The problem now is to extricate him alive and in one piece."

Behind a cloud of pipe smoke, Dulles nodded slowly. "I don't recall your name," he told Leo.

"Kritzky. I'm standing in for—" He named the head of the Soviet Russia Division.

"I like the idea of Torriti explaining the facts of life to the Russians," Dulles announced, eyeing Leo over the top of his glasses. "Coming from the Sorcerer, the menace of reciprocity would carry weight with the Russians; Torriti doesn't play games." Dulles hiked a cuff and glanced at his wrist-watch. "It's early afternoon in Berlin. He might be able to get something off the ground today. Write that up, Kritzky. I'll sign off on it."

Torriti's corpulent body had slowed down over the years but not his head. The deciphered version of Dulles's "Action Immediate" reached his desk when he was slumped over it, snoring off a hangover from a bottle of monastery-aged Irish whiskey he'd finally gotten around to cracking open; it had been a gift from the Rabbi to celebrate the Jewish New Year. ("May 5717 bring you fame, fortune and a defector from the Politburo," he had written on the tongue-in-cheek note that accompanied the bottle. "Barring that, may you at least live to see 5718.") Shaking himself out of a stupor, fitting on a pair of spectacles that he had begun to use to read printed matter, the Sorcerer digested Dulles's orders, then bawled through the half open door to Miss Sipp, "Get ahold of McAuliffe—tell him to get his butt down here pronto."

"From Washington, it probably looked like a cakewalk," Jack—now the second-in-command at Berlin Base—remarked when he'd read through the Action Immediate. "One of our people's fallen into the hands of the AVH in Budapest. We're going to hold the KGB's feet to the flame if anything happens to him. So far, so good. But Jesus H. Christ, how does Dulles expect us to get in touch with the KGB *rezident* at Karlshorst on such short notice—I mean, it's not as if you could pick up the phone and dial his number and invite him over to West Berlin for tea and sympathy."

"Knew you'd come up with a creative idea," Torriti said. He dragged the telephone across the desk, then laced the fingers of both hands through his thinning hair to make himself presentable for the phone conversation he hoped to engage in. From the pocket of his rumpled trousers he produced a small key attached to the end of a long chain anchored to his belt. Squinting, he inserted the key in the lock of the upper right-hand desk drawer, tugged it open and rummaged among the boxes of ammunition until he found the small notebook German children used to keep track of class schedules, which he used as an address book. "Does Karlshorst begin with *C* or *K*?" he asked Jack.

"*K*, Harvey."

"Here it is. Karlshorst *rezidentura*." The Sorcerer fitted his trigger finger into the slots on the phone and dialed the number. Jack could hear the phone pealing on the other end. A woman babbling in Russian answered.

Torriti spoke into the phone cautiously, articulating every syllable. "Get me some-one who speaks A-mer-i-can Eng-lish." He repeated the words "American English" several times. After a long while someone else came on the line. "Listen up, friend," Torriti said as patiently as he could. "I want you to go and tell Oskar Ugor-Zhilov that Harvey Torriti wants to speak to him." Pleats of skin formed on the Sorcerer's brow as he spelled his name. "T-O-R-R-I-T-I." There was another long wait. Then: "So, Oskar, how the fuck are you? This is Harvey Torriti. Yeah, *the* Harvey Torriti. I think we need to talk. No, not on the phone. Face to face. Man to man. I got a message from my summit that I want you to deliver to your summit. The sooner, the better." Torriti held the phone away from his ear and grimaced. Jack could make out the tinny sound of someone with a thick Russian accent struggling to put a coherent sentence together in English. "You have to be making a joke," Torriti barked into the phone. "No way am I going to put a foot into East Berlin. I got another idea. Know the playground in the Spandau Forest in the British Sector? There's an open-air ice-skating rink that sits smack on the border. I'll meet you in the middle of the rink at midnight." The KGB *rezident* grunted something. Torriti said, "You can bring as many of your thugs as you like long as you come out onto the ice alone. Oh, yeah, and bring two glasses. I'll supply the whiskey," he added with a titter.

The Sorcerer dropped the phone back onto the receiver. Jack asked, "So how do you figure on playing it, Harvey?"

Torriti, cold sober and thinking fast, eyed Jack. "Not for laughs," he said.

The full moon flitting between the clouds had transformed the ice on the skating rink into Argentine marble. At the stroke of midnight two phantoms emerged from the woods on either side and started across the ice in short, cautious flat-footed steps. Oskar Ugor-Zhilov, a wiry man in his middle fifties, wearing baggy trousers tucked into rubber galoshes and a fur shapka with the earflaps raised and jutting, carried two wine glasses in one hand and a bulky Russian walkie-talkie in the other. The Sorcerer, bareheaded, held his ankle-length green overcoat closed with both hands (two buttons were missing) and clutched a bottle of PX booze under an armpit. As the two men warily circled each other in the center of the rink, a giant US Air Force transport plane roared over the tree tops on its way to Tegel Airport in the French Sector of Berlin.

"We're right under the air corridor," Torriti shouted to his Russian counterpart.

Ugor-Zhilov raised the walkie-talkie to his mouth and muttered something into it. There was an ear-splitting squeal by way of an answer. The Sorcerer waved the bottle. Nodding, the Russian held out the two glasses and Torriti filled them with whiskey. He grabbed one of the glasses by its stem and, saluting the KGB *rezident*, drank it off as if it were no more potent than apple juice. Not to be outdone by an American, Ugor-Zhilov threw back his head and gulped down the contents of his glass.

"You got a family?" Torriti inquired, skating from one side of the Russian to the other and back again on the balls of his shoes. He was mesmerized by the small tuft of curly hair growing under Ugor-Zhilov's lower lip.

Torriti's question amused the Russia. "You meet me at midnight in the middle of nowhere to find out if I have family?"

"I like to get to know the people I'm up against."

"I am married man," the Russian said. "I have two sons, both living in Moscow. One is senior engineer in the aeronautics industry, the other is journalist for *Pravda*. Or you, *Gospodin* Harvey Torriti—you have family?"

"Had a wife once," the Sorcerer said wistfully. "Don't have one any more. She didn't appreciate the line of work I was in. She didn't appreciate my drinking neither. Say, Oskar—you don't mind me calling you Oskar, right?—you wouldn't want to defect, would you?" When the Sorcerer spotted the scowl on the Russian's face, he laughed out loud. "Hold your water, sport, I was only pulling your leg. You know, kidding, teasing. Hey, you Russians need to loosen up. You need to be able to let your hair down. Take a joke." Suddenly Torriti turned serious. "The reason I ask about your family, Oskar, baby," he said, his head angled to one side as if he were sizing the Russian up for a coffin, "is..."

Torriti offered Ugor-Zhilov a refill but was waved off with an emphatic shake of the head. He refilled his own glass and carefully set the bottle down on the ice. "Suppose you were to kick the bucket, Oskar—that's American for cash in your chips, bite the dust, push up the daisies, buy the farm, *die*— would your family get a pension?"

"If you are threatening me, I inform you that two sharpshooters have your head in telescopic sights even as we talk."

Torriti's lips twisted into a lewd smirk. "If I don't make it off the ice, sport, you can bet you won't make it off the ice neither. Listen up, Oskar, I wasn't threatening you. I was talking hypothetically. I'm *concerned* about what would happen to your family if we were to start killing each other off. We being the KGB and the CIA. I mean, we're not vulgar Mafia clans, right? We are civilized organizations on two sides of a divide who don't see eye to eye on things like what makes a free election free and due process due, stuff like that. But we are careful not to—"

The throaty growl of a small propeller plane passing low over Spandau drowned out the Sorcerer.

"Yeah, like I was saying, we are careful, you and me, your KGB and my CIA, not to start hurting each other's people."

Ugor-Zhilov looked puzzled. "As far as I know we are not hurting any CIA people."

"You don't know very far," the Sorcerer retorted icily. "Fact is, you have one of our people in custody—"

"I know of no—"

"It's in Budapest, sport. The person in question disappeared from the radar screen twenty-four hours ago."

The Russian actually seemed relieved. "Ah, Hungary. That complicates the problem. The Hungarian AVH are completely autonomous—"

"Autonomous, my ass! Don't hand me that crap, Oskar. The KGB runs the AVH same as it runs every other intelligence service in East Europe. You take a crap, they flush the toilet." Over the Russian's shoulder, a flashlight came on near the edge of the woods and described a circle and then flicked off. Torriti skated closer to Ugor-Zhilov. "What would happen right now if I reached under my jacket and lugged out a handgun and stuck it into your gut?"

The Russian's eyes narrowed; he was clearly a man who didn't scare easily. "You would be doing a big mistake, Torriti," he said softly. "Such a gesture would be a form of suicide."

Nodding, the Sorcerer finished the whiskey in his wine glass and noisily licked his lips and set the glass down on the ice. Then, moving very deliberately, he slid his right hand inside his overcoat and came out with the pearl-handled revolver. The Russian froze. The long barrel glistened in the moonlight as Torriti raised the revolver over his head so that anybody watching from either side of the rink could see it. Ugor-Zhilov held his breath, waiting for the crack of the rifle to echo across the rink. Smiling sourly, the Sorcerer thumbed back the hammer and jammed the business end of the barrel into the Russian's stomach. "Looks like the turkeys backing you up have gone to sleep on the job," he remarked. Then he pulled the trigger.

The hammer fell onto the firing pin with a hollow click.

"Goddamn," Torriti said. "I must've forgotten to load the fucker."

Cursing Torriti in a stream of guttural Russian, Ugor-Zhilov started backing toward his side of the rink.

"If anything happens to our guy in Budapest," Torriti called after him, "I'll load the pistol and come after you. There won't be anyplace in Germany for you to hide. You reading me, Oskar? Like my friend the Rabbi says, our man looses a tooth, you lose a tooth. Our man goes blind, you go blind. Our man stops breathing, your wife starts collecting your KGB pension."

Torriti retrieved the wine glass and the bottle from the ice and poured himself a refill. Ambling in flat-footed steps back toward the woods, humming under his breath, he treated himself to a well-earned shot of booze.

"So how many of the fuckers were there?" the Sorcerer asked Jack. They were squeezed into the back seat of a station wagon filled with agents from Berlin Base. Sweet Jesus was driving. A second station wagon trailed behind them.

"Six. Two with sniper rifles, two with submachine guns, one with binoculars, one with a walkie-talkie."

"Did they put up much of a fight?"

Jack smirked. "They were all very reasonable types, you could see it in their eyes when they spotted our artillery," Jack said. He produced a small pair of Zeiss binoculars from the pocket of his duffle coat and offered them to the Sorcerer. "Thought you might like a trophy."

Torriti, suddenly weary, let his lids close over his eyes of their own accord. "You keep them, Jack. You earned them."

"I'll keep them, Harvey. But we both know who earned them."

5

HANGING FROM A MEAT HOOK EMBEDDED IN THE WALL OF THE refrigerator room, his limbs numb from the cold, Ebby sank into a sleep so shallow he found himself drifting into or out of it with the twitch of an eye. When the lockset on the outside of the door was cranked open, he was wide awake and straining to make out the footfalls of his jailers before they entered the room. He was glad they were finally coming for him; between beatings, he would at least be thawed out by the spotlights in the interrogation chamber. One of the guards grabbed him around the waist and lifted his body while the other, standing on a crate, detached his jacket and shirt from the hook. With his bare feet planted on the icy floor tiles, Ebby raised his elbows so they could grasp him under the armpits and drag him off for another round of questioning. Curiously, the two guards who held him erect did so with unaccustomed gentleness, and Ebby understood that something had changed. The guards steered him, at a pace he set, out of the frigid room and down the corridor to an elevator, which sped him to an upper floor. There he was taken along a carpeted corridor to a heated room with a wooden bed with sheets and a pillow and blankets. Even more astonishingly, the room was equipped with a shaded table lamp that could presumably be switched off at night. There was a flush toilet and a small bathtub at one end, and a window with a slatted shutter on the outside through which Ebby could make out the sounds of traffic.

The honking of a horn in the street below seemed like music to his ears.

A short matronly woman with coarse gray hair and a stethoscope dangling from her neck rapped her knuckles against the open door and walked in. Smiling impersonally at Ebby, she began examining him. She listened to his heart and wedged a thermometer under his tongue and (obviously accustomed to dealing with prisoners being questioned by the AVH) checked to see if any of his bruised ribs were broken. Then she set about massaging his limbs to restore circulation to them. Before she departed, she disinfected the welts on his chest and spread a salve on his swollen lid, and set out on the table a glass of water and two pills, telling him in sign language that he was to take them before going to sleep. Another woman appeared with clean clothing and a tray of food—there was a bowl of clear broth, a slice of bread, a plate of goulash, even a piece of candy wrapped in cellophane. Ebby drank off the broth, which soothed his raw throat, and managed to get down a little of the goulash. Before stretching out on the bed, he hobbled over to the window and stared at the street through the slats. Judging from the fading light he reckoned it was the end of the afternoon. There weren't many automobiles, but the street was packed with young people calling back and forth to each other as they hurried along in one direction. An open truck filled with students shouting what sounded like slogans and holding aloft large Hungarian flags sped past in the same direction.

Steadying himself on the back of a chair piled high with the clean clothing, switching off the light as he passed the table, Ebby made his way back to the bed. Stripping to the skin, dropping his filthy clothes onto the floor, he slid under the sheets and slowly stretched out his aching limbs as he concentrated, once again, on composing pertinent questions.

Why had the AVH started treating him with kid gloves?

He could assume the State Department people at the Gellért had alerted the embassy when he didn't return to the hotel; that the Company chief of station at the embassy had set off alarm bells in Washington. Would the Company have dared to broach the subject of its missing agent with the KGB? He knew there was an unspoken compact between the two intelligence services; there were exceptions, of course, but normally neither side went around shooting the other's people. Had the AVH—an organization with a reputation for brutality—been operating behind the back of the KGB to root out local troublemakers? Had the KGB read the riot act to the AVH? Was he being fattened up for the kill or would he eventually be traded for one of the KGB's officers who had fallen into American hands?

And what about the mob of youngsters flowing through the street under his window? Were they hurrying to a soccer match or a Communist rally? If a Communist rally, how could he explain the bewildering detail that had caught his eye: the Communist coat-of-arms—the hammer and the sheath of wheat at the center of the white-green-and-red Hungarian flag—had been cut from the banners held aloft by the students riding in the truck.

In the early hours of the next morning there was a soft knock on the door. A moment later the table lamp flickered on. Ebby struggled into a sitting position and pulled the blanket up to his unshaven chin. A dwarflike man—Ebby guessed he couldn't be more than five feet tall— who wore a goatee and mustache and dark rimmed eyeglasses on his round face, scraped over a chair. When he sat down his feet barely reached the floor. He snapped open a tin case and offered Ebby a cigarette. When he declined, the visitor selected one for himself, tapped the tobacco down, and thrust it between extraordinarily thick lips. He lit the cigarette and sucked in a lungful of smoke and turned his head away and exhaled. "For purposes of this conversation," he said, turning back, speaking English with what Ebby took to be a Russian accent, "you may call me Vasily. Let me begin by expressing my regret at the—what shall I call it?—the *zeal* with which some of my Hungarian colleagues questioned you. Still, one has to see their side. Insurrection is brewing in Budapest and across the country. It is understandable that my very nervous Hungarian colleagues would want to quickly learn what instructions you brought to the revolutionist A. Zelk, if only to better anticipate the direction he would be likely to lead the masses. You handled yourself with distinction, Mr. Ebbitt. Although we are adversaries, you and I, I offer you—for what it is worth—my esteem." The Russian cleared his throat in embarrassment. "The English national who was taken into custody the same night as you was not able to withstand the persuasive interrogation techniques of the AVH. So we now know the contents of the message you delivered to A. Zelk."

"I saw the *persuasive* techniques of the AVH through a window," Ebby noted caustically.

"Mr. Ebbitt, your clients—your Germans, as opposed to ours—have used similar or even harsher interrogation techniques to persuade captured agents to divulge their small secrets. You are an experienced intelligence officer. Surely we can agree not to quibble over methods of interrogation."

"Is the woman still alive?"

The Russian sucked pensively on his cigarette. "She is alive and continues to be interrogated," he said finally. "My Hungarian colleagues are hoping, with her help, to be able to put their hands on A. Zelk before—"

From somewhere in the city came the crackle of rifle fire; it sounded like firecrackers popping on the Chinese New Year. The Russian laughed bitterly. "Before the situation deteriorates into outright conflict, though it appears we are too late. I can tell you that there is unrest in the city. A. Zelk is reported to have read out revolutionary poems to a crowd of students assembled at the statue of the Hungarian poet Petöfi earlier in the day. Perhaps you saw the rabble of students heading in the direction of the Erzsebet Bridge and the Petöfi statue—"

There was a burst of automatic weapon fire from a nearby intersection. Under Ebby's window a car with a loudspeaker on its roof broadcast the national anthem as it sped through the streets. And it suddenly dawned on Ebby why the hammer and sheath of wheat had been cut out from the center of the national flag: the students were in open revolt against Communist rule in Hungary!

"That's not what I'd call *unrest*, Vasily. There's a revolution underway out there."

A young Hungarian wearing a wrinkled AVH uniform appeared at the door and breathlessly reported something in a kind of pidgin Russian. Grinding out the cigarette under his heel, Vasily went over to the window and, standing on his toes, looked down between the slats of the shutter. He clearly didn't like what he saw.

"Dress quickly, if you please," he ordered. "A mob of students is preparing to assault the building. We will leave by a back entrance."

Ebby threw on clean clothing and, moving stiffly, followed the Russian down four flights of steel steps to a sub-basement garage. The Hungarian who had alerted Vasily moments before, a bony young man with a nervous tic to his eyelids, was hunched behind the wheel of a shiny black Zil limousine, its motor purring. A second Hungarian, a beefy AVH officer with the bars of a captain on his shoulder boards and a machine pistol slung under one arm, slid into the passenger seat. Vasily motioned Ebby into the back of the car and scrambled in beside him. Throwing the car into gear, the young driver inched the Zil up a ramp toward the metal door slowly sliding back overhead. When the opening was clear, the driver came down hard on the gas pedal and the Zil leapt out of the garage onto a darkened and deserted side street. At the first intersection he spun the wheel to the right, skidding the Zil on two wheels around the corner. The headlights fell on a mob of young people marching toward them with raised banners and placards. Vasily barked an order. The driver jammed on the brakes, then threw the car into reverse and started backing up. In the headlights, a young man armed with a rifle could be seen sprinting forward. He dropped to one knee and aimed and fired. The right front tire burst and the Zil, pitching wildly from side to side, slammed back into a lamppost. The AVH officer in the passenger seat flung open his door and, crouching behind it, fired off a clip at the rioters racing toward them. Several figures crumpled to the ground. There was a howl of outrage from the students as they engulfed the Zil. The AVH officer tried desperately to cram another clip into the machine pistol but was cut down by two quick rifle shots. The doors of the car were wrenched open and dozens of hands pulled the occupants into the street. The driver, Vasily and Ebby were dragged across the gutter to a brick wall and thrown against it. Behind him, Ebby could hear rifle bolts driving bullets home. Raising his hands in front of his eyes to shield them from the bullets, he cried into the night, "I am an American. I was their prisoner."

A voice yelled something in Hungarian. In the faint light coming from the street lamps that hadn't been shot out, Ebby could make out the mob parting to let someone through.

And then Arpád Zelk appeared out of the darkness. He was wearing a black leather jacket and a black beret and black leggings, and carried a rifle in his hand. He recognized Ebby and shouted an order. A young man holding a wine bottle with a cloth wick sticking from its throat darted forward and pulled Ebby away from the two Russians. Behind him, the young AVH driver sank onto his knees and started pleading in disjointed phrases for his life. The dwarflike Vasily, smiling ironically, calmly pulled the cigarette case from the pocket of his jacket and snapped a cigarette between his lips. He struck a match and held the flame to the end of the cigarette but didn't live long enough to light it.

A line of students, formed into an impromptu firing squad, cut down the two men with a ragged volley of rifle fire.

Arpád came up to Ebby. "Elizabet—do you know where she is?" he asked breathlessly. The question came across as half plea, half prayer.

Ebby said he had caught a glimpse of her in prison. He explained that there was an entrance to the sub-basement garage under the prison on a nearby side street. Brandishing the rifle over his head, Arpád shouted for the students to follow him and, gripping Ebby under an arm, headed for the AVH prison. As they approached the garage, they could hear the demonstrators massed around the corner in front of the main entrance chanting slogans as they tried to break through a steel fence. The student who had retrieved the machine pistol from the dead AVH officer in the car stepped forward and shot out the lock on the garage door. Eager hands tugged at the metal door and pushed it open overhead. From inside the garage pistol shots rang out. A girl with long dark hair plaited with strands of colorful wool turned to stare with lifeless eyes at Ebby and then collapsed at his feet. The students spilled down the ramp into pitch darkness. Ebby tried to keep up with Arpád but lost him in the melee. Shots reverberated through the garage. A Molotov cocktail detonated under a car and the gas tank caught fire and exploded. Flames licked at the concrete ceiling. In the shimmering light, Ebby saw some students herding half a dozen men in disheveled AVH uniforms against a wall. The students stepped back and formed a rough line and Arpád shouted an order. The whine of rifle shots echoed through the garage. The AVH men cowering against each other melted into a heap on the floor.

With Arpád leading the way and Ebby at his heels, the students flooded up the steel staircase and spread out through the building, cutting down any AVH men they discovered, opening cells and liberating prisoners. In a basement toilet, the insurrectionists discovered three AVH women, including the one who looked like a sumo wrestler, hiding in stalls; they pulled them out and forced them into urinals and finished them off with pistol shots to the necks. Ebby pulled Arpád through a heavy double door that separated the administrative offices from the cells. Finding himself in a corridor that seemed familiar, he started throwing bolts and hauling open doors. Behind one door he recognized his own cell with the plank bed and the window high in the wall. At another room he spun a chrome wheel to retract the lockset and swung open a thick door and felt the chill from the refrigerated chamber.

Against one wall, Elizabet was dangling from a meat hook spiked through the collar of a torn shirt, her bare legs twitching in a macabre dance step. Her mouth opened and her lips formed words but the rasps that emerged from the back of her throat were not human. Arpád and Ebby lifted her free of the meat hook and carried her from the room and laid her on the floor. Arpád found a filthy blanket in a corner and drew it over her to hide her nakedness.

Two young men—one Ebby recognized as Mátyás, the angry student who had been at the meeting in the Buda safe house—appeared at the end of the hall, prodding ahead of them the woman doctor with coarse gray hair and an older man with the gold bars of a colonel general on the shoulder boards of his AVH uniform. One of his arms hung limply from his shoulder and he was bleeding from the nose. Ebby told Arpád, "She is a doctor."

Jumping to his feet, Arpád gestured for the woman to attend to Elizabet. Only too glad to be spared the fate of the other AVH people in the building, she dropped to her knees and began to feel for a pulse. Arpád pulled a pistol from his waistband and motioned for Mátyás to bring the prisoner closer. The AVH officer stared at Ebby and said, in English, "For the love of God, stop him." A gold tooth in his lower jaw glistened with saliva. "I have information that could be of great value to your Central Intelligence Agency."

Ebby recognized the voice—it was the one that had emerged from the darkness of the interrogation chamber to ask him, "Be so kind as to state your full name."

"His name is Száblakó," Arpád informed Ebby, the pupils of his eyes reduced to pinpricks of hate. "He is the commandant of this prison, and well-known to those of us who have been arrested by the AVH."

Ebby stepped closer to the AVH colonel general. "How did you know I was CIA? How did you know I work for Wisner? How did you know I worked in Frankfurt?"

Száblakó clutched at the straw that could save his life. "Take me into your custody. Save me from them and I will tell you everything."

Ebby turned to Arpad. "Let me have him—his information can be of great importance to us."

Arpád, wavering, looked from Elizabet on the floor to Száblakó, and then at Mátyás, who was angrily shaking his head no. "Give him to me," Ebby whispered, but the muscles around the poet's eyes slowly contorted, disfiguring his face, transforming it into a mask of loathing. Suddenly Arpád jerked his head in the direction of the refrigerator room. Mátyás understood instantly. Ebby tried to step in front of the colonel general but Arpád, rabid, roughly shoved him to one side. Száblakó, seeing what was in store for him, began to tremble violently. "It was the Centre that told us," he cried as Arpád and Mátyás dragged him into the cold room. A shriek of terror resounded through the basement corridor, followed by the mournful whimpering a coyote would make if one of its paws had been caught in the steel teeth of a bear trap. The whimpering continued until Arpád and Mátyás emerged from the refrigerator room and swung the heavy door shut. They spun the chrome wheel, driving home the spikes on the lockset.

Once outside the room, Arpád cast a quick look at Elizabet, stretched out on the floor. For a fleeting moment he seemed to be torn between staying with her and dashing off to lead the revolution. The revolution won; grabbing his rifle, Arpád strode away with Mátyás. The prison doctor busied herself disinfecting Elizabet's wounds and, with Ebby's help, dressed her in a man's flannel shirt and trousers that were tugged up high and tied around her waist with a length of cord. Elizabet eyes flicked open and she stared dumbly into Ebby's face, unable at first to place him. Her tongue measured the gap in a chipped front tooth. Then her right hand clutched her left breast through the fabric of the shirt and her stiff lips pronounced his name.

"Elliott?"

"Welcome back to the world, Elizabet," Ebby whispered.

"They hurt me..."

Ebby could only nod.

"The room was so cold—"

"You're safe now."

"I think I told them who you were—"

"It doesn't matter."

Ebby noticed a filthy sink with a single faucet at the far end of the hallway. He tore off a square of cloth from the tail of his shirt and wet it and sponged her lips, which were caked with dried blood.

"What has happened?" she asked weakly.

"The insurrection is underway," Ebby said.

"Where is Árpád?"

Ebby managed a bone-weary grin. "He's trying to catch up with the revolution so he can lead it."

As streaks of gray tinted the sky in the east, rumors spread through the city that Russian tanks from the 2nd and the 17th Mechanized Divisions had already reached the outskirts of the capital. Ebby spotted the first T-34 tank, with the number 527 painted in white on its turret, lumbering into position at an intersection when he and Elizabet were being taken in a bread delivery van to the Corvin Cinema on the corner of Ulloi and Jozsef Avenues. A skinny girl named Margit, with veins of rust bleached into her long blonde hair, was behind the wheel of the van. Ebby sat next to her, Elizabet lay curled up on a mattress in the back. On Kalvin Square, five tanks with Russian markings stenciled on the turrets had formed a circle with their guns pointing outward and their commanders surveying the surrounding streets through binoculars from their open hatches. Ebby noticed that three of the tanks had small Hungarian flags attached to their whip antennas; the Russians clearly weren't looking for a scrap with the students, many of whom were armed with Molotov cocktails.

Ebby scribbled down an address on Prater Street that he had memorized back in Washington—it was the apartment of the Hungarian cutout equipped with a radio and ciphers—and Margit managed to make it there using only side streets and alleyways, avoiding the intersections controlled by Russian tanks. The cutout turned out to be a happy-go-lucky young gypsy named Zoltan with sickle-shaped sideburns that slashed across his smallpox-scarred cheeks and two steel teeth that flashed when he smiled. Ebby had no difficulty convincing Zoltan to come along with him; the gypsy didn't have anything against Communism but he was aching to get into a fight with the Russians who occupied his country. He brought along a backpack with a transceiver in it, a long curved knife that his father's father had used in skirmishes against the Turks and a violin in a homemade canvas case.

"I understand about the radio and the knife," Ebby told him as they squeezed into the front seat of the van. "But why the violin?"

"Not possible to make war without a violin," Zoltan explained seriously. "Gypsy violinists led Magyars into battle against goddamn Mongols, okay, so it damn good thing if gypsy violinist, yours truly, leads Hungarians into battle against goddamn Russians." He crossed himself and repeated the same thing to Margit in Hungarian, which made her laugh so hard it brought tears to her eyes.

On Rákóczi Street the van was suddenly surrounded by students who had thrown up a roadblock of overturned yellow trolley cars placed in such a way that an automobile had to zigzag through the gaps between them. Overhead, electric cables dangled from their poles. The students wore armbands with the Hungarian colors and brandished large naval pistols, antiquated World War I German rifles and, in one case, a cavalry sword. They must have recognized Margit because they waved the van through. From the sidewalk, an old woman raised her cane in salute. *"Eljen!"* she cried. "Long life!" On the next corner, more students were carrying out armloads of suits from a big clothing emporium and piling them on the sidewalk. A young woman wearing the gray uniform of a tram conductor, her leather ticket pouch bulging with hand grenades, shouted to a group of passing students that anyone joining them would be given a suit and five Molotov cocktails. Half a dozen students took her up on the offer.

The Corvin Cinema, a round blockhouse-like structure set back from the wide avenue, had been transformed into a fortress and command post for the five hastily organized companies of the so-called Corvin Battalion. A poster in the lobby advertised a film entitled *Irene, Please Go Home*;

someone had crossed out "Irene" and substituted "Russki." In the basement, girls manufactured Molotov cocktails by the hundreds, using petrol from a nearby gas station. The movie theater itself, on the ground floor of a four-story block of flats, had been turned into a freewheeling assembly patterned after the popular "Soviets" that had sprung up in Petrograd during the Bolshevik Revolution. Delegates from schools and factories and Hungarian Army units came and went, and raised their hands to vote while they were there. At any given moment a speaker could be heard arguing passionately that the object of the uprising was to put an end to the Soviet occupation of Hungary and rid the country of Communism; merely reforming the existing Communist government and system would not satisfy the people who flocked to Corvin.

Students wearing Red Cross armbands carried Elizabet off on a stretcher to a makeshift infirmary on the third floor. Ebby and his gypsy radioman set up shop in an office on the top floor of an adjoining apartment house that was connected to the Corvin Cinema by a jury-rigged passage through the walls of the buildings. "If goddamn Russian tanks start shooting, this safest place to be," Zoltan explained with an ear-to-ear grin. "Because those cannons on the goddamn T-34's, they can't aim so high in narrow streets, right." Zoltan shinnied up a stovepipe on the roof to string the shortwave antenna, then set about enciphering Ebby's first bulletin to the Company listening post in Vienna. It reported briefly on his arrest and the arrival of a KGB officer who tried to spirit him away from the AVH station, only to wind up in front of an impromptu firing squad as the insurrectionists raided secret police buildings. Ebby described sighting the first Russian tanks and the telling detail that many of them displayed Hungarian flags. He also pointed out that the Russian armor that had taken up positions in Budapest was not accompanied, as far as he could see, by ground troops, which meant that the Russians were incapable of putting down the revolution without the assistance of the Hungarian army and regular 40,000-strong uniformed police force. And as of dawn on this second day of the insurrection, he said, the Hungarian army and the regular Budapest police had either gone over to what Ebby called the freedom fighters (a phrase that would be picked up by the press) or had declared neutrality.

6

VIENNA, MONDAY, OCTOBER 29, 1956

A S REBELLION ROCKED HUNGARY, CIA REINFORCEMENTS POURED INTO
Vienna from Company stations across Europe. Jack McAuliffe, on
detached duty from Berlin, reported to the dingy six-story hotel that
the Company had leased on the edge of the Danube Canal in the blue collar
suburb of Landstrasse. Directing a task force working out of a warren of rooms
on the fourth floor, Jack began to set up an infrastructure for screening the
refugees starting to trickle across the Austro-Hungarian frontier; if the situation
deteriorated, that trickle was expected to turn into a flood and the Company had
to be ready to deal with it. The Austrian Red Cross had opened reception centers in villages near the frontier. Jack's brief was to make sure that middle or high
level Communists, as well as ranking military and police officers, were weeded
out and interrogated; to make sure, also, that the Company kept an eye peeled
for refugees who might be recruited as agents and sent back into Hungary.

Late in the afternoon of the 29th, Jack received word that his refugee
screening net had pulled in its first big fish: a regular army colonel who had been
attached to the Hungarian general staff as liaison with the Soviet 2nd
Mechanized Division had come across the frontier with his family during the
night and had exhibited a readiness to trade information for the promise of
political asylum in America. Jack was signing off on an in-house memo on the
subject when one of his junior officers, fresh out of the S.M. Craw Management course in Alexandria, Virginia, stuck his head in the door. There was going
to be a briefing on the latest developments in Hungary in twenty minutes.

Jack was settling into one of the folding metal chairs at the back of
the banquet hall on the hotel's top floor when a young woman pushed
through the swinging doors from the kitchen. The officer sitting next to him

whistled under his breath. "Now that's someone I wouldn't kick out of the rack," he said.

"If she's the new briefing officer," a meteorologist quipped, "they'd better rent another truckload of seats for the hall."

Jack pushed up his tinted aviator's sunglasses with a forefinger and peered under them to get a closer look at her. The young woman seemed vaguely familiar. She was wearing a soft blue skirt that fell to the tops of her ankle-length boots, a white shirt with a ruffled front and a riding jacket that flared at the waist. Her mouth was painted with raspberry-pink lipstick. She strode across the room to the podium, propped up her briefing folder and scratched a very long and very painted fingernail across the microphone to see if it was turned on. Then she stared out at the ninety or so Company officers crowded into the banquet hall. "My name," she announced, her take-charge voice cutting through the background noise of unfinished conversations, "is Mildred Owen-Brack."

Of course! Owen-Brack! A lifetime ago, back at the posh Cloud Club in the Chrysler building in Manhattan, Jack had been dumb enough to make a pass at her but she hadn't been in the market for a one-night stand. Bye-bye, John J. McAuliffe, and good luck to you, she'd said, batting eyelashes that were so long he'd imagined they were trying to cool his lust.

At the podium Owen-Brack was providing a rundown on the latest news from Hungary. The Stalinist old guard in Budapest had been booted out and Imre Nagy, the former Hungarian premier who had once been imprisoned as a "deviationist," had emerged as the new head of government. Nagy, who favored a system that Communist intellectuals dubbed Marxism with a human face, had informed the Russians that he couldn't be held responsible for what happened in Hungary unless Soviet troops were pulled out of Budapest. Within hours the Soviet tanks guarding the major intersections had kicked over their engines and started to re-deploy. A long line of ammunition carriers pulling field kitchens, some with smoke still corkscrewing up from their stovepipes, had been spotted heading east through the suburbs. The population, convinced that the revolution had triumphed, had spilled into the streets to celebrate. Nagy, under pressure from militant anti-Communists, appeared willing to test the limits of Russian patience; one of the uncensored newspapers quoted Nagy as saying privately that he would abolish the one-party system and organize free elections. The political counselor at the American embassy guessed that, in a genuinely free election, the Communists would be lucky to poll ten percent of the vote, which would spell the end of Socialism in Hungary. This same counselor had heard rumors that Nagy was toying with the idea of pulling Hungary out of the Soviet-dominated Warsaw Military Pact.

The $64,000 question, Owen-Brack suggested, was: Would the Soviets sit on their hands while Nagy eased Hungary out of the Soviet orbit? Were the Russians pulling the 2nd and 17th Mechanized Divisions out of Budapest in order to buy time—time for Soviet reinforcements, known to be massing in the Ukraine, to cross the pontoon bridges over the Tisza and reoccupy the entire country?

After the briefing, Jack lingered to discuss some of the finer points of the refugee screening program with his younger staffers, then wandered over to the bar at the back of the banquet hall. Owen-Brack was already there, chatting with two visiting firemen from the House Armed Services Committee. Jack ordered a whiskey sour, then edged closer to Owen-Brack. Turning toward the bar for a pretzel, she caught him sizing her up.

"Crying shame to come all the way up to the top floor of the hotel and not take in the view," he remarked. "From the window over there you can catch a glimpse of the blue Danube flowing toward Hungary."

Owen-Brack looked hard at Jack, trying to place him. Then she snapped her fingers. "New York. The Cloud Club. I don't remember your name but I do remember you had a middle initial that didn't stand for anything." She laughed. "To tell the truth, I wouldn't have recognized you without the mustache...you've changed."

"In what way?"

"You seem older. It's your eyes..." She let the thought trail off.

"Older and wiser, I hope."

"If you mean by wiser, less cocky," she said with a musical laugh, "you had no place to go but up."

Jack smiled. "Last time we met I offered you a cup of Champagne. You saw right through that—you said I wanted to get you into bed, and you were damn right."

Owen-Brack gnawed on the inside of her cheek. "Tell you what," she said. "I'll take you up on that drink you offered me in New York." She held out a hand. "I'm Millie to my friends."

Jack took it. "John McAuliffe. Jack to you."

He bought her a daiquiri and they drifted across the hall to the floor-to-ceiling windows for a view of the Danube. Because of the chandeliers behind them the only thing they could see was their own reflection. "What've you been up to since that day at the Cloud Club?" she inquired, talking to his image in the window.

"This and that."

"Where did you do your this and that?"

"Here and there."

Owen-Brack's brown eyes crinkled into a smile. "Hey, I'm cleared for top secret, eyes-only. I can read anything Allen Dulles can read."

Jack said, "I've been stationed in Germany. In Berlin."

"You work with that character Torriti?"

"Yeah. I'm his XO."

"Berlin's supposed to be a tough beat."

"So they say."

"Now I understand why your eyes look older."

Jack turned away from their reflection to gaze at her directly. He liked what he saw. "Harvey Torriti suffers from stomach cramps, loss of appetite, a more or less permanent ache in the solar plexus. Me, too. I guess you could write it off as occupational afflictions. But so far I've had Lady Luck on my side—I've managed to survive the skirmishes that killed your husband."

Millie was very moved. "Thanks for remembering that," she said softly.

They clinked glasses and drank to the skirmishes inside and outside the office they'd both survived. Jack asked her if she wanted to sample something beside hotel fare and when she said "Sure, why not," he took her to dinner at a small Viennese restaurant two blocks away with a covered terrace jutting over the Danube Canal. They ordered trout fresh from the kitchen tank and grilled over an open fire, and washed it down with a bottle of chilled Rhine wine. Gradually Jack loosened up. He talked about his childhood in Pennsylvania and his education at Yale which, in hindsight, seemed like the four best years of his life. He talked about varsity rowing; how the few worries he might have had vanished when he concentrated on the intricate business of pulling a twelve-foot blade.

By the time they cracked the second bottle of wine, Millie was rambling on about her adolescence in Santa Fe, where she'd spent most of her free time on horseback, exploring the endless ranges and canyons. There had been something that passed for an education at a state college and four years of law at a university in Colorado, then a chance meeting with a reckless man in his thirties who introduced her to a world that was a world away from the mysterious Anasazi canyons of New Mexico. There had been a wild trek across Thailand and Laos, an abortion, an angry separation, an emotional reconciliation. Because of his experiences in the Far East and his ability to speak Mandarin Chinese, her husband had been recruited by the Company, which is how she'd gotten her foot in the Pickle Factory door; for security reasons, the CIA liked to employ the wives of officers because it tended to keep the secrets in the family. Then one unforgettable day the DD/O, Allen Dulles, and his deputy, Frank Wisner, had turned up at the cubbyhole where she was busy writing contracts and had delivered some awful news: her husband had been ambushed and killed running saboteurs into China from Burma. Wisner had taken the new widow under his wing and she'd wound up working at various jobs in the DD/O. And here she was, briefing officers on the situation in Hungary while she waited for her boss, the Wiz, currently on a tour of European stations, to show up in Vienna.

It was after eleven when Jack called for the check and started to count out bills from his wallet. Suddenly he raised his eyes and looked directly into hers. "I guess this is where I get to ask, your room or mine?"

Millie caught her breath. "Are you dead sure you're not pushing your luck?"

"It's not my luck I'm pushing."

She sipped the last of her wine. "I haven't changed my mind about one-night stands."

"I have." Jack came around to sit next to her on the banquette and reached down to finger the hem of her skirt. "I'm not as interested in them as I used to be."

It was easy to see she was tempted. "Look, I just met you. I mean, for all I know you could be a serial killer." She laughed a little too loudly. "So are you, Jack? A serial killer?"

He focused on the smudge of raspberry lipstick on the rim of her wine glass. It reminded him of the color of Lili's lips the night he met her at the ballet and bought her a *Berliner Weisse mit Schuss.* Jack was still haunted by the memory of the slim dancer who had survived American bombs and rampaging Russian soldiers and the winter of '47 but not the East German Stasi pounding on the locked door of the toilet; in his mind's eye he could see her filling her mouth with water and inserting the small caliber pistol between her thin raspberry-pink lips.

"I have killed," he announced, his eyes never wavering from hers, "but not serially."

His answer irritated her. "If that's your idea of a joke," she retorted, "you're registering zero on my laugh meter." Then she noticed the faraway look in his eyes and she realized that he was telling her a truth.

"God damn it!" she moaned.

"What's the matter?"

"Every New Year's Eve I vow I'll never get involved with someone who works for the Company."

Jack reached across to touch her knuckles. "We make New Year's resolutions," he said solemnly, "in order to have the satisfaction of breaking them."

7

BUDAPEST, FRIDAY, NOVEMBER 2, 1956

FROM THE FIRST HOURS OF THE REVOLT TEN DAYS EARLIER, BANDS OF armed students had been combing the city in the blood hunt for members of the loathed Hungarian secret police. Tracked like animals to their hiding places in basements or subway tunnels, AVH men had been dragged out into the street and executed on the spot; sometimes their bodies were hung head-down from trees, with their pay slips (showing they earned many times more than the average worker) pinned to their trousers. Shortly after midnight on Friday, Arpád personally led a foray against a group of AVH men who had gone to ground in an abandoned police post in one of the Pest suburbs; there were rumors that two particularly brutal district Communist bosses were hiding there, too. Ebby, eager to take the temperature of the city for what had become his daily report to the Company station in Vienna, talked the poet into letting him tag along.

Piling into six taxicabs parked in the alleyway behind the Corvin Cinema, borrowing an armored car from the rebel Hungarian soldiers occupying the Kilian Barracks across the intersection, the raiding party headed down Jozsef Avenue and onto Stalin Avenue. Ebby could see evidence of fierce fighting everywhere: shattered store windows, pitted façades, thousands of spent bullets, heaps of cobblestones that had been pried up and used to construct anti-tank strongpoints, the burned out carcasses of automobiles and yellow trolley cars, the black bunting draped from apartment windows in sign of a recent death in the family. At Hero's Park, the caravan skirted the giant statue of Stalin, now sprawling in the gutter. It had been cut down with acetylene torches in the early hours of the revolution; only Stalin's hollow boots, filled with Hungarian flags, remained on the pink pedestal.

At the other side of the giant city park, on a dark street lined with entrepôts and automobile repair garages, the taxis pulled up in a semicircle facing an ugly two-story cinderblock building that had served as a neighborhood AVH station, their headlights illuminating the darkened windows. The armored car sighted its cannon on the front door. From a radio in one of the taxis came the tinny sound of an accordion playing "Que Será, Será." Standing behind the open door of his vehicle, Arpád raised a battery-powered megaphone and called out an ultimatum in Hungarian. As his voice reverberated through the street, he fixed his eyes on his wristwatch. The hand-rolled cigarette glued to his lips burned down until the embers scorched the skin but he barely noticed the pain.

Moments before Arpád's three-minute deadline expired, the front door swung open and a puffy AVH officer with crew-cut gray hair emerged, his hands thrust so high over his head that his white shirt cuffs protruded from the sleeves of his shapeless uniform jacket. Six other AVH men filed out behind him. Blinded by the headlights, the officer shaded his eyes with one hand.

"*Polgátárs*," he shouted.

Arpád, his eyes ablaze with pent-up fury, spit the butt of the cigarette into the street. "After nine years of Communist rule we have suddenly become *citizens*," he called over to Ebby.

The AVH officer made an appeal in Hungarian, and then laughed nervously. A tall AVH man behind him held up a framed photograph of his three children and pleaded for mercy. Arpád looked over to the next taxicab and nodded at Ulrik, whose left arm was bound in a blood-soaked bandage. Ulrik, in turn, muttered something to the riflemen near him. Half a dozen of them steadied their weapons on the tops of open taxi doors. Ebby, watching from behind the open door of the last taxicab in the semicircle, turned away as the shots rang out. When he looked back, the seven AVH members lay crumpled on the ground.

Several more men appeared at windows and began firing at the students. The windshield of Ebby's taxicab splintered; flying shards scored the right side of his face. He pressed a handkerchief to his cheek to stop the bleeding as the students returned the fire, shattering windowpanes and pockmarking the cinderblocks around them. A headlight on one of the taxicabs exploded with a loud hiss. The cannon on the armored car blasted away at the front door of the building, filling the frosty night air with the stinging odor of cordite. A sole figure appeared through the haze of dust and rubble at the front door waving an umbrella with a square of white cloth tied to the tip. The shooting broke off. Seven AVH men and two AVH women in disheveled uniforms emerged to cower against the front of the building.

"For God's sake," Ebby shouted to Arpád, "take them prisoner."

Suddenly an AVH major materialized in the doorway. He was holding a pistol to the head of a terrified girl and prodding her ahead of him. With tears streaming from her eyes, the girl, who couldn't have been more than twelve, cried out shrilly in Hungarian. The AVH major, a thin man wearing sunglasses with only one lens still intact, waved for the students to clear a path for him.

He made the fatal mistake of waving with the hand that held the pistol. The girl ducked and scampered away. From behind the blinding glare of the headlights, a rifle whispered. Clutching his throat, the major stumbled back drunkenly and then fell onto his back, stone dead. Behind him the other AVH agents panicked and started running in different directions only to be gunned down by rifle and pistol fire. One of the women had almost reached Ebby's taxicab when a burst of automatic fire hit her skull, shearing off the top of it.

From inside the police station came the muffled reports of individual pistol shots; Ebby guessed that the Communist Party district bosses remaining in the building had committed suicide. Students stormed through the front door and returned minutes later dragging out two bodies by their arms. Both were dressed in civilian clothing. One of them was bleeding from a superficial head wound but still very much alive. Ulrik and several others tied a rope around his ankles and hauled him across the street to one of the city's ornate pre-war gas lampposts. Flinging the end of the rope over an iron curlicue on the lamppost, they strung him head-down above the sidewalk. American twenty-dollar bills spilled from the pockets of his suit jacket. The students piled the money, along with leaves and twigs and pages torn from a magazine, on the sidewalk under his head and touched a match to them. As the flames leaped up to singe his hair the man cried hysterically, "Long live world Communism."

A mad gleam dilating the pupils of his eyes, Arpád strode over to the torso twisting at the end of the rope. Holding his rifle with one hand, he forced the tip of the barrel into the man's mouth and jerked the trigger. Turning away, the poet casually brushed fragments of bone and brain off of his leather jacket with the back of a hand.

A ghostly calm—the kind that exists in its purest form at the eye of a hurricane—gripped Budapest. A light snow had blanketed the Buda hills during the night, dampening the churr of the yellow trolley cars that had been put back into service. In the morning, glaziers began fitting new glass into store windows shattered during the fighting; it was a point of pride among Hungarians that, despite the broken windows, there had been almost no looting. In churches across the city candles burned to mark All Souls' Day, when the practicing Catholics of this largely Catholic country offered prayers for the souls of the dead in purgatory.

By midday, the sun had melted the snow in Buda and blunted the whetted rawness of the wind sweeping off the Danube. Bundled in borrowed duffle coats, strolling along the embankment on the Pest side of the river, Ebby and Elizabet could hear church bells across the city tolling the end of the morning's All Souls' services. To Elizabet, at least, it sounded as if the bells were celebrating the triumph of the revolution and the start of a new epoch for Hungary, and she said as much.

Ebby was less optimistic. There had been too much killing, he told her. It was true that the two Russian divisions had pulled back from Budapest. But if the Russians returned in force, the AVH and the Communists would come back with them, and there would be a bloody reckoning.

Elizabet bridled. "For years they tortured us, they imprisoned us, they slaughtered us," she said with great passion, "and you talk of them settling scores with us!" Since her imprisonment she tended to break into tears easily and took several deep breaths to head them off now.

Stepping around open suitcases on the sidewalk, set out to collect donations for the wounded, they strolled on past walls plastered with poems and caricatures and the omnipresent slogan *"Nem Kell Komunizmus"*—"We don't want Communism!" At one corner, Elizabet stopped to chat with two young journalists who were handing out free copies of one of the four-sheet independent newspapers that had sprung up in the early days of the revolution. Coming back to Ebby, she held up the hand-set *Literary Gazette* and translated the headline over the front page editorial: "'In revolution, as in a novel, the most difficult part is to invent the end'—de Tocqueville." Crossing a street, Elizabet stopped to look at the two rows of fresh graves in a small triangle of grass at the middle of the intersection; each of the dozen or so mounds of earth was piled high with flowers and red-white-and-green ribbons. Tacked to sticks hammered into the ground at the heads of several graves were photographs of smiling young boys and girls, some dressed in school uniforms, others in makeshift battle fatigues.

"The Russians won't invade," Elizabet predicted emotionally, "for the same reason they didn't invade Yugoslavia all these years: because they know our young people are ready to die for the revolution, and they'll take a lot of Russian soldiers with them." Again her eyes teared; again she flung the tears away with the back of her finger. She looked across the river at the statue of the martyred Archbishop Gellért, his crucifix raised high, atop one of the Buda hills. "Purgatory is not big enough to contain all the Russian soldiers who will go to hell if the Soviets make the mistake of returning," she said.

She slipped a hand inside the duffle coat to massage her mutilated breast. Again her eyes filled with tears. "The truth is that I am afraid to cry," she confessed.

"You've earned the right to a good cry," Ebby said.

"Never," she said, spitting out the word. "I am terrified that if I start I will never be able to stop."

While the wound on her breast cicatrized, Elizabet took to prowling the Corvin Cinema. She sat in on Council sessions in the movie theater or impromptu committee meetings in the rooms off it, or pulled Ebby after her down the long tunnel that connected Corvin with the Kilian Barracks across the street to chat with the officers of the 900-man construction battalion that had gone over to the revolution. Evenings they listened (with Elizabet providing a running translation) to the endless bull sessions raging in hallways that had been transformed into dormitories for the hundreds of students crowded into Corvin. Arpád occasionally was called upon to read one of his poems, but for the most part the discussions revolved around how fast and how far the students and workers dared push the new leadership, headed by the reformer Nagy, to break with the Soviet Union and the country's Communist past.

According to the radio, negotiations were already underway concerning the departure of all Soviet forces from Hungary; the Russian delegation, headed by the tall, humorless Soviet Ambassador, Yuri Andropov, and the Soviet Politburo idealogue, Mikhail Suslov, was demanding only that the troops be allowed to quit the country with their banners flying and bands playing to avoid humiliation. In the hallways of Corvin, the few voices brave enough to question the wisdom of withdrawing from the Warsaw Pact and calling for free elections, two moves that were bound to test the patience of Moscow, were shouted down. The revolution had triumphed, Arpád proclaimed during one of the hallway discussions. What was the point of making concessions that undermine this triumph?

"What if the Russians decide we have gone too far and invade Hungary?" a boy with long blond hair asked.

"We will defeat them again," Arpád responded.

"And if they return with two thousand tanks?" another student persisted.

"The Americans," Arpád promised, stabbing the air with a hand-rolled cigarettes to emphasize his point, "will come to our assistance. NATO planes will bomb the Russian tanks before they reach Budapest. NATO airdrops will supply us with anti-tank weapons to deal with the few that get through the bombardment." Arpád gazed over the heads of the students to stare defiantly at Ebby. "If we don't lose our nerve," he said, "we will soon live in a free and democratic Hungary." Then, his Roman face burning with pious fervor, he pumped his fist in the air. *"Ne Bántsd a Magyart!"* he cried. And the students, clapping in unison, took up the refrain.

"With soldiers like these," Elizabet shouted into Ebby's ear, "how can we possibly lose?"

Ebby could only shake his head. He hoped to God that Arpád had gotten it right; hoped to God the Russians stayed in Russia. If they did come back, they would return in overwhelming numbers and with overwhelming fire power. And the world would not lift a finger to help as Arpád and others like him led the courageous Hungarian lambs to the slaughter.

In the darkness one night, Ebby could hear Elizabet flinging herself from one side of the mattress to the other in the hunt for a position that would ease the ache of her injury. He wondered what time it was. A cheerful young mason with a bandaged ear had bricked in the sniper's hole in the wall, which had the advantage of making the room less drafty but the disadvantage that Ebby was no longer woken up by the daylight. From time to time he could hear members of the Corvin Battalion stirring in the hallway, but that didn't necessarily mean it was sunup; small groups of them came and went through the night, relieving others on guard duty or heading out to patrol the city on foot or in one of the commandeered taxi cabs. On the other side of the room, Elizabet scraped her mattress across the floor and propped half of it against the wall to create a makeshift chair; she seemed to suffer less pain when she slept in a sitting position.

"Elliott—"

Ebby propped himself up on elbow. "What is it?"

"It hurts. I hurt. Can't sleep. Can't not sleep. Worried sick."

Ebby pulled his mattress over to the wall alongside hers. He felt her hand groping for his in the darkness and twined his fingers through hers.

"I'm glad you're here," she confided in a whisper.

"Want to talk?" he asked.

"I have a child...a daughter..."

"What's her name?"

"Her Christian name is Nellie. She will be six in January."

"Is Arpád her father?"

"Yes." Ebby could hear her brushing tears from her eyes. I was still living with my husband when Arpád and I...when we..."

"You don't need to go into details," Ebby said. "Where is your husband—what was his name again?"

"Németh. Nándor Németh. His father was a high-ranking Communist. When we married, Nándor was an undersecretary in the Ministry for External Affairs. He was posted to the Hungarian embassy in Moscow two years ago. He knew about Arpád by then. I decided not to go with him..."

"What happened to Nellie?"

"She's living with Nándor's sister on a collective farm near Györ, about ninety kilometers from Budapest. Until all this started"—Elizabet sighed into the darkness—"I used to drive out to see her every other weekend. Before Arpád went underground, the AVH used to pick him up once or twice a month; sometimes they would question him for an entire week. When Arpád was in prison, I used to bring Nellie back with me to Budapest for days at a time."

"Why didn't you bring her to Budapest when Arpád was here?"

Elizabet thought about that for a moment. "You have to understand Arpád—he is an ardent fighter for the freedom of people in general, but individual freedoms, the right to bring your daughter to live with you, are subject to his veto." She cleared a lump from her throat. "The fact is he doesn't like children around. I was free to leave him, of course. I tried to several times. But in the end I always came crawling back. I am addicted to Arpád—he is like a drug habit that is impossible to kick..."

The hollowness Ebby detected in the timbre of Elizabet's voice frightened him. To distract her he told her he had a son three years older than Nellie. "His name is Manny, which is short for Immanuel. He's a bright boy, bright and serious. He lives with my former wife...I don't really know him all that well...I spend so much time abroad."

"It must be difficult for you—"

Ebby didn't say anything.

Elizabet tightened her grip on his hand. "When all this is finished—the revolution, the killing, the hurting, the exhilaration—we must both of us spend more time with our children."

"Yes. We'll find a way to do that."

"You look like you've been run over by a steam roller," the young embassy counselor Jim Doolittle remarked to Ebby. It was Friday evening and the two were gazing out of a window on the second floor of the Parliament building, which had a splendid view of the vast square. There had been a furnace of a sunset earlier in the evening; now the last pigments of color in the sooty sky had been blotted up by the darkness. A bonfire burned in the middle of the square and a pick-up Tzigane orchestra stood around it playing gypsy melodies. Every now and then a small open truck would pull up and the gypsies would unload chairs swiped from neighborhood Communist Party offices, smash them on the pavement and feed the wood into the fire. Ebby could make out Zoltan dancing around the flames as he sawed away at the violin jammed into his collarbone.

Did Zoltan have his own sources of information? Was the gypsy violinist warming up to lead the Hungarians into battle against the Russians?

Doolittle turned away from the window to watch the American ambassador, along with his political chargé d'affaires (Doolittle's immediate superior) and the Company's chief of station talking in urgent undertones with the Hungarian premier, Nagy, on the other side of the large mirrored reception hall. In a corner one of Nagy's aides fed documents into the fire burning in a marble fireplace. "Washington ought to have warned us you were Company," Doolittle told Ebby. "We could have kept closer tabs on you. When you went missing we could have started ringing the gong sooner."

Ebby touched his eye, which was still tender. "Wouldn't have changed anything," he remarked.

"I guess not," Doolittle conceded.

Arpád and a tall, lanky officer in a crisp uniform of the armored corps appeared at the double doors of the reception room and walked in lockstep across the marble floor to join Nagy and the Americans.

"Who's the guy with Zelk?" Ebby asked.

"That's Nagy's minister of defense, Pal Maléter, the commander of the Kilian Barracks. He's the one who's been negotiating the Soviet pullout with the Russians."

The chief of station waved for Ebby to join them. Nagy was talking to Maléter in Hungarian. The premier turned to the Americans. "If you please, Mr. Ambassador, tell him what you told me."

The ambassador, an old-school diplomat who agonized over the situation in Hungary, tugged a message blank from the inside pocket of his double-breasted suit jacket. Pasted across the paper in strips was a deciphered top secret cable that had come into the embassy earlier in the day. "We have reports—" he began. He cleared his throat; he felt as if he were reading out a death sentence. "—reports that two trains filled with the latest model Soviet tank, the T-54, crossed the Hungarian frontier at Zahony, then offloaded and dug in around Szolnok and Abony. We have intelligence that the old Soviet T-34 tanks that pulled out of Budapest a few days ago went no further than Vecses, nine miles from the city, where they turned around and blocked roads. French diplomats who flew out of Budapest in the last twenty-four hours reported seeing Soviet tanks closing in on the three Budapest airports—Ferihegy, Budaörs, and Tokol. Finally, one of our own reconnaissance aircraft flying from a base in Austria spotted two hundred tanks and a long column of new Soviet armored personnel carriers, designated BTR-152, heading in the direction of Budapest near Vac and Cegledopen."

Nagy puffed agitatedly on an American cigarette. Ashes tumbled onto one of the lapels of his brown suit jacket but he didn't appear to notice. "We also have had information," he told the ambassador, "indicating that a great many Soviet tanks have crossed the Tisza into Hungary." He turned to his Minister of Defense and, speaking in English for the benefit of the Americans, asked, "Did you raise the subject of these sightings with the Soviet side at tonight's negotiations?"

"I did, Mr. Prime Minister," Maléter replied. "Ambassador Andropov became enraged—he claimed it was a provocation of the American CIA designed to ignite full scale fighting between the Russian side and the Hungarian side before we could conclude the terms of the Soviet withdrawal. He cautioned us against falling into the American trap."

"Whom do you trust," Ebby asked bluntly, "Andropov or us?"

Maléter sized up Ebby. "I can say that we are obliged to trust him. The alternative is too tragic to contemplate. If the Soviets invade Hungary we will of course fight. But for us there can be only one issue—death with honor."

Arpád Zelk added grimly, "We harbor no illusions about surviving—without American intervention we have no possibility of defeating the Russians if it comes to full scale war."

"Do you, sir, believe the Russians will invade?" the American chargé d'affaires asked Nagy.

The premier took his time before answering. "If one judges from history," he said finally, "the response must be yes. The Russians always come in."

"Let us look at this realistically," Maléter said. "There are bound to be some in the Soviet superstructure who will argue that if Hungary is permitted to remove itself from the Soviet sphere, other satellite states will follow."

Nagy became aware of the ashes on his lapel and flicked them away with his fingernails. "History will judge us harshly if we went too far, too fast," he confided in a gruff voice. He concentrated on his cigarette for a moment. "It comes down to this: In the event of war what will the Americans do?"

"We have been clear about this from the start," the ambassador said. "Mr. Ebbitt here, at great personal risk, brought an unambiguous message to Mr. Zelk. The day you assumed the powers of premier, I delivered the same message to you, Mr. Nagy. Neither the Americans nor NATO are prepared to intervene in Hungary."

"What if we were to provide a casus belli for the Western powers to intervene by taking Hungary out of the Warsaw Pact and declaring neutrality?"

The ambassador said, "It would not alter anything—except perhaps infuriate the Soviets even more."

"Our only hope, then, rests on the Russians being unsure of the American attitude," Maléter said. "As long as they are in doubt, there is always a chance that Khrushchev and the doves on the Soviet politburo will restrain Zhukov and his hawks."

As the Americans were leaving the Parliament building, the chief of station pulled Ebby into a vestibule. "I think it might be wise if you came back to the embassy with me. We'll supply you with diplomatic cover—"

"What about Zoltan, my radioman? What about Elizabet Németh?"

"If word gets out that we're giving asylum to Hungarians we'll be swamped—mobs will beat down our doors."

"A lot of these people went out on the limb for us."

"What they were doing, they were doing for Hungary, not for us. We don't owe them anything."

Ebby said, "That's not how I see things. I'll stay with them."

The chief of station hiked his shoulders. "I can't order you. Officially, I don't even know you're in Budapest—you're reporting directly to the DD/O. For the record, if the Russians do invade I strongly urge you to change your mind."

"Thanks for the advice."

"Advice is cheap."

Ebby nodded in agreement. "The advice you gave me is cheap."

8

WASHINGTON, DC, SATURDAY, NOVEMBER 3, 1956

AT SUNUP, BERNICE SHIFTED ONTO HER SIDE IN THE NARROW BED, pressing the large nipples of her tiny breasts into Eugene's back. The previous night he had turned up at her third-floor walkup later than usual—the candles she always lit when she knew he was coming had almost burned down to their wicks—and their love-making had lasted longer than usual. He hadn't wanted to do any peyote; he seemed to be walking on air without it.

"So are you awake?" Bernice whispered into his neck. "I think there's something you need to know, baby."

Stirring lazily, Eugene opened an eye and, squinting, played with the sunlight streaming through slits in the window shade. "What do I need to know?"

"I figured out where you don't come from."

"Where don't I come from?"

"Canada is where you don't come from, baby."

Eugene maneuvered onto his back and Bernice crawled on top of him, her long bony body light as a feather, her fingers reaching down to comb through his pubic hair.

"If I don't come from Canada, where do I come from?"

The tip of her tongue flicked at the inside of his ear. "You come from ...Russia, baby. You're Russian."

Both of Eugene's eyes were wide open now. "What makes you think that?"

"You mutter things in your sleep, things I don't understand, things in a foreign language. "

"Maybe I'm speaking Canadian."

Bernice's body trembled with silent laughter. "You said something like *knigi.*"

"*Knigi* sounds Canadian to me."

"Max speaks pigeon Russian from when he visited Moscow before the war. Hey, don't worry—I told him I overheard two customers speaking what I thought was Russian. Max says I must have been right—he says *knigi* means 'book' in Russian."

"Book?"

"Yeah, baby. *Book!* So don't act innocent. You say other Russian-sounding things, too. You say something that sounds like *starik*. Max says *starik* is Russian for 'old man.' He says *Starik* with a capital *S* was Lenin's nickname. Almost everyone around him was younger and called him 'the old man.' Honest to God, Eugene, it gives me goose pimples thinking about it—I mean, actually *talking* to Comrade Lenin in your sleep!"

Eugene tried to pass it off as a joke. "Maybe I was Russian in a previous incarnation."

"Maybe you're Russian in this incarnation. Hey, there's more. Reasons why I think you're Russian, I mean."

Eugene propped himself up in bed, his back against a pillow, and reached for a cigarette on the night table. He lit it and passed it to Bernice, who sat up alongside him. He lit a second one for himself.

"So you want to hear my reasons?"

"Anything for a laugh."

"Remember when Max lent us the station wagon two weeks ago and we drove down to Key West? You did something real funny before we left—after you packed your valise you sat down on it."

"I was trying to lock it."

"It was locked when you sat down on it, Eugene, baby."

Eugene sucked pensively on the cigarette.

"After we left, you remembered you'd forgotten the antenna for your Motorola. Shows how dumb I am, I didn't even know Motorolas needed antennas. Long as we were going back, I went up to pee. You found the antenna in the closet and then you did something funny again—you looked at yourself in the full-length mirror on the wall next to the john."

"That doesn't make me Russian, Bernice. That makes me narcissistic."

"Remember me telling you about my grandfather coming from Vilnus? Well, he always used to sit on his valise before setting out on a trip—us kids used to kid him about it. He said it brought good luck. He flat-out refused to go back across the threshold once he started out—he said it meant the trip would end badly. And if he absolutely had to, like the time when my grandmother forgot the sulfa pills for her heart, he did what you did—he looked at himself in the mirror before starting out again." She reached across Eugene's stomach to flick ashes into a saucer on the night table. "I don't know how you got to talk American with a Brooklyn accent but if you're not Russian, Eugene, I'm a monkey's uncle."

Eugene regarded his girlfriend of five years. "This started out as a joke, Bernice, but it has stopped being funny."

Leaning toward him, Bernice pressed her lips against his ear and whispered into it. "When I was vacuuming your apartment over the store yesterday, I discovered the hiding place under the floorboards in the closet. I found the antenna. I found packs of money. Lots and lots of it. More money than I've ever seen before. I found *stuff*—a miniature camera, rolls of film, a small gizmo that fits in your palm and looks like some kind of microscope. I found matchbooks with grids of numbers and letters on the inside covers." Bernice shuddered. "I'm so proud of you, Eugene, I could die. I'm proud to be your friend. I'm proud to fuck you." She reached down with her right hand and cupped it protectively over his testicles. "Oh, baby, it takes my breath away when I think of it. It's the bee's knees. It's the cat's pajamas. It's completely *colossal*! You're a spy for Soviet Russia, Eugene! You're a Communist warrior battling on the front line against capitalism." She began sliding down his body, sucking on his nipples, planting moist kisses on his stomach, pulling his penis up toward her lips and bending to meet it. "You don't need to worry, Eugene. Bernice would die before she tells a soul about you being a spy for the Motherland."

"Even Max, Bernice. Especially Max."

Tears of joy streamed from Bernice's shut eyes. "Even Max, baby," she whispered breathlessly. "Oh my God, I love you to death, Eugene. I love what you are, I love you the way a woman loves a soldier. This secret will be an engagement ring between us. I swear it to you."

She rambled on about the permanent revolution that would bring Marxism to the world and the dictatorship of the proletariat that would follow. She kept talking but gradually her words became garbled and he had difficulty understanding them.

Eugene had met SASHA the previous night at the rendezvous marked as

X O X

O X O

O O X

in the tic-tac-toe code: the McClellan statue on California Avenue. A face-to-face meeting between an agent and his handler was a rare event; when the

matter was more or less routine, Eugene usually retrieved films and enciphered messages from dead drops. Both SASHA and Eugene had taken the
usual precautions to make sure they weren't being followed; doubling back
on their tracks, going the wrong way on one-way streets, ducking into stores
through a main entrance and leaving through a side door. Despite the chilly
weather, two old men were playing chess under a streetlight on a nearby park
bench. SASHA nodded toward them but Eugene shook his head no. He'd
reconnoitered the site before leaving the coded tic-tac-toe chalk marks on
the mailbox near SASHA's home; the same two old men, bundled in overcoats and scarves, had been playing chess then, too.

"Know anything about General McClellan?" Eugene asked, looking up
at the statue.

"He won a battle during the Civil War but I don't remember which
one," SASHA said.

"It was what the North called Antietam, after a creek, and the South
called Sharpsburg, after the town. McClellan whipped Lee's ass but he was
too cautious for Lincoln when it came to exploiting the victory. Lincoln
grumbled that 'McClellan's got the slows' and fired him."

"Khrushchev's got the slows, if you ask me," SASHA said moodily. "If
he doesn't go into Hungary and put down the goddamn insurrection, all of
Eastern Europe will break away. And there will be no buffer zone left
between the Soviet Union and NATO forces in the west."

"If Khrushchev's dragging his feet, it's because he's worried about starting a world war," Eugene guessed.

"There won't be a world war," SASHA said flatly, "at least not over
Hungary. That's why I phoned in the order to the girl at the liquor store.
That's why I asked for this meeting." He held out a small brown paper bag
filled with peanuts. "Under the peanuts you'll find two rolls of microfilms
that will change history. There are contingency papers, there are minutes of
a high-level telephone discussion, there are messages from Vienna Station,
there's even a copy of a CIA briefing to President Eisenhower on American
military preparedness in Europe in the event of war. I sat in on the briefing.
When it was finished Eisenhower shook his head and said, 'I wish to God I
could help them, but I can't.' Remember those words, Eugene. They're not
on any of the microfilms but they're straight from the horse's mouth."

"'I wish to God I could help them, but I can't.'"

"Starik's been peppering me with interrogatives since this business in
Budapest exploded. Here's his answer: The Americans won't move a tank or
a unit to assist the Hungarians if Khrushchev takes the leash off Zhukov."

Eugene plucked a peanut from the bag, cracked it and popped the nuts into his mouth. Then he accepted the bag. "I'll have the remark from Eisenhower in Starik's hands in two hours."

"How will I know it's been delivered?" SASHA asked.

"Watch the headlines in the *Washington Post*," Eugene suggested.

Philip Swett had a hard time rounding up the usual movers and shakers for his regular Saturday night Georgetown bash. Sundry stars of the Washington press corps, senior White House aides, Cabinet members, Supreme Court justices, members of the Joint Chiefs, State Department topsiders and Pickle Factory mavens had asked for rain checks; they were all too busy following the breaking news to socialize. Joe Alsop, who had popularized the domino theory in one of his columns, dropped by but fled in mid-cocktail when he received an urgent phone call from his office (it seemed that Moscow had just threatened to use rockets if the Israelis didn't agree to a Middle East ceasefire and the British and French continued to menace Egypt). Which left Swett presiding over a motley crew of under-secretaries and legislative assistants and the stray guest, his daughter Adelle and his son-in-law Leo Kritzky among them. Putting the best face on the situation, he waved everyone into the dining room. "Looks like Stevenson is going down in flames next Tuesday," he announced, motioning for the waiters to uncork the Champagne and fill the glasses. "Latest polls give Ike fifty-seven percent of the popular vote. Electoral college won't even be close."

"Adlai never had a chance," a State Department desk officer observed. "No way a cerebral governor from Illinois is going to whip General Eisenhower, what with a full-fledged revolution raging in Hungary and the Middle East in flames."

"People are terrified we'll drift into world war," remarked a Republican speechwriter. "They want someone at the helm who's been tested under fire."

"It's one thing to be terrified of war," maintained a Navy captain attached to the Joint Chiefs. "It's another to sit on the sidelines when our allies—the British and French and Israelis—attack Egypt to get back the Suez Canal. If we don't help out our friends, chances are they won't be there for us when we need them."

"Ike is just being prudent," explained the State Department desk officer. "The Russians are already jittery over the Hungarian uprising. The Israeli invasion of Sinai, the British and French raids on Egyptian airfields, could lead Moscow to miscalculate."

"In the atomic age it would only take one teeny miscalculation to destroy the world," declared Adelle. "Speaking as the mother of two small girls, I don't fault an American president for being cautious."

Leo said, "Still and all, there's such a thing as being too cautious."

"Explain yourself," Swett challenged from the head of the table.

Leo glanced at Adelle, who raised her eyebrows as if to say: For goodness sake, don't let him browbeat you. Smiling self-consciously, Leo turned back to his father-in-law. "The data I've seen suggests that Khrushchev and the others on the Politburo have lost their taste for confrontation." he said. "It's true they rattle their sabers from time to time, like this threat to intervene in the Suez matter. But we need to look at their actions, as opposed to their words—for starters, they pulled two divisions out of Budapest when the Hungarians took to the streets. If we play our cards right, Hungary could be pried out of the Soviet sphere and wind up in the Western camp."

"Russians believe in the domino theory as much as we do," said a much-published think tank professor who made a small fortune consulting for the State Department. "If they let one satellite break away others are bound to follow. They can't afford to run that risk."

"Is that what you're telling the State Department—that you think the Red Army will invade Hungary?" Swett asked.

"Count on it, the Red Army will be back, and in force," the professor predicted.

"If the Russians do invade Hungary," Leo said, "America and NATO will be hard put to sit on their hands. After all these years of talking about rolling back Communism, we'll have to put up or shut up if we want to remain credible."

Adelle, who worked as a legislative assistant for Senate Majority Leader Lyndon Johnson, looked surprised. "Are you saying we ought to go to war to keep our credibility?" she asked.

Before Leo could answer, the State Department desk officer said, "Mark my words, nobody's going to war over Hungary. Knowing Ike, knowing John Foster Dulles, if push comes to shove my guess is we'll back down."

"I hope you're wrong," Leo persisted earnestly. "I hope, at the very least, they have the nerve to bluff the Russians. Look, if the Russians can't be sure how America will react, then the doves on the Politburo, Khrushchev among them, might be able to keep the hawks in line."

The grandfather clock was closing in on midnight by the time the last of the guests had departed. With only family remaining—since the birth of his twin granddaughters, two years before, Philip Swett grudgingly included

Leo under 'family'—the host broke out a bottle of very aged and very expen-sive Napoleon cognac and filled three snifters. "To us," he said, raising his glass. A grunt of pure pleasure escaped his lips after he swallowed the first sip of cognac. Turning the snifter in his fingers, he gazed sideways at his son-in-law. "Knew you were an ardent anti-Communist, Leo—suppose you wouldn't be in the Company if you weren't—but never thought you were madcap about it. This Hungary business brings out the gung-ho in you."

"There is something exhilarating about a slave nation breaking free," Leo admitted.

"I've got nothing against a slave nation breaking free long as it doesn't bring the world down around our ears."

"Each of us has his own idea of where American national interest lies—" Leo started to say.

"By golly, it's not in America's national interest to bring on a nuclear war which could reduce America to volcanic ashes!" Swett squinted at Leo. "You appear to be pretty damn sure of yourself when you say Khrushchev and Company went and lost their taste for confrontation. What do you know that's not in the newspapers? Has that Pickle Factory of yours got a spy in the Politburo?"

Leo smiled uncomfortably. "It's just an educated guess."

Swett snorted. "Ask me, sounds more like an *un*educated guess."

"I don't agree with what he's saying any more than you do, Daddy," Adelle said, "but Leo's entitled to his opinion."

"Not saying he isn't. Just saying he's full of crap."

Swett was grinning as he spoke, which made it impossible for Leo to take offense. "On that note," he said, setting the snifter on a table, pushing himself to his feet, "we ought to be heading home to relieve the baby-sitter." He nodded at his father-in-law. "Phil."

Swett nodded back. "Leo."

Adelle sighed. "Well, at least the two of you know each other's name."

Leaning over the small table in the inner sanctum off the library of the Abakumov mansion outside of Moscow, matching the numbers on the message to the letters on the grid of the one-time pad, Starik meticulously deciphered the bulletin from his agent in Rome; he didn't want messages dealing with KHOLSTOMER passing through the hands of code clerks. The several sums of US dollars, transferred over the past six months to a Swiss bank from SovGaz and the Soviet Import-Export Cooperative, then discreetly paid out to various shell companies in Luxembourg that channeled the money on to the Banco Ambrosiano, Italy's largest private bank, and finally to the Vatican Bank itself, were accounted for.

Starik burned the enciphered message and the one-time pad in a coal bucket, then inserted the deciphered message in the old-fashioned file box with an iron hasp. The words *Soversheno Sekretno* ("Top Secret") and KHOLSTOMER were written in beautiful Cyrillic script across the oak cover. He placed the box on the shelf of the large safe that was cemented into the wall behind the portrait of Lenin, enabled the destruction mechanism, closed the heavy door and carefully double-locked it at the top and at the bottom with the only existing key, which he kept attached to the wrought silver chain hanging around his neck.

Then he turned his attention to the next message, which the code clerks working in the top floor room-within-a-room had just broken out of its cipher. It had come in marked "Urgent Immediate" fourteen minutes earlier. The clerk who had delivered the deciphered version to Starik mentioned that the Washington *rezidentura*, using emergency contact procedures, had come on the air outside its regularly scheduled transmissions, which underscored the importance of the matter.

As Starik read through SASHA's brief message—"I wish to God I could help them, but I can't." —his eyes brightened. He reached for the phone and dialed the gatehouse. "Bring my car around to the front door immediately," he ordered.

Starik extracted the last of the hollow-tipped Bulgarian cigarettes from the packet and thrust it between his lips. He crumpled the empty packet and tossed it into the corrugated burn bin on his next turn around the anteroom. One of the half-dozen KGB heavies sitting around on wooden benches reading photo magazines noticed Starik patting his pockets and offered a light. Bending over the flame, Pasha Semyonovich Zhilov sucked the cigarette into life.

"How long have they been at it?" he called across the room to the secretary, a dreary-faced young man wearing goggle-like eyeglasses, who was sitting behind the desk next to the door.

"Since nine this morning," he answered.

"Seven hours," one of the bodyguards grunted.

From behind the shut door of the Politburo conference room came the muffled sound of riotous argument. Every now and then someone would raise his voice and a phrase would be audible: "Simply not possible to give you a written guarantee." "No choice but to support us." "Matter of days at the most." "Weigh the consequences." "If you refuse the responsibility will be on your head."

Starik stopped in front of the male secretary. "Are you certain he knows I am here?"

"I placed your note in front of him. What more can I do?"

"It is vital that I speak to him before a decision is taken," Starik said. "Ring through to him on the phone."

"I am under strict instructions not to interrupt—"

"And I am instructing you *to* interrupt. It will go badly for you if you refuse."

The young man was caught in an agony of indecision. "If you give me another written message, Comrade Colonel General, I can attempt to delivered it in such a way as to ensure that he has read it."

Starik scribbled a second note on a pad and ripped it off. The secretary filled his lungs with air and plunged into the room, leaving the door partly open behind him. "Run unacceptable risks if we do not intervene." "Still recovering from the last war." "Only thing counterrevolutionists understand is force."

The door opened wider and the secretary returned. The round figure of Nikita Sergeyovich Khrushchev materialized behind him. The six heavies lounging around the room sprang to their feet. Starik dropped his cigarette on the floor and stubbed it out with the toe of one of his soft boots.

Khrushchev was in a foul mood. "What the devil is so important that it cannot wait until—"

Starik produced a plain brown envelope from the inside pocket of his long peasant's jacket, pulled several sheets of paper from it and held them out to Khrushchev. "These speak for themselves."

The First Secretary of the Soviet Communist Party fitted on a pair of steel-rimmed reading glasses and started to skim the documents. As he finished the first sheet, his thick lips parted. From time to time he would glance up and pose a question.

"How sure are you of the source of these reports?"

"I would stake my life on him."

"These appear to be minutes of a meeting—"

"There was a three-way conversation on a secure telephone line between CIA Director Dulles; his brother, John Foster Dulles, who is recuperating in a Washington hospital; and Secretary of Defense Charles Wilson. A stenographer in the office of CIA Director Dulles recorded the conversation."

Khrushchev chuckled. "I will not ask you how these records came into your possession."

Starik did not smile. "I would not tell you if you did."

Khrushchev bristled. "If I instruct you to tell me, you will tell me."

Starik stood his ground. "I would quit first."

Nikolai Bulganin, the one-time mayor of Moscow who, on Khrushchev's insistence, had been named premier the previous year, appeared at the door behind the First Secretary.

"Nikita Sergeyevich, Marshal Zhukov is pressing for an answer—"

Khrushchev passed the pages he'd already read to Bulganin. "Look through these, Nikolai Aleksandrovich," he ordered crisply. He read through the remaining pages, reread two of them, then looked up. His small eyes danced excitedly in his round face. "The parenthetical observation at the top," he said, lowering his voice, "suggests that these words were spoken in the White House."

Starik permitted himself a faint smile.

Khrushchev showed the last document to Bulganin, then returned the papers to Starik. "My thanks to you, Pasha Semyonovich. Of course, this permits us to assess the situation in a different light." With that, both the First Secretary and the Soviet premier returned to the conference room, closing the door behind them.

The KGB heavies settled back onto the benches. The young secretary breathed a sigh of relief. Behind the thick wooden door the storm seemed to have abated, replaced by the droning of unruffled men moving briskly in the direction of a rational decision.

9

BUDAPEST, SUNDAY, NOVEMBER 4, 1956

ON THE STAGE OF THE CORVIN CINEMA, AMID A CLUTTER OF orange peels and empty sardine tins and broken ammunition crates and discarded clothing and heaps of mimeographed tracts and assorted weaponry, the players in the drama waited for the curtain to rise on the third act. Half a dozen teenage girls fitted machine gun bullets, smuggled in from a Hungarian Army base the previous night, into cartridge belts as they giggled over boys who had caught their eye. Several older women, sitting in a semicircle under the stage, filled empty beer bottles with petrol and then stuffed cloth wicks into them. In a corner, Zoltan, Ebby's gypsy radioman, sharpened the long curved blade of his father's father's knife on a snakestone, testing it every now and then against the ball of his thumb. A young squad leader, just back from patrolling the Pest bank of the Danube, stripped off his bandolier, leather jacket and knitted sweater and crawled onto a pallet alongside his sleeping girlfriend, a freckle-faced teenager with blonde pigtails; she stirred and turned and buried her head in the boy's neck, and the two whispered for several minutes before falling asleep in each other's arms. In the back of the auditorium Ebby dozed on one of the folding wooden seats, his head propped against a window curtain rolled into a makeshift pillow. Elizabet lay stretched across three seats in the row behind him, a Hungarian Army greatcoat covering her body, a sailor's watch cap pulled over her eyes and ears shutting out the light and sound, but not the tension.

Shortly before four in the morning Arpád lumbered through the double door of the theater and looked around. He spotted Ebby and strode across the auditorium to sink wearily onto the seat next to him.

Ebby came awake instantly. "Are the rumors true?" he demanded.

Arpád, his eyes swollen from lack of sleep, nodded gloomily. "You must radio the news to your American friends in Vienna. Pál Maléter and the other members of the delegation were invited to continue the negotiations at the Russian command post on the island of Tokol in the Danube. Sometime after eleven last night, Maléter phoned to say everything was in order. An hour later his driver turned up at the Parliament and reported that Maléter and the others had been arrested. The KGB burst into the conference room during a coffee break. Maléter's driver was napping in the cloakroom. In the confusion he was overlooked. Later he managed to slip out a back door. He said the Russian general negotiating with Meléter was furious with the KGB. He'd given him his word as a soldier that the Hungarian delegation would be safe. The leader of the KGB squad took the general aside and whispered something in his ear. The general waved his hand in disgust and stalked out of the room. The KGB threw burlap sacks over the heads of our negotiators and led them away."

"This can only mean one thing," Ebby whispered.

Arpád nodded grimly. "We are betrayed by everyone," he said dully. "There is nothing left for us except to die fighting."

From beyond the thick walls of the Corvin Cinema came the dry thud of cannon fire; it sounded like someone discreetly knocking on a distant door. Somewhere in Pest several artillery shells exploded. Around the auditorium students were climbing to their feet in alarm. A shell burst on Ulloi Avenue, shaking the building. Everyone started talking at once until an Army officer clambered onto a stepladder and shouted for silence. He began issuing orders. Grabbing their weapons, filling their overcoat pockets with Molotov cocktails, the students headed for the exits.

Elizabet was on her feet in the row behind Ebby and Arpád, shivering under the greatcoat pulled over her shoulders like a cape. Clutching her mutilated breast, she listened for a moment to the distant thunder and the explosions. The blood drained from her already pale lips. "What is happening?" she whispered.

Arpád stood up. "The Russians have come back, my dear Elizabet. They have declared war on our revolution." He started to say something else but his voice was lost in the burst of a shell between the Corvan Cinema and the Kilian Barracks across the street. The explosion cut off the electricity. The lights in the cinema blinked out as a fine powdery dust rained down from the ceiling.

Around the auditorium flashlights flickered on. Ebby buttonholed

Zoltan and the two of them made their way by flashlight to the makeshift passageway that had been cut in the walls between the Cinema and the adjoining apartment building, and climbed up to the top floor room that had been turned into a radio shack. With the stub of a pencil Ebby started printing out a CRITIC to Vienna Station. "Don't bother enciphering this," he told Zoltan. "The most important thing now is—"

The whine of Russian MiGs screaming low over the rooftops drowned out Ebby. As the planes curled away, he heard the dry staccato bark of their wing cannons. Racing to a window, he saw flames leaping from the roof of the building next to the Kilian Barracks across the intersection. Zoltan, his face creased into a preoccupied frown, wired the transceiver to an automobile battery and fiddled with the tuning knob until the needle indicated he was smack on the carrier signal. Then he plugged in the Morse key. Ebby finished the message and passed it to Zoltan, and then held the flashlight while the gypsy radioman tapped out his words:

soviet artillery on buda hills began shelling pest 4 this morning explosions heard throughout city one shell landed street outside corvin soviet jets strafing rebel strongpoints according unconfirmed report kgb arrested nagy defense minister pal meleter and other members hungarian negotiating team last night hungarians at corvin preparing for house to house resistance but unlikely prevail this time

Bending low over the Morse key, working it with two fingers of his right hand, Zoltan signed off using Ebby's code name. Ebby caught the sound of tank engines coughing their way down Ulloi. He threw open the window and leaned out. Far down the wide avenue, a long line of dull headlights could be seen weaving toward the Cinema. Every minute or so the tanks pivoted spastically on their treads and shelled a building at point blank range. As Zoltan had predicted when they installed the radio shack on the top floor, the Russian tanks were unable to elevate their cannons in the limited space of the streets. So they were simply shooting the ground floors out from under the buildings, and letting the upper floors collapse into the basements.

"I think we'd better get the hell out of here," Ebby decided.

Zoltan didn't need to be told twice. While Ebby retrieved the antenna attached to the stovepipe on the roof, he stuffed the battery and the transceiver into his knapsack. The gypsy led the way back through the deserted corridors to the apartment that connected to the Corvin Cinema. The first Russian tanks started blasting away at the ground floor of their building as they ducked through the double hole in the bricks and made their way down a narrow staircase to the alleyway behind the cinema. The clouds overhead had turned rose-red from the fires raging around the city. Groups of Corvin commandos, boys and girls wearing short leather jackets and black berets and red-white-and-green armbands, crouched along the alleyway, waiting their turn to dash out into the street to hurl Molotov cocktails at the tanks that were blasting away at the thick concrete walls of the Cinema and the fortress-like façade of the massive barrack building across the avenue. Someone switched on a battery-powered radio and, turning up the volume, set it atop a battered taxi sitting on four flat tires. For a moment the sound of static filled the alleyway. Then came the hollow, emotional voice of the premier, Imre Nagy.

Gesturing with both hands as if he himself were giving the speech, Zoltan attempted a running translation. "He says us that Soviet forces attack our capital to overthrow the legal democratic Hungarian government, okay. He says us that our freedom fighters are battling the enemy. He says us that he alerts the people of Hungary and the entire world to these goddamn facts. He says us that today it is Hungary, tomorrow it will be the turn of—"

There were whistles of derision from the crouching students waiting their turn to fling themselves against the Russian tanks; this was not a crowd sympathetic to the plight of a bookish Communist reformer caught between the Soviet Politburo and the anti-Communist demands of the great majority of his own people. One of the young section-leaders raised a rifle to his shoulder and shot the radio off the roof of the taxi. The others around him applauded.

There were sporadic bursts of machine gun fire from the avenue. Moments later a squad of freedom fighters darted back into the alleyway, dragging several wounded with them. Using wooden doors as stretchers, medical students wearing white armbands carried them back into the Corvin Cinema.

The students nearest the mouth of the alleyway struck matches and lit the wicks on their Molotov cocktails. The freckled girl with pigtails, who looked all of sixteen, burst into tears that racked her thin body. Her boyfriend tried to pry the Molotov cocktail out of her fist but she clutched it tightly. When her turn came she rose shakily to her feet and staggered from the alleyway. One by one the others got up and dashed into the street. The metallic tick of Russian machine guns drummed in the dusty morning air. Bullets chipped away at the brick wall across the alleyway and fell to the ground.

Zoltan picked up a bullet and turned it in his fingers; it was still warm to the touch. He leaned close to Ebby's ear. "You want an opinion, okay, we need to get our asses over to the American embassy."

Ebby shook his head. "We'd never make it through the streets alive."

In the stairwell inside the doorway to the cinema Arpád and Elizabet were arguing furiously in Hungarian. Several times Arpád started to leave but Elizabet clung to the lapel of his leather jacket and continued talking. They stepped back to let two medical students haul a dead girl—the freckled sixteen-year-old who had broken into tears before she ran into the street—down the stairs to the basement morgue. Arpád waved an arm in dismay as they carried the body past, then shrugged in bitter resignation. Elizabet came over to kneel behind Ebby. "Remember the tunnel that runs under the street to the Kilian Barracks? I talked Arpád into going with us—there are hundreds of armed freedom fighters still in the barracks, plenty of ammunition. The walls are three meters thick in places. We can hold out there for days. Even if the rest of the city falls we can keep the ember of resistance alive. Perhaps the West will come to its senses. Perhaps the Western intellectuals will oblige their governments to confront the Russians." She nodded toward the knapsack on Zoltan's back. "You absolutely must come with us to send reports of the resistance to Vienna. They will believe messages from you."

Zoltan saw the advantages immediately. "If things turn bad at Kilian," he told Ebby, "there are tunnels through which you can escape into the city."

"The reports I send back won't affect the outcome," Ebby said. "At some point someone with an ounce of sanity in his brain has to negotiate a truce and stop the massacre."

"You must send back reports as long as the fighting continues," Elizabet insisted.

Ebby nodded without enthusiasm. "I'll tell them how the Hungarians are dying, not that it will change anything."

The four of them descended the steel spiral stairs to the boiler room and then made their way single file along a narrow corridor into a basement that had been used to store coal before the cinema switched to oil, and had been transformed into a morgue. Behind them the medical orderlies were carrying down still more bodies and setting them out in rows, as if the neatness of the rows could somehow impose a shred of order on the chaos of violent and obscenely premature death. Some of the dead were badly disfigured by bullet wounds; others had no apparent wounds at all and it wasn't obvious what they had died of. The smell in the unventilated basement room was turning rancid and Elizabet, tears streaming from her eyes, pulled the rolled collar of her turtleneck up over her nose.

Threading their way through the bodies, the group reached the steel door that led to the narrow tunnel filled with thick electric cables. On one large stone someone had carefully chiseled "1923" and, under it, the names of the workers on the construction site. About forty meters into the tunnel—which put them roughly under Ulloi Avenue—they could hear the treads of the tanks overhead fidgeting nervously from side to side as they hunted for targets. Arpád, in the lead, pounded on the metal door blocking the end of the tunnel with the butt of his pistol. Twice, then a pause, then twice more. They could hear the clang of heavy bolts being thrown on the inside, then the squeal of hinges as the door opened. A wild-eyed priest with a straggly gray beard plunging down his filthy cassock peered out at them. Several baby-faced soldiers wearing washed-out khaki and carrying enormous World War I Italian bolt-action naval rifles trained flashlights on their faces. When the priest recognized Arpád, he gave a lopsided smile. "Welcome to Gehenna," he cried hysterically, and with a flamboyant gesture he licked his thumb and traced an elaborate crucifix on the forehead of each of them as they passed through the door.

10

THE DEPUTY DIRECTOR FOR OPERATIONS HAD LANDED RUNNING. Moving in with his old Georgetown chum, Llewellyn Thompson, now the American ambassador to Austria, the Wiz had set up a war room in the embassy's paneled library and started poring over every scrap of paper he could get his hands on. Millie Owen-Brack commandeered a tea wagon to ferry in the reams of Company and State Department cables and wire service ticker stories; pushing the wagon through the swinging double doors of the library, she would pile up the material on the table in front of Wisner until he disappeared behind the mountain of paper. Groggy from lack of sleep, his bloodshot eyes darting, his shirt damp with perspiration, the Wiz attacked each new pile with a melancholy intensity, as if merely reading about what was going on across a border a few dozen miles away would allow him to dominate the situation. The day before, Dwight Eisenhower had won a second term in a landslide but the Wiz had barely noticed. "Mongolian units are reportedly searching neighborhoods block by block, house by house, hunting for the ringleaders of the rebellion," he read aloud from one operational cable that had originated with the political officer at the Budapest embassy. "Thousands of freedom fighters are being thrown into boxcars and carried off in the direction of the Ukraine." Wisner crushed the cable in his fist and added it to the small mountain of crumpled messages on the floor. "Mother of God," he moaned, noisily sucking in air through his nostrils. "Here's another one from Ebbitt dated five November. 'Kilian Barracks still holding out. Teenagers are tying sticks of industrial dynamite around their waists and throwing themselves under the treads of Soviet tanks. Ammunition running low. Spirits also. Freedom fighters have propped up dead comrades next to windows to draw Russian fire in hope they'll run out of ammunition. Everyone asks where is United Nations, when will American aid arrive. What do I tell them?'"

Tears clouding his eyes, Wisner waved Ebbitt's cable at Owen-Brack. "For six years—*six years!*—we encouraged the suckers in the satellites to rebel against their Soviet masters. We spent millions creating covert capabilities for just such an occasion—we stockpiled arms across Europe, we trained émigrés by the thousands. My God, the Hungarians in Germany are breaking down the doors of their case officers to be sent in. And what do we do? *What do we do, Millie?* We offer them goddamn pious phrases from Eisenhower: 'The heart of America goes out to the people of Hungary.' Well, the heart may go out but the hand remains stashed in its pocket..."

"Suez changed the ball game," Owen-Brack said softly but the Wiz, plowing through the next message, didn't hear her.

"Oh, Jesus, listen to this one. It's a cable from the Associated Press correspondent in Budapest. 'UNDER HEAVY MACHINE GUN FIRE. ANY NEWS ABOUT HELP? QUICKLY, QUICKLY. NO TIME TO LOSE.' Here's another. 'SOS SOS. THE FIGHTING IS VERY CLOSE NOW. DON'T KNOW HOW LONG WE CAN RESIST. SHELLS ARE EXPLODING NEARBY. RUMOR CIRCULATING THAT AMERICAN TROOPS WILL BE HERE WITHIN ONE OR TWO HOURS. IS IT TRUE?'" Wisner threw the cables aside and plucked the next one off the stack, as if he couldn't wait to hear how the story would turn out. "'GOODBYE FRIENDS. GOD SAVE OUR SOULS. THE RUSSIANS ARE NEAR.'" The Wiz rambled on, reading disjoined bits of messages, flinging them to the floor before he had finished them, starting new ones in the middle. "'Summary executions...flame throwers...charred corpses...dead washed with lime and buried in shallow graves in public parks...Nagy, hiding in Yugoslav embassy on Stalin Square, lured out with promise of amnesty and arrested...'"

Ambassador Thompson pushed through the doors into the library. "You need a break, Frank," he said, wading through the swamp of crumpled papers scattered on the floor, coming around the side of the table and putting an arm over the Wiz's shoulder. "You need a square meal under your belt, a few hours shut-eye. Then you'll be able to think more clearly."

The Wiz shook off his arm. "Don't want to think more clearly," he shouted. Suddenly the energy seemed to drain from his body. "Don't want to think," he corrected himself in a harsh whisper. He drew another pile of papers toward him with both hands, as if they were a stack of chips he'd just won at a roulette table, and held up the first cable, this one with deciphered sentences pasted in strips across a blank form. It was from the Director of

Central Intelligence, Allen Dulles. "Here's the word from Washington," Wisner snarled. "'HEADQUARTERS ADVISING VIENNA STATION THAT COMPANY POLICY IS NOT TO INCITE TO ACTION.' Not to incite to action! We're witnessing the Mongol invasion of Western civilization but we're not to incite to action! The Hungarians were incited to action by our pledge to roll back Communism. The Russians were incited to action by the Hungarians taking us at our word. We're the only ones not *incited to action*, for Christ's sake."

Thompson looked at Owen-Brack. "Don't bring him any more paper," the ambassador told her.

Wisner climbed to his feet and reared back and kicked the wire wastepaper filled with crumpled cables across the room. Thompson's mouth fell open. "You run the goddamn embassy," the Wiz told his friend icily, pointing at him with a forefinger as his hand curled around an imaginary pistol. I run the CIA operation here." He gestured with his chin toward the tea wagon. "Bring more cables," he ordered Owen-Brack. "Bring me everything you can put your hands on. I need to read into this...get a handle on it...find an angle." When Owen-Brack looked uncertainly at the ambassador, Wisner glared at her. "Move your ass!" he roared. He stumbled back into the chair. "For God's sake, bring me the paper," he pleaded, blinking his eyes rapidly, breathing hard, clutching the edge of the table to steady himself. Then he pitched forward and buried his head in a heap of cables and silently wept.

Out of the blue the Wiz announced that he wanted to see the Hungarian refugees streaming across the frontier into Austria for himself. Heartache, like the common cold, needed to be fed, he said. The chief of station, alerted by the ambassador, gave him the runaround but finally provided wheels when the phone calls from the Wiz turned ugly. Millie Owen-Brack persuaded Jack McAuliffe, the officer who had laid in the screening operation at the Austrian Red Cross reception centers, to tag along as chaperon.

The exodus from Hungary had started out as a trickle but had quickly turned into a torrent when the Russians came back in force. Each night hundreds of Hungarians braved the minefields and the Russian paratroopers who, in some sectors, had replaced the regular Hungarian Army border patrols because they tended to look the other way when they spotted refugees.

Twenty-five minutes out of Vienna, the car-pool Chevy and its chase car (filled with Company security men) pulled up at the first in a string of reception centers. This particular one had been set up in the lunchroom of a small-town *Gymnasium*. The roughly two hundred Hungarians who had come across the previous night—young men and woman for the most part, some with children, a few with aging parents—were stretched out on mattresses lined up on the floor. Many sucked absently on American cigarettes, others stared vacantly into space. In a corner, Austrian Red Cross workers in white aprons handed out bowls of soup and bread, steaming cups of coffee and doughnuts. At the next table a nineteen-year-old American volunteer, wearing a nametag on his lapel that identified him as B. Redford, was helping refugees fill out embassy requests for political asylum. The Hungarian-speakers that Jack had recruited wandered through the crowded lunchroom armed with clipboards and questionnaires. They knelt now and then to talk to the men in quiet whispers, jotting down tidbits on specific Soviet units or materiel, occasionally inviting someone who expressed an interest in "settling accounts with the Bolsheviks" to a private house across the street for a more thorough debriefing.

The Wiz, bundled into an old winter coat, the collar turned up against nonexistent drafts, a University of Virginia scarf wound around his neck, took it all in. Shaking his head, he uttered the words déjà vu—he'd seen it all before, he said. It had been at the end of the war. He'd been the OSS chief in Bucharest when the Red Army had started rounding up Rumanians who had fought against them and shipping them in cattle cars to Siberian concentration camps. Did anyone here know Harvey Torriti? he inquired, looking around with his twitching eyes. When Jack said he worked for the Sorcerer, the Wiz perked up. Good man, Torriti. Thick-skinned. Needed thick skin to survive in this business, though there were times when thick skin didn't help you all that much. Harvey and he had winced when the screams of the Rumanians reached their ears; with their own hands Harvey and he had buried prisoners who had killed themselves rather than board the trains. Déjà vu, Wisner murmured. History was repeating itself. America was abandoning good people to a fate literally worse than death. Rumanians. Poles. East Germans. Now Hungarians. The list was obscenely long.

A small boy wearing a tattered coat several sizes too large for him came up to the Wiz and held out a small hand. "*A nevem* Lórinc," he said.

One of Jack's Hungarian-speakers translated. "He tells to you his name is Lórinc."

The Wiz crouched down and shook the boy's hand. "My name is Frank."

"*Melyik foci csapatnak drukkolsz?*"

"He asks to you which football team you support?"

"Football team? I don't get to follow football much. I suppose if I had to pick one team I'd pick the New York Giants. Tell him the New York Giants are my favorite team. And Frank Gifford is my favorite player."

Wisner searched his pockets for something to give to the boy. The only thing he could come up with was a package of Smith Brothers cough drops. Forcing one of his gap-toothed smiles onto his stiff lips, he held out the box. The boy, his eyes wide and serious, took it.

"He'll think it's candy," Wisner said. "Won't hurt him any, will it? Hell, we can't hurt him more than we already have."

The smile faded and the Wiz, rolling his head from side to side as if the heartache was more than he could bear, straightened up. Jack and Millie Owen-Brack exchanged anxious looks. The Wiz glanced around in panic. "I can't breath in here," he announced with compelling lucidity. "Could someone kindly show me how one gets outside?"

The Hungarian restaurant, in a glass-domed garden off Prinz Eugenstrasse, one of Vienna's main drags, was abuzz with the usual after-theater crowd when the Wiz and his party turned up after the tour of the border. Corks popped, Champagne flowed, the cash register next to the cloakroom clanged. Viennese women in Parisian dresses with plunging necklines, their musical laughter pealing above the din of conversation, leaned over candle flames to light thin cigars while the men pretended not to notice the swell of their bosoms. The Wiz, presiding over an L-shaped table in the corner, knew Vienna well enough to remind his guests—they included Ambassador Thompson, Millie Owen-Brack, Jack McAuliffe, a correspondent from the Knight-Ridder newspapers whose name nobody could remember and several CIA station underlings—where they were: where they were, Wisner announced, stifling a belch with the back of his hand, was a stone's throw from the infamous Kammer für Arbeiter und Angestellte, where Adolf Eichmann ran what the Nazis euphemistically called the "Central Office for Jewish Emigration." The Wiz swayed to his feet and rapped a knife against a bottle of wine to propose a toast.

"I've had too much to drink, or not enough, not sure which," he began, and was rewarded with nervous laughter. "Let's drink to Eisenhower's victory over Stevenson—may Ike's second four years turn out to be gutsier than his first four." Ambassador Thompson began to climb to his feet to deliver a toast but Wisner said, "I'm not finished yet." He collected his thoughts.

"Drinking their health may violate State Department guidelines but what the hell—here's to the mad Magyars," he cried, raising his glass along with his voice. "It'll be a great wonder if any of them are left alive."

"The mad Magyars," the guests around Wisner's table repeated, sipping wine, hoping that would be the end of it; the Wiz's sudden shifts in mood had them all worried.

Several of the diners at nearby tables glanced uncomfortably in the direction of the boorish Americans.

Wisner cocked his head and squinted up at the dome, searching for inspiration. "Here's to a commodity in short supply these days," he plunged on. "Different folks call it by different names—coolness under fire, gallantry, mettle, courage of one's convictions, stoutness of one's heart but, hell, in the end it all boils down to the same thing." Stretching the vowel, Southern-style, he offered up the word in a gleeful bellow. *"Balls!"*

Jack said solemnly, "Damnation, I'll drink to balls."

"Me, too," Millie agreed.

Wisner leaned across the table to clink glasses with them. Jack and Millie toasted each other; the three of them were on the same wavelength. Nodding bitterly, the Wiz tossed off the last of his wine. "Where was I?" he inquired, his eyes clouding over as he slipped into a darker mood.

Ambassador Thompson signalled for the bill. "I think we ought to call it a day," he said.

"Let's do that," Wisner agreed. "Let's call it a day. And what a day it's been! *A Day at the Races*, featuring the brothers Marx—no relation to Karl, Senator McCarthy. A day in the life of Dennis Day. A day that will live in infamy." He melted back into his seat and turned the long stem of a wine glass between his fingers. "Problem with the world," he muttered, talking to himself, slurring his words, "men think, for their ship to come in, all they need to do is put to sea. Lost the capacity for celestial navigation. Lost true north."

11

BUDAPEST, THURSDAY, NOVEMBER 8, 1956

IN THE SMALL CHAPEL OFF THE CENTRAL COURTYARD OF THE KILIAN
Barracks, Elizabet, gaunt and drawn, wearing woolen gloves with the
fingertips cut off, stirred the cauldron simmering over an open fire.
Every once in a while she would feed pieces of furniture into the flames to
keep them going. This was the third soup she had made from the same
chicken bones. From time to time, one or two of the eighty-odd survivors
would make their way down to the "Kilian Kitchen" and fill their tin cups
from the cauldron. Crouching next to the fire to absorb some of its warmth,
they would sip the thin broth and crack jokes about the restaurant Elizabet
would open once the Russians had been kicked out of Budapest. The day
before they had killed the last dog in the barracks, a pye-mongrel nicknamed
Szuszi; one of the boys had held its front paws while another cut its throat
so as not to waste a bullet. A soldier who had been raised on a farm skinned
and eviscerated it, and roasted the meat on a grill. Talk of trapping rats in
the sub-basements under Kilian ended when the soldiers discovered that the
Russians had flooded the tunnels with sewage. Elizabet was just as glad. She
could barely swallow the dog meat, she said.

In an inside room under the roof, Ebby scratched out another message
for Vienna on a blank page torn from a manual on close order drill and
passed it to Zoltan, who tuned the radio to the weak carrier signal. The car
battery was running down and the gypsy radioman figured this would be
their last dispatch. In any case it was clear that Kilian—completely ringed by
Russian paratroopers, pounded by tank cannon, raked by machine gun fire—
could not hold out much longer. Zoltan began working the Morse key:

situation no longer desperate now hopeless scraping barrel bottom for food ammunition pain killers russian loudspeakers promising amnesty for those who lay down arms survivors debating whether to fight to finish or negotiate surrender everyone agrees russians after betrayal of nagy maleter not trustable but options narrowing if they surrender I plan to pass myself off—

The power indicator on Zoltan's transceiver flickered for a moment and then blinked out; the battery had run dry. The gypsy picked it up and shook it and tightened the contacts, and then tried the Morse key again. He shook his head grimly. "Goddamn battery gone dead on us, okay," he announced.

From the avenue outside came the whine of a single high-powered sniper bullet. On the hour, the nine tanks facing the barracks fired off two rounds each at the thick walls and then, backing and filling in the wide avenue, ceded their places to another line of tanks; given the thickness of the barrack walls, the Russians had long since abandoned the idea of bringing the structure down on the heads of the defenders but they wanted to make sure that none of them got any sleep. Which was why, when they weren't shooting, they continued broadcasting appeals to surrender from a loudspeaker mounted on one of the tanks.

While sharpshooters kept the Russian paratroopers at bay by firing at anything that moved in the street, most of the survivors, including the walking wounded, assembled in the courtyard outside the chapel. His thick hair matted, his eyes receding into his skull with fatigue, Arpád passed out cigarettes to those who wanted a smoke, and rolled one for himself with the last of his tobacco. Lighting up, he hoisted himself onto a railing and searched the anxious faces. Then, speaking quietly in Hungarian, he summarized the situation.

"He is telling them that the Corvin Cinema fell to the Russians last night," Elizabet translated for Ebby. "Firing can be heard in the city, which suggests that hit-and-run squads are still operating out of basements, though with each passing hour there seems to be less shooting. He says to us falls the honor of being the last pocket of organized resistance in the city. We have run out of food. We have hundreds of Molotov cocktails left but only twelve rounds of ammunition for each fighter. The inevitable question can no longer be put off. With the tunnels flooded, escape is cut off. Which narrows the choices down to fighting to the end or taking the Russians at their word and seeking amnesty."

There was an angry exchange between several of the young soldiers, which Elizabet didn't bother translating—it was clear from the tone that some of them thought the time had come to lay down their arms while the others wanted to go on fighting. Two of the soldiers almost came to blows and had to be separated. Arpád kept his own counsel, watching the young fighters through the haunted eyes of someone who had made tragic miscalculations. Finally he signaled for quiet.

"He is calling for a show of hands," Elizabet explained.

By twos and threes the hands went up. Arpád concentrated on his cigarette; he was obviously against surrendering. Elizabet kept her hands tightly at her sides; she had no illusions about the Russians and preferred a fight to the finish to a Communist prison.

Arpád looked over at Ebby. "You have earned the right to vote here," he said.

Ebby raised his hand. "I belong to the live-to-fight-another-day school."

One of the young soldiers climbed onto a crate and counted the votes.

"The majority wants to test the Russians," Elizabet told Ebby; it was clear that she was bitterly disappointed. "Arpád will go out under a white flag and negotiate the terms of the amnesty. Then he'll take out the wounded. If all passes well the rest of us will surrender tomorrow."

From the far corners of the enormous barracks, the wounded were brought to the arched enceinte leading to the narrow passageway with the steel door set in a bend, back from the street. Many limped along on makeshift crutches. Those who could walk aided those who couldn't. Arpád attached a soiled white undershirt to a pole. Several of the freedom fighters, blinded by tears, turned away as Arpád, with a last ferocious glance at Elizabet, threw the bolts on the armor-plated door and slipped around the bend in the passageway, out into the street.

Ebby and Elizabet hurried up to the third floor to watch through a narrow slit in the wall. A Russian officer wearing a long gray greatcoat with gold glittering on the shoulder boards stepped out from behind a tank and met Arpád halfway. The Russian offered the poet a cigarette, then shrugged when he refused. The two men talked for several minutes, with the Russian shaking his head again and again; he obviously wasn't giving ground. Finally the poet nodded his assent. The Russian held out his hand. Arpád looked at it for a long moment in disgust, then, thrusting his own hands deep into the pockets of his leather jacket, turned on a heel and made his way back to the barracks.

Moments later he emerged into the street again, this time at the head of a straggly procession of wounded fighters, some of them carried on chairs, others dragging their feet as comrades pulled them toward the line of Russian tanks. The gray-bearded priest, his head swathed in bloody bandages, leaned on a girl wearing a Red Cross armband. Halfway to the line of tanks Arpád stopped in his tracks and the others drew up behind him. Several sank to the pavement in exhaustion. From the slit in the wall, Ebby could see Arpád angrily stabbing the air in the direction of the Russians on the roofs across the avenue; several dozen of them could be seen steadying rifles fitted with telescopic sights on the parapets. Arpád shook his head violently, as if he were awakening from a deep sleep. He tugged the heavy naval pistol from a jacket pocket and stepped forward and pressed the tip of the long barrel to his forehead. *"Eljen!"* he cried out hoarsely. *"Long life!"* and he jerked the trigger. A hollow shot rang out, blowing away the lobe of the poet's brain where speech originated. Arpád sprawled backward into the gutter, one ankle folded under his body at a grotesque angle, blood gushing from the massive wound in his head. The wounded milling around him started to back away from the body. From the roof across the street a whistle shrilled. Then a sharp volley of sniper fire cut them all down. The several who were sitting on chairs were knocked over backward. It was over in a moment. Elizabet, too stunned to utter a word, turned away from the slit and stood with her back pressed against the wall, white and trembling. There was a moment of deathly silence. Then a primal animal howl emerged from the slits and windows of the barracks. Several of the young Hungarians began shooting at the snipers on the roof until someone yelled for them not to waste ammunition.

"But why?" Elizabet breathed. "Where is the logic to all this death?"

"The Russians must have panicked when they heard the shot," Ebby guessed grimly.

Hugging herself tightly, Elizabet stared out at the body of Arpád lying on the gutter in a pool of blood. She recalled the line of Persian poetry that had inspired one of his early poems, and sought what comfort was to be had in the words. "The rose blooms reddest where some buried Caesar bled," she murmured. She pulled the ancient Webley-Fosbery from her belt and spun the cylinder. "I have four bullets left—three are for the Russians, the last is for me. I could not face torture again..."

Ebby went over to a body covered with pages of newspaper and retrieved the rifle next to it. He batted away flies as he searched the pockets of the dead soldier for bullets. He found two, inserted one and, working the bolt, drove it home. "I will fight alongside you," he said.

From somewhere above their heads came the melancholy moan of a gypsy violin; it was Zoltan, summoning the Hungarian freedom fighters in the Kilian Barracks to the last stand against the invading Mongols.

Somewhere around two forty-five in the morning Ebby, dozing fitfully with his back against a wall and the rifle across his thighs, felt a hand gently shake his shoulder. Opening his eyes, he discovered Zoltan crouching next to him.

"There is a way to escape," the gypsy whispered excitedly. "Through the tunnels."

Curled up in a blanket on the cement floor next to Ebby, Elizabet came awake with a start. "Why do you wake us?" she said angrily. "The tanks haven't fired off their three o'clock rounds."

"Zoltan thinks we can get out," Ebby whispered.

"The boys and me, we been working with crowbars for hours," Zoltan said. His white teeth flashed in a proud grin. "We broke through the bricks at the lowest point in one of the narrow back tunnels and drained off most of the sewage into the basements, okay. In a quarter of an hour it will be possible to pass through. Everyone is getting ready to slip away in the night. How did you say it when we voted, Mr. Ebbitt? We will all live to fight a different day, right? Don't make noise. Follow me."

Feeling his way in the darkness, Zoltan led them down a series of winding steel staircases into the bowels of the barracks, and then through a hatch and down a wooden ladder into what had been the Kilian magazine when the barracks was first constructed. The cavernous hall, illuminated by several railroad kerosene lamps, was bare except for wooden crates once used to transport cannon powder. The brick walls were green with moisture. Gradually the last of the Kilian defenders made their way down to the magazine. Twelve Russian deserters who had been hiding in an oubliette used for prisoners at the turn of the century were brought over; each had been given civilian clothing stripped from dead fighters, Hungarian identity cards and money, along with road maps marked with routes to the Yugoslav frontier. The Russians, their eyes dark with dread, leapt at the chance to make a run for Yugoslavia; they would certainly be put before firing squads if they were captured alive.

Dividing into groups of five and moving at five-minute intervals, the surviving fighters and the Russian deserters climbed down what looked like a brick-walled well at one end of the magazine. From the avenue outside the barracks came the dull crump of the Russians firing off their three A.M. rounds. Zoltan, Ebby, Elizabet and two deserters made up the next-to-last group. Descending hand over hand into the well, Zoltan came out into a tunnel awash with thick ankle-deep sewage that reeked of feces. Elizabet, sandwiched between Zoltan and Ebby, covered her mouth and nose with her forearm but the stench made her dizzy. Ebby noticed her reeling from side to side, her shoulders slamming into the brick walls, and took a firm grip on her belt to steady her. Zoltan, up ahead with a kerosene lamp, the curved knife tucked into his belt, the violin case slung across his back on a rope, plunged on. They must have gone a hundred and fifty meters when the level of the sewage began mounting. Elizabet cried out in fear. Zoltan quickened the pace, wading through the slop that had now risen to his knees. From behind them came the panicky gasps of the last group pushing through the rising waters.

The sewage had risen to their waists by the time the tunnel curled to the right and a steel ladder appeared in the sallow beams of Zoltan's kerosene lamp. The rungs, driven individually into the bricks of the wall, disappeared into the darkness high above their heads. Zoltan threw himself onto the ladder and reached back to tug Elizabet onto the first rung visible above the water level in the tunnel. One by one the five of them began to claw their way up the ladder. Every time they came to a rung that had rusted away, Zoltan reached back to pull Elizabet over the gap. From far below came the spluttering gasps of other escapees struggling through the sewage, and then frantic splashing and sounds of choking.

Resting on a rung, Zoltan hollered down in Hungarian. A rasping voice shouted back. Zoltan said, "Only two made it out," then turned and continued climbing.

Above their heads, a light flickered and soft voices called encouragement in Hungarian. Strong arms reached down and pulled them over the top and they collapsed onto a dirt floor. The two young Russian deserters—so young it was impossible to tell they hadn't shaved in weeks—settled down next to them. Around the room the surviving freedom fighters who had arrived before them from the Kilian Barracks rested with their backs against the walls.

"Where are we?" Ebby asked.

One of the fighters who spoke some English said, "We come out to sub-basement of old building converted to industrial bakery. Listen."

Sure enough, from above came the low rumble of machinery. Zoltan consulted with several of the fighters, then returned to sit with Ebby and Elizabet. "They say we have two and a half hours left of darkness, okay. We going to catch our breath for a minute, then split up into small groups and put space between us and Kilian before the Russians figure out we are escaped. Students who know Pest will guide us out."

"Where are we going?" Elizabet asked.

Zoltan grinned. "Austria."

She turned to Ebby. "Surely you can take refuge in the American embassy."

He shook his head. "The Russians will have circled it with troops to prevent Hungarians from seeking asylum there." He smiled at her. "My best bet is to go with you to Austria."

The twelve Russian deserters, who had the most to lose if they were captured, started out first. One of them turned back at the door to deliver a quick speech in Russian. Bowing from the waist to the freedom fighters, he managed a brave half-smile before turning away and disappearing up a wooden staircase. Minutes later Ebby and Elizabet and Zoltan joined a group and made their way out a loading ramp, then climbed over a wall into a soccer field behind a school. A cold dry wind was blowing in from the Danube, and Elizabet angled her face toward it, inhaling in deep gulps. In the distance flames licked at the night sky over the city. The National Archives building across the river on Castle Hill in Buda was ablaze. The Rokus Hospital was a smoldering ruins. Fires raged over Csepel, Ujpest and Köbánya. The student leading their group, a thin-faced bespectacled young man with an old rifle slung over a bony shoulder, led them through a maze of back alleys toward the southern suburbs of Pest. The trek took them across well-kept gardens behind mansions, over brick walls and chain-link fences, through warehouses filled with silent women and children, down narrow streets. At one point they came to the main avenue leading, further up, to a square. As far as the eye could see apartment houses on both sides of the avenue had been reduced to heaps of rubble. The pavement underfoot was strewn with debris and dry yellow autumn leaves. Peering around the corner of a building, they could make out Russian paratroopers in short capes warming their hands around a fire blazing in the middle of the street near the square. Close by, the branches of trees were stark against the matte red of the blistering sky.

Hanging from the branches, twisting slowly in the currents of air from the Danube, were the bodies of twelve freedom fighters. In the street near the bodies was a human figure, his arms splayed, one leg tucked underneath, the other awry at the knee. On first glace it looked as if a large rag doll had been flattened onto the gutter by the treads of a Russian tank. But it quickly became obvious that the figure had once consisted of flesh and bones.

Ebby realized the horrible truth before the others. "Don't look," he whispered fiercely, dragging Elizabet back.

Sick at heart, she lurched against the side of a building and held her head in her hands.

Bent low and running, the Kilian survivors crossed the avenue in twos and threes without attracting the attention of the Russians around the fire. After a while Elizabet, short of breath and pushing herself through a fog of nervous exhaustion, began to lag behind. Ebby threw an arm around her waist and pulled her along. By the time the first wisps of gray were visible in the east, they were deep into the southern suburbs of Pest. To the left the first fields appeared, the dark earth plowed and glistening with dew. Below Csepel, they found tourist pedal boats chained to a pier. They broke the locks and slid the chains free and pedaled the boats over to the other bank of the Danube, then started down a dirt road that ran parallel to the river. Two kilometers on they came to the crude wooden arch marking the entrance to the Red Banner Farm, a dairy collective known to be sympathetic to the rebels. With the sky completely light now, a bearded night watchman hustled them into a storage shed. Within minutes everyone was stretched out on bales of hay, sound asleep.

During the day more refugees joined the group in the shed: an aging university professor and his emaciated wife, the conductor of Budapest Philharmonic, a puppeteer carrying two enormous suitcases filled with marionettes, a famous sportscaster with his blonde girlfriend, and the equally famous goalie of the Hungarian national soccer team with his wife and baby. At midday several women from the collective carried over hampers filled with bread and cheese, which the refugees attacked ravenously; for many it was their first meal in days. At dusk the collective's ancient Skoda diesel truck was brought around. Elizabet took the driver aside and whispered to him in urgent undertones for a moment. When he seemed to hesitate, she found a roadmap in the glove compartment and, flattening it against the hood of the truck, traced the route for him. Folding the map away, she took his hand in hers and repeated the request. The driver glanced at his wristwatch and nodded without enthusiasm and Elizabet, blinking tears out of her eyes, thanked him profusely.

The nineteen refugees crowded into a cavity hollowed out of the load of hay in the back of the truck. The farmers set planks over their heads and then lowered bales of hay onto the planks. In the darkness Elizabet, drained despite having slept for most of the day, leaned her head on Ebby's shoulder. He put an arm around her and pulled her closer. Huddled against each other, they heard the Skoda's motor backfire and finally crank over.

For the better part of three hours the truck meandered across the country-side in a westerly direction, skirting towns and villages as it jounced over dirt roads. Shifting from side to side inside their hiding place to ease their cramps, the refugees clung to each other. The professor, who turned out to be a Talmudic scholar, muttered an occasional prayer in Hebrew under his breath. The conductor took out a small pocket flashlight and an orchestral score and distracted himself by reading through the music; every once in a while he would hum a particularly melodic passage in a strained falsetto.

Around ten the passengers could feel the truck swerve sharply onto a paved road and, moments later, pull up. The motor died. Men could be heard climbing up the sides of the truck. Hands pulled away the bales of hay overhead, and then the planks. Suddenly a cloudless sky riddled with stars became visible, the Milky Way cutting a broad swath across it. The passengers climbed out to stretch their limbs for a few minutes. Several disappeared into the darkness to urinate. The truck was parked inside the hangar of a collective farm; workers in overalls formed a chain and began filling plastic jerry cans from an overhead diesel reservoir, pouring the contents into the truck's gas tank. Elizabet looked around anxiously. A thickset woman appeared at the door of the hangar. She was clutching the hand of a slim lit-tle girl with cropped dirty-blonde hair. The girl, dressed in a boy's overcoat and clutching a doll, spotted Elizabet and, crying out, bolted into her arms. The two hugged each other tightly. As soon as the fuel tank was topped off, the driver announced that they had no time to lose; they had to be at the border-crossing rendezvous no later than three. The heavy woman dropped to one knee and hugged the little girl to her. Then she and Elizabet embraced. Ebby lifted the girl onto the truck and lowered her into the hol-low space in the middle of the hay. As the last of the bales were set over their heads, Elizabet leaned toward Ebby and whispered, "This is my daughter, Nellie. Nellie, sweet pea, this is a very nice man called Elliott."

Nellie hugged the doll to her. "Hi," she said shyly. "Do you like hiding in hay?"

"It's great fun," Ebby replied.

"Will the bad people find us?"

Ebby took her small hand in his. He could feel her tenseness. "Not much chance of that," he told her.

"What if they do?"

"They won't."

She seemed to accept that. After a while she said, "Elliott?"

"Yes."

"Are you afraid of the dark?"

"I used to be," Ebby said. "I'm not any more."

"Me, too, I used to be when I was four. Now I'm practically six, so I'm not afraid anymore," she said in a surprisingly grown-up voice.

"Whatever happens," Elizabet told the girl, "you must promise not to complain."

"I promise," Nellie said.

"Good girl," Ebby said.

Nellie went to sleep on Elizabet's lap; Elizabet dozed on Ebby's shoulder. The minutes dragged by as the truck, back on dirt roads, continued westward. From time to time someone would switch on a flashlight and Ebby would catch a glimpse of his ghostlike companions, some asleep, others staring straight ahead with wide-open eyes. Just after one in the morning, the truck drew to a stop and the refugees inside the hay came awake. They could hear voices talking to the driver outside. Elizabet, scarcely breathing, passed her Webley-Fosbery to Ebby in the darkness. He fingered the bullets in the cylinder to make sure one was under the firing pin. Zoltan whispered in his ear, "Hungarian Army roadblock, not Russian, okay. Not to worry. Driver said him don't search under hay because it will wake everyone up. The soldiers laugh and ask how many. Driver tells him eighteen, not counting one child and one baby. Soldier asks for cigarettes, tells us to watch out for Russians patrolling the frontier, wishes us luck."

Bumping over the potholes, the truck continued westward. At two twenty-five in the morning it pulled off the dirt road and eased to a stop next to a stream. Once again the hay was removed and the refugees climbed out. Elizabet wet a kerchief in the stream and rinsed Nellie's face, then her own.

"I'm hungry," Nellie said. Overhearing her, the elderly professor came over and offered her what was left of a sandwich. "Oh, what stories you will tell your children when you are older," he told her. "They will think you made it all up to impress them."

Twenty minutes later Ebby heard the muffled sound of hooves on the dirt path. Moments later a lean, middle-aged man wearing knee-high riding boots and breeches and a leather jacket appeared leading a dun-colored stallion, its hooves wrapped in thick cloth. Speaking Hungarian, he introduced himself as Marton. The refugees gathered around him as he spoke in low tones.

"He says it is forty minutes by foot to the border," Elizabet told Ebby. "In principle we will cross an area patrolled by Hungarian Army units. If they spot us it is hoped they will look the other way. He instructs the young couple to give sleeping powder to their baby. He argues with the others—he says luggage will only slow us down. But the puppeteer insists—he says his whole life is in the valises. Without them he would not be able to make a living in the West. Marton tells him, If you fall behind it's your problem. He tells us we are to walk double file directly behind him and the horse. He knows the way through the mine fields. He has been through every night for weeks. Each person is instructed to walk in the footsteps of the person before him. The little girl will not be able to keep up, he says. Someone must carry her."

"Tell him I will."

Marton supplied a vial of sleeping powder, and the young couple broke the end of the capsule and poured it into the baby's mouth. Those with luggage removed the objects that were valuable and threw the rest aside. When they started out, with Marton in the lead, Ebby saw the puppeteer struggling with his two enormous valises. He reached down and took one from him.

The elfin man, his face taut with anxiety, attempted to smile at him. "Thanks to you, Mister," he whispered.

A low ground fog closed in on the refugees as they left the safety of the clump of trees. Walking in a double file behind Martin and his horse, they cut across the tarmac of Highway 10, the Budapest-Vienna road, and headed into the countryside. Each field they came to was bordered by low stone walls—for centuries the peasants who guarded the flocks had been obliged to build a meter of stone wall a day. Scrambling over the walls, the group trudged through fields that were dark and empty and still. An icy wind knifed through layers of clothing, chilling everyone to the bone. Hoarfrost on the ground crackled underfoot. The women wearing city shoes began to complain of frostbitten toes but there was nothing to do but trudge on. Off to the right a dog bayed at the moon threading through lace-like clouds. Other dogs further afield howled in response. A star shell burst silently high over Highway 10 and floated back toward the earth on a parachute. Marton's horse, visible in the sudden daylight, snorted through his nostrils and pawed softly at the ground. The refugees froze in their tracks. Marton, alert to sounds in the night, climbed onto a low wall and concentrated on the horizon, then muttered something.

"He tells that the Russians are probably hunting for other refugees trying to cross further north," Zoltan explained to Ebby.

When the light from the star shell faded, Marton motioned them forward. The orchestra conductor, immediately in front of Ebby, turned with a long drawn face. His ankle-length leather coat was dripping with fog. "Are you by any chance familiar with Mahler's *Kindertotenlieder?*" he asked. When Ebby shook his head, the conductor removed his beret and cleaned his eyeglasses on the fabric as he hummed the melody in a quiet falsetto. "I was supposed to conduct it in Budapest tonight," he remarked. The jowls in his cheek vibrated as he shook his head in disbelief. "Who would have thought it would come to this?" He turned back to continue on through the icy fields.

Nellie, astride Ebby's shoulders, tapped him on the head. "I am quite cold," she whispered. "I'm not complaining. I'm just giving you information."

"We're almost there," Elizabet told the girl. "Aren't we almost there?" she asked Ebby, a note of alarm in her voice.

"It can't be much further," he agreed.

They tramped on for another half hour. Then, far across a field that sloped gently toward a stand of trees, they saw the white stucco of a farmhouse. It materialized out of the ground fog like a mirage. Marton gathered the refugees around him and began to talk to them in an undertone. Several reached out to shake his hand.

"He says this is where we part company," Elizabet translated. "The farmhouse is immediately inside Austria. There will be hot soup waiting. When we've rested, there will be a two kilometer walk down a dirt road to an Austrian Red Cross center in a village."

Starting to retrace his steps, Marton passed close to Ebby. The two regarded each other for a moment and Ebby reached out to offer his hand. "Thank you," he said.

Marton took it and nodded and said something in Hungarian. Elizabet said, "He tells you: Remember Hungary, please, after you leave it."

"Tell him I will never forget Hungary—or him," Ebby replied.

Marton swung onto his horse in an easy motion. Clucking his tongue at the stallion, pulling its head around, he set it walking back into Hungary. Zoltan took over the lead and started toward the stuccoed farmhouse. The group was halfway across the sloping field when there was a disturbance up ahead. Five figures in hooded arctic greatcoats loomed out of a drainage ditch. Each carried a rifle at the ready in mittened hands. Zoltan reached for the handle of his curved knife. Ebby lifted Nellie off his shoulders and set her down behind him, then pulled Elizabet's English revolver from his overcoat pocket. In the stillness he could make out the Jewish professor mumbling a Hebrew prayer. One of the five soldiers came up to Zoltan and asked him something.

Elizabet breathed deeply in relief. "He speaks Hungarian," she said. "He says there are no Russians in this sector tonight. He asks if we have cigarettes. He wishes us Godspeed."

The soldiers saluted the refugees with stiff-armed waves as they lumbered off to finish patrolling the zone.

Four young Austrians emerged from the farmhouse to help the refugees over the last fifty meters. Inside, a fire was burning in an old pot-bellied stove and soup was simmering in a cast-iron pot on top of it. The refugees, massaging their frozen toes, warmed themselves with cup after cup of soup. Before long, four more refugees made it to the house. And still later, two couples with three children joined them. Zoltan thawed out his hands in front of the stove, then slipped on woolen gloves with the fingertips cut off and began playing sentimental gypsy melodies on his fiddle. Gradually the tenseness on the faces around the room faded into tired smiles. Hours later, with the eastern sky ablaze with a fiery dawn, one of the Austrians guided them all down a sunken dirt path toward the village. Ebby, carrying Nellie on his shoulders and the puppeteer's enormous valise in one hand, had just caught sight of the church steeple when he spotted figures standing on a rise.

One of them raised a hand and waved at him. "Ebby!" he called, scrambling down the rise to the road.

"Jack!" Ebby said. The two men thumped each other on the back.

"The Wiz is up there—" Jack turned to call up the rise. "It *is* him." He turned back to Ebby. "Frank's taking this very personally," he said, gesturing with his chin toward the refugees stumbling down the rut of a road. "We've been coming out here mornings hoping against hope...damnation, are you a sight for sore eyes." He grabbed the valise from Ebby. "Here, let me give you—Jesus H. Christ, Ebby, what do you have in here?"

"You won't believe me if I tell you."

Jack, falling into step alongside him, laughed happily. "Try me, pal."

"Marionettes, Jack." Ebby turned to look back in the direction of Hungary. "Marionettes."

12

THE COMPANY'S COUNTERINTELLIGENCE BAILIWICK HAD GROWN BY quantum leaps since James Jesus Angleton set up the shop in the early years of the decade. Three full-time secretaries now guarded the door to his office; in the last twelve months alone thirty-five CIA officers had been added to Mother's ever-expanding roster. Despite the chronically severe shortage of office space on Cockroach Alley, counterintelligence had managed to pull off what in-house wags nervously referred to as "Angleton's *Anschluss*"— it had commandeered a large windowless stockroom across the hall and crammed it full of unpickable Burmah-lock diamond safes to accommodate the paper trails that Angleton's prodigies hacked through the tangled Central Intelligence copse. Despite this expansion, the heart of the heart of counterintelligence was still Angleton's permanently dusky sanctum sanctorum (one school of thought held that Mother's Venetian blinds had been *glued* closed), with its spill of three-by-five index cards flagged with red priority stickers.

"Nice of you to stop by on such short notice," Angleton told Ebby, steering him through the maze of boxes to the only halfway decent chair in the room.

"Except for the pour with Dulles late this afternoon, I have no pressing engagements," Ebby said.

"Jack Daniel's?" Angleton asked, settling behind the desk, peering around the Tiffany lamp at his visitor. The last vestiges of a migraine that had kept him up most of the night lurked in the furrows of his brow.

"Don't mind."

Angleton poured two stiff drinks into kitchen tumblers and pushed one across the desk. "To you and yours," he said, hiking his glass.

"To the Hungarians who were naive enough to fall for all that malarkey about rolling back Communism," Ebby shot back, his voice a low rumble of crankiness as he clinked glasses with Mother. Sipping his bourbon, he winced at the memory of the Torkoly that had scalded the back of his throat the first time he met Arpád Zelk. Angleton's Jack Daniel's was a lot tamer. Everything in Washington was a lot tamer.

"You sound bitter—"

"Do I?"

Angleton was always uncomfortable with small talk but he made a stab at it anyway. "How was your plane ride back?"

"How it was, was long—twenty-seven hours, door to door, not counting the day and a half holdover in Germany while the Air Force cured a coughing propeller."

"I heard on the grapevine you came back with a woman—"

"A woman and a kid. A girl. She's practically six and not afraid of the dark. The woman is practically thirty-three and very much afraid of the dark. Of the light, too, come to think of it."

"Manage any R and R after you got out of Hungary?"

"The Wiz laid on ten days in a *Gasthaus* near Innsbruck for the three of us. Long walks in the Bavarian Alps. Quiet evenings by a roaring fire. While we were there another twelve thousand Hungarian refugees came across."

Angleton's well of small talk dried up. He lit a cigarette and vanished for a moment behind a bank of smoke. "I read through"—there was a hacking cough—"through the notes the debriefing team made in Vienna..."

"Thought you might."

"Especially interested in your suspicions about a Soviet mole—"

"What I have isn't suspicions—it's certainty."

"Uh-huh."

"I told the debriefing people pretty much all I knew."

"Want to walk me through it once more?"

"I went in under deep cover—I was backstopped at my old law firm in New York in case anybody tried to check up on me. The AVH people picked me up—"

"After or before you made contact with Arpád Zelk?"

"It was after."

Angleton was thinking out loud. "So you could have been betrayed by one of the Hungarians around Zelk."

"Could have been. Wasn't. The AVH colonel general who interrogated me seemed familiar with my Central Registry file. He knew I was assigned to Frank Wisner's Operations Directorate; he knew I was in the DD/O's Soviet Russia Division. He knew I'd worked out of Frankfurt station running émigrés into Poland and Soviet Russia and Albania."

Behind the smoke screen, Angleton's eyes were reduced to slits of concentration.

"Then there was the business about Tony Spink," Ebby said.

"There's no mention of Spink in the transcript of your debriefing."

"It came back to me during one of those long walks in the Alps—I went over and over the interrogation in my head. When I slept, I dreamed about it—dreamed I was back in that room, back on the stool, back in the spotlight, back at the window watching them torture Elizabet..."

Angleton tugged the conversation back to where he wanted it to go. "You were talking about Spink."

"Spink, yes. Comrade Colonel General knew that Tony Spink was my immediate superior at Frankfurt Station. He knew that I was kicked upstairs to run agent ops when Spink was rotated back to Washington in 1954."

"He knew the date?"

"Yeah. He said 1954." Ebby closed his eyes. "Just before Arpád Zelk dragged him into the refrigerator room and hung him from a spike, the colonel general cried out that the Centre had told them about me..."

Angleton leaned forward. "In the wide world of intelligence there are many Centers."

"He meant Moscow Centre."

"How could you know that?"

"I just assumed—" Ebby shrugged.

Angleton scribbled notes to himself on a three-by-five card flagged with a red sticker. One of the telephones on his desk purred. He wedged the receiver between a shoulder and his ear and listened for a moment. "No, it's not a rumor," he said. "My *Cattleya* cross flowered, and eighteen months ahead of my wildest dreams. It's a raving beauty, too. Listen, Fred, I have someone with me. Let me get back to you." He dropped the phone back onto its cradle.

"What's a *Cattleya* cross?"

Angleton smiled thinly. To Ebby, eyeing him from across the desk, the Company's edgy counterintelligence chief almost looked happy. "It's a hybrid orchid," Angleton explained with unaccustomed bashfulness. "I've been trying to breed one for years. Son of a gun flowered over the weekend. I'm going to register it under my wife's name—it's going into the record books as the Cicely Angleton."

"Congratulations."

Angleton didn't hear the irony. "Thank you." He nodded. "Thank you very much." He cleared his throat and glanced down at the index card. When he spoke again there was no hint of the orchid in his voice. "Anything else you forgot to tell the debriefing people in Vienna?"

"I can think of a lot else. Most of what I can think of comes across as questions."

"Such as?"

"Such as: Why did all those émigré drops go bad *after* June 1951, which is when Maclean and Burgess skipped to Moscow and Philby got sacked? Why did we lose those double agents in Germany two years ago? How did the KGB know which of the diplomats working out of our Moscow embassy were Company officers servicing dead drops? The list is a long one. Where did the leaks come from? How could the Hungarian colonel general be so sure I worked for the Wiz? How did he know I'd stepped into Spink's shoes when he was called home? If he was tipped off by the KGB, how did the Russians find out?"

Angleton, his shoulders bent under the weight of secrets, stood up and came around the desk. "Thanks for your time, Elliott. Glad to have you back safe and sound."

Ebby laughed under his breath. "Safe maybe. I'm not so sure about sound."

When Ebbitt had gone, Angleton slumped back into his chair and helped himself to another dose of Jack Daniel's. Ebbitt was right, of course; the Russians had a mole in the CIA, most likely in the Clandestine Service, maybe even in the heart of the Clandestine Service, the Soviet Russia Division. Angleton pulled the index card on Anthony Spink from a file box and attached a red sticker to the corner. Spink intrigued him. Unbeknownst to Ebbitt and the others at Frankfurt Station, Spink hadn't been rotated back to Washington in 1954—he'd been pulled back by Angleton because he was sleeping with a German national who had a sister living in East Germany. At the time Spink had passed the polygraph test, but if you took enough tranquilizers anybody could get past a polygraph. It wouldn't hurt to bring Spink in and flutter him again. As long as he was taking another look at Spink, he might as well flutter the two desk officers who had known about Spink's affair and covered for him at the time. And there was the deputy head of station in Prague who had deposited $7,000 in his wife's account in an upstate New York bank. And the cipher clerk in Paris who had made seven telephone calls to Istanbul, supposedly to speak to a vacationing daughter. And the secretary in Warsaw who had received flowers from a Polish national she'd met at a concert. And the Marine guard at the Moscow embassy who changed dollars into rubles on the black market to pay for the services of a Russian prostitute. And the contract employee in Mexico City who had been spotted coming out of a transvestite nightclub that the local KGB was known to use for secret meetings. And the young officer working under diplomatic cover in Sofia who had smuggled three priceless icons back to the States in a diplomatic pouch. And then, of course, there was E. Winstrom Ebbitt II. What if he had been "turned" in prison? What if he had never been in prison? If Ebbitt himself were the Soviet mole, the spymaster Starik might have instructed him to raise the specter of a Soviet mole in the CIA—*to tell Angleton what he already knew!*—in order to divert attention from himself? Clearly, this was a possibility that had to be looked into.

Angleton brought his palms up and pressed them against his ears. He had detected the distant drumbeat of the migraine—a primitive tattoo summoning Starik's specter to prowl the lobes of his brain, keeping sleep and sanity at bay for the time the visitation lasted.

Drifting with postcoital languidness, Bernice hiked herself onto a counter stool at the Peoples Drugstore, a short stroll from her apartment. "So what are you hungry for?" she asked Eugene as he slid onto the next stool.

"You."

"Me you just had," Bernice said. "I'm talking supper, baby."

"Maybe sausages," Eugene decided. He called over to the Greek behind the counter. "Sausages, Lukas. A frying pan full of them. With hash browns and one of your Greek omelets with lots of eggs and onions. And coffee."

"Looks like you two lovebirds worked up an appetite again," Lukas said with a lecherous smirk. He'd seen them at the counter often enough to know they were always ravenously hungry after they had sex. "What about the little lady?"

"Ditto for me except for the hash browns," Bernice told the Greek. "I'll have a Coke with, and a raspberry milkshake after."

"Coming up," Lukas said, neatly cracking eggs into a bowl with one hand.

Thirty-five minutes later Lukas collected the empty plates and Bernice attacked the milkshake, noisily sucking it through two straws. When she came up for air she raised her head and squinted sideways at Eugene. "You've been looking pretty pleased with yourself the last few weeks, baby. It makes me happy to see you happy."

Eugene glanced at the Greek, who was scouring frying pans at the far end of the counter. "There's a lot to be happy about. Counterrevolution got a bloody nose in Hungary. Colonialism got a drubbing in Egypt. It was a good month for socialism."

"Oh, you kill me, Eugene—even out of bed you're passionate. I've known a lot of socialists in my life but you're the cat's whiskers." She took another sip of milkshake. "Eugene, baby, correct me if I'm wrong," she said, her expression suddenly very intent, "but when communism triumphs, when America goes socialist, you'll be heading home."

Eugene stirred sugar into his second cup of coffee. "I suppose so."

"So can you?"

"What do you mean, can I?"

"After living here all these years, after getting accustomed to all this"—she waved at the bumper-to-bumper traffic on the avenue behind them—"can you go back to communal living?"

"I haven't been corrupted by materialism, Bernice."

"I didn't say you were, baby. I only mean, like, the transition could be hard." She smiled at a thought. "You ought to go back slowly, like a deep-sea diver coming up to the surface."

He had to laugh at the image. "You're something else, Bernice. I'm not a deep-sea diver!"

"In a way, you are. You're a *Russian* deep-sea diver, braving sharks and stingarees to explore the capitalist wreckage in the murky depths." She spotted the scowl in his eyes and said quickly, "Hey, Lukas can't hear us." She smiled wistfully. "Pretty please—take me with you, Eugene, when you go home." She checked on the Greek and, turning back, went on in a whisper, "I want to live with you in Mother Russia, baby. It's my dream."

"It's not the way you think it is," he said quietly.

"How is it?"

"There's a big housing shortage—two or three families sometimes share one apartment. There are long lines in stores—you have to stand in three of them before you can buy anything." He tried to think of what else he could say to discourage her. If he ever did go back, who knows, he might be able to pick up where he'd left off with Azalia Isanova. Assuming she wasn't married. Assuming she remembered him. Even after all these years he could still reproduce her voice in his head. *We will together explore whether your lust and my desire are harmonious in bed.* "Another thing you wouldn't like, Bernice," he added seriously, "there's no jazz in Russia."

Unfazed, she murmured, "But the proletariat owns the means of production, which means the workers aren't exploited by the capitalist classes. The way I see it, having to share a toilet is a small price to pay. Anyway, the communal apartments and the lines and the no jazz, that'll all get straightened out once they've moved past socialism to actual communism. Isn't that so, baby?"

"They may fix the apartments and the lines. I don't know if they can fix the jazz."

"I'd be willing to go cold turkey on jazz if it meant I could live in the Socialist motherland," she said gravely. "It's a hypothetical, sure, but it's important to me, Eugene. So yes or no, will you take me with you when you go back?"

Eugene could see she wouldn't let go until he gave her an answer. "Both of us are under Party discipline, Bernice. Which means that even if America goes communist, the Centre might not want you to abandon your post. They'll need people like you here to keep track of things."

Bernice looked miserable. "So I might have to stay in America for the rest of my life, is that what you're saying?"

"You and Max are front-line soldiers," Eugene explained. "When America goes communist, streets will be named after you. Hell, you'll probably be promoted to important positions in the superstructure."

"Like what?"

"Someone with your track record could be assigned to the White House, for all I know."

Bernice brightened. "You're not just saying that to cheer me up?"

"No, honest to God, really, I think it's a possibility."

Bernice swayed away from Eugene and shook her head and laughed and then swayed back toward him, as if she were high on milkshake. "What I'm going to do now is tell you something I never told a living soul. I talk about permanent revolution and the dictatorship of the proletariat and exploitation and alienation and all that gobbledygook, but deep down I don't really understand it."

"What is communism for you, Bernice?"

She thought about this. "For me," she finally said, "communism is resistance to indifference. It's caring about people more than you care about yourself."

Eugene leaned over and kissed her on the mouth. "You are one hell of a comrade in arms, Bernice."

"You, also, Eugene, baby."

The DCI's six-thirty pour was running late. Several of the Company's senior people, Leo Kritzky among them, had been held up at the old State, War and Navy Building next to the White House, waiting for Vice President Richard Nixon to turn up for a briefing on the situation in Hungary. Allen

Dulles himself had been closeted with a team of Company psychiatrists, trying to figure out what to do about Frank Wisner. The Wiz's erratic behavior
had set tongues wagging. The failure of the Hungarian uprising had obviously hit him hard. At first the old DD/O hands attributed his violent mood
swings to stress and exhaustion; they hoped that, with time, his spirits would
pick up. Dick Helms, Wisner's chief of operations, had been covering for his
boss; gradually the Clandestine Service officers began bypassing Wisner and
bringing their problems and projects to him. Helms, a patient bureaucrat
who instinctively mistrusted risky operations, drew the appropriate conclusions from the Hungarian debacle and closed down "rollback." The émigré
paramilitary units in Germany were disbanded, secret arms caches were
scrapped. Radio Free Europe and Radio Liberty were put on short leashes;
the days when they would broadcast lessons on how to fabricate Molotov
cocktails and incite the "captive nations" to riot were over. Under Helms, the
Central Intelligence Agency hunkered down and concentrated on the
tedious business of collecting and interpreting intelligence on its principal
adversary, the Soviet Union.

Dulles, shuffling into the DCI's private dining room in his bedroom
slippers, turned up for the pour twenty minutes past the appointed hour.

"Look at his feet," Elizabet whispered to Ebby as the Director worked
the room, chatting up the officers nibbling on canapés and drinking
Champagne.

"He has gout," Ebby told her. "He wears slippers around the office
because his feet swell."

"Gout is an upper-class Englishman's disease," Elizabet said with a
straight face. She moistened her lips on the Champagne in her glass. "Your
Mr. Dulles is an American. He can't possibly have gout."

"I'm sure he'll be relieved to hear that," Ebby told her.

Dulles made his way over to Ebby and offered a hand. "Lot of water's
flowed under the bridge since we met in the Alibi Club."

"Wasn't water flowing under the bridge, Director," Ebby replied. "It was
blood. I don't believe you know Elizabet Németh?"

The Director eyed Ebby for a moment, trying to decipher his observation. Turning to the slim woman at his side, he immediately brightened.
Dulles was known to have an eye for the ladies; office scuttlebutt had it that
he consoled his wife every time he started a new affair by sending her off to
Cartier's for a fresh ration of jewelry. "I have read all about your heroism,
young lady," he declared in his booming voice, turning on the charm, sand-
wiching her hand between both of his, showing no inclination to let go of

it. "If you worked for the Agency we'd be giving you one of our medals today as well as Ebbitt here."

"Elliott was serving American interests and earned his medal," she said. She slipped her hand free. "I was serving Hungarian interests," she murmured. A parody of a smile appeared on her lips. "Someday, perhaps, a free and democratic Hungary will remember its dead sons and daughters."

"I'm sure it will," Dulles agreed enthusiastically.

The low rumble of conversation gave way to a strained silence. Looking past the Director, Ebby saw that the Wiz had appeared at the door. As he strode across the carpet to snatch a glass of Champagne from the table, his eyes flitted wildly around the room. Draining his drink in one long gulp, he grabbed a second glass and then ambled over, with a sailor's rolling gait, to the Director and Ebby.

"Well, now, Frank, what's the word from inside the beltway?" Dulles asked.

"In recognition of my contributions to world socialism," the Wiz announced, rolling his *R*s, hardening the *G*s in a good imitation of a Russian speaking English, "the Kremlin has promoted me to colonel general in its KGB." He raised his glass to salute the DCI. "Comrade Director," he plunged ahead, "you and your staff have performed in the highest tradition of socialist surrealism. Marx, Engels, the *nomenklatura* that rules in their name, are proud of you. The phantom of Vladimir Ilyich Lenin will pin on you the Order of Aleksandr Nevsky. The ghost of Yosef Vissarionovich Stalin proclaims you a Hero of the Soviet Union. Without encouragement from the Company, the misguided peasants and workers of the Hungàrian Banana Republic would never have risen up against their fraternal brothers in the Red Army. If you and your comrades had not pulled rug out from under them, who knows? they might have succeeded in their anti-socialist *folie*."

Dulles looked around anxiously. "You've had too much to drink, Frank," he said under his breath.

"Bull's-eye," Wisner agreed. "Alcohol's the problem. Soon as I dry out things will fall into perspective. The twenty thousand dead Hungarians, the two hundred thousand who fled the country—that was only our opening bid. We'll up the ante. We'll send more people off to die for us." He chewed on his lower lip, then punched Ebby lightly on the shoulder. "You fucked up, chum. You didn't stop them. What went wrong?"

"You tell me."

"Sure I'll tell you. What went wrong is nobody, me included, had thought it through—"

The Champagne glass slipped out of the Wiz's hand and clattered to the floor without breaking. He kicked it under a table with the side of his shoe. "Out of sight, out of mind," Wisner said. His jaw continued to work but no words emerged. He used his forefinger like a rapier, thrusting and circling as he drove home points that existed in his head. Around the dining room people looked away in embarrassment.

Several of the Barons managed to steer the Wiz into a corner and Dulles hurried through the ceremony. The citation was brief and to the point: E. Winstrom Ebbitt II was being given the Distinguished Intelligence Medal, the Agency's second-highest award, for courage far above and far beyond the call of duty; he had performed in the highest tradition of the clandestine service and, in so doing, had brought honor on the country and on the Company. Dulles offered some tongue-in-cheek remarks about where Ebbitt could wear the award; since CIA medals were, by nature, secret, they were known as jock-strap decorations. Glasses around the room were raised in tribute. Ebby was asked to say a few words. He took a step forward and stood there for a moment, gazing down at the medal in the palm of his hand. Images blinded him—the rag doll of a figure ground into the gutter by a Russian tank, the twelve bodies twisting slowly from branches above it. Breathing hard, he looked up.

"Remember Hungary, please." He caught Elizabet's eye. She wiped away a tear with the back of her fist and nodded imperceptibly. "For God's sake, remember where we went wrong so we don't go wrong in the same way again."

Waiting for an elevator in the corridor afterward, Ebby looked pale as death. When the elevator arrived, Leo stepped into it with Elizabet and him and, turning to face the doors, punched the lobby button. The elevator whirred downward. Leo glanced sideways at Ebby.

"You look like you've seen a ghost," he said. "You okay?"

Ebby shook his head. "I'm not okay. I have the bends. From coming up too fast."

Leo didn't understand. "Coming up from where?"

Ebby remembered the wild-eyed priest guarding the door when he and Arpád and Elizabet emerged from the tunnel into the Kilian Barracks. "Coming up from Gehenna," he told Leo.

PART THREE

VICIOUS CIRCLES

*There was something very queer about the water,
[Alice] thought, as every now and then the oars
got fast in it, and would hardly come out again.*

Snapshot: an amateur photograph, taken at sea from the bridge of an American destroyer, shows sailors scrambling down cargo netting to rescue a man in a drenched khaki uniform from a half-inflated rubber raft. As the image is fuzzy and the figure is bearded, the Pentagon didn't raise objections to the publication of the photograph in the late April 1961 edition of Time *magazine as long as the person rescued wasn't identified as an American national.*

1

I F YOU PUT IT INTO ONE OF YOUR BOOKS," DICK BISSELL RAGED TO E. Howard Hunt, a full-time CIA political action officer and occasional writer of espionage potboilers, "nobody would believe it." Bissell, a tall, lean, active-volcano of a man who had replaced the ailing Wiz as Deputy Director for Operations, loped back and forth along the rut he'd worn in the government-issue carpeting, his hands clasped behind his back, his shoulders stooped and bent into the autumn cat's-paw ruffling through the open windows of the corner room. Hunt, a dapper man who had been assigned to kick ass down in Miami until the 700-odd anti-Castro splinter groups came up with what, on paper at least, could credibly pass for a government in exile, kept his head bobbing in eager agreement. "Someone who shall remain nameless," Bissell continued, "came up with the harebrained scheme of flooding Cuba with rumors of a Second Coming. The idea was for one of our subs to surface off the Cuban coast and light up the night sky with fireworks to establish that the Second Coming was at hand, at which point the Cuban Catholics would identify Castro as the Antichrist and send him packing."

"Elimination by illumination," Hunt quipped.

Shaking his head in disgust, Bissell said, "The God-awful part is that this happens to be one of the better schemes that made it as far as my in-box."

The intercom on Bissell's desk squawked. The DD/O lunged for the button as if it were an alarm clock that needed to be turned off before it woke anyone. "He's here," a woman's high-pitched voice could be heard bleating. "If you want to see him I'm afraid you'll have to go down to the lobby and rescue him."

Bissell, in shirtsleeves and suspenders, discovered the Sorcerer in the room behind the reception desk where the uniformed security guards played pinochle; cards, obviously discarded in haste, were scattered across the table. Two of the guards, holding drawn and cocked automatics with both hands, had the intruder pinned to the wall while the third guard, working up from the ankles, frisked him. When the guard reached the shapeless sports jacket, he gingerly unbuttoned it and reached in to extract Torriti's pearl-handled revolver from the sweat-stained holster under his armpit. The Sorcerer, a smudge of a smile plastered on his bloated face, puffed away on a fat Havana as he kept track of the proceedings through his beady eyes.

"You must be Harvey Torriti," Bissell said.

"You got to be Dick Bissell," the Sorcerer replied.

"He stormed through the lobby like gangbusters," one of the guards blurted, preparing a retreat in case the intruder turned out to be someone important. "When we went and asked him for Company ID, he waved a wrinkled piece of paper in our faces and headed for the elevator."

"We could tell he was carrying," another guard insisted, "from the way his shoulder sagged."

Bissell glanced at the wrinkled piece of paper in question. It was a deciphered copy of the Operational Immediate, addressed to Alice Reader (the Sorcerer's in-house cryptonym), summoning Harvey Torriti back to Washington from Berlin Station.

"In addition to which, he don't look like no one named Alice," the third guard put in.

"Okay. Nobody's going to second-guess you for going by the book," Bissell assured the guards. "I'll vouch for Alice, here," he added, a laugh tucked away in the spaces between his words.

He crossed the room and held out a hand to the Sorcerer. Soft sweaty fingers give it a perfunctory shake. Torriti retrieved his revolver and started to follow Bissell. At the door he pirouetted back with the nimbleness of a ballet dancer, sending the hem of his jacket swirling around his hips. "You need to demote these clowns to janitors," he told Bissell. Leaning down, he hiked one leg of his trousers and, in a blur of a swipe, came up with the snub-nosed .38 Detective Special taped to an ankle. "They missed this fucker," he announced gleefully. He smiled into the livid faces of the three guards. "No shit, if looks could kill I'd be dead meat now."

"You really shouldn't have baited them the way you did," Bissell said once they were safely past the gawking secretaries and back in his office.

Torriti, rolls of body fat spilling out of a chair, one arm draped over its high wooden back, the other caressing the cigar, wanted to get the relationship with the DD/O off on the right track. "Don't appreciate being hassled," he announced.

"Asking you for a laminated identity card doesn't come under the category of hassling, Harvey," Bissell suggested mildly.

"They weren't asking. They were ordering. Besides which I long ago lost any goddamn ID I might have had. Didn't need any in Berlin. Everybody knew me."

"I can see everybody here is going to know you, too." Bissell nodded toward a sideboard filled with bottles of alcohol. "Can I offer you some firewater?"

Peering through the cigar smoke, the Sorcerer studied the sideboard. The DD/O's stash of whiskey seemed to have Gaelic brand names and boasted of having been aged in barrels for sixteen years; he supposed that they'd been bottled and put on the market as a last resort when the family-owned breweries faced bankruptcy. For Torriti, it was one thing to be a consenting alcoholic, another to actually drink this upper-class piss. Good whiskey burned your throat. Period. "Today's Friday," he finally said. "It's a religious thing. Fridays, I go on the wagon."

"Since when?"

"Since I noticed the labels on your whiskey. Your booze's too ritzy for my tastes."

The Sorcerer eyed the DD/O across the desk, determined to get a rise out of him. He was familiar with Bissell's pedigree—Yale by way of Groton, an economist by training, an academic at heart, an officer and a gentleman by lineage, a risk-runner by instinct. It was the risk-runner who had attracted Dulles's attention when the Director (bypassing the Wiz's chief of operations, Dick Helms) shopped around for someone to replace Frank Wisner, who had been diagnosed as a manic-depressive and was said to have retreated to his farm on the eastern shore of Maryland, where he spent his waking hours staring off into space.

Bissell absently tortured a paperclip out of shape between his long fingers. "Your reputation precedes you, Harvey."

"And I race after the son of a bitch trying my goddamnedest to live up to it."

"Sounds like the tail wagging the dog," Bissell remarked. He stuck an end of the paperclip between his lips and gnawed on it. "I'm running a new project, Harvey. That's why I brought you in. I want to offer you a piece of the action. It's big. Very big. I'll give you three guesses."

The Sorcerer was having second thoughts about Bissell's fancy Gaelic whiskeys but he didn't know the DD/O well enough to admit it. "Cuba, Cuba and Cuba."

Bissell nodded happily. "Khrushchev recently boasted to the world that the Monroe Doctrine has died a natural death. I'm going to prove him wrong. President Eisenhower has authorized me to develop a covert action capability against the Castro regime. We're going to base it on the Guatemala model but the scale will be larger—we're going to spread rumors of multiple landings and uprisings and frighten Castro out of Cuba the way we frightened Arbenz out of Guatemala. The plan calls for the creation of a government-in-exile, an intensive propaganda offensive, cultivating resistance groups inside Cuba and training a paramilitary force outside of Cuba for an eventual guerrilla action. The whole package goes under the code name JMARC."

The Sorcerer puffed on his cigar. "Where do I fit in?"

The DD/O slipped around to the front of the desk and unconsciously lowered his voice. "I brought you back in order to put another arrow in our quiver, Harvey. I want you to set up a general capability within the Company for disabling foreign leaders. We're going to call this capability 'executive action.' The in-house cryptonym for executive action will be ZR/RIFLE. ZR/RIFLE's first order of business will be to assassinate Fidel Castro. If you succeed it will make the military option superfluous, or at the very least, simpler."

"Don't tell me you haven't already tried to kill Castro."

Bissell began patrolling the rut in the carpet. "The people who up to now have been in charge of that particular show tend to move their lips when they read. If I told you about some of the plots—"

"Tell me, if only so I won't make the same mistakes."

"We had an asset in a hotel ready to dust Fidel's shoes with thallium salts to make his beard fall out, but he never put them out to be shined. We contaminated a box of his favorite Cohiba cigars with botulism toxin and smuggled it in to another asset who was being paid to deliver it to him. Our man took the money and ditched the cigars and disappeared. The Technical Service elves toyed with the idea of fouling the ventilating system of Castro's broadcasting studio with LSD so his speech would slur and he'd ramble on during one of his marathon orations to the Cuban people. There were other schemes that never got off the drawing boards—dusting Castro's wet suit with fungus spores that would give him chronic skin disease, filling his underwater breathing apparatus with tuberculosis bacilli, planting an exotic seashell on the ocean floor where Castro liked to skin-dive that would explode when he opened it."

One of the four phones on Bissell's desk rang. He snatched it off the hook, listened for a moment, then said "Put him through on the secure line." Wagging a finger in Torriti's direction to indicate he wouldn't be long, he grabbed the red phone off of its hook. "Listen, Dave, the problem is your act's too slick. It smells American, which means it can be traced back to the

Company. The trick is to make everything look less professional and more Cuban. I'm talking about lousy grammar when your Cubans deliver the news, I'm talking about needles getting stuck in grooves when they play their theme songs, I'm talking about starting the programs several minutes early or late. Rough edges, Dave, are the secret for this kind of operation...That's the ticket, Dave...I know you will."

Bissell flung the phone back onto its cradle. "Ever hear of Swan Island, Harvey? It's a mound of guano off Honduras with a fifty-kilowatt medium-wave transmitter broadcasting propaganda to Cuba."

Torriti said, "Am I reading you right, Dick? You're complaining that the propaganda show is too professional and the executive action show is too amateur."

Bissell had to laugh. "You're reading me right, Harvey. The only rule is that there are no rules." He plunked himself down behind his desk again and began screwing a chrome-plated nut onto and off of a chrome-plated bolt. "You still speak the Sicilian dialect?"

"It's not something you forget. I'm half-Sicilian on my mother's side."

"You were the OSS's point man with the Mafia in Sicily during the war."

The Sorcerer hiked his shoulders in a disgruntled shrug. "You can't judge a man by the company he keeps if he works for an intelligence organization."

"I want you to keep company with the Mafia again, Harvey."

Torriti leaned forward; his sports jacket sagged open and the pearl handle of his revolver came into view. "You want the Cosa Nostra to hit Fidel!"

Bissell smiled. "They've been known to engage in this sort of activity. And they have a reputation for being good at it. Also for keeping their mouths shut after the fact."

"What's in it for them?"

"Cold cash, to begin with. The man I want you to start with—Johnny Rosselli—entered the United States illegally when he was a teenager. He faces deportation. We can fix that if he cooperates with us. Before Castro came down from the mountains Rosselli ran the Cosa Nostra's casinos in Havana. Now he has a finger in the Las Vegas gambling pie and represents the Chicago mob on the West Coast."

"You got a time frame in mind for JMARC?"

"We don't want to start anything before the November election. We don't like Nixon all that much—the last thing we want is for him to get credit for overthrowing Castro and win the election on the strength of it. I'll tell you a state secret, Harvey—the Vice President's not our sort of fellow. Allen Dulles is close to Jack Kennedy. He wants him to be the next President. He wants him to owe the Company a favor."

"The favor being we waited for his watch to start before we went after Castro."

"Precisely. On the other hand we have to get something going before, say, next summer. Castro's got fifty Cuban pilots training to fly Russian MiGs in Czechoslovakia. The planes will be delivered, the pilots will be operational, the summer of '61."

"Does Kennedy know about JMARC?"

"Only in the vaguest terms."

"So what guarantee you got he'll sign off on the op if he's elected President?"

"You're asking the right questions, Harvey. We consider it unlikely that the next President will back off from a paramilitary operation initiated by that great American war hero, Dwight Eisenhower. It would leave him open to all sorts of political flak. The Republicans would say he had no balls."

"The people around Kennedy might talk him out of it."

Bissell screwed up his lips. "Kennedy comes across as smart and tough. The people around him take their cue from his toughness more than his smartness."

"Does that great American war hero Eisenhower know about executive action?"

The DD/O shook his head vehemently. "That's simply not a subject we would raise in the White House."

Torriti tugged a rumpled handkerchief from a jacket pocket and mopped his brow. Now that they had exchanged confidences he felt he knew the DD/O better. "Could I—" He tossed his head in the direction of the sideboard.

"For God's sake, please. That's what it's there for, Harvey. You'll find ice in the bucket."

The Sorcerer grasped a bottle with an unpronounceable Gaelic word on the label and helped himself to four fingers of alcohol. He dropped in an ice cube, stirred it with a swizzle stick, tinkling the cube against the sides of the glass. Then he drained off two fingers' worth in one long swig.

"Smooth stuff, isn't it?"

"Too smooth. Good whiskey, like good propaganda, needs to have rough edges." Torriti ambled over to the window, parted the blinds with his trigger fingers and stared out at what he could see of Washington. It wasn't a city he felt comfortable in—there were too many speed-readers who knew it all, too many fast talkers who never said what they meant, who expected you to read between the lines, then left you holding the bag if anything went wrong. Bissell had earned his grudging respect. There was a downside to the DD/O—Bissell'd never run a goddamn agent in his life, never run a Company station for that matter. On the other hand he had a reputation for getting the job done. He had gotten the U-2 reconnaissance plane—a glider with a jet engine and cameras that could read Kremlin license plates from 70,000 feet—off the drawing boards and into the stratosphere over Russia in eighteen months, something that would have taken the Air Force eight years. Now this DD/O out of Groton-Yale with a taste for swanky whiskey wanted someone whacked and he fucking came right out and said it in so many words. He didn't beat around the goddamn mulberry bush. Torriti turned back to Bissell. "So I accept," he said.

The DD/O was on his feet. "I'm delighted—"

"But on my terms."

"Name them, Harvey."

Torriti, dancing back across the office, set his glass down on the top-secret papers in Bissell's in-box and ticked the points off on his fingers.

"First off, I want good cover."

"As far as the Company is concerned you're the new head of Staff D, a small Agency component dealing with communications intercepts."

"I don't want James Jesus fucking Angleton breathing down my goddamn neck."

"You have a problem with him, you bring it to me. If I can't fix it I'll bring it to the Director. Between us we'll keep him off your back."

"You want me to push the magic button on Fidel, fine. But I don't want any other government agencies in on this. And inside the Company every fucking thing needs to be done by word of mouth."

"No paper trail," Bissell agreed.

"Executors of ZR/RIFLE need to be foreign nationals who never resided in America or held US visas. The 201 files in Central Registry need to be forged and backdated so it looks like anyone I recruit is a long-time agent for the Soviets or Czechs."

Bissell nodded; he could see bringing Torriti back from Berlin had been a stroke of genius.

The Sorcerer ticked off his fifth finger but he couldn't remember the fifth item on his list.

"What else, Harvey?" Bissell asked encouragingly.

"What else?" He racked his brain. "A lot else. For starters, I want an office in the basement. I'm like a mole—I'm more comfortable working underground. It needs to be big—something like what the President of Yale would get if he worked here. I want the housekeepers to sweep it for bugs once in the morning and once in the afternoon. I want an endless supply of cheap whiskey and a secure phone line and a phonograph so I can play operas while I'm talking on it in case the housekeepers fuck up. I want my secretary from Berlin, Miss Sipp. I want a car that's painted any color of the spectrum except motor-pool khaki. I want my Rumanian gypsies, Sweet Jesus and the Fallen Angel, to ride shotgun for me. What else I want? Yeah. I need to get ahold of a goddamn laminated identity card with my photo on it so I can waltz past the clowns at the door."

"You've got it, Harvey. All of it."

The Sorcerer, breathing as if he'd run the hundred-meter low hurdles, nodded carefully. "I think you and me, we're going to get along real fine, Dick."

"Push the magic button for me, Harvey, and you can write your own ticket."

"Don't know many folks who hang ordinary garden variety shovels over their fireplaces," observed Philip Swett. "You'd think it was a family heirloom."

"It sort of is, Daddy," Adelle explained. "It happens to be the shovel Leo bought the day we met—the day we buried his dog and my cat on a hill in Maryland. Leo came across it when he was cleaning out the basement last month. We decided it'd be fun to put it up."

The twins, Tessa and Vanessa, aged six years and five months, had just planted wet kisses on the scratchy cheek of their grandfather and raced out the kitchen door, their pigtails flying, to catch the school bus in front of the small Georgetown house that Swett had bought for his daughter when his granddaughters were born. Adelle, one eye on the kitchen clock, the other on the toaster, set her father's favorite marmalade on the table.

"So where's that first husband of yours," growled Swett.

"First and only, Daddy," Adelle groaned, tired of his old gag; her father would be the last person on earth to admit it but he had grown fond of Leo over the years. "Leo's on the phone, as usual." There was a note of pride in her voice. "He's been promoted, you know. For God's sake, don't tell him I told you—he'd flay me alive. He's been filling in as Dick Bissell's troubleshooter for several months now. At one point he had to fly out to LA and actually met Frank Sinatra. Last Friday they told him he'd been named Bissell's deputy on a permanent basis. It means a raise. It means a full-time secretary." She sighed. "It also means more phone calls in the middle of the night. That Dick Bissell never sleeps..."

Sour Pickles, the cat with the gnarled snout that LBJ had given Adelle as a wedding present, appeared at the door of the mud room. She'd been sleeping on the laundry that had been piling up for the Negro lady who came three afternoons a week. Adelle spilled some milk into a small dish and set it on the floor, and the cat began lapping it up. Leo Kritzky pushed through the kitchen door, a tie flapping loose around his collar. Adelle brushed away with a forefinger a speck of shaving cream on his earlobe. Leo shook hands with his father-in-law and sat down across from him in the breakfast nook.

"Girls get off on time?" he asked.

"They'd still be here if they didn't," Swett growled.

"How are you, Phil?" Leo asked.

"Dog-tired. Bushed. You think raising money for a Catholic candidate is easy as falling off a log, guess again."

"I thought his father was bankrolling him," Leo said.

"Joe Kennedy saw him through the primaries, especially the early ones. Now it's up to the big ticket Democrats to cough up. Either that or watch Tricky Dick take an option on the White House."

Adelle filled two giant coffee cups from a percolator and pushed them across the table to the men. "Where's Kennedy today?" she asked her father.

Swett buttered a slice of toast and helped himself generously to marmalade. "Jack's starting another swing through the Midwest. He'll be sleeping at my place in Chicago tonight, which is why I invited myself over for breakfast—got to get up there by early afternoon and organize an impromptu fund raiser for him. What's Lyndon up to?"

Adelle, who was coordinating the pollsters working for Lyndon Johnson's vice presidential campaign, removed a tea bag from the small china pot and filled her cup. "He's off campaigning in Texas and California," she said. "He figures they can't win without both those states. Did you see the story in the *Washington Post* where Lyndon blasted the Eisenhower administration over that toy submarine—"

Swett laughed out loud. "I did. I did."

"What toy submarine?" Leo asked.

"And you're supposed to be in the intelligence racket," Swett said. "Some toy company or other put a damn-near-perfect scale model of our new Polaris submarine on the market. Russians don't need spies any more. All those geezers got to do is shell out two ninety-eight for the model sub. I read where it shows the atomic reactor, the two Polaris missiles, down to the last detail."

"Getting Lyndon to raise the subject—to use it as another example of the Eisenhower administration's bungling—was my idea, Daddy. I found the story in the back pages of the *Baltimore Sun* and showed it to one of our speech writers."

"Want to know what I think, I think it's a crying shame handing them the Polaris on a silver platter." Swett blew noisily on his coffee and swallowed a mouthful. "If I worked for that Company of yours, Leo, I'd send out signals to get the KGB thinking we manufactured the model to mislead them?"

Leo smiled. "Life isn't that simple, Phil. If we try to convince the KGB we planted it, they'll figure out we're trying to convince them it's false and assume it's true."

"Then what we have to do," Adelle said brightly, "is drop hints it's true. That way they'll think we're trying to convince them it's true and come to the conclusion it's false."

Leo shook his head. "That might work, unless of course the KGB has some bright USA analyst who says, 'Look, boys, the CIA's dropping hints the toy sub's true, which means they think we'll think they're trying to convince us it's true and we'll assume it's false. Which means it must be true.'"

"Oh, dear, that's much too convoluted for me," Adelle said.

Swett said, "I remember back when you wouldn't even admit you worked for the Pickle Factory, Leo." He regarded his son-in-law across the breakfast table. "What's cooking with Cuba?" he asked suddenly.

Leo glanced quickly at Adelle, then said, "Only thing I know about Cuba is what I read in the newspapers."

"Leo, Leo, remember me? Phil Swett? I'm the guy who used to eat breakfast with Harry Truman. I'm the guy who's on a first name basis with Dwight Eisenhower. I'm the guy who came up with the idea that Lyndon Johnson was fed up with being Senate majority leader and would say 'Hell, why not?' if Jack Kennedy offered him the vice presidency. If Lyndon brings in Texas and Jack squeaks into the Oval Office, folks'll be lining up to shake my hand. Least you could do is stop treating me like a Russian spy, or a dimwit. Everybody and his uncle knows something's going on in the Caribbean. It's an open secret in Jack's campaign that he's been briefed on some kind of anti-Castro operation that's supposed to be in the works."

Leo looked his father-in-law in the eye. "Phil, all I can tell you is that you know more than I do."

Adelle's eyes sparkled with merriment. "The idea that Leo might know things you don't drives you up the wall, doesn't it, Daddy?"

Swett was on the verge of losing his temper. "By golly, Harry Truman and Ike and Jack Kennedy treat me like a patriotic American. But my own son-in-law treats me like I'm working for the Kremlin."

"Phil, believe me, if I knew something about a Cuban operation, I'd tell you. Far as I'm concerned, if Jack Kennedy can be briefed so can you. You've got to understand that the Company is very compartmented. I'm just not involved in that area of the world. Okay?"

Swett growled, "I guess you don't know spit about Cuba. I pride myself on being able to read folks real well—I could see the surprise in your eyes when I told you about the open secret in Jack's campaign."

"Leo wouldn't lie, Daddy. Not to you."

"Fact is, I was surprised," Leo admitted.

Leo waited while the security guard verified his ID in the lobby of Quarters Eye, a former WAVE barrack off Ohio Drive in downtown Washington that Bissell had commandeered for JMARC, his scare-Castro-out-of-Cuba operation. Pinning on his red badge, he made his way down the narrow, dimly lit ground floor corridor to a green door marked "Access Strictly Limited to Authorized Personnel." Under it someone had chalked: "No Exceptions Whatsoever." Leo dialed the code number into the box on the wall and heard the soft buzz of electric current as the lock sprang open. Inside Bissell's Cuba war room the windows had been blacked out. Two walls were covered with enormous maps, one of the island of Cuba, the other of the Caribbean; each of the maps was fitted with a plastic overlay on which tactical details could be noted using various colored grease pencils. A third wall was filled with blown-up photographs of prime targets: Castro's three principal military air strips with his T-33 jet trainers and Sea Furies parked in rows on the runways; Point One, the Cuban military nerve center located in a luxurious two-story villa in the Nuevo Vedado suburb of Havana; various Army and militia bases, as well as motor pools crammed with Russian tanks and American army-surplus trucks and Jeeps. Leo's secretary, a matronly gray-haired woman named Rosemary Hanks, was sorting the overnight traffic at her desk immediately outside Leo's cubicle off the war room. She plucked a Kleenex from an open box on the desk to blow her nose.

"Are you allergic, Mrs. Hanks?" Leo asked.

"I am. To bad news," she announced in a dry Montana drawl. She waved a cable in the air. "Which is what we just received from Helvetia," she said, referring to the coffee plantation in Guatemala's Sierra Madre Mountains where the CIA had set up a training camp for the Cuban exile brigade that would eventually be infiltrated into Cuba. "We've had our first casualty. One of the Cubans fell to his death from a cliff during a training exercise yesterday. His name was Carlos Rodríguez Santana. His comrades decided to adopt the dead man's number—2506—as the brigade's formal designation."

"I wish you'd start my day with the good news for a change," Leo said.

She shook her head resolutely. "Mr. Bissell always wants the bad news first—get it out of the way and move on, that's his theory. Here's the good news: we've found more B-26 bombers than you could shake a stick at. There's an entire fleet of them mothballed outside of Tucson, Arizona."

"That is good news," Leo agreed. He took the cable and pushed through the door marked "ADD/O/A" (Assistant Deputy Director Operations for Action) into his office, draped his suit jacket over the back of a chair and settled down at his desk to read it. Bissell had decided to use vintage World War II B-26 bombers as the main aircraft in the brigade's small air force because hundreds of them had been sold as surplus around the globe after the war, which meant that Washington could plausibly deny that it had supplied the planes to the Cuban exiles. The problem now would be to pry a dozen or so of the B-26s loose from the Pentagon's tightfisted paper-pushers without telling them what they were for. The Alabama Air National Guard pilots who had been sheepdipped to JMARC would sanitize the planes—remove all numbers and insignias that could reveal where they came from—and then fly them down to the runway being constructed below the Helvetia base, at Retalhuleu. The Alabama air crews could then begin training the Cuban pilots, recruited from the exile community in Miami, for combat missions over Cuba.

Leo went through the overnight folder, cable by cable, routing several to the JMARC desk officers in the building; forwarding the good news about the mothballed B-26s in Arizona to Bissell with a note attached asking how he planned to approach the Pentagon brass—perhaps Dulles would want to take the matter up directly with the Chairman of the Joint Chiefs, General Lemnitzer, Leo suggested. Mrs. Hanks brought in the loose-leaf news book prepared by the night watch, and Leo read through every item concerning Castro or Cuba that had appeared in the national press or wire services in the past twenty-four hours. He added three eyewitness reports on conditions inside Cuba to Bissell's pouch; one of them suggested that more and more Cubans were attending Mass on Sundays, and interpreted this as a sign of growing passive resistance to Castro's Communist regime. That out of the way, Leo attacked the metal folder with the red slash across the cover. This morning it contained only one item, a deciphered cable from one of the Company's assets in Havana. The cable passed on a story that the asset had picked up at a cocktail party for Fidel Castro's brother, Raoul. According to this account, Ernesto "Che" Guevara, the Argentine doctor who fought the revolution alongside Castro and emerged as the second most powerful figure in Cuba, had just returned from Moscow, along with Castro's American-educated chief of the Dirección Generale de Inteligencia, the bearded and elegant Manuel Piñeiro. Both men boasted about meeting Nikita Khrushchev, as well as a mysterious Russian who was said to be a leading figure in the KGB known by the nickname Starik, the Old Man; the Cubans jokingly referred to their Russian interlocutor as "White Beard" to distinguish him from Piñeiro, who was known as "Barba Roja" or "Red Beard."

The asset's cable, too, was earmarked for Bissell.

Leo called through the open door for Mrs. Hanks to come collect the pouch and hand-deliver it to Bissell's bailiwick on the top floor of Quarters Eye. His morning housekeeping chores out of the way, Leo swiveled around to the locked file cabinet against one windowless wall, spun the dial and pulled open the top drawer. Rummaging through the files, he found the one he was looking for and opened it on his desk. When his father-in-law had asked about Cuba that morning, Leo *had* been startled. *It's an open secret in Jack's campaign that he's been briefed on some kind of anti-Castro operation.* In fact, it was Leo who had briefed the Democratic Presidential candidate. He'd caught up with Senator Kennedy in his Miami hideaway, which turned out to be the sprawling home of Frank Sinatra. Kennedy and three of the five members of the legendary Hollywood Rat Pack—Sinatra, Dean Martin and Sammy Davis—had been lounging around the pool behind the house, along with a short, balding man who went by the name of Sam Flood and a stunningly beautiful young brunette who had not been introduced. (Only later, when Leo managed to buttonhole one of the Secret Service agents assigned to the candidate, did he discover her identity: she was a sometime Sinatra girlfriend named Judy Exner.) Leo had been taken aback to find himself in the presence of the Rat Pack; he and Adelle had seen them the previous month in *Ocean's Eleven*, an entertaining film about a caper in Las Vegas. Oh, how Leo had relished the look on Adelle's face when he described Sinatra himself handing him a drink and chatting him up while Senator Kennedy took a phone call.

Back at Quarters Eye in Washington, Leo had drawn up a summary of the briefing for Bissell and kept a copy for his own files. Rereading it now he realized how vague he had been; perhaps it was Sinatra and Sammy Davis and Dean Martin and Judy Exner, boozing it up just out of earshot, that had inhibited him. Kennedy, according to Leo's notes, had remarked that the subject must be important for him to have come all that way to brief him. Leo had said it was CIA policy to keep the major candidates informed on current events. Kennedy, looking fit and relaxed in white flannel slacks and an open-collared shirt, had fixed himself another gin and tonic and had clinked glasses with Leo. I'm all ears, the candidate had said. It's about Cuba, Leo had begun. Kennedy had nodded. Thought it might be, he had said. Leo had started to talk in very general terms about the Cuban exiles being trained in a secret CIA base on a remote coffee plantation in Central America. Had Eisenhower signed off on the operation? Kennedy had wanted to know. Absolutely, Leo had replied; this wasn't the sort of project the CIA would undertake without presidential authorization. If things went according to plan, he had continued, the infiltration of the exile brigade into Cuba would coincide with the formation of a Cuban provisional government, as well as the acceleration of guerrilla activities in the various provinces of the island. You want to be careful, Kennedy had remarked, not to make so much noise that everybody in the world will know the US is behind this. The noise level, Leo had assured the candidate, would be low enough to avoid that particular pitfall and high enough to trigger an island-wide rebellion against Cuba's Marxist dictator. Is there a timetable? Kennedy had asked very casually. Leo had glanced at Sinatra, who was cracking up over one of Dean Martin's stories. Vice President Nixon was pushing the CIA to put the show on the road before the November election, he had informed the Senator.

Will you?

We don't think that's practical.

Hmmmm. I see. Kennedy had scratched at an earlobe. Anything else I need to be aware of? he had asked.

Leo had shaken his head. For the moment, that's it. Needless to say, Senator, the information I gave you this morning is highly classified and must not to be shared with anyone, including members of your staff.

That goes without saying, Kennedy had said. He had offered his hand. I appreciate the briefing.

That night Leo had caught the Senator on TV tearing into the Eisenhower administration for permitting the Iron Curtain to come within ninety miles of the American coastline and not doing anything about it. *Not doing anything about it!* Kennedy knew they were doing something about it; knew also that Nixon couldn't defend himself for fear of compromising the entire operation. His face a mask of sincerity, Kennedy had gone on to vow that, if elected, he would support the Cuban freedom fighters in their efforts to bring democracy to Cuba.

The briefing of Kennedy had taken place in July. Looking up from the file now, Leo was surprised by how much the profile of the Cuban operation had changed in the past two months. What had started out on the drawing boards as a series of guerrilla pinpricks designed to panic Castro into fleeing had become, thanks to Bissell and his top-floor planning staff, a World War II-style amphibious landing on a beach near the Cuban city of Trinidad, involving up to 750 guerrillas and an armada of B-26s overhead to provide air cover. It was not Leo's job to weigh in on the pros and cons of the operation but he could sense that JMARC was spiraling out of control. And he thought he knew why. In theory, Bissell presided over the entire Clandestine Service: fifty undercover stations around the world, hundreds of covert operations, not to mention the "candy"—$100 million in unvouchered funds to finance the operations. In practice, however, he left it all to his second-in-command, Dick Helms, while he focused on what had become an obsession for him: bringing down the avowed Marxist who ran Cuba, Fidel Castro.

The interoffice phone on Leo's desk purred. Bissell's voice came booming down the line. "Great work, finding those B-26s, Leo. I'll speak to the Director straight away about borrowing some of them from Lemnitzer."

"While you're on the phone," Leo said, "I think there's something you should know."

"Shoot."

Leo told the DD/O about the rumor Phil Swett had picked up from one of Kennedy's staffers. "I just looked at my briefing notes," he added. "I warned the Senator the material was highly classified. I specifically asked him not to share it with anybody, including his campaign staff."

Leo could almost hear the shrug of Bissell's stooped shoulders on the other end of the phone line. "We can't get into a flap over every rumor making the rounds of Georgetown—"

"Dick, the Guatemala newspaper *La Hora* ran a story a few weeks ago about a heavily guarded CIA base near Retalhuleu. Luckily for us the American press didn't pick up on it. But one of these days there's going to be one rumor too many. The *Times* or the *Post* or someone else is going to put two and two together..."

"I'll be seeing Kennedy at a Georgetown dinner tonight," Bissell said. "If I can get him off into a corner I'll raise the subject."

To Leo's ear Bissell sounded half-hearted. Dulles's retirement wasn't far off and Bissell had high hopes of succeeding Dulles as Director Central Intelligence. Clearly, he didn't want to rub the Democratic presidential candidate the wrong way. You never knew—despite the political handicap of being Catholic, Kennedy might conceivably squeak through and win the election.

Four hours out of the secret CIA air strip at Opa-Locka in suburban Miami, Jack McAuliffe came awake in the belly of the unmarked C-54, violently airsick. The drumfire of the engines reverberated through his jaw bone. The crew chief, a Cuban who went by the nickname Barrigón because of his remarkable beer belly, stumbled back into the passenger compartment with a glass of neat whiskey and spiked it with powdered Dramamine when he saw Jack holding his head in his hands. "You gonna vomit, vomit in the vomit-bag," he yelled over the drone of the engines. He stirred in the Dramamine with a thick pinky and handed the drink to Jack, the only passenger on the weekly mail run to Guatemala. Grinning from ear to ear —people who weren't air sick tended to enjoy the misery of those who were—Barrigón watched as Jack gulped down the concoction.

"You gotta know it's worse without the noise," the Cuban shouted.

Jack shuddered. "Jesus H. Christ, how could it be worse?" he yelled back.

"No noise, no engines," the Cuban explained. "No engines, we'd come to a sudden stop—like against a mountain." Barrigón tapped a dirty fingernail against his balding skull, as if he had just delivered a nugget of aviation folklore. Waddling down the aisle formed by the packing crates, he headed back toward the cockpit.

Jack had been loath to leave Washington so soon after the birth of his redheaded son, christened Anthony McAuliffe, but he didn't want to pass up a plum assignment. Anthony had come into the world three years to the week after he and Millie Owen-Brack tied the knot in a small civil ceremony in Virginia. Jack's college roommate Leo Kritzky, who had been best man at the wedding, was the boy's godfather; Ebby's wife, Elizabet, who had become a close friend of Millie's after her escape from Hungary, was his godmother. Elizabet's daughter, Nellie, had cracked everyone up when she appeared at Anthony's baptism holding hands with Ebby's boy, Manny, the two of them wide-eyed and serious and looking like a dwarf couple. The priest—fascinated by Anthony's curious birthmark, a dark welt forming a cross on the little toe of his right foot—anointed the baby's head with holy water and everyone had stepped outdoors into the sunlight for a group photograph. A framed copy of it hung now over Jack's worktable in his Arlington apartment; Millie could be seen cradling her infant son as she gazed lovingly up at the profile of her husband.

The whiskey and Dramamine had a soothing effect and Jack, stiff from dozing in the cramped seat, wandered up to the cockpit to stretch his legs. Off to the right he could make out the low folds of a coastline. "That there's Texas," called the pilot, an Alabama air national guardsman working as a CIA contract employee. "We'll be hitting the Gulf of Honduras in an hour fifteen minutes, give or take. After that it's a cakewalk into the strip you dudes put down at Retalhuleu."

"Don't miss the landing—it's worth seeing," the co-pilot shouted to Jack. "We come in under a volcano. Scenery'll knock your eye out."

Jack glanced at the dozens of dials and knobs in the cockpit. Many of them had small plaques over them with Chinese writing. "What's with the Chinese?" he called.

The co-pilot, who was smoking a reefer, laughed. "Plane's on loan from the Formosan Air Force," he explained. "Someone in your shop forgot to sanitize it."

"Maybe they left it on purpose," quipped Barrigón, sitting on a stool near the radio and swigging beer out of a can. "We go down over Cuba, Fidel'll figure he's being attacked by the Chinks."

The landing at Retalhuleu turned out to be every bit as exciting as the co-pilot had said. The volcano, which was still active and named Santiaguita, towered over the sprawling coffee plantation that had been carved out of the wilderness of the Sierra Madre Mountains. The C-54 banked around it, then plunged through a thick mist so rapidly that Jack's heart rose to his mouth. At the last instant the mist thinned and a long ribbon of tarmac— the CIA's spanking new strip—materialized dead ahead. The transport plane hit the deck hard and bounced and hit again and, with every bolt in the fuselage vibrating, taxied to a stop at the far end of the runway. An antiquated bright orange fire engine and several canvas-topped army trucks and a Jeep came racing down the runway behind the plane and pulled up near the cargo hatch. Jack tossed his duffel out the door of the plane, and then jumped down after it. A thin Cuban in spit-shined combat boots and crisp fatigues stepped forward from the Jeep.

"Habla español?" he demanded.

"Antes hablaba español," Jack replied. "It's kind of rusty now."

"I'm Roberto Escalona," the Cuban announced.

"Jack McAuliffe," Jack said.

"I welcome you to the asshole of the planet earth, known locally as Camp Trax," Escalona said with a twisted grin that conveyed more irony than humor.

"Glad to be here."

Flinging the duffel into the back of the Jeep, Jack climbed in alongside Escalona, the Cuban field commander of Brigade 2506. Escalona let the clutch out and the Jeep shot off the tarmac onto a dirt trail and, ricocheting from one rain-filled chuckhole to the next, jolted its way up hill.

Jack held on for dear life. "You angry at the Jeep or me?" he shouted.

Escalona, a professional army officer who had been jailed for leading a revolt against the Cuban dictator Batista before Castro succeeded in ousting him, glanced sideways at his passenger. "I'm angry at Castro for betraying the *revolución*," he called back. "Since I can't get my hands on him I take it out on my Willys."

"Where'd you learn to speak English so well?" Jack asked.

"Fort Benning, Georgia. I took an advanced course in infantry tactics there once."

The brigade commander skillfully twisted the Jeep through a gully and over a narrow wooden bridge. Arriving at a clearing filled with rows of Quonset huts, he jammed on the brakes and skidded the vehicle to a stop in front of the coffee-grading barn that served as a barrack for the thirty-eight brigade "advisors"—sheepdipped military people posing as civilians. A plank walkway led from the dirt path to the front door of the barn. On either side of the walkway, in carefully weeded patches, the leaves of waist-high marijuana plants trembled in the fresh morning breeze washing down from the volcano. From behind the screen door of the barn came the scratchy sound of Julie London singing "If I'm Lucky."

"You want my shopping list, Mr. McAuliffe?" the Cuban demanded.

"You don't waste time," Jack observed.

"I don't waste ammunition, words or time," the Cuban said matter-of-factly. "All of them are in short supply."

"My orders are to act as a clearing house between you and Washington," Jack said. "You tell me your problems, I'll pass on the ones I think are important enough to need solutions." Jack took out a notebook and a ballpoint pen.

Escalona pulled a small dog-eared pad from the pocket of his shirt and fitted on a pair of reading spectacles. "Yeah. So. First off, the CIA has to screen the recruits in Miami better before it flies them out here. Last week I got one man who is a convicted murderer, I got another who is retarded and thinks Castro is a brand of sofa. Trouble is, once they're out here we can't send them back because they know we exist."

"Screen recruits in Miami," Jack said as he wrote. "What else?"

"I was promised portable showers but so far they never came. Your advisors wash in the *finca* swimming pool but they put up a sign saying 'Officers Only,' which means my Cubans have no place to bath except in the streams, which are ice-cold."

"For starters we'll take down the 'Officers Only' sign at the swimming pool," Jack said. "Then I'll see you get your portable showers."

"We were supposed to have a fully equipped dispensary," Escalona continued. "All they gave us was a trunk filled with Band-Aids and aspirins and insect repellent. These hills are crawling with poisonous snakes—but we don't even have snakebite serum."

Watching Jack scribble in the notebook, Escalona worked his way down the brigade's shopping list. From somewhere in the hills above them came the staccato crackle of rifle fire, each shot followed by a whisper of an echo. A squad of baby-faced Cuban recruits, carrying American M-1s at various angles across their chests, trotted by; an American advisor in khakis and penny loafers, with a paunch to rival Barrigón's beer belly, breathlessly shouted out cadence as he brought up the rear. "Hep-two-hep-two-hep-two."

"Last but not least," Escalona said, "we got a major security problem. On any given day roughly fifteen percent of my people go AWOL."

Jack glanced at the snake-infested mountains around them. "Where do they go AWOL to?" he asked.

"The village of San Felipe, which is nine miles across the mountains."

"How in hell do they get to San Felipe?"

"The ones who can, swipe a Jeep or a truck. The ones who can't hitch a ride, they walk. There and back. In one night."

"What's the big attraction at San Felipe that's worth an eighteen-mile hike across the mountains?"

"Whores."

Jack nodded slowly. "Whores."

"Naturally, we indoctrinate the recruits about not shooting off their mouths—but these girls got to be deaf, dumb and stupid not to know somebody's running a military-type training camp out here at Helvetia. For all I know some of the whores could be spying for Castro."

"That certainly comes under the heading of a problem that badly needs a solution," Jack agreed. "I'll see what I can come up with."

Escalona came around the side of the Jeep and deposited Jack's duffel on the planks of the walkway. Slipping the notebook back into his pocket, Jack slid out of the seat. Escalona eyed Jack for an awkward moment. Then he cleared his throat and looked at his boots. Then he looked up and said, "Listen—"

"I'm listening."

"The people here—the Cuban kids learning to strip M-1s and put them back together blindfolded, the mortar teams learning to bracket a target, me, all of us—we're in this thing for keeps. We are going to win or we are going to die."

"Why are you telling me this?" Jack asked.

Escalona shrugged. "Like that," he said. He started to walk away, then turned back. "I tell you this so you'll know where you are. I tell you this so you'll know who we are—so you won't think this is a summer camp for Cuban boy scouts, which is what it looks like, even to me."

Jack tamed his Cossack mustache with the back of a forefinger. "I've been on front lines before. I recognize one when I see it. I'll do everything I can to help you, Señor Escalona."

"Roberto," Roberto Escalona corrected him.

Jack nodded. "Jack."

The two men shook hands for the first time.

In the days that followed there was a flurry of messages that entertained the handful in Quarters Eye who read them.

TOP SECRET
WARNING NOTICE: SENSITIVE COMPARTMENTED INFORMATION

FROM: Carpet Bagger [Jack McAuliffe's cryptonym]
TO: Ozzie Goodfriend [Leo Kritzky's cryptonym]
SUBJECT: Getting ashes hauled

1. Discovered serious breach of base security due dozens of recruits going AWOL daily to get ashes hauled at nearest village nine miles away. Discreet inquiries in village reveal that ladies of ill-repute are Guatemalan nationals employed by local drug dealer running whorehouse on side. New girls bused in weekly to replace those who worn out or fed up or ill. Thus impossible perform background checks or debriefings to see who learned what from whom.

2. Request permission recruit Portuguese-speaking Brazilian females who won't be able to communicate with Spanish-speaking recruits except through body language, and set up brothel, code-named PROJECT PHOENIX as it will be associated with ashes, just off-base to control situation.

3. For God's sake don't let my wife find out what I'm up to.

TOP SECRET
WARNING NOTICE: SENSITIVE COMPARTMENTED INFORMATION

FROM: Ozzie Goodfriend
TO: Carpet Bagger
SUBJECT: Ash-amed
REF: Your *Getting Ashes Hauled*

1. Raised delicate matter of PROJECT PHOENIX with Kermit Coffin [Dick Bissell's cryptonym], who hit proverbial ceiling. He says there is no question of using taxpayers' money for hauling ashes. He asks you to imagine furor if Congress gets wind of services you propose to provide to recruits. Coffin suggests tighter perimeter patrols of camp would solve problem.

2. Don't worry about your wife. She thinks you are teaching Cubans exiles to be altar boys in local churches.

3. Ball in your court, pal.

TOP SECRET
WARNING NOTICE: SENSITIVE COMPARTMENTED INFORMATION

FROM: Carpet Bagger
TO: Ozzie Goodfriend
SUBJECT: Ashes to ashes

1. Helvetia consists of 5,000 acres with sixty repeat sixty miles of private roads. According to my rough calculation, patrolling perimeter would require entire Washington, DC police force, which is impractical as absence might be noticed by Congress, raising embarrassing questions.

2. Not proposing dip into taxpayers' money to finance brothel. Propose to recruit Brazilians and launch PROJECT PHOENIX using unvouchered funds. Once enterprise is up and running on capitalistic pay-as-you-go profit principle, which is one of the doctrines we are defending in this hemisphere, propose to reimburse unvouchered funds. Propose to use subsequent profits from PROJECT PHOENIX to improve living conditions here.

3. Ball back to you.

TOP SECRET
WARNING NOTICE: SENSITIVE COMPARTMENTED INFORMATION

FROM: Ozzie Goodfriend
TO: Carpet Bagger
SUBJECT: PHOENIX rising from its ashes

1. Kermit Coffin doesn't want to know any more about PROJECT PHOENIX. You were sent down there to make sure recruits were trained and ready for action. If the action they are ready for requires you to make decisions that can only be described as creative, so be it. You are to do whatever in your judgment is necessary to ensure the good health, mental as well as physical, of the brigade.

His shirt drenched in sweat after leading the brigade on a two-day hike over mountain trails, Roberto Escalona found Jack stretched out on the lengths of cardboard covering his army cot (to absorb humidity) in the coffee-grading barn. *"Hombre,"* he said, shaking Jack awake from his siesta.

His Cossack mustache sticky with perspiration, Jack propped himself up on an elbow. "How'd it go, Roberto?"

"Great. Aside from three sprained ankles and a squad that read the map coordinates wrong and missed a rendezvous, everyone came through with flying colors. Having snakebite serum with us made a big difference—the men weren't afraid of walking the trails at night. Coming back, without me saying a word, the pace picked up. It was like horses breaking into a trot when they smell the barn. The men with coupons for your bordello washed in the *finca* pool and made a beeline for the Phoenix Quonset."

"You need to get it into your head that it's not *my* bordello, Roberto."

Escalona sat down on the next cot and started unlacing his boots, which had lost their spit-shine. "It's not just the whorehouse, Jack. It's the refrigerators you got us to keep the Pepsi cold. It's the showers behind the Quonset huts. It's the Hollywood movies you show every night on the big screen in the canteen. It's the crates of M-1 ammunition—everyone's getting two hours of target practice a week now. Morale is soaring. The men are starting to understand we're not alone in this thing. Now that Kennedy's been elected President, they're beginning to think America's behind us. With America behind us we can't lose."

"We can lose, Roberto. America will supply you with B-26s and train your pilots and give you a lifetime supply of M-1 ammunition. But you've got to defeat Castro on your own. If you get into trouble on the beach, America won't lift a finger to get you out of trouble."

Escalona smiled knowingly. "I know the official line as well as you do."

Jack was wide awake now and shaking his head in dismay. "It's not an official line, Roberto. It's official policy. It's the name of the game. We'll help you covertly but not overtly."

"Sure thing, Jack."

"Damnation, I hope to God you don't have to find out the hard way that I'm telling you the truth."

2

W E KNOW THIS JACK KENNEDY INDIVIDUAL AWRIGHT. WE KNOW his father, Joe, awright also," Johnny Rosselli was saying. "What we don't know—" The *consiglière* lazily turned his head and gazed through horn-rimmed shades at the Fallen Angel, who was leaning against the fender of the Sorcerer's dirty-orange Chevrolet parked on President Street outside the small park, his angelic face raised toward the sun, his eyes closed. "What didja say was his name again?"

"I didn't say," Harvey Torriti replied. "His name is Silwan II."

"That don't sound completely American."

"He's Rumanian. We call him the Fallen Angel."

"What'd he do to fall?"

The Sorcerer wondered if Rosselli's interest was purely professional; one killer appreciating another, that kind of thing. Tall, silver-haired, impeccably dressed with a silk handkerchief spilling from his breast pocket, Rosselli looked like someone Hollywood would cast as a mortician. He had started out in the Cosa Nostra working for Al Capone in Chicago; along the way he'd been involved in more than a dozen gangland murders. "It's not the kind of question I'd encourage you to ask him," Torriti finally said. "Curiosity has been known to lower the life expectancy of pussy cats." He nudged the conversation back on theme. "You were talking about Jack Kennedy, you were saying how you knew him—"

"Like I was saying, Jack's got his head screwed on right. What we don't know is his kid brother. Who is this Bobby Kennedy? What ideas are rattling around between his ears, makes him go around the country shooting off his mouth about how he's gonna go and shut down organized crime? Maybe the Micks are jealous of Italians, maybe that's it."

"It's not about race," Torriti said. "It's about politics."

Rosselli shook his head. "I do not understand politics."

"The way I see it," the Sorcerer said, "politics is the continuation of war by other means."

"Come again!"

The Sorcerer surveyed the park. Except for five of Rosselli's hoods scattered around the benches, it was empty, which was odd. It was lunch hour. The sun was shining full-blast. At this time of day old men speaking Sicilian would normally be playing *bocce* on the dirt paths. Which meant that Rosselli, a man with connections in South Brooklyn, had requisitioned the park for the meeting. The hood nearest the Sorcerer leaned forward to scatter breadcrumbs to the pigeons milling around his thick-soled shoes. Under a loud checkered sports jacket, the leather harness of a shoulder holster was visible coming over the narrow collar of the man's shirt; for some reason it reminded Torriti of the times he'd caught a glimpse of Miss Sipp's garter belt.

The meeting with Rosselli was supposed to have taken place in the Plaza Hotel in Manhattan. When the Sorcerer turned up in the lobby, a slight man had approached him. One of his eyes had looked straight at Torriti. The other had stared off over his shoulder.

"You need to be Torriti."

The Sorcerer could feel the Fallen Angel slip around to one side, his right hand fondling a five-inch switchblade in the pocket of his windbreaker. Across the lobby, at the newsstand, Sweet Jesus watched over the top of his newspaper.

"So how'd you pick me out, sport?" Torriti asked.

The slight man's wild eye seemed to take in the Fallen Angel. Not at all intimidated by the presence of Torriti's bodyguard, he said, "Like I was told to look for a gentleman who oughta go on a crash diet real quick." He handed Torriti a note. "PLAN B," it said in block letters. "WAITING FOR YOU IN SOUTH BROOKLYN IN CARROLL PARK CORNER OF SMITH AND CARROLL USE THE GATE ON CARROLL." There was a crude diagram on the reverse side showing how to get there from the Brooklyn Bridge.

Coming off the bridge into Brooklyn, Torriti immediately recognized the turf. Young toughs in leather jackets lounged around on stoops, sizing up with insolent eyes everyone who passed. Brownstones had statues of the Virgin visible in their bay windows. President Street, Carroll Street, Smith Street—this wasn't a low crime neighborhood; this was a *no* crime neighborhood. And it wasn't the police who enforced law and order. At the entrance to Carroll Park one of Rosselli's hoods frisked the Sorcerer (he was obviously looking for wires as well as weapons) just as a blue-and-white patrol car from the 76th Precinct cruised by; the two officers in it kept their eyes fixed straight ahead. Rosselli's hood came away empty-handed. Torriti had left his guns in the Chevrolet. He didn't like people he didn't know fingering them.

"I hope the last-minute switch did not piss you off," Rosselli said now.

"It was good tradecraft," Torriti said.

"What's tradecraft?"

"It's when you take precautions."

Rosselli laughed. "Precautions is how come I am still alive."

"Before the revolution," the Sorcerer said, "you used to run the Sans Souci casino in Havana."

"Nice town, Havana. Nice people, Cubans. All that ended when Castro came down from the Sierra Maestras." Without a change in tone or expression, the *consiglière* added, "I do not know Castro."

"Aside from the fact that he closed down the casinos, what don't you know about him?"

Sunlight glinted off Rosselli's manicured fingernails. "I do not know what makes a Commie tick. I do not know what they got against free enterprise. Free enterprise has been good to we Italians."

Torriti thought he knew what Rosselli meant by free enterprise. After the Chicago period he'd been the mob's man in Hollywood. He'd been caught trying to shake down some film companies and been sent up—for three years, to be exact. These days he ran the ice concession on the Strip in Las Vegas. Judging from the alligator shoes, the platinum band on his wristwatch, the diamond glistening in the ring on his pinkie, he must sell a lot of ice.

"I represent a joker who represents some Wall Street people with nickel interests and properties in Cuba," Torriti said. "My clients would like to see free enterprise restored in the island."

Rosselli watched him, the barest trace of a smile on his lips. It was evident he didn't swallow a word of this. "For that to happen Castro would need to disappear," he said.

"You have contacts in Cuba. You ought to be able to get ahold of someone who could disappear him."

"You want us to knock off Castro!"

"There'd be a packet of money in it for you, for the hit man—"

Rosselli's mournful face wrinkled up in an expression of pained innocence. "I would not pocket a thin dime," he said with vehemence. "The United States of America has been good to me and mine. I am as patriotic as the next guy. If whacking Castro is good for the country, that is good enough for me."

"There might be other ways of showing our appreciation."

Rosselli's muscular shoulders lifted and fell inside his custom-made suit jacket. "I ask for nothing."

"Are you saying you can organize it?"

"I am saying it could be organized. I am saying it would not be a pushover—Castro is no sitting duck. I am saying I might be able to fix you up with a friend who has friends in Havana who could get the job done."

"What is your friend's name?"

Out on President Street a passing car backfired. Rosselli's hoods were on their feet and reaching inside their sports jackets. The pigeons, startled, beat into the air. The *consiglière* raised a forefinger and cocked a thumb and sighted on one and said "Bang bang, you just won a one-way ticket to bird heaven." Turning back to the Sorcerer, he said, "People who are friendly with my friend call him Mooney."

Martin Macy waved a palm as the Sorcerer appeared in the door of La Niçoise, an upper Georgetown restaurant popular with many of the Company's mandarins. Torriti slalomed between the crowded tables, stopping to shake hands with Dick Bissell and his ADD/O/A, Leo Kritzky, before he lowered himself onto a seat across from his old FBI pal.

"So is there life after retirement, Martin?" he inquired. He signaled to the waiter and pointed to Macy's drink and held up two fingers for more of the same.

Macy, a wiry man with a square Dick Tracy jaw and cauliflower ears, the result of a hapless welter-weight college boxing career, shook his head in despair. "My pulse is still beating, if that's what you mean," he said. He threaded his fingers through his thinning hair. "Getting tossed to the dogs after twenty-nine years of loyal service—*twenty-nine years, Harvey*—really hurt."

"No question, you got a rough deal," Torriti agreed.

"You can say that again."

"What'd Hoover hold against you?"

Macy winced at the memory. "One of Bobby Kennedy's people wanted the file on Hoffa and the Teamsters, and I made the mistake of giving it to him without first checking with the front office, which had already refused the request." Macy polished off the last of his drink as the waiter set two new ones on the table. "Hoover hates the Kennedys, Harvey. Anyone who gives them the time of day winds up on his shit list. I had to hire a lawyer and threaten to sue to collect my pension."

"Kennedy wasn't born yesterday. If Hoover hates them so fucking much, why is Jack keeping him on as Director?"

Macy rolled his eyes knowingly.

"He has something on him?" Torriti guessed.

"You didn't hear it from me," Macy insisted.

"What kind of stuff?"

Macy looked around to make sure they couldn't be overheard. "Broads, for starters. There's that Hollywood sex queen, Marilyn Monroe. One of Sinatra's girlfriends, an eyeful name of Exner, is bed-hopping—when she's not holding Kennedy's hand she's thick with the Cosa Nostra boss of Chicago. When the regulars aren't available the President-elect invites the girls who lick envelopes up for tea, two at a time."

"Didn't know Jack was such a horny bastard," Torriti said with a certain amount of admiration; in his book it was horniness that was next to godliness. "What are you up to these days, Martin?"

"I do some consulting for district attorneys who want to make a name for themselves going after local Cosa Nostra dons. If Jack listens to his father and names Bobby Attorney General, I'll do some consulting for him, too—Bobby's going to take out after Hoffa and the Teamsters, bet on it."

Torriti fitted on a pair of reading glasses. "Figured out what you want to eat?" he asked. They glanced at the menu. Torriti crooked a finger and the waiter came over and took their orders.

Macy leaned across the table and lowered his voice. "Isn't that your house paranoid sitting over there?"

The Sorcerer peered over the top of his eyeglasses. Sure enough, James Angleton was holding the fort at his usual table, his back to the restaurant, a cigarette in one fist, a drink in the other, deep in conversation with two men Torriti didn't recognize. While he talked, Angleton kept track of what was going on behind him in the large mirror on the wall. He caught Torriti's eye in the mirror and nodded. The Sorcerer elevated his chins in reply.

"Yeah, that's Angleton, all right," he said.

"Doesn't sound like there's any love lost between you."

"He's ruining the Company with his goddamn suspicions. A lot of good people are being passed over for promotion because they're on Angleton's short list of possible moles, after which they say 'fuck it' and head for the private sector, where they make twice as much money and don't have an Angleton busting their balls. Trust me, Martin, this is not the way to run a goddamn intelligence shop."

For a while they both concentrated on the plates of cassoulet that were set in front of them. Then Macy raised his eyes. "To what do I owe this lunch, Harvey?"

"Do you think you could fit another consulting client into your schedule?"

Macy perked up. "You?"

"My money's as good as Bobby Kennedy's, isn't it?" Torriti uncapped a pen and scratched the dollar sign and a number on the inside of the matchbook, then passed it across the table.

Macy whistled through his teeth. "Retirement's looking rosier by the minute."

"I'll pay you that every time we have a conversation. In cash. No bills. No receipts."

"You could have picked my brain for free, Harvey."

"I know that." The Sorcerer scratched his forehead in embarrassment. "We go back a long way, Martin."

Macy nodded. "Thanks."

"My pleasure. Does the name Mooney mean anything to you?"

Macy's eyes narrowed. "You're not rubbing shoulders with the Mafia rubes again, Harvey? I thought you got that out of your system in Sicily during the war."

The Sorcerer snorted. "I had a conversation with a joker named Rosselli in a park in Brooklyn. He's fixing me up on a blind date with another joker called Mooney."

"Make sure you're armed," Macy advised. "Make sure someone's backing you up. Mooney goes by the alias of Sam Flood but his real name is Sal 'Mo-Mo' Giancana—he's the Cosa Nostra boss of Chicago I told you about, the one who's sharing the Exner woman with Jack Kennedy."

"Like they say in Hollywood, the plot thickens!"

Macy, who had been one of the FBI's experts on the Cosa Nostra, leaned back, closed his eyes and recited chapter and verse: "Giancana, Salvatore, born 1908. On his passport application he listed his profession as motel operator. Motel operator, my foot! He's a foul-mouthed Cosa Nostra hit man who murdered dozens when he was clawing his way up the mob's ladder. Eventually he reached the top of what people in Chicago call The Outfit. He's the godfather of the Chicago Cosa Nostra—they say he has six wards in his hip pocket. Back in the fifties he skimmed millions off mob-run casino operations in Havana and Las Vegas. When he's not in Chicago he hangs out with Sinatra, which is where he met Judy Exner."

The Sorcerer's small eyes burned with interest.

"There's more," Macy said. "We've been bugging Giancana for years—his telephones, his home, his hotel rooms when he's on the road, also a joint called the Armory Lounge, which is where he hangs out when he's in Chicago. We have miles of tape on him. That's what Hoover really has on

Kennedy. It's not the women—even if he leaked it nobody would print it. It's the Giancana tapes."

"I don't get it."

"We have Joe Kennedy on tape asking Mooney to get out the vote for his boy's election. Joe owns the Merchandise Mart in Chicago; when he talks people listen, even people like Giancana. Mooney's hoods turned to in his six wards. Jack Kennedy won Illinois by nine thousand or so votes. He won the election by a hundred thirteen thousand out of sixty-nine million cast. It was no accident that the three states where the Cosa Nostra rule the roost— Illinois, Missouri and Nevada—all wound up in Kennedy's column."

"The mob doesn't work for free. There must have been a quid pro quo."

"Papa Kennedy promised Giancana that if his son became President, he'd appoint Bobby Attorney General. On paper at least, Hoover reports to the Attorney General. Joe indicated that Bobby would take the heat off the Chicago Cosa Nostra." Macy reached for the bottle of Sancerre in the bucket, refilled both of their glasses and took a sip of wine. "Hoover has other tapes. Last August, a few weeks after he won the nomination in Los Angeles, Jack disappeared from the Carlyle Hotel in Manhattan for twenty-four hours. The Secret Service guys assigned to him went crazy. We happened to pick him up on tape—he was in Judy Exner's hotel room. There was the usual screwing around. At one point Jack told Judy that if he didn't win the election he was probably going to split with Jackie. The tryst turned out to be coitus inter- ruptus—the doorman called up to announce a visitor named Flood."

"Kennedy met with Giancana!"

Macy nodded. "It was all very innocent. Judy excused herself to use what she called the facilities. Jack opened the door. The two men chatted in the living room for a few minutes. They talked about the weather. Mooney described Floyd Patterson's knockout of Johansson in the fifth—turns out he had a ringside seat. Jack said he'd heard from his father that Sal—"

"They were on a first-name basis?"

Macy nodded. "Sal, Jack—Jack, Sal, sure. Jack said he'd heard Sal would get out the vote in Chicago. He thanked him for his help. Judy returned and made them drinks. When it came time for Mr. Flood to leave there was talk of a satchel in a closet—Judy was asked to bring it and give it to Sal."

"What was in it?"

"Your guess is as good as mine. Money, probably. To pay off the people who come out to vote early and often in Giancana's six wards."

The Sorcerer stole a glance in Angleton's direction. The counterintelli- gence chief had turned away from the mirror to talk to someone passing next to his table. Torriti produced an envelope and slid it across the table to Macy, who quickly slipped it into a pocket.

"Walk on eggshells," Macy said. "Rosselli, Giancana—these guys play for keeps."

"This is turning into a fucking can of worms," the Sorcerer muttered. "I think we're barking up the wrong tree—we maybe ought to give some serious thought to taking our business elsewhere."

Dick Bissell signed off on a message being dispatched to Jack McAuliffe in Guatemala. He went over to the door and handed it to his secretary. "Doris, start this down the tube right away," he said. He closed the door and made his way back to the seat behind the desk and began torturing a paperclip. "Where'd you get this information, Harvey?"

"I consulted with an old pal from Hoover's shop, is where. Listen, Dick, Johnny Rosselli was only too happy to appear helpful. I'm supposed to meet Mooney in Miami tomorrow afternoon. He's going to sing the same lyrics. These jokers have got nothing to lose, Rosselli and Giancana. Helping us knock off Castro—whether they succeed or not; *whether they actually try or not*—gives them a working immunity against prosecution. Bobby's not going to let a federal prosecutor put them onto a witness stand and make them swear to tell the whole truth and nothing but, for fear they might."

"On the other hand," Bissell said, "the Company doesn't have a pot to piss in when it comes to Cuba. Almost all of our assets have been rolled up. These guys have contacts in Havana. And they have an incentive to help us—with Castro out of the way they'll be able to get back into the casino business. I know it's a long shot, Harvey. But it's a shot. They might just get the job done, if only because they'd have more leverage with the Justice Department if they actually succeeded in knocking off Castro. And without Castro, the road from the invasion beaches to Havana will turn into a cakewalk for the brigade." Bissell rummaged through a drawer and came up with an inhaler. He closed one nostril with a forefinger and breathed in the medication through the other to clear a stuffed sinus. "I was raised in the house in Hartford where Mark Twain wrote *Tom Sawyer* and *The Adventures of Huck Finn*," he said. "Maybe that's why I'm tantalized by the idea of starting down a river on a raft—you have a rudder that can give you a semblance of control over the craft, but basically you go with the current." He shook his head reflectively. "Someone in my shoes has to weigh alternatives. In the great scheme of things, two thugs avoiding prosecution is a small price to pay for neutralizing Castro."

Bissell accompanied the Sorcerer to the door. "They'll probably get knocked off themselves one of these days," he told him. "Keep the raft heading downriver, Harvey—let's see where the current takes you. Okay?"

Torriti touched two fingers to an eyebrow. "Aye, aye, captain."

The Sorcerer couldn't take his eyes off Mooney's fingers. Long and skeletal, with tufts of black hair protruding from the joints below the knuckle and a sapphire ring (a gift from Frank Sinatra) on one pinkie, they drummed across the bar, took a turn around the ashtray overflowing with cigar butts, caressed the side of a tall double Scotch, picked wax out of an ear, then jabbed the air to emphasize the point he was making. "Bobby Kennedy's uh fuckin' four-flusher," Mooney sneered. "He is cross-examinin' me in front of dis fuckin' Senate committee last year, right? I keep uh fuckin' smile plastered on my puss while I take duh fifth like my mouthpiece tells me to, an' what does dis fucker say?"

"What does the fucker say?" Rosselli asked.

"Duh fucker says, 'I thought only little fuckin' girls giggled, Mr. Giancana' is what he says. Out loud. In front of deze fuckin' senators. In front of deze fuckin' reporters. Which makes some of them laugh out loud. Nex thing you fuckin' know, every fuckin' newspaper in duh fuckin' country has uh headline about fuckin' Bobby Kennedy callin' Mooney Giancana uh little fuckin' girl." Giancana's fingers plucked the Havana from his lips and pointed the embers straight at Torriti's eye. "Nobody insults Mooney Giancana. Nobody. I'm gonna fuckin' whack dis little prick one of deze days, fuckin' count on it."

The three of them were sitting on stools at the half-moon bar in a deserted cocktail lounge not far from the Miami airport. Heavy drapes had been drawn across the windows, blotting out the afternoon sunshine and dampening the sound of traffic. Rosselli's people were posted at the front door and the swinging doors leading down a hallway to the toilets and the kitchen. The bartender, a bleached blonde wearing a flesh-pink brassiere under a transparent blouse, had fixed them up with drinks, left the bottle and ice on the bar and vanished.

Rosselli delivered his verdict on Bobby Kennedy. "The cocksucker was grandstanding."

"Nobody fuckin' grandstands at my expense." Giancana chomped on his cigar and sized up the Sorcerer through the swirl of smoke. "Johnny here tells me you're all right," he said.

Rosselli, looking debonair in a double-breasted pinstriped suit, said, "I know people in Sicily who remember him from the war—they say he is okay."

"With a recommendation like that I could have gone to an Ivy League college," Torriti said with a snicker.

The idea seemed to amuse Rosselli. "What would you have done in an Ivy League college?"

"Educate them as to the facts of life."

Giancana, a short, balding man who bared his teeth when something struck him as funny, bared his teeth now; Torriti noticed that several of them were dark with decay. "Dat's uh fuckin' good one," Mooney said. "Go to uh fuckin' college to educate duh fuckin' professors."

The Sorcerer gripped the bottle by its throat and poured himself a refill. "I think we need to lay out some ground rules if we are going to collaborate," he said.

"Lay away," Giancana said cheerfully.

"First off, this is a one-shot arrangement. When it's over we never met and it never happened."

Giancana waved his cigar, as if to say this was so obvious it was hardly worth mentioning.

"Johnny here," the Sorcerer continued, "has already turned down compensation—"

Giancana eyes rolled in puzzlement.

"Like I told you, Mooney, he is ready to pay cold cash but I told him if we decide to get involved, we get involved out of patriotism."

"Patriotism is what dis is all about," agreed Giancana, his hand on his heart. "America has been fuckin'—"

"—fucking good to you," said the Sorcerer. "I know."

"So like you want for us to whack Castro?" Giancana gave a nervous little giggle.

"I was hoping you would have associates in Havana who could neutralize him."

"What's with dis fuckin' *neutralize*?" Giancana asked Rosselli.

"He wants us to rub him out," Rosselli explained.

"Dat's what I said in duh first place—you want us to whack him. You got dates dat are more convenient than other dates?"

"The sooner, the better," said the Sorcerer.

"Deze things take time," Giancana warned.

"Let's say sometime before next spring."

Giancana nodded carefully. "How do deze people you represent see duh hit?"

The Sorcerer understood they had gotten down to the nitty-gritty. "We imagined your associates would figure out Castro's routine and waylay his car and gun him down. Something along these lines..."

Giancana looked at Rosselli. His lower lip curled over his upper lip as he shook his head in disbelief. "You can see duh Wall Street pricks don't have no fuckin' experience in deze matters." He turned back to the Sorcerer. "Guns is too risky. I don't see no one usin' guns on Castro. For duh simple reason dat no one pullin' off duh hit could get away with all doze bodyguards or what have you around. If we specify guns nobody's goin' to volunteer."

"How do you see the hit, Mooney?"

Giancana puffed thoughtfully on his cigar, then pulled it out of his mouth and examined it. "How do I see duh hit? I see duh hit usin' poison. Let's say, for argument's sake, you was to give me uh supply of poison. Castro likes milkshakes—"

Rosselli told Torriti, "Mooney is a serious person. He has given serious thought to your problem."

"I am very impressed," the Sorcerer said.

"Like I was sayin', he has dis thing for milkshakes. Chocolate milkshakes, if you want to know everythin'. He buys them in duh cafeteria of duh Libre Hotel, which was duh Havana Hilton when I was there. He always offers to pay for deze milkshakes but they don't never take his money. Then sometimes he goes to dis Brazilian restaurant—it's uh small joint down on duh port uh Cojímar, which is where dat Hemingway character used to hang out before duh fuckin' revolution. Castro goes there uh lot with his lady friend, uh skinny broad, daughter of uh doctor, name of Celia Sánchez, or with the Argentine, what's his fuckin' name again?"

"Che Guevera," said Torriti.

"Dat's duh guy. Someone with uh fast boat could spike Castro's milkshake in duh hotel or his food in duh restaurant an' get away by sea." Giancana slid off the stool and buttoned the middle button of his sports jacket. He nodded toward the two men guarding the door to the cocktail lounge. "Bring duh car around, huh, Michael." He turned back to the Sorcerer. "How about if we meet again, say around duh middle of January. If you need me Johnny here knows how to get hold of me. I'll nose around Havana an' see what I can see. You nose around Wall Street"—Rosselli smiled knowingly and Giancana giggled again—"an see if your friends can come up with uh poison dat could do duh trick. It needs to be easy to hide—it needs to look like ordinary Alka-Seltzer, somethin' like dat. It needs to work fast before they can get him to uh fuckin' hospital an' pump his fuckin' stomach out."

"I can see I've come to the right place with my little problem," Torriti said.

"You have," Rosselli said. "Mooney here does not fuck around."

"I do not fuckin' fuck around," Giancana agreed.

3

PALM BEACH, TUESDAY, JANUARY 10, 1961

A SWARM OF SECRET SERVICE AGENTS, WEARING DARK GLASSES AND distinctive pins in their lapels, descended on the visitors as they walked up the gravel driveway.

"Would you gentlemen kindly identify yourselves," the section leader said.

Allen Dulles, hobbling along because of an attack of gout, seemed insulted not to have been recognized. "I'm the Director of Central Intelligence," he said huffily. "These gentlemen and I have an appointment with the President-elect."

"We'd appreciate it if you produce IDs," the section leader insisted.

Dulles, Dick Bissell, Leo Kritzky, and the Sorcerer all dragged laminated identity cards from their wallets. The section leader studied each photograph and then looked up to compare it to the face in front of him. "Anyone here carrying?" he wanted to know.

DCI Dulles looked bewildered. Dick Bissell said, "They're asking if we're armed, Allen."

"Holy cow, I haven't had a weapon on me since the war."

Both Bissell and Leo Kritzky shook their heads. Torriti, a bit shame-faced, plucked the pearl-handled revolver from under his armpit and handed it, grip first, to one of the agents, who deposited it in a brown paper bag. Bissell coughed discreetly to attract the Sorcerer's attention. "Oh, yeah, I almost forgot," Torriti said. He pulled the snub-nosed Detective Special from its makeshift ankle holster and gave it to the astonished agent.

At the end of the driveway, a young aide holding a clipboard checked off their names and then led them through Joseph Kennedy's rambling house, across a very manicured garden toward the summer pavilion in the back of the compound. From behind a high hedge came the peal of female laughter and the sound of people splashing in a pool. Passing a gap in the hedge, Leo caught a glimpse of a very slim and suntanned young woman, wearing only the bottom half of a bikini, sunning herself on the diving board. Up ahead he could see Jack Kennedy sitting in a wicker rocking chair, his shirt sleeve rolled up, looking off to one side as a woman administered an injection.

Bissell, trailing behind with Leo, murmured, "Penicillin shots for chronic nongonorrheal urethritis."

"That's a venereal disease," Leo whispered. "How do you know that?"

"Keep my ear to the ground. Want to wager the first words out of his mouth have to do with the *New York Times*?"

"It's a sucker's bet."

The doctor who had given Kennedy the injection said, "See you next Tuesday in Washington, then" as she turned to leave.

Kennedy rose from the chair to greet Dulles. "I take it you saw the article in the *Times*," he said, clearly peeved. He pulled a copy off a stack of newspapers on a low wicker table. "Front page, no less. 'US Helps Train Anti-Castro Force at Secret Guatemalan Base.' My God, Allen, they've even printed a map of the camp! Castro doesn't need spies in America. He's got the *New York Times*!" He shook hands with the CIA men. "Dick, good to see you again. Kritzky, I remember you briefed me last summer."

Bissell introduced the Sorcerer. "This is Harvey Torriti, a key member of our team."

Kennedy held on to Torriti's hand. "I've heard about you—you're supposed to be our James Bond."

The Sorcerer laughed under his breath. "As you can see, Mr. Kennedy, I am not equipped for some of Bond's more daring sexual escapades."

Kennedy waved the CIA people to seats. His brother Bobby and his father, Joe Kennedy, wandered over from the pool. Jack bunched his hand into a fist and his father wrapped his fingers around it. The two smiled into each other's eyes. Joe Kennedy took the last folding chair. Bobby sat on the ground with his back against one of the pavilion stanchions. Jack settled into the wicker rocker. "Why don't you begin, Allen," he said.

"Mr. President-elect," Dulles said, opening the briefing, "ten days from today you will be taking the oath of office as President of the United States, at which point, as Harry Truman liked to say, the buck will stop at your desk. It's obviously vital to bring you up to snuff on the details of the operation that General Eisenhower"—Dulles's use of the word *General*, as opposed to *President*, wasn't lost on anyone—"authorized."

"It's my understanding, Director, that *President* Eisenhower authorized the CIA to work up plans and an infrastructure for an operation, as opposed to actually authorizing the operation itself," commented Kennedy.

Dulles cleared his throat. "I thought that that was what I conveyed, Jack."

Kennedy, rocking gently in his chair, said softly, "I wanted to be sure we're on the same wavelength, Allen." He motioned for Dulles to go on.

Dulles, rattled, looked at the notes he had jotted on the back of an envelope. "Make no mistake about it, Mr. President-elect, Moscow has installed a Communist puppet regime ninety miles off the coast of Florida. Castro has rigged elections, muzzled the press and nationalized sugar plantations and industry, most of which, I might add, belonged to Americans. He has executed more than five hundred political opponents and jailed thousands of others, he's surrounded himself with Marxist advisors and turned to the Soviet Union for weapons. He currently has fifty Cuban pilots training to fly Soviet MiGs in Czechoslovakia. These planes are expected to become operational by next summer. And if all this isn't reason enough to go after him, the CIA has developed intelligence proving that Castro is dispatching teams to stir up revolutions in the Dominican Republic, in Panama, in Haiti and in Nicaragua. Working hand in glove with the Kremlin, Castro's ultimate aim is to surround the United States with a string of Communist satellites and isolate us in our own hemisphere."

Bobby Kennedy rubbed at an eye. "No one doubts that Castro's a pain in the butt, Mr. Dulles," he said, dragging out the vowels in a lethargic New England drawl. "Question is: What is the Kennedy administration"—Bobby managed to linger over the words *Kennedy administration*—"going to decide to do about it?"

Dulles said, "The anti-Castro operation, code named JMARC, is directed by Dick Bissell here. Dick, why don't you run with the ball."

Bissell, in his element, casually uncrossed his legs and, speaking without notes, his toe drumming impatiently on the floor, began walking the three Kennedys through what he called "the new paramilitary concept of the Trinidad plan." "We are thinking along the lines of putting somewhere between six and seven hundred fifty men from the brigade ashore at Trinidad, a shore city in southern Cuba that has a reputation as a hotbed of anti-Castro sentiment. The dawn landing will be preceded by a series of air strikes starting on D-day minus two. The strikes will be flown by Cuban pilots now being trained to fly surplus B-26s out of a secret airfield in Guatemala."

Bobby mumbled, "The airstrip's less secret today than it was yesterday."

Bissell wasn't accustomed to being interrupted. He turned toward

Bobby, who at thirty-five had honed the fine art of playing bad cop to Jack's good cop, and asked coolly, "Did you say something, Mr. Kennedy?"

Jack Kennedy said quickly, "Please go on, Dick."

Bissell kept his gaze on Bobby for a moment, then turned back to Jack. "As you are surely aware, Mr. President-elect, we don't expect the brigade, even with tactical air support, to defeat Castro's two-hundred-thousand-man army in combat. But we do expect the landing, which will coincide with the establishment of a provisional government on Cuban soil, to spark a general uprising against the Castro regime. It's our estimate that the brigade will double in size in four days, at which point it will break out of the beachhead. We have intelligence estimates that seventy-five to eighty percent of Cuban army personnel disagree with Castro's political system. A great percentage of the officers are believed to be ready to rebel against the government and take their troops with them. The peasant populations of several provinces, especially in western Cuba, are likely to rise up as soon as the first shots are fired. Castro's political prisoners on the Isle of Pines can be counted on to join the brigade."

"How are you going to arm all these peasants and political prisoners if they do rise up?" Jack Kennedy asked.

Leo Kritzky, who was monitoring the brigade's logistical profile for Bissell, said, "The ships carrying the Cuban exiles to the landing site will be crammed with arms packages—there'll be enough recoilless rifles, mortars, ammunition, grenades, walkie-talkies to supply fifteen hundred men."

"How long can the brigade survive if it doesn't double in size and break-out?" the President-elect wanted to know.

"We figure that, with the air umbrella overhead, it could hold out on its own for four days," Bissell said.

Jack Kennedy abruptly stopped rocking. "Then what happens?"

"You're talking worst-case scenario," Dulles put in.

"Expect the worst, that way you're tickled pink when it doesn't happen," Joe Kennedy snapped.

"In the worst case, Mr. President-elect," Bissell said, "the brigade will take to the hills—in this case the Escambray Mountains—and go guerrilla. We'll be able to keep them supplied by air. They'll join forces with existing bands of guerrillas. If nothing else, Castro will have difficulty exporting his revolution to Latin America if he's putting down a counterrevolution in Cuba."

Jack Kennedy resumed his rhythmic rocking. The CIA men exchanged looks; it was hard to judge how the briefing was going. From beyond the high hedge came the shriek of someone being thrown into the pool, and then the splash. "Teddy's pushing the girls in again," Jack Kennedy said with a chuckle.

"Naturally we don't expect you to react until you've had an opportunity to mull JMARC over," Dulles said.

Kennedy kept the rocker in motion. He nodded to himself. He looked down at Bobby, who raised his eyebrows. "Too noisy," the President-elect finally said.

Dulles leaned forward. "How's that, Jack?"

"I am fully aware that the smaller the political risk, the greater the military risk," Kennedy said. "The trick is to find the prudent balance between the two. Trinidad is too spectacular, too loud. The whole thing sounds too much like a full-fledged World War II invasion. I want you to reduce the noise level. I would feel more comfortable signing off on this if it were a quiet landing on a remote beach, and preferably at night. By dawn I'd want the ships that brought them there to be out of sight over the horizon. That way we can plausibly deny any American involvement—a group of Cuban exiles landed on a beach, some war surplus B-26s flown by pilots who defected from Castro's air force are providing them with air cover, that sort of thing."

Joe Kennedy shook his head. "What are you people doing about Castro? He ought to be assassinated before the invasion or it will fail."

There was an embarrassed silence. Torriti opened his mouth to say something but Bissell touched his arm and he shut it. Jack Kennedy told his father, very gently, "Dad, that is just not the kind of thing we want to get into."

Joe Kennedy got the message. "Of course, of course. I withdraw the question."

The President elect asked about the nuts and bolts of JMARC. Bissell provided answers. The few details he couldn't come up with, Leo Kritzky had at his fingertips. Yes, Castro had a small air force, he said: a few dozen planes that could get off the ground, old Sea Furies and a few T-33 jet trainers, possibly jury-rigged with cannon, that the United States had given to Batista. Absolutely, the brigade's B-26s could be expected to control the skies over the invasion beaches without assistance from American jets flying from aircraft carriers. No question about it, brigade morale was high and the exiles' combat proficiency excellent; each recruit had fired off more rounds than the average GI in an American army boot camp. Yes, it was true that there had been a minor uprising in Oriente province but it had been crushed by the Cuban army. Yes, the CIA did have raw reports from Camaguey Province that the Castro regime was on the ropes, that civil strife and even anarchy were a real possibility, which is why they believed that the brigade landing and the establishment of a provisional government would lead to a massive uprising.

As the briefing dragged on, Bobby looked at his watch and reminded his brother that, in ten minutes, he would be talking on the telephone with Charles de Gaulle. Kennedy thanked the CIA men for coming down and asked Allen Dulles to accompany him back to the main house. "Eisenhower urged me to go ahead with this," he told Dulles, who limped along beside him. "But I want you to remember two things, Allen. Under no circumstance will I authorize American military intervention. Everything we're trying to do in Latin America, my entire Alliance for Progress initiative, will go down the drain if we're seen beating a tiny country over the head. The brigade has to sink or swim on its own. Also, I reserve the right to cancel the landings right up to the last moment if I judge the risks unacceptable."

"When the time comes to decide, Jack, bear in mind that we'll have a disposal problem if we stand down."

"What do you mean, a disposal problem?"

"What do we do with the brigade if we cancel? If we demobilize them in Guatemala, it could turn into a nightmare. They might resist being disarmed, they might invade on their own. We can't have them wandering around Latin America telling everyone what they've been doing. If word got around that we'd backed down it could trigger a domino effect— Communist uprisings elsewhere."

Kennedy stopped in his tracks and touched Dulles's shirtfront with a fingertip. "You're not going to back me into a corner on this, Allen."

"That wasn't my intention, Jack. I'm only alerting you to problems that we'll have to deal with if you decide to cancel."

Across the garden Bobby led Bissell, Leo and the Sorcerer through his father's house to the bar and offered them one for the road. He knew that Bissell was being groomed to step into Dulles's shoes as DCI when the veteran spy master retired, which made Bissell a mover and shaker in Washington. Bobby didn't want to get off on the wrong foot with him. At the same time he wanted to make sure that Bissell, like the Washington pundits, understood that he was the second most important man in the capitol. "I think your briefing was effective," he told Bissell now. "My brother likes the CIA—he always says, if you need something fast the Pickle Factory is the place to go. The pencil pushers over at the State Department take four or five days to answer a question with a simple yes or no."

Through a partly open door, Jack Kennedy could be seen talking animatedly on the telephone while his father stood by, his arms folded across his chest, listening to the conversation. "Let's be clear about one thing," Bobby went on. "Cuba is my brother's top priority. Everything else plays second fiddle. No time, no money, no effort, no manpower is to be spared. We want you to get rid of Castro one way or another." Bobby's eyes suddenly turned to ice; his voice became soft and precise. "We're in a hurry, too. We want to start the Kennedy administration off with a grand slam." He looked hard at Bissell. "Frankly, we're concerned that the CIA will lose its nerve."

The Sorcerer, feeling better with alcohol in his veins, let a satanic smile work its way onto his lips. Bobby's arrogance had rubbed him the wrong way. "We won't lose our nerve," he muttered, crunching ice between his teeth. "But we're worried you might."

Bobby's eyes narrowed. "Iron the wrinkles out of your plan, my brother will sign off on it. Like my father suggested, it'd certainly make the decision easier if Castro were out of the picture."

In a Company limousine on the way to the airport, where a private plane was waiting to fly them back to Washington, the four CIA men were lost in contemplation. Leo finally broke the silence. "Bobby sure is a sinister little bastard."

"Trouble is," Dulles remarked, "every time he uses the imperial *we,* you don't know if he's speaking for Jack or just trying to sound important."

"I thought I was brought along so I could brief Jack on Executive Action," the Sorcerer said.

"Jack obviously doesn't want to talk about Executive Action in front of witnesses," Bissell said. "In any case, your presence on the team was more eloquent than a briefing."

"Bobby didn't mince words," Dulles noted. *"Get rid of Castro one way or another.* It's evident the Kennedys won't shed any tears if we can manage to neutralize Fidel."

"I hope to hell that that's not a condition for giving the green light to JMARC," Bissell said.

"Jack's nobody's fool," Dulles told him. "Getting rid of Castro would certainly be the icing on the cake. But I can't believe he's counting on it."

Bissell, worried sick about his project, gazed out the window of the speeding car. After a while Dulles said, "I remember dining with Jack in his home on N Street right after he was elected to the Senate. After dinner the men went off to smoke cigars. The conversation turned to American presidents—it turned out that Jack was especially fascinated with Abraham Lincoln and Franklin Roosevelt. My brother, Foster, asked him, why these two. Jack replied that they were the two greatest presidents. Then he said"—Dulles shut his eyes in an effort to recapture the scene—"he said, 'In order to be a great president you have to be a wartime president.'" He opened his eyes and punched Bissell playfully in the elbow. "He'll go ahead with JMARC, Dick. Mark my words."

The Technical Service elves, as they were known in-house, lived in a world of their own: a sealed-off warren of top-floor rooms in one of the Company's "temporary" World War II buildings on the Reflecting Pool. The single entrance off the stairwell to their shop, protected by a hermetically sealed door with a skull and crossbones stenciled on it, was manned day and night by armed security guards. The elves themselves, stooped men with a tendency toward thick eyeglasses and thinning hair, favored white lab coats, the pockets of which were usually filled with disposable syringes. Some of the rooms were climate-controlled, with the temperatures hovering in the greenhouse range because of the spoors germinating on moist cotton in petri dishes. Cardboard labels were propped up everywhere: bacteria, fungi, algae, neurotoxins were growing like weeds. The man who directed the division, Dr. Aaron Sydney, a cantankerous five foot two biochemist with tufts of wiry hair on his cheekbones, had worked for a giant pharmaceutical firm before joining the Company. His most recent triumph had been the development of the infected handkerchief that the CIA mailed to General Abdul Karim al-Kassem, the Iraq military strongman who had fallen afoul of the wonks who masterminded American foreign policy. "Oh, my, no, we certainly don't expect it to kill the poor man," Dr. Sydney was supposed to have told Dulles when he brought him the finished product. "With any luck, it will only make him ill for the rest of his life."

"I didn't catch your name when Mr. Bissell called to arrange the appointment," Dr. Sydney told the Sorcerer when he turned up in his office.

"Torriti, Harvey."

"What can we do for you, Mr. Harvey?"

The Sorcerer looked around the room with a certain amount of discomfort. The walls were lined with shelves filled with sealed jars containing white mice and the occasional small monkey preserved in formaldehyde. Each jar was carefully labeled in red ink: *clostridium botulinum, toxoplasma gundii,* typhus, small pox, bubonic plague, Lupus. Torriti repeated the question to jump-start the answer. "What can you do for me? You can give me an Alka-Seltzer."

"Oh, dear, do you have an upset stomach?"

"I want to arrange for someone else to have an upset stomach."

"Ahhhhh. I see. Male or female?"

"Does it make a difference?"

"Indeed it does. Matter of dosage."

"Male, then."

Dr. Sydney uncapped a fountain pen and jotted something on a yellow legal pad. "Would it be asking too much to give me an idea of his age, height, weight and the general state of his health?"

"He's in his early thirties, tall, on the solid side, and in excellent health as far as I know."

"Excellent...health," Dr. Sydney repeated as he wrote. He ogled the Sorcerer through his reading glasses. "Just how upset do you want his stomach to become?"

Torriti was beginning to get a kick out of the conversation. "I want his stomach to stop functioning."

Dr. Sydney didn't miss a beat. "Suddenly or slowly?"

"The suddener, the better."

Dr. Sydney's brows knitted up. "Is that a word, *suddener*?"

"It is now."

"*Suddener*. Hmmmm. Which would suggest that you don't want to give anyone time to pump his stomach."

"Something along those lines, yeah."

"Will the product need to be disguised in order to get past an inspection at a border?"

"That'd be a smart idea. Yes. The answer is yes."

"Obviously, you won't want a powder—police at borders of certain countries tend to get all hot under the collar when they see powders. A pill, perhaps?"

"An Alka-Seltzer would be about right."

"Oh, dear, Mr. Harvey, I can see you are a novice at this. Alka-Seltzer is far too big. I'm afraid you'll want something smaller. The smaller it is, the easier it will be for the perpetrator to slip it into a liquid without anyone noticing. You do want the perpetrator to get away with the crime, I take it."

"I suppose so."

"You only suppose?"

"To tell the truth, I haven't given it much thought." The Sorcerer scratched at his nose. "Okay. I've thought about it. I want the perpetrator to get away with the crime."

"How many specimens will you require, Mr. Harvey?"

Torriti considered this. "One."

Dr. Sydney seemed surprised. "One?"

"Is something not right with one?"

"We generally supply more than one in case something goes wrong during the delivery process, Mr. Harvey. To give you a for-instance, the product might be dropped into the wrong glass. Or it might be delivered to the right glass which, for one reason or another, is not consumed. If the perpetrator possessed a backup supply, he—or, why not? she—could get a second shot." Dr. Sydney aimed a very nasty smile in the Sorcerer's general direction. "If at first you don't succeed—"

"Skydiving is not for you."

"I beg your pardon?"

"That was a joke. Listen, right, I hadn't thought about a backup supply. As long as you're going to all this trouble you might as well give me a bunch of pills."

"How does three sound to you?"

"Three sounds fine to me."

Dr. Sydney scratched the number three on the pad. "May I ask if you are working on a tight schedule, Mr. Harvey."

"Let's say I'm hurrying without rushing."

"Dear me, that's nicely put; oh, nicely put, indeed. The hustle without the bustle. The haste without the waste." Dr. Sydney rose to his feet and looked up at the Sorcerer. "Would that everyone in the Pickle Factory functioned the way you do, Mr. Harvey. Mr. Bissell generally wants things done by yesterday. If you could manage to drop by again in, say, four days, chances are I will have what you need."

Leo Kritzky was in the process of tacking the photographs to the wall when Dick Bissell and his Cuba task force people trooped into the war room on the ground floor of Quarters Eye. "How does it shape up?" Bissell demanded. He hooked a pair of dark-rimmed spectacles over his ears and, leaning forward on the balls of his feet, examined the black-and-white blow-ups. Taken from a height of 70,000 feet during the previous day's U-2 mission over the southern coast of Cuba, they showed what appeared to be a long stretch of beach, part of which was filled with tiny one-room bungalows set in neat rows.

"If anything," Leo said, "it looks even better than Trinidad."

Waving everyone to wooden seats pulled up in a semicircle facing the wall, Bissell nodded. "Walk us through this, will you, Leo?"

"Dick, gentlemen, what you're looking at is the Bahia de Cochinos—in English, the Bay of Pigs. It's a stretch of beach roughly thirteen miles long and averaging four miles in depth. On one side is the bay and, beyond that, the Caribbean. On the other are the Zapata swamps, which for all practical purposes are impassable—they're crawling with marabu bushes with long thorns that'll flay the skin off you, poisonous guao plants, the occasional deadly snake, not to mention the *cochinos cimarrónes*, the wild pigs that have been known to attack humans and give their name to the bay."

"Sounds like a description of Capitol Hill," someone quipped.

"There are three ways across the Zapata, three causeways"—Leo traced them with a pointer—"built up from land fill and rising above the swamp."

"Do we have an idea what Castro has down there in the way of troops?" Bissell asked.

Leo pointed out what looked like four long low structures next to an unpaved road behind the town of Girón, which consisted of a few dozen wooden buildings set back from a wide main street. "There are roughly a hundred militiamen from the 338th Militia Battalion stationed in these barracks. Notice the antennas on the third building—it must be the radio shack. Here is a blow-up of their motor pool—we can read the license plates so we know these are militia trucks. Seven, all told. No armor, no artillery in sight."

E. Winstrom Ebbitt, who recently had been brought in as Bissell's deputy chief of planning in charge of logistics, leaned forward. People who knew Ebby well understood that he had grave doubts about JMARC but tended, like everyone else, to nibble around the edges of the operation to avoid a head-on confrontation with Bissell and his gung-ho top-floor planning staff. "That looks like more barracks—down there, Leo, more to the left, north of the road that runs parallel to the beach."

"No, that's civilian housing, according to our photo interpreters," Leo said. "The construction workers who are building the Playa Girón bungalow resort down at the beach"—Leo pointed out the neat rows of one-room structures—"live up there. Again, you can read the license plates on the Jeeps and trucks and the two earth movers parked in the field behind the housing—it's all civilian. Judging from the sign on the roof of the shack near the pier—it says 'Blanco's'—this must be the local watering hole. The two piers here appear to be in good condition—one is made of concrete, the other of wood pilings and planks. Between them there is what amounts to a small harbor, which appears to be deep enough to accommodate landing craft. There is some evidence of seaweed but no serious obstacles. I'm getting our people to work up tide charts—"

Bissell interrupted. "It's the airport that attracts me."

"The strip, it goes without saying, is a godsend," Leo said. His pointer traced the runway angling off to the left beyond Girón. "That's a Piper parked next to the control tower. Working from that we were able to calculate the length of the runway. It's long enough to handle B-26s, which means that the air strikes could plausibly look Cuban from D-day onward. Once we secure the beachhead and get fuel ashore, planes could actually fly from the runway."

"Have we had a reaction from the Joint Chiefs?" someone asked.

"We ran it by them late yesterday," Leo reported. "They said it looked okay to them."

"They weren't bursting with enthusiasm," Ebby remarked.

"This isn't a Joint Chiefs operation," Bissell said, "so they're keeping their distance—they're not going to come straight out for or against anything. That way, if JMARC falls on its face they can say, 'we told you so.'"

"I like the causeways," one of Bissell's military planners, a marine colonel sheepdipped to the Company for the Cuban project, commented. "If the brigade can seize and hold the points where they reach the beach area, Castro's columns will be trapped on the causeways and sitting ducks for the B-26s."

Ebby shook his head. "There's a downside to your Bay of Pigs," he told Leo. "We'll be losing the guerrilla option if things turn sour."

"How's that?" someone asked.

Ebby walked over to the giant map of Cuba on the next wall. "Trinidad is at the foot of the Escambray Mountains. From your Bay of Pigs, the mountains are"—he stepped off the distance with his fingers and measured it against the scale—"roughly eighty miles away across impassable swamps. If the B-26s can't break Castro's grip on the causeways, the brigade won't have the guerrilla option available. They'll be trapped on the beaches."

"There's an upside to your downside," Bissell said. "Havana will be nearer when the brigade breaks out of the beachhead."

"There's no fallback if the brigade air strikes don't destroy Castro's armor," Ebby insisted.

Bissell bridled. "The brigade won't need a fallback."

"Things can go wrong..."

"Look," Bissell said, "we'll have a carrier off the coast. If the B-26s can't hack it, we'll fly strikes from the carrier. One way or another Castro's forces will be cut to ribbons."

"Kennedy specifically told Director Dulles he'd never authorize overt American intervention," Leo noted in a flat voice.

"If push comes to shove," said Bissell, "he'll have to, won't he?" He stood up. "I like it, Leo. Except for a handful of militiamen and some construction workers, it's uninhabited, which will make it less noisy than Trinidad, which is what Kennedy wants. Let's all head back to the drawing boards and work up an operation order predicated on early April landings at the Bay of Pigs. As for the business about going guerrilla, I see no reason to raise the matter again when we brief the President, one way or the other."

Squatting in front of the office safe to hide the combination lock with his body, Dr. Sydney twirled the dials and pulled open the heavy door. He took a metal box from the safe and placed it on the desk. Producing a key from the pocket of his lab coat, he inserted it into the Yale lock on the lid and opened the box. Fitted into a bed of Styrofoam was a small half-filled bottle of what appeared to be ordinary Bayer aspirin. Dr. Sydney removed the bottle and set it on the desk. "Looks like garden-variety aspirin, doesn't it, Mr. Harvey?" he said proudly. "In point of fact, all but three of the tablets *are* ordinary aspirin."

"How will the perpetrator know which three are extra-ordinary?" Torriti asked.

"Child's play," said Dr. Sydney. He unscrewed the cap, spilled the pills onto the blotter and separated them with a spatula. "Go ahead. See if you can spot them," he challenged.

The Sorcerer fitted on his reading glasses and poked through the pills with the tips of his fingers. After a while he shook his head. "Damn things all look alike to me."

"That would be the reaction of a custom's inspector or policeman," Dr. Sydney agreed. He bent over the blotter. "If you study my precious pills attentively, Mr. Harvey, you will discover that on three of them the word *Bayer* is misspelled *Bayar*." The head of the Technical Service Division set three pills apart from the others. Torriti picked one up and inspected it. Sure enough, the lettering across the pill spelled out *Bayar*.

"The pill you are holding, along with its two companions, contains a botulism toxin that I personally tested on three monkeys—all were clinically dead within minutes. I obtained the poison from the Army Chemical Corps stockpile at Fort Detrick in Maryland. I don't mind telling you that I had the run of their biological warfare laboratory. They offered me the bacterium *Francisella tularensis* that causes tularemia, which you know as rabbit fever. They offered me *brucellae*, which causes undulant fever. Oh, I did have a choice, I promise you. I could have had tuberculosis or anthrax or smallpox, I could have had *encephalitis lethargica*, better known as sleeping sickness. But I preferred to stick with the tried-and-true botulism toxin, which cause paralysis of the respiratory muscles and suffocation. There are several things you should take note of. These particular aspirins should not be used in boiling liquids—I am thinking of soup or coffee or tea. They can be used in water, beer, wine—"

"How about milkshakes?"

"Yes, yes, milkshakes would be ideal. But I must caution you that the potency will not last forever."

"How long have I got?"

"I would highly recommend that my little treasures be employed inside of three months. Anything longer and the pills risk becoming unstable— they might disintegrate in your fingers before you could use them, they might lose enough potency to produce only severe stomach cramps."

"You did a terrific job," the Sorcerer said. He carefully popped the pill with the word *Bayar* back into the bottle. "Anything else I need to know, doctor?"

"Let me see…Oh, dear, yes, Mr. Harvey, there is one more thing—you will want to wash your hands very thoroughly before going out to lunch."

Rising with excruciating slowness, the large freight elevator worked its way up to the third floor of the warehouse on Chicago's Printer's Row, south of the Loop. Through the steel grating over his head, the Sorcerer could make out the giant spool reeling in the cable. The disfigured man operating the elevator worked the control knob and brought it, in a series of small jerks, flush with the floor. Two of Giancana's boys, wearing gray coveralls with "Southside Gym" emblazoned on their chests, pulled open the double grilled doors as if they were parting a curtain and Torriti ambled off the elevator into the most enormous room he'd ever been in. Except for several hundred cartons of alcohol marked "Duty Free Only" stacked against one wall, the space was empty. A football field away, or so it seemed to Torriti, he could see Mooney Giancana sitting behind the only piece of furniture in view, a very large table that once might have served for cutting fabric. Behind Giancana, gossamer threads of light pierced the grimy window-panes. Several men wearing sports jackets with shoulder padding—or was that their natural build?—lounged against iron stanchions, their eyes glued to the television set on one end of the table.

At the elevator, one of the men in coveralls held out a shoebox and nodded toward the Sorcerer's chest and ankle. Torriti removed his hand guns and deposited them in the box. "You jokers going to give me a baggage check?" he asked, an irritable smirk squirming onto his face.

One of the Southside gymnasts took the question seriously. "You're duh only one here—we ain't gonna mix nothin' up."

From across the room Giancana called, "Come on duh fuck over. Kennedy's gettin' sworn in on duh TV."

The Sorcerer moseyed across the room. Giancana, smoking a thick Havana as he watched the television screen through dark glasses, pointed to a chair without looking at it or his visitor. One of Giancana's heavies splashed Champagne into a plastic cup and handed it to Torriti.

"You celebrating something, Mooney?" the Sorcerer inquired.

"Fuckin' right—I'm celebratin' Kennedy movin' into duh fuckin' White House." Giancana laughed. The heavies laughed along with him.

On the television, Kennedy, bareheaded and dressed in formal tails, could be seen standing at the podium and delivering, in the clipped nasal voice that Torriti instantly recognized, his inaugural address. "Let the word go forth, from this time and place, to friend and foe alike..."

"Who would have thought Joe's kid would become President?" one of the heavies said.

"I thought, is who fuckin' thought," Giancana said.

"...born in this century, tempered by war, disciplined by a hard and bitter peace..."

"To fuckin' Jack," Giancana said, raising his plastic glass to the TV. *"Salute."*

"I didn't know you were interested in politics, Mooney," the Sorcerer said with a straight face.

"You're pullin' my fuckin' leg," Giancana said. "I voted for duh fucker. Uh bunch of times. You could even say I campaigned for him. If it wasn't for me he wouldn't be in duh fuckin' White House."

"...every nation know, whether it wishes us well or ill, that we shall pay any price..."

"You got out the vote," the Sorcerer said.

Giancana glanced sideways at Torriti. "Fuckin' right I got out duh vote. I got out so many votes he won Illinois."

"...support any friend, oppose any foe, to ensure the survival and the success of liberty."

"Enough of dis bullshit aready," Giancana muttered.

"You want for me to turn it off, Mooney?" one of the heavies asked.

"Turn duh sound off, leave duh pitcher on." Giancana scraped his chair around so that he was facing Torriti across the vast expanse of table. "So what brings you to duh Windy City?"

"Sightseeing." He glanced at the four leather dog collars screwed into the wood of the table, wondering what they could be used for. "People tell me Lake Michigan is worth seeing."

Giancana snickered. "I seen it so many times I don't fuckin' see it no more when I look."

Torriti held out his glass for a refill. Giancana exploded. "For cryin' out loud, you guys are supposed to fill his fuckin' glass *before* he asks. Where were you brought up, in uh fuckin' garbage dump?"

One of the heavies lurched over and filled the Sorcerer's glass. Torriti drained off the Champagne as if it were water, then waved off another refill. "Do you think you could—" He tossed his head in the direction of the hoods listening to the conversation.

"Leave duh fuckin' bottle an' take uh powder," Giancana ordered.

The men retreated to the other side of the warehouse floor.

"So have you made any progress in our little matter?" Torriti inquired.

"Yeah, you could say dat. I got uh guy who works in duh Libre Hotel in Havana. In duh cafeteria, as uh matter of fact, which is where Castro goes once, twice uh week for his milkshakes."

"What's your friend's name?"

Giancana's eyes rolled in their sockets. "Don't be uh fuckin' wise guy."

It hit Torriti that the dog collars could be used to tie down the wrists and ankles of a wise guy spread-eagled on the table. "At least tell me something about him," he said. "Why's he willing to take the risk..."

"He owes me uh favor."

"That's some favor."

Giancana flashed a brutal smile. "Favors is what makes duh world go round." He puffed on the cigar and blew a perfectly round circle of smoke into the air, then a second one and giggled with pleasure. "So do you got duh Alka-Seltzer?"

Torriti pulled the half-filled aspirin bottle from the pocket of his jacket. "There are three aspirins at the bottom of the bottle—any one of them can kill a horse."

Giancana kept his eye on the bottle as he sucked thoughtfully on his cigar. "How will duh guy in Havana know which three are spiked?"

Torriti explained about the word *Bayer* being spelled wrong.

Giancana's face actually creased into a smile. "Awright," he said. "We're in business."

The Sorcerer pushed himself to his feet. "So when do you figure this can be taken care of?"

The Cosa Nostra boss of Chicago turned to watch Kennedy on the television screen. "I used to know uh guy who could read lips even though he wasn't deaf," he said. "He told me he learned how in case he went deaf. Duh moral of duh story is you got to plan ahead." He looked back at Torriti. "Like I told you in Miami, deze things take time. I got to get deze aspirins to Havana. I got to organize duh fast boat dat'll pick up my friend afterwoods. After dat he's got to find' duh right occasion."

"So what are we talking about?"

Giancana tittered. "You tell me what'd be convenient for your Wall Street friends."

"We're January twentieth," Torriti said. "You need to make sure that the friend pays back the favor he owes anytime before, say, ten April."

"Ten April," Giancana repeated. "Dat ought to work out awright."

Philip Swett came away from the luncheon with Jack Kennedy feeling mighty pleased with himself. It had been a private affair in a small dining room off the President's living quarters on the second floor. Dean Rusk, Kennedy's Secretary of State, and McGeorge Bundy, the President's special assistant for national security, had joined them. CIA Director Allen Dulles, who had been conferring with Bundy and his staff in the basement of the White House all morning, was invited at the last minute when Kennedy discovered he was still in the building. Presiding over a light lunch of cold Virginia ham, cucumber salad, and white wine, Kennedy had gone out of his way to publicly thank Swett for his fund-raising efforts. "My father always said he was willing to buy me the election," Kennedy had joked, "but he flat-out refused to pay for a landslide, which is why the vote was so close. Kidding aside, you made a big difference, Phil."

"Believe me, Mr. President," Swett had responded, "a lot of people, me included, sleep better at night knowing it's your hand that's on the helm, and not Nixon's."

Over coffee and mints the talk had turned to Cuba. Rusk had filled in the President on the contents of an overnight cable from Moscow: the American embassy's political officer had been told by a Soviet journalist with close ties to the Politburo that Khrushchev would respond to any overt American attack on Cuba by closing off access routes into Berlin and constructing a great wall separating East and West Germany. Kennedy had pulled a long face and, paraphrasing the opening line from T.S. Eliot's "The Waste Land," had remarked, "April is going to be the cruelest month after all." To which Dulles had remarked, in a booming voice, "Assuming he's still around to see it, the Bay of Pigs will go down in history as Fidel Castro's Waterloo, Mr. President. I can promise you that."

Kennedy had favored Dulles with a wintry smile. "You and Bissell have countersigned the check, Allen."

McGeorge Bundy had caught the President's eye and had gestured imperceptibly with his head in Swett's direction. Kennedy had gotten the message and had changed the subject. "Anyone here had a chance to read the Heller novel, *Catch-22*? I think it may be the best damn book to come out of the war. He has this character named Yossarian who decides to live forever or die in the attempt."

Speeding away from the White House in the limousine, Swett sat back and lit up the fat cigar that Kennedy had slipped into his breast pocket after the lunch. He had noticed Bundy warning the President off the subject of Cuba. Even without the gesture, Swett would have understood he had overheard things that were not common knowledge in the nation's capitol; his own son-in-law, for Christ's sake, worked for the CIA and still didn't have the foggiest idea what Bissell and Dulles were cooking up. But Swett had put two and two together: at some point in *the cruelest month*, April, Cubans trained and armed by the CIA would land at a place known as the Bay of Pigs. *Assuming he's still around to see it!* Swett chuckled into the haze of cigar smoke swirling through the back of the car. Of course! How could he have missed it? Dulles and his people would have to be horses' asses not to get rid of Castro before the fireworks started.

By golly, the people over at the Pickle Factory were many things, Swett reflected. But his son-in-law aside, they were certainly not horses' asses.

4

EUGENE, WHO HAD BEEN DELIVERING LIQUOR SINCE LATE AFTERNOON, decided to go straight to Bernice's without touching base at his studio apartment over the store. He parked Max's station wagon on a side street in Georgetown, locked the doors and started down Wisconsin toward his girl-friend's. He sensed something was *different* as soon as he turned the corner into Whitehaven. It was nine-twenty, a time when the residential street was nor-mally deserted. Now it seemed to crawl with activity. A man and a woman, both dressed in duffel coats, stood talking on a brownstone stoop diagonally across from Bernice's building; from a distance they could have been lovers making up after a quarrel. A middle-aged man Eugene had never seen before in all the years he'd been sleeping with Bernice was walking a dog he'd never seen before either. Further along, Eugene passed a white panel truck with "Slater & Slater Radio-TV" printed on its side parked in front of a fire hydrant. Why would the Messrs. Slater leave their vehicle in front of a hydrant for the entire night when there were parking spaces to be had on the side streets off Wisconsin? Up ahead, near the intersection with 37th Street, he spotted a gray four-door Ford backed into a driveway; the area was well-lit and Eugene could make out two figures in the front seat and a long antenna protruding from the rear bumper. Out of the corner of his eye, he could see the bay windows of Bernice's third-floor walkup across the street. They were awash with light, which was curious; when Bernice was expecting him she made a fetish of switching off the electric lights and illuminating the room with candles.

Eugene could hear his own footsteps echoing in the wintry night as he made his way along Whitehaven. With an effort he mastered the riot of panic rising to his gorge. Bits and pieces of basic training at the First Chief Directorate's compound in the woods at Balashikha came back to him: *inno-*

cent people act innocently, which was to say they didn't break into a sprint at the first whiff of peril. It was lucky he'd taken the precaution of parking the car *before* he got to Whitehaven; if the FBI had staked out Bernice's apartment, they would surely be looking for him to arrive in Max's station wagon. He was lucky, too, to be walking down the wrong side of the street—it would raise doubts in their minds. They would be wary of stopping the wrong person for fear the right person might round the corner, spot the stakeout and be frightened off. Willing himself to remain calm, Eugene pulled his woolen cap down across his forehead, buried his chin in his turned-up collar and continued on his way—past the man walking the dog, past Bernice's bay windows, past the two lovers making up after a quarrel, past the four-door Ford with the two men in the front seat and the whip antenna on the back. He could feel the eyes of the men in the Ford following him down the street; he thought he heard the quick burst of static a radio produces when you switch it on. At the corner he turned right and made his way down 37th. Where it met Calvert, he walked back up Wisconsin until he came to the Peoples Drugstore that he and Bernice often went to when they became famished after making love.

Pushing through the door, Eugene waved to the Greek behind the lunch counter. "Hey, Loukas, how's tricks?"

"Not bad, considering. Where's your lady friend?"

"Sleeping it off."

The Greek smiled knowingly. "You want I should maybe cook you up something?"

Eugene hadn't had anything to eat since lunch. "How about sunnysides over easy with bacon and a cup of coffee."

Loukas said, "Over easy, with, coming up."

Eugene went around the side to the phone on the wall opposite the rest room. He fed a dime into the slot and dialed Bernice's number. Maybe he was jumping at shadows. Philby's nerves had been shot toward the end, he remembered. On the other hand, the last thing he wanted was to finish up like the Russian colonel he'd met in the Brooklyn Botanical Garden when he first arrived in America in 1951. Rudolf Abel's arrest by the FBI six years later had made headlines across the country and sent a shiver up Eugene's spine; unless he were lucky enough to be exchanged for an American spy caught by the Soviets, Colonel Abel would probably spend the rest of his life in prison.

Eugene could hear the phone ringing in Bernice's floor-through. This, too, was bizarre; when she knew he would be coming over and he didn't turn up on time, she always answered on the first or second ring. After the seventh ring he heard her pick up the phone.

"Hello," she said.

"Bernice?"

"That you, Eugene?" Her voice seemed strained. There was a long pause, which Eugene didn't try to fill. "Where are you?" she finally asked.

"I stopped for gas. Everything all right?"

She laughed a little hysterically. "Sure everything's all right. It's all right as rain." Then she yelled into the mouthpiece, "Run for it, baby! They pinched Max. They found the stuff in your closet—"

There was the scrape of scuffling. Bernice shrieked in pain. Then a man's voice came through the earpiece. He spoke quickly, trying to get his message across before the line went dead. "For your own good, Eugene, don't hang up. We can cut a deal. We know who you are. You can't run far. We won't prosecute if you cooperate, if you change sides. We can give you a new iden—"

Eugene slammed his finger down on the button, cutting off the speaker in mid-word. Then he said "Fuck you, mac," to the dead line that surely had a tracer on it. Back at the cash register, he pulled out two dollar bills from his wallet and a quarter from his pocket and put them on the counter. "Something's come up, Loukas," he muttered.

"At my counter you don't pay for what you don't eat," Loukas said, but Eugene left the money next to the cash register anyway. "Next time your over easy is on the house," the Greek called after him.

"I'll remember that," Eugene called just before the heavy door closed behind him.

Outside, the night seemed suddenly icier than before and Eugene shivered. There would be no next time, he realized. Everything that was part of his old life—Max, Bernice, his delivery job, his studio apartment over Kahn's Wine and Beverage, his identity as Eugene Dodgson—had slipped into a fault; the various crusts of his life were moving in different directions now. Even Max's station wagon was of no use to him anymore.

He started walking rapidly. He needed to think things through, to get them right; there would be no margin for errors. A bus passed him and pulled up at the next corner. Eugene broke into a sprint. The driver must have seen him in the sideview mirror because he held the door open and Eugene swung on board. Out of breath, Eugene nodded his thanks, paid for the ticket and lurched to the back of the nearly empty bus.

He looked up at the ads. One of them, featuring the Doublemint twins, reminded Eugene of the twin sisters at Yasenovo, Serafima and Agrippina, drilling him day after day on his two legends: the first one, Eugene Dodgson, he would be using; the second, Gene Lutwidge, he would fall back on if the first identity was compromised. "You must shed your identity the way a snake sheds its skin," Serafima had warned him. "You must settle into each legend as if it were a new skin."

Only a new skin could save him from Colonel Abel's fate.

But how had the FBI stumbled across Eugene Dodgson? Max Kahn had severed his ties with his Communist Party friends when he went underground. Still, Max might have run into someone he knew by chance, or telephoned one of them for old time's sake. The person he contacted might have become an informer for the FBI or the line may have been tapped. Once the FBI agents latched onto Max they would have become curious about his two employees, Bernice and Eugene; would have taken photographs of them from their panel truck through a small hole in the *O* of the word "Radio." They would have searched Bernice's floor-through and his studio over the liquor store the first chance they got.

"They found the *stuff* in your closet," Bernice had cried before being dragged away from the phone. Discovery of Eugene's espionage paraphernalia—the Motorola antenna (and, eventually, the short-wave capabilities of the Motorola itself), the microdot viewer, the ciphers, the carefully wrapped wads of cash—would have set off alarm bells. The FBI would have realized that it had stumbled across a Soviet agent living under deep cover in the nation's capitol. They would have assumed that Max and Bernice and Eugene were all part of a larger spy ring. The Feds had probably decided not to arrest them immediately in the hope of identifying other members of the ring. J. Edgar Hoover himself would have supervised the operation, if only to be able to take the credit when the spies were finally arrested. Eventually, when the Soviet spies working out of Kahn's Wine and Beverage didn't lead them to anyone—Max and Bernice had no one to lead them to; Eugene hadn't contacted SASHA in weeks—Hoover must have decided that it would be better to take them into custody and, playing one off against the other with a combination of threats and offers of immunity, break them. By sheer luck Eugene had avoided the trap. And Bernice, courageous to the end, had given him the warning he needed to run for it. Now, grainy mug shots of Eugene Dodgson, taken with one of the FBI's telephoto lenses, would circulate in Washington. They would show an unshaven, long-haired, stoop-shouldered young man in his early thirties. The local police would be covering the train and bus stations and the airports; flashing the photograph at night clerks, they would make the rounds of motels and flophouses. If Eugene was apprehended, the FBI would compare his fingerprints to the samples lifted from the studio over Kahn's liquor store. Eugene's arrest, like Colonel Abel's before him, would make headlines across America.

Eugene had long ago worked out what to do if his identity was blown. As a precaution against the proverbial rainy day he had hidden ten fifty-dollar bills, folded and refolded lengthwise and ironed flat, in the cuffs of his chinos; the $500 would tide him over until he could make contact with the *rezident* at the Soviet embassy. The first order of business was to go to ground for the night. In the morning, when the city was crawling with people heading for work, he would mingle with a group of tourists, take in a film in the afternoon and then retrieve the box he had squirreled away in the alley behind the theater. Only then would he make the telephone call to alert the *rezident*, and eventually Starik, that his identity had been discovered and his ciphers had fallen into the hands of the FBI.

Changing buses twice, Eugene made his way downtown to New York Avenue. Prowling the back streets behind the intra-city bus station, he noticed several prostitutes huddled in doorways, stamping their feet to keep them from turning numb.

"Cold out tonight," he remarked to a short, plump bleached-blonde wearing a shabby cloth coat with a frayed fur collar and Peruvian mittens on her hands. Eugene guessed she couldn't have been more than seventeen or eighteen.

The girl pinched her cheeks to put some color into them. "I can warm it up for you, dearie," she replied.

"How much would it set me back?"

"Depends on what you want. You want to hump and run, or you want to go 'round the world?"

Eugene managed a tired smile. "I've always loved to travel."

"A half century'll buy you a ticket 'round the world. You won't regret it, dearie."

"What's your name?"

"Iris. What's yours?"

"Billy, as in Billy the Kid." Eugene produced one of the folded $50s from his jacket pocket and slipped it inside the wristband of her mitten. "There's a second one with your name on it if I can hang out with you until morning."

Iris hooked her arm through Eugene's. "You got yourself a deal, Billy the Kid." She pulled him into the street and stepped out ahead of him in the direction of her walk-up down the block.

Iris's idea of "around the world" turned out to be a more or less routine coupling, replete with murmured endearments that sounded suspiciously like a needle stuck in a groove ("Oh my god, you're so big...oh, baby, don't stop") whispered over and over in his ear. In the end the prostitute had other talents that interested her client more than sex. It turned out that she had worked as a hairdresser in Long Branch, New Jersey, before moving to Washington; using a kitchen scissors, she was able to cut Eugene's neck-length locks short, and then, as he bent over the kitchen sink, she dyed his hair blond. And for another half-century bill she was talked into running an errand for him while he made himself breakfast; she returned three-quarters of an hour later with a used but serviceable black suit and an overcoat bought in a second hand shop, along with a thin knitted tie and a pair of eyeglasses that were weak enough for Eugene to peer through without giving him a headache. While she was out Eugene had used her safety razor to shorten his sideburns and to shave. At midmorning, dressed in his new finery and looking, according to Iris, like an unemployed mortician, he ventured into the street.

If he had owned a valise he would have sat on it for luck; he had the sensation that he was embarking on the second leg of a long voyage.

Strolling around to the front of Union Station, he made a point of walking past two uniformed policemen who were scrutinizing the males in the crowd. Neither gave him a second glance. Eugene picked up a *Washington Post* at a newsstand and carefully checked to see if there was a story about a Russian spy ring. On one of the local pages he found a brief item copied from a precinct blotter announcing the arrest of the owner of Kahn's Wine and Beverage, along with one of his employees, on charges of selling narcotics. They had been arraigned the night before; bail had been denied when it was discovered that both the girl and Kahn had been living for years under assumed names, so the article reported.

To kill time, Eugene bought a ticket for a bus tour that started out from Union Station to visit historical houses dating back to Washington's Washington. When the tour ended in mid-afternoon, he ate a cheese sandwich at a coffee shop and then made his way on foot to the Loew's Palace on F Street. He sat through Alfred Hitchcock's *Psycho*, which he had seen with Bernice the previous week. Remembering how she had turned away from the screen and buried her head in his shoulder when Janet Leigh was hacked to death in the shower, he had a pang of regret for what Bernice must be going through now. She had been a good trooper and he had become attached to her over the years; chances were she would wind up doing time in prison for aiding and abetting a Soviet agent. Eugene shrugged into the darkness of the theater; the front line soldiers like Max and Bernice were the cannon fodder of the Cold War.

The film ended and the houselights came on. Eugene waited until the theater had emptied and then pushed through a fire door at the back into the alleyway. It was already dark out. Heavy flakes of snow were beginning to fall, muffling the sounds of traffic from the street. Feeling his way along the shadowy alley, he came to the large metal garbage bin behind a Chinese take-out restaurant. He put his shoulder to the bin and pushed it to one side, and ran his hand over the bricks in the wall behind it until he came to the one that was loose. Working it back and forth, he pried it free, then reached in and touched the small metal box that he had planted there when he first came to Washington almost ten years before. He had checked it religiously every year, updating the documents and identity cards with fresh samples provided by the KGB *rezident* at the Soviet Embassy.

Grasping the packet of papers—there was a passport in the name of Gene Lutwidge filled with travel stamps, a Social Security card, a New York State driver's license, a voter registration card, even a card identifying the bearer as a member in good standing of the Anti-Defamation League—Eugene felt a surge of relief; he was slipping into his second skin, and safe for the time being.

The phone call to the Soviet embassy followed a carefully rehearsed script. Eugene asked to speak to the cultural attaché, knowing he would fall on his secretary, who also happened to be the attaché's wife. (In fact, she was the third-ranking KGB officer at the embassy.)

"Please to say what the subject of your call is," intoned the secretary, giving a good imitation of a recorded announcement.

"The subject of my call is I want to tell the attaché"—Eugene shouted the rest of the message into the phone, careful to get the order right—"fuck Khrushchev, fuck Lenin, fuck Communism." Then he hung up.

In the Soviet embassy, Eugene knew, the wife of the cultural attaché would report immediately to the *rezident*. They would open a safe and check the message against the secret code words listed in Starik's memorandum. Even if they hadn't noticed the item in the police page of the *Washington Post*, they would understand instantly what had happened: Eugene Dodgson had been blown, his ciphers were compromised (if the FBI tried to use them to communicate with Moscow Centre, the KGB would know the message had not originated with Eugene and act accordingly), Eugene himself had escaped arrest and was now operating under his fallback identity.

Precisely twenty-one hours after Eugene's phone call to the wife of the cultural attaché, a bus chartered by the Russian grade school at the Soviet embassy pulled up in front of Washington's National Zoological Park. The students, who ranged in age from seven to seventeen and were chaperoned by three Russian teachers and three adults from the embassy (including the attaché's wife), trooped through the zoo, ogling the tawny leopards and black rhinoceroses, leaning over the railing to laugh at the sea lions who ventured into the outdoor part of their basin. At the Reptile House, the Russians crowded around the boa constrictor enclosure while one of the teachers explained how the reptile killed its prey by constriction, after which its unhinged jaw was able to open wide enough to devour an entire goat. Two of the Russian teenagers in the group were carrying knapsacks loaded with cookies and bottles of juice for a late afternoon snack; a third teenager carried a plastic American Airlines flight bag. In the vestibule of the reptile house, the Russians crowded around as the cultural attaché's wife distributed refreshments from the knapsacks. Several of the boys, including the one carrying the flight bag, ducked into the toilet. When the boys emerged minutes later the flight bag was nowhere to be seen.

Its disappearance was not noticed by the two FBI agents monitoring the school outing from a distance.

When the Russians returned to their bus outside, dusk was settling over Washington. Eugene, coming through the reptile house from the other direction, stopped to use the toilet. A moment later he retraced his steps, going out the other door and heading in the opposite direction from the Russians visiting the zoo.

He was carrying an American Airlines flight bag.

Back in the tiny apartment he had rented over the garage of a private house in the Washington suburb of Tysons Corner, he unpacked its contents. There was a small General Electric clock radio and instructions on how to transform it into a shortwave receiver; an external antenna coiled and hidden in a cavity inside the back cover; a microdot viewer concealed as the middle section of a working fountain pen; a deck of playing cards with ciphers and new dead drop locations, along with their code designations, hidden between the faces and the backs of the cards; a chessboard that could be opened with a paperclip to reveal a spare microdot camera and a supply of film; a can of Gillette shaving cream, hollowed out to cache the rolls of developed film that would be retrieved from SASHA; and $12,000 in small-denomination bills bunched into $1,000 packets and secured with rubber bands.

That night Eugene tuned into Radio Moscow's 11 P.M. shortwave English language quiz program. He heard a contestant identify the phrase "Whiffling through the tulgey wood" as a line in Lewis Carroll's *Through the Looking-Glass*. "Whiffling through the tulgey wood" was one of Gene Lutwidge's personal code phrases. At the end of the program Eugene copied down the winning lottery number, then took his lucky ten-dollar bill from his wallet and subtracted the serial number from the lottery number, which left him with a Washington phone number. At midnight, he dialed it from a phone booth.

"Gene, is that you?" the woman asked. To Eugene's ear, she sounded half a world and half a century away, a delicate bird whose wings had been clipped by age. She spoke English with a heavy Eastern European accent. "I placed an advertisement in the *Washington Post* offering for sale a 1923 Model A Duesenberg, the color of silver, in mint condition, one of only one hundred and forty sold that year."

"I understand," Eugene said. Starik was notifying SASHA that Eugene Dodgson had dropped from sight and Gene Lutwidge had taken his place; the cryptic advertisement would automatically activate an entirely different set of dead drops, as well as the code names identifying them.

"I received nine responses," the woman continued. "One of the nine inquired whether I would be interested in trading the Duesenberg for a black 1913 four-door Packard in need of restoration."

"What did you say?"

The woman on the other end of the phone line sighed. "I said I would think about it. The caller said he would phone again in two days' time to see if I agreed to the trade. The appointed hour passed at seven this evening but he never called."

Eugene said, "I hope you find a customer for your Duesenberg." Then he added, "Goodbye and good luck to you."

The woman said, "Oh, it is for me to wish you good luck, dear child," and hung up.

Back in his apartment, Eugene consulted his new list of dead drops. *A black 1913 four-door Packard in need of restoration*—that was the code phrase indicating that SASHA would be leaving four rolls of microfilm, fifty exposures to a roll, in a hollowed-out brick hidden in the bushes behind the James Buchanan statue in Meridian Hill Park.

Bone-tired, Eugene set the clock radio's alarm for six and stretched out on the bunk bed. He wanted to be at the park by first light and gone by the time people started walking their dogs. He switched off the light and lay there for a long time, concentrating on the silence, staring into the darkness. Curiously, the specter of his mother, a ghostly figure seen through a haze of memory, appeared. She was speaking, as she always did, in a soft and musical voice, and using their secret language, English; she was talking about the genius and generosity of the human spirit. "These things exist as surely as

greed and ruthlessness exist," she was saying. "It is for Lenin's heirs, the soldiers of genius and generosity, to vanquish Lenin's enemies."

The battle was, once again, joined. Eugene Dodgson had disappeared
from the face of the earth. Gene Lutwidge, a Brooklyn College graduate who
had been raised in the Crown Heights section of Brooklyn and was struggling to make a living writing short stories, had taken his place and was now
operational.

The tall, rangy Russian with a scraggy pewter beard ducked through the door
of the Ilyushin-14 and, blinded by the brilliant Cuban sunlight, hesitated on
the top step of the portable stairs. The thin metal dispatch case in his left hand
was attached to his left wrist by a stainless steel wire. Descending the steps, the
Russian caught sight of a familiar figure leaning against the door of the gleaming black Chrysler idling near the tail of the plane. As the other passengers
headed in the direction of the customs terminal, the Russian broke ranks and
started toward the Chrysler. Two Cuban policemen in blue uniforms ran over
to intercept him but the man at the car barked something in Spanish and they
shrank back. The Cuban stepped forward from the Chrysler and embraced the
Russian awkwardly. Tucking an arm behind his visitor's elbow, he steered him
into the back seat of the car. A bodyguard muttered a code phrase into a walkie-
talkie and climbed into the front seat alongside the driver. The Cuban translator and a middle-aged secretary settled onto jump seats facing the Russian
and his Cuban host. The driver threw the Chrysler into gear and sped across
the tarmac and the fields beyond toward an airport gate guarded by a squad of
soldiers. Seeing the Chrysler approaching they hauled the gate open. A lieutenant snapped off a smart salute as the Chrysler whipped past. The car jounced
up an embankment onto an access road and roared off in the direction of the
Havana suburb of Nuevo Vedado. Its destination: the tree-shaded villa two
houses down the street from Point One, Castro's military nerve center.

Speeding along a broad boulevard lined with flame trees and bougain-
villea, Manuel Piñeiro, the chief of Castro's state security apparatus, instructed
the translator to tell their guest how pleased the Cubans were to welcome Pavel
Semyonovich Zhilov on his first visit to Communist Cuba. Starik caught sight
of a group of elderly men and women doing calisthenics in a lush park and
nodded his approval; this was the Cuba he recognized from dozens of Soviet
newsreels. Turning back to Piñeiro, he offered an appropriate response: it went
without saying that he was delighted to be here and eager to be of service to
the Cuban revolution. The two men filled the quarter-hour ride to Nuevo

Vedado with small talk, chatting—through the interpreter, a diffident young man hunched forward on his seat and nodding at every word—about what they'd been up to since they'd last met in Moscow. They brought each other up to date on common acquaintances: the German spy chief Marcus Wolf, who had achieved considerable success infiltrating Reinhard Gehlen's West German intelligence organization; a former Soviet ambassador to Cuba, who had fallen afoul of Khrushchev and been sent off to manage a shoe factory in Kirghizstan; a gorgeous Cuban singer, who was rumored to be having a lesbian affair with the wife of a member of the Soviet Central Committee. Piñeiro, an early and ardent *Fidelista* who had been educated at New York's Columbia University before joining Castro and his guerrillas in the Sierra Maestras, wanted to know if the stories in the American press about Leonid Brezhnev, currently chairman of the presidium of the Supreme Soviet, were accurate. Had Brezhnev set his sights on succeeding Khrushchev as First Secretary of the Party? Did he have supporters in the Politburo? How would the tug-of-war between the two factions affect Soviet policy toward Cuba?

It was only when the two men and the young translator were alone in the "secure" room-within-a-room on the top floor of Piñeiro's villa that they got down to the serious business that had brought Starik to Cuba.

"I have come to alert you to the critical danger that confronts the Cuban revolution," Starik announced. Producing a small key, he unlocked the stainless steel bracelet, opened the dispatch case and took out four manila folders with security notations marked on the covers in Cyrillic. He opened the first folder, then, eyeing the translator, frowned uncertainly. Piñeiro laughed and said something in Spanish. The young translator said in Russian, "He tells you that I am the son of his sister, and his godson."

Piñeiro said, in English, "The boy is my nephew. It is okay to speak in front of him."

Starik sized up the translator, nodded and turned back to Piñeiro. "The information we have developed is too important, and too secret, to risk sending it through the usual channels for fear the Americans may have broken our ciphers, or yours. For reasons that will be apparent to you we do not want them to know that we know. The American Central Intelligence Agency"—Starik remembered Yevgeny teaching him the English words for *glavni protivnik*, and used them now—"*the principal adversary...*" He reverted to Russian. "...is arming and training a force of Cuban exiles, recruited in Miami, for the eventual invasion of Cuba. This force includes a brigade of ground troops and several dozen pilots of B-26s expropriated from a fleet of mothballed bombers near the city of Tucson in the state of Arizona. The

CIA's B-26 bombers differ from your Cuban air force B-26s in as much as they are fitted with metal nose cones where yours have plastic nose cones."

Piñeiro extracted some deciphered cables from a thick envelope and ran his thumb nail along lines of text. "What you say does not come as news to us, my dear Pasha," he said. "We have, as you can imagine, made an enormous effort to develop assets in Miami; several of them actually work for the CIA's Miami Station, located on the campus of the University of Miami. According to one of my informants the Cuban mercenaries, known as Brigade 2506, are being trained by the Americans at Retalhuleu in the Sierra Madre Mountains of Guatemala and now numbers four thousand."

Starik, an austere man who, in a previous incarnation, might have been a monk, permitted a weak smile onto his lips; the expression was so rare for him that it somehow looked thoroughly out of place. "The number of four thousand is inaccurate," he told Piñeiro. "This is because they began numbering the exiles starting with twenty-five hundred to mislead you. The mercenary bearing the number twenty-five-oh-six was killed in a fall from a cliff and the brigade adopted his number as its official name."

"There are only fifteen hundred, then? Fidel will be happy to learn of this detail."

"The invasion is scheduled for early in the month of April," Starik said. "Current plans call for three civilian freighters to ferry half the brigade of mercenaries, some seven hundred and fifty men, to Cuba, though it is not excluded that this number could increase to fifteen hundred if more ships are brought into the operation."

Piñeiro pulled another of the deciphered cables from the pile. "We have an agent among the longshoremen loading one of the freighters, the *Río Escondido*, at its anchorage on the Mississippi River. The ship is carrying a communications van, large stores of ammunition and a quantity of aviation gasoline."

"A portion of the aviation gasoline is in tanks below deck, the rest in two hundred fifty-five-gallon drums lashed to the decks topside," Starik told the Cuban. "With all this gasoline on the main deck the *Río Escondido* will be a juicy target for your planes. Note, too, that the brigade's B-26 bombers will strike three times before the landings, once on D-day minus two, a second time on D-day minus one, a third on the morning of the landings. The principal targets of the first two raids will be the airplanes parked at your air bases, and the air base facilities themselves. The third raid will attack any of your planes that survived the first two raids, plus your command-and-control centers, your communications facilities and any armor or artillery spotted by the U-2 overflights near the invasion site."

"We know that the Americans plan to send the Cuban counterrevolu-tionists ashore at Trinidad," Piñeiro said. He was anxious to impress his guest with the work of the Cuban intelligence community. "They selected Trinidad because of its proximity to the Escambray Mountains. They rea-soned that if the landing failed to spark a general uprising or an Army mutiny and the invaders then failed to break out of the beachhead, they could slip away into the mountains and form guerrilla bands that, sustained by air drops, could prove to be a thorn in the side of the revolution."

Starik consulted a second folder. "It is true that the CIA originally targeted Trinidad but, at the insistence of the new President, they recently moved the landings to a more remote area. Even Roberto Escalona, the leader of the brigade, has not yet been informed of the change. The plan now calls for the establishment of a bridgehead on two beaches in a place called the Bay of Pigs."

Piñeiro had assumed that the KGB had excellent sources of information in America but he had never quite realized how excellent until this moment. Though he was too discreet to raise the subject, it was clear to him that Starik must be running an agent in the upper echelons of the CIA, perhaps someone with access to the White House itself.

"The Zapata swamps, the Bay of Pigs," he told Pasha excitedly, "is an area well known to Fidel—he goes down there often to skin-dive." He pulled a detailed map of southern Cuba from a drawer and flattened it on the table. "The Bay of Pigs—it is difficult for me to believe they could be so foolish. There are only three roads in or out—causeways that can be easily blocked."

"You must be careful to move your tanks and artillery down there in ones and twos, and at night, and camouflage them during the day, so that the CIA does not spot them and realize you have anticipated their plans."

"Fidel is a master at this sort of thing," Piñeiro said. "The mercenaries will be trapped on the beach and destroyed by artillery and tank fire."

"If the American Navy does not intervene."

"Do you have information that it will?"

"I have information that it will *not*." Starik opened yet another folder. "The Americans will have the aircraft carrier *Essex* and a destroyer squadron standing off your coast, not to mention the air-bases available in Key West, fifteen min-utes flying time from Cuba. The young Kennedy has specifically warned the CIA that he has no intention of committing American forces overtly, even if things turn against the Cuban mercenaries on the beaches. But the CIA people in charge of the operation believe that, faced with the destruction of the Cuban brigade on the Bay of Pigs, the President will give in to the logic of the situation and, to avoid a debacle, commit American planes and ships to the battle."

"What is your assessment?"

"The young President will come under enormous pressure from the CIA and the military clique to intervene if disaster threatens. My feeling, based on nothing more than instinct, is that he will resist this pressure; that he will write off his losses and move on to the next adventure."

They discussed various details of the CIA operation that the Russians had knowledge of: the arms and ammunition that would be available to the Cuban invaders on the beach, the communications channels that would be used from the beach to the American flotilla off the coast, the makeup of the Cuban government in exile that would be flown to the invasion site if and when the beachhead was secured. Piñeiro asked what the Soviet reaction would be if the American President gave in to the pressure and used American ships and plans overtly. Starik himself had briefed Nikita Khrushchev on the CIA plans to mount an invasion of Cuba, he told his Cuban colleague. They had not discussed what the Soviet side would do in the event of overt—as opposed to covert—American aggression; that was a subject that Fidel Castro would have to take up with First Secretary Khrushchev, either directly or through diplomatic channels. Again, all exchanges between the two sides should be limited to letters carried by hand in diplomatic pouches, lest the America code-breakers learn that the CIA plans had leaked. Pressed, Starik offered his personal opinion: in the event of overt American intervention, the best that the Soviet side could do would be to threaten similar intervention in, say, Berlin. This would focus the attention of the American President on the risks he was running.

Piñeiro pointed with his chin toward Starik's manila folders. "There is a fourth folder you haven't yet opened," he said.

Starik kept his eyes fixed on Piñeiro's. "Hand in glove with the invasion," he said, "the CIA is planning to assassinate Castro."

The young translator winced at the word "assassinate." Piñeiro's high brow furrowed. The red beard on his chin actually twitched as his Russian visitor pulled a single sheet from the fourth folder and began reading from it aloud. Piñeiro's nephew translated the words phrase by phrase. The CIA had summoned home its Berlin Base chief of many years, a Sicilian-American who had been in contact with the Mafia during the war, and ordered him to develop a capability to neutralize foreign leaders who obstructed American foreign policy. Castro was the first target on the list. The former Berlin Base chief, whose name was Torriti, had immediately contacted various American Cosa Nostra figures, including the head of the Chicago Cosa Nostra, Salvatore Giancana. Giancana, in turn, had come up with a Cuban on the island willing to slip poison into one of Castro's drinks.

Giancana had refused to identify the killer even to the CIA, so the Russians were unable to pass his name on to the Cubans. "We know only that sometime in the next month he will be given a bottle filled with aspirins, three of which will contain deadly botulism toxin," Starik said.

Piñeiro asked how the poison pills could be distinguished from the ordinary aspirin. Starik had to admit that he was unable to provide an answer to that crucial question. Piñeiro, feverishly jotting notes on a pad, wanted to know if any other details of the plot, however small, were available. The Russian reread his sheet of paper. There was one other thing, he said. The Cosa Nostra apparently expected to exfiltrate the killer from Cuba after the assassination by means of a fast boat. To Piñeiro, this seemed to be a telling detail and he said so. It indicated that the attempt on Castro's life would be made not far from a port.

Starik could only shrug. "I leave it to your service," he said, "to fill in the missing pieces of the puzzle."

Piñeiro said with a cold glint in his eye, "We will."

Minutes after eleven there was a soft drumbeat on the door of the suite on the top floor of the hotel in a Havana suburb. His spidery legs jutting from a coarse nightshirt, Starik padded over to the door and looked through the fisheye lens of the peephole. Three little girlies, their thin bodies squat and foreshortened in the lens, stood giggling outside the door. Starik threw the bolt and opened it. The girls, wearing white cotton slips, their bare feet dark with grime, filed silently past into the hotel room. The tallest of the three, whose dyed blonde hair curled around her oval face, started to say something in Spanish but Starik put a finger to his lips. He circled around the girls, taking in their jutting shoulder blades and flat chests and false eyelashes. Then he raised the hem of their slips, one by one, to inspect their crotches. The bleached-blonde turned out to have pubic hair and was immediately sent away. The two others were permitted into the enormous bed planted directly under the mirrors fixed in the ceiling.

In the immutable dusk of his corner office on the Reflecting Pool in Washington, James Jesus Angleton crawled like a snail across "Eyes-Only" cables and red-flagged index cards and hazy black-and-white photographs, leaving behind a sticky trail of conjecture.

Lighting a fresh cigarette, Angleton impatiently whisked ashes off the open file folder with the back of his hand. (His two-and-a-half pack a day habit had left his fingertips stained with nicotine, and his office and everything in it saturated with tobacco smoke; people who worked in Angleton's counterintelligence shop liked to say they could sniff the paperwork and tell from the odor whether a given document had already passed through the chief's hands.) He reached again for a magnifying glass and held it above one of the photographs. It had been taken with a powerful telephoto lens from a rooftop half a mile from the airport and enlarged several times in one of the Company's darkrooms, leaving a grainy, almost pointillistic, image of a man emerging from the dark bowels of an Ilyushin freshly landed at José Martí Airport after one of the twice-weekly Moscow-Havana runs. The man appeared to shrink away from the dazzling burst of sunlight that had struck him in the face. Speckles of light glanced off something metallic in his left hand. A dispatch case, no doubt; standard KGB procedures would require that it be chained to the courier's wrist.

But this was clearly no run-of-the-mill courier. The figure in the photo was tall, his face thin, his eyes hooded, his hair thinning, his civilian suit badly cut and seriously in need of a pressing. A long, unkempt wispy white beard trickled off of his chin.

Angleton shuffled through a pile of top-secret cables and dragged one out onto his blotter. A Company asset in Havana had reported on a conversation overheard at a cocktail party; Che Guevara and Manuel Piñeiro had been describing a meeting in Moscow with a bearded KGB chief known to the Russians as Starik. The Cubans, always quick to assign nicknames to people, had taken to calling him White Beard.

The cigarette glued to Angleton's lower lip trembled at the possibility—at the likelihood even!—that he was, after all these years, looking at a photograph, albeit a blurred one, of his nemesis, the infamous Starik.

Angleton stared intently at the photograph. The word KHOLSTOMER came to his lips and he uttered them aloud into the silence of his office. Recently, one of the legal assistants in the Public Prosecutor's office in Rome— a middle-aged paper pusher who, unbeknownst even to the Rome CIA station, was on Angleton's personal grapevine—reported hearing rumors that the Institute for Religious Works, the Vatican bank, may have been laundering large amounts of hard currency being siphoned out of the Soviet Union and Eastern Europe. The original tip had come from an Italian Communist who worked as an informer for the Prosecutor's Office; according to the informer the money-laundering operation, some of it tied to loans to the Banco Ambrosiano, Italy's largest private bank, went under a code name known only to a handful of the bankers involved: KHOLSTOMER. The sums of money mentioned had so many digits that the Public Prosecutor had actually laughed in derision when the rumors were brought to his attention. A very junior prosecutor had been assigned to the case, nevertheless; his investigation had been cut short when a speedboat he was riding in capsized while crossing the lagoon off Venice and he drowned. Soon after the Communist tipster was found floating face down in the Tiber, the apparent victim of a drug overdose. The Public Prosecutor, unmoved by the coincidence of these deaths and convinced that the whole affair was political propaganda, had decided to drop the matter.

Angleton shifted the magnifying glass to a second photograph. Like the first, it had been enlarged many times and was slightly out of focus. Piñeiro himself could be seen reaching up awkwardly to embrace the taller man. The fact that Piñeiro, the chief of Cuban intelligence, had personally come to the airport to greet the Russian reinforced the idea that the visitor, and the visit, must have been extraordinarily important.

Grabbing the bottle, Angleton poured himself a refill and gulped down a dose of alcohol. The warm sensation in the back of his throat steadied his nerves; these days he needed more than the usual amount of alcohol in his blood to function. Assuming, for the moment, that the man in the photograph was Starik, what was he doing in Havana? Angleton peered into the twilight of his office, looking for the thread that would lead him in the direction of answers. The only thing that would bring Starik himself to Cuba was to deliver intelligence that he didn't want to trust to other hands or send by cipher for fear that American cryptoanalysts would be able to read his mail. Castro already knew what every Cuban in Miami knew (the *New York Times* had, after all, published the details): the Company was training Cuban exiles on a coffee plantation in Guatemala with the obvious intention of infiltrating them into Cuba in the hope of sparking a counterrevolution. What Castro didn't know was where and when the exiles would strike. Within the CIA itself this information was closely held; there weren't more than half a hundred people who knew where, and two dozen who knew when.

Over the years, American cryptographers had broken out snippets of clear text from enciphered Soviet messages and discovered garbled references which, when pieced together, seemed to point to the existence of a Russian operating under deep cover in Washington using the code name SASHA. Assuming, as Angleton did, that SASHA was a Russian mole in the heart of the Company, one had to presume the worst case: that he was among the happy few who knew the date and precise target of the Cuban operation. SASHA might even have caught wind of the super-secret ZR/RIFLE, the executive action program being organized by Harvey Torriti to assassinate Castro. In his mind's eye Angleton could follow the chain links: SASHA to a cutout to Starik to Piñeiro to Castro.

The existence of a cutout intrigued Angleton. Weeks before he had been on the receiving end of a private briefing from one of Hoover's underlings. The department had unearthed an old Communist named Max Cohen, who had changed his identity and gone underground in 1941, probably on orders from his KGB handler. Kahn, as he was now called, wasn't giving the FBI the time of day: he claimed his arrest was a case of mistaken identity; claimed also that he knew nothing about the young man named Dodgson who delivered liquor for him, or the cache of espionage paraphernalia the FBI discovered under the floorboards of the closet in Dodgson's studio apartment over the store.

The FBI had stumbled across Kahn by chance. He had mailed a greeting card to an old Party friend on the twenty-fifth anniversary of his marriage; Kahn had been the best man at the wedding. The card, which the FBI intercepted, had been signed "Your old comrade-in-arms who has never forgotten our friendship or abandoned the high road, Max." Fingerprints on the envelope and the card matched those of the Max Cohen who had dropped from sight in 1941. The card had been mailed from Washington, DC. Working from the cancellation stamp on the envelope the FBI had been able to pin down the post office, then (on the assumption that Max Cohen might have kept his given name) went over the phone book looking for white males with the given name of Max in that neck of the Washington woods. There turned out to be a hundred and thirty-seven Maxes in that particular postal zone. From there it was a matter of dogged legwork (photographs of the young Max Cohen were doctored to see what he might look like twenty years later) until the FBI narrowed the search down to Max Kahn of Kahn's Wine and Beverage. Agents had shadowed him and his two employees for weeks before they decided to risk searching the suspects' homes when they were out. It was then that the FBI hit pay dirt: in the studio over the store, the agents discovered a cache of ciphers and microfilms, a microdot reader, a small fortune in cash, along with a radio that could be tuned to shortwave bands. Hoover had hoped that one of three Soviet agents would lead him to Americans who were spying for the Soviet Union but, after ten days, he lost his nerve; fearful that one of the three might have spotted the FBI surveillance, he decided to take them into custody. The one who went by the name of Dodgson—a male Caucasian, age 31, medium height, sturdy build with sandy hair—had somehow slipped through the FBI net. When he phoned the girl she managed to blurt out a warning. After that he simply vanished, which indicated to Angleton that he must have been meticulously trained and furnished with a fallback identity. Although Eugene Dodgson was said to speak American English without a trace of a foreign accent, Angleton didn't rule out the possibility that he might be a Russian passing himself off as an American.

Angleton would have given up cigarettes for the rest of his life to interrogate this Dodgson character. Agonizing over the problem, he reflected once again on the central reality of counterintelligence: everything was related in some way to everything else. A North Vietnamese defector who asked for asylum in Singapore was related to the fragment of a message that MI6 had deciphered from the London KGB *rezident* to Moscow Centre, which in turn was related to the disappearance in Germany of a secretary who worked part time for Gehlen's organization. Hoping to stumble across missing pieces of the puzzle, Angleton had asked the FBI for a list of Kahn's customers since the liquor store opened for business in the early 1940s. Philby's name had leapt off the page. *On several occasions in 1951 Eugene Dodgson had delivered liquor to Philby's address on Nebraska Avenue.* Suddenly it all made sense: Philby had been too valuable to let the KGB people at the Soviet embassy, constantly surveilled by FBI agents, come into contact with him. Starik would have set up a cutout operation, using someone living under deep cover. Dodgson, whether Russian or American, had been the link between Philby and his Soviet handler from the time he came to work at Kahn's. Which meant that Dodgson was also the cutout between the Soviet mole SASHA and the KGB.

Going over Kahn's list of deliveries since Philby quit Washington with a fine-tooth comb, Angleton discovered last names that corresponded to the names of one hundred sixty-seven current full-time CIA employees and sixty-four contract employees.

Fortifying his blood with another shot of alcohol, he started working down the list...

5

DO I HAVE IT RIGHT?" JACK KENNEDY ASKED DICK BISSELL AFTER the DD/O finished bringing the President and the others in the room up to date on the invasion of Cuba. "For the first air strike, sixteen of the brigade's B-26s, flying from Guatemala, are going to attack Castro's three principal airports. An hour or so later two other B-26s filled with cosmetic bullet holes will land in Miami. The Cubans flying the two planes will claim that they defected from Castro's air force and strafed his runways before flying on to Miami to ask for political asylum."

Bissell, cleaning his eyeglasses with the tip of his tie, nodded. "That's the general idea, Mr. President."

Kennedy, his eyes wrinkling at the corners with tension, his brow furrowing in concentration, shook his head slowly. "It won't wash, Dick. Presumably—hopefully—your sixteen planes will inflict sixteen planes' worth of damage on Castro's air force. Castro will surely have footage of the damage. He may even have footage of the attack. How in heaven's name can you hope to pass off the raids as if they were done by *two* planes? Nobody will swallow it."

"The notion that we can plausibly deny American involvement will be compromised from the start," agreed Dean Rusk, the Secretary of State.

Decked out in a sports jacket, slacks and an open-necked shirt, Jack Kennedy presided from the head of a long oval table cluttered with coffee cups and packs of cigarettes, the saucers doubling as ash trays. The President had gone over to State late in the afternoon to witness the swearing-in of Anthony Drexel Biddle as ambassador to Spain, then ducked into the small conference room tucked away behind Rusk's office immediately after the

5:45 ceremony. It was D-day minus thirteen. A dozen people were already crammed into the room. Some had been waiting for hours; in order not to attract attention to the meeting, they had been instructed to arrive by side doors throughout the afternoon. Now Bissell and Dulles exchanged knowing looks. Leo Kritzky underlined two sentences on a briefing paper and passed it to Bissell, who glanced at it, then turned back to Jack Kennedy. "Mr. President, it's obvious that the key to the invasion is the success of the landings. And the key to the success of the landings, as we've pointed out before, is complete control of the air space over the beaches. Castro has a small air force—we count two dozen machines which are air worthy and sixteen which are combat-ready. It is essential to the success of our project that they be destroyed on the ground before D-day. If the cover story is bothering you—"

"What's bothering me," Kennedy snapped, "is that no one in his right mind is going to believe it. We can count on the Communist bloc to raise a stink at the United Nations. The world will be watching. Adlai Stevenson has to sound convincing when he denies—"

"Perhaps we could fly some additional B-26s into Miami—" Dulles started to suggest.

"Replete with bullet holes in the wings," Kennedy commented ironically.

Rusk leaned forward. "Let's face it, no cover story is going to hold water until your Cubans have captured the runway at the Bay of Pigs. Only then can we argue convincingly that Cuban freedom fighters or Castro defectors are flying from an air strip that has nothing to do with the United States."

Kennedy asked, "Is there any way you scale back the raid, Dick, in order to make the story of the two B-26 defectors look plausible?"

Bissell could see which way the wind was blowing; if he didn't give way there would be no air attacks at all before D-day. "I could conceivably cut it back to six planes—two for each of Castro's three airports. Anything we don't destroy on the D-minus-two raid we could still get on the D-minus-one raid."

Kennedy seemed relieved. "I can live with six planes," he said.

The President glanced at Rusk, who nodded reluctantly. "I'd prefer no planes," the Secretary of State said, "but I'll buy into six."

The people gathered around the table started shooting questions at Bissell. Was the Cuban brigade motivated? Was its leadership up to the challenge? Had the Company's people in Miami cobbled together a credible provisional government? How much evidence was there to support the idea that large segments of Castro's army would refuse to fight? That the peasants would flock to join the freedom fighters?

Bissell handled the concerns with a combination of gravity and cool confidence. The brigade was motivated and straining at the leash. When the moment of truth came the provisional government in Miami would pass muster. The latest CIA intelligence report—CS-dash-three-slant-four-seven-zero—that had been distributed earlier in the morning showed that Castro was losing popularity steadily: sabotage was frequent, church attendance was at record highs and could be taken as a benchmark of opposition to the regime. Disenchantment of the peasants had spread to all the regions of Cuba. Castro's government ministries and regular army had been penetrated by opposition groups that could be counted on to muddy the waters when the actual landing took place.

From the far end of the table, Paul Nitze, Kennedy's Assistant Secretary of Defense for International Security Affairs, asked what would happen to the brigade if the invasion was called off. Kennedy caught Dulles's eye and smiled grimly. Bissell admitted that the Company would have a disposal problem. The 1,500 members of the brigade couldn't be brought back to Miami; they would have to be dumped somewhere out of sight of the American press.

"If we're going to dump them," Kennedy remarked with sour fatality, "there's something to be said for dumping them in Cuba."

At the last minute the President had invited Senator Fulbright to join the briefing; Fulbright had gotten wind of JMARC and had sent Kennedy a long private memorandum outlining why he was dead set against the operation. Now Kennedy turned to the Senator, who was sitting next to him, and asked what he thought. Fulbright's mastery of foreign affairs won respect even from those who disagreed with him. He sat back in his chair and eyed Bissell across the table. "As I understand your strategy, Mr. Bissell, your brigade is supposed to break out of the beachhead and march on Havana, with supporters swelling its ranks as it goes."

Bissell nodded warily; he wasn't at all pleased to discover that Fulbright was a member of the President's inner circle when it came to the Cuban project.

Fulbright favored the DD/O with a wan smile. "Sounds like the game plan for Napoleon's return from Elba in 1815."

"Napoleon started out with fifteen hundred men also," Bissell shot back. "When he reached Paris he had an army."

"It only lasted a hundred days," Fulbright noted. He turned to the President. "Forgetting for a moment whether this adventure can or will succeed, let me raise another aspect of the problem, namely that the invasion of Cuba clearly violates several treaties, as well as American law. I'm talking about Title 18, US code, Sections 958 through 962, I'm talking about Title 50, Appendix, Section 2021, which specifically prohibits the enlistment or recruitment for foreign military service in the United States, the preparation of foreign military expeditions, the outfitting of foreign naval vessels for service against a country with which we are not at war."

Rusk waved a hand. "In my view success is self-legitimizing. It legitimized Castro when he seized power. It legitimized the founding fathers of this country when they rebelled against British rule. I've always taken it for granted that Jefferson and Washington would have been hanged as traitors if the revolution had failed."

Fulbright shook his head angrily. "The United States is forever condemning Moscow for meddling in the internal affairs of sovereign countries, Mr. President. Intervention in Cuba will open the door to Soviet intervention anywhere in the world—"

Dulles said, "The Soviets are already intervening anywhere in the world, Senator."

Fulbright didn't back off. "If we go ahead with this, if we invade Cuba, we won't have a leg to stand on when we condemn them."

"You're forgetting that the operation is going to look indigenous," Bissell remarked.

Fulbright fixed him with an intense gaze. "No matter how Cuban the operation is made to appear, everyone on the planet is going to hold the United States—hold the Kennedy administration—accountable for it." The Senator turned back to the President. "If Cuba is really so dangerous to the national interest we ought to declare war and send in the Marines."

Kennedy said, "I'd like to go around the room—I'd like to see what everyone thinks."

He looked to his right at Adolf Berle, the State Department's Latin-American specialist. Berle, an old Liberal warhorse who had served under Franklin Roosevelt, began weighing the pros and cons. Kennedy cut him short. "Adolf, you haven't voted. Yes or no?"

Berle declared, "I say, let 'er rip, Mr. President!"

Rusk, who had been in on the planning of guerrilla operations in the China-Burma theater during World War II, wasn't convinced that the Company's operation would succeed but he felt that the Secretary of State had to close ranks behind his President, and he did so now with a lukewarm endorsement of the operation. Secretary of Defense Robert McNamara; National Security Adviser McGeorge Bundy; Bundy's deputy, Walt Rostow, all voted for JMARC. The Chairman of the Joint Chiefs, Lyman Lemnitzer, and the Chief of Naval Operations, Arleigh Burke, voiced reservations about whether the operation could be plausibly disavowed; when pressed, both conceded that the CIA and the President were better judges of this aspect than the military chiefs. Nitze said he thought the chances of success were fifty-fifty, but Bissell had made a convincing case that the Cuban people would join the freedom fighters, which prompted him to come down on the side of the project.

Kennedy glanced at his wristwatch. "Look, I know everyone is grabbing their nuts over this." He turned to Bissell. "Do you know Jack Benny's line when a mugger sticks a gun in his stomach and demands, 'Your money or your life?'" Bissell looked blank. "When Benny doesn't answer," Kennedy went on, "the mugger repeats the question. 'I said, your money or your life?' At which point Benny says, 'I'm thinking about it.'"

Nobody in the room so much as cracked a smile. The President nodded heavily. "I'm thinking about it. What's the time frame for my decision?"

"The ships put to sea from Guatemala on D-minus-six, Mr. President. The latest we can shut things down is noon on Sunday, D-minus-one."

Jack Kennedy's eyes narrowed and focused on a distant thought; in a room crowded with people he suddenly looked as if he were completely alone. "Noon," he repeated. "Sixteen April."

The Mosquito Coast was little more than a memory on the horizon astern as the five dilapidated freighters, half a day out of Puerto Cabezas, Nicaragua, steamed north in a line, one ship plodding through the silvery-gray wake of another, toward the island of Cuba. Sitting on the main deck of the lead ship, the *Río Escondido*, his back propped against a tire of the communications van, Jack McAuliffe caught a glimpse through binoculars of the distinctive bed-spring airsearch radar antenna atop the mast of an American destroyer, hull down off to starboard. The aircraft carrier *Essex*, loaded with AD-4 Skyhawk jet fighters, would be out there beyond the escorting destroyers. It was reassuring to think the US Navy was just over the horizon, shadowing the dilapidated freighters and the 1,453 Cuban freedom fighters crowded onto them. Overhead, on the flying bridge, a merchant officer was lining up the mirrors of his sextant on the first planet to appear in the evening sky. Around the deck, amid the drums of aviation fuel lashed with rusting steel belts to the deck, the hundred and eighty men of the sixth battalion of La Brigada lay around on sleeping sacks or army blankets. Some of them listened to Spanish music on a portable radio, others played cards, still others cleaned and oiled their weapons.

"D-day minus six," Roberto Escalona said, settling down next to Jack. "So far, so good, pal."

Up on the fo'c's'le forward of the foremast, some of the Cubans were lobbing empty number ten cans into the water and blasting away at them with Browning automatic rifles or M-3 submachine guns. Shrieks of pleasure floated back whenever someone hit one of the targets. From a distance the Cubans looked like kids trying their luck at the rifle range of a county fair, not warriors headed into what the brigade priest had called, in the evening prayer, the valley of the shadow of death.

"D-minus-six," Jack agreed. "So far, so bad."

"What's your problem, *hombre?*"

Shaking his head in disgust, Jack looked around. "The logistics, for starters, Roberto—logistically, this operation is a keg of gunpowder waiting to explode. When's the last time you heard of a troop ship going into combat crammed with a thousand tons of ammunition below decks and two hundred drums of aviation fuel on the main deck?"

"We've been over this a hundred times," Roberto said. "Castro has only sixteen operational warplanes. Our B-26s are going to destroy them on the ground long before we hit the beaches."

"They might miss one or two," Jack said. "Or Castro might have stashed a few more planes away for a rainy day."

Roberto groaned in exasperation. "We'll have an air umbrella over the *Bahia de Cochinos*," he said. "Any of Castro's planes that survive the initial strikes will be shot out of the skies by carrier jets flown by pilots who don't speak a word of Spanish."

"You still think Kennedy's going to unleash the Navy if things heat up," Jack said.

Roberto clenched his fingers into a fist and brought it to his heart. "I believe in America, Jack. If I didn't I wouldn't be leading my people into combat."

"I believe in America, too, Roberto, but America hasn't told me how we're supposed to wrestle four-hundred-pound drums of gasoline off the ship and onto the beach. If we don't get them ashore, our B-26s won't be able to operate from the Bay of Pigs strip after you capture it."

Roberto only smiled. "When my kids get a whiff of victory in their nostrils they'll move mountains."

"Forget about moving mountains," Jack said. "I'll settle for drums of gasoline."

One of the mess boys made his way forward carrying a wooden tray filled with tumblers of *Anejo*, a distilled rum that was taken with coffee in

Cuba but sipped neat on the *Río Escondido* because the electric coffee machine in the galley had broken down. Roberto clanked glasses with Jack and tossed back some of the rum. "Did you get to speak with your wife before we left?" he asked.

"Yeah. The loading master at Puerto Cabaezas let me use his phone. I got through to her right before we put to sea."

Jack turned away and grinned at the memory: "Oh, Jack, is that really you? I can't believe my goddamn ears," Millie had cried into the telephone. "Where are you calling from?"

"This isn't a secure line, Millie," Jack had warned.

"Oh, Christ, forget I asked. Anyhow, I know where you are. Everyone in the shop knows where you are. Everyone knows what you're doing, too."

"I'm sorry to hear that," Jack had said, and he had meant it. He had heard scuttlebutt about the *New York Times* story on the CIA's operation in Guatemala. "How's my boy? How's Anthony?"

"He's only incredible, honey. He celebrated his eight-month birthday yesterday by standing up all by himself for the first time. Then he fell down all by himself, too. But he didn't cry, Jack. He picked himself up all over again. Oh, honey, I just know the first words out of his mouth's going to be your family motto—*once down is no battle!*"

"What about you, sweetheart? You hanging in there?"

The phone had gone silent for a moment. Jack could hear Millie breathing on the other end of the line. "I'm surviving," she had finally said. "I miss you, Jack. I miss your warm body next to mine in bed. I miss the tickle of your mustache. I get horny remembering the time you touched the hem of my skirt back in Vienna..."

Jack had laughed. "Jesus H. Christ, if this were a secure line I'd tell you what I miss."

"Screw the line, tell me anyhow," Millie had pleaded.

The loading master had pointed to the *Río Escondido* tied to the pier. Through the grimy office window Jack could see the sailors singling up the heavy mooring lines. "I've got to go, sweetheart," Jack had said. "Give Anthony a big kiss from his old dad. With luck, I ought to be home soon."

Millie had sounded subdued. "Come home when you can, Jack. Just as long as you come home safe and sound. I couldn't bear it if—"

"Nothing's going to happen to me."

"I love you, Jack."

"Me, too. I love you, too, Millie." He had listened to her breathing a moment longer, then had gently placed the receiver back on its cradle.

"There's something I've been wanting to ask you, *hombre*," Roberto was saying now.

"What's stopping you?"

"I know why I'm here. I know why they're here," he said, waving toward the Cubans sprawled around the deck. "I don't know what you're doing here, Jack."

"I'm here because I was ordered to come out and hold your hand, Roberto."

"That's horseshit and you know it. I heard you volunteered."

"This is a hot assignment for a young officer looking for a promotion."

"More horseshit, *hombre*."

The shooting on the fo'c's'le had stopped. Darkness had fallen abruptly, as it does in the Caribbean. Stars were still-dancing over the tips of the swaying masts. The bow wave, filled with phosphorescent seaweed, washed down the sides of the ancient hull. Jack polished off his rum. "In the beginning," he told Roberto, "it was inertia. I was in motion—been in motion since they sent me off to Berlin ten years ago. And a body in motion tends to continue in motion. Then it was curiosity, I suppose. Where I come from you're brought up to test yourself." He thought of Anthony. "You climb to your feet, you fall down, you climb to your feet again. It's only by testing yourself that you discover yourself."

"So what have you discovered?"

"A center, a bedrock, a cornerstone, the heart of the heart of the matter. On one level I'm the son of an Irish immigrant buying into America. But that's only part of the story. I came down here hoping to find the beginning of an answer to the eternal question of what life is all about. To give it a name, Roberto, I guess what I discovered was something worth rowing for besides speed."

Dick Bissell's Cuba war room on the ground floor of Quarters Eye had been transformed for what one Company clown had billed as a *pre*mortem autopsy on the cadaver known as JMARC, the last global review scheduled before the Cuban freedom fighters hit the beaches. Fifty or so folding chairs had been set up in semicircular rows facing a lectern. Folding metal tables off to one side were filled with sandwiches, soft drinks and electric coffee urns. There was a handwritten sign posted on the inside of the door advising participants that they could make notes for the purposes of discussion, but they were obliged to deposit them in the burn bin when they left the room. Dick Bissell, his shirtsleeves rolled up, his tie hanging loose around his neck, had been talking nonstop for one and a quarter hours. Now, turning to the wall behind him, he tapped the grease pencil marks on the plastic overlay to bring everyone up to date on the progress of the five freighters ferrying Brigade 2506 toward the beaches designated Blue and Red at the Bay of Pigs. "We're at D-minus-three and counting," he said. "Planes from the *Essex*, patrolling the airspace between Cuba and the invasion fleet, have seen no indication of increased air or sea activity on the part of Castro's forces. We haven't stepped up the U-2 overflights for the obvious reason that we don't want to alert Castro. The single overflight on D-minus-four showed no unusual activity either."

A Marine colonel sheepdipped to JMARC said from the front row, "Dick, the communications people on Swan Island did pick up a sharp increase in coded traffic between Point One and several militia units on the island. And the Pentagon is reporting more radio traffic than usual between the Soviet embassy in Havana and Moscow."

Leo raised a finger. "There's also that report from the Cuban government in exile in Miami about the two Cuban militiamen who fled in a fishing boat to Florida last night—the militiamen, from the 312th Militia Battalion stationed on the Isle of Pines, reported that all leaves have been cancelled until further notice."

Bissell took a sip of water, then said, "So far we've been unable to confirm the report from the militiamen, nor is there evidence of leaves being cancelled anywhere else in Cuba. As for the increase in Cuban military traffic, I want to remind you all that we've known since late February that the Cuban General Staff was planning to call a surprise alert sometime in late March or early April to test the readiness of the militia to respond to an emergency situation. The alert even had a code name—"

Leo said, "The Cubans were calling it Operation Culebras."

"That's it," Bissell said. "*Culebras*. Snakes."

"Which leaves the Russian traffic," Ebby noted from the second row.

Bissell worked a cap on and off of a fountain pen. "If you take the traffic between any given Soviet embassy in the world and Moscow, you'll see that it fluctuates from week to week and month to month. So I don't see what conclusions we can draw from an increase in Russian diplomatic traffic. For all we know, a Russian code clerk in the Havana embassy could be having a hot love affair with a code clerk in Moscow."

"That's not very convincing," Ebby muttered.

Bissell stared hard at him. "How would you read these particular tea leaves, Eb?"

Ebby looked up from some notes he had jotted on a scrap of paper. "It's the nature of the beast that every morsel of intelligence can have several interpretations. Still, every time we see a detail that would appear to warn us off JMARC, we somehow manage to explain it away."

And there it was, out in the open for everyone to see: the visceral misgivings of one of the Company's most respected middle-level officers, a veteran of the CIA's unsuccessful efforts to infiltrate agents behind the Iron Curtain in the early fifties, a holder of the Distinguished Intelligence Medal for his exploits in Budapest in 1956. The room turned still—so still that it was possible to hear a woman in the back scratching away on a cuticle with a nail file. Bissell said, very quietly, "Your *every time we see a detail* covers an awful lot of territory, Eb. Are you suggesting that we're institutionally incapable of criticizing an operation?"

"I guess I am, Dick. I guess I'm saying it is an institutional problem— the Company has the action in Cuba, so it has become the advocate, as opposed to the critic, of the action it has. What criticism I've seen always seems to be confined to this or that detail, never to whether the operation itself is flawed."

"D-minus-three seems to me to be pretty late in the game for second thoughts."

"I've had second thoughts all along. I did raise the problem of our losing the so-called guerrilla option when we switched the landing site from Trinidad to the Bay of Pigs. When I was brought in on the logistics end of the operation, I wrote a paper suggesting that the obsession with being able to plausibly deny an American role in the invasion had adversely influenced the choice of materiel—we are using old, slow cargo ships with limited storage space below decks, we are using antiquated B-26 bombers flying from air bases in Central America instead of southern Florida, giving them less time over target." Ebby, tormented by the possibility that the Company was treating the Cubans freedom fighters the way it had treated the Hungarians five years before, shut his eyes and massaged the lids with the thumb and third finger of his right hand. "Maybe I should have raised these points more forcefully—"

Bissell swatted at the air with a palm as if he were being strafed by an insect. "If those are your only objections—"

Ebby bristled. "They're not my only objections, not by a long shot—"

"Mr. Ebbitt seems to forget that we pulled off this kind of operation in Guatemala," a young woman working on the propaganda team commented from the back row.

Ebby was growing angrier by the second. "There's been nothing but repression in Guatemala since we got rid of Arbenz," he said, twisting around in his seat. "Ask the Mayan *campesinos* if we succeeded. Ask them if—"

Bissell tried to calm things down. "Okay, Eb. That's what we're here for. Let's hear your objections."

"For starters," Ebby began, "it's an open question whether the so-called Guatemala model will work in Cuba. Castro won't scare off the way Arbenz did in Guatemala simply because we land a brigade of émigrés on one of his beaches. He's made of sterner stuff. Look at his track record. He and a handful of guerrilla fighters sailed to Cuba on a small yacht, took to the mountains and survived everything Batista could throw at them, and finally walked into Havana when Batista lost his nerve and ran for it. Today Castro is thirty-two years old, a confident and vigorous man on the top of his game, with zealous supporters in the military and civilian infrastructure."

Ebby pushed himself to his feet and walked around to one of the tables and drew himself a cup of coffee. Behind him, nobody uttered a word. He dropped two lumps of sugar into the cup and stirred it with a plastic spoon as he turned back to face Bissell. "Look at the whole thing from another angle, Dick. Even if the invasion does succeed, the whole world will see this for what it is: a CIA operation from start to finish. The fact of the matter is that JMARC is likely to cripple the Company for years to come. We're supposed to steal secrets and then analyze the bejesus out of them. Period. Using the Company to do covertly what the government doesn't have the balls to do overtly is going to make it harder for us to collect intelligence. What business do we have mounting an amphibious invasion of a country because the Kennedys are pissed at the guy who runs it? We have an Army and a Navy and the Marines and an Air Force— they're supposed to handle things like invasions." Ebby opened his mouth to say something else, then, shrugging, gave up.

At the lectern, Bissell had been toying with his wedding ring, slipping it up and back on his finger until the skin was raw. "Whoever called this a *pre*mortem certainly knew what he was talking about," he said uneasily. Nervous laughter rippled through the war room. "Anyone who assumes that we haven't agonized over the points Ebbitt raised would be selling us short. What you're saying, Eb—what we've said to ourselves so many times the words ring in my brain like a broken record—is that there are risks no matter what we do. There are risks in not taking risks. Risks in moving the invasion site to the more remote Bay of Pigs. Risks in using obsolete B-26s instead of Skyhawks. Risks in calculating how the Cuban people and the Cuban Army will respond to the landings. Our job up on the top floor is to calculate these risks and then weigh them against the downside. Which, believe me, is what we've done." Bissell's voice was hoarse and fading fast. He took another gulp of water. Then he straightened his stooped shoulders as if he were a soldier on a parade ground. "Let me be clear—I believe in the use of power, when it's available, for purposes that I regard as legitimate. Ridding the hemisphere of Castro, freeing the Cuban people from the oppression of Communism, is clearly legitimate. So we'll go forward, gentlemen and ladies, and win this little war of ours ninety miles from the coast of Florida."

The Marine colonel hammered a fist into the air. A dozen or so people in the room actually applauded. Bissell, embarrassed, shuffled through his notes. "Now I want to say a word about the bogus coded messages we're going to broadcast from Swan Island..."

Later in the day, after the premortem, a number of old hands went out of their way to stop Ebby in the hallway and tell him that they shared some of his reservations on JMARC; they had gone along, they admitted, out of a kind of group-think that tended to confuse criticism with disloyalty. At one point Ebby ran across Tony Spink, his old boss from Frankfurt, in the men's room. Spink, who had been put in charge of air drops to anti-Castro guerrillas holed up in the mountains of Cuba, remarked that Bissell and the topsiders seemed so fucking sure of themselves, he'd begun to suspect there had to be an aspect of JMARC he didn't know about, something that would tilt the scales in favor of going ahead. What are we talking about? Ebby wondered; what could tilt the scales, in your opinion? Maybe Kennedy has quietly signalled Bissell that he's ready to send in American forces if it looked as if Castro was getting the upper hand. Ebby thought about this for a moment. Bissell may be *calculating* that Kennedy, faced with defeat, will relent and send in the Skyhawks, Ebby said. But if this is what Bissell was thinking he was deluding himself; why would Kennedy go to all the trouble and expense of unleashing a *covert* operation if, in the end, he planned to bail it out with *overt* intervention? It just didn't make sense. You've got to be right, Spink said. It had to be something else, something such as...Spink, who was nearing retirement age and looking forward to returning to civilian life, screwed up his face. Didn't you work for Torriti in Berlin before you came to Frankfurt Station? he asked. Yes I did, Ebby acknowledged, I worked for him until something I said about his alcohol consumption got back to him. So what's the Sorcerer doing here in Washington? Spink asked. And he answered his own question: he's running something called Staff D, which is supposed to be dealing with communications intercepts. Ebby got his point. The Sorcerer wasn't a communications maven, he said. Spink nodded in agreement. He was liaising with the Mafia on Sicily at the end of the war, Spink remembered.

It dawned on Ebby what his friend was driving at. He smiled grimly. No, he said. It's just not possible. Even Bissell wouldn't do that. Can you imagine the stink if it ever leaked. No.

Spink raised his eyebrows knowingly. Maybe.

No. No.

But the idea was planted in Ebby's head and he couldn't dislodge it.

Returning near midnight to the small house he and Elizabet rented in Arlington, Ebby found his wife sitting on the couch in the living room, one weak bulb burning in a lamp, her legs tucked under her, a Scotch in one hand, the half-empty bottle on the floor. "Elliott, my sweet love, you are not going to believe what happened to me today," Elizabet announced.

Ebby threw off his suit jacket and sank wearily onto the couch next to her; she stretched out with her head on his thigh. "Try me," he said.

"The school phoned me up at State late this afternoon," she began. "Nellie was at it again. She was caught fighting with a boy. This one was a year older and a head taller but that didn't faze her. I found her in the infirmary with wads of cotton stuffed in her nostrils to stop the bleeding. The principal warned me the next time she picked a fight they would treat her like a juvenile delinquent and call in the police. Parents were starting to complain, he said. My God, Elliott, the way he talked about her you would have thought Nellie was a hardened criminal." Elizabet laughed nervously. "She'll be the first eleven-year-old to make it onto the FBI's ten most wanted list. Naturally, Nellie's version of the fight was different from the principal's. She said the boy, whose name was William, had been teasing her because she spoke English with an accent. When she said she came from Hungary and spoke Hungarian to prove it, he announced to everyone within earshot that she was a dirty Communist. At which point Nellie socked him in the face. Which is when this William, bleeding from a cut lip, punched her in the nose. I have to admit, the first time this sort of thing happened I thought it was rather funny but I've stopped laughing, Elliott. What am I going to do with her? She can't go through life socking someone every time she gets pissed at him, can she?"

Ebby said grimly, "I don't see why not. That's how our government operates."

The cold fury in his voice made Elizabet sit up. She scrutinized what she could see of his face in the shadows of the living room. "Elliott, my love, I'm sorry—something's very wrong, and here I've been carrying on about Nellie. What's happening? What's happened?"

Ebby let his fingers drift from her waist to the breast that had been injured in prison. She pressed her palm over the back of his hand, validating the complicity between them.

After a moment she said, very softly, "Want to tell me about it?"

"Can't."

"Another of your goddamned secrets?"

He didn't say anything.

"How serious is it?"

"The people I work for are involved in something that's going to blow up in their faces. I don't want to be part of it. I've decided to resign from the Company. I've already written the letter. I would have given it to Dulles today but he'd gone by the time I got over to his office. I'm going to put the letter in his hands tomorrow morning."

"You ought to sleep on it, Elliott."

"Sleeping on it isn't going to change anything. I have to resign in protest against what they're doing. When the word gets around maybe others will do the same thing. Maybe, just maybe, we can head Bissell off—"

"So it's Bissell?"

"I shouldn't have said that."

"As usual, I don't have a need to know."

"You're a Company wife, Elizabet. You know the rules."

Elizabet was not put off. "If it's Bissell that means we're talking about Cuba. Those Cubans who have been training in Guatemala are going to be turned loose. Oh my God, they're going to invade Cuba!" Elizabet immediately thought of the Hungarian revolution. "Is Kennedy going to order American planes to protect them?"

"Bissell's probably counting on it. He thinks he can force Kennedy's hand."

"What do you think?"

"I think...I think it's liable to be Hungary all over again. People are going to climb out on a limb, then the limb will be cut off and they will be obliged to fend for themselves, and a lot of them are going to wind up very dead."

Elizabet folded herself into his arms and buried her lips in his neck. "Surely you can make them see the light—"

"They've told themselves over and over that it's going to work. If you repeat something often enough, it sounds possible. Repeat it some more and it begins to sound like a sure thing."

"You should still sleep on it, my love. Remember what you told Arpád at Kilian the day you voted in favor of surrendering to the Russians? You belong to the live-to-fight-another-day school. Who will speak out against things like this if you're not around?"

"What's the good of speaking out if nobody listens?"

"There's always somebody listening to the voice of sanity," Elizabet said. "If we don't hold on to that, we're really lost."

Sleeping on it, however, only reinforced Ebby's determination to resign in protest; he *had* lived to fight another day, and fought—and nothing seemed to change. The CIA was still sending friendly nationals off to fight its wars, and watching from the safety of Fortress America to see how many would survive. At ten in the morning Ebby strode past two secretaries and a security guard and pushed through a partly open door into Dulles's spacious corner office. The Director, looking more drawn than Ebby remembered, sat hunched over his desk, studying a profile on him that was going to appear in the *New York Times Magazine.* "Ebbitt," he said, looking up, making no effort to hide his irritation; only the several Deputy Directors and the head of counterintelligence, Jim Angleton, had no-knock access to the DCI's sacristy. "To what do I owe the pleasure?"

"Director, I wanted to deliver this to you personally," Ebby said, and he dropped an envelope on the DCI's blotter.

"What is it?"

"My resignation."

Dulles pulled the paper from the envelope and read through it quickly. He folded the letter back into the envelope and tapped it on the desk impatiently. "You serve at the pleasure of the DCI," Dulles said with a scowl. "I refuse to accept your resignation. And I don't appreciate people abandoning ship just when we're going into battle."

"I don't deserve that—" Ebby started to say.

The red phone on Dulles's desk rang. He picked it up and listened for a moment before exploding, "He wants to what?" He listened again. "Tell Hunt that's out of the question," he said gruffly. "The Provisional Government will hold a press conference when we tell them to, and not a minute sooner. Until then we'll stick to the scenario we worked out...That's correct. Hunt will release bulletins in their name."

Dulles dropped the phone back on the hook and looked up at his uninvited visitor. "There are two possibilities, Ebbitt. Possibility number one:

This thing is going to succeed, in which case your resignation will look awfully stupid. Possibility number two: This thing is going to fail. If it fails Kennedy's not going to blame Eisenhower for starting JMARC up, or himself for switching the landing site to the Bay of Pigs because Trinidad seemed too noisy. Kennedy is going to blame the CIA, and that's as it should be. When things go wrong someone has to take the fall. And that someone cannot be the President or the institution of the Presidency. So I'll be washed up, which is right and proper. Dick Bissell will be finished, too. The press will howl for the Company's hide. Congress will form killer committees to investigate where we went wrong; the fact that we went wrong trying to combat Communism in this hemisphere and abroad will get lost in the shuffle. If JMARC is a debacle the Company will need people like you to pick up the pieces, to save what can be saved, to get on with the always tedious and often dangerous business of defending the country. God help the United States of America if the Central Intelligence Agency is gutted at the height of this Cold War. America needs a first line of defense, however imperfect it turns out to be. Are you following me, Ebbitt?"

"I'm hanging on your words, Director."

"Fine. Don't let go of them." He thrust the envelope back at Ebby. "Now get the hell out of my office and go back to work."

"I love nothing better, believe me, but it's simply not possible."

The woman's voice on the other end of the phone line said, "It used to be possible."

"You have to understand," Jack Kennedy insisted. "We just can't be together as often as we'd both like. Especially here. This place is a goldfish bowl. Hold on a second, will you?" He must have covered the phone with a hand because his words were muffled. She thought she heard him say, "Tell him I can't come to the phone just now. Tell him I'll have to think about it. Then get Bobby over here. Make sure he understands it's important." The man's voice came across loud and clear again. "You still there?"

"I'm always here, your handy doormat—"

"That's not fair and you know it."

"How's your back?"

"Quiet for the moment. Jacobson came up from New York the day before yesterday and gave me one of his feel-good shots."

"I worry about you. I worry about whether you should be taking all those amphetamine injections."

"Jacobson's a bona fide doctor. He knows what he's doing. Listen, I have to go to New York on Saturday for a fund-raiser."

"Is your wife going with you?"

"She hates these political road shows. She's decided to take the children up to Hyannisport to spend the weekend with my parents."

"Any chance of me coming to New York?"

"You took the words out of my mouth, Judy. I'll have a room booked for you in the Carlyle under your maiden name."

"What time does the fund-raiser finish up?"

"Around eleven-thirty."

"By midnight the last thing on your mind will be your backache."

"Just thinking about your coming to New York takes my mind off my backache." He cleared his throat. "Sal around?"

"He's in the living room."

"He alone?"

"Sal's never alone. He's got what the hoi polloi calls an entourage."

"Could you get him to come to the phone? Don't say who's calling in front of the others."

"I wasn't born yesterday. Hold on, huh? See you Saturday."

After a while a door could be heard slamming and the footsteps of a heavy man could be heard approaching.

"So what's duh good word?"

"How are things, Sal?"

"I can't complain. How's with you, Jack?"

"I'm all right. What's the weather like in Chicago?"

"Windy, like always. If I didn't have business interests here I'd move to Vegas in uh minute. I'm goin' there next weekend—duh Canary'll be in town. Frank'd be tickled pink to see you. Why don't you drop what you're doin' an' join us?"

"What with one thing or another I don't have much time for friends these days. But I haven't forgotten who my friends are. You get the satchel, Sal?"

"Judy gave it to me soon as she got off duh train. Thanks, Jack."

"Listen, Sal, what's happening with that little matter you were involved in?"

"You mean duh business duh fat man asked me to take care of?"

Jack was confused. "What fat man?"

Sal laughed. "Duh one dat talks Sicilian. Duh one dat drinks without never gettin' drunk. I wish I knew how duh fuck he does it."

The penny dropped. "I see whom you're talking about now."

"I thought you would. So about dat little matter—it's in duh bag, Jack."

"You're sure? I've got decisions to make. A lot depends on that."

"What's dat mean, *am I sure?* There's only two things sure, pal, death an' taxes." Sal let out a belly laugh. "Hey, no kiddin' aside, Jack, it's buttoned up."

"For when is it?"

"For anytime now."

"I don't need to hedge my bets?"

Sal sounded insulted. "Jack, Jack, would I lead you down duh garden path on somethin' like dis?"

"There's a lot at stake."

"There's always uh lot at stake, Jack. Everywhere. All duh time."

"All right."

"Awright. So did you catch what duh fuckin' Russians did duh other day, puttin' dat cosmonaut character Gagarin into orbit?"

Jack commented wryly, "There are people here who keep me up to date on things like that, Sal."

"I dunno...you seem to be takin' dis pretty calmly. I would've thought us Americans would've creamed duh Russians when it comes to things like sendin' rockets around duh earth. Now it's us with egg on our kisser."

"You take care of that business we spoke about, Sal, it'll be Khrushchev who'll wind up with egg on his face."

"Awright. So what's dis I hear about your brother being out to screw Hoffa."

"Where'd you pick that up?"

"Uh little bird whispered in my ear. Listen up, Jack, I don't give uh shit what he does to Hoffa, long as he sticks to duh deal your father an' me worked out. Your brother can fuck with Detroit till he's blue in duh balls. Chicago is off-limits."

"Don't lose sleep over Bobby, Sal."

"I'm glad to hear I don't need to lose sleep over your kid brother. I'm relieved, Jack. No shit."

Jack laughed pleasantly. "Say hello to Frank for me when you see him."

"Sure I will. You want to talk to Judy some more?"

"No. I'm pretty busy. Take it easy, Sal."

"Yeah, I will. I always take it easy. Dat's what I do best. You take it easy, too, Jack."

"So long, Sal."

"Yeah. Sure thing. So long."

Arturo Padrón pedaled his heavy Chinese "Flying Pigeon" through the seedy back streets of downtown Havana, then turned onto the road behind the Libre Hotel where rich Cubans used to live before Castro hit town. Nowadays the houses, set back from the street and looking like wrecked hulks that had washed up on a shore, were filled with squatters who simply moved on when the roofs collapsed. The wraparound porches sagged into the tangled worts and bindweeds of the cat-infested gardens. At the rear of the once-fashionable hotel, Padrón, a middle-aged man who wore his thinning hair long over his oversized ears, double-chained his bicycle to a rusty iron fence, then walked through the employees' entrance and down a long flight of steps to the locker room. He opened the locker and quickly changed into the tan uniform and black shoes with "Made in China" stamped in English on the inside of the tongues. The shoes were too tight and squeaked when he walked, and he had been promised a new pair when the next shipment arrived. He tied his black bow tie as he made his way upstairs to the sprawling kitchen off the hotel's cafeteria. Pushing through the double swinging door into the kitchen, he called a greeting to the four short-order cooks who were sweating over the bank of gas stoves. One of them, an old man who had worked at the Libre when it was called the Havana Hilton, looked hard at Padrón as if he were trying to convey a message. Then the old man gestured with his chin toward the door of the manager's office. Padrón thrust out both of his palms, as if to ask, *What are you trying to tell me?* just as the door to the office opened and two policemen wearing green Interior Ministry uniforms motioned for him to come in. For an instant Padrón thought of running for it. Glancing over his shoulder, he saw two more Interior Ministry police push through the double door into the kitchen behind him; both had opened holster flaps and rested their palms on the butts of revolvers. Padrón forced a smirk of utter innocence onto his long mournful face and sauntered past the two policemen into the office. He heard the door close behind him. An elegantly dressed man with a neatly trimmed reddish beard stood behind the manager's desk.

"Padrón, Arturo?" he asked.

Padrón blotted a bead of perspiration on his forehead with the back of his wrist. "It's me, Padrón, Arturo."

"You have a cousin named Jesús who owns a thirty-two foot Chris Craft cabin cruiser with twin gas engines, which he keeps tied up in the port of Cojímar. For a price he has been known to run Cubans to Miami."

Padrón experienced a sharp pain in the chest, a sudden shortness of breath. He had seen photographs of the man behind the desk in the newspapers. It was none other than Manuel Piñeiro, the head of the regime's secret police. "My cousin, he has a boat, *señor*," he said. "What he does with it is not known to me."

Piñeiro crooked a forefinger and Padrón, prodded forward by one of the policemen, his shoes squeaking with each step, approached the desk. "Your cousin Jesús has admitted that he was instructed to keep the gas tank of his boat and spare jerry cans filled; that he was to remain next to his telephone every evening this week waiting for a signal. When a caller quoted a certain sentence from Corinthians—'For if the trumpet give an uncertain sound, who shall prepare to the battle?'—he was to immediately put to sea and pick you up on the beach of Miramar, minutes from here by bicycle. He was then instructed to run you across to Miami. For this he was to be paid twelve thousand five hundred American dollars."

By now the blood had literally drained from Padrón's face.

"I am not a religious man," Piñeiro continued, his head tilted to the side and back, his tone reassuringly amiable, "though in my youth, to gratify my grandparents, I was obliged to attend church services. I recall another sentence from the Holy Book, this one from the Gospel According to Saint Matthew: 'Woe unto that man by whom the Son of man is betrayed! It had been good for that man if he had not been born.'" His tone turned hard. "Empty your pockets on the desk."

With shaky hands Padrón did as he was told. Piñeiro separated the items with the tips of his fingers: a pocketknife, some loose change, several sticks of chewing gum, a crumpled handkerchief, some toothpicks, a depleted roll of dental floss, two lumps of sugar wrapped in the cafeteria's distinctive brown paper, an unopened pack of Russian cigarettes, a book of matches, a wristwatch without a strap, a lottery ticket, two small keys fitting the locks securing the "Flying Pigeon" to the iron fence behind the hotel, a half-empty bottle of Bayer aspirins, a frayed photograph of a child in a crib and another of a woman with listless eyes attempting to find a smile for the camera, an internal identity card with a photograph of a younger and thinner Padrón peeling away from the pasteboard. "I will now pose several questions," Piñeiro informed the waiter, who was gnawing on his lower lip. "One: How much were you to be paid for the assassination of Fidel Castro?"

"I know nothing of this," the waiter breathed. "I swear it on the tomb of my mother. I swear it on the head of my son."

"Two: Who gave you your orders?"

"I received no orders—"

"Three: Who else in Havana is in on the plot?"

"As God is my witness there is no plot."

Piñeiro greeted the denials with a bemused smile. Using the back of a finger, the chief of the secret police separated the bottle of aspirin from the rest of the pile. Then he unscrewed the lid and spilled the tablets onto the desk. Bending over the pills, he opened Padrón's pocketknife and used the blade to sort through them. At first he was unable to detect any difference between them. He glanced up and saw the terror that had installed itself in the waiter's eyes and began again, examining the pills one by one. Suddenly Piñeiro's mouth opened and the words "So that's it!" escaped his lips. He pushed one of the pills off to the side, then a second, then a third. Then he straightened and, looking the waiter in the eye, said, "It will be good for you if you had not been born."

Padrón understood that it was a sentence worse than death.

Piñeiro signalled for the two policemen to advance. As they started forward, Padrón's hand shot out and he snatched one of the aspirins and turning and crouching, shoved it into his mouth and with a sob bit down hard on it. The two policemen lunged for him, seizing his arms as his body went limp. They held him up for a moment, then lowered the dead weight to the floor and looked at their chief, fearful that he would blame them.

Piñeiro cleared his throat. "It saves us the trouble of executing him," he remarked.

His garish silk tie askew and stained with Scotch, his shirt unchanged in days and gray under the collar, his reading glasses almost opaque with grime and sliding down his nose, the Sorcerer leaned over the United Press ticker installed in a corner of the war room, monitoring the bulletins slipping through his fingers. "Anything coming out of Havana?" Dick Bissell called from the cockpit, the command-and-control well facing the plastic overlays filled with up-to-date tactical information. On the giant map, the five freighters carrying Brigade 2506 had inched to within spitting distance of the Cuban coast. The two American destroyers that would guide the invasion force into the Bay of Pigs that night, assuming the President didn't call off the operation, were just over the horizon. Two CIA Landing Ship Docks—filled with the smaller LCUs and LCVPs that would swim out of the LSDs and ferry the invaders to the beaches—were closing in on the rendezvous point off the coast.

"The usual weekend bullshit," Torriti called back. Stooping, he retrieved the bottle of mineral water filled with vodka and poured another shot onto the coffee grounds in his plastic cup. "There's one about the joys of deep sea fishing off Havana, another about a Cuban family that's been making cigars for five generations."

Bissell resumed his obsessive pacing, prowling back and forth between the water cooler against one wall and the easel on which all the operational codes

water cooler against one wall and the easel on which all the operational codes had been posted for fast reference. Other members of the war room team came and went as the morning dragged on. Topsiders appeared with last-minute glitches to be ironed out and cables to be initialed. Leo Kritzky brought over the press clippings on Cuba for the past twenty-four hours; Castro had delivered another of his marathon speeches, this one to the air raid wardens association in Havana, extolling the virtues of Socialism. Leo's secretary, Rosemary Hanks, turned up with a hamper of fresh sandwiches and a supply of toothbrushes and toothpaste for staffers who were sleeping over and had forgotten theirs. Allen Dulles checked in on a secure phone from time to time to see if Jack Kennedy had come through with the final go-ahead. The big clock on the wall ticked off the seconds with a maddening clatter; the minute hand seemed to emit a series of dull detonations as it climbed the rungs toward high noon, the deadline Bissell had given the President for calling off the invasion of Cuba.

JMARC had gotten off to a rotten start the day before when post-strike reports from the initial D-minus-two raids against Castro's three principal air bases started to filter through. The damage assessment photos, rushed over from the Pentagon after a U-2 overflight, confirmed that only five of Castro's aircraft had been destroyed on the ground; several Sea Furies and T-33 jet trainers appeared to have been hit, but the photo interpreters were unable to say whether they were still operational. And they could only guess at how many planes had been parked inside hangers or nearby barns and escaped altogether. To make matters worse, Adlai Stevenson, the American ambassador to the United Nations, was bitching to Rusk that he, Stevenson, had been made to seem a horse's ass; when the Russians raised a storm at the UN over the attack on Cuba, Stevenson had held aloft a wire service photograph of the two B-26s that had landed in Miami and had sworn that pilots defecting from Castro's air force, and not American-backed anti-Castro Cubans, had been responsible for the air strike. The cover story, which Stevenson (thanks to a vague CIA briefing) really believed, had quickly fallen apart when journalists noticed the tell-tale metal nose cones on the two B-26s in Miami and concluded the planes hadn't defected from Cuba after all; Castro's B-26s were known to have plastic noses. Stevenson, livid at being "deliberately tricked" by his own government, had vented his rage on Rusk. By Sunday morning shock waves from the affair were still reverberating through the administration.

Bissell's noon deadline came and went but the DD/O didn't seem alarmed, and for good reason: he had informed the President that the freighters would cross the line of no return at noon on Sunday, but he had built in a margin of error. The real deadline was four o'clock. Around the war, room people stared at the red phone sitting on a table in the command-and-control well as the clock batted away the seconds. Ebby and Leo poured coffee from one of the Pyrex pots warming on the hot plate and drifted into Leo's cubbyhole office off the war room. "I was ready to quit over this," Ebby confided to his friend, sinking into a wooden chair in near-exhaustion. "I actually delivered a letter of resignation to the Director."

"What happened?"

"He pretty much made the case that this wasn't the moment to abandon ship."

Leo shook his head. "I don't know, Ebby—JMARC could succeed."

"It would take a miracle."

Leo lowered his voice. "The news Bissell's waiting for from Havana—it could change the ball game."

Ebby sipped his coffee. "Doesn't it worry you, Leo—the United States of America, the most powerful nation on the face of the earth, trying to assassinate the bellicose leader of a small island-country because he's thumbing his nose at his Yankee neighbor? It's a classic case of the elephant swatting a mosquito, for Christ's sake."

Leo sniffed. "At my pay grade we don't deal in moral niceties."

"It doesn't seem as if moral niceties are the subject of conversation at any pay grade," Ebby griped.

Settling onto the edge of the desk, Leo absently poked through some papers with the tips his fingers. "Say that Castro survives," he said, talking to himself. "The operation could still succeed."

"Balls! The landing might succeed if we provide air cover. But then what? Castro and his brother, Raoul, and their buddy Che Guevara aren't about to opt for early retirement in Soviet Russia. If things turn against them they'll retreat into the Sierra Maestras and go guerrilla. Tito did the same thing against the Germans in the mountains of Yugoslavia, and he held out for years. With Castro in the mountains and a CIA-supported Provisional Government in Havana, there'll be a slow simmering civil war. Jesus, it could go on for ten, twenty years."

"I hope to hell you're wrong," Leo said.

"I'm terrified I'm right," Ebby said.

Outside in the war room the red telephone buzzed. Conversations ended abruptly as every head turned to stare at it. The Sorcerer abandoned the UP ticker and ambled over. Ebby and Leo rushed to the doorway. Controlling himself with an effort, Bissell, his shoulders hunched, walked slowly across the room to stand over the phone. He looked at it, then reached down and picked it up.

"Bissell," he said.

He listened for a long moment. Gradually his features relaxed. "Right, Mr. President," he said. "You bet," he said. "Thank you, Mr. President." Then he hung up and, grinning, turned to flash the thumbs-up sign to the staffers around the room.

"So what did he have to say?" Torriti asked.

"Why, he said, 'Go ahead.'" Bissell laughed. And then he swung into high gear. "All right, let's put the show on the road. Leo, pass the coded signal on to the *Essex* and to Jack McAuliffe on the lead freighter. Also get the word down to Swan Island so the propaganda machine starts humming. And get Hunt off his duff in Miami—I want those bulletins from the Provisional Government on the air as soon as the first Cubans hit the beaches. Gentlemen and ladies, we are about to breathe new life into the Monroe Doctrine."

And then everyone began talking at once. The war room churned with activity. For the first time in days the dull detonations from the minute hand stumbling across the face of the wall clock were inaudible. At the overlay of the giant map of the Caribbean, two young woman edged the five freighters closer to Cuba. Bissell, riding a second wind, huddled with several photo interpreters, going over the prints from the post-attack U-2 overflight, circling runways and hangars and fuel depots with a red pencil. Two generals from the Pentagon were called in for consultation in midafternoon. By late afternoon a revised target op order had been enciphered and dispatched to the CIA air base at Retalhuleu, where the brigade's B-26s would be loading up with bombs and ammunition for the crucial D-minus-one raid.

In the early evening, Bissell took a call from Rusk and the two chatted for several minutes about Adlai Stevenson. Bissell mentioned that they were gearing up for the all-important second strike. The phone line went silent. Then Rusk said, "Let me get back to you on that."

Bissell was startled. "What do you mean, get back to me?"

"I have a call in to the President at Glen Ora, where he's spending the weekend," Rusk explained. "There's been some discussion about whether the second strike is wise."

"It's already been authorized—"

"I'll call right back," Rusk insisted. Minutes later the Secretary of State came on the line again to say that the President had decided, in light of the fiasco at the UN, to cancel the second raid. There would be no more air strikes, he explained, until the brigade captured the Bay of Pigs runway and America could credibly argue that the B-26s were flying from Cuban soil.

Rusk's announcement set off a fire storm inside the war room. Ebby led the charge of those who felt the CIA was betraying the brigade. "It would be criminal to go ahead with the landings under these conditions," he cried, raising his voice, slamming a fist into a wall. "They cut back the first raid from sixteen B-26s to six. Now they're cancelling the second raid. The brigade won't have a ghost of a chance if Castro can put planes over the beaches."

Tempers flared. Rank was forgotten as junior officers pounded tables to emphasize the points they were making. As the argument raged in the cockpit, staffers dropped what they were doing and gathered around to watch. In the end the agonizing went nowhere: most of those present felt, like Bissell, that the die was cast; it was too late for the ships, by now sneaking into the Bay of Pigs behind two US destroyers, to turn back.

With Leo in tow, Bissell charged over to State to talk Rusk and Kennedy into changing their minds. The Secretary listened patiently to their arguments and agreed to call the President. Rusk stated Bissell's case fairly to Kennedy: the CIA was pleading to reinstate the strike because the freighters carrying the brigade, and the brigade itself, would be sitting ducks for any of Castro's planes that had survived the first raid. Then Rusk added, "In my view, Mr. President, operations of this sort do not depend nearly so heavily on air cover as conventional amphibious operations did in World War II. I am still recommending, in view of the uproar at the United Nations over the first raid, that we cancel." Rusk listened for a moment, then covered the mouthpiece with a palm. "The President agrees with me." He held out the telephone. "Would you like to speak to him yourself?"

Bissell, dog-tired after days of napping on a cot in the bunkroom of Quarters Eye, looked at Leo, then, thoroughly disheartened, shook his head. "If the President's mind is made up," he said wearily, "there's really no point, is there?"

Back at the war room Bissell tried to put the best face on the situation. There was a good chance that the bulk of Castro's combat aircraft had been neutralized. Some T-33s may have survived, true. But the T-bird was a relatively tame training plane—the CIA wasn't even sure they were armed. There was a bottom line, Bissell added: the President wasn't dumb. He had given the go-ahead for the operation, which meant he would have to relent and allow jets from the *Essex* to fly air cover if Castro's planes turned up over the beaches.

"And if Kennedy doesn't relent?" Ebby demanded.

Bissell turned away and, his shoulders sagging, resumed patrolling the corridor between the water cooler and the easel. "Anything on the wire?" he called to the Sorcerer, who was slumped over the UP ticker.

Torriti kicked at the long reams of paper collecting in the cardboard box at his feet. "Nothing yet," he mumbled.

"Goddamn it, I can't hear you."

"NOTHING YET!" Torriti shouted at the top of his lungs.

Shortly before midnight Bissell took another phone call from a very edgy Secretary of State. The President wanted to know where they were at, Rusk said. Bissell checked the coded phrases on the message board against the operational codes posted on the easel. The brigade's frogmen had gone ashore to mark the way with blinking landing lights. The two LSDs had gone ballast down to flood the well deck; the three LCUs and the four LCVPs inside would have swum out and started picking up the troops on the freighters. The first wave would form up in fifteen minutes and start out for the beaches designated Red and Blue. By first light all 1,453 members of Brigade 2506 would be ashore.

Rusk mumbled something about the need for the five merchant ships to be out of sight by sunup. Then, almost as an afterthought, the Secretary of State said that Kennedy was concerned about one other detail of the invasion. The President wanted to double-check that there would be no Americans hitting the beaches with the Cubans.

Bissell provided the necessary assurance. Sending Americans ashore was the last thing he'd do, he promised.

6

BLUE BEACH, THE BAY OF PIGS, MONDAY, APRIL 17, 1961

THE MEN IN THE FIRST WAVE, THEIR FACES BLACKENED WITH SOOT from galley stoves, slung web belts filled with spare ammunition clips across their chests, then bowed their heads and crossed themselves as the brigade priest blessed them and their crusade. "*In nomine Patris, et Filii, et Spiritui Sancti, Amen,*" he intoned. With that, the Cubans of the Sixth Battalion began clambering down the rope ladders into the LCU bobbing in the water under the *Río Escondido.* Two LCVPs, loaded down with tanks and trucks, chugged past, groundswells slapping against their blunt bows.

Jack, dressed in camouflage khakis and paratrooper boots, a .45 strapped to his waist, his Cossack mustache stiff with salt and quivering in the gusts from sea, was the last one down the ladder. He'd been planning the coup for weeks. To come this far with Roberto Escalona and the brigade and then (following explicit orders from Bissell) to remain on the freighter, watching the invasion through night binoculars—it was simply not possible. Not for the descendant of a bare-knuckle fighter, the undefeated McAuliffe whose name was still a legend in County Cork. There was also the little matter of showing the freedom fighters that America was confident enough in the venture to send one of its own ashore with them. The message wouldn't be lost on Roberto or the rank and file grunts of the brigade.

In the LCU, a hand gripped Jack's arm. "*Hombre,* what do you think you're doing?" Roberto Escalona demanded.

"I'm landing with you," Jack said.

"No," Roberto said. "Don't misunderstand me. I'm grateful for all your help but this part belongs to us now."

"Believe me, you're going to be on your own," Jack said. "I'm planning to stay on the beach long enough to take a look around so I can report first-hand to Washington. I'm coming right back."

"Still rowing for something besides speed?" guessed Roberto.

"I suppose you could say that," confessed Jack.

In the darkness, Roberto grunted. Several of the men who knew Jack murmured greetings in Spanish; it was easy to see they weren't sorry to see him tag along. Turning, Roberto waved to the sailors. The LCUs' crewmen pushed off from the tires hanging against the rusting hull of the freighter and the stubby landing craft lurched into the choppy waters, heading for the red lights twinkling on the shoreline.

Crouching in the midst of the Cuban fighters, Jack listened to them bantering back and forth nervously in Spanish. Looking over his shoulder, he could make out Roberto standing next to the helmsman, his hand raised over his eyes to shield it from the salt spray. Roberto stabbed the air off to the right and the helmsman eased the LCU over toward the blinking red light at the end of the rock jetty. "A hundred yards to go," Roberto shouted over the splashing waves and the wind.

Suddenly, there was a terrible grinding under the vessel. Shards of coral sliced through the double hull. The man crouching next to Jack gagged and clutched at his foot as the LCU pitched forward dizzily and then stopped dead in the water. Someone snapped on a flashlight and trained it on the moaning man, sitting on the deck. Anaesthetized with shock, the soldier followed the beam of light down to the stump of his foot. The razor-sharp coral had amputated his leg above the ankle. Blood gushed from the open wound. Nearby, a paratrooper boot with raw meat protruding from it floated in the bilge. A medic whipped off his belt and tightened it around the wounded man's calf but the blood continued to stream out. Around them, the hull was slowly filling with sea water, which swished gently back and forth as the LCU rolled with the swells. Cursing under his breath, Roberto leaped down into the hold. "Your people swore the smudge on the photos was seaweed, not a reef!" he shouted into Jack's ear.

"Jesus H. Christ, cut the goddamned motor," Jack yelled up to the helmsman. Roberto called to the men, "Quick, over the side. We're eighty yards off the beach—the water won't be deep here."

"*Qué haremos con él?*" the medic asked, clinging to the belt around the stump of leg as the soldier slumped to the deck. Sea water stained with syrupy red splotches swirled around the two men. Roberto reached down to the wounded man's neck and felt for a pulse. Then he shook his head furiously. "*Muerto!*" he said.

In twos and threes, the Cubans slipped over the side of the sinking vessel, their weapons raised above the heads. Jack found himself in waist high-water as he and the shadowy figures around him waded toward the shore. They were still some forty yards out when they heard the shriek of brakes from the beach. A truck filled with militiamen had roared up. As the militiamen spilled out, the truck backed and came forward again until its headlights played across the bay, illuminating the brigade fighters. The men in the water, pinned in the headlights, froze. Jack snatched a BAR from the nearest man's hands and fired off the magazine; every third round was a tracer, so it was easy to see that the truck was being riddled with bullets. Other brigade fighters began shooting. On the shore, there were flashes of fire as the militiamen shot back. Then, dragging the wounded and the dead, they began retreating toward a dense stand of woods on the other side of the gravel road that ran along the waterfront. The truck's headlights popped out, one after the other. In the darkness, Roberto shouted for the men to cease firing, and they struggled through the water and up onto the beach.

Another battalion on the right had already seized the rock jetty and was racing inland, the men shooting from the hip as they ran toward the building with the neon sign sizzling on the roof that advertised "Blanco's." Off to the left, still another battalion waded ashore from a sinking LCVP and, firing furiously, charged across the sand toward the rows of box-like bungalows at the edge of the beach. One brigade fighter dropped to his knees near Jack, who was crouching behind a stack of wheelbarrows. The Cuban aimed a .75 recoilless rifle at a bungalow with firefly-like sparks in the windows, and pulled the trigger. The shot burst on the roof, setting it aflame. In the saffron glow of the dancing flames, the last of Castro's militiamen could be seen disappearing across the fields.

And then the night turned deathly still; crickets could be heard chirping in the woods, a generator murmured somewhere behind the bungalows. At the head of the jetty, Roberto scooped up a fistful of sand and made a brief speech. The members of the brigade who could hear him cheered hoarsely. Then they started inland to secure the road and the town of Girón, and the three causeways over the Zapata swamp. One squad discovered an ancient Chevrolet parked behind a bungalow and, cranking up the motor, set off to capture the airstrip.

Jack took a turn around the beach area. Several wounded brigade fighters were being carried into the makeshift infirmary set up in one of the concrete bungalows. Roberto Escalona had scratched "G-2" on the door of another bungalow and was using it as his headquarters. Behind the bungalows, Jack found the bodies of three of Castro's soldiers with 339th Militia Battalion insignias on their sleeves lying face down in the sand, blood oozing from wounds. He gazed at the dead men for a while, trying to recollect in the heat of the moment what the issues were that had brought the brigade to Cuba; trying to weigh whether the issues vindicated the killers and the killed.

There were no easy answers. Suddenly the Cold War—the romp of great powers turning around great ideas—was reduced to bodies on a beach, to blood being sponged up by sand.

Making his way along the beachfront, Jack came across a brigade corporal—more a boy than a man—with a bulky radio strapped to his back. He was cowering behind a wrecked Jeep, cradling the head of a dead brigade officer in his arms. Jack gently pulled the body free and, motioning for the radioman to follow him, headed for Blanco's Bar. Inside, the jukebox was still feeding 45-rpm records into the playing slot; the grating voice of Chubby Checkers could be heard belting out "Twist again like you did last sum-mer." Cans of Cuban beer, sets of dominoes, were scattered around the tables, evidence that the bar had been hastily abandoned. The small *fogón*, a stove that burned the local charcoal, lay on its side, riddled with bullets. Righting a chair, Jack collapsed into it; he hadn't realized how exhausted he was until he sat down. He motioned for the young corporal to set up his equipment.

"*Debes tener un nombre, amigo,*" he asked the radioman.

"Orlando, *señor.*"

"*De dónde eres?*"

The boy pointed in the general direction of the swamp. "*Soy de aquí. De Real Campiña, qué está al otro lado de Zapata.*"

"Welcome home, Orlando." Jack handed him a slip of paper listing two emergency frequencies monitored by the aircraft carrier *Essex*. The radioman, proud to be of assistance to the only Yankee on the beach, strung the antenna and tuned in the frequency. With an effort, Jack pushed himself out of the chair and stood there swaying like a drunk. He shook his head to get the cobwebs out, then stumbled across the room. "Maybe you can tell me what the fuck I'm doing here," he said.

The radioman didn't understand English. "*Qué dice, señor?*"

Jack had to laugh. He patted the young man on his bony shoulder. "All right, pal. Whatever we're doing here, we'd better get it right." Grasping the small microphone, he called: "Whistlestop, this is Carpet Bagger, do you read me? Over."

There was a burst of background static. Gradually a voice speaking

English with a lazy Southern accent filtered through it. "Roger, Carpet Bagger. This heah's Whistlestop. Ah'm readin' you loud and clear. Over."

"Whistlestop, please pass the following message on to Kermit Coffin: Phase one of operation completed. Initial objectives are in our hands. Casualties are light. At least one LCU and one LCVP with heavy equipment and spare ammunition hit a coral reef and sank offshore. Now we're waiting for the offloading of ammunition and mobile communication van from *Río Escondido*, and the field hospital from the *Houston*."

Jack started to sign off when the radio operator on the *Essex* told him to stand by; a message was coming through for him. Then he read it: "Combat information center reports that Castro still has operational aircraft. Expect you'all gonna be hit at dawn. Unload all troops and supplies and take your ships to sea as soon as possible."

Jack shouted into the microphone, "What about the goddamned air umbrella that's supposed to be over the beach?"

The *Essex* radioman, unfazed, repeated the message. "I say again, you'all gonna be hit at dawn. Unload all troops and supplies and take your ships to sea as soon as possible."

"Whistlestop, how are we supposed to unload all troops and supplies? The LCUs and the LCVPs that are still afloat won't be able to get over the coral reef until high tide, which isn't due until midmorning. Over."

"Wait one, Carpet Bagger."

A full three minutes later the radio operator came back on. "Kermit Coffin says there must be some mistake—there is no coral reef, only seaweed. Over."

Jack's sentences came with deliberate gaps between the words. "Whistlestop, this is Carpet Bagger. Kindly pass the following question on to Kermit Coffin: When's the last time you heard of seaweed cutting through a hull and severing a man's leg?"

Using his thumb, Jack flicked off the microphone.

Bissell, reputed to be unflappable, blew his stack when Leo brought him the message board from the *Essex*. What annoyed him wasn't what Jack McAuliffe was saying but where he was saying it from. "He's gone ashore!" he cried incredulously.

"He's with the Sixth Battalion on Blue Beach, Dick," Leo said.

"Who in God's name authorized him to land?"

"It seems to have been a personal initiative—"

The DD/O got a grip on himself. "All right. Get the *Essex* to pass the following order on to him. Keep the radio channel to the *Essex* open until the mobile communication van is offloaded from the *Río Escondido* and we can establish a direct link with the beaches. As for McAuliffe, he's to get his hide back to the ship pronto, even if he has to swim out to it."

Glancing at the wall clock, Bissell turned back to the giant overlay. He didn't like what he saw. First light would be seeping over the invasion beaches, but the five freighters that had brought Brigade 2506 to Cuba were still positioned inside the narrow confines of the Bay of Pigs. By now they should have offloaded their precious cargoes and headed out to the safety of the open sea. Staring at the wall map, Bissell thought he detected the distant, dull whine of disaster—the sound seemed to come from somewhere deep inside his ear. And it wouldn't go away.

In Miami, Howard Hunt locked the Cuban Provisional Government inside a safe house and issued "Bulletin Number 1" in its name: "Before dawn today, Cuban patriots began the battle to liberate our homeland from the desperate rule of Fidel Castro."

From Swan Island in the Caribbean, the powerful CIA transmitter beamed calls for the Cuban army to revolt against Castro. "Take up strategic positions that control roads and railroads! Take prisoner or shoot those who refuse to obey your orders! All planes must remain on the ground." Between calls for insurrection, the radio—as part of JMARC's psychological warfare campaign designed to convince Castro that an insurrection was underway—began broadcasting what appeared to be coded messages to Cuban underground units: "The hunter's moon will rise before dawn. I repeat, the hunter's moon will rise before dawn. The forest is blood red with flames. I repeat, the forest is blood red with flames. The Caribbean is filled with jellyfish. I repeat, the Caribbean is filled with jellyfish."

At high tide, the LCUs and the LCVP started ferrying equipment and supplies over the coral reef to the beach. Roberto actually kissed the first of the three tanks to roll off the landing craft, and then sent them off to beef up the units blocking the causeways. Shirtless young men were tossing cartons of Spam and tins of ammunition from hand to hand up the beach to one of the bungalows that had been turned into a depot. Up the bay, in the direction of Red Beach some twenty miles to the north, a thin plume of smoke rose into the crystalline sky. At first light, a lone Sea Fury had come in at sea level and hit one of the freighters, the *Houston*, on the waterline amidships with a rocket. The Second Battalion had already been offloaded onto Red Beach but the Fifth Battalion and the field hospital, and tons of spare ammunition, were still on board when the *Houston*, ablaze and taking water fast, settled stern down into the bay. Dozens of fighters in the Fifth Battalion drowned trying to swim to shore; the ones who made it were no longer fit for combat.

At the end of the jetty on Blue Beach, a fighter manning one of the few antiaircraft guns ashore scanned the sky to the north through binoculars. Suddenly he stiffened. "Sea Fury!" he shouted. Along the beach, others took up the cry as they dove into hastily dug slit trenches. "Sea Fury! Sea Fury!"

Jack, catnapping on the floor of Blanco's Bar, heard the commotion and raced out onto the porch in time to see two of Castro's planes roar in low from the Zapata Swamp. One peeled off and, circling, came down the shoreline, raking the beach with machine gun fire. Jack dove into a hole he'd scooped out in the sand under the porch. Fighters lying on their backs in the slit trenches fired BARs at the plane, which sped past over their heads and banked to come around for a second run. The second Sea Fury, skimming the waves, headed straight for the port side of the *Río Escondido*, two miles out in the bay. The plane fired eight rockets and then climbed at a steep angle and banked away to escape the .50-caliber machine guns blazing away from the side of the freighter. Seven of the Sea Fury's rockets splashed into the sea, short of the target. The eighth struck the ship under the bridge. The explosion ignited several of the drums of aviation gasoline lashed to the deck. In an instant the fire skidded forward. From his shelter in the sand, Jack could see sailors trying to fight the blaze with hand extinguishers but he knew they would be useless against a gasoline fire. Minutes later there was a small explosion. Then a giant explosion racked the freighter as the stores of ammunition below deck went up. Men in orange life vests could be seen leaping into the sea as flames shot hundreds of feet into the air. Smoke obscured the ship for several minutes. When it drifted clear, Jack saw the *Río Escondido*'s stern jutting straight up, the two screws slowly churning in air as the freighter slid down into the oily waters of the Bay of Pigs.

Black smoke streamed from the stacks of the two other freighters in sight as they got up steam and headed to sea.

The two Sea Furies made a last pass over the beach, shooting up Jeeps and trucks that had been offloaded, then disappeared back over the swamp. Inside the bar, Jack had his Cuban corporal raise the *Essex* on the radio. "Whistlestop, Whistlestop, this is Carpet Bagger. Two bogies just attacked the beach and the ships. The *Río Escondido* was hit and has sunk. I repeat, the *Río Escondido* was sunk before it could offload its aviation fuel or the communication van, or the spare ammunition. The other freighters, the ones carrying ammunition, have hauled ass and are putting to sea." Jack smiled at a thought. "Do me a favor, Whistlestop, pass word on to Kermit Coffin that I can't go back on board the *Río Escondido* because it's underwater."

The laconic voice from the *Essex* filtered back over the wavelength. "Roger, Carpet Bagger. In the absence of the communication van we'll need to keep this channel open. The only reports we're getting from Blue Beach are coming from you." There was a buzz of static. Then the *Essex*, with just a hint of breathlessness, said, "Combat information center has a sighting from one of our Skyhawks. An enemy battalion estimated at nine hundred men, I repeat, nine hundred men was spotted approaching the middle causeway that leads to Girón and the airstrip. Our pilot counted sixty, I repeat, sixty vehicles, including a dozen or so Stalin Three tanks."

Jack said, "Whistlestop, when can we expected the air cover you promised?"

"Carpet Bagger, we are reporting three brigade B-26s seventy-five miles out and approaching. Good luck to you."

Jack said, "We'll need more than luck," and cut the microphone. He stepped onto the porch again and gazed into the shimmering waves of heat rising off the Zapata on the horizon. He could hear the dull boom of cannon as Castro's column closed in on the unit blocking the middle causeway. In the haze, he could make out swarms of birds circling high over the battlefield.

The young corporal came up behind him and pointed at the birds. *"Buitres,"* he whispered.

Jack caught his breath. "Vultures," he repeated.

In Washington, Millie Owen-Brack gave a good imitation of someone at work. She was supposed to be preparing a briefing paper for Allen Dulles. The idea was for the Director to give an off-the-record interview to a columnist considered friendly to the CIA; in it Dulles would make it clear that, while America sympathized with the Cuban rebels who were trying to overthrow Castro, the Company had not organized the Bay of Pigs landings or aided the Cuban brigade in any way, shape or form during the actual invasion. Millie, her mind wandering, reworked the second paragraph for the tenth time, changing "way, shape or form" to "overtly," then crossing that out and trying "militarily." She left "militarily" and added "or logistically," and then sat back to reread it. She had difficulty focusing on the sentences and turned her head to stare out the window. The cherry blossoms had appeared on the mall the week before but there was no sense of spring in the air; in her heart, either.

The two other women who shared the office glanced up from their desks and then looked at each other; they both knew that Millie was worried sick about her husband, who was somehow involved in this Bay of Pigs business.

Late in the morning a topside secretary phoned down to ask one of the women if Millie Owen-Brack happened to be at her desk. "Why, yes, as a matter of fact she is," the woman confirmed.

Millie looked up. "Who was that?"

"Someone was asking if you were in the office."

The question struck Millie as ominous. "This is a Monday. Where else would I be, for heaven's sake?"

A few moments later the footfalls of a man walking as if he wasn't eager to get where he was going could be heard in the corridor. Millie drew a quick breath and held it. She vividly remembered the day twelve years before when Allen Dulles, then DD/O, and Frank Wisner, his deputy, had come into her tiny office to announce that her husband had been shot dead on the China-Burma border. Dulles, a smooth man in public but awkward when it came to dealing with emotions, had turned his head away and covered his eyes with a hand as he searched for comforting words. He never found them. It was Wisner who had put an arm over her shoulder and said how sorry they all were that things had turned out like this. He had assured she would have nothing to worry about materially; the Company took care of its widows.

The soft scrape of a knuckle on the door brought Millie back to the present. "Yes?" she called.

The door opened and Allen Dulles stepped into the office. He had aged a great deal in the last months, and grown visibly tired. The jubilant spring to his step, the optimistic pitch to his voice were long gone. Now he slouched noticeably as he shuffled across the room to Millie's desk. "Please don't get up," he told her. He sank slowly into a seat and sucked for a moment on a dead pipe. His gaze finally lifted and he noticed the look of absolute dread in Millie's eyes. "Oh, dear," he said. "I should have told you immediately—I don't have bad news, if that's what you're thinking."

Millie let herself breathe again, though her heart was still beating wildly.

"I don't have good news either," Dulles went on. He glanced across the room at the two women. "I wonder if I could trouble you ladies..."

The women grabbed their purses and hurriedly left the room.

"Yes, well, here it is. Castro's planes sank two ships this morning. The

Río Escondido, which is the one Jack was riding, was one of them. But Jack wasn't on it—he apparently took it upon himself to go ashore with the first wave. It's just as well he did. The brigade's communication van went down with the *Río Escondido*, so the only first-hand news we're getting off the beach is from an impromptu hookup Jack established with the *Essex*."

"When's the last time you heard from him?" Millie asked.

Dulles looked at his watch, then absently began winding it. "About three-quarters of an hour ago. That's how we learned about the *Río Escondido*."

"What's the situation on the beach?"

"Not good." Dulles shut his eyes and massaged the brows over them. "Terrible, in fact. Castro's columns are closing in. The brigade never managed to offload ammunition from the freighters."

"It's not too late—"

"The ships that weren't sunk headed for the open sea—"

Millie was keenly aware of the ludicrousness of the situation: here she was, a public relations flack, discussing operational details with the head of the Central Intelligence Agency. "Surely you can organize air drops—"

"Not while Castro has planes in the air. Jack Kennedy has flatly refused..." Dulles let the sentence trail off.

"If things get really bad," Millie said, "you'll extricate Jack, won't you?"

"Of course we will," Dulles said, a trace of the old heartiness back in his voice. "We certainly don't want a CIA officer to fall into Castro's hands. Look, I know you've been through this before." The Director cleared his throat. "I wanted to bring you up to date—you were bound to hear about the sinking of the two ships and start worrying that Jack might have been on one of them."

Millie came around the desk and offered her hand to Dulles. "You were very thoughtful, Director. With all the things you have to think of—"

Dulles stood up. "Dear lady, it was the least I could do, all things considered."

"You'll keep me posted on what's happening to Jack?"

"Yes."

"Thank you, Director."

Dulles nodded. He tried to think of what else he could say. Then he pursed his lips and turned to go.

Early on Tuesday morning, Jack—running on catnaps and nervous energy—shared some dry biscuits and muddy instant coffee with Roberto Escalona in his G-2 bungalow as they took stock of the situation. Castro's heavy artillery was starting to zero in on the beaches; his tanks and mortars would soon come within range. The brigade's makeshift infirmary was overflowing with wounded; the makeshift mortuary behind it was filled with dead bodies and pieces of bodies. Ammunition was running perilously low; if the freighters didn't return to the Bay of Pigs and offload supplies, the brigade would run out of ammunition in the next twenty-four hours. And then there was the eternal problem of air cover. Unless American Navy jets off the *Essex* patrolled overhead, the brigade's antiquated B-26s, lumbering in from Guatemala, were no match for Castro's T-33s and Sea Furies; three of them had been shot down that morning trying to attack Castro's forces on the causeways. The brigade blocking units there were taking heavy casualties; Roberto wasn't sure how long they could hold out without air support. Once they pulled back, there would be nothing to stop Castro's heavy Stalin III tanks from rolling down to the water's edge.

Jack waited for a lull in the shelling, then jogged back across the sand to Blanco's Bar. Orlando, his radioman, raised the *Essex* and Jack called in the morning's situation report. At midmorning he went out onto the porch and scanned the bay with binoculars. There was still no sign of the freighters. He climbed onto the porch railing and then up to the roof. Sitting on the edge of an open skylight, his feet dangling down into the bar, he watched the contrails high overhead thicken and dissipate. Then he trained his binoculars on the horizon to the northeast, where the battle was raging for control of the middle causeway. "It was a dirty trick," he muttered, talking to himself, shaking his head dejectedly.

The dirty trick he had in mind was the one he'd pulled on Millie when he came ashore with the brigade. It was one thing not to resist the demon that drives you to live on the edge, quite another not to protect your wife from becoming, once again, a widow.

A voice boomed, "Ladies and gentlemen, the President and Mrs. Kennedy!"

Elegant in white tie and tails, Jack Kennedy strode into the East Room of the White House as the Marine band, decked out in red dress uniforms, struck up "Mr. Wonderful." Jackie, wearing green earrings and a pleated floor-length sea-green gown that bared one shoulder, clung to the President's elbow. The eighty or so guests around the room applauded. Smiling broadly, looking as if he didn't have a care in the world, Jack gathered his wife in his arms and started off the dancing.

As the gala dragged on the couple separated to work the room. "Oh,

thank you," Jackie, slightly breathless, told a congressman who compli-
mented her on the bash. "When the Eisenhowers were here we used to get
invited to the White House. It was just unbearable. There was never anything served to drink and we made up our minds, when we moved to the
White House, that nobody was ever going to be as bored as we'd been."

Jack was chatting with Senator Smathers from Florida when Bobby, also
in white tie, motioned to him from the door. The two brothers met half
way. "The shit has hit the fan," Bobby told the President in a low voice.
"The whole thing has turned sour in ways you won't believe. Bissell and his
people are coming over." Bobby glanced at his wristwatch. "I've rounded up
the usual suspects—everyone'll be in the Cabinet Room at midnight."

Jack nodded. Forcing a smile onto his face, he turned to chat up the wife
of a syndicated columnist.

At two minutes to midnight the President, still in his tails, pushed
through the doors into the Cabinet Room. Other guests from the evening
gala were there already: Vice President Johnson, Secretaries Rusk and
McNamara. General Lemnitzer and Admiral Burke, trailing after the
President from the East Room and wearing formal dress uniforms with rows
of medals glistening on their breasts, closed the doors behind them. A dozen
or so aides from the White House, Defense and State had been summoned
from their homes by the White House switchboard; most of them had
thrown on corduroys and sweatshirts and looked as if they had been roused
from a deep sleep. The CIA men—Bissell and Leo Kritzky and a handful of
others—were unshaven and dressed in the same rumpled clothing they'd
been sleeping in for days. They all climbed to their feet while the President
made his way around to the head of the table. When Kennedy sank into a
chair everyone except Bissell followed suit.

"Mr. President, gentlemen, the news is not good," the DD/O began.

"That may be the understatement of the century," Bobby Kennedy
remarked. "This administration is ninety days old and you people—"

Jack said patiently, "Let him tell us what's happening."

Bissell, barely controlling his emotions, brought everyone up to date on
the situation. Castro's tanks and mortars had closed to within range of the
two landing beaches. Casualties were heavy. The units blocking the causeways
were running desperately low on ammunition. Roberto Escalona was
rationing what was left—commanders begging for five mortar shells were
lucky to get two. If the blocking units gave way, Castro's tanks would roll
down to the beaches in a matter of hours. The ships carrying spare ammunition had fled the bay after the two freighters were sunk. The Navy had talked

them into returning but didn't expect them to get there in time to save the situation. To complicate matters several members of the provisional government, under lock and key in a Miami hotel, were threatening to commit suicide if they weren't allowed to join their comrades in the Bay of Pigs. In Guatemala, the Company liaison officers at the Retalhuleu airstrip were complaining that the pilots and crews, flying nonstop since Monday morning, were too exhausted to respond to the brigade's appeals for air cover. A handful of American advisors, sheep-dipped from Alabama Air National guard units, were begging for permission to take the B-26s out in their place.

"I trust you didn't say yes," Kennedy snapped.

"I sent them a four-word response, Mr. President: 'Out of the question.'"

Secretary McNamara and General Lemnitzer pressed Bissell for details. When the DD/O, who hadn't slept in days, hesitated, Leo, sitting next to him, scratched answers on a pad and Bissell, his memory refreshed, responded as best he could. There were roughly a hundred dead, twice that number of wounded, he said. Yes, there were brigade tanks on the beach but, due to the shortage of fuel, they had dug in and were being used as fixed artillery positions.

"That is," Bobby put in, "as long as their ammunition lasts."

"Thank you for the clarification, Mr. Attorney General," Bissell said.

"Any time," Bobby shot back.

"The bottom line, Mr. President," Bissell said, trying to ignore Bobby, "is that the operation can still be saved."

"I'd certainly like to know how," Kennedy said.

"It can be saved if you authorize jets from the *Essex* to fly combat missions over the beaches. It would take them forty-five minutes to clean out the causeways."

Bissell found an unlikely ally in Admiral Burke. "Let me have two jets and I'll shoot down anything Castro throws at us," declared the gruff Chief of Naval Operations.

"No," Kennedy said flatly. "I want to remind you all of what I said over and over—I will not commit American armed forces to combat to save this operation."

Bobby remarked, "The problem, as I see it, is that the CIA and Admiral Burke are still hoping to salvage the situation. The President wants to find a way to cut our losses. There's a whole world out there waiting to rub our noses in this if we let them."

Burke shook his head in disbelief. "One destroyer opening fire from the bay could knock the hell out of Castro's tanks. It could change the course of the battle—"

Jack Kennedy's eyes narrowed. "Burke, I don't want the United States involved in this. Period."

Arleigh Burke wasn't ready to give up yet. "Hell, Mr. President, we *are* involved."

Secretary of State Rusk jotted some words on a pad and passed the slip of paper to Kennedy. On it he had written: "What about the hills?"

Kennedy looked across the table at Bissell, still the only person in the room on his feet. "Dick, I think the time has come for the brigade to go guerrilla, don't you?"

Everyone in the room appeared to be hanging on the answer to the President's question. Leo glanced at his chief out of the corner of an eye; Bissell was terribly alone, a bone-weary emotional wreck of a man. Swaying slightly as he shifted his weight from one foot to the other, he seemed close to tears. "Mr. President, going guerrilla is not possible—"

Kennedy appeared confused. "I always thought...you assured me..." He looked around the table for support.

General Lemnitzer leveled an accusing finger at Bissell. "You specifically said that, in a worst-case scenario, the brigade could fade into the Escambray Mountains and go guerrilla."

Bissell, barely audible now, said, "That was a worst-case option in the Trinidad plan, which we shelved at the request of the President. From the Bay of Pigs, the brigade would have to fight its way across eighty miles of swamp to get to the mountains." Bissell looked around desperately and saw the chair behind him and collapsed back into it. "Mr. President—"

"I'm listening, Dick."

"Mr. President, to put a fine point on it, our people are trapped on the beaches. Castro has massed twenty thousand troops in the area. If we can keep Castro's forces—keep his tanks—at bay, keep them pinned to the causeways, why, we could bring in the ammunition ships, couldn't we? The brigade could regroup, get a second wind." Around the table people were starting to stare at the walls or the ceiling. Bissell, too, was getting a second wind. "The Provisional Government could set up shop, Mr. President. We'd have our foothold on the island—"

"You mean *toehold*—" Bobby interrupted, but Bissell, oblivious to the sarcasm, rushed on.

"Once the Provisional Government is in place Castro's troops will desert in droves. It's all down here in black and white, isn't it, Leo? Where's that briefing paper we worked up?" Leo went through the motions of riffling through a pile of file folders. Bissell, impatient, began quoting from memory.

"Sabotage is frequent, for God's sake. Church attendance is at record highs and can be interpreted as opposition to the regime. Disenchantment of the peasants has spread to all the regions of Cuba. Castro's government ministries and regular army have been penetrated by opposition groups. When the time comes for the brigade to break out of the beachhead, they can be counted on to muddy the waters..." Bissell looked around the table. "Muddy the waters," he repeated weakly. Then he shut his mouth.

A leaden silence filled the Cabinet Room. The President cleared his throat. "Burke, I'll let you put six jet fighters over the beach for one hour tomorrow morning on the absolute condition that their American markings are painted out. They are not to attack ground targets—"

"What if they're fired on, Mr. President?" asked Admiral Burke.

"There's no reason for them to be fired on if they stay out of range of Castro's antiaircraft batteries. Dick, you can bring in the brigade's B-26s from Guatemala during that hour. The jets off the *Essex* will cover them. If any of Castro's T-33s or Sea Furies turn up the jets have permission to shoot them down. Just that. Only that."

"Aye-aye, sir," Burke said.

"Thank you for that, Mr. President," Bissell mumbled.

As the meeting was breaking up, a National Security aide rushed up to the President with a message board. Kennedy read it and, shaking his head in disbelief, passed the board on to Bobby. Sensing that something important had happened, several of the participants gathered around the President and his brother. Bobby said, "Jesus! Four of those Alabama National Guard pilots who were training the Cubans in Guatemala have taken matters into their own hands— they flew a sortie in two B-26s. Both bombers were shot down over Cuba."

"What happened to the pilots?" asked General Lemnitzer.

"Nobody knows," Bobby said. The President's brother turned on Bissell. "Those American pilots had better goddamned well be dead," he fumed, his voice pitched high into a hatchet man's killer octave.

By midday Wednesday what was left of the units blocking the causeways had began pulling back toward Girón. When word of this reached the beaches, panic spread. Castro's tanks, pushing down the road from the airport, were firing at line-of-sight targets. Blanco's Bar was bracketed and Jack and his radioman decided the time had come to join Roberto Escalona, who was crouching with a handful of fighters at the water's edge. Shells were bursting around them, kicking up gusts of sand and dust that blotted out the sun but causing relatively few injuries because the beach tended to dampen the explosions.

"Darkness at noon," Jack called over the din of combat.

Roberto, clutching a BAR with two almost empty ammunition belts crisscrossing his chest, stared out to sea through the sooty air. An American destroyer, its hull number painted out, was patrolling a mile off shore. Jack shouted, "I can get them to come in close and take us all off."

Roberto shook his head. "If it has to end, let it end here."

The brigade's fate had been sealed earlier in the morning when Bissell's topside planners in Washington, dazed from lack of sleep, forgot there was a one-hour difference in time zones between Cuba and Guatemala. The six carrier-based A4Ds with their American markings painted out had turned up over the beaches an hour early for the rendezvous with the B-26s flying in from Retalhuleu. When the brigade's planes did show up, the American jets were on the way back to the *Essex* and Castro's T-birds had a field day, shooting down two more B-26s.

At the water's edge a half-crazed Cuban fighter crouching near Jack screamed obscenities at the American destroyer, then leveled his rifle at the hull and managed to shoot off two rounds before Roberto punched the barrel down. On either side, as far as the eye could see, men were scurrying in every direction, leaping in and out of shallow craters gouged in the dunes by the bursting shells. Orlando, monitoring the radio through earphones, grabbed Jack's arm to get his attention. *"Quieren hablar con usted, señor,"* he cried. Jack pressed one of the earphones to an ear. A static-filled squeal made him wince. Then a voice forced its way through the static: "Carpet Bagger, this is Whiskey Sour patrolling off Blue Beach. Do you read me?"

Jack grasped the microphone and waded into the water, with Orlando right behind him. "Whiskey Sour, this is Carpet Bagger. I read you. Over."

"Carpet Bagger, I have orders for you from Kermit Coffin. You are instructed to leave the beach immediately. I repeat—"

Jack interrupted. "Whiskey Sour, no way am I leaving this beach by myself."

Roberto came up behind Jack. "Get your ass out of here," he yelled. "You can't help us anymore."

"Jesus H. Christ, I'll leave when everyone leaves."

Two shells exploded, one hard on the heels of the other, scooping shallow craters on either side of the group. For a moment the sandstorm obscured everything. As it settled, a bearded fighter, blood spilling from a gaping wound where his ear had been, stumbled toward them, then fell face down in the sand. Another soldier rolled the wounded man onto his back, looked over toward Roberto and shook his head. Jack became aware of a sticky wetness on his thigh. Looking down, he saw that shrapnel had grazed his leg, shredding his trousers, lacerating the skin. Roberto, cracking like porcelain, snatched the .45 from the holster on Jack's web belt and pointed it at the American's head. "Castro captures you," he cried, his voice breaking, tears of frustration streaking his sand-stained cheeks, "he'll tell the world we were led by American officers. For Christ's sake, Jack, don't take away our dignity. It's the last thing we have left. Okay, Jack? You hearing me, Jack? I swear to you—I'll kill you before I let you fall into their hands alive."

Jack backed away. Water swirled around his knees. "You're a shit," he yelled at Roberto.

"*Gringo carajo!* I'll blow your head off, you'll be just another body floating in the surf."

Jack turned and waded deeper into the water, then lost his footing and began to dogpaddle away from the beach. From time to time he glanced back. The first of Castro's Stalin III tanks, their cannons spurting flames, were lumbering through the lanes between the concrete bungalows. One of the brigade tanks dug into the sand exploded; the mangled turret slid off to one side and its cannon nosed into the sand. Troops, running low and shouting in Spanish, poured onto the dunes behind the tanks. Along the beach, men were emerging from holes and slit trenches with their hands stretched high over their heads. Jack turned back and went on paddling. He saw a raft up ahead, partially inflated and half submerged, and made for it. Squirming onto it, he lay there for a long time, his face turned toward the sun, his eyes tightly shut. Visions of riot clashed with images of Millie slithering slowly up his body, cauterizing his wounds with her burning lips.

Jack lost track of time. He raised himself on an elbow and looked back at the beach. The shooting had stopped. Lines of men, their hands clasped on their heads, were being prodded at bayonetpoint up the dunes. Floating not far from the raft was a broken plank—it must have come from the wooden benches in one of the sunken LCUs. Jack retrieved it and, lying flat so he couldn't be seen from the beach, began to paddle out to sea. After a while blisters formed on his hands and burst, and the makeshift paddle became slick with blood. Slivers of sunlight glancing off the bay blinded him. When he was able to see he caught a glimpse of the destroyer riding on its inverted reflection. The sun scorched the back of his neck. From time to time, despite the heat, he shivered uncontrollably, calming down only when he summoned images of Millie's long body fitted against his. He could hear her voice in his ear: *Come home when you can, Jack. I couldn't bear it if...*

When he looked up again, the destroyer was near enough to make out the fresh paint on the bow where the hull number had been blotted out. On the fantail sailors were shouting encouragement at him. He guessed that there was enough distance between the raft and the beach for him to sit up now. Punctuating each stroke with a rasping grunt, Jack made a clean catch and felt his blade lock onto a swell of sea water. A splinter of pain stabbed at the rib that had mended and broken and mended again. His head reeled. He thought he heard hoarse shrieks from the students lining the banks of the river. Coiling and uncoiling his limbs in long fluid motions, he caught sight of the finish line ahead.

And then the plank in Jack's hands became stuck in the water and it dawned on him that he wasn't rowing in a sleek-sculled eight on the Charles after all. He tugged at the plank but couldn't pull it free. He looked over the side—there was something queer about the water. It was a dirty red and washing through a mass of greenish gulfweed. And then he saw that the tip of the plank had embedded itself in the stomach of a bloated corpse that was tangled in the weed. Jack let go of the plank and gagged and turned and vomited, and vomited again in long spasms, the pain searing his throat, until he felt that nothing could be left inside him—no heart or lungs or stomach or intestines.

This sense of perfect emptiness overwhelmed him and he blacked out.

Ebby rang up Elizabet from his office in mid afternoon. "Have you been listening to the news?" he asked.

"Everyone at State's glued to the radio," she said. "UPI is talking about hundreds of casualties and more than a thousand taken prisoner."

"All hell's broken loose here," Ebby said. "I can't talk now. Leo and I think it might be a good idea for you to pick up Adelle and drive over to Millie's to hold her hand."

"How come she's home?"

"She called in sick this morning. She said there was nothing wrong physically—given what's happening she just couldn't concentrate."

Elizabet didn't dare breath. "Is there bad news?"

"There's no news," Ebby told her. "But there could be bad news."

"Oh, Elliott, it's turning out the way you said it would—it's Budapest revisited."

Adelle was waiting at the curb when Elizabet came by. The two had grown very close over the years but they barely uttered a word on the way over to Millie's. They went around to the back and, pushing through a screen door, found Jack's wife sitting in the kitchen. She was staring at a daytime television quiz program, waiting for it to be interrupted with the latest news bulletin. An open bottle of Scotch was within arm's reach. There was a mountain of unwashed dishes in the sink, dirty laundry heaped on the floor in front of the washing machine.

Millie jumped up and looked at her friends with dread in her eyes. "For God's sake don't beat around the bush," she pleaded. "If you know something, tell me."

"We only know what's on the news," Elizabet said.

"You swear to God you're not hiding anything?"

"We know it's a disaster," Adelle said. "Nothing more."

"Jack's on the beach," Millie said.

The three women hugged each other. "You can bet they'll move heaven and earth to get him off," Adelle assured her.

"There's been no mention of an American in the bulletins," Adelle pointed out. "Surely Castro would be boasting to the world by now if he had captured one of ours."

"Where's Anthony?" Elizabet asked.

"My mother came around and took him and Miss Aldrich over to her place the minute she heard what was happening."

Millie poured out three stiff shots of Scotch and clinked glasses.

"Here's to the men in our lives," Elizabet said.

"Here's to the day they're so fed up working for the Company they get nine-to-five jobs selling used cars," Millie said.

"They wouldn't be the same men we married if they worked nine-to-five selling used cars," Adelle said.

The women settled down around the kitchen table. On the television screen, four housewives were trying to guess the price of a mahogany bedroom set; the one who came closest would win it.

"The Company really screwed up this time," Millie said. "Dick Bissell and the Director are going to be drawing unemployment."

To take her mind off the Bay of Pigs fiasco, Elizabet asked Millie how she and Jack had met. Millie smiled at the memory as she described the brash young six-footer sporting a Cossack mustache and wearing a three-piece linen suit who had made a pass at her on the sixty-sixth floor of the Chrysler Building. I thought you met in Vienna during the Budapest business, Adelle said. He propositioned me in New York, Millie said. I said yes in Vienna five years later. Never hurts to keep 'em waiting, Adelle said with a laugh. They talked for a while about Elizabet's daughter, Nellie, and about Ebby's boy by his first marriage, Manny, who had turned fourteen and was at the top of his class in Groton.

Adelle described how her twin girls had giggled when they caught sight of a pregnant woman in a store the week before. When Adelle started telling them about the birds and the bees, Vanessa had interrupted. Oh, mommy, we know all about thingamabobs turning hard and getting shoved into thingamagigs and the whatsit swimming up to fertilize the egg and stuff like that. Where on earth did you learn about thingamabobs and thingamagigs? Adelle had inquired with a straight face. The two girls had explained how their school chum Mary Jo had swiped a Swedish sex education book filled with photographic illustrations of naked people actually "doing it" from an older stepsister, and then spent the weekend poring over the pages with a magnifying glass. Oh, they do grow up fast these days, Elizabet said. Don't they, though, Adelle agreed.

And then the phone rang. Elizabet and Adelle exchanged looks. Millie lifted the receiver. The blood drained from her lips when she heard Dulles's voice.

"Yes, speaking," she said..."I see," she said..."You're absolutely sure? There's no chance you're wrong?"

On the television screen a woman was laughing deliriously because she had won the bedroom set. Adelle went over and snapped off the set. The pinpricks of light disappeared as if they had been sucked down a drain.

Millie said into the phone, "No, I'll be fine, Director. I have two friends here with me...Thank you, Director. I *am* proud of Jack. Very. Yes. Goodbye."

Millie turned to her friends. Tears welled in her eyes. She was too choked up to speak. Adelle, sobbing, came around the table and hugged her tightly.

"It's not what you think," Millie finally managed to say. "Jack's safe and sound. They got him off the beach. A destroyer picked him up from a raft—" Tears were streaming down her cheeks now. "His paratrooper boots turned white from the salt water. His hands were covered with blisters. He has shrapnel wounds—the Director swears they're scratches, nothing more." She began laughing through her tears. "He's alive. Jack's alive!"

Lights blazed late in the West Wing of the White House Wednesday night. A very tired secretary dozed at a desk immediately outside the President's office. Even the four Secret Service agents posted in the corridor were swallowing yawns. Inside, silver trays with untouched finger sandwiches filled a sideboard. Committee chairmen trudged in and huddled with a shaken President and departed, wondering aloud how such a smart man could have gotten sucked into such a cockamamie scheme in the first place. Shortly after eleven Leo came by with the most recent situation report. Jack Kennedy and his brother Bobby were off in a corner, talking with McGeorge Bundy, the

National Security Advisor. Waiting inside the door, Leo caught snatches of conversation. "Dulles is a legendary figure," the President was saying. "It's hard to operate with legendary figures—he'll have to fall on his sword."

"Bissell will have to go, too," Bobby said.

"I made a mistake putting Bobby in Justice," Kennedy told Bundy. "He's wasted there. Bobby should be over at CIA."

"That's about as logical as closing the barn door after the horse has headed for the hills," Bobby observed.

Bundy agreed with Bobby but for another reason. "To get a handle on a bureaucracy you need to know what makes it tick. The CIA has its own culture—"

"It's a complete mystery to me," Bobby admitted.

"You could figure it out," Kennedy insisted.

"By the end of your second term I ought to be able to," Bobby quipped.

The President spotted Leo at the door and motioned for him to come in. "What's the latest from Waterloo, Kritzky?"

Leo handed him a briefing paper. Kennedy scanned it, then read bits aloud to Bobby and Bundy, who had come up behind him. "A hundred fourteen dead, eleven hundred thirteen captured, several dozen missing." He looked up at Leo. "Any chance of some of these missing being rescued?"

Leo recognized the PT-109 commander from World War II brooding over the safety of his men. "Some of our Cubans made it into the swamps," he replied. "The destroyers have been picking them off in ones and twos. A bunch escaped in a sailboat and were rescued at sea."

As Kennedy sighed aloud Leo heard himself say, "It could have been worse, Mr. President."

"How?" Bobby challenged; he wasn't going to let the CIA off the hook anytime soon.

Leo screwed up his courage. "It might have succeeded."

Kennedy accepted this with a dispirited shake of his head. "A new President comes to the job assuming that intelligence people have secret skills outside the reach of mere mortals. I won't make the same mistake twice."

"The problem now is Khrushchev," Bobby said. "He's going to read you as a weak leader, someone who doesn't have the nerve to finish what he starts."

"He's going to assume you can be bullied," Bundy agreed.

Kennedy turned away. Leo, waiting at the door to see if the President wanted anything else from the CIA that night, heard him say, "Well, there's one place to prove to Khrushchev that we can't be pushed around, that we're ready to commit forces and take the heat, and that's Vietnam."

"Vietnam," Bobby said carefully, "could be the answer to our prayers."

The President plunged his hands deep into the pockets of his suit jacket and strolled through the French doors into the garden. There was the distant murmur of traffic and, curiously, the first unmistakable scent of spring in the air. Kennedy tramped off into the darkness, lost in thought as he tried to come to terms with the first political disaster of his life.

7

BOBBY KENNEDY, HIS SHIRTSLEEVES ROLLED UP, A LAMINATED SECURITY pass flapping on the outside of his breast pocket, was picking Leo's brain in the war room on the ground floor of Quarters Eye. The giant maps of Cuba and the overlays with tactical information had been removed. Enlarged U-2 reconnaissance photos of the beaches on the Bay of Pigs taken after the debacle were tacked to the walls in their place. They showed shattered tanks and trucks and Jeeps half-buried in drifts of sand, the wreckage of several LCUs awash in the surf off shore and an enormous Cuban flag streaming from the neon sign atop Blanco's Bar. Bobby had spent most of the last ten days at the CIA, trying to read into the *culture*; Jack Kennedy had abandoned the idea of having his brother run the Company, but he had decided it would be prudent if an emissary from the Kennedy clan took a closer look at its inner workings.

"My own feeling," Leo was saying, "is that we're in a Catch-22 situation. If we reach out for more opinions, what we gain in expertise we lose on security. When too many people know about an operation you can be certain it will leak."

"If you'd brought more people in on the Bay of Pigs could the disaster have been avoided?" Kennedy wanted to know.

Leo shook his head. "Look, can I speak frankly?"

Kennedy nodded. "If you don't we're both in trouble."

Leo scratched behind an ear. "The big problem wasn't a lack of expertise—we had plenty of that even though we limited access drastically. There was dissent expressed, and vigorously, in this room. The big problem was that the President, having inherited an Eisenhower operation that he was then reluctant to cancel, was half-hearted. Dick Bissell, on the other hand, was one-and-a-half hearted. The nature of the beast was that there would have to be compromises if the two visions were to be compatible. Compromises killed the operation, Mr. Attorney General. Moving the landings from Trinidad was a compromise. Using those old surplus B-26s was a compromise. Cutting back on the first air strike was a compromise. Cancelling the second air strike was a tragic compromise. I think I understand why the President was tailoring the operation; as the commander in chief he's obliged to take a global view of the Cold War. If he committed American planes or ships in Cuba, Khrushchev might move against Berlin. Our problem here was that, at some point, someone should have bitten the bullet and said we've made one compromise too many. The risk-benefit scale has tipped in favor of the risks. The whole thing ought to be cancelled."

Bobby fixed his ice blue gaze on Leo; he thought he had tapped into the Company *culture* at last. "What stopped you?"

Leo considered the question. "There are two mentalities cohabiting under one roof here. There are those who think we've been put on earth to steal the other side's secrets and then analyze the secrets we steal. Implicit in this mindset is the belief that you can discover the enemy's intentions by analyzing his capabilities. Why would Hitler mass barges on the English Channel if he didn't intend to invade England? Why would the Chinese mass troops on the Yalu if they didn't plan to attack the Americans in North Korea? That sort of thing. Then there are others who want this organization to impact events, as opposed to predict them—rig elections, sap morale, promote rebellions, bribe officials in high places to throw monkey wrenches into the works, eventually eliminate political figures who frustrate us. The people holding this second view ran the show during the Bay of Pigs. Once the cards were dealt, once they drew a halfway interesting hand, they weren't about to fold."

"And which side do you belong to?"

Leo smiled. He had heard scuttlebutt that Bobby, during his ten-day short course, had become intrigued with clandestine operations; with the gadgets and the dead drops and the safe houses. "I have a foot in each camp," he finally told the Attorney General.

"Playing it safe?"

"Playing it smart. Why fight the Cold War with one hand tied behind your back?"

Bobby's eyebrows arched. "You've given me food for thought, Kritzky." He looked at the wall clock, then got to his feet and strolled across the war room to join several staffers who were watching a television set with the sound turned down low. Earlier in the day, Commander Alan Shepard had rocketed off from Cape Canaveral in a Mercury capsule to become the first American in space; assuming that Shepard was recovered alive, the United States—*the Kennedy administration*—could take credit for catching up with the Russians in the space race. On the TV screen Walter Cronkite was reporting that Shepard had reached the apogee of the flight, a hundred and sixteen miles up. A wire ticker next to the television set was spitting out a long tongue of paper. Bobby absently let it slip through his fingers, then, intrigued, leaned over the machine to read the text. The plain language message had been routed, using a secure intra-Company channel, from the communications center in another building on the Reflecting Pool, where the original cable had been deciphered.

TOP SECRET
WARNING NOTICE: SENSITIVE COMPARTMENTED INFORMATION
Intelligence sources and methods involved

FROM: Mexico City Station
TO: Kermit Coffin
SUBJECT: Rumors from Castro-land

1. Mexico City station has gotten wind of rumors circulating in left-wing circles in Latin America that Castro might be willing to trade prisoners captured at Bay of Pigs for $50 million, repeat, $50 million, worth of food and medicine.

2. Cuban cultural attaché here overheard on tapped phone line telling Cuban wife of left-wing publisher that deal could be negotiated with private humanitarian groups if this arrangement more palatable to Kennedy administration.

Excited by this nugget of intelligence, Bobby ripped the communiqué off the ticker and started toward the door.

Harvey Torriti, just back from one of his two-martini coffee breaks and in a foul mood, noticed the Attorney General heading for the exit with the top secret message in his hand. He planted his body in the doorway. "Hey, where you going with that?" he demanded.

Bobby, his eyes smoldering, stared at the obese man blocking the exit. "Who the fuck do you think you're talking to?"

The Sorcerer's jowls sagged into a sneer. "I'm talking to you, sport.

Newspapers say you're the second most powerful man in the District of Columbia, which may or may not be true. Whichever, you're not getting out of here carrying paperwork crawling with Company indicators and operational codes. No fucking way, pal."

"I don't like your tone, Torriti—"

The Sorcerer duck-swaggered closer to Bobby, grabbed his wrist with one hand and pulled the message free with the other. Around the war room people froze in their tracks, mesmerized by the dispute. Leo came rushing across the floor. "Harvey, you're overreacting—the Attorney General knows the rules—"

"You and your brother fucked up," Torriti snapped at Bobby. "The Bay of Pigs was your fault. The Cuban freedom fighters are rotting in Castro's prisons because of you."

Bobby's face had turned livid. "You're out," he snarled. He turned on Leo. "I want him out of this building, out of this city, out of the country."

"Fuck you," the Sorcerer shot back. He waved five fat fingers in Bobby's direction as if he were trying to flag down a taxi. "Fuck him," he told the staffers in the war room. He belched into his fist. Then, with his flanks scraping the sides of the jambs, he pushed through the doorway and lumbered off down the corridor.

"You ought to have seen it," Jack whispered to Millie. "It was like Moses catching a glimpse of the Promised Land he would never live in. Everyone understands Dulles's head has to be lopped off. All the same a lot of us felt bad for him."

Scabs had formed over the shrapnel wounds on Jack's thigh. Millie ran her fingers lightly over them in the darkness of the bedroom, then fitted herself against his lanky body. "I haven't slept through the night once since you're back," she whispered in his ear. "I keep waking up and checking to make sure you're actually here, and not a figment of my imagination."

Jack held her tightly. "I wasn't a figment of your imagination tonight, was I?"

She ran the tip of her tongue along the inside of his ear. "I love it when you're inside me, Jack. I wish you'd stay there forever."

"I want it to last forever. Orgasms are the enemy. They remind me of *The End* that flashes onto the screen when the movie's over."

"We can always start again."

"*You* can always start again. Mere mortals like me need to rest up for a few hours."

"There are things I can do to bring you to a boil sooner."

"Like what?"

Millie could feel him getting hard. "Like talking about the things I can do to bring you to a boil."

They laughed softly into each other's necks. Over the intercom Jack had strung between bedrooms they could hear Anthony tossing in his sleep. Millie said, "You started to describe Dulles."

"He put on a good show. He was the perfect gentleman. You'd never have known that he was about to be replaced by some rich Catholic ship-builder friend of JFK's. He took Kennedy around the new digs, pointing things out with the stem of his pipe—"

"What's it like out at Langley?"

"Very modern, very elaborate. After all these years on Cockroach Alley we'll be able to spread our wings. Every division's going to have its own suite. Soviet Russia's on the fourth and fifth floors. Your office will be one flight down from the topsiders on the seventh floor." Jack snickered. "They like to keep the public relations folks close by."

"We're their security blanket," Millie said.

"Yeah. Although I don't know why. All you ever say on the record is *No comment.*"

"It's the way we say it, Jack."

"Langley's going to be easier to work in," he went on. "The DCI suite has several waiting rooms so that visitors won't run in to each other. You can send documents from one office to another through pneumatic tubes. They've set up a parallel phone system so we'll all have numbers with a State or Defense exchange—calls to these numbers will come in on an outside line, bypassing the regular Company switchboard; they'll be answered by operators pretending to be secretaries in other government offices." Jack mimicked a secretary. *"I'm terribly sorry but Mr. McAuliffe is away from his desk. But I'd be glad to take a message?"*

Millie listened to Jack's breathing for awhile; it occurred to her that this was the most reassuring sound she had ever heard in her life. "That was a great homecoming barbecue this afternoon," she said. "It was really sweet of Adelle to go to all that trouble."

"Leo and I go back a long way," Jack said drowsily.

"Leo and Ebby and you—this Bay of Pigs business really brought you closer together, didn't it?"

"We see eye to eye on a lot of things. Some people are starting to call us the 'Three Musketeers' because we hang out together so much. We work together. We break for lunch together. We party together weekends." Jack was silent for a moment. "I like Ebby an awful lot—he's the best the Company has, the cream of our generation. He can wade into the thick of the action, like he did in Budapest, or he can hang back and think things out for himself. He's not afraid to speak his mind. He was the perfect choice to take over the Soviet Russia Division. Something tells me he's going to go a long way..."

"What did Adelle's father mean when he told you and Leo that he'd heard it from the horse's mouth? And what did he hear?"

"Phil Swett gets invited to the White House pretty regularly. He said that all the Kennedy brothers could talk about at a lunch last week was Vietnam. Adelle picked up the same thing in the Vice President's office. Lyndon Johnson has her working up a position paper on Vietnam."

"What's going on in Vietnam, Jack?"

"So far, not much. There's a Communist insurgency but it's back burner stuff. After what happened in Cuba, Kennedy apparently feels he needs to convince Khrushchev he can be tough. Tough and unpredictable at the same time. And Vietnam is going to be the showcase. The Company is beefing up its station there. JFK's going to send over a few hundred Green Berets to help train the anti-Communist forces."

"He'd better be careful not to get sucked in. I don't think the American people will support a war in Asia."

"Vietnam's too far away." Jack yawned into a pillow. "Nobody will notice."

The two newcomers and the two who had been living at the mansion for half a year were squatting in a circle on the parquet floor, playing jacks. None of the four wore a stitch of clothing. "I am up to five-zees," announced the bony girl whose long golden tresses plunged halfway down her naked back. She tossed the small ball into the air, deftly scooped up the six-pointed pieces and snatched the ball out of the air an instant before it bounced.

"You throw the ball so very high," one of the new girls complained, "it's no wonder you manage to win all the time."

"There is no regulation about how high one can throw it," the golden-haired girl maintained.

"There is," insisted another.

"Is not."

"Is."

"Do come over, Uncle, and decide which of us is correct," called the girl with the golden hair.

"Too busy right now, girlies," Starik muttered from across the room.

"Oh, pooh," fumed the new girl. "If you don't set things straight she'll only go on winning."

At the worktable, Starik sipped scalding tea through a sugar cube wedged between his teeth as he reread the text of the latest lode from SASHA. One of his newcomers, a scrawny thing who walked with her toes turned out like a ballet dancer's, came across the room and draped herself over Starik's shoulders. "What an awfully pretty book you have there, Uncle," she murmured into his ear.

"It is called a world atlas," he instructed her; he prided himself on the fact that his nieces, when they left him, were more educated than the day they arrived.

"And what in the world is an atlas?" inquired the girl, slipping a thin hand over his shoulder and down under the front of his rough peasant shirt.

"The atlas *is* the world. Look here—on every page there are maps of all the different countries."

"Are there enough countries in the world to fill a book, then?"

"More than enough, dearie."

"And what country is on the page open before you, Uncle?"

"Why, it is called Vietnam."

The girl giggled into his ear. "I have never heard anyone speak of a country with the name of Vietnam."

"Rest assured, you will," Starik said.

The Sorcerer's tour as Chief of Station, Rome, began on a mortifying note when he dozed off during his first round-table with the American ambassador. The embassy's political officer, a myopic John Hopkins Ph.D. with the unfortunate habit of sniffling whenever he came to the end of a sentence, was droning on about the latest nuance in the speeches of the Italian Communist Party chief, Palmiro Togliatti; according to the political attaché, Togliatti had started down the slippery slope of independence from Big Brother in the Kremlin, and this breach between the Italian and Soviet Communists ought to be encouraged and exploited. The political officer was midway through the presentation when the Sorcerer's head nodded onto his chest and he slumped to one side in the seat. His checkered sports jacket flapped open, the pearl-handled revolver slipped out of the shoulder holster and clattered to the floor.

"Are we keeping you up?" the ambassador inquired as the Sorcerer jerked awake.

"I'm resting my eyes but not my brain," Torriti shot back, leaning over to retrieve the hand gun. "I was hanging on his every word."

"How much more convincing you would be if you could manage to hang on his every word with your eyes open," the ambassador remarked dryly.

"Why Rome?" the ambassador cabled back to Foggy Bottom in Washington when, a few days later, Torriti turned up drunk at an embassy reception for the Italian foreign minister. "There are dozens of embassies around the world where he could be hidden away from Bobby Kennedy."

The Sorcerer, for his part, had been dragged into exile kicking and complaining. "Torriti, the patriot, is deported to Italy while the Cosa Nostra pricks, Rosselli and Giancana, get to live in America," he had muttered into the microphone at the discreet farewell party the outgoing DD/O, Dick Bissell, organized for him in the executive dining room on the eve of his departure for Rome. There had been a ripple of laughter from the handful of people who knew what Torriti was talking about. Angleton, thinner and darker and more brooding than anyone remembered, had emerged from the polar-darkness of his counterintelligence shop to give a going-away present to the man everyone knew he detested. It was a leather holster he had personally handcrafted for Torriti's .38 Detective Special. "Jesus, James, I don't know what to say," sputtered the Sorcerer, for once at a loss for words.

"It's not *Jesus* James," Angleton, scowling, corrected him. "It's James *Jesus*."

Torriti had peered at James Jesus Angleton to see if the counterintelligence chief had stepped out of character to make a joke. It was obvious from the cantankerous expression on his face that this was not the case. "Sorry, sorry," the Sorcerer had said, nodding obsequiously as he fitted his ankle gun into the holster. "James Jesus. Right."

In Rome, the Sorcerer made a stab at actually running the Station for several months but the situation gradually deteriorated. A colonel in the *carabinieri* took him on a tour of the Yugoslav frontier only to discover Torriti snoring away in the back seat of the Fiat. There were all-night binges that were hushed up, a fling with an Italian actress that found its way into the gossip columns of several Roman newspapers, a very public clash with the ambassador that wound up on the desk of the Secretary of State. There were two minor traffic accidents, one involving an embassy car, the second involving an automobile that a used car dealer swore had been stolen and Torriti claimed to have bought, though he was unable to put his hand on the receipt for the cash payment he claimed to have made. The matter was hushed up when some unvouchered Company funds changed hands. By the time July rolled around the Sorcerer had taken to flying off for sentimental weekend visits to Berlin. Accompanied by one or two old hands who had served under him when he was the head of Berlin Base, he'd make the rounds of the bars where his name was still a legend, then wander through the shadowy side streets near Checkpoint Charlie to get a whiff of the action, as he put it. On one memorable occasion he drank whiskey at a pub in the British Sector and had to be forcibly restrained from strolling into the Soviet zone for a chaser. At two in the morning one Sunday during the second week of August, he trudged with his old Mossad pal, Ezra Ben Ezra, to the roof of an apartment building to watch as Soviet tanks wheeled into position and East German troops strung barbed wire blocking the frontier between the two Germanies. Behind the tanks and troops came an armada of bulldozers, their headlights tunneling through the dust and darkness as they cleared a broad no-man's land that would later be mined. "This rates a nine on my Richter scale," the Rabbi told his old friend. "My sources tell me this is Khrushchev's answer to the Bay of Pigs—they are going to build a Great Wall of China across Germany, sealing off the Communist zone from the free world." The Sorcerer pulled a hip flask from a pocket and offered the Rabbi a swig. Ben Ezra waved away the alcohol. "There is nothing here to celebrate," he said mournfully. "It will be next to impossible to get Jews out now."

Returning to Rome that night, Torriti found a bottle of cheap whiskey and two kitchen tumblers set out on his desk and Jack McAuliffe stretched out on the couch waiting for him. A table lamp in a corner etched shadows onto the café-au-lait walls as the two sat drinking and reminiscing into the early hours of Monday morning. The Sorcerer, his eyes puffy, pulled out his pearl-handled revolver, spun the cylinder and set the weapon on his knees, with the barrel pointing directly at Jack's stomach. "I wasn't born yesterday, sport," he grumbled. "You weren't sent all this way to chew the fat. What aren't you saying to me?"

"What I'm not saying, Harvey, is you're an embarrassment to the Company."

"Who says so?"

"The American ambassador to Rome says so. The new DD/O, Dick Helms, agrees with him. The new DCI, John McCone, also."

"Fuck them all."

"What I'm not saying, Harvey, is you've been around a long time. You've pulled your weight and then some."

"What you're not saying is I ought to call it a day, right?"

"All things considered, that would probably be the best thing to do, Harvey."

"I'm glad it was you they sent, Jack." The Sorcerer, suddenly sober, straightened in the chair. "Do they want me to hang in here until the new Chief of Station comes out?"

"I'm the new Chief of Station, Harvey."

Torriti nodded listlessly. "At your pleasure, sport."

The Sorcerer organized his own farewell bash in the ballroom of the Rome Hilton. For background music there were recordings of arias sung by Luciano Pavarotti, an Italian tenor who had made a scintillating debut earlier in the year. Liquor flowed. Speeches were delivered. The phrase "end of an era" came back like a refrain. Around midnight Jack finally managed to get a call through to Millie in Washington; she and Anthony would be flying over the following week, their furniture would be coming out on an MSTS freighter at the end of the month, she said. Had Jack found an apartment yet? Jack promised he'd start looking first thing Monday.

Returning to the ballroom, Jack discovered that the Hilton's night manager had turned off the air conditioning. The handful of people remaining drifted toward the exits. Two secretaries were fending off a very soused Torriti, who was trying to talk them into transporting the party, or what was left of it, to "a more reputable hotel than the Hilton." At two in the morning Jack and his old boss from Berlin Base stumbled out onto the sidewalk in front of the hotel. A stifling August heat wave struck them in the face.

Jack gasped. "We need air conditioning."

"We need booze," Torriti agreed. Hanging on to each other's arms, the two stumbled down the street to the Excelsior on Via Veneto and managed to bribe the bartender into giving them one for the road.

Munching an olive, Torriti squinted at Jack. "So you loved her, didn't you, sport?"

"Who?"

"The German broad. The dancer. The one that went by the code name RAINBOW. The one that filled her mouth with water and shot herself."

"You mean Lili. Yeah, Harvey. I did love her."

"I figured." Torriti threw back some more whiskey. "She wasn't one of my barium meals, Jack."

"That's what you said at the time. I never thought otherwise."

"There was a war on but there are lines I don't cross."

"I know that, Harvey."

"You believe me, don't you, kid?"

"Sure I do."

"Cause if you didn't, if you thought she'd been one of my goddamn barium meals, it would hurt real bad, you see what I mean?"

"I never blamed you."

The Sorcerer punched Jack in the shoulder. "That means a lot to me, sport." He signaled for a refill.

"Last one, please," implored the bartender as he refilled their glasses. "I have this second job, it starts at eight-thirty, which leaves me five and a half hours to sleep."

Torriti clinked glasses with Jack. "My barium meals paid off, sport. It was yours truly who smoked out Philby when fucking Jesus James you-know-who was buying him lunch at La Niçoise."

"The Company owes you, Harvey."

Torriti leaned so far toward Jack that he would have fallen off the barstool if he hadn't grabbed the brass rail. "There's another Russian mole in the Company," he murmured, the liquor breath stirring the air around his companion's face. "The famous SASHA. And I know who it is."

"You know the identity of SASHA!"

"Fucking A. I'll let you in on a little secret, kid. SASHA is none other than Jesus James fucking Angleton himself." When Jack started to smile Torriti turned ornery. "I've given this a lot of thought, pal. Okay, the evidence is circumstantial, I'm the first to admit it. Look at it this way: If the KGB actually has a mole inside the Company he couldn't do more damage than Angleton."

"I'm not sure I follow you—"

"Angleton's been turning the CIA inside out for the last ten years looking for moles, right? Tell me something, sport—has he ever found one? The answer is negative. But he's crippled the Soviet Russia division with his suspicions. He's got everyone looking over everyone else's shoulder. I know guys who're afraid to bring in a defector for fear Angleton will think they're vouching for a KGB plant because they're a KGB plant. I made a head count once—Jesus James's ruined the careers of something like a hundred officers. He sits on the promotion board—"

"I didn't know that."

"Well, I know that. He's blackballed dozens of promotions, he's forced good people into early retirement. One Soviet Russia division officer on Angleton's shit list went and passed a lie detector, at which point he was reassigned to Paris as Chief of Station. You know what Angleton did?"

"What did he do, Harvey?"

"Fucking Jesus James flew to Paris and personally warned the French counterintelligence people that the CIA station chief was a Soviet mole. The fucking frogs immediately cut off all contact with the station. Holy shit, Angleton's going around telling anyone in Congress who'll listen that the Sino-Soviet split is KGB disinformation designed to lull the West into letting down its guard. Ditto for Tito in Yugoslavia."

The bartender finished rinsing glasses. "Gentlemen, have a heart. I need to close now."

The Sorcerer slid off the seat and hiked his baggy trousers high up on his vast waist. "Remember where you heard it first, sport," he said. "Jesus James fucking Angleton is SASHA."

"I won't forget, Harvey."

"Fucker thought he'd buy me off with a holster but I'm one jump ahead of him. Shit, I may go around in vicious circles but I go around one jump ahead of everyone."

Outside the Excelsior, Torriti looked up and down the deserted avenue, trying to figure out which way to go and what to do with the rest of his life. With Jack trailing behind, he staggered off in the direction of the American embassy, a block away. As he drew abreast of the gate, the young Marine on duty in the glass booth recognized him.

"Morning to you, Mr. Torriti, sir."

"No fucking way," the Sorcerer called over his shoulder to Jack as he waddled past the Marine down the walkway toward the main entrance. "RAINBOW wasn't one of my barium meals." He reached the wall and unzipped his fly and flexed his knees and began to urinate against the side of the embassy. "I'd remember if she was, sport. Something like that'd lodge in your skull like a goddamn tumor."

Jack caught up with the Sorcerer. "I can see how it would, Harvey." He conjured up a vision of Roberto and Orlando and the other Cubans jammed into one of Castro's dark dungeons. Blinking hard to stifle the image, he opened his fly and began to relieve himself against the embassy, too.

Torriti didn't appear to notice the puddle of urine forming around his scuffed shoes. "You're still the Sorcerer's Apprentice, right, sport?"

"I am, Harvey. The Sorcerer's Apprentice. And proud to be."

PART FOUR

SLEEPING DOGS

*She tried to fancy what the flame of a candle
looks like after the candle is blown out.*

Snapshot: a black-and-white photograph, taken in the dead of night with ASA 2,000 film using available light from wrought iron lampposts, shows two figures passing each other in the middle of a deserted bridge. They appear to have stopped for a moment to exchange words. The older of the two, a haggard man with thick eyeglasses that have turned fuliginous in the overhead light, is threading long bony fingers through his thinning hair. The gesture conveys anxiety. The other man, younger and taller than the first and wearing a shapeless raincoat, seems to be smiling at a private joke. The photograph was snapped by a journalist from Der Spiegel *who had staked out the bridge after being tipped off by the Gehlen Organization in Pullach. Before* Der Spiegel *could go to press with the photo, the CIA got wind of its existence and arranged for the negative and prints to be seized by a German state prosecutor. The negative and all existing copies of the photograph were turned over to the chief of Berlin Base, who shredded everything but the single copy that was filed away in the station's archives. Stamped diagonally across the photograph are the words "Top Secret" and "Archives Only."*

1

O N TELEVISION, WORKERS FROM THE RED STAR CHEMICAL FERTILIZER Plant Number Four in Nizhnevartovsk on the Ob River could be seen streaming into Red Square carrying a giant papier-mâché head of Leonid Brezhnev, the First Secretary of the Communist Party of the USSR. As Brezhnev's head, bobbing above a sea of people, came abreast of the reviewing stand atop Lenin's Tomb, a slip of a girl wearing gold lamé tights and a silver tank top detached herself from the marchers to skip up the stairs at the side of the tomb and present the First Secretary, his face thick with makeup for the television cameras, with a bouquet of red and pink carnations. "Oh, she is awfully cute, don't you think?" exclaimed one of the girls glued to the TV screen, a twelve-year-old Chechen with guileless eyes. "If Uncle were watching he would certainly pick up the telephone and ask her name."

Uncle was watching—he'd been invited by the First Secretary to join the head of the Komitét Gosudárstvennoi Bezopásnosti and several senior Directorate chiefs in his private suite in the Kremlin, where they could observe the May Day parade on a giant television screen while sipping Champagne and snacking on *zakuski*. In Uncle's apartment in the Apatov Mansion near Cheryomuski, the nieces—they were reduced to five now; the sixth, a Uighur from the Xinjiang Uigur region of Central Asia, had been sent home when it was discovered, during bath hour, that she had started menstruating—grew bored with the parade, which still had four hours to run, and decided to play hide-and-seek. Crouching behind Uncle's bathrobes in a closet in the bedroom, the Cuban girl, Revolución, discovered a toy revolver loaded with toy bullets in a shoebox. "Girls, girls," she cried, emerging from her hiding place, "come see what I've found."

The weather had turned unseasonably warm but nobody had thought to turn off the mansion's central heating. Uncle's bedroom was like a sauna. The five girls stripped to their cotton underpants and undershirts and settled in a circle on Uncle's great bed, and Revolución taught them a new game she had heard about in Havana. First she removed the make-believe bullets until only one was left in the revolver. Looking up, she recited from memory a passage from Uncle's favorite book. "'I'll be judge, I'll be jury,' said cunning old Fury. 'I'll try the whole cause, and condemn you to death.'" Then she spun the cylinder and, closing her eyes, inserted the tip of the long barrel between her thin lips. Holding the revolver with both hands, she pushed against the trigger with her thumb. There was an audible click as the hammer came down on an empty chamber. Smiling innocently, she passed the handgun to the Kazakh niece on her right. When the girl seemed uncertain about what exactly she was expected to do, Revolución guided her—she spun the cylinder and inserted the barrel in the girl's mouth and showed her how to trip the trigger with her thumb. Once again there was a loud click.

The Chechen, who was next in the circle, shook her head. "Oh, dear, I really don't wish to play this game," she announced.

"But you must," Revolución insisted. "Once a game's begun there can be no turning back. It's like Alice and her friends, don't you see? Everybody shall win and all shall have prizes."

"I don't know," the Chechen said uncertainly.

"Play, play," pleaded the others in chorus. The Chechen girl picked up the gun reluctantly. She spun the cylinder and, pouting to better suck on the barrel, inserted the tip ever so slightly into her mouth.

"Do go ahead and play, for it's only a game," Revolución said impatiently.

"Play, play," the others taunted when she still hesitated. Screwing up her eyes, the Chechen sighed and tripped the trigger with a jerk of her thumb.

There was a deafening report as the back of her skull exploded, spattering the girls and the wall behind the bed with blood and flecks of bone and brain.

Uncle found the body of the Chechen when he returned from Moscow that evening. He was distressed for the longest time, and calmed down only after men in white coveralls enshrouded the dead girl in the blood-drenched sheets and took her away. The nieces, beside themselves with fright, were all made to bathe while Uncle himself sponged the wall behind the bed clean of blood and brain tissue. Revolución was given a scolding about the perils of playing with firearms and sent off without supper, and was not permitted to participate in the hugging and fondling that always followed the nightly reading from the worn pages of Uncle's now blood-speckled bedside book.

The next afternoon a new child appeared at the doorway of Uncle's suite in the Apatov Mansion. Her name turned out to be Axinya. She came from the city of Nizhnevartovska on the Ob River, and was wearing gold lamé tights and a silver tank top.

Moving like phantoms through the pre-dawn stillness, the seven members of the hit team, dressed in identical black trousers and turtleneck sweaters and sneakers, assaulted the house in Oak Park near Chicago. Three of the attackers cut the telephone lines and the electricity cables, then came over the high brick wall with shards of glass cemented into the top, dropped lightly down onto the grass and broke into the gatehouse. Using aerosol cans filled with an experimental Soviet nerve gas, they subdued the three body-guards sleeping on Army cots before they could raise an alarm. Two other attackers cut the glass out of a basement window and, slipping through the frame, landed in what had once been the coal bin before the house was switched over to oil. Making their way to the small service apartment at the back of the basement, they bound and gagged the Korean couple in their beds. The leader of the hit team and another attacker scrambled up a trellis to a second-floor terrace, jimmied open French doors with a short crowbar that had been ground down to a thin wedge at the end, then padded through a room filled with round tables and wicker chairs to the hallway. The bodyguard on night duty had nodded off in an easy chair. He was neutralized with nerve gas and lowered soundlessly to the parquet floor. Gripping their Czech 7.65 pistols fitted with silencers, the two invaders pushed through a door into a large bedroom that reeked from the cigar butts heaped in a glass ashtray on a night table. Startled out of a sound sleep, a short, balding man wearing striped pajamas sat upright in bed to find himself pinned in the beams of two flashlights.

"What duh fuck—"

A young woman with long dyed hair and heavy breasts slid naked from the sheets and cowered in a corner, shielding her body with the hem of the window curtain. One of the invaders nodded toward the bathroom door. The woman, only too glad to escape, darted across the room and locked her-self in the bathroom.

From the bed the man croaked, "Who duh fuck sent you?"

The hit team leader produced lengths of nylon cord and began tying the man's wrists and ankles to the four bedposts. The second attacker kept a flashlight and pistol trained on the man's face.

"Holy shit, you're makin' uh big fuckin' mistake. You know who I am? Fuck, dis can't be happenin' to me."

The last length of nylon was slipped over his left ankle and pulled tight against a bedpost. The man in pajamas, spread-eagled on the bed, began to panic.

"Wait, wait, listen up, whatever whoever's payin' you pays you, I'll pay you double. I swear to Christ. Double! Triple, even. Sure, triple." He twisted his head toward the door. "Charlie, where duh fuck are you?" He turned back to his captors. "Why not triple? Do not laugh uh gift horse in duh mouth. You need to be smart, dis is uh opportunity to make big bucks. Jesus Christ, don't just stand there lookin' at me like dat, say something."

The hit team leader removed a pillow from the bed. *"Hubiese sido mejor para ustedes de no haber nacido nunca,"* he murmured.

"Oh, Jesus, I don't know Spanish. Why duh fuck are you talkin' Spanish?"

"I'm talking Cuban," the leader told the man spread-eagled on the bed. "I am telling you: *It will be good for you if you had not been born.*"

"Holy Mother of God, I'm ain't goin' to croak. I won't do it. I refuse."

The hit team leader slowly lowered the pillow over the victim's face. Wrenching his head from side to side, pulling on the bindings until the nylon cord bit into his wrists, the short balding man spit out half-stifled phrases. "...please don't...beggin' you...love of God...please, oh, please... mercy on...I'm on my fuckin' knees...I'm pleadin' with you..."

The other attacker pressed the tip of the silencer attached to his Czech pistol deep into the pillow and shot seven bullets through it into the man's face.

The self-propelled garbage scow that normally serviced ships anchored off North Miami Beach cut across Dumfoundling Bay after midnight. The sea was flat, the offshore breeze barely able to stir the worn company pennant flying from a halyard on the mast. Astern of the scow headlights flickered playfully along the low Florida coastline. Overhead, a gibbous moon burned through the haze, churning up flecks of silver in the vessel's wake. In the well of the scow, a tall, silver-haired man with a mournful face stood ankle-deep in garbage, his legs spread for balance. Four men wearing black trousers, turtleneck sweaters and rubber boots kept Czech pistols trained on him. The silver-haired man took off his blazer and, folding it inside out, set it down on the garbage. Then he undid his tie and removed a pair of silver cufflinks and set them on the blazer. Gripping the side of the scow, he kicked off one alligator loafer and then the other, then pulled off his socks and the garters that kept them up on his calves. He undid the silver buckle on his belt and the buttons on his fly, dropped his trousers to his ankles and gingerly stepped out of them, trying to avoid placing his bare feet in the more revolting garbage. He unbuttoned his shirt and added it to the pile of clothing. He removed the watch on his wrist and the diamond ring on his pinkie and tossed them overboard. Then he looked up at the leader of the hit team, who was watching from the open pilot house.

The leader gestured with a finger toward the man's white skivvy shorts. Without a word the silver-haired man slipped them off and folded them onto the pile. He straightened and stood there, stark naked and hugging his hairy chest because of the chill.

"Awright, just tell me who wants me whacked," the naked man called up to the pilot house.

"*Hubiese sido mejor para ustedes de no haber nacido nunca,*" the hit team leader shouted back.

The naked man, who spoke Spanish, shook his head in disgust. "Whoever, you tell him for me to go fuck himself," he said.

The other men moved in to attach his wrists and ankles with telephone line, which they tightened with pliers until the wire cut into the skin, drawing blood. The naked man didn't utter a word as he was lifted into an empty oil drum and forced down until he was seated in it with his knees jammed up against his chin. The top of the barrel was screwed on and locked in place with several blows from a sledgehammer. The four men in turtleneck sweaters wrestled the barrel up onto the shelf that ran from stem to stern above the garbage well. A length of heavy anchor chain was wrapped around the barrel and secured with thick wire. The team leader nodded. The four men rolled the barrel to the edge of the scow. Just before it was pushed overboard a hollow voice could be heard crying out, "The fucker should go fuck himself."

The barrel, with the anchor chain around it, hit the water and floated for a moment before it began to sink with excruciating slowness into the sea.

2

WASHINGTON, DC, SUNDAY, MAY 12, 1974

THE ANNUAL SOVIET DIVISION (THE ANACHRONISTIC APPELLATION "Russia" finally had been dropped from the nomenclature) BYOB barbecue on the back lawn of Leo Kritzky's newly purchased Georgetown house had been called on account of rain and the party had moved indoors, sprawling across the kitchen and dining room into the living room, finally spilling down into the basement rumpus room when a handful of the younger officers showed up with their wives or girlfriends. Leo, the current division chief, and his wife, Adelle, meandered through the rooms distributing hot dogs to the troops. Ebby, in his second year as DD/O, was pushing through knots of people to hand out fresh bottles of Beaujolais when he noticed his son, Manny, arguing in a corner with Elizabet's daughter, Nellie. The two hadn't seen each other in nineteen months. Fresh out of Harvard Law, Nellie, now a bewitching twenty-three-year-old with a willowy figure and her mother's dark impatient eyes dancing under a mop of dirty-blonde hair, had gone to work for an insurance firm in Hong Kong and only just come back for job interviews in Washington. Manny, a reserved, slightly stooped young man with a solemn mien, had been recruited into the Company soon after he was graduated from Yale with honors in Central Asian studies; he was fluent in Russian, could converse with an Afghan in Pashto and haggle in pidgin Tajik in a souk.

"Vietnam is the wrong war in the wrong place at the wrong time," Manny, now twenty-eight and a junior officer in Leo's Soviet Division, was saying.

"You're forgetting about the goddamn dominoes," Nellie shot back. She popped a cigarette into her mouth and, knowing Manny didn't smoke, grabbed the elbow of a passing young man. "Do you have fire?" He was only too happy to produce a lighter, She rested a hand lightly on his wrist and pulled the flame to the tip of the cigarette. "So, thanks," she said, dismissing him and turning back to Manny. "If Vietnam falls, believe me, Laos, Cambodia, Thailand won't be far behind. Hellfire, all of Southeast Asia will go Communist, leaving Japan out on a limb, leaving American interests in Asia in a limbo. It doesn't take much political savvy to understand that we need to draw the line somewhere."

"You sound like Joe Alsop," Manny remarked. "You miss the same point he misses—the war in Vietnam is a political problem that requires a political solution, not a military solution."

Nellie decided to tack toward the port she hoped to dock in. "I may sound like Joe Alsop but I don't look like Joe Alsop," she observed sweetly.

Manny flashed a tight grin; somehow Nellie always managed to get under his skin. "Nellie, what happened between us..." Manny looked around nervously, then lowered his voice. "What I'm trying to say is that we're practically brother and sister."

Nellie tucked her arm under Manny's elbow and pushed her breast lightly into his arm. "So like the Bible tells us, incest is best, Manny."

"Be serious, for once."

"Don't be misled by the smile—I'm always serious. Look, if God had been dead set against incest he would have started things off with two couples in two gardens. Which leads me to suspect he wasn't convinced incest was all that bad. So why don't we give it the old college try? Our one-night stand lasted one month. If we shoot for a one-month stand, who knows? It might last a year."

Squirming uncomfortably, Manny tried to pass the idea off as a joke. "It's out of the question, Nellie. I'm allergic to cigarettes. I don't see myself dating someone who smokes."

Nellie tightened her grip on his elbow. "If you loved me even a teensy bit you'd smoke, too. What do you say we take in the new Mel Brooks flick tonight. *Young Frankenstein* sounds like it ought to be required viewing for CIA spooks."

"I can't—I have the night watch from eight to eight."

"Want a rain check?"

"I don't understand you, Nellie. You walk into a room, men—hell, women, too—stop in mid-sentence to follow you with their eyes. Someone lights your cigarette, next thing you know he's head over heels in love with you. Why me?"

Nellie contemplated Manny for a moment. "Believe me, I ask myself the same question. Maybe it's because of the one-night stand that stretched into a month. There was something...different about it."

Manny raised his eyebrows in acknowledgement. "You scare the shit out of me, Nellie."

"If it's any consolation I scare the shit out of me, too. So what about that rain check?"

"Sure. Why not?"

"Tuesday?"

"Tuesday."

In the narrow pantry next to the kitchen Jack's gangly fourteen-year-old son, Anthony, finally managed to buttonhole his godfather, Leo Kritzky. "Are you following the Judiciary Committee's hearings?" the boy asked.

"You'd have to be deaf, dumb and blind not to," Leo said.

"You think they'll actually impeach Nixon?"

"It's beginning to look like a possibility. Especially if the Supreme Court rules against the President on the tapes."

"Explain me something, Leo." Anthony shook a shock of flaming-red hair out of his eyes. "Why would Nixon be dumb enough to record all his conversations in the Oval Office, including the ones that show he was involved in the Watergate business?"

Leo shrugged a shoulder. "Has to do with his personality, I suppose. Nixon feels the Eastern establishment hates him. He tends to pull up the drawbridges and hunker down in the White House, agonizing about his enemies, real or imagined. The tapes may have been his way of agonizing for posterity."

"Have you actually met Nixon, Leo?"

"Several times. I was called in to brief him on specific Soviet Division areas of interest."

"Like what?"

Leo had to smile; he was extremely fond of his godson and had a sneaking admiration for his lively curiosity even when the questions were off-base. "You ought to know better than to ask me something like that, Anthony."

"I'm not a Russian spy, Chrissakes. You can trust me?"

"I don't think you're a Russian spy. But I'm still not going to tell you things that you don't need to know. That's how we operate in the Company."

"I've pretty much decided to join the Company when I finish college," the boy said. "With both my parents working there, I ought to breeze in."

"First finish high school, buddy. Then get your warm body into a good college. Then graduate. After which we'll see about your breezing into the Company."

Jack McAuliffe pushed through the kitchen door looking for more booze. He waved to Anthony in the pantry, grabbed two bottles of Beaujolais by their throats and headed back toward the rumpus room. Jack, who was Ebby's Chief of Operations, still sported his flamboyant Cossack mustache, but his dark hair had begun to thin out on the crown of his head and his once-lanky body had thickened noticeably around the middle. To the younger generation of Company officers he was something of a legend: the man who had defied orders and gone ashore at the Bay of Pigs—and escaped only when the Brigade commander threatened to shoot him if he remained.

"Where were we?" Jack asked as he spilled wine into outstretched tumblers.

"We were on the beaches of the Bay of Pigs," a newcomer to the Soviet Division reminded him.

"That's not anyplace you'd want to go for R and R," Jack quipped. The young officers scraping up chairs around him in the rumpus room laughed appreciatively.

"Would the invasion have succeeded if Kennedy hadn't cut back on the first air strike and called off the second?" an intense young woman inquired.

"Probably not," Jack said thoughtfully. "But Khrushchev might have thought twice about installing missiles in Cuba if he hadn't been convinced Kennedy was chicken-shit."

"Are you saying the Cuban missile crisis was Kennedy's fault?" another officer wanted to know.

Jack swivelled on his stool. "It was Khrushchev's fault for trying to upset the balance of power in the hemisphere by installing missiles in Cuba. It was Kennedy's fault for letting Khrushchev think he might be able to get away with it."

Ebby wandered down to join the impromptu bull session. One of the mid-level officers, a crateologist who specialized in analyzing packages from their shape, size, weight and markings, asked the DD/O about the CIA's role in the 1956 Hungarian Revolution. Ebby, sitting on the edge of the ping-pong table, explained how he had been sent into Budapest to talk the anti-Communist Hungarians out of an uprising, at least until the groundwork for the revolution could be laid. Jack described the day when he and Millie had spotted Ebby coming across the Austrian border with a group of refugees. "Frank Wisner was the DD/O at the time," he said. "He had tears in his eyes when he realized Ebby had made it out alive."

"What ever happened to Wisner?" someone asked.

Jack and Ebby avoided each other's eye. "Hungary broke him," Ebby finally said. "He became moody. The moodiness turned into dark depressions. Eventually things got serious enough for him to check into a private psychiatric hospital near Baltimore, where he was diagnosed for psychotic mania—which is roughly a manic-depressive with dreams of grandeur. The doctors even thought his grand schemes—the idea of rolling back Communism in Eastern Europe—might have been early symptoms of the mania. The Wiz was given shock therapy, which brought an end to a given depression but couldn't prevent a new one. By the time he retired—"

"That was back in 1962," Jack said.

"—he wouldn't eat in the same restaurant twice for fear it had been staked out by the KGB. Then, nine years ago—"

Jack finished the story for Ebby. "In 1965 the Wiz was living on his farm in Maryland. The family had hidden his firearms...one day he found a shotgun"—Jack inhaled through his nostrils—"and he went and killed himself."

"It was the Wiz who recruited me," Ebby told the young officers. "It was the Wiz who gave me a boot in the backside when I lost sight of the goal posts. He was a passionate man with a great intellect and boundless energy. I'm proud to have known him—proud to have fought the Cold War alongside him."

"He's one of America's unsung heroes," Jack agreed.

In the early evening the rain let up and the Soviet Division officers and their ladies wandered off to movie theaters. Manny headed back to Langley for the night watch in the Operations Center. Leo and Jack and Ebby broke out some whiskey for a last drink in Leo's den on the second floor of the house. Downstairs, their wives could be heard tidying up. Leo glanced at his two friends. "Who's going to be the first to raise the subject?" he asked.

Ebby said, "You mean Giancana, I suppose."

"Harvey Torriti phoned me up from Santa Fe when he saw the story in the paper," Jack said.

"What did he think?" Ebby asked.

"It sure looks like a mob hit—prying up the manhole to cut the alarm system, the clockwork precision of the break-in, subduing everyone in the house with an unidentified nerve gas, Giancana tied to the bed with a pillow covering his face and seven bullet holes in the pillow."

"I can hear the *but* coming," Leo said.

"There was a *but*," Jack said. "It's Rosselli's disappearance. The Sorcerer said it was too much of a coincidence to be a coincidence—the two Cosa

Nostra dons who were trying to knock off Castro for us getting whacked at the same time."

"He's assuming Rosselli's dead," Ebby noted.

Jack snickered. "Jesus H. Christ, guys like Rosselli don't drop from sight like that. He left a woman's apartment at midnight. Miami police found his car abandoned in a parking lot near the docks in North Miami Beach. The doors were wide open, the key was in the ignition, a Saturday Night Special was in the glove compartment. The Sorcerer said the word on the street was Rosselli'd bought it, too."

"Could be Castro," Ebby remarked.

"Fidel knew the Company was trying to nail his hide to the wall," Leo said. "He knew who our middlemen were."

Ebby said, "If Castro is behind Giancana's murder and Rosselli's disappearance, it raises ominous possibilities—"

One of the two telephones on Leo's desk purred. Leo picked up the receiver. "Kritzky." He reached over and hit the button marked "Scramble," then listened for a moment. "Add it to the President's Book but flag it to say that HUMINT sources are involved so he won't think it came from a cipher breakout." He listened again. "We're flying out of Dulles tonight. Unless World War III starts I'll be out of the loop for two weeks...Thanks, I plan to." Leo rang off. "Vienna Station's got a Russian journalist claiming that India's going to test a ten kiloton atomic device before the month is out."

"That'll put nuclear proliferation on the front burner," Ebby guessed. "We'll get the usual flurry of 'drop whatever you're doing' queries from Kissinger's shop in the White House basement."

"Let's get back to your ominous possibilities," Jack said quietly.

"Remember what Castro is supposed to have said after the Bay of Pigs?" Ebby asked. "Something along the lines of United States leaders should bear in mind that if they were sending terrorists to eliminate Cuban leaders, they themselves would not be safe."

"I can feel the sand shift under my feet every time we get onto this subject," Leo admitted.

"It's a mystery we'll never get to the bottom of," Jack said.

"Maybe it's better that way," Ebby said. "There's something to be said for letting sleeping dogs lie."

"Adelle once repeated something Lyndon Johnson told her days after Kennedy was shot in Dallas," Leo said. He stirred the ice cubes in his drink with the blade of a letter opener. "'Kennedy was trying to kill Castro but Castro got him first.'"

"If Johnson had a shred of hard evidence it would have come out when the Warren Commission investigated the assassination," Ebby said. "I think he was going on gut feelings."

"Warren Commission was a joke," Jack said. "Remember when Harvey Torriti testified at a closed session? He never breathed a word about the Company's Cosa Nostra connections and the various attempts to knock off Castro. He never told them that Oswald had been spotted visiting the Soviet embassy in Mexico City before he killed Kennedy; or that Oswald saw a KGB 13th Department wetwork specialist named Valery Kostikov, who had connections to people close to Castro." Jack had to laugh. "I once asked Harvey how come he never told Warren's people about that stuff. You know what he said? He said he didn't tell them because they didn't ask."

Ebby shook his head uncomfortably. "Assuming Castro got to Giancana and Rosselli, the question is: Did he get to John Kennedy, too?"

"Maybe Fidel'll write his memoirs some day," Leo said. "Maybe he'll tell us the answer then."

Ebby looked at Leo. "Where are you and Adelle going?"

"Changing the subject," Jack accused Ebby.

"We're off to the Loire Valley," Leo said. "We're biking from one chateau to another. You get to eat these fantastic French meals, then you pedal all day to work them off."

"When's the last time you took a holiday?" Ebby asked.

"We spent ten days biking through Nova Scotia the September before last," Leo said. "What's that? Twenty months ago."

"You've earned a break," Ebby said.

"Tessa and Vanessa going with you?" Jack asked.

"The twins' idea of a vacation is holding the fort while the parents are away," Leo said.

Ebby climbed to his feet and stretched. "I guess we'd better assign a team to the Giancana-Rosselli thing," he told Jack. "Just in case Castro left some fingerprints lying around."

"The absence of fingerprints is a fingerprint," Leo noted.

"You're supposed to be on vacation," Jack said.

Manny settled into the catbird seat in the pit of the spacious Operations Center, kicked off his loafers and hiked his stockinged feet up on a desk crammed with sterile telephones. The night watch, which came his way once every twenty-one days, was not his idea of a sexy way to spend an evening;

he would have preferred to take in *Young Frankenstein* with Nellie. Catching up on operational reports made the first hour or two pass quickly enough but then tedium inevitably set in; to get through the night the dozen or so hands on deck would resort to reading very tattered copies of Cold War spy novels that were stacked in a bookcase near the water cooler.

Tonight looked as if it would be no exception to the rule. First, Manny leafed through the blue-bordered *National Intelligence Daily* hot off the basement press and due to be circulated (to a very restricted audience) the following morning. Behind him, technicians from the Office of Security, dressed in pristine white overalls, were inspecting the devices that vibrated the glass panes in the windows to prevent the KGB from eavesdropping on conversations with laser beams. Television sets lined up on a shelf were tuned to the major networks to monitor breaking news stories. Junior officers from various directorates sat around an enormous oval table keeping track of overnight cables pouring in from stations around the world, sorting them according to security classification and dropping the more urgent ones into the duty officer's in-box. Manny glanced at the wall clock—he still had ten and a half hours to go on the twelve-hour shift—and, swallowing a yawn, attacked the pile in the in-box to see if anybody on the seventh floor of Langley needed to be rousted out of bed.

The first batch of cables all looked as if they could wait until people showed up for work the following morning. There was a report from Cairo Station about a shake-up in the Muhabarat, the Egyptian intelligence service, with President Anwar el-Sadat bringing in people known for their personal loyalty to him. Beirut Station had weighed in with still another warning that Lebanon was moving toward the brink of civil war between Islamic fundamentalists and Christian Arabs; Yasir Arafat's Palestine Liberation Organization, firmly implanted in the country's sprawling Palestinian refugee camps, was stockpiling arms and boasting of turning northern Lebanon into a launching pad for raids into Israel. Saigon Station was ringing the gong (as Company argot had it): the situation in Vietnam was unraveling faster than anyone had expected; CIA was working with the Navy to develop plans to evacuate 1,500 American civilians by helicopter if regular Army units from the North broke through South Vietnamese lines and made a dash for the capital. Paris Station was predicting that the Gaullist Valéry Giscard d'Estaing would defeat the Socialist François Mitterand in the run-off round of the election in a week's time. Lisbon Station was concerned that Communists in the leftist military junta that seized power in a coup d'état the previous month might leak NATO secrets to Moscow.

At ten P.M. the green light over the door to the Operations Center flickered. The armed guard on duty looked through the one-way window, then called out, "Coffee's on." The dozen duty officers and secretaries, delighted to be diverted for even a few minutes, filed through the partly open door to the corridor and returned carrying doughnuts and cups of steaming coffee. Manny slipped into his shoes and lined up behind the cart. He drew a mugful of coffee and helped himself to a jelly doughnut, then made his way back to the pit. Across the room the young woman at the telephone switchboard pulled off her earphones and announced, "Mr. Ebbitt, sir, I have a call on an open line from a lady asking to speak to the person in charge. She says it's a matter of life or death."

"Put it through on my outside line," Manny said. He picked up the green phone. "Yes?"

The caller's edgy voice came through the earpiece. "There has to be someone in charge at night. I need to talk to him, and fast."

"Could you kindly state your name and your business—" Manny began but the woman cut him off. "For crying out loud, don't pussyfoot around with me. A man's life is hanging on this call. We don't have much time—he has to be back at his embassy by eleven. Pass me over to someone who can make things happen."

Manny sat up in his chair and hit the "record" button on the tape recorder plugged into the phone. "You're speaking to the night duty officer, ma'am."

On the other end of the line the woman took a deep breath. "Okay, here's the deal. My name's Agatha Ept. That's *E-P-T*, as in *inept* but without the *in*. I work for the government Patent Office. A week ago Friday I met this Russian diplomat at a reception at the Smithsonian—they were giving a sneak preview of a show honoring a hundred years of American inventions. The Russian said he was a political attaché. He obviously knew a lot about inventions and we got to talking. He asked me if we could meet again and I thought, where's the harm? So we met for lunch last Sunday at one of the restaurants in the Kennedy Center." The woman covered the mouthpiece with her hand and spoke to someone in the room. Manny heard her say, "I'm coming to that part." She came back on the line. "Where was I?"

Manny liked the sound of her voice—she was in some sort of bind but she was cool enough. He even caught a hint of humor in her tone, almost as if she were enjoying the situation; enjoying the adventure of phoning up the CIA. "You were having lunch in the Kennedy Center," he said.

"Right. So my Russian acquaintance—"

"You want to give me his name?"

"He specifically asked me not to do that over the phone. So we talked about this and that and then we each went our merry ways. Then tonight, out of the blue, it was around eight-thirty, I got a buzz on the intercom. Lo and behold, there he was! He'd found my address, you see, though I don't really know how since my phone is unlisted. He was in the lobby downstairs. He begged me to let him come up. He said it was a matter of life or death which, given his situation, I suppose isn't an exaggeration. I let him in and up he came. Well, the long and the short of it is he wants political asylum. He said Russians didn't get to meet many Americans. He said I was the only person he could turn to. He asked me to get in touch with the CIA on his behalf—he wants to stay in America, in return for which he's ready to give you information."

"What sort of information?"

Ept could be heard repeating the question to the Russian. "He wants to know what sort of information you can give him."

Manny could hear a man with a thick accent whispering urgently behind her. The woman said, "He says he has a lot of secrets to offer. Okay, what do I do now?"

Manny said, "What you do now is you give me your phone number and your address. Then you sit tight. You brew up a pot of coffee, you make small talk until I get there. Okay?"

"It has to be okay. I mean, it's not as if I have a wide range of options to choose from, is it?"

Manny scratched her name and address on a pad, then read it back to her to confirm them. Agatha wanted to know his name. He told her she could call him Manny. She laughed and said she would have preferred his real name but would settle for Manny. She asked him what his birth sign was and when he told her he was a Capricorn, she breathed an audible sigh of relief. The Russian in her apartment was a Virgo, she said. She herself was a Taurus with Capricorn rising, which meant the three of them were earth signs and would get along real fine. Manny was in luck, she added: Jupiter just happened to be in Taurus and was about to form a sextile with Venus in Virgo, which meant that any project they undertook together in the next ten days was bound to work out. Manny told her, "I like your style, Agatha. Hang in there."

He cut the connection and bellowed out, "Marv, I want two cars and six men from the Office of Security, armed and wearing civilian clothes, waiting in the garage in ten minutes. Waldo, get me a read-out on a female American name of Ept, I'm spelling that *E-P-T*, first name, Agatha, she works for the US Patent Office." He reached for the red phone and the clipboard filled with unlisted numbers that even the phone company couldn't locate and dialed one of them. After four rings the DD/O's Chief of Operations, Jack McAuliffe, came on the line. "Mr. McAuliffe, this is Manny Ebbitt, the night duty officer in the Operations Center—"

"What's with the Mr. McAuliffe, Manny?"

"I'm calling on official business, Jack, so I thought—"

"You thought wrong. What's up?"

"Looks as if we've got a walk-in." He explained about the call from the American woman who said she worked for the patent office; about the Russian attaché asking for political asylum in exchange for unspecified information. Waldo came across the room on the run and shoved a paper under Manny's eyes. "I'm getting a confirmation on the American woman, Jack— Ept, Agatha, forty-two, divorced, an associate researcher at the US Patent Office for the past nine years. Normally I'd check with my division chief but Leo's on a plane heading for Europe. You probably know that. So I decided to check in with you."

Jack, who had seen his first defector in a Berlin safe house over a movie theater a lifetime ago and had personally handled half a dozen since, was all business. "All right. I'll authorize you to talk to the Russian. Make sure he's not some journalist playing footsie with the Company. If he's really Russian, if he's really a diplomat, if he really has access to secrets, string him along. See if you can get an idea of what he has to offer. See what he wants in return. Don't commit yourself. Don't commit the Company. Bear in mind that if he is the genuine article the optimum solution, from our point of view, is to talk him into remaining as an agent in place inside the Soviet embassy, at least until his tour of duty expires. Bear in mind, too, that even if he looks like the genuine article he could still be a dispatched agent sent to feed us malarkey. If you're satisfied, instruct him to phone the Ept woman at midweek. Since all Russian diplomats work for the KGB, directly or indirectly, he could claim he's having an affair with this woman from the patent office, or trying to, in order to get hold of American patents. We could eventually supply him with some. The Russians who look over everyone's shoulder at the embassy ought to swallow that."

Marv came back into the Operations Center and gestured with two fingers to indicate that the cars were waiting in the basement. "Okay. I'm on my way," Manny said.

"You're taking security with you?"

"Two cars. Six people."

"Spread them around to make sure you're not walking into a nest of vipers. Take one man inside with you just in case. Tape the conversation with the Russian if he lets you. Call me as soon as you come out. I'll alert your father and counterintelligence. Angleton will want to be brought in on this. We'll meet in the DD/O's office first thing tomorrow to see if we want to pursue the matter."

Manny waved for Waldo to take over the catbird seat, grabbed his sports jacket off the back of a chair and a small battery-powered tape recorder from a shelf and headed for the door.

For once, the long night watch had turned out to be more intriguing than one of those Cold War spy novels.

Agatha Ept lived in a no-frills six-story apartment house constructed, according to the date over the door, in 1946, a time when returning GIs were flooding into the Washington area after the war. Located in the heart of a lower-middle-class neighborhood outside the Beltway a stone's throw from Rockville, with ugly fire escapes clinging like limpets to its brick sides, the building was saved from falling into the category of a flophouse by a conspicuous neatness. There were trimmed hedges on either side of a heavy glass outer door leading to a straightforward well-lit vestibule, leading to a heavy glass inner door that could only be opened if you had a key or someone in the building buzzed you through. Five of Manny's shadows from the Office of Security, checking with each other on small walkie-talkies, had quietly spread out around the building, covering the front and back entrances, the underground garage and the poorly lit bushy areas under the two fire escapes. The sixth shadow hovered behind Manny as he pushed the chrome button next to the name "Ept, A."

Almost instantly a woman's voice burst over the intercom. "Who's there?" she demanded.

"It's the person you spoke to earlier this evening," Manny replied.

"Marty?"

Manny realized he was dealing with a smart cookie. "Not Marty. Manny."

"What's your birth sign, Manny?"

The shadow from Security tapped a forefinger against his forehead to suggest that the woman was off her rocker. Manny said, "I'm a nonpracticing Capricorn."

"You don't know what you're missing out on. I'm on the fifth floor, second door to your right when you get off the elevator."

The lock in the glass door buzzed. Manny and his shadow pushed through into the building. Agatha, standing at the door of her apartment when they emerged from the elevator, turned out to be a tall, reedy woman with bright eyes and delicate features. When she flashed a nervous smile she looked as if she had more than her share of teeth. "Which one of you is the nonpracticing Capricorn? And who the hell is the one who isn't?" she wanted to know.

"I'm Manny, he's my security blanket," Manny explained.

"He can't come in," Agatha declared categorically. "My Russian said he'll talk to you and no one else."

"Let me take a quick look around," the security man said. "If everything looks kosher I'll wait out here."

"Do I have a choice?" Agatha asked Manny.

He screwed up his face.

"All right. Just a quick look."

Agatha let the two men in and locked the door behind them with the safety chain. The security man ignored the Russian, who was watching from the kitchenette, and proceeded to throw open doors and run his hand under the tops of tables and along the arms of chairs. He disappeared into the bedroom, then came out and nodded at Manny. "I'll be in the hallway if you need me," he said.

Manny walked over to the political attaché and offered his hand. "My name is—" he started to say in Russian.

The Russian gripped it firmly and answered in Russian. "It's you, the Manny from the telephone conversation. I am Sergei Semyonovich Kukushkin."

Manny set the portable recorder down on a coffee table and started to open the leather flap. "What are you doing with the machine?" the Russian demanded.

"I'd like to record the conversation."

The Russian shook his head emphatically; his long, vaguely blond hair, already disheveled, flew off in all directions. "*Nyet, nyet*. If you please, I am not wanting that."

Manny looked at Agatha. "Would you mind?" he asked, nodding toward the bedroom door.

"I'd mind if I thought someone would notice." She smiled encouragingly at the Russian and disappeared into the bedroom.

Kukushkin snatched a glass filled with an orange liquid from the kitchenette counter. "Juice of carrot," he said, holding it up. "You want some?"

Manny shook his head. "I was hoping it might be whiskey."

The Russian said unhappily, "The lady is vegetarian."

Manny motioned him toward a couch and settled into a chair facing him. He decided to see how well Kukushkin spoke English. "Where do the KGB watchdogs at the Soviet embassy think you are right now?"

Kukushkin looked confused. "What means *watchdog*?"

"Your security people? Your SK?"

"Ahhh. Watchdogs. I sign out going to movie theater."

"What film are you supposed to be seeing?"

"*Young Frankenstein.*"

"What time does it finish?"

"Ten-forty. Bus takes me back to embassy by eleven, eleven-fifteen."

Manny looked at his wristwatch. "That gives us forty minutes if we drop you at a bus stop near the theater. Do you know the plot of *Young Frankenstein*?"

"I know enough—I read criticism of film in newspaper."

Manny studied the Russian. He was forty-five, give or take a few years, of medium height, handsome in a rough way with the heavy shoulders and thick body of a wrestler. His gaze was straightforward and unwavering. The only outward sign of uneasiness was his habit of flicking the nail of his middle finger back and forth against his thumbnail.

Manny had the queasy feeling that he was dealing with a professional. He switched back to Russian. "Agatha said you were a political attaché..."

Kukushkin produced a sour grin. "Political attaché is my diplomatic cover. My real name is Klimov. Sergei Klimov. I have temporary rank of captain in KGB." The Russian's fingernails clicked like a metronome. "To speak openly, I was expecting the meeting to be with someone more senior. You are too young. If I need brain surgery I would not want a young surgeon." He added in English, "Same reasonment is holding true for spies."

"I'm senior enough to deal with this, I promise you. You want to give me a brief rundown on your background?"

Kukushkin nodded reluctantly. "My pedagogic background is study of capitalist political model. Before assignment in Washington I was attached to Directorate S of the First Chief Directorate, which responsible for running KGB officers and agents operating abroad under deep cover. During that assignment many many cables passed through my hands. Arrived Washington fourteen months ago. Principal job in Washington is analyzing relationship between your White House and the two branches of your Congress. Seven months remain on normal tour, though sometimes tour stretching to two and a half, three years if SK agree."

"You want to come over to our side?" Manny said carefully.

"I want political asylum in America." The Russian looked as if he were about to throw up. "For me," Kukushkin added. "For my wife. For my seven-years daughter."

"Why?"

"I do not understand your *why*."

"What made you decide to come over?"

"Look, I understand motive is important so you can make judgment if I am genuine or false defector, but we are not having much time for this tonight. I will say you that one of ironies of Cold War is that KGB operatives, especially those who have been posted to the West, have a better understanding of the capitalist world's strengths and weaknesses than average Russian. I am living proof of this. I am disillusioned with corruption, with inefficiency of our Soviet Socialist model. I believe in Mother Russia, not Soviet Russia." Kukushkin leaned forward and spoke with stifled passion. "I will say you honestly there exists another reason. My wife is heart sick—she was taking medicine before many years. She is treated by Russian doctor at embassy. I want to have her American doctor and American medicine."

"How long have you been disillusioned?"

One of Kukushkin's large hands floated off his lap, palms up. "Disillusion is something not growing like mushroom over one night. Many, many years it grows until your brain and your heart are poisoned."

"Were you disillusioned when you arrived in Washington fourteen months ago? Was your wife in need of medical help when you came here?"

The Russian nodded warily; he wasn't sure where this line of questioning was leading.

Manny pushed himself to the edge of the chair. "Why didn't you come over fourteen months ago?"

Kukushkin's gaze wavered from Manny's for the first time. *"Ne vozmozhno!"* he said, lowering his voice and uttering the words with great intensity.

Manny persisted. "Why was it impossible?"

His nails clicking into the silence, the Russian considered the question for a moment. "KGB *rezident* in Washington, Borisov, is schoolmate from Lomonosov University—for two years we roomed together. *Rezident* is very open with me, telling me many things when we drink whiskey in his office late at night. From him I know that KGB has what you call a mole inside your

CIA with code name SASHA. This SASHA, he is having very important position"—one of Kukushkin's thick hands measured off rungs on a ladder—"somewhere high up in your organization. Impossible to come over when SASHA in Washington—he would be one of first in CIA to find out, he would alarm our SK people. The Russian trying to come over, his family"—he slashed a forefinger across his throat—"kaput."

Assuming Kukushkin was the real McCoy, Manny knew that he had gotten his hands on a gold nugget. "Are you saying that SASHA is *not* in Washington?"

The Russian nodded grimly. "Borisov is telling me that both SASHA and his cutout are out of the city."

Manny asked quietly, "Can you identify SASHA?"

Kukushkin's fingernails fell silent. "I do not think even *rezident* knows his identity, only that he exists. But you already know that SASHA is not in Washington. I am able provide other particulars...I am able to say you another time when he is not in Washington. I am able to say you the first initial of his family name, along with one other important biographical detail. In return for political asylum for me, for my family, I am ready to help you narrow list of suspects."

"You two know each other?" the DCI, Bill Colby, asked as the Company's legendary chief of counterintelligence, James Jesus Angleton, carefully folded his brittle body into a chair at the head of the table.

"We've never met," Angleton murmured.

Jack McAuliffe did the honors. "This is Manny Ebbitt—one of the rising stars in the Soviet Division."

"It's a honor to meet you, Mr. Angleton," Manny volunteered.

Angleton peered down the table at Manny, fixing his brooding Mexican eyes on him. "So you're Elliott's boy," he said.

From his place alongside Colby, Ebby remarked testily, "Yes, he is."

"Everyone has a cross to bear," Jack quipped, hoping to lighten the atmosphere. Nobody smiled.

Suppressing a chain-smoker's hacking cough, Angleton bent his head and lit a cigarette from the stump of another that had burned down to his dehydrated lips. "I'd like to get started," he said impatiently. "I'm supposed to be briefing the President's Foreign Intelligence Advisory Board at eleven."

Manny was more than a little intimidated to be in the presence of the institutional legend who went by the in-house code name of Mother. For more than twenty years Angleton had kept his lonely vigil, turning over stones and looking for worms of treason; he traced every operational failure to the presence of a Soviet mole inside the Company, every operational success to Starik's diabolical efforts to advance the mole's career. In Manny's Soviet Division, people spoke about Mother in hushed tones. Someone would brag of having caught a glimpse of him in a corridor, a drawn, gray, hunched specter prowling Langley with his hands clasped behind his back and a faraway gleam in his eyes. Scuttlebutt had it that Angleton was past his prime, living on borrowed time, incapable after a four-martini lunch of working his way through the mountain of cables and files heaped on his desk. At regular topsider staff meetings on the seventh floor of what Company hands now called the "Campus," Angleton was said to rant about his latest theory. One week he would claim that the Sino-Soviet split and the seeming independence of Dubček in Czechoslovakia or Ceaucescu in Rumania or Tito in Yugoslavia were the dirty work of KGB disinformation specialists trying to lure the West into thinking the Soviet monolith was breaking up. Another time he would ramble on about how his nemesis, Philby, who fled to Moscow in the early 1960s after finally having been exposed as a Soviet spy, had recast the posture and character of the Soviet intelligence service. Under Philby's stewardship, Angleton would claim, it had become more subtle; more stiletto than blunderbuss. Angleton went so far as to see Philby's handiwork when KGB operatives traded in their easy-to-spot baggy trousers and wide cuffs for tailored suits. Inside the Company, there were caustic complaints that Angleton's paranoid hunt for moles had paralyzed Soviet ops; that he'd hurt the Company more than any Soviet mole could. Angleton still had his defenders, though their ranks seemed to thin out with each passing year. Every intelligence organization needed a resident paranoid, they would argue; Angleton was the Company's. And the fact that he hadn't uncovered a single Soviet mole inside the CIA didn't mean there wasn't one.

Colby sat back and crossed his legs and regarded Manny over his eyeglasses. "Why don't you begin," he said.

"Yes, sir. I received the phone call from the woman named Ept, Agatha, at approximately nine thirty-two—"

"Nine thirty would be *approximately*," Angleton remarked. "Nine thirty-two is *precisely*."

Manny looked up from his notes, the faintest of smiles pasted on his lips. "I take your point, sir. The Ept woman claimed to work for the US Patent Office, a fact I was able to verify—"

"You were able to verify that someone named Ept, Agatha, was on the Patent Office payroll," Angleton interjected. "You did not verify, nor, as far as I know, have you verified, that the woman claiming to be Ept, Agatha, was in fact the same Ept, Agatha employed by the US Patent Office."

Ebby kept his mouth shut. Colby glanced at Angleton. "You're nitpicking, Jim. Why don't we let him finish."

"Nitpicking is what I do for a living, Bill," Angleton said.

It was clear there was no love lost between the two men, and for good reason. Soon after he became DCI in 1973 Colby had terminated one of Angleton's pet operations, code named HT/LINGUAL, which had his counterintelligence people reading all first-class mail to and from the Soviet Union that passed through New York; Colby had argued that the CIA's charter prohibited operations inside the continental United States. Adding injury to insult the Director had whittled away at Angleton's empire, reducing his staff from three hundred to eighty. Now, the Director eyed his counterintelligence chief. "Do me a favor, Jim," he told him. "Nitpick on your own time and in your own shop." Colby turned back to Manny and nodded.

"A Russian political attaché that Ept had met at a Smithsonian reception weeks before had turned up at her door."

Angleton closed his eyes and puffed on the cigarette. "Ept has an unlisted phone. How did the Russian know where she lived?"

Jack caught Ebby's eye and signalled with a palm for him to simmer down.

Manny looked directly at Angleton. "Ept told me on the phone that she had met the Russian for lunch at the Kennedy Center a week ago Sunday. When I asked him directly how he managed to turn up at her door, given that her phone was unlisted, he claimed that he knew her address because he had followed her home after the lunch."

Ebby said coldly, "That explains that."

Manny wondered if all topside meetings were this nerve-racking. "Jack here—Mr. McAuliffe—gave me verbal authorization to proceed with the initial meeting. I interviewed the Russian, whom I assigned the random cryptonym AE-slant-PINNACLE, in the living room of Ept's apartment near Rockville. Ept was not present during the meeting. The Russian specifically asked me not to record the conversation."

Angleton looked up. "SOP for dispatched agents. The people who sent him over don't want me nitpicking before you swallow the bait."

"For Christ's sake, Jim, Manny went by the book," Ebby blurted out. "A genuine defector is putting his life on the line. He's bound to be skittish. It's SOP to go along with his wishes as long as security isn't compromised."

"Thank you for this illuminating instruction on how to handle defectors," Angleton said in a flat voice.

Colby said grimly, "Manny, I'd take it as a favor if you would go on with your presentation."

"Yes, sir. AE/PINNACLE identified himself as a Soviet political attaché named Kukushkin, Sergei Semyonovich, on assignment in Washington to monitor the relationship between the White House and Congress. He quickly got around to telling me that he was really a temporary captain in the KGB named Klimov, Sergei"—Manny turned to another page of his notes—"who, in addition to his political attaché duties, works on general assignment for the *rezidentura*. I consulted the 201 in Central Registry early this morning. We have a file on a Klimov, Sergei, born 1927, which would make him forty-seven, which matches Kukushkin's appearance. According to our 201, Klimov, Sergei, successfully completed a four-year course at Lomonosov University in Moscow; he passed the Marxist-Leninism boilerplate course with a three out of possible five and graduated with honors in comparative political models. His wrote his senior thesis on the American republican model and the system of checks and balances between the various branches of government. At the end of the four-year course, graduates routinely appear before selection committee composed of representatives from various departments and ministries—Foreign Affairs, Trade, the Trade Unions, TASS, KGB, GRU, what have you. Klimov must have been selected by the KGB, because the next time we see him he's working for the First Chief Directorate, analyzing American signal intercepts that deal with the political situation, as well as political articles in the American press and magazines. At some point during this tour he married the daughter of an Artillery colonel-general who was area commander of intercontinental ballistic missiles bases in Kazakhstan. Curiously, there is no mention in our 201 of the birth of a daughter, though if she is seven, as AE/PINNACLE told me, she would have been born around this time. Klimov was next posted to Directorate S—which, as you know, runs Soviet illegals abroad—after which we lose track of him. The man claiming to be Klimov told me he had worked for Directorate S of the First Chief Directorate. If we decide to go back at him we can prepare questions to confirm this—ask him to pick out from lists the names of classmates at Lomonosov University, as well as colleagues and superiors who worked with him in Directorate S."

Angleton sat there slowly shaking his head.

Colby asked, "What's wrong now, Jim?"

"If your Kukushkin is a genuine defector, which is extremely unlikely, he will know the answers to these questions. If he is a dispatched agent he will also know the answers. The fact that he knows the answers tells us nothing."

Jack teased his Cossack mustache with a forefinger. "Jim's right, of course," he observed. He turned to Manny. "What reason did Kukushkin-Klimov give for wanting to cross over?"

"There is the usual disillusionment with the Communist system—" Manny began.

Angleton snorted. "Sounds like someone sent over from central casting."

"There's more," Manny insisted. "He claimed that his wife suffers from a heart ailment—that she's had it for years. He wants to have her treated by American doctors. This is a detail that can be verified. She won't be able to fake a heart disorder."

Colby said, "The ultimate test will be the information he gives us."

Angleton was still shaking his head. "A dispatched agent will always give us a certain amount of true information in order to convince us he is not a dispatched agent."

"Let's move on to the *get*," Colby suggested.

Manny looked at the notes he had scribbled as soon as they had dropped the Russian a block from a downtown bus stop the night before. "I only had enough time with him to scratch the surface," he reminded everyone. "But AE/PINNACLE gave me to understand that once we'd put in the plumbing for the defection, he'd come over with a briefcase filled with secrets. Here I take Mr. Angleton's point—some or all of these serials could be true even if the defector turns out to be a dispatched agent. All right. I'll start at the base camp and work my way up to the summit." Manny wished his division chief, Leo Kritzky, were sitting in on the session to lend him moral support; Angleton's bloodshot eyes, staring across the table through curlicues of cigarette smoke, were beginning to unnerve him.

"For openers he's offering the order of battle at the Soviet embassy in Washington—we can expect to get from him names, ranks, serial numbers. Plus particulars of local KGB tradecraft—locations of dead drops, for instance, along with the variety of signals, including classified ads in newspapers, indicating that the dead drops have been filled or emptied."

Angleton shrugged his bony shoulders in derision. "Chickenfeed," he said crabbily.

"AE/PINNACLE claimed that Moscow Centre has recently created a special Disinformation Directorate, designated Department D, to coordinate a global disinformation campaign. He said it was staffed by fifty officers who were area or country specialists with field experience. He said he knew of the existence of the Disinformation Directorate, which is supposed to be closely held and highly secret, only because he himself had been recruited into its ranks due to his expertise on the American political model. But AE/PINNACLE was determined to remain abroad. Since he would have had to return to Moscow if he was transferred to the Disinformation Directorate, he asked his wife's father to use his considerable influence to have the assignment cancelled."

Manny had finally come up with something that impressed Angleton. The chief of counterintelligence straightened in his chair. "Does your Russian have specifics on the Directorate's product? Did he mention the Sino-Soviet split? Did he talk about Dubček or Ceaucescu or Tito?"

"We won't know whether AE/PINNACLE has heard of specific projects associated with Department D until we arrange for additional debriefings," Manny said.

"What else is he offering, Manny?" Jack asked.

"He claims to have information on the current British Prime Minister, Harold Wilson, but when I pressed him he became very vague—all he would say was that serials concerning Wilson had passed through the hands of a KGB officer who shared an office with him in Moscow."

"He's playing hard-to-get," Colby commented.

"He's negotiating his retirement package," Ebby said. "If he gives us everything at once he'll lose his leverage."

Manny looked again at his notes. "I'm halfway to the summit. AE/PIN-NACLE claims that approximately a year ago he picked up office scuttlebutt that the *rezidentura* was running a walk-in from the National Security Agency with a *habit*—the walk-in apparently had a weakness for women and gambling and needed money badly. To avoid unnecessary risks, all of the face-to-face debriefings with the NSA walk-in were organized while he was vacationing abroad. The contacts in Washington were through dead drops. The KGB lieutenant colonel who ran the defector was awarded the Order of the Red Banner in a private embassy ceremony last December. AE/PINNACLE took this as an indication of how important the NSA defector was. In mid-January—on January sixteenth, to be exact, which was a Wednesday—the KGB *rezident* asked Kukushkin to stand in for this same lieutenant colonel, who had come down with the flu. He was instructed to service a dead drop in the men's room of the Jefferson Hotel in downtown Washington. Because he was filling in for the lieutenant colonel who had won the Red Banner, Kukushkin concluded that the message he was delivering was intended for the mole inside NSA. The *rezident* gave Kukushkin an enciphered note rolled up inside the top of a fountain pen and, defying regulations, laughingly told him what was in it. Once we know the contents of this note, so Kukushkin claims, we will be able to identify the traitor in the NSA. As the operation was tightly compartmented inside the Soviet *rezidentura*, AE/PINNACLE never heard anything more about it."

Colby whistled through his teeth. The National Security Agency, which, among other things, eavesdropped on Soviet communications and broke Russian codes, was so secret that few Americans were aware of its existence; an in-house joke held that the initials NSA stood for "No Such Agency." If the KGB actually had an agent inside the NSA it would mean that America's most closely held Cold War secrets were hemorrhaging. If Kukushkin's defection could lead to the unearthing of the NSA mole, it would be a major blow to the KGB.

Angleton sniffed at the air as if he had detected a foul odor. "*Timeo Danaos et donna ferentis*—I am wary of Greeks bearing gifts."

"I hate to think what you're saving for your last-but-not-least if your next-to-last is a Soviet mole inside the NSA," Jack commented.

"Time to take us up to the summit," Colby told Manny.

Manny caught his father's eye across the table. Ebby nodded once to encourage him; Manny could tell from his expression that the briefing was going well, that his father was pleased at the way he had handled himself. "The summit, Mr. Colby," Manny said. He flipped to the last page of his hand-written notes. "The last item on my list—" Manny stole a look at Angleton, who was preoccupied lighting another cigarette from the old one—"has to do with SASHA."

Angleton's drowsy eyes flicked open.

"AE/PINNACLE claims that Moscow Centre—not the Washington *rezidentura*—directly runs an agent in place inside the Company code named SASHA. The mastermind behind this operation is someone known only by the nickname Starik, which means 'old man' in Russian. Word of mouth inside the *rezidentura* is that this Starik is supposed to be the same person who ran Philby. There is no direct contact between the *rezidentura* and SASHA—everything passes by a cutout who is living under deep cover in America."

"Pie in the sky," Angleton groused, but it was evident that Manny's story had hit a nerve.

"Kukushkin claims that the KGB *resident*, the chief of the embassy's consular section named Kliment Yevgenevich Borisov, is an old chum from Lomonosov University. The two often drink together late at night in the *rezident's* office. Kukushkin says he decided to defect at this moment in time when he learned, during a casual conversation with the *rezident,* that both SASHA and his cutout were out of town. He claims that no defection is possible while SASHA is in Washington because he would be one of the first to get wind of it and alert the SK people at the Soviet embassy. Kukushkin says we must move rapidly because the window of opportunity, which is to say the period of time that SASHA will be absent from Washington, is very narrow—two weeks, to be precise. Once we have brought him and his wife and daughter to safety, AE/PINNACLE is prepared to give us the first initial of SASHA's family name, along with an important biographical detail and another specific period when SASHA was away from Washington. With that information, so he says, we ought to be able to identify him."

Angleton swatted the cigarette smoke away from his eyes. It was an article of faith with him that all Soviet walk-ins worldwide were dispatched agents, since the Soviet mole inside the Company would have warned Moscow Centre the moment he got wind of a defection, and a genuine defector would be eliminated before he could organize the defection. Now he had finally heard a single plausible detail that intrigued him: it was possible for a walk-in to be genuine *if SASHA were somehow absent from Washington and therefore couldn't immediately learn about the defection.* Angleton's smoker's rasp drifted across the table. "Did your Russian provide details on the cutout?"

"I pressed him, Mr. Angleton. He said only that the cutout who serviced SASHA was away on home leave; the summons back to Russia had been passed on to the cutout by a woman who freelances for the *rezidentura* and serves as a circuit breaker between the *rezidentura* and the cutout. AE/PINNACLE is not sure whether the cutout went away because SASHA was away, or vice versa. As for the biographical details and the date of SASHA's previous absence from the Washington area, all he would say was he came across that information when he was attached to Directorate S of the First Chief Directorate in Moscow Centre; SASHA's previous absence from Washington corresponded with a trip abroad by the handler known as Starik."

The men around the table were silent for some minutes, digesting Manny's report. Lost in thought, Ebby nodded to himself several times; he had been convinced there was a Soviet mole inside the Company since he was betrayed into the hands of the Hungarian secret police in 1956. Colby climbed to his feet and began circling the table. "Did you set up a second meeting with your Russian friend?" he asked.

Manny said, "No. I assumed I would need authorization to do that."

Ebby said, "How is he going to contact you?"

"I took my cue from something Mr. McAuliffe said when he authorized the initial contact—I told AE/PINNACLE to telephone Agatha Ept on Thursday evening. I suggested that he tell his SK people that, following a chance meeting at the Smithsonian, he was trying to become her lover in the hope of gaining access to American patents. If she invites him over for dinner, then he'll know we are willing to continue the dialogue. If she gives him the cold shoulder it will mean we don't want to pursue the matter."

Angleton scraped back his chair but remained sitting in it. "Obviously, counterintelligence needs to take over from here," he announced.

Jack bristled. "It's obvious to you but not to me. The Soviet Division has the competence to deal with this."

Settling back into his seat, Colby pulled at an earlobe. "Let the battle for turf begin."

Angleton reached for an ashtray and corkscrewed his cigarette into it. "There's an outside chance that this could be a genuine defection," he said carefully. "But it's equally likely that the KGB—that Starik himself—is dangling some bait in front of our noses."

"Let's take the worst case," Colby said. "Kukushkin is bait. He's offering us some odds and ends about a Disinformation Directorate and God knows what about the British Prime Minister, and some juicy morsels—a mole inside NSA, SASHA inside the CIA. You've always said that a false defector would have to bring over true information to establish his *bona fides*, to make us swallow the false information. If we play our cards carefully we ought to be able to separate the wheat from the chaff."

"Almost impossible to do," Angleton replied, "without assigning an experienced counterintelligence team. There's a lot at stake here. If AE/PINNACLE is genuine, we'll need to wade through a maze of serials. If he's a dispatched agent, it means the KGB is going to a great deal of trouble and we'll need to find out why." Angleton, suddenly short of breath, wheezed for a moment. Then he addressed Ebby directly. "Your boy did a good job, I'm not suggesting otherwise, Elliott. He didn't put a foot wrong as far as I can see. But he's too young, too inexperienced, to run with this. Debriefing a defector is an art in itself—it's not only a matter of asking the right questions but of not asking them too soon; questions bring answers and answers bring closure to the process of thinking, and that's not something you want to rush."

Jack said to Colby, "Manny wouldn't be alone, Bill. He'll have the considerable resources of the Soviet Division behind him."

Ebby turned to the DCI. "I'll remove myself from the decision, for obvious reasons."

Jack said, "Well, I won't. If Leo Kritzky were here he'd be saying the same thing as me. The Soviet Division, under the aegis of the DD/O, ought to be handling this. Counterintelligence has a long history of turning away defectors, some of whom—many of whom—could well be genuine."

"If counterintelligence discourages defections," Angleton retorted hotly, "it's to protect the Company from dispatched agents—"

"All right," Colby said. "Jim, we both know that a familiar face is worth its weight in gold to a would-be defector. And you yourself said that Manny here didn't put a foot wrong." He turned to Ebby. "I want the DD/O to form a task force to handle this defection. Keep it down to a happy few, which is to say the people in this room and their principal aides and secretaries. All paper is to be stamped NODIS. I don't want the fact that we're dealing with a walk-in to become known outside this small circle. I want the task force's recommendation in my hand within thirteen days, which not incidentally is the time frame that has SASHA away from Washington. Manny, you'll be the point man—you'll meet with AE/PINNACLE and gain his confidence and bring home the bacon. Jim, you'll represent counterintelligence on the task force. If you have operational qualms that you can't iron out with the DD/O or his deputy, you can bring them directly to me. Once we've milked the Russian you can file a dissenting opinion with me if you don't reach the same conclusions as the DD/O." Colby shot out a cuff and looked at his watch. "Jim, if you don't shake a leg, you're going to stand up the President's Foreign Intelligence Advisory Board."

"It's all right. Really. Nooooo problem."

"I can tell from your voice it's a problem."

"Hey, it's not as if I can't scare up a date for *Young Frankenstein*. Afterwards we can meander back to my place, crack a bottle of California red, turn down the lights, put on some Paul Anka. You know from personal experience how one thing has a way of leading to another. Next thing you know we could be into what Erica Jong calls the Zipless Fuck."

"I'm really sorry, Nellie. Something important's come up—"

"With you guys something important's always coming up. That's what my mother says. Elizabet says you have to be stark raving to fall for someone who works for the CIA because you start out a Company widow and it's all downhill from there."

Manny slipped another coin into the slot. "Are you saying you've fallen for someone who works for the Company?"

"I've fallen for the opposite of the Zipless Fuck, which, so far, I've unfortunately for me only experienced with you."

"You put a lot of emphasis on the physical side of a relationship—"

"Yeah, I do, don't I? Pay attention, Manny, because I'm going to fill you in on my theory about lasting relationships. My theory is you need to start someplace and the bedroom is as good a venue as any. So do you or don't you want to hear the good news?"

"You got the job!"

"I did, I did. Oh, Manny, I'm really delirious. I waved my Harvard diploma under their noses and they cracked. The firm's small but it's one of the hottest items in DC. Two ex-senators and a former Cabinet Secretary. And I'm the first woman they've ever hired who wasn't there to take dictation. It'll be a scream—all those three-piece suits and me in my miniskirt!"

"That's fantastic, Nellie. I knew you'd wow them—"

"You want to hear how much they're paying me a month?"

"I don't think so."

Nellie had a sudden thought. "Hey, you don't have a hang-up about dating girls who make more than you, I hope."

"No. My only hang-up is about incest."

Nellie's laughter pealed down the phone line. "I'll admit I'm relieved. A hang-up over money could have been a serious hurdle. So when do you get to see me again?"

"Maybe this weekend. Maybe."

"What's with the maybe?"

"I told you, something important's on a front burner."

"Okay. I suppose there's nothing for me to do but masturbate until then."

"Nellie, you're impossible—"

"You've got it ass-backwards, Manny. What I am is *possible*."

The AE/PINNACLE task force set up shop in an empty office down the hall from the DD/O. The housekeepers swept the room for bugs, then brought in a safe with a Burmah lock, a shredding machine, a burn bag and assorted office furniture. Jack McAuliffe was put in charge, reporting directly to Ebby, the DD/O, who in turn reported directly to the DCI, Bill Colby. Angleton himself (his interest piqued by the would-be defector's mention of SASHA) sat in on the informal meetings, which were held every second day.

With Jack looking over his shoulder, Manny set about putting in the plumbing for the defection that might or might not take place. Agatha Ept, thrilled to let a little excitement into her dreary nine-to-five existence, announced that she was game; sure, she'd be willing to go through the motions of having an illicit affair with a married Russian diplomat if it was in the interests of national security. The superintendent of Ept's apartment building, a retired chief petty officer who had painted the basement spaces battleship gray, went out of his way to be helpful. As a matter of fact, he said, there would be a vacant apartment down the hall from 5D at the end of the month; the homosexual couple living in 5F had signed a lease on a floor-through in Annandale. Manny knocked on the door of 5F and flashed a laminated card identifying him as a State Department security officer. When he offered to foot the bill for the move if the tenants vacated immediately, the couple jumped at the opportunity. The first night after 5F was free a crew from the Office of Security moved in electronic equipment, along with two army cots and a percolator. Working out of the vacated apartment they wired every room in Ept's apartment, and rigged the phone and the doorbell so that both rang simultaneously in 5D and 5F. Then they set up a tape recorder and a backup machine, and settled in for the duration.

Back in Langley, Manny took a shot at getting the head of the US Patent Office to give them some recent patent applications that a junior patent officer such as Ept might have access to. He ran into a brick wall and had to pass the matter up the chain of command. Eventually the DD/O put in a call to Yale classmate who worked as a legislative aide on the Senate Armed Services Committee and explained the problem. Three quarters of an hour later, the head of the Patent Office called to tell Ebby he would be sending over three raw reports on pending patents for relatively unimportant industrial gadgets. Now that he understood what was a stake, he would be delighted to supply more of the same if and when they were needed.

Angleton, meanwhile, produced a six-page, single-spaced typewritten list of questions (with the answers in parentheses) that he wanted Manny to throw at AE/PINNACLE; the list was designed to determine if the defector Kukushkin was, in fact, the Sergei Klimov on the Central Registry 201 and not someone pretending to be him. The questions ranged from "What was the name and nickname of the person who taught 'Bourgeois Democracy—a Contradiction in Terms' at Lomonosov University?" to "What was the nickname of the fat woman who served tea in the First Chief Directorate's third-floor canteen at Moscow Centre?" Angleton instructed Manny on the seven layers of meaning that could be coaxed out of any given set of facts. Take his list of questions: a genuine defector would not be able to answer all the questions correctly. But then, a dispatched agent who had been coached by a KGB maestro would be careful not to answer all the questions correctly. Manny asked: Assuming that Kukushkin answers some of the questions incorrectly, how will we know if he is genuine or a dispatched agent?

From behind a cloudbank of cigarette smoke, Angleton's rasped: Welcome to the wilderness of mirrors.

It was Angleton, nursing a persistent migraine that had reduced his eyes to brooding slits, who worked out Manny's modus operandi for the second meeting with AE/PINNACLE. The first priority would be to establish the defector's *bona fides*, hence the six-page list of questions. The peculiar situation that the defector found himself in—he and his family had to come over before SASHA returned to Washington—gave the Company, in Angleton's considered opinion, some very strong leverage. Assuming Kukushkin-Klimov passed muster, Manny's second priority would be to talk him into immediately delivering the several serials that would lead them to SASHA. AE/PINNACLE needed to be informed that, in the best of all possible worlds, a defection would take time to organize. The Russian would be encouraged to deliver the SASHA serials for his own safety, and that of his family; if SASHA remained operational, so Manny was instructed to argue, he would certainly learn of the defection when he returned to Washington and promptly betray Kukushkin to the SK people at the embassy. Angleton pointed out that if the Company could identify and apprehend SASHA on his return to Washington, there was a good possibility that Manny would then be able to talk AE/PINNACLE into spying in place until the end of his tour of duty at the embassy. This could be achieved through judicious use of carrots (a sizable lump-sum payment when he finally came over, a new identity for himself and his family, first-class medical help for his wife, a high-paying consultancy contract from the Company) and sticks (hinting that he would not be granted political asylum except on Company terms, and thus his wife would not have access to American medical help).

As the meeting was ending Manny raised the possibility that AE/PINNACLE might be wired for sound. Angleton's lips twisted into scowl. "If AE/PINNACLE is a genuine defector, he won't be wired," he told Manny. "If he's a dispatched agent, he won't be wired so as not to give himself away."

On Thursday evening a very weary Manny was drinking lukewarm coffee in 5F with two men from the Office of Security when the phone rang. One of the men flicked on the tape recorder and tripped a button on a loud speaker. Agatha Ept could be heard picking up the phone in her apartment.

"Hello?" she said, her voice rising to transform the word into a question.

"Hello to you."

Manny nodded at the second security man, who picked up a phone hooked to a permanently open line and said quietly, "He's called—see if you can trace it."

"Oh, it's you," Agatha said with a suggestion of breathlessness; Manny hoped she wouldn't ham it up too much. He wondered if the SK people at the embassy were recording the conversation on their end. "I guess I oughtn't to admit it but I was hoping you'd call," she added.

AE/PINNACLE seemed relieved. "I am hoping you are hoping such a thing."

Agatha was playing her role—eager, yet fearful of appearing too eager—to the hilt. "I was wondering...I mean, if you're free...What I'm driving at is, well, what the hell, would you like to come for supper tomorrow."

The Russian cleared his throat. "So: I am free tomorrow—I will come happily, of course."

"Do you remember where I live?"

AE/PINNACLE laughed excitedly; he, too, was playing his role well—but what was his role? "It is not something I am forgetting easily," he said.

"Where are you calling from?" Agatha asked.

"A public phone near the...near where I work."

"They traced the call—he's calling from the Soviet embassy," the security man on the open line told Manny.

"Well, that's settled," Agatha said. "About six-thirty would be fine. I get back from the Patent Office at five-thirty"—she had worked the Patent Office into the conversation as Manny had asked—"which will give me time to make myself presentable."

"You are very presentable," AE/PINNACLE said.

Agatha caught her breath. "Tomorrow, then?"

"Yes. Tomorrow. Goodbye to you, presentable lady."

"Goodbye, Sergei."

A moment later the phone rang in 5F. Manny snatched it off the hook. "He's coming," Agatha announced excitedly.

"I know. I heard the conversation."

"How'd I do?"

"You were great. You ought to think of getting into the acting business."

Agatha laughed nervously. "To tell the truth I had my heart in my mouth—I was so frightened."

"The thing now, Agatha, is to go about your life as if nothing out of the ordinary is happening. We'll be monitoring your apartment all day to make sure nobody from their side breaks in to plant microphones. If you have any unusual contacts—if anybody calls you whom you don't know—you phone the number I gave you and report it immediately."

"You'll be here when he shows up?"

"I'll be outside your door when he gets off the elevator."

Despite Angleton's assurances that AE/PINNACLE would not be wired, Manny decided it wouldn't hurt to check. As the Russian emerged from the elevator Manny signalled with a forefinger to his lips for him to remain silent, then held up an index card with the words, written in Russian: "Are you wired for sound?"

"Not wired for sound, Manny," Kukushkin replied in English. He raised his arms and spread his legs. "You may search me if you wish. My *rezident* very happy when I tell him of this contact. He always ready to boast to Moscow Centre about new sources of information."

Manny gestured for him to lower his arms and follow him. He produced a key, opened the door to 5D and locked it when they were both inside Ept's apartment.

Agatha came across the room. "Hello," she said, shyly offering a hand, which the Russian vigorously shook.

"Hello to you, presentable lady," he said with a smirk.

"Not that it matters," she said, "but today happens to be a propitious time for intercourse between Capricorns and Virgos. Both parties will tend to be wary at first but once they break the ice great things will follow. I'd explain why but judging from the way you're both looking at me it would take more time than you want to invest. So unless I hear dissenting opinion...no one? Then I'll leave you gentlemen to yourselves now." Turning on a heel she disappeared into the bedroom.

Manny motioned Kukushkin to sit on the couch and settled down on a chair facing him. The Russian loosened his tie and grunted something that Manny recognized as a curse in Tajik. "You speak Tajik?" Manny asked in surprise.

"I do not speak it—I curse in it," Kukushkin said. "My grandfather on my father's side was a Tajik. How is it you recognize Tajik?"

"I studied Central Asian languages in college." He pulled a thick wad of typed pages from his breast pocket. "Question and answer time, Sergei," he announced.

"I am knowing the rules of this terrible game we are playing. You are wanting to make certain I am who I say."

"Something like that." Manny eyed the Russian. "When you phoned Agatha yesterday you told her you were calling from a public phone. Were you?"

Kukushkin looked around. "Where are microphones?"

Manny said, "All over the place."

Kukushkin nodded grimly. "I am phoning from embassy, not public phone. The *rezident*, Kliment Borisov, is listening on extension. SK is recording conversation. Borisov is telling me to tell I using public phone, since I am supposed to be starting love affair outside of marriage and not wanting wife, not wanting people at embassy, to know." The Russian crossed his legs, then uncrossed them and planted his large feet flat on the floor. "Are you having patent documents I can take back."

Manny put on a surgeon's glove and pulled the photocopies of the three raw patent reports from a manila envelope. He handed them to Kukushkin, who glanced quickly at the pages. "Her fingerprints are being on them?" he asked.

"You think of everything," Manny said, removing the glove. "I had her read through the reports and put them into the envelope."

The Russian folded the papers away in his inside breast pocket. "It is you who are thinking of everything, Manny."

"Time to put the show on the road," Manny said. He looked at the first question typed in Cyrillic on the top sheet. "What was the name and nickname of the person who taught 'Bourgeois Democracy—a Contradiction in Terms' at Lomonosov University?"

Kukushkin closed his eyes. "You are having very good biography records at your CIA. Teacher of 'Bourgeois Democracy' is Jew named Lifshitz. He is losing an eye escorting British convoys from Murmansk during Great Patriotic War and wearing black patch over it, so students are calling him Moshe Dayan behind his back."

Reading off the questions in Russian, Manny worked his way down the list. Speaking in English, Kukushkin answered those that he could. There were a handful that he couldn't answer—the man's name had slipped his mind, he said—and several that he answered incorrectly, but he got most of them right. Agatha brought them cups of steaming tea at one point and sat with them while they drank it. Kukushkin asked her where she worked in the Patent Office and what kind of documents passed through her hands; Manny understood that he was gathering details for the report he would be obliged to write for the SK people. When they returned to Manny's list of questions, Kukushkin corrected one of the inaccurate answers he had given and remembered the nickname of the fat woman who had served tea in the third floor canteen in Moscow Centre: because of the mustache on her upper lip and her habit of wearing men's shirts, everyone had taken to calling her "Dzhentlman Djim." Manny was halfway through the last of Angleton's six pages when the telephone on the sideboard rang. Both the Russian and Manny stared at it. Agatha appeared in the bedroom doorway; behind her the television set was tuned to *Candid Camera*. "It could be my mother," she said hopefully.

"Answer it," Manny said.

"What do I say if it's not?"

"You don't say anything. You're starting an illicit affair with a married man. That's not the kind of thing you'd tell someone over the phone while he was here."

Agatha gingerly brought the telephone to her ear. "Hello?" Then: "What number are you calling?"

She looked at Manny and mouthed the words *search me*. "Well, you have the right number but there's no one here by that name...You're welcome, I'm sure." She hung up. "He wanted to speak to someone named Maureen Belton." She batted her eyes nervously and retreated to the bedroom.

Manny went over to the sideboard and picked up the phone. "Were you able to trace it?" He listened for a moment, then replaced the receiver and came back to his seat. "Too quick to trace. It was a man—he spoke with an accent."

"The SK is having her phone number. Maybe they checking to see if there is a woman here."

"That may be it," Manny agreed.

"So how am I doing with your questions and my answers?" Kukushkin asked when Manny reached the end of the six pages.

"You did just fine," Manny said.

"So we may talk now of how I can come over?"

Manny shook his head. "If only it was that easy, Sergei. Successful defections aren't organized in one night. Your answers must be analyzed by our counterintelligence staff—"

"By your Mr. Angleton," Kukushkin said.

"You know of Mr. Angleton?"

"Everybody at our embassy knows of your Mr. Angleton."

"If counterintelligence gives us the go-ahead, then we need to set up a safe house in the countryside and staff it, and then organize the actual coming over—we will need a time when you and your wife and your daugh-ter leave the Russian compound together on a pretext. You must be able to fill that briefcase with the secrets you promised us and spirit it out of the embassy. We must be able to bring you over and hide you away before the SK people know you are missing."

Kukushkin face darkened. "How long?"

"If all goes well it could be done in five to six weeks."

The Russian exploded out of his chair. "SASHA is back in Washington before five weeks!" He strode over to the window, parted the curtain and studied the dark street below. "In five weeks, Manny, I am a dead man."

"Calm down, Sergei. There is a way out of this."

"There is no way out of a coffin."

Manny joined Kukushkin at the window. "There will not be a coffin, Sergei, if you give me the SASHA serials now—give us the first initial of SASHA's family name, give us the biographical detail, tell us when SASHA was absent from Washington."

Kukushkin turned away and prowled back and forth behind the couch, a caged panther looking for a way out of the trap he had fallen into. "So: how are you feeling when you play this blackmail game with me?"

Manny avoided Sergei's eye. "Lousy. I feel lousy, is how I feel. But we all have our jobs to do..."

The Russian grunted. "Being in your shoes I am doing the same. You and me, we are being in a lousy business."

"I didn't invent SASHA, Sergei," Manny said from the window. "I didn't create the situation where he returns to Washington in a little more than a week."

"How can I be sure you are not throwing me away like old rag after I deliver SASHA serials?"

"I give you my word, Sergei—"

"Your Mr. Angleton is not bound by your word."

"You have other things we want—most especially, we want to discover the identity of your mole inside the NSA."

The Russian settled onto the couch again, defeated by the logic of the situation. "What about medical help for my wife?"

"We can have her examined by specialists within days. If she needs treat-ment we can provide it."

"How examined within days?"

"The Russians at the embassy all get their teeth fixed in America—they use that Bulgarian dentist near the Dupont Circle subway stop who speaks

Russian and doesn't charge a lot. If your wife suddenly had a toothache she would make an appointment. If she were going to have root canal, she would need three or four appointments over a period of three or four weeks. We could organize to have a heart specialist in another office in the same building."

"And the Bulgarian dentist?"

"He would cooperate. He could pretend to do actual work on her and nobody would be the wiser."

"How are you being sure he cooperating?"

Manny only smiled.

AE/PINNACLE thought about it. Manny came across the room and sat on the back of the couch. "Trust me, Sergei—give me the SASHA serials. If we can identify SASHA your troubles are over. We'll bring you and your wife and your daughter across under conditions that are as near to risk-free as we can make them. Then we'll make you an offer that will knock your eyes out. You won't regret it."

3

TIME WAS RUNNING OUT ON THE SOVIET POLITICAL ATTACHÉ Kukushkin. His two-week window of opportunity had forty-eight hours left on the clock; if his information was correct, SASHA would return to Washington on Sunday and be back at his desk the following morning. Despite the task force's efforts to limit distribution of its product, SASHA would be bound to pick up rumors of a high-level defection in the works, after which he could be expected to alert the SK people at the Soviet embassy.

At the start Angleton had been wary of AE/PINNACLE. But his natural tendency to assume the worst case, when it came to defectors, started to crack the day Manny mentioned the serial concerning Moscow Centre's newly created Department D, the Disinformation Directorate in charge of coordinating the KGB's global disinformation campaign. Angleton had long ago inferred the existence of such a directorate from the fact that the world in general, and the American media in particular, had swallowed whole the rumors of a Sino-Soviet split, as well as the stories of Dubcek and Ceausescu and Tito seeking to distance themselves from Moscow. Angleton, who prided himself on being able to distinguish between KGB disinformation and real political events in the real world, knew intuitively that these were planted stories designed to lull the West into cutting military and intelligence budgets.

The SASHA serials that Manny brought back from his second rendezvous with AE/PINNACLE made Angleton's head swim with possibilities. For the better part of two years he had been closing in on SASHA, gradually narrowing the list of suspects using a complex process of elimination that involved analyzing operations that had gone bad, as well as operations that had been successful. He felt that it was only a matter of months before he would be able to figure out, with near-certainty, the identity of SASHA. During those months, of course, SASHA could still do a great deal of damage. Which was why the AE/PINNACLE serials, used in conjunction with Angleton's own painstaking work, were so crucial. Back in his own shop, Angleton assigned a team of counterintelligence experts to each serial.

—SASHA, according to AE/PINNACLE, would be away from Washington until Sunday, May 26, which probably meant that he would be back at Langley on Monday, the twenty-seventh.

—he was a Russian-speaker.

—his last name began with the letter *K*.

—when Kukushkin worked in Directorate S of the First Chief Directorate in Moscow Centre, he reported directly to Starik. In September of 1972, Kukushkin was asked to provide Starik with logistical support—highway and city maps, bus and train schedules, locations of car rental agencies—for one of his rare trips abroad, this one to the province of Nova Scotia in eastern Canada. In a casual conversation that took place when Kukushkin personally delivered the file to Starik's private apartment, located in a villa known as the Apatov Mansion near a village called Cheryomuski, Starik intimated that he was going abroad to meet someone. Only later, when Kukushkin became aware of the existence of a high-level KGB penetration of the CIA, code named SASHA, did he put two and two together; only SASHA would have been important enough to lure Starik overseas.

Even with these serials, identifying SASHA would be tantamount to stumbling across the proverbial needle in the haystack. The Company had something in the neighborhood of 22,000 regular employees and another 4,000 contract employees. The Clandestine Service alone had roughly 5,000 staffers worldwide; 4,000 of them worked in Washington and another thousand were spread across stations around the globe.

While counterintelligence went about the tedious business of searching the Central Registry—they had to sort through thousands of files by hand—Manny organized the medical visit for Kukushkin's wife, a short, heavy woman whose close-cropped hair was beginning to turn white...with worry, Manny supposed. Her name was Elena Antonova. On cue, she complained of a toothache and asked the Russian nurse at the embassy to suggest a dentist. The nurse gave her the phone number of the Russian-speaking Bulgarian dentist near Dupont Circle whom everyone at the embassy used.

Miraculously, someone had canceled and there was an opening on the following day. The dentist, actually a Company contract employee, had given Mrs. Kukushkin a formal written diagnosis without even examining her—she was suffering from an abscess at the root of the lower first bicuspid, which would require between three and four appointments for root canal work, at a cost of $45 per visit.

Manny was loitering in the corridor when Elena Antonova emerged from the dentist's office, an appointment card in her hand. He gestured for her to follow him up two flights to an office with the words "Proffit & Proffit, Attorneys at Law" stenciled on the glass door. Inside, Manny introduced Kukushkin's wife to a heart specialist, a Company contract employee with a top secret security clearance. The doctor, who went by the name M. Milton when he moonlighted for the CIA's Office of Medical Services, was fluent in Russian. He led her into an inner office (equipment had been rushed in the night before) for an examination that lasted three quarters of an hour. Then, with Manny present, the doctor delivered his prognosis: in all likelihood, Elena Antonova was suffering from angina pectoris (he would make a definitive diagnosis when her blood tests came back from the laboratory), the result of a high cholesterol count that was causing a narrowing of the arteries carrying blood to her heart. Dr. Milton proposed to treat the problem with a combination of beta-blocking agents to decrease the work of the heart and slow the pulse rate, and vasodilators designed to increase coronary circulation. If the condition persisted, Mrs. Kukushkin might eventually require coronary bypass surgery but that decision could be made at a later date.

Manny accompanied Mrs. Kukushkin to the elevator and, speaking Russian in an undertone, promised her that on her next visit to the dentist, the doctor will have prepared the necessary medicine disguised as ordinary over-the-counter pills that women used to alleviate menstrual cramps. *Bolshoe spasibo*, she whispered. She tried to smile. "I will tell you—I am terrified. If they find out about this it will be terrible for us: for Sergei, for me, for our daughter, Ludmilla."

"We will do everything under the sun to prevent them from finding out," Manny promised her.

At Langley Angleton emerged from a sick bed—he had come down with Asian flu and was running a fever—to attend the regular afternoon task force meeting down the hall from the DD/O's office. Wrapped in an overcoat and a scarf, he settled sluggishly into his habitual seat at the head of the table. The skin on his wrists and face was almost translucent, his shirtfront was drenched in sweat; beads of perspiration trickled down the side of his nose. For the first time in memory he didn't immediately light a cigarette. "My people have gone over the serials with a fine-tooth comb," he announced, his voice low and strained. "And we've added a serial of our own that has been on a back burner for years. My tentative conclusion is that AE/PINNACLE could be the rarest of orchids, a genuine defector bearing real secrets."

Colby looked across the table at his DD/O, Elliott Ebbitt. It was easy to see that both men were stunned.

"Are you telling us that you've identified SASHA?" Jack asked.

Angleton only said, "You're not going to like it."

"You want to walk us through it," Colby said impatiently. He doodled with the point of a number two pencil on a yellow legal pad, creating an endless series of linked circles.

Angleton's lanky body could be seen trembling under the overcoat. "Working from AE/PINNACLE's four serials," he began, "my people have narrowed the list of suspects dramatically. I'll start with the first three serials. There are one hundred and forty-four Russian speaking Company employees whose last name begins with K and are expected to be away from Washington until Sunday. Of these hundred and forty-four, twenty-three were also out of Washington at some point during the period Kukushkin claims SASHA was away, which was in September of 1972."

Colby designed a very elaborate "twenty-three" on his pad, replete with curlicues. From his place at the far end of the table, Manny watched Angleton slouch back into his seat, almost like an animal gathering itself for a kill.

"Which brings me to the serial that I've kept on a back burner now for thirteen years." Angleton's mask of a face twisted into an anguished smile; his dark eyes seemed to be laughing at some long-forgotten joke. "*Thirteen years!* You need the patience of a saint to breed orchids. It can take twelve months for the seedpod to develop, another year or two for the seed to grow as big as your thumb. The flowering, if there is a flowering, could take another five years, even eight or ten. Counterintelligence is like that—you nurture seeds in small jars for years, you keep the temperature moist and hot, you hope the seeds will flower one day but there's no guarantee. And all the while you hear the voices whispering behind your back. Mother's obsessed, they say. He's paranoid, they say. Mother is a conclusion searching for confirmatory evidence." Angleton shivered again and chewed on his lower lip. "Believe me, I heard every word. And every word hurt."

Colby tried to gently nudge Angleton back on track. "The fifth serial, Jim."

"The...fifth...serial," Angleton said, dolling out the words as if he had decided to toy with his audience. "In 1961 the FBI stumbled across an old Communist named Max Cohen who had gone underground twenty years earlier. You recall the incident, don't you, Bill? Cohen, using the alias Kahn, had set up a wine and beverage store in Washington. Kahn provided the perfect front for the Soviet cutout who lived above the store and delivered liquor to hundreds of clients in the Washington area. The cutout went by the name of Dodgson, which, curiously, happened to have been the real name of Lewis Carroll, the author of *Alice in Wonderland*; it makes you wonder if the KGB spymaster who ran Philby, who *runs* SASHA, isn't, like Dodgson, creating worlds within worlds within worlds for us to get lost in." Angleton shut his eyes and appeared to meditate for a moment before going on. "When the FBI searched Kahn's store they discovered ciphers and microfilms, a microdot reader, wads of cash bound in rubber bands and a shortwave radio, all of it hidden under the floorboards in Dodgson's closet. Dodgson himself somehow slipped through the FBI's fingers when they arrested Kahn and a female employee. But I never forgot him. Not for a moment. All these years. Nurturing the seeds, keeping the temperature moist and hot, hoping against hope that the seeds would burst into flower." His voice trailed off and a glazed look came into his eyes.

Colby tugged on the rein again. "The fifth serial?"

"The fifth serial...I checked Kahn's invoices for the previous ten years and discovered that, at one point in the early fifties, Dodgson had been delivering liquor to"—Angleton spit out the words—"my former colleague Adrian Philby; I myself was at Adrian's house one evening when Dodgson brought over two bottles of Lagavulin Malt Whisky. At the time, of course, it seemed perfectly natural and I thought nothing of it. Only now do I understand how close I was to..." The sentence trailed off. Angleton shook his head in frustration. "With Philby gone," he plunged on, "it seemed logical to suppose that this same Dodgson would act as the cutout for Philby's replacement; for SASHA." Angleton reached into a jacket pocket and extracted a pack of cigarettes, which he set on the table. The sight of the cigarettes seemed to revive him. "Checking through Kahn's clients who had been on the receiving end of deliveries during the previous ten years, I was able to identify the names of one hundred and sixty-seven full-time Company employees and sixty-four contract employees."

Jack jumped ahead. "You matched the Kahn client list against the twenty-three names you teased out of the Kukushkin serials."

"It seemed too good to be true," Angleton admitted. "And it was. None of the names on Kahn's delivery list matched any of the twenty-three names derived from Kukushkin's four serials."

"It sounds as if you reached another dead end after all," Colby said.

Angleton extracted a cigarette from the pack and turned it in his fingers.

"Oh, it may have looked like a dead end to the ordinary eye. But not to mine. I knew the identity of SASHA was buried there—somewhere in the overlap of the two lists." He clamped the cigarette between his chapped lips without lighting it. "Last weekend," he continued, his voice a throaty growl, the unlit cigarette twitching on his lower lip, "I overheard my wife on the phone making hotel reservations for us in New Haven—Cicely and I were going up to attend a Robert Lowell reading at Yale. As a security precaution—we don't want the opposition keeping track of my movements, do we? —I always have my wife make reservations or purchases using her maiden name. And all of a sudden it hit me—my God, how did I miss it?—SASHA could have had a wife. To put as much distance between himself and Dodgson, he could have had his *wife* order the liquor from Kahn's using her maiden name. With this in mind I sent my people back to the drawing boards. We checked the maiden names of the wives of the twenty-three people we teased out of Kukushkin's serials, and then went back to Kahn's clients—to the people the cutout Dodgson had delivered liquor to between the hasty departure of Philby and Kahn's arrest ten years later."

By now everyone in the room was hunched forward, their eyes fixed on Angleton's lips almost as if they expected to *see* the name emerging from his mouth before they could hear it.

"And?" Colby whispered.

"The only maiden name that turned up on both lists was...Swett," Angleton said.

Both Jack and Ebby recognized the name instantly. "Adelle Swett is Philip Swett's daughter," Jack said.

"And Leo Kritzky's wife," Angleton murmured.

"You're way off base, Jim—" Ebby started to say.

"Are you suggesting that Leo Kritzky is SASHA?" Jack demanded incredulously.

Manny said, "This has got to be a blind alley—"

Jack's palm came down hard on the table. "I've known Leo since Yale. We crewed together. We roomed together. He's the godfather of my boy. I'd stake my life on him—"

Angleton produced a lighter and brought the flame to the tip of the cigarette. He inhaled deeply and let the smoke stream from his nostrils. "You don't want to do that, Jack. You'd lose it."

Colby scratched at the stubble on his cheek, deep in thought. "How can you be sure that the Swett who ordered liquor at Kahn's wasn't Adelle's father, Philip Swett?"

"Or anyone else named Swett," Jack snapped.

The fix of nicotine had soothed Angleton; the shivering had let up and a hint of color had seeped back into his skin. Even his voice was stronger. "Question of addresses," he explained. "In the early fifties Dodgson delivered the Swett order to an apartment on Bradley Lane behind the Chevy Chase Club, which is where Kritzky lived when he married Adelle. Starting in 1954 the Swett order was delivered to the small house on Jefferson, in Georgetown, which Philip Swett purchased for his daughter when his twin granddaughters were born."

"I'm at a loss for words," Colby admitted. "I'm staggered. If it's true...good God, if Leo Kritzky has been spying for the Soviets all these years do you realize what it means? He was in on Wisner's roll-back strategy in the early fifties—he would have known about all of the Wiz's Soviet-targeted ops. Kritzky knew about your mission to Budapest, Eb. He was Bissell's ADD/O/A during the Bay of Pigs business—he knew the time and place of the landings, he knew the Brigade's order of battle, he knew which ships were loaded with munitions and fuel. The possibility that the man who's running the Soviet Division might be a KGB mole..."

"It happened before," Angleton reminded Colby. "Don't forget that Philby ran MI6's anti-Soviet counterintelligence show after the war."

Colby thought of something else. "His wife, Swett's daughter Adelle, was a White House legislative aide during the Johnson Presidency. Imagine the inside stuff he could have gotten from her! It makes me sick to my stomach."

"I'm not buying into this," Ebby announced. "Leo's a loyal American—"

Angleton, puffing away on his cigarette, seemed to grow calmer as the others became agitated. "It all fits like the pieces of an elaborate puzzle," he said. "Leo Kritzky is a Russian speaker whose last name begins with *K*. In September of 1972 he vacationed in Nova Scotia for two weeks. On a number of occasions the cutout Dodgson—who had delivered liquor to Philby's address on Nebraska Avenue—also delivered liquor to a client named Swett, who turns out to be Kritzky's wife." Angleton concentrated on Colby. "The evidence is overwhelming, Bill. Kritzky's due back from a two-week bicycle trip in France on Sunday afternoon—"

"Jesus," Manny exclaimed from his end of the table. He was horrified at the conclusion Angleton had drawn from the AE/PINNACLE serials. "What are you going to do, arrest him?"

"That seems like the obvious place to start," Angleton remarked.

"The evidence is circumstantial," Jack insisted. "The case is full of holes. It won't hold water when we take a closer look at it."

Colby doodled another circle into the chain on his yellow pad. "We'd have to be horses' asses not to take a closer look at it," he decided. "Let's not forget that AE/PINNACLE is out there on a limb—if Kritzky *is* SASHA, we can't afford to let him back into Langley." He turned to Angleton. "The ball's in your court, Jim. Run with it."

Jack blurted out, "Damnation, Bill, you're giving him a blank check."

Angleton gathered up his papers. "This isn't a garden party, gentlemen."

Colby said, "A blank check, within limits."

Jack said, "Whose limits?"

Manny rang again. When nobody answered, he tried the door of Nellie's top-floor loft. It was unlocked. He stuck his head inside. "Anybody home?" he called. "Nellie, you there?" He went in, kicked the door closed and looked around. The long, narrow living room was aglow with flickering candlelight. Sheets of typing paper, each with a bare footprint traced on it, were set out on the floorboards. With a laugh, Manny followed the footprints and wound up in front of a not-quite-closed door at the end of the corridor. On the floor in front of it was an open bottle of Dom Perignon in a silver bucket filled with crushed ice, and two glasses. He eased the door open with an elbow. Candles set into two candelabras bathed the misty room in sulfurous hues. Stretched languorously in a bathtub filled with steaming water was Nellie; only her head and a single toe broke the surface. Overhead, a three-quarters moon could be seen through the condensation on the skylight. "You're ten minutes late," she announced in a throaty whisper. "The ice was starting to melt. Me, too."

"For Christ's sake, Nellie—"

"I'm not naked as a jaybird for *Christ's* sake, I'm doing this for your sake." She grinned lewdly at him. "So why don't you slip into something more comfortable, like your birthday suit, and we'll guzzle Champagne in the tub while you try to fend off my advances."

Manny filled the two glasses with Champagne and handed one to her as he settled onto the edge of the tub. He looked down at her body. Her brown nipples and blonde pubic hair were visible under the crystal-clear water.

Nellie sipped her Champagne. "So what do you think are my physical flaws?" she inquired. "Be brutal. Don't be afraid to hurt my feelings."

Manny toyed with the stem of his glass. "Your nose is too big, for starters. Your nipples are too prominent, your thighs are too thin, too girl-like as opposed to woman-like, your shoulders are too bony, your pubic hair is too sparse—"

"I pluck it, dodo, so it won't show when I climb into my yellow-polka dot bikini."

"Your pubis looks like a teenage girl's—there's no meat on your pelvis bone. Your feet are too gangly, your eyes are set too far apart, your belly button is too conspicuous..." His voice grew thicker. "Your skin in the moonlight is gorgeous, your body takes my breath away..."

"Come on in," she murmured, "I'll give you mouth-to-mouth resuscitation."

Manny gulped down some of his drink. "You don't leave a guy much room to maneuver."

"You don't have to look so grim about it. Elizabet says working for the Company can be dangerous for your mental health. I talked to her on the phone tonight—Mom said your father came back from the office looking like death warmed over; looking pretty much the way you look now, come to think of it. You guys have problems?"

"We always have problems," Manny said vaguely.

"Want to share them?"

"Can't."

"Try."

He shook his head.

"Give me a hint. Is the earth going to collide with an asteroid? Are the Russians going to launch a preemptive first strike? Is Congress going to reduce your budget by a billion or two?"

"Psychologically speaking, all of the above and then some. Someone I know—someone I like and respect—is in trouble..." He let the sentence trail off.

"Is it going to spoil our night together?"

"There isn't going to be a night together, Nellie. That's what I came to tell you. I thought you'd understand if I told you in person...Do you understand?"

Nellie polished off her Champagne and thrust it out for a refill. She gulped that down, too, then splashed out of the tub. Wrapping herself in an enormous white towel, she stomped from the bathroom. Carrying the bottle, Manny followed her wet footprints. "So how do you expect a girl to understand when you don't say anything?" she fumed, flinging herself onto a couch, her legs spread wide, the towel parting to reveal a bony hip and a white thigh.

Manny said, "Look, I need to be somewhere in three quarters of an hour. It's an all-hands-on-deck situation. I'd stay and talk some more–"

"If you could, but you can't."

Manny set the bottle down at her feet. He bent over to kiss her but she leaned away.

"I was just getting used to the idea that you had a crush on me," he said.

"I don't have a crush on you, Manny. I love you."

"Right now you look as if you hate me."

She turned back to him. "I hate the part of you I don't love."

"I'll call as soon as I can."

"Do that. Just don't think I'll be satisfied with the crumbs you throw my way. I want a whole loaf, Manny. That or nothing."

The Air France Airbus touched down at Dulles International minutes after four in the afternoon. Leo and Adelle, stiff from the long flight, queued at the passport control counter, then tugged two bags off the conveyor belt and made their way down the "Nothing to Declare" passageway toward the exit. They could see Vanessa waving to them from behind the glass partition.

"Oh, Daddy, Mom, welcome back," she cried, kissing her mother and then flinging herself into her father's arms. "How was the trip?"

"Great, except for the time your father didn't turn up at the chateau until eleven at night."

"I took a wrong turn and wound up in a village with a name I couldn't pronounce," Leo explained sheepishly. "And I didn't know the name of the chateau we were supposed to be going to."

"So what happened?"

"We actually called the police," Adelle said. "They found him drinking Calvados at a bistro twenty-two kilometers away. Was he red in the face when they brought him and his bicycle back in one of their *fourgons*."

"You guys are something else," Vanessa said admiringly. "When I tell my friends my parents are *bike riding* through France, they flip out."

Leo noticed a young man in a belted Burberry regarding him from the street door. The man approached. "Sir, are you Mr. Kritzky?" he asked.

Leo was suddenly wary. "Who are you?"

"Sir, I have a letter for Mr. Kritzky from his office."

"Why don't you mail it?"

The young man never cracked a smile. "I was told to deliver it by hand, sir."

Leo said, "All right, I'm Kritzky."

"Sir, could I see your passport."

Leo fished the passport out of his pocket. The young man looked at the photograph and then at Leo's face, and returned the passport. He handed Leo a sealed envelope.

"What's all this, Daddy?" Vanessa asked.

"Don't know yet." He tore open the envelope and unfolded the letter with a flick of the wrist. His eye went immediately to the signature: *Bill* was scrawled in blue ink over the words *William Colby, DCI.* "Dear Leo," the letter began.

> Sorry to hit you over the head with business as you step off the plane, but something important has come up that needs your immediate attention. Would you come straight out to the campus—I'll fill you in when you get here.

"Sir," the young man said. "I have transportation waiting."

Leo studied the young man. "You know what's in the letter?"

"Sir, I only know what I'm told. What I'm told is to have a car and driver waiting to take you to the person who wrote the letter."

Adelle asked, "What's happening, Leo?"

"Bill Colby's asked me to come over to Langley," he said in a low voice. "Vanessa, you take your mother home. I'll make it back on my own steam. If I'm going to be delayed I'll call."

"Sir, if you'll follow me..."

Leo kissed his daughter on each cheek and smiled at Adelle, then fell into step alongside the young man in the raincoat. "Which Division do you work for?" he asked.

"The Office of Security, sir."

The young man pushed a door open for Leo and followed him through it. A gray four-door Ford sedan was waiting at the curb. The driver held the back door open for Leo, who ducked and settled onto the back seat. To his astonishment a burly man squeezed in next to him, pushing him over to the middle of the seat. To his left, the door opened and another man with the bruised face of a prizefighter climbed in the other side.

"What's go—"

The two men grabbed Leo's arms. One of them deftly clamped handcuffs onto each wrist and snapped them closed. Outside the car, the young man in the Burberry could be seen talking into a walkie-talkie. Up front, the driver slid behind the wheel and, easing the car into gear, pulled out into traffic. "Lean forward, with your head between your knees," the burly man instructed Leo. When he didn't immediately do as he was told the prizefighter delivered a short, sharp punch to his stomach, knocking the wind out of his lungs. Leo doubled over and threw up on his shoes. "Oh, shit," the burly man groaned as he pressed down on the back of Leo's neck to keep him hunched over.

The Ford was obviously caught in traffic. Leo could hear horns blowing around them. His back began to ache from his cramped position but the hand pushing down on his neck didn't ease up. Forty minutes or so later he felt the car turning off a thoroughfare and then slipping down a ramp. A garage door cranked open and must have closed behind them because they were suddenly enveloped in darkness. The burly man removed his hand from the back of Leo's neck. He straightened and saw that they were in a dimly lit underground garage. Cars were scattered around in the parking spaces. The Ford drew up in front of a service elevator. The burly man got out and hauled Leo out after him. The prizefighter came up behind them. The elevator door opened and the three men entered the car. The prizefighter hit a button. The motor hummed. Moments later the doors opened and Leo was pulled down a dark hallway and pushed into a room painted in a creamy white and lit by an overhead battery of surgical lights. Two middle-aged women dressed in long white medical smocks were waiting for him. The prizefighter produced a key and removed the handcuffs. As Leo massaged his wrists, the two men took up positions on either side of him.

"Do precisely as you are told," one of the women ordered. "When we tell you to, you will remove your clothing item by item, and very slowly. All right. Begin with your left shoe."

"What are you looking for?" Leo managed to ask.

The burly man slapped him sharply across the face. "Nobody said nothing about you talking, huh? The shoe, Mr. Kritzky."

His cheek stinging and tears brimming in his eyes, Leo stooped and removed his left shoe and handed it to the man who had struck him, who passed it on to one of the women. She inspected it meticulously, turning it in her hands as if she had never seen this particular model before. Working with pliers she pried off the heel, then with a razor blade cut open the leather to inspect the inside of the sole and the underside of the tongue. Finding nothing, she cast Leo's left shoe aside and pointed to his right shoe. Item by item, the two women worked their way through every stitch of clothing on Leo until he was standing stark-naked under the surgical lights. One of the women fitted on a pair of surgeon's latex gloves. "Spread your legs," she ordered. When Leo was slow to comply the prizefighter kicked his legs apart. The woman knelt on the floor in front of him and began feeling around between his toes and under his feet. She worked her way up the inside of his crotch to his testicles and his penis, probing all the folds and creases of his groin. Leo chewed on his lip in humiliation as she inspected his armpits and threaded her fingers through his hair. "Open wide," she ordered. She thrust a tongue depressor into his mouth and, tilting his head toward the surgical lights, inspected his teeth. "All rightie, let's take a gander at your anus, Mr. Kritzky."

"No," Leo said. The word emerged as a sob. "I demand to see—"

"Your asshole, asshole," the prizefighter said. He punched Leo hard in the stomach and folded him over with a deft judo lock on one arm. The woman stabbed a gloved finger into a jar of Vaseline and, kneeling behind him, probed his anus.

When he was permitted to straighten up, Leo gasped, "Water."

The burly man looked at the woman wearing the surgical gloves. When she shrugged, he went out and came back with a paper cup filled with water. Leo drained it, then, panting, asked, "Am I still in America?"

The prizefighter actually laughed. "This is like the Vatican, pal—it's extraterritorial. Habeas corpus don't exist."

One of the women dropped a pair of white pajamas and two scuffs onto the floor at Leo's feet. "You want to go and put them on," she said in a bored voice.

Leo pulled on the pajama bottoms; there was no elastic band and he had to hold them up. One by one, he slipped his arms into the top. His hands were trembling so much he had trouble buttoning the buttons with his free hand. Finally the prizefighter did it for him. Then, clutching the waist of the pajamas and shuffling along in the backless slippers, Leo followed the burly man through a door and down a long dark corridor to another door at the far end. The man rapped his knuckles on it twice, then produced a key, unlocked the door and stepped back. Breathing in nervous gasps, Leo made his way past him.

The room in which he now found himself was large and windowless. All the walls, and the inside of the door, were padded with foam rubber. Three naked electric bulbs dangled at the ends of electric cords from a very high ceiling. A brown army blanket was folded neatly on the floor next to the door. A lidless toilet was fixed to one wall and a tin cup sat on the floor next to it. In the middle of the room stood two chairs and a small table with a tape recorder on it; the table and both chairs were bolted to the floor. James Jesus Angleton sat in one of the chairs, his head bent over the loose-leaf book open before him. A cigarette dangled from his lips; an ashtray on the table overflowed with butts. Without looking up, he waved Leo toward the seat opposite him and hit the "record" button on the tape machine.

"You're Yale, class of fifty, if I'm not mistaken," Angleton remarked.

Leo sank onto the seat, mentally exhausted. "Yale. Fifty. Yes."

"What college?"

"I was in Timothy Dwight for two years, then I lived off campus."

"I was Silliman but that was before your time," Angleton said. He turned to another page in the loose-leaf book to check something, then flipped back to the original page. "How about if we begin with your father."

Leo leaned forward. "Jim, it's me, Leo. Leo Kritzky. These goons abducted me from the airport. They roughed me up. I was strip-searched. What's going on?"

"Start with your father."

"Jim, for God's sake..." Leo glanced at the whirring reels of the tape recorder, then, shuddering, took a deep breath. "My father's name was Abraham. Abraham Kritzky. He was born in Vilnus, in the Jewish Pale, on the twenty-eighth of November 1896. He emigrated to America during the 1910 pogroms. He got a job in the Triangle Shirtwaist factory sewing bands inside hats—he was there when the famous fire broke out in 1911, killing almost a hundred and fifty seamstresses. My father got out with his sewing machine strapped to his back when firemen hacked open a locked fire door leading to an alleyway."

"Did the experience make him bitter?"

"Of course it made him bitter."

"Did it turn him against capitalism?"

"What are you looking for, Jim? I went over all this when I was recruited. There are no secrets hidden here. My father was a Socialist. He worshipped Eugene Debs. He joined Debs's Socialist Party when it was formed in 1918. He picketed when Debs was jailed, I think it was around 1920. He read the *Jewish Daily Forward*. His bible was the 'Bintel Brief' letters-to-editor column, where people poured out their troubles; he used to read the letters aloud to us in Yiddish. My father was a bleeding heart, which wasn't a federal offense until the House Un-American Activities Committee came along."

"You were born on the twenty-ninth of October 1929—"

Leo laughed bitterly. "The day the stock market crashed. Are you going to read something into that?"

"Your father had a small business by then." Angleton turned to another page in his loose-leaf book. "He manufactured and repaired hats at an address on Grand Street in Manhattan. The crash wiped him out."

"The banks called in his loans—he'd bought the brownstone on Grand Street. We lived upstairs. His business was on the ground floor. He lost everything."

"And then what happened?"

"Can I have some water?"

Angleton nodded toward the tin cup on the floor next to the toilet. "There's water in the bowl."

Leo shook his head in dismay. "You're out of your goddamn mind, Jim. You're crazy if you think I'm going to drink out of a toilet."

"When you're thirsty enough, you will. What happened after the stock market crash?"

When Leo didn't respond Angleton said, "Let's understand each other. You're going to stay in this room until you've answered all my questions, and many times. We're going to go over and over your life before and after you joined the Company. If it takes weeks, if it takes months, it's no skin of my nose. I'm not in any particular hurry. You want to go on now or do you prefer that I come back tomorrow?"

Leo whispered, "Son of a bitch."

Angleton started to close the loose-leaf book.

"Okay. Okay. I'll answer your damn questions. What happened after the stock market crash was that my father killed himself."

"How?"

"You know how."

"Tell me anyway."

"He jumped off the Brooklyn Bridge. They found his body washing around under the docks under Brooklyn Heights the next morning."

"What was the date?"

"March 1936."

Angleton said, "Seven March, to be exact. Between the stock market crash and his suicide, did your father become a Communist, or was he one already when he came over from Russia?"

Leo laughed under his breath. "My father was a Jew who believed, like the Prophet Amos—writing eight centuries before Jesus Christ—that you were a thief if you had more than you needed, because what you owned was stolen from those who didn't have enough. Luckily for Amos there was no Joe McCarthy around in those days." Leo looked away. In his mind's eye he could see his father reading from a worn Torah, and he quoted the passage from memory. "'For they know not to do right, saith the Lord, who store up violence and robbery in their palaces.' That's Amos 3:10, if I remember correctly, Jim."

"You seem fixated on Joe McCarthy."

"He was a shit."

"Did you agree with Amos and with your father? Did you think that what you own is stolen from those who don't have enough?"

"In an ideal world such a sentiment might have a shred of validity. But I long ago moved on into the imperfect world."

"Did capitalism kill your father?"

"My father killed himself. Capitalism, as it was practiced in America in the twenties and thirties, created conditions that caused a great many people to kill themselves, including the capitalists who threw themselves out of Wall Street windows in 1929."

Angleton lit a fresh cigarette. There was a fragment of a smile clinging limply to one corner of his mouth and volcanic ash in the pupils of his eyes. Leo remembered that Angleton was a devoted angler; the word was that he would spend endless hours working the Brule in the upper watershed of northern Wisconsin, casting with a flick of his wrist a nymph fly he had tied with his own fingers and letting it drift back downstream, waiting with infinite patience to snare the mythical brown trout that was rumored to hide in the currents of the river. It hit Leo that the counterintelligence chief was working another river now; casting hand-made flies in front of Leo in the hope that he would snap at the hook, fudge a truth, lie about a detail, after which he would carefully reel in the line.

Flipping through the pages of his loose-leaf Angleton ticked off an item here, underlined a phrase there, scratched out a word and wrote a new one above it. He wanted to know how Leo felt about Soviet Russia during the Second World War. He was only a kid then, Leo said; he didn't remember thinking about Soviet Russia one way or the other. "You joined Ethical Culture after the war," Angleton noted. He'd never actually joined Ethical Culture, Leo replied; he'd gone to evening meetings in Brooklyn, mostly to play chess. "What kind of people did you meet there?" Leo had to laugh. He'd met chess players, he said. "You met a girl there, didn't you?" Angleton asked. "Named"—he moistened a finger and skipped ahead several pages—"named Stella." Yes, Leo agreed. He remembered Stella. She had the infuriating habit of taking a move back after she took her hand off the piece; eventually he'd been the only one who would play with her. Angleton asked, "Do you recall her family name?" Leo thought a moment. No, he said, he didn't. The fragment of a smile turned up again on Angleton's face. "Could it have been Bledsoe?" he wanted to know. That rings a bell, Leo agreed. Bledsoe sounds familiar.

Angleton's voice was reduced to a purr now as he worked the rod, letting the fly skid across the surface of the water. "There was a Bledsoe, Stella, named by Whittaker Chambers as a fellow traveler whom he'd met at Communist Party meetings after the war." When Leo didn't say anything Angleton looked up from his notes. "Was Stella Bledsoe a Communist?" Leo snickered. She was a social worker, and a lot of social workers were Socialists, so she might have been, too. If she was a Communist when I first met her in the forties I never knew it. Sucking away on his cigarette, Angleton said, "She espoused the party line—unilateral nuclear disarmament, abandoning Berlin to the Russians—which makes her a Communist, wouldn't you agree?"

"Does it matter if I agree?"

"It doesn't, Leo. But it would make things easier."

"For whom?"

"For yourself. For me. For the Company."

Pushing himself to his feet, clutching the waistband on the pajama bottoms, Leo shuffled over to the toilet and stared down at the water in the bowl. He swallowed hard to relieve his parched throat and returned to the chair. "Where are we here?" he asked, waving toward the padded walls. He thought he knew; there was a former Naval Hospital on 23rd Street, a group of yellow buildings across from the State Department, which the CIA used for secret research. Because the place was so secure the Company occasionally debriefed defectors there.

Angleton looked up at Leo. "As far as you're concerned we could be on another planet," he said. There was no malice in his voice, only cold information.

"My wife will start asking questions when I don't turn up at home."

Angleton glanced at his wristwatch. "By now," he said, "the Director will have phoned up Adelle and apologized profusely for packing you off to Asia on such short notice. 'Something has come up,' he will have told her. 'You'll understand if he didn't provide details.' Your wife will have taken the news bravely; will have surely inquired when she might expect you to return home. The Director would have been vague. 'It could take time,' he would have said. 'He has no clothing,' your wife will have remarked. 'Can you pack a bag and I'll send a car around to pick it up,' the Director will have said. 'Will he call me?' Adelle might have asked. 'I've instructed him to maintain radio silence,' the Director would have answered. 'But rest assured I'll personally call you when I have more to tell you.' 'Will he be in any kind of danger?' Adelle would want to know. 'None whatsoever,' the Director would tell her. 'You have my personal word for that.'"

Leo felt as if the wind had been knocked out of him again. "I never really understood until now what a bastard you are," he murmured.

Unperturbed, Angleton turned back to the first page in the loose-leaf book and stared at the single word printed on it. Leo concentrated on the capital letters, trying to read them upside down. The letters swam into focus. The word was: SASHA.

Angleton closed the loose-leaf book and stopped the tape recorder. He put them and the ash tray into a brown paper shopping bag and, without a word, went to the door. He rapped twice against it with his free hand. The prizefighter opened the door and let him out and closed it again. Leo found himself regretting that Angleton had gone. At least he was someone to talk to. He spread the blanket and doubled it and tried to doze. The three naked bulbs were brighter than before—Leo realized that they worked on a rheostat and had been turned up to deprive him of sleep. Lying there on the blanket, curled up in a fetal position, he lost track of time. At one point the door opened and someone slid a tin plate inside, then the door slammed closed again. Clutching his waistband, Leo shuffled over to the door and stuffed bits of cold cooked cabbage into his mouth with his fingertips. Tears came to his eyes when he realized that the cabbage had been salted. For a long time he stood staring at the toilet. Finally he went over to it and dipped the tin cup into the water and sipped it. He gagged and crouched, jamming his head between his legs and breathing deeply to keep from vomiting. When he felt better he stood up and urinated into the toilet and flushed it, and stretched out again on the blanket, his eyes wide open, thinking.

SASHA.

Agatha Ept was categoric: Today was not the moment for a Capricorn and a Virgo to undertake new projects. "I'd be thrilled to explain why," she said," backing toward the bedroom. "To begin with, Pluto is squaring Mars—okay, okay, I can take a hint." And she disappeared through the door.

"She is a crazy American lady," Sergei Kukushkin told Manny when they were alone, "if she is seriously thinking that stars decide our fate."

Manny had come to like Kukushkin. His open features, the worry lines that creased his brow whenever they talked about his wife or daughter, even the anxiety betrayed by the metronome-like clicking of his fingernails—they all appeared to support the notion that AE/PINNACLE was a genuine defector bearing genuine information. Manny wished it were otherwise; wished that Sergei wouldn't look him straight in the eye when he talked, wished that he could detect in his handshake a holding back, a hesitation, a hint of something other than forthrightness. Because if Kukushkin was genuine and Jim Angleton was right, Leo Kritzky was SASHA.

"Did Elena Antonova pick up the pills this morning?" he asked Kukushkin now.

A smile lurked in the Russian's eyes. "She took the first two immediately she returned to the embassy," he said. "Elena said me that she felt relief in minutes." Kukushkin's fingernails fell silent, a sign that a particularly important question was on his tongue. "And SASHA? What has happened with SASHA?"

With an effort Manny kept his eyes on Kukushkin. "Mr. Angleton claims he has discovered his identity."

The Russian asked in a whisper, "And has SASHA been taken into custody?" Manny nodded.

"You do not look happy about this."

"Arranging meetings with you, establishing codes and signals that you can use if the circumstances change, relaying questions and bringing back your answers, this is my job. What happens with the serials you give me is in the hands of others."

"And do you honestly think, Manny, that the SASHA in custody is the real SASHA?"

"It's Thursday," Manny said. "According to your information SASHA has been back at his desk at Langley since Monday. It is true that only a handful of our people know your identity. But a number of people from various departments are involved in this—monitoring phone lines, disguising pills for your wife, watchers and handlers keeping track of you and your wife, that kind of thing. Word that there is a high-level defection in the works is bound to seep out. If you are right about SASHA—if he is someone important—he would have heard about it by now. Did you notice your SK people taking any particular precautions?"

Kukushkin shook his head.

"Did your wife think she was followed when she went to the dentist this morning?"

"If she was followed I am not sure she would see it."

"We would see it, Sergei. She was clean when she came out of the subway at Dupont Circle. She was clean when she went back into the subway. Have you noticed anything out of the ordinary at the embassy? Anyone paying particular attention to you?"

"The *rezident* called me in and opened a bottle of Scotch whiskey and offered me a drink."

"He's pleased with the patent reports you bring back?"

Kukushkin thought about this. "I would say he is satisfied, yes. He was in trouble with Moscow Centre last December. A KGB officer at the embassy was recalled to Moscow for claiming he ran an American defector who gave him radar secrets—it developed that this same information was available in aviation magazines. A month later a KGB colonel, working under diplomatic cover, wrote a ten-page report on a conversation he had with your Secretary of Defense Schlesinger when he only shook his hand in a receiving line." The Russian raised his palms. "We are all under great pressure to produce secrets."

Manny judged the time had come to pose the question he had been instructed to ask. "How about it, Sergei? Will you risk it? Will you stay in place now that SASHA is no longer a menace to you?"

"And if I agree..."

Manny understood that the Russian wanted to hear the terms again. "We'll bring you all over at Christmas when you and your family go down to visit Disney World in Florida. There will be a lump sum payment of two hundred fifty thousand dollars sitting in a bank account, and a monthly consultant's stipend of fifteen hundred for a minimum of ten years. There will be a completely new identity and American citizenship, and a two-story house in a residential area of Florida to be decided on by you. There will be a four-door Oldsmobile parked in the driveway."

"What if I sense that they are closing in on me before December?"

"We'll devise emergency signals and procedures to pull you and your family out immediately."

Kukushkin inspected his fingernails, then looked up. "I think I am crazy like the American lady in the bedroom, Manny, but I trust you. I do not think you would lie to me. I do not think you would betray me. I will do it—not for the money, although I will be happy to provide security to my family. I will do it to prove to your organization that I am who I say I am— that I am loyal to America."

Manny reached over and the two men shook hands. "You won't regret it, Sergei. I promise you." He looked at his wristwatch. "We still have three quarters of an hour."

Kukushkin himself started the tape recorder and pulled the microphone to the edge of the kitchen table. "I will begin today by telling you what was in the message that I deposited in the men's room of the Jefferson Hotel for the agent that the *rezidentura* is running inside your National Security Agency." When the Russian hesitated, Manny smiled encouragingly. "So,

I have already told you that the *rezident* gave me an enciphered note rolled up inside the top of a fountain pen. Because the contents did not concern operational information, Borisov boasted to me what was in it. The message said, '*Congratulations on the Second Man.*' You must apprehend that KGB agent-handling guidelines call for paying careful attention to the personal lives of American agents. The contents of this particular message suggests that the wife of the American spying inside your NSA gave birth to a second son, probably sometime early in the month of January..."

4

MOSCOW, SUNDAY, JUNE 9, 1974

ASIDE FROM THE WRINKLES FANNING OUT FROM HIS EYES AND THE eight or ten pounds around his waist, PARSIFAL hadn't changed all that much since Yevgeny had met him on the Gettysburg battlefield twenty-three years before. "Awfully good of you to stop by," mumbled Harold Adrian Russell Philby, leading his visitor down a narrow corridor that smelled of disinfectant to the glass doors opening onto a small living room crammed with furniture and piles of books and magazines. A Westinghouse air conditioner fixed into the bottom of one window hummed in the background. "B-b-bloody things make a hell of a racket but at least they keep the corpus from overheating. Do I have it right? Last time our p-p-paths crossed you were called Eugene. What do I call you now?"

"The Russian equivalent—Yevgeny."

"Well, old b-b-boy, you haven't gone to seed like some people I know, I'll give you that. Been living in America all these years, have you?"

Yevgeny raised his eyebrows apologetically.

"Oh, dear, there I g-g-go again! Sorry, sorry, so very sorry," Philby muttered. "Ropey thing to ask a spy, isn't it, old chap?" It was not yet four and Philby's breath reeked of alcohol. "Starik send you by to see how I was holding up, did he?"

"As a matter of fact," Yevgeny lied, "I asked him where I could find you. Though it might be fun to compare notes."

"Right. I'll b-b-bet. Compare notes with old PARSIFAL." Squinting, he grabbed a half empty-bottle of Lagavulin and measured out a shot for Yevgeny before refilling his own glass to the brim. "Ice? Water? Both? Neither?"

"Ice, thanks. Lagavulin is what I used to deliver to your door on Nebraska Avenue. How do you manage to find good malt whiskey in Moscow?"

Philby unbuttoned his booze-stained blazer and carefully lowered himself into a shabby armchair that squeaked on its rusty springs. "Find anything I need in Moscow," he grumbled. "Easy as falling off a log. I draw up a shopping list—m-m-mango chutney from Harrods, custom tailored b-b-blazer from Savile Row, beluga from the shallow end of the Caspian, olives from Italy, *Tinker, Tailor, Soldier, Spy* from Hayward Hill, *Times* of London seven days late by air mail, you name it, my minders supply it."

"And do you mind your minders?" Yevgeny inquired, settling onto a ratty settee with an outrageously loud floral pattern. He had come across Philby's minders when he entered the run-down building on Patriarch's Pond; the one in the lobby had checked his identity card and ticked his name off a list, the one sitting behind a small table on the fourth floor landing had favored him with a surly nod, the one standing in front of the door of Philby's seedy three-room flat had wanted to see his ID again.

Philby snickered. "Law of nature, isn't it, old boy? One always minds one's b-b-bloody minders. If you get used to them, means you've got one foot in the grave, doesn't it? They tell me I need round-the-clock minding to prevent MI6 from knocking me off. What they're really afraid of is that Jimbo Angleton may have turned me into a triple agent. Christ, there's a ripe idea—I managed the double agent stint all right but triple would keep me up nights trying to figure out which side I really worked for." And he laughed uproariously at what he thought was a joke.

Yevgeny sipped at his whiskey. "What was it like," he asked, studying Philby over the rim of his glass. "Coming home after all those years."

"Told you in Gettysburg when you wanted me to run for it. No state secret. England was my home, old boy, not Russia," Philby said with undisguised bitterness. "Russia was merely where my loyalties were since I saw the light at Cambridge. In my wildest imagination I never dreamed I'd wind up *living* here. If you can call this living. Mind you, it's more upscale than your average English slammer." He forced another laugh through his clenched jaw.

Philby's new wife—after he'd fled to Moscow in 1963, one jump ahead of the Brits who had finally come up with proof that he had spied for the Soviets, he had courted and married Donald Maclean's wife—stuck her head in the room. "Will your friend be staying for tea, then, Kim?" she asked. "Do stay," she said to Yevgeny. Her cheery voice seemed out of place in this dreary setting; she could have been the spouse of a Midlands squire chatting up her husband's chums.

"Will you, old b-b-boy?" Philby asked hopefully.

"Afraid I'll have to take a rain check," Yevgeny said.

"Tea for three, three for tea another time, so the gentleman says," Philby chirped, waving his wife out of the room. He fixed his bloodshot eyes on his visitor. "They don't trust me, old boy, do they?"

"Nobody told me."

"Course they did. B-b-brecht once said something about how a good Communist had quite a few dents in his helmet, and some of them were the work of the enemy." Philby scrubbed his lips with the back of his hand. "Starik's on the fence, doesn't know which way to jump. KGB pinned the Order of Lenin on my b-b-blazer when I came in—at the time I thought it roughly equivalent to one of the better K's handed out by HM Elizabeth II, but I have my doubts now. The KGB *Oberführer*, Comrade Chairman Andropov, keeps me at arm's length—never even had the d-d-decency to give me the rank of a KGB officer. Far as he's concerned I'm still a lowly agent. Trots me out Friday nights to brief people whose faces are carefully kept in the shadows. I lecture them on what life is like in England and the States; I tell them how to tip; I tell them to be careful to order two for the road when the warning bell rings; I advise them to butter up your average American by talking about money, your average Brit by talking about the last war." Philby closed his eyes for a moment. "I tell them how James Jesus Angleton's mind works. I'm the in-house expert on Jimbo, aren't I, chum? Biggest asset we have in the states is Jimbo Angleton. Thanks to yours truly he suspects absolutely everyone, so nobody takes him very seriously."

Philby took a swig of Lagavulin, tilted back his head and tossed it down. "Tell you a secret, sport, if you swear you won't repeat it to too many people. After I came over Jimbo had a note delivered to me—it took the form of a handwritten inscription on the title page of a book I'd ordered from London. Bugger signed it, too—with a big fat *J* for Jimbo."

"What did he say in the note?"

"*Amicitia nostra dissoluta est.* That's Latin for *Our friendship is dissolved.* S'what Nero wrote to Seneca when he wanted his old fart of a tutor to bugger off and commit suicide." Philby giggled like a schoolgirl. "Bit out of touch with the real world, wasn't he, old boy, if Jim actually imagined I'd slit my wrists because he'd put paid to our friendship?"

Philby fell into a moody silence. After a moment Yevgeny said, "Do you ever think about going back?"

"Wouldn't tell you if I did, would I, sport? Not stark raving yet." He gulped down some more alcohol. "Truth is, even if I could, I'd never give the shits the satisfaction."

They chatted on for another half hour. Philby was following the Nixon impeachment business closely. He was particularly intrigued by the presence of the one-time CIA hand E. Howard Hunt at the heart of the White House "plumbers" who had pulled off the Watergate break-in; he wondered aloud if the CIA didn't know more about the caper than they let on. Oh, Brezhnev was a jammy b-b-bastard, all right; doesn't say much for the Communist system when a sod like him makes it to the top of the heap. Yes, he'd read about the Russian dissidents in the English press; he'd ordered a copy of Solzhenitsyn's *Gulag Archipelago* from his favorite London bookstore, Hayward Hill, expected it any day now. One of Andropov's lackeys had come round with a letter condemning dissident writers and invited him to sign but Philby had sent the bugger packing; told them they ought to be fighting real criminals instead of persecuting dissidents.

Later, lumbering down the dark hallway toward the front door, a drink in one soft paw, the palm of the other brushing the wall to steady himself, Philby said in a slurred mutter, "Bit schizo, these Russians, don't you think? I have a theory about it—I reckon it's because a Russian, Peter the Great, tried to turn them into Germans, and a German, Catherine the Great, tried to turn them into Russians." At the door, which had Philby's original Soviet code name—SYNOK, TOM—written under the apartment number, Philby hung on to Yevgeny's lapel. "Heard the news? The Brits are thinking of making a film about me. It's all very hush-hush. They say M-m-michael York's going to play me. Rotten choice, that's my view. Don't see how in b-b-bloody hell he could pull it off. M-m-michael York's not a gentleman, is he, old boy?"

Yevgeny had been servicing SASHA's dead drops on the average of once every three or four weeks with such regularity that the possibility of home leave had never crossed his mind. Then one night, a month or so before his reunion with Philby, he'd strung the antenna from picture frame hooks on the walls of his tiny apartment over the garage in Tysons Corner and had tuned the General Electric clock radio to Radio Moscow's 11 P.M. English-language shortwave quiz program. When he recognized one of his personal code phrases—"I don't like belonging to another person's dream"—he had subtracted the serial number of his lucky ten-dollar bill from the winning lottery number and had wound up with a Washington phone number. At the stroke of midnight he had dialed it from an outdoor pay phone in a local shopping center. The ancient woman who spoke English with a thick Eastern European accent had answered immediately.

"Gene?"

"Yes, it's me."

"Ah, dear boy"—he could hear her exhaling in relief—"it is a comfort to hear your voice, a comfort to know that you are alive and well."

As a matter of pure tradecraft Yevgeny never liked to stay on the telephone too long; you couldn't be sure who might be listening in, who might be tracing the call. But his cutout to the *rezident* had wanted to talk. And he liked the sound of her voice.

"Do you realize, dear Gene, that this will be our seventeenth conversation in twenty-three years?"

Yevgeny had laughed. "I wasn't counting, to tell the truth."

"I was," the woman had said emphatically. "You are all I do, Gene—you are the reason I remain in this godforsaken America. Sometimes I think you are the reason I remain alive. Seventeen conversations in twenty-three years! After each telephone call I am obliged to relocate—to move to another address and another phone number. And I settle in and wait to be contacted; wait to be told you will be calling; wait to be instructed what information to pass on to you."

"You are a vital link—" Yevgeny started to say, but the woman rushed on.

"Over the years I have come to feel as if I know you, Gene. I have come to think of you as the son I lost to the fascists in Poland a lifetime ago."

"I didn't know. I'm sorry for that—"

The woman must have realized that she had been running on. "You must pardon me, Gene—the truth is I am quite alone in the world. The only times I am not alone is when I speak with you." She cleared her throat abruptly. "I am, I beg you to believe me, very grieved to be the bearer of distressing news. Your father had surgery ten days ago—two knee operations to correct a condition which, uncorrected, would have left him confined to a wheelchair. The anesthesia lasted seven hours. His heart must have been weaker than the surgeons thought because, two days later, he suffered a stroke. His right side is paralyzed. He can hear but he cannot speak. Your mentor, the Old Man, arranged to be alone with him and told him at long last what you were doing. It appears that your father, hearing this, opened his eyes and nodded with pleasure. He was elated to learn that you were following in his footsteps, and—like me, I may add—extraordinarily proud of you."

Cornered in a foul-smelling phone booth, Yevgeny had started to sort through emotions; he had discovered that the principal emotion was a lack of emotion where there should have been one. He had never loved his father, had barely liked him; he felt closer to the unidentified woman speaking to him on the phone than to his own father. Now that he himself was leading the shadowy life of an undercover agent, he could understand that his father—who had worked undercover for the KGB, for Starik, while posted to the United Nations Secretariat—must have had strong nerves and a certain amount of courage. "For Gene, from his Dad, on his eighth birthday," the handwritten message on the lucky ten-dollar bill read. As far as Yevgeny could remember, Alexsandr Timofeyivich Tsipin had never given him anything in his life other than criticism: when he did badly at school he had been told he should have done well; when he did well he had been told he should have done better. End of conversation.

"Gene, are you on the line?"

"I'm still here."

"Please bear with me if I talk business at such a moment."

"Life goes on."

"Oh, it must, mustn't it?" the woman had agreed with quivering vehemence. "There can be no turning back, no alternative but to go forward with the work in progress. We are, both of us, the servants of history."

"I never thought otherwise."

"Given the precarious state of your father's health, given other considerations which neither you nor I can be party to, your mentor has decided that this is a convenient moment for you to return for home leave. Do you hear me, Gene? You are long overdue for a vacation—"

Yevgeny had almost laughed into the phone. The mere mention of a vacation had made it seem as if he held a dull nine-to-five job at a bank. "I'm not sure...It's been twenty-three years..."

"Oh, dear boy, you must not be afraid to go home."

"You're right, of course. In any case I always follow the suggestions of my mentor. Tell me what I must do."

The extraction had been simple enough: Yevgeny had packed a beat-up valise, spit over his shoulder for luck, then sat on the valise for a moment before heading for the airport and a charter flight to Paris. From there he had caught an overnight train across central Europe to Vienna, then (using a Canadian passport with a new identity) a Hungarian steamer down the Danube to Budapest. In a Pest tearoom near the quai, the Allamvédelmi Hatóság, the Hungarian secret police, had handed him on to the local KGB *rezidentura*, which had provided him with an Australian passport and had put him aboard an Aeroflot flight bound for Moscow. A black Zil with two men in civilian clothes standing next to it had been waiting at the curb when Yevgeny emerged from the passenger terminal at Sheremetyevo

International. One of the men stepped forward and relieved Yevgeny of his valise. "The *general polkovnik* is waiting for you," he said.

Forty-five minutes later the car had turned onto the narrow road with a sign at the edge reading "Center for Study—No Admittance." The armed guards at the small brick gatehouse had waved the car through. Up ahead, at the end of the gravel driveway, loomed the Apatov Mansion that Yevgeny had first come to in the early 1950s. Three little girls in loose-fitting bathing suits were splashing around in a small plastic pool. Their shrieks of pleasure had echoed across the manicured lawns. Moments later, Pavel Semyonovich Zhilov himself had pulled open the second floor door leading to his apartment and had drawn Yevgeny into an awkward embrace.

"Welcome back, Yevgeny Alexandrovich," he murmured. "Welcome home."

"Home," Yevgeny repeated. "The trip back, being here, has the unreal quality of a dream to me."

Starik had grown more brittle with the passage of time. The skin on his face and neck and on the back of his long peasant hands had become spotted and leathery. His once-pewter beard had turned white and grown sparser. But the flame in his brooding eyes was just as Yevgeny remembered; when his eyes narrowed intently and he concentrated, he made you think he could light the wick of a candle by merely staring at it.

"You have served our cause, and me, nobly," Starik was saying as he led Yevgeny through several rooms to the spacious wood-paneled library filled with hundreds of leather-covered volumes and several dozen small gold- and silver-inlaid icons.

Two little girls in short cotton dresses were squatting on the parquet playing pick-up-sticks. "Oh, it did move, I swear it," one of them whined. Frowning, she looked up. "Do stop Axinya from cheating, Uncle."

"Out, away from here, the both of you," Starik cried playfully, waving toward the door, swatting Axinya on the rump to hurry her along as they scampered past him. "Peace and quiet at last," he said to Yevgeny. Pointing to a seat across from him at the large wooden table in the center of the room, he filled two glasses with Narzan mineral water, added a twist of lemon and pushed one across to his guest. "I salute you," he said, raising his glass in toast. "Few have been as unwavering and as unselfish in the service of our great crusade, few have contributed more to the struggle to preserve and promote the genius and generosity of the human spirit. Few have been as true as you to the vision we share in the capacity of the human race, once freed from capitalist exploitation and alienation, to create a truly egalitarian society."

"Few are given the opportunity to serve," Yevgeny declared.

Starik moistened his lips with the mineral water. "You are certain to be exhausted—"

Yevgeny smiled. "I'm getting my second wind."

"When you have had time to settle in—there is an apartment at your disposal on the Lenin Hills—we will talk about operational matters at great length. For now, I would like to ask you..."

When Starik seemed to hesitate, Yevgeny said, "Please ask anything you like."

Starik bent forward, his eyes burning into Yevgeny's. "What is it like?" he inquired in a solemn voice.

"What is *what* like?"

"America. What is America really like? I have been to the German Democratic Republic and to Cuba and, once, to Canada, but never to America. Everything I know about that country comes to me filtered. And so I ask you, Yevgeny: describe America to me."

It struck Yevgeny as a strange question, coming from a man who had access to all kinds of secret intelligence documents; who could read the daily translation of the *New York Times* circulated by the KGB. "Americans are a great people," Yevgeny began, "trapped in a terrible system that brings out the worst in them, in the same sense that our system brings out the best in us. The capitalist system emphasizes acquisition and accumulation. People are conditioned to judge themselves and others by the quantity of material wealth they possess; as they know others will judge them the same way, they have a predisposition to flaunt the symbols of their material wealth. This explains the preoccupation, on almost every level of society, with trophies— large and flashy automobiles, diamond engagement rings, Rolex wristwatches, younger and slimmer second wives, suntans in the winter, designer clothing, the psychoanalyst's couch."

"And how would you describe the attitude of Americans toward life in general?"

"They laugh at the drop of a hat, and loudly, which I take to mean that they are frightened."

"Of?"

"Frightened of losing everything they have accumulated, I suppose. Frightened, as a country, of not being the biggest and the best. Nothing in recent years has had more of an impact on the American psyche than when we put Yuri Gagarin into orbit before their John Glenn."

"And what are their superior qualities, Yevgeny?"

"Americans are bright and open and imaginative and innocent. Their openness makes it relatively easy for an espionage agent to function, since your average American is ready to accept people at face value. Their innocence results in a kind of mental blindness; they are raised to believe that their system is the best in the world, and they are unable to see evidence to the contrary—they don't see the twenty-five million Americans who go to bed hungry every night, they don't see how Negroes live in the ghettos, they don't see how the working classes are exploited for the sake of higher profits for the few who own the means of production."

From the garden below came the stifled yelps of girls leaping into the makeshift pool. Starik strolled over to the window and looked down at them. "Your Americans sound curiously like the principal character in the stories I read to my nieces," he remarked. "She, also, is bright and open and imaginative and innocent."

Yevgeny joined his mentor at the window. "Why do you ask me about America?"

"When you are engaged, as we are, in a conflict, there is a tendency to demonize your enemy."

"The Americans certainly demonize the Soviet Union," Yevgeny agreed.

"It is a great mistake to reduce your enemy to a demon," Starik said. "It leaves you at a distinct disadvantage when you are attempting to outwit him."

The face of Moscow had been lifted during the years Yevgeny had been away. Gazing down from the small balcony of an apartment perched high on the Lenin Hills, he scrutinized the sprawling cityscape spread out below him. The downtown wart, once renowned for its ponderous Stalin-Gothics, was pockmarked with modern high-rise towers that dwarfed the onion-shaped domes of abandoned churches. The relentless drone of traffic seeping through broad arteries rose from the city. On the drive back from the Apatov Mansion, the Zil carrying Yevgeny had actually become caught in heavy traffic on Gorky near Pushkin Square; drivers, ignoring the several policewomen frantically blowing whistles, leaned on their horns, as if the cacophony itself could magically untie the knot. "In general Russians are a disciplined people," Yevgeny's chauffeur, a sleepy-eyed Lithuanian attached to the KGB motor pool, had reflected. "Their idea of rebellion is eating ice cream in the dead of winter. All this changes when they climb behind the wheel of a car. The experience is too new, you see, and so they become slightly crazed."

Yevgeny's visit to his father the next day had come off better than he anticipated, which wasn't saying much because he had expected the worst. His kid brother, Grinka, had turned up at the clinic with his second wife; Grinka, a Party *apparatchik* who worked in the superstructure, had grown heavy with importance. He had been carefully briefed by a KGB colonel not to mention Yevgeny's twenty-three year absence, and so the two brothers shook hands as if they had dined together the week before. "You look well enough," Grinka said. "Meet my wife, Kapitolina Petrovna."

"Do you have children?" Yevgeny asked as they walked toward their father's room though a hallway that reeked of cooked cabbage.

"Two by my first marriage. Both girls, thank God. I named the older one Agrippina, after our mother." Grinka took hold of Yevgeny's elbow. "Father is dying, you know."

Yevgeny nodded.

"I have been instructed not to ask you where you have been all these years. But you must understand, the burden of caring for him—of driving him back and forth to the dacha, of looking after his pension—fell on me." Grinka lowered his voice. "What I am driving at is that father's flat in the Lenin Hills is state-owned, put at his disposal during his lifetime for services rendered. But the dacha in Peredelkino is his. And it cannot conveniently be divided between two families."

"If that's what you are worried about," Yevgeny muttered, "forget it. I don't want the dacha. In any case I won't be in Russia long enough to make use of it."

"Ah, Yevgeny, I told Kapitolina you were a sensible man."

A male nurse, an Azerbaijani wearing a sooty white knee-length jacket and a colorful skull cap, knocked twice on a door, then threw it open and stood back so the two brothers could enter. "Father, look who has come to visit you," Grinka exclaimed.

Aleksandr Timofeyevich's right eye flicked open and he tried to force through his lips the sounds welling up from the back of his throat. "Yev...Yev..." Saliva trickled from a corner of his mouth. The nurse brought a second pillow from the closet and lifted the old man until his head, which fell over to one side, was raised and he could stare at his elder son. "Sit in this chair," the nurse instructed Yevgeny. "He will see you better."

The soft gray skin clung to the old man's face, giving it the appearance of a death mask. His mouth sagged open and his lips trembled. Yevgeny reached for one of his hands and, taking it in his own, stroked the back of it. "It seems that Pavel Semyonovich has filled your ears with stories about me..."

Aleksandr Timofeyevich's bony fingers dug into Yevgeny's palm with surprising strength. The only emotion Yevgeny was able to muster was pity

for the shipwreck of a man who had foundered on a hospital bed in the special KGB clinic in Pekhotnaya Street. He wondered if his father was hanging on to his son, or to life?

"Pro...prou...proud," Aleksandr Timofeyevich managed to say.
"Lo...lone...lonely."

"Yes, it is a lonely life." He smiled into his father's good eye. "But there
is satisfaction to be had from it, as you know from your own experience."

A corner of the old man's mouth drooped, almost as if he were trying to
work the muscles that produced a smile. "Where?" he managed to say.
"Wh...when?"

Yevgeny understood the question. "The same place as before. Soon."

The eye fixed intently on Yevgeny blinked and several tears welled from
it. The nurse touched Yevgeny on the shoulder. "You must not tire him," he
whispered. Yevgeny gave a last squeeze to his father's now limp-hand. The
lid closed slowly over the open eye. The only sound in the room was the
nasal wheezing of his father sucking air through congested nostrils.

The days passed quickly. Starik monopolized Yevgeny's mornings, going
over and over every detail of his meetings with SASHA, reviewing the tight
security precautions that built a fire wall between the Washington *rezidentura* and the Polish circuit breaker; between the Polish circuit breaker and
Yevgeny; and that kept Yevgeny isolated from SASHA in all but the most
extraordinary circumstances. A trusted technician turned up at the Apatov
Mansion one afternoon to introduce Yevgeny to a new generation of espionage gadgets: a microdot projector hidden inside a Kodak box camera that
was actually able to take photographs; a shortwave transmitter disguised as
an electric razor that could send coded messages from perforated tape in
bursts; a one-shot pistol hidden in an ordinary lead pencil that fired a 6.35
millimeter bullet straight from the cartridge buried under the eraser.

Evenings, Yevgeny prowled the streets of Moscow, drifting through the
masses of people hurrying home from work, studying their faces—he was curious to see if they were eager to get where they were going, which he took to be
a barometer-reading of whether the system worked. Afterward he would catch a
bite to eat, dining in the Chinese restaurant in the Hotel Peking one night, the
Prague restaurant complex near Arbat Square another. One evening, fresh from
a visit to his father in the clinic, Yevgeny was invited to join Starik and a handful of KGB brass at a private restaurant on the top floor of the Ukraine Hotel.
Settling down for a banquet that began with bowls of black beluga caviar and
French Champagne, Yevgeny found himself sitting next to none other than the
illustrious Chairman of the KGB, Yuri Vladimirovich Andropov, who, as Soviet

Ambassador to Hungary in 1956, had masterminded the Russian assault on Budapest and the arrest of Imre Nagy. The conversation was banal enough— Andropov seemed more interested in gossip about American film stars than in the Watergate scandal or Nixon's chances of being impeached. Was it true that John Kennedy had slept with Marilyn Monroe, he wanted to know. Had the famous ladies' man Errol Flynn really lived on a yacht off Cannes with a sixteen-year-old girl? Was there any truth to the rumor that the marriage of so and so— here he named a notorious Hollywood couple—was a sham organized by one of the film studios to obscure the fact that both were homosexuals?

The dishes were cleared away and a four-star Napoleon brandy was set out, after which the two waiters disappeared and the double door was locked from the inside. Andropov, a tall, humorless man who was said to write melancholy poems about lost love and the regret of old age, climbed to his feet and tapped a knife against a snifter. *"Tovarishi,"* he began. "To me falls the pleasure—I may say the honor—of celebrating tonight, in this necessarily restricted company, the remarkable career of one of our preeminent operatives. For reasons of security I must keep my remarks vague. Suffice it to say that the comrade sitting on my right, Yevgeny Alexandrovich Tsipin, has blazed a trail through the espionage firmament, equaling, perhaps surpassing, the accomplishments of the legendary Richard Sorge, who, as we all know, played a crucial role in the Japanese theater during the Great Patriotic War. If anything, the stakes are higher today. I can say to you that when the time comes for Yevgeny Alexandrovich to come in, his portrait will take its place alongside other Soviet intelligence heroes in the Memory Room of the First Chief Directorate." Reaching into the pocket of his suit jacket, Andropov produced a small flat box, which he clicked open. It was lined in blue velvet and contained a Soviet medal and ribbon. He motioned for Yevgeny to rise. "Acting in my capacity as Chairman of the KGB, I award you this Order of the Red Banner." The general lowered the ribbon over Yevgeny's head and straightened it around his collar so that the round metal badge rested against his shirtfront. Then he leaned forward and kissed him on both checks. The eight people around the room tapped their knives against their glasses in salute. Yevgeny, embarrassed, looked at Starik across the table.

His mentor, too, was tapping his knife and nodding his approval. And it hit Yevgeny that his approval meant far more to him than his father's; that in a profound sense, Starik—who had started out as his Tolstoy—had become the father he always wanted to have: the authoritarian idealist who could point him in the right direction, after which all he had to do was concentrate on his forward motion.

Grinka phoned Yevgeny at the apartment the next morning to announce the bad news: their father had slipped into a coma during the early morning hours and breathed his last just as the sun was rising over Moscow. The body was to be cremated that morning and the ashes would be entrusted to Grinka, who proposed driving his brother to the dacha at Peredelkino and scattering them in the white birch woods surrounding the house. To Grinka's surprise, Yevgeny declined. "I am preoccupied with the living and have little time to devote to the dead," he said.

"And when will I see you again?" Grinka asked. When Yevgeny didn't answer, Grinka said, "You haven't forgotten about the dacha—there will be papers to sign."

"I will leave instructions with people who will arrange things to your liking," he said. And he hung up the receiver.

There was one other base that Yevgeny wanted to touch before he left Moscow. For that he needed to get his hands on a Moscow-area phone book, an item that was not available to the general public. One afternoon when he was roaming through the narrow lanes behind the Kremlin, he stopped by the Central Post Office on Gorky Street. Flashing a laminated card that identified him as a GRU officer on detached duty, he asked a functionary for the directories, which were classified as a state secret and kept under lock and key. Which letter do you require? the woman, a prissy time-server, demanded. Yevgeny told her he was interested in the *L*'s. Moments later he found himself in a private room leafing through a thick volume. Running his thumb down the column filled with Lebowitzes, he came across an A.I. Lebowitz. He jotted the phone number on a scrap of paper, then stuffed kopeks into a public phone on the street and dialed it. After two rings a musical voice came on the line.

"Is it you, Marina? I have the documentation on your—" The woman answering the phone hesitated. "Who is on the line?"

"Azalia Isanova?"

"Speaking."

Yevgeny didn't know how to explain the call to her; he doubted whether he could explain it to himself. "I am ghost from your past," he managed to say. "Our life lines crossed in a previous incarnation—"

On the other end of the phone line, Azalia gasped. "I recognize the tentativeness of your voice," she breathed. "Are you returned from the dead, then, Yevgeny Alexandrovich?"

"In a manner of speaking, yes. Would it be possible...can we talk?"

"What is there to say? We could explore what might have been but we can never go back and pick up the thread of our story as if nothing had happened; as if the thread had not been broken."

"I was not given a choice at the time—"

"To allow yourself to be placed in a position where you have no choice *is* a choice."

"You're right, of course...Are you well?"

"I *am* well, yes. And you?"

"Are you married?"

She let the question hang in the air. "I was married," she said finally. "I have a child, a beautiful girl. She is going to be sixteen this summer. Unfortunately my marriage did not work out. My husband was not in agreement with certain ideas that I hold, certain things that I was doing...The long and short of it is that I am divorced. Did you marry? Do you have children?"

"No. I have never married." He laughed uneasily. "Another choice, no doubt. What kind of work do you do?"

"Nothing has changed since...I work for the Historical Archives Institute in Moscow. In my free time I still like to translate from the English language. Do you know a writer by the name of A. Sillitoe? I am translating something he wrote entitled *The Loneliness of the Long Distance Runner*."

"The title is intriguing."

"Are you a long-distance runner, Yevgeny Alexandrovich?"

"In a manner of speaking."

A cement truck roared down Gorky, causing Yevgeny to miss what she said next. He plugged his free ear with a fingertip and pressed the phone harder against the other one. "I didn't hear you."

"I asked if you were lonely?"

"Never more so than right at this moment. My father just died."

"I am sorry to hear that. I remember him at the garden party that day at the dacha in Peredelkino—an old man was pressing a bottle filled with bees against the bare skin of his back when Comrade Beria introduced me to him. You must be melancholy..."

"That's the problem. I am not at all melancholy, at least not at the death of my father. I barely knew him and barely liked what I knew. He was a cold fish..."

"Well, at least he lived into old age. My father and mother died after the war."

"Yes. I remember your telling me about their disappearance—"

"They didn't disappear, Yevgeny. They were murdered."

"In his last years, Stalin strayed from the Socialist norm—"

"Strayed from the Socialist norm! In what ostrich hole have you been hiding your head? He was a murderer of peasants in the early thirties, he murdered his Party comrades in the mid and late thirties, he suspended the killings during the war but resumed them immediately afterward. By then it was the turn of the Jews—"

"It was not my intention to get into a political discussion, Aza."

"What was your intention, Yevgeny Alexandrovich? Do you know?"

"I only intended...I thought..." He was silent for a moment. "The truth is I was remembering—"

"Remembering what?"

"Remembering the gap between your two front teeth. Remembering also how my lust and your desire turned out to be harmonious in bed."

"It is indelicate of you to raise the subject—"

"I mean no offense..."

"You *are* from a previous incarnation, Yevgeny Alexandrovich. I am not the same person who lived in the apartment of Comrade Beria. I am no longer innocent." And she quickly added, "I am not speaking of sexual matters, it goes without saying. I am speaking of political matters."

"I wish things could have been otherwise—"

"I don't believe you."

A woman waiting to use the pay phone tapped a finger against the crystal on her wristwatch. "How long do you intend to monopolize the line?" she cried.

"Please believe me, I wish you well. Goodbye, Azalia Isanova."

"I am not sure I am glad you called. I wish you had not stirred memories. Goodbye to you, Yevgeny Alexandrovich."

A dark scowl passed across Starik's eyes. "I won't tell you again," he scolded the two nieces. "Wipe the smirks off your faces, girlies."

The nieces found Uncle unusually short-tempered; they were not at all sure what he did to gain money but, whatever it was, they could tell he was preoccupied by it now. He switched on the klieg lights and adjusted the reflectors so that the beams bathed the bodies of the two angelic creatures posing for him. Returning to the tripod, he peered down into the ground glass of the Czech Flexaret. "Revolución, how many times must I tell you, throw your arm over Axinya's shoulders and lean toward her until your heads are touching. Just so. Good."

The two girls, their long gawky feet planted casually apart, their pubic bones jutting pugnaciously, stared into the camera. "Do take the photograph, Uncle," Axinya pleaded. "Even with all these lights I am quite chilly."

"Yes, take the picture before I catch my death of cold," Revolución said with a giggle.

"I will not be rushed, girlies," Starik admonished them. "It is important to focus correctly, after which I must double check the exposure meter." He bent his head and studied the image on the ground glass; the klieg lights had scrubbed the pink out of the naked bodies until only the eye sockets and nostrils and oral cavities of the girls, and their rosebud-like nipples, were visible. He took another reading on the light meter, set the exposure, then moved to one side and regarded the girls carefully. They were staring into the lens, painfully conscious of their nudity. He wanted to achieve something incorporeal, something that could not be associated with a particular time and place. He thought he knew how to distract them.

"Girlies, imagine you are innocent little Alice lost in Wonderland—transport yourselves into her magical world for a moment."

"What is Wonderland *really* like?" Axinya asked shyly.

"Is Wonderland in the socialist camp, Uncle?" Revolución, always pragmatic, wanted to know. "Is it a workers' paradise, do you think?"

"It is a paradise for little girls," Starik whispered. He could make out the ethereal expressions creeping onto the faces of the two little nieces as they were transported to the whimsical world where, at any moment, the White Rabbit might appear, splendidly dressed, with a pair of white kid gloves in one hand and a large fan in the other. Satisfied, Starik tripped the plunger. Opening the aperture to heighten the washed-out effect, he took several more shots. Finally he waved toward the door. "Enough for today," he said grumpily. "You may go outside and play until suppertime."

The nieces, only to happy to flee his moodiness, tugged sleeveless cotton shifts over their heads and, arm in arm, scampered from the room. Starik could hear their shrieks as they skipped down the wide steps toward the front door of the Apatov Mansion. He turned off the klieg lights, rewound the film and stuck the exposed roll in the pocket of his long shirt. Deep in thought, he returned to the library and poured himself a glass of mineral water.

What should he make of Philby, he wondered. He liked the man personally; Yevgeny had come away from their meeting saying that the Englishman was an embittered drunk and incapable of the intricate mental compartmentalization that would be required of a triple agent. Andropov, on the other hand, was absolutely convinced that Philby had been turned by Angleton; that somewhere along the way Philby had switched his ultimate loyalties to the CIA. How else explain the fact, so Andropov reasoned, that Philby had never been arrested? How else explain that he had been allowed to slip away from

Beirut, where he had been working as a journalist, after the British came up with irrefutable evidence that he had betrayed his country? Starik's gut view, which found few supporters within the KGB hierarchy, was that Angleton would have been only too happy to see Philby escape; might even have made sure whispers of an impending arrest reached the Englishman's ears so that he could head for Moscow one jump ahead of the MI6's agents come to fetch him home to London. The last thing Angleton wanted was for Philby to tell the world about all those lunches with the American counterintelligence chief at La Niçoise, about all the state secrets he'd swiped directly from the man charged with protecting state secrets. When Philby had turned up in Moscow in 1963, Starik had spent weeks screening the serials he'd sent from Washington during the years he'd been meeting regularly with Angleton. All of them had seemed true enough, which meant...which meant what? If Angleton *had* turned Philby into a triple agent, he would have been shrewd enough to continue feeding him real secrets to keep the KGB from suspecting the truth. That was what Starik had done over the years; was still doing, in fact: sending over false defectors with real secrets and real defectors with false secrets was all part of the great game.

Sipping the mineral water, Starik slipped through the narrow door in the wood paneling into his small inner sanctum. Locking the door behind him, he disabled the destruction mechanism on the large safe cemented into the wall behind the portrait of Lenin, then opened it with the key he kept attached to the wrought silver chain hanging around his neck. He pulled out the old-fashioned file box with the words *Soversheno Sekretno* and KHOL-STOMER written in Cyrillic across the oak cover, and set it on the small table. He opened the box and extracted from a thick folder the cable that had been hand-delivered to the Apatov Mansion the previous night. The KGB *rezident* in Rome was alerting Directorate S to rumors circulating in Italian banking circles: The Patriarch of Venice, Cardinal Albino Luciani, was said to be looking into reports that the Vatican Bank, known as the Institute for Religious Works, was involved in money-laundering trans-actions. Luciani, whom some touted as a possible successor to the current Pope, Paul VI, had apparently been alerted to the existence of a fourteen-year-old investigation by a Roman public prosecutor into a money-laundering operation bearing the code name KHOLSTOMER, and had dispatched two priests with accounting skills to review the handwritten ledgers gathering dust in the archives of the Institute for Religious Works.

Starik looked up from the cable, his eyes dark with apprehension. Fortunately, one of the two priests came from a Tuscan family with strong ties to the Italian Communist Party; working closely with the Italian Communists, the *rezident* in Rome would be able to keep track of what information the priests sent back to Albino Luciani in Venice.

If the Patriarch of Venice came too close to the flame he would have to be burned. Nothing could be allowed to interfere with KHOLSTOMER. Now that the American economy was in a recessionary spiral and inflation was soaring, Starik intended to present the scheme first to KGB Chairman Andropov and, if he approved it, to the secret Politburo Committee of Three that scrutinized intelligence operations. By year's end, Starik hoped that Comrade Brezhnev himself would sign off on KHOLSTOMER and the stratagem that would bring America to its knees could finally be launched.

Starik's thoughts drifted to Yevgeny Alexandrovich. He bitterly regretted his decision to bring him back to Russia on home leave. The fatal illness of Yevgeny's father had clouded Starik's thoughts, lured him into the realm of sentimentality; he owed a last debt to the elder Tsipin, whom Starik had controlled when he worked in the United Nations Secretariat. Now that the debt was paid—Tsipin's ashes had been scattered amid the birches of Peredelkino the previous afternoon—it was time for Yevgeny Alexandrovich to return to the war zone. Time, also, for Starik to get on with his cat-and-bat game with the declining but still dangerous James Jesus Angleton.

"Do cats eat bats? Do bats eat cats?" he recited out loud.

He made a mental note to read that particular chapter to the girlies before they were tucked in for the night.

5

WASHINGTON, DC, THURSDAY, JULY 4, 1974

THE DARK GOVERNMENT OLDSMOBILE, OUTFITTED WITH BULLETPROOF windows and anti-mine flooring, threaded through the heavy beltway traffic in the direction of Langley. Riding shotgun up front next to the driver, the security guard fingered the clips taped back to back in the Israeli Uzi across his knees as he talked on the car radio to the chase car. "Breakwater Two, that there green Ford pickup two cars backa us been round for a spell—"

There was blast of static from the speaker in the dashboard. "Breakwater One, been eyeballing him since we crossed the Potomac. Two Caucasian males with Raybans up front."

"Breakwater Two, ah'd certainly 'preciate you cuttin'em off if they was to try to tuck in behind us."

"Breakwater One, wilco."

In the backseat the Director of Central Intelligence, Bill Colby, was reading through the "Eyes-Only" overnight cables bound in a metal folder with a red slash across it. There had been a dry spell in the last several weeks—Angleton had run into a stone wall in his interrogation of Leo Kritzky, Jack McAuliffe hadn't had any joy in identifying the Soviet mole inside the National Security Agency, Manny Ebbitt was scraping the bottom of the barrel at the weekly debriefing of the Russian defector AE/PINNACLE. Which made downright good news all the more welcome. Colby initialed a cable from Teheran Station (reporting on the feebleness of the Islamic fundamentalist opposition movements in Iran) and added it to the thin batch that would be routed on to Secretary of State Kissinger once the Company indicators and operational codes were expunged. Teheran Station's assessment reinforced recent estimates from the Deputy Director/Intelligence predicting that Iran's pro-Western monarch, Muhammad Reza Shah Pahlevi, would rule into the next century; that Islamic fundamentalists would not menace Persian Gulf stability, or Western oil supplies, in the foreseeable future.

The red telephone in the console buzzed. Colby lifted the receiver. "Yes?" He listened for a moment. "I'll be at my desk at the stroke of eight—tell him to stop by."

Minutes later Colby was pushing a steaming cup of coffee across the table toward Jack McAuliffe, the chief of operations for the Deputy Director/Operations, Elliott Ebbitt. "It seemed pretty straightforward," Jack explained. "Manny went back at AE/PINNACLE with the wording to make sure he got it right. There's no mistake. The KGB *rezident* deposited a message, addressed to the NSA mole, behind the radiator in the men's room of the Jefferson Hotel. The message said: 'Congratulations on the Second Man.'"

Colby gazed out the window of the seventh floor office. The wooded Virginia countryside stretched away as far as the eye could see, conveying a sense of serenity that contrasted sharply with the mood inside the CIA's sprawling Langley campus. "Maybe the mole's second son was born in December rather than January," Colby suggested.

"Tried that," Jack said. "I went over the NSA roster with their chief of security. There are ten thousand people making and breaking codes over at Fort Meade. Of these ten thousand, fourteen had second sons in January, eight in December, eighteen in November."

"That ought to give you something to work on—"

Jack shook his head. "Remember what AE/PINNACLE told Manny. All contact between the *rezidentura* and the mole in Washington were through dead drops. The face-to-face debriefings took place when their mole was vacationing abroad—Paris during Christmas of '72, Copenhagen during Christmas of '73, Rome during Easter of this year. None of the fathers of second sons fit into this vacation pattern."

"How about working backward from the vacation pattern?"

"Tried that, too. Got swamped. Half of NSA takes off for Christmas, the other half for Easter, and the security people don't have a systematic breakdown on where people went during vacations. If I give them a name they could find out—from phone logs, from discreet inquiries at their travel office, from office scuttlebutt. But I'm obliged to start with a suspect. We need the second son to narrow the field."

"What does Elliott think?"

"Ebby says that the answer is probably staring us in the face, that it's just a matter of coming at the problem from the right direction."

"All right. Keep looking. Anything else?"

"As a matter of fact, there is, Director." Jack cleared his throat.

"Spit it out, Jack."

"It's about Leo Kritzky—"

"Thought it might be."

"Jim Angleton's had him on the carpet for five weeks now."

Colby said coldly, "I can count as well as you."

"When Angleton turns up for a meeting of the AE/PINNACLE task force, which isn't often these days, Ebby and I ask him how the interrogation is going."

"He probably tells you what he tells me," Colby said uncomfortably.

"He says these things take time. He says Rome wasn't built in a day. He says he's convinced AE/PINNACLE is a genuine defector, which means that Leo Kritzky is SASHA."

"What do you want me to do, Jack?"

"Put a time limit on the interrogation. God knows what Angleton's people are doing to Leo. If you let Angleton have him long enough he'll confess to anything."

Colby pulled a manila envelope from a bulging briefcase and dropped it onto the table in front of Jack. "Jim polygraphed Kritzky."

"You can't flutter someone who's been in solitary confinement for five weeks. His nerves will be shot. He'll send the stylus through the roof when he gives his full name."

"Look, Jack, for better or for worse, Jim Angleton is the head of counterintelligence. Counterintelligence is supposed to detect Soviet penetrations of the Company. Angleton thinks he has detected such a penetration."

"All based on the fact that SASHA's last name begins with the letter *K*, that he is a Russian speaker, that he's been out of the country at such and such a date. That's pretty thin gruel, Director. On top of which AE/PINNACLE's second serial—the Soviet mole inside the NSA—hasn't worked out. If the second serial is wrong there's a good chance the first is, too."

Colby eyed Jack across the low table. "Are you sure you want the second serial to work out?"

The question stunned Jack. "What's that supposed to mean?"

"If you find the NSA mole it will establish that AE/PINNACLE is genuine. If AE/PINNACLE is genuine, Leo Kritzky is SASHA."

"Damnation, Director, I'd give my right arm for there to be no mole in NSA. But if there is a mole I'll find the son of a bitch. Count on it."

"If I wasn't convinced of that, Jack, you wouldn't be in my office this morning. Look, the case Angleton's building against Kritzky rests on more than the AE/PINNACLE serials. Jim claims to have discerned a pattern to the SASHA business—a long list of operations that went bad, a short list of operations that came off and boosted Kritzky's career. He's saying he was closing in on Kritzky even without the AE/PINNACLE serials."

Jack pushed away the cup of coffee and leaned forward. "Jim Angleton has been chasing shadows since Philby was exposed as a Soviet agent. He's convinced the Sino-Soviet split is phony. He thinks half the leaders of the Western world are KGB agents. He's decimated the Company's Soviet Division in his manhunt for SASHA. We don't even know for sure that SASHA exists outside of Angleton's head, for Christ's sake."

"Simmer down, Jack. Put yourself in the catbird seat. Maybe AE/PIN-NACLE is a dispatched agent. Maybe Leo Kritzky is clean as a whistle. Maybe SASHA is a figment of Angleton's imagination. But we can't take the risk of ignoring Jim Angleton's worst-case scenario." Colby stood up. Jack rose, too. The Director said, "Track down the father of the second man, Jack. Or bring me proof that he doesn't exist."

In the corridor, Jack hiked his shoulders in frustration. "How can you prove something doesn't exist?"

The words, uttered in a hoarse whisper, were almost inaudible. "I don't have any recollection of that."

"Let me refresh your memory. The Russian journalist was recruited in Trieste, given some elementary tradecraft training on a farm in Austria, then sent back to Moscow. Less than a week later he was pushed under the wheels of a subway train—"

"Moscow Station said he'd been drinking—".

"Ah, the story's coming back to you now. Moscow Station passed on the police report printed in *Pravda*, which mentioned a high alcohol level in the dead man's blood. A journalist who worked at the same radio station said our man was perfectly sober when he was picked up by two strangers the night before. The next morning the women cleaning the subway found his body on the tracks. The NODIS file describing the initial recruitment of the journalist has your initials on it. And you want to chalk it up to coincidence—"

"I haven't been able to...to move my bowels in days. I suffer from stomach cramps. I would like to see a doctor—"

James Angleton glanced up from the loose-leaf book, a soggy cigarette stuck between his lips. "In August of 1959, two six-man frogmen teams from Taiwan were caught as they came ashore on mainland China and shot the next morning. Do you remember that incident?"

"I remember the incident, Jim. I told you that last time you asked. The time before, also. I just don't remember initialing the op order on its way up to the DD/O."

Angleton unhinged the loose-leaf spine and pulled a photocopy of the op order from the book. "The *LK* in the upper right hand corner look familiar?" he inquired, holding it up.

Leo Kritzky swayed on his seat, trying to concentrate. The overhead lights burned through his lids even when they were closed, causing his eyes to smart. An unruly stubble of a beard covered his face, which was pinched and drawn. His hair had started to turn white and came out in clumps when he threaded his fingers through it. The skin on the back of his hands had taken on the color and texture of parchment. His joints ached. He could feel a pulse throbbing in his temple, he could hear a shrill ringing in his right ear. "I have difficulty...focusing," he reminded Angleton. Trembling with fatigue, Leo bit his lip to fight back the sobs rising from the depths of his body. "For God's sake, Jim, please be patient..."

Angleton waved the paper in front of Kritzky's eyes. "Make an effort."

Leo willed one of his eyes open. The *LK* swam into focus, along with other initials. "I wasn't the only one to sign off on that op order, Jim."

"You weren't the only one to sign off on the one hundred and forty-five op orders that ended with agents being arrested and tried and executed. But your initials were on all one hundred and forty-five. Should we chalk them all up to coincidence?"

"We lost something like three hundred and seventy agents between 1951 and now. Which means my name wasn't associated with"—simple arithmetic was beyond Leo and his voice trailed off—"a great many of them."

"Your name wasn't associated with two hundred twenty-five of them. But then a lot of paperwork never passed through your hands, either because you were too far down the ladder or out of town or out of the loop or sidetracked on temporary assignments."

"I swear I've told you the truth, Jim. I never betrayed anybody to the Russians. Not the Russian journalist who died in Moscow. Not the Nationalist Chinese who went ashore on the mainland. Not the Polish woman who was a member of the Central Committee."

"Not the Turk who smuggled agents into Georgia?"

"Not the Turk, no. I never betrayed him. Our investigators concluded that the Russians had been tipped off by his wife's brother when he failed to come up with the bride price he'd promised to the wife's family."

"You didn't betray the Cubans at the Bay of Pigs."

"Oh, God, no. I never betrayed the Cubans."

"You never passed word to the Russians that the landing had been switched from Trinidad to the Bay of Pigs?"

Kritzky shook his head.

"Somebody passed word to the Russians, because Castro's tanks and artillery were waiting on the other side of the Zapata swamps when the brigade came ashore."

"The Joint Chief's postmortem raised the possibility that Castro's forces were there on a training exercise."

"In other words, chalk it up to coincidence?"

"A coincidence. Yes. Why not?"

"There were a lot of coincidences over the years." Angleton remembered the E.M. Forster's dictum, which had been posted over Philby's desk back in the Ryder Street days: "Only connect!" That's what he was doing now. "You never gave the Russians the brigade's order of battle but the Cuban fighters who were released from Castro's prisons said their interrogators knew it. You never told them that Kennedy had ruled out overt American intervention under any circumstances?"

"No. No. None of it's true."

"Let's set the clock back to 1956 for a moment. The current DD/O, Elliott Ebbitt, was sent into Budapest under deep cover. Within days he'd been arrested by the Hungarian AVH."

"Chances are he was betrayed by a Soviet spy inside the Hungarian resistance movement."

Angleton shook his head. "The AVH Colonel who interrogated Elliott seemed to be familiar with his Central Registry file: he knew Elliott worked for Frank Wisner's Operations Directorate, he knew that he organized émigré drops behind the Iron Curtain out of Frankfurt Station, he was even able to identify Elliott's superior at Frankfurt Station as Anthony Spink."

Leo's chin nodded onto his chest and then jerked up again.

"You are one of the thirty-seven officers in Washington whose initials turn up on paper work relating to Ebbitt's mission. I suppose you want to chalk that up to coincidence, too."

Leo said weakly, "What about the other thirty-six," but Angleton had already turned the page and was struggling to decipher his own handwriting. "You were present in early November of 1956 when the DCI and the DD/O briefed President Eisenhower in the White House on American military preparedness in Europe in the event of war."

"I recall that, yes."

"What did Eisenhower tell our people?"

"He said he wished to God he could help the Hungarians, but he couldn't."

"Why couldn't he?"

"He and John Foster Dulles were afraid American intervention would trigger a ground war in Europe, for which we weren't prepared."

"There's a lot of internal evidence to suggest that the Soviet Politburo was divided on intervention and Khrushchev was sitting on the fence. Then, out of the blue, he came down on the side of intervention. It wasn't because you passed on Eisenhower's comment, was it?"

"I never passed anything on to the Russians," Leo insisted. "I am not a Russian spy. I am not SASHA."

"You denied these things when you were hooked up to the polygraph."

"Yes. I denied them then. I deny them now."

"The experts who read the polygraph decided you were lying."

"They're mistaken, Jim." One of Leo's hands waved in slow motion to dispel the cigarette smoke accumulating between the two men. "I am agitated. I am exhausted. I don't know whether it's night or day. I've lost track of time. Sometimes I say things to you and, a moment later, I can't remember what I said. The words, the thoughts, slip away from me. I reach for them but they are illusive. I have to sleep, Jim. Please let me sleep."

"Only tell me the truth and I'll turn out the lights and let you sleep as long as you like."

A spark of bitterness flared for a moment. "You don't want the truth. You want me to authenticate lies. You want me to vindicate all these years you've been turning the Company inside out looking for SASHA. You've never actually caught a mole, have you? But you've wrecked the careers of more than a hundred Soviet Division officers looking for one." Leo licked dried blood from his lips. "I won't crack, Jim. This can't go on forever." He looked up wildly; the lights blazing in the ceiling brought tears to his eyes, blinding him momentarily. "You're recording this. I know you are. Somebody somewhere will read the transcript. In the end they're going to become convinced I'm innocent."

Angleton flipped to another page in the loose-leaf. "Do you remember the Russian trade attaché in Madrid who offered to sell us the Soviet diplomatic cipher key, but was drugged and hustled onto a Moscow-bound Aeroflot plane before he could deliver?"

Millie kissed Anthony goodnight, then made her way downstairs to find Jack in the living room fixing himself a stiff whiskey. Lately he always made a bee-line for the bar when he came home. "Sorry," he muttered, and he waved his hand to take in all the things he was sorry for: returning from Langley, once again, at an ungodly hour; getting back too late to help Anthony with his homework or take Millie downtown for a film; being down in the dumps.

"Don't tell me—let me guess: You had another hard day at the office," Millie remarked testily. It was written on his face, inscribed in the worry lines around his eyes. Millie had compared notes with Elizabet over lunch that afternoon; Elizabet's husband, Jack's boss, Ebby Ebbitt, had been in a sour mood for weeks, leading the two women to suspect the worst. They teased out various possibilities from the clues they had: the DD/O was being shaken up; one or both of their husbands had been fired or transferred to the Company equivalent of an Arctic listening post; the Company had suffered an operational setback; some friend or colleague was dead or dying, or rotting in a Communist prison somewhere in the world. Both women agreed the worst part was that you couldn't talk to them about their troubles. Raise the subject and they clammed up and went back to the bar for a chaser. "Jack," Millie whispered, sinking down onto the couch next to him, "how long is this going to go on?"

"What?"

"You know. Something's very wrong. Is it us? Is it our life together, our marriage?"

"Oh, Christ, no," Jack said. "It has nothing to do with you and me. It's Company stuff."

"Bad stuff?"

"Terrible stuff."

"Remember me, Jack? Millie Owen-Brack, your wife for better or for worse? I'm the guy who writes speeches and press releases for the Director," she reminded him. "I'm cleared for anything you're cleared for."

Jack tossed back half his drink. "You don't have a need to know, Millie. Even if you knew I don't see how you could help."

"Wives are supposed to be sharers of troubles, Jack. Just sharing will lighten the load. Try."

She could see he was tempted. He actually opened his mouth to say something. Then he blew air through his mustache and clamped his mouth shut again. He threw an arm over Millie's shoulder and drew her against him. "Tell me about your day," he said.

Millie leaned her head against his shoulder. "I spent most of my time working up a press kit on this Freedom of Information act. Jesus, if Congress actually passes the damn thing, people will be able to sue the CIA to get their 201 records."

Jack nursed his drink. "Always has been, always will be a tension between an intelligence agency's need to keep its secrets and the public's right to know what's going on."

"What if the American Communist Party sues the FBI to find out if their phones are being tapped? What then?"

Jack laughed quietly. "We'll draw the line where national security is at stake."

"You surprise me, Jack—I thought you'd be against this Freedom of Information business."

"As long as there are safeguards built in, hell, I don't see what's so God-awful about it."

"Hey, you're turning into a flaming liberal in your old age."

Jack's gaze drifted to a framed photograph on the wall of two men in their early twenties, wearing sleeveless undershirts with large *Y*'s on the chests, posing in front of a slender racing shell. A thin woman in a knee-length skirt and a man's varsity sweater stood off to one side. The faded caption on the scalloped white border of the photograph, a copy of which was on Leo's living room wall, read: *Jack & Leo & Stella after The Race but before The Fall.* "I believe in this open society of ours," Jack said. "God knows I've been fighting for it long enough. I believe in habeas corpus, I believe every man has a right to his day in court, I believe he has the right to hear the accusations against him and confront his accuser. We sometimes forget that this is what separates us from the goons in the Kremlin."

Millie sat up and caressed the back of Jack's neck. She had never heard him wax passionate about the American system. "Say, Jack, what *is* going on at your shop?"

He decided to change the subject. "You still short-handed over in PR?"

Millie sighed. "Geraldine's decided to take that private sector job. And Florence is out on maternity leave—hey, she had an ultrasonograph yesterday and found out the baby is a girl. She was disappointed—her husband was hoping for a boy—but I told her she ought to count her blessings."

Jack was barely following the conversation. "Why's that?" he asked absently.

"I told her I was speaking from experience—it's hard enough to live with one man, two is twice as difficult. I mean, first off, when you have two men under the same roof they outnumber you—"

Jack was suddenly gaping into Millie's eyes. "What did you say?"

"I said two men in the house outnumber you—"

"Two men outnumber the wife?"

"What's wrong, Jack?"

"And the two men who outnumber the wife—one is the husband and the other is the *firstborn* son!"

"Well, yeah. It was just a joke, Jack."

"So if Florence were to give birth to a baby boy, I could send her a note saying 'Congratulations on the Second Man?'"

"Well, sure. If you count the husband as the first man."

Ebby had been on target: the answer *was* staring him in the face, it *was* just a matter of coming at the problem from the right direction. Jack bounded from the couch, plucked his sports jacket off the back of it and headed for the front door.

"Where are you going, Jack?"

"To find the first man."

Adelle was at her wit's end. She'd spoken with Director Colby twice in the past five weeks. The first time, he'd phoned her to apologize for hustling Leo off to Asia on such short notice; he'd asked her to pack a suitcase and had sent a car around to pick it up. When three weeks had gone by without word from Leo, Adelle had put in a call to the Director. It had taken her three more calls and two days to get past the gatekeepers. Not to worry, Colby had said when she finally managed to speak with him. Leo was fine and engaged in vital work for the Company; with Leo's help, Colby had said, he had high hopes that some extremely important matters might be cleared up. He was sorry he couldn't tell her more. Naturally he counted on her discretion; the fewer people who knew Leo was out of town, the better. Adelle had asked if she could get a letter through to her husband; the Director had given her a post-office box number that she could write to and had promised to call her the moment he had more news.

Her two letters sent to the post-box had gone unanswered.

Now, five weeks after their return from France, she still had no direct word from Leo. Vanessa was starting to ask questions; Daddy had never disappeared before like this, she noted. Another week and he'd miss Philip Swett's eightieth-birthday shindig, a Georgetown bash that was expected to attract Congressmen and Cabinet members and Supreme Court justices, perhaps even the Vice President. Vanessa, who doted on her father, looked so worried that Adelle swore her to secrecy and told her Leo had been sent to Asia on an extremely important mission. Why would the Company pack the Soviet Division chief off to Asia? Vanessa wanted to know. It wasn't logical, was it? It wasn't necessarily *illogical*, Adelle said. Soviet Russia stretched across the continent to Asia; according to the newspapers, there were Soviet submarine and missile bases on the Kamchatka Peninsula that would be of great interest to the Central Intelligence Agency.

The answer satisfied Vanessa but it left Adelle with the queasy feeling that Colby was being less than straightforward with her. She decided then and there to see if her father could find out where Leo had been sent to, and why.

Philip Swett had grown hard-of-hearing with age and Adelle had to repeat the story several times before her father grasped the problem. "You trying to tell me you haven't seen hide nor hair of that husband of yours in five weeks?" he demanded.

"Not a word, Daddy."

"And that Colby fellow said he'd packed him off to Malaysia?"

"Not Malaysia, Daddy. Asia."

"By golly, I'll get to the bottom of this," Swett swore. And he put in a call to Henry Kissinger over at the State Department.

Kissinger returned the call within the hour. "Phil, what can I do for you?" he asked.

Swett explained that his son-in-law, Leo Kritzky, who happened to be the Soviet Division chief over at Langley, seemed to have dropped from sight. Colby was giving his daughter a song and dance about Kritzky being off on a mission to Asia.

"Where's the problem?" Kissinger demanded. Here he was, trying to trim American foreign policy sails to weather the Presidential impeachment tempest brewing in Congress; he didn't have the time or the energy to track down missing CIA personnel.

"Tarnation, Henry, the boy's been gone for five weeks and there hasn't been a letter, a phone call, nothing."

Kissinger's office rang Swett back that afternoon. One of the Secretary's aides had checked with Langley. It seemed as if Kritzky was on a personal mission for the DCI. The Company had declined to give out any further information and had made it clear that it didn't appreciate inquiries of this nature.

Swett recognized a brush off when he saw one. By golly, he was going to have a word with that Colby fellow if he ran into him. There had been a time when Harry Truman tried out his speeches on Swett, when Dwight Eisenhower sought his advice, when young John Kennedy ruminated aloud in his presence about the imbecility of allowing the Central Intelligence Agency to organize an invasion of Cuba. Come to think of it, Charles de Gaulle had put his finger on the problem before he died four years before: Old age was a shipwreck, he'd said. This time next week Swett would be pushing eighty from the wrong side. Pretty soon folks wouldn't even return his calls.

Stretching out on the couch, Philip Swett made a mental note to phone his daughter when he woke up from his afternoon nap. Chances were Kritzky was off in Malaysia, just as Colby said; chances were he'd be back in time for Swett's damn birthday party. Swett wouldn't lose any sleep if he didn't show up. Always wondered what the devil his mule of a daughter saw in Kritzky. Recently she'd dropped hints that their marriage wasn't all that swell. Well, if she decided to divorce that Jewish fellow, he for one wouldn't shed any tears...

Philip Swett's lids twitched shut over his eyes with a strange weightiness, blotting out the light with such finality he wondered if he would ever see it again.

A filament of moonlight stole through the gap between the curtains on the window and etched a silver seam into the wooden planking on the floor. Wide-awake on the giant bed, Manny pressed his ear against Nellie's spinal column and eavesdropped on her breathing. The night before, high on daiquiris and Beaujolais Nouveau, they had wandered back to her apartment from a small French restaurant in Georgetown. Manny had been quieter than usual. Kicking off her shoes and curling up on the couch next to him, Nellie had sensed he was preoccupied with something other than her. I could take your mind off it, she had murmured, teasingly pressing her lips into his ear, her breast into his arm. And shrugging off the shoulder straps of the silky black mini-dress, she'd done just that. There had been an impatient exploration of possibilities on the couch. Then they'd padded into the bedroom and made love a second time with lazy premeditation, spread-eagled across fresh sheets scented with lilac. Afterward, losing all sense of time, they had talked in undertones until traffic ceased to move through the street below Nellie's apartment.

In the early hours of the morning Nellie had gotten around to the subject that was mystifying her. "So why?"

"Why what?"

"Why tonight? Why did you fuck me?"

"I didn't *fuck* you, Nellie. I made love to you."

"Oh, you certainly did, Manny. But you haven't answered the question. Why tonight?"

"I figured out that the object of intercourse is intimacy, and not the other way round. For reasons I can't explain it suddenly seemed very important—I needed a close friend close."

"That may be the nicest thing a man's ever said to me, Manny," she had whispered in the slow, husky rasp of someone slipping into delicious unconsciousness. "Incest definitely beats...masturbation."

Now, while she slept, Manny's thoughts drifted back to his most recent session with AE/PINNACLE. Late in the afternoon he'd debriefed Kukushkin in the living room of Agatha's apartment near Rockville, scribbling furiously even though the tape recorder was capturing every word the Russian uttered. Kukushkin seemed edgier than usual, prowling the room as he delivered the latest batch of serials.

—Moscow Centre had forged the letter from Chinese Premier Minister Chou En-lai, published in an African newspaper the previous month, which seemed to suggest that Chou considered the Cultural Revolution to have been a political error.

—the KGB was financing a costly world-wide campaign in support of ratification of the Revised ABM Treaty, limiting the Soviet Union and the United States to one anti-ballistic missile site each.

—the Russians, convinced that Nixon was lying when he claimed to have cancelled the American biological weapons program in the late 1960s, had gone ahead with their own program, with the result that they were now capable of arming intercontinental ballistic missile warheads with anthrax bacteria and smallpox viruses.

—the Kremlin had reason to believe that Taiwan was attempting to buy nuclear technology from South Africa, developed over the past few years in partnership with Israel.

—the KGB had buried bugs inside the electric typewriters used in the American embassy in Moscow while the typewriters were being shipped from Finland on Soviet trains; the bugs transmitted what was being typed to a nearby listening post in short bursts and on a frequency used by television transmitters so that security sweeps through embassy detected nothing out of the ordinary.

"So, Manny, there it is—your weekly ration of secrets."

"Is everything normal at the embassy?"

Kukushkin had settled onto the couch and had looked at his wristwatch; he wanted to be back at the embassy when his wife returned from the dentist. "I think so."

"You only think so?"

"No. I can be more positive. Everything appears normal to me, to my wife also." The Russian had flashed a lopsided smile. "I appreciate you worry about me, Manny."

"If anything were to happen...if there were to be an emergency, you have the safety razor with the numbers on the handle."

Kukushkin nodded wearily; they had been over this before. "I twist the grip to adjust the setting of the blade. If I set the grip precisely between number two and number three and twist counterclockwise, a hidden chamber in the bottom of the handle snaps open. Inside is a frame of microfilm containing emergency procedures for establishing contact in both Washington and Moscow."

"Are you still on good terms with your *rezident*, Borisov?"

"It would seem so. He invited me into his office for a cognac late last night. When I said him he looks gloomy he laughed a Russian laugh—which, for your information, is a laugh with more philosophy than humor in it. He said Russians are born gloomy. He is blaming it on the winters. He is blaming it on the immensity of Russia. He says we are afraid of this immensity the way children are afraid of the dark—afraid there is a chaos somewhere out there waiting to strangle us in its tentacles. I said him that this explains why we put up with Stalin—our dread of chaos, of anarchy, pushes us to the other extreme: we value order even if it is not accompanied by law."

Manny had watched Kukushkin's eyes as he spoke; they were fixed intently on his American friend and filled with anguish. The nail of his middle finger, flicking back and forth across his thumbnail, had fallen silent. A sigh had escaped from his lips. Was Kukushkin the genuine defector he claimed to be or a consummate actor putting on a good imitation of treason?

Leo Kritzky's fate was riding on the answer to this question.

Kukushkin, suddenly eager to bare his soul, had plunged on. "I am going to tell you something I never before told to a living person, Manny. Not even my wife. There was a Communist, his name was"—even now, even here, Kukushkin had lowered his voice out of habit—"Piotr Trofimovich Ishov, who fought with great heroism in our Civil War and rose to the rank of colonel general. In 1938, I am eleven years old at that moment, Piotr Ishov vanished one evening—he simply did not return to his flat after work. When his much younger wife, Zinaida, made inquiries, she was told that her husband was caught plotting with Trotsky to murder Stalin. There was no trial—perhaps he refused to confess, perhaps he was too beaten to permit him to confess in public. Within days Zinaida and Ishov's oldest son, Oleg, were arrested as enemies of the people and deported to a penal village in the Kara Kum desert of Central Asia. There Zinaida committed suicide. There Oleg died of typhus fever. A youngest son, a child of eleven, was given over for adoption to a distant relative living in Irkutsk. The relative's name was Klimov. I am that child, Manny. I am the son of the enemy of the people Ishov."

Manny had instantly recognized this as the defining moment of their relationship. Reaching over, he had gripped Kukushkin's wrist. The Russian had nodded and Manny had nodded back. The silence between them had turned heavy. Manny had asked, "Why didn't you tell me this before?"

"Before...you were not yet my friend."

One thing had puzzled Manny. "The KGB would never have recruited you if they had known about your past."

"My adopted father, Ivan Klimov, worked as a structural engineer in an aviation plant in Irkutsk. After the Great War he was transferred to Moscow and eventually rose through the *nomenklatura* to become a sub-minister for aviation attached to the Ministry of Armaments. He understood that I would never be admitted to the Party or a university, never be permitted to hold an important job, if my history became known. The Klimovs had lost a son my age in a car accident in 1936. When they were transferred to Moscow, with the help of a nephew who worked in the Irkutsk Central Record department they managed to erase all traces of my past. In Moscow Ivan Klimov passed me off as his legitimate son, Sergei."

"My God," Manny had whispered. "What a story!"

What bothered him most about it was that nobody could have invented it.

Jack fed some coins into the pay phone in the parking lot of the sprawling National Security Agency building at Fort Meade, Maryland. "It's our worst nightmare," Jack confided in Ebby. "I can't say more—this is an open line. I'll be back by three. You'd better convene a war council. Everyone in the task force will want to be in on this."

Colby was the last to turn up for the meeting. "Sorry to be late," he said, settling into an empty seat. "I had to take a call from the White House. That Indian atomic test has them going up the wall." He nodded at Jack "You want to start the ball rolling."

"Director, gentlemen, AE/PINNACLE was on the money," Jack began. "The Russians do have a mole inside the NSA." He noticed a faint smile creeping onto the lips of James Angleton, slouched in his seat at the head of the table. "We came at the 'Congratulations on the Second Man' serial from another angle." Here Jack nodded at Ebby. "If you start from the premise that the husband is the *first* man and the firstborn baby is the *second* man, the pieces fall into place. There were twenty-three NSA employees who had children born in January. Of these twenty-three, seventeen were firstborn sons. Working from phone logs, what records they have in the NSA travel office and the master logs, we were able to establish that the father of one of these seventeen boys was in Paris during Christmas of '72, Copenhagen during Christmas of '73 and Rome during Easter of this year. This, you'll remember, matches the pattern of the KGB's face-to-face debriefings that AE/PINNACLE passed on to us."

"Who is it?" Colby asked. He could tell from the way that his DD/O, Ebbitt, avoided his eye that it was going to be pretty bad.

"His name is Raymond R. Shelton. He's a forty-eight-year-old middle-grade NSA staffer who has been analyzing transcripts of Russian intercepts—"

"That's all we needed," Colby muttered.

Angleton raised the eraser-end of a pencil to get Jack's attention. "Were you able to work up any corroboration aside from the business of the first son and the travel pattern?"

Ebby said, "The answer is affirmative."

Jack provided the details. "AE/PINNACLE also mentioned that the mole had a *habit*, a weakness for women and gambling. The implication was that he couldn't make ends meet on his NSA salary, which in Shelton's case is twenty-four thousand five hundred dollars, and sold out to the Russians for cold cash."

Colby said to himself, "I don't know which is worse—selling out for cash or because you believe in Communism."

"Four years ago," Jack went on, "Shelton's wife filed divorce papers against her husband and named a second woman. The wife eventually reconciled with her husband and dropped the case. The security people looked into it at the time and came across evidence that Shelton, who was a natty dresser with a reputation as a skirt chaser, may have been playing around. They also discovered what they called a 'manageable' poker habit that had him dropping fifty or a hundred on a bad night. Shelton was warned he'd be fired if he continued gambling. He denied the womanizing part and vowed to give up poker, which apparently mollified the security people. In any case, the work he was doing was so important that his section head and the division director both vouched for him."

Colby asked, "Who knows about Shelton outside this room?"

"I had to bring the chief of security at Fort Meade into the picture," Jack explained. "I didn't tell him how we found out about the second-man message or the travel dates."

Angleton was scratching notes to himself on a yellow legal pad. "Who or what's going to keep the NSA security chief from blowing the story to his superiors at Fort Meade?" he asked.

Jack looked across at Angleton. Their eyes met. "I took the liberty of reminding him that Bill Colby wasn't only the CIA director; he was the director of the entire American intelligence establishment, including NSA, and as such would bring the appropriate NSA topsiders in on the situation when he considered it appropriate. For now, the Shelton affair is being closely held."

"Okay," Colby grunted. "Time for the other shoe to drop."

Angleton put a fine point on the question. "What exactly does this Shelton do for a living?"

Jack nodded to himself. "He's in charge of the team assigned to one of NSA's most productive intercept projects, a top-secret BIGOT listed operation code-named IVY BELLS."

"Christ, I walk sterilized chunks of the IVY BELLS product up to the White House from time to time," Colby said.

Ebby said, "I'm sorry, Jack—I'm not familiar with IVY BELLS."

Jack said, "I wasn't either until this morning. Turns out that American submarines have fitted a small waterproof pod onto a Soviet underwater communications cable lying on the ocean floor in the Sea of Okhotsk off the Soviet Union's Pacific coast. The cable is packed with Soviet military lines. The pod is probably the most sophisticated eavesdropping device ever conceived. It wraps itself around the target cable and taps into the lines electronically without actually touching the wires themselves. When the Soviets raise the cables for maintenance, the pod breaks away and sits undetected on the seabed. Tapes in the pod can record Soviet military channels for six weeks, at which point our sub returns, frogmen retrieve the tapes and install new ones. The tapes are sent to NSA for transcription and deciphering. The messages are old but they are brimming with information about Soviet ballistic missile tests—"

"Soviet missiles test fired from the Kamchatka Peninsula land in the Sea of Okhotsk," Colby noted.

"Which means that reports of their successes or failures pass through our pod," Ebby observed.

"The Russians are so confident their underwater lines are untappable that they don't use high-grade cipher systems," Jack went on. "On some of the channels they don't bother enciphering their transmissions at all."

Manny caught Jack's eye. "I'm missing something. If the guy in charge of the NSA team handling the IVY BELLS material is a Soviet agent, it means that the Russians know about the pod—they know their undersea cable is being tapped. So why didn't they shut it down?"

Jack said, "If you were the KGB would you shut it down?"

Manny's mouth opened, then closed. "You're all one jump ahead of me, aren't you? They won't shut it down because they don't want us to walk back the cat and stumble across their mole at NSA."

"There are also advantages to knowing your phone's being tapped," Ebby said. "You can fill it with disinformation."

Colby said, "The Soviets could have been overstating the accuracy of their missiles or the success rate of their tests. We'll have to go back and reevaluate every single IVY BELLS intercept."

Manny said, "When we take Shelton into custody—"

Angleton interrupted. "Arresting Shelton is out of the question."

"But how can we let a Soviet mole operate inside NSA?" Manny asked.

Jack filled in the blanks. "Think it through, Manny. If we pick up Shelton, the KGB will walk back the cat to see how we found out about him. That could lead them to our defector in the Soviet embassy, AE/PIN-NACLE. Besides which, we're better off knowing that they know about IVY BELLS—we can see what they're trying to make us believe, which will give us clues about what's really going on in their missile program."

"On top of that," Colby said, "we have similar pod intercepts on Chinese underwater lines, as well as French undersea cables to Africa. They don't know about the existence of the pod technology. But they will if we blow the whistle on Shelton."

"It's a classic intelligence standoff," Angleton remarked. "The Russians know about our pod but don't close it down so we won't discover Shelton. We know about Shelton but don't close him down so they won't discover AE/PINNACLE. We're dealing with a helix of interlocking secrets—unlock one and we give away secrets we don't want to give away."

"What we need to do now," Ebby said, "is leave some disinformation lying around Shelton's shop that he can pass on to his handlers."

The ashes on Angleton's cigarette grew perilously long but he was too engrossed in the discussion to notice. Squinting down the table at his colleagues, he declared, "Which brings us back to the unfinished business—AE/PINNACLE and SASHA."

Ebby glanced at Jack, then lowered his eyes.

Angleton said, "I take it that nobody in this room doubts that Kukushkin has proven, beyond a shadow of a doubt, his *bona fides.*"

Everyone understood what that meant.

Jack said, "Director, I'd like to speak with Leo—"

"That's a nonstarter," Angleton snapped. "Kritzky has to be kept in total isolation, he has to be brought to the point of despair—"

Colby asked Jack, "What would you hope to accomplish?"

Jack considered the question. "Leo and I go back a long way. I can get him to face up to the reality of the situation he's in—"

Ebby saw possibilities in this approach. "We have to give Leo a way out short of life in prison. The problem isn't to break him—it's to double him back. If we handle Leo skillfully we could turn a disaster into an intelligence triumph—imagine what we can feed the KGB if Leo agrees to work for us."

Angleton, as he often did, began thinking out loud. "In order to double him you'd have to convince him that we have proof of his treason. Which means you'd have to tell him about the existence of AE/PINNACLE. And that breaks every rule in the book—"

"That's why it'd work," Jack said with sudden vehemence. He talked directly to Angleton. "If you go by the book, Jim, this could drag on for God knows how long. It could be the Philby interrogation all over again. His interrogators were the best in the business. They went at him for months. They knew he was guilty but as long as he held out, as long as he insisted on his innocence, they couldn't bring the case into court because, in the end, without a confession, the evidence was circumstantial."

"It might be worth trying," Ebby told Colby.

"It would be coming at the problem from another angle," Jack pleaded.

Angleton puffed away on his cigarette. "Highly unusual," he grumbled. "Not something I'd feel comfortable with."

Colby looked from one to the other. "Let me think about it," he finally said.

At first Jack thought he'd been let into the wrong cell. The man sitting on the floor on an army blanket, his back to the padded wall, didn't seem familiar. He looked like one of those survivors of concentration camps seen in old photographs: thin, drawn, with a wild stubble of a beard and sunken cheeks that made his hollow eyes appear oversized and over-sad. His complexion had turned chalky. He was dressed in pajamas that were too large for him. His teeth gnawed away on his lower lip, which was raw and bleeding. The man brought a trembling hand up to shield his eyes from the three naked electric bulbs dangling from the high ceiling. Words seemed to froth up from his lips. "Slumming in Angleton's dungeons, Jack?"

Jack caught his breath. "Leo, is that you!"

The mask on Leo's face cracked into a lop-sided grimace. "It's me, or what's left of me." He started to push himself to his feet but sank back in exhaustion. "Can't offer you much by way of refreshments except water. You can have water, Jack, if you don't mind drinking from the toilet bowl."

Jack crossed the room and settled onto his haunches facing Leo. "God almighty, I didn't know..." He turned his head and stared at the tin cup on the floor next to the toilet. "None of us knew..."

"Should have found out, Jack," Leo said with stiff bitterness. "Shouldn't have left me in Angleton's clutches. I have diarrhea—I clean the inside of the toilet with my hand so I can drink out of it afterward."

Jack tried to concentrate on the reason for his being there. "Leo, you've got to listen up—this doesn't have to end with you rotting here, or in prison for the rest of your days."

"Why would I go to prison, Jack?"

"For treason. For betraying your country. For spying for the Russian we know as Starik."

"You believe that, Jack? You believe I'm SASHA?"

Jack nodded. "We know it, Leo. There's nothing left for you to do but come clean. If you won't think of yourself, think of Adelle. Think of the twins. It's not too late to redeem yourself—"

Mucus seeped from one of Leo's nostrils. Moving in lethargic slow motion, he raised the arm of his filthy pajamas and wiped the mucus away, then blotted the blood off his lips. "How do you know I'm SASHA?" he asked.

Jack settled back until he was sitting on the floor. He realized how cold the room was. "We have a Russian defector," he said. "We've given him the code name AE/PINNACLE. Ebby's boy, Manny, had the night watch when the Russian made contact. Manny's been running him since."

Leo's eyes burned fiercely into Jack's; it dawned on him that Jack's visit was highly irregular; he was astonished Angleton would sit still for it. "This AE/PINNACLE identified me by name? He said Leo Kritzky is SASHA?"

"He said SASHA's last name began with *K.* He said he was fluent in Russian."

"How did he know these things?"

"The defector worked for Directorate S of the First Chief Directorate in Moscow Centre, the department that runs illegals—"

"Damn it, I know what Directorate S is."

"He reported directly to this Starik character. In September of '72, he laid in the plumbing for a trip Starik took to Nova Scotia to meet an agent."

"He said Starik was going to meet an agent."

"No. We surmised that part. We surmised that the only thing that would lure Starik out of Russia was a face-to-face meeting with his agent SASHA."

"And I was on a bicycle trip to Nova Scotia in September of '72."

"Yes, you were, Leo."

"There has to be more to it. What else do you have?"

"AE/PINNACLE learned from the KGB *rezident* that SASHA was away from Washington for the two weeks ending on Sunday, twenty-six May."

"Which just happens to be when I was in France." What started out as a laugh gurgled up from Leo's throat. "That it?"

"Jesus H. Christ, isn't that enough?"

"Didn't occur to you guys that Starik was feeding you a phony defector with phony serials to frame the wrong person."

"Why would Starik want to frame you, Leo?"

"To distract you from the right person?"

Jack shook his head. "Angleton's worked up a profile on you that is very persuasive—"

Leo managed a sneer. "Every operation that succeeded was designed to advance my career. Every one that failed, failed because I gave it away."

"There's too much overlap for it to be coincidental. Besides which, you flunked Jim's polygraph test. In spades."

"Did anyone flutter this AE/PINNACLE character of yours?"

"Come off it, Leo. You know as well as I do we don't flutter defectors in a safe-house environment. He'll be too uptight, too edgy to get an accurate reading. We'll flutter him when we bring him over for good."

"You can't flutter a defector in a safe house. But Angleton can flutter a prisoner in a padded cell who drinks water out of the toilet and still get good results?" Leo teetered forward. "Pay attention, Jack, I'm going to tell you something you need to remember: AE/PINNACLE will never be fluttered. He'll be run over by a car or mugged in an alleyway or whisked back to Mother Russia for some cockamamie reason that will sound plausible enough. But he won't be fluttered because he won't be brought in. He won't be brought in because he's a dispatched defector sent to convince Angleton I'm SASHA."

Jack shook his head in despair. "If you're not SASHA, Leo, it means that SASHA is still out there somewhere. If that's so, how do you explain the fact that AE/PINNACLE hasn't been put on ice by his embassy's SK people?"

"Jack, Jack, he hasn't been put on ice because your AE/PINNACLE is a dispatched agent and SASHA, if he exists, *knows it.*"

"Look, I didn't come here to argue with you, Leo. I came here to offer you a way out."

Leo whispered hoarsely, "The way out of here is through that padded door, Jack. I'm innocent. I'm not SASHA. I'm Leo Kritzky. I've been fighting the good fight for twenty-four years. And look at the thanks I get—" Suddenly Leo began trembling. He jammed his thumb and third finger into the corners of his eyes and breathed hard through his mouth. "It's so unfair, Jack. So fucking unfair. There has to be someone who believes me—who believes this defector is a dispatched agent, sent to frame me—"

Jack struggled to find the right words. "Leo, I can't tell you how but AE/PINNACLE has proven his *bona fides* beyond any doubt. There is absolutely no possibility of his being a dispatched agent. Which means his serials concerning SASHA are genuine. And they all point to you. Admit you're SASHA, Leo. Tell us what you've given them over the years so we can run a damage assessment analysis. And then come over to our side. We'll double you, we'll run you back *against* the KGB. No one here will forgive you, no one here will shake your hand again. But it can keep you out of prison, Leo. Adelle, the twins won't find out you betrayed your country unless you tell them. When it's all over, you can go off somewhere where people won't know you and live out what's left of your life."

With an effort Leo struggled to his feet and, clutching the waistband of his pajamas, shuffled in short, cautious steps across the room to the toilet. He sank to his knees in front of it and filled the tin cup from the bowl and moistened his lips with the water. He looked over at Jack. Then, with his eyes fixed on him, Leo slowly drank off the rest of the cup. When he finished he set the cup down on the ground and whispered through his raw lips, "Go fuck yourself, Jack."

6

WASHINGTON, DC, TUESDAY, JULY 30, 1974

AND THEN AE/PINNACLE DISAPPEARED FROM THE RADAR SCREEN. "What do you mean, disappeared?" Jack demanded when Manny called in on a secure line from the Watcher's flat down the hall from Agatha Ept's apartment.

"He seems to have vanished, Jack. That's all I can say for the moment."

"Did their SK people somehow tag on to him?"

"Don't know."

Jack was clearly irritated. "What do you know?"

"AE/PINNACLE phoned Ept Friday before she left for work to say he'd come by Monday evening. I just listened to the tape of the conversation. He said he'd appreciate it if she could get her hands on more of the candy that she swiped from the Patent Office from time to time. Which means that, as of Friday morning, he was operational."

"How did he sound?"

"He didn't sound as if he was talking with a gun to his head, if that's what you mean. He was tense—who wouldn't be in his shoes—but he wasn't particularly agitated or anything. "

"When did you see him last?"

"A week ago today. We cut the session short because his daughter was running a fever and he was anxious to get back to the embassy."

"He seem normal?"

"Yeah, Jack, he did. Although for AE/PINNACLE, 'normal' was preoccupied—anxious to unload the material he'd collected, worried about what the future held for him and his family. We chatted for a moment waiting for the elevator—he told me the latest Brezhnev joke, then he said he'd call Ept and let her know when he would be able to come again."

Jack asked "Did you have any trace of him between Tuesday and Friday, when he phoned Ept?"

"The FBI caught him on their surveillance cameras going in and out of the embassy, once on Wednesday afternoon, once on Thursday morning. Both times he was with the chief of the consular section, Borisov, who is the KGB *resident*—they were chatting away as if neither of them had a care in the world. Then we have him on tape Friday morning telling Ept he'd come by on Monday. Then—he dropped from sight."

"I don't like the sound of it, Manny," Jack said. "With all the cameras and Watchers, how does a Russian diplomat drop from sight?"

"It turns out the Russians recently bought several cars with tinted windows—we film them coming into and out of the underground parking but we have no idea who's inside. It's possible AE/PINNACLE could have been in one of these cars."

"Any sign of the wife or daughter?"

"No. And his wife missed a Monday afternoon appointment with the heart man we set up two floors above the Bulgarian dentist. She was supposed to come in for another electrocardiogram. And she never phoned the dentist's office to cancel."

Jack said, "Okay, if AE/PINNACLE and his wife left town, chances are it was by plane, so we ought to have them on surveillance cameras. I'll put the Office of Security onto the problem. You come on in and look over their shoulder when they go through the footage—if anybody can spot Kukushkin or his wife it'll be you."

Manny spent the rest of the morning and all of the afternoon in a Company screening room, studying the clips that the security people projected for him. He started with the footage from Friday afternoon—reel after reel of people boarding international carriers. Several times Manny spotted heavy-shouldered men with light-colored hair. But when the clip was run again in slow motion he could see that none of them was Sergei Kukushkin. Sandwiches and coffee were brought in and he started going through the Saturday morning reels.

At one point, Manny ducked out to phone Nellie and tell her not to count on him that night; they were more or less living together in Nellie's apartment, though Manny hadn't given up his old flat, which was a sore point with Nellie. It's not the two rents that bugs me, she'd told him when the subject came up at breakfast one morning, it's the symbolism; you're afraid to burn your bridges. Incest takes getting used to, he'd explained. At which point they'd laughingly repeated in chorus what had become their credo: No doubt about it, incest is definitely best!

"Hey, are you watching the tube?" Nellie asked now.

"I am otherwise engaged," Manny said dryly.

"Well, you're missing out on history in the making: The House Judiciary Committee just voted the third article of impeachment."

"Nixon will worm out of it," Manny said. "He always does."

"Not this time," Nellie said. "Here's what I think: It has nothing to do with the Watergate break in, it has nothing to do with the Supreme Court ordering Nixon to turn over those sixty-four incriminating tapes to the special prosecutor."

"You always have exotic explanations for current events," Manny noted.

"I see under the surface of things, is all," Nellie said.

Manny took the bait: "And under the surface of Watergate is?"

"Come on, Manny, don't play the innocent," Nellie said. "Under the surface is crude oil at eleven dollars and twenty-five cents a barrel; my law firm negotiates insurance for the tankers, is how I know this. Under the surface is the recession, also the Dow Jones plunging past the six-hundred mark and no bottom in sight. It's not Nixon—he more or less did what Lyndon Johnson did when he ran the Oval Office; it's the economy, stupid."

Back in the screening room, the projectionist brought in the Saturday afternoon reels and Manny started in on them. Halfway through one reel he straightened in his seat and called, "Morris, you want to go back and run that one again." Manny leaned forward. On the screen, a man with the heavy shoulders and thick torso of a wrestler and disheveled, vaguely blond hair had joined the line boarding a Scandinavian Airline flight to Stockholm.

"Oh my God," Manny whispered. He stood up and called, "Freeze that frame and make up some prints." Turning, he hurried from the screening room.

The task force handling the AE/PINNACLE affair convened in the small office down the hall from the DD/O's shop at 5:55 P.M. Present and presiding was Bill Colby. Seated around the table were the other regulars: Ebby Ebbitt, Jack McAuliffe, Jim Angleton, and Manny Ebbitt.

Colby had been under a great deal of pressure in recent months, and looked it. At the moment he was desperately trying to shield the Company from the fallout that would inevitably accompany a Presidential impeachment or resignation. And then there was the lingering bitterness over "the family jewels." In 1973, the CIA had come under fire when it turned out that most of the people involved in the Watergate break-in had CIA ties. When Congress began breathing down the CIA's neck, Colby, then DD/O, had drafted an order instructing CIA employees to report any Company activities that might be "outside the legislative charter of this agency." The result was a 693-page single-spaced brief, which Colby had eventually turned over to Congress. He was convinced that letting out what he called the "bad" secrets would protect the "good" ones—the identity of agents and details of ongoing operations. Angleton, the most outspoken of the Director's many critics inside Langley, told anyone who would listen that Colby couldn't have done more harm to the Company if he'd been a paid Soviet agent. "What we have going for us is the generally accepted notion that we are the good guys," Angleton would say. "Wound this notion and you cripple the Company."

Now, peering wearily through his eyeglasses, Colby studied the grainy photograph that the security people had printed up. "You're positive this is AE/PINNACLE?" he demanded grumpily; the last thing he needed right now was to lose the rare defector-in-place who was spying for the Company from inside the Soviet embassy compound.

"It's Kukushkin, all right," Manny assured him.

"There wasn't a Russian in sight at the airport," Jack noted. "So there is no reason to think he was being coerced into getting on the plane."

Ebby said, "I looked at the footage myself. At any point he could have buttonholed a policeman and demanded political asylum. The fact that he didn't speaks for itself—he was going of his own free will and volition."

Angleton's listless eyes suddenly focused on the DD/O; he knew that, deep down, Elliott Ebbitt and his people were hoping AE/PINNACLE was a phony defector, which would mean Kukushkin's serials were disinformation and Leo Kritzky was innocent. "Do we know what happened to AE/PINNACLE in Stockholm, Elliott?" Angleton inquired.

Ebby pulled a deciphered cable from a file folder. It had originated with the Company's Chief of Station in Stockholm and was stamped "Top Secret" and "Eyes Only." "A Russian matching AE/PINNACLE's description was in transit at Stockholm airport. He purchased two bottles of aquavit before he boarded the early evening Aeroflot flight to Moscow."

"Doesn't sound like someone who's worried about being arrested when he arrives," Colby commented.

"We have some indication that his wife, Elena Antonova, and his seven-and-a-half-year-old daughter, Ludmilla, may have been on the regular Friday afternoon New York-Moscow Aeroflot flight," Jack said. "Two women named Zubina, apparently mother and daughter, were listed on the manifest— Zubina is Elena Antonova's maiden name. Manny is the only one who could really recognize her but he hasn't had a chance to look at the Kennedy Airport surveillance clips. The flight stopped for refueling in Stockholm and the passengers were taken into the airport lounge for coffee and cakes. One of the waitresses there remembers seeing a short, heavy Russian woman with close-cropped hair and a thin girl, aged seven or eight. We've wired mug shots to Stockholm of Elena Antonova and Ludmilla, taken from the State Department forms filed by all foreign diplomats posted to Washington— we're waiting on confirmation now."

"Assuming, for a moment, that Elena Antonova and Ludmilla were on the Friday Aeroflot flight to Moscow," Ebby said, "do we have any idea what prompted them to return?"

Jack and Manny shook their heads. Angleton sucked on a cigarette, then corkscrewed it out of his mouth and said, "My people came across an item in the Soviet military newspaper *Krasnaia Zvezda* which could shed some light on this." Everyone stared at Angleton and he basked in the attention. "The Russian Central Asian high command announced the appointment of a Colonel General Maslov as commander of Soviet missile bases in Kazakhstan," he said. "You'll remember that Kukushkin's father-in-law, a Colonel General Zubin, held this post. The brief communiqué said that Maslov's predecessor had been granted sick leave. The tour of duty for area commanders of missile bases is normally five years; Colonel General Zubin's tour had twenty-two months more to run. Reading between the lines, he would have had to be pretty ill to cut short the tour and bring in a replacement."

Colby said, "So Kukushkin's wife and daughter could have been summoned back to Moscow to be at his bedside."

"The pieces fit, which means we're nibbling at the edge of something that's true," Angleton said. "If Kukushkin's wife and daughter were summoned home on the spur of the moment, he wouldn't have had time to arrange for the three of them to defect."

"And he couldn't have stopped them from going back without arousing suspicion," Manny put in.

"Why would Kukushkin himself have gone back, and on such short notice?" Colby asked.

"He sure went back in a hurry," Jack said. "He didn't wait for the regular weekly Aeroflot direct flight but took the SAS flight to Stockholm and caught a connecting flight to Moscow."

"Maybe the father-in-law bought the farm," Manny said. "Maybe Kukushkin went back for Zubin's funeral."

Angleton said, "I'll have my people who monitor Soviet newspapers keep their eyes peeled for an obit."

The phone on a side table buzzed. Ebby snatched it up, listened for a moment, said "Thanks" and hung up. "You don't have to look through the New York surveillance reels," Ebby told his son. "The waitress in the Stockholm lounge positively identified Kukushkin's wife and daughter from photographs."

"All of which could mean AE/PINNACLE is alive and well in Moscow," Colby said. "That would be a relief."

Manny, whose loyalty to Leo Kritzky was matched by his feelings of responsibility for the defector Kukushkin, didn't look relieved. "I won't breathe easy until AE/PINNACLE's back in Washington and I can personally debrief him."

Angleton shut his eyes, as if his patience were being put to the supreme test. "What makes you think he'll return to Washington?"

"I just assumed—"

"We've noticed that the Russians tend not to fly diplomats and their families across the Atlantic if they have less than six months to serve on station," Angleton remarked. "It's surely connected to budgetary considerations; when it comes to money the KGB has the same problems we have. Kukushkin's tour was due to end in December, which is in five months. And don't forget that they wanted to recruit him for the KGB's new Disinformation Directorate. With his father-in-law sidelined and his tour in Washington running down, he may not be able to weasel out of the posting this time around."

Jack turned to Manny. "You set up emergency procedures for contacting him in Moscow?"

Manny nodded. "We agreed on a primary and a secondary meeting place for the second and fourth Tuesday of every month."

Colby said, "That gives us fourteen days."

Jack said, "We won't really know what the situation is until someone's talked to Kukushkin."

"I suppose we ought to alert one of our people in Moscow," Colby said.

Angleton came awake again. "At AE/PINNACLE's last debriefing, he warned us that the KGB had started coating the shoes of American diplomats with a scent that trained dogs can follow. Which means that our people are tracked when they service dead drops. We'd be running the risk of blowing Kukushkin if we sent one of our embassy-based officers to the rendezvous."

Jack agreed. "Whoever contacts Kukushkin ought to come in from the outside. It should be a one-shot deal. He should come in and meet him and go out again."

Manny and his father exchanged looks. Ebby smiled and nodded; his son had matured into a seasoned CIA officer during the three months that he had been handling the Kukushkin defection. Watching Manny across the table, Ebby was extremely proud of him. And he knew what Manny was going to suggest before he opened his mouth.

"It has to be me," Manny declared, and he quoted something Director Colby had said at the task force's first meeting: "A friendly face is worth its weight in gold."

"I don't like it," Jack said. "The man who goes in to contact him could wind up in one of the KGB's Lubyanka dungeons."

Manny said eagerly, "My going to meet Kukushkin makes sense. Either he'll agree to work for us in Moscow or, alternatively, he may let us bring him out—either way we'll be ahead of the game."

Fidgeting uneasily, Colby glanced at Ebby. "He'd be taking one hell of a risk."

Ebby said, "He's a consenting adult, Director, and a damn good Soviet Division officer who happens to be fluent in Russian."

"Two weeks wouldn't give us time to work up diplomatic cover and immunity," Colby noted. "He'd have to go in naked."

Ebby said, "If we opt for sending a man in from the outside, there's a lot to be said for using someone Kukushkin knows personally, and trusts."

Colby gathered up his notes. "I'll sleep on it," he announced.

"Back up one sentence," Nellie said, her eyes squinting into the duststorm she was about to kick up. "You're going somewhere, right?"

"It's just for a week—"

"You're going somewhere for a week, but you can't take me with you and you won't tell me where you're going?"

Manny shifted his weight from one foot to the other.

"You won't tell me where you're going because it's a secret?"

"That's right."

"How do I know you're not running off with another female of the species?"

"Damn it, Nellie. You're the only woman in my life."

"Is it dangerous? At least tell me that much."

Manny took her hand. "Look, Nellie, if you're going to marry into the Company there are certain thing you need to—"

"Who said anything about *marrying* into the Company?"

"Well, I sort of assumed, what with us more or less living together, what with incest being best, that marriage would be on the agenda."

"Marriage? To each other?"

"That's how it's usually done. I marry you and you marry me."

"You're ready to give up your apartment?"

Manny considered the question, raised his eyebrows and nodded.

Cocking her very pretty head, Nellie said, "Manny, are you proposing to me?"

Manny seemed as surprised as Nellie by the turn the conversation had taken. "I suppose you could make a case that I am."

Nellie brought the flat of a hand up to her solar plexus and collapsed onto the couch. "Well, that sort of changes things," she murmured.

Manny sat down next to her. "I sure hope marriage doesn't change things," he said.

"I'm talking about your trip. I've got this theory, Manny. You need to be possessive of the things you don't possess. But once you possess them you can afford not to be possessive any more."

"I'm not positive I follow you."

Nellie leaned over and kissed Manny hard on the lips. "I accept," she announced in a throaty whisper. "I've wanted to fuck you as far back as I can remember. From puberty onward I wanted to marry you. I never changed my mind, not even when you used to beat me up."

"I never beat you up—"

"What about the time you came back from graduate school and shoved me into a snowdrift?"

"You were throwing snowballs at me—"

"So when's the wedding?"

"I'm leaving Friday afternoon. What's that?"

"The ninth."

"Friday, nine August. Which means I'll be back on Friday the sixteenth. We could find a justice of the peace and do the dirty deed that weekend."

Nellie, suddenly short of breath, said, "You really know how to sweep a girl off her feet." She thought a moment. "So if we're getting married a week from this weekend, that makes us engaged, right?"

"I guess it does."

"If we're actually engaged, nothing would be more natural than for you to tell your bride-to-be where you're going on this trip of yours." When she saw the expression on his face, she started laughing. "Don't tell me, let me guess: Company wives..."

"...don't ask..."

"...dumb questions."

Leo Kritzky experienced a surge of exaltation: *He was not alone in his padded cell!*

His companion was the moth that had slipped in from the bleak corridor when Jim Angleton, turning back on the threshold as he was about to leave, thought of a last question. "You have no recollection of liquor being delivered to your door from Kahn's Wine and Beverage on M Street?"

"You keep coming back to Kahn's Wine and Beverage—" Leo saw the flutter of tiny wings as the moth, possibly attracted to the bulbs suspended from the ceiling, flew past Angleton's knee. For a harrowing moment he was sure Angleton would notice; noticing, he would summon the guards to hunt down the moth and squash it against the padded wall before Leo could savor the pleasure of its company. Determined not to follow the moth with his eyes lest he betray its presence, he concentrated on Angleton. "Adelle was the one who did all the ordering-in—pizza, groceries, liquor, whatever. I didn't even know where she got the liquor and I never asked. I had too many other things to worry about. And I don't remember making out any checks to Kahn's Wine and Beverage."

"You were careful to make sure the orders and the checks were in your wife's maiden name so that nobody would stumble across the link between you and Kahn's delivery boy, who turned out to be a cutout for the KGB."

With his peripheral vision, Leo saw the moth alight on the padding of the wall above the toilet bowl. He couldn't wait for Angleton to leave so he could formally welcome his visitor. "It's another assumption of yours that fits in with what you want to believe," Leo said impatiently. "The only problem is that your assumptions don't add up. Your case is circumstantial and you know it."

"My circumstantial case, as you put it, rests on incontrovertible evidence from an irrefutable witness. There's only one way out of all this for you— admit you're SASHA, then cooperate with us in undoing the damage you've done to the Company." Angleton patted his jacket pocket in search of cigarettes as he turned his back on Leo and left the room. A guard bolted the door behind him.

For several minutes Leo continued sitting on the folded blanket with his back against a wall. He suspected that Angleton would be watching him through the pinhole in the door and he didn't want to put the moth in jeopardy. After a long while he decided the coast was clear and let his eyes drift up to the moth, clinging with spread-eagled wings to the padding of the wall behind the toilet. It was by far the most beautiful creature Leo had ever set eyes on in his life. There was a elegant symmetry to the intricate purple and brown pattern on the back of the wings; a graceful sensuality to the elongated hairy undercarriage and the feathery antennas that probed, like a blind man tapping a cane, the microcosm immediately in front of its head. Leo remembered having a high school chum who collected moths. The prize in his collection, grotesquely (so it had seemed to Leo) pinned to cork under glass, had been a rare species of moth called the Sphinx of Siberia. Leo decided that his moth was every bit as exotic and could qualify as a Sphinx, too. His spirits soared—he took it as an omen, a sign that someone beyond this secret prison and outside of Angleton's immediate circle knew of his predicament and would soon slip into the cell to succor him. He raised a hand in salute to convey to his comrade that they shared not only the same cell, but the same fate.

In the hours and days that followed Leo would make his way to one side of the room or another to visit his fellow prisoner clinging with endless patience to the padded wall. He took to murmuring words of encouragement to it and listened to the message of its body language: with patience, with fortitude, it seemed to be saying, they would both escape from this confinement that could no longer be described as solitary. And as if to drive home the point, from time to time the Sphinx would quit its perch and circle one of the light bulbs for minutes on end, delighting his cellmate by casting large flickering shadows onto the walls.

Angleton noticed the change in his prisoner immediately. Kritzky managed a conspiratorial smile now and then, almost as if he were concealing a delicious secret, and appeared eager to engage Angleton in verbal sparring. He even tittered out loud when the counterintelligence chief raised the possibility that Leo would die of old age in this cell if he didn't cooperate. Suspecting that one of the jailers might have befriended the prisoner, Angleton had all of the guards changed. Still, Leo's morale seemed to grow stronger by the day. "Sure, operations I had a hand in went bad," he admitted to Angleton during one morning session. "For heaven's sake, Jim, operations *you* had a hand in went bad, too, but nobody's accusing you of being a Soviet mole." Leo cast a glance in the direction of the Sphinx of Siberia and then suddenly started to laugh. Soon he was laughing so hard tears trickled from his eyes. "Maybe someone—" Laughter racked his body, laughter hurt his gut. "Maybe someone should, Jim. I mean, what a joke it would be if James Jesus Angleton...turned out to be SASHA. Maybe you're going through the motions...oh, God, it's hilarious...going through the motions of hunting for SASHA...to divert attention from yourself." Doubled over, Leo clutched his stomach and gasped for air between spasms of laughter. "Don't you see the humor of it, Jim? The joke would be on the Company, wouldn't it? Oh, Christ, the joke would be on me."

7

THE REGULAR FRIDAY AEROFLOT FLIGHT TO MOSCOW WAS RUNNING three quarters of an hour late. The plane had been delayed at the gate to repair a leak in a hydraulic system, then held up on the runway by the heavy traffic in and out of JFK. The fifty or so passengers aboard—two dozen wore blue-and-white lapel pins identifying them as clients on Trailblazer Travel's one-week tour of Moscow—were sound asleep, stretched across the vacant seats of the half-empty Tupolev 144. Manny, who had been leafing through Fodor's guide to Russia when he wasn't catnapping, wandered back down the aisle to where the stewards had set up a sandwich bar and helped himself to a ham on black bread and a plastic cup filled with kvass. He opened the sandwich and spread some mustard on the bread.

"What's going to happen now that Nixon has resigned?" the male steward inquired from the pantry. "Will there be a coup d'état?"

Manny had to laugh. "I doubt it," he said. "Gerald Ford's already been sworn into the White House. In America, the transition is spelled out in the constitution." He bit into the sandwich, then talked with his mouth full. "What would happen in Russia if Brezhnev resigned tomorrow?"

"Why would Comrade Brezhnev want to resign?"

"Say he did something illegal like Nixon—say he had his people break into the opposition's headquarters. Say the burglars were caught and Mr. Brezhnev ordered the police not to investigate the case. Say he tried to bribe the burglars into keeping quiet when that didn't work."

Now it was the steward's turn to laugh. "What you are describing couldn't happen in a proletarian democracy," he said earnestly. He tossed his fine blond hair away from his eyes with a snap of his head. "Our Communist Party represents all points of view in the Socialist spectrum, which means there is no political opposition and no headquarters to break into. I can see you are not familiar with the Soviet Union—is this your first visit?"

Manny was vaguely aware that the steward had initiated the conversation and steered it around to this question. "Yeah, as a matter of fact, it is."

"Where are you from?"

"New York. Manhattan, actually. Upper West Side, if you really want to pin me down."

The Company, in fact, had provided Manny with a cover identity and backstopped it so he could pass any but the most exhaustive vetting. Armed with a driver's license, an Upper West Side neighborhood grocery fidelity card, a Yale alumni card, a voter registration card, American Express Travelers Cheques and a very worn three-year-old passport filled with entry and exit stamps to England and Spain and Mexico, he was traveling under the name of Immanuel Bridges. If someone took the trouble to check, he would find an Immanuel Bridges listed in the Manhattan telephone directory on Broadway and Eighty-Second Street. (Anyone who dialed the number would reach an answering machine with Manny's recorded voice saying, "Hi, I can't come to the phone. Now you say something.") Manny, who had once taken a course in business administration, would be passing himself off as a merger consultant; he had been assigned an office in a firm on 44 Wall Street, as well as a parking space two blocks away. (A secretary at the firm would answer all calls coming in on Manny's line with, "I'm sorry, Mr. Bridges is away on vacation. Would you care to leave a message?") A check with the admissions office at Yale would reveal that someone named Bridges, Immanuel, had graduated in 1968 with a degree in business administration. Even the gym card in Manny's wallet had been backstopped; someone phoning up the gym on upper Broadway would hear a gruff voice muttering, "Hang on—I'll see if he's here." A moment later the voice would come back on the line. "No, he ain't here—a guy who works out with Mr. Bridges says he's out of town for the week."

It was twenty-five minutes after high noon, local time, when the Tupolov finally began its descent through dense clouds toward Sheremetyevo Airport northwest of Moscow. As they came out under the clouds, Manny spotted a blue-gray tear in the overcast sky off to the right through which sunlight streamed, illuminating what seemed to be a carpet of white birches. It was his first glimpse of Mother Russia. Moments later a tongue of tarmac materialized below the fuselage and the Tupolov dropped down onto it. Many of the passengers, relieved to be alive, applauded.

Inside the terminal, Manny joined the mob queuing at the passport control lines. Waiting his turn, he thought again of the remarkable conversation he'd had with Ebby the previous afternoon. Ebby had insisted on driving him to the airport. It was Manny who raised a subject that they had nibbled at dozens of times over the years.

The subject was fear.

Whenever Manny had worked up the nerve to ask his father about Budapest '56, Ebby had somehow managed to reply without telling his son anything he didn't already know. Driving Manny to JFK, Ebby had started to reply to his son's perennial question with the usual half answers. Manny, exasperated, had interrupted him. "Dad, we're coming down to the wire here. The Company has supplied me with a cover ID but it hasn't outfitted me mentally. What I want to know—what you need to tell me—is: Were you afraid in Budapest?"

And for the first time Ebby had addressed the subject directly. "Yeah, I was afraid, Manny. I was frightened going into Budapest. I was terrified when they snatched me off the street and started to question me in one of their torture chambers. I was paralyzed with fear when I realized they knew my name and rank and details of my service record."

"How did you deal with the fear?"

"What I'm going to say may sound strange to you—I had an epiphany. It hit me like a bolt of lightening. I wasn't afraid of the pain, I wasn't afraid of the dying. For reasons that had to do with my father and the way he'd died, I was afraid of being afraid, which is another way of saying I was afraid of not living up to my father. And this insight liberated me. It was as if I'd suddenly been sucked into the eye of a hurricane. Everything slowed down—my racing pulse, the thoughts tearing through my skull, the rotation of the earth on its axis. Everything."

As the car was emerging from the Midtown Tunnel, sunlight had turned the window opaque for an instant. Ebby had leaned forward and squinted anxiously and, when he could see again, had followed the signs to the Long Island Expressway. After a while Manny had said, very quietly, "I have a father, too."

Ebby had looked quickly at his son. "You have nothing to prove to me, Manny. You're everything a man could want in a son. When the Judgment Day comes you are the evidence, defense exhibit number one."

"Maybe I have things to prove to myself."

Ebby had considered this for a moment. "When I joined the Company we had an instructor by the name of Andrews. He was OSS and had been to hell and back in the war. He drummed into us that the only sure way to avoid being broken—he called it the eleventh commandment of intelligence work—was to never get caught."

"You broke the eleventh commandment," Manny had remarked.

"I did, didn't I? Concentrate on your tradecraft and make goddamn sure you don't."

Manny had smiled. Ebby had grinned back but his son could see the worry lines distorting the forced smile. And it struck him how courageous his father had been to let him volunteer for this mission. "Thanks, Dad," he said.

Ebby understood that they were communicating between the lines. "Sure. You're welcome."

In the crowded airport hall at Sheremetyevo one of the Trailblazer tourists was prodding Manny. "You're next," he whispered. Snapping out of his reverie, Manny walked up to the booth and slid his passport under the glass partition. A woman with badly bleached hair piled on her head and a completely expressionless face, wearing the gray uniform and shoulder boards of the KGB's elite frontier guards, rifled through it page by page before turning back to the photograph and looking up straight into his eyes to see if he matched the picture. Her gaze flicked over Manny's right shoulder to the mirror planted above and behind him at a forty-five degree angle to give her a view of his feet; in the mirror she could see if he were trying to make himself shorter or taller. She checked his height in the passport and then looked again at him through the partition. Manny knew that there were calibrations etched into her side of the glass so she could tell his exact height at a glance. She flipped through an enormous loose-leaf binder to make sure his name wasn't in it, then stamped the passport and the currency form he'd filled out in the plane and, looking to her right, nodded for the next person.

Manny scarcely let himself breathe—he had passed the very stringent Soviet border control and was inside the belly of the whale. A pulse throbbed in his temple; the rotation of the earth on its axis seemed to have speeded up.

For the rest of Saturday and the two days that followed, Manny found himself being whisked by the Trailblazer chaperons from one tourist site to another. Accompanied by Intourist guides who regurgitated the official Soviet version of history, they visited the Kremlin churches, the onion-domed St. Basil's Cathedral on Red Square and the Lenin Museum on one side of the square, then were taken to the head of the long queue to file past the wax-like corpse of Lenin in the nearby mausoleum. Across from the mausoleum, the side of GUM, a vast show-case department store that they were scheduled to visit Tuesday morning, was draped with giant portraits of the

Soviet leaders: there was Vladimir Ilyich Lenin with a vaguely Kazakh slant to his eyes, Karl Marx hiding behind his unkempt Walt Whitman-like beard, Leonid Brezhnev beaming down like a benevolent alcoholic. The American tourists spent one entire morning at the VDNKh, the Exhibit of the Economic Achievements of the Nationalities (the highlights: Yuri Gagarin's rocket monument and the colossal 'Worker and Kolokhoznik' statue), and an afternoon at a church in Zagorsk that reeked of incense and candle wax. That evening they were taken to the Bolshoi Theater, a stone's throw from the Metropole, to attend a dazzling performançe of *Giselle*. At mealtimes the tourists were bused back to the Hotel Metropole and seated under the stained-glass dome at tables with small American flags on them; the first course (served by waiters who tried to peddle black market caviar on the side) was invariably half a hard-boiled egg covered with wrinkled peas and mayonnaise that had petrified because the food had been prepared hours in advance.

Manny mingled with the others in his group (there were half a dozen bachelor women who regarded the only single man on the tour with open curiosity), fending off their questions with vague replies, and kept his eye peeled for signs that the KGB were paying special attention to him. He knew that all the Russians who had anything to do with foreign tourists—the bus drivers, the Intourist guides, the clerks at the main desk, the *babushkas* stationed on each floor of the hotel who kept the keys to the chambers—reported to the KGB. Before leaving his room Monday morning, Manny was careful to commit to memory the precise position of every item of clothing in his valise and plant a human hair on the cuff of a folded shirt. When he returned that afternoon he checked the valise; as far as he could see, the position of the clothing hadn't changed and the hair was still in place on the cuff.

Tuesday morning a soft rain started falling, turning the streets slick. After breakfast the Trailblazer group followed an Intourist guide with an umbrella held aloft through Red Square and into GUM to visit the department store, two floors of boutiques teeming with Muscovites as well as Russians who came in from the countryside to buy things that weren't available locally. "You absolutely must stay together," the guide called nervously as she shooed the Americans past the black-market moneychangers lurking in doorways.

Manny lagged behind to talk to one of them. "How much?" he asked a bearded man with a loud striped shirt hanging outside his jeans.

"I give you six times the official rate, three rubles to the dollar," the man shot back, barely moving his lips as he spoke. He kept his eyes on the street, looking for policemen or plainclothes detectives who would have to be paid off if he were caught in the act.

"There's a waiter at the hotel who is offering four-to-one."

"Take it," the man advised with a sneer. "You want to sell anything—shoes, blue jeans, wash-and-wear shirts, a wristwatch, a camera? I give you a great price."

"How much for these shoes?"

The man glanced at Manny's feet. "Fifty rubles."

"How much for a pair of jeans?"

"Are they in good condition?"

"Like new."

"Seventy-five rubles. You won't get a better deal nowhere else. You can always find me around GUM before noon. Ask anyone where is Pavlusha."

Manny figured the group would be far enough ahead of him by now. "I'll think about it, Pavlusha," he said, and he pushed through the heavy inner door into the store. The last Americans were disappearing down one of the passageways. He trailed lazily after them, stopping from time to time to inspect shop windows filled with Czech crystal or East German appliances; to use the windows as mirrors to see what was going on behind him. Gradually he fell further and further behind the Trailblazer group. At one intersection he looked around as if he were lost, then, moving rapidly, ducked down a side passageway and cut through a fabric store that straddled the area between two passageways and had doors on both; he went in one door and out the other and waited to see if anyone came trotting out after him. Convinced that he was clean, he made his way down another passage and pushed through a door into a side street behind GUM. He looked at his watch—he still had an hour and a quarter before the primary rendezvous, in the Pushkin Museum at noon on the second Tuesday of the month. Mingling with groups of East German tourists, he strolled through Red Square and around the side of the Kremlin Wall. The East Germans stopped to watch the changing of the guard at the Tomb of the Unknown Soldier. Hugging the Kremlin Wall, Manny continued on south. When he reached the Borovistkaya Tower at the southern end of the wall, he darted through traffic across the wide boulevard and ducked into the Borovistkaya metro station next to the Lenin Library. He bought two tickets at a machine for ten kopecks—if AE/PINNACLE didn't turn up at the Pushkin Museum, Manny would take the metro to the secondary rendezvous. He went north one stop, then hurried through a maze of tunnels until he came to the Red Line and took the subway south. He got off at the first stop, Kropotkinskaya, emerging into a drizzle not far from the Pushkin Museum. He still had three quarters of an hour to kill. Concentrate on your tradecraft,

Ebby had said; that's what he did now. He spent the time meandering through a labyrinth of nearly empty back streets behind the Pushkin to see if any individuals or automobiles seemed to be following him. With a quarter of an hour remaining he made his way into the museum, bought a ticket and began wandering through the spacious rooms, stopping now and then to admire a Picasso or a Cézanne. At the stroke of noon he entered the room filled with Bonnards and began to scrutinize the paintings one by one. If Kukushkin turned up at the appointed hour, it would be here in the Bonnard room.

Noon came and went, and then twelve thirty. Various scenarios occurred to Manny—Kukushkin had been caught, the time and place of the rendezvous had been forced out of him under torture—as he checked out the adjoining rooms, then returned to the Bonnards. There was still no sign of AE/PINNACLE. At a quarter to one he decided that the rendezvous had been aborted. He retraced his steps to the Kropotkinskaya station and, using the second ticket, headed south again on the Red Line. He got off at Sportivnaya and roamed through the nearly deserted streets in the general direction of the Novodievitchi Monastery. When he finally reached it, he followed the wall around to the left until he came to the cemetery. At the window he purchased a ticket for ten kopecks. Walking through the main gate, he began strolling along the gravel lanes, stopping now and then to read the inscriptions on the tombs. He noticed two young couples off to his right standing around the tombstone of Stalin's wife, Nadezhda Alliluyeva, who had shot herself after a stormy argument with her husband; apologists for Stalin claimed that his grief over Nadezhda's suicide, in 1932, was what led to the great purges of the thirties and the Gulag prison camps. Passing the tombs of Bulgakov, Stanislavsky, Chekhov and Gogol, Manny returned to the main walkway and headed away from the main gate toward the tomb of Nikita Khrushchev at the far end of the path. Between the tombstones he could make out three men deep in conversation on a parallel path, and two younger men copying the inscriptions off some old tombs with tracing paper and sticks of charcoal. None of them seemed to be paying the slightest attention to him. Reaching Khrushchev's tomb, Manny gazed at the bust of the late Soviet leader. Etched into the stone were the dates of his birth and death: 1894–1971; his round Ukrainian peasant face stared into the distance and there was a suggestion of bitterness in the faint smile crinkling his eyes.

"He was the one who first denounced the excesses of Joseph Stalin," a voice said. Startled, Manny turned quickly. Sergei Kukushkin appeared from behind a black marble tombstone. He was bareheaded and dressed in a light raincoat; his hair was disheveled and glistening with rain. "Do you know the story, Manny? It was at the Twentieth Party Congress in 1956. Khrushchev stunned everyone by denouncing the crimes of Stalin. According to the story, which is obviously apocryphal, someone passed a note up to the podium which said, 'Where were you when all this happened?' Khrushchev, so the story goes—ah, even in apocrypha there is what you Americans call gospel truth—Khrushchev turned livid when he read the note. Waving the scrap of paper over his head, he shouted, 'Who wrote this? Who wrote this?' When nobody stood up to acknowledge authorship, he said, 'That's where I was, comrades.'" Kukushkin took Manny's elbow and the two of them began to walk along a narrow path between tombstones. "That's where I was, too, my friend. From the time I joined the KGB I saw what was going on but I was afraid to raise my voice. Nothing has changed since Tolstoy described life in Russia: 'Stench, stone, opulence, poverty, debauchery.'" Kukushkin, looking more drawn than Manny remembered him, said, "I knew you would be the one to come, Manny. Thank you for that."

"What happened in Washington, Sergei?"

"I returned to our quarters to find my wife and my daughter packing their valises. Her father had suffered a stroke and was under intensive care in a Kremlin hospital. An embassy car was waiting to rush them to New York to catch the Friday evening Aeroflot flight. Impossible to delay the trip without arousing the suspicions of the SK people. The next morning I received a cable from the First Chief Directorate saying that Elena's father had died before she arrived and giving me permission to return to Moscow immediately for the funeral. Once again I could not appear to hesitate for fear the SK would become suspicious of me. My *rezident* was very considerate—he personally authorized the expenditure of hard currency for the Scandinavian Airline ticket—so I did not believe that they had become suspicious of my activities. I was afraid to call the emergency number you gave me from the embassy. The *rezident* himself accompanied me to the airport. Once I had checked through the gate I was afraid to use a public telephone—they could have had someone inside watching me." Kukushkin shrugged. "And so I returned."

"Since you're back have you observed anything out of the ordinary?"

Kukushkin shook his large head vigorously, as if he were trying to shake off any last doubts he might have had. "We were given a three-room apartment in a hotel reserved for transient KGB officers. The funeral was held two days after my return—many high-ranking officers from the missile forces attended. They paid their respects to my wife and several, knowing I was in the KGB, made a point of asking my opinion of the attempt to impeach your President Nixon. At the office I was invited to take tea with the head of the

First Chief Directorate, who spoke of seconding me to that new Division D. In short, everything seemed normal and my initial fears subsided."

On a parallel pathway the two young men tracing inscriptions unrolled sheets of paper and attacked another tombstone.

"You had fears initially?"

"I am human, Manny. Like everyone I see ghosts lurking in shadows. But I calculated that, if the story of my father-in-law's stroke had been invented to lure me home to Moscow, the SK would have sent me back with my wife and daughter, and not afterward."

"Not necessarily."

Kukushkin's English syntax broke down under the strain. "Which isn't not necessarily?" he demanded angrily. "Where can you be knowing better than me what is not necessarily?"

"Sergei, let's try to look at the situation coldly," Manny suggested.

"I am coldly looking," Kukushkin, clearly agitated, muttered.

"If the SK suspected you, they would have had to devise a scheme to get you back to Moscow without your knowing they suspected you. If they had sent you back with your wife and daughter, the three of you could have asked for political asylum at the airport. The fact that they sent you back separately—"

"You interpret that as a bad omen?"

"I don't think you can interpret it either way. I'm just trying to explore different possibilities, Sergei."

Kukushkin considered this. "I hate Russia," he announced with sudden vehemence. "Everybody I meet is nostalgic for something—for revolution, for war, for snow, for empire, for Stalin even. Would you believe it, Manny? People at the Lubyanka canteen still talk in undertones about the good old days. Roosevelt wore braces on his legs, they say, but he would push himself to his feet when Stalin walked into the room." He stopped in his tracks and turned on Manny. "I will not spy for you in Moscow, if that is what you have come to ask me to do. I barely had the nerve to do it in Washington. Here it is out of the question."

"I didn't come all this way to ask you to work for us here. I came because we owe you something. We can smuggle you out. Exfiltrations have been organized before."

"From Russia?"

"From the Crimea, where you can easily go on your first vacation."

"And my wife and my daughter?"

"We can arrange for them to come out also."

"And my wife's sister and her son, and their old mother, now a widow?"

The two resumed walking. "We could charter a plane," Manny quipped dryly.

Neither man laughed.

Manny said, "Think about it carefully, Sergei. It may be years before you are posted abroad again."

"The competition to go abroad is heavy. I may never again get such a posting."

"I'll give you a phone number to memorize. K 4-89-73. Repeat it."

"K 4-89-73."

"When someone answers, cough twice and hang up. That will activate the primary and secondary rendezvous on the second and fourth Tuesdays of the month. The person who meets you will carry a copy of *Novi Mir* under an arm and tell you simply that he is a friend of Manny's."

Kukushkin repeated the number twice more. Then he asked what Manny would do now.

"I came in only to speak to you. I'll head home as soon as I can."

The two circled back onto the main walkway leading to the cemetery gate. Kukushkin started to thank Manny again for coming to Moscow. "I will tell Elena that you raised the possibility of an exfil—" The Russian broke off in mid word and caught his breath. Manny followed his gaze. A hoard of men, some in uniform and carrying machine pistols, others in dark civilian suits, had appeared at the cemetery gate. Fragments of thoughts tore through Manny's skull: they couldn't have been following me, it just wasn't possible, which meant that they had followed Kukushkin...if they had followed Kukushkin it meant that they suspected him of working for the CIA...had summoned home his wife and daughter, and then Kukushkin, because of these suspicions...which would, dear God, be confirmed if they caught him with an American.

At the gate the men in uniform trotted off in either direction along side paths, the civilians started up the central walkway toward them. "Quick," Kukushkin whispered, "I know where is an opening in the fence." Manny spun around and followed him as Kukushkin dodged between the tombstones of Scriabin and Prokofiev. Behind them a voice over a bullhorn bellowed in broken English, "Stopping where are you. The cemetery is closed by militia on all sides. You are in the impossibility of escaping." The pulse hammering in Manny's temple almost drowned out the howl of the bullhorn. Glancing to his left, he saw the two young men who had been copying inscriptions off tombstones running toward them and he could make out dark metallic objects in their hands. The two couples who had been studying the tomb of Stalin's wife, along with the three men who had been deep in conversation, were racing along parallel paths to cut them off from the fence. Somewhere in the cemetery firecrackers exploded. Only when stone chips splintered off a tomb and scratched his arm did it dawn on Manny that shots had been fired. Ahead, he caught a glimpse of the shoulder-high cemetery fence laced with ivy. Kukushkin, moving with surprising nimbleness for his size, darted toward a segment where one of the uprights had rusted away, leaving a space through which a man could slip. He was about to wedge his body through it when a line of soldiers, machine pistols leveled at their hips, appeared from behind the bushes in the lot on the other side. Kukushkin's mouth jerked open as if he intended to scream. He turned back toward Manny and said in a wooden voice, "So: it is going to end as I suspected it must—with my execution."

Feet pounded up the gravel path behind them.

"Oh, God, I'm sorry, Sergei."

"Me, also, I am being sorry, Manny."

There was a glint of smugness in the inquisitor's unblinking eyes, a know-it-all smirk on his colorless lips. "We have been led to believe," he said in flaw-less English, "that a CIA officer taken into custody is authorized to answer three questions—his name, his pay grade and his parking space number at Langley." A thin, middle-aged functionary with a shaven head, steel-rimmed spectacles and bad teeth, he came around to Manny's side of the large table and stared down at him. "Your name, or at least the one you gave to the trai-tor Kukushkin, I know. I can take an educated guess as to your pay grade—given your age, given that you were designated to be the controlling officer of the traitor Kukushkin, you are probably GS-15, which is the highest grade for a middle-level CIA officer and roughly equivalent to a colonel in the army. But tell me, if you please, what is your parking space number?"

Curiously, the fact of his arrest had given Manny a measure of liberation. The worst had happened—it was to be regretted but no longer dreaded. Now he understood what his father had meant when he said that he felt as if he had been sucked into the eye of the hurricane; Manny, too, discovered that the pulse pounding in his temple, the thoughts tearing through his skull, the rotation of the earth on its axis, had all slowed down. Looking up at the inquisitor, he managed a tight smile. "I want to speak to someone from the American embassy," he announced.

One of the several telephones on the table rang shrilly. Returning to his seat, the Russian plucked the phone off of its hook. He listened for a moment, murmured "*Bolshoe spasibo*," and hung up. He leaned back in the wooden swivel chair, his hands folded behind his head. Light from the overhead fixture glinted off his spectacles like a Morse signal; Manny supposed that if he could decode the message it wouldn't be good news. "I will tell you something you already know," the inquisitor said. "The telephone number K 4-89-73 rings in the American embassy guard room manned twenty-four hours a day, seven days a week by US Marines."

Manny understood that the interrogation had taken an ominous turn. His inquisitor could only have gotten the phone number from Kukushkin, which suggested that Sergei had been forced to talk. "The United States and the Soviet Union are obliged by international treaty to allow embassy officials access to citizens who are detained—" Manny started to say.

"You are not detained, my friend." The man's tone had turned patronizing. "You are arrested for espionage. You will be prosecuted and convicted of espionage. The Procurator will demand the supreme penalty. Whether the judge sentences you to execution by hanging will depend on the degree to which you cooperate with our investigative organs."

"If you're trying to frighten me you've certainly succeeded," Manny admitted. He was absolutely determined to play innocent, not only for his own sake but for Kukushkin's. "Listen, I am who I say I am. If you took the trouble to check up on Immanuel Bridges, you would see that."

The inquisitor seemed to enjoy the game. "Tell me again what you were doing in the cemetery of the Novodievitchi Monastery?"

"I lost sight of my group during a visit to GUM—"

The Russian rummaged through papers in a file folder. "Trailblazer Travel."

"Trailblazer. Exactly. Look, I'll admit something to you—I lost the group because I was trying to change US dollars on the black market. There was a guy in the GUM doorway. His name was Pavlusha."

"Did you change dollars?"

"No. He was only offering three rubles to the dollar. A waiter at the hotel had mentioned the possibility of four to a dollar—"

"Three is the correct black market exchange rate. The story of the waiter offering you four-for-one is invented. I know this because the waiters and waitresses all work for our service—when they exchange money at black-market rates or sell caviar, it is reported to us."

"Maybe some of the waiters free-lance."

The inquisitor only smiled. "What happened after you lost touch with your group?"

"To tell the truth, I wasn't sorry. The tour is too organized for my taste. We never get to talk to any honest-to-God Russians. So I decided to strike out on my own for the rest of the day. I took the subway to Kropotkinskaya and walked over to the Pushkin Museum. After that I decided to see the famous tombs in the Novodievitchi cemetery—Stalin's wife, Bulgakov, Chekhov, Gogol."

"And Khrushchev."

"Right. Khrushchev."

"And you happened to strike up a conversation with a man who was passing next to the tomb of Khrushchev. And this man, by a complete coincidence, turned out to be the traitor Kukushkin."

Manny retorted, "He wasn't wearing a nametag that said 'the traitor Kukushkin.' He was just a guy who happened to be there and spoke English. And so we chatted for a few minutes."

"About what?"

"When he realized I was a foreigner he asked what my impressions were of the Soviet Union."

"When he saw the police and the militia coming toward him he tried to escape, and you fled with him."

"Put yourself in my shoes," Manny pleaded. "I was talking to a complete stranger. Then suddenly I see an armed gang heading my way and the stranger starts to run. I thought I was going to get mugged so I ran with him. How was I to know these people were policemen?"

"You and the traitor Kukushkin conversed in English."

"English. Right."

"*Vui gavorite po-Russki?*"

Manny shook his head. "I studied Russian at Yale. For one year, actually. I can catch a word here and there but I don't speak it."

"The traitor Kukushkin told us you speak fluent Russian."

"I want to talk to someone from the American embassy."

"Who at the embassy do you want to see? The Chief of Station Trillby?"

Manny glanced around the room, which was on the top floor of Lubyanka and spacious and filled with functional wooden furniture. The jailer who had brought him up from the cell, a bruiser wearing a crisp blue uniform at least one size too small for his bulky body, stood with his back to the wall and his arms folded across his chest. The windows were double-glazed and barred on the outside. A portrait of Lenin and another of KGB Chairman Andropov hung on the wall over a sideboard containing a samovar and bottles of mineral water. Looking back at the Russian, Manny played dumb. "I don't know anyone at the embassy by name or title, so I don't know whom you're talking about."

The Russian nodded to himself as if he were savoring a good joke. His inter-office buzzer sounded. The melodious voice of a woman could be heard saying, "Comrade Arkiangelskiy is here."

"Send him in," the Russian ordered. He eyed Manny across the table, shook his head and smiled again. "The game is up, my friend."

The door to the office opened and a short man dressed in the white coveralls of a technician pushed a dolly into the room. On it was a bulky tape-recorder. He wheeled the dolly up to the table, then unraveled the electric cord and plugged it into a wall socket. Straightening, he turned to the inquisitor, who said, "Play the tape for him."

The technician bent over the machine and pressed a button. The tape began to whir through the playback head and onto the pickup spool. At first the sound was muffled. The technician turned up the volume and increased the treble. A voice became audible. The entire conversation was in Russian.

"...would debrief me in the apartment of the Ept woman who worked for the Patent Office."

"What about the patents that you gave to the *rezident*?"

"Manny supplied them."

"Did he give you money?"

"Never. Not a penny. He offered to organize medical treatment for my wife's heart condition. I accepted that—"

"Did he promise to give you money when you defected?"

"There was talk of compensation but that wasn't why I—"

"What were your motivations?"

Kukushkin could be heard laughing bitterly. "The Americans were also interested in my motivation."

"You haven't responded to the question."

"The system under which we live is inefficient and corrupt, the people who preside over this system are unscrupulous. They are only interested in one thing, which is power. It is not an accident that our word for power— *vlast*—is also our word for authority."

"And this distorted reasoning induced you to betray your country?"

Kukushkin muttered something unintelligible.

"Of course you betrayed your country. You betrayed its secrets, you betrayed the operatives who are defending it into the hands of the Central Intelligence—"

"Fast forward to the rendezvous in the cemetery," the inquisitor ordered.

Manny said, "Why are you playing this for me? I don't understand a word he's saying."

Hunched in his chair, concentrating on the tape recorder, the inquisitor remarked, "You understand every word."

The technician hit the fast-forward button and regarded the numbers on the counter. When it reached the place he wanted he pressed "Play." Kukushkin's voice came on in mid-sentence. "...primary meeting place in the Pushkin Museum at noon on the second and fourth Tuesday of any given month. I went there immediately before the appointed hour but decided it was too crowded. Manny arrived at the secondary meeting place, the tomb of Nikita Khrushchev in the Novodievitchi cemetery. There were nine people in the cemetery but they looked innocent enough and so I went ahead with the meeting."

"What did the American tell you?"

"That the CIA could smuggle my wife and myself and our daughter out of the Soviet Union from the Crimea."

"How were you to get in touch with the CIA if you decided to accept?"

"I was to call a phone number in Moscow—K 4-89-73—and cough twice and hang up. This would activate the primary meeting place in the Pushkin Museum and the secondary meeting place next to Khrushchev's tomb in the Novodievitchi cemetery on the second or fourth Tuesday of every month."

The inquisitor waved his hand and the technician touched another button, cutting off the recording. He unplugged the electric cord and rolled it up and, pushing the cart ahead of him, left the room.

"As you yourself can see, the traitor Kukushkin has admitted to everything," the Russian told Manny. "He has agreed to plead guilty in the trial that will start in a week's time. With this in mind, would you care to make an official declaration that will relieve the judge of the obligation of imposing the maximum sentence when you come to trial?"

"Yeah," Manny said. "I guess I ought to." He spotted the smirk creeping back onto the inquisitor's lips. "Hotel—twenty-three."

The Russian's eyes flashed with triumph. "Ah, that must be your parking space number at Langley."

Curled up in the eye of his storm, Manny thought of the story that had plagued him as far back as he could remember—the one about his father telling the Hungarian interrogators to go to hell. He had heard it as a child, had memorized it and repeated it to himself whenever he found himself in a tight corner. "Hotel—twenty-three is the space assigned to me in the parking lot two blocks down from 44 Wall Street," he said. "Which is where I work when I'm not dumb enough to come as a tourist to the Soviet Union."

For Manny, time slipped past in a series of hazy and curiously detached vignettes. Basic training on The Farm—he'd been locked in an icy room and deprived of food, water and sleep for several wintery days—had not prepared him for the hard reality of a KGB prison. The anxiety he felt wasn't a result of physical abuse (the KGB actually did lay on a bare minimum of creature comforts); it came from the stifling uncertainty of what would happen next, and how the game would play out. He was decently fed and allowed to shower daily and questioned again and again; the sessions with the persistent inquisitor sometimes lasted into the early hours of the morning, at which point Manny would be led back to his cell and permitted to sleep for six hours. Two days after his arrest he was taken to a room to talk to a Miss Crainworth, who flashed a laminated card identifying her as a vice-counsel from the American embassy. She reported that the Secretary of State had summoned the Soviet embassador in Washington and demanded an explanation for the arrest of an American tourist. The Russians, the vice-counsel explained, were claiming that Manny was an officer of the CIA sent to Moscow to contact a recently returned diplomat who had defected to the American side in the States. The CIA had vehemently denied that it employed anyone named Immanuel Bridges or had had any contact with a Soviet diplomat named Kukushkin. Miss Crainworth said that the embassy had hired an English-speaking Soviet attorney to represent him.

The attorney, whose name was Robespierre Pravdin, was permitted to spend an hour with his client that evening. Pravdin, an anxious man with a facial twitch and sour breath, assured Manny that the Soviet system of justice would be lenient with him if he admitted what the KGB could prove: that he was, in fact, an agent of the Central Intelligence Agency. When Manny persisted in his denials, Pravdin told him, "I have seen a typescript of the traitor Kukushkin's confession, which implicates you. I will be able to help you get a lighter sentence only if you plead guilty and throw yourself on the mercy of the court."

The next morning Manny was roused from a deep sleep as daylight penetrated the open slit of a window high in the wall of his cell. He was permitted to shave with an East German electric razor that worked on batteries and given a clean pair of trousers and shirt. Sitting on the edge of the bunk waiting for the guards to fetch him, he stared at the small porthole to the world high above his head, listening to the jeers and catcalls of prisoners kicking around a soccer ball in the courtyard below. A conversation he'd had with his father when he was very young came back to him; he could hear his father's voice in his ear and he smiled at the memory. They'd been returning to Manhattan on the subway after an outing to Coney Island.

Mommy says you work for a Center Intelligence Agency. She says that's why you spend so much time outside America.

I work for the American government—

So what kind of stuff do you do for the government?

I help protect America from its enemies.

Why does America have enemies?

Not every country sees eye to eye on things.

What things?

Things like the existence of different political parties, things like honest trials and free elections, things like the freedom of newspapers to publish what they want, things like the right of people to criticize the government without going to jail. Things like that.

When I grow up, I'm going to protect America from its enemies same as you—if it still has any.

"When I grow up," Manny said aloud. He didn't finish the sentence because he knew the cell would be bugged.

Soon afterward Manny was handcuffed and taken down in a freight elevator to a basement garage. There he was seated between two guards in the back of a closed bread delivery van, which drove up a ramp, threaded its way through traffic and eventually came to stop in another basement garage. He was escorted up a fire staircase to the second-floor holding room, where his handcuffs were removed and he was offered coffee and a dry doughnut. Before long Pravdin and the vice-counsel Crainworth turned up. Pravdin explained that the traitor Kukushkin's trial was about to start; that there was a possibility Manny would be summoned as a witness. Pravdin removed his eyeglasses, fogged the lenses with his foul breath and wiped the lenses on the tip of his tie. Manny's chances of eventually being treated leniently by the Soviet judicial system, he repeated, depended on his cooperating with the prosecution in the Kukushkin case. Manny stuck to his cover story. Miss Crainworth, clearly in over her head, merely looked from one to the other as if she were watching a ping-pong match.

At five minutes to ten Manny was escorted into what looked like a ballroom, an enormous high-ceilinged chamber with glittering chandeliers and white Corinthian columns set against light blue walls. On one side were rows of plain wooden benches filled with working-class people who looked uncomfortable in city clothing. Several seemed to know who he was and pointed him out to the others when he entered. Flashbulbs exploded in his face as he was steered into a pew with a brass railing around it. Pravdin, the muscles in his cheeks atwitch, settled into a seat in front of him. Miss Crainworth squeezed onto a front-row bench and opened a notebook on her lap. Two judges in dark suits sat behind a long table on a raised stage. At the stroke of ten the accused appeared through a narrow door at the back of a wire enclosure. Kukushkin, surrounded by KGB security troops in tunics and peaked caps, looked gaunt and dazed. His face was expressionless, his eyes tired and puffy; he closed them for long periods and conveyed the impression of someone who was sleepwalking. He was dressed in rumpled suit and tie and, judging from the mincing steps he took when he entered the courtroom, wearing ankle cuffs. At one point he looked in Manny's direction but gave no indication that he recognized him. There was an angry murmur from the crowd when Kukushkin turned up in the prisoner's box. Flashbulbs burst, causing him to raise a forearm over his eyes. One of the guards gripped his wrist and pried it away. The chief judge, wearing a black robe and a red felt cap, appeared from a door at the back of the stage. Everyone in the courtroom stood. Manny was nudged to his feet. The chief judge, a white-haired man with red-rimmed eyes and the jowls of a heavy drinker, took his place between the assistant judges. *"Sadityes pojalusta,"* the bailiff called. The audience on the benches, along with the lawyers and stenographers settled onto their seats. The security troops guarding the prisoners continued to stand. The State Procurator, a young man wearing a beautifully-tailored blue suit, climbed to his feet and began to read the charges against Kukushkin.

"The traitor Kukushkin, the accused in criminal case Number 18043, is an opportunist," he began, his voice suffused with outrage, "a morally depraved person who betrayed his country. He was recruited by agents of the imperialist espionage service while he served in the Soviet embassy in Washington. There he committed treason with the intent to overthrow the Soviet regime, dismember the Soviet Union and restore capitalism in what would be left of the country. Returning to Moscow on home leave, he was caught in the act of meeting an agent of this imperialist espionage service. Confronted with irrefutable evidence by the representatives of the state security organs, the traitor Kukushkin had no choice but to admit to his crimes and sign a confession. It is this document, respected judges, that you now have before you."

Manny leaned forward and tapped Pravdin on the shoulder. "What did he say?"

Pravdin twisted around in his chair; Manny got another whiff of his bad breath when the lawyer whispered, "The Procurator explains that the traitor Kukushkin has confessed to his crimes. If you want to save yourself, so, too, must you."

Across the courtroom the Procurator sat down. The bailiff rose and demanded, "How does the accused plead?"

Kukushkin stood up. "I confirm I am guilty of espionage but my intent was not to dismember the Soviet Union or restore capitalism. My intent was to save the Soviet Union from an oppressive ruling class that is ruining the country economically and distorting the Communist ideal politically."

The Procurator leaped to his feat and waved a copy of Kukushkin's confession. "How is it you admitted to these charges in writing?"

"I was forced to."

There was an astonished rumble from the benches. The Procurator turned to the judges. "In light of this recantation I request a recess."

"Granted," the chief judge growled.

Manny was taken back to the holding room and offered coffee from a thermos and a sandwich filled with a meat he couldn't identify. Two hours later he found himself back in the courtroom. The bailiff addressed the prisoner. "How does the accused plead?"

Kukushkin, his shoulders hunched, mumbled something. The chief judge ordered him to speak louder. "I plead guilty to all the charges," the prisoner said. "I admit everything."

The Procurator said, "What, then, was the meaning of the statement you made two hours ago?"

"I could not bring myself to admit my guilt before the world," Kukushkin said. "Mechanically, I sidestepped the truth in the hope of presenting my treachery in a better light. I beg the court to take note of the statement which I now make to the effect that I admit my guilt, completely and unreservedly, on all the charges brought against me. I assume full responsibility for my criminal and treacherous behavior."

The Procurator accepted this with a nod of satisfaction. "The accused Kukushkin admits that he delivered state secrets into the hands of an agent of the Central Intelligence Agency?"

"I openly and unrestrainedly admit it."

"The accused Kukushkin admits that he met in Moscow at a prearranged place and at a prearranged time with this same agent of the Central Intelligence Agency?"

"Yes, yes. I admit it."

The Procurator shuffled through what looked like cue cards. "The question inevitably arises: How can it be that a man like the traitor Kukushkin, which is to say someone born and brought up and educated during the years of Soviet power, could so completely lose the moral qualities of a Soviet man, lose his elementary sense of loyalty and duty and end up committing treason?"

As if reading from a prepared script, Kukushkin answered: "It was the base qualities in me which brought me to the prisoner's dock: envy, vanity, the love of an easy life, my affairs with many women, my moral decay, brought on in part by the abuse of alcohol. All of these blotches on my moral character led to my becoming a degenerate, and then a traitor."

The chief judge asked, "Is the agent of the Central Intelligence Agency you met present in this courtroom?"

"Yes." Kukushkin raised a finger and pointed at Manny without looking at him. "He is sitting over there."

"Look at him to be sure of the identification," the chief judge ordered.

Kukushkin reluctantly turned his head. His eyes met those of Manny, then dropped. "I confirm the identification."

The Procurator said, "Respected judges, the agent from the Central Intelligence Agency is not protected by diplomatic immunity and will be tried in a separate proceeding. The American agent denies the obvious—that he was sent to Moscow to establish contact with the traitor Kukushkin so that he could continue his perfidious behavior here in the capital of the Motherland. The American agent denies also that he speaks fluent Russian, though a child can see, as he looks from one speaker to the other, that he is able to follow the conversation."

The chief judge addressed Manny directly. "Do you know the traitor Kukushkin?"

Pravdin twisted around and repeated the question in English, then whispered urgently, "This is your opportunity to impress the judges by your truthfulness. The traitor Kukushkin is condemned out of his own mouth. Save yourself."

Manny rose to his feet. "Your honor," he began. "I do know the accused." The spectators in the audience stirred, the American vice-counsel looked up from her notebook. The chief judge brought his gavel down sharply. "I am a tourist, your honor," Manny continued. "The truth is that

I was separated from my group and, wanting to see some of the interesting sites that were not on the itinerary, wound up in the Novodievitchi cemetery. It was there that I met the accused for the first and only time in my life. Taking me for a foreign tourist, he asked me in English for my impressions of the Soviet Union. As for my being a member of the Central Intelligence Agency—nothing could be further from the truth."

A frail elderly woman sitting behind the judge had been scribbling notes in shorthand as Manny spoke, and now translated his testimony into Russian. The chief judge said, "Let the record show that the American denies that he is an intelligence agent." He nodded at the Procurator. "You may deliver your summation."

The Procurator rose. "I call upon the respected judges, however reluctant they may be, to deliver a verdict of guilty and a sentence of execution. An example must be made of the traitor Kukushkin. The weed and the thistle will grow on the grave of this execrable traitor. But on us and our fortunate country the sun will continue to shine. Guided by our beloved leader and the Communist Party, we will go forward to Communism along a path that has been cleansed of the sordid remnants of the past."

Kukushkin's defense lawyer stood up to address the court. "Respected judges, confronted with the confession of the accused Kukushkin, I can only echo my colleague's remarks. I invite the court's attention to the fact that the confession of the accused was wholehearted, if belated, and should be weighed on the scales of justice in deciding on a sentence appropriate to the crime."

Twenty-five minutes later the three judges filed back into the courtroom. The chief judge ordered the accused to rise. "Do you have a last statement before I pass judgment?"

Kukushkin intoned woodenly, "My own fate is of no importance. All that matters is the Soviet Union."

The judge removed his red cap and replaced it with a black one. "Sergei Semyonovich Kukushkin," he intoned, "degenerates and renegades like you evoke a sentiment of indignation and loathing in all Soviet people. One can take comfort from the fact that you are a passing phenomenon in our society. But your example shows clearly what danger lurks in the vestiges of the past, and what they might develop into if we do not act with ruthless determination to uproot them. I pronounce you guilty of all the charges brought against you and sentence you to be shot. Court adjourned."

The spectators on the benches applauded the verdict vigorously. "So finish all traitors to the Motherland," a man called from a back row. Kukushkin's expressionless gaze drifted over the room and came to rest for a fleeting moment on Manny. The barest trace of an ironic smile disfigured his lips. One of his guards tapped him on the arm. Kukushkin turned and held out his wrists and handcuffs were snapped on. Walking in short steps because of the ankle bracelets, he shuffled from the prisoner's box and disappeared through the door.

Sometime in the pre-dawn stillness, Manny was startled out of an agitated sleep by the sound of a metal door clanging closed in the corridor, followed by footsteps outside his cell. The overhead light came on. A key turned in the lock and Kukushkin appeared at the door. Manny sat up on the army cot and pulled the blanket up to his chin. Still wearing ankle bracelets, Kukushkin walked slowly across the cell and sat down at the foot of the cot. "Hello to you, Manny," he said, his voice reduced to a rasp.

Manny knew that the conversation would be recorded, perhaps even filmed. He chose his words carefully. "I gather things didn't go well for you. I want you to know..." His voice trailed off.

Kukushkin's heavy shoulders sagged. "I am to be executed at dawn," he announced.

The news struck Manny with the force of a fist. "I wish...if only I could do something—"

"You can."

"What?"

"For me it's over. For Elena, for my daughter—"

Manny could see the torment in Sergei's eyes.

"In Soviet Russia, the immediate relations of enemies of the people are made to suffer. I have denied it, of course, but they assume that my wife, even my daughter, were aware of my...activities. They will be sent to a Gulag camp for fifteen years. With her heart condition Elena will not survive fifteen days. And my daughter will not survive the loss of her mother."

"I don't see—"

"Look, Manny, I'll come to the point. They have sent me to offer you a deal. It is important to them, vis-à-vis international opinion, that you admit publicly to being a CIA officer."

"But I'm not—"

Kukushkin raised the palm of his hand. "In return for your cooperation they have promised that Elena and my child will not be punished. So, like it or not, their fate is in your hands." Kukushkin turned away and chewed on his lip. When he had regained his composure he said, "You owe it to me,

Manny. And I ask you to pay this debt. I beg you. I will go to my death with a firmer step, with a lighter conscience, if you do this thing for me."

Manny had the crazed feeling that he could feel the earth picking up speed in its rotation around its axis. Thoughts ripped through the lobes of his skull. He looked at the wreck of a man hunched at the foot of the bunk bed. Then he nodded miserably. "Okay," he whispered. "I'll do what has to be done."

Kukushkin nodded back and brought the palm of his hand to his chest. "I thank you from my heart," he said.

Manny remained awake for the rest of the night, his eyes riveted on the slit of a window high in the wall, his ears straining for the slightest groan or grate from the massive tomb of Lubyanka. He thought of Leo Kritzky, isolated in Angleton's private dungeon; as far as Manny was concerned Leo could rot in prison for the rest of his natural life. The Company owed Kukushkin that much. When dawn broke into his own cell he heard death stirring in the courtyard below. A cart on steel-rimmed wheels was rolled into position. A short while later a door opened and a squad of men could be heard marching in lockstep across the cobblestones. A command echoed off the stone walls. The men halted and slammed their boots and the butts of rifles onto the ground. Another door was thrown open and three men walked slowly from the far end of the courtyard toward the squad waiting at parade rest. Moments later two of them walked away. More orders were barked, one on the heels of the other. In his cell, Manny folded his knees up to his chin and caught his breath. Below the window rifle bolts were thrown. A voice that Manny only recognized when he reproduced it in his brain was heard to yell, "You owe it to me, Manny." A volley of rifle shots rang out. On the roof of the prison wave after wave of pigeons beat into the ash-streaked sky. As the men marched off in lockstep, the whiplash of a single pistol shot reverberated through Manny's cell. The steel-rimmed wheels of the cart rolled back across the courtyard. A jet of water from a high-powered hose scoured the cobblestones. And then a silence as suffocating as any Manny had heard in his life filled his grieving skull.

The inquisitor asked if the prisoner would like to read the confession in English before he signed both the Russian and English versions. "Why not?" Manny said. He held the sheet of single-spaced typewriting up to the light.

I, the undersigned, Immanuel Ebbitt, hereby acknowledge the following particulars to be true and factual: One: that I am a full-time employee of the American Central Intelligence Agency on active duty. Two: that I was the controlling officer of the Soviet traitor Sergei Semyonovich Kukushkin, who defected to the American side while serving as a political attaché in Washington. Three: that I was sent under the cover of a tourist to contact the traitor Kukushkin after he was recalled to Moscow in order to convince him to continue spying for the Central Intelligence Agency.

Manny skimmed the rest of the paper—it followed exactly the Russian version. He'd agreed to acknowledge his connection to Kukushkin but drawn the line when it came to revealing operational information or the identities of Company officers and agents; the KGB, realizing that half a loaf was better than nothing, had settled for that. Manny reached for the fountain pen that the inquisitor had set on the desk and scrawled his name across the bottom of both versions. "Now what?" he asked.

"Now we will prepare for your public trial."

"Can I ask for a favor?"

"You can ask."

"I'd like a different lawyer."

"Comrade Pravdin is one of the most competent defense attorneys in Moscow—"

"I'm not challenging his competence," Manny said. "It's his bad breath that I can't stand."

8

ANGLETON LOOMED LIKE AN APPARITION BEHIND THE CIGARETTE smoke. "*Pravda* published a photograph of the confession alongside the story about the execution of 'the traitor Kukushkin,'" he noted. "My people checked the signature—they're convinced it's Manny's handwriting."

"He must have been drugged," Ebby said. "There's no other way to explain it."

Jack put his hand on Ebby's shoulder. "There are other possibilities," he said quietly. "He may have been...forced. I mean physically. Or he could have been trading the confession for..."

Jack couldn't bring himself to finish the sentence. Angleton finished it for him. "For his life. That's what you wanted to say, isn't it, Jack?"

"Thank you for your bluntness," Ebby said coldly.

Angleton jammed another cigarette between his lips and, crumpling the empty pack, tossed it into the burn bag. "As you pointed out to me, Elliott, your son's a consenting adult—he went into Russia with his eyes open."

"Yes, he did," Ebby conceded. "Now the problem is to get him out—with his eyes open."

When the American named Immanuel Bridges failed to turn up for supper at the Metropole the evening of the visit to GUM, the Trailblazer representative leading the tour had phoned the US embassy. The embassy people weren't unduly alarmed; from time to time a visiting fireman had gone off with one of the hookers who frequented the underpasses near the Kremlin, only to turn up a day or two later with a roaring hangover and a missing wallet. Still, the embassy had covered the appropriate bases, checking with the city militia and the hospitals. When there was still no trace of the Trailblazer tourist the next morning, an undersecretary had formally notified the Soviet Ministry of the Interior and the Department of State in Washington. The embassy's cable to Foggy Bottom was routinely routed ("for information only") to the CIA. At which point the alarm bells had gone off at Langley. The Kukushkin task force had gathered in Ebby's office. For the moment all they had were hypothetical questions. Had Manny succeeded in meeting with AE/PINNACLE at either the primary or secondary rendezvous? Had the KGB become suspicious of Manny and trailed him despite his tradecraft precautions? Or had they somehow figured out that Kukushkin was spying for the Americans? Had the father-in-law's illness and demise been staged to get his wife and daughter, and then Kukushkin, to return to Moscow before the CIA could bring the family to safety? If Kukushkin had in fact been arrested, would he break under questioning? Would he implicate Manny?

Two days after Manny's disappearance, the Soviet Interior Minister had informed the embassy that an American national by the name of Bridges, Immanuel, had been caught in the act of meeting clandestinely with a Soviet diplomat and had been taken into custody. A vice-counsel, Elizabeth Crainworth (actually a CIA officer assigned to the Company's Moscow Station under diplomatic cover) had been dispatched to Lubyanka prison to interview the American in question. Unaware (for reasons of security, Moscow Station had been left out of the loop) that she was dealing with a CIA agent on a one-time mission in Moscow, she'd reported back that Bridges had denied the Soviet charges and had maintained he was an ordinary tourist.

The Pravda account of Kukushkin's execution and Manny's confession had been picked up by the Associated Press. The switchboard at the Company's public relations office lit up as newspapers across America tried to pry a statement out of the CIA; those that managed to get through to one of Millie Owen-Brack's public relations flacks came away with the usual "The Central Intelligence Agency does not comment on stories of this nature." Director Colby was spirited into the White House through a side entrance to explain to an irate President Ford (who had just stirred up a storm by issuing a full pardon to Richard Nixon for all federal crimes "he committed or may have committed" while in office) why the Company had sent an officer into the Soviet Union without diplomatic cover. Inside Langley, the corridors were abuzz with rumors of what looked like an intelligence fiasco. As word of Kukushkin's execution and Manny's confession spread, the veteran agents and officers on the seventh floor closed ranks; many dropped by Ebby's shop to offer moral support. Jack and Ebby huddled with some of the more experienced field hands to see if they couldn't come up with a game plan. It was at one of these sessions that a possible solution surfaced. The brainstorming had reached a dead end when Jack suddenly jumped to his feet. "Damnation," he exclaimed, "it's been staring us in the face. The way to spring Manny is to exchange him for someone the KGB wants."

"Exchange Manny for whom?" Bill Colby inquired when the full task force met to consider the idea.

Ebby glanced at Jack, then looked uncertainly at Bill Colby. "Spit it out, Elliott," the Director ordered.

"If I'm reading the tea leaves correctly," Ebby finally said, "Kukushkin's trial and execution...what I'm driving at is there appears to be no room left for doubt that AE/PINNACLE was a genuine defector, which means that his serials were true serials."

Jack said, "It's not easy for me to say this but Jim got it right—Leo Kritzky is SASHA."

Angleton was following the conversation with heavy-lidded eyes. "Hang on," he said. "I can see where this is headed. The answer is: Over my dead body."

Ebby turned on Angleton. "Let me ask you something, Jim—have you broken Leo? Has he admitted to being a Soviet agent?"

"Not yet."

"Not yet," Jack repeated, looking at Colby. "Jim's had Leo on ice for more than three months, Director. I went to see him a while back and I can tell you he's not in a luxury hotel. He's drinking water out of a toilet bowl. If he hasn't cracked by now chances are he's not going to. He'll rot to death in Jim's private dungeon proclaiming his innocence."

"I can see you've never been fly fishing," Angleton said lazily. "Doesn't surprise me—you don't have the patience. Count on it, Kritzky will break. In the end they all do. When he does I'll tap into a counterintelligence gold seam—what he gave away during all these years, the identity of the controlling officer known as Starik, details of the operation known as KHOLSTOMER—"

"What are you going to do if he doesn't break?" Jack asked Angleton.

Ebby said, "You don't have many alternatives, Jim. You can bring him to trial—but without a confession and a guilty plea, this would involve calling witnesses and exposing Company secrets. Or you could keep him in prison for the rest of his life, something that would eventually present moral and legal problems. Imagine the stink if someone in Congress or the press broke the story: 'CIA jails suspected Soviet mole for life without giving him his day in court.' Talk about scandals, it would make Watergate look like a parking infraction." Ebby turned to Colby. "The KGB, on the other hand, might jump at the chance to trade Manny for Kritzky—"

Colby slowly shook his head. "I'm just thinking out loud," he said, "but if we handed Kritzky over to the Soviets, what would prevent them from trotting him out in front of a pack of Western journalists for a propaganda triumph. He could still deny he worked for the Russians, he could tell them how he was illegally incarcerated in a CIA prison for three months under humiliating conditions. He would come across angry and bitter, which would explain why he'd decided to reveal the good secrets I've managed to keep out of the hands of Congress—the identity of our agents and descriptions of our ongoing operations, not to mention the operations he's been party to for the past twenty-three years—Iran, Guatemala, Cuba for starters." The Director saw the pain on Ebby's face. "Let me be clear—in principle I'm not against the idea of trading one of theirs for one of ours. But trading Kritzky is a nonstarter."

Ebby got up and walked over to stare out a window. Colby started to collect his papers. Jack focused on Angleton across the table. "There's more than one way to skin a cat," he muttered.

"You have another idea?" Colby inquired.

"As a matter of fact, yeah. I know someone else we could trade for Manny."

A very thin, nattily dressed man in his late forties ducked into the men's room off the lobby of the Hay-Adams Hotel on 16th Street. He urinated in one of the stalls, then rinsed his hands and dried them on a paper towel, which he threw into the bin. He removed his thick eyeglasses, cleaned them with a handkerchief and carefully hooked them back over his ears. Studying himself in the mirror, he adjusted his bow tie, then tried to pick food particles from between his teeth with a fingernail. The Puerto Rican janitor finished washing the floor and, gathering his mop and pail, departed, leaving the man alone in the lavatory. Opening the middle cubicle, he climbed onto the toilet seat, reached into the cistern and removed the package sheathed in a condom. On the way to the door, he discarded the condom in the bin filled with used paper towels and slipped the package into the pocket of his suit jacket. Stepping out into the lobby, he discovered half a dozen men in dark three-piece suits waiting for him. Off to one side a cameraman filmed the proceeding. One of the men stepped forward and, flipping open a small wallet containing a laminated card and a silver badge, identified himself as agent Sibley of the Federal Bureau of Investigation. Another agent expertly snapped handcuffs on the man's wrists. Behind them, in the lobby, guests and employees of the Hay-Adams stopped what they were doing to watch.

"Raymond Shelton, we are arresting you for passing classified information to a foreign intelligence service with intent to harm the United States," agent Sibley announced.

Shelton, clearly terrified, sputtered, "This has to be a case of mistaken identity—"

This seemed to amuse the FBI agent. "You are the Raymond W. Shelton employed by the National Security Agency?"

"Yes, I am. But I don't understand—"

"You will in a moment."

With the camera zooming in, agent Sibley reached into Shelton's pocket and took out the package he had recovered from the cistern. He opened it on camera and spilled the contents onto a table. There was a wad of five-hundred-dollar bills, four tiny microfilm canisters and a blank piece of paper which the agent handled gingerly so as not to eradicate the secret writing believed to be on it. There were also two matchbooks with one-time code grids hand-drawn under the matches. Another agent pulled an index card from his breast pocket and began to read from it. "I advise you that you have the right to remain silent. Anything you say may be used against you in subsequent legal proceedings. You have the right to legal counsel. If you can't afford legal counsel, one will be appointed by a court of law..."

"Oh, dear, Ardyn, what *is* going on?" a gray-haired woman whispered to the concierge standing behind the reception desk.

"Well, you're not going to believe this, Mrs. Williams, but I think the FBI's just captured a criminal."

"In the Hay-Adams! My goodness, how thrilling," the woman said. "Will I have something to tell my children when I get back to Memphis!"

When word of Manny's disappearance reached Langley, two of his closest friends in the Soviet Division stopped by Nellie's law office to break the news to her: Manny had gone into Moscow as a tourist and failed to show up for supper at the Hotel Metropole the previous evening. So far they had no idea what had happened to him. The embassy people were on the case, checking with the police and hospitals to see if he had been involved in an accident. Of course the Company would let Nellie know the instant there was any news.

Ebby phoned her soon after. She would have to understand that he couldn't tell her much over the phone. All they knew for sure was that Manny hadn't returned to the hotel. When Ebby told her they were still hoping the disappearance would have an innocent explanation, Nellie exploded: You mean he might have been mugged and is lying unconscious in some alleyway, as opposed to arrested? Then she got a grip on her emotions. She was terribly sorry; she understood this must be as hard for Ebby as it was for her. It's hard on all of us, Ebby agreed, and she could tell from his voice that he was worried sick. Before he hung up he said, Look, when you get off work, why don't you move back in with us until this blows over.

Ebby never made it home from Langley that night. Elizabet and Nellie sat up until after two, knocking down frozen daiquiris. The only light came from a late-night film, *Five Easy Pieces*, flickering on the television screen with the sound switched off. To break the long silences, Nellie got her mother onto the subject of Hungary. Elizabet, under the spell of the daiquiris, let down her guard and began to talk about Nellie's father, the poet Arpád Zelk. "I'm told that young people still recite his poems in the university," she said.

"How long were you together?" Nellie wanted to know.

Elizabet smiled in the flickering darkness. "We were never together, Arpád and I. Our paths crossed, sometimes several times during a day, more often than not in bed. He was what you might call an ardent despot, tyrannical in the pursuit of poetry and liberty for the masses. Individual freedom—my freedom—was not high on his agenda."

"And he was killed in the revolution."

"The revolution—the Russians—in a manner of speaking killed him. He and his poetry had helped suck the Hungarian people into a tragedy. When he realized this he did what had to be done—he shot himself."

Nellie whispered, "You told me he'd died but you never said he'd killed himself." She gulped down what was left in the glass, then chewed on some crushed ice. "Did you love him?" she asked.

Elizabet thought about that. "I don't remember," she said.

This annoyed Nellie. "How can you say that? How can you say you don't remember if you loved my father?"

"It's an honest answer. I must have thought I loved him—why else would I have been with him? But when I fell in love with Elliott it eradicated the several loves that went before."

"If something happens to Manny..." Nellie brought a fist up to her solar plexus. When the pain in her chest subsided she finished the sentence. "If something happens I will never forget how much I love him. Nothing...no one...no amount of time will eradicate the memory."

Elizabet held out her arms and Nellie came into them. Soundless sobs racked the girl's body and a torrent of tears spilled from her eyes.

The news that Manny had been arrested came as a relief to both women—at least it meant that he wasn't dying in an alleyway. Ebby showed up late one afternoon but he only stayed the time it took to shower and shave and change into fresh clothing, at which point he headed straight back to Langley to stay on top of the situation.

It was Jack who eventually phoned up with the good news. "I think it's going to work out," he told Nellie.

She covered the mouthpiece. "Jack thinks things will work out," she told her mother. Elizabet took the phone when Nellie chocked up with emotion. "Jack, are you sure?"

"We won't be sure until he's on our side of the Iron Curtain," he said. "But I think the fix is in."

Nellie grabbed the phone back. "How are you going to get him out?"

"Can't tell you that, Nellie. Bear with us. Pack a bag and be ready to leave at a moment's notice."

"Where am I going?"

"Stop asking dumb questions. Ebby wanted you both to know that we're working on something, that it's looking good. When Manny comes out we thought you'd like to be there."

"Goddamn it, I would. Like to be there. Thanks, Jack."

"Sure."

A film of fog blanketed the Havel River separating West Berlin from Potsdam in the Soviet Zone, deadening the hollow knell from a distant steeple on the eastern bank. Soon after midnight, seven Jeeps and a lorry with mud-splashed Red Army stars on its doors pulled up on the Potsdam side of the Glienicke Bridge. The lead Jeep flashed its lights twice. From the American end of the bridge came two answering flashes. Russian soldiers lowered the lorry's tailgate and a tall, slightly stooped man wearing a shapeless raincoat jumped down onto the road. The Russian colonel checked the luminous dial of his wristwatch, then nodded at two soldiers, who took up position on either side of the man in the raincoat. They accompanied him past the raised barrier onto the suspension bridge. A quarter of the way along it, the two Russian soldiers stopped in their tracks and the tall civilian kept walking. A figure could be seen heading toward him from the far end. He was wearing thick glasses that had turned fuliginous in the light from the bridge's wrought-iron lampposts. The two men slowed as they approached each other in the middle of the bridge. Regarding each other warily, they stopped to exchange a few words.

"You speak Russian?" asked the younger man.

The second man, appearing disoriented, worked his bony fingers through his thinning hair. "No."

The younger man found himself smiling at a private joke. "Unfortunately for you, you'll have the rest of your life to learn."

As the bespectacled man approached the Soviet side the Russian colonel started forward to greet him. "Welcome to freedom," he called.

"I'm damned glad to be here."

On the American side, a man and a young woman were waiting impatiently in front of a line of Jeeps. The man was peering through binoculars. "It's him, all right," he said.

The woman darted forward to meet the young man approaching under the wrought-iron lampposts. "Are you all right?" she breathed as she flung herself into his arms.

The two clung to each other. "I'm fine," he said.

The man with the binoculars came up behind her. The two men shook hands emotionally. "I broke the eleventh commandment," said the young man.

"We don't think it was your fault," the other man replied. "The way they pulled out his wife and daughter on a moment's notice, then brought him home a day later—given how the game played out it all begins to look very premeditated. They must have become suspicious of him in Washington and then just outplayed us. You were sent on a wild-goose chase."

"I lost my Joe, Dad. He's dead. Jim Angleton was right—I was too green. I must have gone wrong somewhere—"

The three started toward the Jeeps. "I know how you feel," remarked the man with binoculars. "I've been there a bunch of times. It's the downside of what we do for a living."

"Is there an upside?" the girl demanded.

"Yes, there is," he shot back. "We're doing a dirty job and we get it right most of the time. But there's no way you can get it right every time." The fog was rolling in off the river, imparting a pungent sharpness to the night air. "What keeps us going, what keeps us sane," he added, talking to himself now, "is the conviction that if something's worth doing, it's worth doing badly."

9

SANTA FE, SATURDAY, OCTOBER 12, 1974

JACK CAUGHT AN EARLY MORNING FLIGHT FROM DULLES TO ALBUQUERQUE, then rented a car at the airport and drove an hour up the interstate to Santa Fe. Following the Sorcerer's fuzzy directions as best he could, stopping twice at gas stations to ask directions, he finally found East of Eden Gardens east of the city, on the edge of a golf course. In a billboard planted halfway down the access road, East of Eden Gardens was advertised as a promoters' vision of what paradise must be like, though Jack had a sneaking suspicion the promoters didn't actually live there themselves. Smart folks. The sprawling condominium community, semi-attached bungalows made of fake adobe and set at weird angles to each other, was surrounded by a no-nonsense chain-link fence topped with coils of Army surplus concertina wire to keep the Hispanics from nearby Española out. For all Jack knew, there could have been a minefield under the belt of Astroturf inside the fence. His identity was controlled at the gatehouse by an armed and uniformed guard wearing Raybans. "Got a message for you from Mista Torriti," he said, checking Jack's name off the list on the clipboard. "If you was to get here after eleven and before four, you'll find him at the clubhouse." Following the guard's instructions, Jack drove through an intestinal tangle of narrow streets named for dead movie stars, past a driving range, past a communal swimming pool shaped to look like the most fragile part of a promoter's body, the kidney.

"Jesus H. Christ, Harvey, I didn't know you'd taken up golf," Jack exclaimed when he found the Sorcerer nursing a Scotch on the rocks at the empty bar.

"Haven't taken up golf," Torriti said, squeezing his Apprentice's hand with his soft fingers, punching him playfully in the shoulder. "Taken up drinking in golf clubs. Everyone who owns a condo is a member. Members get happy-hour prices all day long. All night, too."

The Sorcerer bought Jack a double Scotch and another double for himself, and the two carried their drinks and a bowl of olives to a booth at the back of the deserted clubhouse.

"Where's everybody?" Jack asked.

"Out golfin'," Torriti said with a smirk. "I'm the only one here who doesn't own clubs." He waved toward the adobe condominiums on the far side of the kidney-shaped pool. "It's a retirement home, Jack. You get free maid service, you can order in from the club kitchen, faucet drips and you got a handyman knocking at your door by the time you hang up the phone. Half a dozen ex-Langley types live out here; we got an all-Company dealer's-choice game going Monday nights."

"Aside from drinking and poker, how do you make time pass in the middle of nowhere?"

"You won't believe me if I tell you."

"Try me."

"I read spy stories. I finished one yesterday called *The Spy Who Came in from the Cold* by someone name of le Carré."

"And?"

"He gets the mood right—he understands that Berlin was a killing field. He understands that those of us who lived through it were never the same again. People could learn more about the Cold War reading le Carré than they can from newspapers. But he loses me when he says spies are people who play cowboys and Indians to brighten their rotten lives. What a load of bullshit! How about you, sport? How's tricks?"

"Can't complain," Jack said.

"So what brings you to Santa Fe? Don't tell me you were just passing through and wanted to chew the fat. Won't swallow that."

Jack laughed. "I wanted to see how retirement was treating the honcho of Berlin Base, Harvey."

Torriti's red-rimmed eyes danced merrily, as if he had heard a good joke. "I'll bet. What else?"

"You read the newspapers?"

"Don't need to. Anything concerning my ex-employer turns up in the news, one of my poker pals fills me in." The Sorcerer plucked an ice cube from the glass and massaged his lids with it. "I heard about the joker from NSA you traded for one of ours, if that's what you want to know. Newspapers said he was a low-level paper pusher, but I wasn't born yesterday."

Jack leaned forward and lowered his voice. "He was a mid-level analyst working on Russian intercepts—"

"Which means the Ruskies knew what we were intercepting, which means they were filling it with shit."

Jack took a sip of Scotch. He wondered if the Sorcerer broke down and ordered solids at lunchtime. "But they didn't know we knew. Now they do."

"How'd you trip to him?"

"We got a walk-in at the Russian embassy. He wanted to defect but we talked him into spying in place until his tour was up. He gave us two important things, Harvey—the NSA mole and a series of serials that led Jim Angleton to SASHA."

The Sorcerer rolled his head from side to side, impressed. "Where's the problem?"

"What makes you think there's a problem?"

"You wouldn't be here if there wasn't."

"Something's bothering me, Harvey. I thought, if your twitching nose was still functioning, you might help me sort through it."

"Try me."

"Like I was saying, based on the walk-in's serials, Angleton identified SASHA. He told us he'd been closing in on him, that it was only a matter of time before he narrowed it down to two or three. The walk-in's serials speeded up the inevitable, that's what Mother said."

"You want to go whole-hog."

Jack was whispering now. "It's Kritzky. Leo Kritzky."

A whistle seeped through Torriti's lips. "The Soviet Division chief! Jesus, it's Kim Philby redux, only this time it's in our shop."

"Angleton's been giving Leo the third degree for four months and then some, but he hasn't cracked. Leo claims he's innocent and Angleton hasn't been able to make him admit otherwise."

"Seems open and shut, sport—everything depends on the walk-in inside the Russian embassy. Flutter him. If he's telling the truth"—Torriti's shoulders heaved inside a very loud sports jacket—"eliminate SASHA."

"Can't polygraph the walk-in," Jack said. He explained how Kukushkin's wife and daughter had suddenly flown home to be with her dying father; how Kukushkin had followed them back to Moscow the next day.

"Did the father die?"

"As far as we can tell, yes. There was a funeral. There was an obituary." Torriti waved these tidbits away.

"That's what we thought, too, Harv. So we sent Kukushkin's controlling officer to Moscow to speak to him."

"Without diplomatic cover."

"Without diplomatic cover," Jack conceded.

"And he was picked up. And then he confessed to being CIA. And then you traded the NSA mole to get him back."

Jack concentrated on his drink.

"Who was the controlling officer?"

"Elliott Ebbitt's boy, Manny."

Torriti pulled a face. "Never did like that Ebbitt fellow but that's neither here nor there. What did Manny have to say when he came in?"

"He was at Kukushkin's trial. He heard him confess. He heard the verdict. Kukushkin turned up in his cell to ask him to acknowledge being CIA in order to save his family. That's what Manny's so-called confession was all about—it was in return for an amnesty for the wife and kid. That night he heard the firing squad execute Kukushkin—"

"How did he know it was Kukushkin being executed?"

"He cried out right before. Manny recognized his voice."

The Sorcerer munched on an olive, spit the pit into a palm and deposited it in an ashtray. "So what's bothering you, kid?"

"My stomach. I'm hungry."

Torriti called over to the Hispanic woman sitting on a stool behind the cash register. *"Dos BLT's sobre tostado,* honey," he called. *"Dos cervezas también."*

Jack said, "I didn't know you spoke Spanish, Harvey."

"I don't. You want to go and tell me what's really bothering you?"

Jack toyed with a saltcellar, turning it in his fingers. "Leo Kritzky and I go back a long way, Harv. We roomed together at Yale. He's my son's godfather, for Christ's sake. To make a long story shorter, I visited him in Angleton's black hole. Mother has him drinking water out of the toilet bowl."

The Sorcerer didn't see anything particularly wrong with this. "So?"

"Number one: He hasn't broken. I offered him a way out that didn't involve spending the rest of his life in prison. He told me to fuck off."

"Considering the time and money you spent to come here, there's got to be a number two."

"Number two: Leo said something that's been haunting me. He was absolutely certain our walk-in would never be fluttered." Jack stared out the window as he quoted Leo word for word. "He said Kukushkin would be run over by a car or mugged in an alleyway or whisked back to Mother Russia for some cockamamie reason that would sound plausible enough. But he wouldn't be fluttered because we would never get to bring him over. And he wouldn't be brought over because he was a dispatched defector sent to convince Angleton that Kritzky was SASHA and take the heat off the real SASHA. And it played out just the way Leo said it would."

"Your walk-in wasn't polygraphed because he rushed back to Moscow for a funeral. After which he was arrested and tried and executed."

"What do you think, Harvey?"

"What do I think?" Torriti considered the question. Then he tweaked the tip of his nose with a forefinger. "I think it stinks."

"That's what I think, too."

"Sure that's what you think. You wouldn't be here otherwise."

"What can I do now? How do I get a handle on this?"

The Hispanic woman backed through a swinging door from the kitchen carrying a tray. She set the sandwiches and the beers down on the table. When she'd gone Torriti treated himself to a swig of beer. "Drinking a lot is the best revenge," he said, blotting his lips on a sleeve. "About your little problem—you want to do what I did when I ran up against a stone wall in my hunt for Philby."

"Which is?"

"Which is get ahold of the Rabbi and tell him your troubles."

"I didn't know Ezra Ben Ezra was still among the living."

"Living and kicking. He works out of a Mossad safe house in a suburb of Tel Aviv. Saw him eight months ago when he was passing through Washington—we met in Albuquerque and he picked my brain, or what was left of it." The Sorcerer took a bite out of his sandwich, then produced a ballpoint pen and scratched an address and an unlisted phone number on the inside of an East of Eden Gardens matchbook. "A word to the wise—it's not polite to go empty- handed."

"What should I bring?"

"Information. Don't forget to say *shalom* from the Sorcerer when you see him."

"I'll do that, Harvey."

The midday Levantine sun burned into the back of Jack's neck as he picked his way through the vegetable stalls in the Nevei Tsedek district north of Jaffa, a neighborhood of dilapidated buildings that dated back to the turn of the century when the first Jewish homesteaders settled on the dunes of what would become Tel Aviv. The sleeves of his damp shirt were rolled up to the elbows, his sports jacket hung limply from a forefinger over his right shoulder. He double-checked the address that the Sorcerer had scribbled inside the matchbook, then looked again to see if he could make out house numbers on the shops or doorways. "You don't speak English?" he asked a bearded man peddling falafel from a pushcart.

"If I don't speak English," the man shot back, "why do you ask your question in English? English I speak. Also Russian. Also Turkish, Greek and enough Rumanian to pass for someone from Transylvania in Bulgaria, which is what saved my life during the war. German, too, I know but I invite Ha-Shem, blessed be He, to strike me dead if a word of it passes my lips. Yiddish, Hebrew go without saying."

"I'm looking for seventeen Shabazi Street but I don't see any numbers on the houses."

"I wish I had such eyes," remarked the falafel man. "To be able to see there are no numbers! And at this distance, too." He indicated a house with his nose. "Number seventeen is the poured-concrete Bauhaus blockhouse with the second-hand bookstore on the ground floor, right there, next to the tailor shop."

"Thanks."

"Thanks to you, too, Mister. Appreciate Israel."

The stunning dark-haired young woman behind the desk raised her imperturbable eyes when Jack pushed through the door into the bookstore. "I need help," he told the young woman.

"Everybody does," she retorted. "Not many come right out and admit it."

Jack looked fleetingly at the old man who was browsing through the English language books in the back, then turned to the woman. "I was led to believe I could find Ezra Ben Ezra at this address."

"Who told you that?"

"Ezra Ben Ezra, when I called him from the United States of America. You've heard of the United States of America, I suppose."

"You must be the Sorcerer's Apprentice."

"That's me."

The woman seemed to find this amusing. "At your age you should have become a full-fledged Sorcerer already. Remaining an apprentice your whole life must be humiliating. The Rabbi is expecting you." She hit a button under the desk. A segment of wall between two stands of shelves clicked open and Jack ducked through it. He climbed at long flight of narrow concrete steps that bypassed the first floor and took him directly to the top floor of the building. There he came across a crewcut young man in a dirty sweat suit strip cleaning an Uzi. The young man raised a wrist to his mouth and muttered something into it, then listened to the tinny reply coming through the small device planted in one of his ears. Behind him, still another door clicked open and Jack found himself in a large room with poured concrete walls and long narrow slits for windows. The Rabbi, looking a decade older than his sixty-one years, hobbled across the room with the help of a cane to greet Jack.

"Our paths crossed in Berlin," the Rabbi announced.

"I'm flattered you remember me," Jack said.

Ben Ezra pointed with his cane toward a leather-and-steel sofa and, with an effort, settled onto a straight-backed steel chair facing his visitor. "To tell you the terrible truth, I am not so great at faces any more but I never forget a favor I did for someone. You were running an East German code-named SNIPER, who turned out to be a professor of theoretical physics named Löffler. Ha, I can see by the expression on your face I hit the hammer on the head. Or should that be nail? Löffler finished badly, if my memory serves, which it does intermittently. His cutout, RAINBOW, too." He shook his head in despair. "Young people today forget that Berlin was a battleground."

"There were a lot of corpses on both sides of the Iron Curtain back then," Jack allowed. "When we met in Berlin you were dressed differently—"

Ben Ezra rolled his head from side to side. "Outside of Israel I dress ultra-religious—I wear ritual fringes, the works. It is a kind of disguise. Inside Israel I dress ultra-secular, which explains the business suit. Can I propose you a glass of freshly squeezed mango juice? A yoghurt maybe? Iced tea, with or without ice?"

"Tea, with, why not?"

"Why not?" Ben Ezra agreed. "Two teas, with," he hollered into the other room where several people could be seen sitting around a kitchen table. Behind them two tickertape machines chattered unrelentingly. The Rabbi focused on his American guest. "So what brings you to the Promised Land, Mr. Jack?"

"A hunch."

"That much I know already. The Sorcerer called me long-distance, charges reversed, to say that if I heard from someone claiming to be you, it was." The Rabbi produced a saintly smile. "Harvey and me, we cover each other's backsides. He said you had a tiger by the tail."

A dark-skinned Ethiopian girl, wearing a khaki miniskirt and a khaki Army sweater with a revealing V-neck, set two tall glasses of iced tea tinkling with ice cubes on the thick glass of the coffee table. A slice of fresh orange was embedded onto the rim of each glass. She said something in Hebrew and pointed to the delicate watch on her slim wrist. Ben Ezra scratched absently at the stubble of a beard on his chin. *"Lama lo?"* he told her. He pulled the slice of orange off of the glass and began sucking on it. "So you want to maybe tell the Rabbi what's bothering you?"

Jack wondered if Ben Ezra was recording the conversation. His career would come to a sudden stop if the Rabbi played the tape for Angleton, who had run the Mossad account for years and still had admirers here. The Rabbi saw him hesitating. "You are having second thoughts about sharing information. I am not indifferent to such scruples. If you would feel more comfortable taking a rain check on this conversation..."

In his mind's eye Jack could see Leo Kritzky scooping water out of the toilet bowl with a tin cup and deliberately drinking from it. He could hear the defiance in Leo's voice as he rasped, "Go fuck yourself, Jack." What the hell, he thought. I've come this far. And he began to walk the Rabbi through the circumstances surrounding the defection of Sergei Klimov (a.k.a. Sergei Kukushkin). "When Kukushkin was suddenly recalled to Moscow, we sent someone in to contact him—"

"Ah, I am beginning to see the handwriting on the wall," the Rabbi declared. "That explains what some crazy bones was doing in Moscow without diplomatic cover. Your someone was arrested, Klimov-Kukushkin was tried and executed, you swapped the Company arrestee for the NSA mole at the Glienicke *Brücke*." Ben Ezra pointed to the two glasses of iced tea. "We should drink up before they get warm." He raised one to his lips. *"L'chaim*—to life," he said and sipped noisily. "You think the trial and execution of this Klimov-Kukushkin could have been staged?"

"He wasn't polygraphed," Jack insisted.

"I am not sure how you think I can help."

"Look, Angleton is convinced Kukushkin was caught and tried and executed, which makes him genuine and his serials accurate. You people have assets in Russia that we only dream about. I thought you might take a second look. If Kukushkin was executed there ought to be a grave somewhere, there ought to be a grief-stricken wife and daughter scraping to make ends meet."

"If he was not executed, if the whole thing was theater, there ought to be a Klimov-Kukushkin out there somewhere."

"Exactly."

"Where in your opinion should one start one's inquiries?"

"Just before the two of them were arrested, Kukushkin told our guy he was living in a three-room apartment in a hotel reserved for transient KGB officers."

Wrinkled lids closed over the Rabbi's bulging eyes as he searched his memory. "That would be the Alekseevskaya behind the Lubyanka on Malenkaia Lubyanka Street. I suppose, correct me if I am wrong, you have brought with you photographs of this Klimov-Kukushkin and his wife and daughter."

Jack pulled an envelope from his breast pocket. "These are copies of the State Department forms filed by foreign diplomats when they arrive in Washington—I've thrown in several FBI telephoto mug shots for good measure. If your people came up with anything I would be very grateful."

Ben Ezra's eyes flicked open and focused intently on his visitor. "How grateful?"

"I've heard that one of the Nazis on the Mossad's ten most wanted list is Klaus Barbie—"

The Rabbi's voice came across as a wrathful growl now. "He was the Gestapo chief in Lyons during the war—many thousands of Jews, kiddies, women, old men, innocents every last one of them, were dragged off to the death camps because of him. The Butcher of Lyons, as he is known here, worked for the US Army in Germany after the war. He fled Europe one jump ahead of our agents—where we don't know. Yet."

"A file has passed through my hands...in it was the name of the Latin-American country where Barbie is believed to be living."

The Rabbi pushed down on his cane, levering himself to his feet. "You would not like to make a down payment for services certain to be rendered?" he inquired. "It is not as if your people and mine are strangers to each other."

Jack stood, too. "Barbie is in Bolivia."

Ben Ezra pulled an index card and a ballpoint pen from a pocket and offered them to Jack. "Write, please, a private phone number where I can reach you in Washington, Mr. Jack. We will for sure be in touch."

Sometime after midnight a frail, gray-haired woman wearing faded silk Uzbek leggings under her ankle-length skirt pushed the cleaning cart through the double doors into the lobby of the Hotel Alekseevskaya. She emptied the ash trays into a plastic bucket and wiped them clean with a damp cloth, rearranged the chairs around the coffee tables, replaced the dessert menus that were torn or stained, polished the mirrors hanging on the walls. Using a skeleton key attached to her belt, she opened a closet and took out the hotel's old Swedish Electrolux. Plugging it into a wall socket, she started vacuuming the threadbare carpets scattered around the lobby. Gradually she worked her way behind the check-in counter and began to vacuum the rugs there, too. The night porter, an elderly pensioner who worked the graveyard shift to supplement his monthly retirement check, always went to the toilet to sneak a cigarette while the Uzbek woman vacuumed behind the counter. Alone for several minutes, she left the Electrolux running and rummaged in the wooden "Mail to be forwarded" bin on one side of the switchboard. She found the small package easily; she'd been told it would be wrapped in brown paper and tied with a length of yellow cord. The package, which had been dropped off by a courier too late to be forwarded that day, was addressed to a recent resident, Elena Antonova Klimova, Hotel Alekseevskaya, Malenkaia Lubyanka Street, Moskva. At the bottom left of the package someone had written in ink: "*Pereshlite Adresatu*—please forward." The day clerk at the hotel's reception desk had crossed out "Hotel Alekseevskaya" and written in an address not far from the Cistyeprudnyi metro stop. The cleaning woman slipped the small package into her waistband and went back to vacuuming.

When she quit work at eight the next morning, she brought the package to the small used-clothing store on a side street off the Arbat run by the Orlev brothers. It was the older of the two, Mandel Orlev, dressed in the dark suit and dark raincoat associated with operatives of the KGB, who had delivered the package to the hotel the previous afternoon. Mandel, elated to discover that their scheme appeared to have worked, collected his briefcase and made his way to Cistyeprudnyi by metro and then on foot to the address written on the package. Taking a book from the briefcase, he sat reading for hours in the small neighborhood park separated by a low fence from the entrance to number 12 Ogorodnaia. A dozen people came and went but none of them resembled the description of Klimov-Kukushkin or his wife, Elena, or their daughter, Ludmilla. When it started to grow dark Mandel's brother, Baruch, relieved him and hung around until after ten, by which time he was too cold to remain any longer. The next day, and the day following, the two brothers spelled each other watching the entrance to number 12 Ogorodnaia. It wasn't until the morning of the fourth day that their patience was rewarded. A Zil driven by a chauffeur pulled up in front of the door and a man with long, vaguely blond hair and the heavy shoulders and thick body of a wrestler emerged from the back seat. He used a key to open the front door of the building and disappeared inside. Three quarters of an hour later he reappeared, followed by a short, heavy woman with close-cropped hair that was beginning to turn white. The two talked for a moment on the sidewalk until a slender girl of about eight came running out of the building behind them. The parents laughed happily.

In the park, Mandel Orlev positioned his battered briefcase and tripped the shutter of the West German Robot Star II camera hidden under the flap.

10

OUTSIDE, RAZOR-EDGED GUSTS CURLING OFF THE CHESAPEAKE flayed the trees, giant waves lashed the shoreline. From his room on the third floor of the private sanatorium, Leo Kritzky watched nature's riot through the storm window. His wife, Adelle, was brewing up a pot of coffee on the electric plate. "You look much better," she was saying as she cut the banana cake she'd baked and handed him a wedge. "The difference is night and day."

"No place to go but up," Leo said.

"You planning to tell me what happened?" she asked, her back toward him.

"We've been through all that," Leo said. "Can't."

Adelle turned to face Leo. She had suffered also, though nobody seemed much concerned about that. "The United States Congress passed the Freedom of Information Act over President Ford's veto today," she told him. Try as she might she couldn't keep the anger out of her voice. "Which means ordinary citizens can sue the CIA to get at your secrets. But my husband disappears for four months and one week and turns up looking like he survived the Bataan death march and nobody—not you, not the people who work with you—will tell me what's going on."

Leo said, "That's the way it has to be, Adelle."

From things Jack had said—and not said—Adelle had figured out that the Company had done this to Leo. "You can't let them get away with it," she whispered.

Leo stared out the window, wondering how trees could be pushed so far over and still not break. He had been pushed over, too; like the trees, he had not broken. There had been days when he'd been tempted to sign the confession that Angleton left on the table during the interrogations; the morning he discovered the dead body of the Sphinx of Siberia, he would have killed himself if he could have figured out how to do it.

It was one month to the day since Jack and Ebby had turned up in his padded cell, a doctor and a nurse in tow, to set him free. "You've been cleared, old buddy," Jack had said. His voice had choked with emotion. "Angleton, all of us, made a horrible mistake."

Tears had welled in Ebby's eyes and he had had to look away while the doctor examined Leo. His hair, or what was left of it, had turned a dirty white, his bruised eye sockets had receded into his skull, a scaly eczema covered his ankles and stomach.

"Where are we here—Gestapo headquarters?" the doctor had remarked as he was taking Leo's pulse. He had produced a salve for the eczema and a concoction of vitamins in a plastic container, which Leo began sipping through a straw. "What in God's name did you guys think you were doing?"

Leo had answered for them. "They were defending the Company from its enemies," he had said softly. "They only just discovered I wasn't one of them."

"We were led up the primrose path," Ebby had said miserably. "Somehow we have to make it up to you."

Leo had plucked at Jack's sleeve while they were waiting for the nurse to return with a wheelchair. "How'd you figure it out?" he had asked.

"You figured it out," Jack had said. "You predicted the walk-in would never be fluttered. He wasn't. The Russians pulled him back to Moscow on a pretext, just the way you said they would. Then they arrested him. There was a trial and an execution. Only it all turned out to be theater. We found out the walk-in was still among the living, which meant his serials were planted. For some reason they wanted Angleton to decide you were SASHA."

"Trying to throw him off the scent of the real SASHA," Leo had guessed.

"That's as good an explanation as I've heard," Jack had said.

"And Angleton? Does he admit—"

"His days are numbered. Colby is offering him a Chief of Station post to get him out of Washington. Angleton's hanging on to counterintelligence with his fingernails. He's mustering his troops but there aren't many of them left. Skinny is the Director's trying to work up the nerve to fire him."

"Not Angleton's fault," Leo had said.

Leo's lucidity had unnerved Ebby. "After what you've been through how can you, of all people—"

"Heard you say it more than once, Eb. If something's worth doing, worth doing badly. Can't run counterintelligence wearing kid gloves. It's a dirty job. Mistakes inevitable. Important not to be afraid of making them." Leo had been helped to his feet by Jack and Ebby. Before allowing himself to be taken from the room, he had shuffled over to the toilet and reached down behind the pipes to recover the corpse of the moth he had hidden there. "If only you'd held out a bit longer," he had whispered, "you would have been set free."

Now, in the third-floor room of the private sanatorium, Adelle filled two cups with steaming coffee. She gave one to Leo at the window and pulled over a chair to sit next to him. "I wasn't going to hit you over the head until you'd had a chance to mend," she said. "But I think we have to talk about it—"

"Talk about what?"

"Your attitude. Jack let slip that the legal people came by to offer you a package settlement."

"Jack ought to learn to keep his lips buttoned."

"He and the others—they're all kind of awed by your attitude. You seem to have waived any claim to compensation."

"In any combat situation soldiers are wounded or killed by friendly fire all the time. I've never heard of any of them suing the government."

"There's no war on, Leo—"

"Dead wrong, Adelle. You were close enough to Lyndon Johnson to know there's a hell of a war raging out there. I was wounded by friendly fire. As soon as I'm well enough I plan to return to the battle."

Adelle shook her head incredulously. "After what you've been through—after what *they* put you through—after what I and the girls have been through!—you still refuse to quit the Company." She gazed out the window. After a while she said, "We honeymooned not far from here."

Leo nodded slowly. "We watched the sun rising over Chesapeake Bay..."

"Our life together began with two deaths—your dog and my cat. And then we turned our backs on death and went forward toward life." She started to choke up. "Everything happening at once...my father dying...you disappearing without a trace. I couldn't sleep, Leo...I stayed up nights wondering if you were alive, wondering if I'd ever see you again. All those nights, all those weeks, I felt that death was right behind me, looking over my shoulder. It can't go on like this, Leo. You have to choose—"

"Adelle, this conversation is a terrible mistake. You're too emotional. Give it time—"

"You can only have one of us, Leo—the Company or me."

"Please don't do this."

"I've made up my mind," she announced. "I tried to bring up the subject several times before you disappeared for four months. With you recovering in this clinic, I was only waiting for the right moment."

"There is no right moment for such conversations."

"That's true enough. So here we are, Leo. And I'm asking you the wrong question at the wrong moment. But I'm still asking. Which will it be?"

"I'll never quit the Company. It's what I do for a living, and what I do best—protecting America from its enemies."

"I loved you, Leo."

He noticed the past tense. "I still love you."

"You don't love me. Or if you do, you love other things more." She stood up. "You can keep the house—I'll move into Daddy's. If you have a change of heart..."

"My heart won't change—it's still with you, Adelle. With you and with the girls."

"But you've got this zealot's head on your shoulders and it overrules your heart—that's it, isn't it, Leo?" She collected her duffle coat from the foot of the bed and headed for the door. She looked back at the threshold to see if he would say something to stop her. They eyed each other across the chasm that separated them. Behind Leo nature's riot whipped angrily at the panes of the storm window. Flicking tears away with a knuckle, Adelle turned on a heel and walked out of her twenty-three year marriage.

Nellie, looking radiant in a flaming-orange body-hugging knee-length dress with long sleeves and a high collar, clung to Manny's arm as the Justice of the Peace carefully moistened the official seal with his breath, and then stamped and signed the marriage certificate. "Reckon that 'bout does it," he announced. "Never could figure out at which point in the ceremony you're actually hitched but you sure as shootin' are now. You want to put the certificate into one of these leather frames, it'll run you ten dollars extra."

"Sure, we'll take the frame," Manny said.

Nellie turned to her mother and Ebby, who were standing behind them. "So the dirty deed is done," she told them with a giggle.

Jack, Millie, and their son, Anthony, came up to congratulate the newly-weds. Half a dozen of Manny's friends from the Soviet Division, along with their wives or girl friends, crowded around. Leo, on a day's furlough from the private sanatorium, waited his turn, then kissed the bride and shook Manny's hand. He nodded at them and it took a moment or two before he could find words. "I wish you both a long and happy life together," he said softly.

Elizabet called out, "Everyone's invited back to our place for Champagne and caviar."

"I'm going to get high on Champagne," Anthony announced.

"No, you're not, young man," Jack said.

Anthony, showing off for his godfather, persisted, "Don't tell me you never got drunk when you were a teenager."

"What I did when I was fourteen and what you do when you're fourteen are two different kettles of fish," Jack informed his son.

Elizabet handed out sachets of birdseed (on the instructions of Nellie, who had heard that rice swelled in the stomachs of birds and killed them), and the guests bombarded the newlyweds as they emerged from the front door. The wedding guests brought around their cars and, horns honking, followed Manny's Pontiac with the empty beer cans trailing from the rear bumper back toward Ebby's house. In the last car, Anthony eyed his godfather's white hair, which had grown back into a stubbly crew cut. "Dad says you've been through the ringer, Leo," the boy said. "How much can you tell me?"

Leo, concentrating on the road, said, "Jack's already told you more than I would have,"

"I don't have a need to know, right?"

"You're making progress, Anthony."

"Yeah, well, as I plan to make the CIA my life's work I've got to learn the ropes early." He watched Leo drive for a while, then said, "There are four or five of us at my school who have parents working at Langley. Sometimes we get together after school and trade information. Naturally, we make sure nobody can overhear us—"

With a straight face, Leo asked, "Do you sweep the room for microphones?"

Anthony was taken aback. "You think we ought to?"

"I wouldn't put it past the KGB—bug the kids in order to find out what the parents are up to."

"Do you guys do that in Moscow with the kids of KGB people?" Anthony waved a hand. "Hey, sorry. I don't have a need to know. So I take back the question."

"What did you find out at these bull sessions of yours?"

"We read about Manny being traded for the low-level Russian spy in the papers, so we kicked that around for a while. One kid whose dad forges signatures said he'd overheard his father telling his mother that the Russian spy was much more important than the CIA let on. A girl whose mother works as a secretary on the seventh floor told her husband that a task force had been set up to deal with something that was so secret they stamped all their paperwork NODIS, which means no distribution whatsoever except to the Director Central Intelligence and a designated list of deputies."

Leo said, "I know what NODIS means, Anthony." When he returned to Langley he would have to circulate a toughly worded all-hands memorandum warning Soviet Division officers not to talk shop at home. "What else did your group discuss?"

"What else? A girl I know's father who is a lie detector specialist said that someone code-named Mother had called him in to polygraph a high-ranking CIA officer who was being held in a secret—"

Suddenly Anthony's mouth opened and his face flushed with embarrassment.

"Held in a secret what?"

Anthony went on in an undertone. "In a secret cell somewhere in Washington."

"And?"

"And the person's hair had become white as snow and started to fall out in clumps—"

A stoplight on the avenue ahead turned red. The car in front ran it but Leo pulled up. He looked at his godson. "Welcome to the frontier that separates childhood from adulthood. If you really plan on joining the CIA some day, this is the moment to cross that frontier. Right here, right now. The problem with secrets is that they're hard to keep. People let them slip out so that others will be impressed by how much they know. Learn to keep the secrets, Anthony, and you might actually have a shot at a CIA job. We're not playing games at Langley. What you've figured out—nobody has a need to know."

Anthony nodded solemnly. "My lips are sealed, Leo. Nobody will hear it from me. I swear it."

"Good."

Ebby and Elizabet were handing out long-stemmed glasses filled with Champagne when Leo and Anthony finally arrived. Leo helped himself to a glass and handed a second one to Anthony. Jack said, "Hey, Leo, he's only a kid—he shouldn't be drinking."

"He was a kid when he started out this afternoon," Leo replied. "On the way here he crossed the line into manhood."

"To the bride and groom," Ebby said, raising his glass.

"To the bride and groom," everyone repeated in chorus.

Leo clicked glasses with Anthony. The boy nodded and the two of them sipped Champagne.

Later, as Manny was struggling to open another bottle, Ebby came back downstairs from his den. He was carrying a small package wrapped in plain brown paper, which he handed to his son. "This is my wedding present to you," he told him. With everyone looking on, Manny tore the paper off the package to reveal a beautifully crafted mahogany box that Ebby had had made to order years before. Manny opened the box. Fitted into the red felt was a British Webley Mark VI revolver with "1915" engraved in the polished wood of the grip. Manny knew the story of the weapon—it was the revolver that the young Albanians had presented to Ebby before they set off on their fatal mission to Tiranë. He hefted the weapon, then looked up at his father. Watching from the side, Elizabet brought the back of a fist to her mouth.

"Consider this a sort of passing of the torch," Ebby said.

Manny said, "Thanks, Dad. I know what this gun means to you. I will never forget where you got it. And I will always be true to it."

Anthony whispered to Leo, "Where did he get the gun, Leo?" He spotted the knowing smile on his godfather lips and smiled back. "Hey, forget I asked, huh?"

Leo drove down Dolly Madison Boulevard in McLean, Virginia, past the "CIA Next Right" sign that was swiped so often by souvenir hunters the Company ordered replacements by the dozen, and turned off at the next intersection. Braking to a stop at the gatehouse, he rolled down the window and showed the laminated card identifying him as a CIA officer to one of the armed guards. (Leo's appearance had altered so drastically that Jack had taken the precaution of providing him with new ID bearing a more recent photograph.) Driving slowly down the access road, he saw the statue of Nathan Hale (put there on the initiative of Director Colby) outside the front entrance as he pulled around to the ramp leading to the basement garage reserved for division heads and higher. Leo reached for his laminated card but the guard manning the control booth waved to indicate he recognized the Soviet Division chief. "Glad to see you back, Mr. Kritzky," he called over the loudspeaker. "The Director asked for you to come straight on up to his office when you got in."

Waiting for the Director's private elevator to descend, Leo could hear the secret printing press humming in a room at the back of the garage; at the height of the Cold War it had worked twenty hours a day turning out birth certificates, foreign passports and driver's licenses, along with bogus copies of newspapers and propaganda handbills. When the doors opened, Leo stepped in and hit the only button on the stainless steel panel, starting the elevator up toward the Director's seventh floor suite of offices. His head was bowed in thought as the elevator slowed. He was a bit nervous about what he'd find on this first day back on the job. Jack had filled him in on the storm brewing over Angleton's HT/LINGUAL mail opening operation; a *New York Times* reporter named Seymour Hersh had gotten wind of the illegal project, which had been running for twenty years before Colby finally closed it down in 1973, and was going to break the story any day now. Everyone topside was bracing for the explosion and the inevitable fallout.

The elevator doors slid open. Leo heard a ripple of applause and raised his eyes and realized that he had walked into a surprise party. Colby, Ebby and Jack stood in front of half a hundred or so staffers, including many from Leo's own Soviet Division. Jack's wife and Manny were off to one side, applauding with the others and smiling. Few of those present knew where Leo had been, but they only had to catch a glimpse of the reed of a man coming off the elevator to realize that he had returned from a hell on earth. He had lost so much weight that his shirt and suit were swimming on him. Shaken, Leo looked around in bewilderment. He spotted dozens of familiar faces—but Jim Angleton's was not among them. Leo's personal secretary and several of the women from the Soviet Division had tears in their eyes. The Director stepped forward and pumped his hand. The applause died away. "On behalf of my colleagues, I want to take this opportunity to welcome back one of our own," Colby said. "Leo Kritzky's devotion to duty, his loyalty to the Company, his grace under fire, have set a high standard for us and for future generations of CIA officers. It is in the nature of things that only a handful here are aware of the details of your ordeal. But all of us"—the Director waved an arm to take in the crowd—"owe you a debt of gratitude."

There was another ripple of applause. When the crowd had quieted down Leo spoke into the silence. His voice was husky and low and people had to strain to hear him. "When I came aboard what we used to call Cockroach Alley, some twenty-four years ago, it was with the intention of serving the country whose system of governance seemed to offer the best hope to the world. As a young man I imagined that this service would take the form of initiating or becoming involved in dramatic feats of espionage or counterespionage. I have since come to understand that there are other ways of serving, no less important than reporting to the trenches of the espionage war. As the poet John Milton said, 'They also serve who only stand and wait.' Director, I appreciate the welcome. Now I think I'd like to get back to my division and my desk, and get on with the tedious day-to-day business of winning the Cold War."

There was more applause. The Director nodded. People drifted away. Finally only Jack and Ebby remained. Ebby stood there shaking his head in admiration. Jack opened his mouth to say something, thought better of it and raised a finger in salute. He and Ebby headed back toward the DD/O's shop on the seventh floor.

Leo took a deep breath. He was home again, and relieved to be.

Angleton was on the carpet, figuratively as well as literally. "What did you tell this Hersh fellow?" he demanded.

Colby had come around the side of his enormous desk and the two men, standing toe to toe, confronted each other. "I told him HT/LINGUAL was a counterintelligence program targeting the foreign contacts of American dissidents, that it had been fully authorized by the President, that in any case the whole mail-opening program had been terminated."

Angleton said bitterly, "In other words you confirmed that we opened mail."

"I didn't need to confirm it," Colby said. "Hersh knew it already."

"He didn't know it was a counterintelligence program," Angleton snapped. "You pointed the finger at me."

"Correct me if I'm wrong, Jim, but HT/LINGUAL was *your* brainchild. Your people opened the envelopes. Your people indexed the names of three hundred thousand Americans who sent or received mail from the Soviet Union over a period of twenty years."

"We had reason to believe the KGB was using ordinary mail channels to communicate with their agents in America. We would have been chumps to let them get away with this because of some silly laws—"

Colby turned away. "These *silly* laws, as you call them, are what we're defending, Jim."

Angleton patted his pockets, hunting for cigarettes. He found one and jammed it between his lips but was too distracted to light up. "It is inconceivable that a secret intelligence arm of the government has to comply with all the overt orders of that government."

Colby peered out a window at the Virginia countryside. A thin haze seemed to rise off the fields. From the seventh floor of Langley it looked as if the earth were smoldering. "Let's be clear, Jim. The role of counterintelligence is to initiate penetrations into the Russian intelligence services and to debrief defectors. As for uncovering Soviet penetrations within the CIA, well, we have the entire Office of Security to protect us. That's their job.

Now, how many operations are you running against the Soviets? I never heard of a single one. You sit in that office of yours and, with the exception of Kukushkin, shoot down every single Soviet defector who is recruited by luck or good intelligence work. And the one you don't shoot down turns out to be a dispatched agent dangling false serials. The situation is quite impossible." Colby turned back to face Angleton. "The *Times* is running the Hersh story on your domestic spying operation the day after tomorrow. This is going to be tough to handle. We've talked about your leaving before. You will now leave, period."

Angleton snatched the unlit cigarette from between his bloodless lips. "Am I to understand that you are firing me, Director?"

"Let's just say that I'm retiring you."

Angleton started toward the door, then turned back. His lips moved but no sounds emerged. Finally he managed, "Philby and the KGB have been trying to destroy me for years—you're serving as their instrument."

"Counterintelligence will still exist, Jim."

"You're making a tragic mistake if you think anybody else can do what I do. To *begin* to thread your way through the counterintelligence quagmire, you need eleven years of continuous study of old cases. Not ten years, not twelve but precisely *eleven*. And even that would make you only a journeyman counterintelligence analyst."

Colby returned to his desk. "We'll do our best to muddle through without you, Jim. Thanks for stopping by on such short notice."

The Deputy Director/Intelligence and his second-in-command, the Deputy Director/Operations (Ebby) and his Chief of Operations (Jack), the various area division chiefs, Angleton representing counterintelligence, along with senior representatives from the Office of Security, the Office of Technical Services and the Political Psychological Division had crowded into the small conference room across from the DCI's office for the regular Friday nine o'clock *tour de horizon*. The deputy head of the Political Psychological Division, a dead pipe clenched in his jaws, was winding up a thumbnail portrait of the Libyan dictator Muammar Al-Qaddafi, who had recently pushed world crude prices up by cutting back on oil exports. "Popular belief to the contrary not withstanding," he was saying, "Qaddafi is certainly not psychotic, and for the most part is in touch with reality. He has what we would call a borderline personality disorder, which means that the subject behaves crazily one day and rationally the next."

"Strikes me as a fairly accurate description of some of us," the Director quipped, drawing a chuckle from the troops around the table.

"If the KGB has a psychological division, that's exactly how they would have diagnosed Nixon when he invaded Cambodia in 1970," remarked Leo, who was sitting in on his first regular topside session since his return to Langley.

"Seems to me that this is precisely the kind of personality a leader needs to project," Ebby pointed out. "That way the opposition can't count on being able to predict what he'll do in any given situation."

Jack said, "The question is: Are the Qaddafis and the Nixons suffering from borderline personality disorders—or just trying to convince each other that they are?"

The Director, presiding from the head of the table, glanced at his watch. "We'll put that intriguing question on a back burner for now. I have one more matter to raise before we break up. I want to announce, to my great regret, the retirement of Jim Angleton here. I don't need to tell anyone in this room that his contributions to the Company in general, and counterintelligence in particular, are nothing short of legendary. His service to the United States, which goes back to his days at Ryder Street in London during the war, are a matter of record. I accepted Jim's resignation with deep regret. But he's an old warhorse and if anyone deserves a pasture, he does."

Colby's announcement was greeted with stunned silence; an earthquake under the foundations of Langley wouldn't have shaken the people gathered around the table more. Ebby and Jack studiously avoided looking at each other. Several of the Barons couldn't resist glancing at Leo Kritzky, who was staring out a window, lost in thought. The Director smiled across the table at the chief of counterintelligence. "Would you care to say a word, Jim?" he asked.

Angleton, a lonely and skeletal figure of a man at the bitter end of a long and illustrious career, slowly pushed himself to his feet. He raised one palm to his forehead to deal with the migraine lurking behind his eyes. "Some of you have heard my *Nature of the threat* presentation before. For those who haven't I can think of no more appropriate swan song." Angleton cleared his throat. "Lenin once remarked to Feliks Dzerzhinsky: 'The West are wishful thinkers, so we will give them what they want to think.'" Avoiding eye contact with the Company Barons around the table, Angleton droned on. "When I worked at Ryder Street," he said, "I learned that the key to playing back captured German agents was orchestration—where layer upon layer of confirming disinformation supports the deception. This is what the Soviets have been doing for years—as part of a master plan they've been feeding layer upon layer of mutually reinforcing disinformation to the wishful thinkers in the West. They achieve this through the sophisticated use of interlocking agents-in-place and dispatched defectors. I have determined that the British Labor leader Hugh Gaitskell, who died in 1963 of *lupus disseminata*, was murdered by KGB wetwork specialists. They employed the Lupus virus as an assassination weapon so that Moscow could insert its man, Harold Wilson, into the top Labor post and position him to become Prime Minister, which is the job he holds today. Wilson, who made many trips to the Soviet Union before becoming Prime Minister, is a paid agent of the KGB. Olaf Palme, the current Swedish Prime Minister, is a Soviet asset recruited during a visit to Latvia. Willy Brandt, the current West German chancellor, is a KGB agent. Lester Pearson, the Canadian Prime Minister until two years ago, is a KGB agent. Roger Hollis, the head of MI5, is a longtime Soviet agent. Averell Harriman, the former ambassador to the USSR and the former governor of New York State, has been a Soviet agent since the 1930s. Henry Kissinger, the National Security Adviser and Secretary of State under Nixon, is objectively a Soviet agent. What these agents-in-place have in common is that they all advocate and defend, which is to say *orchestrate*, the Soviet strategy of détente. Make no mistake about it, gentlemen, détente, along with such Soviet-inspired chimera as the Sino-Soviet split, the Yugoslav or Rumanian deviations, the Albanian defection, the Italian Communist Party's presumed independence from Moscow, are part of a master disinformation scheme designed to destabilize the West, to lure us into thinking that the Cold War has been won."

Several of the Barons around the table glanced uneasily at the Director. Colby, who had anticipated a short valedictory, didn't have the heart to interrupt Angleton.

"Dubček's so-called Prague Spring," Angleton plunged on, "was part of this disinformation campaign; the 1968 Soviet invasion of Czechoslovakia was worked out by Brezhnev and Dubček in advance. The differences between Moscow and the so-called Euro-Communists in Western Europe are phony, part of the KGB Disinformation Department's global theater." The counterintelligence chief scoured his bone-dry lips with the back of a hand. "If the facts I have outlined have been questioned at the highest level within our own intelligence organization, it can be said that this is the handiwork of the Soviet mole inside the CIA code named SASHA, who has twisted the evidence and caused many in this room to overlook the obvious menace. Which brings me to the greatest Soviet plot of all—one designed to ravage the economies of the Western industrial nations, bringing on civil unrest that will ultimately result in the triumph of the Moscow-oriented left in national elections. I have determined that the mastermind of this long-term KGB plot is none other than the almost mythical controlling officer who directed the activities of Adrian Philby, and today directs the activities of SASHA. He is known only as Starik—in Russian, the Old Man. The plot he has been concocting for at least the last ten years, and possibly longer, involves siphoning off hard currency from the sale of Soviet gas and oil and armaments abroad, and laundering these sums in various off-shore banking institutions against the day when he will use the vast sum that he has accumulated to attack the dollar. Ha, don't suppose that I can't see your reactions—you think this is far-fetched." Angleton's eyelids began to flutter. "I have discovered that the Patriarch of Venice, Cardinal Albino Luciani, is investigating reports that the Vatican Bank has been receiving mysterious deposits and sending the money on to a variety of off-shore accounts. The money-laundering operation bears the Russian code name KHOLSTOMER. The English equivalent is STRIDER—it's the nickname of the piebald gelding in Tolstoy's 'Strider: The Story of a Horse.'"

Shaking himself out of a near-trance, Angleton opened his eyes and began to speak more rapidly, as if he were running out of time. "Obviously these serials—Gaitskell, Wilson, Palme, Brandt, Pearson, Hollis, Harriman, Kissinger, Starik, KHOLSTOMER—weren't handed to me on a silver platter. Far from it. I teased them out of the wilderness of mirrors during thousands of hours of painstaking attention to the minutiae that nobody else bothers with. The process, like the art of fly-fishing, requires infinite patience. Oh, some people would have you think that all you have to do is go out there and toss a fly onto the river and you'll wind up with a trout. But it's not that way at all, gentlemen. You can take my word for it. The first thing you have to do if you want to catch the mythical brown giant of a trout that swims the upper reaches of the Brule is to observe what the fish are feeding on." Angleton was leaning over the table now, eager to share his professional secrets with his colleagues. "You catch a small trout, you slit it open, you empty the contents of the stomach into a celluloid cup. And when you see what it's been feeding on, you fashion a fly that resembles it. You can give the *illusion* of a real fly with the coloring of your hackle and wings and all the feathers you put on it. And it will float down the river with its hackles cupped up, and if you do it correctly, the trout really believes that it is a fly. And that, gentlemen," he announced triumphantly, "is how you get a strike..."

The Director stood up and said, very quietly, "Thank you, Jim."

Looking preoccupied, Colby turned and walked out of the room. One by one the others followed him until only Leo and Angleton were left.

"I know it's you," Angleton murmured. His brow was pleated in pain. "I see the whole thing clearly now—you really are SASHA. Kukushkin was sent over by Starik to feed me serials that would lead me to you because he knew it was only a matter of time before I teased your identity out of the wilderness. Then Starik organized the mock trial and execution knowing we would walk back the cat and discover that Kukushkin was still alive. Which would free you and undermine my credibility. The whole thing was a KGB plot to ruin me before I could identify SASHA...before I could expose KHOLSTOMER."

Leo scraped back his chair and rose. "I bear you no hard feelings, Jim. Good luck to you."

As Leo walked out the door, Angleton was still talking to himself. "The trick, you see, is to cast as far as you can and let the fly float back down stream with its hackles cupped up, and from time to time you give it a little twitch"—his wrist flicked an imaginary rod—"so that it dances on the surface of the water. And if you are subtle enough and deft enough, above all if you don't rush things, why, the son of a gun will snap at it and you'll have your trout roasting on the spit for supper..."

His voice faded as he settled heavily into the chair and braced himself for the lesser pain of the inevitable migraine.

The red bulb burning in the darkroom had turned Starik's skin fluorescent—for an instant he had the eerie feeling that his hands resembled those on the embalmed corpse of Lenin in the mausoleum on Red Square. Under Starik's lucent fingers, details began to emerge on the twelve-by-fifteen black-and-white print submerged in the shallow pan filled with developer. Using a pair of wooden tongs, he pulled the paper out of the bath and held it up to the red light. It was underexposed, too washed out; the details that he had hoped to capture were barely visible.

Developing the film and printing enlargements had calmed Starik down. He had returned from the showdown in the Kremlin in a rage, and had actually spanked one of the nieces on her bare bottom for the minor transgression of wearing lipstick. (He had fired the maid who had given it to her.) Leonid Ilyich Brezhnev, the First Secretary of the Communist Party and the rising star in the Soviet hierarchy, had lost his nerve, and no amount of persuasion could induce him change his mind. Starik had first briefed Brezhnev on KHOLSTOMER the year before. The First Secretary had been impressed with the meticulous planning that had gone into the project over a twenty-year period; impressed also by the fact that sizable sums of hard currency had been squirreled away with infinite patience and in relatively small doses so as not to attract the attention of the Western intelligence services. The potential of KHOLSTOMER had staggered Brezhnev, who suddenly saw himself presiding over the demise of the bourgeois capitalist democracies and the triumph of Soviet Socialism across the globe. The history books would elevate him to a position alongside Marx and Lenin; Brezhnev would be seen as the Russian ruler who led the Soviet Union to victory in the Cold War.

All of which made his current reticence harder to fathom. Starik had gotten approval for the project from his immediate superior, KGB Chairman Yuri Andropov, as well as the Committee of Three, the secret Politburo panel that vetted intelligence initiatives, then gone to the Kremlin to clear the final hurdle. He had argued his case to Brezhnev with cool passion. American inflation was soaring and consumers were feeling the pinch: sugar, for instance, had doubled to thirty-two cents a pound. The Dow Jones industrial average had plummeted to 570, down from 1003 two years earlier. The hike in crude oil prices after the 1973 Middle East war (to $11.25 a barrel, up from $2.50 at the beginning of that year) made the American economy particularly fragile; an attack on the dollar stood a good chance of accelerating the crisis and throwing the economy into a recessionary spiral from which it would never recover. On top of everything, the single American who might have exposed Soviet intentions had been discredited and sent into retirement. Conditions for launching KHOLSTOMER couldn't be more propitious.

Tucked into a wicker wheelchair with a blanket drawn up to his armpits and a small electric heater directed at his feet, wearing a fur-lined silk dressing gown buttoned up to the neck, Brezhnev had heard Starik out and then had slowly shaken his massive head. Khrushchev had attempted to destabilize the Americans when he installed medium-range missiles in Cuba, the First Secretary had reminded his visitor. Starik knew as well as he did how that episode had ended. John Kennedy had gone to the brink of war and a humiliated Khrushchev had been forced to withdraw the missiles. The Politburo—Brezhnev in the forefront—had drawn the appropriate conclusions and, two years later, had packed Khrushchev off into forced retirement.

Brezhnev had kicked aside the electric heater and had wheeled himself out from behind his vast desk equipped with seven telephones and a bulky English dictaphone. His bushy eyebrows arched in concentration, his jowls sagging in anxiety, he had informed Starik that he didn't intend to end up like

Khrushchev. He had given KHOLSTOMER his careful consideration and had become convinced that an economically weakened America would react to an attack on the dollar like a cornered cat, which is to say that Washington would provoke a war with the Soviet Union in order to save the American economy. Don't forget, he had lectured Starik, it was the Great War that had saved the American economy from the Great Depression that followed the stock market crash of 1929. When the economy needed boosting, so the Kremlin's Americanologists argued, the capitalists invariably turned to war.

Brezhnev had not closed the door entirely on KHOLSTOMER. Perhaps in five or seven years, when the Soviet Union had built up its second strike capacity to the point where it could deter an American first strike, he would be willing to take another look at the project. In any case it was a good card to keep up his sleeve, if only to prevent the Americans from one day attacking the Soviet economy in a similar way.

Now, in his attic photography shop at Apatov Mansion in Cheryomuski, Starik set the timer on the Czech enlarger to seven seconds, then exposed the photographic paper and slipped it into the pan filled with developer. After a while details began to emerge. First came the nostrils, then the eye sockets and oral cavities, finally the rosebud-like nipples on the flat chests of the bony klieg-scrubbed bodies. Using wooden tongs, Starik extracted the print from the bath and slipped it into a pan of fixative. Studying the washed-out enlargement, he decided that he was reasonably pleased with the finished product.

In a curious way photography had a lot in common with intelligence operations. The trick with both was to visualize the picture before you took it, then attempt to come as close as possible to what had been in your imagination. To succeed required endless patience. Starik consoled himself with the notion that his patience would pay off when it came to KHOL-STOMER, too. Brezhnev wouldn't be around forever. He had suffered a series of mild strokes earlier in the year (caused, according to a secret KGB report, by arteriosclerosis of the brain) that left him incapacitated for weeks on end. Since then an ambulance manned by doctors who specialized in resuscitation accompanied him everywhere. Andropov, who had been head of the KGB since 1967 and a member of the Politburo since 1973, had already confided to Starik that he saw himself as Brezhnev's logical successor. And Andropov was an ardent champion of KHOLSTOMER.

The first December blizzard was howling outside the storm windows when Starik settled onto the great bed that night to read the nieces their bedtime story. Electricity cables, heavy with ice, had sagged to the ground, cutting all power to the Apatov Mansion. A single candle burned on the night table. Angling the frayed page toward the flickering light, Starik came to the end of another chapter.

"Alice ran a little way into the wood, and stopped under a large tree. 'It can never get at me here,' she thought: 'it's far too large to squeeze itself in among the trees. But I wish it wouldn't flap its wings so—it makes quite a hurricane in the wood.'"

The nieces, snuggling together in a tangle of limbs, sighed as if with one voice. "Oh, do read us a tiny bit more," begged Revolución.

"Yes, uncle, you must because we are too frightened by what was chasing Alice to fall asleep," Axinya insisted.

"If you will not read to us," pleaded the angelic blonde Circassian who had been spanked for wearing lipstick, "at least remain for a long while with us."

Starik moved to get up from the bed. "I am afraid I still have files to read," he said.

"Stay, stay, oh, do stay," the girls cried altogether. And they clutched playfully at the hem of his nightshirt.

Smiling, Starik tore himself free. "To become drowsy, girlies, you must plunge deeper into the wonder of Alice's Wonderland."

"How in the world can we do that if you will not read to us?" Revolución inquired.

"It is not terribly difficult," Starik assured them. He leaned over the night table and blew out the candle, pitching the room into utter darkness. "Now you must try, all of you, each in her own imagination, to fancy what the flame of a candle would look like after the candle is blown out."

"Oh, I can see it!" exclaimed the blonde Circassian.

"It is ever so pretty," Revolución agreed, "drifting across the mind's eye."

"The flame after the candle is blown out looks awfully like the light of a distant star with planets circling around it," Axinya said dreamily. "One of the planets is a wonderland where little nieces eat looking-glass cakes and remember things that happened the week after next."

"Oh, let's do go there quickly," Revolución cried eagerly.

"Only close your eyes, girlies," Starik said gruffly, "and you will be on your way to Alice's planet."

THE CALABRIAN

Alice thought with a shudder, "I wouldn't have been the messenger for anything!"

A T 6:40 A.M., UNDER A BLEAK SKY, SAILORS ON THE FIVE-THOUSAND-ton *Vladimir Ilyich* singled up all lines and cast off from the pier. The moment the ship was no longer attached to land, a whistle sounded. The deckhand standing at the stern pole lowered the Soviet flag as a signalman raised another on a halyard. An Italian tug pulled the bow out and cast off the hawser, and the freighter, loaded with a cargo of Fiat engines, heavy lathes and refrigerators, slipped out on the morning tide toward the open sea. On the flying bridge, atop the wheel house, a reed-like figure with a wispy white beard watched as the Italian coast transformed itself into a faint smudge on the horizon. Starik had been up since midnight, drinking endless cups of instant espresso in the dockside warehouse as he waited for the messenger to bring word that the threat to KHOLSTOMER had been eliminated. Seventeen minutes after three, a dirty yellow Fiat minicab had drawn up before the side door. The Calabrian, walking with a perceptible limp, had come into the room. A man of few words, he had nodded at Starik and had said, *"La cosa e fatta."* Starik's niece, a wafer-thin half-Italian, half-Serbian creature called Maria-Jesus, had translated into Russian. "He tells you," she said, thrilled to be useful to Uncle, "the thing is done."

From the deep pockets of a Dominican cassock, the Calabrian retrieved the small metal kit with the syringe, the tumbler with traces of doped milk, the phial that had contained uncontaminated milk, the surgeon's gloves and the lock-pick, and set them on a table. Then he handed the Russian a brown dossier with the words KHOLSTOMER printed in Roman letters on the cover. Starik motioned with a finger and the girl handed the Calabrian a sailor's canvas duffle bag containing $1 million in used bills of various denominations. The Calabrian opened the flaps and fingered the packets of bills, each bound by a thick rubber band. "If you again need my services," he said, "you will know how to find me."

Standing in the wheel house of the *Vladimir Ilyich* at first light, Starik had watched as the Master worked his way down the checklist for getting underway. The engine room telegraph was tested. The rudder was swung from port to starboard and back to midships. Sailors posted at the windlass phoned up to the bridge to say they were ready to trip the riding pawls and let go the anchors if an emergency arose. Deckhands in black turtleneck sweaters and oilskins prepared to single up the heavy lines dipped onto the bollards and retrieve the fenders.

While these preparations were going on, a small fishing boat fitted with powerful diesel engines quit a nearby quay. Once clear of the breakwater it turned due south in the direction of Palermo. Both the Calabrian and his Corsican taxi driver with the broken, badly set nose were on board. Peering through binoculars, Starik spotted them standing on the well deck; one was cupping the flame of a match so that the other could light a cigarette. Over the radio speaker in the pilothouse, a program of early morning Venetian mandolin music was interrupted for an important announcement. Maria-Jesus provided a running translation. There were reports, so far unconfirmed, that Pope John Paul I, known as Albino Luciani when he was the Patriarch of Venice, had suffered a cardio-something attack during the night. The last rites of the church had been administered, leading some to speculate that the Pope, after a reign of only thirty-four days, was either dead or near death. Cardinals were said to be rushing to the Vatican from all over Italy. When the regular program resumed, the station switched to solemn funereal music. As the lines were being singled up on the *Vladimir Ilyich*, Starik raised the binoculars to his eyes again. The fishing boat was hull down already; only the lights on its mast and tackle were visible. Suddenly there was a muffled explosion, no louder than a distant motor coughing before it caught. Through the binoculars Starik could see the mast and tackle tilt crazily to one side, and then disappear altogether.

Filling his lungs with sea air, Starik fondled the back of Maria-Jesus's long neck. He craved one of his Bulgarian cigarettes; on the advice of a Centre doctor he had recently given up smoking. He comforted himself with the thought that there were other pleasures to be taken from life. Like Alice, he had run fast enough to stay in the same place; the messenger had been buried at sea and the Pope, who had made no secret of his intention to crack down on the money-laundering activities of the Vatican bank, would take the secrets of KHOLSTOMER with him to the grave. And in five days time Starik would be home with his adopted nieces, reading to them from the fable that taught the importance of believing six impossible things after breakfast.

PART FIVE

BLIND ALLEY

"Look, look!" Alice cried, pointing eagerly.
"There's the White Queen running across the country!
She came flying out of the wood over yonder—
How fast those Queens can run!"
"There's some enemy after her, no doubt," the
King said, without even looking round.
"That wood's full of them."

Snapshot: the amateur black-and-white photograph, which made front pages around the world, shows the two American hostages being held somewhere in Afghanistan by Commander Ibrahim, the legendary leader of the fundamentalist splinter group Islamic Jihad. The young woman, the well-known television journalist Maria Shaath, regards her captors with an impatient smile; one of her producers in New York said she looked as if she were worried about missing a deadline. Standing next to her, his back to a poster of the Golden Dome Mosque in Jerusalem, is the young American whom Islamic Jihad identified as a CIA officer and the US government insists is an attaché assigned to the American consulate in Peshawar, Pakistan. The American stares into the camera with a detached, sardonic grin. Both prisoners appear pale and tired from their weeks in captivity.

1

S O MUCH DUST HAD BEEN KICKED UP ON THE DIRT FIELD NEXT TO THE sprawling Kachagan Refugee Camp that the spectators in the wooden bleachers heard the hoofbeats before they saw the horses. "The Pashtun tribesmen call the game *buzkashi*—literally 'goat-grabbing,'" Manny explained. He had to shout into Anthony's ear to be heard over the clamor of the crowd. On the field, twenty horsemen wheeled in a confused scrimmage, pushing and punching each other as they leaned from saddles to reach for something that had fallen to the ground. "Think of it as a rougher version of polo," Manny went on. "They toss a headless goat onto the field. Anything goes short of using knives. Your team gets points when you wrestle the carcass away from the other team and drop it into the scoring circle."

"How long does this go on?" inquired Anthony, newly arrived from Islamabad and still wearing the sweat-stained khaki suit and Clark boots he had traveled in.

Manny had to laugh. "It goes on nonstop until the horses or the riders collapse from exhaustion."

Anthony McAuliffe was a gangly twenty-three-year-old six-footer with open, rugged features and a mop of flaming-red hair, the spitting image of his father, Jack. He gazed across the field at the scores of young men sitting on a low wooden fence, passing joints (so Manny had said) from hand to hand as they egged on the riders of their favorite team. Suddenly Cornell's fraternity parties, basic training at the Farm, his initial tour of duty at Langley all seemed like images from a previous incarnation. Behind the bleachers, half-naked kids fought over a dead chicken as they imitated the adults on horseback. Beyond the playing field, Anthony could make out a

mass of low mud houses stretching off as far as the eye could see. Back in
Islamabad, the briefing book for officers posted to Peshawar said that so
many refugees had come over the mountain passes from Afghanistan since
the start of the jihad against the Soviet invasion, almost four years before,
that the international agencies had given up trying to count them.

Manny must have noticed the expression on Anthony's face. "Culture
shock is curable," he observed. "In a week or two all this will seem perfectly
ordinary to you."

"That's one of the things I'm worried about," Anthony shot back.

A roar went up from the crowd as a rider wrenched the goat's carcass
from the hands of an opponent and spurred his horse away. With a whoop,
the opposing team tore after him in hot pursuit. Once again the riders were
lost in the dust billowing from the playing field. One of Manny's two bodyguards, a bearded tribesman wearing a thick woolen vest with a jeweled knife
in his belt and a double-barreled shotgun under one arm, pointed to his
watch. Manny led Anthony off the bleachers and the two started toward the
parking lot. The second bodyguard, a giant of a man with a black turban
around his head, brought up the rear. Manny's driver, slouched behind the
wheel of an old Chevrolet, a joint sticking out of his mouth, came awake.
"Where to, chief man?" he asked.

"Khyber Tea Room in Smugglers' Bazaar," Manny ordered as he and
Anthony settled onto the rear seat. One of the bodyguards slid in next to
Manny, the other rode shotgun up front.

"Where'd you scrounge these guys?" Anthony asked under his breath.
"Central casting?"

"They're both Afridis, which is the tribe that controls the Khyber Pass,"
Manny said. "The one with the knife in his belt used to slit the throats of
Russians the way Muslims slaughter goats for holy day feasts."

"How can you be sure he won't slit ours?"

"You can't." Manny patted the shoulder holster under his bush jacket.
"Which is why I keep Betsy around."

Honking nonstop at bicycles and mobilettes and donkey carts and men
pulling wheelbarrows filled with television sets or air conditioning units or
electric typewriters, the driver turned west onto the Grand Trunk Road.
They passed an ancient German bus, its red paint faded to a washed-out
pink, the original sign ("Düsseldorf-Bonn") still visible above the front window, and several diesel trucks whose bodies had been repaired so often they
resembled old women who had had one face lift too many. Manny pointed
at the road ahead. "Khyber Pass starts twenty or so kilometers down there—

Darius's Persians, Alexander's Greeks, Tamerlane's Tartars, Babur's Moguls all came through here."

"Now it's our turn," Anthony said.

Infantrymen armed with automatic rifles waved the car to a stop at a checkpoint. At the side of the road, a soldier in the back of a Toyota pickup truck trained a needle-thin machine gun on the Chevrolet. "Pakis," Manny murmured. "They control the road but their authority ends fifty meters on either side of it. Beyond that it's the mountain tribesmen who rule the roost."

"*Shenasnameh*," a Pak subaltern with the waxed whiskers and long side-burns of a British sergeant major barked. "Identity papers."

Manny produced a fistful of crisp twenty-dollar bills from a pocket and cracked the window enough to pass them through. The Pak soldier took the money and, moistening a thumb, slowly counted it. Satisfied, he saluted and waved the car through.

Smugglers' Bazaar, a warren of shack-like stalls selling everything under the sun, was swarming with tribesmen in *shalwar qamiz*—the traditional Afghan long shirt and baggy trousers. Wherever Anthony looked there was evidence of war: men with missing limbs hobbled on wooden crutches, a teenage girl tried to flag down a passing taxi with the stump of an arm, Pajero Jeeps crammed with bearded mujaheddin brandishing weapons roared off toward the Khyber Pass and Afghanistan, makeshift ambulances filled with the wounded and the dying raced with screaming sirens back toward Peshawar. In an empty lot between shacks, gun dealers had spread their wares on tarpaulins. There were neat rows of Israeli Uzis and American M-1s and both the Russian and Chinese versions of the AK-47, and every kind of pis-tol imaginable. Two Syrians had set up World War II machine guns on straw mats. Next to them, on another straw mat, a man wearing the dark flowing robes of a desert Bedouin was selling camouflage fatigues, cartridge belts and black combat boots. Mules loaded with green ammunition boxes were tied to a fence near a trough filled with muddy water. Afghan warriors with assault rifles slung over their shoulders strolled through the open-air market, inspecting weapons and haggling over the prices.

The Chevrolet turned onto a pitted side lane and bumped its way down it to a two-story wooden house with a sign over the door that read, in English: "Last drinkable tea before the Khyber Pass." Manny signaled for the bodyguards to remain with the car. He and Anthony crossed a narrow bridge over what smelled like an open sewer. "We're here to meet the Lion of Panjshir, Ahmed Shah Massoud," Manny explained. "He's a Tajik from the Panjshir Valley, which knifes north of Kabul all the way to the Tajik border.

His people bear the brunt of the fighting against the Russians—the six other resistance groups spend a lot of their time fighting each other."

"So why don't we funnel the arms directly to him?" Anthony asked.

"The Pak Intelligence Directorate, the ISI, cornered the market on handing out American largess. Basically, they have other fish to fry—they want the war to end with a fundamentalist Afghanistan to strengthen their hand against India."

"I can see I've got a lot to learn," Anthony said.

"The Company has a lot to learn," Manny said. "I hope the report you'll write will open their eyes to a great many things."

Inside, a woman dressed in a shroud-like *burqa* squatted before a chimney and worked the bellows, heating the kettles suspended above the wood fire. In an alcove off to one side, an itinerant dentist was drilling into the tooth of an Afghan fighter who had come through the Khyber Pass with Massoud the night before. A teenage boy pedaling a bicycle welded into a metal frame ran the lathe that turned the drill in the dentist's fist. "Don't get a toothache here," Manny warned. "They fill cavities with molten shotgun pellets."

They climbed the narrow steps to the private room on the second floor. Two of Massoud's bodyguards stood outside the door. For some reason both of them had ear-to-ear grins splashed across their faces. The taller of the two cradled a vintage German MP-44 in his arms, the other had an enormous Czech pistol tucked into his waistband and held a small bamboo cage containing a yellow canary.

"The canary is the Afghan resistance's early warning system," Manny said.

"Against what?"

"The bird'll keel over at the first whiff if the Russians use chemical or biological weapons."

Massoud, a thin, bearded man with a direct gaze and an angelic smile, rose off the prayer rug to greet the Company's Chief of Station at Peshawar. "Manny, my friend," he said, shaking his hand warmly and drawing him into the room. He gestured toward the prayer rugs scattered on the floor. "I am deeply glad to see you again."

Manny saluted Massoud in Dari, then switched to English so his American friend could follow the conversation. "Meet a comrade, Anthony McAuliffe," Manny said. Massoud nodded once at him but didn't offer to shake hands. As the visitors settled cross-legged onto the rugs, a teenage girl with a shawl draped over her head shyly approached and filled two tin cups with *khawa*, the watery green tea that was standard fare in the tribal area.

Massoud made small-talk for a quarter of an hour—he brought Manny up to date on the shifting front lines inside Afghanistan and the Soviet order of battle, gave him the names of fighters he knew who had been killed or wounded in the three months since they last met, described a daring attack he had led against a Soviet air base in which three helicopters had been blown up and a Russian colonel had been taken prisoner. Manny wanted to know what had happened to the Russian. We offered to trade him for the two mujaheddin who were taken prisoner in the raid, Massoud said. The Russians sent them back alive and strapped to the saddles of pack animals, each with his right hand cut off at the wrist. Massoud shrugged. We returned their colonel missing the same number of hands.

At dusk, wood-burning stoves were lighted in the stalls and a sooty darkness settled over the bazaar area. Massoud accepted another cup of green tea as he got down to business. "It is this way, Manny," he began. "The modern weapons that you give to the Pakistani Intelligence Directorate finish up in the hands of the Pakistani Army, which then passes down its old hardware to the mujaheddin. We go into battle against the Soviet invaders at a great disadvantage. The situation has gotten worse in the last months because the Russians are starting to employ spotter planes to direct the firepower of their helicopters."

"There are portable radars that could detect the helicopters."

Massoud shook his head. "They fly through the valleys at the height of the tops of trees and fall upon us without warning. Our anti-aircraft guns, our machine guns are of no use against their armor plating. A great many mujaheddin have been killed or wounded this way. Radar will not improve the situation. Heat-seeking Stingers, on the other hand—" He was referring to the shoulder-fired ground-to-air missile that could blow planes or helicopters out of the sky at a distance of three miles.

Manny cut him off. "Stingers are out of the question. We've asked our Pentagon people—they're afraid the missiles will wind up in the hands of Islamic fundamentalists once the war is won."

"Give them to me, Manny, and the fundamentalists will not rule Afghanistan when the Russians are defeated." Massoud leaned forward. "The group which defeats the Russians will decide the future of Afghanistan—if the United States of America wants a free and democratic state, you must support me."

"Your Tajiks are a minority ethnic group. You know as well as I do that we can't give you high-tech weapons without upsetting the delicate balance between the various resistance groups."

"If not the Stinger," Massoud pleaded, "then the Swiss Oerlikon—it has the fire power to bring down the Russian helicopters."

"The Oerlikon is the wrong weapon for a guerrilla war. Its armor-piercing ammunition is expensive, the guns themselves are very sophisticated and require complicated maintenance. Our people say the Oerlikon wouldn't be operational after the journey over the Khyber Pass."

"So what is left?" Massoud asked.

"Conventional weapons."

"And the most conventional of all weapons is the surrogate who fights your war for you."

"It's your country that was occupied by the Russians. It's your war."

"Bleeding the Soviets is in your interest—"

"Is there anything else on your shopping list?"

Throwing up a palm in defeat, Massoud pulled a scrap of paper from the pocket of his woolen pants. "Medical supplies, especially anesthesia and antibiotics. Artificial limbs, also—unless, of course, your Pentagon worries that they will end up on the bodies of fundamentalists when the Russians are defeated."

Manny scribbled notes to himself in a small spiral notebook. "I'll do what I can," he said.

Massoud rose gracefully to his feet. "I, too, will do what I can, Manny." He threw an arm over Manny's shoulder and steered him off to one side. "I have heard it said that the Peshawar KGB *rezident*, Fet, is trying to establish contact with Islamic fundamentalist groups, for what purpose I do not know. I thought this information would be of interest to you."

Manny said thoughtfully, "It is."

The Lion of Panjshir turned to Anthony and regarded him with a cheerless half-smile. "Afghanistan was once an unbelievably beautiful country," he said. "With the war a kind of gangrene has infected its arteries. Newcomers have a hard time seeing beyond the infection." The half-smile brightened into a full-blown smile; small lines fanned out from the corners of his eyes. "Try anyhow."

Anthony stood up. "I will," he vowed.

As the Chevrolet passed the airport on the way back to Peshawar, Manny pointed to the runway, visible behind a chain-link fence draped with Turkistan carpets, Bukhara silks and Kurdistan lambskins set out by street vendors. "Gary Powers's U-2 took off from here in 1960," he remarked.

"That's the year I was born," Anthony noted.

"I was thirteen at the time," Manny said. "I remember Ebby coming back from work looking as if he'd seen a ghost. When Elizabet asked him what'd happened, my father switched on the radio and we listened to the news bulletin in the kitchen—Francis Gary Powers had been shot down by a Soviet ground-to-air missile over Sverdlovsk. That's when I learned the expression 'When the shit hits the fan.'"

They stopped at the fortress-like American consulate in the British Cantonment long enough for Manny to check the incoming traffic, then headed down Hospital Road, turned left onto Saddar and pulled up in the lot behind Dean's Hotel, the local watering hole for Peshawar's diplomats and journalists and visiting firemen. The armed *chowkidar* at the entrance, a clean-shaven Pashtun disfigured with napalm burn scars, recognized Manny and waved him and Anthony in but stopped the two Saudi civilians behind them to inspect their diplomatic passports. Manny led the way through the seedy lobby into the courtyard restaurant, snared a table just vacated by three Pakistanis and ordered an assortment of Chinese appetizers and two Murree beers from the Afghan boy waiting on tables. The appetizers were sizzling on the plates when a young woman with dark hair cut boyishly short slipped uninvited into a vacant chair. She was wearing khaki riding trousers tucked into soft ankle-high boots and a long, tight collarless cotton shirt buttoned up to the soft pale skin of her neck. She plucked some fried lamb from a plate with her fingertips and popped it into her mouth. "What did Massoud have to tell you that I don't already know?" she demanded.

"How do you know I saw Massoud?" Manny asked.

The young woman raised her very dark eyes, which were brimming with laughter. "I heard it from a rabid fundamentalist name of Osama bin Laden when I was drinking watered-down whiskey at the Pearl bar." She produced a pack of Lucky Strike cigarettes and, when the two men declined, stabbed one into her mouth and lit it with a small silver lighter. "Have our paths crossed?" When Manny shook his head no, she said, "Doesn't surprise me—he loathes the West as much as he loathes Russians, and America symbolizes the West. Bearded guy, thirtyish, gaunt, with a gleam of icy charm where his eyes ought to be. He's a full-time fund raiser for several of the mujaheddin groups. You guys might want to save string on him—the word on bin Laden is he inherited a few hundred million from his Saudi father and has big plans about how to spend it."

Manny flashed a knowing look in Anthony's direction. "Say hello to Maria Shaath, who has more balls than a lot of her male colleagues. She's famous for turning to the camera on a battlefield and saying: 'Afghanistan is a place where armed children with long memories set out to right wrongs done to the great-grandfathers of their grandfathers.' Maria, meet Anthony McAuliffe."

Anthony said, "I've seen you on TV."

Maria fixed her straightforward gaze on Anthony. "Another spook?" she asked sweetly.

Anthony cleared his throat. "I'm an attaché at the American consulate."

"Yeah, sure, and I'm Maria Callas, come to entertain the mujaheddin at the Khyber Pass with arias from Italian operas." She turned back to Manny. "He's green behind the ears—tell him the score."

"He's been flown in to work up a report on the weapon pipeline— the people who pay our salaries want to know how much of what they send to the Pak ISI is getting through to the folks actually shooting at Russians."

Maria helped herself to Anthony's mug of beer, then wiped her lips on the back of her small fist. "I could have saved you the trip out," she said. "The answer is precious little. Buy me dinner and I'll let you pick my brain." And she smiled a tight-lipped smile.

"Afghanistan is a can of worms," she said over a bowl filled with what the menu billed as chop suey. "It's a place where you can trade a copy of *Playboy* for a bottle of fifteen-year-old Scotch whiskey, and get your throat cut if you're caught sleeping with your feet pointed toward Mecca. Actually, there are a lot of overlapping wars going on: ethnic wars, clan wars, tribal wars, drug wars, religious wars, the Iranian Shi'ites versus the Afghan Sunni *taleb* studying the Koran in their Pak *medressas* versus the Afghan diaspora in the secular universities, Massoud's Tajiks versus everyone, Saudi Wahhabi versus the Iraqi Sunnis, capitalists with a small *C* versus Communists with a capital *C*, Pakistan versus India."

"You left out the last but not least," Manny said. "The Afghan freedom fighters versus the Russians."

"There's that war, too, though sometimes it gets lost in the shuffle. Look, the truth of the matter is that the Americans only vaguely understand what's going on and, more often than not, wind up backing the wrong horse. You need to stop looking for quick fixes to long-term problems."

"We're not going to give them Stinger missiles, if that's what you mean," Manny insisted.

"You will," Maria predicted. "In the end the itch to get even for Vietnam will overwhelm sweet reason. Then, when the war's over the bin Ladens will turn whatever weapons you give them against you."

Anthony asked, "What would you do if you were the American President?"

"First off, I'd stop supplying weapons to the former Peugeot salesman who claims to be a descendant of the Prophet. I'd give the cold-shoulder to splinter groups which want to create the perfect Islamic state modeled after the seventh-century Caliphate."

"Are you saying Russian rule in Afghanistan is the lesser of two evils?" Anthony wanted to know.

"I'm saying you're laying the groundwork for the next disaster by settling for the quickest solution to the last disaster. I'm saying hang in there. I'm saying the journey isn't over until you've copulated with the camel."

Manny pulled a face. "Copulating with a camel is a high price to pay for getting where you're going."

Maria batted her slightly Asian eyes. "Don't knock it if you haven't tried it."

Manny said, "Are you speaking from experience?"

Maria shot back, *"Bilagh!"*

Manny translated for Anthony. "That's the Persian equivalent of 'fuck you.'"

Laughing to herself, Maria went off to mooch a cup of coffee from Hippolyte Afanasievich Fet, the local KGB *rezident*. Fet, a mournful middle-aged man with sunken cheeks, was the laughing stock of Peshawar because of his uncanny resemblance to Boris Karloff. He was dining at a corner table with his much younger and deliciously attractive wife, and two male members of his staff.

Maria caught up with Manny and Anthony in the parking lot three quarters of an hour later. "Can I bum a lift back to University Town?" she asked.

"Why not?" Manny said.

The two bodyguards squeezed in next to the driver and Maria settled into the back of the car between Manny and Anthony. "What did Boris Karloff have to say?" Manny inquired.

"Hey, I don't tell him what you say to me," she remarked.

"But he asks?"

"Of course he asks."

Manny got the point. "I withdraw the question," he said.

The sun was dipping below the Suleiman Range as the car swung off Jamrud Road west of the airport and cut through the quiet, grid-like streets filled with consulates and plush private homes rented by US-AID officials and Pakistani brass and Afghan resistance leaders. The Company had a high-walled villa sandwiched between the estate of a Pashtun drug dealer and a warehouse filled with artificial limbs. Maria shared a house with half a dozen other journalists one street over. The Chevrolet slowed at an intersection to let a bus filled with children pass. A sign at the side of the road said, in English: "Drive with care and seek help from Almighty Allah." "There are two kinds of experts in Afghanistan," Maria was saying. "Those who have been here less than six weeks and those who have been here more than six months."

"Which category do you fall into?" Anthony asked.

Up ahead, a cart pulled by oxen was blocking the street. Two men wearing long shirts and baggy trousers appeared to be wrestling with a broken axle. "I'm in the second category," Maria started to explain. "I've been here for seven months—"

In the front of the Chevrolet, the driver looked around nervously as he pulled up twenty meters from the cart. "Don't like this," he muttered. The bodyguard with the turban around his head tugged a .45 automatic from his shoulder holster. From behind them came the screech of brakes. Three Jeeps skidded to a stop, pinning the Chevrolet in their headlights. *"Dacoit,"* cried the driver. "Bandits." The bodyguard with the shotgun flung open the door and dove for the ground and rolled once and fired both barrels at the nearest Jeep. One of the headlights sizzled out. The staccato rattle of automatic fire filled the night. Glass shattered. Dark figures loomed around the car. The driver, hit in the chest, slumped forward onto the wheel. The car's horn shrieked. The turbaned bodyguard fell to the right, his torso hanging half out of the open door. On the road, a man kicked the shotgun out of the hands of the bodyguard and rammed the muzzle of a rifle into his back and pulled the trigger. The bodyguard twitched, then lay still. In the Chevrolet, Manny wrestled Betsy from his shoulder holster. Before he could throw the safety hands reached in and dragged him from the back seat. Bearded men hauled Anthony and Maria out the other door toward one of the two tarpaulin-covered trucks behind the Jeeps. Behind them, one of the assailants bent over the turbaned bodyguard to make sure he was dead. The bodyguard twisted and pointed his pistol and pulled the trigger at point-blank range, and a .45 caliber bullet with grooves hand-etched into its soft head shattered his attacker's shoulder. Another man wearing combat boots kicked the bodyguard hard in the head, then reached down and slit his throat with a razor-sharp Turkish *yataghan.* In the back of the tarpaulin-covered truck, the three prisoners were shoved to the floor and their hands were lashed behind their backs with leather thongs. Foul-smelling leather hoods were pulled over their heads. Maria's muffled voice could be heard saying, "Oh, shit, this is all I needed." Under their bodies, the truck vibrated as the driver floored the gas pedal and rattled off down a side street. Minutes later the two trucks, running without headlights, bounced onto a dirt track and headed cross-country in the direction of the Khyber Pass.

Hippolyte Afanasievich Fet made his way through the maze of alleyways of the Meena Bazaar to the tattoo shop above the Pakistani acupuncturist with the colorful sign out front that read, "Eyes, Ears, Nose, Throat & Sexual Problems." The two bodyguards, unzipping their jackets so they could get at their shoulder holsters quickly, went up the creaking stairs first to inspect the premises. One emerged to say it was safe for Fet to enter. He went inside and sat down in the red barber's chair in the middle of the room, which was illuminated by a single forty-watt overhead electric bulb. Shadows danced on the woven straw mats covering the wooden walls. The floor was smudged with green from the *naswar*—the small balls of tobacco, lime and spices Pakistanis kept tucked under their lower lip—that had been expectorated by clients. From outside came the sound of two mountain tribesmen, high on hashish, urinating into the stream of sewage running along the curb. Fet glanced at the telephone on the table and then at his wristwatch.

One of the bodyguards said, "Maybe your watch is fast."

"Maybe it didn't come off," said the second bodyguard from the door.

"Maybe you should keep your opinions to yourselves," Fet growled.

At three minutes after midnight the phone rang. Fet snatched it off the hook. A voice on the other end of the line said, in heavily accented English, "Ibrahim is on his way to Yathrib. He is not alone."

Fet muttered *"Khorosho"* and severed the connection with his forefinger. He dialed the number of the duty officer in the Soviet consulate. "It's me," he said. "I authorize you to send the coded message to Moscow Centre."

The truck had been climbing a steep mountain track for the better part of three hours. At first light the driver, downshifting and veering to avoid shell holes filled with rainwater, steered the vehicle onto a level clearing and cut the motor. The tarpaulin was unlaced and flung back, the tailboard was lowered and the three prisoners, their wrists bound behind their backs, were prodded onto solid ground. Hands pulled the leather hoods off their heads. Filling his lungs with fresh mountain air, Anthony looked around. They were obviously in some sort of guerrilla encampment high in the mountains—though it was impossible to say whether they were still in Pakistan or had crossed into Afghanistan. Layers of blue-gray mountain ridges fell away to a cinereous horizon stained with veins of tarnished silver. Anthony had the feeling you could see for centuries, and said so.

"You're confusing time and space," Maria remarked sourly.

"I thought they were pretty much the same thing," Anthony insisted.

"Two sides of the same coin," Manny agreed.

"Exactly," said Anthony.

Around the guerrilla camp bearded men, some with blankets over their shoulders, others wearing surplus US Army coats, were loading arms and ammunition onto donkeys and camels. Nearby, yelping dogs brawled over a bone. Next to a long low mud-brick structure, a bearded mullah wearing a white skull cap read from the Koran to a circle of men sitting cross-legged in the dirt. At the edge of the clearing, a teenage boy fired a bazooka into a tree at point blank range, felling it in a shower of splinters. Then he dragged over a wheelbarrow and began to collect firewood.

Its engine straining, black exhaust streaming from the tailpipe, the second truck came up the mountain track and pulled to a stop on the flat. A lean and graceful figure emerged from the passenger seat. He was wearing a black turtleneck under a soiled knee-length Afghan tunic, thick English corduroy trousers, hand-made Beal Brothers boots and a brown Pashtun cap with an amulet pinned to it to ward off sniper bullets. His skin was fair, the hair under his cap long and matted, his short beard tinted reddish-orange with henna. He had the dark, intense eyes of a hunter, with shadowy hollows under them that didn't come from lack of sleep. The fingers of his left hand worked a string of ivory worry beads as he approached the captives. He gazed out over the hills. "Five years ago," he said, speaking English with the high-pitched, rolling accent of a Palestinian, "I was standing on this mountain top watching Russian tanks come down that road in the valley. My men and me, we sat on these stones all morning, all afternoon, all evening, and still the tanks came. We stopped counting after a time, there were so many of them. Many of the new recruits to the jihad came from the mountains and had never seen an automobile before, but Allah gave them the strength to war against tanks. They fired rockets at the tanks using hammers when the percussion mechanisms on the launchers broke down. Since then, many tanks have been destroyed and many mujaheddin have died. Against the tanks we are still making war."

From far below came the distant whine of jet engines, though no planes were visible. The men on the hilltop stopped what they were doing to stare down into the murky depths of the valleys. Flares burst noiselessly, illuminating the low ground haze more than the ground. Green and red tracer bullets intersected in the sky and napalm canisters exploded into bright flames on a thread of road that ran parallel to a stream. The fingers of the tall guerrilla leader kneaded the worry beads as he turned to face the three prisoners. "I am Commander Ibrahim. You are on my territory. Pakistani law is behind us, Afghan law is ahead of us. Here *Pashtunwali*—the Pashtun moral code—is the highest law and I am its custodian."

Four mujaheddin pulled a stretcher from the back of the second truck and started toward the low mud-brick building carrying the warrior who had been shot by the bodyguard in the attack on the Chevrolet. What remained of his shoulder was held in place with a blood-soaked bandanna knotted across his chest. His body quaking, the wounded man groaned in agony. Ibrahim scooped brackish rainwater from a puddle with a rusty tin can and, propping up the wounded man's head, moistened his lips. Then he and the three captives trailed after the stretcher. Anthony ducked under a low lintel into a dark room that was filled with smoke and smelled of hashish. Half a dozen guerrillas too young to grow beards sat around a small potbellied stove sucking on hookahs. Two old men tended to the wounded man, who had been stretched out on a narrow wooden plank. One held an oil lamp above his shattered shoulder while the other peeled away the bandanna and coated the raw wound with honey. The prisoners followed Ibrahim into a second room. Here a young boy cut the thongs binding their wrists and, motioning them toward straw-filled pillows set on the floor, offered each a bowl of scalding apple tea. Ibrahim drank in noisy gulps. After a while the boy returned with a copper tray filled with food—each of the prisoners and Ibrahim was given a piece of *nan*, a flat unleavened bread baked in a hole in the ground, and a small wooden bowl filled with a greasy goat stew and sticky rice. Ibrahim began eating with the fingers of his left hand—Manny noticed that he hardly used his right arm, which rested in his lap. The prisoners, eyeing one another, ate hungrily. When he'd finished his bowl, Ibrahim belched and leaned back against the wall. "While you are with me," he said, "you will be treated, in so far as it is possible, as guests. I counsel you to rest now. At sunset we will set out on a long journey." With that, Ibrahim removed his cap and, drawing his knees up to his chin, curled up on two cushions. Within moments, so it seemed, he was sound asleep.

Maria pulled a pad from a pocket and filled a page with tiny handwriting. Manny caught Anthony's eye and, nodding toward the two small windows covered with thick iron grilling, mouthed the word "escape." The two leaned their heads back against the wall but sleep was impossible. From the next room came the unrelenting moaning of the wounded man, and from time to time a muffled cry of *"lotfi konin"* repeated again and again.

Near midnight, one of the old men who had been tending the wounded man came into the room and touched Ibrahim's elbow. *"Rahbar,"* he said, and he bent down and whispered something in the commander's ear. Sitting up, Ibrahim lit a foul-smelling Turkish cigarette, coughed up the smoke after the first drag, then climbed to his feet and followed the old man out of the room. The wounded man could be heard pleading *"Khahesh mikonam, lotfi konin."* Manny explained to the others, "He says, *'I beg you, do me a kindness.'"*

The voice of Ibrahim intoned, *"Ashadu an la ilaha illallah Mohammad rasulullah."* The wounded man managed to repeat some of the words. There was a moment of silence. Then the sharp crack of a low-caliber revolver echoed through the building. Moments later Ibrahim strode back into the room and settled heavily onto the straw-filled pillow.

"He was a virtuous Muslim," he declared, "and a *shaheed*—what we call a war martyr. He will certainly spend eternity in the company of beautiful virgins."

Maria asked from across the room, "What happens when a virtuous Muslim woman dies?"

Ibrahim considered the question. "She will surely go to heaven, too. After that I cannot be sure."

Well before the first breath of dawn reached the clearing, the three prisoners were shaken awake and offered dried biscuits and tin cups filled with strong tea. Ibrahim appeared at the door. "You will be locked in the room while we bury our comrade," he said. "After which our journey will begin." When he'd gone, bolting the door behind him, Manny sprang to his feet and went over to one of the small windows covered with iron mesh. He could make out four men carrying the corpse, which was shrouded in a white sheet and stretched out on a plank, across the clearing. Walking two abreast, a long line of mujaheddin, some holding gas lamps or flashlights, followed behind. The cortege disappeared over the rim of the hill. Anthony tried the door but it didn't give. Maria whispered, "What about the grille on the windows?"

Manny laced his fingers through the grille and tugged at it. "It's cemented into the bricks," he said. "If we had a knife or screwdriver we might be able to work it out."

Anthony spotted a can of insecticide in a corner. He picked it up and shook it—there was still some fluid left in it. "Give me your cigarette lighter," he ordered Maria.

Manny saw instantly what he was up to. He took the lighter and thumbed the wheel, producing a flame, and held it near the grille. Anthony raised the can's nozzle up to the lighter and sprayed the insecticide through the flame, turning it into a jury-rigged flame-thrower that slowly melted the grille. When three sides of a square had been melted, Manny bent the grille out.

"You go first," Anthony said.

Manny didn't want to waste time arguing. He hiked himself up on the sill and worked his body through the small opening. Ragged ends of the grille tore his clothing and scratched his skin. Anthony pushed his feet from behind and Manny squirmed headfirst through the window and tumbled to the ground outside. Anthony squatted and Maria stepped onto his shoulder and started to wriggle through the opening. She was half out when the bolt of the door was thrown and Ibrahim appeared on the threshold.

Anthony cried out, "Run for it, Manny!"

Ibrahim shouted an alarm. Feet pounded in the clearing outside the mud-walled building as the mujaheddin raced to cut off Manny. Cries rang out. Jeeps and trucks roared up to the lip of the clearing and played their headlights on the fields dropping away to a ravine. Shots were fired. In the room, Maria slipped back through the opening into Anthony's waiting hands. Her shoulders and arms bleeding from a dozen scratches, she turned to face Ibrahim. He motioned with a pistol for them to quit the building and came out into the clearing behind them. The manhunt ended abruptly. The headlights on the Jeeps and trucks flicked out one after the other. One of the bearded fighters ran over and said something to Ibrahim in a low voice. Then he joined the others kneeling for the first prayer of the day. Rows of men prostrated themselves in the dirt facing Mecca. Ibrahim turned to Anthony as two of his men tied the prisoners' wrists behind their backs. "My fighters tell me the escaped prisoner is for sure dead." He stared out over the praying mujaheddin to the glimmer of light touching the top of the most distant mountain ridge, hunched like the spine of a cat. "So I think," he added, "but God may think otherwise."

2

THAT'S A LOT OF CRAP, SENATOR," DIRECTOR CASEY GROWLED INTO the phone. He dipped two fingers into the Scotch and soda and slicked back the last few strands of white hair on his scalp. "If there was a shred of truth to any of it I'd submit my resignation tomorrow." He listened for a while, screwing up his lips and tossing his head the way the senator did when he presided over the Select Committee on Intelligence. "Look," Casey finally said, cutting into the soliloquy, "everyone and his brother knows I ran the President's campaign. But what's-his-name in the *Washington Post* is out to lunch when he suggests I'm running his reelection campaign from Langley." Casey held the phone away from his ear and let the senator drone on. He'd heard it all before: the motivating force in the White House was the President's popularity; the search for popularity drove policy; the best-kept secret in the capitol was that Reagan and his senior White House people were ignoramuses when it came to foreign affairs; the President had a hearing problem so you couldn't be sure, when you briefed him, that you were getting through to him; he never came right out and said no to anything, it was always *Yes, well* or *Sounds all right to me but, uh*, after which the sentence trailed off; decisions, when you managed to get any, filtered down from the White House staff and it wasn't certain where they came from; for all anybody knew Nancy Reagan could have been running the country. The terrible part was that it was all true, though Casey wasn't about to tell the senator that; Reagan had never fully recovered from the bullet that John Hinckley had pumped to within an inch of the President's heart two and a half years before. "The story that he can't locate his chief of staff's office—it's a bad rap, senator," he said, forever loyal to his old pal, Ron. "Reagan's a big picture man but he's been on top of everything

I've brought up to the White House, up to and including the downing of the Korean 747 that strayed into Soviet air space two weeks ago."

Casey's daughter, Bernadette, stuck her head in the door of the den and pointed upstairs: the people her father was expecting had turned up. "Senator, let me get back to you—I've got some Company business to attend to." He listened for another moment, then mumbled "Count on it" and hung up. "Tell them to come on in," he told his daughter.

Ebby, Bill Casey's Deputy Director Central Intelligence, had met the plane carrying Manny at McGuire Air Force Base and driven his son (after a hurried phone call to Nellie) straight out to the Director's new tan brick house in the posh development carved out of the old Nelson Rockefeller estate off Foxhall Road in northwest Washington. As they made their way down half a level and through the three sitting rooms, he told Manny, "Jack may turn up, too. He's worried sick about Anthony—if you have any gory details, for crying out loud keep them to yourself. No point in alarming him more than we have to."

"Anthony wasn't hurt or anything," Manny said. "It was plain bad luck that he and the Shaath woman didn't make it through the window. I still kick myself for going first—"

"No one faults you so don't fault yourself." He stepped into the den and Casey came off the couch to seize his hand. "This is my boy, Manny," Ebby said.

Casey waved both of them to leather-covered easy chairs. "I don't need to tell you how glad I am you got your ass out of there," he remarked. Sinking back onto the couch, he asked Manny about the escape.

"Anthony gets the credit," Manny said, and he went on to explain how Jack's son had turned a can of insecticide into a blowtorch to burn away the wire mesh on the window. "I'd slipped through and Maria Shaath was halfway out when the guerrilla leader—"

Casey, renowned for his photographic memory, had read the cable that Manny filed from Islamabad. "The one who calls himself Commander Ibrahim?" he said.

"Commander Ibrahim, right. They'd just buried the fighter who'd been shot in the attack and Ibrahim turned up at the door and gave the alarm. In the darkness I scrambled down into a ravine and up the other side. Headlights came on above me, illuminating the area. There were shots. I threw up my arms as if I'd been hit and fell over the lip of a bluff. Then I just let myself roll downhill. After that it was a matter of walking for three days in the general direction of the rising sun."

The DCI, a lawyer by training who had been chief of the Special

Intelligence Branch of the OSS at the end of World War II, savored the cloak-and-dagger side of intelligence operations. "You make it sound easy as falling off a log," he said, leaning forward. "What did you do for food and water?"

"Water was no problem—I came across streams and rivulets. As for food, I took a refresher survival course at the Farm before I went out to Peshawar, so I knew which roots and mushrooms and berries were edible. Three days after my escape I spotted a campfire. It turned out to be an Afridi camel caravan running contraband over the Khyber from Afghanistan. I gave them the five hundred-dollar bills hidden in my belt. I promised them that much again when they delivered me to Peshawar."

When Jack turned up Manny had to go through the escape again for him. Director Casey, whose lack of patience was legendary, fidgeted on the couch. Jack, his face tight with worry, asked, "What condition was Anthony in when you last saw him?"

"He wasn't wounded in the kidnapping, Jack," Manny said. "He was in great shape, and very alert."

The Director said, "As far as I'm aware, we don't have string on a Commander Ibrahim."

Jack said, "There was nothing in Central Registry. The Afghanistan desk at State never heard of him. The National Security people have no string on him either."

"Which means," Ebby said, "that he's just come out of the woodwork."

"Aside from the physical description Manny's provided, what do we know about him?" the Director asked.

"He spoke English with what I took to be a Palestinian accent," Manny offered. "Which could mean he was brought up in the Middle East."

"He might have cut his teeth in one of the Hezbollah or Hamas training camps," Jack said. He turned to the Director. "We ought to bring the Israelis in on this—they keep close tabs on Islamic fundamentalists in the Palestinian ranks."

"That's as good a place as any to start," Casey agreed. "What about the report from the Kalasha informant?"

Jack, quick to clutch at any straw, said, "What report are we talking about?"

Ebby said, "This came in late last night. We have an informant among the Kalasha, which is an ancient tribe of non-Muslims living in three valleys along the Afghanistan frontier, who claims that a Palestinian named Ibrahim had been running arms into Pakistan and selling them in Peshawar. According to our Kalasha, Ibrahim has made a trip every two months—he bought automatic weapons in Dubai, crossed the Gulf and Iran in trucks, then smuggled the stuff into Pakistan and up to the Tribal Areas on pack animals."

"Did your informant provide a physical description?" Jack asked.

"As a matter of fact, yes. The Kalasha said Ibrahim was tall and thin, with long hair and an amulet on his cap to protect him from sniper bullets. His right arm was partially paralyzed—"

"That's Commander Ibrahim," Manny said excitedly. "He ate, he manipulated his worry beads with his left hand. His right arm hung limply at his side or lay in his lap."

"That's a start," Casey said. "What else did the Kalasha have on this Ibrahim character?"

"He described him as a rabid fundamentalist in search of a jihad," Ebby said. "He dislikes Americans only slightly less than he despises Russians."

"Well, he's found his jihad," Manny commented.

"Which brings us to the fax that landed in the American consulate in Peshawar," Casey said, impatient to move on. His expressionless eyes regarded Ebby through oversized glasses. "Are we sure it came from this Ibrahim character?"

"The fax appears to be authentic," Ebby said. "It was hand-printed in English, in block letters. There were two grammatical mistakes—verbs that didn't agree with their subjects—and two misspellings, suggesting that English was not the writer's native language. There was no way to trace where the fax originated, of course. It came in sometime during the night. Our people found it in the morning. It spoke of three hostages—Manny would have escaped by then but Commander Ibrahim probably thought he'd been killed and didn't want to advertise the fact, which makes sense from his point of view."

"They want Stingers," Jack said.

"Everybody out there wants Stingers," Manny noted.

"Not everybody who wants Stingers has hostages," Jack observed glumly.

Casey said, "I'm all for giving them Stingers—I'm for anything that makes the Russians bleed—but the praetorians around the President are chickenshit. They're afraid to escalate. They're afraid to make the Russians mad." The Director's head bobbed from side to side with the futility of it all. "How is it that we always wind up fighting the Cold War with one hand tied behind our back? Everything we do has to be so goddamned licit. When are we going to fight fire with fire? The Contra guerrillas in Nicaragua are a case in point. I have some creative ideas on the subject that I want to throw at you, Ebby. If we could get our hands on some cash that the Senate Committee on Intelligence doesn't know about—"

The red phone next to the couch purred. Casey snatched it off the hook and held it to his ear. "When'd you get back, Oliver?" he asked. "Okay, let me know as soon as the payment is transferred. Then we'll work out the next step." He listened again. "For Christ's sake, no—you tell Poindexter that the President has signed off on this so there's no need to bring the details to his attention. If something goes wrong he has to be able to plausibly deny he knew anything about it." Casey snorted into the phone. "If that happens you'll fall on your sword, then the Admiral will fall on his sword. If the President still needs another warm body between him and the press, I'll fall on my sword."

"Where were we?" Casey said when he'd hung up. "Okay, let's plug into the Israeli connection to see if Commander Ibrahim's Palestinian accent leads anywhere. Also, let's see if the people who read satellite photos can come up with something—your report, Manny, mentioned two tarpaulin-covered trucks, a bunch of Jeeps and about sixty Islamic warriors. If a snail leaves a trail on a leaf, hell, these guys ought to leave a trail across Afghanistan. To buy time we'll instruct Peshawar Station to respond to the fax—"

"They're supposed to put an ad in the personal column of the Islamabad English-language *Times*," Jack said.

"Let's establish a dialogue with the kidnappers, however indirect. Let them think we're open to trading Stingers for the hostages. But we want proof that they're still alive. The thing to do is stall them as long as we can and see where this goes."

Nellie cleared the dishes and stacked them in the sink. Manny refilled the wine glasses and carried them into the living room. He sank onto the couch, exhausted both physically and mentally. Nellie stretched out with her head on his thigh. From time to time she lifted her long-stemmed glass from the floor and, raising her head, took a sip of wine. On the radio, a new pop singer named Madonna Louise Ciccone was belting out a song that was starting to make its way up the charts. It was called "Like a Virgin." "The Mossad guy brought over seven loose-leaf books filled with mug shots," Manny said. "I saw so many Islamic militants my eyes had trouble focusing."

"So did you find this Ibrahim individual?"

"Nellie?"

Nellie laughed bitterly. "Whoops, sorry. I must have been out of my mind to think that just because my occasional lover and absentee husband was shanghaied by an Islamic crazy he'd let me in on Company secrets, such as the identity of the Islamic crazy in question. I mean, I might go and leak it to the *New York Times*."

"We live by certain rules—"

"It's a damn good thing I love you," Nellie said. "It's a damn good thing I'm too relieved you're back to pick a fight." She put on a good show but she was close to tears; she'd been close to tears since he returned home. "I hate that fucking Company of yours," she said with sudden vehemence. "One of the reasons I hate it is because you love it."

In fact, Manny *had* come across Ibrahim in the Mossad books. Two hours and twenty-minutes into the session one mug shot had leapt off the page—Ibrahim was younger and leaner and wearing his hair short but there was no mistaking him. Curiously, this earlier version of Ibrahim had the eyes of someone who was hunted—not the hunter. The Israelis identified the man in the photograph as Hajji Abdel al-Khouri and quickly came up with a profile on him. Al-Khouri, born in September 1944 in Jidda, Saudi Arabia, turned out to be half-Saudi, half-Afghan, the youngest son of Kamal al-Khouri, a Yemeni-born Saudi millionaire who had founded a construction empire that built roads and airports and shopping malls in the Middle East and India. The second of his three wives, the ravishing seventeen-year-old daughter of a Pashtun prince he met in Kabul, was Hajji's mother. In his late teens Hajji, then an engineering student at King Abdul-Aziz University in Jidda, abandoned his studies, assumed the nom de guerre of Abu Azzam and moved to Jordan to join Fatah, the forerunner of the Palestine Liberation Organization. Arrested by the Israelis in Hebron on the West Bank of the Jordan for the attempted murder of a Palestinian suspected of collaborating with the Israeli Shin Bet, Abu Azzam spent two years in a remote Negev prison. After his release (for lack of evidence) in 1970 he broke with the PLO when he became convinced that its leader, Yasser Arafat, was too willing to compromise with the Israelis. In the early 1970s the PLO sentenced Abu Azzam to death in absentia for vowing to kill Arafat and King Hussein of Jordan, at which point the Fatah renegade fled to Baghdad, founded the Islamic Jihad and masterminded a series of terrorist actions against Israeli and Arab targets, including the 1973 occupation of the Saudi Embassy in Paris. When the Soviet Union invaded Afghanistan in 1979 Abu Azzam assumed still another identity—henceforth he was known as Ibrahim—and moved the Islamic Jihad to the

Hindu Kush Mountains east of the Afghan capital of Kabul. Making use of an estimated hundred million dollars that he had inherited from his father, he established secret recruiting and training centers around the Arab world and forged links with Pakistan's radical Islamic Tablighi Jama'at, Gulbuddin Hekmatyar's Hezb-i-Islami and other extremist Islamic splinter groups in the Middle East. What all these groups shared was a fanatic loathing of both the Soviet invaders of Afghanistan and the Americans who were using Islamic warriors as cannon fodder to oppose them; Ibrahim and the others associated Westernization with secularization and a rejection of Islam's dominant role in defining the cultural and political identity of a country. Ibrahim in particular looked beyond the Soviet defeat and the Afghan war to the establishment of strict Koranic rule in Afghanistan and the overthrow of the feudal Saudi ruling family; if oil rich Saudi Arabia were to fall into the hands of the fundamentalists, so Ibrahim reasoned, Islam— by controlling the quantity of petrol pumped out of the ground, and the price—would be in a strong position to defend the faith against Western infidels.

Jack was exultant when he learned that Manny had succeeded in identifying Ibrahim. "Jesus H. Christ, you're one hundred percent sure?" he demanded on a secure intra-Company line, and Manny could hear the sigh of relief escape Jack's lips when he told him there was no doubt about it. Jack raced down one flight to Millie's suite of offices—she was now, in addition to her regular public relations chores, the Company's senior spokesperson—and pulled his wife into the corridor to share the hopeful news out of earshot of the half-dozen assistants and secretaries in her shop. "It's the first step in the right direction," he told her, grasping her clammy hand in both of his giant paws, nodding stubbornly as if he were trying to convince himself that the story would have a happy ending. Thanks to the Israelis, he whispered, the Company now had a mug shot to go with Manny's description. A top-secret Action Immediate was on its way to all Stations, signed by the DCI himself, William Casey, and countersigned by the Deputy Director/ Operations, yours truly, John J. McAuliffe, using my middle initial, which is something I never do, to emphasize its importance. The Company, it said, considered the identification and eventual infiltration of Islamic Jihad's recruiting and training centers in the Middle East to be of the highest priority. A Company officer's life was on the line. Any and all potential sources with ties to Islamic groups should be sounded out, IOU's should be called in, the expenditure of large sums of money was authorized. No stone should be left unturned. The quest to find

Commander Ibrahim and his two hostages should take priority over all other pending business.

"What do you think, Jack?" Millie asked. She could see how drawn he looked; she knew she didn't look much better. "Is there any possibility of getting Anthony out of this alive?"

"I promise you, Millie...I swear it..."

Millie whispered, "I know you'll do it, Jack. I know you'll succeed. You'll succeed because there is no alternative that you and I can live with."

Jack nodded vehemently. Then he turned and hurried away from the woman whose eyes were too full of anguish to look into.

Jack buttonholed Ebby at the end of the workday. The two sat knee to knee in a corner of the DDCI's spacious seventh-floor office, nursing three fingers of straight Scotch, talking in undertones. There was a hint of desperation in Jack's hooded eyes; in his leaden voice, too. "I stumbled across an Israeli report describing how the Russians dealt with a hostage situation," he said. "Three Soviet diplomats were kidnapped in Beirut by a Hezbollah commando. The KGB didn't sit on their hands, agonizing over what they could do about it. They abducted the relative of a Hezbollah leader and sent his body back with his testicles stuffed in his mouth and a note nailed— *nailed*, for Christ's sake—to his chest warning that the Hezbollah leaders and their sons would suffer the same fate if the three Soviets weren't freed. Within hours the three diplomats were released unharmed a few blocks from the Soviet embassy." Jack leaned forward and lowered his voice. "Look, Ebby, we've identified the kidnapper—this Ibrahim character has to have brothers or cousins or uncles—"

There was an embarrassed silence. Ebby studied his shoelaces. "We're not the KGB, Jack," he finally said. "I doubt if our Senate custodians would let us get away with employing the same tactics."

"We wouldn't have to do it ourselves," Jack said. "We could farm it out—Harvey Torriti would know who to go to."

Ebby said, "I know how scared you must be, Jack. But this is a nonstarter. The CIA is an endangered species as it is. There's no way I'm going to sign off on something like this." He looked hard at Jack. "And there's no way I'm going to let my Deputy Director/Operations sign off on it, either." Ebby climbed tiredly to his feet. "I want your word you won't do anything crazy, Jack."

"I was just letting off steam."

"Do I have your word?"

Jack looked up. "You have it, Ebby."

The DDCI nodded. "This conversation never took place, Jack. See you tomorrow."

Keeping one eye on the odometer, Tessa jogged along the treadmill in the Company's makeshift basement gymnasium at Langley. "I prefer to run down here," she told her twin sister, Vanessa, "than on the highway where you breath in all those exhaust fumes."

Vanessa, an IBM programmer who had been hired by the Company the previous year to bring its computer retrieval systems up to date, was lying flat on her back and pushing up a twenty-pound bar to strengthen her stomach muscles. "What's new in the wide world of counterintelligence?" she asked.

A stocky woman wearing a sweat suit with a towel around her neck, something of a legend for being the first female Station Chief in CIA history, abandoned the other jogging machine and headed for the shower room. Tessa waited until she was out of earshot. "Actually, I stumbled across something pretty intriguing," she said, and she proceeded to tell her sister about it.

In part because she was the daughter of Leo Kritzky, Jack McAuliffe's current Chief of Operations, in part because of an outstanding college record, Tessa had been working in the counterintelligence shop since her graduation from Bryn Mawr in 1975. Her most recent assignment had been to pore through the transcripts of English-language radio programs originating in the Soviet Union, looking for patterns or repetitions, or phrases or sentences that might appear to be out of context, on the assumption that the KGB regularly communicated with its agents in the Americas by passing coded messages on these programs. "Seven months ago," she said, "they gave me the transcripts of Radio Moscow's nightly shortwave English-language cultural quiz program, starting with the first broadcast made in the summer of 1950."

Sliding over to sit with her back against a wall, Vanessa mopped her neck and forehead with a towel. "Don't tell me you actually found a coded message in them?" she said.

"I found something in them," Tessa said. She glanced at the odometer and saw that she'd run five miles. Switching off the treadmill, she settled down next to her sister. "You remember how I adored *Alice in Wonderland* and *Through the Looking Glass* when I was a kid. I read them so many times I practically knew both books by heart. Well, at the end of every quiz program they give a line from some English-language classic and ask the contestant to identify it. In the thirty-three years the program has been on the air—that's something in the neighborhood of twelve thousand fifteen-minute broadcasts—they used Lewis Carroll quotations twenty-four times. They naturally caught my eye because they were the only questions I could personally answer." Tessa cocked her head and came up with some examples. "'The more there is of mine, the less there is of yours.' Or 'If I'm not the same, who in the world am I?' Or 'Whiffling through the tulgey wood.' And 'I don't like belonging to another person's dream.'"

Vanessa said, "I don't really see how you could decode these sentences—"

"I studied Soviet and East European code systems at the NSA school in Fort Meade," Tessa said. "Some KGB codes are merely recognition signals—special sentences that alert the agent to something else in the program that is intended for him."

"Okay, for argument's sake let's say that the twenty-four references to *Alice* or *Looking Glass* are intended to alert an agent," Vanessa said. "The question is: Alert him to what?"

"Right after the quotes they always announce the winning lottery number," Tessa said.

"How many digits?"

"Ten."

"That's the number of digits in a telephone number if you include the area code." Vanessa thought a moment. "But the lottery number itself couldn't be a phone number—it would be too obvious."

"At the NSA code school," Tessa said, "they taught us that East German agents operating in West Germany in the early 1950s were given American ten-dollar bills—they used the serial numbers on the bill as a secret number, which they subtracted from the lottery number broadcast from East Germany to wind up with a phone number."

Vanessa looked puzzled. "You said there were twenty-four references to *Alice* and *Looking Glass*—if you're right about all this, it means there were twenty-four lottery numbers that translated into twenty-four phone numbers over a period of thirty-three years. But why would a Soviet agent have to be given a new phone number to call all the time?"

Tessa said, "KGB tradecraft calls for cutouts to keep on the move. So the agent might be getting in touch with a cutout who periodically changes his phone number."

"Did you show your boss what you'd found?"

"Yeah, I did. He said it could easily be a coincidence. Even if it wasn't, he didn't see how we could break out a phone number from a lottery number, since there were an infinite number of possibilities for the secret number."

Vanessa said, "Hey, computers can deal with an infinite number of possibilities. Let me take a crack at it."

Vanessa, who was programming an IBM mainframe, stayed after work to play with the twenty-four lottery numbers that had been broadcast after the Lewis Carroll quotations. She checked with the CIA librarian and found out that area codes had been introduced in the early 1950s, about the time the Moscow Radio quiz program began, so she started with the assumption that the ten-digit lottery number hid a ten-digit phone number that included a low-numbered East Coast area code. She began with the winning lottery number broadcast after the first use of an *Alice* quotation ('And the moral of that is—the more there is of mine, the less there is of yours') on April 5, 1951: 2056902023. Running a series of equations through the computer, she discovered there was a high probability that an eight-digit secret number beginning with a three and a zero, subtracted from the ten-digit lottery number, would give you a ten-digit phone number that began with the 202 area code for Washington, DC, which was where the girls assumed a cutout would live. Using an eight-digit secret number that began with a three and a zero, Vanessa was also able to break out the 202 area code from the other twenty-three lottery numbers.

The results were hypothetical—but the statistical probability of this being a fluke were slim.

Starting with a three and a zero still left six digits in the secret number. The problem stymied Vanessa for the better part of a week. Then, one evening, she and her lawyer boyfriend happened to be eating at a Chinese restaurant two blocks from the apartment the sisters shared in Fairfax outside the Beltway. The boyfriend went off to pay the cashier with his Visa card and asked her to leave the tip. Vanessa pulled two dollar bills from her purse and flattened them on the table. Her head was swimming with the numbers that the computer had been spitting out for the past ten days. As she glanced at the dollar bills the serial numbers seemed to float off the paper. She shook her head and looked again. Tessa's story of how East Germans spies operating in the West had used the serial numbers on American ten-dollar bills to break out telephone numbers came back to her. The first Moscow quiz lottery number had been broadcast on April 5, 1951, so the Soviet agent on the receiving end of the code would have been in possession of a ten-dollar bill printed before that date. The serial numbers on American bills ran in series, didn't they? Of course they did! What she needed to do now was find out the serial numbers that were in circulation from, say, the end of the war until April 1951, and run them through the computer.

First thing next morning, Vanessa made an appointment with a Treasury Department official and turned up at his office that afternoon. Yes, serial numbers on all American bills did run in series. No problem, he could supply her with the series that were in circulation from 1945 until April 1951, it was just a matter of checking the records. If she would care to wait he could have his assistant retrieve the log books and photocopy the appropriate pages for her.

That evening, with a very excited Tessa looking over her shoulder, Vanessa went down the list of ten-dollar bill serial numbers in circulation before April, 1951 until she found one that began with the telltale three and zero. In 1950, the Treasury had printed up $67,593,240-worth of ten-dollar bills with serial numbers that started with a letter of the alphabet, followed by 3089, followed by four other numbers and another letter of the alphabet.

Going back to her mainframe, Vanessa started to work with the number 3089; subtracting 3089 from the first winning lottery number broke out a Washington area code and exchange that existed in the early 1950s: 202 601. And that, in turn, left a mere 9,999 phone numbers to check out.

"What we're looking for," Tessa reminded her sister, "is someone who had a phone number corresponding to 201 601 and then moved out of that house or apartment in the week after April 5, 1951." Tessa was almost dancing with excitement. "Boy, oh boy," she said. "Do you think this is actually going to work?"

KGB housekeepers had drawn the Venetian blinds and transformed the third-floor Kremlin suite into a working clinic. It was staffed around the clock by doctors and nurses specially trained in hemodialysis, and fitted with an American-manufactured artificial kidney machine to deal with acute kidney failure. Yuri Vladimirovich Andropov—the former Soviet Ambassador to Budapest at the time of the 1956 Hungarian uprising, head of the KGB from 1967 to 1982, and since the death of Leonid Brezhnev in 1982 the General Secretary of the Communist Party and the Soviet Union's undisputed leader—was the clinic's only patient. Ten months in power, Andropov, at 69, was suffering from chronic kidney disease and kept alive by regular sessions of hemodialysis that filtered noxious waste out of his blood stream. Living on borrowed time (doctors gave him six months at most), pale and drawn, capable of concentrating for only relatively short periods, Andropov sat propped up in bed, an electric blanket tucked up to his gaunt neck. "I'm fed up with the bickering," he told Starik. "The Army brass, their chests sagging under the weight of medals, come here every day or two to swear to me that the war is winnable, it is only a question of having the stamina to stick with it despite the losses."

Starik said something about how his particular service concentrated on the Principal Adversary but Andropov rushed on. "Then the KGB people drop by with their latest assessment, which is the same as the previous assessment: the war in Afghanistan is unwinnable, the Islamic fundamentalists can never be defeated, the Army must be instructed to cut its losses, at which point the fundamentalists can be manipulated in such a way as to turn them against US interests." Shaking his head in frustration, Andropov glanced at the yellow appointments card. "It is written here you requested an appointment to talk about KHOLSTOMER."

"The Politburo's Committee of Three has split down the middle, Yuri Vladimirovich," Starik explained. "One member is for the project, one against, one undecided."

"And who is against it?" Andropov inquired.

"Comrade Gorbachev."

Andropov snickered. "Mikhail Sergeyevich is supposed to be a specialist on agricultural questions, though even that is not sure—all he mumbles about lately is the need for *glasnost* and *perestroika*, as if *openness* and *restructuring* were magic potions for all of our economic troubles." He waved for the male nurse sitting next to a window to leave the room. Once they were alone he said to Starik, "This KHOLSTOMER project of yours—is it the same as the one I signed off on when I ran the KGB? The one that Brezhnev subsequently vetoed?"

"There have been slight modifications since Comrade Brezhnev's time—the project has been fine tuned to take into account the ability of the American Federal Reserve Board to allocate currency resources and deal with a massive attack on the dollar."

Andropov reached with trembling fingers to turn up the heat on the electric blanket. "Refresh my memory with the details," he ordered.

"Since the middle 1950s the KGB has been siphoning off hard currency from the sales of our national gas company, GazProm, as well as armament and oil sales abroad. We quietly created what are called shell companies in various tax havens—on the Isle of Man, on Jersey and Guernsey in the Channel Islands, in Switzerland and the Caribbean. Typically, a shell company is owned by two other companies, which in turn is owned by a Geneva- or Bermuda-based company, which in turn—"

Andropov waved a hand listlessly. "I get the point."

"At the present moment we control roughly sixty-three billion in American dollars in these shell companies. The beauty of KHOLSTOMER is that all the dollars are physically held in corresponding banks in the city of New York. These New York banks are unable to identify the ultimate owner of the dollars. Now, on any given day, somewhere between five and six hundred billion United States dollars change hands in New York on what currency traders call the spot market—which means that the sales of these dollars are executed immediately."

"How can you expect to undermine the American dollar if you only have a fraction of the six hundred billion available?"

"We calculate that if we handle the affair shrewdly, which is to say if we plant articles in the world's newspapers about the intrinsic weakness of the dollar and then manipulate the market cleverly, the sudden sale of our sixty-three billion will suck in people and institutions—speculators, insurance companies, private banks, retirement funds and, most especially, European and Asian Central Banks—in the general panic of the moment. We estimate that the panic money will be ten times the original sixty-three billion, which will mean that the total sum of dollars dumped onto the market will be the neighborhood of six hundred billion dollars—and this will be in addition to the regular sale of dollars on that day. A movement of this nature will inevitably have a snowball effect. The American Central Bank, which is called the Federal Reserve Bank, would naturally intervene to buy up dollars in an effort to stabilize the American currency. But our guess is that, on the condition that we catch them by surprise, this intervention will come too late and be too little to prevent the dollar from spiraling downward. We estimate that seventy percent of the foreign currency holdings of the Central Banks of Japan, Hong Kong, Taiwan and Malaysia are in US dollars; we are talking about a sum in the neighborhood of one thousand billion. Ninety percent of this one thousand billion is held in the form of US Treasury bonds and bills. We have agents of influence in these four territories, people in key posts in the Central Banks, as well as a German agent close to the West German Chancellor Helmut Kohl. At the first sign of a steep downward spiral of the US dollar our agents will push their respective Central Banks, as a hedge against further deterioration of their holdings, to sell off twenty percent of their Treasury bond dollar assets. At that point, in addition to the downward spiral of the American currency, the American bond market would collapse and this, in turn, would lead to panic and collapse on Wall Street; one could expect the Dow Jones industrial average, now in the twelve hundred range, to plummet. The European stock markets would plunge in turn. Europeans who hold dollar assets would join the panic, selling off their American holdings in their haste to switch personal and corporate assets into gold."

Andropov's right eyelid twitched. "Can you predict the long term effects of KHOLSTOMER on the Principal Adversary?"

"Interest rates in the United States, and then Europe and Asia, would climb sharply in response to the collapse of the bond market. As interest rates soar prices would rise, which would mean that American companies would sell less, both domestically and abroad, leading to a dramatic increase in the American trade deficit. This would result in inflationary pressures, an economic slowdown, a sharp rise in unemployment. The chaos in the American economy would, it goes without saying, have political repercussions, most especially in France and Italy, where the powerful Communist parties could offer alternatives that freed their countries from American economic domination and led to closer cooperation and eventually alignment with the Soviet bloc. West Germany, Spain and Scandinavia could be expected to follow suit to avoid being isolated."

There was a soft knock on the door. A young male nurse wheeled a stainless steel cart to the side of the bed. "Time for your vitamins, Comrade Andropov," he said. The General Secretary pulled the blanket away from his left arm and shut his eyes. The nurse rolled back the left sleeve of the patient's bathrobe and pajama top and deftly injected 20 cc of a milky solution into a vein. After his arm was safely back under the heated blanket and the nurse gone from the room, Andropov kept his eyes closed. For a few moments Starik wondered if he had dozed off. Then Andropov eyes drifted open and he broke the silence. "For the past six months I have been obsessed with the American President's Strategic Defense Initiative—what the American press has called 'Star Wars.' I have never believed Reagan seriously imagined that the United States, at a staggering cost, could build and position satellites capable of shooting down one hundred percent of the incoming missiles with lasers. Which led me to conclude that he has one of two motives. First, he may think that by escalating the arms race and moving it into outer space, he will oblige us to commit enormous sums to keep up with the Americans, both in terms of offense and defense. This would have the effect of sabotaging our already delicate economic situation, which would undermine the power and prestige of our ruling Communist Party."

Andropov gazed hard at his interlocutor and it appeared as if he had lost the thread of the conversation.

"And the second motive, Yuri Vladimirovich," Starik prompted.

"Yes, the second motive...which I consider the more likely, is that Reagan's Star Wars proposals of last March were designed to prepare the American people psychologically for nuclear war, and more specifically, for what our military planners refer to as *Raketno yadenoye napadeniye*—an American nuclear first strike on the Soviet Union."

Startled, Starik looked up to find the anxious eyes of the General Secretary fixed on him. "Army intelligence has broken a NATO cipher system and discovered," Andropov continued, his voice barely audible, "that a secret NATO exercise, designated ABLE ARCHER 83, is scheduled to be held before the end of the year. Its stated purpose is to practice nuclear release procedures. It is apparent to me that this so-called NATO exercise could well be a cover for the imperialist powers to launch a nuclear first strike."

"If what you say is true—"

"It is a worst-case scenario," Andropov said, "but I believe that the imperial ambitions of Reagan, aggravated by his tendency to view us as an evil empire, to use his own words, justify a worst-case conclusion." Andropov's right hand appeared from under the blanket. He leaned over the bedside table and scratched the words "Approved and sanctioned," and, in a clumsy script, his full name on the bottom of the six-line authorization order designated, 127/S-9021, that Starik had prepared. "I consent to KHOLSTOMER," he announced in a gruff whisper. "I instruct you to launch the operation before the end of November."

The General Secretary's head sank back into the pillow in exhaustion. Starik said, softly, "I will do it, Yuri Vladimirovich."

3

SOMEWHERE IN AFGHANISTAN, SUNDAY, OCTOBER 23, 1983

IBRAHIM'S BAND, SOME SIXTY IN ALL, TRAVELED BY NIGHT, SOMETIMES ON foot, sometimes on donkeys, occasionally in canvas-covered trucks driving without headlights not only as a matter of security, but because Afghans believed vehicles used less gasoline when they ran without headlights. Everywhere they went, peasants offered them shelter and shared the meager rations of food left to them after the passage of Russian commando units. Everyone recognized Ibrahim and he seemed to know dozens by name. The group would turn off the trail as soon as the first silver-gray streaks of light transformed the tops of the mountains high above them into murky silhouettes. Closely guarded by the mujaheddin, Anthony and Maria were led along narrow tracks marked by whitewashed stones. Scrambling up footpaths, they would reach one of the half-deserted, half-destroyed hamlets clinging to the sides of steep hills. Each hamlet had its mosque, surrounded by the stone houses that had not been destroyed in Russian air raids, and the rubble of those that had been hit. Inside common rooms fires blazed in soot-blackened chimneys. Calendars with photographs of the Kaaba at Mecca or the Golden Dome Mosque in Jerusalem were tacked to unpainted plastered walls next to the mihrab—the niche that marked the direction of Mecca. Pistachios and *nabidth*, a mildly alcoholic drink made of raisons or dates mixed with water and allowed to ferment in earthenware jugs, would be set out on linoleum-covered wooden tables. One morning, after a particularly arduous night-long march, a boy set a porcelain bowl filled with what looked like cooked intestines in front of Maria. She made a face and pushed it away. When Ibrahim taunted her, Maria—who had been raised in Beirut by her

Lebanese-American father—retorted with an old Arab proverb, *"Yom asal, yom basal"*—"One day honey, one day onions."

Ibrahim, a moody man who could explode in rage if he thought Islam was being mocked, spit out, "What do you Westerners know of onions? Here everyone has suffered, and deeply, at one time or another."

Hoping to draw biographical details out of Ibrahim, Anthony asked, "Are you speaking from personal experience?"

His eyes clouding over, Ibrahim stared out a window; clearly the story was distressing to him. "It was in the middle seventies," he recounted. "The Iranian SAVAK arrested me when I was transiting Tehran in the mistaken belief that I worked for Iraqi intelligence. This was before the start of the Iran-Iraq war when tension between the intelligence services ran high. The terrible part was that I did not know the answers to their questions so I was powerless to stop the torture, which lasted for three days and three nights. There are still moments when I feel the pliers biting into the nerves on my right arm and the pain shooting to my brain, and I must clamp my lips shut to keep from screaming." Beads of sweat materialized on Ibrahim's upper lip as he sipped *nabidth* from a tin cup. "I live with the memory of searing pain," he continued. Ibrahim retreated into himself for some time. Then, almost as if he were talking to himself, he picked up the thread of the story. "Believe me, I do not hold it against the Iranians. In their place I would have done the same. I have been in their place, here in Afghanistan, and I *have* done the same. When I convinced the SAVAK of my innocence they again became my comrades in the struggle against imperialism and secularism."

A thin boy who had lost a leg to a mine hobbled in on one crude wooden crutch deftly balancing a straw tray filled with small cups of green tea. Ibrahim distributed the cups and sat down cross-legged on a frayed mat to drink one himself. From high above the hamlet came the whine of jet engines. A mujahed darted into the room and reported something to Ibrahim. He muttered an order and his men quickly extinguished all their gas lamps and candles, and the small fire in the chimney. From another valley came the dull thud of exploding bombs. In the darkness Ibrahim murmured a Koranic verse. From the corners of the room, some of the fighters joined in.

On the evening of the tenth day of the journey, Ibrahim led his band and the two prisoners to the edge of a riverbed that cut through a valley. A rusted Soviet tank lay on its side, half submerged in the water. In twos and threes, the mujaheddin crossed the gushing torrent in a bamboo cage suspended from a thick wire and tugged across by hand. Maria clutched Anthony's arm as the two of them were pulled over the raging river. Once on the other side, Ibrahim set out in the pale light cast by a quarter moon, clawing up steep tracks filled with the droppings of mountain goats. After hours of relentless climbing they reached a narrow gorge at the entrance to a long canyon. Steep cliffs on either side had been dynamited so that the only way into and out of the canyon was on foot. Inside the gorge, the trail widened and the terrain flattened out. Hamlets of one-story stone houses lay half-hidden in the tangle of vines that grew over the slate roofs. Vintage anti-aircraft cannon covered with camouflage netting could be seen in the ruins of a mosque and the courtyard of a stable. In the pre-dawn murkiness men holding gas lamps emerged from doorways to wave scarfs at Ibrahim. The Pashtun headman of one hamlet buttoned a Soviet military tunic over his Afghan shirt, buckled on an artificial leg and hobbled over to shake hands with the mujaheddin as they passed in single file. "Your courage is a pearl," he intoned to each. Further up the trail, the group reached a mud-walled compound with a minaret rising from a mosque in the middle and a line of mud-brick houses planted with their backs against a sheer cliff. Smoke spiraled up from chimneys, almost as if Ibrahim and his warriors were expected. A young woman appeared at the doorway of one of the houses. When Ibrahim called to her, she lowered her eyes and bowed to him from the waist. Two small children peeked from behind her skirt.

"We are arrived at Yathrib," Ibrahim informed his prisoners.

Lighting a gas lamp, Ibrahim led Anthony and Maria up to an attic prison. "This will be your home until the Americans agree to deliver missiles in exchange for your freedom. Food, tea, drinking and washing water will be brought to you daily. The ceramic bowl behind the curtain in the corner is to be used as a toilet. You will lack for nothing."

"Except freedom," Maria said scornfully.

Ibrahim ignored the comment. "For one hour in the morning and another in the afternoon you will be permitted to walk in the compound. Guards will accompany you at a distance. If you hear the wail of a hand-cranked siren, it means Russian planes or helicopters have been spotted so you must take shelter. I wish you a good night's sleep." He looked hard at Anthony. "Tomorrow, God willing, we will begin your interrogation," he said softly. "Prepare yourself." With that Ibrahim backed down the ladder, lowering the trapdoor behind him.

Anthony looked across the room at his companion. Her collarless shirt was soaked with sweat and plastered against her torso just enough for him to make out several very spare ribs. Maria removed her boots and stretched her feet straight out and, unbuttoning the top two buttons of her shirt, absently began to massage the swell of a breast. Shivering in her damp clothes, she shed for the first time the tough exterior that she had gone to great pains to project—the ballsy female journalist who could hold her own in a male-dominated profession. Out of the blue she said, "We're fooling ourselves if we think we're going to get out of this alive."

Anthony watched the flame dancing at the end of the wick in the gas lamp. The truth was that the mention of an interrogation had shaken him. He remembered Ibrahim's account of being tortured by the Iranian intelligence service. *In their place I would have done the same. I have been in their place, here in Afghanistan, and I have done the same.* Anthony wondered how much pain he could stand before he cracked; before he admitted to being a CIA officer and told them what he knew about the Company's operations in Pakistan and Afghanistan.

Glancing again at Maria, he saw how miserable she was and tried to raise her spirits. "Man is a victim of dope in the incurable form of hope," he recited. He smiled in embarrassment. "I had a lit teacher at Cornell who made us memorize Ogden Nash—he said it would come in handy when we were trying to impress girls."

She smiled weakly. "Are you trying to impress me, Anthony?"

He shrugged.

She shrugged back. "If we ever get out of here—"

"Not *if.* When. When we get out of here."

"*When* we get out of here we'll start from scratch. You'll quote Ogden Nash and I'll be suitably impressed, and we'll see where it goes."

As Ibrahim made his way across the compound toward the two prisoners the next morning, a beardless young man wearing a dirty white skullcap fell in behind him. He had a dagger wedged into the waistband of his trousers and an AK-47 with spare clips taped to the stock slung from a shoulder. A yellow canary, one of its legs attached to a short leash, perched on his forearm.

Anthony had noticed the lean young man hovering near Ibrahim on the long trek across the mountains and had nicknamed him the Shadow. "Why do you need a bodyguard in your own village?" he asked him now.

"He is not here to guard my body," Ibrahim replied, "He is here to make sure that it does not fall alive into the hands of my enemies." He gestured with a toss of his head. "Come with me."

Maria and Anthony exchanged anxious looks. He tried to smile, then turned to follow Ibrahim and his Shadow toward the low building at the far end of the compound. Pushing through a narrow door, he found himself in a whitewashed room furnished with a long and narrow wooden table and two chairs. A 1979 Disneyland calendar was tacked to one wall. Three of Ibrahim's young fighters, scarves pulled across their faces so that only their eyes were visible, leaned impassively against the walls. Ibrahim's Shadow closed the door and stood with his back to it next to a pail filled with snow that had been brought down from the mountains earlier that morning. Ibrahim settled onto one of the chairs and motioned for Anthony to take the other one. "Do you have any distinguishing marks on your body?" he asked his prisoner.

"That's a hell of a question."

"Answer it. Do you have any tattoos or scars from accidents or operations or birth marks?"

Anthony assumed Ibrahim wanted to be able to prove to the world that the diplomat named McAuliffe was really in his custody. "No tattoos. No scars. I have a birthmark—a dark welt in the form of a small cross on the little toe of my right foot."

"Show me."

Anthony stripped off his sock and Clark boot and held up his foot.

Ibrahim leaned over the table to look at it. "That will serve nicely. We are going to amputate the toe and have it delivered to your American Central Intelligence Agency in Kabul."

The blood drained from Anthony's lips. "You're making a bad mistake," he breathed. "I'm not CIA. I'm a diplomat—"

Ibrahim's Shadow drew the razor-edged dagger from his waistband and approached the table. Two of the warriors came up behind the prisoner and pinned his arms against their stomachs.

Anthony started to panic. "What happened to that famous Pashtun moral code you told us about?" he cried.

Ibrahim said, "It is because of the moral code that we brought snow down from the heights. We do not have anesthetics so we will numb your toe with snow. That's how we amputate the limbs of wounded fighters. You will feel little pain."

"For God's sake, don't do this—"

"For God's sake, we must," Ibrahim said.

The last of the warriors brought over the pail and jammed Anthony's bare foot into the snow. Ibrahim came around the table. "Believe me, when the thing is accomplished you will feel proud of it. I counsel you not to struggle against the inevitable—it will only make the amputation more difficult for us and for you."

Anthony whispered hoarsely, "Don't hold me down."

Ibrahim regarded his prisoner, then nodded at the two warriors pinning his arms. Very slowly, very carefully, they loosened their grip. Anthony filled his lungs with air. Tears brimmed in his eyes as he turned away and bit hard on his sleeve. When it was over Ibrahim himself pressed a cloth to the open wound to stop the bleeding. "*El-hamdou lillah,*" he said. "You could be Muslim."

Five days later, with Anthony hobbling on a makeshift crutch next to Maria during one of their morning walks, Ibrahim's prisoners witnessed the arrival of the gun merchant. A swarthy-skinned man with a long pointed beard, he wore opaque aviator's sunglasses and a Brooklyn Dodgers baseball cap with a handkerchief hanging off the back to protect his neck from the sun. He and two black Bedouins drove a line of mules charged with long wooden crates through the main gate and began unpacking their cargo onto woven mats. In short order they had set out rows of Chinese AK-47 assault rifles, American World War II bazookas, German Schmeisser MP-40s, as well as piles of green anti-tank mines with American designations stenciled on them. As the morning wore on, mujaheddin drifted up to the compound from the hamlets spread out below it and began to inspect the weapons. Some of the younger fighters looked as if they had stumbled into a candy store. Calling to his friends, a teenager wearing camouflage fatigues rammed a clip into an AK-47 and test fired a burst at some tin cans atop the back wall, causing the mules to bray in fright. Ibrahim, followed by his everpresent bodyguard, appeared from one of the stone houses set against the cliff to talk with the gun merchant. Tea was brought and they settled onto a mat to haggle over the prices, and the currency in which they would be paid. The two men came to an agreement and shook hands on it. Rising to his feet, the gun merchant noticed the two prisoners watching from a distance and apparently asked his host about them. Ibrahim looked across the compound, then said something that caused the gun merchant to turn his head in Anthony's direction and spit in the dirt.

"I don't think Ibrahim's visitor likes us," Anthony told Maria.

"He's a Falasha, judging from the look of him," Maria said. "I wonder what an Ethiopian Jew is doing so far from home."

The delicate woman who spoke English with a thick Eastern European accent kept Eugene on the phone as long as she dared. He had to understand, she said, that his calls were moments of grace in an otherwise bleak existence. Aside from her friend, Silvester, she was utterly alone in the world. When the phone rang and Eugene's voice came over the line, well, it was as if the sun had appeared for a fraction of a second in a densely overcast sky and you had to squint to keep the light from hurting your eyes. Oh, dear, no, she didn't mind having to find another furnished apartment after every phone call. Over the years she had more or less become used to the routine. And she understood that, to protect Eugene, it was important for him never to reach her at the same number twice. Thank you for asking, yes, she was well enough, all things considered...What she meant by that was: considering her age and the dizzy spells and nausea that followed the radiation treatments and her miserable digestion and of course the tumor eating away at her colon, though the doctors swore to her that cancers progressed very slowly in old people...Oh, she remembered back to some hazy past when men would say she was exceptionally attractive, but she no longer recognized herself when she looked at the curling sepia photographs in the album—her hair had turned the color of cement, her eyes had receded into her skull, she had actually grown shorter. She didn't at all mind his asking; quite the contrary, Eugene was the only one to take a personal interest in her...Please don't misunderstand, she didn't expect medals but it would not have been out of place, considering the decades of loyal service, for someone to drop a tiny word of appreciation from time to time...Alas, yes, she supposed they must get down to business...She had been instructed to inform Eugene that his mentor required him to organize a face-to-face meeting with SASHA...the sooner, the better...He would discover why when he retrieved the material left in SILKWORM one seven...Oh, how she hoped against hope that he would take care of himself...Please don't hang down yet, there was one more thing. She knew it was out of the realm of possibility but she would have liked to meet him once, just once, only once; would have liked to kiss him on the forehead the way she had kissed her son before the Nazi swines hauled him off to the death camp...Eugene would have to excuse her, she certainly hadn't intended to cry...He would! Why, they could meet in a drug store late at night and take tea together at the counter...Oh, dear child, if such a thing could be organized she would be eternally grateful...It could be a week or so before she found a suitable furnished apartment so he could ring back at this number...She would sit next to the phone waiting for him to call...Yes, yes, goodbye, my dear.

They came to the rendezvous marked as

```
O   X   X

X   X   O

O   X   O
```

in the tic-tac-toe code from opposite directions and met just off the Mall between 9th and 10th Streets under the statue of Robert F. Kennedy. "There were people in the Company who broke out Champagne and celebrated when he was gunned down," SASHA recalled, gazing up at Bobby, who had been assassinated by a Palestinian in the kitchen of a Los Angeles hotel just after winning the 1968 California Democratic Presidential primary.

"You knew him, didn't you?" Eugene asked.

The two men turned their backs on the statue and on the woman who was setting out the skeletons of fish on newspaper for the wild cats in the neighborhood, and strolled down 10th street toward the Mall. "I don't think anybody knew him," SASHA said. "He seemed to step into different roles at different periods of his life. First he was Black Robert, Jack Kennedy's hatchet man. When JFK was assassinated he became the mournful patriarch of the Kennedy clan. When he finally threw his hat into the ring and ran for President, he turned into an ardent defender of the underprivileged."

"From Black Robert to Saint Bobby," Eugene said.

SASHA eyed his cutout. "What's your secret, Eugene? You don't seem to grow older."

"It's the adrenalin that runs through your veins when you live the way we do," Eugene joked. "Every morning I wonder if I'll sleep in my bed that night or on a bunk in a cell."

"As long as we're vigilant, as long as our tradecraft is meticulous, we'll be fine," SASHA assured him. "What Starik has to tell me must be pretty important for you take the trouble—"

"You mean *the risk*."

SASHA smiled faintly. "—for you to take the risk of personally meeting me."

"It is." Eugene had deciphered the document he'd retrieved from SILK-WORM one seven, and then spent a long time trying to figure out how to come at the subject with SASHA. "It's about your recent replies to Starik's query of September twenty-second—you left messages in dead drops at the end of September and the first week of October. Comrade Chairman Andropov is absolutely positive that he has analyzed the situation correctly. He was furious when Starik passed on your reports—he even went so far as to suggest that you had been turned by the CIA and were feeding Moscow Centre disinformation. That was the only explanation he could see for your failing to confirm that ABLE ARCHER 83 is covering an American first strike."

SASHA burst out, "We're really in hot water if Andropov has become the Centre's senior intelligence analyst."

"Don't get angry with me. I'm just the messenger. Look, Comrade Andropov is convinced the Americans are planning a preemptive first strike. With final preparations for KHOLSTOMER being put in place, it's only natural that Andropov and Starik want to pin down the date of the American attack—"

SASHA stopped in his tracks. "There is no American preemptive strike in the works," he insisted. "The whole idea is pure nonsense. The reason I can't come up with the date is because there is none. If there were a preemptive strike on the drawing boards I'd know about it. Andropov is an alarmist."

"Starik is only suggesting that you are too categoric. He asks if it isn't possible for you to report that you are *unaware* of any plans for a preemptive strike, as opposed to saying there are no such plans. After all, the Pentagon could be planning a strike and keeping the CIA in the dark—"

SASHA resumed walking. "Look, it's simply not possible. The Russians have a mobile second-strike capacity on board railroad flatcars—twelve trains, each with four ICBMs, each ICBM with eight to twelve warheads, shuttling around the three hundred thousand miles of tracks. Without real-time satellite intelligence, the Pentagon couldn't hope to knock these out in a first strike. And the CIA provides the guys who interpret the satellite photographs." SASHA shook his head in frustration. "We have a representative on the committee that selects targets and updates the target list. We keep track of Soviet missile readiness; we estimate how many warheads they could launch at any given moment. Nobody has shown any out-of-the-ordinary interest in these estimates."

An overweight man trotting along with two dogs on long leashes overtook them and then passed them. Eugene kept an eye on the occasional car whizzing down Pennsylvania Avenue behind them. "I don't know what to tell you," he finally said. "Starik obviously doesn't want you to make up stories to please the General Secretary. On the other hand, you could make his life easier—"

"Do you realize what you're saying, Eugene? Jesus, we've come a long way together. And you're out here asking me to cook the intelligence estimates I send back."

"Starik is asking you to be a bit more discreet when you file reports."

"In another life," SASHA remarked, "I'm going to write a book about spying—I'm going to tell the fiction writers what it's really all about. In theory, you and I and the *rezidentura* have enormous advantages in spying against the Principal Adversary—Western societies, their governments, even their intelligence agencies are more open than ours and easier to penetrate. But in practice, we have enormous disadvantages that even James Angleton, in his heyday, wasn't aware of. Our leaders act as their own intelligence analysts. And our agents in the field are afraid to tell their handlers anything that contradicts the preconceptions of the leaders; even if we tell the handlers, they certainly won't put their careers on the line by passing it up the chain of command. Stalin was positive the West was trying to promote a war between the Soviet Union and Hitler's Germany, and any information that contradicted that—including half a hundred reports that Hitler was planning to attack Russia—was simply buried. Only reports that appeared to confirm Stalin's suspicions were passed on to him. At one point the Centre even concluded that Kim Philby had been turned because he failed to find evidence that Britain was plotting to turn Hitler against Stalin. Our problem is structural—the intelligence that gets passed up tends to reinforce misconceptions instead of correcting them."

"So what do I tell Starik?" Eugene asked.

"Tell him the truth. Tell him there isn't a shred of evidence to support the General Secretary's belief that America is planning a preemptive nuclear strike against the Soviet Union."

"If Andropov believes that, there's a good chance he may cancel KHOLSTOMER."

"Would that be such a bad thing?" SASHA demanded. "If KHOLSTOMER succeeds hundreds of millions of ordinary people are going to lose their life's savings." After a while SASHA said, "A long time ago you told me what Starik said to you the day he recruited you. You remember?"

Eugene nodded. "I could never forget. He said we were going to promote the genius and generosity of the human spirit. It's what keeps me going."

SASHA stopped in his tracks again and turned to face his comrade in the struggle against imperialism and capitalism. "So tell me, Eugene: what does KHOLSTOMER have to do with promoting the genius and generosity of the human spirit?"

Eugene was silent for a moment. "I'll pass on to Starik what you said—ABLE ARCHER 83 is not masking an American preemptive strike."

SASHA shivered in his overcoat and pulled the collar up around his neck. "It's damn cold out tonight," he said.

"It is, isn't it?" Eugene agreed. "What about KHOLSTOMER? You're still supposed to monitor the Federal Reserve preparations to protect the dollar. What do we do about that?"

"We think about it."

Eugene smiled at his friend. "All right. We'll think about it."

Tessa was incoherent with excitement so Vanessa did most of the talking. Tessa's unit supervisor, a saturnine counterintelligence veteran appropriately named Moody, listened with beady concentration as she led him through the solution. It had been a matter, she explained impatiently, of plying back and forth between the lottery numbers, various telephone numbers and the serial number on a ten-dollar bill. Tessa could tell Mr. Moody was perplexed. If you start with the area code 202, she said, and subtract that number from the lottery number broadcast with the first Lewis Carroll quotation on April 5, 1951, you break out a ten-dollar bill serial number that begins with a three and a zero. You see?

I'm not sure, Moody admitted, but Vanessa, caught up in her own story, plunged on. Using a three and a zero, I was also able to break out the 202 area code from the other twenty-three lottery numbers broadcast by Radio Moscow after an *Alice* or *Looking Glass* quotation. There was no way under the sun this could be an accident.

So far, so good, Moody—one of the last holdovers from the Angleton era—muttered, but it was evident from the squint of his eyes that he was struggling to keep up with the twins.

Okay, Vanessa said. In 1950 the US Treasury printed up $67,593,240 worth of ten-dollar bills with serial numbers that started with a three and a zero, followed by an eight and a nine.

Moody jotted a three and a zero and an eight and a nine on a yellow pad.

Vanessa said, Subtracting the 3089 from that first lottery number gave us a telephone number that began with 202 601, which was a common Washington phone number in the early 1950s.

Tessa said, At which point we checked out the 9,999 possible phone numbers that went with the 202 601.

What were you looking for? Moody wanted to know. He was still mystified.

Don't you see it? Vanessa asked. If Tessa's right, if the quotations from *Alice in Wonderland* and *Through the Looking Glass* alerted the Soviet agent to copy off the lottery number, and if the lottery number was a coded telephone number, the fact that they were changing it all the time meant that the cutout was moving all the time.

Moody had to concede that that made sense; when the agent being contacted was important enough, counterintelligence knew of instances where KGB tradecraft required cutouts to relocate after each contact.

So, Vanessa continued, what we were looking for was someone whose phone number began with 202 601, and who moved out soon after April 5th, 1951.

Tessa said, It took us days to find anyone who even knew that old telephone records existed. We eventually found them buried in dusty boxes in a dusty basement. It turns out there were one hundred and twenty-seven phones that started with the number 202 601 that were taken out of service in the week following April 5th, 1951.

After that it was child's play, Vanessa said. We subtracted each of the hundred and twenty-seven phone numbers from that first lottery number, which gave us a hundred and twenty-seven possible eight-digit serial numbers for the Soviet agent's ten-dollar bill. Then we went to the second time the Moscow quiz program used a Lewis Carroll quote, and subtracted each of the hundred and twenty-seven possible serial numbers from it, giving us a hundred and twenty-seven new phone numbers. Then we waltzed back to the phone records and traced one of these phone numbers to an apartment rented by the same person who had been on the first 202 601 list.

Tessa came around the desk and crouched next to the unit supervisor's wooden swivel chair. The serial number on the agent's ten-dollar bill is 30892006, Mr. Moody. Five days after Radio Moscow broadcast the second coded lottery number, which is to say five days after the Soviet agent in America phoned that number, this person relocated again.

Vanessa said, We tested the serial number on all the lottery numbers broadcast by Radio Moscow when an *Alice* or a *Looking Glass* quote turned up in the quiz. Every time we subtracted the eight-digit serial number from the winning lottery number, it led to a Washington-area phone number in an apartment rented by the same woman. In every case the woman relocated within a week or so of the Moscow Radio broadcast.

So the cutout's a woman! Moody exclaimed.

A Polish woman by the name of—Tessa retrieved an index card from the pocket of her jacket—Aida Tannenbaum. We got our hands on her naturalization papers. She is an Auschwitz survivor, a Jewish refugee from Poland who emigrated to America after World War II and became an American citizen in 1951. She was born in 1914, which makes her sixty-nine years old. She never seems to have held a job and it's not clear where she gets money to pay the rent.

Vanessa said, She's changed apartments twenty-six times in the past thirty-two years. Her most recent address—which we traced when we broke out the most recent lottery signal from Moscow Radio—is on 16th Street near Antioch College. If she sticks to the pattern she'll move out in the next two or three days.

Mr. Moody was beginning to put it all together. She moves out a week or so after she's contacted by the Soviet agent in America, he said.

Right, Tessa said.

Vanessa said, When she moves, all we have to do is get the phone company to tell us when someone named Aida Tannenbaum applies for a new phone number—

Tessa finished the thought for her: Or wait for the Moscow quiz program to come up with an *Alice* or a *Looking Glass* quotation, then subtract the serial number from the lottery number—

Moody was shaking his head from side to side in wonderment. And we'll have her new phone number—the one that the Soviet agent will call.

Right.

That's it.

It looks to me, Moody said, as if you girls have made a fantastic breakthrough. I must formally instruct both of you not to share this information with anybody. By anybody I mean *any-body, without exception.*

As soon as the twins were gone, Moody—who, like his old mentor Angleton, was reputed to have a photographic memory—opened a four-drawer steel file cabinet and rummaged through the folders until he came to an extremely thick one marked "Kukushkin." Moody had been a member of the crack four-man team that Angleton had assigned to work through the Kukushkin serials. Now, skimming the pages of the dossier, he searched anxiously for the passage he remembered. After a time he began to wonder whether he had imagined it. And then, suddenly, his eye fell on the paragraph he'd been looking for. At one point Kukushkin—who turned out to be a dispatched agent but who had delivered a certain amount of true information in order to establish his *bona fides*—had reported that the cutout who serviced SASHA was away from Washington on home leave; the summons back to Russia had been passed on to the cutout by a woman who freelanced for the Washington *rezidentura*.

A woman who freelanced for the rezidentura!

In other words, SASHA was so important that one cutout wasn't sufficient; the KGB had built in a circuit breaker between the *rezidentura* and the cutout who serviced SASHA. Could it be this circuit breaker that the Kritzky twins had stumbled across? He would get the FBI to tap Aida Tannenbaum's phone on 16th Street on the off-chance the cutout who serviced SASHA called again before she moved on to another apartment, at which point they would tap the new number.

Barely able to conceal his excitement, Moody picked up an intra-office telephone and dialed a number on the seventh floor. "This is Moody in counterintelligence," he said. "Can you put me through to Mr. Ebbitt...Mr. Ebbitt, this is Moody in counterintelligence. I know it's somewhat unusual, but I'm calling you directly because I have a something that requires your immediate attention..."

4

TWO MEN IN WHITE JUMP SUITS WITH "CON EDISON" PRINTED ON THE backs showed laminated ID cards to the superintendent of the apartment building on 16th Street off Columbia, within walking distance of Antioch College. Quite a few Antioch undergraduates lived in the building, three or four to an apartment. The old woman with the heavy Eastern European accent in 3B had given notice, so the super said. She was obliged to move in with a sister who was bedridden and needed assistance; the old woman, whose name was Mrs. Tannenbaum, didn't seem overly concerned when she discovered that she would lose the two-months' security she had deposited with the real estate company. No, the super added, she didn't live alone; she shared the furnished apartment with someone named Silvester.

Using penlights, the two technicians found where the telephone cable came into the basement and followed it along the wall to the central panel near a wire mesh storage space filled with baby carriages and bicycles. The shorter of the two men opened a metal tool kit and took out the induction tap and cable. The other man unscrewed the cover on the central panel. Inside, the connections were clearly labeled by apartment number. He touched 3B and, following the wire up with a fingertip, separated it from the others. Then he attached the induction clamp to the line; the device tapped into a phone without touching the wire, which made it difficult to detect. The two men wedged a small battery-powered transmitter between a metal beam and the ceiling, then ran the black cable from the induction tap up behind a pipe and plugged the end into the transmitter. They connected one end of an antenna wire to the terminal and, unreeling it, taped it to the side of the beam, then activated the transmitter and hit the "Test" button.

Inside the white panel truck with "Slater & Slater Radio-TV" printed on the side, a needle on a signal reception meter registered "Strong." The two FBI agents manning the truck, which was parked in front of a fire hydrant further down 16th Street, gave each other the thumb's up sign. From this point on, all incoming and outgoing calls to 3B would be picked off the phone line by the induction clamp and broadcast to the white panel truck, where they would be recorded on tape and then rushed over to a joint command post staffed by FBI agents and Moody's people from counterintelligence.

The President was extremely proud of his long-term memory. "I recall, uh, this grizzly old sergeant looking out at the new recruits, me among them," he was saying, "and he growled at us, you know, the way sergeants growl at new recruits: 'I'm going to tell you men this just once but trust me—it'll stay with you for the rest of your lives. When you come out of a brothel the first thing you want to do is wash your, uh, private parts with Dial soap. The way you remember which soap to use is that Dial spelled backwards is laid.'" Reagan, who liked to think of himself as a stand-up comic manqué, grinned as he waited for the reactions. They weren't long in coming. "*Dial* spelled backward is *laid*!" one of the White House staffers repeated, and he and the others in the room howled with laughter. Reagan was chuckling along with them when his chief of staff, James Baker, stuck his head in the door of the second-floor office in the Presidential hideaway, the four-story brick townhouse on Jackson Place that Reagan had worked out of during the transition and still used when he wanted to get away from the darned goldfish bowl (as he called the Oval Office). "Their car's arriving," Baker snapped. He looked pointedly at the aides. "You have five minutes before I bring them up." With that, he disappeared.

"Remind me who's, uh, coming over," Reagan said amiably.

A young aide produced an index card and hurriedly started to brief the President. "Bill Casey is coming to see you with two of his top people. The first person he's bringing along is his deputy director, Elliott Ebbitt II, Ebby for short. You've met him several times before."

"Did I, uh, call him Elliott or Ebby?"

"Ebby, Mr. President. The second person is the Deputy Director for Operations, Jack McAuliffe. You've never met him but you'll pick him out immediately—he's a six-footer with reddish hair and a flamboyant mustache. McAuliffe is something of a legendary figure inside the CIA—he's the one who went ashore with the Cuban exiles at the Bay of Pigs."

"Ashore with the Cuban exiles at the Bay of Pigs," Reagan repeated.

"McAuliffe's boy, Anthony, is the CIA officer who is being held hostage in Afghanistan, along with the Shaath woman."

Reagan nodded in concern. "The father must be pretty, uh, distressed."

"You were briefed about the boy's toe being amputated and delivered to the CIA station in Kabul."

"I remember the business with the toe," Reagan said cheerily. "They were able to identify it because of a birthmark."

"They're coming to see you," another aide added, "because they've discovered where this Commander Ibrahim is holding the hostages. They want a Presidential *finding* to mount a commando-style raid to free them."

Bill Clark, the President's National Security Advisor, came over to Reagan, who seemed lost in an enormous leather chair behind the large mahogany desk. Photographs of Nancy and himself, along with several of his favorite horses, were spread across the desk. "There are pros and cons to a commando raid," Clark said. "The one your predecessor, President Carter, mounted to free the hostages in Iran went wrong. US servicemen were killed. And of course the raiders never got anywhere near the hostages. Carter looked inept—the press was very critical. On the other hand, the Israelis mounted a commando raid to free the Jewish hostages being held by airline hijackers in Entebbe and pulled it off. They got a terrific press. The whole world applauded their audacity."

An appreciative smile worked its way onto Reagan's tanned features. "I remember that. Made quite a splash at the time."

There were two quick raps on the door, then Baker came in and stepped aside and three men walked into the room. Reagan sprang to his feet and came around the side of the desk to meet them half way. Grinning, he pumped Casey's hand. "Bill, how are you?" Without waiting for a response, he shook hands with Casey's deputy director, Elliott Ebbitt. "Ebby, glad to see you again," he said. The President turned to the DD/O, Jack McAuliffe and gripped his hand in both of his. "So, you're the famous Jack McAuliffe I've, uh, heard so much about—your reputation precedes you. You're the one who went ashore with the Cuban exiles at the Bay of Pigs."

"I'm flattered you remember that, Mr. President—"

"Americans don't forget their heroes. At least this American doesn't." He pulled Jack toward the couch and gestured for everyone to sit down. The aides hovered behind the President.

"Can I offer you boys something to wet your whistles?"

"If you don't mind, Mr. President, we're in a bit of a time bind," Casey said.

Reagan said to Jack, "I was briefed about the toe with the birthmark—you must be pretty distressed."

"Distressed is not the word, Mr. President," Jack said. "This Ibrahim fellow is threatening to cut off more of his toes unless the negotiations—" He couldn't continue.

Reagan's eyes narrowed in sincere commiseration. "Any father in your situation would be worried sick."

"Mr. President," Bill Casey said, "we've come over because there have been new developments in the hostage situation."

Reagan turned his gaze on Casey and stared at him in total concentration. "Our KH-11 has come up with—"

The President leaned back toward an aide, who bent down and whispered in his ear, "Sir, KH-11 is a photo reconnaissance satellite."

"Our KH-11 has come up with some dazzling intelligence," Casey said. "You'll remember, Mr. President, that the Russians and everyone else fell for the disinformation we put out—they think the KH-11 is a signals platform. As they don't suspect there are cameras on board, they don't camouflage military installations or close missile silo doors when the satellite passes overhead. The KH-11 has an advanced radar system to provide an all-weather and day-night look-down capability—using computers, our people are able to enhance the radar signals and create photographs. Thanks to this we've been able to track the Ibrahim kidnappers across Afghanistan. We've traced them to a mountain fortress two hundred and twenty miles inside Afghanistan." Casey pulled an eight-by-ten black-and-white photograph from a folder and handed it to Reagan. "We even have a daytime shot of the Shaath woman and Jack's son, Anthony, walking inside the compound."

The President studied the photograph. "I can make out the two figures but how can you, uh, tell who they are."

"We determined that one is a woman by her chest. And as neither is dressed the way the tribesmen dress, we concluded that they are Westerners."

Reagan handed the photograph back. "I see."

Ebby said, "Mr. President, we have independent confirmation that Anthony McAuliffe and Maria Shaath are, in fact, being held in Ibrahim's stronghold. We arranged for our Israeli friends to send in an agent masquerading as a gunrunner. This happened four days ago. The Mossad's report reached us this morning. The gunrunner saw the two prisoners with his own eyes and subsequently picked out the young McAuliffe and Maria Shaath from a group of photographs that we faxed to the Israelis."

"While this was going on, Mr. President," Casey said, "we've been buying time by negotiating with this fellow Ibrahim by fax. As you know, he originally wanted a hundred and fifty Stinger ground-to-air missiles. In the course of the negotiations we've managed to talk him down to fifty—"

Reagan was shaking his head in disagreement. "I don't see why you're being so stingy," he said. "Far as I'm concerned Afghanistan's the right war at the right time. I told Jim Baker here that the, uh, money you boys allocated to the freedom fighters was peanuts." The President repeated the word "peanuts." The others in the room dared not look at each other. Reagan slapped a knee. "By gosh, there were fifty-eight thousand Americans killed in Vietnam. Afghanistan is payback time."

The National Security Advisor coughed into a palm and Reagan looked up at him. "Mr. President, you decided some time ago that giving Stingers to the Islamic fundamentalists could backfire on us, in the sense that after the Russians leave Afghanistan the fundamentalists could turn the Stingers on the West. Perhaps you would like to review this policy—"

"Well, I just, uh, hate to see the gall darn Commies squirm off the hook, and so forth."

"It's a piece of policy I could never understand," Casey said, hoping to sway the President. He avoided looking at Baker, whom he suspected of bad-mouthing him behind his back; the two were barely on speaking terms. "Putting Stingers into the hands of the mujaheddin," Casey added, "would tilt the scales against the Russians—"

"We could have the National Security shop take another look at the Stinger question," Baker told the President. "But I don't see what's changed since you made your determination that it was too risky."

"We're not afraid of taking risks," Reagan said, searching for a formulation that would accommodate everyone's point of view. "On the other hand, we certainly wouldn't want the Islamists turning the Stingers on us when this war is, uh, over."

Baker, who organized Reagan's schedule and controlled what paperwork reached his desk, took his cue from the last thing the President said. "Until the President changes his mind," he instructed the aides, "we'll leave the Stinger decision stand."

Casey shrugged; another skirmish lost in the behind-the-scenes infighting that went on around the disengaged President. "Now that we know where the hostages are," Casey mumbled, "we'd like to explore with you the possibility of organizing a commando-style raid to free them."

Jack said earnestly, "What we have in mind, Mr. President, is to farm out the operation to the Israelis. We've already sounded out the Mossad's deputy director, Ezra Ben Ezra, the one they call the Rabbi—"

Reagan looked bemused. "That's a good one—a Rabbi being deputy director of the Mossad!"

"The Israelis," Jack rushed on, "have an elite unit known as the Sayeret Matkal—it was this unit that pulled off the Entebbe raid, Mr. President."

"I'm, uh, familiar with the Entebbe raid," Reagan said.

"The game plan," Ebby said, "is for us to agree to exchange the hostages for fifty Stingers. Then a dozen or so members of this Israeli unit—Jews who were born in Arab countries and look like Arabs—"

"And speak perfect Arabic," Jack put in.

"The Sayeret Matkal team," Ebby continued, "would go in with a string of pack animals carrying crates filled with Stingers that have been modified to make them unworkable. Once they're inside Ibrahim's compound—"

Baker interrupted. "What's in it for the Israelis?"

Casey talked past Reagan to Baker. "They're willing to lend a helping hand in exchange for access to KH-11 photos of their Middle East neighbors."

The aides studied the patterns in the carpet underfoot. Baker kept nodding. Clark chewed pensively on the inside of his cheek. Their underlings were waiting to see which way the wind would blow. Finally the President said, very carefully, "Well, it, uh, sounds interesting to me, boys."

Later, waiting outside number 716 Jackson Place for the Company car to pick them up, Jack turned on Casey. "Jesus, Bill, we came away without an answer."

Casey smiled knowingly. "We got an answer."

Ebby said, "If we got an answer it went over my head."

"We all heard him say the idea was interesting, didn't we? That was his way of saying okay."

Ebby could only shake his head. "It's a hell of a way to run a government!"

Aida Tannenbaum snatched the phone off the hook after the first ring.

"Yes?"

When no one responded, Aida became anxious. In her heart she knew who was breathing into the phone on the other end of the line. "Is that you, Gene?" she whispered, hoping to lure his voice through the miles of wire and into her ear. "If it is, please, please say so."

"It's me," Eugene finally said. His voice was strained; he obviously felt uneasy. "I promised I'd call back—"

"Dear child," Aida said, "I knew you would."

"It violates basic tradecraft but I'll do it—I will meet you for a drink, if you like."

"Where?" she asked impatiently. "When?"

"How about the bar of the Barbizon, on Wyoming off Connecticut? At eleven if that's not too late for you."

"The Barbizon at eleven," she said. "You don't mind if I bring Silvester?"

Eugene's voice turned hard. "If you are with anyone I won't show up."

"Dear, dear Gene, Silvester is a *cat*."

He laughed uneasily. "I didn't understand...sure, bring Silvester if you want to. It'll be a recognition signal—I'll look for a woman with a cat. You look for an overweight middle-aged man with hair the color of sand carrying a copy of *Time* under his left arm—"

"Even without the magazine I would know you immediately. Until tonight, then?"

"Until tonight."

Eugene made his way across the half-empty lounge to the bird-like woman sitting next to a small table at the back. She was wearing clothing that he'd seen in old black-and-white motion pictures: a square hat was planted atop her silvery hair and a black lace veil fell from it over her eyes, a paisley form-fitting jacket with padded shoulders hugged her delicate rib cage, a heavy black satin skirt plunged to the tops of sturdy winter walking shoes. Her eyes were watering, whether from age or emotion he couldn't tell. A wicker shopping basket containing a ratty old cat with patches of pink skin where his hair had fallen out was set on the chair next to her.

"I don't even know your name," Eugene said, looking down at the woman.

"I know yours, dear Eugene."

A skeletal hand encased in a white lace glove floated up to him. Eugene took hold of it and, recalling the etiquette lessons his mother had given him when he was twelve years old, bent from the waist and brushed the back of her hand with his lips. He removed his overcoat and threw it across the back of a chair and settled onto a seat across from her.

"I will have a daiquiri," the woman informed him. "I had one immediately after I arrived in America in 1946 in a very elegant cocktail lounge the name of which has since slipped my mind."

Eugene signaled to the waiter and ordered a daiquiri and a double cognac. The old woman appeared to sway on her seat, then steadied herself by gripping the edge of the table. "My name," she said, "is Aida Tannenbaum."

"It is an honor to make your acquaintance," Eugene told her, and he meant every word. He knew of few people who had given as much to the cause.

The waiter set two drinks on the table and tucked a check upside down under an ashtray. Eugene said, "So this is Silvester."

Aida lifted the veil with one gloved hand and sipped the daiquiri. She swallowed and winced and shuddered. "Oh, dear, I don't remember the daiquiri being so strong. Yes, this is Silvester. Silvester, say hello to a comrade-in-arms, Eugene." She swayed toward Eugene and lowered her voice. "I was instructed to live alone and never told anyone about Silvester. I found him on the fire escape of an apartment I rented in the early 1970s. You don't think they would mind, do you?"

"No. I'm sure it's all right."

She seemed relieved. "Tell me about yourself, Eugene. How did an American—I can tell from your accent that you are from the East Coast; from New York in all probability—how did you become involved in the struggle..."

"I was led to believe that I could contribute to the fight to defend the genius and generosity of the human spirit."

"We are doing exactly that, dear child. Of course I don't know what it is that you do with the messages I pass on to you, but you are a Socialist warrior on the front line."

"So are you, Aida Tannenbaum."

"Yes." Her eyes clouded over. "Yes. Though I will admit to you I am fatigued, Eugene. I have been fighting on one or another front line as far back as I can remember. Before the war, there were some who believed that only the creation of a Zionist state in Palestine could shield the Jews, but I was in the other camp—I believed that the spread of Socialism would eradicate anti-Semitism and protect the Jews, and I joined the struggle led by the illustrious Joseph Stalin. If I were a religious person, which I am not, I would certainly think of him as a saint. During the war I fought against the Fascists. After the war—" She sipped the daiquiri and shuddered again as the alcohol burned her throat. "After the war I was mystified to find myself still alive. In order to make what life I had left worth living, I joined the ranks of those battling alienation and capitalism. I dedicated the fight to the memory of my son, assassinated by the Nazis. His name was Alfred. Alfred

Tannenbaum, aged seven at the time of his murder. Of course I don't believe there is a word of truth in the things they have said about Stalin since—I am absolutely certain it is all capitalist propaganda."

Three young men in three-piece suits and a young woman, all slightly inebriated, entered the lounge. They argued over whether to sit at the bar or a table. The bar won. Sliding onto stools, depositing their attaché cases on the floor, they summoned the bartender and loudly ordered drinks. At the small table Eugene inspected the newcomers, then turned back to Aida. "You are what Americans would call an unsung heroine. The very few people who know what you do appreciate you."

"Perhaps. Perhaps not." Aida dabbed a tear away from the corner of an eye with the paper napkin. "I have rented a furnished apartment at number forty-seven Corcoran Street off New Hampshire, not far from Johns Hopkins University. I am moving there tomorrow. I prefer to live in buildings with college students—they are always very kind to Silvester. And they often run errands for me when I am too nauseous or too dizzy to go out in the street." She managed a tight-lipped smile. "Perhaps we could meet again from time to time."

"This was probably a bad idea. We must not take the risk again."

"If they haven't found us out during all these years I doubt they will do it now," she said.

"Still—"

"Once every six months, perhaps? Once a year even?" Aida sighed. "What we do, the way we do it, is terribly lonely."

Eugene smiled back at her. "At least you have Silvester."

"And you, dear child. Whom do you have?" When he didn't answer she reached across the table and rested her fingers on the back of his hand. She was so frail, her hand so light, he had to look down to be sure she was touching him. She pulled back her hand and, opening a small snap purse, took out a minuscule ballpoint pen and scratched a phone number on the inside of a Barbizon Terrace matchbook. "If you change your mind before—" She laughed softly. "If you change your *heart* before our friends broadcast a new lottery number you can reach me at this number."

Outside, a cold wind was seeping in off the Tidal Basin. Aida was wearing a cloth coat with an imitation fur collar. Eugene offered to flag down a taxi for her but she said she preferred to walk home. She tucked the thick piece of cloth in the basket around Silvester and buttoned the top button of her overcoat. Eugene held out his hand. Ignoring it, she reached up and placed her fingers on the back of his neck and, with a lover's gesture perfected fifty years before, gently pulled his head down and kissed him on the lips. Spinning quickly away, she walked off into the night.

As soon as she was out of sight Eugene pulled the matchbook from his pocket and ripped it so that the phone number was torn in half. He dropped half of the matchbook in the gutter and the other half in a garbage pail he found two blocks up the street.

He would never again set eyes on Aida Tannenbaum.

Casey, bored to tears, was auditing a high-level symposium that had been convened to reconcile the differences between CIA forecasts for the Soviet Union and those from a "B" team panel of outside economists. CIA specialists maintained that Soviet per capita income was on a par with Britain's; the "B" team had calculated that it was roughly equal to Mexico's. To make matters more complicated, the "B" team insisted that the Company's projections of Soviet strategic forces was also on the high side. The argument raged back and forth across the table as economists on both sides of the divide dredged up statistics to support their conclusions. Swallowing each yawn as it bubbled up from the depths of his weary soul, Casey gazed listlessly out the window. Darkness had fallen and the lights that illuminated the security fence around Langley were flickering on. Casey knew what the number crunchers didn't: that the CIA had in fact detected signs of a slowdown in the Soviet economy but continued to overstate its size and the growth rate to appease Reagan's people, who grew livid when anyone raised the possibility that the Soviet economy and Soviet military spending were flattening out. Team players, so the Reagan people contended, didn't challenge the logic behind the President's decision to build the B-1 bomber or recommission two World War II battleships and budget for a 600-ship navy: military-wise, the Soviet Union was nipping at our heels and we had to throw immense amounts of money at the problem to stay ahead. Period. End of discussion.

"The Soviet Union," one of the independent economists was arguing, "is an Upper Volta with rockets." He waved a pamphlet in the air. "A French analyst has documented this. The number of women who die in childbirth in the Soviet Union has been decreasing since the Bolshevik Revolution. Suddenly, in the early seventies, the statistic bottomed out and then started to get worse each year until the Russians finally grasped how revealing this statistic was and stopped reporting it."

"What in God's name does a statistic about the number of women who die in childbirth have to do with analyzing Soviet military spending?" a Company analyst snarled across the table.

"If you people knew how to interpret statistics, you'd know that everything is related—"

Elliott Ebbitt, Casey's DDCI, appeared at the door of the conference room and beckoned the Director with a forefinger. Casey, only too happy to flee the debate, slipped out into the corridor with Ebby. "Will Rogers once said that an economist's guess is liable to be as good as anybody else's," Casey grumbled, "but I'm beginning to have my doubts."

"I thought you'd want to be in on this," Ebby told him as they started toward the DCI's suite of offices. "There's been a breakthrough in the SASHA affair."

Moody from counterintelligence, along with two FBI agents, were waiting in the small conference room across from the DCI's bailiwick. Waving a paw at the others to go on with the conversation, Casey flopped into a seat.

Moody picked up the thread. "Director, thanks to the ingenious work of Leo Kritzky's daughters, we've identified what we call the circuit breaker between the Soviet *rezidentura* and the cutout that runs SASHA."

"What makes you think the cutout runs SASHA?" Casey wanted to know.

Moody explained about the Kukushkin serial involving the woman who freelanced for the *rezidentura* and the cutout who worked SASHA. "Kukushkin was a dispatched agent," he said, "but he gave us true information in order to convince us he was a genuine defector. It looks as if the tidbit about the woman freelancer and the cutout could have been true information."

The FBI agent wearing a nametag that identified him as A. Bolster said, "We're not a hundred percent sure why, but the circuit breaker, an old Polish woman by the name of Aida Tannenbaum, met the cutout late last night at the Barbizon Terrace."

Casey nodded carefully. "How can you be sure the person Tannenbaum met was not simply a friend?"

Bolster said, "We have a tap on her phone. The person who called her earlier in the evening told her: 'It violates basic tradecraft but I'll do it—I will meet you for a drink, if you like.'"

"He said that?" Casey inquired. "He used the word *tradecraft*?"

"Yes, sir."

Moody said, "It was short notice but we managed to get a team into the lounge when they were halfway through their little tête-à-tête. One of our people had a directional mike hidden in an attaché case, which he put on the floor pointing at them. The sound quality wasn't very good but our technicians enhanced it and we came up with a transcript of their conversation." Moody passed two typed sheets across to the Director, then read aloud from his own copy. "We can hear him saying, and I'm quoting: 'You are what Americans would call an unsung heroine. The very few people who know what you do appreciate you.' And she answers, and again I'm quoting: 'Perhaps. Perhaps not.' Then she can be heard saying: '*I have rented a fur-nished apartment on number forty-seven Corcoran Street off New Hampshire, not far from Johns Hopkins University. I am moving there tomorrow. I prefer to live in buildings with college students—they are always very kind to Silvester. And they often run errands for me when I am too nauseous or too dizzy to go out in the street. Perhaps we could meet again from time to time.*'"

"Who's Silvester?" Casey asked.

The second FBI agent, F. Barton, said, "We think it's the woman's cat, Director."

Jack McAuliffe turned up at the door, a preoccupied frown etched onto his forehead; he'd been over at the Pentagon laying in the plumbing for the Israeli commando raid on Ibrahim's mountain compound, and was worried sick they weren't assigning enough helicopters. "Director, Ebby, gentlemen," he said, sliding into a free seat next to Moody, "what's this I hear about a breakthrough in the SASHA business?"

While Moody brought the Deputy Director for Operations up to date in a hurried whisper, Ebby said, "Director, taken together, the phone con-versation and the conversation in the Barbizon seem to suggest that, in violation of standard tradecraft precautions, the Polish woman talked the cutout into a face-to-face meeting. If, as we suspect, she's been acting as his circuit breaker for decades, she may have fantasized about him; may have even fallen in love with him. As for the cutout—"

"Maybe he felt sorry for her," Moody suggested.

"What do you think, Jack?" Ebby asked.

Jack looked up. "About what?"

"About why the cutout violated standard tradecraft precautions."

Jack considered this. "He's been leading a dreary life," he guessed. His eyes were heavy lidded, his face pale and drawn; it wasn't lost on Ebby and the Director that the DD/O could have been describing himself. "Maybe he just needed to talk to someone to get through one more night," Jack added.

"Either way," Ebby said, "he agreed to meet her this one time."

Bolster said, "On Moody's recommendation we laid on a tiered surveil-lance. Twelve vehicles—six private automobiles, three taxis, two delivery vehicles, one tow truck—were involved, one peeling off as another came on line. The cutout flagged down a taxi and took it to Farragut Square, then caught a bus to Lee Highway, where he got off and changed to another bus going up Broad Street to Tysons Corner. He got off there and walked the last half-mile to an apartment over the garage of a private home—"

Barton said, "When he emerged from the Barbizon he tore up a matchbook and threw the different halves in different places. Our people recovered them—the phone number of the apartment the Polish woman moved into today was written inside."

Casey, always impatient, snapped, "Who is the cutout?"

Moody said, "He's renting the apartment under the name of Gene Lutwidge, which is obviously an operational identity."

Bolster said, "We've put a tap on Lutwidge's line from the telephone exchange. And we've created a special fifty-man task force—he'll be tailed by rotating teams every time he leaves the apartment. With any luck, it'll only be a matter of time before he leads us to your famous SASHA."

Casey asked, "What does this guy do for a living?"

Barton said, "He doesn't go to an office, if that's what you mean. People in the neighborhood are under the impression that he's some kind of writer—"

"Has Lutwidge published anything?" Casey demanded.

"We checked the Library of Congress," Barton said. "The only thing that surfaces when you look up the name Lutwidge is *Alice in Wonderland* and *Through the Looking Glass*—"

"They're by Lewis Carroll," Casey said.

"Lewis Carroll was the pseudonym for Charles Lutwidge Dodgson," Bolster explained.

"Did you say *Dodgson*?" Moody exclaimed.

Everyone turned to stare at Moody. Bolster said, "What do you remember that we don't?"

Moody said, "In 1961—that was before your time, Archie—the FBI arrested a man named Kahn who ran a liquor store in the Washington area. You also arrested the girl who worked for him, name of Bernice something-or-other. Both Kahn and Bernice were American communists who had gone underground, and were providing infrastructure for the Soviet agent who was the cutout between Philby and his controlling officer. We think this same cutout serviced SASHA after Philby was no longer operational. The FBI agents who raided the liquor store came across evidence of the cutout's presence: ciphers and microfilms, a microdot reader, lots of cash and a radio that could be calibrated to shortwave bands, all of it hidden under the floorboards of a closet in the apartment above the store, which is where the cutout lived. The cutout smelled a rat and assumed another identity before he could be apprehended. The name he was operating under was Eugene *Dodgson*."

Casey was starting to see the connection. "Dodgson. Lutwidge. The *Alice* or *Looking Glass* quotes on the Moscow quiz program. Someone in the KGB is obsessed with *Alice in Wonderland*."

Bolster asked Moody, "Do you remember what the man posing as Dodgson looked like?"

"The FBI report described him as a Caucasian male, aged thirty-one in 1961—which would make him fifty-three today. He was of medium height, with a sturdy build with sandy hair. There will be photographs of him in your files taken during the weeks he was under surveillance."

Bolster extracted an eight-by-ten photograph from an envelope and handed it across the table to Moody. "This was snapped by a telephoto lens from the back of a delivery vehicle as Lutwidge passed under a street light. The quality is piss-poor but it'll gives you a rough idea of what he looks like."

Moody studied the photograph. "Medium height, what looks like light hair. If this is the man we knew as Dodgson, his hair has grown thin and his body has thickened around the middle."

Moody passed the photo on to Ebby, who said, "It's been twenty-two years since the FBI described him as sturdy. All of us have thickened around the middle."

"The trick," Casey quipped, "is not to thicken around the brain."

Ebby handed the photograph on to Jack, who fitted a pair of reading glasses over his ears and peered at the photograph. His mouth fell open and he muttered, "It's not possible—"

Ebby said, "What's not possible?"

"Do you recognize him?" Moody asked.

"Yes...Maybe...It couldn't be...I'm not sure...It looks like him but he's changed..."

"We've all changed," Ebby commented.

"It looks like whom?" Casey demanded.

"You're not going to believe this—it looks like the Russian exchange student I roomed with my senior year at Yale. His name was Yevgeny Tsipin. His father worked for the United Nations Secretariat..."

Moody turned to Casey. "The Tsipin who worked for the UN Secretariat in the 1940s was a full-time KGB agent." He fixed his eyes on Jack. "How well did your Russian roommate speak English?"

Jack, still puzzled, looked up from the photograph. "Yevgeny graduated from Erasmus High in Brooklyn—he spoke like a native of Brooklyn."

Moody flew out of his chair and began circling the table. "That would explain it—" he said excitedly.

"Explain what?" Casey asked.

"The Eugene Dodgson who worked at Kahn's Wine and Beverage spoke English like an American—there was no trace of a Russian accent. But Jim Angleton never ruled out the possibility that he was a Russian who had somehow perfected his English."

Shaking his head in amazement, Jack gaped at the photograph. "It could be him. On the other hand it could be someone who looks like him." He stared at the photograph. "I know who'll know," he said.

5

S TARIK'S NIECES HAD TAKEN TO TIPTOEING AROUND THE SECOND-FLOOR apartment in the Apatov Mansion as if it were a clinic and Uncle was ailing, which was how he looked. His disheveled appearance—the scraggly white beard tumbling in matted knots to his cadaverous chest, the bloodshot eyes sunken into the waxen face and conveying permanent trepidation, the odor of an old man's secretions emanating from his unwashed carcass—frightened the girlies so much that the bedtime cuddle in the great bed in which the Chechen girl blew out her brains had become a nightly ordeal. Unbeknownst to Uncle, the girlies had taken to drawing lots to see who would be obliged to crawl under the hem of his sweaty peasant's shirt.

"If you please, Uncle, do read more quickly," implored the blonde Ossete when he lost his place and started the paragraph over again. Starik absently stroked the silken hair of the newly arrived niece from Inner Mongolia; even now, approaching the age of seventy, he was still moved by the innocence of beauty, by the beauty of innocence. Behind his back the Ossete reached beneath the undershirt of the Latvian and pinched one of her tiny nipples. The girl squealed in surprise. Uncle turned on the Latvian in vexation. "But she pinched my nipple," whined the girl, and she pointed out the culprit.

"Is that the way to treat a cousin?" Starik demanded.

"It was meant to be a joke—"

Uncle's hand shot out and he cuffed her hard across the face. His long fingernails, cut square in the style of peasants, scratched her cheek. Blood welled in the wounds. Sobbing in fright, the Ossete peeled off her sleeveless cotton undershirt and held it against the welts. For a moment nobody dared to utter a word. Then the muffled voice of the Vietnamese girl could be heard from beneath Uncle's shirt, "What in the world is happening up there?"

Adjusting his spectacles, Uncle returned to the book and started the paragraph for the third time. "'Look, look!' Alice cried, pointing eagerly. 'There's the White Queen running across the country! She came flying out of the wood over yonder—How fast those Queens can run!' 'There's some enemy after her, no doubt,' the King said, without even looking round. 'That wood's full of them.'"

Starik's voice trailed off and he cleared a frog from his throat. His eyes turned misty and he was unable to continue. "Enough for tonight," he barked, tugging the Vietnamese girl out from under the nightshirt by the scruff of her neck. He slid off the bed and padded barefoot to the door, leaving the room without so much as a "sleep tight, girlies." The nieces watched him go, then looked at one another in bafflement. The Ossete's sobbing had turned into hiccups. The other girls set about trying to scare the hiccups away with sharp cries and hideous expressions on their faces.

In the inner sanctum off the library, Starik poured himself a stiff Bulgarian cognac and sank onto the rug with his back against the safe to drink it. Of all the passages he read to the girls this one unnerved him the most. For Starik—who saw himself as the Knight with the mild blue eyes and the kindly smile, the setting sun shining on his armor—could discern the black shadows of the forest out of which the White Queen had run, and they terrified him. "'There's some enemy after her,' the King said. 'The wood's full of them.'" Starik had long ago identified the enemy lurking in the woods: It was not death but failure.

When he was younger he had believed with all his heart and all his energy in the inevitability of success; if you fought the good fight long enough you were bound to win. Now the sense of quest and crusade were gone, replaced by the presentiment that there was not even a remote possibility of triumph; the economy of Greater Russia, not to mention the social structure and the Party itself, was coming apart at the seams. Vultures like that Gorbachev fellow were circling overhead, waiting to feast off the pieces. Soviet control over Eastern Europe was unraveling. In Poland, the independent trade union Solidarity was gaining ground, making a joke out of the Polish Communist Party's claim to represent the Polish proletariat. In East Germany, the "concrete heads"—the nickname for the old Party hacks who resisted reform— were clinging to power by their fingertips.

Clearly the genius, the generosity of the human spirit would shrivel, replaced by the rapaciousness of the unrestrained *Homo economicus*. If there was consolation to be had, it was in the certainty that he would wreck the capitalist edifice even as socialism went down to defeat. The Germans had an expression for it: the twilight of the gods, Götter-dämmerung! It was the last gasp of gratification for those who had battled and failed to win.

Andropov had been dozing, an oxygen mask drawn over the lower half of his face, when Starik turned up at the third-floor Kremlin suite earlier in the day. The Venetian blinds had been closed; only low-wattage bulbs burned in the several shaded lamps around the room. The General Secretary had just completed another grueling session of hemodialysis on the American artificial kidney machine. Male nurses bustled around him monitoring his pulse, changing the bedpan, checking the drip in his forearm, applying rouge to his pasty cheeks so that the afternoon's visitors would not suppose they were in the presence of a corpse.

"*Izvinite,* Yuri Andropov," Starik had whispered. "Are you awake?"

Andropov had opened an eye and had managed an imperceptible nod. "I am always awake, even when I sleep," he had mumbled from behind his oxygen mask. His left hand had levitated off the blanket and two fingers had pointed toward the door. The nurses had noticed the gesture and departed, closing the door behind them.

Andropov understood what Starik was doing there. This was to be the General Secretary's final briefing before KHOLSTOMER was initiated. All the elements were in place: the accounts in off-shore banks were set to dump 63.3 billion US dollars onto the spot market; at the first sign of the downward spiral of the dollar, KGB's agents of influence in Japan, Hong Kong, Taiwan and Malaysia, along with a German economist who was close to West German Chancellor Helmut Kohl, would press their central banks into selling off dollar Treasury bond holdings to protect their positions, resulting in the collapse of the bond market.

Prying away the oxygen mask, breathing hard, Andropov had started firing questions: Had the KGB come up with evidence confirming America's intention of launching a preemptive nuclear strike on the Soviet Union? If so, where had the evidence originated? Was there an indication of a time frame?

It had become obvious to Starik that the fate of KHOLSTOMER was intricately bound to Andropov's assumption that the NATO exercise, designated ABLE ARCHER 83, was intended to cover the preemptive strike. If the General Secretary began to have doubts about American hostile intentions, he—like Brezhnev before him—would step back from the brink. The operatives around the world waiting for the final coded message to launch KHOLSTOMER would have to stand down. The CIA might get wind of what had almost happened from a disgruntled agent. Once the secret was out KHOLSTOMER would be dead. And so Starik did what he had never done in his forty-three years of running spies: he fabricated the report from one of his agents in place.

"*Tovarish* Andropov, I have the response from SASHA to your most recent queries." He held out a sheet filled with typescript, knowing that the General Secretary was too ill to read it for himself.

Andropov's eyes twitched open and something of the old combativeness glistened in them; Starik caught a glimpse of the unflinching ambassador who had put down the Hungarian uprising and, later, run the KGB with an iron hand.

"What does he say?" the General Secretary demanded.

"The Pentagon has asked the CIA for real-time satellite intelligence updates on the twelve trains filled with ICBMs that we keep shuttling around the country. Their Joint Chiefs have also requested a revised estimate of Soviet missile readiness; they specifically wanted to know how long it would take us to launch ICBMs from missile silos once an American attack was spotted and the order to shoot was given and authenticated."

Andropov collapsed back into the pillows of the hospital bed, drained of hope that his analysis of Reagan's intentions had been wrong. "SASHA's information has always been accurate in the past..."

"There is more," Starik said. "We have deciphered a cable to American detachments guarding medium-range nuclear missile bases in Europe cancelling all leaves as of twenty-fifth November. The NATO exercise designated ABLE ARCHER 83 has been advanced two weeks and is now scheduled to commence at three A.M. on December first."

Andropov reached for the oxygen mask and held it over his mouth and nose. The act of breathing seemed to take all his strength. Finally he tugged the mask away from his lips, which were bluish and caked with sputum. "The only hope of avoiding a nuclear holocaust is if KHOLSTOMER can damage them *psychologically*—if the capitalist system collapses around them Reagan and his people may lose their nerve. The world would accuse them of starting a war to divert attention from the economic crisis. Under these circumstances they may hesitate."

"There could be widespread unrest, even riots," Starik agreed. He was starting to believe the scenario that Andropov had invented and he had confirmed. "It is not out of the realm of possibility that their military establishment will be too preoccupied with maintaining order to wage war."

The General Secretary scraped the sputum off his lips with the back of his arm. "Do it," he wheezed. "KHOLSTOMER is our last hope."

From his corner table near the back of the courtyard restaurant in Dean's Hotel, Hippolyte Afanasievich Fet, the gloomy KGB *rezident*, kept an eye on the CIA officers drinking bottles of Murree beers at the first table off the seedy lobby. The Americans talked in undertones but laughed boisterously—so boisterously no one would have guessed that there was a war raging beyond the Khyber Pass, half an hour by car down the road. At half past seven, the Americans divided up the bill and counted out rupees and noisily pushed back their chairs to leave. Fet's two table companions—one was the *rezidentura's* chief cipher clerk, the other a military attaché at the Soviet consulate—exchanged smutty comments about the comportment of Americans abroad. You could tell Americans, one of them remarked, the minute they walked into a room. They always acted as if the country they were in belonged to them, the other agreed. Fet said, They throw rupees around as if they were printing them in the back room of the CIA station. Maybe they are, said the military attaché. All three Russians laughed at this. Fet excused himself to go to the lavatory. Get the bill and pay it but don't tip like an American—the Pakistanis overcharge as it is, he instructed the cipher clerk.

Fet ambled across the restaurant to the lobby. Walking past the door to the lavatory, he continued on out the front door and made his way to the parking lot behind the hotel. The Americans were lazily climbing into two Chevrolets. Fet walked around to the passenger side of one and motioned for the acting chief of station to roll down the window.

"Well, if it isn't Boris Karloff in the flesh," the American commented. "Got any state secrets you want to sell, Fet?"

"As a matter of fact, I do."

The smile was still plastered across the American's face but his eyes were bright with curiosity. Sensing that something unusual was occurring, he signaled with a hand. The others spilled out of the cars and surrounded the Russian. Two of them walked off a few paces and, turning their backs on Fet, peered into the parking lot to see if there were other Russians around.

"Okay, Fet, what's all this about?" demanded the acting chief of station.

"I wish to defect. Do not attempt to talk me into defecting in place. I will come across here and now, or not at all." He patted his jacket pockets, which were stuffed with thick manila envelopes. "I have all the correspondence between the Centre and the *rezidentura* for the last month in my pockets. And I have many other secrets in my head—secrets that will surprise you."

"What about your wife?" one of the Americans asked. "Things will go badly for her if you skip out?"

A cruel smile stole across Fet's sunken cheeks; it made him look even more like Boris Karloff. "My wife last night announced to me that she has fallen in love with the young head of our consulate, a prick if there ever was one. She asked me for a separation. I will give her a separation she will never forget."

"I think he's serious," said one of the Americans.

"I am very serious," Fet assured them.

The acting station chief weighed the pros and cons. Inside the kitchen of the restaurant one of the Chinese chefs could be heard yelling at another in high-pitched Mandarin. Finally the American made up his mind; if for some reason Langley didn't like what they had hooked, hell, they could always toss Fet back into the pond. "Quickly, get in the car," he told Fet.

Moments later the two Chevrolets roared out of the parking lot and swung onto Saddar Road, heading at high speed toward the fortress-like American Consulate across town.

Bundled in a sheepskin jacket with a printed Sindhi shawl wound around her neck like a scarf, Maria Shaath sat hunched over the crude wooden table, scratching questions on a pad by the shimmering light of the single candle burning on the table. From time to time she would look up, the eraser end of the pencil absently caressing her upper lip as she stared intently into the yellow-blue flame. As new questions occurred to her, she bent back to the pad to note them down.

Anthony and Maria had been strolling around the compound that morning when Ibrahim emerged from his dwelling. The air was sharp; snow was falling in the mountains, lowering visibility for Russian helicopters that were said to be marauding through the labyrinth of valleys. In the hamlet below two skinny boys were pulling a hump-backed cow along the dirt trail. A group of fundamentalist fighters back from a three-day patrol, their long shirts and long beards and fur-lined vests caked with dust, could be seen filing up the road, Kalashnikovs casually perched on their shoulders. From a firing range in a hidden quarry came the sound of hollow metallic drumbeats, each one containing its own echo. Just inside the great double doors of the compound, which were open during the day, an old man wearing plastic sunglasses to protect his eyes from sparks was sharpening knives on a stone wheel turned by a girl hidden in a dark brown *burqa*.

"You are a remarkable man," Maria had said. She looked at him intently. "Why don't you let me interview you?"

"Interview me?"

"Well, that's what I do for a living. You have all this gear around—surely you can come up with a television camera."

Ibrahim seemed interested. "And what would you ask me in such an interview?"

"I would ask you where you come from and where you're going. I would ask you about your religion, your friends, your enemies. I would ask you why you fight the Russians, and what will be your next jihad when the Russians are gone."

"What makes you think there will be another jihad?"

"You are in love with holy war, Commander Ibrahim. It's written on your face. Cease-fire, peace—they bore you. I've met people like you before. You will go from one war to the next until you get your wish—"

"Since you know so much about me, what is my wish?"

"You want to become a martyr."

Maria's comments had amused Ibrahim. "And what would you do with the tape of an interview if I consent," he had asked.

"You could arrange for it to be delivered to my office in Peshawar. Within twenty-four hours it would be on the air in New York—what you say would be picked up and broadcast around the world."

"Let me think about it," Ibrahim had said. And with his Shadow trailing two-steps behind him, he had stridden past the knife-sharpener and out of the compound in the direction of the barracks at the edge of the hamlet below.

Maria had turned to Anthony. "Well, he didn't say no, did he?"

At dusk Ibrahim had sent word that he consented to the interview, which would take place in the room under the attic at midnight. Included in the note was a list of things he would refuse to talk about: questions concerning his real identity and his past were prohibited, along with anything that might reveal the location of the mountaintop he called Yathrib.

When Maria and Anthony climbed down the ladder at a quarter to midnight, they found that the communal kitchen had been transformed into a crude studio. Two kleig lights, running off a generator humming away outside the house, illuminated the two kitchen chairs set up in front of the chimney. A beardless young man holding a German Leica motioned for the two prisoners to stand with their backs to a poster of the Golden Dome Mosque in Jerusalem and then snapped half a dozen shots of them. (It was this photo that turned up on front pages around the world a few days later.) Maria regarded the camera with an impatient smile; she was eager to get on with the interview. Anthony managed an uncomfortable grin that editorialists later described as sardonic. With the photo op out of the way Ibrahim, wearing an embroidered white robe that grazed the tops of his Beal Brothers boots, appeared at the door and settled onto one of the chairs. His long hair had been combed and tied back at the nape of his neck, his short henna-tinted beard had been trimmed. A bearded mujahed wearing thick eyeglasses fiddled with the focus of a cumbersome Chinese camera mounted on a homemade wooden tripod. Maria, pulling the Sindhi shawl over her shoulders, took her place in the second chair. A red light atop the camera came on. Maria looked into the lens. "Good evening. This is Maria Shaath, broadcasting to you from somewhere in Afghanistan. My guest tonight—or should I say my *host*, since I am his guest, or more accurately, his prisoner—is Commander Ibrahim, the leader of the commando unit that kidnapped me and the American diplomat Anthony McAuliffe from the streets of Peshawar in Pakistan." She turned toward Ibrahim and favored him with a guileless smile. "Commander, it's hard to know where to begin this interview, since you have given me a list of things you refuse to talk about—"

"Let us start by correcting an error. Anthony McAuliffe is posing as an American diplomat, but he is actually a CIA officer attached to the CIA station in Peshawar at the time of his...apprehension."

"Even if you're correct, it's still not clear why you kidnapped him. I thought the American Central Intelligence Agency was helping Islamic fundamentalist groups like yours in the war against the Soviet occupation of Afghanistan."

Ibrahim's fingers kneaded the worry beads. "The American Central Intelligence Agency could not care less about Afghanistan. They are supplying antiquated arms to Islamic fundamentalists in order to bleed the Soviet enemy, much as the Soviets supplied arms to the North Vietnamese to bleed their American enemy in Vietnam."

"If the situation were reversed, if you were fighting the Americans, would you accept aid from the Soviet Union?"

"I would accept aid from the devil to pursue the jihad."

"If you drive out the Soviet occupiers—"

"*When* we drive out the Soviet occupiers—"

Maria nodded. "Okay, will the war be over *when* you drive out the Russians?"

Ibrahim leaned forward. "We are engaged in a struggle against colonialism and secularism, which are the enemies of Islam and the Islamic state we will create in Afghanistan, as well as other areas of the Muslim world. The war will go on until we have defeated all vestiges of colonialism and secularism and inaugurated a Muslim commonwealth based on the pure faith—the Islam—of the Prophet you call Abraham and we call Ibrahim. Such a state, governed by Koranic principles and the example of the Messenger Muhammad, would be characterized by total submission to God. This I believe."

Casey and his deputy, Ebby, stood in front of the enormous television set in the Director's office on the seventh floor of Langley, drinks in their fists, watching the interview.

On the screen Maria was glancing at her notes. "Let me ask you some personal questions. Are you married?"

"I have two wives and three sons. I have several daughters also."

Casey tinkled the ice cubes in his glass. "Surprised the son-of-a-bitch even bothered mentioning the female children."

Maria could be heard asking, "What is you favorite film?"

"I have never seen a motion picture."

"He's trying to qualify for Islamic sainthood," Casey quipped.

"Which political figures do you admire most?"

"Living or dead?"

"Both. Historical as well as living figures."

"Historically, I admire and respect the Messenger Muhammad—he was not only a holy man who lived a holy life, he was a courageous warrior who inspired the Islamic armies in their conquest of North Africa and Spain and parts of France. Historically I admire, too, Moses and Jesus, both prophets who brought the word of God to the people but were ignored. I also hold in high esteem the sultan of Egypt, Saladin, who defeated the first colonialists, the Crusaders, and liberated the sacred city of Jerusalem."

"Too bad he's holding one of our people," Casey decided. "This is the sort of guy who could really bloody the Russians."

On the television screen Maria asked, "How about living figures?"

"She is certainly a handsome woman," Reagan said as he and his National Security Advisor, Bill Clark, watched TV on the second floor of the White House. "Remind me what her, uh, name is?"

"Maria Shaath," Clark said. "The Ibrahim character is the one who thinks we've agreed to trade Shaath and the CIA fellow for fifty Stingers."

"Living figures," Ibrahim was telling Maria, "are more difficult."

"Why is that?" she inquired.

"Because it will be fifty or a hundred years before you can have enough historical perspective to weigh what a leader has done."

"You take a long view of history?"

"I measure things in centuries."

"Go out on a limb," Maria insisted. "Give it your best shot."

Ibrahim smiled faintly. "I admire Qaddafi for not being intimidated by the colonial powers. I respect Iraq's Saadam Hussein and Syria's Hafez al-Assad for the same reasons. On the other hand, I despise Jordan's King Hussein and Egypt's Mubarak and Saudi Arabia's entire royal family for their failure to stand up to the colonial and secular West. They have in fact been co-opted by the secular West. They have become agents of secularism in the Islamic world."

Reagan asked, "What did I, uh, decide about those Stingers, again, Bill?"

"You felt it would be a mistake to supply them to Islamic fundamentalists like this Ibrahim character. So the Stingers we're sending in with the Israeli raiding party have had their firing mechanisms removed."

"You speak often about colonialism and secularism," Maria was asking on the screen. "What about Marxism?"

"I hate Marxism!" Reagan muttered to himself.

"Marxism is as bad as capitalism," Ibrahim replied. "Marxism is colonialism with a secular packaging."

Reagan perked up. "Well, he's not a Marxist!" he decided.

"He certainly isn't," agreed the National Security Advisor.

"I don't see what we have to lose by arming him with, uh, Stingers if he uses them against the Marxists," Reagan said.

"A lot of Senators are saying the same thing," Clark observed.

Reagan stared with troubled sincerity at his National Security Advisor. "Are you suggesting that supplying Stingers to the, uh, Afghan freedom fighters would be popular in Congress?"

"I suppose it would be," Clark conceded.

"Well, maybe we need to take another look at this, uh, Stinger business after all," Reagan ventured. "I'm not saying we should give them Stingers. On the other hand, if they use them to shoot down Russian planes... Hmmmmmm."

Leo Kritzky had just returned from Baltimore, where he'd personally debriefed Hippolyte Fet, the former KGB *rezident* in Peshawar who had been spirited out of Pakistan immediately after his defection, flown to America and installed in a Company safe house. Pulling into his Georgetown driveway after dark, Leo was surprised to see a familiar gray Plymouth already parked there. Jack was slouched in the driver's seat, the radio on and tuned to a station that gave the news every hour on the hour. Both drivers emerged from their cars at the same moment. "Jack," Leo said. "What brings you out at this hour?"

"I badly need a drink," Jack moaned as they headed toward the front door of Leo's home. He glanced at his old Yale roommate and scull-mate. Physically, Leo had pretty much recovered from Angleton's draconian inquisition nine years before; his hair had grown back ash-colored and was worn in a brush cut popular with Army officers. The gauntness had given way to a sturdy leanness. If there were vestiges of the ordeal, they were to be found in Leo's dark eyes, which still looked haunted, more so tonight than usual, or so it seemed to Jack, who said, "You look as if you could use a dose of alcohol, too, old buddy."

"We've both come to the right place," Leo said. He let himself in with a latch key and flicked on lights. The two men threw their coats over the backs of chairs. Leo made a beeline for the bar across the living room. "What's your pleasure, Jack?"

"Whiskey, neat. Don't stint."

Leo half-filled two thick jelly glasses (Adelle had taken the crystal after the divorce) with Glenfiddich. "Any news from the raiding party?" Leo asked, handing one glass to Jack, hiking his own in salute.

"The last we heard they'd transited the Nameh Pass, north of the Khyber." Jack frowned. "They're crossing unmarked mountain trails now and maintaining radio silence, so we won't know more until they've reached Ibrahim's hilltop."

"When's D-day?"

"Hard to say how long it will take them to get over the mountains with pack animals. For the rendezvous with the helicopters we're calculating a minimum of five, a maximum of eight days."

"Must be tough on Millie," Leo guessed.

"Tough is not the word," Jack said. "On the other hand, if it ends well—"

"It will, Jack."

"Yeah, I keep telling myself that but I haven't been able to convince myself." He took a sip of whiskey and shivered.

"Did you catch the Shaath interview?" Leo asked.

"They supplied us with a preview tape. We ran it in the office."

"I heard it on the radio driving back," Leo said. "The part where Ibrahim says he'll defend Islam from colonial oppression in other parts of the world once the Russians are out of the way—it made my hair stand on end."

"Yeah. The Shaath woman didn't beat around the bush with him, either."

"You mean when she asked him if he was issuing a declaration of war?" Leo said. He waved Jack to the sofa and settled tiredly onto a rocking chair at right angles to him. "Ibrahim's talking about Saudi Arabia, of course," he added. "That's next on the fundamentalists' menu when the Russians cut their losses and pull out of Afghanistan." Leo drank his whiskey thoughtfully. "It's not a pretty picture. About this Fet fellow—"

"Yeah, I meant to ask you. What goodies has he brought with him?"

"Mind you, Jack, we haven't fluttered him yet so we can't say for sure he's not feeding us a load of bull. On the other hand—"

"On the other hand?"

"He claims that the guys who run the KGB are ready to write off Afghanistan. Inside the KGB this information is being closely held. As far as they're concerned the war is lost—it's only a matter of time, and casualties, before the Soviet military gets the message and figures out how to wind down the war."

"Wow! If it's true—"

"Fet claims he was under orders to open back-channels to the various fundamentalist splinter groups—the KGB is already looking beyond the war to the postwar period when the fundamentalists will have taken over Afghanistan and turned their attention elsewhere."

"Elsewhere being Saudi Arabia?"

"The KGB, according to Fet, thinks it can harness the hatred the fundamentalists have for America and turn it against American interests in the Middle East. If the Saudi royal family is overthrown—"

Jack filled in the blanks. "The Russians are an oil-exporting nation. If the fundamentalists tighten the spigot, Moscow will be able to buy the allegiance of European countries that rely on Saudi oil."

"The possibilities for manipulation are limited only by a lack of imagination," Leo said.

"And the KGB's schemers have never been known to lack imagination."

"No," Leo said, frowning thoughtfully. "They haven't." Something was obviously disturbing him. "They are far more cynical than I imagined."

"When Fet says he was under orders to establish contact with fundamentalists, what exactly does that mean?"

"It means that Fet and the KGB decided that Ibrahim was worth cultivating. It means they fingered Manny and my godson, Anthony. It means they urged Ibrahim to kidnap them—Maria Shaath happened to be in the car, so she was a wild card—and hold them against the delivery of the Stingers that will boost Ibrahim's chances of winding up at the head of the fundamentalist pack."

"But the Stingers will shoot down Russian aircraft," Jack said.

"According to Fet, that's the short term price and the KGB is willing to pay it. Stingers in the hands of fundamentalists, so Fet's superiors told him, will convince the Soviet brass that the war can't be won. The sooner the war ends, the sooner the fundamentalists, with the KGB pulling the strings behind the scenes, can turn their attention to the Saudi oil fields."

Jack polished off his whiskey and went over to the bar to help himself to more. He held the bottle up but Leo waved away a refill. "You're the DD/O's Chief of Operations, pal," Jack said. "Do you swallow this story?"

Leo said carefully, "There was a detail in the Shaath interview that seems to give Fet's story plausibility. Remember where she asks Ibrahim how come, with Soviet planes and helicopters crisscrossing the countryside, his mountaintop fortress hasn't been attacked, at least since she's been there?"

"Yeah, I do remember. His answer was kind of feeble."

"He said they had too many anti-aircraft guns around and the Russians knew it," Leo said. "But you and I know that anti-aircraft guns are almost useless against modern jets or helicopters hugging the ground and coming in fast."

"Which is why they want Stingers," Jack said.

"Which is why," Leo agreed.

"Which could mean," Jack said, "that the KGB—which has a hand in drawing up the target lists, same as we do—has put Ibrahim's real estate off limits."

"That's what Fet says," Leo confirmed.

They concentrated on their drinks for a while, each following his own train of thoughts. Eventually Leo glanced up at his old friend. "When are you going to get around to what really brought you over at this time of night?" he asked.

. Jack shook his head in distress. "There's a photo I want you to take a look at."

"What kind of photo?"

"I'm glad you're sitting down," Jack said. He pulled the photograph from the inside breast pocket of his sports jacket and held it out. Leo rocked forward and took it. Fitting on a pair of reading glasses, he held the photograph up to the light.

Jack saw his friend catch his breath. "So it *is* Yevgeny," Jack whispered.

"Where did you get this?" Leo demanded.

"We have your girls to thank for it," Jack said, and he explained how Tessa and Vanessa had come up with the Washington phone number of the old Polish woman who was acting as a circuit breaker for a KGB cutout, who went by the name of Gene Lutwidge. "I've always wondered what became of our Russian roommate," Jack said. "Now we know."

Breathing irregularly, Leo rocked back in his chair. The photo of Yevgeny had obviously shaken him.

"I couldn't believe it either at first," Jack said. "The FBI's assigned a fifty-man task force to Yevgeny. If we're patient enough he'll lead us to SASHA. If we grow impatient we'll pick him up and wring it out of him." Jack leaned forward. "You should be very proud of Tessa and Vanessa...Hey, Leo, you all right?"

Leo managed to nod. "Vanessa told me they had scored a breakthrough but she didn't give me details. I should have guessed it concerned Yevgeny..."

Jack, puzzled, asked, "How could you have guessed that?"

Leo pushed himself to his feet and, dropping the photo onto the rocking chair, made his way to the bar. Crouching behind it, he hunted for something in a cupboard. Then, standing, he splashed some whiskey into a new tumbler and carried it back across the room. This time he settled onto the couch across from Jack.

Leo's anxious eyes were fixed on his oldest friend. He had come to a decision: From here on there would be no turning back. "This is what the bullfighters and the fiction-writers call the moment of truth," he said. His voice was too soft; the softness conveyed menace. "Yevgeny doesn't have to lead you to SASHA," he went on. "You're looking at him."

Jack started to come out of his seat when the automatic materialized in Leo's hand. For an instant Jack's vision blurred and his brain was incapable of putting the riot of thoughts into words. He sank back onto the cushions in confusion. "Damnation, you wouldn't shoot to kill," was all he could think to say.

"Don't misread me," Leo warned. "I'd shoot to wound. I don't plan to spend the rest of my life in a federal penitentiary."

"You're SASHA!" It began to dawn on Jack that this wasn't a joke or a dream. "Jim Angleton was right all along!"

"Do us both a favor, keep your hands where I can see them," Leo ordered. He tossed a pair of handcuffs onto the couch next to Jack. "Attach one end to your right wrist. Don't make any sudden moves—now sit on the floor with your back against the radiator. Okay, lock the other end of the cuffs onto the pipe at the side of the radiator. Good." Leo came across and sat down where Jack had been sitting. "Now we'll talk, Jack."

"How did you do it—how did you get past all the lie detector tests?"

"Tranquilizers. I was so relaxed I could have told them I was female and it wouldn't have stirred the stylus. The only lie detector test I failed was the one Angleton gave me in his dungeon—and I was able to explain it away because I'd been locked up for so long."

Leo's treachery was starting to sink in. "You bastard! You *prick*! You betrayed everyone, your country, your wife, your girls, the Company. You betrayed *me*, Leo—when you drank that water from Angleton's toilet bowl, Jesus H. Christ, I fell for it. I thought you could actually be innocent. It was your old buddy Jack who didn't let the matter drop when Kukushkin was supposed to have been executed. It was me who set the wheels turning to see if he might still be alive."

"I was manning the ramparts of the Cold War, Jack, but on the other side. Remember when I came off the elevator and you were all waiting there to welcome me back after my incarceration? I said something about how I was serving the country whose system of governance seemed to offer the best hope to the world. I wasn't lying. That country, that system of governance, is the Soviet Union."

The air in the room was suddenly charged with emotion. It was almost as if two longtime lovers were breaking up. "So when did you start to betray your country, Leo?"

"I never *betrayed* my country, I fought for a better world, a better planet. My allegiance to the Soviet Union goes all the way back to Yale. Yevgeny wasn't a KGB agent when he roomed with us but, like all Russians abroad, he was an unofficial spotter. He told his father, who *was* a KGB agent, about me: about how my family had been ruined by the depression and my father had jumped to his death from the Brooklyn Bridge; about how I had inherited from my father the Old Testament belief that what you own was stolen from those who don't have enough."

"Then what?"

"Yevgeny's father alerted the New York *rezident*, who sent an American Communist named Stella Bledsoe to recruit me."

"Your girlfriend Stella!" Jack gazed across the room at the framed black-and-white photograph hanging on the wall, the one taken after the 1950 Harvard-Yale boat race. He couldn't make out the caption but since he'd written it, he recollected it: *Jack & Leo & Stella after The Race but before The Fall.* Now he said with a sneer, "I remember Stella slipping into my room that night—"

"She snuck into your room and screwed you so I would have a plausible explanation for breaking off with her. Moscow Centre wanted to put some distance between Stella and me in case the FBI discovered her connection with the American Communist Party, which is what happened when Whittaker Chambers identified her as a fellow traveler he'd met at Party meetings after the war."

Jack tugged angrily on the handcuff and the metal bit into the skin on his wrist. "What a sap I was to trust you."

"It was Stella who instructed me to go out for Crew when they learned that Coach Waltz was a talent scout for the new Central Intelligence Agency. The idea was for me to get close to him. The rest of the story you know, Jack. You were there when he made his pitch to us."

Jack looked up suddenly. "What about Adelle? Was she *planned*, too?"

Leo turned away. "Adelle's not the part of the story I'm the most comfortable with," he admitted. "The Centre wanted me to marry into the Washington establishment, both to further my career and to give me other sources of intelligence. The *rezidentura* more or less picked Adelle out because she worked for Lyndon Johnson, also because her father was rich and powerful and had access to the White House. They arranged for our paths to cross."

"But you met by chance at a veterinarian," Jack remembered.

Leo nodded grimly. "When Adelle was away at work, they broke into her apartment and dropped her cat out a fourth-floor window. I picked up an old dog at the pound and fed him enough rat poison to make him sick. I took him to her vet knowing Adelle would show up with her cat. If that hadn't worked out we would have figured another way to make our paths cross."

Jack, stunned, sat there shaking his head. "I almost feel sorry for you, Leo."

"The truth is I grew to love her," Leo said. "I adore my girls..." Then he blurted out, "I never accepted a penny, Jack. I risked my neck for peace, for a better world. I didn't betray a country—I have a higher loyalty...an international conception of things."

"Just for the record, explain the AE/PINNACLE caper, Leo. Kukushkin was a dispatched defector—but weren't they taking a big risk accusing you of being SASHA? We might have believed it."

"It's not very complicated," Leo said. "Angleton was slowly narrowing down the list of suspects through a careful analysis of failed and successful operations, and who was associated with them. My name was on all the overlaps. Moscow Centre—or more precisely, my controlling officer— decided Angleton was getting uncomfortably close, so he organized AE/PINNACLE to lure Angleton into accusing me. Kukushkin would have been unmasked as a dispatched agent even if you hadn't brought the Israelis in. Once Kukushkin was discredited, the case against me would fall apart. And Angleton would be ruined. We killed two birds with one stone."

"Where do you go from here, Leo? Yevgeny is being watched twenty-four hours a day. You'll never get away."

"I'll get away and so will Yevgeny. We have contingency plans for situations like this. All we need is a head start, which is what those handcuffs will buy me. Tomorrow morning I'll phone Elizabet and tell her where you are."

"So this is how it all ends," Jack said bitterly.

"Not quite. There's one more piece of business, Jack. I want to pass some secrets on to you." Leo couldn't restrain a grim smile when he spotted the incredulity in Jack's eyes. "The Soviet Union is coming apart at the seams. If it weren't for oil exports and the worldwide energy crisis, the economy would probably have collapsed years ago. The Cold War's winding down. But there are people on my side who want it to wind down with a bang. Which brings me to the subject of KHOLSTOMER—"

"There is a KHOLSTOMER! Angleton was right again."

"I'll let you in on another secret, Jack. I've had qualms about KHOLSTOMER all along, but I wasn't sure what to do about it until I talked with Fet today. When I learned about the KGB plotting to put Stingers in the hands of people who would shoot them at Russian pilots, not to mention their role in my godson's kidnapping—" Leo, his face contorted, whispered, "For me, it's as if the KGB amputated Anthony's toe, Jack. That was the last straw. Enough is enough. Listen up."

Jack's sense of irony was returning. "Consider me your captive audience," he remarked dryly.

"Andropov is dying, Jack. From what I hear—both from Company sources and from Starik—the General Secretary is not always lucid—"

"You mean he's off his rocker."

"He has periods of lucidity. He has other periods where his imagination takes hold and the world he sees is cockeyed. Right now he's in one of his cockeyed phases. Andropov is convinced that Reagan and the Pentagon are planning to launch a preemptive nuclear strike against the Soviet Union—"

"That's preposterous and you know it," Jack burst out.

"I've sent back word that it's not true. But I have reason to believe my reports have been doctored to feed into Andropov's paranoia."

"How could you know that from Washington?"

"I surmise it from the queries I get from Moscow Centre—they're focused on ABLE ARCHER 83, they want to know if the Pentagon could be keeping the CIA in the dark about plans for a preemptive strike. I've told them it's out of the realm of possibility but they keep coming back with the same questions. They say I must be missing something, they instruct me to look again."

"Where does KHOLSTOMER fit in?" Jack asked.

"KHOLSTOMER is Moscow's response to ABLE ARCHER 83. Believing the US is going to launch a preemptive war on December first, Andropov has authorized Starik to implement KHOLSTOMER—they plan to flood the spot market with dollars and cause the American currency, and ultimately the American economy, to crash."

"I'm not an economist," Jack said, "but they'd need an awful lot of greenbacks to make a dent in the market."

"They have an awful lot of dollars," Leo said. "Starik has been siphoning off hard currency for decades. He has slightly more than sixty billion dollars sitting in off-shore banks around the world. On top of that, he has agents of influence in four key countries ready to push the central banks into selling off US bonds once the dollar starts to nosedive. On D-day I'm supposed to monitor the Federal Reserve's reaction and the movement in the bond market. The thing could spiral out of control—the more the dollar goes down, the more people will panic and sell off dollars and US bonds to protect their positions. At least that's what Starik is counting on."

"Can you identify the agents of influence?"

"No. But I know which countries they're supposed to be operating in. Our stations—"

A half smile crept onto Jack's face. *"Our?"*

Leo grinned back. "I've been leading a double life for a long time. *Your* stations ought to be able to figure out which one of the people close to the central bank of any given country might be a Soviet agent of influence."

"If in doubt," Jack said, "we could always neutralize the three or four leading candidates. That's how the KGB operates, isn't it?"

Leo exploded, "Don't be so pious, Jack! *Your* stations trained the secret police in Vietnam, Argentina, the Dominican Republic, Chile, Iraq, Iran—the list is as long as my arm. *You* looked the other way when *your* clients arrested and tortured and assassinated their political opponents. The Phoenix Operation in Vietnam, with its tiger cages on Con Son Island, killed or crippled some twenty thousand Vietnamese suspected—only *suspected*, Jack, not convicted!—of being pro-Communist."

"The Company was fighting fire with fire—" Jack insisted.

"Fire with fire!" Leo repeated scornfully. "*You* financed and equipped and trained armies of agents and then abandoned them—the Cubans in Miami, the Khambas in Tibet, the Sumatran colonels in Indonesia, the Meos in Laos, the Montagnards in Vietnam, the National Chinese in Burma, the Ukrainians in Russia, the Kurds in Iraq."

Jack said, very quietly, "You're the last person on earth who ought to climb on a moral high horse, buddy."

Leo rose to his feet. "I've admired you all of my adult life, Jack. Even before you made it off the beach at the Bay of Pigs, you were a hero to me—it didn't matter that we were on different sides of the fence. I still have that mug shot of you in the senior yearbook—'Jack McAuliffe, mad, bad and dangerous to know.' You were always mad, you were sometimes bad—but you were never dangerous to know." Leo shrugged tiredly. "I'm sorry, Jack." His lips tightened and he nodded once. "Sorry that our friendship had to end this way..."

Jack had a vision of Leo filling the tin cup from Angleton's toilet and drinking off the water, and then turning to him to whisper through his raw lips *Go fuck yourself, Jack.* It was on the tip of his tongue to tell him, "You too, Leo—go fuck yourself, huh?" But he stopped himself and said instead: "You're eating into your head start, buddy."

"Yeah, I am." Leo retrieved a plastic airline bag from a closet, then switched on the radio and turned up the volume. "Listen up, Jack," he called from the door. "My Russian friends aren't going to publicize my defection if I can help it—I want to protect the girls and my ex-wife. Also, I haven't told Moscow Centre about the Israeli raid. I hope to God it works out."

Jack couldn't bring himself to thank SASHA; he would have gagged on the words if he had tried. But he lifted his free paw to acknowledge this last favor.

The skinny black kid, decked out in a tight red jump suit with the name "Latrell" embroidered over the breast pocket, shook his head emphatically. Hell, there couldn't be no mistake, he insisted. No way. He leafed through the packet of order forms and came up with one. Looka here, mister, he said. One Neapolitan without olives. The orderer is—he named a street in Tysons Corner, a house number. The apartment over the garage at the end of the driveway, that's you, ain't it?

That's me, Yevgeny admitted. What's the name on the order?

The black kid held the form up to the light seeping through the partly open door. Dodgson, he said. You Dodgson?

Yevgeny reached for the pizza. How much do I owe you?

Five-fifty.

Yevgeny came up with a five and two ones and told the kid to keep the change. He shut the door and stood with his back pressed against it until the pounding in his chest subsided. A pizza delivered to Dodgson, the name Yevgeny had abandoned when his identity had been blown twenty-two years before, was SASHA's emergency signal. It meant the world had come to an end. It meant the Americans had somehow managed to identify the cutout who serviced SASHA. FBI agents were probably watching him day and night. Gradually, a semblance of calm seeped back into Yevgeny's thought process. Start with a single fact and follow the logic of it, he told himself. Fact: they hadn't arrested him yet, which was a good omen—it must mean they were hoping he would lead them to SASHA. Which meant that they didn't know who SASHA was. Which in turn suggested that the weak link was between the KGB's Washington *rezident* and Yevgeny: Aida Tannenbaum.

Fortunately for Yevgeny, SASHA had learned about the breakthrough and had now warned Yevgeny the only way he could. Okay. The next thing he had to do was go through the motions of going to bed—leave enough of the window shades halfway up so that anyone watching through binoculars would see that he didn't have a worry in the world.

Yevgeny cut out a wedge of pizza and forced himself to eat it while he watched the end of a movie on the small portable TV set. He changed into pajamas and brushed his teeth and, switching out the lights in the other rooms, retreated to the small bedroom. He sat up in bed for a quarter of an hour going through the motions of reading Philip Roth's *The Anatomy Lesson*. The truth of the matter was that his eyes were incapable of focusing on the words; that the pulse throbbing in his forehead made thinking difficult. Yawning, he set the book down, wound his clock and checked the alarm. Almost as an afterthought, he padded over to the window and pulled down the shade. Climbing under the covers, he switched off the light on the night table.

In the total darkness, the sounds from the neighborhood seemed amplified. Every quarter hour or so he could make out the bus coming down Broad Street, two blocks away. Sometime after midnight he caught the scrape of a garage door opening and a car backing down a driveway. At 12:25 he heard the next door neighbor calling to his dog to pee already, for Christ's sake. His brain awash with scenarios, Yevgeny lay there motionless until the luminous hour hand on the alarm clock clicked onto three. Then, moving stealthily, he slipped into his clothing and overcoat and, carrying his shoes, made his way to the bathroom in his stockinged feet. He flushed the toilet—they might have planted a microphone in the apartment—and while the water was gushing through the pipes, eased open the small window that gave out onto the sloping roof of the toolshed attached to the back of the garage. Once on the roof, he let himself down the incline and climbed down the trellis to the ground. Here he put his shoes on and tied the laces and, crouching in the shadows, listened. The night was cold; with each breath he expelled a small cloud of vapor. From the back bedroom of a nearby house came the sound of a hacking cough. A bed lamp flicked on, then was switched off again. After a long while Yevgeny rose to his feet and crossed the yard, moving in the shadow of the high wooden fence that separated the back garden from the next door neighbor's paved basketball court. At the end of the garden he climbed over a wooden fence and, moving sideways, squeezed through the space between two garages. Halfway to the end, under a boarded up window, he felt for the chipped brick and, working it loose, plunged his hand into the cavity to retrieve the package wrapped in layers of plastic.

Twenty minutes later Yevgeny ducked into an all-night drugstore a mile or so up Broad Street. He ordered a coffee and a doughnut and made his way to the phone booths at the back. He had thrown away Aida's new phone number but he remembered the address: 47 Corcoran Street. He dialed information and requested the number of a party named Tannenbaum at that address. He dialed the number and heard the phone ring. After a dozen rings the breathless voice of Aida came on the line.

"Who is this?" she demanded.

Yevgeny knew they would be tapping her phone. As long as he didn't remain on the line long enough for the call to be traced, it didn't matter. Nothing mattered. "It's me, lovely lady."

He could hear a frightened gasp. "Something must be very wrong for you to call at this hour," Aida whispered.

"Yes. Something is wrong."

"Oh!"

"I have to hang up before they trace the call."

"Is it that bad, then?"

"You are a great lady, a great fighter, a heroine. I hold you in high esteem." Yevgeny hated to break the connection. He blurted out, "I wish there were something I could do for you."

"There is. Hang up quickly. Run fast, dear child. Save yourself. And remember me as I remember you."

Aida cut the line. Yevgeny listened to the dial tone ringing in his ear for several seconds, then hung up and, swaying unsteadily, stumbled back to the counter to nurse his coffee and doughnut. He glanced at his wristwatch. He still had two and a half hours to kill before he met SASHA at the prearranged site.

Aida knew she should have been terrified but the only emotion she could detect was relief. After all these years it was finally going to end. She wedged a chair under the knob of the front door and went down the hallway into the narrow kitchen. She wedged a chair under the knob of that door, too, and stuffed the gap under the door with newspaper, then turned on the four gas burners and the oven. Lifting Silvester out of the basket lined with an old nightdress, she sat at the small linoleum-covered table and began to stroke his neck. She smiled when the old cat started to purr. She thought she heard a car pull up on the street somewhere under the window. It reminded her of the night the Gestapo had raided the warehouse where the Communist underground kept the printing press, and her dear, dear son, Alfred, was torn screaming from her arms. Was that the grind of the elevator starting up or just her imagination? She felt terribly, terribly tired. Fists were pounding on the door of the apartment. She rested her head on one arm and tried to summon an image of her son, but all she saw was her lover, Yevgeny, bending to kiss the back of her gloved hand.

With a crash, the front door burst open against its hinges.

Savoring the thought that she had finally run out of time, Aida reached for the box of safety matches.

6

YATHRIB, FRIDAY, NOVEMBER 18, 1983

THE STRING OF CAMELS—THREE OF THEM CARRYING BURLAP SADDLE sacks filled with food, drinking water and ammunition; the twenty-five others loaded with long wooden crates, two to an animal—made their way across the fast-flowing stream. The twelve Arab herdsmen, all heavily armed, all wearing *kiffiyeh* drawn over their noses against the dust kicked up by the camels, had strung a thick cord from the rusted Russian tank awash in the water to a tree on the far bank and had posted themselves at intervals along the cord to steady any camel that lost its footing. Once on the other side the men paused for a lunch break. The practicing Muslims in the group prostrated themselves in the direction of Mecca and began to pray. The non-practicing among the herders brewed green tea in a beat-up casserole propped over a small fire. Chunks of stale bread, baked the previous day in shallow holes scooped out of the ground, and tins of humus were passed around, along with raw onions. If anyone noticed the two Pashtuns inspecting them through binoculars from a cliff high above, he didn't call attention to the fact. When lunch was finished most of the men sat with their backs to trees, dozing or sucking on cigarettes. Five minutes before the hour the headman, a slim Egyptian wearing khaki fatigues and mirrored sunglasses, climbed to his feet and, calling in Arabic, began rounding up the camels that had wandered off to graze. When the line was formed up and each animal was attached to the one in front, the herders flicked the birch switches against the flanks of the camels and the pack train started up the steep tracks. After several hours the caravan reached the narrow gorge. During another break for prayers, two Pashtuns and an Iraqi came through the gorge on horseback. Speaking in Arabic, the Iraqi exchanged greetings with the herders and chatted up the headman while the Pashtuns pried open several crates attached to the camels at random—each crate contained a spanking-new ground-to-air Stinger with American markings stenciled on the side, along with a handbook printed in English. The headman and several of the herders had been trained by the CIA in the working of the weapon and would remain for a week or ten days to instruct the tribesmen after the Stingers had been delivered. Satisfied, the Pashtuns preceded the pack train through the gorge into a long canyon. As the trail widened and flattened out, the herders passed the ruins of hamlets lost in tangles of vines. Toward sundown, they arrived at the walled compound at the bitter end of the trail. A mud-brick minaret rose from the mosque inside; from the top a muezzin was summoning the faithful to evening prayers. Pashtuns emerged from the stone houses built against the cliffs. The ones who were devout crowded into the mosque; the others, along with a swarm of teenage boys, came over to look at the Stinger that had been set out on an Army blanket.

Ibrahim, wearing a sheepskin vest and his Pashtun cap with the amulet to ward off sniper bullets pinned to it, strode across the compound. Behind him, his children watched from a doorway. Smiling jubilantly, Ibrahim greeted the Egyptian headman and offered him the creature comforts of the camp for as long as he and his comrades remained. The headman replied in elaborate Arabic that he appreciated his host's hospitality and would go to great lengths not to abuse it. Ibrahim retorted that his guest need not worry about abusing his hospitality—on the contrary, hospitality needed to be abused in order to measure its depth and the spirit in which it was offered.

Ibrahim turned away to join the fighters squatting around the Stinger. They looked like children inspecting a new toy as they gingerly reached out to caress the fins of the missile that would destroy Russian planes and helicopters so far away you could only hear them, not see them. No one paid attention when, in the gathering darkness, one of the Arab herdsmen swung closed the great double door to the compound. The others unslung their automatic weapons from their shoulders and nonchalantly started to fan out on either side of the men huddled around the Stinger. Several of the Arabs strolled over to a trough facing the door of the mosque. Two others started to meander across the compound toward the building that housed Ibrahim's prisoners.

Suddenly Ibrahim sniffed at the icy air and, threading his worry beads through the fingers of his left hand, rose slowly to his feet. It hit him that the great double doors, normally left open so that mujaheddin praying in the mosque could return to the hamlet, had been closed. Squinting into the duskiness, he noticed that the Arab herdsmen had spread out around the compound. He muttered something to his Shadow, who stepped behind him and closed his fingers over the hilt of the dagger in his waistband. In ones and twos, the Pashtuns, infected with Ibrahim's edginess, stood and peered into the shadowy stillness of the compound.

From over the rim of the hill came the distinctive thwak-thwak of helicopter rotors. Ibrahim shouted a warning as the Arab herdsmen opened fire. One of the first shots caught Ibrahim in the shoulder, spinning him into the arms of the Shadow. With a flutter of wings the yellow canary scampered free, dragging its leash behind it. Brilliant lights in the bellies of two giant insects overhead illuminated the compound as the helicopters sank straight down. Gatling guns spit bullets from open ports. One of the helicopters settled onto the ground, kicking up a squall of dust, the other hovered above the mosque and bombarded the hamlet below the compound, and the path coming up from the hamlet, with phosphorus shells. From the doorways and windows of the buildings women shrieked in terror. The mujaheddin who bolted out of the dust cloud were cut down by rifle fire. The Egyptian headman knelt and fired and methodically changed clips and fired again at the Pashtuns spilling out of the mosque. Then, calling orders to his commandos in Hebrew, he started toward the fallen Ibrahim. "Take him alive!" someone shouted in English.

The Shadow drew his knife and, leaning over Ibrahim, looked questioningly into his eyes. "Recall your vow," Ibrahim pleaded. There was another staccato burst of automatic fire—to Ibrahim's ear it sounded like a distant tambour announcing his arrival in paradise. Soon he would be sitting on the right hand of the Prophet; soon he would be deep in conversation with the one true God. He could see the Prophet Ibrahim raising the sacrificial knife to the throat of his son Isma'il on the black stone at the heart of the Kaaba. The vision instructed him on what he had to do. Murmuring *"Khahesh mikonam, lotfi konin*—I beg you, do me a kindness," he gripped the bodyguard's wrist with his good hand and coaxed the razor-whetted blade down toward his jugular.

In the attic prison, Anthony had drawn Maria Shaath into a corner when they heard gunfire in the compound. Moments later people broke into the room under their feet. "It's a commando raid," Anthony said. "But who will reach us first—Ibrahim or the raiders?" Someone set a ladder against the wall and began climbing the rungs. Anthony grabbed the small charcoal stove by its legs and positioned himself on the blind side of the trap door as it was pushed up on its hinges. A man fingering the trigger of a stubby Israeli Uzi, his face sheathed in a *kiffiyeh*, appeared. Maria screamed. Anthony raised the charcoal stove over his head and was about to bring it crashing down on the intruder when he said, in cheerful and flawless English, "Anyone here interested in hitching a helicopter ride to Pakistan?"

At the Company's high-walled villa off Jamrud Road in Peshawar, a young radioman sat in front of the transceiver with a crystal inserted, locking it onto a given frequency. He and his buddies had been monitoring the static twenty-four hours a day for the past week. Now, unexpectedly, what sounded like a human voice seeped through the background noise, repeating a single sentence.

"He promised me earrings but he only pierced my ears. I say again. He promised me earrings but he only pierced my ears."

The radioman ran his thumb nail down the list of code phrases in his notebook until he found the one he was looking for. He raced through the corridors and stuck his head in the door of the chief of station who had replaced Manny Ebbitt after the kidnapping. "The copters have broken radio silence," he blurted out.

"And?"

"They've sent a 'mission accomplished' message. They're in the air and on the way back."

"Encipher the message and send it on to Washington," the chief of station ordered. He sat back in relief. Jesus, the Israelis had pulled it off after all. The Champagne would flow at Langley when they learned that the helicopters were heading home. Thank goodness the naysayers had been wrong—it hadn't ended like Carter's raid to free the American hostages in Teheran after all.

The mujaheddin who had survived the Israeli raid were in for another surprise. When they tried to use the Stingers they would discover that the firing mechanisms had been removed, which made the weapons about as valuable as lengths of piping in a junkyard.

They met at first light in the back row of the First Baptist Church on 16th Street, not far from Scott Circle. There were only three early-morning worshipers in the church when Yevgeny slid into the pew and sat down next to Leo. For a moment neither said a word. Then, glancing at his cutout, Leo whispered harshly, "We always knew it had to end one day."

"It's been a long Cold War," Yevgeny said. He was thinking of Aida Tannenbaum. He could hear her voice in his ear: *I will admit to you I am fatigued, Eugene. I have been fighting on one or another front line as far back as I can remember.*

Leo reached down, unzipped the airline bag between his feet and handed Yevgeny a small package. "I've had this stashed in a closet for years—it's a Company disguise kit. We'll go out as priests—there are black shirts, white collars, a goatee for me, a gray beard for you, wigs, rimless eyeglasses. Your own brother wouldn't recognize you."

"My own brother barely recognize me when I was in Moscow on home leave," Yevgeny remarked. He took a manila envelope from his overcoat pocket. "Passports, driver's licenses, and cash," he said.

"We'll change in the vestry," Leo said. "With any luck the Company'll concentrate on the hunt for my Chevrolet. We'll go by subway to the Greyhound terminal, take a bus to Baltimore, then a train to Buffalo, where we'll cross into Canada. I have an emergency address in Toronto where we can stay until they can smuggle us onto a cargo ship."

"What did you do with your car?" Yevgeny asked.

"I buried it in the long-term parking lot at Dulles and came back in a shuttle. We'll be far away by the time they find it."

Yevgeny asked, "Any idea how they tagged us?"

Leo didn't see any need to bring his daughters into it, so he answered vaguely. "They got on to your Polish lady," he said.

Yevgeny slapped his forehead. "She's dying of cancer, Leo. She begged me to meet her—"

"What's done is done. They snapped a photograph of you. Jack thought he recognized it. He came over tonight to show it to me."

"What did you do with Jack?"

"I left him handcuffed to a radiator."

"If he came over to show you the photograph," Yevgeny whispered, "he didn't suspect you were SASHA."

"I told him," he said. "I was also getting tired of the game."

"There must be more to it than that..."

"Reagan and the Pentagon aren't planning a preemptive strike, Yevgeny," Leo explained wearily. "Andropov is over the hill if he thinks they are. And I don't want to see Starik and Andropov bring the whole world crashing down around our ears."

"You never could stomach KHOLSTOMER. I could see it in your eyes when we talked about it."

"The Cold War is winding down. Our side is losing—the Soviet economy is rotted to the core. KHOLSTOMER doesn't make sense—ruining economies, pushing the Third World back into the Middle Ages, causing hundreds of millions to suffer. For what? I don't see the point."

"Ours was the best side," Yevgeny said flatly. "We were the good guys,

Leo. I still believe the Socialist system, with all its terrible faults, is a better model for the planet earth than anything the West can offer. Capitalism is intrinsically decadent—it brings out the worst in people."

Leo, his eyes burning, turned to Yevgeny. "Did you ever have a shadow of a doubt?"

"Only once," Yevgeny admitted. "It was when I met Philby in Gettysburg to tell him Burgess had run for it with Maclean. Starik wanted Philby to run for it, too, but he refused. He said he could bluff it out. He said as long as he didn't confess they could never lay a glove on him. Those were his exact words. *Lay a glove on him.* I used to replay this conversation in my skull—it was as if a needle had gotten stuck in a groove. It raised a question that I was afraid to ask, because if I asked it I'd have to answer it."

"Answer it now."

Yevgeny recalled a snatch of the phone conversation he'd had with Aza Isanova the last time he'd been in Moscow. *In what ostrich hole have you been hiding your head,* she had berated him. *Stalin was a murderer of peasants in the early thirties, he murdered his Party comrades in the mid and late thirties, he suspended the killings during the war but resumed them immediately afterward. By then it was the turn of the Jews.*

"The system Philby was spying for would not have had a problem getting a confession out of someone like Philby," Yevgeny admitted.

"The system Philby was spying for wouldn't have needed a confession to haul him down to the basement of Lubyanka and put a bullet into the nape of his neck," Leo said.

"The Socialist revolution has been under siege from day one," Yevgeny said. "It was fighting for its life against ruthless enemies—"

Leo cut him off. "We've made too many excuses for ourselves. We justify our shortcomings and condemn those of our opponents." Leo glanced at his wristwatch. "It's going to get light soon. We have the rest of our lives for postmortems. We ought to start moving."

"Yeah," Yevgeny agreed. And he declared bitterly, *"Za uspiekh nashevo beznadiozhnovo diela!"*

Leo, nodding fatalistically, repeated Yevgeny's old Yale slogan in English. "To the success of our hopeless task!"

At midmorning, Leo dialed Jack's home from a public booth outside the Baltimore Greyhound terminus. Jack's wife answered.

"Millie, it's me, Leo."

"Oh, Leo, you've heard—"

"Heard what?"

"Ebby called me with the news ten minutes ago. He just rang off. The helicopters have landed in Peshawar. Anthony is safe." Leo could hear Millie's voice breaking on the other end of the phone line. "He's all right, Leo," she added weakly. "He's coming home."

"That's just great. I love that kid of yours. I'm elated he's out of harm's way. I'll tell you something, I hope you remember it in the days ahead: I think this is the happiest moment of my life."

"You've been a swell godfather to him, Leo."

Leo started to say, "I'm not so sure of that," but Millie was rushing on. "The funny part is that nobody seems to know where Jack is. When he didn't come home last night I just assumed he'd stayed at Langley to monitor the raid, but Ebby said he wasn't there." Millie had a sudden thought. "Should I be worried about Jack, Leo?"

"No, you shouldn't be. Actually, that's why I called—Jack spent the night at my place. He's still there."

"Put him on, for God's sake."

"I'm not calling from home."

"Where are you calling from? Hey, what's going on, Leo?"

"I'm going to tell you something. After which there's no point in your asking questions because I won't answer them."

Millie laughed uncomfortably. "You sound awfully mysterious."

"As soon as I hang up, call Ebby. Don't speak to anyone else, only Ebby. Tell him that Jack's at my house. He's not hurt or anything. But he's hand-cuffed to a radiator."

"Have you been drinking, Leo? What's all this about?"

Leo said patiently, "You don't have a need to know, Millie."

"Jack'll tell me."

"Jack won't tell you. Chances are nobody will. I got to go. Take care of yourself. Take care of Jack, too. Goodbye, Millie."

"Leo? Leo? Well, how do you like that?"

Jack examined the postmark on the letter. It had been mailed from Baltimore three days before and only just arrived at the apartment the girls shared in Fairfax. "For heaven's sake, what is he talking about?" Vanessa demanded. She glanced at her sister, than looked back at Jack. "Why in the world is he going to Russia? And why did Dad want us to show the letter to you first?"

Jack cleared his throat. "I'm glad you're both sitting down," he said. "Your father—" What he was going to say seemed so monstrous that Jack had to start over again. "It seems that Leo has been spying for the Soviet Union."

Vanessa gasped. Tessa whispered, "It's not true. You're out of the loop, Jack—they didn't tell you. He must have been sent to Russia on an assignment—"

Jack could only shake his head in misery. "He hasn't been *sent* to Russia—he's *fled* to Russia. If he manages to get there—mind you, we're doing everything to stop him, but they have escape routes prepared—it'll be to seek political asylum in the country he's worked for...the country he's loyal to." Jack sank dejectedly into a chair facing the girls. "I got my information from the horse's mouth. Leo himself told me four days ago."

Vanessa blurted out, "What's going to happen to us, Jack?"

"Why should anything happen to you. You haven't done anything wrong."

Tessa said, "How could Dad have done such a thing? You were his oldest and best friend, Jack. How do you explain it?"

"It goes back to the 1929 Crash, to the Great Depression, to his father's suicide. Don't forget your grandfather emigrated from Russia after the Bolshevik Revolution—it's possible he was a Bolshevik and a Chekist to begin with, or became one in the early 1930s. In any case the son inherited his father's radicalism, this disenchantment with capitalism, this certitude that the socialist model was better than the capitalist model."

"You think Dad actually believed in communism!"

"Leo didn't spy for the Russians for money, Tessa. To give him the benefit of the doubt, I suppose you could say he was an idealist—only his ideals were different from the ones we hold to be self-evident."

Vanessa said, "If what you say is true—"

"Unfortunately, it is."

"When it becomes known—"

"When it hits the newspapers—" Tessa added.

"It's not going to hit the newspapers, not if we can help it. That's why Leo wanted you to show the letter to me. As far as the Company is concerned, Leo Kritzky retired after thirty-odd years of loyal and honorable service. After his retirement he disappeared into the woodwork. Look, the truth is that we don't want to wash our dirty linen in public. If the Company-killers on the congressional oversight committees discover that the one-time head of the Soviet Division, the man in charge of spying on Russia, was actually a Russian mole—Jesus H. Christ, they'll make mincemeat of us, budget-wise and otherwise. We have enough trouble convincing the public that we serve a useful purpose as it is."

"But won't the Russians spill the beans?" Tessa asked.

"We don't think so. We think Leo will oblige them to keep his defection under wraps to protect you guys and your mother. He told me as much—"

Vanessa interrupted. "How will Dad be able to *oblige* the KGB?"

"For one thing, he'll dose out what he knows over a period of years. They won't have any choice in the matter if they want him to cooperate."

Tessa had a sudden doubt. "Did Dad's going to Russia have any connection with the phone numbers we broke out of the Russian lottery numbers?"

"None whatsoever. The two aren't connected."

"Swear it, Jack," Tessa said.

Jack didn't hesitate. "I swear it." He could hear the Sorcerer, back at Berlin Base in the early '50s, swearing on his mother's grave that SNIPER and RAINBOW hadn't been one of the barium meals he'd used to unmask Philby...how effortlessly lies came to the lips of spies. "You have my word," he added now. "Honestly."

Tessa seemed relieved. "Thank goodness for that. It would have been hard to deal with."

Vanessa turned to her sister and announced, very calmly, "I think I hate him!"

"No, you don't," Tessa said. "You're angry with him. You're angry with yourself because you still love him and you think you shouldn't." A faraway look appeared in Tessa's eyes. "It's as if he died, Vanessa. We'll go into mourning. We'll rend our garments and grieve for what might have been but isn't."

Tears streamed down Vanessa's cheeks. "Nothing will ever be the same."

Jack was staring out a window. "It won't be the same for any of us," he muttered.

Reagan's professional instincts surfaced when he spotted the television cameras. Deftly steering Anthony and Maria Shaath across the Oval Office, he positioned himself and them so that the light from the silver reflectors washed out the shadows under their eyes. "Good lighting can take ten years off your age," he said to no one in particular. Squinting, he glanced around the room. "Can someone close the curtains," he called. "We're getting too much backlight." He turned to his visitors. "For the photo op," he told them, "you'll want to keep your eyes on me and, uh, smile a lot while we chat, and so forth." He turned to the cameras. "All right, boys, roll 'em."

And he grasped Maria's hand in both of his and exclaimed, in that utterly sincere and slightly breathless voice that the entire country loved, "Gosh, are we suckers for happy endings, especially where Americans are concerned."

"Can we have another take, please, Mr. President?" one of the television producers called from the bank of cameras.

"Sure thing. Tell me when you gents are ready."

"Do we have to have so many people in the room?" the line producer complained. "It's distracting to the principals."

The President's press secretary shooed several secretaries and one of the two Secret Service men out of the Oval Office.

"Okay, Mr. President. Here we go."

Reagan's eyes crinkled up and a pained smile illuminated his ruggedly handsome features. "Gosh, are we suckers for happy endings, especially where, uh, Americans are concerned."

"Great!"

"Fine."

"I got what I wanted," the producer told the press secretary.

"Thanks for coming around, fellows," Reagan told the television people as he escorted Anthony and Maria to the door.

Bill Casey caught up with the President in the small room off the Oval Office that Reagan retreated to after photo sessions. "Congratulations, Bill," Reagan said, swiveling toward his Director of Central Intelligence. "You people did a swell job on this raid thing. My pollster tells me that my, uh, positive job rating leaped six points."

"You're only getting your just desserts, Mr. President," Casey said. "It took moxie to sign off on the venture."

Reagan's long term-memory kicked in. "My father, rest his soul, loved the taste of Moxie—he drank a glassful when he got up in the morning, another before going to bed, swore the, uh, gentian root in it was a purgative." He noticed the bewildered glaze in the eyes of his aides. "I, uh, guess Moxie Nerve Food was before your time, boys."

"Bill's come over to brief you on this KHOLSTOMER business," the President's chief of staff, James Baker, reminded Reagan.

Bill Clark said, "KHOLSTOMER's the code designation of the Soviet plot to undermine the US currency and destabilize our economy."

Reagan raised a hand to Casey, inviting him to go on.

"As you know, Mr. President, the CIA worked up intelligence on KHOLSTOMER, so it didn't come as a surprise to us. On D-day, the Federal Reserve was ready and waiting to support the dollar the instant there were signs of a sell-off on the spot market. We knew that the Russians only had sixty-three billion available, and it wasn't difficult for the Fed to sponge it up. The danger was in the panic money that might come in behind the sixty-three billion if fund managers and central banks and foreign entities got the impression that the dollar was in free fall. Importantly, we flooded the media with inside stories of the Federal Reserve's resolve to support the dollar, and its almost unlimited ability to do so. The result was that the panic money the Russians were counting on never materialized."

Reagan nodded solemnly. "So the panic money never, uh, materialized."

"On top of that, we worked up intelligence revealing that Soviet agents of influence close to the central banks of Japan, Hong Kong, Taiwan and Malaysia, along with an economist close to West German chancellor Kohl, were set to press their central banks into a sell-off of dollar Treasury bond holdings."

Reagan, who tended to become ornery when he was deluged with details, said, "Sounds like one of Hitchcock's McGuffins. Cut to the chase, Bill."

"We managed to neutralize these agents of influence. One was arrested on charges of molesting a minor, the other four were encouraged to go off on vacation for a month or two. All five, I might add, will be job hunting. On D-day, we brought our own pressure to bear on the central banks in question to make sure there would be no panic sell-off. The bottom line, Mr. President, is that Andropov's scheme to destabilize our currency and our economy turned into out to be a blind alley for him."

Reagan's eyes narrowed. "You think Andropov was personally behind this, uh, KHOLSTOMER business?"

"We take the view that the KGB would not have gone ahead with it in the absence of a specific order from the General Secretary," Casey said.

"Hmmmmm." Reagan was clearly peeved. "Makes me downright angry when I think that Andropov had the gumption to attack our currency."

Casey, always alert to the possibility of nudging Reagan into action, perked up. "It would be a dangerous precedent," he agreed, "to let him get away with it."

"Can't argue with Bill there," Reagan said.

Casey homed in on the President. "Andropov needs to be reminded that you don't attack the Reagan administration with impunity."

Reagan was still brooding. "My father always said, don't get angry, get, uh, even."

Casey recognized an opening when he saw one. "Getting even—that's the ticket, Mr. President. We could hit Andropov where he's most vulnerable—"

James Baker was on his feet. "Hold on, now, Bill."

"We don't want to do anything rash," Bill Clark chimed in.

But it was Casey who had Reagan's attention. "Where is Andropov vulnerable?" the President asked.

"In Afghanistan. If we supplied Ibrahim's freedom fighters with Stingers, Andropov would hurt."

"This Ibrahim fellow is certainly no Marxist," Reagan remembered. "And Andropov is."

"Ibrahim is dead," Bill Clark noted, but the remark went over the President's head.

"The beauty of it," Casey said, driving home the point, "is that we don't have to deliver Stingers to the freedom fighters. *They have them already*—fifty of them, to be precise. All we have to do is supply the firing mechanisms that we took out before the Stingers were delivered."

"You'll want to think about this very carefully, Mr. President," James Baker said uneasily.

"It would be a hell of a way to get even for what they did to us in Vietnam," Casey persisted. "We lost more than nine hundred planes there, many of them to Russian SAMs."

Reagan fitted the knuckles of his right hand against his cheek with the little finger extended under his nose as if it were a mustache. "Looking at the big picture," he said, nodding carefully, "I think Bill here may be on to something."

The President glanced at Baker and then at Clark. Each in turn averted his eyes. They had been outmaneuvered by Casey and they knew it.

"If that's what you want, Mr. President—" Clark said.

Casey, who had been trying to get Stingers into the hands of the mujaheddin for months, favored Baker and Clark with one of his famous deadpan stares. "You fellows can leave the details to me."

Before anyone could utter a word he had quit the room.

A nippy wind was sweeping the leaves across Pennsylvania Avenue outside the White House as Anthony, walking with a slight limp, and Maria headed for a French restaurant on 17th Street.

"So what was your impression of our President?" Anthony asked.

Maria shook her head. "To the naked eye, he looks more like the stand-in for the President than the actual President. He goes through motions, he recites lines of dialogue that have been written for him. God only knows how decisions are made in there. What about you? What did you think?"

For answer, Anthony recited a poem:

Whether elected or appointed
He considers himself the Lord's anointed,
And indeed the ointment lingers on him
So thick you can't get your fingers on him.

"Where's that from?" Maria asked with a laugh.

"Ogden Nash."

She stepped in front of him, blocking his path. "Anthony McAuliffe, are you trying to impress me?"

"I guess you could make a case that I am. Is it having the desired effect?"

The smile evaporated from her face and her eyes turned very solemn. "I think so," she said.

Wearing a threadbare overcoat with its collar turned up and a moth-eaten cashmere scarf wrapped around his gaunt neck, James Jesus Angleton wheeled the chair back so that the sun wouldn't be in his eyes. "Had to happen eventually," he remarked in a feeble voice. "Too many packs of cigarettes a day for too many decades. Gave them up, along with alcohol, but it was too damn late. Death sentence. Cancer of the lungs, that's what they're telling me. They put me on painkilling drugs that seem to work a bit less each day." He wheeled the chair closer to Ebby, who had taken off his overcoat and loosened his tie and pulled over a broken wicker stool. "Funny thing is you get used to pain. Don't remember what it was like without it." Angleton swung his wheelchair left, then right. "I spend a lot of time out here," he went on. "The heat, the humidity, seem to help me forget."

"Forget what?" Ebby asked.

"The pain. How much I miss cigarettes and alcohol and Adrian Philby. The great mole hunt. The AE/PINNACLE serials that pointed to SASHA. All the mistakes I made, and I made my share, as you no doubt know."

Ebby let his eyes wander around the greenhouse, set in the back yard of Angleton's Arlington home. Clay pots, small jars, gardening tools, bamboo work tables, and wicker furniture had been piled helter-skelter in a corner. Several panes in the roof had been shattered by hailstones the previous winter and left unrepaired. The sun, high overhead, had scorched the half dozen or so orchids still in pots scattered around the floor. The earth in the pots looked bone dry. Obviously nobody was watering them.

"Nice of you to come by," Angleton mumbled. "Don't see many Company people these days. Come to think of it, don't see any. Doubt if the new generation even knows who Mother is."

"I thought someone from Langley ought to come out and brief you," Ebby said.

"Brief me on what?"

"You were right all along, Jim. The KGB did have a mole inside the Company. You identified him but nobody believed you. When AE/PIN-NACLE turned out to be alive after his supposed execution, your suspect went free."

Angleton made eye contact with his visitor for the first time. "Kritzky!"

Ebby nodded.

"You've incarcerated him?"

"Like Philby, like Burgess and Maclean, he fled the country before we could get our hands on him."

"Gone home to Soviet Russia, no doubt."

Ebby shrugged. "We don't expect him to surface—the days when the KGB trots out its spies for the press are long gone. Everyone's better off keeping the lid on this kind of thing."

Angleton's lower lip trembled. "Knew it was Kritzky—told him so to his face. You have to hand it to him, he had a lot of balls, bluffing it out until you all swallowed his line. Playing the innocent. A lot of balls."

"You were right about something else, too, Jim. There was a Soviet master plan to undermine our currency and ruin the economy. They called it KHOLSTOMER."

"KHOLSTOMER," Angleton groaned. He brought a hand up to his migraine-scarred forehead. "Warned you about that, too. One of my biggest mistakes—squandered my credibility warning about too many people. When I got it right nobody was listening."

Ebby said, "Well, I thought you ought to know. I thought we owed it to you."

Both men were at a loss for conversation. Finally Ebby said, "Where do you go from here, Jim? Isn't there something you can do about your...?"

"No place to go from here. This is the last stop, the terminus, the ultima Thule. I'm going to go into the woods on my own and deal with the end of my life, like an Apache." Drawing the overcoat around his wasted body, Angleton shut his eyes and began intoning what sounded like an Indian death chant.

He didn't appear to notice when Ebby retrieved his overcoat and got up to leave.

PART SIX

DEAD RECKONING

*. . . there would be no harm, she thought, in asking
if the game was over. "Please, would you tell me—"
she began, looking timidly at the Red Queen.*

Snapshot: a glossy Polaroid color print of Jack McAuliffe and Leo Kritzky strolling along the sun-saturated bank of the Rhone River in Basel, Switzerland. Jack, his Cossack mustache and thinning hair ruffled by the breeze blowing off the river, is wearing prescription sunglasses, a khaki safari jacket and khaki chinos. Leo, his face thin and drawn, is dressed in a light Russian windbreaker and a peaked worker's cap. Both men are so absorbed in their conversation they don't appear to notice the street photographer who stepped into their path and snapped the picture. Leo reacted violently. Jack calmed him down and quickly purchased the photograph for twenty Swiss francs, which was twice the normal price. Leo wanted to destroy it but Jack had another idea. Uncapping a pen, he scrawled across the face of the picture, "Jack and Leo before The Race but after The Fall," and gave it to Leo as a memento of what was to be their last encounter.

1

MOSCOW, THURSDAY, FEBRUARY 28, 1991

L EO KRITZKY COULD NEVER QUITE GET USED TO THE RUSSIAN WINTER. It had taken him seven years and eight winters to figure out why. It wasn't so much the arctic temperatures or the drifts of dirty snow piled against dirty buildings or the permanent film of black ice on the sidewalks or the enormous stripped chimneys spewing chalk-white smoke into the eternal twilight or the fume of humidity trapped between the double windows of his apartment, making you feel as if you were marooned in a pollution-filled cloud chamber. No, it was more the unrelenting bleakness of everybody in sight—the grim expressions frozen onto the faces of pensioners peddling razor blades on street corners to buy a handful of tea, the emptiness in the eyes of the prostitutes selling themselves in metro stations to feed their children, the resignation in the voices of the gypsy cabbies who weren't sure they could make enough working a fifteen-hour shift to repair their battered cars.

In winter every bit of bad news or bad luck or bad temper seemed to take on tragic proportions. Come spring, so went the saw to which all sensible Muscovites (including Leo) subscribed, life had to get better because there was no way it could get worse.

Thirty-two days to go until All Fools' Day, Leo told himself as he made his way across Taganskaya Square in the flatfooted shuffle that veterans of the Russian winter employed to keep from slipping on the ice. He saw the Commercial Club up ahead on Bolshaya Kommunisticheskaya—the posh watering hole for the nouveau riche (unofficial motto: better nouveau than never) would have been difficult to miss. Pulled up on the curb in brazen illegality were two dozen or so of the latest model BMWs or Mercedes-Benzes or Jeep Cherokees, their motors running to keep the broad-shouldered body-guards (almost all of them Afghan veterans) warm as they catnapped in the front seats. Once inside the club, Leo checked his wool-lined duffle coat (a birthday present from Tessa) in the cloakroom and walked across the lobby to the visitors desk, where he was politely but firmly invited to produce an identity card, after which his name was checked against a list on a comput-er screen. "*Gospodin* Tsipin is waiting for you in the private baths, door number three," a white-jacketed flunkey said as he led Leo down a freshly painted corridor and, using one of the passkeys attached to a large ring, let him into the bath.

Yevgeny, a soggy sheet wrapped around the lower half of his body, was sitting on a wooden bench, flaying his back with a birch branch. "What kept you?" he cried when he caught sight of Leo.

"The Vyhino-Krasnopresneskaja line was down for half an hour," Leo told him. "People said that a man fell in front of a train."

Yevgeny snorted. "This is Gorbachev's Russia," he said. "Which means there's a good chance he was pushed."

"You used to be a stubborn optimist," Leo said. "Has Russia trans-formed you into an incorrigible cynic?"

"I spent thirty years fighting for Communism," Yevgeny said, "before I returned home to a Mother Russia run by the *vorovskoi mir*. What's that in English, Leo? *The thieves' world.*" The smile on Yevgeny's lips only served to emphasize his disenchantment. "It's good to see you again after all this time."

"I'm pleased to see you, too, Yevgeny."

The moment turned awkward. "If I'd known you were coming by metro," Yevgeny said, "I would have sent one of my cars around to fetch you."

"Cars, plural?" Leo asked. Feeling self-conscious, he turned his back on Yevgeny and peeled off his clothes, handing them to the attendant who gave him a white sheet, which he quickly wrapped around his waist. "How many cars do you have?"

Yevgeny, who had put on weight during his seven years in Moscow, filled two small glasses with iced vodka. "*Nazdorovie*," he said, and he threw his back in one brisk gulp. "Personally, I don't own anything more than the shirt on my back. On the other hand, my organization has several BMWs, a Volvo or two and a Ferrari, not to mention the Apatov mansion near the village of Cheryomuski. Beria kept an apartment there until his execution in 1953, Starik used it as a home and office before his illness; it was in the wood-paneled library on the second floor that he first recruited me into the service. I bought the mansion from the state for one million rubles; with inflation being what it is, it turned out to be a steal." Yevgeny pursed his lips. "So where have you been hiding, Leo? I heard you'd settled in Gorky after we came back, but by the time I persuaded someone to give me your address you'd moved. Two years ago a friend told me you were living on a houseboat without a telephone at the end of the metro line at Rechnoi Vokzal—I sent one of my drivers around half a dozen times but the boat was always deserted. I figured you were out of the city, or out of the country. Finally I got an old KGB colleague at Lubyanka to tell me where your pension check was being sent. Which is how I found the address on Frunzenskaya Embankment—number fifty, entrance nine, apartment three seventy-three."

Leo said quietly, "I had a lot of ghosts to exorcise. I've more or less become a hermit—a hermit lost in a city filled with hermits."

Yevgeny peeled off the sheet and pulled Leo into the steam room. The thermometer on the wall read eighty-five centigrade. The heat scalded Leo's throat when he tried to breathe. "I'm not used to this—don't know how long I can stand it."

Yevgeny, his face growing beet-red, splashed a ladle full of cold water onto the hot coals. A haze of vapor sizzled into the moist air. "You become used to it," he whispered. "The trick is to store up enough heat in your body to see you through the winter months."

Leo abandoned the steam room when the sand ran out of the glass. Yevgeny came out behind him and the two dipped in a tiled pool. The water was so icy it took Leo's breath away. Later, wrapped in dry sheets, they settled onto the bench and the attendant wheeled over a cart loaded with *zakuski*—herring, caviar, salmon, along with a bottle of iced vodka.

"I'm not sure I can afford this on my KGB pension," Leo remarked. "The ruble doesn't go as far as it used to."

"You are my guest," Yevgeny reminded him.

"How did you get so rich?" Leo asked.

Yevgeny looked up at his friend. "You really want to know?"

"Yeah. I see all these characters in their foreign cars and leather coats with bleached blondes clinging to their arms. I'm curious how they do it."

"It's not a state secret," Yevgeny said. "After I returned to Moscow the Centre gave me a job in the USA section of the First Chief Directorate, but I could see I was going nowhere fast. When Gorbachev came on the scene in 1985, I decided to strike out on my own. All those years I spent in the Mecca of free enterprise must have rubbed off on me. I rented a dilapidated indoor pool and gymnasium for a song—ha! my English is still pretty good—and transformed it into a sports center for the new Russian rich. With the profit I organized a financial information center for foreign investors. With the profit from that I bought a Communist Party printing press and started a financial newspaper. Then I branched out. I started buying and selling raw materials in Siberia and trading them for finished products—Japanese VCRs, Hong Kong computers, American blue jeans—which I imported. Tell me if this is boring you."

"On the contrary."

"I sold the VCRs and computers and blue jeans in Russia for a huge profit. All the while I was working out of the back seat of a car and renting a relatively small apartment behind the Kremlin from an opera singer for a thousand US dollars a month—she'd fired the housekeeper and moved into her attic room. I needed a larger apartment and a corporate center, which is why I bought the Apatov mansion. It solved all my problems. Now people come to me with ideas and I give them seed money in return for a fifty percent interest in the *bizness*. And I'm in the process of setting up my own private bank. I'm calling it the Greater Russian Bank of Commerce. We are opening our doors this week, with branch offices in Leningrad and Kiev and Smolensk, as well as Berlin and Dresden to plug into the international banking scene." Yevgeny helped himself to some herring on a dry biscuit and washed it down with vodka. "Tell me what you've been doing, Leo."

Leo sniggered in derision. "There's not much to tell. The Centre kept me on ice for several years when I came in. The address in Gorky was a decoy—it was supposed to throw off the CIA if they came looking for me, which of course they didn't. I went through endless debriefings. Case officers would bring me questions, area specialists would seek my opinion on this or that senator or congressman, they'd ask me to read between the lines of the latest Presidential speech. When my conclusions reinforced the views held in the superstructure they were passed on. When they didn't they were shelved."

Yevgeny said, "It's an old story—an intelligence organization functioning in a country that doesn't tolerate dissent has a tendency to ignore dissenting information."

Leo shrugged listlessly. "The middle-level analysts seemed to think I had a magic key that could unlock American mysteries and kept coming back for more. In the last few years, as Gorbachev opened things up and information began to circulate more freely, they finally began to lose interest in my opinions—"

"And the CIA never acknowledged that you'd been a mole?"

Leo shook his head. "They had nothing to gain and everything to lose by revealing that they'd been penetrated, and on such a high level. The press would have had a field day, heads would have rolled, budgets would have been cut, for all I know the CIA might have been broken up. At one point early on the Centre proposed to trot me out in front of the international press to embarrass the Company, but I managed to talk them out of it—I made them understand that they couldn't count on my cooperating with the debriefers if they went public. Since then the CIA has taken in a handful of KGB defectors without publicly rubbing it in, so I suppose it's a standoff."

"Do you hear from your family?"

For a while Leo didn't respond. "Sorry—what did you say?"

"Your family, the twins—have you been in touch with them?"

"Both girls quit the Company in the aftermath of my...retirement. Vanessa flatly refuses to have anything to do with me. My ex-wife became an alcoholic—one winter night, Adelle drank herself senseless and curled up in a hole on a hill in Maryland not far from where we'd buried my dog and her cat the day we met. A farmer found her body covered with snow the next morning. Vanessa said it was all my fault, which it obviously was, and swore she'd never communicate with me again as long as she lived. She married and had a baby boy, which I suppose makes me a grandfather. I wrote her a letter of congratulations but she never replied. Tessa got a job in Washington covering intelligence agencies for *Newsweek*. She married a journalist and divorced him three years later. She writes me every month or so and keeps me up to date. I've encouraged her to come over for a visit but she says she's not ready for that yet. I keep hoping Tessa will turn up at my door one day." Leo caught his breath. "I miss the twins..."

The two concentrated on the *zakuski*. Yevgeny refilled their glasses with vodka. "What's your personal life like?" he asked Leo.

"I read a great deal. I became friendly with a woman who illustrates children's books—she's a widow. We keep company, as they used to say in America. When the weather permits we go for long walks. I've gotten to know Moscow quite well. I read *Pravda* every day, which improves my Russian and instructs me on what Gorbachev's been up to the last twenty-four hours."

"What do you think of him?"

"Gorbachev?" Leo reflected for a moment. "He's made an enormous difference—he was the first person to openly challenge the Communist establishment and eat away at the power of the Party and build up democratic institutions. But I can't figure out whether he wants to reform the Communist Party or eventually do away with it."

"They want to patch it so that it lasts until their careers are over," Yevgeny guessed "They want an office to go to when they wake up in the morning."

"I wish Gorbachev were a better judge of people," Leo said. "He surrounds himself with right-wingers whom I don't trust—Kryuchkov, the KGB chairman, for instance."

"The Minister of Defense, Yazov, the Interior Minister, Pugo—I wouldn't trust them either," Yevgeny said. "For me, for the new class of entrepreneurs, Gorbachev is the lynchpin to economic reform. If he's overthrown it will set Russia back fifty years."

"Someone ought to warn him—"

"He has been warned," Yevgeny said. "I heard that Boris Yeltsin specifically alerted him to the possibility of a right-wing coup, but Gorbachev despises Yeltsin and doesn't believe anything that comes from him."

"Gorbachev doesn't know who his real friends are," Leo said.

"Well, you can't say we don't live in fascinating times," Yevgeny declared with a low laugh. "I heard on the car radio that the Americans are pulverizing Saddam Hussein's army. Do you think they would have gone to war if the principal export of Kuwait was carrots instead of oil?" He raised his glass and clinked it against Leo's. *"Za uspiekh nashevo beznadiozhnovo diela!"*

Leo smiled. For an instant he almost seemed happy. "To the success of our hopeless task!"

Later, outside in the street, Yevgeny signalled for his car. Down the block a polished black BMW backed off the sidewalk onto the street and drew up parallel to the curb. A man with a livid scar running from his ear to his jaw jumped out of the passenger seat and held open the back door.

"Let me drop you someplace," Yevgeny offered.

"I think I'll walk back," Leo said. "I lead a very sedentary life. I could use the exercise."

"I hope our paths cross again," Yevgeny said.

Leo studied his friend's face. "I never asked you—are you married?"

Yevgeny shook his head. "There was someone once—but too much time has passed, too much water has flowed under the bridge."

"You could try to pick up where you left off. Do you know where she is?"

"I read about her in the newspapers from time to time—she is one of the reformers around Yeltsin. In certain circles—amongst the reformers, in the ranks of the KGB—she is quite well known."

"Get in touch with her."

Yevgeny kicked at a tire. "She wouldn't give me the time of day."

"You never know, Yevgeny."

When Yevgeny looked up, a sad half-smile was disfiguring his lips. "I know."

"Turn onto the Ring Road," Yevgeny told the driver. "There's less traffic at this time of day."

He melted back into the leather of the seat and watched the shabby automobiles and shabby buses and shabby buildings parade past the window. At a red light, the BMW pulled up next to a Saab with a chauffeur and a bodyguard up front and two small boys in the back. The sight of the children liberated a flood of memories. As children, Yevgeny and his brother, Grinka, had often been driven out to the dacha in Peredelkino in his father's shiny Volga. My God, he thought, where have all those years gone to? Nowadays, when he shaved in the morning, he caught himself staring at the image that peered back at him from the mirror. Its face seemed only vaguely familiar, a distant cousin from the Tsipin side of the family tree with a suggestion of his father's high forehead and squint and stubby chin. How was it possible to be sixty-two years old? Leo, who had always appeared younger than his years, had aged. But Yevgeny, to his own eye, had actually grown old.

In the front of the BMW, Yevgeny's driver and the bodyguard were busy trashing Gorbachev. It wasn't his economic or political reforms that annoyed them so much as the *sukhoi zakon*—the dry laws he'd put into effect to reduce chronic alcoholism in the workplace and boost production. On Gorbachev's orders vodka factories had been shut down, grapevines in Georgia and Moldavia had been bulldozed. "Under Brezhnev," the driver remembered, "the standard half-liter bottle of vodka was three rubles sixty-two. The price never went up and it never went down, not so much as a kopeck. It got so that you didn't use the word vodka—you asked for a three sixty-two and everyone knew what you were talking about. Today people who work in factories can't even afford ersatz vodka—"

Yevgeny asked jokingly, "How can a Russian get through the day without vodka?"

The bodyguard with the livid scar on his face twisted around in his seat. "They concoct substitutes, Yevgeny Alexandrovich," he said.

"Tell him the recipes," the driver insisted.

"In Afghanistan, we used to mix one hundred grams of Zhigulev beer, thirty grams of *Sadko the Rich Merchant* brand shampoo, seventy grams of a Pakistani anti-dandruff shampoo and twenty grams of insect repellent. The result was rotgut but it would take your mind off the war. The trick was to drink it in quick gulps, otherwise you could burn your throat."

The driver called over his shoulder, "I have a friend in the militia who says the kids have taken to eating shoe polish sandwiches."

"And what is a shoe polish sandwich?" Yevgeny asked.

"You spread shoe polish on a thick slice of white bread—"

"If you can find white bread," quipped the bodyguard.

"You let it sit for fifteen minutes while the bread absorbs the alcohol in the shoe polish. Then you skim off as much of the shoe polish as you can and eat the bread. They say four slices will put you out of your misery for the day."

The bodyguard glanced over his shoulder again. "Brown shoe polish is supposed to be the best," he added.

"Thanks for the tip," Yevgeny remarked dryly.

The two men in the front seats grinned. Yevgeny leaned forward and tapped the driver on the arm. "Turn right after the light—the clinic is on the right at the end of the block."

The private KGB clinic, set back from the street with a tarnished gold hammer and sickle over the revolving door, was a dingy four-story brick building with a solarium on the roof. Inside, sounds—plaintive cries for a nurse, the shrill ringing of telephones, cryptic announcements on the public address system—echoed through the enormous domed entrance hall. Both elevators were out of order, so Yevgeny climbed the fire staircase to the fourth floor. Two peasant women wearing layers of sweaters and rubber boots were mopping the corridor with filthy water. Yevgeny knocked once on the door with a scrap of paper taped to it marked "Zhilov, Pavel Semyonovich," then opened it and looked inside. The room—there was a metal hospital bed, a night table, mustard-color paint peeling from the walls, a toilet without a lid and two sleet-streaked windows without shades or blinds—was unoccupied. Yevgeny woke the nurse dozing at a desk at the end of the corridor. She ran her painted thumbnail down a list and pointed with her chin toward the roof. "He is taking the sun," she said sullenly.

About thirty or so former KGB employees, all of them old and ill, were scattered around one end of the rooftop solarium—the other end was filled with drafts from the panes that had been broken in a hailstorm the previous winter and never repaired. Yevgeny found Starik slumped in a wheelchair, his wispy white beard on his chest, his eyes closed. A tattered blanket with dried vomit stains had slipped down around his ankles and nobody had bothered to tuck it back up to his gaunt neck. Transparent tubes from an intravenous drip suspended from a jury-rigged bar attached to the back of the wheelchair disappeared through a slit in his sweatshirt into a catheter implanted in his chest. From behind the wheelchair came the soft hum of a battery-powered pump. Nearby, two retired KGB colonels who would have groveled before Starik in his prime played backgammon, slamming the checkers down onto the wooden board, indifferent to the racket they were making.

Yevgeny studied the man in the wheelchair. Whoever took responsibility for the intensive-care patients had stripped him of whatever dignity was left to him after he had been diagnosed with primitive arterial pulmonary hypertension and, barely able to breathe as his lungs filled with fluid, rushed to the clinic the previous month. Starik was dressed in a pair of faded red sweat pants and a soiled white sweatshirt. There were fresh urine stains around his crotch. As if mocking his glorious record of services to the Motherland, four medals were pinned to his chest. Yevgeny recognized the rosettes—there was the Hero of the Soviet Union, the Order of the Red Banner, the Order of Alexandr Nevsky, the Order of the Red Star. When his father had been dying in the Kremlin clinic, Yevgeny remembered turning away to hide his lack of emotion. But even in decrepitude, the Tolstoyan figure of Starik managed to stir feelings in him.

Yevgeny squatted next to the wheelchair and pulled the blanket up around his mentor's armpits. "Pavel Semyonovich," he whispered.

Starik's eyes twitched open. He stared at his visitor in bewilderment. His jaw trembled when he realized who it was. "Yevgeny Alexandrovich," he mumbled through one side of his half-paralyzed mouth. Each intake of breath was accompanied by a pained rasp. "Tell me if you can...do cats eat bats...do bats eat cats?"

"Are you feeling any better?" Yevgeny inquired. As soon as he said it he realized what a stupid question it was.

Starik nodded yes but muttered the word no. "Life is torment...since they inject me with this French drug Flolan twenty-four hours a day, I have lost all appetite...unable eat...mealtimes they push carts past my open door... the smell of food nauseates me."

"I will speak to the director—"

"That's not worst." Between phrases sickening sounds gurgled up from the back of Starik's throat. "I am washed...shaved...diaper changed... ass wiped...by grown women who bathe once a month and *menstruate*... their body odors are unbearable." A tear welled in the corner of one of his bloodshot eyes. "The night nurse is a *zhid*...she flaunts her name... Abramovna...Oh, where...where have my girlies gone to?"

"They were put in orphanages when you took sick."

One of the KGB colonels rolled double sixes and roared with triumph as he cleared his last pieces off the board.

Grasping Yevgeny's wrist, Starik swayed toward his visitor. "Is Cold War still being waged?" he demanded.

"It is winding down," Yevgeny said.

"Who will be seen as the victor?"

"History will record that the Principal Adversary, America, won the Cold War."

Startled, Starik tightened his grip on Yevgeny's wrist. "How can this be? We won every battle...beat them at every turn...Philby, Burgess, Maclean, Kritzky—endless list." Starik swung his skeletal head from side to side in dismay. "Tolstoy turning in grave...Communism betrayed by the Jews." He gasped for breath. "Cold War may be winding down...but there is an end game. In Tolstoy's story, the death of the horse KHOLSTOMER serves a purpose—the she-wolf and her cubs feed off of his carcass. We, also, will feed off what is left of KHOLSTOMER. Essential for us to—"

His breath gave out and he wheezed dangerously for a moment. Yevgeny was on the verge of shouting for a doctor when Starik regained control of himself. "Essential to look beyond Communism...to nationalism and purifi- cation...must get rid of the Jews once and for all...finish what Hitler started." Starik's eyes blazed with wrath. "I have had contacts with...people have come to see me...messages have been exchanged...I have given out your name, Yevgeny Alexandrovich...someone will be in touch." His slender reserve of energy spent, Starik collapsed back into the wheel chair. "Do you still recall...Tolstoy's last words?"

"The truth—I care a great deal," Yevgeny murmured.

Starik blinked several times, pressing tears out onto his parchment-brit- tle cheeks. "That will serve as a code phrase...whoever speaks it...comes to you with my blessing."

Looking like a Swiss banker in his three-piece Armani, Yevgeny worked the room.

"Happy you could make it, Arkhip," he told one of the senior econo- mists from the Central Bank, pumping his hand. He lowered his voice. "How determined is Gorbachev to support the ruble?"

"He's going to hold the line as long as he can," the economist said. "The big question mark is inflation."

"Inflation has an upside," noted an aide to the Minister of Finance who overheard the conversation. "It weeds out the factories and businesses and banks that don't have the resources or the will to adapt. It's like Mao's Long March—only the strongest survive. Which means that they are better able to cope with the capitalist reality that is imposing itself on the Socialist model."

"That's one way of looking at it," Yevgeny conceded. "On the other hand, a lot of the new entrepreneurs are struggling to keep their heads above water."

"Congratulations, Yevgeny Alexandrovich," gushed a tall man who kept a forefinger on his hearing aide. He carried the business section of *Izvestia* folded into his jacket pocket. "My father and I wish you every success with your Greater Russian Bank of Commerce."

"Thank you, Fedya Semyonovich," Yevgeny said. "I am sorry your father could not make it today. I would like to talk to you both about the hard-currency services we plan to offer import-export companies."

Several waitresses carrying trays filled with triangles of white bread covered with black caviar from the Caspian Sea threaded their way through the crowded ballroom that Yevgeny had rented for the afternoon. Wondering how many in the room knew about the existence of shoe polish sandwiches, Yevgeny plucked a triangle from a passing doily and popped it into his mouth. He helped himself to another glass of French Champagne from the long table and looked around. In front of the thick curtains drawn across a high window, two very elegant women in low-cut cocktail dresses were holding court, surrounded by semicircle of men. Yevgeny recognized the older of the two women—she was the wife of a notorious press baron, Pavel Uritzky. Making his way across the room, he leaned toward her and grazed the back of her gloved hand with his lips. A painful image rushed to his skull—he could make out the bird-like figure of Aida Tannenbaum peering up at him through watery eyes in the Barbizon lounge some seven years earlier. Shaking off the vision, he shook hands with the other woman and each of the men. "We are all in agreement," one of them told Yevgeny, "Russia must have massive doses of outside investment in order to survive. The problem is how to attract capital, given the political and monetary uncertainty—"

"Gorbachev is responsible for both," the older woman said flatly. "If only we had an iron hand on the helm..."

"If she had her way, Mathilde would have us go back to the Brezhnev era," one of the men said with a laugh.

"As long as we are going back, I would have us return to the Stalin era," the woman maintained. "People conveniently forget that the economy *worked* under Stalin. The shelves in the stores were filled. Nobody went hungry. Everyone who wanted to work was employed."

"True, nobody in Moscow went hungry," one of the men said. "But it was different in the countryside. Remember the old aphorism: *The shortage shall be divided among the peasants.*"

"Under Stalin there was no dissent," a man said. "Nowadays, there are twenty opinions on every matter under the sun."

"There was no dissent," Yevgeny remarked, "because the Gulag camps were filled with the dissenters."

"Exactly," said the older woman, misunderstanding which side of the issue Yevgeny was on. She focused her bright eyes on him. "I have heard it said, Yevgeny Alexandrovich, that you were a spy for the KGB in America? Is there any truth to this?"

"It is no secret that I was a Chekist for many years," he replied. "You will forgive me if I do not reveal to you what I did, or where I did it."

"Tell us, then, how one goes about opening a private bank these days," the younger woman asked.

"It is not all that difficult," Yevgeny said with a twinkle in his eyes. "First you must convince people that you have a hundred million American dollars. Once you do that the rest is child's play."

"Oh, you are a naughty man," the older woman remarked. "Everyone knows you have much more than a hundred million American dollars."

A young Russian businessman who had made a fortune exporting second-hand Soviet weapons—the word was he could supply everything from a Kalashnikov to a nuclear submarine—pulled Yevgeny aside. "What do you make of the rumors of a coup d'état against Gorbachev?" he demanded.

"I have heard them, of course," Yevgeny said. "And common sense would suggest that if you and I heard them, Gorbachev has heard them, too. Mikhail Sergeyevich is many things but stupid is not one of them. He will surely take precautions—"

"A coup would be bad for business," the young Russian decided. "What forward dollar rate are you giving against the ruble?"

Smiling, Yevgeny extracted a small embossed business card from his breast pocket. "Call me for an appointment, Paval. I have reason to believe that the Greater Russian Bank of Commerce can be of assistance to you."

Later, as the cocktail party thinned out and the guests were calling for their cars, the wife of the press baron buttonholed Yevgeny in the antechamber off the ballroom. "Yevgeny Alexandrovich, my husband is eager to make your acquaintance. It appears the two of you have a mutual friend who speaks very highly of you."

"I would be honored to meet your husband."

Mathilde slipped a perfumed visiting card from her small embroidered purse and handed it to Yevgeny. An address in Perkhushovo, a village off the Mozhaysk Highway, a date at the end of February, and hour, were written in ink on the back of it. "You are invited to join a select gathering. My husband and a group of his friends and associates are meeting to discuss"—the woman flashed a knife-edged smile—"Count Leo Nikolayevich Tolstoy. Our mutual friend, the person who speaks of you in glowing terms, has said you were greatly influenced by Tolstoy in your youth—that you once adopted as an alias the name Ozolin, who of course was the stationmaster at Astapovo, where the great Tolstoy died."

Yevgeny hardly dared breathe. He had assumed Starik's talk of a code phrase was the ranting of a half-crazed old man. He managed to murmur, "I am stunned by how much you know about me."

The barest trace of a smile vanished from the woman's painted lips. "My husband has been told that you are one of the rare people who remembers the Count's last words: 'The truth—I care a great deal.' Do you, like the immortal Tolstoy, care about the truth, Yevgeny Alexandrovich?"

"I do."

"Then you will share that obsession with my husband and his friends when you honor us with your presence."

Mathilde offered the back of her gloved hand. Yevgeny bent forward and brushed her fingers with his lips. When he straightened and opened his eyes, she was gone.

Room SH219 in the Hart Office Building, home to the House and Senate Select Committees on Intelligence, was reputed to contain the most secure suite of offices in a town obsessed with security. The unmarked door opened into a foyer guarded by armed Capitol Hill policemen. The conference room was actually a room suspended inside a room so that the walls and floor and ceiling (all made of steel to prevent electromagnetic signals from penetrating) could be inspected for bugs. Even the electrical supply was filtered. Inside, mauve chairs were set around a horseshoe-shaped table. On one wall hung a map of the Intelligence Committees' area of interest: the world. Elliott Winstrom Ebbitt II, the Director of Central Intelligence since Bill Casey's death in 1987, had barely settled into a catbird seat when the assault began.

"Mawning to you, Di-rector," drawled the Texan who chaired the Senate Select Committee on Intelligence. He had a smile plastered across his jowls but it didn't mislead anyone; the Senator had been quoted in the *New York Times* the previous week saying there were some in Congress who favored breaking up the Company into component parts and starting over again. "Won't waste your time 'n ours pussyfootin' 'round," he began. He looked through bifocals at some notes he'd scrawled on a yellow legal pad, then peered sleepily over the top of the glasses at the Director. "No secret, folks in Congress are pissed, Ebby. Been almost two years since the last Russian soldier quit Afghanistan. Still can't figure out what the CIA could've been thinkin' 'bout when it delivered Stinger missiles to Islamic fundamentalists. Now that we're bombin' the bejesus out of Saddam Hussein, chances are good some of them-there Stingers will wind up bein' shot at our aircraft."

Ebby said, "I would respectfully remind the Senator that giving Stingers to the mujaheddin was a Presidential decision—"

"Casey recommended it," a Republican Congressman from Massachusetts told the Director. "You could make a case that he talked Reagan into it."

"How many Stingers are still out there and what are you doing to get them back?" another Congressman asked.

"We reckon roughly three hundred and fifty are unaccounted for, Congressman. As for recuperating them, we're offering a no-questions-asked bounty of one hundred thousand dollars a Stinger—"

The Chairman snapped his head to one side to clear the mane of white hair out of his eyes. "I expect an Islamist could get more for a Stinger in the Smugglers' Bazaar in Peshawar. The long an' the short of it, Ebby, is that everyone's patience is wearin' rice-paper thin. Here we are, shellin' out somewhere in the neighborhood of twenty-eight billion dollars of the taxpayers money a year on intelligence. And the single most important event since the end of the Second World War—I'm talkin' 'bout the dee-cline 'n' fall of the Soviet empire—goes unpredicted. Hellfire, the CIA didn't give us a week's warnin'."

A Senator from Maine rifled through a folder and came up with a report stamped "Top Secret." "A couple of months ago you personally told us, in this very room, Mr. Ebbitt, that—and I'm quoting your words—'the most likely outcome for 1991 is that the Soviet economy will stagnate or deteriorate slightly.'"

"It sure as hell deteriorated slightly!" scoffed the Chairman. "The Berlin wall came tumblin' down November of '89; Gorbachev let the satellites in East Europe squirm off the Soviet hook one by one; Lithuania, Latvia, Estonia, Armenia, Azerbaijan, Georgia, the Ukraine are talkin' autonomy—

and we're settin' here twenty-eight billion poorer and readin' 'bout these earth-quaking events in the newspaper."

A Democratic Congressman from Massachusetts cleared his throat. "Senator, in all fairness to Mr. Ebbitt, I think we are obliged to acknowledged that he's done a lot to clean up the CIA's act since Director Casey's day. I don't think I need to remind anyone in this room that, in Casey's time, we had him testifying into a microphone and we listened on earphones trying to decipher his mumblings. And we didn't succeed. Mr. Ebbitt, on the other hand, has been very open and straightforward with us—"

"I 'preciate that much as you do," the Chairman said. "But the problem of gettin' a handle on intelligence—the problem of gettin' some early warnin' for our bucks—remains. We woulda been a hell of a lot better off if'n the CIA'd apprised us of Saddam Hussein's dishonorable intentions vis-à-vis Kuwait."

"Senator, Senators, Congressmen, we've been moving in the right direction on these matters," Ebby said, "but Rome wasn't built in a day and the CIA isn't going to be reconstructed in a year or two. We're dealing with a culture, a mindset, and the only thing that's going to change that over the long run is to bring in new blood, which, as you gentlemen know, is what I've been doing. As far as drawing an accurate portrait of the Soviet Union's leadership, I want to remind the Senators and Congressmen that you've put pressure on the CIA over the years to cut back on covert operations—nowadays we run roughly a dozen programs a year, compared with hundreds in the fifties and sixties. One of the results of this policy is that we don't have assets in Moscow capable of telling us what Gorbachev and the people around him are up to. We don't even know what information they're getting. As for the stagnation of the Soviet economy, Gorbachev himself didn't put his hands on reasonably accurate economic statistics until two or three years ago, and it seems unfair to criticize us for not knowing what he himself didn't know. Looking back, we can see that when he finally discovered how bad things really were, he decided the only way to rejuvenate a stagnating command economy was to move to a market-oriented economy. Just how fast and how far he plans to move is something that Gorbachev himself probably hasn't figured out."

"And how does the Company assess his chances of arresting the downward spiral of the Soviet economy?" inquired a Republican Congressman.

"It's a good bet that things will get worse before they get better," Ebby replied. "In Russia there are individuals, communities, organizations, factories, entire cities even, that have no rational economic reason to exist. Pruning them away is as much a social problem as an economic problem. Then there is the challenge of meeting the raised expectations of the workers—coal miners in the Kuzbass or the Don Basin, to give you one example, want to find more on the pharmacy shelves than jars filled with leeches. It's anybody's guess whether Gorbachev, with his talk of *perestroika* and *glasnost*, will be able to satisfy their expectations. It's anybody's guess whether he'll be able to buck the vested interests—buck the KGB and the military establishment, buck what's left of the Communist Party which fears Gorbachev will reform them out of existence. It's anybody's guess whether the revolution—and there will be a revolution, gentlemen—will come from below or from above."

"What do you make of all this talk in the papers 'bout a putsch?" the Chairman demanded.

"There are people in the Soviet superstructure who would obviously like to set the clock back," Ebby said. "Speaking frankly, we don't know how serious the rumors of a coup are."

"I think we need to give Mr. Ebbitt credit," the Congressman from Massachusetts remarked. "He doesn't bull his way through these briefings. I for one appreciate that when he doesn't know something, he says he doesn't know."

"I second the motion," said a Republican Congressman.

"Still 'n' all, these rumors need to be checked out," the Chairman persisted. "Is there a clique workin' behind the scenes to undermine Gorbachev? How strong are they? What kind of support can they expect from the military? What can we do to support Gorbachev or undermine his opponents? And what should we make of those rumors 'bout the KGB having large amounts of foreign currencies stashed away somewhere in the West?"

"There is sketchy evidence that sizable amounts of Soviet foreign currency holdings may be finding their way into German banks," Ebby confirmed. "The front man handling the mechanics of the operation is said to be someone in the Central Committee—his identity remains a mystery. Who is giving the orders, to what use this money will be put has yet to be determined."

"What role do you see Yeltsin playing in all this?" asked one of the Congressman who had remained silent up to now.

"Yeltsin is coming at Gorbachev from the other direction," Ebby said. "The two men detest each other—have ever since Gorbachev expelled Yeltsin from the Politburo in '87; in those days the Party was above criticism and Yeltsin made the fatal mistake of ignoring this cast-iron rule. Nowadays, Yeltsin openly attacks Gorbachev for slowing down the pace of reforms. I think it can be said with some assurance that Yeltsin, who was elected Russian President by the Russian Republic's Supreme Soviet last year and thus has a strong power base, sees himself as the logical successor to Gorbachev. Our reading is that he wouldn't mind seeing Gorbachev shunted aside on the condition that he's the one doing the shunting."

"Which pretty much pits Yeltsin against the KGB and the military and the Communist Party hacks who are squeamish about reforms," someone said.

"He has more than his share of enemies," Ebby agreed.

The briefing went on for another three-quarters of an hour, with most of the time devoted to a discussion of Saddam Hussein's ability to wage chemical or biological warfare in the wake of his stunning defeat in the Gulf War. At noon, when the meeting finally broke up, even those who tended to be critical of the Company conceded that Ebby had a firm grasp of current events and was doing his level best to shape the CIA into an organization that could cope with the post-Cold War world.

"How'd it go?" Jack asked quietly.

"As well as could be expected," Ebby told his Deputy Director, "all things considered."

"What does that mean?"

"It means that the policy wonks still don't understand the limitations on intelligence gathering. They spend twenty-eight billion a year and they don't feel they're getting their money's worth if questions go unanswered or events go unanticipated."

"They don't give us credit for the ones we call right," Jack griped.

"They give us credit," Ebby said. "But they want us to get it right a hundred percent of the time."

The two stood off to one side in the executive dining room at the Company's Langley headquarters watching as Manny, Deputy Director/ Operations since the previous summer, presented gold wristwatches to three veteran case officers who had been encouraged to take early retirement. (Encouraged, in the sense that all three had been offered new assignments, two in listening posts in the Cameroon Republic, the third in a one-man Company station in the Canary Islands.) The chairs and tables had been pushed against one wall to make room for the hundred or so Operations personnel at the ceremony. Manny, at forty-four the youngest DD/O in memory, blew into the microphone to make sure it was alive. "It's always painful to see old hands take their leave," he began. "John, Hank, Jerry, I speak for everyone in the DD/O when I tell you that we'll miss not only your expertise but your company. Between the three of you, there's exactly seventy-six years of experience—seventy-six years of manning the ramparts of the Cold War. These wristwatches are a token of our esteem and the country's appreciation for your long and meritorious service."

There was a smattering of applause. Several voices from the back cried, "Speech, speech."

"What bullshit," Jack muttered to Ebby. "These jokers were never interested in scoring. They sat around various stations waiting for opportunities to fall into their laps. Even then they always played it safe."

The oldest of the three retirees, a corpulent man with bushy eyebrows fixed in a permanent scowl, stepped up to the microphone. Bitterness was draped across his face like a flag. "Thought I'd pass on a joke that may or may not be about the Central Intelligence Agency," he said. Manny, standing at his side, shifted his weight from one foot to another in discomfort. "Goes like this: A Federal census taker comes across a family of hillbillies living in a shack in Tennessee. Barefoot kids everywhere. The adults have rifles in one hand and moonshine jugs in the other. The father says there are twenty-two in the family. He whistles with his thumb and middle finger and everyone comes a-running."

Some of the DO people began to titter—they had heard the story before.

"The census taker counts heads but finds only twenty-one. Turns out that Little Luke is missing. Then someone shouts from the outhouse—Little Luke has fallen through the privy hole. Everyone runs over to take a look. The father shrugs and wanders off. The census taker can't believe his eyes. 'Aren't you going to pull him out?' he shouts. 'Shucks no,' the father calls back. 'It'll be easier to have another than clean him up.'"

Half the DO staffers burst into laughter. Others raised their eyebrows. Manny gazed at the floor. The officer who told the joke turned his head and looked across the room directly at the DCI.

"Jesus H. Christ," Jack moaned angrily. He would have strode over to have it out with the retiring officer then and there if Ebby hadn't put a hand on his arm.

"These guys were hotshots when they started, but they're burnt out," Ebby said in a low voice.

"That doesn't give him the right—"

"Getting rid of the deadwood is a painful experience for everyone concerned. Grin and bear it, Jack."

Later, in the DCI's seventh-floor Holy of Holies, Jack flopped into a seat across the desk from Ebby. "What he said back there—there may be some truth to it," he moaned. "There are people in Congress who'd prefer to start from scratch rather than give us a chance to clean up the mess Casey left behind him."

"Ran into several of them when I testified this morning," Ebby said.

Jack leaned forward. "I've given this a lot of thought, Ebby. Fighting Colombian drug lords or Islamic terrorists or Russian arms merchants is too much of a sideshow to justify the twenty-eight billion spent on intelligence every year. Look at it another way: How are we going to recruit the best and the brightest if our archenemy is Cuba?"

"You have another idea of what we should be doing?"

"As a matter of fact, I do." Jack got up and strolled over to the door, which was ajar, and kicked it closed. He came around behind Ebby and settled onto on a windowsill.

Ebby swiveled around to face him. "Spit it out, Jack."

"I nibbled around the edges of the subject with you when Anthony was kidnapped by the fundamentalists in Afghanistan. We were in a no-win situation then, we're in a no-win situation now. Congress ties our hands with oversight and budget restrictions and strict limitations on Presidential Findings—my God, Ebby, it's actually against the law for us to target a foreign leader, it doesn't matter that he may be targeting us."

"I remember that conversation—at the time I told you that the CIA was an endangered species and couldn't afford to get involved in what you had in mind."

"At the time," Jack retorted in annoyance, "I told you that we wouldn't have to get involved. We could get others to do the dirty work for us—"

"It would be a violation of our charter—"

"Take this Gorbachev thing—even if we knew what was going on we'd be helpless to do anything about it."

"I'm not sure I want to have this conversation—"

"You're having the conversation—"

"What do you mean by doing something about it?"

"You know what I mean? We could get Torriti to put a toe in the water. Ezra ben Ezra still runs the Mossad—he could be counted on to contribute resources to an enterprise that keeps Gorbachev in power and Jewish emigration from Russia going."

Ebby turned sarcastic. "Contribute to an enterprise—you make it sound so congenial. You make it sound almost legal."

"Those dollars being stashed in Germany by the Russians—if we could get our hands on some of them, the enterprise could become a self-financing entity operating outside of Congressional appropriations and oversight."

"Casey tried to pull that off by selling arms to the Iranians and using the money to support the contra rebels in Nicaragua. I don't need to remind you that it blew up in his face."

"We're supposed to be a shadowy organization, Ebby. I'm only suggesting that we start to operate in the shadows."

Ebby sighed. "Look, Jack, we've fought the same wars, we bear the same scars. But you're wide of the mark now. Because the enemy doesn't have scruples is no excuse for the Company not having scruples. If we fight the wars their way, even if we win, we lose. Don't you see that?"

"What I see is that ends justify means—"

"That's a meaningless catch phrase unless you weigh each case on its merits. Which ends? Which means? And what are the chances of a particular means achieving a particular end?"

"If we don't score, and soon, they'll break up the Company," Jack said.

"So be it," Ebby said. "If you want to continue working for me," he added, "you'll do so on my terms. There will be no *enterprise* as long as I'm running the show. I'm the custodian of the CIA. I take that responsibility very seriously. You read me, Jack?"

"I read you, pal. Like the man says, you're right from your point of view. But your point of view needs work."

2

W E HAVE IRREFUTABLE EVIDENCE," ASSERTED THE KGB CHAIRMAN, Vladimir Kryuchkov, "that the American CIA has succeeded in infiltrating its agents into Gorbachev's inner circle."

At the end of the table, the Minister of Defense, Marshal Dmitri Yazov, a dull, plodding old soldier with a broad chunky face, demanded, "Name names."

Kryuchkov, happy to comply, identified five figures known to be intimate with the General Secretary. "Any idiot can see that Gorbachev is being manipulated by the CIA—it is part of an American plot to sabotage first the Soviet administration, and after that the economy and scientific research. The ultimate goal is the destruction of the Communist Party and the Union, the crushing of Socialism and the elimination of the Soviet Union as a world power capable of holding American arrogance in check."

The eighteen men and one women seated around the long outdoor picnic table listened in consternation. Yevgeny, taking in the scene from a place half way down the table, decided that the last time he had seen so many VIPs in one place was when the television cameras panned to the reviewing stand atop Lenin's Tomb during Red Square May Day parades. At midmorning, the limousines had started arriving at the stately wooden dacha on the edge of the village of Perkhushovo off the Mozhaysk Highway. The guests had sipped punch and had chatted amiably in a large room overheated by a tiled stove as they waited for the latecomers to turn up. One ranking member of the Politburo secretariat had complained about the cost of sending a daughter to a Swiss boarding school and the people listening had nodded in empathy. Eventually everyone had pulled on overcoats—the last snow of the winter had melted but the air was still chilly—and trooped outside to thwart any microphones that might have been installed inside the dacha. Vladimir Kryuchkov's guests hunted for their nametags and took the places assigned to them around the long picnic table set up under a stand of Siberian spruce. Beyond the trees, the lawn sloped down to a large lake on which several dozen teenagers were racing small sailboats. From time to time shrieks of exaltation drifted up hill as the helmsmen wheeled around the buoys marking the course. To the left, through the trees, armed guards could be seen patrolling the electrified fence that surrounded the property.

Mathilde, sitting directly opposite Yevgeny, dispatched a smile of complicity across the table, then turned to whisper in the ear of her husband, Pavel Uritzky. An austere man who made no secret of his deep aversion for Jews, he nodded in agreement and addressed Kryuchkov, presiding from the head of the table. "Vladimir Alexandrovich, the story of CIA spies within Gorbachev's inner circle may be the drop that causes the bucket to overflow. It is one thing to disagree with Gorbachev, as we all do; to reproach him for abandoning the fraternal Socialist states of Eastern Europe, to criticize him for spitting on our Bolshevik history, to fault him for plunging headlong into economic reforms without having the wildest idea of where he was taking the country. It is quite another to accuse him of being manipulated into doing the dirty work of the American CIA. Have you exposed your charges directly to the General Secretary?"

"I attempted to warn him during our regular briefings," Kryuchkov replied. "I can tell you that he invariably cuts me short and changes the subject. He obviously does not want to hear me out; the few times I have managed to get a word in, he has waved a hand in the air as if to say that he does not believe my information."

"Knowingly or unknowingly, Gorbachev is selling the Soviet Union to the devil," Mathilde declared with great passion.

"The country is facing famine," claimed the Soviet prime minister, Valentin Pavlov, from the other end of the table. "The economy has been reduced to total chaos. Nobody wants to carry out orders. Factories have cut production because they lack raw materials. The harvest is disorganized. Tractors sit idle because there are no spare parts."

"Our beloved country is going to the dogs," agreed Valentin Varennikov, the general in charge of all Soviet ground forces. "Tax rates are so prohibitive no one can pay and remain in business. Retired workers who have devoted their lives to Communism are reduced to brewing carrot peelings because they can no longer afford tea on their miserable pensions."

Mathilde's husband slapped the table with the palm of his hand. "It's the fault of the Jews," he insisted. "They bear collective responsibility for the genocide of the Russian people."

Mathilde said, "I wholeheartedly agree with my husband—I hold the view that Jews must be forbidden to emigrate, and most especially to the Zionist entity of Israel, until a tribunal of the Russian people has had a chance to weigh their fate. After all, these Jews were born and educated here at state expense—it is only fitting that the state be compensated."

One of the foreign ministry *apparatchiki*, Fyodor Lomov, the great-grandson of a famous old Bolshevik who served as the first People's Commissar of Justice after the 1917 revolution, spoke up. "It is well known that Jewish architects designed Pushkin Square so that the great Pushkin had his back turned to the motion picture theater, the Rossiya. The symbolism escaped no one." Lomov, a bloated figure of a man with yellowish liquor stains in his snow-white goatee, added, "The *zhids* and Zionists are responsible for rock music, drug addiction, AIDS, food shortages, inflation, the decline in the value of the ruble, pornography on television, even the breakdown of the nuclear reactor at Chernobyl."

As the meeting went on, the plotters (as Yevgeny began to think of them) exposed their resentments and fears. Emotions ran high; there were moments when several people were talking at once and Kryuchkov, like a teacher managing an unruly classroom, had to point to someone so the others would give way to him.

"Gorbachev deceived us into thinking he intended to tinker with the Party structure. He never let on that he intended to destroy it."

"Malicious mockery of all the institutions of the state is commonplace."

"I speak from experience—authority on all levels has lost the confidence of the population."

"The state's coffers are empty—the government is regularly late in paying military salaries and pensions."

"The Soviet Union has, in effect, become ungovernable."

"Soviet arms were humiliated by Gorbachev's decision to retreat from Afghanistan."

"The drastic cuts in the military budget, and the inability to come up with the sums that are budgeted, have left us badly positioned to deal with the Americans after their hundred-hour triumph in the Gulf War."

Kryuchkov searched the faces around the table and said, very solemnly, "The only hope is to declare a state of emergency."

"Gorbachev will never consent to a state of emergency," Paval Uritzky observed.

"In that case," Kryuchkov said, "we will have to consent to a state of emergency for him. I ask those who agree with this analysis to raise a hand."

Around the table nineteen hands went up.

From the lake far below came the howling of a teenager whose boat had capsized. The other boats closed in on the boy from all directions and dragged him out of the water. One of the young girls watching from the shoreline shouted uphill, "They've got him—he's all right."

"When it comes time to launch our project," remarked Uritzky, "we must not be squeamish about people falling overboard." He arched his brows knowingly. Many around the table chuckled.

Later, when the meeting broke up and the guests began drifting toward the limousines, Kryuchkov took Yevgeny aside. "We have a mutual friend who speaks highly of you," the KGB Chairman said. "Your work in the Centre is known to me, your devotion to our cause is legendary within a closed circle of colleagues."

Yevgeny said, "I did my duty, Comrade Chairman, nothing more."

Kryuchkov permitted a humorless smile onto his face. "There are fewer and fewer who use the term *Comrade* since Gorbachev took power." He steered Yevgeny into the bathroom and turned on the two faucets full blast. "One amongst us—a senior official responsible for the Central Committee finances—has managed over the years to move important sums of foreign currency into Germany and convert them, with the complicity of what the Germans call the *Devisenbeschaffer*—the currency acquirer—into dollars and gold. If we are to sideline Gorbachev and declare a state of emergency, we will need large amounts of cash to finance our movement. Once we are successful, it will be of paramount importance to immediately stock the shelves of the food and liquor stores in the major cities to demonstrate our capacity to bring order out of Gorbachev's chaos—we'll reduce the prices of staples, and most especially of vodka. We'll also send out back pension checks to retired people who haven't been paid in months. To accomplish this will require an immediate infusion of capital."

Yevgeny nodded. "I am beginning to understand why I was invited—"

"Your Greater Russian Bank of Commerce has a branch in Germany, I am told."

"Two, in fact. One in Berlin, one in Dresden."

"I ask you bluntly—can we count on your help, Comrade?"

Yevgeny nodded vigorously. "I have not fought for Communism my entire life to see it humiliated by a reformer who is manipulated by the Principal Adversary."

Kryuchkov gripped Yevgeny's hand in both of his and, gazing deep into his eyes, held it for a moment. "The Central Committee official responsible for finances is named Izvolsky. Nikolai Izvolsky. Commit his name to memory. He will get in touch with you in the next few days. He will act as an intermediary between you and the German *Devisenbeschaffer*—together you will organize the repatriation of funds through your bank. When the moment comes you will make these funds available to our cause."

"I am glad to be back in harness," Yevgeny said, "and proud to be working again with like-minded people to protect the Soviet Union from those who would dishonor it."

The day after the meeting in Perkhushovo Yevgeny stopped off for a drink in the piano bar of the Monolith Club, a private hangout where the new elite met to trade tips on Wall Street stocks and off-shore funds. He was wondering what he had gotten himself into and agonizing over what he should do about it—somehow he had to warn Gorbachev—when an effete man with transparent eyelids and a jaw that looked as if it were made of porcelain turned up at the door. He appeared out of place in his synthetic fiber Soviet-era suit with wide lapels and baggy trousers that dragged on the floor; the regulars who frequented the club favored English flannel cut in the Italian style. Yevgeny wondered how the *Homo Sovieticus*, as he immediately dubbed him, had made it past the ex-wrestlers guarding the entrance. The man peered through the swirls of cigar smoke in the dimly lit bar as if he had a rendezvous with someone. When his eyes fixed on Yevgeny, sitting at a small table in a corner, his mouth fell open in recognition. He came straight across the room and said, "It is you, Y. A. Tsipin?"

"That depends on who is asking?"

"I am Izvolsky, Nikolai."

The club's young house photographer caught Yevgeny's eye and held up his scrapbook filled with portraits of Sharon Stone and Robert De Niro and Luciano Pavarotti. "Another time, Boris," Yevgeny called, waving him off. He gestured Izvolsky to a seat. "Can I offer you something?" he asked the *Homo Sovieticus*.

"I never touch alcohol," Izvolsky announced with a certain smugness; being a teetotaler obviously gave him a feeling of moral superiority. "A glass of tea, perhaps."

Yevgeny signalled to the waiter and mouthed the word *tchai* and turned back to his guest. "I was told you worked for the Central Committee—"

"We must be discreet—the walls here are said to be filled with micro-phones. An individual of some importance in the superstructure directed me to contact you."

A cup of tea and a china bowl filled with cubes of Italian sugar were set in front of Izvolsky. He pocketed a handful of the sugar cubes and leaned forward to blow on his tea. "I was instructed," he went on, lowering his voice, nervously stirring the spoon around in the cup, "to alert you to the existence of a German nationalist who, in the months ahead, will be deposit-ing sizable sums of US dollars in the Dresden branch of your bank. Like many in our coterie, he is a patriot who has devoted his life to battling the great Satan, international Jewry."

"What is his name?"

"You will know him only by the German sobriquet *Devisenbeschaffer*—the currency acquirer."

"If you can trust me with the money, you can trust me with the identity of this *Devisenbeschaffer*."

"It is not a matter of trust, Comrade Tsipin. It is a matter of security."

Yevgeny accepted this with what he hoped was a professional nod.

Izvolsky retrieved a pen from the breast pocket of his jacket and care-fully wrote a Moscow phone number on a cocktail napkin. "This is a private number monitored by an answering machine that I interrogate throughout the day. You have only to leave an innocuous message—suggest that I watch a certain program on television, for instance—and I will recognize your voice and contact you. For the present, you are to instruct your Dresden branch to open an account in your name. Communicate to me the number of this account. When we wish to repatriate sums that will be regularly deposited in this account, I will let you know, at which point you will trans-fer them to the Moscow branch office of your bank."

Izvolsky brought the cup to his lips and delicately tested the tempera-ture of the tea. Deciding it was cool enough, he drank it off in one long swallow, as if he were quenching a thirst. "I thank you for the hospitality, Comrade Tsipin," he said. And without so much as a handshake or a good-bye, the *Homo Sovieticus* rose from his chair and headed for the door.

Leo Kritzky listened intently as Yevgeny described the visit to Starik in the clinic; the mention of a coded phrase that would put him in touch with a group organizing an "end game," the meeting of the conspirators in Perkhushovo. "I didn't take Starik seriously," Yevgeny admitted. "I thought he was ranting—all that talk about Jews and purification and starting over again. But I was wrong. He hangs onto life by a thread—in his case an intravenous drip into a catheter planted under the skin of his chest—and devises schemes."

Leo whistled through his teeth. "This is a bombshell of a story that you're telling me."

Yevgeny had phoned Leo's number from a public booth late the previous evening to organize a rendezvous. "I could leave a tic-tac-toe code chalked on your elevator door," he had said with a conspiratorial chuckle, "but it would take too long. I must see you tomorrow. In the morning, if possible."

The mention of the coded tic-tac-toe messages identifying meeting places in the Washington area awakened in Leo enigmatic emotions—it transported him back to what now seemed like a previous incarnation, when the dread of tripping up imparted to everyday activities an adrenalin kick that retirement in Moscow lacked. He had agreed at once to the meeting. Yevgeny had said he would start out from the tomb of the unknown soldier at the Kremlin wall and stroll south, and named an hour. Leo immediately understood the implications of the outdoor meeting: Yevgeny wanted to be sure whatever he had to say wouldn't be recorded.

Now the two men drifted past a bank of outdoor flower stalls and, further along, a group of English sightseers listening to an Intourist guide describe how Czar Ivan IV, known as "The Terrible," had murdered his son and heir, as well as several of his seven wives. "A fun guy!" one of the tourists quipped.

"I'm not sure I understand you," the Intourist guide replied in puzzlement.

"So what do you make of it all?" Leo asked when they were alone again.

"The meeting I attended was not a discussion group," Yevgeny said. "Kryuchkov is plotting to take power. He is a meticulous man and is slowly tightening the noose around Gorbachev's neck."

"Your list of plotters reads like a who's who of Gorbachev's inner circle. Defense Minister Yazov, the press baron Uritzky, Interior Minister Pugo, Soviet ground forces chief Varennikov, Lomov from the foreign ministry, Supreme Soviet Chairman Lukyanov, Prime Minister Pavlov."

"Don't forget Yevgeny Tsipin," Yevgeny said with a anxious grin.

"They want to use your bank to bring in enormous sums of money from Germany to finance the putsch—"

"As well as stock the empty shelves in the food and liquor stores and send out pension checks. The plotters are shrewd, Leo. If they can take over quickly, with little or no bloodshed, and buy off the masses with cosmetic improvements, they can probably get away with it."

Leo looked at his friend. "Whose side are we on?" he asked, half in jest.

Yevgeny smiled grimly. "We haven't changed sides. We're for the forces that promote the genius and generosity of the human spirit, we're against right-wing nationalism and anti-Semitism and those who would obstruct the democratic reforms in Russia. In short, we're on the side of Gorbachev."

"What do you expect me to do?"

Yevgeny tucked his arm under Leo's elbow. "There is a possibility that I may be watched by Kryuchkov's henchmen—Yuri Sukhanov, the boss of the KGB's Ninth Chief Directorate, the division responsible for Gorbachev's security, attended the Perkhushovo meeting. The Ninth Directorate has plenty of warm bodies available. My phone could be tapped. The people I employ may be bought off and report on my activities."

Leo saw where the conversation was going. "All those years you acted as my cutout. Now you want to flip the coin—you want me to act as *your* cutout."

"You will be freer—"

"They could be watching us right now," Leo said.

"I drove myself into the city and took some tradecraft precautions before I showed up at the Tomb of the Unknown Soldier."

"Okay. Let's assume I am freer. Freer to do what?"

"For starters, I think you should pass on what I told you—the account of the secret meeting at Perkhushovo, the list of those who attended—to your former friends at the CIA."

"You could accomplish the same thing with an anonymous letter to the Company station in Moscow—"

"We must work on the assumption that the KGB has penetrated the station. If the Americans discuss the letter and their comments are picked up by microphones, it could lead, by a process of elimination, back to me. No, someone should take the story directly to the Company brass in Washington. Logically, that someone has to be you. They'll believe you, Leo. And if they believe you they may be able to convince Gorbachev to clean house, to arrest the conspirators. The CIA has a long arm—they may be able to act behind the scenes to thwart the conspiracy."

Leo scratched at an ear, weighing Yevgeny's suggestion.

"Obviously you can't let them know where your information comes from," Yevgeny added. "Tell them only that you have a mole inside the conspiracy."

"Say I buy your idea. That doesn't exclude your trying to get word to Gorbachev directly—"

"I'm a jump ahead of you, Leo. I know one person I can trust—someone who is close to Yeltsin. I'll see what I can accomplish through her."

The two men stopped walking and stood facing each other for a moment. "I thought the game was over," Leo said.

"It never ends," Yevgeny said.

"Be careful, for God's sake."

Yevgeny nodded. "It would be too ridiculous to survive America and get knocked off in Russia."

Leo nodded in agreement. "Too ridiculous and too ironic."

The auditorium, a drafty factory hall where workers had once dozed through obligatory lectures on the abiding advantages of the dictatorship of the proletariat, was jam-packed. Students sat cross-legged in the aisles or stood along the walls. On a low stage, under a single overhead spotlight, a tall slender woman, whose no-nonsense short dark hair was tucked behind her ears, spoke earnestly into a microphone. Her melodious voice made her sound younger than her fifty-nine years. And she pulled off the orator's hat trick: she managed to convey emotion by playing with the spaces between the words. "When they heard about my index cards," she was saying, "when they discovered that I was collecting the names of Stalin's victims, they hauled me into a overheated room in the Lubyanka and let me know that I was flirting with a prison sentence...or worse. That took place in 1956. Afterward, I learned that I had been branded an SDE. It is a badge I wear with pride—I am, from the point of view of the Communist regime, a Socially Dangerous Element. Why? Because my project of documenting Stalin's crimes—I now have more than two hundred and twenty-five thousand index cards and I've only scratched the surface—threatened to return history to its proper owners, which is to say, return it to the people. When the Communists lose control of history, their party—to borrow Trotsky's expression—will be swept into the dustbin of history."

There was loud applause from the audience. Many of those sitting on the folding chairs stomped on the floor in unison. When the noise subsided the speaker forged on.

"Mikhail Gorbachev has been a leading force behind the return of history to the people—no easy task considering that we, as a nation, never experienced a Reformation, a Renaissance, an Enlightenment. Since Gorbachev came to power in 1985, our television has aired documentaries about Stalin's brutal collectivization of agriculture in the early 1930s, the ruthless purge trials in the mid-1930s, along with details of the millions who were purged without trials, who were summarily executed with a bullet in the neck or sent off to the Gulag camps in Kolyma, Vorkuta and Kazakhastan."

The speaker paused to take a sip of water. In the auditorium there was dead silence. She set down the glass and looked up and, surveying the faces in the audience, continued in an even quieter voice. The students leaned forward to catch her words.

"All that is the positive side of Gorbachev's governance. There is a negative side, too. Gorbachev, like many reformers, has no stomach for what Solzhenitsyn termed the work in the final inch; he is afraid to follow where logic and common sense and an impartial examination of history would lead. Gorbachev argues that Stalin was an aberration—a deviation from the Leninist norm. *Chepukha!*—rubbish! When are we going to admit that it was Lenin who was the genius of state terror. In 1918, when the Bolsheviks lost the election, he shut down the democratically elected Constitutional Assembly. In 1921 he systematically began liquidating the opposition, first outside the party, eventually inside the party. What he created, under the sophism *dictatorship of the proletariat,* was a party devoted to the eradication of dissent and the physical destruction of the dissenters. It was this Leninist model that Stalin inherited." The woman's voice grew even fainter; in the audience people barely breathed. "It was a system which beat prisoners so badly that they had to be carried on stretchers to the firing squads. It was a system that broke Meyerhold's left arm and then forced him to sign a confession with his right. It was a system that sent Osip Mandelstam to the frozen wastelands of Siberia for the crime of writing, and then reading aloud, a poem about Stalin that fell far short of being an encomium. It was a system that murdered my mother and my father and carted off their bodies, along with the nine hundred and ninety-eight others who were executed that day, to the Donskoi Monastery for cremation. I have been told you could often see dogs in the neighborhood fighting over the human bones that they had scratched out of the fields around the monastery." The speaker looked away to collect herself. "I myself have never gained access to the *spetskhran*—the special shelves in the Soviet archives where secret dossiers are stored. But I have reason to believe there are somewhere in the neighborhood of sixteen million files in the archives dealing with arrests and executions. Solzhenitsyn estimates that sixty million—that is a sixty with six zeroes dragging after it like a crocodile's tail—*sixty million* people were victims of Stalinism."

The woman managed a valiant smile. "My dear friends, we have our work cut out for us."

There was a moment of silence before the storm of applause broke over the auditorium. The woman shrank back, as if buffeted by the ovation that soon turned into a rhythmic foot-pounding roar of admiration. Eager supporters surrounded her and it was well after eleven before the last few turned to leave. As the speaker collected her notes and slipped them into a tattered plastic briefcase, Yevgeny made his way from the shadows at the back of the auditorium down the center aisle. Expecting more questions, the woman raised her eyes—and froze.

"Please excuse me for turning up suddenly—" Yevgeny swallowed hard and started over again. "If you consent to talk with me you will understand that it might have been dangerous for me, and for you also, if I had phoned you at your home. Which is why I took the liberty—"

"How many years has it been?" she inquired, her voice reduced to a fierce whisper.

"It was yesterday," Yevgeny replied with feeling. "I was catnapping under a tree in the garden of my father's dacha at Peredelkino. You woke me—your voice was as musical yesterday as it is today—with a statement in very precise English: *I dislike summer so very much.* You asked me what I thought of the novels of E. Hemingway and F. Fitzgerald."

He climbed onto the stage and stepped closer to her. She shrank back, intimidated by the intensity in his eyes. "Once again you take my breath away, Yevgeny Alexandrovich," she confessed. "How long have you been back in the country?"

"Six years."

"Why did it take you six years to approach me?"

"The last time we spoke—I called you from a pay phone—you gave me to understand that it would be better, for you at least, if we never met again."

"And what has happened to make you ignore this injunction?"

"I saw articles about you in the newspapers—I saw an interview with you and Academician Sakharov on the television program *Vzglyad*—I know that you are close to Yeltsin, that you are one of his aides. That is what made me ignore your injunction. I have crucial information that must reach Yeltsin, and through him, Gorbachev."

At the door of the auditorium a janitor called, "*Gospodina* Lebowitz, I must lock up for the night."

Yevgeny said, with some urgency, "Please. I have an automobile parked down the street. Let me take you someplace where we can talk. I can promise you, you will not regret it. I am not overstating things when I say that the fate of Gorbachev and the democratic reformation could depend on your hearing me out."

Azalia Isanova nodded carefully. "I will go with you."

Midnight came and went but the bull session in the Sparrow, a coffeehouse downhill from Lomonosov University on the Sparrow Hills (lately residents had taken to calling the area, known as Lenin Hills, by its pre-revolutionary name), showed no sign of flagging. "Capitalist systems have been transformed into Socialist systems but not vice versa," argued a serious young man with long sideburns and a suggestion of a beard. "There are no textbooks on the subject, which is why we need to proceed cautiously."

"We're writing the textbook," insisted the girl sitting across from him.

"It's like swimming in a lake," another girl said. "Of course you can go in slowly but the pain lasts longer. The trick is to dive in and get it over with."

"People who dive into icy lakes have been known to die of heart attacks," a boy with thick eyeglasses pointed out.

"If Socialism dies of a heart attack," the first boy quipped, "who will volunteer to give it mouth-to-mouth resuscitation?"

"Not me," the girls shot back in chorus.

"Another round of coffee," one of the boys called to the waiter, who was reading a worn copy of *Newsweek* behind the cash register.

"Five Americans, coming up," he called back.

At a small round table near the plate-glass window, Aza mulled over what Yevgeny had just told her. On the avenue outside, the traffic was still thick and the throaty murmur of car motors made it sound as if the city were moaning. "You are certain that Yazov was there?" Aza demanded. "It really would be a stab in the back—Gorbachev plucked him out of nowhere to be Minister of Defense."

"I am absolutely sure—I recognized him from pictures in the newspapers even before someone addressed him as *Minister*."

"And Oleg Baklanov, the head of the military-industrial complex? And Oleg Shenin from the Politburo?"

"Baklanov introduced himself to me in the dacha before we all trooped out to the lawn for the meeting. He is the one who pointed Shenin out to me."

Aza reread the list of names she had jotted on the back of an envelope. "It is terribly frightening. We knew, it goes without saying, that trouble was coming. Kryuchkov and his KGB friends have not made a secret of their opinion of Gorbachev. But we never anticipated a plot would attract so many powerful people." She looked up and studied Yevgeny, as if she were seeing him for the first time. "They were very sure you would be sympathetic to their cause—"

"I worked for the KGB abroad. They assume that anyone with KGB credentials must be against reforms and for a restoration of the old order. Besides, almost all of the people who have set up private banks are gangsters without any political orientation other than pure greed. The conspirators need someone they can trust to repatriate the money in Germany. And I came highly recommended—"

"Who recommended you?"

"Someone whose name is a legend in KGB circles but would mean nothing to you."

"You are very courageous to come to me. If they were to discover your identity—"

"It is for that reason that I don't want anyone, including Boris Yeltsin, to know the source of your information."

"Not knowing the source will detract from its credibility."

"You must say only that it comes from someone you have known a long time and trust." Yevgeny smiled. "After how I deceived you, do you trust me, Aza?"

She considered the question. Then, almost reluctantly, she nodded. "From the start you have always made me hope—and then you have dashed my hopes. I am afraid to hope again. And yet—"

"And yet?"

"Are you familiar with the American title of Nadezhda Mandelstam's book about her husband, Osip? *Hope Against Hope.* If I were to write a book about my life, it would also be an appropriate title. I am a sucker for hope."

Yevgeny turned over the check and glanced at the amount and started counting out rubles. "I will not drive you home—we must not risk being seen together. You remember the formula for meeting me?"

"You will ring my number at home or at work and ask to speak to someone with a name that has the letter *z* in it. I will say there is nobody by that name at this number. You will apologize and hang down. Exactly one hour and fifteen minutes after your call I am to walk west along the north side of the Novy Arbat. At some point a gypsy taxicab will pull up, the driver will wind down the window and ask if I want a ride. We will haggle for a moment over the price. Then I will get into the back seat. You will be the driver of the taxi."

"Each time we meet I will give you a formula for the next meeting. We must vary these signals and meeting places."

"I can see that you have had experience in these matters."

"You could say that I am a maestro when it comes to such things."

Aza said, "There are parts of you I have not yet visited, Yevgeny Alexandrovich." She sensed that the conversation had turned too solemn and attempted to lighten it. "I'll bet you wowed the girls when you were a young man."

"I never had a childhood sweetheart, if that's what you mean."

"I never had a childhood."

"Perhaps when all this is over—"

Blushing, she raised a hand to stop him before he could finish the sentence. He smiled. "Like you, I hope against hope."

Boris Yeltsin, a hulking man with heavy jowls and a shock of gray hair spilling off his scalp, was on congenial territory; he liked giving interviews because it permitted him to talk about his favorite subject: himself. "The first thing journalists always ask me," he told the London reporter, fixing her with a steely stare, "is how I lost the fingers." He raised his left hand and wiggled the stumps of his pinkie and the finger next to it. "It happened in 1942, when I was eleven," he went on. "Along with some friends, I tunneled under the barbed wire and broke into a church that was being used to store ammunition. We came across a wooden box filled with grenades and took several of them to the forest, and like an idiot I tried to open one with a hammer to see what was inside. The thing blew up, mangling my hand. When gangrene set in the surgeons had to amputate two of my fingers."

Yeltsin spoke Russian with a slurred drawl and the British reporter didn't catch every word. "Why did he want to open the grenade?" she asked Aza, who spoke excellent English and often acted as Yeltsin's informal translator.

"To see what was in it," she said.

"That's what I thought he said but it sounded so silly." The journalist turned back to Yeltsin. "Is the story about you being baptized true?"

Yeltsin, sitting behind an enormous desk on the third floor of the White House, the massive Russian parliament building next to the Moscow River, shot a quick look of puzzlement in Aza's direction; he had difficulty understanding Russian when it was spoken with a British accent. Aza translated the question into a Russian that Yeltsin could grasp. He laughed out loud. "It is true I was baptized," he said. "The priest was so drunk he dropped me into the holy water." Yeltsin hefted the bottle of vodka to see if the journalist wanted a refill. When she shook her head no, he refilled his own glass and downed half of it in one gulp. "My parents pulled me out and dried me off and the priest said, *If he can survive that he can survive anything. I baptize him Boris.*"

The interview went on for another half-hour. Yeltsin walked the journalist through his childhood in the Sverdlovsk region ("All six of us slept in one room, along with the goat"), his rise through the ranks of the *apparatchiki* to become the commissar in charge of Sverdlovsk and eventually the Party boss of Moscow. He described his break with Gorbachev three years before. "I had just visited America," he recounted. "They took me to a Safeway supermarket and I prowled through the aisles in a daze. I could barely believe my eyes—there were endless shelves stocked with an endless variety of products. I am not ashamed to say that I broke into tears. It struck me that all of our ideology hadn't managed to fill our shelves. You have to remember we were in the early days of *perestroika* and our Communist Party was above criticism. But I stood up at one of the Central Committee meetings and I did precisely that—I criticized the Party, I said we'd gotten it wrong, I criticized Gorbachev's reforms as being inadequate, I suggested that he ought to step down and transfer power to the collective rule of the republican leaders. Gorbachev turned white with rage. For me it was the beginning of the end of my relationship with him. He had me expelled from the Central Committee and the Politburo. All my friends saw the handwriting on the wall and abandoned me. I can tell you that I almost had a nervous breakdown. What saved me was my wife and my two daughters, Lena and Tanya, who encouraged me to fight for what I believed in. What saved me, also, was my election last year to the Russian Republic's Supreme Soviet, and my election by the Supreme Soviet to the position of President of the Russian Republic."

The London journalist, scrawling notes in a rudimentary shorthand, double-checked several details with Aza. Yeltsin, in his shirt sleeves, glanced at his wristwatch. Taking the hint, the reporter stood up and thanked Yeltsin for letting her have an hour of his precious time. Aza saw her to the door and, closing it behind her, returned to Yeltsin's desk. "Boris Nikolayevich, can I suggest that we go for a stroll in the courtyard."

Yeltsin grasped that she wanted to talk to him about something delicate. His office was swept for microphones every week but the people who did the sweeping worked for Kryuchkov's KGB, so his staffers had taken to holding important conversations in the open inner courtyard of the White House. Draping a suit jacket over his heavy shoulders, Yeltsin led Aza down the fire staircase to street level and pushed through the fire door into the courtyard. A large outdoor thermometer indicated that winter had finally broken, but after several hours in the overheated offices of the White House the air outside seemed quite crisp. Yeltsin drew the jacket up around his thick neck; Aza pulled her Uzbek shawl over her head.

"What do I need to know that you dare not tell me upstairs?" Yeltsin demanded.

"By chance I have an old acquaintance who used to work for the KGB—I believe he served abroad for a great many years. He has since become a successful entrepreneur and has opened one of those private banks that are springing up around Moscow. Because of his KGB background and the existence of his bank, he was invited by the wife of the press baron Uritzky to attend a secret meeting in a dacha at the edge of the village of Perkhushovo."

Yeltsin was one of those politicians who squirreled away a great deal of seemingly useless information—the names of the children of his collaborators, their wedding anniversaries and birthdays and name days, the location of their summer houses. He came up with an item now. "Kryuchkov has a dacha at Perkhushovo."

Aza described the meeting as Yevgeny had described it to her. Producing an envelope, she read off the list of those who had attended. She quoted Kryuchkov's *We will have to consent to a state of emergency for him*, and recounted how everyone present had raised their hands in agreement with this proposition.

Yeltsin stopped in his tracks and surveyed the sky as if it were possible to read in the formations of clouds clues on how the future would turn out. Moscow was overcast, as usual; it had been overcast for so long people tended to forget what sunlight looked like, or felt like on the skin. "And who is your old acquaintance?" he asked Aza, his eyes still fixed on the sky.

"He specifically forbid me to reveal his identity. And he asks you not to reveal that you received this information from me."

"I will, of course, relay the warning to Gorbachev, but if I cannot identify the source he will shrug it off as another attempt by me to drive a wedge between him and the Party loyalists."

Aza said, "But you believe my story, don't you, Boris Nikolayevich?"

Yeltsin nodded. "To tell the truth, I am somewhat surprised by the quantity, and quality, of the people aligning themselves with the putschists, but I don't doubt for a moment that Kryuchkov would oust Gorbachev if he could. You must bear in mind that Kryuchkov had a hand in planning the Red Army assault on Budapest in 1956 and Prague in 1968. He is certainly someone who thinks in the old style—that the correct dose of force, applied in the right spot at the right moment, can stuff the genie back in the bottle." Yeltsin sighed. "The peasants in the village near Sverdlovsk, where I was raised, used to say that there are fruits which rot without ripening. When I grew older I discovered the same holds true for people. Kryuchkov is an excellent illustration of this axiom. Of course I will not mention your name when I warn Gorbachev. For your part, you must stay in touch with this acquaintance of yours who has penetrated to the heart of the conspiracy. His collaboration will be crucial in the weeks and months ahead."

The after-dinner speeches dragged on and on; Russian bureaucrats, fortified with alcohol, tended to get carried away by emotion. And the emotion that carried them away at the Kremlin state dinner honoring Valentina Vladimirovna Tereshkova, the Russian cosmonaut who was the first woman in space, was nostalgia. Nostalgia, if you read between the lines, for the days when the Soviet Union was able to give the United States a run for its money; when hardware produced in the Soviet factories actually worked; when the time servers who minded the Soviet store were still looked on as an aristocracy.

"Valentina Vladimirovna," the head of the space agency declared, blotting the beads of sweat glistening on his forehead with a handkerchief, "demonstrated to the entire world what Soviet courage and Soviet technology and Soviet ideology could accomplish in the never-ending struggle to conquer space. To our guest of honor, Valentina Vladimirovna," the speaker cried, raising his glass in her direction for yet another toast.

Around the horseshoe-shaped banquet table, chairs were scraped back as the guests lunged to their feet and held aloft their own glasses. "To Valentina Vladimirovna," they cried in unison, and they gulped down the Bulgarian Champagne that had long since lost any trace of effervescence.

From her place at the bitter end of one of the wings of the table, Aza studied the ruddy face of Tereshkova, flushed from alcohol and the stuffiness of the Kremlin banquet hall. Aza was careful to merely sip her Champagne at each of the endless toasts, but her own head was growing woozy. She tried to imagine what it must have been like to suit up in a silver cosmonaut outfit and squeeze yourself into a Vostok capsule and be shot, as if from the mouth of a giant cannon, into orbit around the planet earth. Surely there were experiences that, if you survived them, changed your life; nothing could ever be the same afterward. No amount of denying the experience, no amount of trying to diminish it by putting it into some kind of perspective, could alter its effect. Perhaps it was the late hour—the great Kremlin clock had just chimed midnight—or the lack of air or the alcohol content in her blood stream, but Aza understood that the occasional intersection of her lifeline with Yevgeny's were life-altering experiences. Looking back, she could see that she had never really given her first and only husband a chance to measure up before she began talking about divorce. Measure up to what? Measure up to the epiphany that comes when soul communes with soul and the body, tagging along behind, communes with body, and the woman doesn't wind up feeling cheated.

Across the room the speeches and the toasts continued. Aza noticed Boris Yeltsin, stifling a yawn with his fist, push himself to his feet and come behind Tereshkova at the head of the table and whisper something in her ear that made her giggle with pleasure. Yeltsin patted her on the shoulder, then casually moved on to where Mikhail Gorbachev was sitting. Stooping so he could funnel words into his ear, he said something that made Gorbachev twist sharply in his seat. Yeltsin gestured with a toss of his large head. Gorbachev considered, then got up and followed him with obvious reluctance to a far corner of the banquet hall. Aza could see Yeltsin talking intently for several minutes. The General Secretary listened impassively, his head tilted to one side, his eyes almost closed. At one point Yeltsin, to emphasize a point, jabbed a forefinger several times into Gorbachev's shoulder. When Yeltsin finished Gorbachev finally opened his eyes; from her place at the end of the banquet table Aza could see that he was furious. The birthmark curling across his scalp seemed to redden and gleam. His head snapped back and forth in short jerks as he muttered a curt reply. Then he spun away abruptly and strode back to join in another toast to Tereshkova.

Yeltsin watched him go, then caught Aza's eye across the room and hunched his heavy shoulders in defeat.

3

I WASN'T SURE YOU WOULD SHOW UP."

"I almost didn't. I must have changed my mind twenty times before I booked a ticket, and another twenty times before I boarded the plane."

"Well, for what it's worth, I'm glad to see you, Jack."

Currents of moist air from the Rhone ruffled what was left of the once-flamboyant mustache on Jack McAuliffe's upper lip and the strands of ash-red hair on his scalp as he sized up his companion through prescription sunglasses. Leo, clearly ill at ease in the presence of his one-time friend and former Company colleague, looked pallid and thin and dog-tired; he had been plagued by insomnia since Yevgeny alerted him to the impending putsch. Now he tugged the collar of the windbreaker up around his neck and the peaked worker's cap down to his ears, and squinted at the two coxed eights skidding on their inverted reflections along the surface of the river.

"I loved Crew," Jack remarked. For the space of a moment the two men, gazing at the rowers coiling and uncoiling their limbs inside the sleek sculls, were transported back to that last race on the Thames and the triumph over Harvard. "I loved the blisters and the splinters of pain where my rib had mended and broken and mended again," Jack added. "You knew you were alive."

The faint cries of the coxes counting strokes came to them on the breeze. Leo sniggered. "Coach Waltz used to say that rowing was a metaphor for life." With a wistful smile he turned on Jack. "What a lot of crap—rowing wasn't a metaphor for life, it was a substitute. It took your mind off of it for the time you spent rowing. But as soon as you were finished, reality was waiting in ambush."

The two men resumed walking along the path that ran parallel to the Rhone. "And what was your reality, Leo?"

"Stella. Her Soviet handler who gave me my first lesson in one-time pads and dead letter drops and ordered me to stay close to Waltz because he was a talent scout for the Company."

"Did the son of a bitch actually call it *the Company*?"

Leo smiled grimly. "He called it *glavni protivnik*, which is Russian for *principal adversary*." He walked on for some moments in silence. Then he said, "All that's water under the bridge."

"No it's not, pal. It's not water under my bridge. Just because you sign your letter *Gentleman-Ranker* doesn't make you one. You're still a lousy traitor in my book and nothing's going to change that."

"When will you get it into your head that I didn't betray anybody. All along I was fighting for my side."

"Jesus H. Christ, you were fighting for Stalinism. Some side."

"Fuck you, too."

Jack wouldn't let go. "I suppose they gave you a medal when they brought you in."

"They gave me two, as a matter of fact."

The two men, close to blows, glared at each other. Jack stopped in his tracks. "Look, you asked for this meeting. You want to call it off, fine with me."

Leo was still angry. "There are things I need to pass on to you."

"Pass, buddy, and then we'll go our separate ways." Jack dropped his chin and looked at Leo over the top of his sunglasses. "You were pretty goddamn sure we wouldn't have you arrested and extradited when you showed up in Switzerland, weren't you?"

"Who are you kidding, Jack? If you ever brought me in, you'd have to explain why you didn't inform the Congressional oversight committees about me seven and a half years ago."

"You think of all the angles."

Leo shook his head. "Not all. I didn't expect that Adelle would curl up in a ditch on a hill in Maryland to sleep off a hangover."

"A bunch of us attended her funeral," Jack said.

"The twins must have been..."

"They were. Sad and bitter and embarrassed, all rolled into one." Leo's chest heaved. Jack gave an inch. "All things considered," he said, "your girls were brave troopers."

Up ahead, a street photographer positioned herself on the path and, raising a Polaroid to her eye, snapped their picture. Leo strode forward and caught the woman by the arm. "What the hell do you think you're doing?" he cried.

The photographer, a thin young woman wearing torn jeans and a faded sweatshirt, angrily jerked free. Leo lunged for the camera but the woman was too quick for him. Jack rushed up and grabbed the collar on Leo's windbreaker. "Simmer down, pal," he said. To the photographer, who was backing away from them both, he said, "How much?"

"Usually it is ten francs. For you and your crazy friend it is double."

Jack pulled a crisp bill from his wallet and, advancing slowly so as not to frighten the woman, held it out. She snatched the twenty out of his fingers, flung the snapshot at his feet and scampered off down the path. "American bastards," she shouted over a shoulder. "Yankee pricks."

Jack retrieved the photograph and looked at it. Leo said, "Burn it."

"I have another idea," Jack said. He produced a pen and wrote across the faces on the picture, *Jack and Leo before The Race but after The Fall*, and handed it to Leo.

Leo remembered the original only too well. "Another memento of our friendship," he said sarcastically.

"Our friendship ended long ago," Jack shot back. "This is a memento of our last meeting."

The two of them entered a café and made their way to the glassed-in veranda cantilevered over the river. Jack draped his safari jacket over the back of a chair and sat down facing Leo across a small table. He ordered an American coffee, Leo a double espresso. After the coffees arrived Jack waited until the waitress was out of earshot, then announced, "Time to get down to the famous brass tacks."

Leaning over the table, his voice pitched low, Leo said, "I have reason to believe—" and he went on to tell Jack about the plot being hatched against Gorbachev.

When Leo finished Jack sank back into his chair and stared sightlessly at the river. "To know what you know, to name the names you name, you must have a source inside the conspiracy," he finally said.

Leo shrugged noncommittally.

"I take it you won't identify him."

"Or her."

Jack bristled. "Don't play games with me, Leo."

"I'm not playing games. I have a source but the CIA is the last organization I'd confide in. The KGB had you penetrated in my day. For all I know it still does. And the head of the KGB is masterminding the plot."

"What do you expect me to do with this information? Go to the *New York Times* and say that a guy I know has a guy he knows who says Moscow is heading for the waterfall in a barrel. Fat chance."

"For starters we thought—"

"We?"

"I thought you could warn the President, and the President could warn

Gorbachev. Coming from George Bush, the word that there is a putsch afoot might impress him."

"You ought to be able to get word to Gorbachev inside Russia."

"Yeltsin has been warning him in a very general way for months. I've been told that he has now warned him in a very specific way, which is to say he's described meetings and named names. The trouble is that if Yeltsin told Gorbachev it was nighttime, he'd assume he was lying and it was really daytime." Leo turned his espresso cup round and round in its saucer. "Am I wrong in assuming that the United States has a vested interest in seeing Gorbachev stay in power?"

"This is a side of you I'm not familiar with—looking out for the vested interests of the United States."

Leo kept a rein on his temper. "Answer the question."

"The answer is evident. We prefer Gorbachev to Yeltsin, and Yeltsin to Kryuchkov and his KGB chums."

"Then do something about it, dammit."

"Aside from warning Gorbachev I don't see what we can do. Unlike the folks you worked for we don't knock off people."

"What about Salvador Allende in Chile? What about General Abdul Karim Kassem in Iraq?"

"Those days are over," Jack insisted.

"They don't have to be. When the Company wanted to eliminate Castro, it brought in the Sorcerer and he farmed the contract out to freelancers outside the Company. This is important, Jack—a lot is hanging on it."

"The Sorcerer is drinking himself into a grave in East of Eden Gardens." He spotted the puzzled narrowing of Leo's eyes. "That's a retirement village in Santa Fe."

Leo sipped his espresso; he didn't appear to notice that it had grown cold. "What about the *Devisenbeschaffer*? If the putschists don't get Gorbachev on the first try, they'll still have the bankroll in Dresden. They can cause a lot of pain with that amount of money."

Jack brightened. He obviously had an idea. "Okay, I'll see what I can concoct. Give me a meeting place in Moscow. Let's say six P.M. local time one week from today."

"I won't talk to anyone from your Moscow Station—the embassy is riddled with microphones."

"I was thinking more along the lines of sending in someone from the outside."

"Does the person know Moscow?"

"No."

Leo thought a moment, then named a place that anybody ought to be able to find.

Jack and Leo stood up. Jack glanced at the bill tucked under the ash tray and dropped five francs onto the table. Once outside the café, both men looked at the river. The sculls were gone; only a gray skiff with two fishermen in it was visible on the gray surface of the water. Leo held out a hand. Jack looked down at it and slowly shook his head. "There's no way I'm going to shake your hand, pal. Not now. Not ever."

The two men eyed each other. Leo said softly, "I'm still sorry, Jack. About our friendship. But not about what I did." With that he turned on his heel and stalked off.

His shoes propped up on the desk, one thumb hooked under a striped suspender, Ebby heard Jack out. Then he thought about what he'd said. Then he asked, "You believe him?"

"Yeah, I do."

The DCI needed to be convinced. "To our everlasting grief, he's demonstrated his ability to deceive us," he reminded his deputy.

"I don't see what he'd have to gain," Jack said. "He used to work for the KGB—he still may be carried on their books in some sort of advisory capacity. That's what happened to Philby after he fled to Moscow. So it's hard to see why he'd tell us about a KGB plot to oust Gorbachev unless..."

The green phone on Ebby's desk rang. He raised a palm to apologize for the interruption and, picking it up, listened for a moment. "The answer is no," he said. "If a Soviet Oskar-II sub had sortied from Murmansk into the Barents, we would have picked up its signature on our underwater monitors...No way, Charlie—the Barents is a shallow sea so there'd be no possibility of running deep...Anytime. Bye." Ebby looked up. "Pentagon received a report that a Norwegian fishing boat saw a submarine snorkel in the Barents yesterday." He picked up the thread of the conversation. "You don't see why Kritzky would tell us about a KGB plot to oust Gorbachev unless what?"

"I racked my brain for possible motives for hours on the plane home," Jack said. "Here's my reading of Leo Kritzky: in part because of his roots, in part because of what happened to his father, in part because of that eternal chip on his shoulder, he was taken in, like a lot of others, by the utopian rhetoric of Marxism and enlisted in the struggle against capitalism out of a kind of misplaced idealism. His problems began when he reached the Soviet motherland and discovered that it was more of a hell-hole than a workers' paradise. You can imagine his disenchantment—all those years on the firing line, all those betrayals, and for what? To support a Stalinist dictatorship, even if Stalin was no longer alive, that babbled endlessly about equality and then quietly and quickly silenced anyone who suggested that the king was parading through the streets in ratty underwear."

"So the bottom line is that Kritzky feels guilty. That's what you're saying?"

"He feels betrayed, even if he doesn't put it into so many words. And Gorbachev is the last, best hope that he may have been fighting all his life for something worthwhile after all."

"In other words, Kritzky's telling the truth."

"For sure."

"Could the conspirators have taken him into their confidence—is that how he knows what he knows?"

"Not likely. First off, Leo was a KGB agent but the chances are good that, like Philby before him, he was never a KGB officer, which means he was never an insider."

"And he is a foreigner."

"And he is a foreigner, right. In the back of their minds the KGB people must be haunted by the possibility that he might have been turned."

"Who's feeding Kritzky the information on the conspiracy, then?"

"Search me," Jack said. "We can assume that it's someone who trusts him with his life."

"All right. We have true information. I take it to George Bush and I say, Mr. President, there's a putsch being hatched against Gorbachev. Here are the names of some of the plotters. Bush was a director of the CIA back in the seventies, so he knows enough not to ask me how we got our hands on this stuff. He knows I wouldn't tell him if he did ask. If he believes it—a big *if*—the best he can do is to write a letter to Gorbachev. Dear Mikhail, some information fell into my lap that I want to share with you. Blah-blah-blah. Signed, Your friend, George B." Ebby swung his feet to the ground and pushed himself off the swivel seat and came around to settle onto the edge of desk. "See anything else we can do, Jack?"

Jack avoided his friend's eye. "Frankly, I don't, Ebby. Like you always say, we more or less have our hands tied."

Jack checked the little black notebook that he always kept on his person, then pulled the secure phone across the desk and dialed a number. He reached a switchboard that put him through to the clubhouse. The bartender asked him to wait a minute. It turned out to be a long minute, which meant that the Sorcerer had been drinking heavily. When he finally came on the line, his speech was slurred. "Don'tcha know better than t'interrupt someone while he's communing with spirits?" he demanded belligerently.

"I'll bet I can give you the brand name of the spirits," Jack retorted.

"Well, I'll be a monkey's uncle! If it isn't the man his-self, Once-down-is-no-battle McAuliffe! What's up, sport? Is the Sorcerer's Apprentice in over his head again? Need the old Sorcerer to pitch you a lifesaver?"

"You got something to write with, Harvey?"

Jack could hear the Sorcerer belch, then ask the bartender for a pen. "Shoot," Torriti bellowed into the phone.

"What are you writing on?"

"The palm of my hand, chum."

Jack gave him the number of his secure line and then had Torriti read it back. Miraculously, he got it the first time.

"Can you get to a pay phone in Santa Fe?"

"Can I get to a pay phone in Santa Fe?"

"Why are you repeating the question, Harvey?"

"Matter of being sure I have it right."

"Okay, drink a thermos of strong coffee, take a cold shower, when you're dead sober find a pay phone and call this number."

"What's in it for yours truly?"

"A break from the drudgery of retirement. A chance to get even."

"Even with who?"

"Even with the bad guys, Harvey, for all the shit they threw at you over the years."

"I'm your man, sport."

"Figured you would be, Harv."

It was already dark out by the time Jack and Millie picked up Jack's car in the underground garage at Langley and drove over (running two red lights) to Doctor's Hospital off 20th Street. Anthony, all smiles, was waiting for them in the lobby, a dozen long-stemmed red roses in one hand and a box of cigars in the other. "It's a boy," he blurted out. "Six pounds on the nose. We're arguing about whether to call it Emir after her father or Leon after my...well, my godfather."

"The baby's not an *it*," Millie said. "How's Maria?"

"Tired but thrilled," Anthony said, leading them toward the staircase. "Oh God, she was absolutely fantastic. We did the Lamaze thing until the end. The doctor offered her a spinal but she said no thanks. The baby came out wide awake and took one look at the world and burst into tears. Maybe he was trying to tell us something, huh, Dad?"

"The laughter will come," Jack promised.

Maria, now a network anchorwoman, was sitting up in bed breast-feeding. Millie and Maria tried to figure out which of the baby's features had been inherited from the mother's side of the family and which from the father's. Anthony claimed that the only person the baby resembled was Winston Churchill. Jack, a bit flustered at the sight of a woman openly breast-feeding an infant, made a tactical retreat to the corridor to light up one of his son's cigars. Anthony joined him.

"How are things at your shop?" Jack asked his son.

The State Department, impressed by Anthony's experiences in Afghanistan, had lured him away from the Company three years before to run a hush-hush operation that kept track of Islamic terrorist groups. "The White House is worried sick about Saddam Hussein," he said.

"In my shop we're walking a tightrope on this one," Jack said. "Nobody quite knows what we're supposed to be doing about Saddam, and we're not getting guidance from State or the White House."

"It figures," Anthony said. "They'd like to get rid of him, but they're afraid that Iraq will break apart without him, leaving the Iranian fundamentalists with a free hand in the region." Anthony looked curiously at his father. "Were you out of town at the beginning of the week, Dad? I tried to call you a few times to tell you about the countdown but your secretary handed me the standard *He's away from his desk at the moment* routine, and you never called back."

"I had to jump to Switzerland to see a guy."

"Uh-huh."

"What does *un-huh* mean?"

"It means I'm not about to ask any more questions."

Jack had to smile. "I'll answer one of them—but you have to keep it under your hat. Even from Maria. Come to think of it, especially from Maria. The last thing we need is for some journalist to nose around trying to sniff out a story."

Anthony laughed. "I am a tomb. Whatever you tell me goes to the grave with me."

Jack lowered his voice. "I went to Switzerland to meet your godfather."

Anthony's eyes opened wide. "You saw *Leo*? Why? Who initiated the meeting? How did you know where to find him? What did he have to say? How is he? What kind of life does he lead?"

"Whoa," Jack said. "Simmer down. I only wanted to tell you that he is alive and more or less well. I know how attached you were to him."

An attendant pushing a laundry cart came down the hallway. "This here is a no smoking zone," he said. "Whole hospital is, actually. You have to go outside to smoke."

"Oh, sorry," Jack said, and he stubbed out the cigar on the sole of his shoe and then slipped it back into its wrapper so he could smoke it later.

Anthony asked, "How did Leo get out of Russia?"

"Don't know. He could have gone out to Sofia or Prague, say, on his Russian passport, and then flown to Switzerland on a phony Western passport—they're a dime a dozen in Moscow these days."

"Which means he didn't want the KGB to know he was meeting you."

"You're one jump ahead of me, Anthony."

"In my experience, Dad, whenever I reach someplace interesting, you've already been there."

"Flattery will get you everywhere."

"Are you going to see him again?"

"No."

"Never?"

"Never."

"Did he...express any regrets?"

"He's sorry about Adelle. He's sorry about not seeing the twins." Jack took off his eyeglasses and massaged the bridge of his nose with his thumb and middle finger. "I suspect he's sorry he spent thirty years of his life fighting for the wrong side."

"Did he say something to make you think that?"

Jack put his glasses back on. "No."

"So how do you know it?"

"You can't live in the Soviet Union—especially after having lived in the Unites States—and not realize it's the wrong side."

Anthony looked hard at his father; he could see the pain in his eyes. "He hurt you a lot, didn't he?"

"He was my coxswain when I crewed at Yale. He was my best friend then and afterward. He was the best man at my wedding and the godfather of my son. What the hell—I loved the guy, Anthony. And I hate him for betraying the bond that was between us, not to mention his country."

Anthony gripped his father's arm hard, then did something he hadn't done since childhood. He leaned forward and kissed him on the cheek. "I was attached to Leo," he said quietly. "But I love you, Dad. You are one great guy."

Jack was rattled. "Jesus H. Christ."

"You can say that again," Anthony agreed.

Laughing under his breath, Jack did. "Jesus H. Christ."

Walking with the aid of two canes, his bad hip thrusting forward and around and back with each painful step, Ezra Ben Ezra, known to various intelligence services as the Rabbi, approached the fence. Harvey Torriti ambled up behind him and the two stood there inspecting the bombed-out ruins of the Fravenkirche, the Church of Our Lady. "Fire and brimstone was the malediction of Dresden," the Rabbi mused. "The city was burned to the ground in fourteen hundred something, again during the seven year war in seventeen hundred something, then Napoleon had a go at it in eighteen hundred something. In February of '44 the allies transformed the city into a burning fiery furnace with their fire bombs. The Germans, being German, built everything in Dresden back up after the war except this church. This they left as a reminder."

"So what does a Jew feel when he looks at the reminder?" the Sorcerer asked his old comrade-in-arms.

Leaning on his canes, the Rabbi considered the question. "Glee is what he feels. Ha! You expected remorse, maybe. Or worse, forgiveness. The reminder reminds me of the six million who perished in German death camps. The reminder reminds me of the churches that did nothing to stop the killing factories. You see before you a man weighted down with more than bad hips, Harvey. I travel with baggage. It's called the Torah. In it there is a formula that instructs victims on how to survive emotionally. *An eye for an eye, a tooth for a tooth, a burning for a burning.*"

Ben Ezra cranked his body into a hundred and eighty degree turn and started toward the black Mercedes that was circled by Mossad agents busily scrutinizing the rooftops across the street. Torriti winced as he watched his friend struggling with the canes. "I'm sorry to see you in such pain," he said.

"The physical pain is nothing compared to the mental. How many people you know live in a country that may not exist in fifty years? *Genug shoyn!—enough already!* What am I doing here?"

"You're here," the Sorcerer said, "because Israel is getting some fifteen thousand Jews out of the Soviet Union every month. You're here because you don't want this emigration and immigration to dry up. Which it would if Gorbachev is kicked out by a gang of right-wing nationalist thugs, some of whom happen to be anti-Semites to boot."

Torriti walked the Rabbi through the details of the plot to oust Gorbachev. From time to time Ben Ezra interrupted with pointed questions. Why wasn't the CIA approaching the Mossad on a service-to-service basis? What should the Rabbi read into the fact that the Sorcerer, languishing in spirituous retirement, had been summoned back to the wars? Was the Company, or an element inside it, contemplating an operation that was outside the CIA's charter?

"Ha!" snorted Ben Ezra. "I thought so—how far outside?"

The two men reached the limousine and the Rabbi, with considerable difficulty, managed to lower his buttocks onto the rear seat and then swing his legs in, one after the other. The Sorcerer went around to the other side and, wheezing from the exertion, maneuvered his carcass in alongside Ben Ezra. The Mossad agents remained outside, their backs turned to the car, sizing up through opaque sunglasses the people and cars passing on the avenue.

The Rabbi (only months away from retirement; his successor as head of the Mossad had already been designated) sighed. "They are scraping the bottom of the barrel when they recruit us."

"The alcohol at the bottom of the barrel is the most potent," Torriti pointed out.

"Correct me where I have gone wrong," the Rabbi said. "You want us to identify and eventually neutralize a German national known to you only as *Devisenbeschaffer.*"

"For starters, yeah."

"You want us to somehow get a foot in the door of the Dresden branch of the Greater Russian Bank of Commerce in order to take possession of the assets the *Devisenbeschaffer* may have deposited there."

"There's a pretty penny in the bank," Torriti said.

"What do you call a pretty penny?"

"Somewhere between three hundred and five hundred million, give or take."

"Dollars?"

"Would I have come out of retirement for yen?"

The Rabbi didn't blink. "If I succeed in looting the bank we will split the money fifty-fifty, my share going into a fund to finance the continuing immigration of Soviet Jews to Israel via Austria, your share to be deposited in a series of secret Swiss accounts, the numbers of which will be supplied in due time."

One of the Mossad agents rapped his knuckles on the window, pointed to his wristwatch and said something in Hebrew. Ben Ezra wagged a fatherly finger at him. The agent turned away in frustration and barked into a tiny microphone on the inside of his right wrist. "This new generation—they are too impatient," Ben Ezra told Torriti. "They confuse motion with movement. In my day I used to stake out houses in Berlin for weeks on end in the hope of catching a glimpse—a *mere glimpse*, Harvey, nothing more—of a German on Israel's ten most wanted list. Where were we?"

"We are where we always were, my friend," Torriti said with a gruff laugh. "We're trying to figure out how to save the world from itself. There's one more thing you can do for me, Ezra."

"You have arrived at what Americans call your last but by no means least," the Rabbi guessed.

"I hear on the grapevine that there's an underworld in Moscow—a sort of Russian mafia. If it's anything like the mafia in America, which is to say if it's an equal opportunity employer, some of them have got to be Jewish. I figure you could put me in touch with one."

"Exactly what are you're looking for, Harvey?"

"I'm looking for a Russian gangster of Jewish persuasion who is connected with other Russian gangsters who are not afraid of getting their hands dirty."

"Dirty as in dirty or dirty as in bloody?"

"Dirty as in bloody."

The Rabbi attempted to shift his weight on the seat. Grimacing in pain, he murmured, "It is Berlin 1951 redux, Harvey." He tapped a ring against the window to get the attention of the bodyguards and motioned for them to come aboard. "Once again we are neighbors with a common ground—your ceiling is my floor."

After a lifetime of battling against the evil empire from the cortex, Harvey Torriti had finally slipped across the frontier into the heart of darkness. Only just arrived from the airport, he was determined to discover the Russian macrocosm by inspecting the Russian microcosm: in this case, room 505 in one of Moscow's Stalin Gothic monstrosities, the thousand-room Hotel Ukraine on Kutuzovsky Prospekt. Room service (if that was the correct job description for the harassed lady who turned up at the door) had finally gotten around to delivering the bottle of Scotch ordered an hour and a quarter earlier. (The frazzled waitress had forgotten ice but the Sorcerer—passing himself off as a pleasantly inebriated John Deere salesman from Moline, Illinois named T. Harvey—told her to forget it; he had visions of her returning with a block of ice in the middle of the night.) He carefully filled a cracked tumbler just shy of overflowing and, wetting his whistle, began his survey of Socialism in the bathroom.

The toilet seat, made of thin plastic, declined to remain up unless it was blocked by a knee. The once-transparent shower curtain had turned opaque with a film of yellowish scum. Sitting on the pitted sink was the smallest bar of soap the Sorcerer had even set eyes on. The taps on the sink and the bathtub worked but what emerged, with an unsettling human gurgle, was a feces-brown liquid that bore only a passing resemblance to water. In the bedroom the under sheet wasn't large enough to tuck beneath the mattress; the mattress itself looked remarkably like a miniature cross-country terrain for toy four-wheel drive cars. There was a television set that tuned in snow when it was switched on, an inverted bowl-like overhead light fixture which served as a cinerarium for cremated insects and an armoire that opened to reveal—nothing. Not a rod. Not a hanger. Not a hook or a shelf of any shape or kind. Against one wall, next to a desk with nothing in its drawers except mildew, stood a small refrigerator with an extremely large and very dead waterbug in residence. Torriti, crawling on all fours, was unable to locate anything resembling an electrical cord coming out of the refrigerator, which he supposed accounted for its lack of refrigeration. (In the end he flushed the waterbug down the toilet after three tries and used the refrigerator shelves to store his socks and underwear.) On the back of the door to the room were instructions in Russian and English about what to do in case of fire, and a series of arrows showing how the hapless resident of 505 might navigate through the maze of flaming corridors to a fire door. It was easy to see that if you didn't actually have the map in your hand—an unlikely possibility, since it was behind a pane of plexiglass screwed to the back of the door—escape was inconceivable.

"I have seen the future," Torriti muttered aloud, "and it needs work!"

The Sorcerer was still digesting his first impressions—could this really be the Socialist prototype that had threatened to "bury" (to use Khrushchev's term) the Western democracies?—when he thrust his arms into an Aquascutum and ventured out into the cool Moscow evening. He went through some basic tradecraft drills—the KGB was demoralized and underfunded *but it was still there*!—ducking between two buildings on the Arbat and waiting in the shadows of the garbage bin behind one of them to see if he was being followed, then trudging through labyrinthian alleyways crammed with corrugated private garages until he came to a wide boulevard. He stepped off the curb and raised a forefinger. Sure enough a gypsy cab screeched to a stop within seconds. Torriti had a hard time fitting his bulk

through the narrow rear door of the Russian-manufactured Fiat; once inside
he produced the index card with an address written in Cyrillic, along with a
recently minted ten-dollar bill. The driver, a young man who looked as if he
were suffering from terminal acne, turned out to be a Russian kamikaze; he
snatched both items out of Torriti's fingers and, cackling at the fury he
aroused in other drivers as he corkscrewed through traffic, took his passenger
on as wild a ride as the Sorcerer had ever experienced. Jammed into the back
seat, he shut his eyes and fought the queasiness that comes when the viscera
slush like bilge water through the abdominal cavity. After what seemed like
an eternity, he heard the screech of brakes and felt the automobile skid to a
stop. Pushing open the back door, abandoning ship with an adroitness that
came from terror, he sniffed at the burnt rubber in the air. It took a minute
or two before he got his land legs back. He heard the faint sound of Vienna
waltzes booming from loudspeakers a football field away. Pulling a moth-
eaten scarf up around his neck, he started toward the brilliant lights illuminating the Park of Rest and Culture, an immense amusement mall on the
outskirts of the city where, during the winter months, whole avenues were
flooded so that ice skaters could skim along for kilometers on end.

Even after the spring thaw, so Torriti had been informed, there were
barnfires blazing on the edge of the avenues every so often. His insteps were
aching by the time he shambled over to the fourth fire from the right, burning in an enormous industrial drum. A handful of joggers and roller skaters
stood around it, warming their hands, passing around a flask, chatting
amiably. On the avenue, under the blinding lights, teenage girls in thigh-
length skirts and woolen stockings strolled in lock step with other girls, boys
walked backward before their girlfriends, small children tottered along hand
in hand with a parent. A thin man of medium height, wearing a windbreaker and a peaked worker's cap, came over from the avenue and held his
hands over the fire, toasting one side and then the other. After a moment he
looked hard at Torriti. Then, turning, he walked away from the drum. The
Sorcerer pulled a flask from the pocket of the Aquascutum and fortified
himself with a shot of cheap Scotch. Warmed by the alcohol, he backed away
from the group and nonchalantly trailed after the figure in the windbreaker.
He caught up with him in the penumbra between a stand of pitch-dark fir
trees and the blaze of incandescence from a spotlight atop a crane.

"So that you, Kritzky?" Torriti demanded.

Leo was put off by his tone. "You haven't changed," he shot back.

"I've changed, sport. Fatter. Older. Wiser. Lonelier. Nervouser. More
afraid of dying. Less afraid of death."

"I remember you in your heyday," Leo said. "I remember you tearing some secret stuff that came over the ticker out of Bobby Kennedy's hand—it was right after the Bay of Pigs. I remember you telling him where he could shove it."

The Sorcerer blew his nose between two fingers onto the ground. "Made a big mistake," he allowed.

"How's that?"

"Bobby was his brother's son of a bitch, okay, but he wasn't a spy for the Russians. You fucking were. I must have been slowing down not to see it. Ought to have told you where to shove it."

"Yeah. Well, here we are."

"Here is where we are," Torriti acknowledged.

"You still drink your way through the day?"

"You still lie your way through the day?"

Leo managed a forlorn smile. "You always treat your sources this way?"

"My Apprentice said you got ahold of a mole inside this Gorbachev thing. He told me to milk you. He didn't say nothing about climbing into bed with you."

From the loud speakers fixed to telephone poles came the sound of the Red Army chorus bellowing out "It's a Long Way to Tipperary" in what might have been English. Leo stepped closer to the Sorcerer and handed him an old envelope with a grocery list on one side. "I have seven more names to add to the ones I gave Jack," he hollered over the music. "They're written on the inside of the envelope in lemon juice. You pass an iron over it—"

Torriti was offended. "I wasn't born yesterday, sport. I was developing lemon juice before you went to work for the Russians."

"One of the new conspirators is the commander of the elite paratrooper unit in the Ryazan Airborne Division," Leo went on. "Another is the commander of the KGB's Dzerzhinsky Division."

"The plot sickens," Torriti shouted back with a sneer.

"There's more. It's written inside facing the list of names. Are you sober enough to remember—this is important?"

The Sorcerer leaned toward Leo and exhaled into his face. "I was sober enough to make it to this workers' paradise. Sober enough to find you here."

"The plotters have made contact with right-wing nationalist movements across Europe. For starters there's something called the August 21 Group in Madrid. There's Le Pen's National Front in France. There are splinter groups in Germany and Italy and Austria and Serbia and Croatia and Rumania and Poland. They plan to dole out money to these groups, once all the funds have been transferred to the Dresden branch of the Greater Russian Bank of

Commerce. The idea is to orchestrate a wave of international support for the coup against Gorbachev. They plan to present Gorbachev as a bungler who was running Russia into the ground, and the putsch as a patriotic effort to put the country back on its feet. If enough voices across Europe repeat this line the public may begin to think there's some truth in it."

The Sorcerer crumpled the envelope in his fist and stashed it in a pocket. "Where, when do we meet again?" he wanted to know.

"Where are you staying?"

Torriti told him.

"What's your cover?"

"I came armed with a briefcase full of John Deere brochures. Between drinks I'm trying to find someone who wants to import American tractors."

Leo thought a moment. "Okay. If I think we need to meet I'll have a bottle of Scotch delivered to room 505, along with a note thanking you for the John Deere material. The note will be written in ink. Between the lines, in lemon juice, I'll name a time and a place you can find easily."

Torriti started to walk away, then turned back with an afterthought. "Don't send up any of those imported Scotches. I prefer the cheap shit that disinfects the throat."

"Worried about germs?" Leo asked.

"Been inoculated against germs," Torriti snapped. "It's the traitors who make me sick to my stomach."

The Druzhba Hotel made the Ukraine look like the Ritz, or so the Sorcerer decided as he pushed through the mirrored door into the shabby lobby filled with tarnished mirrors and ceiling-to-floor window drapes that must have been put up before the Revolution and hadn't been dry cleaned since. Faded didn't begin to describe them. Pity the poor visitor who might be allergic to dust! Slaloming between ashtrays overflowing with everything but ashes, Torriti approached the main and only desk. "You probably speak English," he told the pasty platinum blonde copying off passport numbers onto a ledger.

The woman, wearing a skin-tight dress made of Army surplus camouflage material, replied without looking up. "Not."

The Sorcerer turned to the half dozen men sitting around the lobby. They were all dressed in identical ankle-length belted leather coats, thick-soled black shoes and dark fedoras with narrow brims. It looked like a casting call for one of Torriti's all-time favorite films, James Cagney's *The Public Enemy*, circa 1931. "Anybody here speak English?" he called.

The woman answered for them. "Not."

"How am I supposed to ask for information if nobody speaks English?" the Sorcerer demanded in exasperation.

"Study Russian," she suggested. "It could be useful in Russia."

"You do speak English!"

"Not."

"Why do I get the feeling I've fallen through the looking glass?" Torriti remarked to nobody in particular.

The woman raised her heavily made-up eyes. "Anybody you want," she ventured, "is not here."

It dawned on the Sorcerer that the thing to do in an insane asylum is humor the inmates. "I don't want anybody," he announced. "I want somebody named Rappaport. Endel Rappaport."

"*Yob tvoyu mat,*" someone called out.

The platinum blonde translated. "He says you, *Fuck your mother.*"

The others giggled at this. Torriti grasped that he was being incited to riot, and a riot would not bring him closer to Endel Rappaport, so he controlled his temper and forced himself to giggle with them.

"Rappaport is a Jew name," one of the extras sitting around the lobby decided.

Torriti pirouetted on a heel to face the speaker. "Is that right?" he said innocently.

The man, a dark-skinned giant with Central Asian eyes, came across the threadbare carpet. "Which sends you to Endel Rappaport?"

"Which which?" the platinum blonde echoed.

"We have a mutual friend. A Rabbi, as a matter of fact, though he has long since given up Rabbi-ing on a daily basis."

"Name?" insisted the man.

"Ezra."

"Ezra his Christian or family name?"

Torriti kept his face expressionless, lest the inmates take offense. Wait till Ezra Ben Ezra learned he had a *Christian* name! "Both."

"Floor number four," the man said, snapping his head in the direction of the ancient elevator next to the ancient staircase.

"Which door?"

"Any doors, all doors," said the blonde. "He rents the floor."

Backing carefully toward the elevator, Torriti pulled the grille open and thumbed the ivory button with a Roman numeral four on it. Somewhere in the bowels of the building a motor groaned into reluctant activity. The elevator jerked several times in aborted departures, then started with infinitesimal slowness to rise. Two men were waiting on the fourth floor. One of them opened the grille. The other frisked the Sorcerer very professionally, checking the small of his back and his ankles (where he carried the snub-nosed .38 Detective Special in his salad days), as well as the creases in his crotch under his testicles. Satisfied, he nodded to his partner, who pulled a latchkey from a pocket and opened an armor-plated door.

Torriti ambled into a spacious, brightly lit room decorated in Finnish imports; stainless steel chairs were gathered around a stainless steel table. Two lean men with vigilant Asian eyes lounged against a lacquered wall. A short, elegantly dressed man with fine white hair leapt from one of the chairs to bow from the waist toward Torriti. His eyes, only half open, fixed themselves intently on the visitor. "You are preceded by your legend, Mr. Sorcerer," he said. "Ben Ezra said me who you used to be. People like me do not meet people like you every day of the week. If you please," he said, nodding toward a chair. "What would give you pleasure?"

Torriti settled heavily into one of the Finnish chairs and discovered it was surprisingly comfortable. "A glass," he said.

Endel Rappaport, who must have been pushing eighty, said something in a strange language and, thrusting a fist out of a cuff, pointed with a pinkie. (Torriti couldn't help but notice that it was the only finger remaining on his hand.) One of the men along the wall sprang to attention and threw open the doors of a closet crammed with liquor bottles and glasses. He brought over a crystal goblet. The Sorcerer pulled his flask from an inside pocket and measured out a short Scotch. Rappaport, his maimed hand buried deep in a blazer pocket, returned to his place at the head of the table. "Any friend of Ben Ezra's—" he said, and waved his good hand to indicate that there was no need to complete the sentence. "In your wildest imagination what do you hope I can do for you?"

Torriti glanced at the bodyguards along the wall. Rappaport pursed his lips, a gesture that made him appear gnome-like. "My guardian angels are Uighurs," he informed the Sorcerer. "They speak only Turkic."

"In my wildest imagination I see you arranging to kill eight or ten people for me."

Rappaport didn't flinch. "I sit in awe in the face of such candidness. In Russia people tend to equivocate. So: the going price to have someone killed is between fifteen and twenty-five thousand American dollars, depending."

"On what?"

"On how important he is, which in turn indicates what kind of protection he is likely to have."

The Sorcerer gnawed on the inside of a cheek. Only half in jest he asked, "You being Jewish, me being a friend of the Rabbi's—doesn't that get me a discount?"

"The fee I accept from you will be used to compensate those who could not care less that I am Jewish and you were sent by the Rabbi," Rappaport said quietly. "When it comes time to calculate my honorarium, I will deal directly with Ben Ezra."

Torriti couldn't quite get a handle on Rappaport. How had such an obviously genteel man become a *caid* in the Moscow underworld? He decided it would help if he knew more about his host. "They had a go at you at some point," he remarked. He pointed with his chins. "I saw the fingers."

"What you saw was the absence of fingers. What a quaint expression you employ—yes, they had a *go* at me. To begin to understand Russia, you need to know that the average Russian anti-Semite is only remotely related to anti-Semites in the West. Here they are not satisfied with harassing Jews or persecuting Jews, with expelling them from music schools or apartments or cities or even the country. Here they are only satisfied if they can whet an ax and personally sink it into your flesh." Rappaport started to elaborate, then gestured with his good hand; again the sentence didn't need to be finished. "Regarding your request: you will surely have a list."

Torriti produced a picture postcard. One of the bodyguards carried it around the table and set it down before Rappaport. He looked at the photograph, then turned the card over and squinted at the names written on the back. "You are a serious man with a serious project," he said. "Permit me to pose several questions."

"Pose. Pose."

"Must the people on this list be killed simultaneously or would results spread over a period of days or weeks be acceptable?"

"The results could safely be spread over a period of minutes."

"I see."

"What do you see?"

"I see that all the people on your list are connected to each other in a way that I can only guess at."

"Guess. Guess."

"They are most likely associates in a complot. You want to avoid a situation where the death of one alerts the others to the danger of assassination. You want the assassinations to preempt the complot."

"You read an awful lot into a list of names."

"I read even more."

"Read. Read."

"Since you come to me, as opposed to another person of influence, since you arrive with the blessing of Ezra Ben Ezra, it must mean that the complot in question is one that will be inconvenient to the state of Israel. The single thing that would be most inconvenient to Israel would be the shutting down of the emigration of Russian Jews to Israel, which would leave the Jewish state at a permanent demographic disadvantage vis-à-vis their Palestinian neighbors."

The Sorcerer was impressed. "All that from one small list!"

"I have only scratched the surface. Since it is Mikhail Gorbachev who is behind the policy that permits the emigration of Russian Jews, the complot must be aimed at removing him from a position of power. In short, what we have here is a putsch against the existing government, and an attempt by the American Central Intelligence Agency and the Israeli Mossad to nip it in the bud with a series of surgical assassinations of the ringleaders."

"At this point I think you know more than I do."

Endel Rappaport waved his good hand again; the Sorcerer's remark was so absurd it didn't need to be denied. "A last question: do you require that the deaths be made to appear to be suicides or accidents?"

"To the degree that that would discourage anyone from walking back the cat and tracing the deaths to you, and eventually to me, suicides, accidents would be suitable. Either, or."

"I am not familiar with the expression *walking back the cat* but I am able to divine its meaning. Let me sleep on your list," he told Torriti. "Given the names involved, given the requirement that the deaths should appear to be suicides or accidents, the cost per head will be much closer to one hundred thousand dollars than twenty-five. There are two, even three names that will be still more expensive. Something in the region of a quarter of a million American dollars. In all cases payment will be in cash deposited in Swiss accounts, the numbers of which I will supply. One-half of each contract is payable on verbal acceptance by the executor, the remaining half payable when the executee has been executed. Can I assume that the sums I have mentioned, along with the terms, are acceptable to you?"

"Assume. Assume."

"You are staying in the Hotel Ukraine, room 505, if I am not mistaken."

"I am beginning to see you in a new light," the Sorcerer conceded.

"I have been told that it is an unpleasant hotel."

Torriti smiled. "It's not that good."

Rappaport rose to his feet and Torriti followed suit. "The rumors about an international Jewish conspiracy are true," Rappaport said.

"The Rabbi told me the same thing in Berlin many years ago," the Sorcerer said. He remembered Ben Ezra's words: *There is an international Jewish conspiracy, thanks to God it exists. It's a conspiracy to save the Jews.* "I believed him then. I believe you now."

Rappaport bowed again from the waist. "Take it for granted that I will be in touch when I have something concrete to tell you."

4

DRESDEN, THURSDAY, AUGUST 1, 1991

THE *DEVISENBESCHAFFER*, A MIDDLE-AGED FUNCTIONARY WITH A toothbrush mustache and a toupee that had fallen off in the scuffle when he was abducted, never lost his composure. He was strapped onto an ordinary kitchen chair in a sub-basement storage room of an abandoned meat-packing factory on the outskirts of the city. Two spotlights burned into his anemic face, making the skin on his cheeks, crisscrossed with fine red veins, look diaphanous. He had been tied to the chair so long that he had lost track of time, lost all feeling in his extremities. When he asked, with elaborate German politeness, to be allowed to use the water closet, his captors exchanged mocking comments in a language he didn't understand. The currency acquirer controlled his sphincter as long as he could. Then, unable to contain himself any longer, he mumbled profuse apologies as he defecated and urinated in his trousers. The odors didn't appear to distress the young men who took turns grilling him. From time to time a doctor would press a stethoscope to his chest and listen intently for a moment, then, satisfied, would nod permission for the interrogation to continue. "Please believe me, I know absolutely nothing about funds being transferred to a local Russian bank," the prisoner insisted. He spoke German with a guttural Bavarian growl that originated in his chest. "It is a case of mistaken identity—you are confusing me with someone else."

The Rabbi, following the interrogation over an intercom from an office on an upper floor, was growing impatient. It was ten days since his team had recruited the Jewish bookkeeper who worked in the Dresden branch of the Greater Russian Bank of Commerce; five days since the teller had alerted him to the daily deposits of anywhere between five and ten million dollars in a special account; two days since the Rabbi had been able to trace the deposits back to a private German bank and its manager, the illustrious *Devisenbeschaffer*. Now, as the interrogation dragged on, the team's doctor, on loan from an elite commando unit, started to hedge when Ben Ezra asked if there was any possibility of the prisoner dying on them. "Eighteen hours of stress is a long time even for a healthy heart," the doctor said. "He looks perfectly composed but his heart is starting to beat more rapidly, suggesting he's not as calm as he seems. If his heart continues to speed up it could end in a cardiovascular episode."

"How much time do we have?"

The young doctor shrugged. "You guess is as good as mine."

The response irritated Ben Ezra. "No. Your guess is better than mine. That's why you are here."

The doctor refused to be intimidated. "Look, if you want to err on the safe side, give him a night's sleep and start again in the morning."

The Rabbi weighed the alternatives. *"Beseda,"* he said reluctantly. "We will do as you suggest."

"This place holds many memories for me," Yevgeny was saying. He examined what countryside you could still see from the roof of the Apatov mansion. "When I first came here—it was before we met at my father's dacha party—I was fresh out of an American university and at loose ends. I had no idea what I wanted to do with my life."

"Do you know now?" Aza asked with her usual directness.

Yevgeny smiled. "Yes."

She smiled back at him. "It is a source of pain to me, dear Yevgeny, to think of all the years we wasted."

He threw an arm over her shoulder and drew her closer. "We will make up for lost time."

"It is a delusion to think you can make up for lost time," she said. "The best you can hope for is not to lose any more."

She wandered over to the southeast corner of the roof. Yevgeny came up behind her. "There were stands of white birches and plowed fields where those apartment buildings and the recycling plant are," he said. "The farmers from the Cheryomuski collective used to spread manure from horse-drawn carts. When the wind was wrong, you had to keep the windows closed if you wanted to survive." He shaded his eyes with a hand. "There used to be a secret runway beyond the fields. That's where my plane landed when I was brought home from America. The airstrip was shut down five years ago after Gorbachev cut the military budget. Gangs of kids race souped-up cars on the runway now. Depending on the winds, you can sometimes here their motors revving." Yevgeny hiked himself onto the balustrade and looked down at the entrance to the three-story mansion. "The first time I came up that gravel driveway there were two little girls playing on a seesaw—they were the nieces of the man I'd come to see."

"The one in the hospital?" Aza said. "The one you will not speak about?"

Yevgeny, deep into his own thoughts, stared off toward the horizon without answering.

"I am very hot," Aza said abruptly. "Let us return to the room that is air-conditioned."

He led her down the stairs to the wood-paneled library on the second floor, and gave her a glass of iced mineral water. She produced an embroidered handkerchief from a small purse, dipped half of it in the glass and patted the back of her neck with it. "Is it safe to talk here?" she asked.

"I have technicians who sweep the rooms for microphones."

"Imagine *sweeping* a room for a microphone! We live in different worlds."

"Thank goodness it's not true," Yevgeny shot back. "Thank goodness we live at last in the same world."

"What transpired at the meeting?"

"Valentin Varennikov—he's the general in charge of all Soviet ground forces—reported that the KGB's Dzerzhinsky Division, along with units from the Kantemirov Division and the Taman Guards, would occupy key sites in the city—the television tower at Ostankino, newspaper offices, bridges, rail stations, intersections on the main arteries, the university and the heights around it—on the first of September. At the same time paratrooper units of the Ryazan Airborne Division will move into Moscow under cover of darkness and stand ready to overwhelm any pockets of resistance. The KGB, meanwhile, has stockpiled two hundred fifty thousand pairs of handcuffs, printed up three hundred thousand arrest forms, cleared two floors of Lefortovo Prison and secretly doubled all KGB pay. The Minister of Defense Yazov, along with the Interior Minister Pugo, are pushing for an earlier date for the putsch—they want to launch it around the middle of this month, while Gorbachev is vacationing in the Crimea. But Kryuchkov and General Varennikov argued that anything before the first of September will involve greater risks, since logistical preparations and tactical orders will not be completed. Also the German *Devisenbeschaffer* needs more time to collect the funds, scattered through banks in Germany and Austria, and funnel them into my bank in Dresden so I can bring them to Moscow and make them available to the plotters."

"So the putsch will take place on the first of September," Aza said grimly.

"You must warn Yeltsin," Yevgeny said. "He must contact the commanders of units that might remain loyal to the government."

"It is a perilous business, sounding out supporters. People could panic. Word could reach the plotters and they could arrest the loyalists. In any case, aside from some scattered tank units and groups of Afghan veterans, Boris Nikolayevich is not at all sure whom he can muster to defend the Parliament's White House."

"He must muster the people," Yevgeny suggested.

"Yes, by all means, the people. They are our secret weapon, Yevgeny. They understand that Boris Nikolayevich takes the business of reforming Russia seriously. He takes the June election seriously—for the first time in our thousand-year history, Russians went to the voting places and *elected* a President. When the crisis comes Russians will remember Patriarch Alexy, with his flowing robes and flowing beard, blessing Yeltsin. *By the will of God and the choice of the Russian people, you are bestowed with the highest office in Russia.* Yeltsin's response will ring in everyone's ears. *Great Russia is rising from its knees.*"

"I hope you're right, Aza. I hope Yeltsin has the nerves for this kind of affair. I hope he doesn't abandon the race at the first hurdle."

Aza came around the table and, leaning over Yevgeny, kissed him hard on the lips. Blushing noticeably, she backed away. "All hurdles grow smaller when confronted by your lust and my desire."

Yevgeny, speechless with emotion, could only nod in agreement.

The Sorcerer bought a ticket at the window, squeezed through the turnstile, and stepped gingerly onto the escalator ferrying passengers down to the Arbatsko-Pokrovskaya line in the bowels of the earth. He looked over the head of the woman in front—the Smolenskaia quays seemed to be at the bottom of a sink hole. To make time pass he studied the people passing on the up-escalator, an arm's length away. Some had their faces buried in folded newspapers; others stared dumbly into space, their minds (judging from their expressions) clouded by fatigue or worry or resignation or all of the above. One old woman knitted. A middle-aged woman talked angrily to the back of the head of the teenage boy in front of her. Two young lovers stood facing each

other, the girl on the higher step so that their heads were level, gazing word-
lessly into each other's eyes. Ahead, at the bottom of the escalator, a stern-faced
woman in an ill-fitting uniform surveyed traffic from a small booth, her hands
on controls that could stop the escalator in an emergency.

The Sorcerer landed on the quays and let himself be carried along in the
river of people flowing toward the trains. Half way down the station platform he spotted Leo Kritzky, exactly where his message—written in lemon
juice between the lines of a *Thank you for the John Deere material* note—said
he would be. He was sitting on a plastic bench reading a copy of the English-
language *Moscow News*. He looked up as a train eased into the station. His
eyes passed over the fat figure of the Sorcerer without a flicker of recognition. Torriti had to hand it to Kritzky; however much he detested him, he
was a thorough professional. Kritzky got up and, dropping the newspaper in
an open trash bin, walked quickly toward the train, lunging inside just as
doors closed. Back on the quay, Torriti nonchalantly fished the newspaper
out of the bin and glanced at the headlines while he waited for the train to
arrive on the eastbound track. BANK OF COMMERCE AND CREDIT INTERNA-
TIONAL INDICTED FOR MONEY LAUNDERING. GORBACHEV OFF TO CRIMEA
FOR SUMMER HOLIDAY. When the train finally pulled in, the crowd, with
Torriti lost in its midst, surged toward the doors.

The Sorcerer changed trains several times, making sure he was the last
person off and the last on as the doors closed. He eventually rode another
escalator to the street, ducked into a toy store with nearly empty shelves and
emerged through a back door into an alleyway that led to another street.
There he flagged down a gypsy cab and made his way back to the fifth-floor
room in the Hotel Ukraine. Locking himself in the bathroom, he tore out
the upper right-hand quarter of page four and heated it over a naked light
bulb. Within seconds writing in lemon juice began to emerge.

D-day is 1 Sept. General in charge of ground forces, Varennikov, working out of KGB complex in Mashkino, is drawing up plans to infiltrate
KGB's Dzerzhinsky Division, units from the Kantemirov Division and the
Taman Guards and paratroop elements from Ryazan Airborne Division into
Moscow to control strategic points. Gorbachev to be isolated under house
arrest while plotters declare state of emergency and take control of government organs. For God's sake, somebody do something before it's too late.

Torriti copied the pertinent details in a minuscule handwriting onto
a slip of paper and hid it under the instep of his left shoe. He burned the

quarter page of newspaper in an ashtray and flushed the cinders down the toilet. Moments later, at a public booth around the corner from the hotel, he fed a coin into the slot and dialed the number the Rabbi had given him if he needed to communicate with the Israelis in Dresden quickly.

A woman answered the phone. *"Pazhalista?"*

"I have been told you sell rare Persian carpets at rock bottom prices," Torriti said.

"Please, who said you this information?"

"A little birdie name of Ezra."

"Ezra, bless his heart! He is from time to time sending clients. Sure thing, you come by and we are showing you Persian carpets until your head spins dizzy. You are having my address?"

"I am having your address, lady."

Torriti set the phone back down on its hook, treated himself to a restorative shot of booze from his nearly empty flask and, pulling up the collar of a rumpled sports jacket that had been washed and worn to death, headed for the Arbat.

The Rabbi snared the intercom speaker with one of his canes and dragged the small wooden box closer so he wouldn't miss a word. He held his breath and listened, but all he heard was absolute silence. Then a primeval curdling whimper filled the room. It originated at the bottom of a deep pit of physical pain. Ben Ezra winced: he had to remind himself that ends did justify means; that the ends, continuing to get hundreds of thousands of Jews out of Russia, vindicated the torture of one man who was involved in a plot to prevent it. Gradually the whimper faded and one of the young men could be heard repeating the question.

What is the secret identification number that provides access to the account?

When the *Devisenbeschaffer* didn't immediately respond, the low buzz of what sounded like an electric razor came over the speaker. Then words detonated like Chinese firecrackers set off in series.

Nicht-das—schalte-es-aus—Ich-werde-es-Dir-sagen!

Enough, a voice ordered. *Switch it off.*

The buzzing stopped.

The numbers came across sandwiched between sobs and whimpers. *Seven-eight-four-two*, then the word *Wolke*, then *nine-one-one.*

The Rabbi scratched the numbers and the word on a pad. Seven-eight-four-two, then *Wolke* or *cloud*, then nine-one-one. He filled his lungs with air and looked up. It was a given in the world of espionage that everyone broke sooner or later. Ben Ezra knew of Jews on mission who had been instructed to hold out long enough to permit the others in their network to escape; sometimes they had, enduring torture for two, two-and-a-half days, sometimes they broke sooner. The Rabbi's own son had been caught in Syria in the mid-1970s and tortured for thirty-four hours before he cracked, at which point he had been sponged and dressed in white pajamas and hanged from a crude wooden gibbet. The German had absorbed more punishment than most; his rage at Jews had numbed him to a portion of the pain he was suffering. But he had broken.

What remained, now, was to test the numbers—and assuming, as he did, that they were correct, to take control of the *Devisenbeschaffer*'s deposits, divert the funds into various bank accounts in Switzerland and send the pre-arranged message to Jack McAuliffe informing him the dirty deed was done.

At which point it would be up to the Sorcerer to fulfill his part of the pact.

Ben Ezra had received the Sorcerer's message the previous evening: the putsch was set for 1 September. Using a scrambled telephone in a Mossad safe house, talking cryptically as an added precaution, the Rabbi had passed this detail on to Jack McAuliffe in Washington. Our mutual friend, Ben Ezra had said, reminds us that we must get our applications in before the first of September if we hope to win any fellowships; any later will be too late. The first of September, Jack had noted on his end of the line, doesn't leave us much time to get recommendations from the eight or ten key figures in Moscow; does our mutual friend think he can contact these people before the deadline? He has started the ball rolling, the Rabbi had replied. He expects to have the eight or ten recommendations in hand by the last week in August. That's cutting it pretty fine, Jack had shot back; any possibility of speeding up the process? Getting recommendations from eight or ten people at more or less the same time is a complicated process, Ben Ezra had cautioned Jack; and we are obliged, for obvious reasons, to get it right the first time, there's no going back for a second try. Okay, Jack had said reluctantly, I'll settle for the last week in August. Now, sitting at a table in the upper floor office of the meatpacking factory, the Rabbi turned the intercom speaker around to unplug the cord. Peering through the thick lenses of his spectacles, his eyes glazed with the pain that was his constant companion, he saw, in the open back of the box, a tiny red-and-black spider dancing across tendrils that were so fine they were invisible to the naked eye. The spider, appearing suspended in space, froze when Ben Ezra touched one of the strands with his thumbnail. It waited with endless patience, trying to determine if the vibrations it had picked up signaled danger. Finally it risked a tentative movement, then swiftly clawed across its invisible web and vanished into the cavernous safety of the intercom speaker.

Something resembling a scowl surfaced on Ben Ezra's bone-dry lips. His time was growing short. Soon he, too, would claw his way across an invisible web, his bad hip thrusting forward and around and back with each painful step, and vanish into the cavernous safety of the land that the Lord God had bequeathed to the descendants of the Patriarch Abraham.

The siren atop the guard tower sounded high noon at the KGB complex in the village of Mashkino, a series of two-story, L-shaped brick satellites connected by covered passageways to the nuclear headquarters building. In the small air-conditioned conference room on the second floor of this building, the KGB Chairman, Vladimir Kryuchkov, in the best of times a testy man who tended to see the cup half empty rather than half full, stared grimly out a window. Behind him the voice of Fyodor Lomov, the foreign ministry *apparatchik*, droned on as he read aloud from the file that had accompanied the photographs rushed over that morning by motorcycle courier.

It seemed that the Israeli desk of the Second Chief Directorate had a surveillance team watching a husband and wife of Jewish origin who sold Oriental carpets in a hole-in-the-wall shop on a side street off the Arbat. The couple was known to have provided safe house and communication services for the Israeli Mossad in the past. The surveillance team, working out of a vacant apartment diagonally across the street from the carpet store, systematically photographed everyone going in or out of the shop. These photographs were developed every night and delivered to the Second Chief Directorate's Israeli desk in the morning. On this particular morning the photographs were still being sorted—the mug shots of visitors who could be identified were labeled and pasted into a scrapbook, the others were stored in a wire basket marked *unidentified*—when Yuri Sukhanov, the cranky head of the Ninth Chief Directorate, one of the core group of plotters working closely with KGB Chairman Kryuchkov, stopped by with a disturbing photograph that the Dresden *rezident* had pouched to Moscow Centre. It showed a twisted old man struggling with the aid of two canes toward a limousine surrounded by bodyguards. Dresden had tentatively identified the old man as Ezra Ben Ezra, the infamous Rabbi who was winding up a seven year tour as head of the Israeli Mossad. Walking next to him was a corpulent figure that the Dresden *rezidentura* had not been able to identify—but Sukhanov, a veteran KGB officer who had begun an illustrious career at the East Berlin Karlshorst *rezidentura* in the mid 1950s, recognized instantly: the man accompanying Ben Ezra was none other than the Rabbi's old friend from Berlin, the legendary one-time chief of the CIA's Berlin Base, H. Torriti, a.k.a.

the Sorcerer. The question on everyone's lips, of course, was: why was the head of the Mossad meeting Harvey Torriti in Dresden? Was it possible that their presence had something to do with the sums of hard currency being transferred by the *Devisenbeschaffer* to the Dresden branch of the Greater Russian Bank of Commerce? Or worse still, something to do with the sudden disappearance of the *Devisenbeschaffer* himself?

The intriguing subject was being kicked around at an informal brain-storming session when Sukhanov noticed a pile of mug shots in the wire basket labelled *unidentified*. Absently leafing through them, he suddenly held one up to the light. Where did you get this? he demanded excitedly. The desk officer explained that it had been taken the previous day by the team watching a Jewish couple that from time to time provided field services to the Israelis. But this is the same man photographed with the Rabbi in Dresden! It's the American Torriti, the head of the Ninth Directorate said. Sukhanov took Torriti's presence first in Dresden, then in Moscow, as an ominous omen—it could only mean that the CIA, bypassing its Moscow station, had slipped an old professional into the Soviet capital from the outside. And that, in turn, could only mean that the Americans suspected a putsch was in the works.

It was at this point that the photographs of Ben Ezra and Torriti in Dresden, and Torriti in Moscow, were biked out to the KGB complex at Mashkino and Kryuchkov was alerted. The premonition of the head of the Ninth Directorate caused consternation among the putschists. A war council with the leading plotters was quickly convened. Lomov finished reading through the file. The Minister of Defense, Yazov, who along with the Interior Minister, Pugo, had originally pushed for a mid-August coup d'état, argued for moving up the date from 1 September in light of this latest information. General Varennikov, the ground forces chief and the man responsible for mustering the troops that would seize control of Moscow, had previously been against the idea because military preparations couldn't be completed that early. Now, albeit reluctantly, he saw the logic of a mid-August date. The head of the Ninth Chief Directorate, whose agents would be responsible for quarantining Gorbachev during the first hours of the coup, reminded the others that the General Secretary was in his summer residence near the Crimean town of Foros until the twentieth. Which didn't leave much time.

Everyone looked at Kryuchkov, who was still staring out the window. He remarked that there was a brownish smog hovering over the fields surrounding the village of Mashkino. It had been there for the better part of a week. Superstitious peasants, he noted, believed that evil spirits lurking in the smog could cause stillbirths in pregnant women who ventured out on days like this.

In short, it was not an auspicious moment to launch new projects. Happily, he, Kryuchkov, was not superstitious. Turning to his colleagues, looking particularly somber, he announced that he, too, was now in favor of moving up the date of the uprising, even if it meant that all the preparations—including the importation of large amounts of foreign currency to Moscow in order to stock the stores immediately after the coup—could not be completed in time.

"How about the nineteenth?" Kryuchkov said.

"Nineteen August sounds fine to me," Defense Minister Yazov commented. The others in the room nodded in agreement.

"So it is decided," Kryuchkov said. "We will declare a state of emergency, isolate Gorbachev and take control of the government one week from today."

Trying to walk off a chronic angst, Leo Kritzky spent the afternoon exploring the narrow streets behind the Kremlin filled with small Orthodox churches. Over the years he had become so Russian-looking that the ever-present hustlers who waylaid foreigners with offers to buy dollars or sell caviar no longer gave him a second glance. He stopped for tea and a dry cupcake in a workers' canteen, then queued at a pharmacy for a bottle of Polish cough syrup and dropped it off at his lady friend's apartment; she'd been battling a chest cold with herbal infusions but it had only gotten worse. He lingered for half an hour looking at the sketches she'd done for a children's book on Siberian elves and fairies, then took the subway back to Frunzenskaya Embankment. Hanging on to an overhead strap, swaying from side to side as the train plunged through a tunnel, his eyes fell on what he took to be a relic of seventy years of Communism: a small metal plaque at the head of the subway car with the words "October Revolution" engraved on it. He wondered how many people noticed this reminder of things past; how many of those who noticed still believed in the promise of the October Revolution. There were days when he himself thought it might be better to start over again; there were other days when he tried not to think about it at all.

Arriving at Frunzenskaya Embankment number 50, entrance 9, he climbed the steps to the third floor. The janitor still had not gotten around to replacing the light bulb at the end of the corridor near his apartment, number 373. As he crouched to insert the latch key in the lock an agitated voice called from the darkness. "Sorry, sorry, but I don't suppose you happen to understand English." When Leo didn't immediately respond, the person sighed. "I didn't think so—it would have been too good to be true."

Leo squinted into the shadows. "As a matter of fact—"

"Oh, thank goodness," the woman exclaimed in relief. She materialized out of the shadows and approached Leo. "Sorry again, but I don't suppose you'd know which of these apartments Leon Kritzky lives in?"

Leo's face turned numb as stone. "Who are you?" he demanded. He raised his fingertips to his cheek and felt only dead skin.

The woman drew closer and peered at Leo. He could hear her catch her breath. "Daddy?" she whispered in a child's anguished voice.

"Tessa? Is that you?"

"Oh, Daddy," she moaned. "It is me. It's me, it's me."

Leo felt time and place and regret and heartache fall away. He opened his arms and Tessa, quaking with sobs, collapsed into them.

It was a long while before either of them could utter a word. They stood there in the shadows clinging to each other until Tessa's tears had saturated the lapel of Leo's windbreaker. Later, neither could remember how they had gotten into the apartment or who had opened the bottle of Bulgarian wine or where the open sandwiches spread with roe had come from. They gazed at each other across the folding table. Every now and then Leo would reach over and touch his daughter and her eyes, riveted on his, would brim with tears. Tessa had checked into a hotel off Red Square but there was no question of her going back to it; they would collect her valise and the package of books she had brought for Leo the next morning. They spread a sheet on the couch for her and propped up pillows on either end of it and talked in soft voices husky with emotion into the early hours of the morning. Tessa, a thin, handsome woman closing in on forty, had just ended another in a series of love affairs; she always seemed to fall for men who were already married or leery of committing themselves to permanent relationships. And as her sister constantly reminded her, the biological clock was ticking. Tessa was toying with the idea of getting pregnant by her next lover even if the affair never went anywhere; she'd at least wind up with a child, which is what she wanted more than anything.

Vanessa? Oh, she was fine. Yes, she was still married to the same fellow, an assistant professor of history at George Washington University; their son, who had been named Philip after his grandfather, was a strapping four-year-old who already knew how to work a computer. Why hadn't she warned Leo she was coming? She hadn't wanted to get his hopes up. Hers either. She was afraid she might chicken out at the last moment, afraid of what she would find—or what she wouldn't find. She hadn't even told Vanessa where she was going. Oh, Daddy, if only...

If only?

If only you hadn't...

He understood what she couldn't bring herself to say. I had allegiances and loyalties that went back to before I joined the CIA, he told her. I was true to these allegiances and loyalties.

Do you have any regrets?

The regrets that had fallen away in the corridor flooded back. Your mother, he said; I bitterly regret what I did to Adelle. Your sister; I regret that she can't bring herself to talk to me. You; I regret that I can't share your life and you can't share what's left of mine.

When I first saw you in the hallway, Daddy, I had the terrible feeling that you weren't glad to see me.

No, it's not true—

I saw it in your eyes.

Seeing you here is the most wonderful thing that's happened to me in seven and a half years. It's only—

Only what?

This isn't the best time to be in Moscow, Tessa.

With Gorbachev in power, I thought it'd be a fascinating time to be in Moscow.

That's just it. Gorbachev may not be in power long.

Is there going to be a coup d'état? Gosh, that would be fun—to be in the middle of a real revolution. Suddenly Tessa looked hard at her father. Do you know something, Daddy, or are you only repeating rumors?

A coup is a real possibility.

Excuse me for asking but do you still work for the KGB?

He tried to smile. I'm retired. I draw a pension. I get what information I have from the newspapers.

Tessa seemed relieved. Predicting coups is like predicting the weather, she said. Everybody knows the newspapers get it wrong most of the time. So if they say there's going to be a coup d'état, chances are things will be quiet as hell. Too bad for me. I could have used some excitement in my life.

5

FLYING INTO THE WHITEWASHED BULL'S-EYE HELIPAD IN A GIANT BUG-like Army helicopter, Yevgeny saw the onion-domed Church of Foros clinging to the granite cliffs and the surf breaking against the jagged shoreline far below it. Moments later Mikhail Gorbachev's compound on the southern Crimean cliffs overlooking the Black Sea came into view. There was a three-story main house, a small hotel for staff and security guards, a separate guest house, an indoor swimming pool and movie theater, even a long escalator to the private beach under the compound. As soon as the helicopter had touched down, the delegation from Moscow—Yuri Sukhanov representing the KGB, General Varennikov representing the Army, Oleg Baklanov representing the military-industrial complex, Oleg Shenin from the Politburo, Gorbachev's personal assistant and chief of staff Valery Boldin, Yevgeny Tsipin representing the powerful banking sector—was rushed over to the main house in open Jeeps. As the group made its way through the marble and gilt central hall, the head of the compound's security detachment whispered to Sukhanov that he had cut off Gorbachev's eight telephone and fax lines at four thirty, as instructed. "When I informed him that he had unexpected visitors, he picked up the phone to see what it was all about," recounted the officer. "That's when he discovered the lines were dead. He even tried the direct phone to the commander in chief—the one that's kept in a box. He must have understood immediately what was happening because he turned deathly pale and summoned his family—his wife, Raisa Maksimovna, his daughter, his son-in-law. They are all with him now in the living room. Raisa was particularly shaken—I heard her say something to her husband about the Bolsheviks murdering the Romanov family after the October revolution."

Pushing through double doors, the delegation found Gorbachev and his family standing shoulder to shoulder in the middle of the grand living room. There was a breathtaking view of the cliffs and the sea through the picture window behind them. The General Secretary, barely able to control his rage, stared at his chief of staff, Boldin. *"Et tu, Brute?"* he said with a sneer. Gorbachev eyed the others. "Who sent you?" he asked with icy disdain.

"The committee appointed in connection with the emergency," Sukhanov told him.

"I didn't appoint such a committee," Gorbachev shot back. "Who is on it?"

Yevgeny went up to Gorbachev and handed him a sheet of onionskin on which the names of the members of the State Committee for the State of Emergency had been typed. The Secretary General fitted on a pair of eyeglasses and looked at the list. "Kryuchkov! Yazov—my God, I plucked him out of nowhere to be Minister of Defense! Pugo! Varennikov! Uritzky!" Gorbachev's head rocked from side to side in disgust. "Do you really think the people are so tired that they will follow any dictator?"

General Varennikov stepped forward. "You don't have much choice in the matter, Mikhail Sergeyevich. You must go along with us and sign the emergency decree. Either that or resign."

Gorbachev glanced at Raisa and saw that she was shivering with fear. He rested a hand on her shoulder, then told the delegation, "Never—I refuse to legalize such a decree with my signature."

In a barely audible voice Raisa asked her husband, "Yeltsin—is his name on the list?"

Sukhanov said, "Yeltsin will be arrested."

Gorbachev and his wife stared into each other's eyes. Their daughter moved closer to her mother and took her hand. Gorbachev smiled grimly at both of them; they all understood that there was a strong possibility of ending up in front of a firing squad. He turned back to the delegation. "You are adventurers and traitors," he said in an even voice. "You will destroy the country. Only those who are blind to history could now suggest a return to a totalitarian regime. You are pushing Russia to civil war."

Yevgeny, conscious of having a role to play, remarked, "You are the one pushing Russia to civil war. We are trying to avoid bloodshed."

Sukhanov said, "Mikhail Sergeyevich, in the end we ask nothing from you. You will remain in Foros under house arrest. We will take care of the dirty work for you."

"Dirty work is what you will be doing," Gorbachev agreed bitterly.

"There is nothing more we can accomplish here," Sukhanov told the other members of the delegation. He approached Gorbachev and thrust out his hand; the General Secretary and the head of the KGB's Ninth Chief Directorate had been on close terms for years. Gorbachev looked down at the hand, then with a contemptuous sneer turned his back on him. Shrugging off the insult, Sukhanov led the way out of the room.

Heading back in the helicopter to Belbek airport, where a Tupolev-154 was waiting to fly them to Moscow, Sukhanov issued instructions over the radiophone to the head of the security detachment at Foros; the General Secretary and the members of his family were to be cut off from the world. No person and no news was to be allowed in or out. Understood?

The words *Your orders will be carried out* crackled over the radio.

Baklanov produced a bottle of cognac from a leather satchel and, filling small plastic cups to the brim, handed them around. Everyone started to drink. "You have to hand it to him," General Varennikov shouted over the whine of the rotors. "Anyone else in his shoes would have signed the fucking decree."

Sukhanov leaned his head back against the helicopter's bulkhead and shut his eyes. "Everything now depends on isolating Boris Yeltsin," he shouted. "Without Gorbachev, without Yeltsin, the opposition will have nobody to rally around."

Yevgeny agreed. "Yeltsin," he said, his thoughts far away, "is definitely the key."

Returning to Moscow well after midnight, Yevgeny rang Aza's apartment from a public phone in the airport parking lot. Using a prearranged code phrase, he summoned her to a quick meeting in a garage across the alleyway from the back door of her building. He found her waiting in the shadows when he got there and they fell into each other's arms. After a moment Yevgeny pushed her away and, in short disjointed sentences, explained what had happened: the putschists had unexpectedly moved up the date of the uprising; he and some others had flown down to Foros to try to browbeat Gorbachev into signing the decree establishing the State Committee for the State of Emergency; Gorbachev had flatly refused and was being held prisoner in the Foros compound. Even as they spoke, Marshal Yazov was promulgating Coded Telegram 8825 putting all military units on red alert. Within hours detachments of tanks and half-tracks loaded with combat troops would occupy strategic positions in Moscow, at which point the public would be informed that Gorbachev had suffered a stroke and resigned, and all governmental power was now in the hands of the State Committee for the State of Emergency.

Aza took the news calmly. The events were not unexpected, she noted, only the timing came as a surprise. She would borrow a car from a neighbor and drive out to warn Boris Nikolayevich immediately, she said. Yeltsin would undoubtedly barricade himself inside the massive Russian parliament building on the Moscow River known as the White House and try to rally the democratic forces to resist. If the White House phones were not cut off, Yevgeny might be able to reach her at the unlisted number in Yeltsin's suite of offices that she had given him. In the darkness she caressed the back of his neck with her hand. Take care of yourself, Yevgeny Alexandrovich, she said, and she whispered a coda from their fleeting romance so many, many years before: *Each time I see you I seem to leave a bit of me with you.*

The line, which Yevgeny instantly recognized, left him aching with regret at what might have been; aching with hope at what still could be.

Aza threaded the small Lada through the deserted streets of the capital. She turned onto Kutuzovsky Prospekt and headed out of Moscow in the direction of Usovo, the village where Boris Yeltsin had his dacha. She had stopped for a red light—the last thing she wanted was to be pulled over by the police for a traffic violation—when she realized that the ground was shaking under the wheels of the car. It felt like the foreshock of an earthquake. She heard the rumbling at the same moment she saw what was causing it. To her stupefaction, a long column of enormous tanks heading toward downtown Moscow hove into view on the avenue. A soldier wearing a leather helmet and goggles stood in the open turret of each tank. Suddenly the trembling of the earth matched the rhythm of Aza's heart; until this instant the putsch had been a more or less abstract concept, but the sight of the tank treads grinding along the cobblestones into Moscow made it painfully real. The tankers didn't stop for the red light, which struck Aza as outrageous. Who did they think they were! And then it hit her; it was preposterous to think that tanks heading for a putsch would obey traffic regulations. One soldier must have noticed there was a woman behind the wheel of the Lada because he made a gallant gesture as he rolled past, doffing an imaginary top hat in her direction.

The instant the light turned green Aza threw the car into gear and, racing past the line of tanks, sped toward Usovo. On the outskirts of Moscow, the buildings gave way to fields with ornate entrances to collective farms or factories set back from the road. Gorki-9, just before Usovo, was deathly still when she drove down the single paved street and turned onto a dirt lane and braked to a stop in front of a walled compound. The two soldiers on duty, country boys from the look of them, were dozing in the guardhouse when she rapped on the window. One of them recognized her and hurried out to open the gate.

"Kind of early for you, isn't it, little lady?" he said.

"I wanted to put Moscow behind me before traffic jammed the streets," she replied.

"If I had a car," the soldier remarked, "wouldn't bother me none being caught in traffic. I'd listen to American rock 'n' roll music on the radio."

Parking around the side of the ill-proportioned wood-and-brick dacha, Aza made her way to the back door inside the screened-in porch. In the woods around the house, the birds had still not started to chirp. She took the skeleton key from its hiding place under a pot of geraniums and let herself into the kitchen. Climbing the wooden steps with the painted balusters, she went down the hallway and knocked softly on the door at the end of it. When there was no response she rapped more insistently. A gruff voice called from inside, "What the devil is going on?"

"Boris Nikolayevich, it's me, Azalia Isanova. I absolutely must speak to you."

Down the hall, several doors opened and Yeltsin's daughters, Lena and Tanya, quite frightened to be awakened at this hour, stuck their heads out. "What is happening?" asked Tanya, the younger of the two.

Yeltsin, wearing trousers with the suspenders dangling and a nightshirt, carrying a large-bored pistol in one hand, pulled open the door of the room. "Go back to bed," he called over Aza's head to his daughters. "Come in," Yeltsin told Aza. He knew that it wasn't good news that had brought her out from Moscow at dawn. He set the pistol down on the night table next to a nearly empty bottle of cognac. Pointing to a chair, pulling another over to it, he sat down facing her. "So you've had word from your informant?" he demanded.

Aza nodded. "He came to see me around one-thirty," she said, and she repeated what Yevgeny had told her: the putsch was underway, Gorbachev had refused to cooperate and was being held prisoner in the Crimea, Army and paratroop units had been ordered to take up positions in the capital. She had seen one of them, a long line of giant tanks, heading into Moscow with her own eyes.

Yeltsin threaded the three thick fingers of his left hand through a shock of graying hair and stared at the floor, brooding. Then he shook his head several times, as if he were arguing with himself. "How did you get out here?" he asked.

"I borrowed a Lada from a neighbor."

He looked away, a preoccupied frown pasted on his face; Aza knew him well enough to realize that he was sorting through scenarios. "It is essential for me to return to the White House," he finally said, thinking out loud. "I'm sure to be on the KGB's list of those to be arrested. By now they'll have set up roadblocks around Moscow. If I go back in my limousine, surrounded by bodyguards, they are bound to recognize me and that will be the end of it. I have a better chance of getting through the checkpoints if I drive back with you. It could be dangerous—are you willing to take the risk?"

"I am, Boris Nikolayevich."

"You are a spunky woman, Azalia Isanòva."

Yeltsin jumped to his feet and switched on a small radio tuned to an all-night Moscow station. It was playing a recording of *Swan Lake*, which was a sinister sign; Soviet stations always switched to *Swan Lake* in times of trouble. Then an announcer, his voice quivering with nervousness, interrupted the music to read a news bulletin: "Mikhail Gorbachev has stepped down for reasons of health. At this grave and critical hour, the State Committee for the State of Emergency has assumed power to deal with the mortal danger that looms over our great Motherland." Hearing the commotion, Lena and Tanya came flying into their father's bedroom. Yeltsin waved for them to be quiet. "The policy of reforms, launched at Mikhail Gorbachev's initiative and designed to insure the country's dynamic development," the voice on the radio was saying, "has entered into a blind alley. The country is sinking into the quagmire of violence and lawlessness. Millions of people are demanding measures against the octopus of crime and glaring immorality."

Yeltsin snapped off the radio. "Millions of people are demanding democratization, not a new dictatorship of the proletariat," he declared. Peeling the nightshirt off over his head, he began to strap on a bulletproof vest. He put on a white shirt and adjusted the suspenders, slipped into a brown suit jacket and dropped the pistol into a pocket. Turning to his daughters, he instructed them to phone their mother in the family's apartment in the city. "The line is certain to be tapped," he told them. "Say only that I heard the radio and left immediately by car for Sverdlovsk. Nothing more."

Outside, a particularly large shooting star etched a fiery path through Ursa Major. "Make a wish," Yeltsin ordered his daughters. He himself was not a religious man but he did believe in destiny; clearly the moment was at hand to fulfill his. Gazing up at the cloudless August sky he made a wish, then settled into the passenger's seat of Aza's Lada.

"Papa, only keep calm," Lena said as she closed the car door. "Remember that everything depends on you."

At first the ringing seemed far away and Jack McAuliffe integrated it into his dream; through a haze of memory, he could see himself handcuffing Leo Kritzky to a radiator as a bicycle bell reverberated through a dilapidated wooden hulk of a building to remind everyone that coffee and doughnuts were available in the hallway. Surfacing with infinite languidness from the depths of the dream, Jack realized where he was and what was ringing. In the darkness he groped for the telephone on the nightstand. Millie got to it first.

"Yes?"…"Who did you say you were?"…Out of long habit she murmured, "I'll see if he's here."

She smothered the mouthpiece in the pillow and whispered to Jack, "It's the Langley night duty officer, Jack. Are you here?"

Jack, breaking the surface, grumbled, "Where else would I be in the middle of the night except in bed with my wife." He found Millie's shoulder, then followed the arm to her hand and the telephone. Taking it from her, he growled, "McAuliffe speaking."

Wide awake now, Jack sat up in bed and shifted the phone to his other ear. "Jesus H. Christ, when did this come in?"…"Okay, dispatch an *Action Immediate* to Moscow Station ordering all hands off the streets until the situation stabilizes. We don't want any of our people killed in crossfires. Sign my name to it. Next, track down Director Ebbitt—he's on a sailboat named *Gentleman Rankers* somewhere off Nantucket."…"Alert the Coast Guard if you can't raise him on the radio. Also notify the DD/O, Manny Ebbitt. Tell him to come straight in to the situation room. I'll be there in three quarters of an hour. I'll decide then whether we wake the President immediately or hold it for a morning briefing."

Jack felt around in the dark until he found the light switch. The sudden brightness blinded him and he covered his eyes with a forearm as he hung up the phone. "Balloon's gone up in Russia," he told Millie. "Leo got it wrong. Goddamn plotters launched their putsch twelve days ahead of schedule. Russian Army's occupying strategic positions in Moscow. Gorbachev's either dead or under arrest in the Crimea."

"Maybe I ought to go in with you, Jack, to get the public relations angle sorted out—*Washington Post*'ll be breaking down our door in the morning to know why we didn't give the President some advance warning of a coup."

"As usual we can't tell them we did." He glanced at Millie—she looked every bit as appetizing as the day he first laid eyes on her in the Cloud Club. "Anyone ever told you you're one hell of a beautiful broad?" he asked.

"You have, Jack." She reached over and smoothed his disheveled mustache with the tips of her fingers. "Tell me one more time, I might begin to believe it."

"Believe it," he said. "It's gospel truth." Frowning in preoccupation, he pushed himself out of the bed. "Fucking Russians," he groaned. "If this coup succeeds it'll put them right back into the Bolshevik ice age."

Curled up on the couch in the living room, Tessa slept through the sound of Leo's alarm and the flushing of the toilet and the water cascading through the pipes in the wall. She finally opened an eye when the odor of percolating coffee reached her nostrils.

"Rise and shine, baby," Leo called from the kitchenette. "We want to get on the road at a decent hour if we're going to go to Zagorsk."

"I can handle the *rise* part," Tessa moaned. "*Shine* is beyond my diminished capacities."

The two of them had been covering Moscow like a blanket (as Tessa liked to say), visiting every nook and cranny of the Kremlin, St. Basil's Cathedral, the labyrinthian halls of GUM, the Novodievitchi Monastery and cemetery (where Manny Ebbitt had been nabbed seventeen years ago this month), the Pushkin Museum. In the waning light of the late afternoons, they had explored lengths of the Moscow River embankment and segments of the Sadovaya Ring. Leo, at sixty-four, seemed to have a bottomless well of energy to draw on; it was Tessa, at thirty-seven, who ultimately cried uncle and asked if they couldn't put off seeing the rest of Moscow until tomorrow.

"Three more days," Leo said now, buttering a toasted bun (he did all his shopping at a special KGB store whose shelves were filled to overflowing) and handing it across to his daughter.

"I'll be back, Daddy."

"Will you?"

"You know I will. Maybe next time I can convince Vanessa..." She let the sentence trail off.

"I'd like that," Leo said quietly. "I'd like it a lot."

The telephone in the living room rang and Leo got up to answer it. Tessa could hear him talking to someone in urgent tones when a low throaty rumble rose from the street. She went over to the open window and parted the curtains and looked out to see the most startling sight of her life: a long column of monstrously large tanks lumbering down Frunzenskaya Embankment.

Behind her Leo was almost shouting into the phone. "What happened to the first of September, for God's sake? Twelve days ahead of schedule will throw any plans Torriti may have made into the garbage heap."

On the avenue, the tanks were splitting up into smaller formations and wheeling off in different directions. Two of the tanks remained behind at an intersection, the barrels of their cannons twitching as if they were searching for something to shoot at.

Leo could be heard saying, "How do they know Yeltsin fled to Sverdlovsk?" Then: "Without Yeltsin the democratic forces will have no one to lead them." Coming back into the kitchen, he heard the coughing of diesel motors on the Embankment and joined Tessa at the window.

"What's going on, Daddy?" she asked anxiously.

Shaking his head in disgust, he took in the scene. "The putsch has begun," he said.

It wasn't lost on Tessa that her father seemed to be extremely well informed. "Who's rebelling against whom?" she asked.

"The KGB, the military-industrial interests, the Army want to get rid of Gorbachev and set the clock back."

Tessa retrieved the 35-mm Nikon from her canvas carryall, fitted on a telescopic lens and took several shots of the two tanks at the intersection. People heading for work had gathered around them and seemed to be arguing with the commanders who stood in the turrets. "Hey, let's go down there," Tessa said, throwing some rolls of film and her camera in the carryall.

"The smartest thing would be for us to stay put."

"Daddy, I work for an American newsmagazine. I'm not about to hide in a closet if there's a real live coup d'état going on."

Leo looked out the window again; he, too, was curious to see what was happening. "Well, as long as nobody's shooting, I suppose we could take a look."

Muscovites were streaming into the streets when Leo and Tessa emerged from Number 50 into the brilliant August sunlight. Knots of people had gathered at corners to exchange information. A large group swarmed around the two tanks at the intersection. Students bending under the weight of backpacks filled with textbooks kicked at the treads. "Make a U-turn and go back to your barracks," one of them cried.

"We have been given orders and we are obliged to follow them," the young officer in the turret tried to explain, but he was shouted down.

"How can you carry out orders to shoot at your own people?" pleaded a young woman balancing an infant on her hip.

"Answer if you can," an old woman challenged.

"Yes, Yes, answer!" others cried in chorus.

An old man shook his cane at the tanks. "Shame on you, shame on the parents who raised you," he called hoarsely.

"Pozor! Pozor!" the crowd chanted.

"Shame! Shame on anyone who shoots Russian bullets at Russian citizens," someone else shrieked.

"We are shooting at no one," declared the officer, visibly shaken.

Tessa circled the crowd, snapping pictures of the officer in the turret and the students shaking their fists at the tank. She reloaded her camera and, tugging at her father's elbow, headed in the direction of the Kremlin walls. At another intersection soldiers had formed a circle around two trucks and a Jeep, their Kalashnikovs slung under their arms. Three young girls wearing short summer skirts that swirled around their bare thighs spiked the stems of roses into the barrels of the rifles, to the cheers of the bystanders. At the Kremlin tower, a soldier could be seen hauling down the Russian tricolor from a flagpole and raising the red hammer-and-sickle standard in its place. A bearded man in a wheelchair watched with tears streaming down his cheeks. "We thought we'd seen the last of the Communists," he complained to everyone within earshot. A teenage boy on roller skates balanced a portable radio on a fire hydrant and turned up the volume. People clustered around. The distinctive voice of Boris Yeltsin's filled the air. "...soldiers and officers of the army, the KGB, and the troops of the Interior Ministry! At this difficult hour of decision remember that you have taken an oath to your people, and your weapons cannot be turned against them. The days of the conspirators are numbered. The elected government is alive and well and functioning in the White House. Our long-suffering masses will find freedom once again, and for good. Soldiers, I believe at this tragic hour you will make the right decision. The honor of Russian arms will not be covered with the blood of the people."

Leo pulled his daughter to one side and said breathlessly, "Yeltsin didn't run away to Sverdlovsk! He's broadcasting from the White House. There still may be a shred of hope."

"What is the White House, Daddy?"

"The Russian parliament building on the Moscow River."

"Then that's where we ought to go."

Around them others were beginning to get the same idea. "To the White

House," a girl with pigtails cried excitedly. As if drawn by a magnet, dozens drifted in the direction of the Arbat, the broad artery that led to the Kalinin Bridge and the Moscow River. With rivulets of Russians streaming into the Arbat, the march to the river thickened to hundreds. By the time the massive white Parliament building at the end of the Arbat came into view, the crowd had swelled to thousands. Leo, bobbing in currents of people, had the sensation of being caught up in a maelstrom; his feet didn't seem to touch the ground as he was carried along with the horde. All of a sudden protecting Yeltsin and the last bastion of democratization, the White House, seemed like a sacred mission, one that would vindicate his life-long allegiance to the Soviet Union.

At the White House, Afghan veterans wearing bits of their old uniforms and armed with anything that came to hand—kitchen knives, socks filled with sand, occasionally a pistol—were directing the students in the construction of barricades. Some were overturning automobiles and a city bus, others were felling trees or dragging over bathtubs stolen from a nearby building site, still others were prying up cobblestones with crowbars. The crewmen of the ten Taman Guard tanks drawn up in a semicircle around the White House sat on their vehicles, smoking and watching but not intervening. Minutes after bells in the city pealed the noon hour, a cheer rose from the hot asphalt and gradually grew louder until it appeared as if the ground itself was erupting. "Look," Leo yelled, pointing to the front doors of the Parliament building. The bulky figure of a tall man with a shock of gray hair could be seen standing on the top step, his arms thrust high over his head, his fingers splayed into V-for-victory signs. "It's Yeltsin," Leo shouted into his daughter's ear.

Scrambling onto the hood of a car, Tessa took several photographs, then elbowed her way through the crowd to get a closer look. Leo trailed after her. At the White House, Yeltsin descended the steps and clambered onto a T-72 with the number 110 stenciled on the side of the turret. The crowd grew silent. Journalists held out microphones to capture what he said. "Citizens of Russia," he bellowed, his voice booming over the heads of the demonstrators, "they are attempting to remove the legally elected president of the country from power. We are dealing with a right-wing anti-constitutional coup d'etat. Accordingly we proclaim all decisions and decrees of this State Committee to be illegal."

Yeltsin's short speech was greeted with wild applause. He climbed down from the tank and chatted for a moment with one of the Taman Guard officers. Surprisingly, the officer snapped off a smart salute. Beaming, Yeltsin made his way up the steps, through supporters who thumped him on the back or pumped his hand, and disappeared into the building.

The motors on the ten Taman Guard tanks revved and black fumes belched from their exhausts. And to everyone's utter astonishment, the gunners in the tanks swiveled their cannons away from the Parliament building. A raw cry of pure joy rose from the masses as people realized that the Taman tankers, moved by Yeltsin's speech, had decided to defend the White House, not attack it.

As the afternoon wore on, thousands more spilled into the plaza around the Parliament building. Estimates picked up from bulletins on portable radios put the crowd at fifteen thousand, then twenty thousand, then twenty-five thousand. The Taman officers and the Afghan veterans began to impose order on what many were calling the counterrevolution. The barricades grew higher and thicker and sturdier. Students on motorcycles were sent out to reconnoiter the city and report back with news of troop movements. Girls, some of them prostitutes who worked the underground passages near the Kremlin, hauled cartons of food and drink and distributed them to the demonstrators blocking the approaches to the White House with their bodies.

At one point Tessa noticed antennas on the roof of the building. "Do you think the phones are still working?" she asked.

Leo looked up at the antennas. "The ones that work off satellites probably are."

"If I could get to a phone, I might be able to call Washington and give my editors a first-hand account of what's happening here. It could help turn world opinion against the coup."

Leo immediately saw the advantages in what she was suggesting. "It's worth a try."

Pushing through the crowd, the two of them went around to entrance number twenty-two at the side of the building. The doors were guarded by some tough-looking Afghan veterans armed with two machine guns and a handful of pistols. One of the veterans was peering through binoculars at the hotel across the street. "Stay alert—there are snipers taking up positions in the upper windows," he called. Leo quickly explained in Russian that the young woman with him was an American journalist. One of the guards glanced at Tessa's press card, which he was unable to read, and waved them through.

Inside, couriers scurried through the corridors delivering messages attached to clipboards. Secretaries pushed carts loaded with Molotov cocktails or sheets ripped into strips to make bandages. Young guards from

private security companies were teaching university students how to load
and fire Kalashnikovs. In one room on the third floor, down the hall from
Yeltsin's command bunker, they found a woman faxing Yeltsin's denunciation of the putsch to Party organizations and factories and local governments around the country. Leo explained that the American journalist
with him needed a telephone to call out the story of the counterrevolution.
The woman stopped what she was doing and took them into a smaller
office with a phone on a table. "This one works off a satellite," she told
Tessa in careful English. "If you get through to America keep the line open.
When we are attacked, you must lock yourself in and let the world know
what is happening."

The woman turned to stare out a window, a faraway look in her eyes. "I
have always disliked summers," she remarked in Russian. "This one is no
exception." She looked back at Leo. "What is your name?"

"Kritzky," he replied. "She is my daughter."

"Mine is Azalia Isanova Lebowitz. An assault could come at any
moment. We are short of guards for Yeltsin's office. Will you volunteer?"

"Of course I will."

Leo left Tessa dialing a number and went down the corridor to the
double door leading to Yeltsin's command bunker. From inside, phones
could be heard ringing insistently. From time to time Yeltsin's booming voice
echoed through the rooms. "The Ukrainian KGB chief, Golushko, phoned
to say he didn't support the coup," he cried. In the hallway, Leo helped himself to a Kalashnikov and several clips of ammunition from a carton on the
floor and joined a heavy man standing sentry duty at the door, an AK-47 in
his strong hands.

"Do you know how to work that thing?" the man inquired in Russian.

"Not really," Leo answered.

"Here, I'll show you. It's not very complicated. You drive home the clip
until you hear a solid click. If you intend to shoot you must work the first
round into the barrel. Then there is nothing left but to aim and squeeze the
trigger. I'll put it on single action firing so the gun won't climb up on you,
which is what happens when you shoot in bursts. Do you think you have it?"

"Work the first round into the barrel, aim, squeeze the trigger."

The man smiled warmly. "Pity the counterrevolution that relies on the
likes of us to defend it." He held out his hand. "Rostropovich, Mstislav," he
said, bowing slightly as he introduced himself.

Leo took the hand of the world-famous Russian cellist. "Kritzky, Leo,"
he said.

"It all comes down to this moment in this place—the struggle to change Russia," Rostropovich remarked.

Leo nodded in fervent agreement. The two of them turned and, planting their backs against the wall, surveyed the traffic in the corridor.

Wedged into a folding aluminum garden chair in the rooftop solarium, one empty and one full bottle of Scotch within arm's reach on the deck, Harvey Torriti enjoyed a bird's-eye view of the events unfolding in the streets around the White House, across the river from the Hotel Ukraine. He had swapped his Swatch for a pair of Red Army binoculars before taking the elevator to the twenty-ninth floor late in the afternoon and hauling his carcass up the last staircase, an exertion that left him vowing to start smoking again since he couldn't see what stopping had done for his respiration. Moscow had cooled down once the sun dipped below the industrial haze on the horizon and the lights of the city had flickered on peacefully enough. It was only when the Sorcerer peered through the binoculars that the scene began to look more ominous. The concierge at the desk in the lobby had been vague about what was going on outside. There was some sort of military exercise under way, he guessed. Certainly nothing to be alarmed about. Russia, after all, was a civilized country where the rule of law prevailed. What about the mob at that white building on the other side of the river? Torriti had asked. Pensioners, the concierge had explained with a contemptuous wave of his hand, bitching about inflation.

The pensioners bitching about inflation, some fifty thousand strong if you believed the British journalists in the lobby, had settled down for the night around the white building. Through the binoculars Torriti could make out clusters of them huddled around dozens of campfires. The light from the flames illuminated shadowy figures who were laboring to pile desks and park benches and potbellied stoves onto the already towering barricades.

Torriti uncapped the last bottle of Scotch and treated himself to one for the road even though he had no intention of hitting the road. It was a crying shame—a few more days and his gnomelike friend Rappaport, surrounded by Uighur guardian angels, might have been able to fulfill the contracts that Torriti had put out on ten of the leaders of the uprising. No plotters, no putsch. The Sorcerer wondered what had pushed them to advance D-day. He'd probably never know. Well, what the hell—you win some, you lose some, in the end it pretty much evened out.

He brought the binoculars back up to his red-rimmed eyes. Near the Kremlin, on the Lenin Hills, along several of the wider boulevards visible from the Ukraine's roof, long lines of hooded headlights could be seen snaking in one direction or another. "Tanks," the Sorcerer muttered to himself. He wondered where Leo Kritzky was at this moment. Probably locked himself in his apartment until the tempest passed. It crossed the Sorcerer's mind that he might not be safe here on the roof—he remembered Ebbitt telling him once how Soviet tanks invading Budapest in '56 had shot out the lower floors of buildings to bring the upper floors crashing down on them. Torriti had gotten off to a sour start in Berlin with Ebbitt—Jesus, that was a lifetime ago!—but he'd turned out to be a good brick after all. And when it came to Russian tanks, Ebbitt knew what he was talking about—he'd witnessed the Budapest fiasco with his own eyes. Still, if the tanks attacked, it wouldn't be the Hotel Ukraine with all the foreigners inside. It would be the white building across the street. But to get close enough to shoot out the bottom floors the tanks would have to crush a lot of warm bodies blocking the streets.

Would the generals and the KGB conspirators lose their nerve when it came down to shedding Russian blood? Would the demonstrators in the streets break and run, if and when the kettle boiled over?

From far below, an indistinct cry rose from the gutters around the white building. Heaving himself out of the chair, Torriti shambled over to the guardrail and angled his ear in the direction of the sound. Words seemed to impregnate the currents of cool air drifting in from the river. *Ross*-something. *Rossiya!* That was it. *Rossiya! Rossiya!* It spread through the streets and came back again like an echo. *Rossiya! Rossiya! Rossiya!*

Torriti scratched at his ass with a fat knuckle. He had frittered away the best years of his life locked in combat with this *Rossiya*. And here he was, boozing it up on a Moscow rooftop and rooting for it to survive.

Go figure!

Azalia Isanova was running on raw nerves and nervous energy. Aside from an occasional catnap on a sofa, she spent most of her waking hours keeping the fax machines humming with Yeltsin's ringing proclamations declaring the putsch not only illegal but downright evil. The barrage of faxes dispatched to the far corners of the immense Soviet empire was starting to bear fruit. Pledges of loyalty to the elected central government trickled in from local Party organizations. Collective farms in the Caucuses, regional dumas in Central Asia, veteran groups as far away as the Kamchaka Peninsula telexed their support. Yeltsin himself was jubilant when Aza brought word that 100,000 people had rallied in Sverdlovsk's main square to denounce the putschists. Now, on the second night of the coup d'état, as the war of nerves dragged on, rumors became rampant. Such-and-such a tank unit was said to have been ordered to come down from the Lenin Hills and clear the approaches to the White House. Elite KGB troops had been spotted boarding helicopters at an airbase near Moscow. The KGB chairman, Kryuchkov, was reported to have assembled his lieutenants in a Lubyanka conference room and given them an ultimatum: Crush the counterrevolution within twenty-four hours.

During a lull on the second night of the putsch, Aza abandoned her bank of fax machines for a few minutes and wandered over to an open window for a breath of fresh air. Three floors below, demonstrators were breaking up enough furniture to feed the campfires for another long night. On a makeshift stage, middle-level government officials loyal to Yeltsin were taking turns at a microphone, boosting morale of the counterrevolutionists as best they could. Then Yevgeny Yevtushenko could be seen striding up to the microphone. His piercing poet's voice, familiar to every Russian, reverberated through the plaza from speakers fixed to lampposts. *"Nyet!"* he cried.

> Russia will not fall again
> on her knees for interminable years.
> With us are Pushkin, Tolstoy.
> With us stands the whole awakened people.
> And the Russian Parliament,
> like a wounded marble swan of freedom,
> defended by the people,
> swims into immortality.

The cheers were still ringing in Aza's ears when the telephone she kept in a drawer of her desk buzzed. She bolted over, yanked open the drawer and plucked the phone from its cradle. "Of course it's me," she breathed. "I am the only one to answer this phone...For me it is the same. Every time you call my heart leaps with an elation that defies description. I only worry that someone will catch you calling...When this is over, dear heart...Yes, yes, with all my soul and all my body, yes...When is this to happen?...You are sure it is only a probing action, not the advance guard for a full-blown attack?...And they suspect nothing?...I pray to heaven it is true. Only be careful. Call when you have news but not more often. Protect yourself...If only it turns out that way. Hang up, I beg you...Then I will do it for you. Goodbye for now."

Aza forced herself to cut the line. She stood for a long moment listening to the dial tone. Then, sighing deeply, she went down the hall to Yeltsin's command center. Boris Nikolayevich, his hair unkempt, his eyes rimmed with red from sleeplessness and anxiety, prowled back and forth in an inner office dictating yet another proclamation to an exhausted secretary. He stopped in mid-phrase when he noticed Aza. She took him aside and quickly told him what she had learned from her source. Yeltsin summoned one of the Afghan veterans and passed the information on to him. The officer hurried down to the second-floor canteen that had been transformed into a dormitory; people who served as guards at the White House doors or inside the building slept in shifts on blankets folded on the floor. The officer buttonholed the group just coming off duty and explained the situation. Three T-72s had been ordered to probe a barricade on the Garden Ring Road and test the will of the defenders. It was vital that the Yeltsin loyalists put up a strong show of force, because conclusions about the counterrevolution's will to resist would obviously be drawn by the putschists. The Afghan officer called for volunteers. Seven students and six veterans, as well as an older man who had been standing shifts outside the command center, raised their hands.

The squad members, jamming spare clips into their pockets and grabbing several cartons filled with Molotov cocktails, commandeered three taxis in the basement garage and, after inching through the masses of people in the plaza, headed into the city. The taxis turned off the Arbat onto the Ring Road and sped along it until they reached the barricade. It was half an hour to midnight and most of the defenders had melted away to snatch some sleep. Only a handful of students, half of them girls, remained. The Afghan officer distributed the Molotov cocktails, two to each man, and posted his volunteers on either side of the street up from the barricade.

At midnight three large tanks with hooded headlights swung into view and crawled toward the barricade, grinding up the pavement under their treads. When they came abreast of the defenders hiding in alleyways off the Ring Road, the Afghan officer blew shrilly on a whistle. From both sides of the road, dark figures grasping wine bottles with burning wicks wedged in the necks darted toward the tanks. The tankers must have been equipped with night-vision goggles because the turrets immediately swiveled to the sides and machine guns raked the street. The first two students were cut down before they got within throwing distance. The other fighters, shooting at the tanks from the alleyways, diverted the attention of the gunners in the turrets. In the confusion two more defenders scurried onto the Ring Road. The first one got close enough to fling a Molotov cocktail at the treads of the lead tank, causing it to veer into a fire hydrant. The gunner in the turret pitched forward and his machine gun, silenced, fell off to one side. At that moment the second fighter, crouching low, lumbered in from the blind side and scrambled onto the back of the tank and pitched his Molotov cocktail directly down through the open hatch. There was a flash of flames, against which the fighter was silhouetted. The Afghan officer screamed from the side, "Run!" The fighter turned to jump off the burning tank—too late. The gunner on the second tank jerked the guncarriage around and opened fire at the silhouetted figure. Impaled on the bullets stabbing into his chest, the fighter was flung back against the burning turret. The ammunition inside the vehicle began to explode as the fighter's body slid sideways off the tank into the street. A burst of radio static from the second tank filled the night. The drivers of the two remaining vehicles revved their engines and the tanks reversed away from the burning hulk. A roar went up from the barricade and the alleyways.

The probe had been turned back.

The volunteers recovered the bodies of their three dead comrades and brought them to the White House, where they were laid out on the makeshift stage. Women, their eyes awash with tears, sponged away the blood as best they could and covered the corpses with flowers. The Afghan veterans, caps in hand, filed past to pay their respects. An Orthodox priest wearing a black pope's hat and robes placed a small wooden cross on the heart of each dead man.

Tessa was sound asleep at a desk, her head buried in her arms, when Azalia Isanova shook her awake.

"Has the attack begun?" Tessa demanded when she saw the tears streaming down Azalia's cheeks.

"It is about your father," Aza said so softly that Tessa wasn't sure she had heard correctly.

"My father?"

"There was an attack on the Ring Road...three tanks...volunteers went out to stop them...destroyed the first and turned back the others...heavy price...three of our defenders were killed. Your father was one of them."

Tessa was too numb to cry. "I must see him," she whispered.

Aza took her by the hand and led her past the students and Afghan veterans lining the corridors and staircase to the great entrance of the White House, and up onto the makeshift stage outside its doors. The masses of people lost in the darkness of the plaza were perfectly still as Tessa sank to her knees next to the body of her father. At first she was afraid to touch him for fear of hurting him even more. Leo's chest looked as if it had been crushed by a sledgehammer. The ankle of one foot was turned out at an angle that could only mean the bone had been pulverized. His face, grown ten years older in twenty-four hours, appeared swollen and colorless. His eyes were shut. Dried blood stained one lid. And yet...and yet he looked, to Tessa's anguished eyes, as if he had finally found a semblance of peace.

She removed the cross from her father's broken chest and handed it to the priest. "He wasn't Christian, you see," she pointed out. "He wasn't really Jewish, either. He was—" Her voice faltered. It suddenly seemed important to provide a requiem. "He was an honorable man doing what he thought was right."

During a break in the tense late-night sessions at Kryuchkov's Lubyanka war room, Yevgeny wandered down the corridor to a canteen where sandwiches and beer had been set out and helped himself to a snack. On the way back to the conference hall, he passed the open door of an office in which a KGB captain was monitoring the pirate radio station broadcasting from the White House. Listening from the door, Yevgeny heard a female announcer reading Boris Yeltsin's latest defiant proclamation. In mid-sentence she interrupted the program with an important bulletin—sources at the White House were reporting that a pitched battle had taken place in the early hours of the morning between forces loyal to the State Committee for the State of Emergency and Yeltsin's counterrevolutionists. The KGB captain turned up the volume and scrawled notes on a pad. Yevgeny, munching on a sandwich, moved closer.

"...three tanks sent by the putschists were stopped by freedom fighters when they tried to break through an outer barricade on the Garden Ring Road. The lead tank was destroyed in the action but at great cost. Three of the gallant fighters laid down their lives. All honor to the heroes Dmitri Komar, Ilya Krichevsky and Leon Kritzky—"

Yevgeny, dazed, asked, "Did she say Kritzky?"

The captain looked at his notes. "Leon Kritzky. Yes. You know him?"

"I know someone named Kritzky," Yevgeny said, thinking fast, "but his first name isn't Leon. And my Kritzky is against Yeltsin."

Yevgeny found his way to the men's room and threw some cold water on his face. He swayed forward until his forehead was touching the mirror. How could such a thing have happened? How could Leo, who had risked his life for thirty years in the service of the Socialist state, have become a victim of the State Committee for the State of Emergency? All he had to do was lock himself in his Embankment apartment. What on earth had lured him into the streets at a time like this? What the hell was he doing at his age defending a barricade?

The irony of Leo's death staggered Yevgeny. Straightening, he stared at his reflection in the mirror and caught a glimpse of a death mask. And he felt a filament of sanity unravel somewhere in his skull.

He knew what had to be done to avenge Leo's death.

Retrieving his car from the basement garage, Yevgeny drove through the deserted streets to the private KGB clinic. As he pushed through the revolving door with the tarnished gold hammer and sickle over it, he realized that he had no memory of how he had gotten there. In the early hours of the morning, only an old, half-blind porter was on duty in the main hall. He touched his cap when he noticed the shadow of a man heading for the staircase.

"If you please, your name?" he called. "I am required to log visitors in my register."

"Ozolin," Yevgeny said.

"And how are you spelling Ozolin?"

"O-Z-O-L-I-N."

Moving as if in a dream where the most extraordinary events came across as perfectly unremarkable, Yevgeny made his way down the hallway on the fourth floor to the door with the scrap of paper taped to it that read, "Zhilov, Pavel Semyonovich." Inside, yellowish light from the street splashed the ceiling. In the undulating darkness, he could detect the purr of a battery-powered pump and the labored breathing of the ghostly figure in the metal hospital bed. Moving closer, Yevgeny's eyes fell on the clipboard at the foot of the bed. Written in ink across it was the notation, "Chest pains compatible with enlarged heart." He moved around to the side of the mattress and stared down at the skeletal body covered with a urine-stained sheet. Small bubbles of air seemed to burst in Starik's throat as his medication flowed through the intravenous drip attached to the catheter in his chest.

So this is what Tolstoy looked like, stretched out on a wooden bench at the Astapovo Station, his straggly beard matted with phlegm and coughed-up blood, his jaw gnashing, the petrified stationmaster Ozolin leaning over him, praying the famous fossil of a man would live long enough to die somewhere else. Starik stirred and a moan escaped his lips. He must have sensed the presence of another human being because his bony fingers reached out and wrapped themselves around Yevgeny's wrist.

"Please," he wheezed, forcing the words out the side of his mouth that wasn't paralyzed. "Tell me...is the game over?"

"Despite all your efforts to keep it going, it is ending, Pavel Semyonovich. Your side is going to lose."

Starik heaved himself onto an elbow and gaped through crazed eyes at the paint peeling from a wall. "Do you see it?" he cried.

"See what?"

"The Red Queen! She is running into the wood where things have no name. *Faster! Faster before it catches you!*" Spent, Starik collapsed back onto the mattress.

Yevgeny reached down to the shelf of the night table and groped around until he found the line connecting the small pump to the battery. He gripped it and yanked it out of the socket. The murmur of the pump broke off abruptly.

With the pump no longer injecting the French drug Flolan into Starik's body, his lungs would gradually fill with fluid. By the time the nurse on the morning shift came around to check him, he would be long dead. Already his breathing was more labored. When he spoke again, ranting about the Red Queen, there was a shallow metallic rasp between each word as he struggled to suck in air.

Yevgeny backed away from the bed of the drowning man until he could no longer make out his voice. Turning, he hurried from the clinic. There were still things he had to do before the sweet tide of insanity ebbed.

Yeltsin hadn't closed his eyes since the start of the putsch. Physically exhausted, mentally drained, he slumped in a chair, his jaw wedged in a palm, desperately trying to focus on Aza's mouth and the words coming out of it. "Say again more slowly," he instructed her. She started from the beginning. Her source in Lubyanka had phoned again to report that KGB Chairman Kryuchkov was pushing for a decisive attack that night. The stratagem, dubbed Operation Thunder by the military planners, was straightforward: before dawn the protesters around the White House would be dispersed by water cannons and tear gas, at which point elite KGB and paratroop units would penetrate the area and blast through the building's doors with grenade launchers. At precisely the same moment helicopter gunships would deposit troops on the roof. The two forces would spread out and comb the building for Yeltsin, who would be killed resisting arrest. If the operation went according to plan the whole thing would be over in minutes.

Yeltsin let the information sink in. He mumbled something about how it was a godsend to have a spy at the heart of the putsch. Then he summoned the Afghan officers and had Aza repeat what she had told him. The group brainstormed for several minutes, after which Yeltsin issued his orders. Buckets of water were to be placed in the plaza around the White House so that demonstrators could wet pieces of cloth and use them as masks to protect themselves from the tear gas. The barricades were to be reinforced, additional Molotov cocktails were to be distributed to stop the water cannons. The roof of the White House was to be immediately strewn with office furniture to make it more difficult for the helicopters to land. Yeltsin himself, along with his senior aides, would retreat to a sub-basement bunker and lock himself behind a fifty-centimeter-thick steel door. "The flame of resistance burns as long as I am alive," he said tiredly.

At the Lubyanka, the debate raged on around the oval table. Some of the middle-level field commanders who had been assigned to lead Operation Thunder were having second thoughts. At first the reservations were couched in mundane operational terms:

"How are we to land helicopters on a roof piled high with furniture?"

"What if Yeltsin manages to slip away in the confusion?"

"We have to consider worst-case scenarios. What will happen if we kill several thousand defenders and still don't capture Yeltsin?"

"What if Yeltsin escapes to the Urals and goes through with his threat to form a shadow government?"

"What if our troops refuse to fire on the people manning the barricades? What then?"

"Worse still, what if our troops attack and are turned back?"

As the discussion dragged on the criticism became more pointed. Sensing that the balance was slowly tilting against them, the putsch leaders tried desperately to save the day. They argued that the stalemate worked for the counterrevolutionists; as long as the White House held out people would continue to rally to Yeltsin. And if Yeltsin were permitted to prevail, the careers, *the lives* of all those who had sided with the putsch would be in jeopardy.

A combat general who had been for the attack when it was first proposed wavered. "I don't know—if this blows up in our faces, it's the Army's reputation that will bear the stain."

"The Party leadership walks away when things turn sour—the war in Afghanistan is the most recent example," complained another war hero.

The press baron Uritzky pleaded with the field commanders. If Gorbachev and Yeltsin retained power, they would slash military budgets and humiliate the once-proud Soviet army. Gorbachev's military adviser, Marshal Akhromeyev, who had rushed back to Moscow from vacation to join the coup, insisted that it was too late to back down; once the putsch had been launched the plotters had no option but to go forward, if only to preserve the Army's credibility.

"We have something more important than credibility—we have the respect of the masses," observed an older officer who had remained silent up to now. "All that goodwill will disappear overnight if we fire on our brothers and sisters in the streets of the capital."

One senior commander headed for the door in disgust. "They want to smear the Army in blood. I for one will not storm the White House."

A much-decorated Air Force commander agreed. "I categorically refuse to send my helicopters into the air. You'll have to get somebody else to issue the order."

Under the noses of the ringleaders the putsch began to unravel in a flurry of recriminations. Watching from the sill of a window, Yevgeny concluded that the senior military commanders had lost their nerve. As the mood deteriorated, bottles of liquor appeared on the conference table and the putschists began the serious business of drinking themselves into a stupor. Yevgeny joined two others who were heading for the toilet, then slipped into a small office with a telephone on the desk. He lit the green-shaded desk lamp and dialed a number and listened to the phone ringing in a drawer on the other end. When Aza finally came on the line Yevgeny could barely repress the triumph in his voice.

"Yeltsin can go to sleep," he told her. "They have called off the attack....No, the leaders were willing to take the risk. In the end it was the field commanders who didn't have the appetite for bloodshed...I think it's over. Without the army behind them, the putschists have no way of swaying the masses. Yeltsin has won...To tell the truth I can hardly believe it either. In a few hours the sun will rise on a new Russia. Things will never be the same...Let us meet at—" Yevgeny stiffened as his ear caught a faint echo in the phone. "Is someone else on this line?" he asked quietly. "Not to worry. It must be my imagination. We will meet at your flat at the end of the afternoon...Yes. For me, too. We will slow down the time left to us so that each instant lasts an eternity."

When he heard Aza hang up, Yevgeny kept the phone pressed to his ear. Twenty seconds went by. Then there was a second soft click on the line that caused him to catch his breath. Perhaps he was jumping at shadows; perhaps it originated with the telephone exchange or the central switchboard operator. Turning off the desk lamp, he walked into the outer office. He stood for a moment waiting for his eyes to become accustomed to the darkness. Hearing the rustle of fabric, he peered into the shadows and realized that someone was in the doorway.

A woman's voice, seething with pent-up fury, hissed, "So it was you, Yevgeny Alexandrovich, the traitor in our ranks who betrayed us to the counterrevolution."

He knew the voice—it belonged to Mathilde, the wife of the press baron Uritzky. An overhead light snapped on and she stepped out of the shadows to confront him. Buried in her fist was a metallic object so small that he thought it could only be a lipstick.

"It was not lost on us that at every turn the counterrevolutionists seemed to know what we were doing. My husband told Kryuchkov there was a traitor in our midst but he didn't pay attention. He was so sure Yeltsin would cave in once he realized the hopelessness of his position."

"He miscalculated," Yevgeny remarked.

"So did you!"

Mathilde stepped closer and raised the object in her fist and pointed it at Yevgeny's forehead. It dawned on him what she was holding and he understood there would be no time left to slow down. "To the success," he murmured, "of our hopeless—"

All of Moscow erupted in a paroxysm of jubilation. On the sweating asphalt avenues around the Kremlin, long convoys of tanks and armored personnel carriers headed out of the city, cheered on by women tossing carnations and roses up to the laughing soldiers. Bystanders lining the route applauded the departing troops who, clearly relieved to be heading back to their barracks, applauded back. "Thanks to God, we're going home," one officer shouted from the turret of a tank. Outside the Central Committee building, thousands of demonstrators chanted defiantly, "Dissolve the Party" and "Smash the KGB." Communist functionaries could be seen fleeing from side entrances carting off everything that wasn't bolted down—fax machines, computers, television sets, video recorders, air conditioners, lamps, desk chairs. Word spread that the *apparatchiki* still inside were feeding mountains of paperwork into shredders; in their panic to destroy evidence of the putsch the Communists neglected to remove the paperclips, causing the machines to break down. When a portable radio at a kiosk blared the news that Yeltsin was said to be preparing a decree suspending the activities of the Russian Communist Party, effectively ending seventy-four years of Bolshevik dictatorship, people linked arms and danced euphorically. In parks and squares around the city, construction workers armed with crowbars pried the statues of Old Bolsheviks from their pedestals and smashed them against the ground. In the great square outside the Lubyanka, a crane lifted the enormous statue of Feliks Dzershinsky off its base. For a few delicious minutes Dzerzhinsky, the cruel Pole who in 1917 created the Cheka, the precursor of the despised KGB, hung from the cable around his neck while the crowd cheered hoarsely.

Sleepwalking through streets teeming with people celebrating the victory of something they barely understood and the defeat of something they understood only too well, Aza happened to witness what newspapers would call "the execution of the executioner." But even that brought her no relief from the ache of the emptiness that would fill the rest of her life.

Only the notion that she might somehow find a way to speed time up gave her a measure of comfort.

The Uighurs checked the stairwell off the fifth floor of the Hotel Ukraine and waved to Endel Rappaport to tell him the coast was clear. Rappaport went in first and held the door for the Sorcerer. "We can talk here," he told Torriti as the heavy fire door swung closed behind him.

"Who's he?" asked the Sorcerer, eyeing the short, slender Russian leaning against a wall; in his early forties and dressed in a smart business suit, he certainly wasn't one of Rappaport's Uighurs. There was a deadpan expression in his humorless eyes; to Torriti, the stranger looked as if he could be bored to death by an assassin.

Rappaport chuckled. "Vladimir is a business associate from Dresden."

"Hello to you, Vladimir," ventured Torriti.

Vladimir didn't crack a smile or respond.

Rappaport asked Torriti, "When are you flying out?"

"This afternoon."

Rappaport, wearing a double-breasted blazer with gold buttons and carrying a walking stick with a golden dog's head on top, waggled his pinkie in the Sorcerer's face. "The country you are leaving is not the same as the one you came to."

"For sure," Torriti conceded. "Yeltsin will pack Gorbachev off into retirement and destroy the Communist Party, so far so good. Sixty-four thousand dollar question is, what's going to take its place?"

"Anything will be better than what we had," Rappaport contended.

"Hey, you got to live here, pal, not me."

Rappaport cleared his throat. "About those contracts." When Torriti glanced at the dour Russian against the wall, Rappaport said, "You can speak in front of him—I have no secrets from Vladimir."

"About those contracts," the Sorcerer agreed.

"Given who you are, given whom you represent, my associates are eager to do the right thing. In light of the fact that the contracts were supposed to be fulfilled *before* the recent events, they are ready to cancel the contracts and return the sums deposited in Switzerland."

The Sorcerer jowls quivered with the comedy of the situation. "In the United States of America," he said, "people have been heard to say, *Better late than never.*"

"Do I understand you correctly, Mr. Sorcerer? Despite the lateness of the hour, you still wish my associates to deliver on these contracts?"

"Look at the situation from my point of view, friend. My clients want to make sure Yeltsin won't have the same jokers diddling with him this time next year."

The gnome-like Russian looked up at the Sorcerer. "You are one in a thousand, Mr. Sorcerer." He thrust out a hand and the Sorcerer gave it a limp shake.

"It's a pleasure to do business with you, Endel. You don't mind I call you Endel? I feel as if we've know each other for weeks. Listen, I'm concerned about your remuneration. I wouldn't want you to come away from all this without a little something for your troubles."

"I am moved almost but not quite to tears by your concern, Mr. Sorcerer. Rest assured, I have been in touch with the Rabbi, who has been in touch with someone who goes by the appellation of *Devisenbeschaffer*—"

Torriti was startled. "You know of the existence of the currency acquirer?"

Endel Rappaport's thick lips curled into a sheepish smirk. "The legendary Rabbi Hillel, who made something a name for himself in the second century, is said to have posed the ultimate question: *If I am not for myself, who is for me?* Vladimir here has been tracking the *Devisenbeschaffer*'s pecuniary activities in Dresden for me. A third of what the Rabbi gets from the currency acquirer will wind up in Swiss accounts that I control."

"People like me do not meet people like *you* every day of the week," Torriti said seriously. "A third of what the Rabbi gets is a pretty penny. What are you going to do with all that money?"

The smirk froze on Rappaport's face. "Before they cut off my fingers I was a student of the violin. Since then I have not been able to listen to music. What I am going to do with my share of the money is get even."

"Even with who?"

"Russia."

"Yeah, well, I'm glad we never got to cross paths during the Cold War. Your premature death would have weighed on my conscience."

Rappaport's brow wrinkled in pain. "I feel the same about you. Do have a good trip back to wherever it is you are going."

"I'm heading home," Torriti said. "The end of the line is East of Eden, a paradise on earth for golfers and/or alcoholics."

Merriment danced in Rappaport's eyes. "I need not ask which category you fall into."

Torriti had to concede the point. "No, I don't suppose you do."

The deaths were all listed on police blotters as accidents or suicides.

Nikolai Izvolsky, the Central Committee's financial wizard who had siphoned Party funds to the *Devisenbeschaffer* in Germany, fell to his death from the roof of a Moscow apartment house while taking the air late one night. A crotchety old woman in the next building later told police that she had seen four men on the roof next door moments before she heard the scream and the police sirens. As the woman was well known in the local precinct for inventing stories of Peeping Toms on the roofs of adjacent buildings, the state procurator discounted her testimony and ruled the death an accident.

The press baron Pavel Uritzky and his wife, Mathilde, were discovered asphyxiated in their BMW parked in the private garage behind their *kottedzhi* on the edge of Moscow. One end of a garden hose had been inserted into the exhaust pipe, the other end run into the ventilation tubing under the hood. The nurse in the ambulance responding to the frantic call from the couple's butler broke the car window with a hammer, switched off the motor, dragged the bodies outside and administered oxygen, but it was too late. In his subsequent declaration to the authorities, the nurse mentioned having detected the pungent odor of chloroform in the garage. The first policemen on the scene made no mention of this and the question of chloroform was relegated to a footnote in the official report. The state procurator noted that the car doors had been locked on the inside, with the remote door control device attached to the key in the ignition. The second remote device, normally in Mathilde's possession, was never found but no conclusions were drawn from this. Careful examination revealed no bruises on the corpses and no evidence under the fingernails to indicate there had been a struggle. No suicide note was found. Pavel Uritzky had been one of the ringleaders of the putsch and deeply depressed at its failure. Mathilde was linked to the shooting of the banking magnate Tsipin and said to be terrified of being prosecuted. The deaths of the Uritzkys were listed as a double suicide and the case was closed.

Moscow neighbors of Boris Pugo heard what sounded like a shot and summoned the police, who broke down the door and discovered the Interior Minister slumped over the kitchen table, a large-caliber pistol (obviously fallen from his hand) on the linoleum floor and brain matter seeping from an enormous bullet wound in his skull. A note addressed to his children and grandchildren said, "Forgive me. It was all a mistake." Pugo's old father-in-law was found cowering in a clothes closet muttering incoherently about assassination squads, but police psychiatrists decided the father-in-law was suffering from dementia and the state procurator eventually ruled that Pugo's wound was self inflicted.

The body of Gorbachev's military adviser, Marshal Akhromeyev, was found hanging from a noose attached to an overhead lighting fixture in his office. People in adjacent offices told police they had heard what sounded like furniture being moved and objects being thrown on the floor, but had not become suspicious because they knew that, in the aftermath of the aborted putsch, the Marshal had been retired from active duty and assumed he was simply moving out his personal affairs. The various noises were further explained away by Akhromeyev's typed suicide note, which said: "I am a poor master of preparing my own suicide. The first attempt didn't work—the cord broke. I will try with all my strength to do it again. My age and all I have done give me the right to leave this life."

The foreign ministry *apparatchik* Fyodor Lomov, one of the key putschists, fled Moscow to avoid arrest and was never heard from again. He left behind a cryptic note saying the only thing he regretted was that the coup against Gorbachev had failed. Clothing later identified as belonging to Lomov were discovered neatly folded on a bank of the Moscow River upstream from the capital. The river was dragged but Lomov's body was never found; his disappearance was carried on the police books as a "swimming accident."

Newspapers reported other mysterious deaths: two in the city that used to be called Leningrad but had changed its name back to Saint Petersburg (the dead men, killed when their car went over a cliff, were KGB generals who had plotted to oust the elected mayor and take control of the city in the name of the State Committee for the State of Emergency); one in the Crimea (a senior KGB officer from the Ninth Chief Directorate who had commanded the unit keeping Gorbachev prisoner in Foros died in the explosion of a kitchen gas canister); one in the Urals Military District (an Army general who, at the height of the putsch, had ordered the local KGB to round up "cosmopolitans," a Stalinist code word for Jews, was knifed to death in a banal mugging).

Alerted by the rash of accidental deaths and suicides, the authorities decided to take extraordinary precautions with the putsch ringleaders already in custody, KGB Chairman Kryuchkov and Defense Minister Yazov being the most prominent among them. Visitors were required to communicate through a glass window; shoelaces, belts and sharp objects were removed from the cells and the accused were put on under round-the-clock surveillance.

With all eyes on Russia, few noticed the small item that appeared on a back page in the Dresden press: early-morning joggers had discovered the body of the *Devisenbeschaffer* hanging under a bridge across the Elbe. Sometime before dawn he had attached one end of a thick rope to a stanchion and tied the other end around his neck, and jumped to his death. He was wearing a neatly pressed conservative three-piece suit that showed no evidence of a struggle. A typed and signed note was found in his inside breast pocket; detectives eventually established that the typeface matched the deceased's computer printer. The note asked his wife and three children to forgive him for taking the easy way out, and went on to say that he had decided to kill himself because he had siphoned funds into Russia to finance the aborted putsch and was now sure he would be exposed and punished. The police report noted that the *Devisenbeschaffer* had failed to specify which accounts in Russia the money had been sent to, and they held little hope of ever finding out; for all intents and purposes the funds had vanished into thin air.

Turning their backs on the main drag crawling with narrow trolley cars and lined with banks, the Sorcerer and his Apprentice strolled across the footbridge at the end of Lake Geneva and went to ground in an open air café. Attractive young women wearing white aprons over gauze-thin blouses and peasant skirts waited on tables. Jack summoned one of them and inquired, "What do people order when they're celebrating?"

"Champagne cups," she said without hesitation.

"Oh, Jesus, not Champagne," Torriti whined. "The goddamn bubbles give me gas."

"Two Champagne cups," Jack told the waitress. When Torriti pulled a face, Jack said, "You've been drinking cheap booze so long you think it's an elixir. Besides which, we've got to launch the Enterprise in style."

Torriti nodded grudgingly. "It's not everybody who waltzes into a Swiss bank and finds out he's got $147 million and change stashed in a secret account. When you got up to leave I thought the clown in the three-piece suit was going to shine your shoes with his tongue."

"It's so much money I have trouble thinking of it as money," Jack told his friend.

"Actually, I thought this *Devisenbeschaffer* character had squirreled away a lot more in Dresden. You sure Ezra Ben Ezra isn't holding out on you?"

"The Rabbi took expenses off the top. To start with, there was your mafia chum in Moscow—"

"The inimitable Endel Rappaport, who's going to make Mother Russia pay through the nose for the fingers that got lopped off."

"He got a share of the money. Another chunk wound up in the pocket of a shadowy individual who may be sponsoring the career of a little known KGB lieutenant colonel named Vladimir Vladimirovich Putin. The individual in question worked with Putin in Dresden and knew his way around well enough to siphon off some of the *Devisenbeschaffer's* loot before the Rabbi could get to it."

"Funny thing, there was a Russian named Vladimir with Rappaport the last time our paths crossed."

"The Rabbi said this Putin quit the KGB the day after the coup against Gorbachev began, then turned up in something called the Federal Security Service, which is the successor to the KGB."

"Nimble footwork," Torriti commented. "Putin." He shook his head. "Name doesn't ring a bell."

"It will," Jack said. "With roughly a hundred fifty million to spread around, he's bound to surface eventually."

The waitress set the Champagne cups on the table and tucked the bill under the ashtray. "Here's to Swiss banks," Torriti said, and wincing in apprehension, he warily tested his cocktail.

"Here's to the Enterprise," Jack said. He drank off half the Champagne as if it were seltzer water. "You want to know something, Harvey. I feel like Mr. Rockefeller must have felt when he set up his foundation. My big problem now is to figure out how to give away the seven or so million the account generates a year."

"Read the newspapers and send out money orders to deserving causes."

"How would you define deserving causes?"

Torriti said with utter seriousness, "That's not complicated—deserving causes knock off deserving people."

Sniffing the air, Torriti smiled at a thought. Jack asked, "What is it?"

"Funny thing, Kritzky cashing in his chips like that. You want a second opinion, he got what was coming to him."

Jack gazed at the lake without seeing it. He could make out Leo's voice in his ear. *I'm still sorry, Jack. About our friendship. But not about what I did.* "He set out to fix the world," Jack said. "He didn't realize it wasn't broken."

Torriti could see that his Apprentice needed cheering up. "Well, don't let it go to your head, sport, but the fact is I'm proud of you. No kidding aside, I am. You're the best thing since sliced bread."

"I had a great teacher."

Torriti hiked his glass. "To you and me, sport, the last of the Cold War Mohicans."

"The last of the Cold War Mohicans," Jack agreed.

The Company pulled out all the stops for Jack's official going away bash in the seventh-floor dining room at Langley. A banner bearing the McAuliffe family mantra ("Once down is no battle") had been strung over the double doors. The *Time* magazine photo of Jack being rescued from a half-inflated rubber raft off the Bay of Pigs had been blown up larger than life and taped to one wall. Much to Jack's embarrassment and Millie's delight, the secret citations that accompanied his many "jockstrap" medals ("...for courage above and beyond the call of duty...highest tradition of the clandestine service...honor on the country and on the Company") had been printed up poster-size and tacked to the remaining walls. The speeches—beginning with Manny's tribute and ending with Ebby's—had been interminable. "All Central Intelligence officers have the right to retire when they're pushing sixty-five," the DCI told the several hundred men and women crowded into the executive dining room, "especially after forty years of dedicated service to the flame of liberty. But with Jack's departure, we're losing more than a warm body who happens to be the Deputy Director of Central Intelligence. We're losing the heart and the soul and the brain and the expertise and the instincts of a warrior who has fought all the battles, from the rooftops of East Berlin to Cuba to the recent attempt at a putsch in Russia. In the process, he survived the bloodletting and earned the kudos and taught us all that once down is no battle. Forty years ago I sat with Jack in a cabaret in Berlin called Die Pfeffermühle and we drank more than our share of beer and wound up singing the Whiffenpoof song. And there's a stanza in it—correct me if I screw this up, Jack—that says:

> And the measure of our torment is the measure of our youth,
> God help us, for we knew the worst too young!

"For those of us who were around then and, like you, Jack, knew the worst too young, that about says it all. Except, perhaps, good luck and Godspeed."

The Company officers, a great many of whom hadn't been born when Jack and Ebby were hanging out in Die Pfeffermühle, applauded enthusiastically; Jack was extremely popular with the rank and file and the truth was they were sorry to see him go. It was, as one section head put it, the end of an era. To everyone's delight, Millie, sobbing openly, rushed up and planted a kiss on Jack's Cossack mustache. Elizabet and Nellie and Manny crowded around him. Jack's son, Anthony, and his daughter-in-law, Maria, hugged him affectionately.

And then the liquor started flowing.

"How did things go in Room SH219?" Jack asked when he managed to buttonhole Ebby in a corner.

"For once they gave us grudging credit for anticipating the putsch and getting the President to warn Gorbachev, even if the warning fell on deaf ears," Ebby recounted. "They asked about you, Jack. I told them you were starting a private security consultancy called the Enterprise. They wanted to know who was bankrolling you." Ebby raised his half-empty whiskey glass and clinked it against Jack's. "Who *is* bankrolling you, old buddy?"

"Clients," he said.

"You sure are tight-lipped about the whole thing."

"A security consultancy needs to be tight-lipped if it wants to have credibility," Jack retorted.

"I suppose," Ebby said. "Funny thing happened at today's session—our congressional watchdogs went to great pains to remind me that political assassination is prohibited by a 1976 executive order. They kept coming back to that rash of accidents and suicides after the putsch—they asked me several times if I knew anything about them."

"What did you say?"

"I told them the truth, Jack. I told them I'd read about the deaths in the newspapers. I told them that there was no way under the sun the Company would be involved in this sort of thing on my watch." Ebby tilted his head and sized up his retiring DDCI. "You don't happen to know anything about these deaths that you haven't told me, do you, Jack?"

"I'm clean as a whistle on this," he replied.

Jack had learned how to lie from a virtuoso. Every inch the Sorcerer's Apprentice, he summoned up a perfectly guileless smile and, looking Ebby squarely in the eye, repeated what Harvey Torriti said when Jack had raised the subject of RAINBOW's death in Berlin a dozen or so wars back. "Hey, pal, I swear it to you. On my mother's grave."

POSTLUDE

THE ANATOMY OF AN INFILTRATION

"Tut, tut, child!" said the Duchess.
"Everything's got a moral, if only you can find it."

VIENNA, VIRGINIA, SUNDAY, AUGUST 6, 1995

HIGH OVER THE CITY, A MARE'S TAIL DRIFTED ACROSS THE GREAT Bear so languorously it looked as if the motion picture had been slowed down. On a deserted street running along one side of Nottoway Park in Fairfax County, Virginia, a crow's mile from the town of Vienna, a broad-shouldered fiftyish-something man known to his Russian handlers only by his code name, Ramon, surveyed the neighborhood through prism binoculars that could see in the dark. Sitting motionless in the back seat of his Isuzu Trooper, he'd been keeping an eye on the streets and paths since midnight. He'd watched several people impatiently walking dogs, a couple of homosexuals who stopped in their tracks every few seconds to bicker, an inebriated woman of uncertain age tottering on spiky heels that dispatched sharp echoes into the still summer night. Then absolute silence. Just after two in the morning he'd spotted the dark four-door Ford with two men in it cruising the area. It vanished down a side street and materialized ten minutes later from another direction. On its fourth pass around the area the car eased to a stop at the curb near the park's main entrance on Old Courthouse Road. The headlights flickered out. For a long while the two men remained in the Ford. From time to time one of them would light a fresh cigarette from the glowing embers of the last one. At a quarter to three the men finally emerged from the car and made their way through the park to the wooden footbridge. The one smoking the cigarette turned his back on the bridge and stood guard. The other crouched quickly and tugged a green plastic trash bag from its hiding place under the end of the bridge, and wedged a paper shopping bag into the cranny in its place. On their way back to their automobile, the two men stripped off the white adhesive tape pasted vertically across a "pedestrian crossing" sign (indicating that Ramon was ready to receive the package) and replaced it with a horizontal length of tape (indicating that the dead drop had been serviced). With a last look around, they got back into their car and, accelerating cautiously, drove off.

Ramon waited another twenty minutes before making his move. He had been spying for the Russians for ten years now, and long ago decided that this was the only really perilous moment in the game. His Russian handlers had no idea who he was. They would have figured out from the documents he supplied that he was deeply involved in Russian counterintelligence and just assumed he worked for the CIA; it would never have crossed their minds that he actually worked for the FBI. Which meant that even if the Americans got their hands on a mole or a highly placed Russian defector, they couldn't discover Ramon's identity from the Russians *because the Russians didn't know it.* On his end, he was senior enough in his shop to have access to computer codes and files that would give him early warning if anybody raised the specter of an American mole working for the Russians.

Ramon, meticulous and experienced when it came to tradecraft, had examined the operation from every point of the compass. As far as he could see there was no way he could be caught—except in the act of picking up the payload in the dead drop. Which was why he went to such lengths to survey the park before retrieving what his Russian handlers had left for him.

Back in the mid-1980s, when he'd delivered his first plastic trash bag filled with secrets, the motive had been money. The people around him—his college classmates, his neighbors, lawyers and stock brokers he ran into at cocktail parties—were pulling down enormous salaries and year-end bonuses and stock options worth a fortune. Ramon's government payroll check permitted him and his family to live comfortably, but he didn't see how he would pay for the college education of the three children he already had and the fourth that was on its way. He didn't see how he could live with a measure of self-indulgence when the time came to retire. Unless...unless he came up with a scheme to augment his income. And the only scheme that seemed within the realm of possibility was peddling state secrets to the state's principal adversary, Russia. He carefully studied the case histories of previous moles to make sure he didn't fall into the same traps that eventually led to their downfall. He was careful not to change his lifestyle, something that was sure to attract the attention of the security mavins. He drove the same beat-up cars and lived in the same middle-class home in Virginia and vacationed at the same modest resorts on mainland America. Curiously, it was only after he'd delivered the first few packets to the Russians that he realized the money wasn't the only reward.

There was an enormous kick to be had from beating the system; the adrenalin flowed when he outsmarted the counterintelligence teams that had been created to prevent someone from doing what he was doing. The fact that he was a member of such a team only made the exploit sweeter. His drab life, which was filled with dreary routines and tedious paperwork and rigorous pecking orders, suddenly seemed a lot more glamorous.

Ramon could feel the pulse pounding in his temple as he let himself out of the Isuzu. Walking soundless on rubber soles, he approached the footbridge and, squatting, worked the paper bag free from the cranny. He could make out the wads of bills, used twenties and fifties bound together with rubber bands, through the paper; his Russian handlers will have left him $50,000 in all, compensation for the payload he'd left the month before that included the identities of two Russian diplomats serving in Washington who were spying for the CIA. Back in the car, he jammed the paper bag up under the dashboard behind the radio and started the motor. Threading his way through the empty streets in the direction of home, he felt the throb in his temple gradually returning to something approaching normal and experienced the liberating serenity familiar to the mountaineer coming down from an alp.

The God-awful truth was he had become an adrenalin junkie; the double game had become the only game worth playing.

Minutes before 5 A.M. an ambulance eased down the ramp of the Veterans Administration hospital on San Pedro Drive in Albuquerque, New Mexico. Hunched over the wheel of a rented car parked in an outdoor space reserved for doctors, Jack McAuliffe watched the automatic door rise and began ticking off the seconds. At three one-hundredth he was jogging down the ramp as the taillights of the ambulance disappeared into the vast basement garage. At nine one-hundredth he ducked under the overhead door as it started closing behind him. Threading his way between parked cars to a locked door, he worked a thin metal wedge down the jamb until the dead bolt clicked open. Picking the lock gave him a lot of satisfaction; he hadn't done this sort of thing since S.M. Craw Management initiated him into the joys of tradecraft. Taking the stairs two at a time, he climbed to the fourth floor. Winded, he leaned on the banister to catch his breath; the body had aged more than the mind wanted to admit. Checking to make sure the coast was clear, he loped down the hospital corridor to the locker room, which was precisely where the nurse said it would be. He snatched a pair of white trousers and a knee-length white coat from the laundry bin, along with two white canvas shoe sheaths, and quickly pulled everything on. For good measure, he pinched a stethoscope from a peg on the wall and hung it around his neck. Moments later he made his way down to the third floor and pushed through the doors of the special ward the Company maintained for former officers and agents. There was an imperious red-lettered sign splashed across the inner doors that warned "Absolutely No Visitors."

Out of the corner of an eye Jack noticed a nurse at the far end of the unit glance in his direction as he approached the third cubicle. He made a show of studying the chart attached to the partition. Moving around to the side of the bed, he reached down to take the patient's pulse. Harvey Torriti, wearing a sleeveless hospital gown and looking like a beached whale, opened one damp eye and then the other. He sniffed in pleasure as he recognized his visitor.

"Goddamn, Harvey, how did you wind up here?" Jack whispered.

"With all the painkillers I take, they're worried about me babbling Company secrets," Torriti said. "So they sentenced me to death in this sterile VA brig. Only immediate family are allowed to visit. As I have no family, immediate or otherwise, nobody gets in to see me." The sight of his Apprentice had obviously cheered the Sorcerer. "How'd you get past the guards?" he demanded in a voice raw from disuse.

"Exfiltrations, infiltrations, I learned it all at the foot of the master," Jack said.

Jack could make out the shrapnel wound that had decapitated the naked lady tattooed on Torriti's arm; he remembered Miss Sipp fainting dead away when the Sorcerer peeled off his shirt to show it to her. He leaned closer until his face was hovering above Torriti's. "So how are you doing, Harvey?"

"What can I say, kid? I'm not doing so good. I'm dog-tired when I go to sleep, I'm bushed when I wake up. Let's face it, I'm on my last legs. I think this is where I get to buy the farm."

"These days the doctors can pull off miracles—"

Torriti waved away the idea with a limp hand. "Don't fuck with me, pal. We've come too far together for you to fling bullshit on a dying man." He turned his head on the pillow to make sure the nurse was still at the far end of the ward. "You wouldn't by any chance have a pick-me-up on you to help a buddy over the Great Divide?"

"Funny you should mention it—"

Jack produced the hip flask filled with cheap whiskey. Torriti brightened as his Apprentice lifted his head and tilted the flask to his lips. The alcohol burned. There was a rattle in the back of his throat as he sucked in air to douse the fire. "Just what the doctor ordered," he murmured as he sank back onto the pillow. "Suppose you read about those two Russian diplomats who were caught spying for the CIA and shot."

"What about them, Harvey?"

"You need to be dumb and blind not to see it, kid. Anybody could stumble across one mole, but two at a time—it set my nose to twitching. Want an educated guess, means the Russians have got themselves a mole of their own somewhere, probably in counterintelligence, since he knew about the two diplomats we'd turned."

"The Cold War may be over but the great game goes on," Jack said.

"Nature of the beast," Torriti grunted. "Long as the *Homo politicus* is addicted to adrenalin highs, spies will keep on spying." The Sorcerer, in pain, opened his mouth wide and breathed deeply. When the pain had subsided, he said, "Read about Endel Rappaport in the papers from time to time."

"I never saw Rappaport's name—"

"They don't mention him by name. They just talk about the home-grown Russian mafia taking over this or that banking syndicate or oil cartel."

Jack started to say something but Torriti plunged on, "I've been following that Vladimir Putin fellow, too. In case you haven't noticed, which I doubt, he's the deputy mayor of St. Petersburg. Folks who keep track of these things say he's close to Yeltsin and conspicuously upwardly mobile and has a filthy rich patron, so they say." The Sorcerer's eyes widened playfully. "I read about you, too, Jacko."

"You read about *me*!"

"I wasn't born yesterday, kiddo. Every now and then the good guys score and I figure your Enterprise could be behind it. The assassination of that drug tsar in Colombia, the disappearance of that Communist journalist in Egypt, the bomb that went off under the car of that neo-Nazi in Austria. You still got all that money stashed in Switzerland?"

"Loose lips sink ships, Harvey."

Torriti's eyes focused on the past. "I remember the day you showed up in Berlin Base, I remember the night we met that poor son of a bitch Vishnevsky in the safe house over the movie theater—you were one hell of a circus act, Jack, with those splotches of green behind the ears and a cannon of a pistol tucked into the small of your back. No harm telling you now, I wasn't positive you'd survive."

"Thanks to you, Harvey, I survived. Thanks to you, we made a difference."

"You think so, Jack? I tell myself we made a difference. Nowadays people have short memories—they forget the goddamn Goths were at the goddamn gate. You and me, kid—we put our warm bodies on the firing line and turned them back. Fuck, something like the Cold War has to have a moral. Otherwise what was it all about?"

"It was about the good guys beating the bad guys," Jack said softly.

The Sorcerer snorted. "We sure screwed up an awful lot in the process."

"We screwed up less than they did. That's why we won."

"Never could figure out how the frigging Soviets lasted as long as they did."

"Russia wasn't a country," Jack said. "It was a metaphor for an idea that may have looked good on the drawing boards but in practice was deeply flawed. And flawed metaphors are harder to slay than flawed countries. But we clobbered them in the end."

Torriti's inflamed lids drifted over his eyes. Jack burst out, "Jesus H. Christ, Harvey, I hope you're not planning to die on me. The least you could do is wait until I'm gone."

The remark drew a feeble grin from the Sorcerer. With an effort he forced his eyes open and said, "All these years I been wondering what the hell that H in Jesus H. Christ stands for."

"Hey, it's like a lot of middle initials," Jack explained. "They don't stand for anything. They're tacked on to dress up the name. The *H* in Jesus H. Christ. The *J* in Jack J. McAuliffe. The *S* in Harry S. Truman."

Torriti coughed up a crabby snicker. "I read what you're saying, sport. It's like the *I* in CIA—that doesn't mean nothing neither."

Jack had a last laugh; he didn't see himself laughing again, ever. "You may be on to something, Harv."